DICK FRANCIS

DICK FRANCIS

FOR KICKS
ODDS AGAINST
FLYING FINISH
BONECRACK
IN THE FRAME

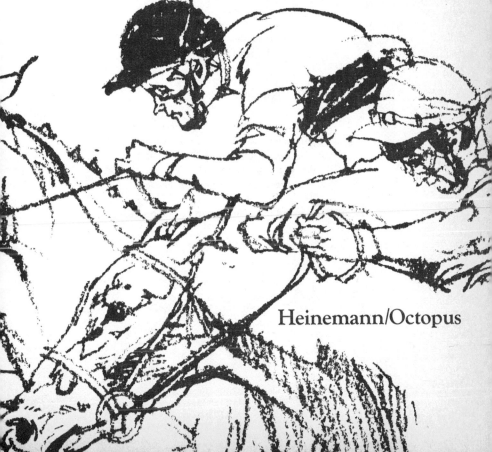

Heinemann/Octopus

For Kicks first published in Great Britain
in 1965 by Michael Joseph Ltd
Odds Against first published in Great Britain
in 1965 by Michael Joseph Ltd
Flying Finish first published in Great Britain
in 1966 by Michael Joseph Ltd
Bonecrack first published in Great Britain
in 1971 by Michael Joseph Ltd
In the Frame first published in Great Britain
in 1976 by Michael Joseph Ltd

This edition first published in Great Britain in 1983
jointly by

William Heinemann Limited   Martin Secker & Warburg Limited
10 Upper Grosvenor Street   54 Poland Street
London W1   London W1

and

Octopus Books Limited
59 Grosvenor Street
London W1

ISBN 0 905712 71 4

Printed and bound in Great Britain by Collins Glasgow

CONTENTS

FOR KICKS

Chapter One

The Earl of October drove into my life in a pale blue Holden which had seen better days, and danger and death tagged along for the ride.

I noticed the car turn in through the gateposts as I walked across the little paddock towards the house, and I watched its progress up our short private road with a jaundiced eye. Salesmen, I thought, I can do without. The blue car rolled to a gentle halt between me and my own front door.

The man who climbed out looked about forty-five and was of medium height and solid build, with a large well-shaped head and smoothly brushed brown hair. He wore grey trousers, a fine wool shirt, and a dark, discreet tie, and he carried the inevitable brief case. I sighed, bent through the paddock rails, and went over to send him packing.

'Where can I find Mr. Daniel Roke?' he asked. An English voice, which even to my untuned ear evoked expensive public schools; and he had a subtle air of authority inconsistent with the opening patter of representatives. I looked at him more attentively, and decided after all not to say I was out. He might even, in spite of the car, be a prospective customer.

'I,' I said, without too much joy in the announcement, 'am Daniel Roke.'

His eyelids flickered in surprise.

'Oh,' he said blankly.

I was used to this reaction. I was no one's idea of the owner of a prosperous stud-farm. I looked, for a start, too young, though I didn't feel it; and my sister Belinda says you don't often meet a business man you can mistake for an Italian peasant. Sweet girl, my sister. It is only that my skin is sallow and tans easily, and I have black hair and brown eyes. Also I was that day wearing the oldest, most tattered pair of jeans I possessed, with unpolished jodhpur boots, and nothing else.

I had been helping a mare who always had difficulty in foaling: a messy job, and I had dressed for it. The result of my – and the mare's – labours was a weedy filly with a contracted tendon in the near fore and a suspicion of one in the off fore too, which meant an operation, and more expense than she was likely to be worth.

My visitor stood for a while looking about him at the neat white-railed paddocks, the L-shaped stable-yard away ahead, and the row of cedar-shingled foaling boxes off to the right, where my poor little newcomer lay in the straw. The whole spread looked substantial and well-maintained, which it was; I worked very hard to keep it that way, so that I could reasonably ask good prices for my horses.

The visitor turned to gaze at the big blue-green lagoon to the left, with the snow-capped mountains rising steeply in rocky beauty along the far side of it. Puffs of cloud·like plumes crowned the peaks. Grand and glorious scenery it was, to his fresh eyes.

But to me, walls.

'Breathtaking,' he said appreciatively. Then turning to me briskly, but with some hesitation in his speech, he said, 'I ... er ... I heard in Perlooma that you have ... er ... an English stable hand who ... er ... wants to go back home ...' He broke off, and started again. 'I suppose it may sound surprising, but in certain circumstances, and if he is suitable, I am willing to pay his fare and give him a job at the other end ...' He tailed off again.

There couldn't, I thought, be such an acute shortage of stable boys in England that they needed to be recruited from Australia.

'Will you come into the house?' I said. 'And explain?'

I led the way into the living-room, and heard his exclamation as he stepped behind me. All our visitors were impressed by the room. Across the far end a great expanse of window framed the most spectacular part of the lagoon and mountains, making them seem even closer and, to me, more overwhelming than ever. I sat down in an old bentwood rocker with my back to them, and gestured him into a comfortable arm-chair facing the view.

'Now, Mr. ... er?' I began.

'October,' he said easily. 'Not Mister. Earl.'

'October ... as the month?' It was October at the time.

'As the month,' he assented.

I looked at him curiously. He was not my idea of an earl. He looked like a hard-headed company chairman on holiday. Then it occurred to me that there was no bar to an earl being a company chairman as well, and that quite probably some of them needed to be.

'I have acted on impulse, coming here,' he said more coherently. 'And I am not sure that it is ever a good thing to do.' He paused, took out a machine-turned gold cigarette case, and gained time for thought while he flicked his lighter. I waited.

He smiled briefly. 'Perhaps I had better start by saying that I am in Australia on business – I have interests in Sydney – but that I came down here to the Snowies as the last part of a private tour I have been making of your main racing and breeding centres. I am a member of the body which governs National Hunt racing – that is to say, steeplechasing, jump racing – in England, and naturally your horses interest me enormously ... Well, I was lunching in Perlooma' he went on, referring to our nearest township, fifteen miles away, 'and I got talking to a man who remarked on my English accent and said that the only other pommie he knew was a stable-hand here who was fool enough to want to go back home.'

'Yes,' I agreed. 'Simmons.'

'Arthur Simmons,' he said, nodding. 'What sort of man is he?'

'Very good with horses,' I said. 'But he only wants to go back to England when he's drunk. And he only gets drunk in Perlooma. Never here.'

'Oh,' he said. 'Then wouldn't he go, if he were given the chance?'

'I don't know. It depends what you want him for.'

He drew on his cigarette, and tapped the ash off, and looked out of the window.

'A year or two ago we had a great deal of trouble with the doping of racehorses,' he said abruptly. 'A very great deal of trouble. There were trials and prison sentences, and stringent all-round tightening of stable security, and a stepping-up of regular saliva and urine tests. We began to test the first four horses in many races, to stop doping-to-win, and we tested every suspiciously beaten favourite for doping-to-lose. Nearly all the results since the new regulations came into force have been negative.'

'How satisfactory,' I said, not desperately interested.

'No. It isn't. Someone has discovered a drug which our analysts cannot identify.'

'That doesn't sound possible,' I said politely. The afternoon was slipping away unprofitably, I felt, and I still had a lot to do.

He sensed my lack of enthusiasm. 'There have been ten cases, all winners. Ten that we are sure of. The horses apparently look conspicuously stimulated – I haven't myself actually seen one – but nothing shows up in the tests.' He paused. 'Doping is nearly always an inside job,' he said, transferring his gaze back to me. 'That is to say, stable lads are nearly always involved somehow, even if it is only to point out to someone else which horse is in which box.' I nodded. Australia had had her troubles, too.

'We, that is to say, the other two Stewards of the National Hunt Committee, and myself, have once or twice discussed trying to find out about the doping from the inside, so to speak . . .'

'By getting a stable lad to spy for you?' I said.

He winced slightly. 'You Australians are so direct,' he murmured. 'But that was the general idea, yes. We didn't do anything more than talk about it, though, because there are many difficulties to such a plan and frankly we didn't see how we could positively guarantee that any lad we approached was not already working for . . . er . . . the other side.'

I grinned. 'And Arthur Simmons has that guarantee?'

'Yes. And as he's English, he would fade indistinguishably into the racing scene. It occurred to me as I was paying my bill after lunch. So I asked the way here and drove straight up, to see what he was like.'

'You can talk to him, certainly,' I said, standing up. 'But I don't think it will be any good.'

'He would be paid far in excess of the normal rate,' he said, misunderstanding me.

'I didn't mean that he couldn't be tempted to go,' I said, 'but he just hasn't the brain for anything like that.'

He followed me back out into the spring sunshine. The air at that altitude was still chilly and I saw him shiver as he left the warmth of the house. He glanced appraisingly at my still bare chest.

'If you'll wait a moment, I'll fetch him,' I said, and, walking round the corner of the house, whistled shrilly with my fingers in my teeth towards the small bunk-house across the yard. A head poked enquiringly out of a window, and I shouted 'I want Arthur.'

The head nodded, withdrew, and presently Arthur Simmons, elderly, small, bow-legged and of an endearing simplicity of mind, made his crab-like way towards me. I left him and Lord October together, and went over to see if the new filly had taken a firm hold on life. She had, though her efforts to stand on her poor misshapen foreleg were pathetic to see.

I left her with her mother, and went back towards Lord October, watching him from a distance taking a note from his wallet and offering it to Arthur. Arthur wouldn't accept it, even though he was English. He's been here so long, I thought, that he's as Australian as anyone. He'd hate to go back to Britain, whatever he says when he's drunk.

'You were right,' October said. 'He's a splendid chap, but no good for what I want. I didn't even suggest it.'

'Isn't it expecting a great deal of any stable lad, however bright, to uncover something which has got men like you up a gum-tree?'

He grimaced. 'Yes. That is one of the difficulties I mentioned. We're scraping the bottom of the barrel, though. Any idea is worth trying. Any. You can't realise how serious the situation is.'

We walked over to his car, and he opened the door.

'Well, thank you for your patience, Mr. Roke. As I said, it was an impulse, coming here. I hope I haven't wasted too much of your afternoon?' He smiled, still looking slightly hesitant and disconcerted.

I shook my head and smiled back and he started the car, turned it, and drove off down the road. He was out of my thoughts before he was through the gate-posts.

Out of my thoughts; but not by a long way out of my life.

He came back again the next day at sundown. I found him sitting patiently smoking in the small blue car, having no doubt discovered that there was no one in the house. I walked back towards him from the stable block where I had been doing my share of the evening's chores, and reflected idly that he had again caught me at my dirtiest.

He got out of the car when he saw me coming, and stamped on his cigarette.

'Mr. Roke.' He held out his hand, and I shook it.

This time he made no attempt to rush into speech. This time he had not come on impulse. There was absolutely no hesitation in his manner: instead, his natural air of authority was much more pronounced, and it struck me that it was with this power that he set out to persuade a boardroom full of hard directors to agree to an unpopular proposal.

I knew instantly, then, why he had come back.

I looked at him warily for a moment: then gestured towards the house, and led him again into the living-room.

'A drink?' I asked. 'Whisky?'

'Thank you.' He took the glass.

'If you don't mind,' I said, 'I will go and change.' And think, I added privately.

Alone in my room I showered and put on some decent trousers, socks and house-shoes, and a white poplin shirt with a navy blue silk tie. I brushed back my damp hair carefully in front of the mirror, and made sure my nails were clean. There was no point in entering an argument at a social disadvantage. Particularly with an earl as determined as this.

He stood up when I went back, and took in my changed appearance with one smooth glance.

I smiled fleetingly, and poured myself a drink, and another for him.

'I think,' he said, 'that you may have guessed why I am here.'

'Perhaps.'

'To persuade you to take the job I had in mind for Simmons,' he said without preamble, and without haste.

'Yes,' I said. I sipped my drink. 'And I can't do it.'

We stood there eyeing each other. I knew that what he was seeing was a good deal different from the Daniel Roke he had met before. More substantial. More the sort of person he would have expected to find, perhaps. Clothes maketh man, I thought wryly.

The day was fading, and I switched on the lights. The mountains outside the window retreated into darkness; just as well, as I judged I would need all my resolution, and they were both literally and figuratively ranged behind October. The trouble was, of course, that with more than half my mind I wanted to take a crack at his fantastic job. And I knew it was madness. I couldn't afford it, for one thing.

'I've learned a good deal about you now,' he said slowly. 'On my way from here yesterday it crossed my mind that it was a pity you were not Arthur Simmons; you would have been perfect. You did, if you will forgive me saying so, look the part.' He sounded apologetic.

'But not now?'

'You know you don't. You changed so that you wouldn't, I imagine. But you could again. Oh, I've no doubt that if I'd met you yesterday inside this house looking as civilised as you do at this moment, the thought would never have occurred to me. But when I saw you first, walking across the paddock very tattered and half bare and looking like a gypsy, I did in fact take you for the hired help . . . I'm sorry.'

I grinned faintly. 'It happens often, and I don't mind.'

'And there's your voice,' he said. 'That Australian accent of yours . . . I know it's not as strong as many I've heard, but it's as near to cockney as dammit, and I expect you could broaden it a bit. You see,' he went on firmly, as he saw I was about to interrupt, 'if you put an educated Englishman into a stable as a lad, the chances are the others would know at once by his voice that he wasn't genuine. But they couldn't tell, with you. You look right, and you sound right. You seem to me the perfect answer to all our problems. A better answer than I could have dreamt of finding.'

'Physically,' I commented dryly.

He drank, and looked at me thoughtfully.

'In every way. You forget, I told you I know a good deal about you now. By the time I reached Perlooma yesterday afternoon I had decided to . . . er . . . investigate you, one might say, to find out what sort of man you really were . . . to see if there were the slightest chance of your being attracted by such a . . . a job.' He drank again, and paused, waiting.

'I can't take on anything like that,' I said. 'I have enough to do here.'
The understatement of the month, I thought.

'Could you take on twenty thousand pounds?' He said it casually,
conversationally.

The short answer to that was 'Yes'; but instead, after a moment's
stillness, I said 'Australian, or English?'

His mouth curled down at the corners and his eyes narrowed. He was
amused.

'English. Of course,' he said ironically.

I said nothing. I simply looked at him. As if reading my thoughts he
sat down in an arm-chair, crossed his legs comfortably, and said 'I'll tell
you what you would do with it, if you like. You would pay the fees of
the medical school your sister Belinda has set her heart on. You would
send your younger sister Helen to art school, as she wants. You would
put enough aside for your thirteen-year-old brother Philip to become a
lawyer, if he is still of the same mind when he grows up. You could
employ more labour here, instead of working yourself into an early grave
feeding, clothing, and paying school fees for your family.'

I suppose I should have been prepared for him to be thorough, but I
felt a surge of anger that he should have pried so very intimately into my
affairs. However, since the time when an angry retort had cost me the
sale of a yearling who broke his leg the following week, I had learned
to keep my tongue still whatever the provocation.

'I also have had two girls and a boy to educate,' he said. 'I know what
it is costing you. My elder daughter is at university, and the twin boy
and girl have recently left school.'

When I again said nothing, he continued, 'You were born in England,
and were brought to Australia when you were a child. Your father,
Howard Roke, was a barrister, a good one. He and your mother were
drowned together in a sailing accident when you were eighteen. Since
then you have supported yourself and your sisters and brother by horse
dealing and breeding. I understand that you had intended to follow your
father into the law, but instead used the money he left to set up business
here, in what had been your holiday house. You have done well at it.
The horses you sell have a reputation for being well broken in and
beautifully mannered. You are thorough, and you are respected.'

He looked up at me, smiling. I stood stiffly. I could see there was still
more to come.

He said 'Your headmaster at Geelong says you had a brain and are
wasting it. Your bank manager says you spend little on yourself. Your
doctor says you haven't had a holiday since you settled here nine years
ago except for a month you spent in hospital once with a broken leg.
Your pastor says you never go to church, and he takes a poor view of it.'
He drank slowly.

Many doors, it seemed, were open to determined earls.

'And finally,' he added, with a lop-sided smile, 'the bar keeper of the
Golden Platypus in Perlooma says he'd trust you with his sister, in spite
of your good looks.'

'And what were your conclusions, after all that?' I asked, my resentment a little better under control.

'That you are a dull, laborious prig,' he said pleasantly.

I relaxed at that, and laughed, and sat down.

'Quite right,' I agreed.

'On the other hand, everyone says you do keep on with something once you start it, and you are used to hard physical work. You know so much about horses that you could do a stable lad's job with your eyes shut standing on your head.'

'The whole idea is screwy,' I said, sighing, 'It wouldn't work, not with me, or Arthur Simmons, or anybody. It just isn't feasible. There are hundreds of training stables in Britain, aren't there? You could live in them for months and hear nothing, while the dopers got strenuously to work all around you.'

He shook his head. 'I don't think so. There are surprisingly few dishonest lads, far fewer than you or most people would imagine. A lad known to be corruptible would attract all sorts of crooks like an unguarded gold-mine. All our man would have to do would be to make sure that the word was well spread that he was open to offers. He'd get them, no doubt of it.'

'But would he get the ones you want? I very much doubt it.'

'To me it seems a good enough chance to be worth taking. Frankly, any chance is worth taking, the way things are. We have tried everything else. And we have failed. We have failed in spite of exhaustive questioning of everyone connected with the affected horses. The police say they cannot help us. As we cannot analyse the drug being used, we can give them nothing to work on. We employed a firm of private investigators. They got nowhere at all. Direct action has achieved absolutely nothing. Indirect action cannot achieve less. I am willing to gamble twenty thousand pounds that with you it can achieve more. Will you do it?'

'I don't know,' I said, and cursed my weakness. I should have said, 'No, certainly not.'

He pounced on it, leaning forward and talking more rapidly, every word full of passionate conviction. 'Can I make you understand how concerned my colleagues and I are over these undetectable cases of doping? I own several racehorses – mostly steeplechasers – and my family for generations have been lovers and supporters of racing . . . The health of the sport means more to me, and people like me, than I can possibly say . . . and for the second time in three years it is being seriously threatened. During the last big wave of doping there were satirical jokes in the papers and on television, and we simply cannot afford to have it happen again. So far we have been able to stifle comment because the cases are still fairly widely spaced – it is well over a year since the first – and if anyone enquires we merely report that the tests were negative. But we *must* identify this new dope before there is a widespread increase in its use. Otherwise it will become a worse menace to racing than anything which has happened before. If dozens of undetectably doped winners start turning up, public faith will be destroyed altogether, and steeplechasing will suffer damage which it will take years to recover from, if it ever does. There is much more at stake than a pleasant pastime. Racing is an industry employing thousands of people . . . and not the least of them are stud owners like you. The collapse of public support would mean a great deal of hardship.

'You may think that I have offered you an extraordinarily large sum of money to come over and see if you can help us, but I am a rich man, and, believe me, the continuance of racing is worth a great deal more than that to me. My horses won nearly that amount in prize money last season, and if it can buy a chance of wiping out this threat I will spend it gladly.'

'You are much more vehement today,' I said slowly, 'than you were yesterday.'

He sat back. 'Yesterday I didn't need to convince you. But I felt just the same.'

'There must be someone in England who can dig out the information you want,' I protested. 'People who know the ins and outs of your racing. I know nothing at all. I left your country when I was nine. I'd be useless. It's impossible.'

That's better, I approved myself. That's much firmer.

He looked down at his glass, and spoke as if with reluctance. 'Well . . . we did approach someone in England . . . A racing journalist, actually. Very good nose for news: very discreet, too; we thought he was just the chap. Unfortunately he dug away without success for some weeks. And then he was killed in a car crash, poor fellow.'

'Why not try someone else?' I persisted.

'It was only in June that he died, during steeplechasing's summer recess. The new season started in August and it was not until after that that we thought of the stable lad idea, with all its difficulties.'

'Try a farmer's son,' I suggested. 'Country accent, knowledge of horses . . . the lot.'

He shook his head. 'England is too small. Send a farmer's son to walk a horse round the parade ring at the races, and what he was doing would soon be no secret. Too many people would recognise him, and ask questions.'

'A farm worker's son, then, with a high I.Q.'

'Do we hold an exam?' he said sourly.

There was a pause, and he looked up from his glass. His face was solemn, almost severe.

'Well?' he said.

I meant to say 'No,' firmly. What I actually said was again 'I don't know.'

'What can I say to persuade you?'

'Nothing,' I said. 'I'll think about it. I'll let you know tomorrow.'

'Very well.' He stood up, declined my offer of a meal, and went away as he had come, the strength of his personality flowing out of him like heat. The house felt empty when I went back from seeing him off.

The full moon blazed in the black sky, and through a gap in the hills behind me Mount Kosciusko distantly stretched its blunt snow-capped summit into the light. I sat on a rock high up on the mountain, looking down on my home.

There lay the lagoon, the big pasture paddocks stretching away to the bush, the tidy white-railed small paddocks near the house, the silvery roof of the foaling boxes, the solid bulk of the stable block, the bunk-house, the long low graceful shape of the dwelling house with a glitter of moonlight in the big window at the end.

There lay my prison.

It hadn't been bad at first. There were no relations to take care of us, and I had found it satisfying to disappoint the people who said I couldn't earn enough to keep three small children, Belinda and Helen and Philip, with me. I liked horses, I always had, and from the beginning the business went fairly well. We all ate, anyway, and I even convinced myself that the law was not really my vocation after all.

My parents had planned to send Belinda and Helen to Frensham, and when the time came, they went. I dare say I could have found a cheaper school, but I had to try to give them what I had had ... and that was why Philip was away at Geelong. The business had grown progressively, but so had the school fees and the men's wages and the maintenance costs. I was caught in a sort of upward spiral, and too much depended on my being able to keep on going. The leg I had broken in a steeplechase when I was twenty-two had caused the worst financial crisis of the whole nine years: and I had had no choice but to give up doing anything so risky.

I didn't grudge the unending labour. I was very fond of my sisters and brother. I had no regrets at all that I had done what I had. But the feeling that I had built a prosperous trap for myself had slowly eaten away the earlier contentment I had found in providing for them.

In another eight or ten years they would all be grown, educated and married, and my job would be done. In another ten years I would be thirty-seven. Perhaps I too would be married by then, and have some children of my own, and send them to Frensham and Geelong ... For more than four years I had done my best to stifle a longing to escape. It was easier when they were at home in the holidays, with the house ringing with their noise and Philip's carpentry all over the place and the girls' frillies hanging to dry in the bathroom. In the summer we rode or swam in the lagoon (the lake, as my English parents called it) and in the winter we ski-ed on the mountains. They were very good company and never took anything they had for granted. Nor, now that they were growing up, did they seem to be suffering from any form of teenage rebellions. They were, in fact, thoroughly rewarding.

It usually hit me about a week after they had gone back to school, this fierce aching desperation to be free. Free for a good long while: to go further than the round of horse sales, further than the occasional quick trip to Sidney or Melbourne or Cooma.

To have something else to remember but the procession of profitable days, something else to see besides the beauty with which I was sur-rounded. I had been so busy stuffing worms down my fellow nestlings' throats that I had never stretched my wings.

Telling myself that these thoughts were useless, that they were self-pity, that my unhappiness was unreasonable, did no good at all. I continued at night to sink into head-holding miseries of depression, and kept these moods out of my days – and my balance sheets – only by working to my limit.

When Lord October came the children had been back at school for eleven days, and I was sleeping badly. That may be why I was sitting on a mountain side at four o'clock in the morning trying to decide whether or not to take a peculiar job as a stable lad on the other side of the world. The door of the cage had been opened for me, all right. But the tit-bit that had been dangled to tempt me out seemed suspiciously large.

Twenty thousand English pounds . . . A great deal of money. But then he couldn't know of my restless state of mind, and he might think that a smaller sum would make no impression. (What, I wondered, had he been prepared to pay Arthur?)

On the other hand, there was the racing journalist who had died in a car crash . . . If October or his colleagues had the slightest doubt it was an accident, that too would explain the size of his offer, as conscience money. Throughout my youth, owing to my father's profession, I had learned a good deal about crime and criminals, and I knew too much to dismiss the idea of an organised accident as fantastic nonsense.

I had inherited my father's bent for orderliness and truth and had grown up appreciating the logic of his mind, though I had often thought him too ruthless with innocent witnesses in court. My own view had always been that justice should be done and that my father did the world no good by getting the guilty acquitted, I would never make a barrister, he said, if I thought like that. I'd better be a policeman, instead.

England, I thought. Twenty thousand pounds. Detection. To be honest, the urgency with which October viewed the situation had not infected me. English racing was on the other side of the world. I knew no one engaged in it. I cared frankly little whether it had a good or a bad reputation. If I went it would be no altruistic crusade: I would be going only because the adventure appealed to me, because it looked amusing and a challenge, because it beckoned me like a siren to fling responsibility to the wind and cut the self-imposed shackles off my wilting spirit.

Common sense said that the whole idea was crazy, that the Earl of October was an irresponsible nut, that I hadn't any right to leave my family to fend for themselves while I went gallivanting round the world, and that the only possible course open to me was to stay where I was, and learn to be content.

Common sense lost.

Chapter Two

Nine days later I flew to England in a Boeing 707.

I slept soundly for most of the thirty-six hours from Sydney to Darwin, from Darwin to Singapore, Rangoon and Calcutta, from Calcutta to Karachi and Damascus, and from Damascus to Dusseldorf and London Airport.

Behind me I left a crowded week into which I had packed months of paper-work and a host of practical arrangements. Part of the difficulty was that I didn't know how long I would be away, but I reckoned that if I hadn't done the job in six months I wouldn't be able to do it at all, and made that a basis for my plans.

The head stud-groom was to have full charge of the training and sale of the horses already on the place, but not to buy or breed any more. A firm of contractors agreed to see to the general maintenance of the land and buildings. The woman currently cooking for the lads who lived in the bunk-house assured me that she would look after the family when they came back for the long Christmas summer holiday from December to February.

I arranged with the bank manager that I should send post-dated cheques for the next term's school fees and for the fodder and tack for the horses, and I wrote a pile for the head groom to cash one at a time for the men's food and wages. October assured me that 'my fee' would be transferred to my account without delay.

'If I don't succeed, you shall have your money back, less what it has cost me to be away,' I told him.

He shook his head, but I insisted; and in the end we compromised. I was to have ten thousand outright, and the other half if my mission were successful.

I took October to my solicitors and had the rather unusual appointment shaped into a dryly-worded legal contract, to which, with a wry smile, he put his signature alongside mine.

His amusement, however, disappeared abruptly when, as we left, I asked him to insure my life.

'I don't think I can,' he said, frowning.

'Because I would be . . . uninsurable?' I asked.

He didn't answer.

'I have signed a contract,' I pointed out. 'Do you think I did it with my eyes shut?'

'It was your idea.' He looked troubled. 'I won't hold you to it.'

'What really happened to the journalist?' I asked.

He shook his head and didn't meet my eyes. 'I don't know. It looked like an accident. It almost certainly *was* an accident. He went off the road at night on a bend on the Yorkshire moors. The car caught fire as it rolled down into the valley. He hadn't a hope. He was a nice chap . . .'

'It won't deter me if you have any reason for thinking it was not an accident,' I said seriously, 'but you must be frank. If it was not an accident, he must have made a lot of progress . . . he must have found out something pretty vital . . . it would be important to me to know where he had gone and what he had been doing during the days before he died.'

'Did you think about all this before you agreed to accept my proposition?'

'Yes, of course.'

He smiled as if a load had been lifted from him. 'By God, Mr. Roke, the more I see of you the more thankful I am I stopped for lunch in Perlooma and went to look for Arthur Simmons. Well . . . Tommy Stapleton – the journalist – was a good driver, but I suppose accidents can happen to anyone. It was a Sunday early in June. Monday, really. He died about two o'clock at night. A local man said the road was normal in appearance at one-thirty, and at two-thirty a couple going home from a party saw the broken railings on the bend and stopped to look. The car was still smouldering: they could see the red glow of it in the valley, and they drove on into the nearest town to report it.

'The police think Stapleton went to sleep at the wheel. Easy enough to do. But they couldn't find out where he had been between leaving the house of some friends at five o'clock, and arriving on the Yorkshire moors. The journey would have taken him only about an hour, which left nine hours unaccounted for. No one ever came forward to say he'd spent the evening with them, though the story was in most of the papers. I believe it was suggested he could have been with another man's wife . . . someone who had a good reason for keeping quiet. Anyway, the whole thing was treated as a straightforward accident.

'As to where he had been during the days before . . . we did find out, discreetly. He'd done nothing and been nowhere that he didn't normally do in the course of his job. He'd come up from the London offices of his newspaper on the Thursday, gone to Bogside races on the Friday and Saturday, stayed with friends near Hexham, Northumberland, over the week-end, and, as I said, left them at five on Sunday, to drive back to London. They said he had been his normal charming self the whole time.

'We, that is, the other two Stewards and I – asked the Yorkshire police to let us see anything they salvaged from the car, but there was nothing of any interest to us. His leather briefcase was found undamaged half-way down the hillside, near one of the rear doors which had been wrenched off during the somersaulting, but there was nothing in it besides the usual form books and racing papers. We looked carefully. He lived with his mother and sister – he was unmarried – and they let us search their house for anything he might have written down for us. There was nothing. We also contacted the sports editor of his paper and asked to see any possessions he had left in his office. There were only a few personal oddments and an envelope containing some press cuttings about doping.

We kept that. You can see them when you get to England. But I'm afraid they will be no use to you. They were very fragmentary.'

'I see,' I said. We walked along the street to where our two cars were parked, his hired blue Holden, and my white utility. Standing beside the two dusty vehicles I remarked. 'You want to believe it was an accident ... I think you want to believe it very much.'

He nodded soberly. 'It is appallingly disturbing to think anything else. If it weren't for those nine missing hours one would have no doubt at all.'

I shrugged. 'He could have spent them in dozens of harmless ways. In a bar. Having dinner. In a cinema. Picking up a girl.'

'Yes, he could,' he said. But the doubt remained, both in his mind and mine.

He was to drive the hired Holden back to Sydney the following day and fly to England. He shook hands with me in the street and gave me his address in London, where I was to meet him again. With the door open and with one foot in the car he said, 'I suppose it would be part of your ... er ... procedure ... to appear as a slightly, shall we say, unreliable type of stable lad, so that the crooked element would take to you?'

'Definitely,' I grinned.

'Then, if I might suggest it, it would be a good idea for you to grow a couple of sideburns. It's surprising what a lot of distrust can be caused by an inch of extra hair in front of the ears!'

I laughed. 'A good idea.'

'And don't bring many clothes,' he added. 'I'll fix you up with British stuff suitable for your new character.'

'All right.'

He slid down behind the wheel.

'Au revoir, then, Mr. Roke.'

'Au revoir, Lord October,' I said.

After he had gone, and without his persuasive force at my elbow, what I was planning to do seemed less sensible than ever. But then I was tired to death of being sensible. I went on working from dawn to midnight to clear the decks, and found myself waking each morning with impatience to be on my way.

Two days before I was due to leave I flew down to Geelong to say goodbye to Philip and explain to his headmaster that I was going to Europe for a while; I didn't know exactly how long, I came back via Frensham to see my sisters, both of whom exclaimed at once over the dark patches of stubble which were already giving my face the required 'unreliable' appearance.

'For heaven's sake shave them off,' said Belinda. 'They're far too sexy. Most of the seniors are crazy about you already and if they see you like that you'll be mobbed.'

'That sounds delicious,' I said, grinning at them affectionately.

Helen, nearly sixteen, was fair and gentle and as graceful as the flowers she liked to draw. She was the most dependent of the three, and had suffered worst from not having a mother.

'Do you mean,' she said anxiously, 'that you will be away the whole summer?' She looked as if Mount Kosciusko had crumbled.

'You'll be all right. You're nearly grown up now,' I teased her.

'But the holidays will be so dull.'

'Ask some friends to stay, then.'

'Oh!' Her face cleared. 'Can we? Yes. That would be fun.'

She kissed me more happily goodbye, and went back to her lessons.

My eldest sister and I understood each other very well, and to her alone, knowing I owed it to her, I told the real purpose of my 'holiday'. She was upset, which I had not expected.

'Dearest Dan,' she said, twining her arm in mine and sniffing to stop herself crying, 'I know that bringing us up has been a grind for you, and if for once you want to do something for your own sake, we ought to be glad, only please do be careful. We do . . . we do want you back.'

'I'll come back,' I promised helplessly, lending her my handkerchief. 'I'll come back.'

The taxi from the air terminal brought me through a tree-filled square to the Earl of October's London house in a grey drizzle which in no way matched my spirits. Light-hearted, that was me. Springs in my heels.

In answer to my ring the elegant black door was opened by a friendly-faced manservant who took my grip from my hand and said that as his lordship was expecting me he would take me up at once. 'Up' turned out to be a crimson-walled drawing-room on the first floor where round an electric heater in an Adam fireplace three men stood with glasses in their hands. Three men standing easily, their heads turned towards the opening door. Three men radiating as one the authority I had been aware of in October. They were the ruling triumvirate of National Hunt racing. Big guns. Established and entrenched behind a hundred years of traditional power. They weren't taking the affair as effervescently as I was.

'Mr. Roke, my lord,' said the manservant, showing me in.

October came across the room to me and shook hands.

'Good trip?'

'Yes, thank you.'

He turned towards the other men. 'My two co-Stewards arranged to be here to welcome you.'

'My name is Macclesfield,' said the taller of them, an elderly stooping man with riotous white hair. He leaned forward and held out a sinewy hand. 'I am most interested to meet you, Mr. Roke.' He had a hawk-eyed piercing stare.

'And this is Colonel Beckett.' He gestured to the third man, a slender ill-looking person who shook hands also, but with a weak limp grasp. All three of them paused and looked at me as if I had come from outer space.

'I am at your disposal,' I said politely.

'Yes . . . well, we may as well get straight down to business,' said October, directing me to a hide-covered armchair. 'But a drink first?'

'Thank you.'

He gave me a glass of the smoothest whisky I'd ever tasted, and they all sat down.

'My horses,' October began, speaking easily, conversationally, 'are trained in the stable block adjoining my house in Yorkshire. I do not train them myself, because I am away too often on business. A man named Inskip holds the licence – a public licence – and apart from my own horses he trains several for my friends. At present there are about thirty-five horses in the yard, of which eleven are my own. We think it would be best if you started work as a lad in my stable, and then you can move on somewhere else when you think it is necessary. Clear so far?'

I nodded.

He went on, 'Inskip is an honest man, but unfortunately he's also a bit of a talker, and we consider it essential for your success that he should not have any reason to chatter about the way you joined the stable. The hiring of lads is always left to him, so it will have to be he, not I, who hires you.

'In order to make certain that we are short-handed – so that your application for work will be immediately accepted – Colonel Beckett and Sir Stuart Macclesfield are each sending three young horses to the stables two days from now. The horses are no good, I may say, but they're the best we could do in the time.'

They all smiled. And well they might. I began to admire their staff work.

'In four days, when everyone is beginning to feel over-worked, you will arrive in the yard and offer your services. All right?'

'Yes.'

'Here is a reference.' He handed me an envelope. 'It is from a woman cousin of mine in Cornwall who keeps a couple of hunters. I have arranged that if Inskip checks with her she will give you a clean bill. You can't appear too doubtful in character to begin with, you see, or Inskip will not employ you.'

'I understand,' I said.

'Inskip will ask you for your insurance card and an income tax form which you would normally have brought on from your last job. Here they are.' He gave them to me. 'The insurance card is stamped up to date and is no problem as it will not be queried in any way until next May, by which time we hope there will be no more need for it. The income tax situation is more difficult, but we have constructed the form so that the address on the part which Inskip has to send off to the Inland Revenue people when he engages you is illegible. Any amount of natural-looking confusion should arise from that; and the fact that you were not working in Cornwall should be safely concealed.'

'I see,' I said. And I was impressed as well.

Sir Stuart Macclesfield cleared his throat and Colonel Beckett pinched the bridge of his nose between the thumb and forefinger.

'About this dope,' I said, 'you told me your analysts couldn't identify it, but you didn't give me any details. What is it that makes you positive it is being used?'

October glanced at Macclesfield, who said in his slow rasping elderly voice. 'When a horse comes in from a race frothing at the mouth with his eyes popping out and his body drenched in sweat, one naturally suspects that he has been given a stimulant of some kind. Dopers usually run into trouble with stimulants, since it is difficult to judge the dosage needed to get a horse to win without arousing suspicion. If you had seen any of these particular horses we have tested, you would have sworn that they had been given a big overdose. But the test results were always negative.'

'What do your pharmacists say?' I asked.

Beckett said sardonically, 'Word for word? It's blasphemous.'

I grinned. 'The gist.'

Beckett said, 'They simply say there isn't a dope they can't identify.'

'How about adrenalin?' I asked.

The Stewards exchanged glances, and Beckett said, 'Most of the horses concerned did have a fairly high adrenalin count, but you can't tell from one analysis whether that is normal for that particular horse or not. Horses vary tremendously in the amount of adrenalin they produce naturally, and you would have to test them before and after several races to establish their normal output, and also at various stages of their training. Only when you know their normal levels could you say whether any extra had been pumped into them. From the practical point of view . . . adrenalin can't be given by mouth, as I expect you know. It has to be injected, and it works instantaneously. These horses were all calm and cool when they went to the starting gate. Horses which have been stimulated with adrenalin are pepped up at that point. In addition to that, a horse often shows at once that he has had a subcutaneous adrenalin injection because the hairs for some way round the site of the puncture stand up on end and give the game away. Only an injection straight into the jugular vein is really foolproof; but it is a very tricky process, and we are quite certain that it was not done in these cases.'

'The lab chaps,' said October, 'told us to look out for something mechanical. All sorts of things have been tried in the past, you see. Electric shocks, for instance. Jockeys used to have saddles or whips made with batteries concealed in them so that they could run bursts of current into the horses they were riding and galvanize them into winning. The horses' own sweat acted as a splendid conductor. We went into all that sort of thing very thoroughly indeed, and we are firmly of the opinion that none of the jockeys involved carried anything out of the ordinary in any of their equipment.'

'We have collected all our notes, all the lab notes, dozens of press cuttings, and anything else we thought could be of the slightest help,' said Macclesfield, pointing to three boxes of files which lay in a pile on a table by my elbow.

'And you have four days to read them and think about them,' added October, smiling faintly. 'There is a room ready for you here, and my man will look after you. I am sorry I cannot be with you, but I have to return to Yorkshire tonight.'

Beckett looked at his watch and rose slowly. 'I must be going, Edward.' To me, with a glance as alive and shrewd as his physique was failing, he said, 'You'll do. And make it fairly snappy, will you? Time's against us.'

I thought October looked relieved. I was sure of it when Macclesfield shook my hand again and rasped. 'Now that you're actually here the whole scheme suddenly seems more possible ... Mr. Roke, I sincerely wish you every success.'

October went down to the street door with them, and came back and looked at me across the crimson room.

'They are sold on you, Mr. Roke, I am glad to say.'

Upstairs in the luxurious deep-green carpeted, brass bedsteaded guest room where I slept for the next four nights I found the manservant had unpacked the few clothes I had brought with me and put them tidily on the shelves of a heavy Edwardian wardrobe. On the floor beside my own canvas and leather grip stood a cheap fibre suitcase with rust-marked locks. Amused, I explored its contents. On top there was a thick sealed envelope with my name on it. I slit it open and found it was packed with five-pound notes; forty of them, and an accompanying slip which read 'Bread for throwing on waters.' I laughed aloud.

Under the envelope October had provided everything from under-clothes to washing things, jodhpur boots to rainproof, jeans to pyjamas.

Another note from him was tucked into the neck of a black leather jacket.

'This jacket completes what sideburns begin. Wearing both, you won't have any character to speak of. They are regulation dress for delinquents! Good luck.'

I eyed the jodhpur boots. They were second-hand and needed polishing, but to my surprise, when I slid my feet into them, they were a good fit. I took them off and tried on a violently pointed pair of black walking shoes. Horrible, but they fitted comfortably also, and I kept them on to get my feet (and eyes) used to them.

The three box files, which I had carried up with me after October had left for Yorkshire, were stacked on a low table next to a small arm-chair, and with a feeling that there was no more time to waste I sat down, opened the first of them, and began to read.

Because I went painstakingly slowly through every word, it took me two days to finish all the papers in those boxes. And at the end of it found myself staring at the carpet without a helpful idea in my head. There were accounts, some in typescript, some in longhand, of interviews the Stewards had held with the trainers, jockeys, head travelling-lads, stable lads, blacksmiths and veterinary surgeons connected with the eleven horses suspected of being doped. There was a lengthy report from a firm of private investigators who had interviewed dozens of stable lads in 'places of refreshment', and got nowhere. A memo ten pages long from a bookmaker went into copious details of the market which had been made on the horses concerned: but the last sentence summed it up: 'We can trace no one person or syndicate which has won consistently on these horses, and therefore conclude that if any one person or syndicate is involved, their betting was done on the Tote.' Further down the box I found a letter from Tote Investors Ltd., saying that not one of their credit clients had backed all the horses concerned, but that of course they had no check on cash betting at racecourses.

The second box contained eleven laboratory reports of analyses made on urine and saliva samples. The first report referred to a horse called Charcoal and was dated eighteen months earlier. The last gave details of tests made on a horse called Rudyard as recently as September, when October was in Australia.

The word 'negative' had been written in a neat hand at the end of each report.

The press had had a lot of trouble dodging the laws of libel. The clippings from daily papers in the third box contained such sentences as 'Charcoal displayed a totally uncharacteristic turn of foot,' and 'In the unsaddling enclosure Rudyard appeared to be considerably excited by his success.'

There were fewer references to Charcoal and the following three horses, but at that point someone had employed a news-gathering agency: the last seven cases were documented by clippings from several daily, evening, local and sporting papers.

At the bottom of the clippings I came across a medium sized manilla envelope. On it was written 'Received from Sports Editor, Daily Scope, June 10th'. This, I realised, was the packet of cuttings collected by Stapleton, the unfortunate journalist, and I opened the envelope with much curiosity. But to my great disappointment, because I badly needed some help, all the clippings except three were duplicates of those I had already read.

Of these three, one was a personality piece on the woman owner of Charcoal, one was an account of a horse (not one of the eleven) going berserk and killing a woman on June 3 in the paddock at Cartmel, Lancashire, and the third was a long article from a racing weekly discussing famous cases of doping, how they had been discovered and how dealt with. I read this attentively, with minimum results.

After all this unfruitful concentration I spent the whole of the next day wandering round London, breathing in the city's fumes with a heady feeling of liberation, asking the way frequently and listening carefully to the voices which replied.

In the matter of my accent I thought October had been too hopeful, because two people, before midday, commented on my being Australian. My parents had retained their Englishness until their deaths, but at nine I had found it prudent not to be 'different' at school, and had adopted the speech of my new country from that age. I could no longer shed it, even if I had wanted to, but if it was to sound like cockney English, it would clearly have to be modified.

I drifted eastwards, walking, asking, listening. Gradually I came to the conclusion that if I knocked off the aitches and didn't clip the ends of my words, I might get by. I practised that all afternoon, and finally managed to alter a few vowel sounds as well. No one asked me where I came from, which I took as a sign of success, and when I asked the last man, a barrow-boy, where I could catch a bus back to the West, I could no longer detect much difference between my question and his answer.

I made one purchase, a zip-pocketed money belt made of strong canvas webbing. It buckled flat round my waist under my shirt, and into it I packed the two hundred pounds; wherever I was going I thought I might be glad to have that money readily available.

In the evening, refreshed, I tried to approach the doping problem from another angle, by seeing if the horses had had anything in common.

Apparently they hadn't. All were trained by different trainers. All were owned by different owners: and all had been ridden by different jockeys. The only thing they all had in common was that they had nothing in common.

I sighed, and went to bed.

Terence, the manservant, with whom I had reached a reserved but definite friendship, woke me on the fourth morning by coming into my room with a laden breakfast tray.

'The condemned man ate hearty,' he observed, lifting a silver cover and allowing me a glimpse and a sniff of a plateful of eggs and bacon.'

'What do you mean?' I said, yawning contentedly.

'I don't know what you and his lordship are up to, sir, but wherever you are going it is different from what you are used to. That suit of yours, for instance, didn't come from the same sort of place as this little lot.'

He picked up the fibre suitcase, put it on a stool, and opened the locks. Carefully, as if they had been silk, he laid out on a chair some cotton pants and a checked cotton shirt, followed by a tan coloured ribbed pullover, some drain-pipe charcoal trousers and black socks. With a look of disgust he picked up the black leather jacket and draped it over the chair back, and neatly arranged the pointed shoes.

'His Lordship said I was to make certain that you left behind everything you came with, and took only these things with you,' he said regretfully.

'Did you buy them?' I asked, amused, 'or was it Lord October?'

'His Lordship bought them.' He smiled suddenly as he went over to the door. 'I'd love to have seen him pushing around in that chain store among all those bustling women.'

I finished my breakfast, bathed, shaved, and dressed from head to foot in the new clothes, putting the black jacket on top and zipping up the front. Then I brushed the hair on top of my head forwards instead of back, so that the short black ends curved on to my forehead.

Terence came back for the empty tray and found me standing looking at myself in a full-length mirror. Instead of grinning at him as usual I turned slowly round on my heel and treated him to a hard, narrow-eyed stare.

'Holy hell!' he said explosively.

'Good,' I said cheerfully. 'You wouldn't trust me then?'

'Not as far as I could throw that wardrobe.'

'What other impressions do I make on you? Would you give me a job?'

'You wouldn't get through the front door here, for a start. Basement entrance, if any. I'd check your references carefully before I took you on; and I don't think I'd have you at all if I wasn't desperate. You look shifty ... and a bit ... well ... almost dangerous.'

I unzipped the leather jacket and let it flap open, showing the checked shirt collar and tan pullover underneath. The effect was altogether sloppier.

'How about now?' I asked.

He put his head on one side, considering. 'Yes, I might give you a job now. You look much more ordinary. Not much more honest, but less hard to handle.'

'Thank you, Terence. That's exactly the note, I think. Ordinary but dishonest.' I smiled with pleasure. 'I'd better be on my way.'

'You haven't got anything of your own with you?'

'Only my watch,' I assured him.

'Fine,' he said.

I noticed with interest that for the first time in four days he had failed to punctuate any sentence with an easy, automatic 'sir', and when I picked up the cheap suitcase he made no move to take it from me and carry it himself, as he had done with my grip when I arrived.

We went downstairs to the street door where I shook hands with him and thanked him for looking after me so well, and gave him a five pound note. One of October's. He took it with a smile and stood with it in his hand, looking at me in my new character.

I grinned at him widely.

'Goodbye Terence.'

'Goodbye, and thank you ... sir,' he said; and I walked off leaving him laughing.

The next intimation I had that my change of clothes meant a violent drop in status came from the taxi driver I hailed at the bottom of the square. He refused to take me to King's Cross station until I had shown him that I had enough money to pay his fare. I caught the noon train to Harrogate and intercepted several disapproving glances from a prim middle-aged man with frayed cuffs sitting opposite me. This was all satisfactory, I thought, looking out at the damp autumn countryside flying past; this assures me that I do immediately make a dubious impression. It was rather a lop-sided thing to be pleased about.

From Harrogate I caught a country bus to the small village of Slaw, and having asked the way walked the last two miles to October's place, arriving just before six o'clock, the best time of day for seeking work in a stable.

Sure enough, they were rushed off their feet: I asked for the head lad, and he took me with him to Inskip, who was doing his evening round of inspection.

Inskip looked me over and pursed his lips. He was a stringy, youngish man with spectacles, sparse sandy hair, and a sloppy-looking mouth.

'References?' In contrast, his voice was sharp and authoritative.

I took the letter from October's Cornish cousin out of my pocket and gave it to him. He opened the letter, read it, and put it away in his own pocket.

'You haven't been with racehorses before, then?'

'No.'

'When could you start?'

'Now,' I indicated my suitcase.

He hesitated, but not for long. 'As it happens, we are short-handed. We'll give you a try. Wally, arrange a bed for him with Mrs. Allnut, and he can start in the morning. Usual wages,' he added to me, 'eleven pounds a week, and three pounds of that goes to Mrs. Allnut for your keep. You can give me your cards tomorrow. Right?'

'Yes,' I said: and I was in.

Chapter Three

I edged gently into the life of the yard like a heretic into heaven, trying not to be discovered and flung out before I became part of the scenery. On my first evening I spoke almost entirely in monosyllables, because I didn't trust my new accent, but I slowly found out that the lads talked with such a variety of regional accents themselves that my cockney-Australian passed without comment.

Wally, the head lad, a wiry short man with ill-fitting dentures, said I was to sleep in the cottage where about a dozen unmarried lads lived, beside the gate into the yard. I was shown into a small crowded upstairs room containing six beds, a wardrobe, two chests of drawers, and four bedside chairs; which left roughly two square yards of clear space in the centre. Thin flowered curtains hung at the windows, and there was polished linoleum on the floor.

My bed proved to have developed a deep sag in the centre over the years, but it was comfortable enough, and was made up freshly with white sheets and grey blankets. Mrs. Allnut, who took me in without a second glance, was a round, cheerful little person with hair fastened in a twist on top of her head. She kept the cottage spotless and stood over the lads to make sure they washed. She cooked well, and the food was plain but plentiful. All in all, it was a good billet.

I walked a bit warily to start with, but it was easier to be accepted and to fade into the background than I had imagined.

Once or twice during the first few days I stopped myself just in time from absent-mindedly telling another lad what to do; nine years' habit died hard. And I was surprised, and a bit dismayed, by the subservient attitude every one had to Inskip, at least to his face: my own men treated me at home with far more familiarity. The fact that I paid and they earned gave me no rights over them as men, and this we all clearly understood. But at Inskip's, and throughout all England, I gradually realised, there was far less of the almost aggressive egalitarianism of Australia. The lads, on the whole, seemed to accept that in the eyes of the world they were of secondary importance as human beings to Inskip and October. I thought this extraordinary, undignified, and shameful. And I kept my thoughts to myself.

Wally, scandalised by the casual way I had spoken on my arrival, told me to call Inskip 'Sir' and October 'My lord' – and said that if I was a ruddy communist I could clear off at once: so I quickly exhibited what he called a proper respect for my betters.

On the other hand it was precisely because the relationship between me and my own men was so free and easy that I found no difficulty in becoming a lad amongst lads. I felt no constraint on their part and, once the matter of accents had been settled, no self-consciousness on mine. But I did come to realise that what October had implied was undoubtedly true: had I stayed in England and gone to Eton (instead of its equivalent, Geelong) I could not have fitted so readily into his stable.

Inskip allotted me to three newly arrived horses, which was not very good from my point of view as it meant that I could not expect to be sent to a race meeting with them. They were neither fit nor entered for races, and it would be weeks before they were ready to run, even if they proved to be good enough. I pondered the problem while I carried their hay and water and cleaned their boxes and rode them out at morning exercise with the string.

On my second evening October came round at six with a party of house guests. Inskip, knowing in advance, had had everyone running to be finished in good time and walked round himself first, to make sure that all was in order.

Each lad stood with whichever of his horses was nearest the end from which the inspection was started. October and his friends, accompanied by Inskip and Wally, moved along from box to box, chatting, laughing, discussing each horse as they went.

When they came to me October flicked me a glance, and said, 'You're new, aren't you?'

'Yes, my lord.'

He took no further notice of me then, but when I had bolted the first horse in for the night and waited further down the yard with the second one, he came over to pat my charge and feel his legs; and as he straightened up he gave me a mischievous wink. With difficulty, since I was facing the other men, I kept a dead-pan face. He blew his nose to stop himself laughing. We were neither of us very professional at this cloak and dagger stuff.

When they had gone, and after I had eaten the evening meal with the other lads, I walked down to the Slaw pub with two of them. Half way through the first drinks I left them and went and telephoned to October.

'Who is speaking?' a man's voice inquired.

I was stumped for a second: then I said 'Perlooma,' knowing that that would fetch him.

He came on the line. 'Anything wrong?'

'No,' I said. 'Does anyone at the local exchange listen to your calls?'

'I wouldn't bet on it.' He hesitated. 'Where are you?'

'Slaw, in the phone box at your end of the village.'

'I have guests for dinner; will tomorrow do?'

'Yes.'

He paused for thought. 'Can you tell me what you want?'

'Yes,' I said. 'The form books for the last seven or eight seasons, and every scrap of information you can possibly dig up about the eleven . . . subjects.'

'What are you looking for?'

'I don't know yet,' I said.

'Do you want anything else?'

'Yes, but it needs discussion.'

He thought. 'Behind the stable yard there is a stream which comes down from the moors. Walk up beside it tomorrow, after lunch.'

'Right.'

I hung up, and went back to my interrupted drink in the pub.

'You've been a long time,' said Paddy, one of the lads I had come with. 'We're one ahead of you. What have you been doing – reading the walls in the Gents?'

'There's some remarks on them walls,' mused the other lad, a gawky boy of eighteen, 'that I haven't fathomed yet.'

'Nor you don't want to,' said Paddy approvingly. At forty he acted as unofficial father to many of the younger lads.

They slept one each side of me, Paddy and Grits, in the little dormitory. Paddy, as sharp as Grits was slow, was a tough little Irishman with eyes that never missed a trick. From the first minute I hoisted my suitcase on to the bed and unpacked my night things under his inquisitive gaze I had been glad that October had been so insistent about a complete change of clothes.

'How about another drink?'

'One more, then,' assented Paddy. 'I can just about run to it, I reckon.'

I took the glasses to the bar and bought refills: there was a pause while Paddy and Grits dug into their pockets and repaid me elevenpence each. The beer, which to me, tasted strong and bitter was not, I thought, worth four miles' walk, but many of the lads, it appeared, had bicycles or rickety cars and made the trek on several evenings a week.

'Nothing much doing, tonight,' observed Grits gloomily. He brightened. 'Pay day tomorrow.'

'It'll be full here tomorrow, and that's a fact,' agreed Paddy. 'With Soupy and that lot from Granger's and all.'

'Granger's?' I asked.

'Sure, don't you know nothing?' said Grits with mild contempt. 'Granger's stable, over t'other side of the hill.'

'Where have you been all your life?' said Paddy.

'He's new to racing, mind you,' said Grits, being fair.

'Yes, but all the same!' Paddy drank past the half-way mark, and wiped his mouth on the back of his hand.

Grits finished his beer and sighed. 'That's it, then. Better be getting back, I suppose.'

We walked back to the stables, talking as always about horses.

The following afternoon I wandered casually out of the stables and started up the stream, picking up stones as I went and throwing them in, as if to enjoy the splash. Some of the lads were punting a football about in the paddock behind the yard, but none of them paid any attention to me. A good long way up the hill, where the stream ran through a steep, grass sided gully, I came across October sitting on a boulder smoking a cigarette. He was accompanied by a black retriever, and a gun and a full game bag lay on the ground beside him.

'Doctor Livingstone, I presume,' he said, smiling.

'Quite right, Mr. Stanley. How did you guess?' I perched on a boulder near to him.

He kicked the game bag, 'The form books are in here, and a note book with all that Beckett and I could rake up at such short notice about those eleven horses. But surely the reports in the files you read would be of more use than the odd snippets we can supply?'

'Anything may be useful . . . you never know. There was one clipping in that packet of Stapleton's which was interesting. It was about historic dope cases. It said that certain horses apparently turned harmless food into something that showed a positive dope reaction, just through chemical changes in their body. I suppose it isn't possible that reverse could occur? I mean, could some horses break down any sort of dope into harmless substances, so that no positive reaction showed in the test?'

'I'll find out.'

'There's only one other thing,' I said. 'I have been assigned to three of those useless brutes you filled the yard up with, and that means no trips to racecourses. I was wondering if perhaps you could sell one of them again, and then I'd have a chance of mixing with lads from several stables at the sales. Three other men are doing three horses each here, so I shouldn't find myself redundant, and I might well be given a raceable horse to look after.'

'I will sell one,' he said, 'but if it goes for auction it will take time. The application forms have to go to the auctioneer nearly a month before the sale date.'

I nodded. 'It's utterly frustrating. I wish I could think of a way of getting myself transferred to a horse which is due to race shortly. Preferably one going to a far distant course, because an overnight stop would be ideal.'

'Lads don't change their horses in mid-stream,' he said rubbing his chin.

'So I've been told. It's the luck of the draw. You get them when they come and you're stuck with them until they leave. If they turn out useless, it's just too bad.'

We stood up. The retriever, who had lain quiet all this time with his muzzle resting on his paws, got to his feet also and stretched himself, and wagging his tail slowly from side to side looked up trustingly at his master. October bent down, gave the dog an affectionate slap, and picked up the gun. I picked up the game bag and swung it over my shoulder.

We shook hands, and October said, smiling, 'You may like to know that Inskip thinks you ride extraordinarily well for a stable lad. His exact words were that he didn't really trust men with your sort of looks, but that you'd the hands of an angel. You'd better watch that.'

'Hell,' I said, 'I hadn't given it a thought.'

He grinned and went off up the hill, and I turned downwards along the stream, gradually becoming ruefully aware that however much of a lark I might find it to put on wolf's clothing, it was going to hurt my pride if I had to hash up my riding as well.

The pub in Slaw was crowded that evening and the wage packets took a hiding. About half the strength from October's stable was there – and also a group of Granger's lads, including three lasses, who took a good deal of double-meaning teasing and thoroughly enjoyed it. Most of the talk was friendly bragging that each lad's horses were better than those of anyone else.

'My bugger'll beat yours with his eyes shut on Wednesday.'

'You've got a ruddy hope . . .'

'. . . Yours couldn't run a snail to a close finish.'

'. . . The jockey made a right muck of the start and never got in touch . . .'

'. . . Fat as a pig and bloody obstinate as well.'

The easy chat ebbed and flowed while the air grew thick with cigarette smoke and the warmth of too many lungs breathing the same box of air. A game of darts between some inaccurate players was in progress in one corner, and the balls of bar billiards clicked in another. I lolled on a hard chair with my arm hooked over the back and watched Paddy and one of Granger's lads engage in a needle match of dominoes. Horses, cars, football, boxing, films, the last local dance, and back to horses, always back to horses. I listened to it all and learned nothing except that these lads were mostly content with their lives, mostly good natured, mostly observant and mostly harmless.

'You're new, aren't you?' said a challenging voice in my ear.

I turned my head and looked up at him. 'Yeah,' I said languidly.

These were the only eyes I had seen in Yorkshire which held anything of the sort of guile I was looking for. I gave him back his stare until his lips curled in recognition that I was one of his kind.

'What's your name?'

'Dan,' I said, 'and yours?'

'Thomas Nathaniel Tarleton.' He waited for some reaction, but I didn't know what it ought to be.

'T. N. T.' said Paddy obligingly, looking up from his dominoes. 'Soupy.' His quick gaze flickered over both of us.

'The high explosive kid himself,' I murmured.

Soupy Tarleton smiled a small, carefully dangerous smile: to impress me, I gathered. He was about my own age and build, but much fairer, with the reddish skin which I had noticed so many Englishmen had. His light hazel eyes protruded slightly in their sockets, and he had grown a narrow moustache on the upper lip of his full, moist-looking mouth. On the little finger of his right hand he wore a heavy gold ring, and on his left wrist, an expensive wrist watch. His clothes were of good material, though distinctly sharp in cut, and the enviable fleece-lined quilted jacket he carried over his arm would have cost him three weeks' pay.

He showed no signs of wanting to be friendly. After looking me over as thoroughly as I had him, he merely nodded, said 'See you,' and detached himself to go over and watch the bar billiards.

Grits brought a fresh half pint from the bar and settled himself on the bench next to Paddy.

'You don't want to trust Soupy,' he told me confidentially, his raw boned unintelligent face full of kindness.

Paddy put down a double three, and looking round at us gave me a long, unsmiling scrutiny.

'There's no need to worry about Dan, Grits,' he said. 'He and Soupy, they're alike. They'd go well in double harness. Birds of a feather, that's what they are.'

'But you said I wasn't to trust Soupy,' objected Grits, looking from one to the other of us with troubled eyes.

'That's right,' said Paddy flatly. He put down a three-four and concentrated on his game.

Grits shifted six inches towards Paddy and gave me one puzzled, embarrassed glance. Then he found the inside of his beer mug suddenly intensely interesting and didn't raise his eyes to mine again.

I think it was at that exact moment that the charade began to lose its light-heartedness. I liked Paddy and Grits, and for three days they had accepted me with casual good humour. I was not prepared for Paddy's instant recognition that it was with Soupy that my real interest lay, nor for his immediate rejection of me on that account. It was a shock which I ought to have foreseen, and hadn't: and it should have warned me what to expect in the future, but it didn't.

Colonel Beckett's staff work continued to be of the highest possible kind. Having committed himself to the offensive, he was prepared to back the attack with massive and immediate reinforcements: which is to say that as soon as he had heard from October that I was immobilized in the stable with three useless horses, he set about liberating me.

On Tuesday afternoon, when I had been with the stable for a week, Wally, the head lad, stopped me as I carried two buckets full of water across the yard.

'That horse of yours in number seventeen is going tomorrow,' he said. 'You'll have to look sharp in the morning with your work, because you are to be ready to go with it at twelve-thirty. The horse box will take you to another racing stables, down near Nottingham. You are to leave this horse there and bring a new one back. Right?'

'Right,' I said. Wally's manner was cool with me; but over the week-end I had made myself be reconciled to the knowledge that I had to go on inspiring a faint mistrust all round, even if I no longer much liked it when I succeeded.

Most of Sunday I had spent reading the form books, which the others in the cottage regarded as a perfectly natural activity; and in the evening, when they all went down to the pub, I did some pretty concentrated work with a pencil, making analyses of the eleven horses and their assisted wins. It was true, as I had discovered from the newspaper cuttings in London, that they all had different owners, trainers and jockeys: but it was not true that they had absolutely nothing in common. By the time I had sealed my notes into an envelope and put it with October's notebook into the game bag under some form books, away from the inquiring gaze of the beer-happy returning lads, I was in possession of four unhelpful points of similarity.

First, the horses had all won selling chases – races where the winner was subsequently put up for auction. In the auctions three horses had been bought back by their owners, and the rest had been sold for modest sums.

Second, in all their racing lives all the horses had proved themselves to be capable of making a show in a race, but had either no strength or no guts when it came to a finish.

Third, none of them had won any races except the ones for which they were doped, though they had occasionally been placed on other occasions.

Fourth, none of them had won at odds of less than ten to one.

I learned both from October's notes and from the form books that several of the horses had changed trainers more than once, but they were such moderate, unrewarding animals that this was only to be expected. I was also in possession of the useless information that the horses were all by different sires out of different dams, that they varied in age from five to eleven, and that they were not all of the same colour. Neither had they all won on the same course, though in this case they had not all won on different courses either; and geographically I had a vague idea that the courses concerned were all in the northern half of the country – Kelso, Haydock, Sedgefield, Stafford and Ludlow. I decided to check them on a map, to see if this was right, but there wasn't one to be found chez Mrs. Allnut.

I went to bed in the crowded little dormitory with the other lads' beery breaths gradually overwhelming the usual mixed clean smells of boot polish and hair oil, and lost an argument about having the small sash window open more than four inches at the top. The lads all seemed to take their cue from Paddy, who was undoubtedly the most aware of them, and if Paddy declined to treat me as a friend, so would they: I realized that if I had insisted on having the window tight shut they would probably have opened it wide and given me all the air I wanted. Grinning ruefully in the dark I listened to the squeaking bed springs and their sleepy, gossiping giggles as they thumbed over the evening's talk; and as I shifted to find a comfortable spot on the lumpy mattress I began to wonder what life was really like from the inside for the hands who lived in my own bunk house, back home.

Wednesday morning gave me my first taste of the biting Yorkshire wind, and one of the lads, as we scurried round the yard with shaking hands and running noses, cheerfully assured me that it could blow for six months solid, if it tried. I did my three horses at the double, but by the time the horse box took me and one of them out of the yard at twelve-thirty I had decided that if the gaps in my wardrobe were anything to go by, October's big square house up the drive must have very efficient central heating.

About four miles up the road I pressed the bell which in most horse boxes connects the back compartment to the cab. The driver stopped obediently, and looked enquiringly at me when I walked along and climbed up into the cab beside him.

'The horse is quiet,' I said, 'and it's warmer here.'

He grinned and started off again, shouting over the noise of the engine. 'I didn't have you figured for the conscientious type, and I was damn right. That horse is going to be sold and has got to arrive in good condition . . . the boss would have a fit if he knew you were up in front.'

I had a pretty good idea the boss, meaning Inskip, wouldn't be at all surprised; bosses, judging by myself, weren't as naïve as all that.

'The boss can stuff himself,' I said unpleasantly.

I got a sidelong glance for that, and reflected that it was dead easy to give oneself a bad character if one put one's mind to it. Horse box drivers went to race meetings in droves, and had no duties when they got there. They had time to gossip in the canteen, time all afternoon to wander about and wag their tongues. There was no telling what ears might hear that there was a possible chink in the honesty of the Inskip lads.

We stopped once on the way to eat in a transport café, and again a little further on for me to buy myself a couple of woollen shirts, a black sweater, some thick socks, woollen gloves and a knitted yachting cap like those the other lads had worn that bitter morning. The box driver, coming into the shop with me to buy some socks for himself, eyed my purchases and remarked that I seemed to have plenty of money. I grinned knowingly, and said it was easy to come by if you knew how; and I could see his doubts of me growing.

In mid-afternoon we rolled in to a racing stable in Leicestershire, and it was here that the scope of Beckett's staff work became apparent. The horse I was to take back and subsequently care for was a useful hurdler just about to start his career as a novice 'chaser, and he had been sold to Colonel Beckett complete with all engagements. This meant, I learned from his former lad, who handed him over to me with considerable bitterness, that he could run in all the races for which his ex-owner had already entered him.

'Where is he entered?' I asked.

'Oh, dozens of places, I think – Newbury, Cheltenham, Sandown, and so on, and he was going to start next week at Bristol.' The lad's face twisted with regret as he passed the halter rope into my hand. 'I can't think what on earth persuaded the Old Man to part with him. He's a real daisy, and if I ever see him at the races not looking as good and well cared for as he does now, I'll find you and beat the living daylights out of you, I will straight.'

I had already discovered how deeply attached racing lads became to the horses they looked after, and I understood that he meant what he said.

'What's his name?' I asked.

'Sparking Plug . . . God awful name, he's no plug . . . Hey, Sparks, old boy ... hey, boy ... hey, old fellow ...' He fondled the horse's muzzle affectionately.

We loaded him into the horse box and this time I did stay where I ought to be, in the back, looking after him. If Beckett were prepared to give a fortune for the cause, as I guessed he must have done to get hold of such an ideal horse in so few days, I was going to take good care of it.

Before we started back I took a look at the road map in the cab, and found to my satisfaction that all the race courses in the country had been marked in on it in indian ink. I borrowed it at once, and spent the journey studying it. The courses where Sparking Plug's lad had said he was entered were nearly all in the south. Overnight stops, as requested. I grinned.

The five race courses where the eleven horses had won were not, I found, all as far north as I had imagined. Ludlow and Stafford, in fact, could almost be considered southern, especially as I found I instinctively based my view of the whole country from Harrogate. The five courses seemed to bear no relation to each other on the map: far from presenting a tidy circle from which a centre might be deduced, they were all more or less in a curve from north east to south west, and I could find no significance in their location.

I spent the rest of the journey back as I spent most of my working hours, letting my mind drift over what I knew of the eleven horses, waiting for an idea to swim to the surface like a fish in a pool, waiting for the disconnected facts to sort themselves into a pattern. But I didn't really expect this to happen yet, as I knew I had barely started, and even electronic computers won't produce answers if they are not fed enough information.

On Friday night I went down to the pub in Slaw and beat Soupy at darts. He grunted, gestured to the bar billiards, and took an easy revenge. We then drank a half pint together, eyeing each other. Conversation between us was almost non-existent, nor was it necessary: and shortly I wandered back to watch the dart players. They were no better than the week before.

'You beat Soupy, didn't you Dan?' one of them said.

I nodded, and immediately found a bunch of darts thrust into my hand.

'If you can beat Soupy you must be in the team.'

'What team?' I asked.

'The stable darts team. We play other stables, and have a sort of Yorkshire League. Sometimes we go to Middleham or Wetherby or Richmond or sometimes they come here. Soupy's the best player in Granger's team. Could you beat him again, do you think, or was it a fluke?'

I threw three darts at the board. They all landed in the twenty. For some unknown reason I had always been able to throw straight.

'Cor,' said the lads. 'Go on.'

I threw three more: the twenty section got rather crowded.

'You're in the team, mate, and no nonsense,' they said.

'When's the next match?' I asked.

'We had one here a fortnight ago. Next one's next Sunday at Burndale, after the football. You can't play football as well as darts, I suppose?'

I shook my head. 'Only darts.'

I looked at the one dart still left in my hand. I could hit a scuttling rat with a stone; I had done it often when the men had found one round the corn bins and chased it out. I saw no reason why I couldn't hit a galloping horse with a dart: it was a much bigger target.

'Put that one in the bull,' urged the lad beside me.

I put it in the bull. The lads yelled with glee.

'We'll win the league this season,' they grinned. Grits grinned too. But Paddy didn't.

Chapter Four

October's son and daughters came home for the week-end, the elder girl in a scarlet T.R.4 which I grew to know well by sight as she drove in and out past the stables, and the twins more sedately, with their father. As all three were in the habit of riding out when they were at home Wally told me to saddle up two of my horses to go out with the first string on Saturday, Sparking Plug for me and the other for Lady Patricia Tarren.

Lady Patricia Tarren, as I discovered when I led out the horse in the half light of early dawn and held it for her to mount, was a raving beauty with a pale pink mouth and thick curly eyelashes which she knew very well how to use. She had tied a green head-scarf over her chestnut hair, and she wore a black and white harlequined ski-ing jacket to keep out the cold. She was carrying some bright green woollen gloves.

'You're new,' she observed, looking up at me through the eyelashes. 'What's your name?'

'Dan . . . Miss,' I said. I realized I hadn't the faintest idea what form of address an earl's daughter was accustomed to. Wally's instructions hadn't stretched that far.

'Well . . . give me a leg up, then.'

I stood beside her obediently, but as I leaned forward to help her she ran her bare hand over my head and around my neck, and took the lobe of my right ear between her fingers. She had sharp nails, and she dug them in. Her eyes were wide with challenge. I looked straight back. When I didn't move or say anything she presently giggled and let go and calmly put on her gloves. I gave her a leg up into the saddle and she bent down to gather the reins, and fluttered the fluffy lashes close to my face.

'You're quite a dish, aren't you, Danny boy,' she said, 'with those googoo dark eyes.'

I couldn't think of any answer to her which was at all consistent with my position. She laughed, nudged the horse's flanks, and walked off down the yard. Her sister, mounting a horse held by Grits, looked from twenty yards away in the dim light to be much fairer in colouring and very nearly as beautiful. Heaven help October, I thought, with two like that to keep an eye on.

I turned to go and fetch Sparking Plug and found October's eighteen-year-old son at my elbow. He was very like his father, but not yet as thick in body or as easily powerful in manner.

'I shouldn't pay too much attention to my twin sister,' he said in a cool, bored voice, looking me up and down, 'she is apt to tease.' He nodded and strolled over to where his horse was waiting for him; and I gathered that what I had received was a warning off. If his sister behaved as provocatively with every male she met, he must have been used to delivering them.

Amused, I fetched Sparking Plug, mounted, and followed all the other horses out of the yard, up the lane, and on to the edge of the moor. As usual on a fine morning the air and the view were exhilarating. The sun was no more than a promise on the far distant horizon and there was a beginning-of-the-world quality in the light. I watched the shadowy shapes of the horses ahead of me curving round the hill with white plumes streaming from their nostrils in the frosty air. As the glittering rim of the sun expanded into full light the colours sprang out bright and clear, the browns of the jogging horses topped with the bright stripes of the lads' ear-warming knitted caps and the jolly October's daughters.

October himself, accompanied by his retriever, came up on to the moor in a Land Rover to see the horses work. Saturday morning, I had found, was the busiest training day of the week as far as gallops were concerned, and as he was usually in Yorkshire at the week-end he made a point of coming out to watch.

Inskip had us circling round at the top of the hill while he paired off the horses and told their riders what to do.

To me he said, 'Dan; three-quarter speed gallop. Your horse is running on Wednesday. Don't over-do him but we want to see how he goes.' He directed one of the stable's most distinguished animals to accompany me.

When he had finished giving his orders he cantered off along the broad sweep of green turf which stretched through the moorland scrub, and October drove slowly in his wake. We continued circling until the two men reached the other end of the gallops about a mile and a half away up the gently curved, gently rising track.

'O.K.' said Wally to the first pair. 'Off you go.'

The two horses set off together, fairly steadily at first and then at an increasing pace until they had passed Inskip and October, when they slowed and pulled up.

'Next two,' Wally called.

We were ready, and set off without more ado. I had bred, broken and rebroken uncountable race-horses in Australia, but Sparking Plug was the only good one I had so far ridden in England, and I was interested to see how he compared. Of course he was a hurdler, while I was more used to flat racers, but this made no difference, I found: and he had a bad mouth which I itched to do something about, but there was nothing wrong with his action. Balanced and collected, he sped smoothly up the gallop, keeping pace effortlessly with the star performer beside him, and though, as ordered, we went only three-quarters speed at our fastest, it was quite clear that Sparking Plug was fit and ready for his approaching race.

I was so interested in what I was doing that it was not until I had reined in – not too easy with that mouth – and began to walk back, that I realised I had forgotten all about messing up the way I rode. I groaned inwardly, exasperated with myself: I would never do what I had come to England for if I could so little keep my mind on the job.

I stopped with the horse who had accompanied Sparking Plug in front of October and Inskip, for them to have a look at the horses and see how much they were blowing. Sparking Plug's ribs moved easily: he was scarcely out of breath. The two men nodded, and I and the other lad slid off the horses and began walking them round while they cooled down.

Up from the far end of the gallop came the other horses, pair by pair, and finally a bunch of those who were not due to gallop but only to canter. When everyone had worked, most of the lads remounted and we all began to walk back down the gallop towards the track to the stable. Leading my horse on foot I set off last in the string, with October's eldest daughter riding immediately in front of me and effectively cutting me off from the chat of the lads ahead. She was looking about her at the rolling vistas of moor, and not bothering to keep her animal close on the heels of the one in front, so that by the time we entered the track there was a ten yard gap ahead of her.

As she passed a scrubby gorse bush a bird flew out of it with a squawk and flapping wings, and the girl's horse whipped round and up in alarm. She stayed on with a remarkable effort of balance, pulling herself back up into the saddle from somewhere below the horse's right ear, but under her thrust the stirrup leather broke apart at the bottom, and the stirrup iron itself clanged to the ground.

I stopped and picked up the iron, but it was impossible to put it back on the broken leather.

'Thank you,' she said. 'What a nuisance.'

She slid off her horse. 'I might as well walk the rest of the way.'

I took her rein and began to lead both of the horses, but she stopped me, and took her own back again.

'It's very kind of you,' she said, 'but I can quite well lead him myself.' The track was wide at that point, and she began to walk down the hill beside me.

On closer inspection she was not a bit like her sister Patricia. She had smooth silver blonde hair under a blue head scarf, fair eye lashes, direct grey eyes, a firm friendly mouth, and a composure which gave her an air of graceful reserve. We walked in easy silence for some way.

'Isn't it a gorgeous morning,' she said eventually.

'Gorgeous,' I agreed, 'But cold.' The English always talk about the weather, I thought: and a fine day in November is so rare as to be remarked on. It would be hotting up for summer, at home . . .

'Have you been with the stable long?' she asked, a little further on.

'Only about ten days.'

'And do you like it here?'

'Oh, yes. It's a well run stable . . .'

'Mr. Inskip would be delighted to hear you say so,' she said in a dry voice.

I glanced at her, but she was looking ahead down the track, and smiling.

After another hundred yards she said, 'What horse is that that you were riding? I don't think that I have seen him before, either.'

'He only came on Wednesday . . .' I told her the little I knew about Sparking Plug's history, capabilities and prospects.

She nodded. 'It will be nice for you if he can win some races. Rewarding, after your work for him here.'

'Yes,' I agreed, surprised that she should think like that.

We reached the last stretch to the stable.

'I am so sorry,' she said pleasantly, 'but I don't know your name.'

'Daniel Roke,' I said: and I wondered why to her alone of all the people who had asked me that question in the last ten days it had seemed proper to give a whole answer.

'Thank you,' she paused: then having thought, continued in a calm voice which I realised with wry pleasure was designed to put me at my ease, 'Lord October is my father. I'm Elinor Tarren.'

We had reached the stable gate. I stood back to let her go first, which she acknowledged with a friendly but impersonal smile, and she led her horse away across the yard towards its own box. A thoroughly nice girl, I thought briefly, buckling down to the task of brushing the sweat off Sparking Plug, washing his feet, brushing out his mane and tail, sponging out his eyes and mouth, putting his straw bed straight, fetching his hay and water, and then repeating the whole process with the horse that Patricia had ridden. Patricia, I thought, grinning, was not a nice girl at all.

When I went in to breakfast in the cottage Mrs. Allnut gave me a letter which had just arrived for me. The envelope, postmarked in London the day before, contained a sheet of plain paper with a single sentence typed on it.

'Mr. Stanley will be at Victoria Falls three p.m. Sunday.'

I stuffed the letter into my pocket, laughing into my porridge.

There was a heavy drizzle falling when I walked up beside the stream the following afternoon. I reached the gully before October, and waited for him with the rain drops finding ways to trickle down my neck. He came down the hill with his dog as before, telling me that his car was parked above us on the little used road.

But we'd better talk here, if you can stand the wet,' he finished, 'in case anyone saw us together in the car, and wondered.'

'I can stand the wet,' I assured him, smiling.

'Good . . . well, how have you been getting on?'

I told him how well I thought of Beckett's new horse and the opportunities it would give me.

He nodded, 'Roddy Beckett was famous in the war for the speed and accuracy with which he got supplies moved about. No one ever got the wrong ammunition or all left boots when he was in charge.'

I said 'I've sown a few seeds of doubts about my honesty, here and there, but I'll be able to do more of that this week at Bristol, and also next week-end, at Burndale. I'm going there on Sunday to play in a darts match.'

'They've had several cases of doping in that village in the past,' he said thoughtfully. 'You might get a nibble, there.'

'It would be useful . . .

'Have you found the form books helpful?' he asked, 'have you given those eleven horses any more thought?'

'I've thought of little else,' I said, 'and it seems just possible, perhaps it's only a slight chance, but it does just seem possible that you might be able to make a dope test on the next horse in the sequence *before* he runs in a race. That is to say, always providing that there is going to be another horse in the sequence . . . and I don't see why not, as the people responsible have got away with it for so long.'

He looked at me with some excitement, the rain dripping off the down-turned brim of his hat.

'You've found something?'

'No, not really. It's only a statistical indication. But it's more than even money, I think, that the next horse will win a selling chase at Kelso, Sedgefield, Ludlow, Stafford or Haydock.' I explained my reasons for expecting this, and went on, 'It should be possible to arrange for wholesale saliva samples to be taken before all the selling chases on those particular tracks – it can't be more than one race at each two-day meeting – and they can throw the samples away without going to the expense of testing them if no . . . er . . . joker turns up in the pack.'

'It's a tall order,' he said slowly, 'but I don't see why it shouldn't be done, if it will prove anything.'

'The analysts might find something useful in the results.'

'Yes. And I suppose even if they didn't, it would be a great step forward for us to be able to be on the lookout for a joker, instead of just being mystified when one appeared. Why on earth,' he shook his head in exasperation, 'didn't we think of this months ago? It seems such an obvious way to approach the problem, now that you have done it.'

'I expect it is because I am the first person really to be given all the collected information all at once, and deliberately search for a connecting factor. All the other investigations seemed to have been done from the other end, so to speak, by trying to find out in each case separately who had access to the horse, who fed him, who saddled him, and so on.'

He nodded gloomily.

'There's one other thing,' I said. 'The lab chaps told you that as they couldn't find a dope you should look for something mechanical . . . do you know whether the horses' skins were investigated as closely as the jockeys and their kit? It occurred to me the other evening that I could throw a dart with an absolute certainty of hitting a horse's flank, and any good shot could plant a pellet in the same place. Things like that would sting like a hornet . . . enough to make any horse shift along faster.'

'As far as I know, none of the horses showed any signs of that sort of thing, but I'll make sure. And by the way, I asked the analysts whether horses' bodies could break drugs down into harmless substances, and they said it was impossible.'

'Well, that clears the decks a bit, if nothing else.'

'Yes.' He whistled to his dog, who was quartering the far side of the gully. 'After next week, when you'll be away at Burndale, we had better meet here at this time every Sunday afternoon to discuss progress. You will know if I'm away, because I won't be here for the Saturday gallops. Incidentally, your horsemanship stuck out a mile on Sparking Plug yesterday. And I thought we agreed that you had better not make too good an impression. On top of which,' he added, smiling faintly, 'Inskip says you are a quick and conscientious worker.'

'Heck . . . I'll be getting a good reference if I don't watch out.'

'Too right you will,' he agreed, copying my accent sardonically. 'How do you like being a stable lad?'

'It has its moments . . . Your daughters are very beautiful.'

He grinned, 'Yes: and thank you for helping Elinor. She told me you were most obliging.'

'I did nothing.'

'Patty is a bit of a handful,' he said, reflectively, 'I wish she'd decide what sort of a job she'd like to do. She knows I don't want her to go on as she has during her season, never-ending parties and staying out till dawn . . . well, that's not your worry, Mr. Roke.'

We shook hands as usual, and he trudged off up the hill. It was still drizzling mournfully as I went down.

Sparking Plug duly made the 250 mile journey south to Bristol, and I went with him. The racecourse was some way out of the city, and the horse box driver told me, when we stopped for a meal on the way, that the whole of the stable block had been newly rebuilt there after fire had gutted it.

Certainly the loose boxes were clean and snug, but it was the new sleeping quarters that the lads were in ecstasies about. The hostel was a surprise to me too. It consisted mainly of a creation room and two long dormitories with about thirty beds in each, made up with clean sheets and fluffy blue blankets. There was a wall light over each bed, polyvinyl tiled flooring, under-floor heating, modern showers in the washroom and a hot room for drying wet clothes. The whole place was warm and light, with colour schemes which were clearly the work of a professional.

'Ye gods, we're in the ruddy Hilton,' said one cheerful boy, coming to a halt beside me just through the dormitory door and slinging his canvas grip on to an unoccupied bed.

'You haven't seen the half of it,' said a bony long-wristed boy in a shrunken blue jersey, 'up that end of the passage there's a ruddy great canteen with decent chairs and a telly and a ping pong table and all.'

Other voices joined in.

'It's as good as Newbury.'

'Easily.'

'Better than Ascot, I'd say.'

Heads nodded.

'They have bunk beds at Ascot, not singles, like this.'

The hostels at Newbury and Ascot were, it appeared, the most comfortable in the country.

'Anyone would think the bosses had suddenly cottoned on to the fact that we're human,' said a sharp faced lad, in a belligerent, rabble-raising voice.

'It's a far cry from the bug-ridden doss houses of the old days,' nodded a desiccated, elderly little man with a face like a shrunken apple. 'But a fellow told me the lads have it good like this in America all the time.'

'They know if they don't start treating us decent they soon won't get anyone to do the dirty work,' said the rabble-raiser. 'Things are changing.'

'They treat us decent enough where I come from,' I said, putting my things on an empty bed next to his and nerving myself to be natural, casual, unremarkable. I felt much more self-conscious than I had at Slaw, where at least I knew the job inside out and had been able to feel my way cautiously into a normal relationship with the other lads. But here I had only two nights, and if I were to do any good at all I had got to direct the talk towards what I wanted to hear.

The form books were by now as clear to me as a primer, and for a fortnight I had listened acutely and concentrated on soaking in as much racing jargon as I could, but I was still doubtful whether I would understand everything I heard at Bristol and also afraid that I would make some utterly incongruous impossible mistake in what I said myself.

'And where do you come from?' asked the cheerful boy, giving me a cursory looking over.

'Lord October's,' I said.

'Oh yes, Inskip's, you mean? You're a long way from home . . .'

'Inskip's may be all right,' said the rabble-raiser, as if he regretted it. 'But there are some places where they still treat us like mats to wipe their feet on, and don't reckon that we've got a right to a bit of sun, same as everyone else.'

'Yeah,' said the raw-boned boy seriously. 'I heard that at one place they practically starve the lads and knock them about if they don't work hard enough, and they all have to do about four or five horses each because they can't keep anyone in the yard for more than five minutes!'

I said idly 'Where's that, just so I know where to avoid, if I ever move on from Inskip's?'

'Up your part of the country . . .' he said doubtfully. 'I think.'

'No, further north, in Durham . . .' another boy chimed in, a slender, pretty boy with soft down still growing on his cheeks.

'You know about it too, then?'

He nodded. 'Not that it matters, only a raving nit would take a job there. It's a blooming sweat shop, a hundred years out of date. All they get are riff-raff that no one else will have.'

'It wants exposing,' said the rabble-raiser belligerently. 'Who runs this place?'

'Bloke called Humber,' said the pretty boy, 'he couldn't train ivy up a wall ... and he has about as many winners as tits on a billiard ball ... You see his head travelling lad at the meetings sometimes, trying to pressgang people to go and work there, and getting the brush off, right and proper.'

'Someone ought to do something,' said the rabble-raiser automatically: and I guessed that this was his usual refrain: 'someone ought to do something'; but not, when it came to the point, himself.

There was a general drift into the canteen, where the food proved to be good, unlimited, and free. A proposal to move on to a pub came to nothing when it was discovered both that the nearest was nearly two (busless) miles away and that the bright warm canteen had some crates of beer under its counter.

It was easy enough to get the lads started on the subject of doping, and they seemed prepared to discuss it endlessly. None of the twenty odd there had ever, as far as they would admit, given 'anything' to a horse, but they all knew someone who knew someone who had. I drank my beer and listened and looked interested, which I was.

'... nobbled him with a squirt of acid as he walked out of the bleeding paddock ...'

'... gave it such a whacking dollop of stopping powder that it died in its box in the morning ...'

'Seven rubber bands came out in the droppings ...'

'... Overdosed him so much that he never even tried to jump the first fence: blind, he was, stone blind ...'

'... gave him a bloody great bucket full of water half an hour before the race, and didn't need any dope to stop him with all that sloshing about inside his gut.'

'Poured half a bottle of whisky down his throat.'

'... used to tube horses which couldn't breathe properly on the morning of the race until they found it wasn't the extra fresh air that was making the horses win but the cocaine they stuffed them full of for the operation ...'

'They caught him with a hollow apple packed with sleeping pills ...'

'... dropped a syringe right in front of an effing steward.'

'I wonder if there's anything which hasn't been tried yet?' I said.

'Black magic. Not much else left,' said the pretty boy.

They all laughed.

'Someone might find something so good,' I pointed out casually, 'that it couldn't be detected, so the people who thought of it could go on with it for ever and never be found out.'

'Blimey,' exclaimed the cheerful lad, 'you're a comfort, aren't you? God help racing, if that happened. You'd never know where you were. The bookies would all be climbing the walls.' He grinned hugely.

The elderly little man was not so amused.

'It's been going on for years and years,' he said, nodding solemnly.

'Some trainers have got it to a fine art, you mark my words. Some trainers have been doping their horses regular, for years and years.'

But the other lads didn't agree. The dope tests had done for the dope-minded trainers of the past; they had lost their licences, and gone out of racing. The old rule had been a bit unfair on some, they allowed, when a trainer had been automatically disqualified if one of his horses had been doped. It wasn't always the trainer's fault, especially if the horse had been doped to lose. What trainer, they asked, would nobble a horse he'd spent months training to win? But they thought there was probably *more* doping since that rule was changed, not less.

'Stands to reason, a doper knows now he isn't ruining the trainer for life, just one horse for one race. Makes it sort of easier on his conscience, see? More lads, maybe, would take fifty quid for popping the odd aspirin into the feed if they knew the stable wouldn't be shut down and their jobs gone for a burton very soon afterwards.

They talked on, thoughtful and ribald; but it was clear that they didn't know anything about the eleven horses I was concerned with. None of them, I knew, came from any of the stables involved, and obviously they had not read the speculative reports in the papers, or if they had, had read them separately over a period of eighteen months, and not in one solid, collected, intense bunch, as I had done.

The talk faltered and died into yawns, and we went chatting to bed, I sighing to myself with relief that I had gone through the evening without much notice having been taken of me.

By watching carefully what the other lads did, I survived the next day also without any curious stares. In the early afternoon I took Sparking Plug from the stables into the paddock, walked him round the parade ring, stood holding his head while he was saddled, led him round the parade ring again, held him while the jockey mounted, led him out on to the course, and went up into the little stand by the gate with the other lads to watch the race.

Sparking Plug won. I was delighted. I met him again at the gate and led him into the spacious winner's unsaddling enclosure.

Colonel Beckett was there, waiting, leaning on a stick. He patted the horse, congratulated the jockey, who unbuckled his saddle and departed into the weighing room, and said to me sardonically, 'That's a fraction of his purchase price back, anyway.'

'He's a good horse, and absolutely perfect for his purpose.'

'Good. Do you need anything else?'

'Yes. A lot more details about those eleven horses . . . where they were bred, what they ate, whether they had had any illnesses, what cafés their box drivers used, who made their bridles, whether they had racing plates fitted at the meetings, and by which blacksmiths . . . anything and everything.'

'Are you serious?'

'Yes.'

'But they had nothing in common except that they were doped.'

'As I see it, the question really is what was it that they had in common that made it *possible* for them to be doped.' I smoothed Sparking Plug's nose. He was restive and excited after his victory. Colonel Beckett looked at me with sober eyes.

'Mr. Roke, you shall have your information.'

I grinned at him. 'Thank you; and I'll take good care of Sparking Plug ... he'll win you all the purchase price, before he's finished.'

'Horses away,' called an official: and with a weak-looking gesture of farewell from Colonel Beckett's limp hand, I took Sparking Plug back to the racecourse stables and walked him round until he had cooled off.

There were far more lads in the hostel that evening as it was the middle night of the two-day meeting, and this time, besides getting the talk round again to doping and listening attentively to everything that was said, I also tried to give the impression that I didn't think taking fifty quid to point out a certain horse's box in his home stable to anyone prepared to pay that much for the information was a proposition I could be relied on to turn down. I earned a good few disapproving looks for this, and also one sharply interested glance from a very short lad whose outsize nose sniffed monotonously.

In the washroom in the morning he used the basin next to me, and said out of the side of his mouth, 'Did you mean it, last night, that you'd take fifty quid to point out a box?'

I shrugged. 'I don't see why not.'

He looked round furtively. It made me want to laugh. 'I might be able to put you in touch with someone who'd be interested to hear that – for fifty per cent cut.'

'You've got another think coming,' I said offensively. 'Fifty per cent ... what the hell do you think I am?'

'Well ... a fiver, then,' he sniffed, climbing down.

'I dunno ...'

'I can't say fairer than that,' he muttered.

'It's a wicked thing, to point out a box,' I said virtuously, drying my face on a towel.

He stared at me in astonishment.

'And I couldn't do it for less than sixty, if you are taking a fiver out of it.'

He didn't know whether to laugh or spit. I left him to his indecision, and went off grinning to escort Sparking Plug back to Yorkshire.

Chapter Five

Again on Friday evening I went down to the Slaw pub and exchanged bug-eyed looks with Soupy across the room.

On the Sunday half the lads had the afternoon off to go to Burndale for the football and darts matches, and we won both, which made for a certain amount of back slapping and beer drinking. But beyond remarking that I was new, and a blight on their chances in the darts league, the Burndale lads paid me little attention. There was no one like Soupy among them in spite of what October had said about the cases of doping in the village, and no one, as far as I could see, who cared if I were as crooked as a cork-screw.

During the next week I did my three horses, and read the form books, and thought: and got nowhere. Paddy remained cool and so did Wally, to whom Paddy had obviously reported my affinity with Soupy. Wally showed his disapproval by giving me more than my share of the afternoon jobs, so that every day, instead of relaxing in the usual free time between lunch and evening stables at four o'clock, I found myself bidden to sweep the yard, clean the tack, crush the oats, cut the chaff, wash Inskip's car or clean the windows of the loose boxes. I did it all without comment, reflecting that if I needed an excuse for a quick row and walked out later on I could reasonably, at eleven hours a day, complain of overwork.

However, at Friday midday I set off again with Sparking Plug, this time to Cheltenham, and this time accompanied not only by the box driver but by Grits and his horse, and the head travelling lad as well.

Once in the racecourse stables I learned that this was the night of the dinner given to the previous season's champion jockey, and all the lads who were staying there overnight proposed to celebrate by attending a dance in the town. Grits and I, therefore, having bedded down our horses, eaten our meal, and smartened ourselves up, caught a bus down the hill and paid our entrance money to the hop. It was a big hall and the band was loud and hot, but not many people were yet dancing. The girls were standing about in little groups eyeing larger groups of young men, and I bit back just in time a remark on how odd I found it; Grits would expect me to think it normal. I took him off into the bar where there were already groups of lads from the racecourse mingled with the local inhabitants, and bought him a beer, regretting that he was with me to see what use I intended to make of the evening. Poor Grits, he was torn between loyalty to Paddy and an apparent liking for me, and I was about to disillusion him thoroughly. I wished I could explain. I was tempted to spend the evening harmlessly. But how could I justify passing over an unrepeatable opportunity just to keep temporarily the regard of one slow-witted stable lad, however much I might like him? I was committed to earning ten thousand pounds.

'Grits, go and find a girl to dance with.'

He gave me a slow grin. 'I don't know any.'

'It doesn't matter. Any of them would be glad to dance with a nice chap like you. Go and ask one.'

'No. I'd rather stay with you.'

'All right, then. Have another drink.'

'I haven't finished this.'

I turned round to the bar, which we had been leaning against, and banged my barely touched half pint down on the counter. 'I'm fed up with this pap,' I said violently. 'Hey, you, barman, give me a double whisky.'

'Dan!' Grits was upset at my tone, which was a measure of its success. The barman poured the whisky and took my money.

'Don't go away,' I said to him in a loud voice. 'Give me another while you're at it.'

I felt rather than saw the group of lads further up the bar turn round and take a look, so I picked up the glass and swallowed all the whisky in two gulps and wiped my mouth on the back of my hand. I pushed the empty glass across to the barman and paid for the second drink.

'Dan,' Grits tugged my sleeve, 'do you think you should?'

'Yes,' I said, scowling. 'Go and find a girl to dance with.'

But he didn't go. He watched me drink the second whisky and order a third. His eyes were troubled.

The bunch of lads edged towards us along the bar.

'Hey, fella, you're knocking it back a bit,' observed one, a tallish man of my own age in a flashy bright blue suit.

'Mind your own ruddy business,' I said rudely.

'Aren't you from Inskip's?' he asked.

'Yea . . . Inskip's . . . bloody Inskip's . . .' I picked up the third glass. I had a hard head for whisky, which was going down on top of a deliberately heavy meal. I reckoned I could stay sober a long time after I would be expected to be drunk; but the act had to be put on early, while the audience were still sober enough themselves to remember it clearly afterwards.

'Eleven sodding quid,' I told them savagely, 'that's all you get for sweating your guts out seven days a week.'

It struck a note with some of them, but Blue-suit said, 'Then why spend it on whisky?'

'Why bloody not? It's great stuff – gives you a kick. And, by God, you need something in this job.'

Blue-suit said to Grits, 'Your mate's got an outsized gripe.'

'Well . . .' said Grits, his face anxious, 'I suppose he has had a lot of extra jobs this week, come to think . . .'

'You're looking after horses they pay thousands for and you know damn well that the way you ride and groom them and look after them makes a hell of a lot of difference to whether they win or not, and they grudge you a decent wage . . .' I finished the third whisky, hiccupped and said, 'It's bloody unfair.'

The bar was filling up, and from the sight of them and from what I could catch of their greetings to each other, at least half the customers were in some way connected with racing. Bookmakers' clerks and touts as well as stable lads – the town was stuffed with them, and the dance had been put on to attract them. A large amount of liquor began disappearing down their collective throats, and I had to catch the barman on the wing to serve my fourth double whisky in fifteen minutes.

I stood facing a widening circle with the glass in my hand, and rocked slightly on my feet.

'I want,' I began. What on earth did I want? I searched for the right phrases. 'I want . . . a motor-bike. I want to show a bird a good time. And go abroad for a holiday . . . and stay in a swank hotel and have them running about at my beck and call ... and drink what I like ... and maybe one day put a deposit on a house ... and what chance do I have of any of these? I'll tell you. Not a snowball's hope in hell. You know what I got in my pay packet this morning ...? Seven pounds and fourpence ...'

I went on and on grousing and complaining, and the evening wore slowly away. The audience drifted and changed, and I kept it up until I was fairly sure that all the racing people there knew there was a lad of Inskip's who yearned for more money, preferably in large amounts. But even Grits, who hovered about with an unhappy air throughout it all and remained cold sober himself, didn't seem to notice that I got progressively drunker in my actions while making each drink last longer than the one before.

Eventually, after I had achieved an artistic lurch and clutch at one of the pillars, Grits said loudly in my ear, 'Dan, I'm going now and you'd better go too, or you'll miss the last bus, and I shouldn't think you could walk back, like you are.'

'Huh?' I squinted at him. Blue-suit had come back and was standing just behind him.

'Want any help getting him out?' he asked Grits.

Grits looked at me disgustedly, and I fell against him, putting my arm round his shoulders: I definitely did not want the sort of help Blue-suit looked as though he might give.

'Grits, me old pal, if you say go, we go.'

We set off for the door, followed by Blue-suit, me staggering so heavily that I pushed Grits sideways. There were by this time a lot of others having difficulty in walking a straight line, and the queue of lads which waited at the bus stop undulated slightly like an ocean swell on a calm day. I grinned in the safe darkness and looked up at the sky, and thought that if the seeds I had sown in all directions bore no fruit there was little doping going on in British racing.

I may not have been drunk, but I woke the next morning with a shattering headache, just the same: all in a good cause, I thought, trying to ignore the blacksmith behind my eyes.

Sparking Plug ran in his race and lost by half a length. I took the opportunity of saying aloud on the lads' stand that there was the rest of my week's pay gone down the bloody drain.

Colonel Beckett patted his horse's neck in the cramped unsaddling enclosure and said casually to me, 'Better luck next time, eh? I've sent you what you wanted, in a parcel.' He turned away and resumed talking to Inskip and his jockey about the race.

We all went back to Yorkshire that night, with Grits and me sleeping most of the way on the benches in the back of the horse box.

He said reproachfully as he lay down, 'I didn't know you hated it at Inskip's ... and I haven't seen you drunk before either.'

'It isn't the work, Grits, it's the pay.' I had to keep it up.

'Still there are some who are married and have kids to keep on what you were bleating about.' He sounded disapproving, and indeed my behaviour must have affected him deeply, because he seldom spoke to me after that night.

There was nothing of interest to report to October the following afternoon, and our meeting in the gully was brief. He told me however that the information then in the post from Beckett had been collected by eleven keen young officer cadets from Aldershot who had been given the task as an initiative exercise, and told they were in competition with each other to see which of them could produce the most comprehensive report of the life of his allotted horse. A certain number of questions – those I had suggested – were outlined for them. The rest had been left to their own imagination and detective ability, and October said Beckett had told him they had used them to the full.

I returned down the hill more impressed than ever with the Colonel's staff work, but not as staggered as when the parcel arrived the following day. Wally again found some wretched job for me to do in the afternoon, so that it was not until after the evening meal, when half the lads had gone down to Slaw, that I had an opportunity of taking the package up to the dormitory and opening it. It contained 237 numbered typewritten pages bound into a cardboard folder, like the manuscript of a book, and its production in the space of one week must have meant a prodigious effort not only from the young men themselves, but from the typists as well. The information was given in note form for the most part, and no space had anywhere been wasted in flowing prose: it was solid detail from cover to cover.

Mrs. Allnut's voice floated up the stairs. 'Dan, come down and fetch me a bucket of coal, will you please?'

I thrust the typescript down inside my bed between the sheets, and went back to the warm, communal kitchen-living-room where we ate and spent most of our spare time. It was impossible to read anything private there, and my life was very much supervised from dawn to bedtime; and the only place I could think of where I could concentrate uninterruptedly on the typescript was the bathroom. Accordingly that night I waited until all the lads were asleep, and then went along the passage and locked myself in, ready to report an upset stomach if anyone should be curious.

It was slow going: after four hours I had read only half. I got up stiffly, stretched, yawned, and went back to bed. Nobody stirred. The following night, as I lay waiting for the others to go to sleep so that I could get back to my task, I listened to them discussing the evening that four of them had spent in Slaw.

'Who's that fellow who was with Soupy?' asked Grits. 'I haven't seen him around before.'

'He was there last night too,' said one of the others 'Queer sort of bloke.'

'What was queer about him?' asked the boy who had stayed behind, he watching the television while I in an arm-chair caught up on some sleep.

'I dunno,' said Grits. 'His eyes didn't stay still, like.'

'Sort as if he was looking for someone,' added another voice.

Paddy said firmly from the wall on my right, 'You just all keep clear of that chap, and Soupy too. I'm telling you. People like them are no good.'

'But that chap, that one with that smashing gold tie, he bought us a round, you know he did. He can't be too bad if he bought us a round . . .'

Paddy sighed with exasperation that anyone could be so simple. 'If you'd have been Eve, you'd have eaten the apple as soon as look at it. You wouldn't have needed a serpent.'

'Oh well,' yawned Grits. 'I don't suppose he'll be there tomorrow. I heard him say something to Soupy about time getting short.'

They muttered and murmured and went to sleep, and I lay awake in the dark thinking that perhaps I had just heard something very interesting indeed. Certainly a trip down to the pub was indicated for the following evening.

With a wrench I stopped my eyes from shutting, got out of my warm bed, repaired again to the bathroom, and read for another four hours until I had finished the typescript. I sat on the bathroom floor with my back against the wall and stared sightlessly at the fixtures and fittings. There was nothing, not one single factor, that occurred in the life histories of all of the eleven microscopically investigated horses. No common denominator at all. There were quite a few things which were common to four or five – but not often the same four or five – like the make of saddle their jockeys used, the horse cube nuts they were fed with, or the auction rings they had been sold in: but the hopes I had had of finding a sizeable clue in those packages had altogether evaporated. Cold, stiff, and depressed, I crept back to bed.

The next evening at eight I walked alone down to Slaw, all the other lads saying they were skint until pay-day and that in any case they wanted to watch Z Cars on television.

'I thought you lost all your cash on Sparks at Cheltenham,' observed Grits.

'I've about two bob left,' I said, producing some pennies. 'Enough for a pint.'

The pub, as often on Wednesdays, was empty. There was no sign of Soupy or his mysterious friend, and having bought some beer I amused myself at the dart board, throwing one-to-twenty sequences, and trying to make a complete ring in the trebles. Eventually I pulled the darts out of the board, looked at my watch, and decided I had wasted the walk; and it was at that moment that a man appeared in the doorway, not from the street, but from the saloon bar next door. He held a glass of gently fizzing amber liquid and a slim cigar in his left hand and pushed open the door with his right. Looking me up and down, he said, 'Are you a stable lad?'

'Yes.'

'Granger's or Inskip's?'

'Inskip's.'

'Hmm.' He came further into the room and let the door swing shut behind him. 'There's ten bob for you if you can get one of your lads down here tomorrow night . . . and as much beer as you can both drink.'

I looked interested. 'Which lad?' I asked. 'Any special one? Lots of them will be down here on Friday.'

'Well, now, it had better be tomorrow, I think. Sooner the better, I always say. And as for which lad . . . er . . . you tell me their names and I'll pick one of them . . . how's that?'

I thought it was damn stupid, and also that he wished to avoid asking too directly, too memorably for . . . well . . . for me?

'O.K. Paddy, Grits, Wally, Steve, Ron . . .' I paused.

'Go on,' he said.

'Reg, Norman, Dave, Jeff, Dan, Mike . . .'

His eyes brightened. 'Dan,' he said. 'That's a sensible sort of name. Bring Dan.'

'I am Dan,' I said.

There was an instant in which his balding scalp contracted and his eyes narrowed in annoyance.

'Stop playing games,' he said sharply.

'It was you,' I pointed out gently, 'who began it.'

He sat down on one of the benches and carefully put his drink down on the table in front of him.

'Why did you come here tonight, alone?' he asked.

'I was thirsty.'

There was a brief silence while he mentally drew up a plan of campaign. He was a short stocky man in a dark suit a size too small, the jacket hanging open to reveal a monogrammed cream shirt and golden silk tie. His fingers were fat and short, and a roll of flesh overhung his coat collar at the back, but there was nothing soft in the way he looked at me.

At length he said, 'I believe there is a horse in your stable called Sparking Plug?'

'Yes.'

'And he runs at Leicester on Monday?'

'As far as I know.'

'What do you think his chances are?' he asked.

'Look, do you want a tip, mister, is that what it is? Well, I do Sparking Plug myself and I'm telling you there isn't an animal in next Monday's race to touch him.'

'So you expect him to win?'

'Yes, I told you.'

'And you'll bet on him I suppose.'

'Of course.'

'With half your pay? Four pounds, perhaps?'

'Maybe.'

'But he'll be favourite. Sure to be. And at best you'll probably only get even money. Another four quid. That doesn't sound much, does it, when I could perhaps put you in the way of winning . . . a hundred?'

'You're barmy,' I said, but with a sideways leer that told him that I wanted to hear more.

He leaned forward with confidence. 'Now you can say no if you want to. You can say no, and I'll go away, and no one will be any the wiser, but if you play your cards right I could do you a good turn.'

'What would I have to do for a hundred quid?' I asked flatly.

He looked round cautiously, and lowered his voice still further. 'Just add a little something to Sparking Plug's feed on Sunday night. Nothing to it, you see? Dead easy.'

'Dead easy,' I repeated: and so it was.

'You're on, then?' he looked eager.

'I don't know your name,' I said.

'Never you mind.' He shook his head with finality.

'Are you a bookmaker?'

'No,' he said. 'I'm not. And that's enough with the questions. Are you on?'

'If you're not a bookmaker,' I said slowly, thinking my way, 'and you are willing to pay a hundred pounds to make sure a certain favourite doesn't win, I'd guess that you didn't want just to make money backing all the other runners, but that you intend to tip off a few bookmakers that the race is fixed, and they'll be so grateful they'll pay you say, fifty quid each, at the very least. There are about eleven thousand bookmakers in Britain. A nice big market. But I expect you go to the same ones over and over again. Sure of your welcome, I should think.'

His face was a study of consternation and disbelief, and I realized I had hit the target, bang on.

'Who told you . . .' he began weakly.

'I wasn't born yesterday,' I said with a nasty grin. 'Relax. No one told me.' I paused. 'I'll give Sparking Plug his extra nosh, but I want more for it. Two hundred.'

'No. The deal's off.' He mopped his forehead.

'All right.' I shrugged.

'A hundred and fifty then,' he said grudgingly.

'A hundred and fifty,' I agreed. 'Before I do it.'

'Half before, half after,' he said automatically. It was by no means the first time he had done this sort of deal.

I agreed to that. He said if I came down to the pub on Saturday evening I would be given a packet for Sparking Plug and seventy-five pounds for myself, and I nodded and went away, leaving him staring moodily into his glass.

On my way back up the hill I crossed Soupy off my list of potentially useful contacts. Certainly he had procured me for a doping job, but I had been asked to stop a favourite in a novice 'chase, not to accelerate a dim long priced selling plater. It was extremely unlikely that both types of fraud were the work of one set of people.

Unwilling to abandon Colonel Beckett's typescript I spent chunks of that night and the following two nights in the bathroom, carefully rereading it. The only noticeable result was that during the day I found the endless stable work irksome because for five nights in a row I had had only three hours' sleep. But I frankly dreaded having to tell October on Sunday that the eleven young men had made their mammoth investigation to no avail, and I had an unreasonable feeling that if I hammered away long enough I could still wring some useful message from those densely packed pages.

On Saturday morning, though it was bleak, bitter and windy, October's daughters rode out with the first string. Elinor only came near enough to exchange polite good mornings, but Patty, who was again riding one of my horses, made my giving her a leg up a moment of eyelash-fluttering intimacy, deliberately and unnecessarily rubbing her body against mine.

'You weren't here last week, Danny boy,' she said, putting her feet in the irons. 'Where were you?'

'At Cheltenham . . . miss.'

'Oh. And next Saturday?'

'I'll be here.'

She said, with intentional insolence, 'Then kindly remember next Saturday to shorten the leathers on the saddle before I mount. These are far too long.'

She made no move to shorten them herself, but gestured for me to do it for her. She watched me steadily, enjoying herself. While I was fastening the second buckle she rubbed her knee forwards over my hands and kicked me none too gently in the ribs.

'I wonder you stand me teasing you, Danny boy,' she said softly, bending down, 'a dishy guy like you should answer back more. Why don't you?'

'I don't want the sack,' I said, with a dead straight face.

'A coward, too,' she said sardonically, and twitched her horse away.

And she'll get into bad trouble one day, if she keeps on like that, I thought. She was too provocative. Stunningly pretty of course, but that was only the beginning; and her hurtful little tricks were merely annoying. It was the latent invitation which disturbed and aroused.

I shrugged her out of my mind, fetched Sparking Plug, sprang up on to his back and moved out of the yard and up to the moor for the routine working gallops.

The weather that day got steadily worse until while we were out with the second string it began to rain heavily in fierce slashing gusts, and we struggled miserably back against it with stinging faces and sodden clothes. Perhaps because it went on raining, or possibly because it was, after all, Saturday, Wally for once refrained from making me work all afternoon, and I spent the three hours sitting with about nine other lads in the kitchen of the cottage, listening to the wind shrieking round the corners outside and watching Chepstow races on television, while our damp jerseys, breeches and socks steamed gently round the fire.

I put the previous season's form book on the kitchen table and sat over it with my head propped on the knuckles of my left hand, idly turning the pages with my right. Depressed by my utter lack of success with the eleven horses' dossiers, by the antipathy I had to arouse in the lads, and also, I think, by the absence of the hot sunshine I usually lived in at that time of the year, I began to feel that the whole masquerade had been from the start a ghastly mistake. And the trouble was that having taken

October's money I couldn't back out; not for months. This thought depressed me further still. I sat slumped in unrelieved gloom, wasting my much needed free time.

I think now that it must have been the sense that I was failing in what I had set out to do, more than mere tiredness, which beset me that afternoon, because although later on I encountered worse things it was only for that short while that I ever truly regretted having listened to October, and unreservedly wished myself back in my comfortable Australian cage.

The lads watching the television were making disparaging remarks about the jockeys and striking private bets against each other on the outcome of the races.

'The uphill finish will sort 'em out as usual,' Paddy was saying. 'It's a long way from the last . . . Aladin's the only one who's got the stamina for the job.'

'No,' contradicted Grits. 'Lobster Cocktail's a flyer . . .'

Morosely I riffled the pages of the form book, aimlessly looking through them for the hundredth time, and came by chance on the map of Chepstow racecourse in the general information section at the beginning of the book. There were diagrammatic maps of all the main courses showing the shape of the tracks and the positioning of fences, stands, starting gates and winning posts, and I had looked before at those for Ludlow, Stafford and Haydock, without results. There was no map of Kelso or Sedgefield. Next to the map section were a few pages of information about the courses, the lengths of their circuits, the names and addresses of the officials, the record times for the races, and so on.

For something to do, I turned to Chepstow's paragraph. Paddy's 'long way from the last', was detailed there: two hundred and fifty yards. I looked up Kelso, Sedgefield, Ludlow, Stafford and Haydock. They had much longer run-ins than Chepstow. I looked up the run-ins of all the courses in the book. The Aintree Grand National run-in was the second longest. The longest of all was Sedgefield, and in third, fourth, fifth, and sixth positions came Ludlow, Haydock, Kelso and Stafford. All had run-ins of over four hundred yards.

Geography had nothing to do with it: those five courses had almost certainly been chosen by the dopers because in each case it was about a quarter of a mile from the last fence to the winning post.

It was an advance, even if a small one, to have made at least some pattern out of the chaos. In a slightly less abysmal frame of mind I shut the form book and at four o'clock followed the other lads out into the unwelcome rain-swept yard to spend an hour with each of my three charges, grooming them thoroughly to give their coats a clean healthy shine, tossing and tidying their straw beds, fetching their water, holding their heads while Inskip walked round, rugging them up comfortably for the night, and finally fetching their evening feed. As usual it was seven before we had all finished, and eight before we had eaten and changed and were bumping down the hill to Slaw, seven of us sardined into a rickety old Austin.

Bar billiards, darts, dominoes, the endless friendly bragging, the ingredients as before. Patiently, I sat and waited. It was nearly ten, the hour when the lads began to empty their glasses and think about having to get up the next morning, when Soupy strolled across the room towards the door, and, seeing my eyes on him, jerked his head for me to follow him. I got up and went out after him, and found him in the lavatories.

'This is for you. The rest on Tuesday,' he said economically; and treating me to a curled lip and stony stare to impress me with his toughness, he handed me a thick brown envelope. I put it in the inside pocket of my black leather jacket, and nodded to him. Still without speaking, without smiling, hard-eyed to match, I turned on my heel and went back into the bar: and after a while, casually, he followed.

So I crammed into the Austin and was driven up the hill, back to bed in the little dormitory, with seventy five pounds and a packet of white powder sitting snugly over my heart.

Chapter Six

October dipped his finger in the powder and tasted it.

'I don't know what it is either,' he said, shaking his head. 'I'll get it analysed.'

I bent down and patted his dog, and fondled its ears.

He said 'You do realise what a risk you'll be running if you take his money and don't give the dope to the horse?'

I grinned up at him.

'It's no laughing matter,' he said seriously. 'They can be pretty free with their boots, these people, and it would be no help to us if you get your ribs kicked in . . .'

'Actually,' I said, straightening up, 'I do think it might be best if Sparking Plug didn't win . . . I could hardly hope to attract custom from the dopers we are really after if they heard I had double-crossed anyone before.'

'You're quite right.' He sounded relieved. 'Sparking Plug must lose; but Inskip . . . how on earth can I tell him that the jockey must pull back?'

'You can't,' I said. 'You don't want them getting into trouble. But it won't matter much if I do. The horse won't win if I keep him thirsty tomorrow morning and give him a bucketful of water just before the race.'

He looked at me with amusement. 'I see you've learned a thing or two.'

'It'd make your hair stand on end, what I've learned.'

He smiled back. 'All right then. I suppose it's the only thing to do. I wonder what the National Hunt Committee would think of a Steward conspiring with one of his own stable lads to stop a favourite?' He laughed. 'I'll tell Roddy Beckett what to expect . . . though it won't be so funny for Inskip, nor for the lads here, if they back the horse, nor for the general public, who'll lose their money.'

'No,' I agreed.

He folded the packet of white powder and tucked it back into the envelope with the money. The seventy-five pounds had foolishly been paid in a bundle of new fivers with consecutive numbers: and we had agreed that October would take them and try to discover to whom they had been issued.

I told him about the long run-ins on all of the courses where the eleven horses had won.

'It almost sounds as if they might have been using vitamins after all,' he said thoughtfully. 'You can't detect them in dope tests because technically they are not dope at all, but food. The whole question of vitamins is very difficult.'

'They increase stamina?' I asked.

'Yes, quite considerably. Horses which "die" in the last half mile – and as you pointed out, all eleven are that type – would be ideal subjects. But vitamins were among the first things we considered, and we had to eliminate them. They can help horses to win, if they are injected in massive doses into the bloodstream, and they are undetectable in analysis because they are used up in the winning, but they are undetectable in other ways too. They don't excite, they don't bring a horse back from a race looking as though benzedrine were coming out of his ears.' He sighed. 'I don't know . . .'

With regret I made my confession that I had learned nothing from Beckett's typescript.

'Neither Beckett nor I expected as much from it as you did,' he said. 'I've been talking to him a lot this week, and we think that although all those extensive inquiries were made at the time, you might find something that was overlooked if you moved to one of the stables where those eleven horses were trained when they were doped. Of course, eight of the horses were sold and have changed stables, which is a pity, but three are still with their original trainers, and it might be best if you could get a job with one of those.'

'Yes,' I said. 'All right. I'll try all three trainers and see if one of them will take me on. But the trail is very cold by now . . . and joker number twelve will turn up in a different stable altogether. There was nothing, I suppose, at Haydock this week?'

'No. Saliva samples were taken from all the runners before the selling chase, but the favourite won, quite normally, and we didn't have the samples analysed. But now that you've spotted that those five courses must have been chosen deliberately for their long finishing straights we will keep stricter watches there than ever. Especially if one of those eleven horses runs there again.'

'You could check with the racing calendar to see if any has been entered,' I agreed. 'But so far none of them has been doped twice, and I can't see why the pattern should change.'

A gust of bitter wind blew down the gully, and he shivered. The little stream, swollen with yesterday's rains, tumbled busily over its rocky bed. October whistled to his dog, who was sniffing along its banks.

'By the way,' he said, shaking hands, 'the vets are of the opinion that the horses were not helped on their way by pellets or darts, or anything shot or thrown. But they can't be a hundred per cent certain. They didn't at the time examine all the horses very closely. But if we get another one I'll see they go over every inch looking for punctures.'

'Fine.' We smiled at each other and turned away. I liked him. He was imaginative and had a sense of humour to leaven the formidable big-business-executive power of his speech and manner. A tough man, I thought appreciatively: tough in mind, muscular in body, unswerving in purpose: a man of the kind to have earned an earldom, if he hadn't inherited it.

Sparking Plug had to do without his bucket of water that night and again the following morning. The box driver set off to Leicester with a pocketful of hard-earned money from the lads and their instructions to back the horse to win; and I felt a traitor.

Inskip's other horse, which had come in the box too, was engaged in the third race, but the novice 'chase was not until the fifth race on the card, which left me free to watch the first two races as well as Sparks' own. I bought a race card and found a space on the parade ring rails, and watched the horses for the first race being led round. Although from the form books I knew the names of a great many trainers they were still unknown to me by sight; and accordingly, when they stood chatting with their jockeys in the ring, I tried, for interest, to identify some of them. There were only seven of them engaged in the first race, Owen, Cundell, Beeby, Cazalet, Humber ... Humber? What was it that I had heard about Humber? I couldn't remember. Nothing very important, I thought.

Humber's horse looked the least well of the lot, and the lad leading him round wore unpolished shoes, a dirty rain-coat and an air of not caring to improve matters. The jockey's jersey, when he took his coat off, could be seen to be still grubby with mud from a former outing, and the trainer who had failed to provide clean colours or to care about stable smartness, was a large, bad-tempered looking man leaning on a thick, knobbed walking stick.

As it happened, Humber's lad stood beside me on the stand to watch the race.

'Got much chance?' I asked idly.

'Waste of time running him,' he said, his lip curling. 'I'm fed to the back molars with the sod.'

'Oh. Perhaps your other horse is better, though?' I murmured, watching the runners line up for the start.

'My other horse?' He laughed without mirth. 'Three others, would you believe it? I'm fed up with the whole sodding set up. I'm packing it in at the end of the week, pay or no pay.'

I suddenly remembered what I had heard about Humber. The worst stable in the country to work for, the boy in the Bristol hostel had said: they starved the lads and knocked them about and could only get riff-raff to work there.

'How do you mean, pay or no pay?' I asked.

'Humber pays sixteen quid a week, instead of eleven,' he said, 'but it's not bloody worth it. I've had a bellyful of bloody Humber. I'm getting out.'

The race started, and we watched Humber's horse finish last. The lad disappeared, muttering, to lead it away.

I smiled, followed him down the stairs, and forgot him, because waiting near the bottom step was a seedy, black-moustached man whom I instantly recognised as having been in the bar at the Cheltenham dance.

I walked slowly away to lean over the parade ring rail, and he inconspicuously followed. He stopped beside me, and with his eyes on the one horse already in the ring, he said, 'I hear that you are hard up.'

'Not after today, I'm not,' I said, looking him up and down.

He glanced at me briefly. 'Oh. Are you so sure of Sparking Plug?'

'Yeah,' I said with an unpleasant smirk. 'Certain.' Someone, I reflected, had been kind enough to tell him which horse I looked after: which meant he had been checking up on me. I trusted he had learned nothing to my advantage.

'Hmm.'

A whole minute passed. Then he said casually, 'Have you ever thought of changing your job . . . going to another stable?'

'I've thought of it,' I admitted, shrugging. 'Who hasn't?'

'There's always a market for good lads,' he pointed out, 'and I've heard you're a dab hand at the mucking out. With a reference from Inskip you could get in anywhere, if you told them you were prepared to wait for a vacancy.'

'Where?' I asked; but he wasn't to be hurried. After another minute he said, still conversationally, 'It can be very . . . er . . . lucrative . . . working for some stables.'

'Oh?'

'That is,' he coughed discreetly, 'if you are ready to do a bit more than the stable tells you to.'

'Such as?'

'Oh . . . general duties,' he said vaguely. 'It varies. Anything helpful to, er, the person who is prepared to supplement your income.'

'And who's that?'

He smiled thinly. 'Look upon me as his agent. How about it? His terms are a regular fiver a week for information about the results of training gallops and things like that, and a good bonus for occasional special jobs of a more, er, risky nature.'

'It don't sound bad,' I said slowly, sucking in my lower lip. 'Can't I do it at Inskip's?'

'Inskip's is not a betting stable,' he said. 'The horses always run to win. We do not need a permanent employee in that sort of place. There are however at present two betting stables without a man of ours in them, and you would be useful in either.'

He named two leading trainers, neither of whom was one of the three people I had already planned to apply to. I would have to decide whether it would not be more useful to join what was clearly a well-organized spy system, than to work with a once-doped horse who would almost certainly not be doped again.

'I'll think it over,' I said. 'Where can I get in touch with you?'

'Until you're on the pay roll, you can't,' he said simply. 'Sparking Plug's in the fifth, I see. Well, you can give me your answer after that race. I'll be somewhere on your way back to the stables. Just nod if you agree, and shake your head if you don't. But I can't see you passing up a chance like this, not one of your sort.' There was a sly contempt in the smile he gave me that made me unexpectedly wince inwardly.

He turned away and walked a few steps, and then came back.

'Should I have a big bet on Sparking Plug, then?' he asked.

'Oh . . . er . . . well . . . if I were you I'd save your money.'

He looked surprised, and then suspicious, and then knowing. 'So that's how the land lies,' he said. 'Well, well, well.' He laughed, looking at me as if I'd crawled out from under a stone. He was a man who despised his tools. 'I can see you're going to be very useful to us. Very useful indeed.'

I watched him go. It wasn't from kind-heartedness that I had stopped him backing Sparking Plug, but because it was the only way to retain and strengthen his confidence. When he was fifty yards away, I followed him. He made straight for the bookmakers in Tattersalls and strolled along the rows, looking at the odds displayed by each firm; but as far as I could see he was in fact innocently planning to bet on the next race, and not reporting to anyone the outcome of his talk with me. Sighing, I put ten shillings on an outsider and went back to watch the horses go out for the race.

Sparking Plug thirstily drank two full buckets of water, stumbled over the second last fence, and cantered tiredly in behind the other seven runners to the accompaniment of boos from the cheaper enclosures. I watched him with regret. It was a thankless way to treat a great-hearted horse.

The seedy, black-moustached man was waiting when I led the horse away to the stables. I nodded to him, and he sneered knowingly back.

'You'll hear from us,' he said.

There was gloom in the box going home and in the yard the next day over Sparking Plug's unexplainable defeat, and I went alone to Slaw on Tuesday evening, when Soupy duly handed over another seventy-five pounds. I checked it. Another fifteen new fivers, consecutive to the first fifteen.

'Ta,' I said. 'What do you get out of this yourself?'

Soupy's full mouth curled. 'I do all right. You mugs take the risks, I get a cut for setting you up. Fair enough, eh?'

'Fair enough. How often do you do this sort of thing?' I tucked the envelope of money into my pocket.

He shrugged, looking pleased with himself. 'I can spot blokes like you a mile off. Inskip must be slipping, though. First time I've known him pick a bent penny, like. But those darts matches come in very handy . . . I'm good, see. I'm always in the team. And there's a lot of stables in

Yorkshire ... with a lot of beaten favourites for people to scratch their heads over.'

'You're very clever,' I said.

He smirked. He agreed.

I walked up the hill planning to light a fuse under T.N.T., the high explosive kid.

In view of the black-moustached man's offer I decided to read through Beckett's typescript yet again, to see if the eleven dopings could have been the result of systematic spying. Looking at things from a fresh angle might produce results, I thought, and also might help me make up my mind whether or not to back out of the spying job and go to one of the doped horse's yards as arranged.

Locked in the bathroom I began again at page one. On page sixty-seven, fairly early in the life history of the fifth of the horses, I read 'Bought at Ascot Sales, By D. L. Mentiff, Esq., of York for four hundred and twenty guineas, passed on for five hundred pounds to H. Humber of Posset, County Durham, remained three months, ran twice unplaced in maiden hurdles, subsequently sold again, at Doncaster, being bought for six hundred guineas by N. W. Davies, Esq., of Leeds. Sent by him to L. Peterson's training stables at Mars Edge, Staffs, remained eighteen months, ran in four maiden hurdles, five novice chases, all without being placed. Races listed below.' Three months at Humber's. I smiled. It appeared that horses didn't stay with him any longer than lads. I ploughed on through the details, page after solid page.

On page ninety-four I came across the following: 'Alamo was then offered for public auction at Kelso, and a Mr. John Arbuthnot, living in Berwickshire, paid three hundred guineas for him. He sent him to be trained by H. Humber at Posset, County Durham, but he was not entered for any races, and Mr. Arbuthnot sold him to Humber for the same sum. A few weeks later he was sent for resale at Kelso. This time Alamo was bought for three hundred and seventy-five guineas by a Mr. Clement Smithson, living at Nantwich, Cheshire, who kept him at home for the summer and then sent him to a trainer called Samuel Martin at Malton, Yorkshire, where he ran unplaced in four maiden hurdles before Christmas (see list attached).'

I massaged my stiff neck. Humber again.

I read on.

On page one hundred and eighty, I read, 'Ridgeway was then acquired as a yearling by a farmer, James Green, of Home Farm, Crayford, Surrey, in settlement of a bad debt. Mr. Green put him out to grass for two years, and had him broken in, hoping he would be a good hunter. However, a Mr. Taplow of Pusey, Wilts, said he would like to buy him and put him in training for racing. Ridgeway was trained for flat races by Ronald Streat of Pusey, but was unplaced in all his four races that summer. Mr. Taplow then sold Ridgeway privately to Albert George, farmer, of Bridge Lewes, Shropshire, who tried to train him himself but said he found he didn't have time to do it properly, so he sold him to a man a cousin of his knew near Durham, a trainer called Hedley Humber.

Humber apparently thought the horse was no good, and Ridgeway went up for auction at Newmarket in November, fetching two hundred and ninety guineas and being bought by Mr. P. J. Brewer, of the Manor, Witherby, Lancs . . .'

I ploughed right on to the end of the typescript, threading my way through the welter of names, but Humber was not mentioned anywhere again.

Three of the eleven horses had been in Humber's yard for a brief spell at some distant time in their careers. That was all it amounted to.

I rubbed my eyes, which were gritty from lack of sleep, and an alarm clock rang suddenly, clamorously, in the silent cottage. I looked at my watch in surprise. It was already half past six. Standing up and stretching, I made use of the bathroom facilities, thrust the typescript up under my pyjama jacket and the jersey I wore on top and shuffled back yawning to the dormitory, where the others were already up and struggling puffy-eyed into their clothes.

Down in the yard it was so cold that everything one touched seemed to suck the heat out of one's fingers, leaving them numb and fumbling, and the air was as intense an internal shaft to the chest as iced coffee sliding down the oesophagus. Muck out the boxes, saddle up, ride up to the moor, canter, walk, ride down again, brush the sweat off, make the horse comfortable, give it food and water, and go in to breakfast. Repeat for the second horse, repeat for the third, and go in to lunch.

While we were eating Wally came in and told two others and me to go and clean the tack, and when we had finished our tinned plums and custard we went along to the tack room and started on the saddles and bridles. It was warm there from the stove, and I put my head back on a saddle and went solidly asleep.

One of the others jogged my legs and said, 'Wake up Dan, there's a lot to do,' and I drifted to the surface again. But before I opened my eyes the other lad said, 'Oh leave him, he does his share,' and with blessings on his head I sank back into blackness. Four o'clock came too soon, and with it the three hours of evening stables: then supper at seven and another day nearly done.

For most of the time I thought about Humber's name cropping up three times in the typescript. I couldn't really see that it was of more significance than that four of the eleven horses had been fed on horse cubes at the time of their doping. What was disturbing was that I should have missed it entirely on my first two reading. I realised that I had had no reason to notice the name Humber before seeing him and his horse and talking to his lad at Leicester, but if I had missed one name occurring three times, I could have missed others as well. The thing to do would be to make lists of every single name mentioned in the typescript, and see if any other turned up in association with several of the horses. An electric computer could have done it in seconds. For me, it looked like another night in the bathroom.

There were more than a thousand names in the typescript. I listed half of them on the Wednesday night, and slept a bit, and finished them on Thursday night, and slept some more.

On Friday the sun shone for a change, and the morning was beautiful on the moor. I trotted Sparking Plug along the track somewhere in the middle of the string and thought about the lists. No names except Humber's and one other occurred in connection with more than two of the horses. But the one other was a certain Paul J. Adams, and he had at one time or another owned six of them. Six out of eleven. It couldn't be a coincidence. The odds against it were phenomenal. I was certain I had made my first really useful discovery, yet I couldn't see why the fact that P. J. Adams, Esq. had owned a horse for a few months once should enable it to be doped a year or two later. I puzzled over it all morning without a vestige of understanding.

As it was a fine day, Wally said, it was a good time for me to scrub some rugs. This meant laying the rugs the horses wore to keep them warm in their boxes flat on the concrete in the yard, soaking them with the aid of a hose pipe, scrubbing them with a long-handled broom and detergent, hosing them off again, and hanging the wet rugs on the fence to drip before they were transferred to the warm tack room to finish drying thoroughly. It was an unpopular job, and Wally, who had treated me even more coldly since Sparking Plug's disgrace (though he had not gone so far as to accuse me of engineering it), could hardly conceal his dislike when he told me that it was my turn to do it.

However, I reflected, as I laid out five rugs after lunch and thoroughly soaked them with water, I had two hours to be alone and think. And as so often happens, I was wrong.

At three o'clock, when the horses were dozing and the lads were either copying them or had made quick trips to Harrogate with their new pay packets; when stable life was at its siesta and only I with my broom showed signs of reluctant activity, Patty Tarren walked in through the gate, across the tarmac, and slowed to a halt a few feet away.

She was wearing a straightish dress of soft looking knobbly green tweed with a row of silver buttons from throat to hem. Her chestnut hair hung in a clean shining bob on her shoulders and was held back from her forehead by a wide green band, and with her fluffy eyelashes and pale pink mouth she looked about as enticing an interruption as a hard worked stable hand could ask for.

'Hullo, Danny boy,' she said.

'Good afternoon, miss.'

'I saw you from my window,' she said.

I turned in surprise, because I had thought October's house entirely hidden by trees, but sure enough, up the slope, one stone corner and a window could be seen through a gap in the leafless boughs. It was, however, a long way off. If Patty had recognised me from that distance she had been using binoculars.

'You looked a bit lonely, so I came down to talk to you.'

'Thank you, miss.'

'As a matter of fact,' she said, lowering the eyelashes, 'the rest of the family don't get here until this evening, and I had nothing to do in that barn of a place all by myself, and I was bored. So I thought I'd come down and talk to you.'

'I see.' I leant on the broom, looking at her lovely face and thinking that there was an expression in her eyes too old for her years.

'It's rather cold out here, don't you think? I want to talk to you about something ... don't you think we could stand in the shelter of that doorway?' Without waiting for an answer she walked towards the doorway in question, which was that of the hay barn, and went inside. I followed her, resting the broom against the door post on the way.

'Yes, miss?' I said. The light was dim in the barn.

It appeared that talking was not her main object after all.

She put her hands round the back of my neck and offered her mouth for a kiss. I bent my head and kissed her. She was no virgin, October's daughter. She kissed with her tongue and with her teeth, and she moved her stomach rhythmically against mine. My muscles turned to knots. She smelled sweetly of fresh soap, more innocent than her behaviour.

'Well ... that's all right, then,' she said with a giggle, disengaging herself and heading for the bulk of the bales of hay which half filled the barn.

'Come on,' she said over her shoulder, and climbed up the bales to the flat level at the top. I followed her slowly. When I got to the top I sat looking down at the hay barn floor with the broom, the bucket and the rug touched with sunshine through the doorway. On top of the hay had been Philip's favourite play place for years when he was little ... and this is a fine time to think of my family, I thought.

Patty was lying on her back three feet away from me. Her eyes were wide and glistening, and her mouth curved open in an odd little smile. Slowly, holding my gaze, she undid all the silver buttons down the front of her dress to a point well below her waist. Then she gave a little shake so that the edges of the dress fell apart.

She had absolutely nothing on underneath.

I looked at her body, which was pearl pink and slender, and very desirable; and she gave a little rippling shiver of anticipation.

I looked back at her face. Her eyes were big and dark, and the odd way in which she was smiling suddenly struck me as being half furtive, half greedy; and wholly sinful. I had an abrupt vision of myself as she must see me, as I had seen myself in the long mirror in October's London house, a dark, flashy looking stable boy with an air of deceitfulness and an acquaintance with dirt.

I understood her smile, then.

I turned round where I sat until I had my back to her, and felt a flush of anger and shame spread all over my body.

'Do your dress up,' I said.

'Why? Are you impotent after all, Danny boy?'

'Do your dress up,' I repeated. 'The party's over.'

I slid down the hay, walked across the floor and out of the door without looking back. Twitching up the broom and cursing under my breath I let out my fury against myself by scrubbing the rug until my arms ached.

After a while I saw her (green dress re-buttoned) come slowly out of the hay barn, look around her, and go across to a muddy puddle on the edge of the tarmac. She dirtied her shoes thoroughly in it, then childishly walked on to the rug I had just cleaned, and wiped all the mud off carefully in the centre.

Her eyes were wide and her face expressionless as she looked at me.

'You'll be sorry, Danny boy,' she said simply, and without haste strolled away down the yard, the chestnut hair swinging gently on the green tweed dress.

I scrubbed the rug again. Why had I kissed her? Why, after knowing about her from that kiss, had I followed her up into the hay? Why had I been such a stupid, easily roused, lusting fool? I was filled with useless dismay.

One didn't have to accept an invitation to dinner, even if the appetiser made one hungry. But having accepted, one should not so brutally reject what was offered. She had every right to be angry.

And I had every reason to be confused. I had been for nine years a father to two girls, one of whom was nearly Patty's age. I had taught them when they were little not to take lifts from strangers and when they were bigger how to avoid more subtle snares. And here I was, indisputably on the other side of the parental fence.

I felt an atrocious sense of guilt towards October, for I had had the intention, and there was no denying it, of doing what Patty wanted.

Chapter Seven

It was Elinor who rode out on my horse the following morning, and Patty, having obviously got her to change mounts, studiously refused to look at me at all.

Elinor, a dark scarf protecting most of the silver blonde hair, accepted a leg up with impersonal grace, gave me a warm smile of thanks and rode away at the head of the string with her sister. When we got back after the gallops, however, she led the horse into its box and did half of the jobs for it while I was attending to Sparking Plug, I didn't know what she was doing until I walked down the yard, and was surprised to find her there, having grown used to Patty's habit of bolting the horse into the box still complete with saddle, bridle, and mud.

'You go and get the hay and water,' she said. 'I'll finish getting the dirt off, now I've started.'

I carried away the saddle and bridle to the tack room, and took back the hay and water. Elinor gave the horse's mane a few final strokes with the brush, and I put on his rug and buckled the roller round his belly. She watched while I tossed the straw over the floor to make a comfortable bed, and waited until I had bolted the door.

'Thank you,' I said. 'Thank you very much.'

She smiled faintly, 'It's a pleasure. It really is. I like horses. Especially race horses. Lean and fast and exciting.'

'Yes,' I agreed. We walked down the yard together, she to go to the gate and I to the cottage which stood beside it.

'They are so different from what I do all the week,' she said.

'What do you do all the week?'

'Oh ... study. I'm at Durham University.' There was a sudden, private, recollecting grin. Not for me. On level terms, I thought, one might find more in Elinor than good manners.

'It's really extraordinary how well you ride,' she said suddenly. 'I heard Mr. Inskip telling Father this morning that it would be worth getting a licence for you. Have you ever thought of racing?'

'I wish I could,' I said fervently, without thinking.

'Well, why not?'

'Oh ... I might be leaving soon.'

'What a pity.' It was polite; nothing more.

We reached the cottage. She gave me a friendly smile and walked straight on, out of the yard, out of sight. I may not ever see her again, I thought; and was mildly sorry.

When the horse box came back from a day's racing (with a winner, a third, and an also-ran) I climbed up into the cab and borrowed the map again. I wanted to discover the location of the village where Mr. Paul Adams lived, and after some searching I found it. As its significance sank in I began to smile with astonishment. There was, it seemed, yet another place where I could apply for a job.

I went back into the cottage into Mrs. Allnut's cosy kitchen, and ate Mrs. Allnut's delicious egg and chips and bread and butter and fruit cake, and later slept dreamlessly on Mrs. Allnut's lumpy mattress, and in the morning bathed luxuriously in Mrs. Allnut's shining bathroom. And in the afternoon I went up beside the stream with at last something worthwhile to tell October.

He met me with a face of granite, and before I could say a word he hit me hard and squarely across the mouth. It was a back-handed expert blow which started from the waist, and I didn't see it coming until far too late.

'What the hell's that for?' I said, running my tongue round my teeth and being pleased to find that none of them was broken off.

He glared at me. 'Patty told me ...' He stopped as if it were too difficult to go on.

'Oh,' I said blankly.

'Yes, oh,' he mimicked savagely. He was breathing deeply and I thought he was going to hit me again. I thrust my hands into my pockets and his stayed where they were, down by his side, clenching and unclenching.

'What did Patty tell you?'

'She told me everything.' His anger was almost tangible. 'She came to me this morning in tears ... she told me how you made her go into the hay barn ... and held her there until she was worn out with struggling to get away ... she told the ... the disgusting things you did to her with your hands ... and then how you forced her ... forced her to ...' He couldn't say it.

I was appalled. 'I didn't,' I said vehemently. 'I didn't do anything like that. I kissed her ... and that's all. She's making it up.'

'She couldn't possibly have made it up. It was too detailed ... She couldn't know such things unless they had happened to her.'

I opened my mouth and shut it again. They had happened to her, right enough; somewhere, with someone else, more than once, and certainly also with her willing co-operation. And I could see that to some extent at least she was going to get away with her horrible revenge, because there are some things you can't say about a girl to her father, especially if you like him.

October said scathingly, 'I have never been so mistaken in a man before. I thought you were responsible ... or at least able to control yourself. Not a cheap lecherous jackanapes who would take my money – and my regard – and amuse yourself behind my back, debauching my daughter.'

There was enough truth in that to hurt, and the guilt I felt over my stupid behaviour didn't help. But I had to put up some kind of defence, because I would never have harmed Patty in any way, and there was still the investigation into the doping to be carried on. Now I had got so far, I did not want to be packed off home in disgrace.

I said slowly, 'I did go with Patty into the hay barn. I did kiss her. Once. Only once. After that I didn't touch her. I literally didn't touch any part of her, not her hand, not her dress ... nothing.'

He looked at me steadily for a long time while the fury slowly died out of him and a sort of weariness took its place.

At length he said, almost calmly, 'One of you is lying. And I have to believe my daughter.' There was an unexpected flicker of entreaty in his voice.

'Yes,' I said. I looked away, up the gully. 'Well ... this solves one problem, anyway.'

'What problem?'

'How to leave here with the ignominious sack and without a reference.'

It was so far away from what he was thinking about that it was several moments before he showed any reaction at all, and then he gave me an attentive, narrow-eyed stare which I did not try to avoid.

'You intend to go on with the investigation, then?'

'If you are willing.'

'Yes,' he said heavily, at length. 'Especially as you are moving on and will have no more opportunities of seeing Patty. In spite of what I personally think of you, you do still represent our best hope of success, and I suppose I must put the good of racing first.'

He fell silent. I contemplated the rather grim prospect of continuing to do that sort of work for a man who hated me. Yet the thought of giving up was worse. And that was odd.

Eventually he said, 'Why do you want to leave without a reference? You won't get a job in any of these three stables without a reference.'

'The only reference I need to get a job in the stable I am going to is no reference at all.'

'Whose stable?'

'Hedley Humber's.'

'Humber!' He was sombrely incredulous. 'But why? He's a very poor trainer and he didn't train any of the doped horses. What's the point of going there?'

'He didn't train any of the horses when they won,' I agreed, 'but he had three of them through his hands earlier in their careers. There is also a man called P. J. Adams who at one time or another owned six more of them. Adams lives, according to the map, less than ten miles from Humber. Humber lives at Posset, in Durham, and Adams at Tellbridge, just over the Northumberland border. That means that nine of the eleven horses spent some time in that one small area of the British Isles. None of them stayed long. The dossiers of Transistor and Rudyard are much less detailed than the others on the subject of their earlier life, and I have now no doubt that checking would show that they too, for a short while, came under the care of either Adams or Humber.'

'But how could the horses having spent some time with Adams or Humber possibly affect their speed months or years later?'

'I don't know,' I said. 'But I'll go and find out.'

There was a pause.

'Very well,' he said heavily. 'I'll tell Inskip that you are dismissed. And I'll tell him it is because you pestered Patricia.'

'Right.'

He looked at me coldly. 'You can write me reports. I don't want to see you again.'

I watched him walk away strongly up the gully. I didn't know whether or not he really believed any more that I had done what Patty said; but I did know that he needed to believe it. The alternative, the truth, was so much worse. What father wants to discover that his beautiful eighteen-year-old daughter is a lying slut?

And as for me, I thought that on the whole I had got off lightly; if I had found that anyone had assaulted Belinda or Helen I'd have half killed him.

After second exercise the following day Inskip told me exactly what he thought of me, and I didn't particularly enjoy it.

After giving me a public dressing down in the centre of the tarmac (with the lads grinning in sly amusement as they carried their buckets and hay nets with both ears flapping) he handed back the insurance card and income tax form – there was still a useful muddle going on over the illegible Cornish address on the one October had originally provided me with – and told me to pack my bags and get out of the yard at once. It would be no use my giving his name as a reference he said, because Lord October had expressly forbidden him to vouch for my character, and it was a decision with which he thoroughly agreed. He gave me a week's wages in lieu of notice, less Mrs. Allnut's share, and that was that.

I packed my things in the little dormitory, patted goodbye to the bed

I had slept in for six weeks, and went down to the kitchen where the lads were having their midday meal. Eleven pairs of eyes swivelled in my direction. Some were contemptuous, some were surprised, one or two thought it funny. None of them looked sorry to see me go. Mrs. Allnut gave me a thick cheese sandwich, and I ate it walking down the hill to Slaw to catch the two o'clock bus to Harrogate.

And from Harrogate, where?

No lad in his senses would go straight from a prosperous place like Inskip's to ask for a job at Humber's, however abruptly he had been thrown out; there had to be a period of some gentle sliding downhill if it were to look unsuspicious. In fact, I decided, it would be altogether much better if it were Humber's head travelling lad who offered me work, and not I who asked for it. It should not be too difficult. I could turn up at every course where Humber had a runner, looking seedier and seedier and more and more ready to take any job at all, and one day the lad-hungry stable would take the bait.

Meanwhile I needed somewhere to live. The bus trundled down to Harrogate while I thought it out. Somewhere in the north east, to be near Humber's local meetings. A big town, so that I could be anonymous in it. An alive town, so that I could find ways of passing the time between race meetings. With the help of maps and guide books in Harrogate public library I settled on Newcastle, and with the help of a couple of tolerant lorry drivers I arrived there late that afternoon and found myself a room in a back-street hotel.

It was a terrible room with peeling, coffee coloured walls, tatty printed linoleum wearing out on the floor, a narrow, hard divan bed, and some scratched furniture made out of stained plywood. Only its unexpected cleanliness and a shiny new washbasin in one corner made it bearable, but it did, I had to admit, suit my appearance and purpose admirably.

I dined in a fish and chip shop for three and six, and went to a cinema, and enjoyed not having to groom three horses or think twice about every word I said. My spirits rose several points at being free again and I succeeded in forgetting the trouble I was in with October.

In the morning I sent off to him in a registered package the second seventy-five pounds, which I had not given him in the gully on Sunday, together with a short formal note explaining why there would have to be a delay before I engaged myself to Humber.

From the post office I went to a betting shop and from their calendar copied down all the racing fixtures for the next month. It was the beginning of December, and I found there were very few meetings in the north before the first week in January; which was, from my point of view, a waste of time and a nuisance. After the following Saturday's programme at Newcastle itself there was no racing north of Nottinghamshire until Boxing Day, more than a fortnight later.

Pondering this set-back I next went in search of a serviceable second-hand motor-cycle. It took me until late afternoon to find exactly what I wanted, a souped-up 500 c.c. Norton four years old and the ex-property of a now one-legged young man who had done the ton once too often on the Great North Road. The salesman gave me those details with relish as he took my money and assured me that the bike would still do a hundred at a push. I thanked him politely and left the machine with him to have a new silencer fitted, along with some new hand grips, brake cables and tyres.

Lack of private transport at Slaw had not been a tremendous drawback, and I would not have been concerned about my mobility at Posset were it not for the one obtrusive thought that I might at some time find it advisable to depart in a hurry. I could not forget the journalist, Tommy Stapleton. Between Hexham and Yorkshire he had lost nine hours, and turned up dead. Between Hexham and Yorkshire lay Posset.

The first person I saw at Newcastle races four days later was the man with the black moustache who had offered me steady employment as a stable spy. He was standing in an unobtrusive corner near the entrance, talking to a big-eared boy whom I later saw leading round a horse from one of the best-known gambling stables in the country.

From some distance away I watched him pass to the boy a white envelope and receive a brown envelope in return. Money for information, I thought, and so openly done as to appear innocent.

I strolled along behind Black Moustache when he finished his transaction and made his way to the bookmakers' stands in Tattersalls. As before he appeared to be doing nothing but examining the prices offered on the first race: and as before I staked a few shillings on the favourite in case I should be seen to be following him. In spite of his survey he placed no bets at all, but strolled down to the rails which separated the enclosure from the course itself. There he came to an unplanned looking halt beside an artificial red-head wearing a yellowish leopard skin jacket over a dark grey skirt.

She turned her head towards him, and they spoke. Presently he took the brown envelope from his breast pocket and slipped it into his race card: and after a few moments he and the woman unobtrusively exchanged race cards. He wandered away from the rails, while she put the card containing the envelope into a large shiny black handbag and snapped it shut. From the shelter of the last row of bookies I watched her walk to the entrance into the Club and pass through on to the Members' lawn. I could not follow her there, but I went up on to the stands and watched her walk across the next-door enclosure. She appeared to be well-known. She stopped and spoke to several people . . . a bent old man with a big floppy hat, an obese young man who patted her arm repeatedly, a pair of women in mink cocoons, a group of three men who laughed loudly and hid her from my view so that I could not see if she had given any of them the envelope from her handbag.

The horses cantered down the course and the crowds moved up on to the stands to watch the race. The redhead disappeared among the throng on the Members' stand, leaving me frustrated at losing her. The race was run, and the favourite cantered in by ten lengths. The crowd roared with approval. I stood where I was while people round me flowed down from the stands, waiting without too much hope to see if the leopard-skin redhead would reappear.

Obligingly, she did. She was carrying her handbag in one hand and her race card in the other. Pausing to talk again, this time to a very short fat man, she eventually made her way over to the bookmakers who stood along the rails separating Tattersalls from the Club and stopped in front of one nearest the stands, and nearest to me. For the first time I could see her face clearly: she was younger than I had thought and plainer of feature, with gaps between her top teeth.

She said in a piercing, tinny voice, 'I'll settle my account, Bimmo dear,' and opening her handbag took out a brown envelope and gave it to a small man in spectacles, who stood on a box beside a board bearing the words Bimmo Bognor (est. 1920), Manchester and London.

Mr. Bimmo Bognor took the envelope and put it in his jacket pocket, and his hearty 'Ta, love,' floated up to my attentive ears.

I went down from the stands and collected my small winnings, thinking that while the brown envelope that the red-head had given to Bimmo Bognor *looked* like the envelope that the big-eared lad had given to Black Moustache, I could not be a hundred per cent sure of it. She might have given the lad's envelope to any one of the people I had watched her talk to, or to anyone on the stands while she was out of my sight: and she might then have gone quite honestly to pay her bookmaker.

If I wanted to be certain of the chain, perhaps I could send an urgent message along it, a message so urgent that there would be no wandering among the crowds, but an unconcealed direct line between a and b, and b and c. The urgent message, since Sparking Plug was a runner in the fifth race, presented no difficulty at all; but being able to locate Black Moustache at exactly the right moment entailed keeping him in sight all the afternoon.

He was a creature of habit, which helped. He always watched the races from the same corner of the stand, patronized the same bar between times, and stood inconspicuously near the gate on to the course when the horses were led out of the parade ring. He did not bet.

Humber had two horses at the meeting, one in the third race and one in the last; and although it meant leaving my main purpose untouched until late in the afternoon, I let the third race go by without making any attempt to find his head travelling lad. I padded slowly along behind Black Moustache instead.

After the fourth race I followed him into the bar and jogged his arm violently as he began to drink. Half of his beer splashed over his hand and ran down his sleeve, and he swung round cursing, to find my face nine inches from his own.

'Sorry,' I said. 'Oh, it's you.' I put as much surprise into my voice as I could.

His eyes narrowed. 'What are you doing here? Sparking Plug runs in this race.'

I scowled. 'I've left Inskip's.'

'Have you got one of the jobs I suggested? Good.'

'Not yet. There might be a bit of a delay there, like.'

'Why? No vacancies?'

'They don't seem all that keen to have me since I got chucked out of Inskip's.'

'You got what?' he said sharply.

'Chucked out of Inskip's,' I repeated.

'Why?'

'They said something about Sparking Plug losing last week on the day you spoke to me . . . said they could prove nothing but they didn't want me around no more, and to get out.'

'That's too bad,' he said, edging away.

'But I got the last laugh,' I said, sniggering and holding on to his arm. 'I'll tell you straight, I got the bloody last laugh.'

'What do you mean?' He didn't try to keep the contempt out of his voice, but there was interest in his eyes.

'Sparking Plug won't win today neither,' I stated. 'He won't win because he'll feel bad in his stomach.'

'How do you know?'

'I soaked his salt-lick with liquid paraffin,' I said. 'Every day since I left on Monday he's been rubbing his tongue on a laxative. He won't be feeling like racing. He won't bloody win, he won't.' I laughed.

Black Moustache gave me a sickened look, prised my fingers off his arm, and hurried out of the bar. I followed him carefully. He almost ran down into Tattersalls, and began frantically looking around. The red-headed woman was nowhere to be seen, but she must have been watching, because presently I saw her walking briskly down the rails, to the same spot where they had met before. And there, with a rush she was joined by Black Moustache. He talked vehemently. She listened and nodded. He then turned away more calmly, and walked away out of Tattersalls and back to the parade ring. The woman waited until he was out of sight: then she walked firmly into the Members' enclosure and along the rails until she came to Bimmo Bognor. The little man leant forward over the rails as she spoke earnestly into his ear. He nodded several times and she began to smile, and when he turned round to talk to his clerks I saw that he was smiling broadly too.

Unhurriedly I walked along the rows of bookmakers, studying the odds they offered. Sparking Plug was not favourite, owing to his waterlogged defeat last time out, but no one would chance more than five to one. At that price I staked forty pounds – my entire earnings at Inskip's – on my old charge, choosing a prosperous, jolly-looking bookmaker in the back row.

Hovering within earshot of Mr. Bimmo Bognor a few minutes later I heard him offer seven to one against Sparking Plug to a stream of clients, and watched him rake in their money, confident that he would not have to pay them out.

Smiling contentedly I climbed to the top of the stands and watched Sparking Plug make mincemeat of his opponents over the fences and streak insultingly home by twenty lengths. It was a pity, I reflected, that I was too far away to hear Mr. Bognor's opinion of the result.

My jolly bookmaker handed me two hundred and forty pounds in fivers without a second glance. To avoid Black Moustache and any reprisals he might be thinking of organizing, I then went over to the cheap enclosure in the centre of the course for twenty boring minutes; returning through the horse gate when the runners were down at the start for the last race, and slipping up the stairs to the stand used by the lads.

Humber's head travelling lad was standing near the top of the stands. I pushed roughly past him and tripped heavily over his feet.

'Look where you're bloody going,' he said crossly, focusing a pair of shoe-button eyes on my face.

'Sorry mate. Got corns, have you?'

'None of your bloody business,' he said, looking at me sourly. He would know me again, I thought.

I bit my thumb nail. 'Do you know which of this lot is Martin Davies' head travelling lad?' I asked.

He said, 'That chap over there with the red scarf. Why?'

'I need a job,' I said: and before he could say anything I left him and pushed along the row to the man in the red scarf. His stable had one horse in the race. I asked him quietly if they ran two, and he shook his head and said no.

Out of the corner of my eye I noticed that this negative answer had not been wasted on Humber's head lad. He thought, as I had hoped, that I had asked for work, and had been refused. Satisfied that the seed was planted, I watched the race (Humber's horse finished last) and slipped quietly away from the racecourse via the paddock rails and the Members' car park, without any interception of Black Moustache or a vengeful Bimmo Bognor.

A Sunday endured half in my dreary room and half walking round the empty streets was enough to convince me that I could not drag through the next fortnight in Newcastle doing nothing, and the thought of a solitary Christmas spent staring at coffee-coloured peeling paint was unattractive. Moreover I had two hundred pounds of bookmakers' money packed into my belt alongside what was left of October's: and Humber had no horses entered before the Stafford meeting on Boxing Day. It took me only ten minutes to decide what to do with the time between.

On Sunday evening I wrote to October a report on Bimmo Bognor's intelligence service, and at one in the morning I caught the express to London. I spent Monday shopping and on Tuesday evening, looking civilized in some decent new clothes and equipped with an extravagant pair of Kastle skis I signed the register of a comfortable, bright little hotel in a snow-covered village in the Dolomites.

The fortnight I spent in Italy made no difference one way or another to the result of my work for October, but it made a great deal of difference to me. It was the first real holiday I had had since my parents died, the first utterly carefree, purposeless, self-indulgent break for nine years.

I grew younger. Fast strenuous days on the snow slopes and a succession of evenings dancing with my ski-ing companions peeled away the years of responsibility like skins, until at last I felt twenty-seven instead of fifty, a young man instead of a father; until the unburdening process, begun when I left Australia and slowly fermenting through the weeks of Inskip's, suddenly seemed complete.

There was also a bonus in the shape of one of the receptionists, a rounded glowing girl whose dark eyes lit up the minute she saw me and who, after a minimum of persuasion, uninhibitedly spent a proportion of her nights in my bed. She called me her Christmas box of chocolates. She said I was the happiest lover she had had for a long time, and that I pleased her. She was probably doubly as promiscuous as Patty but she was much more wholesome; and she made me feel terrific instead of ashamed.

On the day I left, when I gave her a gold bracelet, she kissed me and told me not to come back, as things were never as good the second time. She was God's gift to bachelors, that girl.

I flew back to England on Christmas night feeling as physically and mentally fit as I had ever been in my life, and ready to take on the worst that Humber could dish out. Which, as it happened, was just as well.

Chapter Eight

At Stafford on Boxing Day one of the runners in the first race, the selling chase, threw off his jockey a stride after landing in fourth place over the last fence, crashing through the rails, and bolted away across the rough grass in the centre of the course.

A lad standing near me on the draughty steps behind the weighing room ran off cursing to catch him; but as the horse galloped crazily from one end of the course to the other it took the lad, the trainer, and about ten assorted helpers a quarter of an hour to lay their hands on his bridle. I watched them as with worried faces they led the horse, an undistinguished bay, off the course and past me towards the racecourse stables.

The wretched animal was white and dripping with sweat and in obvious distress; foam covered his nostrils and muzzle, and his eyes rolled wildly in their sockets. His flesh was quivering, his ears lay flat on his head, and he was inclined to lash out at anyone who came near him.

His name, I saw from the race card, was Superman. He was not one of the eleven horses I had been investigating: but his hotted up appearance and frantic behaviour, coupled with the fact that he had met trouble at Stafford in a selling chase, convinced me that he was the twelfth of the series. The twelfth; and he had come unstuck. There was, as Beckett had said, no mistaking the effect of whatever had pepped him up. I had never before seen a horse in such a state, which seemed to me much worse than the descriptions of 'excited winners,' I had read in the press cuttings: and I came to the conclusion that Superman was either suffering from an overdose, or had reacted excessively to whatever the others had been given.

Neither October nor Beckett nor Macclesfield had come to Stafford. I could only hope that the precautions October had promised had been put into operation in spite of its being Boxing Day, because I could not, without blowing open my role, ask any of the officials if the pre-race dope tests had been made or other precautions taken, nor insist that the jockey be asked at once for his impressions, that unusual bets should be investigated, and that the horse be thoroughly examined for punctures.

The fact that Superman had safely negotiated all the fences inclined me more and more to believe that he could not have been affected by the stimulant until he was approaching, crossing, or landing over the last. It was there that he had gone wild and, instead of winning, thrown his jockey and decamped. It was there that he had been given the power to sprint the four hundred yards, that long run-in which gave him time and room to overhaul the leading horses.

The only person on the racecourse to whom I could safely talk was Superman's lad, but because of the state of his horse it was bound to be some time before he came out of the stables. Meanwhile there were more steps to be taken towards getting myself a job with Humber.

I had gone to the meeting with my hair unbrushed, pointed shoes unpolished, leather collar turned up, hands in pockets, sullen expression in place. I looked, and felt, a disgrace.

Changing back that morning into stable lad clothes had not been a pleasant experience. The sweaters stank of horses, the narrow cheap trousers looked scruffy, the under-clothes were grey from insufficient washing and the jeans were still filthy with mud and muck. Because of the difficulty of getting them back on Christmas night I had decided against sending the whole lot to the laundry while I was away, and in spite of my distaste in putting them on again, I didn't regret it. I looked all the more on the way to being down and out.

I changed and shaved in the cloakroom at the West Kensington Air Terminal, parked my skis and grip of ski clothes in the Left Luggage department on Euston Station, slept uneasily on a hard seat for an hour or two, breakfasted on sandwiches and coffee from the auto-buffet, and caught the race train to Stafford. At this rate, I thought wryly, I would have bundles of belongings scattered all over London; because neither on the outward nor return journeys had I cared to go to October's London house to make use of the clothes I had left with Terence. I did not want to meet October. I liked him, and saw no joy in facing his bitter resentment again unless I absolutely had to.

Humber had only one runner on Boxing Day, a weedy looking hurdler in the fourth race. I hung over the rails by the saddling boxes and watched his head travelling lad saddle up, while Humber himself leant on his knobbed walking stick and gave directions. I had come for a good close look at him, and what I saw was both encouraging from the angle that one could believe him capable of any evil, and discouraging from the angle that I was going to have to obey him.

His large body was encased in a beautifully cut short camel-hair overcoat, below which protruded dark trousers and impeccable shoes. On his head he wore a bowler, set very straight, and on his hands some pale unsoiled pigskin gloves. His face was large, not fat, but hard. Unsmiling eyes, a grim trap of a mouth, and deep lines running from the corners of his nose to his chin gave his expression a look of cold wilfulness.

He stood quite still, making no unnecessary fussy movements, the complete opposite of Inskip, who was for ever walking busily from side to side of his horse, checking straps and buckles, patting and pulling at the saddle, running his hand down legs, nervously making sure over and over that everything was in order.

In Humber's case it was the boy who held the horse's head who was nervous. Frightened, I thought, was hardly too strong a word for it. He kept giving wary, startled-animal glances at Humber, and stayed out of his sight on the far side of the horse as much as possible. He was a thin, ragged-looking boy of about sixteen, and not far, I judged, from being mentally deficient.

The travelling head lad, middle-aged, with a big nose and an unfriendly air, unhurriedly adjusted the saddle and nodded to the lad to lead the horse off into the parade ring. Humber followed. He walked with a slight limp, more or less disguised by the use of the walking stick, and he proceeded in a straight line like a tank, expecting everyone else to get out of his way.

I transferred myself to the parade ring rails in his wake and watched him give instructions to his jockey, an allowance-claimer who regarded his mount with justified disillusion. It was the head travelling lad, not Humber, who gave the jockey a leg up, and who picked up and carried off with him the horse's rug. Round at the lads' stand I carefully stood directly in front of the head travelling lad and in the lull before the race started I turned sideways and tried to borrow some money from the lad standing next to me, whom I didn't know. Not unexpectedly, but to my relief, the lad refused indignantly and more than loudly enough for Humber's head lad to hear. I hunched my shoulders and resisted the temptation to look round and see if the message had reached its destination.

Humber's horse ran out of energy in the straight and finished second to last. No one was surprised.

After that I stationed myself outside the stable gate to wait for Superman's lad, but he didn't come out for another half an hour, until after the fifth race. I fell into step beside him as if by accident, saying 'Rather you than me, chum, with one like that to look after.' He asked me who I worked for; I said Inskip, and he loosened up and agreed that a cup of char and a wad would go down a treat, after all that caper.

'Is he always that het up after a race?' I said, half-way through the cheese sandwiches.

'No. Usually, he's dog-tired. There's been all hell breaking loose this time, I can tell you.'

'How do you mean?'

'Well, first they came and took some tests on all the runners before the race. Now I ask you, why before? It's not the thing, is it? Not before. You ever had one done before?'

I shook my head.

'Then, see, old Super, he was putting up the same sort of job he always does, looking as if he is going to come on into a place at least and then packing it in going to the last. Stupid basket. No guts, I reckon. They had his heart tested, but it ticks O.K. So it's no guts, sure enough. Anyway, then at the last he suddenly kicks up his heels and bolts off as if the devil was after him. I don't suppose you saw him? He's a nervy customer always, really, but he was climbing the wall when we finally caught him. The old man was dead worried. Well, the horse looked as though he had been got at, and he wanted to stick his oar in first and get a dope test done so that the Stewards shouldn't accuse him of using a booster and take away his ruddy licence. They had a couple of vets fussing over him taking things to be analysed ... dead funny it was, because old Super was trying to pitch them over the stable walls ... and in the end they gave him a jab of something to quieten him down. But how we're going to get him home I don't know.'

'Have you looked after him long?' I asked sympathetically.

'Since the beginning of the season. About four months, I suppose. He's a jumpy customer, as I said, but before this I had just about got him to like me. Gawd, I hope he calms down proper before the jabs wear off, I do straight.'

'Who had him before you?' I asked casually.

'Last year he was in a little stable in Devon with a private trainer called Beaney, I think. Yes, Beaney, that's where he started, but he didn't do any good there.'

'I expect they made him nervous there, breaking him in,' I said.

'No, now that's a funny thing, I said that to one of Beaney's lads when we were down in Devon for one of the August meetings, and he said I must be talking about the wrong horse because Superman was a placid old thing and no trouble. He said if Superman was nervous it must have been on account of something that had happened during the summer after he left their place and before he came to us.'

'Where did he go for the summer?' I asked, picking up the cup of orange-coloured tea.

'Search me. The old man bought him at Ascot sales, I think, for a cheap horse. I should think he will shuffle him off again after this if he can get more than knacker's price for him. Poor old Super. Silly nit.' The lad stared gloomily into his tea.

'You don't think he went off his rocker today because he was doped then?'

'I think he just went bonkers,' he said. 'Stark, staring, raving bonkers. I mean, no one had a chance to dope him, except me and the old man and Chalky, and I didn't, and the old man didn't, because he's not that sort, and you wouldn't think Chalky would either, he's so darn proud being promoted head travelling lad only last month ...'

We finished our tea and went round to watch the sixth race still talking about Superman, but his lad knew nothing else which was of help to me.

After the race I walked the half mile into the centre of Stafford, and from a telephone box sent two identical telegrams to October, one to London and one to Slaw, as I did not know where he was. They read, 'Request urgent information re Superman, specifically where did he go from Beaney, permit holder, Devon, last May approximately. Answer care Post Restante, Newcastle-on-Tyne.'

I spent the evening, incredibly distant from the gaiety of the day before, watching a dreary musical in a three-quarters empty cinema, and slept that night in a dingy bed-and-breakfast hotel where they looked me up and down and asked for their money in advance. I paid, wondering if I would ever get used to being treated like dirt. I felt a fresh shock every time. I supposed I had been too accustomed to the respect I was offered in Australia even to notice it, far less appreciate it. I would appreciate some of it now, I ruefully thought, following the landlady into an unwelcoming little room and listening to her suspicious lectures on no cooking, no hot water after eleven, and no girls.

The following afternoon I conspicuously mooched around in front of Humber's head travelling lad with a hang-dog and worried expression, and after the races went back by bus and train to Newcastle for the night. In the morning I collected the motor-cycle, fitted with the new silencer and other parts, and called at the post office to see if there was a reply from October.

The clerk handed me a letter. Inside, without salutation or signature, there was a single sheet of typescript, which read; 'Superman was born and bred in Ireland. Changed hands twice before reaching John Beaney in Devon. He was then sold by Beaney to H. Humber, Esq. of Posset. Co. Durham, on May 3rd. Humber sent him to Ascot Sales in July, where he was bought by his present trainer for two hundred and sixty guineas.

'Investigations re Superman at Stafford yesterday are all so far uninformative; dope analyses have still to be completed but there is little hope they will show anything. The veterinary surgeon at the course was as convinced as you apparently were that this is another "joker", and made a thorough examination of the horse's skin. There were no visible punctures except the ones he made himself giving the horse sedation.

'Superman was apparently in a normal condition before the race. His jockey reports all normal until the last fence, when the horse seemed to suffer a sort of convulsion, and ejected him from the saddle.

'Further enquiries re Rudyard revealed he was bought four winters ago by P. J. Adams of Telbridge, Northumberland, and sold again within a short time at Ascot. Transistor was bought by Adams at Doncaster three years ago, sold Newmarket Dispersal Sales three months later.

'Enquiries re thirty consecutive five pound notes reveal they were issued by Barclays Bank, Birmingham New Street branch, to a man called Lewis Greenfield, who corresponds exactly to your description of the man who approached you in Slaw. Proceedings against Greenfield and T. N. Tarleton are in hand, but will be held in abeyance until after your main task is completed.

'Your report on Bimmo Bognor is noted, but as you say, the buying of stable information is not a punishable offence in law. No proceedings are at present contemplated, but warning that a spy system is in operation will be given privately to certain trainers.'

I tore the page up and scattered it in the litter basket, then went back to the motor-cycle and put it through its paces down the A1 to Catterick. It handled well, and I enjoyed the speed and found it quite true that it would still do a hundred.

At Catterick that Saturday Humber's head travelling lad rose like a trout to the fly.

Inskip had sent two runners, one of which was looked after by Paddy; and up on the lads' stand before the second race I saw the sharp little Irishman and Humber's head lad talking earnestly together. I was afraid that Paddy might relent towards me enough to say something in my favour, but I needn't have worried. He put my mind at rest himself.

'You're a bloody young fool,' he said, looking me over from my unkempt head to my grubby toes. 'And you've only got what you deserve. That man of Humber's was asking me about you, why you got the kick from Inskip's, and I told him the real reason, not all that eye-wash about messing about with his nibs' daughter.'

'What real reason?' I asked, surprised.

His mouth twisted in contempt. 'People talk, you know. You don't think they keep their traps shut, when there's a good bit of gossip going round? You don't think that Grits didn't tell me how you got drunk at Cheltenham and blew your mouth off about Inskip's? And what you said at Bristol about being willing to put the finger on a horse's box in the yard, well, that got round to me too. And thick as thieves with that crook Soupy, you were, as well. And there was that time when we all put our wages on Sparking Plug and he didn't go a yard . . . I'd lay any money that was your doing. So I told Humber's man he would be a fool to take you on. You're poison, Dan, and I reckon any stable is better off without you, and I told him so.'

'Thanks.'

'You can ride,' said Paddy disgustedly, 'I'll say that for you. And it's an utter bloody waste. You'll never get a job with a decent stable again, it would be like putting a rotten apple into a box of good ones.'

'Did you say all that to Humber's man?'

'I told him no decent stable would take you on,' he nodded. 'And if you ask me it bloody well serves you right.' He turned his back on me and walked away.

I sighed, and told myself I should be pleased that Paddy believed me such a black character.

Humber's head travelling lad spoke to me in the paddock between the last two reaces.

'Hey, you,' he said, catching my arm. 'I hear you're looking for a job.'

'That's right.'

'I might be able to put you in the way of something. Good pay, better than most.'

'Whose stable?' I asked. 'And how much?'

'Sixteen quid a week.'

'Sounds good,' I admitted. 'Where?'

'Where I work. For Mr. Humber. Up in Durham.'

'Humber,' I repeated sourly.

'Well, you want a job, don't you? Of course if you are so well off you can do without a job, that's different.' He sneered at my unprosperous appearance.

'I need a job,' I muttered.

'Well, then?'

'He might not have me,' I said bitterly. 'Like some others I could mention.'

'He will if I put in a word for you, we're short of a lad just now. There's another meeting here next Wednesday. I'll put in a word for you before that and if it is O.K. you can see Mr. Humber on Wednesday and he'll tell you whether he'll have you or not.'

'Why not ask him now?' I said.

'No. You wait till Wednesday.'

'All right,' I said grudgingly. 'If I've got to.'

I could almost see him thinking that by Wednesday I would be just that much hungrier, just that much more anxious to take any job that was offered and less likely to be frightened off by rumours of bad conditions.

I had spent all the bookmaker's two hundred, as well as half of the money I had earned at Inskip's, on my Italian jaunt (of which I regretted not one penny), and after paying for the motor-cycle and the succession of dingy lodgings I had almost nothing left of October's original two hundred. He had not suggested giving me any more for expenses, and I was not going to ask him for any: but I judged that the other half of my Inskip pay could be spent how I liked, and I despatched nearly all of it in the following three days on a motor-cycle trip to Edinburgh, walking round and enjoying the city and thinking myself the oddest tourist in Scotland.

On Tuesday evening, when Hogmanay was in full swing, I braved the head waiter of L'Aperitif, who to his eternal credit treated me with beautifully self-controlled politeness, but quite reasonably checked, before he gave me a little table in a corner, that I had enough money to pay the bill. Impervious to scandalized looks from better dressed diners, I slowly ate, with Humber's establishment in mind, a perfect and enormous dinner of lobster, duck bigarade, lemon soufflé and brie, and drank most of a bottle of Château Leauville Lescases 1948.

With which extravagant farewell to being my own master I rode down the A1 to Catterick on New Year's Day and in good spirits engaged myself to the worst stable in the country.

Chapter Nine

Rumour had hardly done Hedley Humber justice. The discomfort in which the lads were expected to live was so methodically devised that I had been there only one day before I came to the conclusion that its sole purpose was to discourage anyone from staying too long. I discovered that only the head lad and the head travelling lad, who both lived out in Posset, had worked in the yard for more than three months, and that the average time it took for an ordinary lad to decide that sixteen pounds a week was not enough was eight to ten weeks.

This meant that none of the stable hands except the two head lads knew what had happened to Superman the previous summer, because none of them had been there at the time. And caution told me that the only reason the two top men stayed was because they knew what was going on, and that if I asked *them* about Superman I might find myself following smartly in Tommy Stapleton's footsteps.

I had heard all about the squalor of the living quarters at some stables, and I was aware also that some lads deserved no better – some I knew of had broken up and burned their chairs rather than go outside and fetch coal, and others had stacked their dirty dishes in the lavatory and pulled the chain to do the washing up. But even granted that Humber only employed the dregs, his arrangements were very nearly inhuman.

The dormitory was a narrow hayloft over the horses. One could hear every bang of their hooves and the rattle of chains, and through cracks in the plank floor one could see straight down into the boxes. Upwards through the cracks rose a smell of dirty straw and an icy draught. There was no ceiling to the hayloft except the rafters and the tiles of the roof, and no way up into it except a ladder through a hole in the floor. In the one small window a broken pane of glass had been pasted over with brown paper, which shut out the light and let in the cold.

The seven beds, which were all the hayloft held in the way of furniture, were stark, basic affairs made of a piece of canvas stretched tautly on to a tubular metal frame. On each bed there was supposed to be one pillow and two grey blankets, but I had to struggle to get mine back because they had been appropriated by others as soon as my predecessor left. The pillow had no cover, there were no sheets, and there were no mattresses. Everyone went to bed fully dressed to keep warm, and on my third day there it started snowing.

The kitchen at the bottom of the ladder, the only other room available to the lads, was nothing more than the last loose box along one side of the yard. So little had been done to make it habitable as to leave a powerful suggestion that its inmates were to be thought of, and treated, as animals. The bars were still in place over the small window, and there were still bolts on the outside of the split stable door. The floor was still of bare concrete criss-crossed with drainage grooves; one side wall was of rough boards with kick marks still in them and the other three were of bare bricks. The room was chronically cold and damp and dirty; and although it may have been big enough as a home for one horse, it was uncomfortably cramped for seven men.

The minimal furniture consisted of rough benches around two walls, a wooden table, a badly chipped electric cooker, a shelf for crockery, and an old marble wash stand bearing a metal jug and a metal basin, which was all there was in the way of a bathroom. Other needs were catered for in a wooden hut beside the muck heap.

The food, prepared by a slatternly woman perpetually in curlers, was not up to the standard of the accommodation.

Humber, who had engaged me with an indifferent glance and a nod, directed me with equal lack of interest, when I arrived in the yard, to look after four horses, and told me the numbers of their boxes. Neither he nor anyone else told me their names. The head lad, who did one horse himself, appeared to have very little authority, contrary to the practice in most other training stables, and it was Humber himself who gave the orders and who made sure they were carried out.

He was a tyrant, not so much in the quality of the work he demanded, as in the quantity. There were some thirty horses in the yard. The head lad cared for one horse, and the head travelling lad, who also drove the horse box, did none at all. That left twenty-nine horses for seven lads, who were also expected to keep the gallops in order and do all the cleaning and maintenance work of the whole place. On racing days, when one or two lads were away, those remaining often had six horses to see to. It made my stint at Inskip's seem like a rest cure.

At the slightest sign of shirking Humber would dish out irritating little punishments and roar in an acid voice that he paid extra wages for extra work, and anyone who didn't like it could leave. As everyone was there because better stables would not risk employing them, leaving Humber's automatically meant leaving racing altogether. And taking whatever they knew about the place with them. It was very very neat.

My companions in this hell hole were neither friendly nor likeable. The best of them was the nearly half-witted boy I had seen at Stafford on Boxing Day. His name was Jerry, and he came in for a lot of physical abuse because he was slower and more stupid than anyone else.

Two of the others had been to prison and their outlook on life made Soupy Tarleton look like a Sunday-school favourite. It was from one of these, Jimmy, that I had had to wrench my blankets and from the other, a thickset tough called Charlie, my pillow. They were the two bullies of the bunch, and in addition to the free use they made of their boots, they could always be relied upon to tell lying tales and wriggle themselves out of trouble, seeing to it that someone else was punished in their stead.

Reggie was a food stealer. Thin, white faced, and with a twitch in his left eyelid, he had long prehensile hands which could whisk the bread off your plate faster than the eye could follow. I lost a lot of my meagre rations to him before I caught him at it, and it always remained a mystery why, when he managed to eat more than anyone else, he stayed the thinnest.

One of the lads was deaf. He told me phlegmatically in a toneless mumble that his dad had done it when he was little, giving him a few clips too many over the earholes. His name was Bert, and as he occasionally wet himself in bed, he smelled appalling.

The seventh, Geoff, had been there longest, and even after ten weeks never spoke of leaving. He had a habit of looking furtively over his shoulder, and any mention by Jimmy or Charlie about their prison experiences brought him close to tears, so that I came to the conclusion that he had committed some crime and was terrified of being found out. I supposed ten weeks at Humber's might be preferable to jail, but it was debatable.

They knew all about me from the head travelling lad, Jud Wilson. My general dishonesty they took entirely for granted, but they thought I was lucky to have got off without going inside if it was true about October's daughter, and they sniggered about it unendingly, and made merciless obscene jibes that hit their target all too often.

I found their constant closeness a trial, the food disgusting, the work exhausting, the beds relentless, and the cold unspeakable. All of which rather roughly taught me that my life in Australia had been soft and easy, even when I thought it most demanding.

Before I went to Humber's I had wondered why anyone should be foolish enough to pay training fees to a patently unsuccessful trainer, but I gradually found out. The yard itself, for one thing, was a surprise. From the appearance of the horses at race meetings one would have expected their home surroundings to be weedy gravel, broken-hinged boxes and flaked-off paint: but in fact the yard was trim and prosperous looking, and was kept that way by the lads, who never had time off in the afternoons. This glossy window-dressing cost Humber nothing but an occasional gallon of paint and a certain amount of slave driving.

His manner with the owners who sometimes arrived for a look round was authoritative and persuasive, and his fees, I later discovered, were lower than anyone else's, which attracted more custom than he would otherwise have had. In addition some of the horses in the yard were not racehorses at all, but hunters at livery, for whose board, lodging and exercise he received substantial sums without the responsibility of having to train them.

I learned from the other lads that only seven of the stable's inmates had raced at all that season, but that those seven had been hard worked, with an average of a race each every ten days. There had been one winner, two seconds and a third, among them.

None of those seven was in my care. I had been allotted to a quartet consisting of two racehorses which belonged, as far as I could make out, to Humber himself, and two hunters. The two racehorses were bays, about seven years old; one of them had a sweet mouth and no speed and the other a useful sprint over schooling fences but a churlish nature. I pressed Cass, the head lad, to tell me their names, and he said they were Dobbin and Sooty. These unraceman-like names were not to be found in the form book, nor in Humber's list in 'Horses in Training'; and it seemed to me highly probable that Rudyard, Superman, Charcoal and the rest had all spent their short periods in the yard under similar uninformative pseudonyms.

A lad who had gone out of racing would never connect the Dobbin or Sotty he had once looked after with the Rudyard who won a race for another trainer two years later.

But why, *why* did he win two years later? About that, I was as ignorant as ever.

The cold weather came and gripped, and stayed. But nothing, the other lads said, could be as bad as the fearsome winter before; and I reflected that in that January and February I had been sweltering under the midsummer sun. I wondered how Belinda and Helen and Phillip were enjoying their long vacation, and what they would think if they could see me in my dirty down-trodden sub-existence, and what the men would think, to see their employer brought so low. It amused me a good deal to imagine it: and it not only helped the tedious hours to pass more quickly, but kept me from losing my own inner identity.

As the days of drudgery mounted up I began to wonder if anyone who embarked on so radical a masquerade really knew what he was doing.

Expression, speech and movement had to be unremittingly schooled into a convincing show of uncouth dullness. I worked in a slovenly fashion and rode, with a pang, like a mutton-fisted clod; but as time passed all these deceptions became easier. If one pretended long enough to be a wreck, did one finally become one, I wondered. And if one stripped oneself continuously of all human dignity would one in the end be unaware of its absence? I hoped the question would remain academic: and as long as I could have a quiet laugh at myself now and then, I supposed I was safe enough.

My belief that after three months in the yard a lad was given every encouragement to leave was amply borne out by what happened to Geoff Smith.

Humber never rode out to exercise with his horses, but drove in a van to the gallops to watch them work, and returned to the yard while they were still walking back to have a poke round to see what had been done and not done.

One morning, when we went in with the second lot, Humber was standing in the centre of the yard radiating his frequent displeasure.

'You, Smith, and you, Roke, put those horses in their boxes and come here.'

We did so.

'Roke.'

'Sir.'

'The mangers of all your four horses are in a disgusting state. Clean them up.'

'Yes, sir.'

'And to teach you to be more thorough in future you will get up at five-thirty for the next week.'

'Sir.'

I sighed inwardly, but this was to me one of his more acceptable forms of pinprick punishment, since I didn't particularly mind getting up early. It entailed merely standing in the middle of the yard for over an hour, doing nothing. Dark, cold and boring. I don't think he slept much himself. His bedroom window faced down the yard, and he always knew if one were not standing outside by twenty to six, and shining a torch to prove it.

'And as for you.' He looked at Geoff with calculation. 'The floor of number seven is caked with dirt. You'll clean out the straw and scrub the floor with disinfectant before you get your dinner.'

'But sir,' protested Geoff incautiously, 'if I don't go in for dinner with the others, they won't leave me any.'

'You should have thought of that before, and done your work properly in the first place. I pay half as much again as any other trainer would, and I expect value for it. You will do as you are told.'

'But, sir,' whined Geoff, knowing that if he missed his main meal he would go very hungry, 'Can't I do it this afternoon?'

Humber casually slid his walking stick through his hand until he was holding it at the bottom. Then he swung his arm and savagely cracked the knobbed handle across Geoff's thigh.

Geoff yelped and rubbed his leg.

'Before dinner,' remarked Humber: and walked away, leaning on his stick.

Geoff missed his share of the watery half-stewed lumps of mutton, and came in panting to see the last of the bread-and-suet pudding spooned into Charlie's trap-like mouth.

'You bloody sods,' he yelled miserably, 'You bloody lot of sods.'

He stuck it for a whole week. He stood six more heavy blows on various parts of his body, and missed his dinner three more times, and his breakfast twice, and his supper once. Long before the end of it he was in tears, but he didn't want to leave.

After five days Cass came into the kitchen at breakfast and told Geoff, 'The boss has taken against you, I'm afraid. You won't ever do anything right for him again from now on. Best thing you can do, and I'm telling you for your own good, mind, is to find a job somewhere else. The boss gets these fits now and then when one of the lads can't do anything right, and no one can change him when he gets going. You can work until you're blue in the face, but he won't take to you any more. You don't want to get yourself bashed up any more, now do you? All I'm telling you is that if you stay here you'll find that what has happened so far is only the beginning. See? I'm only telling you for your own good.'

Even so, it was two more days before Geoff painfully packed his old army kit bag and sniffed his way off the premises.

A weedy boy arrived the next morning as a replacement, but he only stayed three days as Jimmy stole his blankets before he came and he was not strong enough to get them back. He moaned piteously through two freezing nights, and was gone before the third.

The next morning, before breakfast, it was Jimmy himself who collected a crack from the stick.

He came in late and cursing and snatched a chunk of bread out of Jerry's hand.

'Where's my bloody breakfast?'

We had eaten it, of course.

'Well,' he said, glaring at us, 'you can do my ruddy horses, as well. I'm off. I'm not bloody well staying here. This is worse than doing bird. You won't catch me staying here to be swiped at, I'll tell you that.'

Reggie said, 'Why don't you complain?'

'Who to?'

'Well . . . the bluebottles.'

'Are you out of your mind?' said Jimmy in amazement. 'You're a bloody nit, that's what you are. Can you see me, with my form, going into the cop house and saying I got a complaint to make about my employer, he hit me with his walking stick? For a start, they'd laugh. They'd laugh their bleeding heads off. And then what? Supposing they come here and asked Cass if he's seen anyone getting the rough end of it? Well, I'll tell you, that Cass wants to keep his cushy job. Oh no, he'd say, I ain't seen nothing. Mr Humber, he's a nice kind gentleman with a heart of gold, and what can you expect from an ex-con but a pack of bull? Don't ruddy well make me laugh. I'm off, and if the rest of you've got any sense, you'll be out of it too.'

No one, however, took his advice.

I found out from Charlie that Jimmy had been there two weeks longer than he, which made it, he thought, about eleven weeks.

As Jimmy strode defiantly out of the yard I went rather thoughtfully about my business. Eleven weeks, twelve at the most, before Humber's arm started swinging. I had been there already three: which left me a maximum of nine more in which to discover how he managed the doping. It wasn't that I couldn't probably last out as long as Geoff if it came to the point, but that if I hadn't uncovered Humber's method before he focused his attention on getting rid of me, I had very little chance of doing it afterwards.

Three weeks, I thought, and I had found out nothing at all except that I wanted to leave as soon as possible.

Two lads came to take Geoff's and Jimmy's places, a tall boy called Lenny who had been to Borstal and was proud of it, and Cecil, a far-gone alcoholic of about thirty-five. He had, he told us, been kicked out of half the stables in England because he couldn't keep his hands off the bottle. I don't know where he got the liquor from or how he managed to hide it, but he was certainly three parts drunk every day by four o'clock, and snored in a paralytic stupor every night.

Life, if you could call it that, went on.

All the lads seemed to have a good reason for having to earn the extra wages Humber paid. Lenny was repaying some money he had stolen from another employer, Charlie had a wife somewhere drawing maintenance, Cecil drank, Reggie was a compulsive saver, and Humber sent Jerry's money straight off to his parents. Jerry was proud of being able to help them.

I had let Jud Wilson and Cass know that I badly needed to earn sixteen pounds a week because I had fallen behind on hire purchase payments on the motor-cycle, and this also gave me an obvious reason for needing to spend some time in the Posset post office on Saturday afternoons.

Public transport from the stables to Posset, a large village a mile and a half away, did not exist. Cass and Jud Wilson both had cars, but would give no lifts. My motor-cycle was the only other transport available, but to the lads' fluently expressed disgust I refused to use it on the frosty snow-strewn roads for trips down to the pub in the evenings. As a result we hardly ever went to Posset except on the two hours we had off on Saturday afternoons, and also on Sunday evenings, when after a slightly less relentless day's work everyone had enough energy left to walk for their beer.

On Saturdays I unwrapped the motor-cycle from its thick plastic cocoon and set off to Posset with Jerry perched ecstatically on the pillion. I always took poor simple-minded Jerry because he got the worst of everything throughout the week; and we quickly fell into a routine. First we went to the post office for me to post off my imaginary hire purchase. Instead, leaning on the shelf among the telegram forms and scraps of pink blotting paper, I wrote each week a report to October, making sure that no one from the stables looked over my shoulder. Replies, if any, I collected, read, and tore up over the litter basket.

Jerry accepted without question that I would be at least a quarter of an hour in the post office, and spent the time unsuspiciously at the other end of the shop inspecting the stock in the toy department. Twice he bought a big friction-drive car and played with it, until it broke, on the dormitory floor: and every week he bought a children's fourpenny comic, over whose picture strips he giggled contentedly for the next few days. He couldn't read a word, and often asked me to explain the captions, so that I became intimately acquainted with the doings of Micky the Monkey and Flip McCoy.

Leaving the post office we climbed back on to the motor-cycle and rode two hundred yards down the street to have tea. This ritual took place in a square bare café with margarine coloured walls, cold lighting, and messy table tops. For decoration there were pepsi-cola advertisements, and for service a bored looking girl with no stockings and mousy hair piled into a matted, wispy mountain on top of her head.

None of this mattered. Jerry and I ordered and ate with indescribable enjoyment a heap of lamb chops, fried eggs, flabby chips and bright green peas. Charlie and the others were to be seen doing the same at adjoining tables. The girl knew where we came from, and looked down on us, as her father owned the café.

On our way out Jerry and I packed our pockets with bars of chocolate to supplement Humber's food, a hoard which lasted each week exactly as long as it took Reggie to find it.

By five o'clock we were back in the yard, the motor-cycle wrapped up again, the week's highlight nothing but a memory and a belch, the next seven days stretching drearily ahead.

There were hours, in that life, in which to think. Hours of trotting the horses round and round a straw track in a frozen field, hours brushing the dust out of their coats, hours cleaning the muck out of their boxes and carrying their water and hay, hours lying awake at night listening to the stamp of the horses below and the snores and mumblings from the row of beds.

Over and over again I thought my way through all I had seen or read or heard since I came to England: and what emerged as most significant was the performance of Superman at Stafford. He had been doped: he was the twelfth of the series: but he had not won.

Eventually I changed the order of these thoughts. He had been doped, and he had not won; but was he, after all, the twelfth of the series? He might be the thirteenth, the fourteenth . . . there might have been others who had come to grief.

On my third Saturday, when I had been at Humber's just over a fortnight, I wrote asking October to look out the newspaper cutting which Tommy Stapleton had kept, about a horse going beserk and killing a woman in the paddock at Cartmel races. I asked him to check the horse's history.

A week later I read his typewritten reply.

'Old Etonian, destroyed at Cartmel, Lancashire, at Whitsun this year, spent the previous November and December in Humber's yard. Humber claimed him in a selling race, and sold him again at Leicester sales seven weeks later.

'*But:* Old Etonian went beserk in the parade ring *before* the race; he was due to run in a handicap, not a seller; and the run-in at Cartmel is short. None of these facts conform to the pattern of the others.

'Dope tests were made on Old Etonian, but proved negative.

'No one could explain why he behaved as he did.'

Tommy Stapleton, I thought, must have had an idea, or he would not have cut out the report, yet he could not have been sure enough to act on it without checking up. And checking up had killed him. There could be no more doubt of it.

I tore up the paper and took Jerry along to the café, more conscious than usual of the danger breathing down my neck. It didn't, however, spoil my appetite for the only edible meal of the week.

At supper a few days later, in the lull before Charlie turned on his transistor radio for the usual evening of pops from Luxembourg (which I had grown to enjoy) I steered the conversation round to Cartmel races. What, I wanted to know, were they like?

Only Cecil, the drunk, had ever been there.

'It's not like it used to be in the old days,' he said owlishly, not noticing Reggie filch a hunk of his bread and margarine.

Cecil's eyes had a glazed, liquid look, but I had luckily asked my question at exactly the right moment, in the loquacious half-hour between the silent bleariness of the afternoon's liquor and his disappearance to tank up for the night.

'What was it like in the old days?' I prompted.

'They had a fair there.' He hiccuped. 'A fair with roundabouts and swings and side-shows and all. Bank Holiday, see? Whitsun and all that.

Only place outside the Derby you could go on the swings at the races. Course, they stopped it now. Don't like no one to have a good time, they don't. It weren't doing no harm, it weren't, the fair.'

'Fairs,' said Reggie scornfully, his eyes flicking to the crust Jerry held loosely in his hand.

'Good for dipping,' commented Lenny, with superiority.

'Yeah,' agreed Charlie, who hadn't yet decided if Borstal qualified Lenny as a fit companion for one from the higher school.

'Eh?' said Cecil, lost.

'Dipping. Working the pockets,' Lenny said.

'Oh. Well, it can't have been that with the hound trails and they stopped them too. They were good sport, they were. Bloody good day out, it used to be, at Cartmel, but now it's the same as any other ruddy place. You might as well be at Newton Abbot or somewhere. Nothing but ordinary racing like any other day of the week.' He belched.

'What were the hound trails?' I asked.

'Dog races,' he said, smiling foolishly. 'Bloody dog races. They used to have one before the horse races, and one afterwards, but they've ruddy well stopped it now. Bloody kill-joys, that's all they are. Still,' he leered triumphantly, 'if you know what's what you can still have a bet on the dogs. They have the hound trail in the morning now, on the other side of the village from the race-track, but if you get your horse bedded down quick enough you can get there in time for a bet.'

'Dog races?' said Lenny disbelievingly. 'Dogs won't race round no horse track. There ain't no bloody electric hare, for a start.'

Cecil swivelled his head unsteadily in his direction.

'You don't have a track for hound trails,' he said earnestly, in his slurred voice. 'It's a *trail*, see?' Some bloke sets off with a bag full of aniseed and paraffin, or something like that, and drags it for miles and miles round the hills and such. Then they let all the dogs loose and the first one to follow all round the trail and get back quickest is the winner. Year before last someone shot at the bloody favourite half a mile from home and there was a bleeding riot. They missed him, though. They hit the one just behind, some ruddy outsider with no chance.'

'Reggie's ate my crust,' said Jerry sadly.

'Did you go to Cartmel this year too?' I asked.

'No,' Cecil said regretfully. 'Can't say I did. A woman got killed there, and all.'

'How?' asked Lenny, looking avid.

'Some bloody horse bolted in the paddock, and jumped the rails of the parade ring and landed on some poor bloody woman who was just having a nice day out. She backed a loser all right, she did that day. I heard she was cut to bits, time that crazy animal trampled all over her trying to get out through the crowd. He didn't get far, but he kicked out all over the place and broke another man's leg before they got the vet to him and shot him. Mad, they said he was. A mate of mine was there, see, leading one round in the same race, and he said it was something awful, that poor woman all cut up and bleeding to death in front of his eyes.'

The others looked suitably impressed at this horrific story, all except Bert, who couldn't hear it.

'Well,' said Cecil, getting up, 'it's time for my little walk.'

He went out for his little walk, which was presumably to wherever he had hidden his alcohol, because as usual he came back less than an hour later and stumbled up the ladder to his customary oblivion.

Chapter Ten

Towards the end of my fourth week Reggie left (complaining of hunger) and in a day or two was duly replaced by a boy with a soft face who said in a high pitched voice that his name was Kenneth.

To Humber I clearly remained one insignificant face in this endless procession of human flotsam; and as I could safely operate only as long as that state of affairs continued I did as little as possible to attract his attention. He gave me orders, and I obeyed them: and he cursed me and punished me, but not more than anyone else, for the things I left undone.

I grew to recognise his moods at a glance. There were days when he glowered silently all through first and second exercise and turned out again to make sure that no one skimped the third, and on these occasions even Cass walked warily and only spoke if he were spoken to. There were days when he talked a great deal but always in sarcasm, and his tongue was so rough that everyone preferred the silence. There were occasional days when he wore an abstracted air and overlooked our faults, and even rarer days when he looked fairly pleased with life.

At all times he was impeccably turned out, as if to emphasize the difference between his state and ours. His clothes, I judged, were his main personal vanity, but his wealth was also evident in his car, the latest type of Cunard-sized Bentley. It was fitted with back-seat television, plush carpets, radio telephone, fur rugs, air conditioning, and a built-in drinks cabinet holding in racks six bottles, twelve glasses, and a glittering array of chromiumed cork screws, ice picks and miscellaneous objects like swizzle sticks.

I knew the car well, because I had to clean it every Monday afternoon. Bert had to clean it on Fridays. Humber was proud of his car.

He was chauffeured on long journeys in this above-his-status symbol by Jud Wilson's sister Grace, a hard faced amazon of a woman who handled the huge car with practised ease but was not expected to maintain it. I never once spoke to her: she bicycled in from wherever she lived, drove as necessary, and bicycled away again. Frequently the car had not been cleaned to her satisfaction, but her remarks were relayed to Bert and me by Jud.

I looked into every cranny every time while cleaning the inside, but

Humber was neither so obliging nor so careless as to leave hypodermic syringes or phials of stimulants lying about in the glove pockets.

All through my first month there the freezing weather was not only a discomfort but also a tiresome delay. While racing was suspended Humber could dope no horses, and there was no opportunity for me to see what difference it made to his routine when the racing was scheduled for any of the five courses with long run-ins.

On top of that, he and Jud Wilson and Cass were always about in the stables. I wanted to have a look round inside Humber's office, a brick hut standing across the top end of the yard, but I could not risk a search when any one of them might come in and find me at it. With Humber and Jud Wilson away at the races, though, and with Cass gone home to his midday meal, I reckoned I could go into the office to search while the rest of the lads were eating.

Cass had a key to the office, and it was he who unlocked the door in the morning and locked it again at night. As far as I could see he did not bother to lock up when he went home for lunch, and the office was normally left open all day, except on Sunday. This might mean, I thought, that Humber kept nothing there which could possibly be incriminating: but on the other hand he could perhaps keep something there which was apparently innocent but would be incriminating if one understood its significance.

However, the likelihood of solving the whole mystery by a quick look round an unlocked stable office was so doubtful that it was not worth risking discovery, and I judged it better to wait with what patience I could until the odds were in my favour.

There was also Humber's house, a whitewashed converted farm house adjoining the yard. A couple of stealthy surveys, made on afternoons when I was bidden to sweep snow from his garden path, showed that this was an ultra-neat soulless establishment like a series of rooms in shop windows, impersonal and unlived-in. Humber was not married, and downstairs at least there seemed to be nowhere at all snug for him to spend his evenings.

Through the windows I saw no desk to investigate and no safe in which to lock away secrets: all the same I decided it would be less than fair to ignore his home, and if I both drew a blank and got away with an entry into the office, I would pay the house a visit at the first opportunity.

At last it began to thaw on a Wednesday night and continued fast all day Thursday and Friday, so that by Saturday morning the thin slush was disintegrating into puddles, and the stables stirred with the reawakening of hunting and racing.

Cass told me on Friday night that the man who owned the hunters I looked after required them both to be ready for him on Saturday, and after second exercise I led them out and loaded them into the horse box which had come for them.

Their owner stood leaning against the front wing of a well polished Jaguar. His hunting boots shone like glass, his cream breeches were perfection, his pink coat fitted without a wrinkle, his stock was smooth and snowy. He held a sensible leather-covered riding stick in his hand and slapped it against his boot. He was tall, broad and bare-headed, about forty years old, and, from across the yard, handsome. It was only when one was close to him that one could see the dissatisfied look on his face and the evidence of dissipation in his skin.

'You,' he said, pointing at me with his stick. 'Come here.'

I went. He had heavy lidded eyes and a few purple thread veins on his nose and cheeks. He looked at me with superior bored disdain. I am five feet nine inches tall; he was four inches taller, and he made the most of it.

'You'll pay for it if those horses of mine don't last the day. I ride them hard. They need to be fit.'

His voice had the same expensive timbre as October's.

'They're as fit as the snow would allow,' I said calmly.

He raised his eyebrows.

'Sir,' I added.

'Insolence,' he said, 'will get you nowhere.'

'I am sorry, sir, I didn't mean to be insolent.'

He laughed unpleasantly. 'I'll bet you didn't. It's not so easy to get another job, is it? You'll watch your tongue when you speak to me in future, if you know what's good for you.'

'Yes sir.'

'And if those horses of mine aren't fit, you'll wish you'd never been born.'

Cass appeared at my left elbow, looking anxious.

'Is everything all right, sir?' he asked. 'Has Roke done anything wrong, Mr Adams?'

How I managed not to jump out of my skin I am not quite sure. Mr. Adams. Paul James Adams, sometime owner of seven subsequently doped horses?

'Is this bloody gipsy doing my horses any good?' said Adams offensively.

'He's no worse than any of the other lads,' said Cass soothingly.

'And that's saying precious little.' He gave me a mean stare. 'You've had it easy during the freeze. Too damned easy. You'll have to wake your ideas up now hunting has started again. You won't find me as soft as your master, I can tell you that.'

I said nothing. He slapped his stick sharply against his boot.

'Do you hear what I say? You'll find me harder to please.'

'Yes, sir,' I muttered.

He opened his fingers and let his stick fall at his feet.

'Pick it up,' he said.

As I bent to pick it up, he put his booted foot on my shoulder and gave me a heavy, over-balancing shove, so that I fell sprawling on to the soaking, muddy ground.

He smiled with malicious enjoyment.

'Get up, you clumsy lout, and do as you are told. Pick up my stick.'

I got to my feet, picked up his stick and held it out to him. He twitched it out of my hand, and looking at Cass said, 'You've got to show them you won't stand any nonsense. Stamp on them whenever you can. This one,' he looked me coldly up and down, 'needs to be taught a lesson. What do you suggest?'

Cass looked at me doubtfully. I glanced at Adams. This, I thought, was not funny. His greyish blue eyes were curiously opaque, as if he were drunk: but he was plainly sober. I had seen that look before, in the eyes of a stable hand I had once for a short time employed, and I knew what it could mean. I had got to guess at once, and guess right, whether he preferred bullying the weak or the strong. From instinct, perhaps because of his size and evident worldliness, I guessed that crushing the weak would be too tame for him. In which case it was definitely not the moment for any show of strength. I drooped in as cowed and unresisting a manner as I could devise.

'God,' said Adams in disgust. 'Just look at him. Scared out of his bloody wits.' He shrugged impatiently. 'Well Cass, just find him some stinking useless occupation like scrubbing the paths and put him to work. There's no sport for me here. No backbone for me to break. Give me a fox any day, at least they've got some cunning and some guts.'

His gaze strayed sideways to where Humber was crossing the far end of the yard. He said to Cass, 'Tell Mr. Humber I'd like to have a word with him,' and when Cass had gone he turned back to me.

'Where did you work before this?'

'At Mr. Inskip's, sir.'

'And he kicked you out?'

'Yes, sir.'

'Why?'

'I . . . er . . .' I stuck. It was incredibly galling to have to lay oneself open to such a man; but if I gave him answers he could check in small things he might believe the whopping lies without question.

'When I ask a question, you will answer it,' said Adams coldly. 'Why did Mr. Inskip get rid of you?'

I swallowed. 'I got the sack for er . . . for messing about with the boss's daughter.'

'For messing about . . .' he repeated. 'Good God.' With lewd pleasure he said something which was utterly obscene, and which struck clear home. He saw me wince and laughed at my discomfiture. Cass and Humber returned. Adams turned to Humber, still laughing, and said, 'Do you know why this cockerel got chucked out of Inskip's?'

'Yes,' said Humber flatly. 'He seduced October's daughter.' He wasn't interested. 'And there was also the matter of a favourite that came in last. He looked after it.'

'October's daughter!' said Adams, surprised, his eyes narrowing. 'I thought he meant Inskip's daughter.' He casually dealt me a sharp clip on the ear. 'Don't try lying to me.'

'Mr. Inskip hasn't got a daughter,' I protested.

'And don't answer back.' His hand flicked out again. He was rather adept at it. He must have indulged in a lot of practice.

'Hedley,' he said to Humber, who had impassively watched this one-sided exchange. 'I'll give you a lift to Nottingham races on Monday if you like. I'll pick you up at ten.'

'Right,' agreed Humber.

Adams turned to Cass. 'Don't forget that lesson for this lily-livered Romeo. Cool his ardour a bit.'

Cass sniggered sycophantically and raised goose pimples on my neck.

Adams climbed coolly into his Jaguar, started it up and followed the horse box containing his two hunters out of the yard.

Humber said, 'I don't want Roke out of action Cass. You've got to leave him fit for work. Use some sense this time.' He limped away to continue his inspection of the boxes.

Cass looked at me, and I looked steadily down at my damp, muddy clothes, very conscious that the head lad counted among the enemy, and not wanting to risk his seeing that there was anything but submissiveness in my face.

He said, 'Mr. Adams don't like to be crossed.'

'I didn't cross him.'

'Nor he don't like to be answered back to. You mind your lip.'

'Has he any more horses here?' I asked.

'Yes,' said Cass, 'And it's none of your business. Now, he told me to punish you, and he won't forget. He'll check up later.'

'I've done nothing wrong,' I said sullenly, still looking down. What on earth would my foreman say about this, I thought; and nearly smiled at the picture.

'You don't need to have done nothing wrong,' said Cass. 'With Mr. Adams it is a case of punish first so that you won't do anything wrong after. Sense, in a way.' He gave a snort of laughter. 'Saves trouble, see?'

'Are his horses all hunters?' I asked.

'No,' said Cass, 'but the two you've got are, and don't you forget it. He rides those himself, and he'll notice how you look after every hair on their hides.'

'Does he treat the lads who look after his other horses so shockingly unfair?'

'I've never heard Jerry complaining. And Mr. Adams won't treat you too bad if you mind your p's and q's. Now that lesson he suggested . . .'

I had hoped he had forgotten it.

'You can get down on your knees and scrub the concrete paths round the yard. Start now. You can break for dinner, and then go on until evening stables.'

I went on standing in a rag-doll attitude of dejectedness, looking at the ground, but fighting an unexpectedly strong feeling of rebellion. What the hell, I thought, did October expect of me? Just how much was I to take? Was there any point at which, if he were there, he would say 'Stop; all right; that's enough. That's too much. Give it up.' But remembering how he felt about me, I supposed not!

Cass said, 'There's a scrubbing brush in the cupboard in the tack room. Get on with it.' He walked away.

The concrete pathways were six feet wide and ran round all sides of the yard in front of the boxes. They had been scraped clear of snow throughout the month I had been there so that the feed trolley could

make its usual smooth journey from horse to horse, and as in most
modern stables, including Inskip's and my own, they would always be
kept clean of straw and excessive dust. But scrubbing them on ones knees
for nearly four hours on a slushy day at the end of January was a
miserable, back-breaking, insane waste of time. Ludicrous, besides.

I had a clear choice of scrubbing the paths or getting on the motor-
cycle and going. Thinking firmly that I was being paid at least ten
thousand pounds for doing it, I scrubbed: and Cass hung around the
yard all day to watch that I didn't rest.

The lads, who had spent much of the afternoon amusing themselves
by jeering at my plight as they set off for and returned from the café in
Posset, made quite sure during evening stables that the concrete paths
ended the day even dirtier than they had begun. I didn't care a damn
about that; but Adams had sent his hunters back caked with mud and
sweat and it took me two hours to clean them because by the end of that
day many of my muscles were trembling with fatigue.

Then, to crown it all, Adams came back. He drove his Jaguar into the
yard, climbed out, and after having talked to Cass, who nodded and
gestured round the paths, he walked without haste towards the box where
I was still struggling with his black horse.

He stood in the doorway and looked down his nose at me; and I looked
back. He was superbly elegant in a dark blue pin-striped suit with a
white shirt and a silver-grey tie. His skin looked fresh, his hair well
brushed, his hands clean and pale. I imagined he had gone home after
hunting and enjoyed a deep hot bath, a change of clothes, a drink . . . I
hadn't had a bath for a month and was unlikely to get one as long as I
stayed at Humber's. I was filthy and hungry and extremely tired. I
wished he would go away and leave me alone.

No such luck.

He took a step into the box and surveyed the mud still caked solid on
the horse's hind legs.

'You're slow,' he remarked.

'Yes, sir.'

'This horse must have been back here three hours ago. What have you
been doing?'

'My three other horses, sir.'

'You should do mine first.'

'I had to wait for the mud to dry, sir. You can't brush it out while it's
still wet.'

'I told you this morning not to answer back.' His hand lashed out
across the ear he had hit before. He was smiling slightly. Enjoying
himself. Which was more than could be said for me.

Having, so to speak, tasted blood, he suddenly took hold of the front
of my jersey, pushed me back against the wall, and slapped me twice in
the face, forehand and backhand. Still smiling.

What I wanted to do was to jab my knee into his groin and my fist into
his stomach; and refraining wasn't easy. For the sake of realism I knew
I should have cried out loudly and begged him to stop, but when it came

to the point I couldn't do it. However, one could act what one couldn't say, so I lifted both arms and folded them defensively round my head.

He laughed and let go, and I slid down on to one knee and cowered against the wall.

'You're a proper little rabbit, aren't you, for all your fancy looks.'

I stayed where I was, in silence. As suddenly as he had begun, he lost interest in ill-treating me.

'Get up, get up,' he said irritably. 'I didn't hurt you. You're not worth hurting. Get up and finish this horse. And make sure it is done properly or you'll find yourself scrubbing again.'

He walked out of the box and away across the yard. I stood up, leaned against the doorpost, and with uncharitable feelings watched him go up the path to Humber's house. To a good dinner, no doubt. An arm-chair. A fire. A glass of brandy. A friend to talk to. Sighing in depression, I went back to the tiresome job of brushing off the mud.

Shortly after a supper of dry bread and cheese, eaten to the accompaniment of crude jokes about my day's occupation and detailed descriptions of the meals which had been enjoyed in Posset, I had had quite enough of my fellow workers. I climbed the ladder and sat on my bed. It was cold upstairs. I had had quite enough of Humber's yard. I had had more than enough of being kicked around. All I had to do, as I had been tempted to do that morning, was to go outside, unwrap the motor-cycle, and make tracks for civilization. I could stifle my conscience by paying most of the money back to October and pointing out that I had done at least half of the job.

I went on sitting on the bed and thinking about riding away on the motor-bike. I went on sitting on the bed. And not riding away on the motor-bike.

Presently I found myself sighing. I knew very well I had never had any real doubts about staying, even if it meant scrubbing those dreadful paths every day of the week. Quite apart from not finding myself good company in future if I ran away because of a little bit of eccentric charring, there was the certainty that it was specifically in Mr. P. J. Adams' ruthless hands that the good repute of British racing was in danger of being cracked to bits. It was he that I had come to defeat. It was no good decamping because the first taste of him was unpleasant.

His name typed on paper had come alive as a worse menace than Humber himself had ever seemed. Humber was merely harsh, greedy, bad-tempered and vain, and he beat his lads for the sole purpose of making them leave. But Adams seemed to enjoy hurting for its own sake. Beneath that glossy crust of sophistication, and not far beneath, one glimpsed an irresponsible savage. Humber was forceful; but Adams, it now seemed to me, was the brains of the partnership. He was a more complex man and a far more fearsome adversary. I had felt equal to Humber. Adams dismayed me.

Someone started to come up the ladder. I thought it would be Cecil, reeling from his Saturday night orgy, but it was Jerry. He came and sat on the bed next to mine. He looked downcast.

'Dan?'

'Yes.'

'It weren't ... it weren't no good in Posset today, without you being there.'

'Wasn't it?'

'No.' He brightened. 'I bought my comic though. Will you read it to me?'

'Tomorrow,' I said tiredly.

There was a short silence while he struggled to organise his thoughts.

'Dan.'

'Mm?'

'I'm sorry, like.'

'What for?'

'Well, for laughing at you, like, this afternoon. It wasn't right ... not when you've took me on your motor-bike and all. I do ever so like going on your bike.'

'It's all right, Jerry.'

'The others were ribbing you, see, and it seemed the thing, like, to do what they done. So they would ... would let me go with them, see?'

'Yes, Jerry, I see. It doesn't matter, really it doesn't.'

'You never ribbed me, when I done wrong.'

'Forget it.'

'I've been thinking,' he said, wrinkling his forehead, 'about me Mam. She tried scrubbing some floors once. In some offices, it was. She came home fair whacked, she did. She said scrubbing floors was wicked. It made your back ache something chronic, she said, as I remember.'

'Did she?'

'Does your back ache, Dan?'

'Yes, a bit.'

He nodded pleased. 'She knows a thing or two, does my Mam.' He lapsed into one of his mindless silences, rocking himself gently backwards and forwards on the creaking bed.

I was touched by his apology.

'I'll read your comic for you,' I said.

'You ain't too whacked?' he asked eagerly.

I shook my head.

He fetched the comic from the cardboard box in which he kept his few belongings and sat beside me while I read him the captions of Mickey the Monkey, Beryl and Peril, Julius Cheeser, the Bustom Boys, and all the rest. We went through the whole thing at least twice, with him laughing contentedly and repeating the words after me. By the end of the week he would know most of them by heart.

At length I took the comic out of his hands and put it down on the bed.

'Jerry,' I said, 'which of the horses you look after belongs to Mr. Adams?'

'Mr. Adams?'

'The man whose hunters I've got. The man who was here this morning, with a grey Jaguar, and a scarlet coat.'

'Oh, that Mr. Adams.'

'Why, is there another one?'

'No, that's Mr. Adams, all right.' Jerry shuddered.

'What do you know about him?' I asked.

'The chap what was here before you came, Dennis, his name was, Mr. Adams didn't like him, see? He cheeked Mr. Adams, he did.'

'Oh,' I said. I wasn't sure I wanted to hear what had happened to Dennis.

'He weren't here above three weeks,' said Jerry reflectively. 'The last couple of days, he kept on falling down. Funny, it was, really.'

I cut him short. 'Which of your horses belongs to Mr. Adams?' I repeated.

'None of them do,' he said positively.

'Cass said so.'

He looked surprised, and also scared. 'No, Dan, I don't want none of Mr. Adams' horses.'

'Well, who do your horses belong to?'

'I don't rightly know. Except of course Pageant. He belongs to Mr. Byrd.'

'That's the one you take to the races?'

'Uh huh, that's the one.'

'How about the others?'

'Well, Mickey . . .' His brow furrowed.

'Mickey is the horse in the box next to Mr. Adams' black hunter, which I do?'

'Yeah.' He smiled brilliantly, as if I had made a point.

'Who does Mickey belong to?'

'I dunno.'

'Hasn't his owner ever been to see him?'

He shook his head doubtfully. I wasn't sure whether or not he would remember if an owner had in fact called.

'How about your other horse?' Jerry had only three horses to do, as he was slower than everyone else.

'That's Champ,' said Jerry triumphantly.

'Who owns him?'

'He's a hunter.'

'Yes, but who owns him?'

'Some fellow.' He was trying hard. 'A fat fellow. With sort of sticking out ears.' He pulled his own ears forward to show me.

'You know him well?'

He smiled widely. 'He gave me ten bob for Christmas.'

So it was Mickey, I thought, who belonged to Adams, but neither Adams nor Humber nor Cass had let Jerry know it. It looked as though Cass had let it slip out by mistake.

I said, 'How long have you worked here, Jerry?'

'How long?' he echoed vaguely.

'How many weeks were you here before Christmas?'

He put his head on one side and thought. He brightened. 'I came on the day after the Rovers beat the Gunners. My Dad took me to the match, see? Near our house, the Rovers' ground is.'

I asked him more questions, but he had no clearer idea than that about when he had come to Humber's.

'Well,' I said, 'was Mickey here already, when you came?'

'I've never done no other horses since I've been here,' he said. When I asked him no more questions he placidly picked up the comic again and began to look at the pictures. Watching him, I wondered what it was like to have a mind like his, a brain like cotton wool upon which the accumulated learning of the world could make no dent, in which reason, memory, and awareness were blanketed almost out of existence.

He smiled happily at the comic strips. He was, I reflected, none the worse off for being simple-minded. He was good at heart, and what he did not understand could not hurt him. There was a lot to be said for life on that level. If one didn't realise one was an object of calculated humiliations, there would be no need to try to make oneself be insensitive to them. If I had his simplicity, I thought, I would find life at Humber's very much easier.

He looked up suddenly and saw me watching him, and gave me a warm, contented, trusting smile.

'I like you,' he said; and turned his attention back to the paper.

There was a raucous noise from downstairs and the other lads erupted up the ladder, pushing Cecil among them as he was practically unable to walk. Jerry scuttled back to his own bed and put his comic carefully away; and I, like all the rest, wrapped myself in two grey blankets and lay down, boots and all, on the inhospitable canvas. I tried to find a comfortable position for my excessively weary limbs, but unfortunately failed.

Chapter Eleven

The office was as cold and unwelcoming as Humber's personality, with none of the ostentation of his car. It consisted of a long narrow room with the door and the single smallish window both in the long wall facing down the yard. At the far end, away to the left as one entered, there was a door which opened into a washroom: this was whitewashed and lit by three slit-like, frosted glass windows, and led through an inner door into a lavatory. In the washroom itself there was a sink, a plastic topped table, a refrigerator, and two wall cupboards. The first of these on investigation proved to hold all the bandages, linaments and medicines in common use with horses.

Careful not to move anything from its original position I looked at every bottle, packet, and tin. As far as I could see there was nothing of a stimulating nature among them.

The second cupboard however held plenty of stimulant in the shape of alcohol for human consumption, an impressive collection of bottles with a well stocked shelf of glasses above them. For the entertainment of owners, not the quickening of their horses. I shut the door.

There was nothing in the refrigerator except four bottles of beer, some milk, and a couple of trays of ice cubes.

I went back into the office.

Humber's desk stood under the window, so that when he was sitting at it he could look straight out down the yard. It was a heavy flat-topped knee-hole desk with drawers at each side, and it was almost aggressively tidy. Granted Humber was away at Nottingham races and had not spent long in the office in the morning, but the tidiness was basic, not temporary. None of the drawers was locked, and their contents (stationery, tax tables and so on) could be seen at a glance. On top of the desk there was only a telephone, an adjustable reading lamp, a tray of pens and pencils, and a green glass paper weight the size of a cricket ball. Trapped air bubbles rose in a frozen spray in its depths.

The single sheet of paper which it held down bore only a list of duties for the day and had clearly been drawn up for Cass to work from. I saw disconsolately that I would be cleaning tack that afternoon with baby-voiced Kenneth, who never stopped talking, and doing five horses at evening stables, this last because the horses normally done by Bert, who had gone racing, had to be shared out among those left behind.

Apart from the desk the office contained a large floor-to-ceiling cupboard in which form books and racing colours were kept; too few of those for the space available. Three dark green filing cabinets, two leather arm-chairs, and an upright wooden chair with a leather seat stood round the walls.

I opened the unlocked drawers of the filing cabinet one by one and searched quickly through the contents. They contained racing calendars, old accounts, receipts, press cuttings, photographs, papers to do with the horses currently in training, analyses of form, letters from owners, records of saddlery and fodder transactions; everything that could be found in the office of nearly every trainer in the country.

I looked at my watch. Cass usually took an hour off for lunch. I had waited five minutes after he had driven out of the yard, and I intended to be out of the office ten minutes before he could be expected back. This had given me a working time of three-quarters of an hour, of which nearly half had already gone.

Borrowing a pencil from the desk and taking a sheet of writing paper from a drawer, I applied myself to the drawer full of current accounts. For each of seventeen race-horses there was a separate hard-covered blue ledger, in which was listed every major and minor expense incurred in its training. I wrote a list of their names, few of which were familiar to me, together with their owners and the dates when they had come into the yard. Some had been there for years, but three had arrived during the past three months, and it was only these, I thought, which were of any real interest. None of the horses which had been doped had stayed at Humber's longer than four months.

The names of the three newest horses were Chin-Chin, Kandersteg and Starlamp. The first was owned by Humber himself and the other two by Adams.

I put the account books back where I had found them and looked at my watch. Seventeen minutes left. Putting the pencil back on the desk I folded the list of horses and stowed it away in my money belt. The webbing pockets were filling up again with fivers, as I had spent little of my pay, but the belt still lay flat and invisible below my waist under my jeans: and I had been careful not to let any of the lads know it was there, so as not to be robbed.

I riffled quickly through the drawers of press cuttings and photographs, but found no reference to the eleven horses or their successes. The racing calendars bore more fruit in the shape of a pencilled cross against the name of Superman in the Boxing Day selling chase, but there was no mark against the selling chase scheduled for a coming meeting at Sedgefield.

It was at the back of the receipts drawer that I struck most gold. There was another blue accounts ledger there, with a double page devoted to each of the eleven horses. Among these eleven were interspersed nine others who had in various ways failed in their purpose. One of these was Superman and another Old Etonian.

In the left hand page of each double spread had been recorded the entire racing career of the horse in question, and on the right hand pages of my eleven old friends were details of the race they each won with assistance. Beneath were sums of money which I judged must be Humber's winnings of them. His winnings had run into thousands on every successful race. On Superman's page he had written 'Lost: three hundred pounds.' On Old Etonian's right hand page there was no race record: only the single word 'Destroyed.'

A cross-out line had been drawn diagonally across all the pages except those concerning a horse called Six-Ply; and two new double pages had been prepared at the end, one for Kandersteg, and one for Starlamp. The left-hand pages for these three horses were written up: the right-hand pages were blank.

I shut the book and put it back. It was high time to go, and with a last look round to make sure that everything was exactly as it had been when I came in, I let myself quietly, unnoticed, out of the door, and went back to the kitchen to see if by some miracle the lads had left me any crumbs of lunch. Naturally, they had not.

The next morning Jerry's horse Mickey disappeared from the yard while we were out at second exercise, but Cass told him Jud had run him down to a friend of Humber's on the coast, for Mickey to paddle in the sea water to strengthen his legs, and that he would be back that evening. But the evening came, and Mickey did not.

On Wednesday Humber ran another horse, and I missed my lunch to have a look inside his house while he was away. Entry was easy through an open ventilator, but I could find nothing whatever to give me any clue as to how the doping was carried out.

All day Thursday I fretted about Mickey being still away at the coast.

It sounded perfectly reasonable. It was what a trainer about twelve miles from the sea could be expected to arrange. Sea water was good for horses' legs. But something happened to horses sometimes at Humber's which made it possible for them to be doped later, and I had a deeply disturbing suspicion that whatever it was was happening to Mickey at this moment, and that I was missing my only chance of finding it out.

According to the accounts books Adams owned four of the racehorses in the yard, in addition to his two hunters. None of his racehorses was known in the yard by its real name: therefore Mickey could be any one of the four. He could in fact be Kandersteg or Starlamp. It was an even chance that he was one or the other, and was due to follow in Superman's footsteps. So I fretted.

On Friday morning a hired box took the stable runner to Haydock races, and Jud and Humber's own box remained in the yard until lunch time. This was a definite departure from normal; and I took the opportunity of noting the mileage on the speedometer.

Jud drove the box out of the yard while we were still eating the midday sludge, and we didn't see him come back as we were all out on the gallop furthest away from the stables sticking back into place the divots kicked out of the soft earth that week by the various training activities; but when we returned for evening stables at four, Mickey was back in his own quarters.

I climbed up into the cab of the horse box and looked at the mileage indicator. Jud had driven exactly sixteen and a half miles. He had not, in fact, been as far as the coast. I thought some very bitter thoughts.

When I had finished doing my two racehorses I carried the brushes and pitch forks along to see to Adams' black hunter, and found Jerry leaning against the wall outside Mickey's next door box with tears running down his cheeks.

'What's the matter?' I said, putting down my stuff.

'Mickey . . . bit me,' he said. He was shaking with pain and fright.

'Let's see.'

I helped him slide his left arm out of his jersey, and took a look at the damage. There was a fierce red and purple circular weal on the fleshy part of his upper arm near the shoulder. It had been a hard, savage bite.

Cass came over.

'What's going on here?'

But he saw Jerry's arm, and didn't need to be told. He looked over the bottom half of the door into Mickey's box, then turned to Jerry and said, 'His legs were too far gone for the sea water to cure them. The vet said he would have to put on a blister, and he did it this afternoon when Mickey got back. That's what's the matter with him. Feels a bit off colour, he does, and so would you if someone slapped a flaming plaster on your legs. Now you just stop this stupid blubbing and get right back in there and see to him. And you, Dan, get on with that hunter and mind your own bloody business.' He went off along the row.

'I can't,' whispered Jerry, more to himself than to me.

'You'll manage it,' I said cheerfully.

He turned to me a stricken face. 'He'll bite me again.'

'I'm sure he won't.'

'He tried lots of times. And he's kicking out something terrible. I daren't go into his box . . .' He stood stiffly, shivering with fright, and I realized that it really was beyond him to go back.

'All right,' I said, 'I'll do Mickey and you do my hunter. Only do him well, Jerry, very well. Mr. Adams is coming to ride him again tomorrow and I don't want to spend another Saturday on my knees.'

He looked dazed. 'Ain't no one done nothing like that for me before.'

'It's a swop,' I said brusquely. 'You mess up my hunter and I'll bite you worse than Mickey did.'

He stopped shivering and began to grin, which I had intended, and slipping his arm painfully back inside his jersey he picked up my brushes and opened the hunter's door.

'You won't tell Cass?' he asked anxiously.

'No,' I reassured him; and unbolted Mickey's box door.

The horse was tied up safely enough, and wore on his neck a long wooden barred collar called a cradle which prevented his bending his head down to bite the bandages off his fore legs. Under the bandages, according to Cass, Mickey's legs were plastered with 'blister', a sort of caustic paste used to contract and strengthen the tendons. The only trouble was that Mickey's legs had not needed treatment. They had been, to my eyes, as sound as rocks. But now, however, they were definitely paining him; at least as much as with a blister, and possibly more.

As Jerry had indicated, Mickey was distinctly upset. He could not be soothed by hand or voice, but lashed forwards with his hind feet whenever he thought I was in range, and made equal use of his teeth. I was careful not to walk behind him, though he did his best to turn his quarters in my direction while I was banking up his straw bed round the back of the box. I fetched him hay and water, but he was not interested, and changed his rug, as the one he wore was soaked with sweat and would give him a chill during the night. Changing his rug was a bit of an obstacle race, but by warding off his attacks with the pitchfork I got it done unscathed.

I took Jerry with me to the feed bins where Cass was doling out the right food for each horse, and when we got back to the boxes we solemnly exchanged bowls. Jerry grinned happily. It was infectious. I grinned back.

Mickey didn't want food either, not, that is, except lumps of me. He didn't get any. I left him tied up for the night and took myself and Jerry's sack of brushes to safety on the far side of the door. Mickey would, I hoped, have calmed down considerably by the morning.

Jerry was grooming the black hunter practically hair by hair, humming tonelessly under his breath.

'Are you done?' I said.

'Is he all right?' he asked anxiously.

I went in to have a look.

'Perfect,' I said truthfully. Jerry was better at strapping a horse than at most things; and the next day, to my considerable relief, Adams passed both hunters without remark and spoke hardly a word to me. He was in a hurry to be off to a distant meet, but all the same it seemed I had succeeded in appearing too spineless to be worth tormenting.

Mickey was a good deal worse, that morning. When Adams had gone I stood with Jerry looking over the half-door of Mickey's box. The poor animal had managed to rip one of the bandages off in spite of the cradle, and we could see a big raw area over his tendon.

Mickey looked round at us with baleful eyes and flat ears, his neck stretched forward aggressively. Muscles quivered violently in his shoulders and hind quarters. I had never seen a horse behave like that except when fighting; and he was, I thought, dangerous.

'He's off his head,' whispered Jerry, awestruck.

'Poor thing.'

'You ain't going in?' he said. 'He looks like he'd kill you.'

'Go and get Cass,' I said. 'No, I'm not going in, not without Cass knowing how things are, and Humber too. You go and tell Cass that Mickey's gone mad. That ought to fetch him to have a look.'

Jerry trotted off and returned with Cass, who seemed to be alternating between anxiety and scorn as he came within earshot. At the sight of Mickey anxiety abruptly took over, and he went to fetch Humber, telling Jerry on no account to open Mickey's door.

Humber came unhurriedly across the yard leaning on his stick, with Cass, who was a short man, trotting along at his side. Humber looked at Mickey for a good long time. Then he shifted his gaze to Jerry, who was standing there shaking again at the thought of having to deal with a horse in such a state, and then further along to me, where I stood at the door of the next box.

'That's Mr. Adams' hunter's box,' he said to me.

'Yes, sir, he went with Mr. Adams just now, sir.'

He looked me up and down, and then Jerry the same, and finally said to Cass, 'Roke and Webber had better change horses. I know they haven't an ounce of guts between them, but Roke is much bigger, stronger and older.' And also, I thought with a flash of insight, Jerry has a father and mother to make a fuss if he gets hurt, whereas against Roke in the next-of-kin file was the single word 'none'.

'I'm not going in there alone, sir,' I said. 'Cass will have to hold him off with a pitchfork while I muck him out.' And even then, I thought, we'd both be lucky to get out without being kicked.

Cass, to my amusement, hurriedly started telling Humber that if I was too scared to do it on my own he would get one of the other lads to help me. Humber however took no notice of either of us, but went back to staring sombrely at Mickey.

Finally he turned to me and said, 'Fetch a bucket and come over to the office.'

'An empty bucket, sir?'

'Yes,' he said impatiently, 'an empty bucket.' He turned and gently limped over to the long brick hut. I took the bucket out of the hunter's box, followed him, and waited by the door.

He came out with a small labelled glass-stoppered chemist's jar in one hand and a teaspoon in the other. The jar was three-quarters full of white powder. He gestured to me to hold out the bucket, then he put half a teaspoonful of the powder into it.

'Fill the bucket only a third full of water,' he said. 'And put it in Mickey's manger, so that he can't kick it over. It will quieten him down, once he drinks it.'

He took the jar and spoon back inside the office, and I picked a good pinch of the white powder out of the bottom of the bucket and dropped it down inside the list of Humber's horses in my money belt. I licked my fingers and thumb afterwards; the particles of powder clinging there had a faintly bitter taste. The jar, which I had seen in the cupboard in the washroom, was labelled 'Soluble phenobarbitone', and the only surprising factor was the amount of it that Humber kept available.

I ran water into the bucket, stirred it with my hand and went back to Mickey's box. Cass had vanished. Jerry was across the yard seeing to his third horse. I looked round for someone to ask for help, but everyone was carefully keeping out of sight. I cursed. I was not going into Mickey alone: it was just plain stupid to try it.

Humber came back across the yard.

'Get on in,' he said.

'I'd spill the water dodging him, sir.'

'Huh.'

Mickey's hoofs thudded viciously against the wall.

'You mean you haven't got the guts.'

'You'd need to be a bloody fool to go in there alone, sir,' I said sullenly.

He glared at me, but he must have seen it was no use insisting. He suddenly picked up the pitchfork from where it stood against the wall and transferred it to his right hand and the walking stick to his left.

'Get on with it then,' he said harshly. 'And don't waste time.'

He looked incongruous, brandishing his two unconventional weapons while dressed like an advertisement for *Country Life*. I hoped he was going to be as resolute as he sounded.

I unbolted Mickey's door and we went in. It had been an injustice to think Humber might turn tail and leave me there alone: he behaved as coldly as ever, as if fear were quite beyond his imagination. Efficiently he kept Mickey penned first to one side of the box and then to the other while I mucked out and put down fresh straw, remaining steadfastly at his post while I cleaned the uneaten food out of the manger and wedged the bucket of doped water in place. Mickey didn't make it easy for him, either. The teeth and hooves were busier and more dangerous than the night before.

It was especially aggravating in the face of Humber's coolness to have to remember to behave like a bit of a coward myself, though I minded less than if he had been Adams.

When I had finished the jobs Humber told me to go out first, and he retreated in good order after me, his well-pressed suit scarcely rumpled from his exertions.

I shut the door and bolted it, and did my best to look thoroughly frightened. Humber looked me over with disgust.

'Roke,' he said sarcastically, 'I hope you will feel capable of dealing with Mickey when he is half asleep with drugs?'

'Yes sir,' I muttered.

'Then in order not to strain your feeble stock of courage I suggest we keep him drugged for some days. Every time you fetch him a bucket of water you can get Cass or me to put some sedative in it. Understand?'

'Yes sir,'

'Right.' He dismissed me with a chop of his hand.

I carried the sack of dirty straw round to the muck heap, and then took a close look at the bandage which Mickey had dislodged. Blister is a red paste. I had looked in vain for red paste on Mickey's raw leg; and there was not a smear of it on the bandage. Yet from the size and severity of the wound there should have been half a cupful.

I took Jerry down to Posset on the motor-cycle again that afternoon and watched him start to browse contentedly in the toy department of the post office.

There was a letter for me from October.

'Why did we receive no report from you last week? It is your duty to keep us informed of the position.'

I tore the page up, my mouth twisting. Duty. That was just about enough to make me lose my temper. It was not from any sense of duty that I stayed at Humber's to endure a minor version of slavery. It was because I was obstinate, and liked to finish what I started, and although it sounded a bit grandiose, it was because I really wanted, if I could, to remove British steeple chasing from Adams' clutches. If it had been only a matter of duty I would have repaid October his money and cleared out.

'It is your duty to keep us informed of the position.'

He was still angry with me about Patty, I thought morosely, and he wrote that sentence only because he knew I wouldn't like it.

I composed my report.

'Your humble and obedient servant regrets that he was unable to carry out his duty last week by keeping you informed of the position.

'The position is still far from clear, but a useful fact has been ascertained. None of the original eleven horses will be doped again: but a horse called Six-Ply is lined up to be the next winner. He is now owned by a Mr. Henry Waddington, of Lewes, Sussex.

'May I please have the answers to the following questions:

1. Is the powder in the enclosed twist of paper soluble phenobarbitone?

2. What are in detail the registered physical characteristics of the racehorses Chin-Chin, Kandersteg and Starlamp?

3. On what date did Blackburn, playing at home, beat Arsenal?'

And that, I thought, sticking down the envelope and grinning to myself, that will fix him and his duty.

Jerry and I gorged ourselves at the café. I had been at Humber's for five weeks and two days, and my clothes were getting looser.

When we could eat no more I went back to the post office and bought a large-scale hiker's map of the surrounding district, and a cheap pair of compasses. Jerry spent fifteen shillings on a toy tank which he had resisted before, and, after checking to see if my goodwill extended so far, a second comic for me to read to him. And we went back to Humber's.

Days passed. Mickey's drugged water acted satisfactorily, and I was able to clean his box and look after him without much trouble. Cass took the second bandage off, revealing an equal absence of red paste. However, the wounds gradually started healing.

As Mickey could not be ridden and showed great distress if one tried to lead him out along the road, he had to be walked round the yard for an hour each day, which exercised me more than him, but gave me time to think some very fruitful thoughts.

Humber's stick landed with a resounding thump across Charlie's shoulders on Tuesday morning, and for a second it looked as though Charlie would hit him back. But Humber coldly stared him down, and the next morning delivered an even harder blow in the same place. Charlie's bed was empty that night. He was the fourth lad to leave in the six weeks I had been there (not counting the boy who stayed only three days) and of my original half dozen dormitory companions, only Bert and Jerry remained. The time was getting perceptibly closer when I would find myself at the top of the queue for walking the plank.

Adams came with Humber when he made his usual rounds on Thursday evening. They stopped outside Mickey's box but contented themselves with looking over the half-door.

'Don't go in, Paul,' said Humber warningly. 'He's still very unpredictable, in spite of drugs.'

Adams looked at me where I stood by Mickey's head.

'Why is the gipsy doing this horse? I thought it was the moron's job.' He sounded angry and alarmed.

Humber explained that as Mickey had bitten Jerry, he had made me change places with him. Adams still didn't like it, but looked as if he would save his comments until he wouldn't be overheard.

He said, 'What is the gipsy's name?'

'Roke,' said Humber.

'Well, Roke, come here, out of that box.'

Humber said anxiously, 'Paul, don't forget we're one lad short already.'

These were not particularly reassuring words to hear. I walked across the box, keeping a wary eye on Mickey, let myself out through the door, and stood beside it, drooping and looking at the ground.

'Roke,' said Adams in a pleasant sounding voice, 'what do you spend your wages on?'

'The never-never on my motor-bike, sir.'

'The never-never? Oh, yes. And how many instalments have you still to pay?'

'About – er – fifteen, sir.'

'And you don't want to leave here until you've finished paying them off.'

'No, sir.'

'Will they take your motor-cycle away if you stop paying?'

'Yes sir, they might do.'

'So Mr. Humber doesn't need to worry about you leaving him?'

I said slowly, unwillingly, but as it happened, truthfully, 'No, sir.'

'Good,' he said briskly. 'Then that clears the air, doesn't it. And now you can tell me where you find the guts to deal with an unstable, half-mad horse.'

'He's drugged, sir.'

'You and I both know, Roke, that a drugged horse is not necessarily a safe horse.'

I said nothing. If there was ever a time when I needed an inspiration, this was it: and my mind was a blank.

'I don't think, Roke,' he said softly, 'that you are as feeble as you make out. I think there is a lot more stuffing in you than you would have us believe.'

'No, sir,' I said helplessly.

'Let's find out, shall we?'

He stretched out his hand to Humber, and Humber gave him his walking stick. Adams drew back his arm and hit me fairly smartly across the thigh.

If I were to stay in the yard I had got to stop him. This time the begging simply had to be done. I slid down the door, gasping, and sat on the ground.

'No sir, don't,' I shouted. 'I got some pills, I was dead scared of Mickey, and I asked the chemist in Posset on Saturday if he had any pills to make me brave, and he sold me some, and I've been taking them regular ever since.'

'What pills?' said Adams disbelieving.

'Tranquil something he said. I didn't rightly catch the wood.'

'Tranquillizers.'

'Yes, that's it, tranquillizers. Don't hit me any more sir, please sir. It was just that I was so dead scared of Mickey. Don't hit me any more, sir.'

'Well I'm damned.' Adams began to laugh. 'Well I'm damned. What will they think of next?' He gave the stick back to Humber, and the two of them walked casually away along to the next box.

'Take tranquillizers to help you out of a blue funk. Well, why not?' Still laughing, they went in to see the next horse.

I got up slowly and brushed the dirt off the seat of my pants. Damn it, I thought miserably, what else could I have done? Why was pride so important, and abandoning it so bitter?

It was more clear than ever that weakness was my only asset. Adams had this fearful kink of seeing any show of spirit as a personal challenge to his ability to crush it. He dominated Humber, and exacted instant obedience from Cass, and they were his allies. If I stood up to him even mildly I would get nothing but a lot of bruises and he would start wondering why I stayed to collect still more. The more tenaciously I stayed, the more incredible he would find it. Hire purchase on the motor-bike wouldn't convince him for long. He was quick. He knew, if he began to think about it, that I had come from October's stables. He must know that October was a Steward and therefore his natural enemy.

He would remember Tommy Stapleton. The hyper-sensitivity of the hunted to danger would stir the roots of his hair. He could check and find out from the post office that I did not send money away each week, and discover that the chemist had sold me no tranquillizers. He was in too deep to risk my being a follow-up to Stapleton; and at the very least, once he was suspicious of me, my detecting days would be over.

Whereas if he continued to be sure of my utter spinelessness he wouldn't bother about me, and I could if necessary stay in the yard up to five or six weeks more. And heaven forbid, I thought, that I would have to.

Adams, although it had been instinct with him, not reason, was quite right to be alarmed that it was I and not Jerry who was now looking after Mickey.

In the hours I had spent close to the horse I had come to understand what was really the matter with him, and all my accumulated knowledge about the affected horses, and about all horses in general, had gradually shaken into place. I did by that day know in outline how Adams and Humber had made their winners win.

I knew in outline, but not in detail. A theory, but no proof. For detail and proof I still needed more time, and if the only way I could buy time was to sit on the ground and implore Adams not to beat me, then it had to be done. But it was pretty awful, just the same.

Chapter Twelve

October's reply was unrelenting.

'Six-Ply, according to his present owner, is not going to be entered in any selling races. Does this mean that he will not be doped?

'The answers to your questions are as follows:

1. The powder is soluble phenobarbitone.

2. The physical characteristics of Chin-Chin are: bay gelding, white blaze down nose, white sock, off-fore. Kandersteg: gelding, washy chestnut, three white socks, both fore-legs and near hind. Starlamp: brown gelding, near hind white heel.

3. Blackburn beat Arsenal on November 30th.

'I do not appreciate your flippancy. Does your irresponsibility now extend to the investigation?'

Irresponsibility. Duty. He could really pick his words.

I read the descriptions of the horses again. They told me that Starlamp was Mickey. Chin-Chin was Dobbin, one of the two racehorses I did which belonged to Humber. Kandersteg was a pale shambling creature looked after by Bert, and known in the yard as Flash.

If Blackburn beat Arsenal on November 30th, Jerry had been at Humber's eleven weeks already.

I tore up October's letter and wrote back.

'Six-Ply may now be vulnerable whatever race he runs in, as he is the only shot left in the locker since Old Etonian and Superman both misfired.

'In case I fall on my nut out riding, or get knocked over by a passing car, I think I had better tell you that I have this week realised how the scheme works, even though I am as yet ignorant of most of the details.'

I told October that the stimulant Adams and Humber used was in fact adrenalin; and I told him how I believed it was introduced into the blood stream.

'As you can see, there are two prime facts which must be established before Adams and Humber can be prosecuted. I will do my best to finish the job properly, but I can't guarantee it, as the time factor is a nuisance.'

Then, because I felt very alone, I added impulsively, jerkily, a postscript.

'Believe me. Please believe me. I did nothing to Patty.'

When I had written it, I looked at this *cri de coeur* in disgust. I am getting as soft as I pretend, I thought. I tore the bottom of the sheet of paper and threw the pitiful words away, and posted my letter in the box.

Thinking it wise actually to buy some tranquillizers in case anyone checked, I stopped at the chemist's and asked for some. The chemist absolutely refused to sell me any, as they could only be had on a doctor's or dentist's prescription. How long would it be, I wondered ruefully, before Adams or Humber discovered this awkward fact.

Jerry was disappointed when I ate my meal in the café very fast, and left him alone to finish and walk back from Posset, but I assured him that I had jobs to do. It was high time I took a look at the surrounding countryside.

I rode out of Posset and, stopping the motor-cycle in a lay-by, got out the map over which I had pored intermittently during the week. I had drawn on it with pencil and compasses two concentric circles: the outer circle had a radius of eight miles from Humber's stables, and the inner circle a radius of five miles. If Jud had driven straight there and back when he had gone to fetch Mickey, the place he had fetched him from would lie in the area between the circles.

Some directions from Humber's were unsuitable because of open-cast coal-mines: and eight miles to the south-east lay the outskirts of the sprawling mining town called Clavering. All round the north and west sides, however, there was little but moorland interspersed with small valleys like the one in which Humber's stable lay, small fertile pockets in miles and miles of stark windswept heath.

Tellbridge, the village where Adams lived, lay outside the outer circle by two miles, and because of this I did not think Mickey could have been lodged there during his absence from Humber's. But all the same the area on a line from Humber's yard to Adams' village seemed the most sensible to take a look at first.

As I did not wish Adams to find me spying out the land round his house, I fastened on my crash helmet, which I had not worn since the trip to Edinburgh, and pulled up over my eyes a large pair of goggles, under which even my sisters wouldn't have recognised me. I didn't, as it happened, see Adams on my travels; but I did see his house which was a square, cream-coloured Georgian pile with gargoyle heads adjoining the gate-posts. It was the largest, most imposing building in the tiny group of a church, a shop, two pubs and a gaggle of cottages which made up Tellbridge.

I talked about Adams to the boy who filled my petrol tank in the Tellbridge garage.

'Mr. Adams? Yes, he bought old Sir Lucas' place three-four years ago. After the old man died. There weren't no family to keep it on.'

'And Mrs. Adams?' I suggested.

'Blimey, there isn't any Mrs. Adams,' he said, laughing and pushing his fair hair out of his eyes with the back of his wrist. 'But a lot of birds, he has there sometimes. Often got a houseful there, he has. Nobs, now, don't get me wrong. Never has anyone but nobs in his house, doesn't Mr. Adams. And anything he wants, he gets, and quick. Never mind anyone else. He woke the whole village up at two in the morning last Friday because he got into his head that he'd like to ring the church bells. He smashed a window to get in . . . I ask you! Of course, no one says much, because he spends such a lot of money in the village. Food and drink and wages, and so on. Everyone's better off, since he came.'

'Does he often do things like that – ringing the church bells?'

'Well, not that exactly, but other things, yes. I shouldn't think you could believe all you hear. But they say he pays up handsome if he does any damage, and everyone just puts up with it. High spirits, that's what they say it is.'

But Adams was too old for high spirits of that sort.

'Does he buy his petrol here?' I asked idly, fishing in my pocket for some money.

'Not often he doesn't, he has his own tank.' The smile died out of the boy's open face. 'In fact, I only served him once, when his supplies had run out.'

'What happened?'

'Well, he trod on my foot. In his hunting boots, too. I couldn't make out if he did it on purpose, because it seemed like that really, but why would he do something like that?'

'I can't imagine.'

He shook his head wondering. 'He must have thought I'd moved out of his way, I suppose. Put his heel right on top of my foot, he did, and leaned back. I only had sneakers on. Darn nearly broke my bones, he did. He must weigh getting on for sixteen stone, I shouldn't wonder.' He sighed and counted my change into my palm, and I thanked him and went on my way thinking that it was extraordinary how much a psychopath could get away with if he was big enough and clever and well-born.

It was a cold afternoon, and cloudy, but I enjoyed it. Stopping on the highest point of a shoulder of moorland I sat straddling the bike and looking round at rolling distances of bare bleak hills and at the tall chimneys of Clavering pointing up on the horizon. I took off my helmet and goggles and pushed my fingers through my hair to let the cold wind in to my scalp. It was invigorating.

There was almost no chance, I knew, of my finding where Mickey had been kept. It could be anywhere, in any barn, outhouse or shed. It didn't have to be a stable, and quite likely was not a stable: and indeed all I was sure of was that it would be somewhere tucked away out of sight and sound of any neighbours. The trouble was that in that part of Durham, with its widely scattered villages, its sudden valleys, and its miles of open heath, I found there were dozens of places tucked away out of sight and sound of neighbours.

Shrugging, I put my helmet and goggles on again, and spent what little was left of my free time finding two vantage points on high ground, from one of which one could see straight down the valley into Humber's yard, and from the other a main cross roads on the way from Humber's to Tellbridge, together with good stretches of road in all directions from it.

Kandersteg's name being entered in Humber's special hidden ledger, it was all Durham to a doughnut that one day he would take the same trail that Mickey-Starlamp had done. It was quite likely that I would still be unable to find out where he went, but there was no harm in getting the lie of the land clear in my head.

At four o'clock I rolled back into Humber's yard with the usual lack of enthusiasm, and began my evening's work.

Sunday passed, and Monday. Mickey got no better; the wounds on his legs were healing but he was still a risky prospect, in spite of the drugs, and he was beginning to lose flesh. Although I had never seen or had to deal with a horse in this state before, I gradually grew certain that he would not recover, and that Adams and Humber had another misfire on their hands.

Neither Humber nor Cass liked the look of him either, though Humber seemed more annoyed than anxious, as time went on. Adams came one morning, and from across the yard in Dobbin's box I watched the three of them standing looking in at Mickey. Presently Cass went into the box for a moment or two, and came out shaking his head. Adams looked furious. He took Humber by the arm and the two of them walked across to the office in what looked like an argument. I would have given much to have overheard them. A pity I couldn't lip-read, I thought, and that I hadn't come equipped with one of those long-range listening devices. As a spy, I was really a dead loss.

On Tuesday morning at breakfast there was a letter for me, post-marked Durham, and I looked at it curiously because there were so few people who either knew where I was or would bother to write to me. I put it in my pocket until I could open it in private and I was glad I had, for to my astonishment it was from October's elder daughter.

She had written from her University address, and said briefly,

'Dear Daniel Roke,
    I would be glad if you could call to see me for a few moments sometime this week. There is a matter I must discuss with you.
                                        Yours sincerely,
                                        Elinor Tarren.'

October, I thought, must have given her a message for me, or something he wanted me to see, or perhaps he intended to be there to meet me himself, and had not risked writing to me direct. Puzzled, I asked Cass for an afternoon off, and was refused. Only Saturday, he said, and Saturday only if I behaved myself.

I thought Saturday might be too late, or that she would have gone to Yorkshire for the week-end, but I wrote to her that I could come only on that day, and walked into Posset after the evening meal on Tuesday to post the letter.

Her reply came on Friday, brief again and to the point, with still no hint of why I was to go.

'Saturday afternoon will do very well. I will tell the porter you are coming: go to the side door of the College (this is the door used by students and their visitors) and ask to be shown to my room.'

She enclosed a pencilled sketch to show me where to find the college, and that was all.

On Saturday morning I had six horses to do, because there was still no replacement for Charley, and Jerry had gone with Pageant to the races. Adams came as usual to talk to Humber and to supervise the loading up of his hunters, but wasted no attention or energy on me, for which I was thankful. He spent half of the twenty minutes he was in the yard looking into Mickey's box with a scowl on his handsome face.

Cass himself was not always unkind, and because he knew I particularly wanted the afternoon free he even went so far as to help me get finished before the midday meal. I thanked him, surprised, and he remarked that he knew there had been a lot extra for everyone (except himself incidentally) to do, as we were still a lad short, and that I hadn't complained about it as much as most of the others. And that, I thought, was a mistake I would not have to make too often.

I washed as well as the conditions would allow; one had to heat all washing water in a kettle on the stove and pour it into the basin on the marble washstand; and shaved more carefully than usual, looking into the six-by-eight-inch flyblown bit of looking glass, jostled by the other lads who wanted to be on their way to Posset.

None of the clothes I had were fit for visiting a women's college. With a sigh I settled for the black sweater, which had a high collar, the charcoal drainpipe trousers, and the black leather jacket. No shirt, because I had no tie. I eyed the sharp-pointed shoes, but I had not been able to overcome my loathing for them, so I scrubbed my jodhpur boots under the tap in the yard, and wore those. Everything else I was wearing needed cleaning, and I supposed I smelled of horses, though I was too used to it to notice.

I shrugged. There was nothing to be done about it. I unwrapped the motor-bike and made tracks for Durham.

Chapter Thirteen

Elinor's college stood in a tree-lined road along with other sturdy and learned looking buildings. It had an imposing front entrance and a less-imposing tarmacked drive entrance along to the right. I wheeled the motor-cycle down there and parked it beside a long row of bicycles. Beyond the bicycles stood six or seven small cars, one of which was Elinor's little scarlet two-seater.

Two steps led up to a large oak door embellished with the single words 'Students'. I went in. There was a porter's desk just inside on the right, with a mournful looking middle-aged man sitting behind it looking at a list.

'Excuse me,' I said, 'could you tell me where to find Lady Elinor Tarren?'

He looked up and said 'You visiting? You expected?'

'I think so,' I said.

He asked my name, and thumbed down the list painstakingly. 'Daniel Roke to visit Miss Tarren, please show him her room. Yes, that's right. Come on, then.' He got down off his stool, came round from behind his desk, and breathing noisily began to lead me deeper into the building.

There were several twists in the corridors and I could see why it was necessary to have a guide. On every hand were doors with their occupant or purpose written up on small cards let into metal slots. After going up two flights of stairs and round a few more corners, the porter halted outside one more door just like the rest.

'Here you are,' he said unemotionally. 'This is Miss Tarren's room.' He turned away and started to shuffle back to his post.

The card on the door said Miss E. C. Tarren. I knocked. Miss E. C. Tarren opened it.

'Come in,' she said. No smile.

I went in. She shut the door behind me. I stood still, looking at her room. I was so accustomed to the starkness of the accommodation at Humber's that it was an odd, strange sensation to find myself again in a room with curtains, carpet, sprung chairs, cushions and flowers. The colours were mostly blues and greens, mixed and blending, with a bowl of daffodils and red tulips blazing against them.

There was a big desk with books and papers scattered on it; a bookshelf, a bed with a blue cover, a wardrobe, a tall built-in cupboard, and two easy chairs. It looked warm and friendly. A very good room for working in. If I had had more than a moment to stand and think about it, I knew I would be envious: this was what my father and mother's death had robbed me of, the time and liberty to study.

'Please sit down.' She indicated one of the easy chairs.

'Thank you.' I sat, and she sat down opposite me, but looking at the floor, not at me. She was solemn and frowning, and I rather gloomily wondered if what October wanted her to say to me meant more trouble.

'I asked you to come here,' she started. 'I asked you to come here because . . .' She stopped and stood up abruptly, and walked round behind me and tried again.

'I asked you to come,' she said to the back of my head, 'Because I have to apologise to you, and I'm not finding it very easy.'

'Apologise?' I said, astonished. 'What for?'

'For my sister.'

I stood up and turned towards her. 'Don't,' I said vehemently. I had been too much humbled myself in the past weeks to want to see anyone else in the same position.

She shook her head. 'I'm afraid,' she swallowed, 'I'm afraid that my family has treated you very badly.'

The silver-blonde hair shimmered like a halo against the pale sunshine which slanted sideways through the window behind her. She was wearing a scarlet jersey under a sleeveless dark green dress. The whole effect was colourful and gorgeous, but it was clearly not going to help her if I went on looking at her. I sat down again in the chair and said with some light-heartedness, as it appeared October had not after all despatched a dressing-down, 'Please don't worry about it.'

'Worry,' she exclaimed. 'What else can I do? I knew of course why you were dismissed, and I've said several times to Father that he ought to have had you sent to prison, and now I find none of it is true at all. How can you say there is nothing to worry about when everyone thinks you are guilty of some dreadful crime, and you aren't?'

Her voice was full of concern. She really minded that anyone in her family should have behaved as unfairly as Patty had. She felt guilty just because she was her sister. I liked her for it: but then I already knew she was a thoroughly nice girl.

'How did you find out?' I asked.

'Patty told me last week-end. We were just gossiping together, as we often do. She had always refused to talk about you, but this time she laughed, and told me quite casually, as if it didn't matter any more. Of course I know she's . . . well . . . used to men. She's just built that way. But this . . . I was so shocked. I couldn't believe her at first.'

'What exactly did she tell you?'

There was a pause behind me, then her voice went on, a little shakily. 'She said she tried to make you make love to her, but you wouldn't. She said . . . she said she showed you her body, and all you did was to tell her to cover herself up. She said she was so flamingly angry about that that she thought all next day about what revenge she would have on you, and on Sunday morning she worked herself up into floods of tears, and went and told Father . . . told Father . . .'

'Well,' I said good humouredly, 'yes, that is, I suppose, a slightly more accurate picture of what took place.' I laughed.

'It isn't funny,' she protested.

'No. It's relief.'

She came round in front of me and sat down and looked at me.

'You did mind, then, didn't you?'

My distaste must have shown. 'Yes. I minded.'

'I told Father she had lied about you. I've never told him before about her love affairs, but this was different . . . anyway, I told him on Sunday after lunch.' She stopped, hesitating. I waited. At last she went on, 'It was very odd. He didn't seem surprised, really. Not utterly overthrown, like I was. He just seemed to get very tired, suddenly, as if he had heard bad news. As if a friend had died after a long illness, that sort of sadness. I didn't understand it. And when I said that of course the only fair thing to do would be to offer you your job back, he utterly refused. I argued, but I'm afraid he is adamant. He also refuses to tell Mr. Inskip that you shouldn't have had to leave, and he made me promise not to repeat to him or anyone what Patty had said. It is so unfair,' she concluded passionately, 'and I felt that even if no one else is to know, at least you should. I don't suppose it makes it any better for you that my father and I have at last found out what really happened, but I wanted you to know that I am sorry, very, very sorry for what my sister did.'

I smiled at her. It wasn't difficult. Her colouring was so blazingly fair that it didn't matter if her nose wasn't entirely straight. Her direct grey eyes were full of genuine, earnest regret, and I knew she felt Patty's misbehaviour all the more keenly because she thought it had affected a stable lad who had no means of defending himself. This also made it difficult to know what to say in reply.

I understood, of course, that October couldn't declare me an injured innocent, even if he wanted to, which I doubted, without a risk of it reaching Humber's ears, and that the last thing that either of us wanted was for him to have to offer to take me back at Inskip's. No one in their right mind would stay at Humber's if they could go to Inskip's.

'If you knew,' I said slowly, 'how much I have wanted your father to believe that I didn't harm your sister, you would realise that what you have just said is worth a dozen jobs to me. I like your father. I respect him. And he is quite right. He cannot possibly give me my old job back, because it would be as good as saying publicly that his daughter is at least a liar, if not more. You can't ask him to do that. You can't expect it. I don't. Things are best left as they are.'

She looked at me for some time without speaking. It seemed to me that there was relief in her expression, and surprise, and finally puzzlement.

'Don't you want *any* compensation?'

'No.'

'I don't understand you.'

'Look,' I said, getting up, away from her enquiring gaze. 'I'm not as blameless as the snow. I did kiss your sister. I suppose I led her on a bit. And then I was ashamed of myself and backed out, and that's the truth of it. It wasn't all her fault. I did behave very badly. So please . . . please don't feel so much guilt on my account.' I reached the window and looked out.

'People shouldn't be hung for murders they decide not to commit,' she said dryly. 'You are being very generous, and I didn't expect it.'

'Then you shouldn't have asked me here,' I said idly. 'You were taking too big a risk.' The window looked down on to a quadrangle, a neat square of grass surrounded by broad paths, peaceful and empty in the early spring sunshine.

Risk . . . of what?' she said.

'Risk that I would raise a stink. Dishonour to the family. Tarnish to the Tarrens. That sort of thing. Lots of dirty linen and Sunday newspapers and your father losing face among his business associates.'

She looked startled, but also determined. 'All the same, a wrong had been done, and it had to be put right.'

'And damn the consequences?'

'And damn the consequences,' she repeated faintly.

I grinned. She was a girl after my own heart. I had been damning a few consequences too.

'Well,' I said reluctantly, 'I'd better be off. Thank you for asking me to come. I do understand that you have had a horrible week screwing yourself up for this, and I appreciate it more than I can possibly say.'

She looked at her watch, and hesitated. 'I know it's an odd time of day, but would you like some coffee? I mean, you've come quite a long way . . .'

'I'd like some very much,' I said.

'Well . . . sit down, and I'll get it.'

I sat down. She opened the built-in cupboard, which proved to hold a wash basin and mirror on one side and a gas ring and shelves for crockery on the other. She filled a kettle, lit the gas, and put some cups and saucers on the low table between the two chairs, moving economically and gracefully. Unselfconscious, I thought. Sure enough of herself to drop her title in a place where brains mattered more than birth. Sure enough of herself to have a man who looked like I did brought to her bed-sittingroom, and to ask him to stay for coffee when it was not necessary, but only polite.

I asked her what subject she was reading, and she said English. She assembled some milk, sugar, and biscuits on the table.

'May I look at your books?' I asked.

'Go ahead,' she said amiably.

I got up and looked along her bookshelves. There were the language text books – Ancient Icelandic, Anglo Saxon and Middle English – and a comprehensive sweep of English writings from Alfred the Great's Chronicles to John Betjeman's unattainable amazons.

'What do you think of my books?' she asked curiously.

I didn't know how to answer. The masquerade was damnably unfair to her.

'Very learned,' I said lamely.

I turned away from the bookshelves, and came suddenly face to face with my full-length reflection in the mirror door of her wardrobe.

I looked at myself moodily. It was the first comprehensive view of Roke the stable lad that I had had since leaving October's London house months before, and time had not improved things.

My hair was too long, and the sideburns flourished nearly down to the lobes of my ears. My skin was a sort of pale yellow now that the suntan had all faded. There was a tautness in the face and a wary expression in the eyes which had not been there before: and in my black clothes I looked disreputable and a menace to society.

Her reflection moved behind mine in the mirror, and I met her eyes and found her watching me.

'You look as if you don't like what you see,' she said.

I turned round. 'No,' I said wryly. 'Would anyone?'

'Well . . .' Incredibly she smiled mischievously. 'I wouldn't like to set you loose in this college, for instance. If you don't realize, though, the effect which you . . . you may have a few rough edges, but I do now see why Patty tried . . . er . . . I mean . . .' Her voice tailed off in the first confusion she had shown.

'The kettle's boiling,' I said helpfully.

Relieved, she turned her back on me and made the coffee. I went to the window and looked down into the deserted quad, resting my forehead on the cold glass.

It still happened, I thought. In spite of those terrible clothes, in spite of the aura of shadiness, it could still happen. What accident, I wondered for the thousandth time in my life, decided that one should be born with bones of a certain design? I couldn't help the shape of my face and head. They were a legacy from a pair of neat featured parents: their doing, not mine. Like Elinor's hair, I thought. Born in you. Nothing to be proud of. An accident, like a birth mark or a squint. Something I habitually forgot, and found disconcerting when anyone mentioned it. And it had been expensive, moreover. I had lost at least two prospective customers because they hadn't liked the way their wives looked at me instead of my horses.

With Elinor, I thought, it was a momentary attraction which wouldn't last. She was surely too sensible to allow herself to get tangled up with one of her father's ex-stable lads. And as for me, it was strictly hands off the Tarren sisters, both of them. If I was out of the frying-pan with one, I was not jumping into the fire with the other. It was a pity, all the same. I liked Elinor rather a lot.

'The coffee's ready,' she said.

I turned and went back to the table. She had herself very well controlled again. There was no mischievous revealing light in her face any more, and she looked almost severe, as if she very much regretted what she had said and was going to make quite certain I didn't take advantage of it.

She handed me a cup and offered the biscuits, which I ate because the lunch at Humber's had consisted of bread, margarine, and hard tasteless cheese, and the supper would be the same. It nearly always was, on Saturdays, because Humber knew we ate in Posset.

We talked sedately about her father's horses, I asked how Sparking Plug was getting on, and she told me, very well, thank you.

'I've a newspaper cutting about him, if you'd like to see it?' she said.

'Yes, I'd like to.'

I followed her to her desk while she looked for it. She shifted some papers to search underneath, and the top one fell on to the floor. I picked it up, put it back on the desk, and looked down at it. It seemed to be some sort of quiz.

'Thank you,' she said. 'I mustn't lose that, it's the Literary Society's competition, and I've only one more answer to find. Now where did I put that cutting?'

The competition consisted of a number of quotations to which one had to ascribe the author. I picked up the paper and began reading.

'That top one's a brute,' she said over her shoulder. 'No one's got it yet, I don't think.'

'How do you win the competition?' I asked.

'Get a complete, correct set of answers in first.'

'And what's the prize?'

'A book. But prestige, mostly. We only have one competition a term, and it's difficult.' She opened a drawer full of papers and oddments. 'I know I put that cutting somewhere.' She began shovelling things out on to the top of the desk.

'Please don't bother any more,' I said politely.

'No, I want to find it.' A handful of small objects clattered on to the desk.

Among them was a small chromium-plated tube about three inches long with a loop of chain running from one end to the other. I had seen something like it before, I thought idly. I had seen it quite often. It had something to do with drinks.

'What's that?' I asked, pointing.

'That? Oh, that's a silent whistle.' She went on rummaging. 'For dogs,' she explained.

I picked it up. A silent dog whistle. Why then did I think it was connected with bottles and glasses and . . . the world stopped.

With an almost physical sensation, my mind leaped towards its prey. I held Adams and Humber in my hand at last. I could feel my pulse racing.

So simple. So very simple. The tube pulled apart in the middle to reveal that one end was a thin whistle, and the other its cap. A whistle joined to its cap by a little length of chain. I put the tiny mouthpiece to my lips and blew. Only a thread of sound came out.

'You can't hear it very well,' Elinor said, 'but of course a dog can. And you can adjust that whistle to make it sound louder to human ears, too.' She took it out of my hand and unscrewed part of the whistle itself. 'Now blow.' She gave it back.

I blew again. It sounded much more like an ordinary whistle.

'Do you think I could possibly borrow this for a little while?' I asked. 'If you're not using it? I . . . I want to try an experiment.'

'Yes, I should think so. My dear old sheepdog had to be put down last spring, and I haven't used it since. But you will let me have it back? I am getting a puppy in the long vac, and I want to use it for his training.'

'Yes, of course.'

'All right, then. Oh, here's that cutting, at last.'

I took the strip of newsprint, but I couldn't concentrate on it. All I could see was the drinks compartment in Humber's monster car, with the rack of ice-picks, tongs and little miscellaneous chromium-plated objects. I had never given them more than a cursory glance; but one of them was a small tube with a loop of chain from end to end. One of them was a silent whistle for dogs.

I made an effort, and read about Sparking Plug, and thanked her for finding the cutting.

I stowed her whistle in my money belt and looked at my watch. It was already after half past three. I was going to be somewhat late back at work.

She had cleared me with October and shown me the whistle: two enormous favours. I wanted to repay her, and could think of only one way of doing it.

' "Nowhere either with more quiet or more freedom from trouble does a man retire than into his own soul . . ." ' I quoted.

She looked up at me, startled. 'That's the beginning of the competition.'

'Yes. Are you allowed help?'

'Yes. Anything. But . . .'

'It's Marcus Aurelius.'

'Who?' She was staggered.

'Marcus Aurelius Antoninus. Roman Emperor, 121 to 180 A.D. . . .'

'The Meditations?' I nodded.

'What language was it originally written in? We have to put that too. Latin, I suppose.'

'Greek.'

'This is fantastic . . . just where did you go to school?'

'I went to a village school in Oxfordshire.' So I had, for two years, until I was eight. 'And we had a master who perpetually crammed Marcus Aurelius down our throats.' But that master had been at Geelong.

I had been tempted to tell her the truth about myself all afternoon, but never more than at that moment. I found it impossible to be anything but my own self in her company, and even at Slaw I had spoken to her more or less in my natural accent. I hated having to pretend to her at all. But I didn't tell her where I had come from and why, because October hadn't, and I thought he ought to know his daughter better than I did. There were her cosy chats with Patty . . . whose tongue could not be relied on; and perhaps he thought it was a risk to his investigations. I didn't know. And I didn't tell her.

'Are you really sure it's Marcus Aurelius?' she said doubtfully. 'We only get one shot. If it's wrong, you don't get another.'

'I should check it then. It comes in a section about learning to be content with your lot. I suppose I remember it because it is good advice and I've seldom been able to follow it.' I grinned.

'You know,' she said tentatively, 'It's none of my business, but I would have thought you could have got on a bit in the world. You seem . . . you seem decidedly intelligent. Why do you work in a stable?'

'I work in a stable,' I told her with perfect, ironic truth, 'because it's the only thing I know how to do.'

'Will you do it for the rest of your life?'

'I expect so.'

'And will it content you?'

'It will have to.'

'I didn't expect this afternoon to turn out like this at all,' she said. 'To be frank, I was dreading it. And you have made it easy.'

'That's all right, then,' I said cheerfully.

She smiled. I went to the door and opened it, and she said, 'I'd better see you out. This building must have been the work of a maze-crazy architect. Visitors have been found wandering about the upper reaches dying of thirst days after they were supposed to have left.'

I laughed. She walked beside me back along the twisting corridors, down the stairs, and right back to the outside door, talking easily about her life in college, talking to me freely, as an equal. She told me that Durham was the oldest English University after Oxford and Cambridge, and that it was the only place in Britain which offered a course in Geophysics. She was indeed, a very nice girl.

She shook hands with me on the step.

'Goodbye,' she said. 'I'm sorry Patty was so beastly.'

'I'm not. If she hadn't been, I wouldn't have been here this afternoon.'

She laughed. 'But what a price to pay.'

'Worth it.'

Her grey eyes had darker grey flecks in them, I noticed. She watched me go over and sit on the motor-cycle and fasten on the helmet. Then she waved her hand briefly, and went back through the door. It closed with finality behind her.

Chapter Fourteen

I stopped in Posset on the return journey to see if there were any comment from October on the theory I had sent him the previous week, but there was no letter for me at all.

Although I was already late for evening stables, I stopped longer to write to him. I couldn't get Tommy Stapleton out of my head: he had died without passing on what he knew. I didn't want to make the same mistake. Or to die either, if it came to that. I scribbled fast.

'I think the trigger is a silent whistle, the sort used for dogs. Humber keeps one in the drinks compartment of his car. Remember Old Etonian? They hold hound-trails at Cartmel, on the morning of the races.'

Having posted that, I bought a large slab of chocolate for food, and also Jerry's comic, and slid as quietly as I could back into the yard. Cass caught me, however, and said sourly that I'd be lucky to get Saturday off next week as he would be reporting me to Humber. I sighed resignedly, started the load of evening chores, and felt the cold, dingy, sub-violent atmosphere of the place seep back into my bones.

But there was a difference now. The whistle lay like a bomb in my money belt. A death sentence, if they found me with it. Or so I believed. There remained the matter of making sure that I had not leaped to the wrong conclusion.

Tommy Stapleton had probably suspected what was going on and had walked straight into Humber's yard to tax him with it. He couldn't have known that the men he was dealing with were prepared to kill. But, because he had died, I did know. I had lived under their noses for seven weeks, and I had been careful: and because I intended to remain undetected to the end I spent a long time on Sunday wondering how I could conduct my experiment and get away with it.

On Sunday evening, at about five o'clock, Adams drove into the yard in his shining grey Jaguar. As usual at the sight of him, my heart sank. He walked round the yard with Humber when he made his normal tour of inspection and stopped for a long time looking over the door at Mickey. Neither he nor Humber came in. Humber had been into Mickey's box several times since the day he helped me take in the first lot of drugged water, but Adams had not been in at all.

Adams said, 'What do you think, Hedley?'

Humber shrugged, 'There's no change.'

'Write him off?'

'I suppose so.' Humber sounded depressed.

'It's a bloody nuisance,' said Adams violently. He looked at me. 'Still bolstering yourself up with tranquillizers?'

'Yes, sir.'

He laughed rudely. He thought it very funny. Then his face changed to a scowl, and he said savagely to Humber, 'It's useless, I can see that. Give him the chop, then.'

Humber turned away, and şaid, 'Right, I'll get it done tomorrow.'

Their footsteps moved off to the next box. I looked at Mickey. I had done my best for him, but he was too far gone, and had been from the beginning. After a fortnight what with his mental chaos, his continual state of druggedness, and his persistent refusal to eat, Mickey's condition was pitiable, and any one less stony than Humber would have had him put down long ago.

I made him comfortable for his last night and evaded yet another slash from his teeth. I couldn't say I was sorry not to have to deal with him any more, as a fortnight of looking after an unhinged horse would be enough for anyone; but the fact that he was to be put down the next day meant that I would have to perform my experiment without delay.

I didn't feel ready to do it. Thinking about it, as I put away my brushes for the night and walked across the yard towards the kitchen, I tried to find one good reason for putting it off.

The alacrity with which a good excuse for not doing it presented itself led me to the unwelcome, swingeing realization that for the first time since my childhood, I was thoroughly afraid.

I could get October to make the experiment, I thought, on Six-Ply. Or on any of the other horses. I hadn't got to do it myself. It would definitely be more prudent not to do it myself. October could do it with absolute safety, but if Humber found me out I was as good as dead: therefore I should leave it to October.

That was when I knew I was afraid, and I didn't like it. It took me most of the evening to decide to do the experiment myself. On Mickey. The next morning. Shuffling it off on to October doubtless would have been more prudent, but I had myself to live with afterwards. What had I really wanted to leave home for, if not to find out what I could or couldn't do?

When I took the bucket to the office door in the morning for Mickey's last dose of phenobarbitone, there was only a little left in the jar. Cass tipped the glass container upside down and tapped it on the bucket so that the last grains of white powder should not be wasted.

'That's his lot, poor bastard,' he observed, putting the stopper back in the empty jar. 'Pity there isn't a bit more left, we could have given him a double dose, just this once. Well, get on with it,' he added sharply. 'Don't·hang about looking mournful. It's not you that's going to be shot this afternoon.'

Well, I hoped not.

I turned away, went along to the tap, splashed in a little water, swilled round in it the instantly dissolved phenobarbitone, and poured it away down the drain. Then I filled the bucket with clean water and took it along for Mickey to drink.

He was dying on his feet. The bones stuck out more sharply under his skin and his head hung down below his shoulders. There was still a disorientated wildness in his eye, but he was going downhill so fast that he had little strength left for attacking anyone. For once he made no attempt to bite me when I put the bucket down at his head, but lowered his mouth into it and took a few half-hearted swallows.

Leaving him, I went along to the tack room and took a new head collar out of the basket of stores. This was strictly against the rules: only Cass was supposed to issue new tack. I took the head collar along to Mickey's box and fitted it on to him, removing the one he had weakened by constant fretting during his fortnight's illness and hiding it under a pile of straw, I unclipped the tethering chain from the old collar and clipped it on to the ring of the new one. I patted Mickey's neck, which he didn't like, walked out of his box, and shut and bolted only the bottom half of the door.

We rode out the first lot, and the second lot; and by then, I judged, Mickey's brain, without its morning dose, would be coming out of its sedation.

Leading Dobbin, the horse I had just returned on, I went to look at Mickey over the stable door. His head was weaving weakly from side to side, and he seemed very restless. Poor creature, I thought. Poor creature. And for a few seconds I was going to make him suffer more.

Humber stood at his office door, talking to Cass. The lads were bustling in and out looking after their horses, buckets were clattering, voices calling to each other: routine stable noise. I was never going to have a better opportunity.

I began to lead Dobbin across the yard to his box. Half way there I took the whistle out of my belt and pulled off its cap: then, looking round to make sure that no one was watching, I turned my head over my shoulder, put the tiny mouthpiece to my lips, and blew hard. Only a thread of sound came out, so high that I could hardly hear it above the clatter of Dobbin's feet on the ground.

The result was instantaneous and hideous.

Mickey screamed with terror.

His hooves threshed wildly against the floor and walls, and the chain which held him rattled as he jerked against it.

I walked Dobbin quickly the few remaining yards into his stall, clipped his chain on, zipped the whistle back into my belt, and ran across towards Mickey's box. Everyone else was doing the same. Humber was limping swiftly down the yard.

Mickey was still screaming and crashing his hooves against the wall as I looked into his box over the shoulders of Cecil and Lenny. The poor animal was on his hind legs, seemingly trying to beat his way through the bricks in front of him. Then suddenly, with all his ebbing strength, he dropped his forelegs to the ground and charged backwards.

'Look out,' shouted Cecil, instinctively retreating from the frantically bunching hind-quarters, although he was safely outside a solid door.

Mickey's tethering chain was not very long. There was a sickening snap as he reached the end of it and his backwards momentum was joltingly, appallingly stopped. His hind legs slid forward under his belly and he fell with a crash on to his side. His legs jerked stiffly. His head, still secured in the strong new head collar, was held awkwardly off the ground by the taut chain, and by its unnatural angle told its own tale. He had broken his neck. As indeed, to put him quickly out of his frenzy, I had hoped he might.

Everyone in the yard had gathered outside Mickey's box. Humber, having glanced perfunctorily over the door at the dead horse, turned and looked broodingly at his six ragged stable lads. The narrow eyed harshness of his expression stopped anyone asking him questions. There was a short silence.

'Stand in a line,' he said suddenly.

The lads looked surprised, but did as he said.

'Turn out your pockets,' said Humber.

Mystified, the lads obeyed. Cass went down the line, looking at what was produced and pulling the pockets out like wings to make sure they were empty. When he came to me I showed him a dirty handkerchief, a penknife, a few coins, and pulled my pockets inside out. He took the handkerchief from my hand, shook it out, and gave it back. The whistle at my waist was only an inch from his fingers.

I felt Humber's searching gaze on me from six feet away, but as I studied to keep my face vacantly relaxed and vaguely puzzled I was astonished to find that I was neither sweating nor tensing my muscles to make a run for it. In an odd way the nearness of the danger made me cool and clear headed. I didn't understand it, but it certainly helped.

'Back pocket?' asked Cass.

'Nothing in it,' I said casually, turning half round to show him.

'All right. Now you, Kenneth.'

I pushed my pockets in again, and replaced their contents. My hands were steady. Extraordinary, I thought.

Humber watched and waited until Kenneth's pockets had been innocently emptied: then he looked at Cass and jerked his head towards the loose boxes. Cass rooted around in the boxes of the horses we had just exercised. He finished the last, came back, and shook his head. Humber pointed silently towards the garage which sheltered his Bentley. Cass disappeared, reappeared, and again excitedly shook his head. In silence Humber limped away to his office, leaning on his heavy stick.

He couldn't have heard the whistle, and he didn't suspect that any of us had blown one for the sole purpose of watching its effect on Mickey, because if he had he would have had us stripped and searched from head to foot. He was still thinking along the lines of Mickey's death being an accident: and having found no whistle in any of the lad's pockets or in their horses' boxes he would conclude, I hoped, that it was none of that downtrodden bunch who had caused Mickey's brain-storm. If only Adams would agree with him, I was clear.

It was my afternoon for washing the car. Humber's own whistle was still there, tucked neatly into a leather retaining strap between a cork-screw and a pair of ice tongs. I looked, and left it where it was.

Adams came the next day.

Mickey had gone to the dog-meat man, who had grumbled about his thinness, and I had unobtrusively returned the new head collar to the store basket, leaving the old one dangling as usual from the tethering chain. Even Cass had not noticed the substitution.

Adams and Humber strolled along to Mickey's empty box and leaned on the half door, talking. Jerry poked his head out of the box next door, saw them standing there, and hurriedly disappeared again. I went normally about my business, fetching hay and water for Dobbin and carting away the muck sack.

'Roke,' shouted Humber, 'come here. At the double.'

I hurried over. 'Sir?'

'You haven't cleaned out this box.'

'I'm sorry sir. I'll do it this afternoon.'

'You will do it,' he said deliberately, 'before you have your dinner.'

He knew very well that this meant having no dinner at all. I glanced at his face. He was looking at me with calculation, his eyes narrowed and his lips pursed.

I looked down. 'Yes, sir,' I said meekly. Damn it, I thought furiously; this was too soon. I had been there not quite eight weeks, and I ought to have been able to count on at least three more. If he were already intent on making me leave, I was not going to be able to finish the job.

'For a start,' said Adams, 'you can fetch out that bucket and put it away.'

I looked into the box. Mickey's bucket still stood by the manger. I opened the door, walked over, picked it up, turned round to go back, and stopped dead.

Adams had come into the box after me. He held Humber's walking stick in his hand, and he was smiling.

I dropped the bucket and backed into a corner. He laughed.

'No tranquillizers today, eh, Roke?'

He swung his arm and the knobbed end of the stick landed on my ribs. It was hard enough, in all conscience. When he lifted his arm again I ducked under it and bolted out through the door. His roar of laughter floated after me.

I went on running until I was out of sight, and then walked and rubbed my chest. It was going to be a fair sized bruise, and I wasn't too keen on collecting many more. I supposed I should be thankful at least that they proposed to rid themselves of me in the ordinary way, and not over a hillside in a burning car.

All through that long, hungry afternoon I tried to decide what was best to do. To go at once, resigned to the fact that I couldn't finish the job, or to stay the few days I safely could without arousing Adams' suspicions. But what, I depressedly wondered, could I discover in three or four days that I had been unable to discover in eight weeks.

It was Jerry, of all people, who decided for me.

After supper (baked beans on bread, but not enough of it) we sat at the table with Jerry's comic spread open. Since Charlie had left no one had a radio, and the evenings were more boring than ever. Lenny and Kenneth were playing dice on the floor. Cecil was out getting drunk. Bert sat in his silent world on the bench on the other side of Jerry, watching the dice roll across the concrete.

The oven door was open, and all the switches on the electric stove were turned on as high as they would go. This was Lenny's bright idea for supplementing the small heat thrown out by the paraffin stove Humber had grudgingly provided. It wouldn't last longer than the arrival of the electricity bill, it was warm meanwhile.

The dirty dishes were stacked in the sink. Cobwebs hung like a cornice where the walls met the ceiling. A naked light bulb lit the brick-walled room. Someone had spilled tea on the table, and the corner of Jerry's comic had soaked it up.

I sighed. To think that I wasn't happy to be about to leave this squalid existence, now that I was being given no choice!

Jerry looked up from his comic, keeping his place with his finger.

'Dan?'

'Mmm?'

'Did Mr. Adams bash you?'

'Yes.'

'I thought he did.' He nodded several times, and went back to his comic.

I suddenly remembered his having looked out of the box next to Mickey's before Adams and Humber had called me over.

'Jerry,' I said slowly, 'did you hear Mr. Adams and Mr. Humber talking, while you were in the box with Mr. Adams' black hunter?'

'Yes,' he said, without looking up.

'What did they say?'

'When you ran away Mr. Adams laughed and told the boss you wouldn't stand it long. Stand it long,' he repeated vaguely, like a refrain, 'stand it long.'

'Did you hear what they said before that? When they first got there, and you looked out and saw them?'

This troubled him. He sat up and forgot to keep his place.

'I didn't want the boss to know I was still there, see? I ought to have finished that hunter a good bit before then.'

'Yes. Well, you're all right. They didn't catch you.'

He grinned and shook his head.

'What did they say?' I prompted.

'They were cross about Mickey. They said they would get on with the next one at once.'

'The next what?'

'I don't know.'

'Did they say anything else?'

He screwed up his thin little face. He wanted to please me, and I knew this expression meant he was thinking his hardest.

'Mr. Adams said you had been with Mickey too long, and the boss said yes it was a bad . . . a bad . . . um . . . oh, yes . . . risk, and you had better leave, and Mr. Adams said yes, get on with that as quick as you can and we'll do the next one as soon as he's gone.' He opened his eyes wide in triumph at this sustained effort.

'Say that again,' I said. 'The last bit, that's all.'

One thing Jerry could do, from long practice with the comics, was to learn by heart through his ears.

Obediently he repeated, 'Mr. Adams said get on with that as quick as you can and we'll do the next one as soon as he's gone.'

'What do you want most on earth?' I asked.

He looked surprised and then thoughtful, and finally a dreamy look spread over his face.

'Well?'

'A train,' he said. 'One you wind up. You know. And rails and things. And a signal.' He fell silent in rapture.

'You shall have them,' I said. 'As soon as I can get them.'

His mouth opened.

I said, 'Jerry, I'm leaving here. You can't stay when Mr. Adams starts bashing you, can you? So I'll have to go. But I'll send you that train. I won't forget, I promise.'

The evening dragged away as so many others had done, and we climbed the ladder to our unyielding beds, where I lay on my back in the dark with my hands laced behind my head and thought about Humber's stick crashing down somewhere on my body in the morning. Rather like going to the dentist for a drilling, I thought ruefully: the anticipation was worse than the event. I sighed, and went to sleep.

Operation Eviction continued much as expected, the next day.

When I was unsaddling Dobbin after the second exercise Humber walked into the box behind me and his stick landed with a thud across my back.

I let go of the saddle – which fell on a pile of fresh droppings – and swung round.

'What did I do wrong, sir?' I said, in an aggrieved voice. I thought I might as well make it difficult for him, but he had an answer ready.

'Cass tells me you were late back at work last Saturday afternoon. And pick up that saddle. What do you think you're doing, dropping it in that dirt?'

He stood with his legs planted firmly apart, his eyes judging his distance.

Well, all right, I thought. One more, and that's enough.

I turned round and picked up the saddle. I already had it in my arms and was straightening up when he hit me again, more or less in the same place, but much harder. The breath hissed through my teeth.

I threw the saddle down again in the dirt and shouted at him. 'I'm leaving. I'm off. Right now.'

'Very well,' he said coldly, with perceptible satisfaction. 'Go and pack. Your cards will be waiting for you in the office.' He turned on his heel and slowly limped away, his purpose successfully concluded.

How frigid he was, I thought. Unemotional, sexless and calculating. Impossible to think of him loving, or being loved, or feeling pity, or grief, or any sort of fear.

I arched my back, grimacing, and decided to leave Dobbin's saddle where it was, in the dirt. A nice touch, I thought. In character, to the bitter end.

Chapter Fifteen

I took the polythene sheeting off the motor-cycle and coasted gently out of the yard. All the lads were out exercising the third lot, with yet more to be ridden when they got back; and even while I was wondering how five of them were possibly going to cope with thirty horses, I met a shifty-looking boy trudging slowly up the road to Humber's with a kit bag slung over his shoulder. More flotsam. If he had known what he was going to, he would have walked more slowly still.

I biked to Clavering, a dreary mining town of mean back-to-back terraced streets jazzed up with chromium and glass in the shopping centre, and telephoned to October's London house.

Terence answered. Lord October, he said, was in Germany, where his firm were opening a new factory.

'When will he be back?'

'Saturday morning, I think. He went last Sunday, for a week.'

'Is he going to Slaw for the week-end?'

'I think so. He said something about flying back to Manchester, and he's given me no instructions for anything here.'

'Can you find the addresses and telephone numbers of Colonel Beckett and Sir Stuart Macclesfield for me?'

'Hang on a moment.' There was fluttering of pages, and Terence told me the numbers and addresses. I wrote them down and thanked him.

'Your clothes are still here, sir,' he said.

'I know,' I grinned. 'I'll be along to fetch them quite soon, I think.'

We rang off, and I tried Beckett's number. A dry, precise voice told me that Colonel Beckett was out, but that he would be dining at his Club at nine, and could be reached then. Sir Stuart Macclesfield, it transpired, was in a nursing home recovering from pneumonia. I had hoped to be able to summon some help in keeping a watch on Humber's yard so that when the horse-box left with Kandersteg on board it could be followed. It looked, however, as though I would have to do it myself, as I could visualise the local police neither believing my story nor providing anyone to assist me.

Armed with a rug and a pair of good binoculars bought in a pawn shop, and also with a pork pie, slabs of chocolate, a bottle of vichy water, and some sheets of foolscap paper, I rode the motor-cycle back through Posset and out along the road which crossed the top of the valley in which Humber's stables lay. Stopping at the point I had marked on my previous excursion, I wheeled the cycle a few yards down into the scrubby heathland, and found a position where I was off the sky line, more or less out of sight from passing cars, and also able to look down into Humber's yard through the binoculars. It was one o'clock, and there was nothing happening there.

I unbuckled the suitcase from the carrier and used it as a seat, settling myself to stay there for a long time. Even if I could reach Beckett on the telephone at nine, he wouldn't be able to rustle up reinforcements much before the next morning.

There was, meanwhile, a report to make, a fuller, more formal, more explanatory affair than the notes scribbled in Posset's post office. I took out the foolscap paper and wrote, on and off, for most of the afternoon, punctuating my work by frequent glances through the binoculars. But nothing took place down at Humber's except the normal routine of the stable.

I began . . .

'To The Earl of October.

    Sir Stuart Macclesfield.

    Colonel Roderick Beckett.

Sirs,

The following is a summary of the facts which have so far come to light during my investigations on your behalf, together with some deductions which it seems reasonable to make from them.

Paul James Adams and Hedley Humber started collaborating in a scheme for ensuring winners about four years ago, when Adams bought the Manor House and came to live at Tellbridge, Northumberland.

Adams (in my admittedly untrained opinion) has a psychopathic personality, in that he impulsively gives himself pleasure and pursues his own ends without any consideration for other people or much apparent anxiety about the consequences to himself. His intelligence seems to be above average, and it is he who gives the orders. I believe it is fairly common for psychopaths to be aggressive swindlers: it might be enlightening to dig up his life history.

Humber, though dominated by Adams, is not as irresponsible. He is cold and controlled at all times. I have never seen him genuinely angry (he uses anger as a weapon) and everything he does seems to be thought out and calculated. Whereas Adams may be mentally abnormal, Humber seems to be simply wicked. His comparative sanity may act as a brake on Adams, and have prevented their discovery before this.

Jud Wilson, the head travelling lad, and Cass, the head lad, are both involved, but only to the extent of being hired subordinates. Neither of them does as much stable work as their jobs would normally entail, but they are well paid. Both own big cars of less than a year old.

Adams' and Humber's scheme is based on the fact that horses learn by association and connect noises to events. Like Pavlov's dogs who would come to the sound of a bell because they had been taught it meant feeding time, horses hearing the feed trolley rattling across a stable yard know very well that their food is on the way.

If a horse is accustomed to a certain consequence following closely upon a certain noise, he automatically *expects* the consequence whenever he hears the noise. He reacts to the noise in anticipation of what is to come.

If something frightening were substituted – if, for instance, the rattle of the feed trolley were followed always by a thrashing and no food – the horse would soon begin to fear the noise, because of what it portended.

Fear is the stimulant which Adams and Humber have used. The appearance of all the apparently 'doped' horses after they had won – the staring, rolling eyes and the heavy sweat – was consistent with their having been in a state of terror.

Fear strongly stimulates the adrenal glands, so that they flood the bloodstream with adrenalin: and the effects of extra adrenalin, as of course you know, is to release the upsurge of energy needed to deal with the situation, either by fighting back or by running away. Running, in this case. At top speed, in panic.

The laboratory reports stated that the samples taken from all the original eleven horses showed a high adrenalin content, but that this was not significant because horses vary enormously, some always producing more adrenalin than others. I, however, think that it *was* significant that the adrenalin counts of those eleven horses were uniformly higher than average.

The noise which triggered off their fear is the high note of the sort of silent whistle normally used for training dogs. Horses can hear it well, though to human ears it is faint: this fact makes it ideal for the purpose, as a more obtrusive sound (a football rattle, for instance) would soon have been spotted. Humber keeps a dog whistle in the drinks compartment of his Bentley.

I do not yet know for sure how Adams and Humber frighten the horses, but I can make a guess.

For a fortnight I looked after a horse known in the yard as Mickey (registered name, Starlamp) who had been given the treatment. In Mickey's case, it was a disaster. He returned from three days' absence with large raw patches on his fore legs and in a completely unhinged mental state.

The wounds on his legs were explained by the head lad as having been caused by the application of a blister. But there was no blister paste to be seen, and I think they were ordinary burns caused by some sort of naked flame. Horses are more afraid of fire than of anything else, and it seems probable to me that it is expectation of being burnt that Adams and Humber have harnessed to the sound of a dog whistle.

I blew a dog whistle to discover its effect on Mickey. It was less than three weeks after the association had been planted, and he reacted violently and unmistakably. If you care to, you can repeat this trial on Six-Ply; but give him room to bolt in safety.

Adams and Humber chose horses which looked promising throughout their racing careers but had never won on account of running out of steam or guts at the last fence; and there are of course any number of horses like this. They bought them cheaply one at a time from auction sales or out of selling races, instilled into them a noise-fear association, and quietly sold them again. Often, far from losing on the deal, they made a profit (c.f. past histories of horses collected by officer cadets).

Having sold a horse with such a built-in accelerator, Adams and Humber then waited for it to run in a selling chase at one of five courses: Segefield, Haydock, Ludlow, Kelso and Stafford. They seem to have been prepared to wait indefinitely for this combination of place and event to occur, and in fact it has only occurred twelve times (eleven winners and Superman) since the first case twenty months ago.

These courses were chosen, I imagine, because their extra long run-in gave the most room for the panic to take effect. The horses were often lying fourth or fifth when landing over the last fence, and needed time to overhaul the leaders. If a horse were too hopelessly behind, Adams and Humber could just have left the whistle unblown, forfeited their stake money, and waited for another day.

Selling chases were preferred, I think, because horses are less likely to fall in them, and because of the good possibility of the winners changing hands yet again immediately afterwards.

At first sight it looks as if it would have been safer to have applied this scheme to Flat racing: but Flat racers do not seem to change hands so often, which would lessen the confusion. Then again Humber has never held a Flat licence, and probably can't get one.

None of the horses has been galvanised twice, the reason probably being that having once discovered they were not burnt after hearing the whistle they would be less likely to expect to be again. Their reaction would no longer be reliable enough to gamble on.

All the eleven horses won at very long odds, varying from 10–1 to 50–1, and Adams and Humber must have spread their bets thinly enough to raise no comment. I do not know how much Adams won on each race, but the least Humber made was seventeen hundred pounds, and the most was four thousand five hundred.

Details of all the processed horses, successful and unsuccessful, are recorded in a blue ledger at present to be found at the back of the third drawer down in the centre one of three green filing cabinets in Humber's stable office.

Basically, as you see, it is a simple plan. All they do is make a horse associate fire with a dog whistle, and then blow a whistle as he lands over the last fence.

No drugs, no mechanical contrivances, no help needed from owner, trainer or jockey. There was only a slight risk of Adams and Humber being found out, because their connection with the horses was so obscure and distant.

Stapleton, however, suspected them, and I am certain in my own mind that they killed him, although there is no supporting evidence.

They believe now that they are safe and undetected: and they intend, during the next few days, to plant fear in a horse called Kandersteg. I have left Humber's employ, and am writing this while keeping watch on the yard. I propose to follow the horse box when Kandersteg leaves in it, and discover where and how the heat is applied.'

I stopped writing and picked up the binoculars. The lads were bustling about doing evening stables and I enjoyed not being down there among them.

It was too soon, I thought, to expect Humber to start on Kandersteg, however much of a hurry he and Adams were in. They couldn't have known for certain that I would depart before lunch, or even that day, and they were bound to let my dust settle before making a move. On the other hand I couldn't risk missing them. Even the two miles to the telephone in Posset made ringing up Beckett a worrying prospect. It would take no longer for Kandersteg to be loaded up and carted off than for me to locate Beckett in his Club. Mickey-Starlamp had been both removed and brought back in daylight, and it might be that Humber never moved any horses by night. But I couldn't be sure. I bit the end of my pen in indecision. Finally, deciding not to telephone, I added a postscript to the report.

'I would very much appreciate some help in this watch, because if it continues for several days I could easily miss the horse box through falling asleep. I can be found two miles out of Posset on the Hexham road, at the head of the valley which Humber's stables lie in.'

I added the time, the date, and signed my name. Then I folded the report into an envelope, and addressed it to Colonel Beckett.

I raced down to Posset to put the letter in the box outside the post office. Four miles. I was away for just under six minutes. It was lucky, I think, that I met no traffic on either part of the trip. I skidded to a worried halt at the top of the hill, but all appeared normal down in the stables. I wheeled the motor-cycle off the road again, down to where I had been before, and took a long look through the binoculars.

It was beginning to get dark and lights were on in nearly all the boxes, shining out into the yard. The dark looming bulk of Humber's house,

which lay nearest to me, shut off from my sight his brick office and all
the top end of the yard, but I had a sideways view of the closed doors of
the horse box garage, and I could see straight into the far end row of
boxes, of which the fourth from the left was occupied by Kandersteg.

And there he was, a pale washy chestnut, moving across and catching
the light as Bert tossed his straw to make him comfortable for the night.
I sighed with relief, and sat down again to watch.

The routine work went on, untroubled, unchanged. I watched Humber,
leaning on his stick, make his slow inspection round the yard, and
absent-mindedly rubbed the bruises he had given me that morning. One
by one the doors were shut and the lights went out until a single window
glowed yellow, the last window along the right hand row of boxes, the
window of the lads' kitchen. I put down the binoculars, and got to my
feet and stretched.

As always on the moors the air was on the move. It wasn't a wind,
scarcely a breeze, more like a cold current flowing round whatever it
found in its path. To break its chilling persistence on my back I constructed
a rough barricade of the motor-cycle with a bank of brushwood on its
roadward, moorward side. In the lea of this shelter I sat on the suitcase,
wrapped myself in the rug, and was tolerably warm and comfortable.

I looked at my watch. Almost eight o'clock. It was a fine, clear night,
and the sky was luminous with the white blaze of the stars. I still hadn't
learned the northern hemisphere patterns except for the Great Bear and
Pole Star. And there was Venus dazzling away to the west-south-west.
A pity that I hadn't thought of buying an astral map to pass the time.

Down in the yard the kitchen door opened, spilling out an oblong of
light. Cecil's figure stayed there for a few seconds silhouetted; then he
came out and shut the door, and I couldn't see him in the dark. Off to
his bottle, no doubt.

I ate some pie, and a while later, a bar of chocolate.

Time passed. Nothing happened down in Humber's yard. Occasionally
a car sped along the road behind me, but none stopped. Nine o'clock
came and went. Colonel Beckett would be dining at his Club, and I could
after all have gone safely down to ring him up. I shrugged in the darkness.
He would get my letter in the morning, anyway.

The kitchen door opened again, and two or three lads came out, picking
their way with a torch round to the elementary sanitation. Upstairs in
the hay-loft a light showed dimly through that half of the window not
pasted over with brown paper. Bed-time. Cecil reeled in, clutching the
door post to stop himself from falling. The downstairs light went out,
and finally the upper one as well.

The night deepened. The hours passed. The moon rose and shone
brightly. I gazed out over the primeval rolling moors and thought some
unoriginal thoughts, such as how beautiful the earth was, and how vicious
the ape creature who inhabited it. Greedy, destructive, unkind, power-
hungry old homo sapiens. Sapiens, meaning wise, discreet, judicious.
What a laugh. So fair a planet should have evolved a sweeter-natured,
saner race. Nothing that produced people like Adams and Humber could
be termed a roaring success.

At four o'clock I ate some more chocolate and drank some water, and for some time thought about my stud farm sweltering in the afternoon sun twleve thousand miles away. A sensible, orderly life waiting for me when I had finished sitting on wintry hillsides in the middle of the night.

Cold crept through the blanket as time wore on, but it was no worse than the temperature in Humber's dormitory. I yawned and rubbed my eyes, and began to work out how many seconds had to pass before dawn. If the sun rose (as expected) at ten to seven, that would be a hundred and thirteen times sixty seconds, which made it six thousand seven hundred and eighty ticks to Thursday. And how many to Friday? I gave up. It was quite likely I would be sitting on the hillside, but with a little luck there would be a Beckett-sent companion to give me a pinch when things started moving.

At six fifteen the light went on again in the lads' quarters, and the stable woke up. Half an hour later the first string of six horses wound its way out of the yard and down the road to Posset. No gallops on the moors on Thursday. Road work day.

Almost before they were out of sight Jud Wilson drove into the yard in his substantial Ford and parked it beside the horse box shed. Cass walked across the yard to meet him, and the two of them stood talking together for a few minutes. Then through the binoculars I watched Jud Wilson go back to the shed and open its big double doors, while Cass made straight for Kandersteg's box, the fourth door from the end.

They were off.

And they were off very slickly. Jud Wilson backed the box into the centre of the yard and let down the ramp. Cass led the horse straight across and into the horse box, and within a minute was out helping to raise and fasten the ramp again. There was then a fractional pause while they stood looking towards the house, from where almost instantly the limping back-view of Humber appeared.

Cass stood watching while Humber and Jud Wilson climbed up into the cab. The horse box rolled forward out of the yard. The loading up had taken barely five minutes from start to finish.

During this time I dropped the rug over the suitcase and kicked the brushwood away from the bike. The binoculars I slung round my neck and zipped inside the leather jacket. I put on my crash helmet, goggles and gloves.

In spite of my belief that it would be to the north or the west that Kandersteg would be taken, I was relieved when this proved to be the case. The horse box turned sharply west and trundled up the far side of the valley along the road which crossed the one I was stationed on.

I wheeled the bike on to the road, started it, and abandoning (this time with pleasure) my third clump of clothes, rode with some despatch towards the cross-roads. There from a safe quarter of a mile away I watched the horse box slow down, turn right, northwards, and accelerate.

Chapter Sixteen

I crouched in a ditch all day and watched Adams, Humber and Jud Wilson scare Kandersteg into a lathering frenzy.

It was wicked.

The means they used were as simple in essence as the scheme, and consisted mainly in the special lay-out of a small two-acre field.

The thin high hedge round the whole field was laced with wire to about shoulder height, strong, but without barbs. About fifteen feet inside this there was a second fence, solidly made of posts and rails which had weathered to a pleasant greyish-brown.

At first glance it looked like the arrangement found at many stud farms, where young stock are kept from damaging themselves on wire by a wooden protective inner fence. But the corners of this inner ring had been rounded, so that what in effect had been formed was a miniature race track between the outer and inner fences.

It all looked harmless. A field for young stock, a training place for racehorses, a show ring ... take your pick. With a shed for storing equipment, just outside the gate at one corner. Sensible. Ordinary.

I half-knelt, half-lay in the drainage ditch which ran along behind the hedge, near the end of one long side of the field, with the shed little more than a hundred yards away in the far opposite corner, to my left. The bottom of the hedge had been cut and laid, which afforded good camouflage for my head, but from about a foot above the ground the leafless hawthorn grew straight up, tall and weedy; as concealing as a sieve. But as long as I kept absolutely still, I judged I was unlikely to be spotted. At any rate, although I was really too close for safety, too close even to need to use the binoculars, there was nowhere else which gave much cover at all.

Bare hillsides sloped up beyond the far fence and along the end of the field to my right; behind me lay a large open pasture of at least thirty acres; and the top end, which was screened from the road by a wedge of conifers, was directly under Adams' and Humber's eyes.

Getting to the ditch had entailed leaving the inadequate shelter of the last flattening shoulder of hillside and crossing fifteen yards of bare turf when none of the men was in sight. But retreating was going to be less pulse quickening, since I had only to wait for the dark.

The horse box was parked beside the shed, and almost as soon as I had worked my way round the hill to my present position there was a clattering of hooves on the ramp as Kandersteg was unloaded. Jud Wilson led him round through the gate and on to the grassy track. Adams, following, shut the gate and then unlatched a swinging section of the inner fence and fastened it across the track, making a barrier. Walking past Jud and the horse he did the same with another section a few yards further on, with the result that Jud and Kandersteg were now standing in a small pen in the corner. A pen with three ways out; the gate out of the field, and the rails which swung across like level crossing gates on either side.

Jud let go of the horse, which quietly began to eat the grass, and he and Adams let themselves out and disappeared into the shed to join Humber. The shed, made of weathered wood, was built like a single loose box, with a window and a split door, and I imagined it was there that Mickey had spent much of the three days he had been away.

There was a certain amount of clattering and banging in the shed, which went on for some time, but as I had only a sideways view of the door I could see nothing of what was happening.

Presently all three of them came out. Adams walked round behind the shed and reappeared beyond the field, walking up the hillside. He went at a good pace right to the top, and stood gazing about him at the countryside.

Humber and Wilson came through the gate into the field, carrying between them an apparatus which looked like a vacuum cleaner, a cylindrical tank with a hose attached to one end. They put the tank down in the corner, and Wilson held the hose. Kandersteg, quietly cropping the grass close beside them, lifted his head and looked at them, incurious and trusting. He bent down again to eat.

Humber walked the few steps to where the swinging rail was fastened to the hedge, seemed to be checking something, and then went back to stand beside Wilson, who was looking up towards Adams.

On top of the hill, Adams casually waved his hand.

Down in the corner of the field Humber had his hand to his mouth . . . I was too far away to see with the naked eye if what he held there was a whistle, and too close to risk getting out the glasses for a better look. But even though try as I might I could hear no noise, there wasn't much room for doubt. Kandersteg raised his head, pricked his ears, and looked at Humber.

Flame suddenly roared from the hose in Wilson's hand. It was directed behind the horse, but it frightened him badly, all the same. He sat back on his haunches, his ears flattening. Then Humber's arm moved, and the swinging barrier, released by some sort of catch, sprang back to let the horse out on to the track. He needed no telling.

He stampeded round the field, skidding at the corners, lurching against the inner wooden rail, thundering past ten feet from my head. Wilson opened the second barrier, and he and Humber retired through the gate. Kandersteg made two complete circuits at high speed before his stretched neck relaxed to a more normal angle and his wildly thrusting hind quarters settled down to a more natural gallop.

Humber and Wilson stood and watched him, and Adams strolled down the hill to join them at the gate.

They let the horse slow down and stop of his own accord, which he did away to my right, after about three and a half circuits. Then Jud Wilson unhurriedly swung one of the barriers back across the track, and waving a stick in one hand and a hunting whip in the other, began to walk round to drive the horse in front of him along into the corner. Kandersteg trotted warily ahead, unsettled, sweating, not wanting to be caught.

Jud Wilson swung his stick and his whip and trudged steadily on. Kandersteg trotted softly past where I lay, his hooves swishing through the short grass: but I was no longer watching. My face was buried in the roots of the hedge, and I ached with the effort of keeping still. Seconds passed like hours.

There was a rustle of trouser leg brushing against trouser leg, a faint clump of boots on turf, a crack of the long thong of the whip . . . and no outraged yell of discovery. He went past, and on up the field.

The muscles which had been ready to expel me out of the ditch and away towards the hidden motor-cycle gradually relaxed. I opened my eyes and looked at leaf mould close to my face, and worked some saliva into my mouth. Cautiously, inch by inch, I raised my head and looked across the field.

The horse had reached the barrier and Wilson was unhooking and swinging the other one shut behind him, so that he was again penned into the small enclosure. There, for about half an hour, the three men left him. They themselves walked back into the shed, where I could not see them, and I could do nothing but wait for them to appear again.

It was a fine, clear, quiet morning, but a bit cold for lying in ditches, especially damp ones. Exercise, however, beyond curling and uncurling my toes and fingers, was a bigger risk than pneumonia; so I lay still, taking heart from the thought that I was dressed from head to foot in black, and had a mop of black hair as well, and was crouched in blackish brown rotting dead leaves. It was because of the protective colouring it offered that I had chosen the ditch in preference to a shallow dip in the hillside, and I was glad I had, because it was fairly certain that Adams from his look-out point would at once have spotted a dark intruder on the pale green hill.

I didn't notice Jud Wilson walk out of the shed, but I heard the click of the gate, and there he was, going into the little enclosure and laying his hand on Kandersteg's bridle, for all the world as if he were consoling him. But how could anyone who liked horses set about them with a flame thrower? And Jud, it was clear, was going to do it again. He left the horse, went over to the corner, picked up the hose and stood adjusting its nozzle.

Presently Adams appeared and climbed the hill, and then Humber, limping on his stick, joined Jud in the field.

There was a long wait before Adams waved his hand, during which three cars passed along the lonely moorland road. Eventually Adams was satisfied. His arm languidly rose and fell.

Humber's hand went immediately to his mouth.

Kandersteg already knew what it meant. He was running back on his haunches in fear before the flame shot out behind him and stopped him dead.

This time there was a fiercer, longer, closer burst of fire, and Kandersteg erupted in greater terror. He came scorching round the track . . . and round again . . . it was like waiting for the ball to settle in roulette with too much staked. But he stopped this time at the top end of the field, well away from my hiding place.

Jud walked across the middle of the field to come up behind him, not round the whole track. I sighed deeply with heartfelt relief.

I had folded my limbs originally into comfortable angles, but they were beginning to ache with inactivity, and I had cramp in the calf of my right leg, but I still didn't dare move while all three men were in my sight and I in theirs.

They shut Kandersteg into his little pen and strolled away into the shed, and cautiously, as quietly as I could in the rotting leaves, I flexed my arms and legs, got rid of the cramp, and discovered pins and needles instead. Ah well . . . it couldn't go on for ever.

They were, however, plainly going to repeat the process yet again. The flame thrower still lay by the hedge.

The sun was high in the sky by this time, and I looked at the gleam it raised on the leather sleeve of my left arm, close to my head. It was too shiny. Hedges and ditches held nothing as light-reflecting as black leather. Could Wilson possibly, *possibly* walk a second time within feet of me without coming close enough to the hedge to see a shimmer which shouldn't be there?

Adams and Humber came out of the shed and leaned over the gate, looking at Kandersteg. Presently they lit cigarettes and were clearly talking. They were in no hurry. They finished the cigarettes, threw them away, and stayed where they were for another ten minutes. Then Adams walked over to his car and returned with a bottle and some glasses. Wilson came out of the shed to join them and the three of them stood there in the sun, quietly drinking and gossiping in the most commonplace way.

What they were doing was, of course, routine to them. They had done it at least twenty times before. Their latest victim stood warily in his pen, unmoving, frightened, far too upset to eat.

Watching them drink made me thirsty, but that was among the least of my troubles. Staying still was becoming more and more difficult. Painful, almost.

At long last they broke it up. Adams put the bottle and glasses away and strolled off up the hill, Humber checked the quick release on the swinging barrier, and Jud adjusted the nozzle of the hose.

Adams waved. Humber blew.

This time the figure of Kandersteg was sharply, terrifyingly silhouetted against a sheet of flame. Wilson swayed his body, and the brilliant, spreading jet flattened and momentarily swept under the horse's belly and among his legs.

I nearly cried out, as if it were I that were being burned, not the horse. And for one sickening moment it looked as if Kandersteg were too terrified to escape.

Then, squealing, he was down the track like a meteor, fleeing from fire, from pain, from a dog whistle . . .

He was going too fast to turn the corner. He crashed into the hedge, bounced off, stumbled and fell. Eyes starting out of his head, lips retracted from his teeth, he scrambled frantically to his feet and bolted on, past my head, up the field, round again and round again.

He came to a jolting halt barely twenty yards away from me. He stood stock-still with sweat dripping from his neck and down his legs. His flesh quivered convulsively.

Jud Wilson, whip and stick in hand, started on his walk round the track. Slowly I put my face down among the roots and tried to draw some comfort from the fact that if he saw me there was still a heavily wired fence between us, and I should get some sort of start in running away. But the motor-cycle was hidden on rough ground two hundred yards behind me, and the curving road lay at least as far beyond that again, and Adams' grey Jaguar was parked on the far side of the horse box. Successful flight wasn't something I'd have liked to bet on.

Kandersteg was too frightened to move. I heard Wilson shouting at him and cracking the whip, but it was a full minute before the hooves came stumbling jerkily, in bursts and stamps, past my head.

In spite of the cold, I was sweating. Dear heavens, I thought, there was as much adrenalin pouring into my bloodstream as into the horse's; and I realized that from the time Wilson started his methodical walk round the track I had been able to hear my own heart thudding.

Jud Wilson yelled at Kandersteg so close to my ear that it felt like a blow. The whip cracked.

'Get on, get on, get on there.'

He was standing within feet of my head. Kandersteg wouldn't move. The whip cracked again. Jud shouted at the horse, stamping his boot on the ground in encouragement. The faint tremor came to me through the earth. He was a yard away, perhaps, with his eyes on the horse. He had only to turn his head . . . I began to think that anything, even discovery, was preferable to the terrible strain of keeping still.

Then, suddenly, it was over.

Kandersteg skittered away and bumped into the rails, and took a few more uneven steps back towards the top of the field. Jud Wilson moved away after him.

I continued to behave like a log, feeling exhausted. Slowly my heart subsided. I started breathing again . . . and unclamped my fingers from handfuls of leaf mould.

Step by reluctant step Jud forced Kandersteg round to the corner enclosure, where he swung the rails across and penned the horse in again. Then he picked up the flame thrower and took it with him through the gate. The job was done. Adams, Humber and Wilson stood in a row and contemplated their handiwork.

The pale coat of the horse was blotched with huge dark patches where the sweat had broken out, and he stood stiff legged, stiff necked, in the centre of the small enclosure. Whenever any of the three men moved he jumped nervously and then stood rigidly still again: and it was clearly going to be some long time before he had unwound enough to be loaded up and taken back to Posset.

Mickey had been away three days, but that, I judged, was only because his legs had been badly burned by mistake. As Kandersteg's indoctrination appeared to have gone without a hitch, he should be back in his own stable fairly soon.

It couldn't be too soon for me and my static joints. I watched the three men potter about in the sunlight, wandering between car and shed, shed and horse box, aimlessly passing the morning and managing never to be all safely out of sight at the same time. I cursed under my breath and resisted a temptation to scratch my nose.

At long last they made a move. Adams and Humber folded themselves into the Jaguar and drove off in the direction of Tellbridge. But Jud Wilson reached into the cab of the horse box, pulled out a paper bag, and proceeded to eat his lunch sitting on the gate. Kandersteg remained immobile in his little enclosure, and I did the same in my ditch.

Jud Wilson finished his lunch, rolled the paper bag into a ball, yawned, and lit a cigarette. Kandersteg continued to sweat, and I to ache. Everything was very quiet. Time passed.

Jud Wilson finished his cigarette, threw the stub away and yawned again. Then slowly, slowly, he climbed down from the gate, picked up the flame thrower, and took it into the shed.

He was scarcely through the door before I was slithering down into the shallow ditch, lying full length along it on my side, not caring about the dampness but thankfully, slowly, painfully, straightening one by one my cramped arms and legs.

The time, when I looked at my watch, was two o'clock. I felt hungry, and regretted that I hadn't had enough sense to bring some of the chocolate.

I lay in the ditch all afternoon, hearing nothing, but waiting for the horse box to start up and drive away. After a while in spite of the cold and the presence of Jud Wilson, I had great difficulty in keeping awake; a ridiculous state of affairs which could only be remedied by action. Accordingly I rolled over on to my stomach and inch by careful inch raised my head high enough to see across to Kandersteg and the shed.

Jud Wilson was again sitting on the gate. He must have seen my movements out of the corner of his eye, because he looked away from Kandersteg, who stood in front of him, and turned his head in my direction. For a fleeting second it seemed that he was looking straight into my eyes: then his gaze swept on past me, and presently, unsuspiciously, returned to Kandersteg.

I let my held breath trickle out slowly, fighting down a cough.

The horse was still sweating, the dark patches showing up starkly, but there was a less fixed look about him, and while I watched he swished his tail and restlessly shook his neck. He was over the hump.

More cautiously still, I lowered my head and chest down again on to my folded arms, and waited some more.

Soon after four Adams and Humber came back in the Jaguar, and again, like a rabbit out of his burrow, I edged up for a look.

They decided to take the horse home. Jud Wilson backed the horse box to the gate and let down the ramp, and Kandersteg, sticking in his feet at every step, was eventually pulled and prodded into it. The poor beast's distress was all too evident, even from across the field. I liked horses. I found I was wholly satisfied that because of me Adams and Humber and Wilson were going to be out of business.

Gently I lay down again, and after a short while I heard both the engines – first the Jaguar's and then the horse box's – start up and drive off, back towards Posset.

When the sound of them had died away I stood up, stretched, brushed the leaf mould from my clothes, and walked round the field to look at the shed.

It was fastened shut with a complicated looking padlock, but through the window I could see it held little besides the flame thrower, some cans presumably holding fuel, a large tin funnel and three garden chairs folded and stacked against one wall. There seemed little point in breaking in, though it would have been simple enough since the padlock fittings had been screwed straight on to the surface of the door and its surround. The screwdriver blade of my penknife could have removed the whole thing, fussy padlock intact. Crooks, I reflected, could be as fantastically dim in some ways as they were imaginative in others.

I went through the gate into Kandersteg's little enclosure. The grass where he had stood was scorched. The inside surfaces of the rails had been painted white, so that they resembled racecourse rails. I stood for a while looking at them, feeling a second-hand echo of the misery the horse had endured in that harmless looking place, and then let myself out and walked away, round past my hiding place in the ditch and off towards the motor-cycle. I picked it up, hooked the crash helmet on to the handle bars, and started the engine.

So that was the lot, I thought. My job was done. Safely, quietly, satisfactorily done. As it should be. Nothing remained but to complete yesterday's report and put the final facts at the Stewards' disposal.

I coasted back to the place from where I had kept a watch on Humber's yard, but there was no one there. Either Beckett had not got my letter or had not been able to send any help, or the help, if it had arrived, had got tired of waiting and departed. The rug, suitcase and remains of food lay where I had left them, undistured.

On an impulse, before packing up and leaving the area, I unzipped my jacket and took out the binoculars to have a last look down into the yard.

What I saw demolished in one second flat my complacent feeling of safety and completion.

A scarlet sports car was turning into the yard. It stopped beside Adams' grey Jaguar, a door opened, and a girl got out. I was too far away to distinguish her features but there was no mistaking that familiar car and that dazzling silver blonde hair. She slammed the car door and walked hesitantly towards the office, out of my sight.

I swore aloud. Of all damnable, unforeseeable, dangerous things to happen! I hadn't told Elinor anything. She thought I was an ordinary stable lad. I had borrowed a dog whistle from her. And she was October's daughter. What were the chances, I wondered numbly, of her keeping quiet on the last two counts and not giving Adams the idea that she was a threat to him.

She ought to be safe enough, I thought. Reasonably, she ought to be safe as long as she made it clear that it was I who knew the significance of dog whistles, and not her.

But supposing she didn't make it clear? Adams never behaved reasonably, to start with. His standards were not normal. He was psychopathic. He could impulsively kill a journalist who seemed to be getting too nosy. What was to stop him killing again, if he got it into his head that it was necessary?

I would give her three minutes, I thought. If she asked for me, and was told I had left, and went straight away again, everything would be all right.

I willed her to return from the office and drive away in her car. I doubted whether in any case if Adams were planning to harm her I could get her out safely, since the odds against, in the shape of Adams, Humber, Wilson and Cass, were too great for common sense. I wasn't too keen on having to try. But the three minutes went past, and the red car stood empty in the yard.

She had stayed to talk and she had no notion that there was anything which should not be said. If I had done as I had wanted and told her why I was at Humber's, she would not have come at all. It was my fault she was there. I had clearly got to do my best to see she left again in mint condition. There was no choice.

I put the binoculars in the suitcase and left it and the rug where it was. Then, zipping up the jacket and fastening on the crash helmet, I restarted the bike and rode it down and round and in through Humber's gate.

I left the bike near the gate and walked across towards the yard, passing the shed where the horse box was kept. The doors were shut, and there was no sign of Jud Wilson. Perhaps he had already gone home, and I hoped so. I went into the yard at the top end beside the wall of the office, and saw Cass at the opposite end looking over the door of the fourth box from the left. Kandersteg was home.

Adams' Jaguar and Elinor's T.R.4 stood side by side in the centre of the yard. Lads were hustling over their evening jobs, and everything looked normal and quiet.

I opened the office door, and walked in.

Chapter Seventeen

So much for my fears, I thought. So much for my melodramatic imagination. She was perfectly safe. She held a half empty glass of pink liquid in her hand, having a friendly drink with Adams and Humber, and she was smiling.

Humber's heavy face looked anxious, but Adams was laughing and enjoying himself. It was a picture which printed itself clearly on my mind before they all three turned and looked at me.

'Daniel!' Elinor exclaimed. 'Mr. Adams said you had gone.'

'Yes. I left something behind. I came back for it.'

'Lady Elinor Tarren,' said Adams with deliberation, coming round behind me, closing the door and leaning against it, 'came to see if you had conducted the experiment she lent you her dog whistle for.'

It was just as well, after all, that I had gone back.

'Oh, surely I didn't say that,' she protested. 'I just came to get the whistle, if Daniel had finished with it. I mean, I was passing, and I thought I could save him the trouble of sending it . . .'

I turned to him, 'Lady Elinor Tarren,' I said with equal deliberation, 'does not know what I borrowed her whistle for. I didn't tell her. She knows nothing about it.'

His eyes narrowed and then opened into a fixed stare. His jaw bunched. He took in the way I had spoken to him, the way I looked at him. It was not what he was used to from me. He transferred his stare to Elinor.

'Leave her alone,' I said. 'She doesn't know.'

'What on earth are you talking about?' said Elinor, smiling. 'What was this mysterious experiment, anyway?'

'It wasn't important,' I said. 'There's . . . er . . . there's a deaf lad here, and we wanted to know if he could hear high pitched noises, that's all.'

'Oh,' she said, 'and could he?'

I shook my head. 'I'm afraid not.'

'What a pity.' She took a drink, and ice tinkled against the glass. 'Well, if you've no more use for it, do you think I could have my whistle back?'

'Of course.' I dug into my money belt, brought out the whistle, and gave it to her. I saw Humber's astonishment and Adams' spasm of fury that Humber's search had missed so elementary a hiding place.

'Thank you,' she said, putting the whistle in her pocket. 'What are your plans now? Another stable job? You know,' she said to Humber, smiling, 'I'm surprised you let him go. He rode better than any lad we've ever had in Father's stables. You were lucky to have him.'

I had not ridden well for Humber. He began to say heavily, 'He's not all that good . . .' when Adams smoothly interrupted him.

'I think we have underestimated Roke, Hedley. Lady Elinor, I am sure Mr. Humber will take him back on your recommendation, and never let him go again.'

'Splendid,' she said warmly.

Adams was looking at me with his hooded gaze to make sure I had appreciated his little joke. I didn't think it very funny.

'Take your helmet off,' he said. 'You're indoors and in front of a lady. Take it off.'

'I think I'll keep it on,' I said equably. And I could have done with a full suit of armour to go with it. Adams was not used to me contradicting him, and he shut his mouth with a snap.

Humber said, puzzled, 'I don't understand why you bother with Roke, Lady Elinor. I thought your father got rid of him for ... well ... molesting you.'

'Oh no,' she laughed. 'That was my sister. But it wasn't true, you know. It was all made up.' She swallowed the last of her drink and with the best will in the world put the finishing touches to throwing me to the wolves. 'Father made me promise not to tell anyone that it was all a story, but as you're Daniel's employer you really ought to know that he isn't anything like as bad as he lets everyone believe.'

There was a short, deep silence. Then I said, smiling, 'That's the nicest reference I've ever had ... you're very kind.'

'Oh dear,' she laughed. 'You know what I mean ... and I can't think why you don't stick up for yourself more.'

'It isn't always advisable,' I said, and raised an eyebrow at Adams. He showed signs of not appreciating my jokes either. He took Elinor's empty glass.

'Another gin and campari?' he suggested.

'No thank you, I must be going.'

He put her glass down on the desk with his own, and said, 'Do you think Roke would be the sort of man who'd need to swallow tranquillizers before he found the nerve to look after a difficult horse?'

'Tranquillizers? *Tranquillizers?* Of course not. I shouldn't think he ever took a tranquillizer in his life. Did you?' she said, turning to me and beginning to look puzzled.

'No,' I said. I was very anxious for her to be on her way before her puzzlement grew any deeper. Only while she suspected nothing and learned nothing was she safe enough.

'But you said ...' began Humber, who was still unenlightened.

'It was a joke. Only a joke,' I told him. 'Mr. Adams laughed about it quite a lot, if you remember.'

'That's true. I laughed,' said Adams sombrely. At least he seemed willing for her ignorance to remain undisturbed, and to let her go.

'Oh,' Elinor's face cleared. 'Well ... I suppose I'd better be getting back to college. I'm going to Slaw tomorrow for the week-end ... do you have any message for my father, Daniel?'

It was a casual, social remark, but I saw Adams stiffen.

I shook my head.

'Well ... it's been very pleasant, Mr. Humber. Thank you so much for the drink. I hope I haven't taken too much of your time.'

She shook Humber's hand, and Adams', and finally mine.

'How lucky you came back for something. I thought I'd missed you . . . and that I could whistle for my whistle.' She grinned.

I laughed. 'Yes, it was lucky.'

'Goodbye then. Goodbye Mr. Humber,' she said, as Adams opened the door for her. She said goodbye to him on the doorstep, where he remained, and over Humber's shoulder I watched through the window as she walked across to her car. She climbed in, started the engine, waved gaily to Adams, and drove out of the yard. My relief at seeing her go was even greater than my anxiety about getting out myself.

Adams stepped inside, shut the door, locked it, and put the key in his pocket. Humber was surprised. He still did not understand.

He said, staring at me, 'You know, Roke doesn't seem the same. And his voice is different.'

'Roke, damn him to hell, is God knows what.'

The only good thing in the situation that I could see was that I no longer had to cringe when he spoke to me. It was quite a relief to be able to stand up straight for a change. Even if it didn't last long.

'Do you mean it is Roke, and not Elinor Tarren after all, who knows about the whistle?'

'Of course,' said Adams impatiently. 'For Christ's sake, don't you understand anything? It looks as though October planted him on us, though how in hell he knew . . .'

'But Roke is only a stable lad.'

'Only,' said Adams savagely. 'But that doesn't make it any better. Stable lads have tongues, don't they? And eyes? And look at him. He's not the stupid worm he's always seemed.'

'No one would take his word against yours,' said Humber.

'No one is going to take his word at all.'

'What do you mean.'

'I'm going to kill him,' said Adams.

'I suppose that might be more satisfactory.' Humber sounded as if he were discussing putting down a horse.

'It won't help you,' I said. 'I've already sent a report to the Stewards.'

'We were told that once before,' said Humber, 'but it wasn't true.'

'It is, this time.'

Adams said violently, 'Report or no report, I'm going to kill him. There are other reasons . . .' He broke off, glared at me and said, 'You fooled me. *Me*. How?'

I didn't reply. It hardly seemed a good time for light conversation.

'This one,' said Humber reflectively, 'has a motor-cycle.'

I remembered that the windows in the office's wash room were all too small to escape through. The door to the yard was locked, and Humber stood in front of his desk, between me and the window. Yelling could only bring Cass, not the poor rabble of lads who didn't even know I was there, and wouldn't bother to help me in any case. Both Adams and Humber were taller and heavier that I was, Adams a good deal so. Humber had his stick and I didn't know what weapon Adams proposed to use; and I had never been in a serious fight in my life. The next few minutes were not too delightful a prospect.

On the other hand I was younger than they, and, thanks to the hard work they had exacted, as fit as an athlete. Also I had the crash helmet. And I could throw things . . . perhaps the odds weren't impossible, after all.

A polished wooden chair with a leather seat stood by the wall near the door. Adams picked it up and walked towards me. Humber, remaining still, slid his stick through his hands and held it ready.

I felt appallingly vulnerable.

Adams' eyes were more opaque than I had ever seen them, and the smile which was growing on his mouth didn't reach them. He said loudly, 'We might as well enjoy it. They won't look too closely at a burnt-out smash.'

He swung the chair. I dodged it all right but in doing so got within range of Humber, whose stick landed heavily on top of my shoulder, an inch from my ear. I stumbled and fell, and rolled: and stood up just in time to avoid the chair as Adams crashed it down. One of the legs broke off as it hit the floor, and Adams bent down and picked it up. A solid, straight, square-edged chair leg with a nasty sharp point where it had broken from the seat.

Adams smiled more, and kicked the remains of the chair into a corner.

'Now,' he said, 'we'll have some sport.'

If you could call it sport, I suppose they had it.

Certainly after a short space of time they were still relatively unscathed, while I had added some more bruises to my collection, together with a fast bleeding cut on the forehead from the sharp end of Adams' chair leg. But the crash helmet hampered their style considerably, and I discovered a useful talent for dodging. I also kicked.

Humber, being a slow mover, stayed at his post guarding the window and slashed at me whenever I came within his reach. As the office was not large this happened too often. I tried from the beginning either to catch hold of one of the sticks, or to pick up the broken chair, or to find something to throw, but all that happened was that my hands fared badly, and Adams guessed my intentions regarding the chair and made sure I couldn't get hold of it. As for throwing things the only suitable objects in that bare office were on Humber's desk, behind Humber.

Because of the cold night on the hillside I was wearing two jerseys under my jacket, and they did act as some sort of cushion: but Adams particularly hit very hard, and I literally shuddered whenever he managed to connect. I had had some idea of crashing out through the window, glass and all, but they gave me no chance to get there, and there was a limit to the time I could spend trying.

In desperation I stopped dodging and flung myself at Humber. Ignoring Adams, who promptly scored two fearful direct hits, I grasped my ex-employer by the lapels, and with one foot on the desk for leverage, swung him round and threw him across the narrow room. He landed with a crash against the filing cabinets.

There on the desk was the green glass paper weight. The size of a cricket ball. It slid smoothly into my hand, and in one unbroken movement I picked it up, pivoted on my toes, and flung it straight at Humber where he sprawled off-balance barely ten feet away.

It took him centrally between the eyes. A sweet shot. It knocked him unconscious. He fell without a sound.

I was across the room before he hit the floor, my hand stretching out for the green glass ball which was a better weapon to me than any stick or broken chair. But Adams understood too quickly. His arm went up.

I made the mistake of thinking that one more blow would make no real difference and didn't draw back from trying to reach the paper weight even when I knew Adams' chair leg was on its way down. But this time, because I had my head down, the crash helmet didn't save me. Adams hit me below the rim of the helmet, behind the ear.

Dizzily twisting, I fell against the wall and ended up lying with my shoulders propped against it and one leg doubled underneath me. I tried to stand up, but there seemed to be no strength left in me anywhere. My head was floating. I couldn't see very well. There was a noise inside my ears.

Adams leaned over me, unsnapped the strap of my crash helmet, and pulled it off my head. That meant something, I thought groggily. I looked up. He was standing there smiling, swinging the chair leg. Enjoying himself.

In the last possible second my brain cleared a little and I knew that if I didn't do something about it, this blow was going to be the last. There was no time to dodge. I flung up my arm to shield my undefended head, and the savagely descending piece of wood crashed into it.

It felt like an explosion. My hand fell numb and useless by my side.

What was left? Ten seconds. Perhaps less. I was furious. I particularly didn't want Adams to have the pleasure of killing me. He was still smiling. Watching to see how I would take it, he slowly raised his arm for the *coup de grace.*

No, I thought, no. There was nothing wrong with my legs. What on earth was I thinking of, lying there waiting to be blacked out when I still had two good legs? He was standing on my right. My left leg was bent under me and he took no special notice when I disentangled it and crossed it over in front of him. I lifted both my legs off the ground, one in front and one behind his ankles, then I kicked across with my right leg, locked my feet tight together and rolled my whole body over as suddenly and strongly as I could.

Adams was taken completely by surprise. He overbalanced with wildly swinging arms and fell with a crash on his back. His own weight made the fall more effective from my point of view, because he was winded and slow to get up. I couldn't throw any longer with my numb right hand. Staggering to my feet, I picked the green glass ball up in my left and smashed it against Adams' head while he was still on his knees. It seemed to have no effect. He continued to get up. He was grunting.

Desperately I swung my arm and hit him again, low down on the back of the head. And that time he did go down; and stayed down.

I half fell beside him, dizzy and feeling sick, with pain waking up viciously all over my body and blood from the cut on my forehead dripping slowly on to the floor.

I don't know how long I stayed like that, gasping to get some breath back, trying to find the strength to get up and leave the place, but it can't really have been very long. And it was the thought of Cass, in the end, which got me to my feet. By that stage I would have been a pushover for a toddler, let alone the wiry little head lad.

Both of the men lay in heaps on the ground, not stirring. Adams was breathing very heavily; snoring, almost. Humber's chest scarcely moved.

I passed my left hand over my face and it came away covered with blood. There must be blood all over my face, I thought. I couldn't go riding along the road covered in blood. I staggered into the washroom to rinse it off.

There were some half melted ice cubes in the sink. Ice. I looked at it dizzily. Ice in the refrigerator. Ice clinking in the drinks. Ice in the sink. Good for stopping bleeding. I picked up a lump of it and looked in the mirror. A gory sight. I held the lump of ice on the cut and tried, in the classic phrase, to pull myself together. With little success.

After a while I splashed some water into the sink and rinsed all the blood off my face. The cut was then revealed as being only a couple of inches long and not serious, though still obstinately oozing. I looked round vaguely for a towel.

On the table by the medicine cupboard stood a glass jar with the stopper off and a teaspoon beside it. My glance flickered over it, looking for a towel, and then back, puzzled. I took three shaky steps across the room. There was something the jar should be telling me, I thought, but I wasn't grasping things very clearly.

A bottle of phenobarbitone in powder form, like the stuff I'd given Mickey every day for a fortnight. Only phenobarbitone, that was all. I sighed.

Then it struck me that Mickey had had the last dose in the bottle. The bottle should be empty. Tipped out. Not full. Not a new bottle full to the bottom of the neck, with the pieces of wax from the seal still lying in crumbs on the table beside it. Someone had just opened a new bottle of soluble phenobarbitone and used a couple of spoonfuls.

Of course. For Kandersteg.

I found a towel and wiped my face. Then I went back into the office and knelt down beside Adams to get the door key out of his pocket. He had stopped snoring.

I rolled him over.

There isn't a pretty way of saying it. He was dead.

Small trickles of blood had seeped out of his ears, eyes, nose and mouth. I felt his head where I had hit him, and the dented bones moved under my fingers.

Aghast and shaking, I searched in his pockets and found the key. Then I stood up and went slowly over to the desk to telephone to the police.

The telephone had been knocked on to the floor, where it lay with the receiver off. I bent down and picked it up clumsily left handed, and my head swam with dizziness. I wished I didn't feel so ill. Straightening up with an effort I put the telephone back on the desk. Blood started trickling down past my eyebrow. I hadn't the energy to wash it off again.

Out in the yard one or two lights were on, including the one in Kandersteg's box. His door was wide open and the horse himself, tied up by the head, was lashing out furiously in a series of kicks. He didn't look in the least sedated.

I stopped with my finger in the dial of the telephone, and felt myself go cold. My brain cleared with a click.

Kandersteg was not sedated. They wouldn't want his memory lulled. The opposite, in fact. Mickey had not been given any phenobarbitone until he was clearly deranged.

I didn't want to believe what my mind told me; that one or more teaspoonfuls of soluble phenobarbitone in a large gin and campari would be almost certainly fatal.

Sharply I remembered the scene I had found in the office, the drinks, the anxiety on Humber's face, the enjoyment on Adams'. It matched the enjoyment I had seen there when he thought he was killing me. He enjoyed killing. He had thought from what she had said that Elinor had guessed the purpose of the whistle, and he had wasted no time in getting rid of her.

No wonder he had raised no objections to her leaving. She would drive back to college and die in her room miles away, a silly girl who had taken an overdose. No possible connection with Adams or Humber.

And no wonder he had been so determined to kill me: not only because of what I knew about his horses, or because I had fooled him, but because I had seen Elinor drink her gin.

It didn't need too much imagination to picture the scene before I had arrived. Adams saying smoothly, 'So you came to see if Roke had used the whistle?'

'Yes.'

'And does your father know you're here? Does he know about the whistle?'

'Oh no, I only came on impulse. Of course he doesn't know.'

He must have thought her a fool, blundering in like that: but probably he was the sort of man who thought all women were fools anyway.

'You'd like some ice in your drink? I'll get some. No bother. Just next door. Here you are, my dear, a strong gin and phenobarbitone and a quick trip to heaven.'

He had taken the same reckless risk of killing Stapleton, and it had worked. And who was to say that if I had been found in the next county over some precipice, smashed up in the ruins of a motor-bike, and Elinor died in her college, that he wouldn't have got away with two more murders?

If Elinor died.

My finger was still in the telephone dial. I turned it three times, nine, nine, nine. There was no answer. I rattled the button, and tried again. Nothing. It was dead, the whole telephone was dead. Everything was dead, Mickey was dead, Stapleton was dead. Adams was dead, Elinor . . . stop it, stop it. I dragged my scattering wits together. If the telephone wouldn't work, someone would have to go to Elinor's college and prevent her dying.

My first thought was that I couldn't do it. But who else? If I were right, she needed a doctor urgently, and any time I wasted on bumbling about finding another telephone or another person to go in my stead was just diminishing her chances. I could reach her in less than twenty minutes. By telephoning in Posset I could hardly get help for her any quicker.

It took me three shots to get the key in the keyhole. I couldn't hold the key at all in my right hand, and the left one was shaking. I took a deep breath, unlocked the door, walked out, and shut it behind me.

No one noticed me as I went out of the yard the way I had come and went back to the motor-bike. But it didn't fire properly the first time I kicked the starter, and Cass came round the end of the row of boxes to investigate.

'Who's that?' he called. 'Is that you, Dan? What are you doing back here?' He began to come towards me.

I stamped on the starter fiercely. The engine spluttered, coughed and roared. I squeezed the clutch and kicked the bike into gear.

'Come back,' yelled Cass. But I turned away from his hurrying figure, out of the gate and down the road to Posset, with gravel spurting under the tyres.

The throttle was incorporated into the hand grip of the right hand handle bar. One merely twisted it towards one to accelerate and away to slow down. Twisting the hand grip was normally easy. It was not easy that evening because once I had managed to grip it hard enough to turn it the numbness disappeared from my arm with a vengeance. I damned nearly fell off before I was through the gate.

It was ten miles north east to Durham. One and a half downhill to Posset, seven and a half across the moors on a fairly straight and unfrequented secondary road, one mile through the outskirts of the city. The last part, with turns and traffic and too much change of pace, would be the most difficult.

Only the knowledge that Elinor would probably die if I came off kept me on the motor-bike at all, and altogether it was a ride I would not care to repeat. I didn't know how many times I had been hit, but I didn't think a carpet had much to tell me. I tried to ignore it and concentrate on the matter in hand.

Elinor, if she had driven straight back to college, could not have been there long before she began to feel sleepy. As far as I could remember, never having taken much notice, barbiturates took anything up to an hour to work. But barbiturate dissolved in alcohol was a different matter. Quicker. Twenty minutes to half an hour, perhaps. I didn't know. Twenty minutes from the time she left the yard was easily enough for her to drive back safely. Then what? She would go up to her room: feel tired: lie down: and go to sleep.

During the time I had been fighting with Adams and Humber she had been on her way to Durham. I wasn't sure how long I had wasted dithering about in the washroom in a daze, but she couldn't have been back in college much before I started after her. I wondered whether she would have felt ill enough to tell a friend, to ask for help: but even if she had, neither she nor anyone else would know what was the matter with her.

I reached Durham: made the turns: even stopped briefly for a red traffic light in a busy street: and fought down an inclination to go the last half mile at walking pace in order to avoid having to hold the throttle any more. But my ignorance of the time it would take for the poison to do irreparable damage added wings to my anxiety.

Chapter Eighteen

It was getting dark when I swung into the College entrance, switched off the engine, and hurried up the steps to the door. There was no one at the porter's desk and the whole place was very quiet. I ran down the corridors, trying to remember the turns, found the stairs, went up two flights. And it was then that I got lost. I had suddenly no idea which way to turn to find Elinor's room.

A thin elderly women with pince nez was walking towards me carrying a sheaf of papers and a thick book on her arm. One of the staff, I thought.

'Please,' I said, 'which is Miss Tarren's room?'

She came close to me and looked at me. She did not approve of what she saw. What would I give, I thought, for a respectable appearance at the moment.

'Please,' I repeated. 'She may be ill. Which is her room?'

'You have blood on your face,' she observed.

'It's only a cut . . . please tell me . . .' I gripped her arm. 'Look, show me her room, then if she's all right and perfectly healthy I will go away without any trouble. But I think she may need help very badly. Please believe me . . .'

'Very well,' she said reluctantly. 'We will go and see. It is just round here . . . and round here.'

We arrived at Elinor's door. I knocked hard. There was no answer. I bent down to the low key-hole. The key was in the lock on her side, and I could not see in.

'Open it,' I urged the woman, who was still eyeing me dubiously. 'Open it, and see if she's all right.'

She put her hand on the knob and turned it. But the door didn't budge. It was locked.

I banged on the door again. There was no reply.

'Now please listen,' I said urgently. 'As the door is locked on the inside, Elinor Tarren is in there. She doesn't answer because she can't. She needs a doctor very urgently indeed. Can you get hold of one at once?'

The woman nodded, looking at me gravely through the pince nez. I wasn't sure that she believed me, but apparently she did.

'Tell the doctor she has been poisoned with phenobarbitone and gin. About forty minutes ago. And please, please hurry. Are there any more keys to this door?'

'You can't push out the key that's already there. We've tried on other doors, on other occasions. You will have to break the lock. I will go and telephone.' She retreated sedately along the corridor, still breathtakingly calm in the face of a wild looking man with blood on his forehead and the news that one of her students was half way to the coroner. A tough-minded university lecturer.

The Victorians who had built the place had not intended importunate men friends to batter down the girls' doors. They were a solid job. But in view of the thin woman's calm assumption that breaking in was within my powers, I didn't care to fail. I broke the lock with my heel, in the end. The wood gave way on the jamb inside the room, and the door opened with a crash.

In spite of the noise I had made, no students had appeared in the corridor. There was still no one about. I went into Elinor's room, switched on the light, and swung the door back into its frame behind me.

She was lying sprawled on top of her blue bedspread fast asleep, the silver hair falling in a smooth swathe beside her head. She looked peaceful and beautiful. She had begun to undress, which was why, I supposed, she had locked her door, and she was wearing only a bra and briefs under a simple slip. All these garments were white with pink rosebuds and ribbons. Pretty. Belinda would have liked them. But in these circumstances they were too poignant, too defenceless. They increased my grinding worry.

The suit which Elinor had worn at Humber's had been dropped in two places on the floor. One stocking hung over the back of a chair: the other was on the floor just beneath her slack hand. A clean pair of stockings lay on the dressing table, and a blue woollen dress on a hanger was hooked on to the outside of the wardrobe. She had been changing for the evening.

If she hadn't heard me kicking the door in she wouldn't wake by being touched, but I tried. I shook her arm. She didn't stir. Her pulse was normal, her breathing regular, her face as delicately coloured as always. Nothing looked wrong with her. I found it frightening.

How much longer, I wondered anxiously was the doctor going to be? The door had been stubborn – or I had been weak, whichever way you looked at it – and it must have been more than ten minutes since the thin woman had gone to telephone.

As if on cue the door swung open and a tidy solid-looking middle-aged man in a grey suit stood there taking in the scene. He was alone. He carried a suitcase in one hand and a fire hatchet in the other. Coming in, he looked at the splintered wood, pushed the door shut and put the axe down on Elinor's desk.

'That's saved time, anyway,' he said briskly. He looked me up and down without enthusiasm and gestured to me to get out of the way. Then he cast a closer glance at Elinor with her rucked up slip and her long bare legs, and said to me sharply, suspiciously, 'Did you touch her clothes?'

'No,' I said bitterly. 'I shook her arm. And felt her pulse. She was lying like that when I came in.'

Something, perhaps it was only my obvious weariness, made him give me a suddenly professional, impartial survey. 'All right,' he said, and bent down to Elinor.

I waited behind him while he examined her, and when he turned round I noticed he had decorously pulled down her rumpled slip so that it reached smoothly to her knees.

'Phenobarbitone and gin,' he said. 'Are you sure?'

'Yes.'

'Self-administered?' He started opening his case.

'No. Definitely not.'

'This place is usually teeming with women,' he said inconsequentially. 'But apparently they're all at some meeting or another.' He gave me another intent look. 'Are you fit to help?'

'Yes.'

He hesitated. 'Are you sure?'

'Tell me what to do.'

'Very well. Find me a good-sized jug and a bucket or large basin. I'll get her started first, and you can tell me how this happened later.'

He took a hypodermic syringe from his case, filled it, and gave Elinor an injection into the vein on the inside of her elbow. I found a jug and a basin in the built-in fitment.

'You've been here before,' he observed, eyes again suspicious.

'Once,' I said: and for Elinor's sake added, 'I am employed by her father. It's nothing personal.'

'Oh. All right then.' He withdrew the needle, dismantled the syringe and quickly washed his hands.

'How many tablets did she take, do you know?'

'It wasn't tablets. Powder. A teaspoonful, at least. Maybe more.'

He looked alarmed, but said, 'That much would be bitter. She'd taste it.'

'Gin and Campari . . . it's bitter anyway.'

'Yes. All right. I'm going to wash out her stomach. Most of the drug must have been absorbed already, but if she had as much as that . . . well, it's still worth trying.'

He directed me to fill the jug with tepid water, while he carefully slid a thickish tube down inside Elinor's throat. He surprised me by putting his ear to the long protruding end of it when it was in position, and he explained briefly that with an unconscious patient who couldn't swallow one had to make sure the tube had gone into the stomach and not into the lungs. 'If you can hear them breathe, you're in the wrong place,' he said.

He put a funnel into the end of the tube, held out his hand for the jug, and carefully poured in the water. When what seemed to me a fantastic amount had disappeared down the tube he stopped pouring, passed me the jug to put down, and directed me to push the basin near his foot. Then, removing the funnel, he suddenly lowered the end of the tube over the side of the bed and into the basin. The water flowed out again, together with all the contents of Elinor's stomach.

'Hm,' he said calmly. 'She had something to eat first. Cake, I should say. That helps.'

I couldn't match his detachment.

'Will she be all right?' My voice sounded strained.

He looked at me briefly and slid the tube out.

'She drank the stuff less than an hour before I got here?'

'About fifty minutes, I think.'

'And she'd eaten . . . Yes, she'll be all right. Healthy girl. The injection I gave her – megimide – is an effective antidote. She'll probably wake up in an hour or so. A night in hospital, and it will be out of her system. She'll be as good as new.'

I rubbed my hand over my face.

'Time makes of lot of difference,' he said calmly. 'If she'd lain here many hours . . . a teaspoonful; that might be thirty grains or more.' He shook his head. 'She would have died.'

He took a sample of the contents of the basin for analysis, and covered the rest with a hand towel.

'How did you cut your head?' he said suddenly.

'In a fight.'

'It needs stitching. Do you want me to do it?'

'Yes. Thank you.'

'I'll do it after Miss Tarren has gone to hospital. Dr. Pritchard said she would ring for an ambulance. They should be here soon.'

'Dr. Pritchard?'

'The lecturer who fetched me in. My surgery is only round the corner. She telephoned and said a violent blood-stained youth was insisting that Miss Tarren was poisoned, and that I'd better come and see.' He smiled briefly. 'You haven't told me how all this happened.'

'Oh . . . it's such a long story,' I said tiredly.

'You'll have to tell the police,' he pointed out.

I nodded. There was too much I would have to tell the police. I wasn't looking forward to it. The doctor took out pen and paper and wrote a letter to go with Elinor to the hospital.

There was a sudden eruption of girls' voices down the passage, and a tramp of many scholarly feet, and the opening and shutting of doors. The students were back from their meeting: from Elinor's point of view, too soon, as they would now see her being carried out.

Heavier footsteps came right up to her room and knuckles rapped. Two men in ambulance uniform had arrived with a stretcher, and with economy of movement and time they lifted Elinor between them, tucked her into blankets, and bore her away. She left a wake of pretty voices raised in sympathy and speculation.

The doctor swung the door shut behind the ambulance men and without more ado took from his case a needle and thread to sew up my forehead. I sat on Elinor's bed while he fiddled around with disinfectant and the stitching.

'What did you fight about?' he asked, tying knots.

'Because I was attacked,' I said.

'Oh?' He shifted his feet to sew from a different angle, and put his hand on my shoulder to steady himself. He felt me withdraw from the pressure and looked at me quizzically.

'So you got the worst of it?'

'No,' I said slowly. 'I won.'

He finished the stitching and gave a final snip with the scissors.

'There you are, then. It won't leave much of a scar.'

'Thank you.' It sounded a bit weak.

'Do you feel all right?' he said abruptly. 'Or is pale fawn tinged with grey your normal colouring?'

'Pale fawn is normal. Grey just about describes how I feel,' I smiled faintly. 'I got a bang on the back of the head, too.'

He explored the bump behind the ear and said I would live. He was asking me how many other tender spots I had about me when another heavy tramp of footsteps could be heard coming up the corridor, and presently the door was pushed open with a crash.

Two broad-shouldered businesslike policemen stepped into the room. They knew the doctor. It appeared that he did a good deal of police work in Durham. They greeted each other politely and the doctor started to say that Miss Tarren was on her way to hospital. They interrupted him.

'We've come for him, sir,' said the taller of them, pointing at me. 'Stable lad, name of Daniel Roke.'

'Yes, he reported Miss Tarren's illness ...'

'No, sir it's nothing to do with a Miss Tarren or her illness. We want him for questioning on another matter.'

The doctor said, 'He's not in very good shape. I think you had better go easy. Can't you leave it until later?'

'I'm afraid that's impossible, sir.'

They both came purposefully over to where I sat. The one who had done the talking was a red-headed man about my own age with an unsmiling wary face. His companion was slightly shorter, brown eyed, and just as much on guard. They looked as if they were afraid I was going to leap up and strangle them.

With precision they leaned down and clamped hard hands round my forearms. The red-head, who was on my right, dragged a pair of hand-cuffs from his pocket, and between them they fastened them on my wrists.

'Better take it quietly, chum,' advised the red-head, evidently mistaking my attempt to wrench my arm free of his agonising grip as a desire to escape in general.

'Let ... go,' I said. 'I'm not ... running anywhere.'

They did let go, and stepped back a pace, looking down at me. Most of the wariness had faded from their faces, and I gathered that they really had been afraid I would attack them. It was unnerving. I took two deep breaths to control the soreness of my arm.

'He won't give us much trouble,' said the dark one. 'He looks like death.'

'He was in a fight,' remarked the doctor.

'Is that what he told you, sir?' The dark one laughed.

I looked down at the hand-cuffs locked round my wrists: they were, I discovered, as uncomfortable as they were humiliating.

'What did he do?' asked the doctor.

The red-head answered, 'He ... er ... he'll be helping in enquiries into an attack on a race-horse trainer he worked for and who is still unconscious, and on another man who had his skull bust right in.'

'Dead?'

'So we are told, sir. We haven't actually been to the stables, though they say it's a shambles. We two were sent up from Clavering to fetch him in, and that's where we're taking him back to, the stables being in our area, you see.'

'You caught up with him very quickly,' commented the doctor.

'Yes,' said the red-head with satisfaction. 'It was a nice bit of work by some of the lads. A lady here telephoned to the police in Durham about half an hour ago and described *him*, and when they got the general call from Clavering about the job at the stables someone connected the two descriptions and told us about it. So we were sent up to see, and bingo ... there was his motor-bike, right number plate and all, standing outside the college door.'

I lifted my head. The doctor looked down at me. He was disillusioned, disenchanted. He shrugged his shoulders and said in a tired voice, 'You never know with them, do you? He seemed ... well ... not quite the usual sort of tearaway. And now this.' He turned away and picked up his bag.

It was suddenly too much. I had let too many people despise me and done nothing about it. This was one too many.

'I fought because they attacked me,' I said.

The doctor half turned round. I didn't know why I thought it was important to convince him, but it seemed so at the time.

The dark policeman raised an eyebrow and said to the doctor, 'The trainer was his employer, sir, and I understand the man who died is a rich gentleman whose horses were trained there. The head lad reported the killing. He saw Roke belting off on his motor-bike and thought it was strange, because Roke had been sacked the day before, and he went to tell the trainer about it, and found him unconscious and the other man dead.'

The doctor had heard enough. He walked out of the room without looking back. What was the use of trying? Better just do what the red-head said, and take it quietly, bitterness and all.

'Let's be going, chum,' said the dark one. They stood there, tense again, with watchful eyes and hostile faces.

I got slowly to my feet. Slowly, because I was perilously near to not being able to stand up at all, and I didn't want to seem to be asking for a sympathy I was clearly not going to get. But it was all right: once upright I felt better; which was psychological as much as physical because they were then not two huge threatening policemen but two quite ordinary young men of my own height doing their duty, and very concerned not to make any mistakes.

It worked the other way with them, of course. I think they had subconsciously expected a stable lad to be very short, and they were taken aback to discover I wasn't. They became visibly more aggressive: and I realized in the circumstances, and in those black clothes, I probably seemed to them, as Terence had once put it, a bit dangerous and hard to handle.

I didn't see any sense in getting roughed up any more, especially by the law, if it could be avoided.

'Look,' I sighed, 'like you said, I won't give you any trouble.'

But I suppose they had been told to bring in someone who had gone berserk and smashed a man's head in, and they were taking no chances. Red-head took a fierce grip of my right arm above the elbow and shoved me over to the door, and once outside in the passage the dark one took a similar grip on the left.

The corridor was lined with girls standing in little gossiping groups. I stopped dead. The two policemen pushed me on. And the girls stared.

That old saying about wishing the floor would open and swallow one up suddenly took on a fresh personal meaning. What little was left of my sense of dignity revolted totally against being exhibited as a prisoner in front of so many intelligent and personable young women. They were the wrong age. The wrong sex. I could have stood it better if they had been men.

But there was no easy exit. It was a good long way from Elinor's room to the outside door, along those twisting corridors and down two flights of stairs, and every single step was watched by interested female eyes.

This was the sort of thing one wouldn't be able to forget. It went too deep. Or perhaps, I thought miserably, one could even get accustomed to being hauled around in hand-cuffs if it happened often enough. If one were used to it, perhaps one wouldn't care . . . which would be peaceful.

I did at least manage not to stumble, not even on the stairs, so to that extent something was saved from the wreck. The police car however, into which I was presently thrust, seemed a perfect haven in contrast.

I sat in front, between them. The dark one drove.

'Phew,' he said, pushing his cap back an inch. 'All those girls.' He had blushed under their scrutiny and there was a dew of sweat on his forehead.

'He's a tough boy, is this,' said Red-head, mopping his neck with a white handkerchief as he sat sideways against the door and stared at me. 'He didn't turn a hair.'

I looked straight ahead through the windscreen as the lights of Durham began to slide past and thought how little could be told from a face. That walk had been a torture. If I hadn't shown it, it was probably only because I had by then had months of practice in hiding my feelings and thoughts, and the habit was strong. I guessed – correctly – that it was a habit I would find strength in clinging to for some time to come.

I spent the rest of the journey reflecting that I had got myself into a proper mess and that I was going to have a very unpleasant time getting out. I had indeed killed Adams. There was no denying or ducking that. And I was not going to be listened to as a respectable solid citizen but as a murdering villain trying every dodge to escape the consequences. I was going to be taken at my face value, which was very low indeed. That couldn't be helped. I had, after all, survived eight weeks at Humber's only because I looked like dregs. The appearance which had deceived Adams was going to be just as convincing to the police, and proof that in fact it already was sat on either side of me in the car, watchful and antagonistic.

Red-head's eyes never left my face.

'He doesn't talk much,' he observed, after a long silence.

'Got a lot on his mind,' agreed the dark one with sarcasm.

The damage Adams and Humber had done gave me no respite. I shifted uncomfortably in my seat, and the hand-cuffs clinked. The light-heartedness with which I had gone in my new clothes to Slaw seemed a long long time ago.

The lights of Clavering lay ahead. The dark one gave me a look of subtle enjoyment. A capture made. His purpose fulfilled. Red-head broke another long silence, his voice full of the same sort of satisfaction.

'He'll be a lot older when he gets out,' he said.

I emphatically hoped not: but I was all too aware that the length of time I remained in custody depended solely on how conclusively I could show that I had killed in self-defence. I wasn't a lawyer's son for nothing.

The next hours were abysmal. The Clavering police force were collectively a hardened cynical bunch suppressing as best they could a vigorous crime wave in a mining area with a high unemployment percentage. Kid gloves did not figure in their book. Individually they may have loved their wives and been nice to their children, but if so they kept their humour and humanity strictly for leisure.

They were busy. The building was full of bustle and hurrying voices. They shoved me still hand-cuffed from room to room under escort and barked out intermittent questions. 'Later,' they said. 'Deal with that one later. We've got all night for him.'

I thought with longing of a hot bath, a soft bed, and a handful of aspirins. I didn't get any of them.

At some point late in the evening they gave me a chair in a bare brightly lit little room, and I told them what I had been doing at Humber's and how I had come to kill Adams. I told them everything which had happened that day. They didn't believe me, for which one couldn't blame them. They immediately, as a matter of form, charged me with murder. I protested. Uselessly.

They asked me a lot of questions. I answered them. They asked them again. I answered. They asked the questions like a relay team, one of them taking over presently from another, so that they all appeared to remain full of fresh energy while I grew more and more tired. I was glad

I did not have to maintain a series of lies in that state of continuing discomfort and growing fatigue, as it was hard to keep a clear head, even for the truth, and they were waiting for me to make a mistake.

'Now tell us what really happened.'

'I've told you.'

'Not all that cloak and dagger stuff.'

'Cable to Australia for a copy of the contract I signed when I took on the job.' For the fourth time I repeated my solicitor's address, and for the fourth time they didn't write it down.

'Who did you say engaged you?'

'The Earl of October.'

'And no doubt we can check with him too?'

'He's in Germany until Saturday.'

'Too bad.' They smiled nastily. They knew from Cass that I had worked in October's stable. Cass had told them I was a slovenly stable lad, dishonest, easily frightened and not very bright. As he believed what he said, he had carried conviction.

'You got into trouble with his Lordship's daughter, didn't you?'

Damn Cass, I thought bitterly, damn Cass and his chattering tongue.

'Getting your own back on him for sacking you, aren't you, by dragging his name into this?'

'Like you got your own back on Mr. Humber for sacking you yesterday.'

'No. I left because I had finished my job there.'

'For beating you, then?'

'No.'

'The head lad said you deserved it.'

'Adams and Humber were running a crooked racing scheme. I found them out, and they tried to kill me.' It seemed to me it was the tenth time that I had said that without making the slightest impression.

'You resented being beaten. You went back to get even ... It's a common enough pattern.'

'No.'

'You brooded over it and went back and attacked them. It was a shambles. Blood all over the place.'

'It was my blood.'

'We can group it.'

'Do that. It's my blood.'

'From that little cut? Don't be so stupid.'

'It's been stitched.'

'Ah yes, that brings us back to Lady Elinor Tarren. Lord October's daughter. Got her into trouble, did you?'

'No.'

'In the family way ...'

'No. Check with the doctor.'

'So she took sleeping pills ...'

'No. Adams poisoned her.' I had told them twice about the bottle of phenobarbitone, and they must have found it when they had been at the stables, but they wouldn't admit it.

'You got the sack from her father for seducing her. She couldn't stand the disgrace. She took sleeping pills.'

'She had no reason to feel disgraced. It was not she, but her sister Patricia, who accused me of seducing her. Adams poisoned Elinor in gin and Campari. There are gin and Campari and phenobarbitone in the office and also in the sample from her stomach.'

They took no notice. 'She found you had deserted her on top of everything else. Mr. Humber consoled her with a drink, but she went back to college and took sleeping pills.'

'No.'

They were sceptical, to put it mildly, about Adams' use of the flame thrower.

'You'll find it in the shed.'

'This shed, yes. Where did you say it was?'

I told them again, exactly. 'The field probably belongs to Adams. You could find out.'

'It only exists in your imagination.'

'Look and you'll find it, and the flame thrower.'

'That's likely to be used for burning off the heath. Lots of farmers have them, round here.'

They had let me make two telephone calls to try to find Colonel Beckett. His manservant in London said he had gone to stay with friends in Berkshire for Newbury races. The little local exchange in Berkshire was out of action, the operator said, because a water main had burst and flooded a cable. Engineers were working on it.

Didn't my wanting to talk to one of the top brass of steeplechasing convince them, I wanted to know?

'Remember that chap we had in here once who'd strangled his wife? Nutty as a fruit cake. Insisted on ringing up Lord Bertrand Russell, didn't he, to tell him he'd struck a blow for peace.'

At around midnight one of them pointed out that even if (and, mind you, he didn't himself believe it) even if all I had said about being employed to find out about Adams and Humber were against all probability true, that still didn't give me the right to kill them.

'Humber isn't dead,' I said.

'Not yet.'

My heart lurched. Dear God, I thought, not Humber too. Not Humber too.

'You clubbed Adams with the walking stick then?'

'No, I told you, with a green glass ball. I had it in my left hand and I hit him as hard as I could. I didn't mean to kill him, just knock him out. I'm right handed ... I couldn't judge very well how hard I was hitting with my left.'

'Why did you use your left hand then?'

'I told you.'

'Tell us again.'

I told them again.

'And after your right arm was put out of action you got on a motor-cycle and rode ten miles to Durham? What sort of fools do you take us for?'

'The fingerprints of both my hands are on that paper-weight. The right ones from when I threw it at Humber, and the left ones on top, from where I hit Adams. You have only to check.'

'Fingerprints, now,' they said sarcastically.

'And while you're on the subject, you'll also find the fingerprints of my left hand on the telephone. I tried to call you from the office. My left hand prints are on the tap in the washroom . . . and on the key, and on the door handle, both inside and out. Or at least, they were . . .'

'All the same, you rode that motor-bike.'

'The numbness had gone by then.'

'And now?'

'It isn't numb now either.'

One of them came round beside me, picked up my right wrist, and pulled my arm up high. The hand-cuffs jerked and lifted my left arm as well. The bruises had all stiffened and were very sore. The policeman put my arm down again. There was a short silence.

'That hurt,' one of them said at last, grudgingly.

'He's putting it on.'

'Maybe . . .'

They had been drinking endless cups of tea all evening and had not given me any. I asked if I could have some then, and got it; only to find that the difficulty I had in lifting the cup was hardly worth it.

They began again.

'Granted Adams struck your arm, but he did it in self-defence. He saw you throw the paper-weight at your employer and realized you were going to attack him next. He was warding you off.'

'He had already cut my forehead open . . . and hit me several times on the body, and once on the head.'

'Most of that was yesterday, according to the head lad. That's why you went back and attacked Mr. Humber.'

'Humber hit me only twice yesterday. I didn't particularly resent it. The rest was today, and it was mostly done by Adams.' I remembered something. 'He took my crash helmet off when he had knocked me dizzy. His fingerprints must be on it.'

'Fingerprints again.'

'They spell it out,' I said.

'Let's begin again at the beginning. How can we believe a yob like you?'

Yob. One of the leather boys. Tearaway. Rocker. I knew all the words. I knew what I looked like. What a millstone of a handicap.

I said despairingly, 'There's no point in pretending to be a disreputable, dishonest stable lad if you don't look the part.'

'You look the part all right,' they said offensively. 'Born to it, you were.'

I looked at their stony faces, their hard, unimpressed eyes. Tough efficient policemen who were not going to be conned. I could read their thoughts like glass: if I convinced them and they later found out it was all a pack of lies, they'd never live it down. Their instincts were all dead against having to believe. My bad luck.

The room grew stuffy and full of cigarette smoke and I became too hot in my jerseys and jacket. I knew they took the sweat on my forehead to be guilt, not heat, not pain.

I went on answering all their questions. They covered the ground twice more with undiminished zeal, setting traps, sometimes shouting, walking round me, never touching me again, but springing the questions from all directions. I was really much too tired for that sort of thing because apart from the wearing-out effect of the injuries I had not slept for the whole of the previous night. Towards two o'clock I could hardly speak from exhaustion, and after they had woken me from a sort of dazed sleep three times in half an hour, they gave it up.

From the beginning I had known that there was only one logical end to that evening, and I had tried to shut it out of my mind, because I dreaded it. But there you are, you set off on a primrose path and if it leads to hell that's just too bad.

Two uniformed policemen, a sergeant and a constable, were detailed to put me away for the night, which I found involved a form of accommodation to make Humber's dormitory seem a paradise.

The cell was cubic, eight feet by eight by eight, built of glazed bricks, brown to shoulder height and white above that. There was a small barred window too high to see out of, a narrow slab of concrete for a bed, a bucket with a lid on it in a corner and a printed list of regulations on one wall. Nothing else. Bleak enough to shrink the guts; and I had never much cared for small enclosed spaces.

The two policemen brusquely told me to sit on the concrete. They removed my boots and the belt from my jeans, and also found and unbuckled the money belt underneath. They took off the hand-cuffs. Then they went out, shut the door with a clang, and locked me in.

The rest of that night was in every way rock bottom.

Chapter Nineteen

It was cool and quiet in the corridors of Whitehall. A superbly mannered young man deferentially showed me the way and opened a mahogany door into an empty office.

'Colonel Beckett will not be long sir. He has just gone to consult a colleague. He said I was to apologise if you arrived before he came back, and to ask if you would like a drink. And cigarettes are in this box, sir.'

'Thank you,' I smiled. 'Would coffee be a nuisance?'

'By no means. I'll have some sent in straight away. If you'll excuse me?' He went out and quietly closed the door.

It rather amused me to be called 'sir' again, especially by smooth civil servants barely younger than myself. Grinning, I sat down in the leather chair facing Beckett's desk, crossed my elegantly trousered legs, and lazily settled to wait for him.

I was in no hurry. It was eleven o'clock on Tuesday morning, and I had all day and nothing to do but buy a clockwork train for Jerry and book an air ticket back to Australia.

No noise filtered into Beckett's office. The room was square and high, and was painted a restful pale greenish grey colour, walls, door and ceiling alike. I supposed that here the furnishings went with rank; but if one were an outsider one would not know how much to be impressed by a large but threadbare carpet, an obviously personal lamp-shade, or leather, brass-studded chairs. One had to belong, for these things to matter.

I wondered about Colonel Beckett's job. He had given me the impression that he was retired, probably on a full disability pension since he looked so frail in health, yet here he was with a well established niche at the Ministry of Defence.

October had told me that in the war Beckett had been the sort of supply officer who never sent all left boots or the wrong ammunition. Supply Officer. He had supplied me with Sparking Plug and the raw material containing the pointers to Adams and Humber. He'd had enough pull with the Army to despatch in a hurry eleven young officer cadets to dig up the past history of obscure steeplechasers. What, I wondered, did he supply nowadays, in the normal course of events?

I suddenly remembered October saying, 'We thought of planting a stable lad . . .' not 'I thought', but 'We'. And for some reason I was now sure that it had been Beckett, not October, who had originally suggested the plan; and that explained why October had been relieved when Beckett approved me at our first meeting.

Unexcitedly turning these random thoughts over in my mind I watched two pigeons fluttering round the window sill and tranquilly waited to say goodbye to the man whose staff work had ensured the success of the idea.

A pretty young woman knocked and came in with a tray on which stood a coffee pot, cream jug, and pale green cup and saucer. She smiled, asked if I needed anything else, and when I said not, gracefully went away.

I was getting quite good at left-handedness. I poured the coffee and drank it black, and enjoyed the taste.

Snatches of the past few days drifted idly in and out of my thoughts . . .

Four nights and three days in a police cell trying to come to terms with the fact that I had killed Adams. It was odd, but although I had often considered the possibility of being killed, I had never once thought that I myself might kill. For that, as for so much else, I had been utterly unprepared; and to have caused another man's death, however much he might have asked for it, needed a bit of getting over.

Four nights and three days of gradually finding that even the various ignominies of being locked up were bearable if one took them quietly, and feeling almost like thanking Red-head for his advice.

On the first morning, after a magistrate had agreed that I should stay where I was for seven days, a police doctor came and told me to strip. I couldn't, and he had to help. He looked impassively at Adams' and Humber's widespread handiwork, asked a few questions, and examined my right arm, which was black from the wrist to well above the elbow. In spite of the protection of two jerseys and a leather jacket, the skin was broken where the chair leg had landed. The doctor helped me dress again and impersonally departed. I didn't ask him for his opinion, and he didn't give it.

For most of the four nights and three days I just waited, hour after silent hour. Thinking about Adams: Adams alive and Adams dead. Worrying about Humber. Thinking of how I could have done things differently. Facing the thought that I might not get out without a trial . . . or not get out at all. Waiting for the soreness to fade from the bruises and failing to find a comfortable way of sleeping on concrete. Counting the number of bricks from the floor to the ceiling and multiplying by the length of the walls (subtract the door and window). Thinking about my stud farm and my sisters and brother, and about the rest of my life.

On Monday morning there was the by then familiar scrape of the door being unlocked, but when it opened it was not as usual a policeman in uniform, but October.

I was standing up, leaning against the wall. I had not seen him for three months. He stared at me for a long minute, taking in with obvious shock my extremely dishevelled appearance.

'Daniel,' he said. His voice was low and thick.

I didn't think I needed any sympathy. I hooked my left thumb into my pocket, struck a faint attitude, and raised a grin.

'Hullo, Edward.'

His face lightened, and he laughed.

'You're so bloody tough,' he said. Well . . . let him think so.

I said, 'Could you possibly use your influence to get me a bath?'

'You can have whatever you like as soon as you are out.'

'Out? For good?'

'For good,' he nodded. 'They are dropping the charge.'

I couldn't disguise my relief.

He smiled sardonically. 'They don't think it would be worth wasting public funds on trying you. You'd be certain of getting an absolute discharge. Justifiable homicide, quite legitimate.'

'I didn't think they believed me.'

'They've done a lot of checking up. Everything you told them on Thursday is now the official version.'

'Is Humber . . . all right?'

'He regained consciousness yesterday, I believe. But I understand he isn't lucid enough yet to answer questions. Didn't the police tell you that he was out of danger?'

I shook my head. 'They aren't a very chatty lot, here. How is Elinor?'

'She's well. A bit weak, that's all.'

'I'm sorry she got caught up in things. If was my fault.'

'My dear chap, it was her own,' he protested. 'And Daniel . . . about Patty . . . and the things I said . . .'

'Oh, nuts to that,' I interrupted. 'It was a long time ago. When you said "Out" did you mean "out" now, this minute?'

He nodded. 'That's right.'

'Then let's not hang around in here any more, shall we? If you don't mind?'

He looked about him and involuntarily shivered. Meeting my eyes he said apologetically, 'I didn't foresee anything like this.'

I grinned faintly. 'Nor did I.'

We went to London, by car up to Newcastle and then by train. Owing to some delay at the police station discussing the details of my return to attend Adams' inquest, any cleaning up processes would have meant our missing the seats October had reserved on the non-stop Flying Scotsman, so I caught it as I was.

October led the way into the dining car, but as I was about to sit down opposite him a waiter caught hold of my elbow.

'Here you,' he said roughly, 'clear out. This is first-class only.'

'I've got a first-class ticket,' I said mildly.

'Oh yes? Let's see it, then.'

I produced from my pocket the piece of white cardboard.

He sniffed and gestured with his head towards the seat opposite October. 'All right then.' To October he said, 'If he makes a nuisance of himself, just tell me, sir, and I'll have him chucked out, ticket or no ticket.' He went off, swaying to the motion of the accelerating train.

Needless to say, everyone in the dining car had turned round to have a good view of the rumpus.

Grinning, I sat down opposite October. He looked exceedingly embarrassed.

'Don't worry on my account,' I said, 'I'm used to it.' And I realized that I was indeed used to it at last and that no amount of such treatment would ever trouble me again. 'But if you would rather pretend you don't know me, go ahead.' I picked up the menu.

'You are insulting.'

I smiled at him over the menu. 'Good.'

'For deviousness, Daniel, you are unsurpassed. Except possibly by Roddy Beckett.'

'My dear Edward . . . have some bread.'

He laughed, and we travelled amicably to London together, as ill-assorted looking a pair as ever rested heads on British Railways' starched white antimacassars.

I poured some more coffee and looked at my watch. Colonel Beckett was twenty minutes late. The pigeons sat peacefully on the window sill and I shifted gently in my chair, but with patience, not boredom, and thought about my visit to October's barber, and the pleasure with which I had had my hair cut short and sideburns shaved off. The barber himself (who had asked me to pay in advance) was surprised, he said, at the results.

'We look a lot more like a gentleman, don't we? But might I suggest
. . . a shampoo?'

Grinning, I agreed to a shampoo, which left a high water mark of
cleanliness about midway down my neck. Then, at October's house, there
was the fantastic luxury of stepping out of my filthy disguise into a deep
hot bath, and the strangeness with which I afterwards put on my own
clothes. When I had finished dressing I took another look in the same
long mirror. There was the man who had come from Australia four
months ago, a man in a good dark grey suit, a white shirt and a navy
blue silk tie: there was his shell anyway. Inside I wasn't the same man,
nor ever would be again.

I went down to the crimson drawing-room where October walked
solemnly all round me, gave me a glass of bone dry sherry and said, 'It
is utterly unbelievable that you are the young tyke who just came down
with me on the train.'

'I am,' I said dryly, and he laughed.

He gave me a chair with its back to the door, where I drank some
sherry and listened to him making social chit-chat about his horses. He
was hovering round the fireplace not entirely at ease, and I wondered
what he was up to.

I soon found out. The door opened and he looked over my shoulder
and smiled.

'I want you both to meet someone,' he said.

I stood up and turned round.

Patty and Elinor were there, side by side.

They didn't know me at first. Patty held out her hand politely and
said, 'How do you do?' clearly waiting for her father to introduce us.

I took her hand in my left one and guided her to a chair.

'Sit down,' I suggested. 'You're in for a shock.'

She hadn't seen me for three months, but it was only four days since
Elinor had made her disastrous visit to Humber's. She said hesitantly,
'You don't look the same . . . but you're Daniel.' I nodded, and she
blushed painfully.

Patty's bright eyes looked straight into mine, and her pink mouth
parted.

'You . . . are you really? Danny boy?'

'Yes.'

'Oh,' A blush as deep as her sister's spread up from her neck, and for
Patty that was shame indeed.

October watched their discomfiture. 'It serves them right,' he said, 'for
all the trouble they have caused.'

'Oh no,' I exclaimed, 'it's too hard on them . . . and you still haven't
told them anything about me, have you?'

'No,' he agreed uncertainly, beginning to suspect there was more for
his daughters to blush over than he knew, and that his surprise meeting
was not an unqualified success.

'Then tell them now, while I go and talk to Terence . . . and Patty
. . . Elinor . . .' They looked surprised at my use of their first names and
I smiled briefly, 'I have a very short and defective memory.'

They both looked subdued when I went back, and October was watching them uneasily. Fathers, I reflected, could be very unkind to their daughters without intending it.

'Cheer up,' I said. 'I'd have had a dull time in England without you two.'

'You were a beast,' said Patty emphatically, sticking to her guns.

'Yes . . . I'm sorry.'

'You might have told us,' said Elinor in a low voice.

'Nonsense,' said October. 'He couldn't trust Patty's tongue.'

'I see,' said Elinor, slowly. She looked at me tentatively. 'I haven't thanked you, for . . . for saving me. The doctor told me . . . all about it.' She blushed again.

'Sleeping beauty,' I smiled. 'You looked like my sister.'

'You have a sister?'

'Two,' I said. 'Sixteen and seventeen.'

'Oh,' she said, and looked comforted.

October flicked me a glance. 'You are far too kind to them Daniel. One of them made me loathe you and the other nearly killed you, and you don't seem to care.'

I smiled at him. 'No. I don't. I really don't. Let's just forget it.'

So in spite of a most unpromising start it developed into a good evening, the girls gradually losing their embarrassment and even, by the end, being able to meet my eyes without blushing.

When they had gone to bed October put two fingers into an inner pocket, drew out a slip of paper, and handed it to me without a word. I unfolded it. It was a cheque for ten thousand pounds. A lot of noughts. I looked at them in silence. Then, slowly, I tore the fortune in half and put the pieces in an ash-tray.

'Thank you very much,' I said. 'But I can't take it.'

'You did the job. Why not accept the pay?'

'Because . . .' I stopped. Because what? I was not sure I could put it into words. It had something to do with having learned more than I had bargained for. With diving too deep. With having killed. All I was sure of was that I could no longer bear the thought of receiving money for it.

'You must have a reason,' said October, with a touch of irritation.

'Well, I didn't really do it for the money, to start with, and I can't take that sort of sum from you. In fact, when I get back I am going to repay you all that is left of the first ten thousand.'

'No,' he protested. 'You've earned it. Keep it. You need it for your family.'

'What I need for my family, I'll earn by selling horses.'

He stubbed out his cigar. 'You're so infuriatingly independent that I don't know now how you could face being a stable lad. If it wasn't for the money, why did you do it?'

I moved in my chair. The bruises still felt like bruises. I smiled faintly, enjoying the pun.

'For kicks, I suppose.'

The door of the office opened, and Beckett unhurriedly came in. I stood up. He held out his hand, and remembering the weakness of his grasp I put out my own. He squeezed gently and let go.

'It's been a long time, Mr. Roke.'

'More than three months,' I agreed.

'And you completed the course.'

I shook my head, smiling. 'Fell at the last fence, I'm afraid.'

He took off his overcoat and hung it on a knobbed hat rack, and unwound a grey woollen scarf from his neck. His suit was nearly black, a colour which only enhanced his extreme pallor and emphasized his thinness: but his eyes were as alive as ever in the gaunt shadowed sockets. He gave me a long observant scrutiny.

'Sit down,' he said. 'I am sorry to have kept you waiting. I see they've looked after you all right.'

'Yes, thank you.' I sat down again in the leather chair, and he walked round and sank carefully into the one behind his desk. His chair had a high back and arms, and he used them to support his head and elbows.

'I didn't get your report until I came back to London from Newbury on Sunday morning,' he said. 'It took two days to come from Posset and didn't reach my house until Friday. When I had read it I telephoned to Edward at Slaw and found he had just been rung up by the police at Clavering. I then telephoned to Clavering myself. I spent a good chunk of Sunday hurrying things up for you in various conversations with ever higher ranks, and early on Monday it was decided finally in the office of the Director of Public Prosecutions that there was no charge for you to answer.'

'Thank you very much,' I said.

He paused, considering me. 'You did more towards extricating yourself than Edward or I did. We only confirmed what you had said and had you freed a day or two sooner than you might have been. But it appeared that the Clavering police had already discovered from a thorough examination of the stable office that everything you had told them was borne out by the facts. They had also talked to the doctor who had attended Elinor, and to Elinor herself, and taken a look at the shed with the flame thrower, and cabled to your solicitor for a summary of the contract you signed with Edward. By the time I spoke to them they were taking the truth of your story for granted, and were agreeing that you had undoubtedly killed Adams in self-defence.

'Their own doctor – the one who examined you – had told them straight away that the amount of crushing your right forearm had sustained was entirely consistent with its having been struck by a force strong enough to have smashed in your skull. He was of the opinion that the blow had landed more or less along the inside of your arm, not straight across it, thus causing extensive damage to muscles and blood vessels, but no bone fracture; and he told them that it was perfectly possible for you to have ridden a motor-bike a quarter of an hour later if you had wanted to enough.'

'You know,' I said, 'I didn't think they had taken any notice of a single word I said.'

'Mmm. Well, I spoke to one of the C.I.D. men who questioned you last Thursday evening. He said they brought you in as a foregone conclusion, and that you looked terrible. You told them a rigmarole which they thought was nonsense, so they asked a lot of questions to trip you up. They thought it would be easy. The C.I.D. man said it was like trying to dig a hole in a rock with your finger nails. They all ended up by believing you, much to their own surprise.'

'I wish they'd told me,' I sighed.

'Not their way. They sounded a tough bunch.'

'They seemed it, too.'

'However, you survived.'

'Oh yes.'

Beckett looked at his watch. 'Are you in a hurry?'

'No.' I shook my head.

'Good . . . I've rather a lot to say to you. Can you lunch?'

'Yes. I'd like to.'

'Fine. Now, this report of yours.' He dug the hand-written foolscap pages out of his inside breast pocket and laid them on the table. 'What I'd like you to do now is to lop off the bit asking for reinforcements and substitute a description of the flame-thrower operation. Right? There's a table and chair over there. Get to work, and when it's done I'll have it typed.'

When I had finished the report he spent some time outlining and discussing the proceedings which were to be taken against Humber, Cass and Jud Wilson, and also against Soupy Tarleton and his friend Lewis Greenfield. He then looked at his watch again and decided it was time to go out for lunch. He took me to his Club, which seemed to me to be dark brown throughout, and we ate steak, kidney and mushroom pie which I chose because I could manage it unobtrusively with a fork. He noticed though.

'That arm still troubling you?'

'It's much better.'

He nodded and made no further comment. Instead, he told me of a visit he had paid the day before to an elderly uncle of Adams, whom he had discovered living in bachelor splendour in Piccadilly.

'Young Paul Adams, according to his uncle, was the sort of child who would have been sent to an approved school if he hadn't had rich parents. He was sacked from Eton for forging cheques and from his next school for persistent gambling. His parents bought him out of scrape after scrape and were told by a psychiatrist that he would never change, or at least not until late middle age. He was their only child. It must have been terrible for them. The father died when Adams was twenty-five, and his mother struggled on, trying to keep him out of too disastrous trouble. About five years ago she had to pay out a fortune to hush up a scandal in which Adams had apparently broken a youth's arm for no reason at all, and she threatened to have him certified if he did anything like that again. And a few days later she fell out of her bedroom window and died. The uncle, her brother, says he has always thought that Adams pushed her.'

'Very likely, I should think,' I agreed.

'So you were right about him being psychopathic.'

'Well, it was pretty obvious.'

'From the way he behaved to you personally?'

'Yes.'

We had finished the pie and were on to cheese. Beckett looked at me curiously and said, 'What sort of life did you really have at Humber's stable?'

'Oh,' I grinned. 'You could hardly call it a holiday camp.'

He waited for me to go on and when I didn't, he said, 'Is that all you've got to say about it?'

'Yes, I think so. This is very good cheese.'

We drank coffee and a glass of brandy out of a bottle with Beckett's name on it, and eventually walked slowly back to his office.

As before he sank gratefully into his chair and rested his head and arms, and I as before sat down opposite him on the other side of his desk.

'You are going back to Australia soon, I believe?' he said.

'Yes.'

'I expect you are looking forward to getting back into harness.'

I looked at him. His eyes stared straight back, steady and grave. He waited for an answer.

'Not altogether.'

'Why not?'

I shrugged; grinned. 'Who likes harness?'

There was no point, I thought, in making too much of it.

'You are going back to prosperity, good food, sunshine, your family, a beautiful house and a job you do well . . . isn't that right?'

I nodded. It wasn't reasonable not to want to go to all that.

'Tell me the truth,' he said abruptly. 'The unvarnished honest truth. What is wrong?'

'I'm a discontented idiot, that's all,' I said lightly.

'Mr. Roke.' He sat up slightly in the chair. 'I have a good reason for asking these questions. Please give me truthful answers. What is wrong with your life in Australia?'

There was a pause, while I thought and he waited. When at last I answered, I was aware that whatever his good reason was it would do no harm to speak plainly.

'I do a job which I ought to find satisfying, and it leaves me bored and empty.'

'A diet of milk and honey, when you have teeth,' he observed.

I laughed. 'A taste for salt, perhaps.'

'What would you have been had your parents not died and left you with three children to bring up?'

'A lawyer, I think, though possibly . . .' I hesitated.

'Possibly what?'

'Well . . . it sounds a bit odd, especially after the last few days . . . a policeman.'

'Ah,' he said softly, 'that figures.' He leant his head back again and smiled.

'Marriage might help you feel more settled,' he suggested.

'More ties,' I said, 'Another family to provide for. The rut for ever.'

'So that's how you look at it. How about Elinor?'

'She's a nice girl.'

'But not for keeps?'

I shook my head.

'You went to a great deal of trouble to save her life,' he pointed out.

'It was only because of me that she got into danger at all.'

'You couldn't know that she would be so strongly attracted to you and find you so . . . er . . . irresistible that she would drive out to take another look at you. When you went back to Humber's to extricate her, you had already finished the investigation, tidily, quietly and undiscovered. Isn't that right?'

'I suppose so. Yes.'

'Did you enjoy it?'

'Enjoy it?' I repeated, surprised.

'Oh, I don't mean the fracas at the end, or the hours of honest toil you had to put in,' he smiled briefly, 'But the . . . shall we say, the chase?'

'Am I, in fact, a hunter by nature?'

'Are you?'

'Yes.'

There was a silence. My unadorned affirmative hung in the air, bald and revealing.

'Were you afraid at all?' His voice was matter of fact.

'Yes.'

'To the point of incapacity?'

I shook my head.

'You knew Adams and Humber would kill you if they found you out. What effect did living in perpetual danger have on you?' His voice was so clinical that I answered with similar detachment.

'It made me careful.'

'Is that all?'

'Well, if you mean was I in a constant state of nervous tension, then no, I wasn't.'

'I see.' Another of his small pauses. Then he said, 'What did you find hardest to do?'

I blinked, grinned, and lied. 'Wearing those loathsome pointed shoes.'

He nodded as if I had told him a satisfying truth. I probably had. The pointed shoes had hurt my pride, not my toes.

And pride had got the better of me properly when I visited Elinor in her college and hadn't been strong enough to play an oaf in her company. All that stuff about Marcus Aurelius was sheer showing off, and the consequences had been appalling. It didn't bear thinking of, let alone confessing.

Beckett said idly, 'Would you ever consider doing something similar again?'

'I should think so. Yes. But not like that.'

'How do you mean?'

'Well . . . I didn't know enough, for one thing. For example, it was just luck that Humber always left his office unlocked, because I couldn't have got in if he hadn't. I don't know how to open doors wihout keys. I would have found a camera useful . . . I could have taken films of the blue ledger in Humber's office, and so on, but my knowledge of photography is almost nil. I'd have got the exposures wrong. Then I had never fought anyone in my life before. If I'd known anything at all about unarmed combat I probably wouldn't have killed Adams or been so much battered myself. Apart from all that there was nowhere where I could send you or Edward a message and be sure you would receive it quickly. Communications, in fact, were pretty hopeless.'

'Yes. I see. All the same, you did finish the job in spite of those disadvantages.'

'It was luck. You couldn't count on being lucky twice.'

'I suppose not.' He smiled. 'What do you plan to do with your twenty thousand pounds?'

'I . . . er . . . plan to let Edward keep most of it.'

'What do you mean?'

'I can't take that sort of money. All I ever wanted was to get away for a bit. It was he who suggested such a large sum, not me. I don't think he thought I would take on the job for less, but he was wrong . . . I'd have done it for nothing if I could. All I'll accept from him is the amount it has cost for me to be away. He knows, I told him last night.'

There was a long pause. Finally Beckett sat up and picked up a telephone. He dialled and waited.

'This is Beckett,' he said. 'It's about Daniel Roke . . . yes, he's here.' He took a postcard out of an inner pocket. 'Those points we were discussing this morning . . . I have had a talk with him. You have your card?'

He listened for a moment, and leaned back again in his chair. His eyes were steady on my face.

'Right?' He spoke into the telephone. 'Numbers one to four can all have an affirmative. Number five is satisfactory. Number six, his weakest spot . . . he didn't maintain his role in front of Elinor Tarren. She said he was good mannered and intelligent. No one else thought so . . . yes, I should say so, sexual pride . . . apparently only because Elinor is clever as well as pretty, since he kept it up all right with her younger sister . . . yes . . . oh undoubtedly it was his intellect as much as his physical appearance which attracted her . . . yes, very good looking: I believe you sometimes find that useful . . . no, he doesn't. He didn't look in the mirror in the washroom at the Club or in the one on the wall here . . . no, he didn't admit it today, but I'd say he is well aware he failed on that point . . . yes, rather a harsh lesson . . . it may still be a risk, or it may have been sheer unprofessionalism . . . your Miss Jones could find out, yes.'

I didn't particularly care for this dispassionate vivisection, but short of walking out there seemed to be no way of avoiding it. His eyes still looked at me expressionlessly.

'Number seven . . . normal reaction. Eight, slightly obsessive, but that's all the better from your point of view.' He glanced momentarily down at the card he held in his hand 'Nine . . . well, although he is British by birth and spent his childhood here, he is Australian by inclination, and

I doubt whether subservience comes easily . . . I don't know, he wouldn't talk about it . . . no, I wouldn't say he had a vestige of a martyr complex, he's clear on that. . . . Of course you never get a perfect one . . . it's entirely up to you . . . Number ten? The three B's. I should say definitely not the first two, much too proud. As for the third, he's the type to shout for help. Yes, he's still here. Hasn't moved a muscle . . . yes, I do think so . . . all right . . . I'll ring you again later.'

He put down the receiver. I waited. He took his time and I refrained consciously from fidgeting under his gaze.

'Well?' he said at last.

'If you're going to ask what I think, the answer is no.'

'Because you don't want to, or because of your sisters and brother?'

'Philip is still only thirteen.'

'I see.' He made a weak-looking gesture with his hand. 'All the same, I'd better make sure you know what you are turning down. The colleague who kept me late this morning, and to whom I was talking just now, runs one of the counter-espionage departments – not only political but scientific and industrial, and anything else which crops up. His section are rather good at doing what you have done – becoming an inconspicuous part of the background. It's amazing how little notice even agents take of servants and workmen . . . and his lot have had some spectacular results. They are often used to check on suspected immigrants and political refugees who may not be all they seem, not by watching from afar, but by working for or near them day by day. And recently, for instance, several of the section have been employed as labourers on top-secret construction sites . . . there have been some disturbing leaks of security; complete site plans of secret installations have been sold abroad; and it was found that a commercial espionage firm was getting information through operatives actually putting brick on brick and photographing the buildings at each stage.'

'Philip,' I said, 'is only thirteen.'

'You wouldn't be expected to plunge straight into such a life. As you yourself pointed out, you are untrained. There would be at least a year's instruction in various techniques before you were given a job.'

'I can't,' I said.

'Between jobs all his people are given leave. If a job takes as long as four months, like the one you have just done, they get about six weeks off. They never work more than nine months in a year, if it can be helped. You could often be home in the school holidays.'

'If I am not there all the time, there won't be enough money for fees and there won't be any home.'

'It is true that the British Government wouldn't pay you as much as you earn now,' he said mildly, 'but there are such things as full-time stud managers.'

I opened my mouth and shut it again.

'Think about it,' he said gently. 'I've another colleague to see . . . I'll be back in an hour.'

He levered himself out of the chair and slowly walked out of the room. The pigeons fluttered peaceably on the window sill. I thought of the years I had spent building up the stud farm, and what I had achieved there. In spite of my comparative youth the business was a solid success, and by the time I was fifty I could with a bit of luck put it among the top studs in Australia and enjoy a respected, comfortably-off, influential middle-age.

What Beckett was offering was a lonely life of unprivileged jobs and dreary lodgings, a life of perpetual risk which could very well end with a bullet in the head.

Rationally, there was no choice. Belinda and Helen and Philip still needed a secure home with the best I could do for them as a father substitute. And no sensible person would hand over to a manager a prosperous business and become instead a sort of sweeper-up of some of the world's smaller messes . . . one couldn't put the job any higher than that.

But irrationally . . . With very little persuasion I had already left my family to fend for themselves, for as Beckett said, I wasn't of the stuff of martyrs; and the prosperous business had already driven me once into a pit of depression.

I knew now clearly what I was, and what I could do.

I remembered the times when I had been tempted to give up, and hadn't. I remembered the moment when I held Elinor's dog whistle in my hand and my mind made an almost muscular leap at the truth. I remembered the satisfaction I felt in Kandersteg's scorched enclosure, knowing I had finally uncovered and defeated Adams and Humber. No sale of any horse had ever brought so quiet and complete a fulfilment.

The hour passed. The pigeons defecated on the window and flew away. Colonel Beckett came back.

'Well?' he said. 'Yes or no?'

'Yes.'

He laughed aloud. 'Just like that? No questions or reservations?'

'No reservations. But I will need time to arrange things at home.'

'Of course.' He picked up the telephone receiver. 'My colleague will wish you to see him before you go back.' He rested his fingers on the dial. 'I'll make an appointment.'

'And one question.'

'Yes?'

'What are the three Bs of number ten?'

He smiled secretly, and I knew he had intended that I should ask: which meant that he wanted me to know the answer. Devious, indeed. My nostrils twitched as if at the scent of a whole new world. A world where I belonged.

'Whether you could be bribed or bludgeoned or blackmailed,' he said casually, 'into changing sides.'

He dialled the number, and altered my life.

ODDS AGAINST

Chapter One

I was never particularly keen on my job before the day I got shot and nearly lost it, along with my life. But the .38 slug of lead which made a pepper-shaker out of my intestines left me with fire in my belly in more ways than one. Otherwise I should never have met Zanna Martin, and would still be held fast in the spider-threads of departed joys, of no use to anyone, least of all myself.

It was the first step to liberation, that bullet, though I wouldn't have said so at the time. I stopped it because I was careless. Careless because bored.

I woke up gradually in hospital, in a private room for which I got a whacking great bill a few days later. Even before I opened my eyes I began to regret I had not left the world completely. Someone had lit a bonfire under my navel.

A fierce conversation was being conducted in unhushed voices over my head. With woolly wits, the anaesthetic still drifting inside my skull like puff-ball clouds in a summer sky, I tried unenthusiastically to make sense of what was being said.

'Can't you give him something to wake him up more quickly?'

'No.'

'We can't do much until we have his story, you must see that. It's nearly seven hours since you finished operating. Surely . . .'

'And he was all of four hours on the table before that. Do you want to finish off what the shooting started?'

'Doctor . . .'

'I am sorry, but you'll have to wait.'

There's my pal, I thought. They'll have to wait. Who wants to hurry back into the dreary old world? Why not go to sleep for a month and take things up again after they've put the bonfire out? I opened my eyes reluctantly.

It was night. A globe of electric light shone in the centre of the ceiling. That figured. It had been morning when Jones-boy found me still seeping gently on to the office linoleum and went to telephone, and it appeared that about twelve hours had passed since they stuck the first blessed needle into my arm. Would a twenty-four hour start, I wondered, be enough for a panic-stricken ineffectual little crook to get himself unde-tectably out of the country?

There were two policemen on my left, one in uniform, one not. They were both sweating, because the room was hot. The doctor stood on the right, fiddling with a tube which ran from a bottle into my elbow. Various other tubes sprouted disgustingly from my abdomen, partly covered by a light sheet. Drip and drainage, I thought sardonically. How absolutely charming.

Radnor was watching me from the foot of the bed, taking no part in the argument still in progress between medicine and the law. I wouldn't have thought I rated the boss himself attendant at the bedside, but then I suppose it wasn't every day that one of his employees got himself into such a spectacular mess.

He said, 'He's conscious again, and his eyes aren't so hazy. We might get some sense out of him this time.' He looked at his watch.

The doctor bent over me, felt my pulse, and nodded. 'Five minutes, then. Not a second more.'

The plain clothes policeman beat Radnor to it by a fraction of a second. 'Can you tell us who shot you?'

I still found it surprisingly difficult to speak, but not as impossible as it had been when they asked me that same question that morning. Then, I had been too far gone. Now, I was apparently on the way back. Even so, the policeman had plenty of time to repeat his question, and to wait some more, before I managed an answer.

'Andrews.'

It meant nothing to the policeman, but Radnor looked astonished and also disappointed.

'Thomas Andrews?' he asked.

'Yes.'

Radnor explained to the police. 'I told you that Halley here and another of my operatives set some sort of trap intending to clear up an intimidation case we are investigating. I understand they were hoping for a big fish, but it seems now they caught a tiddler. Andrews is small stuff, a weak sort of youth used for running errands. I would never have thought he would carry a gun, much less that he would use it.'

Me neither. He had dragged the revolver clumsily out of his jacket pocket, pointed it shakily in my direction, and used both hands to pull the trigger. If I hadn't seen that it was only Andrews who had come in to nibble at the bait I wouldn't have ambled unwarily out of the darkness of the washroom to tax him with breaking into the Cromwell Road premises of Hunt Radnor Associates at one o'clock in the morning. It simply hadn't occurred to me that he would attack me in any way.

By the time I realised that he really meant to use the gun and was not waving it about for effect, it was far too late. I had barely begun to turn to flip off the light switch when the bullet hit, in and out diagonally through my body. The force of it spun me on to my knees and then forward on to the floor.

As I went down he ran for the door, stiff-legged, crying out, with circles of white showing wild round his eyes. He was almost as horrified as I was at what he had done.

'At what time did the shooting take place?' asked the policeman formally.

After another pause I said, 'One o'clock, about.'

The doctor drew in a breath. He didn't need to say it; I knew I was lucky to be alive. In a progressively feeble state I'd lain on the floor through a chilly September night looking disgustedly at a telephone on which I couldn't summon help. The office telephones all worked through a switchboard. This might have been on the moon as far as I was concerned, instead of along the passage, down the curving stairs and through the door to the reception desk, with the girl who worked the switches fast asleep in bed.

The policeman wrote in his notebook. 'Now sir, I can get a description of Thomas Andrews from someone else so as not to trouble you too much now, but I'd be glad if you can tell me what he was wearing.'

'Black jeans, very tight. Olive green jersey. Loose black jacket.' I paused. 'Black fur collar and white checked lining. All shabby . . . dirty.' I tried again. 'He had gun in jacket pocket right side . . . took it with him . . . no gloves . . . can't have a record.'

'Shoes?'

'Didn't see. Silent, though.'

'Anything else?'

I thought. 'He had some badges . . . place names, skull and crossbones, things like that . . . sewn on his jacket, left sleeve.'

'I see. Right. We'll get on with it then.' He snapped shut his notebook, smiled briefly, turned, and walked to the door, followed by his uniformed ally, and by Radnor, presumably for Andrew's description.

The doctor took my pulse again, and slowly checked all the tubes. His face showed satisfaction.

He said cheerfully, 'You must have the constitution of a horse.'

'No,' said Radnor, coming in again and hearing him. 'Horses are really quite delicate creatures. Halley has the constitution of a jockey. A steeplechase jockey. He use to be one. He's got a body like a shock absorber . . . had to have to deal with all the fractures and injuries he got racing.'

'Is that what happened to his hand? A fall in a steeplechase?'

Radnor's glance flicked to my face and away again, uncomfortably. They never mentioned my hand in the office if they could help it. None of them, that is except my fellow trap-setter Chico Barnes, who didn't care what he said to anyone.

'Yes,' said Radnor tersely. 'That's right.' He changed the subject. 'Well, Sid, come and see me when you are better. Take your time.' He nodded uncertainly to me, and he and the doctor, with a joint backward glance, ushered each other out of the door.

So Radnor was in no hurry to have me back. I would have smiled if I'd had the energy. When he first offered me a job I guessed somewhere in the background my father-in-law was pulling strings; but I had been in a why-not mood at the time. Nothing mattered very much.

'Why not?' I said to Radnor, and he put me on his payroll as an investigator, Racing Section, ignoring my complete lack of experience and explaining to the rest of the staff that I was there in an advisory capacity, owing to my intimate knowledge of the game. They had taken it very well, on the whole. Perhaps they realised as I did, that my employment was an act of pity. Perhaps they thought I should be too proud to accept that sort of pity. I wasn't. I didn't care one way or the other.

Radnor's agency ran Missing Persons, Guard, and Divorce departments, and also a section called Bona Fides which was nearly as big as the others put together. Most of the work was routine painstaking enquiry stuff, sometimes leading to civil or divorce action, but oftener merely to a discreet report sent to the client. Criminal cases, though accepted, were rare. The Andrews business was the first for three months.

The Racing Section was Radnor's special baby. It hadn't existed, I'd been told, when he bought the agency with an Army gratuity after the war and developed it from a dingy three-roomed affair into something like a national institution. Radnor printed 'Speed, Results, and Secrecy' across the top of his stationery; promised them, and delivered them. A lifelong addiction to racing, allied to six youthful rides in point-to-points, had led him not so much to ply for hire from the Jockey Club and the National Hunt Committee as to indicate that his agency was at their disposal. The Jockey Club and the National Hunt Committee tentatively wet their feet, found the water beneficial, and plunged right in. The Racing Section blossomed. Eventually private business outstripped the official, especially when Radnor began supplying pre-race guards for fancied horses.

By the time I joined the firm 'Bona Fides: Racing', had proved so successful that it had spread from its own big office into the room next door. For a reasonable fee a trainer could check on the character and background of a prospective owner, a bookmaker on a client, a client on a bookmaker, anybody on anybody. The phrase 'O.K.'d by Radnor' had passed into racing slang. Genuine, it meant. Trustworthy. I had even heard it applied to a horse.

They had never given me a Bona Fides assignment. This work was done by a bunch of inconspicuous middle-aged retired policemen who took minimum time to get maximum results. I'd never been sent to sit all night outside the box of a hot favourite, though I would have done it willingly. I had never been put on a racecourse security patrol. If the Stewards asked for operators to keep tabs on undesirables at race meetings, I didn't go. If anyone had to watch for pickpockets in Tattersalls, it wasn't me. Radnor's two unvarying excuses for giving me nothing to do were first that I was too well known to the whole racing world to be inconspicuous, and second, that even if I didn't seem to care, he was not going to be the one to give an ex-champion jockey tasks which meant a great loss of face.

As a result I spent most of my time kicking around the office reading other people's reports. When anyone asked me for the informed advice I was supposedly there to give, I gave it; if anyone asked what I would do in a certain set of circumstances, I told them. I got to know all the operators and gossiped with them when they came into the office. I always had the time. If I took a day off and went to the races, nobody complained. I sometimes wondered whether they even noticed.

At intervals I remarked to Radnor that he didn't have to keep me, as I so obviously did nothing to earn my salary. He replied each time that he was satisfied with the arrangement, if I was. I had the impression that he was waiting for something, but if it wasn't for me to leave, I didn't know what. On the day I walked into Andrews' bullet I had been with the agency in this fashion exactly two years.

A nurse came in to check the tubes and take my blood pressure. She was starched and efficient. She smiled but didn't speak. I waited for her to say that my wife was outside asking about me anxiously. She didn't say it. My wife hadn't come. Wouldn't come. If I couldn't hold her when I was properly alive, why should my near-death bring her running? Jenny. My wife. Still my wife in spite of three year's separation. Regret, I think, held both of us back from the final step of divorce: we had been through passion, delight, dissention, anger and explosion. Only regret was left, and it wouldn't be strong enough to bring her to the hospital. She'd seen me in too many hospitals before. There was no more drama, no more impact, in my form recumbent, even with tubes. She wouldn't come. Wouldn't telephone. Wouldn't write. It was stupid of me to want her to.

Time passed slowly and I didn't enjoy it, but eventually all the tubes except the one in my arm were removed and I began to heal. The police didn't find Andrews, Jenny didn't come, Radnor's typists sent me a get-well card, and the hospital sent the bill.

Chico slouched in one evening, his hands in his pockets and the usual derisive grin on his face. He looked me over without haste and the grin, if anything, widened.

'Rather you than me, mate,' he said.

'Go to bloody hell.'

He laughed. And well he might. I had been doing his job for him because he had a date with a girl, and Andrews' bullet should have been his bellyache, not mine.

'Andrews,' he said musingly. 'Who'd have thought it? Sodding little weasel. All the same, if you'd done what I said and stayed in the washroom, and taken his photo quiet like on the old infra-red, we'd have picked him up later nice and easy and you'd have been lolling on your arse around the office as usual instead of sweating away in here.'

'You needn't rub it in,' I said. 'What would you have done?'

He grinned. 'The same as you, I expect. 'I'd have reckoned it would only take the old one-two for that little worm to come across with who sent him.'

'And now we don't know.'

'No.' He sighed. 'And the old man ain't too sweet about the whole thing. He did know I was using the office as a trap, but he didn't think it would work, and now this has happened he doesn't like it. He's leaning over backwards, hushing the whole thing up. They might have sent a bomb, not a sneak thief, he said. And of course Andrews bust a window getting in, which I've probably got to pay for. Trust the little sod not to know how to pick a lock.'

'I'll pay for the window,' I said.

'Yeah,' he grinned. 'I reckoned you would if I told you.'

He wandered round the room, looking at things. There wasn't much to see.

'What's in that bottle dripping into your arm?'

'Food of some sort, as far as I can gather. They never give me anything to eat.'

'Afraid you might bust out again, I expect.'

'I guess so,' I agreed.

He wandered on. 'Haven't you got a telly then? Cheer you up a bit wouldn't it, to see some other silly buggers getting shot?' He looked at the chart on the bottom of the bed. 'Your temperature was 102 this morning, did they tell you? Do you reckon you're going to kick it?'

'No.'

'Near thing, from what I've heard. Jones-boy said there was enough of your life's blood dirtying up the office floor to make a tidy few black puddings.'

I didn't appreciate Jones-boy's sense of humour.

Chico said, 'Are you coming back?'

'Perhaps.'

He began tying knots in the cord of the window blind. I watched him, a thin figure imbued with so much energy that it was difficult for him to keep still. He had spent two fruitless nights watching in the washroom before I took his place, and I knew that if he hadn't been dedicated to his job he couldn't have borne such inactivity. He was the youngest of Radnor's team. About twenty-four, he believed, though as he had been abandoned as a child on the steps of a police station in a push-chair, no one knew for certain.

If the police hadn't been so kind to him, Chico sometimes said, he would have taken advantage of his later opportunities and turned delinquent. He never grew tall enough to be a copper. Radnor's was the best he could do. And he did very well by Radnor. He put two and two together quickly and no one on the staff had faster physical reactions. Judo and wrestling were his hobbies, and along with the regular throws and holds he had been taught some strikingly dirty tricks. His smallness bore no relation whatever to his effectiveness in his job.

'How are you getting on with the case?' I asked.

'What case? Oh . . . that. Well since you got shot the heat's off, it seems. Brinton's had no threatening calls or letters since the other night. Whoever was leaning on him must have got the wind up. Anyway, he's feeling a bit safer all of a sudden and he's carping a lot to the old man about fees. Another day or two, I give it, and there won't be no one holding his hand at night. Anyway, I've been pulled off it. I'm flying from Newmarket to Ireland tomorrow, sharing a stall with a hundred thousand pounds' worth of stallion.'

Escort duty was another little job I never did. Chico liked it, and went often. As he had once thrown a fifteen stone would-be-nobbler over a seven foot wall, he was always much in demand.

'You ought to come back,' he said suddenly.

'Why?' I was surprised.

'I don't know . . .' he grinned. 'Silly, really, when you do sweet eff-all, but everybody seems to have got used to you being around. You're missed, kiddo, you'd be surprised.'

'You're joking, of course.'

'Yeah ...' He undid the knots in the window cord, shrugged, and thrust his hands into his trouser pockets. 'God, this place gives you the willies. It reeks of warm disinfectant. Creepy. How much longer are you going to lie here rotting?'

'Days,' I said mildly. 'Have a good trip.'

'See you.' He nodded, drifting in relief to the door. 'Do you want anything? I mean, books or anything?'

'Nothing, thanks.'

'Nothing ... that's just your form, Sid, mate. You don't want nothing.' He grinned and went.

I wanted nothing. My form. My trouble. I'd had what I wanted most in the world and lost it irrevocably. I'd found nothing else to want. I stared at the ceiling, waiting for time to pass. All I wanted was to get back on to my feet and stop feeling as though I had eaten a hundredweight of green apples.

Three weeks after the shooting I had a visit from my father-in-law. He came in the late afternoon, bringing with him a small parcel which he put without comment on the table beside the bed.

'Well, Sid, how are you?' He settled himself into an easy chair, crossed his legs and lit a cigar.

'Cured, more or less. I'll be out of here soon.'

'Good. Good. And your plans are ...?'

'I haven't any.'

'You can't go back to the agency without some ... er ... convalescence,' he remarked.

'I suppose not.'

'You might prefer somewhere in the sun,' he said, studying the cigar. 'But I would like it if you could spend some time with me at Aynsford.'

I didn't answer immediately.

'No,' he said. 'She won't be there. She's gone out to Athens to stay with Jill and Tony. I saw her off yesterday. She sent you her regards.'

'Thanks,' I said dryly. As usual I did not know whether to be glad or sorry that I was not going to meet my wife. Nor was I sure that this trip to see her sister Jill was not as diplomatic as Tony's job in the Corps.

'You'll come, then? Mrs. Cross will look after you splendidly.'

'Yes, Charles, thank you. I'd like to come for a little while.'

He gripped the cigar in his teeth, squinted through the smoke, and took out his diary.

'Let's see, suppose you leave here in, say, another week ... No point in hurrying out before you're fit to go ... that brings us to the twenty-sixth ... hm ... now, suppose you come down a week on Sunday, I'll be at home all that day. Will that suit you?'

'Yes, fine, if the doctors agree.'

'Right, then.' He wrote in the diary, put it away and took the cigar carefully out of his mouth, smiling at me with the usual inscrutable blankness in his eyes. He sat easily in his dark city suit, Rear-Admiral

Charles Roland, R.N., retired, a man carrying his sixty-six years lightly. War photographs showed him tall, straight, bony almost, with a high forehead and thick dark hair. Time had greyed the hair, which in receding left his forehead higher than ever, and had added weight where it did no harm. His manner was ordinarily extremely charming and occasionally patronisingly offensive. I had been on the receiving end of both.

He relaxed in the arm-chair, talking unhurriedly about steeplechasing. 'What do you think of that new race at Sandown? I don't know about you, but I think it's framed rather awkwardly. They're bound to get a tiny field with those conditions, and if Devil's Dyke doesn't run after all the whole thing will be a non-crowd puller *par excellence.*'

His interest in the game only dated back a few years, but recently to his pleasure he had been invited by one or two courses to act as a Steward. Listening to his easy familiarity with racing problems and racing jargon, I was in a quiet inward way amused. It was impossible to forget his reaction long ago to Jenny's engagement to a jockey, his unfriendly rejection of me as a future son-in-law, his absence from our wedding, the months afterwards of frigid disapproval, the way he had seldom spoken to or even looked at me.

I believed at the time that it was sheer snobbery, but it wasn't as simple as that. Certainly he didn't think me good enough, but not only, or even mainly, on a class distinction level, and probably we would never have understood each other, or come eventually to like each other, had it not been for a wet afternoon and a game of chess.

Jenny and I went to Aynsford for one of our rare, painful Sunday visits. We ate our roast beef in near silence, Jenny's father staring rudely out of the window and drumming his fingers on the table. I made up my mind that we wouldn't go again. I'd had enough. Jenny could visit him alone.

After lunch she said she wanted to sort out some of her books now that we had a new book-case, and disappeared upstairs. Charles Roland and I looked at each other in dislike, the afternoon stretching drearily ahead and the downpour outside barring retreat into the garden and park beyond.

'Do you play chess?' he asked in a bored, expecting-the-answer-no voice.

'I know the moves,' I said.

He shrugged (it was more like a squirm), but clearly thinking that it would be less trouble than making conversation, he brought a chess set out and gestured to me to sit opposite him. He was normally a good player, but that afternoon he was bored and irritated and inattentive, and I beat him quite early in the game. He couldn't believe it. He sat staring at the board, fingering the bishop with which I'd got him in a classic discovered check.

'Where did you learn?' he said eventually, still looking down.

'Out of a book.'

'Have you played a great deal?'

'No, not much. Here and there.' But I'd played with some good players.

'Hm.' He paused. 'Will you play again?'

'Yes, if you like.'

We played. It was a long game and ended in a draw, with practically every piece off the board. A fortnight later he rang up and asked us, next time we came, to stay overnight. It was the first twig of the olive branch. We went more often and more willingly to Aynsford after that. Charles and I played chess occasionally and won a roughly equal number of games, and he began rather tentatively to go to the races. Ironically from then on our mutual respect grew strong enough to survive even the crash of Jenny's and my marriage, and Charles' interest in racing expanded and deepened with every passing year.

'I went to Ascot yesterday,' he was saying, tapping ash off his cigar. 'It wasn't a bad crowd, considering the weather. I had a drink with that handicapper fellow, John Pagan. Nice chap. He was very pleased with himself because he got six abreast over the last in the handicap hurdle. There was an objection after the three mile chase – flagrant bit of crossing on the run-in. Carter swore blind he was leaning and couldn't help it, but you can never believe a word he says. Anyway, the Stewards took it away from him. The only thing they could do. Wally Gibbons rode a brilliant finish in the handicap hurdle and then made an almighty hash of the novice chase.'

'He's heavy-handed with novices,' I agreed.

'Wonderful course, that.'

'The tops.' A wave of weakness flowed outwards from my stomach. My legs trembled under bedclothes. It was always happening. Infuriating.

'Good job it belongs to the Queen and is safe from the land-grabbers.' He smiled.

'Yes, I suppose so . . .'

'You're tired,' he said abruptly. 'I've stayed too long.'

'No,' I protested. 'Really, I'm fine.'

He put out the cigar, however, and stood up. 'I know you too well, Sid. Your idea of fine is not the same as anyone else's. If you're not well enough to come to Aynsford a week on Sunday you'll let me know. Otherwise I'll see you then.'

'Yes, O.K.'

He went away, leaving me to reflect that I did still tire infernally easily. Must be old age, I grinned to myself, old age at thirty-one. Old tired battered Sid Halley, poor old chap. I grimaced at the ceiling.

A nurse came in for the evening jobs.

'You've got a parcel,' she said brightly, as if speaking to a retarded child. 'Aren't you going to open it?'

I had forgotten about Charles' parcel.

'Would you like me to open it for you? I mean, you can't find things like opening parcels very easy with a hand like yours.'

She was only being kind. 'Yes,' I said. 'Thank you.'

She snipped through the wrappings with scissors from her pocket and looked dubiously at the slim dark book she found inside.

'I suppose it is meant for you? I mean somehow it doesn't seem like things people usually give patients.'

She put the book into my right hand and I read the title embossed in gold on the cover. *Outline of Company Law*.

'My father-in-law left it on purpose. He meant it for me.'

'Oh well, I suppose it's difficult to think of things for people who can't eat grapes and such.' She bustled around, efficient and slightly bullying, and finally left me alone again.

Outline of Company Law. I riffled through the pages. It was certainly a book about company law. Solidly legal. Not light entertainment for an invalid. I put the book on the table.

Charles Roland was a man of subtle mind, and subtlety gave him much pleasure. It hadn't been my parentage that he had objected to so much as what he took to be Jenny's rejection of his mental standards in choosing a jockey for a husband. He'd never met a jockey before, disliked the idea of racing, and took it for granted that everyone engaged in it was either a rogue or a moron. He'd wanted both his daughters to marry clever men, clever more than handsome or well-born or rich, so that he could enjoy their company. Jill had obliged him with Tony, Jenny disappointed him with me: that was how he saw it, until he found that at least I could play chess with him now and then.

Knowing his subtle habits, I took it for granted that he had not idly brought such a book and hadn't chosen it or left it by mistake. He meant me to read it for a purpose. Intended it to be useful to me – or to him – later on. Did he think he could manoeuvre me into business, now that I hadn't distinguished myself at the agency? A nudge, that book was. A nudge in some specific direction.

I thought back over what he had said, looking for a clue. He'd been insistent that I should go to Aynsford. He'd sent Jenny to Athens. He'd talked about racing, about the new race at Sandown, about Ascot, John Pagan, Carter, Wally Gibbons . . . nothing there that I could see had the remotest connection with company law.

I sighed, shutting my eyes. I didn't feel too well. I didn't have to read the book, or go wherever Charles pointed. And yet . . . why not? There was nothing I urgently wanted to do instead. I decided to do my stodgy homework. Tomorrow.

Perhaps.

Chapter Two

Four days after my arrival at Aynsford I came downstairs from an afternoon's rest to find Charles delving into a large packing case in the centre of the hall. Strewn round on the half-acre of parquet was a vast amount of wood shavings, white and curly, and arranged carefully on a low table beside him were the first trophies out of the lucky dip, appearing to me to be dull chunks of rock.

I picked one of them up. One side had been ground into a smooth face and across the bottom of this was stuck a neat lable. 'Porphyry' it said, and beneath, 'Carver Mineralogy Foundation'.

'I didn't know you had an obsessive interest in quartz.'

He gave me one of his blank stares, which I knew didn't mean that he hadn't heard or understood what I'd said, but that he didn't intend to explain.

'I'm going fishing,' he said, plunging his arms back into the box.

So the quartz was bait. I put down the porphyry and picked up another piece. It was small, the size of a squared-off egg, and beautiful, as clear and translucent as glass. The label said simply 'Rock Crystal'.

'If you want something useful to do,' said Charles, 'you can write out what sort they all are on the plain labels you will find on my desk, and then soak the Foundation's label off and put the new ones on. Keep the old ones, though. We'll have to replace them when all this stuff goes back.'

'All right,' I agreed.

The next chunk I picked up was heavy with gold. 'Are these valuable?' I asked.

'Some are. There's a booklet somewhere. But I told the Foundation they'd be safe enough. I said I'd have a private detective in the house all the time guarding them.'

I laughed and began writing the new labels, working from the inventory. The lumps of quartz overflowed from the table on to the floor before the box was empty.

'There's another box outside,' Charles observed.

'Oh no!'

'I collect quartz,' said Charles with dignity, 'and don't you forget it. I've collected it for years. Years. Haven't I?'

'Years,' I agreed. 'You're an authority. Who wouldn't be an authority on rocks, after a life at sea.'

'I've got exactly one day to learn them in,' said Charles smiling. 'They've come later than I asked. I'll have to be word perfect by tomorrow night.'

He fetched the second lot, which was much smaller and was fastened with important looking seals. Inside were uncut gem quartz crystals, mounted on small individual black plinths. Their collective value was staggering. The Carver Foundation must have taken the private detective bit seriously. They'd have held tight to rocks if they'd seen my state of health.

We worked for some time changing the labels while Charles muttered their names like incantations under his breath. 'Chrysoprase, Aventurine, Agate, Onyx, Chalcedony, Tiger-eye, Carnelian, Citrine, Rose, Plasma, Basanite, Bloodstone, Chert. Why the hell did I start this?'

'Well, why?'

I got the blank stare again. He wasn't telling. 'You can test me on them,' he said.

We carried them piece by piece into the dining-room, where I found the glass-doored book shelves on each side of the fire had been cleared of their yards of leather-bound classics.

'They can go up there later,' said Charles, covering the huge dining-room table with a thick felt. 'Put them on the table for now.'

When they were all arranged he walked slowly round learning them. There were about fifty altogether. I tested him after a while, at his request, and he muddled up and forgot about half of them. They were difficult, because so many looked alike.

He sighed. 'It's time we had a noggin and you went back to bed.' He led the way into the little sitting-room he occasionally referred to as the wardroom, and poured a couple of stiffish brandies. He raised his glass to me and appreciatively took a mouthful. There was suppressed excitement in his expression, a glint in the unfathomable eyes. I sipped the brandy, wondering with more interest what he was up to.

'I have a few people coming for the week-end,' he said casually, squinting at his glass. 'A Mr. and Mrs. Rex van Dysart, a Mr. and Mrs. Howard Kraye, and my cousin Viola, who will act as hostess.'

'Old friends?' I murmured, having only ever heard of Viola.

'Not very,' he said smoothly. 'They'll be here in time for dinner tomorrow night. You'll meet them then.'

'But I'll make it an odd number . . . I'll go up before they come and stay out of your way for most of the week-end.'

'No,' he said sharply. Much too vehemently. I was surprised. Then it came to me suddenly that all he had been doing with his rocks and his offer of a place for my convalescence was to engineer a meeting between me and the weekend guests. He offered me rest. He offered Mr. van Dysart, or perhaps Mr. Kraye, rocks. Both of us had swallowed the hook. I decided to give the line a tug, to see just how determined was the fisherman.

'I'd be better upstairs. You know I can't eat normal meals.' My diet at that time consisted of brandy, beef juice, and some vacuum-packed pots of stuff which had been developed for feeding astronauts. Apparently none of these things affected the worst shot-up bits of my digestive tract.

'People loosen up over the dinner table . . . they talk more, and you get to know them better.' He was carefully unpersuasive.

'They'll talk to you just as well if I'm not there – better in fact. And I couldn't stand watching you all tuck into steaks.'

He said musingly, 'You can stand anything, Sid. But I think you'd be interested. Not bored, I promise you. More brandy?'

I shook my head, and relented. 'All right, I'll be there at dinner, if you want it.'

He relaxed only a fraction. A controlled and subtle man. I smiled at him, and he guessed that I'd been playing him along.

'You're a bastard,' he said.

From him, it was compliment.

The transistor beside my bed was busy with the morning news as I slowly ate my breakfast pot of astronaut paste.

'The race meeting scheduled for today and tomorrow at Seabury,' the announcer said, 'has had to be abandoned. A tanker carrying liquid chemical crashed and overturned at dusk yesterday afternoon on a road crossing the racecourse. There was considerable damage to the turf, and after an examination this morning the Stewards regretfully decided that it was not fit to be raced on. It is hoped to replace the affected turf in time for the next meeting in a fortnight's time, but an announcement will be made about this at a later date. And here is the weather forecast . . .'

Poor Seabury, I thought, always in the wars. It was only a year since their stable block had been burned down on the eve of a meeting. They had had to cancel then too, because temporary stables could not be erected overnight, and the national Hunt Committee in consultation with Radnor had decided that indiscriminate stabling in the surrounding district was too much of a security risk.

It was a nice track to ride on, a long circuit with no sharp bends, but there had been trouble with the surface in the Spring; a drain of some sort had collapsed during a hurdle race. The forefeet of one unfortunate horse had gone right through into it to a depth of about eighteen inches and he had broken a leg. In the resulting pile-up two more horses had been ruinously injured and one jockey badly concussed. Maps of the course didn't even warn that the drain existed, and I'd heard trainers wondering whether there were any more antique waterways ready to collapse with as little notice. The executive, on their side, naturally swore there weren't.

For some time I lay day-dreaming, racing round Seabury again in my mind, and wishing uselessly, hopelessly, achingly, that I could do it again in fact.

Mrs. Cross tapped on the door and came in. She was a quiet, unobtrusive mouse of a woman with soft brown hair and a slight outward cast in her grey-green eyes. Although she seemed to have no spirit whatever and seldom spoke, she ran the place like oiled machinery, helped by a largely invisible squad of 'dailies'. She had the great virtue to me of being fairly new in the job and impartial on the subject of Jenny and me. I wouldn't have trusted her predecessor, who had been fanatically fond of Jenny, not to have added cascara to my beef juice.

'The Admiral would like to know if you are feeling well today, Mr. Halley,' said Mrs. Cross primly, picking up my breakfast tray.

'Yes, I am, thank you.' More or less.

'He said, then, when you're ready would you join him in the diningroom?'

'The rocks?'

She gave me a small smile. 'He was up before me this morning, and had his breakfast on a tray in there. Shall I tell him you'll come down?'

'Please.'

When she had gone, and while I was slowly dressing, the telephone bell rang. Not long afterwards, Charles himself came upstairs.

'That was the police,' he said abruptly, with a frown. 'Apparently they've found a body and they want you to go and identify it.'

'Whose body, for heaven's sake?'

'They didn't say. They said they would send a car for you immediately, though. I gathered they really rang here to locate you.'

'I haven't any relatives. It must be a mistake.'

He shrugged. 'We'll know soon, anyway. Come down now and test me on the quartz. I think I've got it taped at last.'

We went down to the dining-room, where I found he was right. He went round the whole lot without a mistake. I changed the order in which they stood, but it didn't throw him. He smiled, very pleased with himself.

'Word perfect,' he said. Let's put them up on the shelves now. At least, we'll put all the least valuable ones up there and the gem stones in the bookcase in the drawing-room – that one with the curtains inside the glass doors.

'They ought to be in a safe.' I had said it yesterday evening as well.

'They were quite all right on the dining-room table last night, in spite of your fears.'

'As the consultant private detective in the case I still advise a safe.'

He laughed. 'You know bloody well I haven't got a safe. But as consultant private detective you can guard the things properly tonight. You can put them under your pillow. How's that?

'O.K.' I nodded.

'You're not serious?'

'Well no . . . they'd be too hard under the pillow.'

'Damn it . . .'

'But upstairs, either with you or me, yes. Some of those stones really are valuable. You must have had to pay a big insurance premium on them.'

'Er . . . no,' admitted Charles. 'I guaranteed to replace anything which was damaged or lost.'

I goggled. 'I know you're rich, but . . . you're an absolute nut. Get them insured at once. Have you any idea what each specimen is worth?'

'No, as a matter of fact . . . no. I didn't ask.'

'Well, if you've got a collector coming to stay, he'll expect you to remember how much you paid for each.'

'I thought of that,' he interrupted. 'I inherited them all from a distant cousin. That covers a lot of ignorance, not only costs and values but about crystalography and distribution and rarity, and everything specialised. I found I couldn't possibly learn enough in one day. Just to be able to show some familiarity with the collection should be enough.'

'That's fair enough. But you ring the Carver Foundation at once and find out what the stones are worth just the same, and then get straight on to your broker. The trouble with you, Charles, is that you are too honest. Other people aren't. This is the bad rough world you're in now, not the Navy.'

'Very well,' he said amicably. 'I'll do as you say. Hand me that inventory.'

He went to the telephone and I began putting the chunks of quartz on the empty bookshelves, but before I had done much the front door bell rang. Mrs. Cross went to answer it and presently came to tell me that a policeman was asking for me.

I put my useless deformed left hand into my pocket, as I always did with strangers, and went into the hall. A tall heavy young man in uniform stood there, giving the impression of trying not to be overawed by his rather grand surroundings. I remembered how it felt.

'Is it about this body?' I asked.

'Yes, sir. I believe you are expecting us.'

'Whose body is it?'

'I don't know, sir, I was just asked to take you.'

'Well . . . where to?'

'Epping Forest, sir.'

'But that's miles away,' I protested.

'Yes, sir,' he agreed, with a touch of gloom.

'Are you sure it's me that's wanted?'

'Oh, positive, sir.'

Well, all right. Sit down a minute while I get my coat and say where I'm going.'

The policeman drove on his gears, which I found tiring. It took two hours to go from Aynsford, west of Oxford, to Epping Forest, and it was much too long. Finally, however, we were met at a cross-roads by another policeman on a motor cycle, and followed him down a twisting secondary road. The forest stretched away all round, bare-branched and mournful in the grey damp day.

Round the bend we came on a row of two cars and a van, parked. The motor cyclist stopped and dismounted, and the policeman and I got out.

'ETA 12.15,' said the motor cyclist looking at his watch. 'You're late. The brass has been waiting twenty minutes.'

'Traffic like caterpillars on the A40,' said my driver defensively.

'You should have used your bell,' the motor cyclist grinned. 'Come on. It's over this way.'

He led us down a barely perceptible track into the wood. We walked on dead brown leaves, rustling . After about half a mile we came to a group of men standing round a screen made of hessian. They were stamping their feet to keep warm and talking in quiet voices.

'Mr. Halley?' One of them shook hands, a pleasant capable looking man in middle age who introduced himself as Chief-Inspector Cornish. 'We're sorry to bring you here all this way, but we want you to see the er . . . remains . . . before we remove them. I'd better warn you, it's a perfectly horrible sight.' He gave a very human shudder.

'Who is it?' I asked.

'We're hoping you can tell us that, for sure. We think . . . but we'd like you to tell us without us putting it into your head. All right? Now?'

I nodded. He showed me round the screen.

It was Andrews. What was left of him. He had been dead a long time, and the Epping scavengers seemed to have found him tasty I could see why the police had wanted me to see him *in situ*. He was going to fall to pieces as soon as they moved him.

'Well?'

'Thomas Andrews,' I said.

They relaxed. 'Are you sure? Positive?'

'Yes.'

'It's not just his clothes?'

'No. The shape of the hair-line. Protruding ears. Exceptionally rounded helix, vestigial lobes. Very short eyebrows, thick near the nose. Spatulate thumbs, white marks across nails. Hair growing on backs of phalanges.'

'Good,' said Cornish. 'That's conclusive, I'd say. We made a preliminary identification fairly early because of the clothes – they were detailed on the wanted-for-questioning list, of course. But our first enquiries were negative. He seems to have no family, and no one could remember that he had any distinguishing marks – no tattoos, no scars, no operations, and as far as we could find out he hadn't been to a dentist all his life.'

'It was intelligent of you to check all that before you gave him to the pathologist,' I remarked.

'It was the pathologist's idea actually.' he smiled.

'Who found him? ' I asked.

'Some boys. It's usually boys who find bodies.'

'When?'

'Three days ago. But obviously he's been here weeks, probably from very soon after he took a pot at you.'

'Yes. Is the gun still in his pocket.'

Cornish shook his head. 'No sign of it.'

'You don't know how he died?' I asked.

'No not yet. But now you've identified him we can get on with it.'

We went out from behind the screen and some of the other men went in with a stretcher. I didn't envy them.

Cornish turned to walk back to the road with me, the driver following at a short distance. We went fairly slowly, talking about Andrews, but it seemed more like eight miles than eight hundred yards. I wasn't quite ready for jolly country rambles.

As we reached the cars he asked me to lunch with him. I shook my head, explained about the diet, and suggested a drink instead.

'Fine,' he said. 'We could both do with one after that.' He jerked his head in the direction of Andrews. 'There's a good pub down the road this way. Your driver can follow us.'

He climbed into his car and we drove after him.

In the bar, equipped with a large brandy and water for me and a whisky and sandwiches for him, we sat at a black oak table, on chintzy chairs, surrounded by horse brasses, hunting horns, warming pans and pewter pots.

'It's funny meeting you like this,' said Cornish, in between bites. 'I've watched you so often racing. You've won a tidy bit for me in your time. I hardly missed a meeting on the old Dunstable course, before they sold it for building. I don't get so much racing now, it's so far to a course. Nowhere now to slip along for a couple of hours in the afternoon.' He grinned cheerfully and went on, 'You gave us some rare treats at Dunstable. Remember the day you rode that ding-dong finish on Brushwood?'

'I remember,' I said.

'You literally picked that horse up and carried him home.' He took another bite. 'I never heard such cheering. There's no mistake about it, you were something. Pity you had to give it up.'

'Yes . . .'

'Still, I suppose that's a risk you run, steeplechasing. There is always one crash too many.'

'That's right.'

'Where was it you finally bought it?'

'At Stratford on Avon, two years ago last May.'

He shook his head sympathetically, 'Rotten bad luck.'

I smiled. 'I'd had a pretty good run, though, before that.'

'I'll say you did.' He smacked his palm on the table. 'I took the Missus down to Kempton on Boxing Day, three or four years ago . . .' He went on talking with enjoyment about races he had watched, revealing himself as a true enthusiast, one of the people without whose interest all racing would collapse. Finally, regretfully, he finished his whisky and looked at his watch. 'I'll have to get back. I've enjoyed meeting you. 'It's odd how things work out, isn't it? I don't suppose you ever thought when you were riding that you would be good at this sort of work.'

'What do you mean, good?' I asked surprised.

'Hm? Oh, Andrews, of course. That description of his clothes you gave after he had shot you. And identifying him today. Most professional. Very efficient.' He grinned.

'Getting shot wasn't very efficient,' I pointed out.

He shrugged. 'That could happen to anyone, believe me . . . I shouldn't worry about that.'

I smiled, as the driver jerked me back to Aynsford, at the thought that anyone could believe me good at detective work. There was a simple explanation of my being able to describe and identify – I had read so many Missing Persons and Divorce files. The band of ex-policemen who compiled them knew what to base identification on, the unchanging things like ears and hands, not hair colour or the wearing of spectacles or a moustache. One of them had told me without pride that wigs, beards, face-padding, and the wearing of or omission of cosmetics made no impression on him, because they were not what he looked at. 'Ears and fingers,' he said, 'they can't disguise those. They never think of trying. Stick to ears and fingers, and you don't go far wrong.'

Ears and fingers were just about all there was left of Andrews to identify. The unappetising gristly bits.

The driver decanted me at Charles' back door and I walked along the passage to the hall. When I had one foot on the botton tread of the staircase Charles himself appeared at the drawing-room door.

'Oh, hullo, I thought it might be you. Come in here and look at these.'

Reluctantly leaving the support of the banisters I followed him into the drawing-room.

'There,' he said, pointing. He had fixed up a strip of light inside the bookcase and it shone down on to the quartz gems, bringing them to sparkling life. The open doors with their red silk curtains made a softly glowing frame. It was an eye-catching and effective arrangement, and I told him so.

'Good. The light goes on automatically when the doors are open . . . nifty, don't you think ?' He laughed. 'And you can set your mind at rest. They are now insured.'

'That's good.'

He shut the doors of the bookcase and the light inside went out. The red curtains discreetly hid their treasure. Turning to me more seriously, he said, 'Whose body?'

'Andrews.'

'The man who shot you? How extraordinary. Suicide?'

'No, I don't think so. The gun wasn't there, anyway.'

He made a quick gesture towards the chair. 'My dear Sid, sit down, sit down. You look like d . . . er . . . a bit worn out. You shouldn't have gone all that way. Put your feet up, I'll get you a drink.' He fussed over me like a mother hen, fetching me first water, then brandy, and finally a cup of warm beef juice from Mrs. Cross, and sat opposite me watching while I despatched it.

'Do you like that stuff?' he asked.

'Yes, luckily.'

'We used to have it when we were children. A ritual once a week. My father used to drain it out of the Sunday joint, propping the dish on the carving fork. We all loved it, but I haven't had it for years.'

'Try some?' I offered him the cup.

He took it and tasted it. 'Yes, it's good. Takes me back sixty years . . .' He smiled companionably, relaxing in his chair, and I told him about Andrews and the long-dead state he was in.

'It sounds,' he said slowly, 'as if he might have been murdered.'

'I wouldn't be surprised. He was young and healthy. He wouldn't just lie down and die of exposure in Essex.'

Charles laughed.

'What time are your guests expected?' I asked, glancing at the clock. It was just after five.

'About six.'

'I think I'll go up and lie on my bed for a while, then.'

'You are all right, Sid, aren't you? I mean, really all right?'

'Oh yes. Just tired.'

'Will you come down to dinner?' There was the faintest undercurrent of disappointment in his casual voice. I thought of all his hard work with the rocks and the amount of manoeuvring he had done. Besides, I was getting definitely curious about his intentions.

'Yes,' I nodded, getting up. 'Lay me a teaspoon.'

I made it upstairs and lay on my bed, sweating. And cursing. Although the bullet had missed everything vital in tearing holes in my gut, it had singed and upset a couple of nerves, and they warned me in the hospital that it would be some time before I felt well. It didn't please me that so far they were right.

I heard the visitors arrive, heard their loud cheerful voices as they were shown up to their rooms, the doors shutting, the bath waters running, the various bumps and murmurs from the adjoining rooms; and eventually the diminishing chatter as they finished changing and went downstairs past my door. I heaved myself off the bed, took off the loose-waisted slacks and jersey shirt I felt most comfortable in, and put on a white cotton shirt and grey suit.

My face looked back at me, pale, gaunt and dark-eyed, as I brushed my hair. A bit of death's head at the feast. I grinned nastily at my reflection. It was only a slight improvement.

Chapter Three

By the time I got to the foot of the stairs, Charles and his guests were coming across the hall from the drawing-room to the dining-room. The men all wore dinner jackets and the women, long dresses. Charles deliberately hadn't warned me, I reflected. He knew my convalescent kit didn't include a black tie.

He didn't stop and introduce me to his guests, but nodded slightly and went on into the dining-room, talking with charm to the rounded, fluffy little woman who walked beside him. Behind came Viola and a tall dark girl of striking good looks. Viola, Charles's elderly widowed cousin, gave me a passing half-smile, embarrassed and worried. In wondered what was the matter: normally she greeted me with affection, and it was only a short time since she had written warm wishes for my recovery. The girl beside her barely glanced in my direction, and the two men bringing up the rear didn't look at me at all.

Shrugging, I followed them into the dining-room. There was no mistaking the place laid for me: it consisted, in actual fact, of a spoon, a mat, a glass, and a fork, and it was situated in the centre of one the sides. Opposite me was an empty gap. Charles seated his guests, himself in his usual place at the end of the table, with fluffy Mrs. van Dysart on his right, and the striking Mrs. Kraye on his left. I sat between Mrs. Kraye and Rex van Dysart. It was only gradually that I sorted everyone out. Charles made no introductions whatever.

The groups at each end of the table fell into animated chat and paid me as much attention as a speed limit. I began to think I would go back to bed.

The manservant whom Charles engaged on these occasions served small individual tureens of turtle soup. My tureen, I found, contained more beef juice. Bread was passed, spoons clinked, salt and pepper were shaken and the meal began. Still no one spoke to me, though the visitors were growing slightly curious. Mrs. van Dysart flicked her sharp china blue eyes from Charles to me and back again, inviting an introduction. None came. He went on talking to the two women with almost over-powering charm, apparently oblivious.

Rex van Dysart on my left offered me bread with lifted eyebrows and a faint non-commital smile. He was a large man with a flat white face, heavy black rimmed spectacles and a domineering manner. When I refused the bread he put the basket down on the table, gave me the briefest of nods, and turned back to Viola.

Even before he brought quartz into the conversation I guessed it was for Howard Kraye that the show was being put on; and I disliked him on sight with a hackle-raising antipathy that disconcerted me. If Charles was planning that I should ever work for, or with, or near Mr. Kraye, I thought, he could think again.

He was a substantial man of about forty-eight to fifty, with shoulders, waist and hips all knocking forty-four. The dinner jacket sat on him with the ease of a second skin, and when he shot his cuffs occasionally he did so without affectation, showing off noticeably well manicured hands.

He had tidy grey-brown hair, straight eyebrows, narrow nose, small firm mouth, rounded freshly shaven chin, and very high unwrinkled lower eyelids, which gave him a secret, shuttered look.

A neat enclosed face like a mask, with perhaps something rotten underneath. You could almost smell it across the dinner table. I guessed, rather fancifully, that he knew too much about too many vices. But on top he was smooth. Much too smooth. In my book, a nasty type of phony. I listened to him talking to Viola.

'. . . So when Doria and I got to New York I looked up those fellows in that fancy crystal palace on First Avenue and got them moving. You have to give the clothes-horse diplomats a lead, you know, they've absolutely no initiative of their own. Look, I told them, unilateral action is not only inadvisable, it's impracticable. But they are so steeped in their own brand of pragmatism that informed opinion has as much chance of osmosing as mercury through rhyolite . . .'

Viola was nodding wisely while not understanding a word. The pretentious rigmarole floated comfortably over her sensible head and left her unmoved. But its flashiness seemed to me to be part of a gigantic confidence trick: one was meant to be enormously impressed. I couldn't believe that Charles had fallen under his spell. It was impossible. Not my subtle, clever, cool-headed father-in-law. Mr. van Dysart, however, hung on every word.

By the end of the soup his wife at the other end of the table could contain her curiosity no longer. She put down her spoon, and with her eyes on me said to Charles in a low but clearly audible voice, 'Who is that?'

All the heads turned towards him, as if they had been waiting for the question. Charles lifted his chin and spoke distinctly, so that they should all hear the answer.

'That,' he said, 'is my son-in-law.' His tone was light, amused, and infinitely contemptuous; and it jabbed raw on a nerve I had thought long dead. I looked at him sharply, and his eyes met mine, blank and expressionless.

My gaze slid up over and past his head to the wall behind him. There for some years, and certainly that morning, had hung an oil painting of me on a horse going over a fence at Cheltenham. In its place there was now an old-fashioned seascape, brown with Victorian varnish.

Charles was watching me. I looked back at him briefly and said nothing. I suppose he knew I wouldn't. My only defence against his insults long ago had been silence, and he was counting on my instant reaction being the same again.

Mrs. van Dysart leaned forward a little, and with waking malice murmured, 'Do go on, Admiral.'

Without hesitation Charles obeyed her, in the same flaying voice. 'He was fathered, as far as he knows, by a window cleaner on a nineteen-year-old unmarried girl from the Liverpool slums. She later worked, I believe, as a packer in a biscuit factory.'

'Admiral, no!' exclaimed Mrs. van Dysart breathlessly.

'Indeed yes,' nodded Charles. 'As you might guess, I did my best to stop my daughter making such an unsuitable match. He is small, as you see, and he has a crippled hand. Working class and undersized . . . but my daughter was determined. You know what girls are.' He sighed.

'Perhaps she was sorry for him,' suggested Mrs. van Dysart.

'Maybe,' said Charles. He hadn't finished, and wasn't to be deflected. 'If she had met him as a student of some sort, one might have understood it . . . but he isn't even educated. He finished school at fifteen to be apprenticed to a trade. He has been unemployed now for some time. My daughter, I may say, has left him.'

I sat like stone, looking down at the congealed puddle at the bottom of my soup dish, trying to loosen the clamped muscles in my jaw, and to think straight. Not four hours ago he'd shown concern for me and had drunk from my cup. As far as I could ever be certain of anything, his affection for me was genuine and unchanged. So he must have a good reason for what he was doing to me now. At least I hoped so.

I glanced at Viola. She hadn't protested. She was looking unhappily down at her place. I remembered her embarrassment out in the hall, and I guessed that Charles had warned her what to expect. He might have warned me too, I thought grimly.

Not unexpectedly, they were all looking at me. The dark and beautiful Doria Kraye raised her lovely eyebrows and in a flat, slightly nasal voice, remarked, 'You don't take offence, then.' It was half-way to a sneer. Clearly she thought I ought to take offence, if I had any guts.

'He is not offended,' said Charles easily. 'Why should the truth offend?'

'Is it true then,' asked Doria down her flawless nose, 'that you are illegitimate, and all the rest?'

I took a deep breath and eased my muscles.

'Yes.'

There was an uncomfortable short silence. Doria said, 'Oh,' blankly, and began to crumble her bread.

On cue, and no doubt summoned by Charles' foot on the bell, the manservant came in to remove the plates, and conversation trickled back to the party like cigarette smoke after a cancer scare.

I sat thinking of the details Charles had left out: the fact that my twenty-year-old father, working overtime for extra cash, had fallen from a high ladder and been killed three days before his wedding day, and that I had been born eight months later. The fact that my young mother, finding that she was dying from some obscure kidney ailment, had taken me from grammar school at fifteen, and because I was small for my age had apprenticed me to a racehorse trainer in Newmarket, so that I should have a home and someone to turn to when she had gone. They had been good enough people, both of them, and Charles knew that I thought so.

The next course was some sort of fish smothered in mushroom coloured sauce. My astronaut's delight, coming at the same time, didn't look noticeably different, as it was not in its pot, but out on a plate. Dear Mrs. Cross, I thought fervently, I could kiss you. I could eat it this way with a fork, single-handed. The pots needed to be held; in my case inelegantly hugged between forearm and chest; and at that moment I would have starved rather than take my left hand out of my pocket.

Fluffy Mrs. van Dysart was having a ball. Clearly she relished the idea of me sitting there practically isolated, dressed in the wrong clothes, and an object of open derision to her host. With her fair frizzy hair, her baby-blue eyes and her rose pink silk dress embroidered with silver, she looked as sweet as sugar icing. What she said showed that she thoroughly understood the pleasures of keeping a whipping boy.

'Poor relations are such a problem, aren't they?' she said to Charles sympathetically, and intentionally loud enough for me to hear. 'You can't neglect them in our position, in case the Sunday papers get hold of them and pay them to make a smear. And it's especially difficult if one has to keep them in one's own house . . . one can't, I suppose, put them to eat in the kitchen, but there are so many occasions when one could do without them. Perhaps a tray upstairs is the best thing.'

'Ah, yes,' nodded Charles smoothly, 'but they won't always agree to that.'

I half choked on a mouthful, remembering the pressure he had exerted to get me downstairs. And immediately I felt not only reassured but deeply interested. This, then, was what he had been so industriously planning, the destruction of me as a man in the eyes of his guests. He would no doubt explain why in his own good time. Meanwhile I felt slightly less inclined to go back to bed.

I glanced at Kraye, and found his greenish-amber eyes steady on my face. It wasn't as overt as in Mrs. van Dysart's case, but it was there: pleasure. My toes curled inside my shoes. Interested or not, it went hard to sit tight before that loathsome, taunting half-smile. I looked down, away blotting him out.

He gave a sound half-way between a cough and a laugh, turned his head, and began talking down the table to Charles about the collection of quartz.

'So sensible of you, my dear chap, to keep them all behind glass, though most tantalising to me from here. Is that a geode, on the middle shelf? The reflection, you know . . . I can't quite see.'

'Er . . .' said Charles, not knowing any more than I did what a geode was. 'I'm looking forward to showing them to you. After dinner, perhaps? Or tomorrow?'

'Oh, tonight, I'd hate to postpone such a treat. Did you say that you had any felspar in your collection?'

'No,' said Charles uncertainly.

'No, well, I can see it is a small specialised collection. Perhaps you are wise in sticking to silicon dioxide.'

Charles glibly launched into the cousinly-bequest alibi for ignorance, which Kraye accepted with courtesy and disappointment.

'A fascinating subject, though, my dear Roland. It repays study. The earth beneath our feet, the fundamental sediment from the Triassic and Jurassic epochs, is our priceless inheritance, the source of all our life and power . . . There is nothing which interests me so much as land.'

Doria on my right gave the tiniest of snorts, which her husband didn't hear. He was busy constructing another long, polysyllabic and largely unintelligible chat on the nature of the universe.

I sat unoccupied through the steaks, the meringue pudding, the cheese and the fruit. Conversations went on on either side of me and occasionally past me, but a deaf mute could have taken as much part as I did. Mrs. van Dysart commented on the difficulties of feeding poor relations with delicate stomachs and choosey appetites. Charles neglected to tell her that I had been shot and wasn't poor, but agreed that a weak digestion in dependants was a moral fault. Mrs. van Dysart loved it. Doria occasionally looked at me as if I were an interesting specimen of low life. Rex van Dysart again offered me the bread; and that was that. Finally Viola shepherded Doria and Mrs. van Dysart out to have coffee in the drawing-room and Charles offered his guests port and brandy. He passed me the brandy bottle with an air of irritation and compressed his lips in disapproval when I took some. It wasn't lost on his guests.

After a while he rose, opened the glass bookcase doors, and showed the quartz to Kraye. Piece by piece the two discussed their way along the rows, with van Dysart standing beside them exhibiting polite interest and hiding his yawns of boredom. I stayed sitting down. I also helped myself to some more brandy.

Charles kept his end up very well and went through the whole lot without a mistake. He then transferred to the drawing-room, where his gem cabinet proved a great success. I tagged along, sat in an unobtrusive chair and listened to them all talking, but I came to no conclusions except that if I didn't soon go upstairs I wouldn't get there under my own steam. It was eleven o'clock and I had had a long day. Charles didn't look round when I left the room.

Half an hour later, when his guests had come murmuring up to their rooms, he came quietly through my door and over to the bed. I was still lying on top in my shirt and trousers, trying to summon some energy to finish undressing.

He stood looking down at me, smiling.

'Well?' he said.

'It is you,' I said, 'who is the dyed-in-the-wool, twenty-four carat, unmitigated bastard.'

He laughed. 'I thought you were going to spoil the whole thing when you saw your picture had gone.' He began taking off my shoes and socks. 'You looked as bleak as the Bering Strait in December. Pyjamas?'

'Under the pillow.'

He helped me undress in his quick neat naval fashion.

'Why did you do it?' I said.

He waited until I was lying between the sheets, then he perched on the edge of the bed.

'Did you mind?'

'Hell, Charles . . . of course. At first anyway.'

'I'm afraid it came out beastlier than I expected, but I'll tell you why I did it. Do you remember that first game of chess we had? When you beat me out of sight? You know why you won so easily?'

'You weren't paying enough attention.'

'Exactly. I wasn't paying enough attention, because I didn't think you were an opponent worth bothering about. A bad tactical error.' He grinned. 'An admiral should know better. If you underrate a strong opponent you are at a disadvantage. If you grossly underrate him, if you are convinced he is of absolutely no account, you prepare no defence and are certain to be defeated.' He paused for a moment, and went on. 'It is therefore good strategy to delude the enemy into believing you are too weak to be considered. And that is what I was doing tonight on your behalf.'

He looked at me gravely. After some seconds I said, 'At what game, exactly, do you expect me to play Howard Kraye?'

He sighed contentedly, and smiled. 'Do you remember what he said interested him most?'

I thought back. 'Land.'

Charles nodded. 'Land. That's right. He collects it. Chunks of it, yards of it, acres of it . . .' He hesitated.

'Well?'

'You can play him,' he said slowly, 'for Seabury Racecourse.'

The enormity of it took my breath away.

'What?' I said incredulously. 'Don't be silly. I'm only . . .'

'Shut up,' he interrupted. 'I don't want to hear what you think you are only. You're intelligent, aren't you? You work for a detective agency? You wouldn't want Seabury to close down? Why shouldn't you do something about it?'

'But I imagine he's after some sort of take-over bid, from what you say. You want some powerful city chap or other to oppose him, not . . . me.'

'He is very much on his guard against powerful chaps in the city, but wide open to you.'

I stopped arguing because the implications were pushing into the background my inadequacy for such a task.

'Are you sure he is after Seabury?' I asked.

'Someone is,' said Charles. 'There has been a lot of buying and selling of the shares lately, and the price per share is up although they haven't paid a dividend this year. The Clerk of the Course told me about it. He said that the directors are very worried. On paper, there is no great concentration of shares in any one name, but there wasn't at Dunstable either. There, when it came to a vote on selling out to a land developer, they found that about twenty various nominees were in fact all agents for

Kraye. He carried enough of the other shareholders with him, and the racecourse was lost to housing.'

'It was all legal, though?'

'A wangle; but legal, yes. And it looks like happening again.'

'But what's to stop him, if it's legal?'

'You might try.'

I stared at him in silence. He stood up and straightened the bedcover neatly. 'It would be a pity if Seabury went the way of Dunstable.' He went towards the door.

'Where does van Dysart fit in?' I asked.

'Oh,' he said, turning, 'nowhere. I met them only a week or two ago. They're on a visit from South Africa, and I was sure they wouldn't know you. And it was Mrs. van Dysart I wanted. She has a tongue like a rattlesnake. I knew she would help me tear you to pieces.' He grinned. 'She'll give you a terrible week-end, I'm glad to say.'

'Thanks very much,' I said sarcastically.

'I was a bit worried that Kraye would know you by sight,' he said thoughtfully. 'But he obviously doesn't, so that's all right. And I didn't mention your name tonight, as you probably noticed. I am being careful not to.' He smiled. 'And he doesn't know my daughter married Sid Halley . . . I've given him several opportunities of mentioning it, because of course none of this would have been possible if he'd known, but he hasn't responded at all. As far as Kraye is concerned,' he finished with satisfaction, 'you are a pathetic cypher.'

I said, 'Why didn't you tell me all this before? When you so carefully left me that book on company law for instance? Or at least this evening when I came back from seeing Andrews, so that I could have been prepared, at dinner?'

He opened the door and smiled across the room, his eyes blank again. 'Sleep well,' he said. 'Good night, Sid.'

Charles took the two men out shooting the following morning, and Viola drove their wives into Oxford to do some shopping and visit an exhibition of Venetian glass. I took the opportunity of having a good look round the Krayes' bedroom.

It wasn't until I'd been there for more than ten minutes that it struck me that two years earlier I wouldn't have dreamed of doing such a thing. Now I had done it as a matter of course, without thinking twice. I grinned sardonically. Evidently even in just sitting around in a detective agency one caught an attitude of mind. I realised, moreover, that I had instinctively gone about my search methodically and with a careful touch. In an odd way it was extremely disconcerting.

I wasn't of course looking for anything special: just digging a little into the Krayes' characters. I wouldn't even concede in my own mind that I was interested in the challenge Charles had so elaborately thrown down. But all the same I searched, and thoroughly.

Howard Kraye slept in crimson pyjamas with his initials embroidered in white on the pocket. His dressing-gown was of crimson brocade with a black quilted collar and black tassels on the belt. His washing things, neatly arranged in a large fitted toilet case in the adjoining bathroom, were numerous and ornate. He used pine scented after-shave lotion, cologne friction rub, lemon hand cream, and an oily hair dressing, all from gold-topped cut-glass bottles. There were also medicated soap tablets, special formula toothpaste, talcum powder in a gilt container, deodorant, and a supersonic looking electric razor. He wore false teeth and had a spare set. He had brought a half full tin of laxatives, some fruit salts, a bottle of mouth wash, some antiseptic foot powder, penicillin throat lozenges, a spot sealing stick, digestive tablets and an eye bath. The body beautiful, in and out.

All his clothes, down to his vests and pants, had been made to measure, and he had brought enough to cover every possibility of a country week-end. I went through the pockets of his dinner-jacket and the three suits hanging beside it, but he was a tidy man and they were all empty, except for a nail file in each breast pocket. His six various pairs of shoes were hand-made and nearly new. I looked into each shoe separately, but except for trees they were all empty.

In a drawer I found neatly arranged his stock of ties, handkerchiefs, and socks: all expensive. A heavy chased silver box contained cuff links, studs, and tie pins; mostly of gold. He had avoided jewels, but one attractive pair of cuff links was made from pieces of what I now knew enough to identify as tiger-eye. The backs of his hairbrushes were beautiful slabs of the gem stone, smoky quartz. A few brown and grey hairs were lodged in between the bristles.

There remained only his luggage, four lavish suitcases standing in a neat row beside the wardrobe. I opened each one. They were all empty except for the smallest, which contained a brown calf attaché case. I looked at it carefully before I touched it, but as Kraye didn't seem to have left any tell-tales like hairs or pieces of cotton attached, I lifted it out and put it on one of the beds. It was locked, but I had learnt how to deal with such drawbacks. A lugubrious ex-police sergeant on Radnor's payroll gave me progressively harder lessons in lock-picking every time he came into the office between jobs, moaning all the while about the damage the London soot did to his chrysanthemums. My one-handedness he had seen only as a challenge, and had invented a couple of new techniques and instruments entirely for my benefit. Recently he had presented me with a collection of fine delicate keys which he had once removed from a burglar, and had bullied me until I carried them with me everywhere. They were in my room. I went and fetched them and without much trouble opened the case.

It was as meticulously tidy as everything else, and I was particularly careful not to alter the position or order of any of the papers. There were several letters from a stockbroker, a bunch of share transfer certificates, various oddments, and a series of typed sheets, headed with the previous day's date, which were apparently an up to the minute analysis of his investments. He seemed to be a rich man and to do a good deal of buying and selling. He had money in oils, mines, property and industrial stocks. There was also a sheet headed simply S.R., on which every transaction was a purchase. Against each entry was a name and the address of a bank. Some names occurred three or four times, some only once.

Underneath the papers lay a large thick brown envelope inside which were two packets of new ten pound notes. I didn't count, but there couldn't have been fewer than a hundred of them. The envelope was at the bottom of the case, except for a writing board with slightly used white blotting paper held by crocodile and gold corners. I pulled up the board and found underneath it two more sheets of paper, both covered with dates, initials, and sums of money.

I let the whole lot fall back into place, made sure that everything looked exactly as I had found it, relocked the case, and put it back into its covering suitcase.

The divine Doria, I found, was far from being as tidy as her husband. All her things were in a glorious jumble, which made leaving them undisturbed a difficult job, but also meant that she would be less likely than her husband to notice if anything were slightly out of place.

Her clothes, though they looked and felt expensive, were bought ready-made and casually treated. Her washing things consisted of a plastic zipped case, a flannel, a tooth brush, bath essence, and a puffing bottle of talc. Almost stark beside Howard's collection. No medicine. She appeared to wear nothing in bed, but a pretty white quilted dressing-gown hung half off a hanger behind the bathroom door.

She had not completely unpacked. Suitcases propped on chairs and stools still held stirred-up underclothes and various ultra feminine equipment which I hadn't seen since Jenny left.

The top of the dressing-table, though the daily seemed to have done her best to dust it, was an expensive chaos. Pots of cosmetics, bottles of scent and hair spray stood on one side, a box of tissues, a scarf, and the cluttered tray out of the top of a dressing-case filled the other. The dressing-case itself, of crocodile with gold clips, stood on the floor. I picked it up and put it on the bed. It was locked. I unlocked it, and looked inside.

Doria was quite a girl. She possessed two sets of false eyelashes, spare finger nails, and a hair piece on a tortoiseshell headband. Her big jewel case, the one tidy thing in her whole luggage, contained on the top layer the sapphire and diamond earrings she had worn the previous evening, along with a diamond sunburst brooch and a sapphire ring; and on the lower layer a second necklace, bracelet, earrings, brooch and ring all of gold, platinum, and citrine. The yellow jewels were uncommon, barbaric in design, and had no doubt been made especially for her.

Under the jewel case were four paper-back novels so pornographic in content as to raise doubts about Kraye's ability as a lover. Jenny had held that a truly satisfied woman didn't need to read dirty sex. Doria clearly did.

Alongside the books was a thick leather covered diary to which the beautiful Mrs. Kraye had confided the oddest thoughts. Her life seemed to be as untidy as her clothes, a mixture of ordinary social behaviour, dream fantasy and a perverted marriage relationship. If the diary were to be believed, she and Howard obtained deeper pleasure, both of them, from him beating her, than from the normal act of love. Well, I reflected, at least they were well matched. Some of the divorces which Hunt Radnor Associates dealt which arose because one partner alone was pain fixated, the other being revolted.

At the bottom of the case were two other objects of interest. First, coiled in a brown velvet bag, the sort of leather strap used by schoolmasters, at whose purpose, in view of the diary, it was easy to guess; and second, in a chocolate box, a gun.

Chapter Four

Telephoning for the local taxi to come and fetch me, I went to Oxford and bought a camera. Although the shop was starting a busy Saturday afternoon, the boy who served me tackled the problem of a one-handed photographer with enthusiasm and as if he had all the time in the world. Between us we sorted out a miniature German sixteen millimetre camera, three inches long by one and a half wide, which I could hold, set, snap and wind with one hand with the greatest ease.

He gave me a thorough lesson in how to work it, added an inch to its length in the shape of a screwed-on photo electric light meter, loaded it with film, and slid it into a black case so small that it made no bulge in my trouser pocket. He also offered to change the film later if I couldn't manage it. We parted on the best of terms.

When I got back everyone was sitting round a cosy fire in the drawing-room, eating crumpets. Very tantalising. I loved crumpets.

No one took much notice when I went in and sat down on the fringe of the circle except Mrs. van Dysart, who began sharpening her claws. She got in a couple of quick digs about spongers marrying girls for their money, and Charles didn't say that I hadn't. Viola looked at me searchingly, worry opening her mouth. I winked, and she shut it again in relief.

I gathered that the morning's bag had been the usual mixture (two brace of pheasant, five wild duck and a hare), because Charles preferred a rough shoot over his own land to organised affairs with beaters. The women had collected a poor opinion of Oxford shop assistants and a booklet on the manufacture of fifteenth-century Italian glass. All very normal for a country week-end. It was my snooping which seemed unreal. That, and the false position Charles had steered me into.

Kraye's gaze, and finally his hands, strayed back to the gem bookshelves. Again the door was opened, Charles' trick lighting working effectively, and one by one the gems were brought out, passed round and closely admired. Mrs. van Dysart seemed much attached to a spectacular piece of rose quartz, playing with it to make light strike sparks from it, and smoothing her fingers over the glossy surface.

'Rex, you must collect some of this for me!' she ordered, her will showing like iron inside the fluff: and masterful looking Rex nodded his meek agreement.

Kraye was saying, 'You know, Roland, these are really remarkably fine specimens. Among the best I've ever seen. Your cousin must have been extremely fortunate and influential to acquire so many fine crystals.'

'Oh, indeed he was,' agreed Charles equably.

'I should be interested if you ever think of realising on them . . . a first option, perhaps?'

'You can have a first option by all means,' smiled Charles. 'But I shan't be selling them, I assure you.'

'Ah well, so you say now. But I don't give up easily . . . I shall try you later. But don't forget, my first option?'

'Certainly,' said Charles. 'My word on it.'

Kraye smiled at the stone he held in his hands, a magnificent raw amethyst like a cluster of petrified violets.

'Don't let this fall into the fire,' he said. 'It would turn yellow.' He then treated everyone to a lecture on amethysts which would have been interesting had he made any attempt at simplicity: but blinding by words was with him either a habit or a policy. I wasn't certain which.

'. . . Manganese, of course occurring in geodes or agate nodules in South America or Russia, but with such a world-wide distribution it was only to be expected that elementary societies should ascribe to it supra rational inherencies and attributes . . .'

I suddenly found him looking straight at me, and I knew my expression had not been one of impressed admiration. More like quizzical sarcasm. He didn't like it. There was a quick flash in his eyes.

'It is symptomatic of the slum mentality,' he remarked, 'to scoff at what it can't comprehend.'

'Sid,' said Charles sharply, unconsciously giving away half my name, 'I'm sure you must have something else to do. We can let you go until dinner.'

I stood up. The natural anger rose quickly, but only as far as my teeth. I swallowed. 'Very well,' I muttered.

'Before you go, Sid,' said Mrs. van Dysart from the depths of a sofa, '. . . Sid, what a deliciously plebeian name, so suitable . . . Put these down on the table for me.'

She held out both hands, one stone in each and another balanced between them. I couldn't manage them all, and dropped them.

'Oh dear,' said Mrs. van Dysart, acidly sweet, as I knelt and picked them up, putting them one by one on the table, 'I forgot you were disabled, so silly of me.' She hadn't forgotten. 'Are you sure you can't get treatment for whatever is wrong with you? You ought to try some exercises, they'd do you the world of good. All you need is a little perseverance. You owe it to the Admiral, don't you think, to *try*?'

I didn't answer, and Charles at least had the grace to keep quiet.

'I know of a very good man over here,' went on Mrs. van Dysart. 'He used to work for the army at home . . . excellent at getting malingerers back into service. Now he's the sort of man who'd do you good. What do you think Admiral, shall I fix up for your son-in-law to see him?'

'Er . . .' said Charles, 'I don't think it would work.'

'Nonsense.' She was brisk and full of smiles. 'You can't let him lounge about doing nothing for the rest of his life. A good bracing course of treatment, that's what he needs. Now,' she said turning to me, 'so that I know exactly what I'm talking about when I make an appointment, let's see this precious crippled hand of yours.'

There was a tiny pause. I could feel their probing eyes, their unfriendly curiosity.

'No,' I said calmly. 'Excuse me, but no.'

As I walked across the room and out of the door her voice floated after me. 'There you are, Admiral, he doesn't *want* to get better. They're all the same . . .'

I lay on my bed for a couple of hours re-reading the book on company law, especially, now, the section on take-overs. It was no easier than it had been in the hospital, and now that I knew why I was reading it, it seemed more involved, not less. If the directors of Seabury were worried, they would surely have called in their own investigator. Someone who knew his way round the stock markets like I knew my way round the track. An expert. I wasn't at all the right sort of person to stop Kraye, even if indeed anyone could stop him. And yet . . . I stared at the ceiling, taking my lower lip between my teeth . . . and yet I did have a wild idea . . .

Viola came in, knocking as she opened the door.

'Sid, dear, are you all right? Can I do anything for you?' She shut the door, gentle, generous, and worried.

I sat up and swung my legs over the side of the bed. 'No thanks, I'm fine.'

She perched on the arm of an easy chair, looked at me with her kind, slightly mournful brown eyes, and said a little breathlessly, 'Sid, why are you letting Charles say such terrible things about you? It isn't only when you are there in the room, they've been, oh, almost sniggering about you behind your back. Charles and that frightful Mrs. van Dysart . . . What has happened between you and him? When you nearly died he couldn't have been more worried if you'd been his own son . . . but now he is so cruel, and terribly unfair.'

'Dear Viola, don't worry. It's only some game that Charles is playing, and I go along with him.'

'Yes,' she said, nodding. 'He warned me. He said that you were both going to lay a smoke screen and that I was on no account to say a single word in your defence the whole week-end. But it wasn't true, was it? When I saw your face, when Charles said that about your poor mother, I knew you didn't know what he was going to do.'

'Was it so obvious?' I said ruefully. 'Well, I promise you I haven't quarrelled with him. Will you just be a dear and do exactly as he asked? Don't say a single word to any of them about . . . um . . . the more successful bits of my life history, or about my job at the agency, or about the shooting. You didn't today, did you, the trip to Oxford?' I finished with some anxiety.

She shook her head. 'I thought I'd talk to you first.'

'Good,' I grinned.

'Oh dear,' she cried, partly in relief, partly in puzzlement. 'Well in that case, Charles asked me to pop in and make sure you would come down to dinner.'

'Oh he did, did he? Afraid I'll throw a boot at him, I should think, after sending me out of the room like that. Well, you just pop back to Charles and say that I'll come down to dinner on condition that he organises some chemmy afterwards, and includes me out.'

Dinner was a bit of a trial: with their smoked salmon and pheasant the guests enjoyed another round of Sid-baiting. Both the Krayes, egged on by Charles and the fluffy harpy beside him, had developed a pricking skill at this novel week-end parlour game, and I heartily wished Charles had never thought of it. However, he kept his side of the bargain by digging out the chemmy shoe, and after the coffee, the brandy, and another inspection of the dining-room quartz, he settled his guests firmly round the table in the drawing-room.

Upstairs, once the shoe was clicking regularly and the players were well involved, I went and collected Kraye's attaché case and took it along to my room.

Because I was never going to get another chance and did not want to miss something I might regret later, I photographed every single paper in the case. All the stockbroker's letters and all the investment reports. All the share certificates, and also the two separate sheets under the writing board.

Although I had an ultra-bright light bulb and the exposure meter to help me to get the right setting, I took several pictures at different light values of the papers I considered the most important, in order to be sure of getting the sharpest possible result. The little camera handled beautifully, and I found I could change the films in their tiny cassettes without much difficulty. By the time I had finished I had used three whole films of twenty exposures on each. It took me a long time, as I had to put the camera down between each shot to move the next paper into my pool of light, and also had to be very careful not to alter the order in which the papers had lain in the case.

The envelope of ten pound notes kept me hoping like crazy that Howard Kraye would not lose heavily and come upstairs for replacements. It seemed to me at the time a ridiculous thing to do, but I took the two flat blocks of tenners out of the envelope, and photographed them as well. Putting them back I flipped through them: the notes were new, consecutive, fifty to a packet. One thousand pounds to a penny.

When everything was back in the case I sat looking at the contents for a minute, checking their position against my visual memory of how they looked when I first saw them. At last satisfied, I shut the case, locked it, rubbed it over to remove any finger marks I might have left, and put it back where I had found it.

After that I went downstairs to the dining-room for the brandy I had refused at dinner. I needed it. Carrying the glass, I listened briefly outside the drawing-room door to the murmurs and clicks from within and went upstairs again, to bed.

Lying in the dark I reviewed the situation. Howard Kraye, drawn by the bait of a quartz collection, had accepted an invitation to a quiet week-end in the country with a retired admiral. With him he had brought a selection of private papers. As he had no possible reason to imagine that anyone in such innocent surroundings would spy on him, the papers might be very private indeed. So private that he felt safest when they were with him? Too private to leave at home? It would be nice to think so.

At that point, imperceptibly, I fell asleep.

The nerves in my abdomen wouldn't give up. After about five hours of fighting them unsuccessfully I decided that staying in bed all morning thinking about it was doing no good and got up and dressed.

Drawn partly against my will, I walked along the passage to Jenny's room, and went in. It was the small sunny room she had had as a child. She had gone back to it when she left me and it was all hers alone. I had never slept there. The single bed, the relics of childhood, girlish muslin frills on curtains and dressing-table, everything shut me out. The photographs round the room were of her father, her dead mother, her sister, brother-in-law, dogs and horses, but not of me. As far as she could, she had blotted out her marriage.

I walked slowly round touching her things, remembering how much I had loved her. Knowing, too, that there was no going back, and that if she walked through the door at that instant we would not fall into each other's arms in tearful reconciliation.

Removing a one-eyed teddy bear I sat down for a while on her pink armchair. It's difficult to say just where a marriage goes wrong, because the accepted reason often isn't the real one. The rows Jenny and I had had were all ostensibly caused by the same thing: my ambition. Grown finally too heavy for flat racing, I had switched entirely to steeplechasing the season before we married, and I wanted to be champion jumping jockey. To this end I was prepared to eat little, drink less, go to bed early, and not make love if I were racing the next day. It was unfortunate that she liked late-night parties and dancing more than anything else. At first she gave them up willingly, then less willingly, and finally in fury. After that, she started going on her own.

In the end she told me to choose between her and racing. But by then I was indeed champion jockey, and had been for some time, and I couldn't give it up. So Jenny left. It was just life's little irony that six months later I lost the racing as well. Gradually since then I had come to realise that a marriage didn't break up just because one half liked parties and the other didn't. I thought now that Jenny's insistence on a gay time was the result of my having failed her in some basic, deeply necessary way. Which did nothing whatsoever for my self-respect or my self-confidence.

I sighed, stood up, replaced the teddy bear, and went downstairs to the drawing-room. Eleven o'clock on a windy autumn morning.

Doria was alone in the big comfortable room, sitting on the window seat and reading the Sunday papers, which lay around her on the floor in a haphazard mess.

'Hello,' she said, looking up. 'What hole did you crawl out of?'

I walked over to the fire and didn't answer.

'Poor little man, are his feelings hurt then?'

'I do have feelings, the same as anyone else.'

'So you actually can talk?' she said mockingly. 'I'd begun to wonder.'

'Yes, I can talk.'

'Well, now, tell me all your troubles, little man.'

'Life is just a bowl of cherries.'

She uncurled herself from the window seat and came across to the fire, looking remarkably out of place in skin-tight leopard printed pants and a black silk shirt.

She was the same height as Jenny, the same height as me, just touching five foot six. As my smallness had always been an asset for racing, I never looked on it as a handicap for life in general, either physical or social. Neither had I ever really understood why so many people thought that height for its own sake was important. But it would have been naïve not to take note of the widespread extraordinary assumption that the mind and heart could be measured by tallness. The little man with the big emotion was a stock comic figure. It was utterly irrational. What difference did three or four inches of leg bone make to a man's essential nature? Perhaps I had been fortunate in coming to terms early with the effect of poor nutrition in a difficult childhood; but it did not stop me understanding why other short men struck back in defensive aggression. There were the pinpricks, for instance, of girls like Doria calling one 'little' and intending it as an insult.

'You've dug yourself into a cushy berth here, haven't you?' she said, taking a cigarette from the silver box on the mantelpiece.

'I suppose so.'

'If I were the Admiral I'd kick you out.'

'Thank you,' I said, neglecting to offer her a light. With a mean look she found a box of matches and struck one for herself.

'Are you ill, or something?'

'No. Why?'

'You eat those faddy health foods, and you look such a sickly little creature . . . I just wondered.' She blew the smoke down her nose. 'The Admiral's daughter must have been pretty desperate for a wedding ring.'

'Give her her due,' I said mildly. 'At least she didn't pick a rich father-figure twice her age.'

I thought for a moment she meant to go into the corny routine of smacking my face, but as it happened she was holding the cigarette in the hand she needed.

'You little shit,' she said instead. A charming girl, altogether.

'I get along.'

'Not with me, you don't.' Her face was tight. I had struck very deep, it seemed.

'Where is everyone else?' I asked, gesturing around the empty room.

'Out with the Admiral somewhere. And you can take yourself off again too. You're not wanted in here.'

'I'm not going. I live here, remember?'

'You went quick enough last night,' she sneered. 'When the Admiral says jump, you jump. But fast, little man. And that I like to see.'

'The Admiral,' I pointed out, 'is the hand that feeds. I don't bite it.'

'Boot-licking little creep.'

I grinned at her nastily and sat down in an arm-chair. I still didn't feel too good. Pea green and clammy, to be exact. Nothing to be done though, but wait for it to clear off.

Doria tapped ash off her cigarette and looked at me down her nose, thinking up her next attack. Before she could launch it, however, the door opened and her husband came in.

'Doria,' he said happily, not immediately seeing me in the arm-chair, 'where have you hidden my cigarette case? I shall punish you for it.'

She made a quick movement towards me with her hand and Howard saw me and stopped dead.

'What are you doing here?' he said brusquely, the fun-and-games dying abruptly out of his face and voice.

'Passing the time.'

'Clear out then. I want to talk to my wife.'

I shook my head and stayed put.

'Short of picking him up and throwing him out bodily,' said Doria, 'you won't get rid of him. I've tried.'

Kraye shrugged. 'Roland puts up with him. I suppose we can too.' He picked up one of the newspapers and sat down in an arm-chair facing me. Doria wandered back to the window-seat, pouting. Kraye straightened up the paper and began to read the front page. Across the back page, the racing page, facing me across the fireplace, the black, bold headlines jumped out.

'ANOTHER HALLEY?'

Underneath, side by side, were two photographs; one of me, and the other of a boy who had won a big race the day before.

It was by then essential that Kraye should not discover how Charles had misrepresented me; it had gone much too far to be explained away as a joke. The photograph was clearly printed for once. I knew it well. It was an old one which the papers had used several times before, chiefly because it was a good likeness. Even if none of the guests read the racing column, as Doria obviously hadn't, it might catch their eye in passing, through being in such a conspicuous place.

Kraye finished reading the front page and began to turn the paper over.

'Mr. Kraye,' I said. 'Do you have a very big quartz collection yourself?'

He lowered the paper a little and gave me an unenthusiastic glance.

'Yes, I have,' he said briefly.

'Then could you please tell me what would be a good thing to give the Admiral to add to his collection? And where would I get it, and how much would it cost?'

The paper folded over, hiding my picture. He cleared his throat and with strained politeness started to tell me about some obscure form of crystal which the Admiral didn't have. Press the right button, I thought ... Doria spoilt it. She walked jerkily over to Kraye and said crossly, 'Howard, for God's sake. The little creep is buttering you up. I bet he wants something. You're a sucker for anyone who will talk about rocks.'

'People don't make fools of me,' said Kraye flatly, his eyes narrowing in irritation.

'No. I only want to please the Admiral,' I explained.

'He's a sly little beast,' said Doria. 'I don't like him.'

Kraye shrugged, looked down at the newspaper and began to unfold it again.

'It's mutual,' I said casually. 'You Daddy's doll.'

Kraye stood up slowly and the paper slid to the floor, front page up. 'What did you say?'

'I said I didn't think much of your wife.'

He was outraged, as well he might be. He took a single step across the rug, and there was suddenly something more in the room than three guests sparring round a Sunday morning fire.

Even though I was as far as he knew an insignificant fly to swat, a clear quality of menace flowed out of him like a radio signal. The calm social mask had disappeared, along with the wordy, phony, surface personality. The vague suspicion I had gained from reading his papers, together with the antipathy I had felt for him all along, clarified into belated recognition: this was not just a smooth speculator operating near the legal border-line, but a full-blown, powerful, dangerous big-time crook.

Trust me, I thought, to prod an anthill and find a hornets' nest. Twist the tail of a grass snake and find a boa constrictor. What on earth would he be like, I wondered, if one did more to cross him than disparage his choice of wife.

'He's sweating,' said Doria, pleased. 'He's afraid of you.'

'Get up,' he said.

As I was sure that if I stood up he would simply knock me down again, I stayed where I was.

'I'll apologise,' I said.

'Oh no,' said Doria, 'that's much too easy.'

'Something subtle,' suggested Kraye, staring down.

'I know!' Doria was delighted with her idea. 'Let's get that hand out of his pocket.'

They both saw from my face that I would hate that more than anything. They both smiled. I thought of bolting, but it meant leaving the paper behind.

'That will do very nicely,' said Kraye. He leant down, twined one hand into the front of my jersey shirt and the other into my hair, and pulled me to my feet. The top of my head reached about to his chin. I wasn't in much physical shape for resisting, but I took a half-hearted swipe at him as I came up. Doria caught my swinging arm and twisted it up behind my back, using both of hers and an uncomfortable amount of pressure. She was a strong healthy girl with no inhibitions about hurting people.

'That'll teach you to be rude to me,' she said with satisfaction.

I thought of kicking her shins, but it would only have brought more retaliation. I also wished Charles would come back at once from wherever he was.

He didn't.

Kraye transferred his grip from my hair to my left forearm and began to pull. That arm was no longer much good, but I did my best. I tucked by elbow tight against my side, and my hand stayed in my pocket.

'Hold him harder,' he said to Doria. 'He's stronger than he looks.' She levered my arm up another inch and I started to roll round to get out of it. But Kraye still had his grasp on the front of my jersey, with his forearm leaning across under my throat, and between the two of them I was properly stuck. All the same, I found I couldn't just stand still and let them do what I so much didn't want them to.

'He squirms, doesn't he?' said Doria cheerfully.

I squirmed and struggled a good deal more; until they began getting savage with frustration, and I was panting. It was my wretched stomach which finished it. I began to feel too ill to go on. With a terrific jerk Kraye dragged my hand out.

'Now,' he said triumphantly.

He gripped my elbow fiercely and pulled the jersey sleeve up from my wrist. Doria let go of my right arm and came to look at their prize. I was shaking with rage, pain, humiliation . . . heaven knows what.

'Oh,' said Doria blankly. 'Oh.'

She was no longer smiling, and nor was her husband. They looked steadily at the wasted, flabby, twisted hand, and at the scars on my forearm, wrist and palm, not only the terrible jagged marks of the original injury but the several tidier ones of the operations I had had since. It was a mess, a right and proper mess.

'So that's why the Admiral lets him stay, the nasty little beast,' said Doria, screwing up her face in distaste.

'It doesn't excuse his behaviour,' said Kraye. 'I'll make sure he keeps that tongue of his still, in future.'

He stiffened his free hand and chopped the edge of it across the worst part, the inside of my wrist. I jerked in his grasp.

'Ah . . .' I said. 'Don't.'

'He'll tell tales to the Admiral,' said Doria warningly, 'if you hurt him too much. It's a pity, but I should think that's about enough.'

'I don't agree, but . . .'

There was a scrunch on the gravel outside, and Charles' car swept past the window, coming back.

Kraye let go of my elbow with a shake. I went weakly down on my knees on the rug, and it wasn't all pretence.

'If you tell the Admiral about this, I'll deny it,' said Kraye, 'and we know who he'll believe.'

I did know who he'd believe, but I didn't say so. The newspaper which had caused the whole rumpus lay close beside me on the rug. The car doors slammed distantly. The Krayes turned away from me towards the window, listening. I picked up the paper, got to my feet, and set off for the door. They didn't try to stop me in any way. They didn't mention the newspaper either. I opened the door, went through, shut it, and steered a slightly crooked course across the hall to the wardroom. Upstairs was too far. I shut the wardroom door behind me, hid the newspaper, slid into Charles' favourite arm-chair, and waited for my various miseries, mental and physical, to subside.

Some time later Charles came in to fetch some fresh cartons of cigarettes.

'Hullo,' he said over his shoulder, opening the cupboard. 'I thought you were still in bed. Mrs. Cross said you weren't very well this morning. It isn't at all warm in here. Why don't you come into the drawing-room?'

'The Krayes . . .' I stopped.

'They won't bite you.' He turned round, cigarettes in hand. He looked at my face. 'What's so funny?' and then more sharply, looking closer. 'What's the matter?'

'Oh, nothing. Have you seen today's *Sunday Hemisphere?*'

'No, not yet. Do you want it? I thought it was in the drawing-room with the other papers.'

'No, it's in the top drawer of your desk. Take a look.'

Puzzled, he opened the drawer, took out the paper, and unfolded it. He went to the racing section unerringly.

'My God!' he said, aghast. 'Today of all days.' His eyes skimmed down the page and he smiled. 'You've read this, of course?'

I shook my head. 'I just took it to hide it.'

He handed me the paper. 'Read it then. It'll be good for your ego. They won't let you die! "Young Finch", he quoted, "showed much of the judgment and miraculous precision of the great Sid". How about that? And that's just the start.'

'Yeah, how about it?' I grinned. 'Count me out for lunch, if you don't mind, Charles. You don't need me there any more.'

'All right, if you don't feel like it. They'll be gone by six at the latest, you'll be glad to hear.' He smiled and went back to his guests.

I read the newspaper before putting it away again. As Charles had said, it was good for the ego. I thought the columnist, whom I'd known for years, had somewhat exaggerated my erstwhile powers. A case of the myth growing bigger than the reality. But still, it was nice. Particularly in view of the galling, ignominious end to the rough-house in which the great Sid had so recently landed himself.

On the following morning Charles and I changed back the labels on the chunks of quartz and packed them up ready to return to the Carver Foundation. When we had finished we had one label left over.

'Are you sure we haven't put one stone in the box without changing the label?' said Charles.

'Positive.'

'I suppose we'd better check. I'm afraid that's what we've done.'

We took all the chunks out of the big box again. The gem collection, which Charles under protest had taken to bed with him each night, was complete; but we looked through them again too to make sure the missing rock had not got among them by mistake. It was nowhere to be found.

'St. Luke's Stone,' I read from the label. 'I remember where that was, up on the top shelf on the right hand side.'

'Yes,' agreed Charles, 'a dull looking lump about the size of a fist. I do hope we haven't lost it.'

'We have lost it,' I remarked. 'Kraye's pinched it.'

'Oh no,' Charles exclaimed. 'You can't be right.'

'Go and ring up the Foundation, and ask them what the stone is worth.'

He shook his head doubtfully, but went to the telephone, and came back frowning.

'They say it hasn't any intrinsic value, but it's an extremely rare form of meteorite. It never turns up in mines or quarrying of course. You have to wait for it to fall from the heavens, and then find it. Very tricky.'

'A quartz which friend Kraye didn't have.'

'But he surely must know I'd suspect him?' Charles protested.

'You'd never have missed it, if it had really been part of your cousin's passed-on collection. There wasn't any gap on the shelf just now. He'd moved the others along. He couldn't know you would check carefully almost as soon as he had gone.'

Charles sighed. 'There isn't a chance of getting it back.'

'No,' I agreed.

'Well, it's a good thing you insisted on the insurance,' he said. 'Carver's valued that boring-looking lump more than all the rest put together. Only one other meteorite like it has ever been found: the St. Mark's Stone.' He smiled suddenly. 'We seem to have mislaid the equivalent of the penny black.'

Chapter Five

Two days later I went back through the porticoed columned doorway of Hunt Radnor Associates, a lot more alive than when I last came out.

I got a big hullo from the girl on the switchboard, went up the curving staircase very nearly whistling, and was greeted by a barrage of ribald remarks from the Racing Section. What most surprised me was the feeling I had of coming home: I had never thought of myself as really belonging to the agency before, even though down at Aynsford I had realised that I very much didn't want to leave it. A bit late, that discovery. The skids were probably under me already.

Chico grinned widely. 'So you made it.'

'Well . . . Yes.'

'I mean, back here to the grindstone.'

'Yeah.'

'But,' he cast a rolling eye at the clock, 'late as usual.'

'Go stuff yourself,' I said.

Chico threw out an arm to the smiling department. 'Our Sid is back, his normal charming bloody self. Work in the agency can now begin.'

'I see I still haven't got a desk,' I observed, looking round. No desk. No roots. No real job. As ever.

'Sit on Dolly's, she's kept it dusted for you.'

Dolly looked at Chico, smiling, the mother-hunger showing too vividly in her great blue eyes. She might be the second best head of department the agency possessed, with a cross-referencing filing-index mind like a computer, she might be a powerful, large, self-assured woman of forty-odd with a couple of marriages behind her and an ever hopeful old bachelor at her heels, but she still counted her life a wasteland because her body couldn't produce children. Dolly was a terrific worker, over-flowing with intensely female vitality, excellent drinking company, and very, very sad.

Chico didn't want to be mothered. He was prickly about mothers. All of them in general, not just those who abandoned their tots in push-chairs at police stations near Barnes Bridge. He jollied Dolly along and deftly avoided her tentative maternal invitations.

I hitched a hip on to a long accustomed spot on the edge of Dolly's desk, and swung my leg.

'Well, Dolly my love, how's the sleuthing trade?' I said.

'What we need,' she said with mock tartness, 'is a bit more work from you and a lot less lip.'

'Give me a job, then.'

'Ah, now.' She pondered. 'You could . . .' she began, then stopped. 'Well, no . . . perhaps not. And it had better be Chico who goes to Lambourn; some trainer there wants a doubtful lad checked on . . .'

'So there's nothing for me?'

'Er . . . well . . .' said Dolly. 'No.' She had said no a hundred times before. She had never once said yes.

I made a face at her, picked up her telephone, pressed the right button, and got through to Radnor's secretary.

'Joanie? This is Sid Halley. Yes . . . back from Beyond, that's it. Is the old man busy? I'd like a word with him.'

'Big deal,' said Chico.

Joanie's prim voice said, 'He's got a client with him just now. When she's gone I'll ask him, and ring you back.'

'O.K.' I put down the receiver.

Dolly raised her eyebrows. As head of the department she was my immediate boss, and in asking direct for a session with Radnor I was blowing agency protocol a raspberry. But I was certain that her constant refusal to give me anything useful to do was a direct order from Radnor. If I wanted the drain unblocked I would have to go and pull out the plug. Or go on my knees to stay at all.

'Dolly, love, I'm tired of kicking my heels. Even against your well-worn desk, though the view from here is ravishing.' She was wearing, as she often did, a cross-over cream silk shirt: it crossed over at a point which on a young girl would have caused a riot. On Dolly it still looked pretty potent, owing to the generosity of nature and the disposal of her arrangements.

'Are you chucking it in?' said Chico, coming to the point.

'It depends on the old man,' I said. 'He may be chucking me out.'

There was a brief, thoughtful silence in the department. They all knew very well how little I did. How little I had been content to do. Dolly looked blank, which wasn't helpful.

Jones-boy clattered in with a tray of impeccable unchipped tea mugs. He was sixteen; noisy, rude, anarchistic, callous, and probably the most efficient office boy in London. His hair grew robustly nearly down to his shoulders, wavy and fanatically clean, dipping slightly in an expensive styling at the back. From behind he looked like a girl, which never disconcerted him. From in front his bony, acned face proclaimed him unprepossessingly male. He spent half his pay packet and his Sundays in Carnaby Street and the other half on week nights chasing girls. According to him, he caught them. No girls had so far appeared in the office to corroborate his story.

Under the pink shirt beat a stony heart; inside the sprouting head hung a big 'So What?' Yet it was because this amusing, ambitious, unsocial creature invariably arrived well before his due hour to get his office arrangements ready for the day that he had found me before I died. There was a moral there, somewhere.

He gave me a look. 'The corpse has returned, I see.'

'Thanks to you,' I said idly, but he knew I meant it. He didn't care, though.

He said, 'Your blood and stuff ran through a crack in the linoleum and soaked the wood underneath. The old man was wondering if it would start dry rot or something.'

'Jones-boy,' protested Dolly, looking sick. 'Get the hell out of here, and shut up.'

The telephone rang on her desk. She picked it up and listened, said, 'All right,' and disconnected.

'The old man wants to see you. Right away.'

'Thanks.' I stood up.

'The flipping boot?' asked Jones-boy interestedly.

'Keep your snotty nose out,' said Chico.

'And balls to you . . .'

I went out smiling, hearing Dolly start to deal once again with the running dog fight Chico and Jones-boy never tired of. Downstairs, across the hall, into Joanie's little office and through into Radnor's.

He was standing by the window, watching the traffic doing its nut in the Cromwell Road. This room, where the clients poured out their troubles, was restfully painted a quiet grey, carpeted and curtained in crimson and furnished with comfortable arm-chairs, handy little tables with ashtrays, pictures on the walls, ornaments, and vases of flowers. Apart from Radnor's small desk in the corner, it looked like an ordinary sitting-room, and indeed everyone believed that he had bought the room intact with the lease, so much was it what one would expect to find in a graceful, six-storeyed, late Victorian town house. Radnor had a theory that people exaggerated and distorted facts less in such peaceful surroundings than in the formality of a more orthodox office.

'Come in, Sid,' he said. He didn't move from the window, so I joined him there. He shook hands.

'Are you sure you're fit enough to be here? You haven't been as long as I expected. Even knowing you . . .' he smiled slightly, with watching eyes.

I said I was all right. He remarked on the weather, the rush-hour and the political situation, and finally worked round to the point we both knew was at issue.

'So, Sid, I suppose you'll be looking around a bit now?'

Laid on the line, I thought.

'If I wanted to stay here . . .'

'If? Hm, I don't know.' He shook his head very slightly.

'Not on the same terms, I agree.'

'I'm sorry it hasn't worked out.' He sounded genuinely regretful, but he wasn't making it easy.

I said with careful calm. 'You've paid me for nothing for two years. Well, give me a chance to earn what I've had. I don't really want to leave.'

He lifted his head slightly like a pointer to a scent, but he said nothing. I ploughed on.

'I'll work for you for nothing, to make up for it. But only if it's real, decent work. No more sitting around. It would drive me mad.'

He gave me a hard stare and let out a long breath like a sigh.

'Good God. At last,' he said. 'And it took a bullet to do it.'

'What do you mean?'

'Sid, have you ever seen a zombie wake up?'

'No,' I said ruefully, understanding him. 'It hasn't been as bad as that?'

He shrugged one shoulder. 'I saw you racing, don't forget. You notice when a fire goes out. We've had the pleasant, flippant ashes drifting round this office, that's all.' He smiled deprecatingly at his flight of fancy: he enjoyed making pictures of words. It wasted a lot of office time, on the whole.

'Consider me alight again, then,' I grinned. 'And I've brought a puzzle back with me. I want very much to sort it out.'

'A long story?'

'Fairly, yes.'

'We'd better sit down, then.'

He waved me to an arm-chair, sank into one himself, and prepared to listen with the stillness and concentration which sent him time and time again to the core of a problem.

I told him about Kraye's dealing in racecourses. Both what I knew and what I guessed. When at length I finished he said calmly, 'Where did you get hold of this?'

'My father-in-law, Charles Roland, tossed it at me while I was staying with him last week-end. He had Kraye as a house guest.' The subtle old fox, I thought, throwing me in at the deep end: making me wake up and swim.

'And Roland got it from where?'

'The Clerk of the Course at Seabury told him that the directors were worried about too much share movement, that it was Kraye who got control of Dunstable, and they were afraid he was at it again.'

'But the rest, what you've just told me, is your own supposition?'

'Yes.'

'Based on your appraisal of Kraye over one week-end?'

'Partly on what he showed me of his character, yes. Partly on what I read of his papers . . .' With some hesitation I told him about my snooping and the photography. '. . . The rest, I suppose, a hunch.'

'Hmm. It needs checking . . . Have you brought the films with you?'

I nodded, took them out of my pocket, and put them on the little table beside me.

'I'll get them developed.' He drummed his fingers lightly on the arm of the chair, thinking. Then, as if having made a decision, said more briskly, 'Well, the first thing we need is a client.'

'A client?' I echoed absent-mindedly.

'Of course. What else? We are not the police. We work strictly for profit. Ratepayers don't pay the overheads and salaries in this agency. The clients do.'

'Oh . . . yes, of course.'

'The most likely client in this case is either Seabury Racecourse executive, or perhaps the National Hunt Committee. I think I should sound out the Senior Steward first, in either case. No harm in starting at the top.'

'He might prefer to try the police,' I said, 'free.'

'My dear Sid, the one thing people want when they employ private investigators is privacy. They pay for privacy. When the police investigate something, everyone knows about it. When we do, they don't. That's why we sometimes get criminal cases when it would undoubtedly be cheaper to go to the police.'

'I see. So you'll try the Senior Steward . . .'

'No,' he interrupted. 'You will.'

'I?'

'Naturally. It's your case.'

'But it's your agency . . . he is used to negotiating with you.'

'You know him too,' he pointed out.

'I used to ride for him, and that puts me on a bad footing for this sort of thing. I'm a jockey to him, an ex-jockey. He won't take me seriously.'

Radnor shrugged a shoulder. 'If you want to take on Kraye, you need a client. Go and get one.'

I knew very well that he never sent even senior operatives, let alone inexperienced ones, to arrange or angle for an assignment, so that for several moments I couldn't really believe that he intended me to go. But he said nothing else, and eventually I stood up and went towards the door.

'Sandown Races are on today,' I said tentatively. 'He's sure to be there.'

'A good opportunity.' He looked straight ahead, not at me.

'I'll try it, then.'

'Right.'

He wasn't letting me off. But then he hadn't kicked me out either. I went through the door and shut it behind me, and while I was still hesitating in disbelief I heard him inside the room give a sudden guffaw, a short, sharp, loud, triumphant snort of laughter.

I walked back to my flat, collected the car, and drove down to Sandown. It was a pleasant day, dry, sunny, and warm for November, just right for drawing a good crowd for steeplechasing.

I turned in through the racecourse gates, spirits lifting, parked the car (a Mercedes S.L.230 with automatic gears, power assisted steering, and a strip on the back saying NO HAND SIGNALS), and walked round to join the crowd outside the weighing room door. I could no longer go through it. It had been one of the hardest things to get used to, the fact that all the changing rooms and weighing rooms which had been my second homes for fourteen years were completely barred to me from the day I rode my last race. You didn't lose just a job when you handed in your jockey's licence, you lost a way of life.

There were a lot of people to talk to at Sandown, and as I hadn't been racing for six weeks I had a good deal of gossip to catch up on. No one seemed to know about the shooting, which was fine by me, and I didn't tell them. I immersed myself very happily in the racecourse atmosphere and for an hour Kraye retreated slightly into the background.

Not that I didn't keep an eye on my purpose, but until the third race the Senior Steward, Viscount Hagbourne, was never out of a conversation long enough for me to catch him.

Although I had ridden for him for years and had found him undemanding and fair, he was in most respects still a stranger. An aloof, distant man, he seemed to find it difficult to make ordinary human contacts, and unfortunately he had not proved a great success as Senior Steward. He gave the impression, not of power in himself, but of looking over his shoulder at power behind: I'd have said he was afraid of incurring the disapproval of the little knot of rigidly determined men who in fact ruled racing themselves, regardless of who might be in office at the time. Lord Hagbourne postponed making decisions until it was almost too late to make them, and there was still a danger after that that he would change his mind. But all the same he was the front man until his year of office ended, and with him I had to deal.

At length I fielded him neatly as he turned away from the Clerk of the Course and forestalled a trainer who was advancing upon him with a grievance. Lord Hagbourne, with one of his rare moment of humour, deliberately turned his back on the grievance and consequently greeted me with more warmth than usual.

'Sid, nice to see you. Where have you been lately?'

'Holidays,' I explained succinctly. 'Look, sir, can I have a talk with you after the races? There's something I want to discuss urgently.'

'No time like the present,' he said, one eye on the grievance. 'Fire away.'

'No, sir. It needs time and all your attention.'

'Hm?' The grievance was turning away. 'Not today, Sid, I have to get home. What is it? Tell me now.'

'I want to talk to you about the take-over bid for Seabury Racecourse.'

He looked at me, startled. 'You want . . .?'

'That's right. It can't be said out here where you will be needed at any moment by someone else. If you could just manage twenty minutes at the end of the afternoon . . .?'

'Er . . . what is your connection with Seabury?'

'None in particular, sir. I don't know if you remember, but I've been connected' (a precise way of putting it) 'with Hunt Radnor Associates for the last two years. Various . . . er . . . facts about Seabury have come our way and Mr. Radnor thought you might be interested. I am here as his representative.'

'Oh, I see. Very well, Sid, come to the Stewards' tea room after the last. If I'm not there, wait for me. Right?'

'Yes. Thank you.'

I walked down the slope and then up the iron staircase to the jockeys' box in the stand, smiling at myself. Representative. A nice big important word. It covered anything from an ambassador down. Commercial travellers had rechristened themselves with its rolling syllables years ago . . . they had done it because of the jokes, of course. It didn't sound the same, somehow, starting off with 'Did you hear the one about the representative who stopped at a lonely farmhouse . . .?' Rodent officers, garbage disposal and sanitary staff: pretty new names for rat-catchers, dustmen and road sweepers. So why not for me?

'Only idiots laugh at nothing,' said a voice in my ear. 'What the hell are you looking so pleased about all of a sudden? And where the blazes have you been this last month?'

'Don't tell me you've missed me?' I grinned, not needing to look round. We went together through the door of the high-up jockeys' box, two of a kind, and stood looking out over the splendid racecourse.

'Best view in Europe.' He sighed. Mark Witney, thirty-eight years old, racehorse trainer. He had a face battered like a boxer's from too many racing falls and in the two years since he hung up his boots and stopped wasting he had put on all of three stone. A fat, ugly man. We had a host of memories in common, a host of hard ridden races. I liked him a lot.

'How's things?' I said.

'Oh, fair, fair. They'll be a damn sight better if that animal of mine wins the fifth.'

'He must have a good chance.'

'He's a damn certainty, boy. A certainty. If he doesn't fall over his god-damned legs. Clumsiest sod this side of Hades.' He lifted his race glasses and looked at the number board. 'I see poor old Charlie can't do the weight again on that thing of Bob's . . . That boy of Plumtree's is getting a lot of riding now. What do you think of him?'

'He takes too many risks,' I said. 'He'll break his neck.'

'Look who's talking . . . No, seriously, I'm considering taking him on. What do you think?' He lowered his glasses. 'I need someone available regularly from now on and all the ones I'd choose are already tied up.'

'Well, you could do better, you could do worse, I suppose. He's a bit flashy for me, but he can ride, obviously. Will he do as he's told?'

He made a face. 'You've hit the bull's eye. That's the snag. He always knows best.'

'Pity.'

'Can you think of anyone else?'

'Um . . . what about that boy Cotton? He's too young really. But he's got the makings . . .' We drifted on in amiable chat, discussing his problem, while the box filled up around us and the horses went down to the start.

It was a three mile chase, and one of my ex-mounts was favourite. I watched the man who had my old job ride a very pretty race, and with half my mind thought about housing estates.

Sandown itself had survived, some years ago, a bid to cover its green tempting acres with little boxes. Sandown had powerful friends. But Hurst Park, Manchester and Birmingham racecourses had all gone under the rolling tide of bricks and mortar, lost to the double-barrelled persuasive arguments that shareholders liked capital gains and people needed houses. To defend itself from such a fate Cheltenham Racecourse had transformed itself from a private, dividend-paying company into a non-profit-making Holdings Trust, and other racecourses had followed their lead.

But not Seabury. And Seabury was deep in a nasty situation. Not Dunstable, and Dunstable Racecourse was now a tidy dormitory for the Vauxhall workers of Luton.

Most British racecourses were, or had been, private companies, in which it was virtually impossible for an outsider to acquire shares against the will of the members. But four, Dunstable, Seabury, Sandown and Chepstow, were public companies, and their shares could be bought on the open market, through the Stock Exchange.

Sandown had been played for in a straightforward and perfectly honourable way, and plans to turn it into suburban housing had been turned down by the local and county councils. Sandown flourished, made a good profit, paid a ten per cent dividend, and was probably now impregnable. Chepstow was surrounded by so much other open land that it was in little danger from developers. But little Dunstable had been an oasis inside a growing industrial area.

Seabury was on the flat part of the south coast, flanked on every side by miles of warm little bungalows representing the dreams and savings of people in retirement. At twelve bungalows to the acre – elderly people liked tiny gardens – there must be room on the spacious racecourse for over three thousand more. Add six or seven hundred pounds to the building price of each bungalow for the plot it stood on, and you scooped something in the region of two million . . .

The favourite won and was duly cheered. I clattered down the iron staircase with Mark, and we went and had a drink together.

'Are you sending anything to Seabury next week?' I asked. Seabury was one of his nearest meetings.

'Perhaps. I don't know. It depends if they hold it at all, of course. But I've got mine entered at Lingfield as well, and I think I'll send them there instead. It's a much more prosperous looking place, and the owners like it better. Good lunch and all that. Seabury's so dingy these days. I had a hard job getting old Carmichael to agree to me running his horse there at the last meeting – and look what happened. The meeting was off and we'd missed the other engagement at Worcester too. It wasn't my fault, but I'd persuaded him that he stood more chance at Seabury, and he blamed me because in the end the horse stayed at home eating his head off for nothing. He says there's a jinx on Seabury, and I've a couple more owners who don't like me entering their horses there. I've told them that it's a super track from the horses' point of view, but it doesn't make much difference, they don't know it like we do.'

We finished our drinks and walked back towards the weighing room. His horse scrambled home in the fifth by a whisker and I saw him afterwards in the unsaddling enclosure beaming like a Halowe'en turnip.

After the last race I went to the Stewards' tea room. There were several Stewards with their wives and friends having tea, but no Lord Hagbourne. The Stewards pulled out a chair, gave me a welcome, and talked as ever, about the racing. Most of them had ridden as amateurs in their day, one against me in the not too distant past, and I knew them all well.

'Sid, what do you think of the new type hurdles?'

'Oh, much better. Far easier for a young horse to see.'

'Do you know of a good young chaser I could buy?'

'Didn't you think Hayward rode a splendid race?'

'I watched the third down at the Pond, and believe me that chestnut took off outside the wings . . .'

'. . . do you think we ought to have had him in, George?'

'. . . heard that Green bust his ribs again yesterday . . .'

'Don't like that breed, never did, not genuine . . .'

'Miffy can't seem to go wrong, he'd win with a carthorse . . .'

'Can you come and give a talk to our local pony club, Sid? I'll write you the details . . . what date would suit you?'

Gradually they finished their tea, said good-bye, and left for home. I waited. Eventually he came, hurrying, apologising, explaining what had kept him.

'Now,' he said, biting into a sandwich. 'What's it all about, eh?'

'Seabury.'

'Ah yes, Seabury. Very worrying. Very worrying indeed.'

'A Mr. Howard Kraye has acquired a large number of shares . . .'

'Now hold on a minute, Sid. That's only a guess, because of Dunstable. We've been trying to trace the buyer of Seabury shares through the Stock Exchange, and we can find no definite lead to Kraye.'

'Hunt Radnor Associates do have that lead.'

He stared. 'Proof?'

'Yes.'

'What sort?'

'Photographs of share transfer certificates.' And heaven help me, I thought, if I've messed them up.

'Oh,' he said sombrely. 'While we weren't sure, there was some hope we were wrong. Where did you get these photographs?'

'I'm not at liberty to say, sir. But Hunt Radnor Associates would be prepared to make an attempt to forestall the takeover of Seabury.'

'For a fat fee, I suppose,' he said dubiously.

'I'm afraid so, sir, yes.'

'I don't connect you with this sort of thing, Sid.' He moved restlessly and looked at his watch.

'If you would forget about me being a jockey, and think of me as having come from Mr. Radnor, it would make things a lot easier. How much is Seabury worth to National Hunt racing?'

He looked at me in surprise, but he answered the question, though not in the way I meant.

'Er . . . well you know it's an excellent course, good for horses and so on.'

'It didn't show a profit this year, though.'

'There was a great deal of bad luck.'

'Yes. Too much to be true, don't you think?'

'What do you mean?'

'Has it ever occurred to the National Hunt Committee that bad luck can be . . . well . . . arranged?'

'You aren't seriously suggesting that Kraye . . . I mean that anyone would damage Seabury on purpose? In order to make it show a loss?'

'I am suggesting that it is a possibility. Yes.'

'Good God.' He sat down rather abruptly.

'Malicious damage,' I said. 'Sabotage, if you like. There's a great deal of industrial precedent. Hunt Radnor Associates investigated a case of it only last year in a small provincial brewery where the fermentation process kept going wrong. A prosecution resulted, and the brewery was able to remain in business.'

He shook his head. 'It is quite ridiculous to think that Kraye would be implicated in anything like that. He belongs to one of my clubs. He's a wealthy, respected man.'

'I know, I've met him,' I said.

'Well then, you must be aware of what sort of person he is.'

'Yes.' Only too well.

'You can't seriously suggest . . .' he began.

'There would be no harm in finding out,' I interrupted. 'You'll have studied the figures. Seabury's quite a prize.'

'How do you see the figures, then?' It seemed he genuinely wanted to know, so I told him.

'Seabury Racecourse has an issued share capital of eighty thousand pounds in fully paid-up one pound shares. The land was bought when that part of the coast was more or less uninhabited, so that this sum bears absolutely no relation to the present value of the place. Any company in that position is just asking for a take-over.

'A buyer would in theory need fifty-one per cent of the shares to be certain of gaining control, but in practice, as was found at Dunstable, forty would be plenty. It could probably be swung on a good deal less, but from the point of view of the buyer, the more he got his hands on before declaring his intentions, the bigger would be his profit.

'The main difficulty in taking over a racecourse company – it's only natural safeguard, in fact – is that the shares seldom come on the market. I understand that it isn't always by any means possible to buy even a few on the Stock Exchange, as people who own them tend to be fond of them, and as long as the shares pay any dividend, however small, they won't sell. But it's obvious that not everyone can afford to have bits of capital lying around unproductively, and once the racecourse starts showing a loss, the temptation grows to transfer to something else.

'Today's price of Seabury shares is thirty shillings, which is about four shillings higher than it was two years ago. If Kraye can manage to get hold of a forty per cent holding at an average price of thirty shillings, it will cost him only about forty-eight thousand pounds.

'With a holding that size, aided by other shareholders tempted by a very large capital gain, he can out-vote any opposition, and sell the whole company to a land developer. Planning permission would almost certainly be granted, as the land is not beautiful, and is surrounded already by houses. I estimate that a developer would pay roughly a million for it, as he could double that by selling off all those acres in tiny plots. There's the capital gains tax, of course, but Seabury shareholders stand to make eight hundred per cent on their original investment, if the scheme goes through. Four hundred thousand gross for Mr. Kraye, perhaps. Did you ever find out how much he cleared at Dunstable?'

He didn't answer.

I went on, 'Seabury used to be a busy, lively, successful place, and now it isn't. It's a suspicious coincidence that as soon as a big buyer comes along the place goes downhill fast. They paid a dividend of only sixpence per share last year, a gross yield of under one and three-quarters per cent at today's price, and this year they showed a loss of three thousand, seven hundred and fourteen pounds. Unless something is done soon, there won't be a next year.'

He didn't reply at once. He stared at the floor for a long time with the half-eaten sandwich immobile in his hand.

Finally he said, 'Who did the arithmetic? Radnor?'

'No . . . I did. It's very simple. I went to Company House in the City yesterday and looked up the Seabury balance sheets for the last few years, and I rang for a quotation of today's share price from a stockbroker this morning. You can easily check it.'

'Oh, I don't doubt you. I remember now, there was a rumour that you made a fortune on the Stock Exchange by the time you were twenty.'

'People exaggerate so,' I smiled. 'My old governor, where I was apprenticed, started me off investing, and I was a bit lucky.'

'Hm.'

There was another pause while he hesitated over his decision. I didn't interrupt him, but I was much relieved when finally he said, 'You have Radnor's authority for seeing me, and he knows what you have told me?'

'Yes.'

'Very well.' He got up stiffly and put down the unfinished sandwich. 'You can tell Radnor that I agree to an investigation being made, and I think I can vouch for my colleagues agreeing. You'll want to start at once, I suppose.'

I nodded.

'The usual terms?'

'I don't know,' I said. 'Perhaps you would get on to Mr. Radnor about that.'

As I didn't know what the usual terms were, I didn't want to discuss them.

'Yes, all right. And Sid . . . it's understood that there is to be no leak about this? We can't afford to have Kraye slapping a libel or slander action on us.'

'The agency is always discreet,' I said, with an outward and an inward smile. Radnor was right. People paid for privacy. And why not?

Chapter Six

The Racing Section was quiet when I went in next morning, mostly because Chico was out on an escort job. All the other heads were bent studiously over their desks, including Dolly's.

She looked up and said with a sigh, 'You're late again.' It was ten to ten. 'The old man wants to see you.'

I made a face at .ier and retraced my way down the staircase. Joanie looked pointedly at her watch.

'He's been asking for you for half an hour.'

I knocked and went in. Radnor was sitting behind his desk, reading some papers, pencil in hand. He looked at me and frowned.

'Why are you so late?'

'I had a pain in me tum,' I said flippantly.

'Don't be funny,' he said sharply, and then, more reasonably, 'Oh . . . I suppose you're not being funny.'

'No. But I'm sorry about being late.' I wasn't a bit sorry, however, that it had been noticed: before, no one would have said a thing if I hadn't turned up all day.

'How did you get on with Lord Hagbourne?' Radnor asked. 'Was he interested?'

'Yes. He agreed to an investigation. I said he should discuss terms with you.'

'I see.' He flicked a switch on the small box on his desk. 'Joanie, see if you can get hold of Lord Hagbourne. Try the London flat number first.'

'Yes, sir,' her voice came tinnily out of the speaker.

'Here,' said Radnor, picking up a shallow brown cardboard box. 'Look at these.'

The box contained a thick wad of large glossy photographs. I looked at them one by one and heaved a sigh of relief. They had all come out sharp and clear, except some of the ones I had duplicated at varying exposures.

The telephone on Radnor's desk rang once, quietly. He lifted the receiver.

'Oh, good morning Lord Hagbourne. Radnor here. Yes, that's right...' He gestured to me to sit down, and I stayed there listening while he negotiated terms in a smooth, civilised, deceptively casual voice.

'And of course in a case like this, Lord Hagbourne, there's one other thing: we make a small surcharge if our operatives have to take out of the ordinary risks... Yes, as in the Canlas case, exactly. Right then, you shall have a preliminary report from us in a few days. Yes... good-bye.'

He put down the receiver, bit his thumb-nail thoughtfully for a few seconds, and said finally, 'Right, then, Sid. Get on with it.'

'But...' I began.

'But nothing,' he said. 'It's your case. Get on with it.'

I stood up, holding the packet of photographs. 'Can I... can I use Bona Fides and so on?'

He waved his hand permissively. 'Sid, use every resource in the agency you need. Keep an eye on expenses though, we don't want to price ourselves out of business. And if you want leg work done, arrange it through Dolly or the other department heads. Right?'

'Won't they think it odd? I mean... I don't amount to much around here.'

'And whose fault is that? If they won't do what you ask, refer them to me.' He looked at me expressionlessly.

'All right.' I walked to the door. 'Er... who...' I said, turning the knob, 'gets the danger money? The operative or the agency?'

'You said you would work for nothing,' he observed dryly.

I laughed. 'Just so. Do I get expenses?'

'That car of yours drinks petrol.'

'It does twenty,' I protested.

'The agency rate is based on thirty. You can have that. And other expenses, yes. Put in a chit to accounts.'

'Thanks.'

He smiled suddenly, the rare sweet smile so incongrous to his military bearing, and launched into another elaborate metaphor.

'The tapes are up,' he said. 'What you do with the race depends on your skill and timing, just as it always used to. I've backed you with the agency's reputation for getting results, and I can't afford to lose my stake. Remember that.'

'Yes,' I said soberly. 'I will.'

I thought, as I took my stupidly aching stomach up two storeys to Bona Fides, that it was time Radnor had a lift installed: and was glad I wasn't bound for Missing Persons away in the rarefied air of the fifth floor. There was a lot more character, I supposed, in the splendidly proportioned, solidly built town house that Radnor had chosen on a corner site in the Cromwell Road, but a flat half-acre of modern office block would have been easier on his staff. And about ten times as expensive, no doubt.

The basement, to start at the bottom, was – except for the kitchen – given over entirely to files and records. On the ground floor, besides Radnor himself and Joanie, there were two interview-cum-waiting rooms, and also the Divorce Section. On the first floor; the Racing Section, Accounts, another interview room and the general secretarial department. Up one was Bona Fides, and above that, on the two smaller top floors, Guard and Missing Persons. Missing Persons alone had room to spare. Bona Fides, splitting at the seams, was encroaching on Guard. Guard was sticking in its toes.

Jones-boy, who acted as general messenger, must have had legs like iron from pounding up and down the stairs, though thanks to a tiny service lift used long ago to take nursery food to top floor children, he could haul his tea trays up from landing to landing instead of carrying them.

In Bona Fides there was the usual chatter of six people talking on the telephone all at once. The department head, receiver glued to one ear and finger stuck in the other, was a large bald-headed man with half-moon spectacles sitting half way down a prominent nose. As always, he was in his shirt sleeves, teamed with a frayed pullover and baggy grey flannels. No tie. He seemed to have an inexhaustible supply of old clothes but never any new ones, and Jones-boy had a theory that his wife dressed him from jumble sales.

I waited until he had finished a long conversation with a managing director about the character of the proposed production manager of a glass factory. The invaluable thing about Jack Copeland was his quick and comprehensive grasp of what dozens of jobs entailed. He was speaking to the glass manufacturer as if he had grown up in the industry: and in five minutes, I knew, he might be advising just as knowledgeably on the suitability of a town clerk. His summing up of a man went far beyond the basic list of honesty, conscientiousness, normality and prudence, which was all that many employers wanted. He liked to discover his subject's reaction under stress, to find out what he disliked doing, and what he often forgot. The resulting footnotes to his reports were usually the most valuable part of them, and the faith large numbers of industrial firms had in him bore witness to his accuracy.

He wielded enormous power but did not seem conscious of it, which made him much liked. After Radnor, he was the most important person in the agency.

'Jack,' I said, as he put down the receiver. 'Can you check a man for me, please?'

'What's wrong with the Racing Section, pal?' he said, jerking his thumb towards the floor.

'He isn't a racing person.'

'Oh? Who is it?'

'A Howard Kraye. I don't know if he has a profession. He speculates on the stock market. He is a rabid collector of quartz.' I added Kraye's London address.

He scribbled it all down fast.

'O.K., Sid. I'll put one of the boys on to it and let you have a prelim. Is it urgent?'

'Fairly.'

'Right.' He tore the sheet off the pad. 'George? You still doing that knitting wool client's report? When you've finished, here's your next one.'

'George,' I said. 'Be careful.'

They both looked at me, suddenly still.

'An unexploded bomb,' I observed. 'Don't set him off.'

George said cheerfully, 'Makes a nice change from knitting wool. Don't worry, Sid. I'll walk on eggs.'

Jack Copeland peered at me closely through the half specs.

'You've cleared it with the old man, I suppose?'

'Yes.' I nodded. 'It's a query fraud. He said to check with him if you wanted to.'

He smiled briefly. 'No need, I guess. Is that all then?'

'For the moment, yes, thanks.'

'Just for the record, is this your own show, or Dolly's, or whose?'

'I suppose . . . mine.'

'Uh-huh,' he said, accenting the second syllable. 'The wind of change, if I read it right?'

I laughed. 'You never know.'

Down in the Racing Section I found Dolly supervising the reshuffling of the furniture. I asked what was going on, and she gave me a flashing smile.

'It seems you're in, not out. The old man just rang to say you needed somewhere to work, and I've sent Jones-boy upstairs to pinch a table from Missing Persons. That'll do for now, won't it? There isn't a spare desk in the place.'

A series of bangs from outside heralded the return of Jones-boy, complete with a spindly plywood affair in a sickly lemon colour. 'How that lot ever find a missing person I'll never know. I bet they don't even find their missing junk.'

He disappeared and came back shortly with a chair.

'The things I do for you!' he said, setting it down in front of me. 'A dim little bird in the typing pool is now squatting on a stool. I chatted her up a bit.'

'What this place needs is some more equipment,' I murmured.

'Don't be funny,' said Dolly. 'Every time the old man buys one desk he takes on two assistants. When I first came here fifteen years ago we had a whole room each, believe it or not . . .'

The rearranged office settled down again, with my table wedged into a corner next to Dolly's desk. I sat behind it and spread out the photographs to sort them. The people who developed and printed all the agency's work had come up with their usual excellent job, and it amazed me that they had been able to enlarge the tiny negatives up to nine by seven inch prints, and get a clearly readable result.

I picked out all the fuzzy ones, the duplicates at the wrong exposures, tore them up, and put the pieces in Dolly's waste paper basket. That left me with fifty-one pictures of the contents of Kraye's attaché case. Innocent enough to the casual eye, but they turned out to be dynamite.

The two largest piles, when I had sorted them out, were Seabury share transfer certificates, and letters from Kraye's stockbroker. The paper headed S.R. revealed itself to be a summary in simple form of the share certificates, so I added it to that pile. I was left with the photographs of the bank notes, of share dealings which had nothing to do with Seabury, and the two sheets of figures I had found under the writing board at the bottom of the case.

I read through all the letters from the stockbroker, a man called Ellis Bolt, who belonged to a firm known as Charing, Street and King. Bolt and Kraye were on friendly terms; the letters referred sometimes to social occasions on which they had met; but for the most part the typewritten sheets dealt with the availability and prospects of various shares (including Seabury), purchases made or proposed, and references to tax, stamp duty, and commission.

Two letters had been written in Bolt's own hand. The first, dated ten days ago, said briefly:

Dear H.
Shall wait with interest for the news on Friday.

E

The second, which Kraye must have received on the morning he went to Aynsford, read:

Dear H.
I have put the final draft in the hands of the printers, and the leaflets should be out by the end of next week, or the Tuesday following at the latest. Two or three days before the next meeting, anyway. That should do it, I think. There would be a lot of unrest should there be another hitch, but surely you will see to that.

E

'Dolly,' I said. 'May I borrow your phone?'
'Help yourself.'
I rang upstairs to Bona Fides. 'Jack? Can I have a run-down on another man as well? Ellis Bolt, stockbroker, works for a firm called Charing, Street and King.' I gave him the address. 'He's a friend of Kraye's. Same care needed, I'm afraid.'
'Right. I'll let you know.'
I sat staring down at the two harmless looking letters.
'Shall wait with interest for the news on Friday'. It could mean any news, anything at all. It also could mean the News; and on the radio on

Friday I had heard that Seabury Races were off because a lorry carrying chemicals had overturned and burned the turf.

The second letter was just as tricky. It could easily refer to a share-holders' meeting at which a hitch should be avoided at all costs. Or it could refer to a race meeting – at Seabury – where another hitch could affect the sale of shares yet again.

It was like looking at a conjuring trick: from one side you saw a normal object, but from the other, a sham.

If it were a sham, Mr. Ellis Bolt was in a criminal career up to his eyebrows. If it was just my suspicious mind jumping to hasty conclusions I was doing an old-established respectable stockbroker a shocking injustice.

I picked up Dolly's telephone again and got an outside line.

'Charing, Street and King, good morning,' said a quiet female voice.

'Oh, good morning. I would like to make an appointment to see Mr. Bolt and discuss some investments. Would that be possible?'

'Certainly, yes. This is Mr. Bolt's secretary speaking. Could I have your name?'

'Halley. John Halley.'

'You would be a new client, Mr. Halley?'

'That's right.'

'I see. Well, now, Mr. Bolt will be in the office tomorrow afternoon, and I could fit you in at three thirty. Would that suit you?'

'Thank you. That's fine. I'll be there.'

I put down the receiver and looked tentatively at Dolly.

'Would it be all right with you if I go out for the rest of the day?'

She smiled. 'Sid, dear, you're very sweet, but you don't have to ask my permission. The old man made it very clear that you're on your own now. You're not accountable to me or anyone else in the agency, except the old man himself. I'll grant you I've never known him give anyone quite such a free hand before, but there you are, my love, you can do what you like. I'm your boss no longer.'

'You don't mind?' I asked.

'No,' she said thoughtfully. 'Come to think of it, I don't. I've a notion that what the old man has always wanted of you in this agency is a partner.'

'Dolly!' I was astounded. 'Don't be ridiculous.'

'He's not getting any younger,' she pointed out.

I laughed. 'So he picked on a broken-down jockey to help him out.'

'He picks on someone with enough capital to buy a partnership, someone who's been to the top of one profession and has the time in years to get to the top of another.'

'You're raving, Dolly dear. He nearly chucked me out yesterday morning.'

'But you're still here, aren't you? More here than ever before. And Joanie said he was in a fantastically good mood all day yesterday, after you'd been in to see him.'

I shook my head, laughing. 'You're too romantic. Jockeys don't turn into investigators any more than they turn into . . .'

'Well, what?' she prompted.

'Into auctioneers, then . . . or accountants.'

She shook her head. 'You've already turned into an investigator, whether you know it or not. I've been watching you these two years, remember? You look as if you're doing nothing, but you've soaked up everything the bloodhounds have taught you like a hungry sponge. I'd say, Sid love, if you don't watch out, you'll be part of the fixtures and fittings for the rest of your life.'

But I didn't believe her, and I paid no attention to what she had said.

I grinned. 'I'm going down to take a look at Seabury Racecourse this afternoon. Like to come?'

'Are you kidding?' she sighed. Her in-tray was six inches deep. 'I could have just done with a ride in that rocket car of yours, and a breath of sea air.'

I stacked the photographs together and returned them to the box, along with the negatives. There was a drawer in the table, and I pulled it open to put the photographs away. It wasn't empty. Inside lay a packet of sandwiches, some cigarettes, and a flat half bottle of whisky.

'I began to laugh. 'Someone,' I said, 'will shortly come rampaging down from Missing Persons looking for his Missing Lunch.'

Seabury Racecourse lay about half a mile inland, just off a trunk road to the sea. Looking backwards from the top of the stands one could see the wide silver sweep of the English Channel. Between and on both sides the crowded rows of little houses seemed to be rushing towards the coast like Gadarene swine. In each little unit a retired schoolmaster or civil servant or clergyman – or their widows – thought about the roots they had pulled up from wherever it had been too cold or too dingy for their old age, and sniffed the warm south salt-laden air.

They had made it. Done what they'd always wanted. Retired to a bungalow by the sea.

I drove straight in through the open racecourse gates and stopped outside the weighing room. Climbing out, I stretched and walked over to knock on the door of the racecourse manager's office.

There was no reply. I tried the handle. It was locked. So was the weighing room door, and everything else.

Hands in pockets, I strolled round the end of the stands to look at the course. Seabury was officially classified in Group Three: that is to say, lower than Doncaster and higher than Windsor when it came to receiving aid from the Betting Levy Board.

It had less than Grade Three stands: wooden steps with corrugated tin roofs for the most part, and draughts from all parts of the compass. But the track itself was a joy to ride on, and it had always seemed a pity to me that the rest of the amenities didn't match it.

There was no one about near the stands. Down at one end of the course, however, I could see some men and a tractor, and I set off towards them, walking down inside the rails, on the grass. The going was just about perfect for November racing, soft but springy underfoot, exactly right for tempting trainers to send their horses to the course in droves.

In ordinary circumstances, that was. But as things stood at present, more trainers than Mark Witney were sending their horses elsewhere. A course which didn't attract runners didn't attract crowds to watch them. Seabury's gate receipts had been falling off for some time, but its expenses had risen; and therein lay its loss.

Thinking about the sad tale I had read in the balance sheets, I reached the men working on the course. They were digging up a great section of it and loading it on to a trailer behind the tractor. There was a pervasive unpleasant smell in the air.

An irregular patch about thirty yards deep, stretching nearly the whole width of the course, had been burned brown and killed. Less than half of the affected turf had already been removed, showing the greyish chalky mud underneath, and there was still an enormous amount to be shifted. I didn't think there were enough men working on it for there to be a hope of its being re-turfed and ready to race on in only eight days' time.

'Good afternoon,' I said to the men in general. 'What a horrible mess.'

One of them thrust his spade into the earth and came over, rubbing his hands on the sides of his trousers.

'Anything you want?' he said with fair politeness.

'The racecourse manager. Captain Oxon.'

His manner shifted perceptibly towards the civil. 'He's not here today, sir. Hey! . . . aren't you Sid Halley?'

'That's right.'

He grinned, doing another quick change, this time towards brotherhood. 'I'm the foreman. Ted Wilkins.' I shook his outstretched hand. 'Captain Oxon's gone up to London. He said he wouldn't be back until tomorrow.'

'Never mind,' I said. 'I was just down in this part of the world and I thought I'd drop in and have a look at the poor old course.'

He turned with me to look at the devastation. 'Shame, isn't it?'

'What happened, exactly?'

'The tanker overturned on the road over there.' He pointed, and we began to walk towards the spot, edging round the dug up area. The road, a narrow secondary one, ran across near the end of the racecourse, with a wide semi-circle of track on the far side of it. During the races the hard road surface was covered thickly with tan or peat, or with thick green matting, which the horses galloped over without any trouble. Although not ideal, it was an arrangement to be found on many courses throughout the country, most famously with the Melling Road at Aintree, and reaching a maximum with five road crossings at Ludlow.

'Just here,' said Ted Wilkins, pointing. 'Worst place it could possibly have happened, right in the middle of the track. The stuff just poured out of the tanker. It turned right over, see, and the hatch thing was torn open in the crash.'

'How did it happen?' I asked. 'The crash, I mean?'

'No one knows, really.'

'But the driver? He wasn't killed, was he?'

'No, he wasn't even hurt much. Just shook up a bit. But he couldn't remember what happened. Some people in a car came driving along after dark and nearly ran into the tanker. They found the driver sitting at the side of the road, holding his head and moaning. Concussion, it was, they say. They reckon he hit his head somehow when his lorry went over. Staggers me how he got out of it so lightly, the cab was fair crushed, and there was glass everywhere.'

'Do tankers often drive across here? Lucky it's never happened before, if they do.'

'They used not to,' he said, scratching his head. 'But they've been over here quite regularly now for a year or two. The traffic on the London road's getting chronic, see?'

'Oh . . . did it come from a local firm, then?'

'Down the coast a bit. Intersouth Chemicals, that's the firm it belonged to.'

'How soon do you think we'll be racing here again?' I asked, turning back to look at the track. 'Will you make it by next week?'

He frowned. 'Strictly between you and me, I don't think there's a bleeding hope. What we needed, as I said to the Captain, was a couple of bulldozers, not six men with spades.'

'I would have thought so too.'

He sighed. 'He just told me we couldn't afford them and to shut up and get on with it. And that's what we've done. We'll just about have cut out all the dead turf by next Wednesday, at this rate of going on.'

'That doesn't leave any time for new turf to settle,' I remarked.

'It'll be a miracle if it's laid, let alone settled,' he agreed gloomily.

I bent down and ran my hand over a patch of brown grass. It was decomposing and felt slimy. I made a face, and the foreman laughed.

'Horrible, isn't it? It stinks too.'

I put my fingers to my nose and wished I hadn't. 'Was it slippery like this right from the beginning?'

'Yes, that's right. Hopeless.'

'Well, I won't take up any more of your time,' I said, smiling.

'I'll tell Captain Oxon you came. Pity you missed him.'

'Don't bother him. He must have a lot to worry about just now.'

'One bloody crisis after another,' he nodded. 'So long, then.' He went back to his spade and his heart-breaking task, and I retraced the quarter mile up the straight to the deserted stands.

I hesitated for a while outside the weighing room, wondering whether to pick the lock and go in, and knowing it was mainly nostalgia that urged me to do it, not any conviction that it would be a useful piece of investigation. There would always be the temptation, I supposed, to use dubious professional skills for one's own pleasure. Like doctors sniffing ether. I contented myself with looking through the windows.

The deserted weighing room looked the same as ever: a large bare expanse of wooden board floor, with a table and some upright chairs in one corner, and the weighing machine itself on the left. Racecourse weighing machines were not all of one universal design. There weren't any left of the old type where the jockeys stood on a platform while weights were added to the balancing arm. That whole process was much too slow. Now there were either seats slung from above, in which one felt much like a bag of sugar, or chairs bolted to a base plate on springs: in both these cases the weight was quickly indicated by a pointer which swung round a gigantic clock face. In essence, modern kitchen scales vastly magnified.

The scales at Seabury were the chair-on-base-plate type, which I'd always found simplest to use. I recalled a few of the before-and-after occasions when I had sat on that particular spot. Some good, some bad, as always with racing.

Shrugging, I turned away. I wouldn't, I thought, ever be sitting there again. And no one walked over my grave.

Climbing into the car, I drove to the nearest town, looked up the whereabouts of Intersouth Chemicals, and an hour later was speaking to the personnel manager. I explained that on behalf of the National Hunt Committee I had just called in passing to find out if the driver of the tanker had fully recovered, or had remembered anything else about the accident.

The manager, fat and fiftyish, was affable but unhelpful. 'Smith's left,' he said briefly. 'We gave him a few days off to get over the accident, and then he came back yesterday and said his wife didn't fancy him driving chemicals any more, and he was packing it in.' His voice held a grievance.

'Had he been with you long?' I asked sympathetically.

'About a year.'

'A good driver, I suppose?'

'Yes, about average for the job. They have to be good drivers, or we don't use them, you see. Smith was all right, but nothing special.'

'And you still don't really know what happened?'

'No,' he sighed. 'It takes a lot to tip one of our tankers over. There was nothing to learn from the road. It was covered with oil and petrol and chemical. If there had ever been any marks, skid marks I mean, they weren't there after the breakdown cranes had lifted the tanker up again, and the road was cleared.'

'Do your tankers use that road often?'

'They have done recently, but not any more after this. As a matter of fact, I seem to remember it was Smith himself who found that way round. Going over the racecourse missed out some bottle-neck at a junction, I believe. I know some of the drivers thought it a good idea.'

'They go through Seabury regularly, then?'

'Sure, often. Straight line to Southampton and round to the oil refinery at Fawley.'

'Oh? What exactly was Smith's tanker carrying?'

'Sulphuric acid. It's used in refining petrol, among other things.'

Sulphuric acid. Dense; oily; corrosive to the point of charring. Nothing more instantly lethal could have poured out over Seabury's turf. They could have raced had it been a milder chemical, put sand or tan on the dying grass and raced over the top. But no one would risk a horse on ground soaked with vitriol.

I said, 'Could you give me Smith's address? I'll call round and see if his memory has come back.'

'Sure.' He searched in a file and found it for me. 'Tell him he can have his job back if he's interested. Another of the men gave notice this morning.'

I said I would, thanked him, and went to Smith's address, which proved to be two rooms upstairs in a suburban house. But Smith and his wife no longer lived in them. Packed up and gone yesterday, I was told by a young woman in curlers. No, she didn't know where they were. No, they didn't leave a forwarding address, and if I was her I wouldn't worry about his health as he'd been laughing and drinking and playing records to all hours the day after the crash, his concussion having cured itself pretty quick. Reaction, he'd said when she complained of the noise, against not being killed.

It was dark by then, and I drove slowly back into London against the stream of headlights pouring out. Back to my flat in a modern block, a short walk from the office, down the ramp into the basement garage, and up in the lift to the fifth floor, home.

There were two rooms facing south, bedroom and sitting-room, and two behind them, bathroom and kitchen, with windows into an inner well. A pleasant sunny place, furnished in blond wood and cool colours, centrally heated, cleaning included in the rent. A regular order of groceries arrived week by week directly into the kitchen through a hatch, and rubbish disappeared down a chute. Instant living. No fuss, no mess, no strings. And damnably lonely, after Jenny.

Not that she had ever been in the place, she hadn't. The house in the Berkshire village where we had mostly lived had been too much of a battleground, and when she walked out I sold it, with relief. I'd moved into the new flat shortly after going to the agency, because it was close. It was also expensive: but I had no fares to pay.

I mixed myself a brandy with ice and water, sat down in an arm-chair, put my feet up, and thought about Seabury. Seabury, Captain Oxon, Ted Wilkins, Intersouth Chemicals, and a driver called Smith.

After that I thought about Kraye. Nothing pleasant about him, nothing at all. A smooth, phony crust of sophistication hiding ruthless greed; a seething passion for crystals, ditto for land; an obsession with the cleanliness of his body to compensate for the murk in his mind; uncon-ventional sexual pleasures; and the abnormal quality of being able to look carefully at a crippled hand and *then hit it*.

No, I didn't care for Howard Kraye one little bit.

Chapter Seven

'Chico,' I said. 'How would you overturn a lorry on a pre-determined spot?'

'Huh? That's easy. All you'd need would be some heavy lifting gear. A big hydraulic jack. A crane, Anything like that.'

'How long would it take?'

'You mean, supposing the lorry and the crane were both in position?'

'Yes.'

'Only a minute or two. What sort of lorry?'

'A tanker.'

'A petrol job?'

'A bit smaller than the petrol tankers. More the size of milk ones.'

'Easy as kiss your hand. They've got a low centre of gravity, mind. It'd need a good strong lift. But dead easy, all the same.'

I turned to Dolly. 'Is Chico busy today, or could you spare him?'

Dolly leaned forward, chewing the end of a pencil and looking at her day's chart. The cross-over blouse did its stuff.

'I could send someone else to Kempton . . .' She caught the direction of my eyes and laughed, and retreated a whole half inch. 'Yes, you can have him.' She gave him a fond glance.

'Chico,' I said. 'Go down to Seabury and see if you can find any trace of heavy lifting gear having been seen near the racecourse last Friday . . . those little bungalows are full of people with nothing to do but watch the world go by . . . you might check whether anything was hired locally, but I suppose that's a bit much to hope for. The road would have to have been closed for a few minutes before the tanker went over, I should think. See if you can find anyone who noticed anything like that . . . detour signs, for instance. And after that, go to the council offices and see what you can dig up among their old maps on the matter of drains.' I told him the rough position of the subsiding trench which had made a slaughterhouse of the hurdle race, so that he should know what to look for on the maps. 'And be discreet.'

'Teach your grandmother to suck eggs,' he grinned.

'Our quarry is rough.'

'And you don't want him to hear us creep up behind him?'

'Quite right.'

'Little Chico,' he said truthfully, 'can take care of himself.'

After he had gone I telephoned Lord Hagbourne and described to him in no uncertain terms the state of Seabury's turf.

'What they need is some proper earth moving equipment, fast, and apparently there's nothing in the kitty to pay for it. Couldn't the Levy Board . . .?'

'The Levy Board is no fairy godmother,' he interrupted. 'But I'll see what can be done. Less than half cleared, you say? Hmm. However, I understand that Captain Oxon assured Weatherbys that the course would be ready for the next meeting. Has he changed his mind?'

'I didn't see him, sir. He was away for the day.'

'Oh.' Lord Hagbourne's voice grew a shade cooler. 'Then he didn't ask you to enlist my help?'

'No.'

'I don't see that I can interfere then. As racecourse manager it is his responsibility to decide what can be done and what can't, and I think it must be left like that. Mm, yes. And of course he will consult the Clerk of the Course if he needs advice.'

'The Clerk of the Course is Mr. Fotherton, who lives in Bristol. He is Clerk of the Course there, too, and he's busy with the meetings there tomorrow and Monday.'

'Er, yes, so he is.'

'You could ring Captain Oxon up in an informal way and just ask how the work is getting on,' I suggested.

'I don't know . . .'

'Well, sir, you can take my word for it that if things dawdle on at the same rate down there, there won't be any racing at Seabury next week-end. I don't think Captain Oxon can realise just how slowly those men are digging.'

'He must do,' he protested. 'He assured Weatherbys . . .'

'Another last minute cancellation will kill Seabury off,' I said with some force.

There was a moment's pause. Then he said reluctantly, 'Yes, I suppose it might. All right then. I'll ask Captain Oxon and Mr. Fortherton if they are both satisfied with the way things are going.'

And I couldn't pin him down to any more direct action than that, which was certainly not going to be enough. Protocol would be the death of Seabury, I thought.

Monopolising Dolly's telephone, I next rang up the Epping police and spoke to Chief-Inspector Cornish.

'Any more news about Andrews?' I asked.

'I suppose you have a reasonable personal interest.' His chuckle came down the wire. 'We found he did have a sister after all. We called her at the inquest yesterday for identification purposes as she is a relative, but if you ask me she didn't really know. She took one look at the bits in the mortuary and was sick on the floor.'

'Poor girl, you couldn't blame her.'

'No. She didn't look long enough to identify anyone. But we had your identification for sure, so we hadn't the heart to make her go in again.'

'How did he die? Did you find out?'

'Indeed we did. He was shot in the back. The bullet ricocheted off a rib and lodged in the sternum. We got the experts to compare it with the one they dug out of the wall of your office. Your bullet was a bit squashed by the hard plaster, but there's no doubt that they are the same. He was killed with the gun he used on you.'

'And was it there, underneath him?'

'Not a sign of it. They brought in "murder by persons unknown". And between you and me, that's how it's likely to stay. We haven't a lead to speak of.'

'What lead do you have?' I asked.

His voice had a smile in it. 'Only something his sister told us. She has a bedsitter in Islington, and he spent the evening there before breaking into your place. He showed her the gun. She says he was proud of having it; apparently he was a bit simple. All he told her was that a big chap had lent it to him to go out and fetch something, and he was to shoot anyone who got in his way. She didn't believe him. She said he was always making things up, always had, all his life. So she didn't ask him

anything about the big chap, or about where he was going, or anything
at all.'

'A bit casual,' I said. 'With a loaded gun under her nose.'

According to the neighbours she was more interested in a stream of
men friends than in anything her brother did.'

'Sweet people, neighbours.'

'You bet. Anyway we checked with anyone we could find who had
seen Andrews the week he shot you, and he hadn't said a word to any
of them about a gun or a "big chap", or an errand in Cromwell Road.'

'He didn't go back to his sister afterwards?'

'No, she'd told him she had a guest coming.'

'At one in the morning? The neighbours must be right. You tried the
racecourses, of course? Andrews is quite well known there, as a sort of
spivvy odd-job messenger boy.'

'Yes, we mainly tried the racecourses. No results. Everyone seemed
surprised that such a harmless person should have been murdered.'

'Harmless!'

He laughed. 'If you hadn't thought him harmless, you'd have kept out
of his way.'

'You're so right,' I said with feeling. 'But now I see a villain in every
respectable citizen. It's very disturbing.'

'Most of them are villains, in one way or another,' he said cheerfully.
'Keeps us busy. By the way, what do you think of Sparkle's chances this
year in the Hennessy . . .?'

When eventually I put the telephone down Dolly grabbed it with a
sarcastic 'Do you mind?' and asked the switchboard girl to get her three
numbers in a row, 'without interruptions from Halley'. I grinned, got
the packet of photographs out of the plywood table drawer, and looked
through them again. They didn't tell me any more than before. Ellis
Bolt's letters to Kraye. Now you see it, now you don't. A villain in every
respectable citizen. Play it secretly, I thought, close to the chest, in case
the eyes looking over your shoulder give you away. I wondered why I
was so oppressed by a vague feeling of apprehension, and decided in
irritation that a bullet in the stomach had made me nervous.

When Dolly had finished her calls I took the receiver out of her hand
and got through to my bank manager.

'Mr. Hopper? This is Sid Halley . . . yes, fine thanks, and you? Good.
Now, would you tell me just how much I have in both my accounts,
deposit and current?'

'They're quite healthy, actually,' he said in his gravelly bass voice.
'You've had several dividends in lately. Hang on a minute, and I'll send
for the exact figures.' He spoke to someone in the background and then
came back. 'It's time you re-invested some of it.'

'I do have some investments in mind,' I agreed. 'That's what I want
to discuss with you. I'm planning to buy some shares this time from
another stockbroker, not through the bank. Er . . . please don't think that
I'm dissatisfied; how could I be, when you've done so well for me. It's
something to do with my work at the agency.'

'Say no more. What exactly do you want?'

'Well, to give you as a reference,' I said. 'He's sure to want one, but I would be very grateful if you would make it as impersonal and as strictly financial as possible. Don't mention either my past occupation or my present one. That's very important.'

'I won't, then. Anything else?'

'Nothing ... oh, yes. I've introduced myself to him as John Halley. Would you refer to me like that if he gets in touch with you?'

'Right. I'll look forward to hearing from you one day what it's all about. Why don't you come in and see me? I've some very good cigars.' The deep voice was amused. 'Ah, here are the figures ...' He told me the total, which for once was bigger than I expected. That happy state of affairs wouldn't last very long, I reflected, if I had to live for two years without any salary from Radnor. And no one's fault but my own.

Giving Dolly back her telephone with an ironic bow, I went upstairs to Bona Fides. Jack Copeland's mud coloured jersey had a dark blue darn on the chest and a fraying stretch of ribbing on the hip. He was picking at a loose thread and making it worse.

'Anything on Kraye yet?' I asked. 'Or is it too early?'

'George has got something on the prelim, I think,' he answered. 'Anybody got any scissors?' A large area of jersey disintegrated into ladders. 'Blast.'

Laughing, I went over to George's desk. The prelim was a sheet of handwritten notes in George's concertinaed style. 'Leg mat, 2 yrs. 2 prev, 1 div, 1 sui dec.' it began, followed by a list of names and dates.

'Oh, yeah?' I said.

'Yeah.' He grinned. 'Kraye was legally married to Doria Dawn, née Easterman, two years ago. Before that he had two other wives. One killed herself; the other divorced him for cruelty.' He pointed to the names and dates.

'So clear,' I agreed. 'When you know how.'

'If you weren't so impatient you'd have a legible typed report. But as you're here ...' He went on down the page, pointing. 'Geologists think him a bit eccentric ... quartz has no intrinsic value, most of it's much too coomon, except for the gem stones, but Kraye goes round trying to buy chunks of it if they take his fancy. They know him quite well along the road at the Geology Museum. But not a breath of any dirty work. Clubs ... he belongs to these three, not over-liked, but most members think he's a brilliant fellow, talks very well. He gambles at Crockfords, ends up about all square over the months. He travels, always first-class, usually by boat, not air. No job or profession, can't trace him on any professional or university lists. Thought to live on investments, playing the stock market, etc. Not much liked, but considered by most a clever, cultured man, by one or two a hypocritical gasbag.'

'No talk of him being crooked in any way?'

'Not a word. You want him dug deeper?'

'If you can do it without him finding out.'

George nodded. 'Do you want him tailed?'

'No, I don't think so. Not at present.' A twenty-four-hour tail was heavy on man-power and expensive to the client, quite apart from the risk of the quarry noticing and being warned of the hunt. 'Anything on his early life?' I asked.

George shook his head. 'Nothing. Nobody who knows him now has known him longer than about ten years. He either wasn't born in Britain, or his name at birth wasn't Kraye. No known relatives.'

'You've done marvels, George. All this in one day.'

'Contacts, chum, contacts. A lot of phoning, a bit of pubbing, a touch of gossip with the local tradesmen . . . nothing to it.'

Jack, moodily poking his fingers through the cobweb remains of his jersey, looked at me over the half-moon specs and said that there wasn't a prelim on Bolt yet because ex-sergeant Carter, who was working on it, hadn't phoned in.

'If he does,' I said, 'let me know? I've an appointment with Bolt at three thirty. It would be handy to know the set-up before I go.'

'O.K.'

After that I went down and looked out of the windows of the Racing Section for half an hour, idly watching life go by in the Cromwell Road and wondering just what sort of mess I was making of the Kraye investigation. A novice chaser in the Grand National, I thought wryly; that was me. Though, come to think of it, I had once ridden a novice in the National, and got round, too. Slightly cheered, I took Dolly out to a drink and a sandwich in the snack bar at the Air Terminal, where we sat and envied the people starting off on their travels. So much expectation in the faces, as if they could fly away and leave their troubles on the ground. An illusion, I thought sourly. Your troubles flew with you; a drag in the mind . . . a deformity in the pocket.

I laughed and joked with Dolly, as usual. What else can you do?

The firm of Charing, Street and King occupied two rooms in a large block of offices belonging to a bigger firm, and consisted entirely of Bolt, his clerk and a secretary.

I was shown the door of the secretary's office, and went into a dull, tidy, fog-coloured box of a room with cold fluorescent lighting and a close-up view of the fire-escape through the grimy window. A woman sat at a desk by the right hand wall, facing the window, with her back towards me. A yard behind her chair was a door with ELLIS BOLT painted on a frosted glass panel. It occurred to me that she was most awkwardly placed in the room, but that perhaps she liked sitting in a potential draught and having to turn round every time someone came in.

She didn't turn round, however. She merely moved her head round a fraction towards me and said 'Yes?'

'I have an appointment with Mr. Bolt,' I said. 'At three thirty.'

'Oh, yes, you must be Mr. Halley. Do sit down. I'll see if Mr. Bolt is free now.'

She pointed to an easy chair a step ahead of me, and flipped a switch on her desk. While I listened to her telling Mr. Bolt I was there, in the quiet voice I had heard on the telephone, I had time to see she was in her late thirties, slender, upright in her chair, with a smooth wing of straight, dark hair falling down beside her cheek. If anything, it was too young a hair style for her. There were no rings on her fingers, and no nail varnish either. Her clothes were dark and uninteresting. It seemed as though she were making a deliberate attempt to be unattractive, yet her profile, when she half turned and told me Mr. Bolt would see me, was pleasant enough. I had a glimpse of one brown eye quickly cast down, the beginning of a smile on pale lips, and she presented me again squarely with the back of her head.

Puzzled, I opened Ellis Bolt's door and walked in. The inner office wasn't much more inspiring than the outer; it was larger and there was a new green square of carpet on the linoleum, but the greyish walls pervaded, along with the tidy dullness. Through the two windows was a more distant view of the fire-escape of the building across the alley. If a drab conventional setting equalled respectability, Bolt was an honest stockbroker; and Carter, who had phoned in just before I left, had found nothing to suggest otherwise.

Bolt was on his feet behind his desk, hand outstretched. I shook it, he gestured me to a chair with arms, and offered me a cigarette.

'No, thank you, I don't smoke.'

'Lucky man,' he said benignly, tapping ash off one he was half through, and settling his pin-striped bulk back into his chair.

He was rounded at every point, large round nose, round cheeks, round heavy chin: no planes, no impression of bone structure underneath. He had exceptionally heavy eyebrows, a full mobile mouth, and a smug self-satisfied expression.

'Now, Mr. Halley, I believe in coming straight to the point. What can I do for you?'

He had a mellifluous voice, and he spoke as if he enjoyed the sound of it.

I said, 'An aunt has given me some money now rather than leave it to me in her will, and I want to invest it.'

'I see. And what made you come to me? Did someone recommend . . .?' He tailed off, watching me with eyes that told me he was no fool.

'I'm afraid . . .' I hesitated, smiling apologetically to take the offence out of the words, 'that I literally picked you with a pin. I don't know any stockbrokers. I didn't know how to get to know one, so I picked up a classified directory and stuck a pin into the list of names, and it was yours.'

'Ah,' he said paternally, observing the bad fit of Chico's second best suit, which I had borrowed for the occasion, and listening to me reverting to the accent of my childhood.

'Can you help me?' I asked.

'I expect so, I expect so. How much is this er, gift?' His voice was minutely patronising, his manner infinitesimally bored. His time, he suspected, was being wasted.

'Fifteen hundred pounds.'

He brightened a very little. 'Oh, yes, definitely, we can do something with that. Now, do you want growth mainly or a high rate of yield?'

I looked vague. He told me quite fairly the difference between the two, and offered no advice.

'Growth, then,' I said, tentatively. 'Turn it into a fortune in time for my old age.'

He smiled without much mirth, and drew a sheet of paper towards him.

'Could I have your full name?'

'John Halley . . . John Sidney Halley,' I said truthfully. He wrote it down.

'Address?' I gave it.

'And your bank?' I told him that too.

'And I'll need a reference, I'm afraid.'

'Would the bank manager do?' I asked. 'I've had an account there for two years . . . he knows me quite well.'

'Excellent.' He screwed up his pen. 'Now, do you have any idea what companies you'd like shares in, or will you leave it to me?'

'Oh, I'll leave it to you. If you don't mind, that is. I don't know anything about it, you see, not really. Only it seems silly to leave all that money around doing nothing.'

'Quite, quite.' He was bored with me. I thought with amusement that Charles would appreciate my continuing his strategy of the weak front. 'Tell me, Mr. Halley, what do you do for a living?'

'Oh . . . um . . . I work in a shop,' I said. 'In the men's wear. Very interesting, it is.'

'I'm sure it is.' There was a yawn stuck in his throat.

'I'm hoping to be made an assistant buyer next year,' I said eagerly.

'Splendid. Well done.' He'd had enough. He got cumbrously to his feet and ushered me to the door. 'All right, Mr. Halley, I'll invest your money safely for you in good long term growth stock, and send you the papers to sign in due course. You'll hear from me in a week or ten days. All right?'

'Yes, Mr. Bolt, thank you very much indeed,' I said respectfully. He shut the door gently behind me.

There were now two people in the outer office. The woman with her back still turned, and a spare, middle-aged man with a primly folded mouth, and tough stringy tendons pushing his collar away from his neck. He was quite at home, and with an incurious, unhurried glance at me he went past into Bolt's office. The clerk, I presumed.

The woman was typing addresses on envelopes. The twenty or so that she had done lay in a slithery stack on her left: on her right an open file provided a list of names. I looked over her shoulder casually, and then with quickened interest. She was working down the first page of a list of Seabury shareholders.

'Do you want something, Mr. Halley?' she asked politely, pulling one envelope from the typewriter and inserting another with a minimum of flourish.

'Well, er, yes,' I said diffidently. I walked round to the side of her desk and found that one couldn't go on round to the front of it: a large old fashioned table with bulbous legs filled all the space between the desk and the end of the room. I looked at this arrangement with some sort of understanding and with compassion.

'I wondered,' I said, 'if you could be very kind and tell me something about investing money, and so on. I didn't like to ask Mr. Bolt too much, he's a busy man. And I'd like to know a bit about it.'

'I'm sorry, Mr. Halley.' Her head was turned away from me, bent over the Seabury investors. 'I've a job to do, as you see. Why don't you read the financial columns in the papers, or get a book on the subject?'

I had a book all right. *Outline of Company Law.* One thing I had learned from it was that only stockbrokers – apart from the company involved – could send circulars to shareholders. It was illegal if private citizens did it. Illegal for Kraye to send letters to Seabury shareholders offering to buy them out: legal for Bolt.

'Books aren't as good as people at explaining things,' I said. 'If you are busy now, could I come back when you've finished work and take you out for a meal? I'd be so grateful if you would, if you possibly could.'

A sort of shudder shook her. 'I'm sorry, Mr. Halley, but I'm afraid I can't.'

'If you will look at me, so that I can see all of your face,' I said, 'I will ask you again.'

Her head went up with a jerk at that, but finally she turned round and looked at me.

I smiled. 'That's better. Now, how about coming out with me this evening?'

'You guessed?'

I nodded. 'The way you've got your furniture organised . . . Will you come?'

'You still want to?'

'Well, of course. What time do you finish?'

'About six, tonight.'

'I'll come back. I'll meet you at the door, down in the street.'

'All right,' she said. 'If you really mean it, thank you. I'm not doing anything else tonight . . .'

Years of hopeless loneliness showed raw in the simple words. Not doing anything else, tonight or most nights. Yet her face wasn't horrific; not anything as bad as I had been prepared for. She had lost an eye, and wore a false one. There had been some extensive burns and undoubtedly some severe fracture of the facial bones, but plastic surgery had repaired the damage to a great extent, and it had all been a long time ago. The scars were old. It was the inner wound which hadn't healed.

Well . . . I knew a bit about that myself, on a smaller scale.

Chapter Eight

She came out of the door at ten past six wearing a neat well cut dark overcoat and with a plain silk scarf covering her hair, tied under her chin. It hid only a small part of the disaster to her face, and seeing her like that, defenceless, away from the shelter she had made in her office, I had an uncomfortably vivid vision of the purgatory she suffered day in and day out on the journeys to work.

She hadn't expected me to be there. She didn't look round for me when she came out, but turned directly up the road towards the tube station. I walked after her and touched her arm. Even in low heels she was taller than I.

'Mr. Halley!' she said. 'I didn't think . . .'

'How about a drink first?' I said. 'The pubs are open.'

'Oh no . . .'

'Oh yes. Why not?' I took her arm and steered her firmly across the road into the nearest bar. Dark oak, gentle lighting, brass pump handles, and the lingering smell of lunchtime cigars: a warm beckoning stop for city gents on their way home. There were already half a dozen of them, prosperous and dark-suited, adding fizz to their spirits.

'Not here,' she protested.

'Here.' I held a chair for her to sit on at a small table in a corner, and asked her what she would like to drink.

'Sherry, then . . . dry . . .'

I took the two glasses over one at a time, sherry for her, brandy for me. She was sitting on the edge of the chair, uncomfortably, and it was not the one I had put her in. She had moved round so that she had her back to everyone except me.

'Good luck, Miss . . .?' I said, lifting my glass.

'Martin. Zanna Martin.'

'Good luck, Miss Martin.' I smiled.

Tentatively she smiled back. It made her face much worse: half the muscles on the disfigured right side didn't work and could do nothing about lifting the corner of her mouth or crinkling the skin round the socket of her eye. Had life been even ordinarily kind she would have been a pleasant looking, assured woman in her late thirties with a loving husband and a growing family: years of heartbreak had left her a shy, lonely spinster who dressed and moved as though she would like to be invisible. Yet, looking at the sad travesty of her face, one could neither blame the young men who hadn't married her nor condemn her own efforts at effacement.

'Have you worked for Mr. Bolt long?' I asked peaceably, settling back lazily into my chair and watching her gradually relax into her own.

'Only a few months . . .' She talked for some time about her job in answer to my interested questions, but unless she was supremely artful, she was not aware of anything shady going on in Charing, Street and King. I mentioned the envelopes she had been addressing, and asked what was going into them.

'I don't know yet,' she said. 'The leaflets haven't come from the printers.'

'But I expect you typed the leaflet anyway,' I said idly.

'No, actually I think Mr. Bolt did that one himself. He's quite helpful in that way, you know. If I'm busy he'll often do letters himself.'

Will he, I thought. Will he, indeed. Miss Martin, as far as I was concerned, was in the clear. I bought her another drink and extracted her opinion about Bolt as a stockbroker. Sound, she said, but not busy. She had worked for other stockbrokers, it appeared, and knew enough to judge.

'There aren't many stockbrokers working on their own any more,' she explained, 'and . . . well . . . I don't like working in a big office, you see . . . and it's getting more difficult to find a job which suits me. So many stockbrokers have joined up into partnerships of three or more; it reduces overheads terrifically, of course, and it means that they can spend more time in the House . . .'

'Where are Mr. Charing, Mr. Street, and Mr. King?' I asked.

Charing and Street were dead, she understood, and King had retired some years ago. The firm now consisted simply and solely of Ellis Bolt. She didn't really like Mr. Bolt's offices being contained inside of those of another firm. It wasn't private enough, but it was the usual arrangement nowadays. It reduced overheads so much . . .

When the city gents had mostly departed to the bosoms of their families, Zanna Martin and I left the pub and walked through the empty city streets towards the Tower. We found a quiet little restaurant where she agreed to have dinner. As before, she made a straight line for a corner table and sat with her back to the room.

'I'm paying my share,' she announced firmly when she had seen the prices on the menu. 'I had no idea this place was so expensive, or I wouldn't have let you choose it . . . Mr. Bolt mentioned that you worked in a shop.'

'There's Aunty's legacy,' I pointed out. 'The dinner's on Aunty.'

She laughed. It was a happy sound if you didn't look at her, but I found I was already able to talk to her without continually, consciously thinking about her face. One got used to it after a very short while. Some time, I thought, I would tell her so.

I was still on a restricted diet, which made social eating difficult enough without one-handedness thrown in, but did very well on clear soup and Dover sole, expertly removed from the bone by a waiter. Miss Martin, shedding inhibitions visibly, ordered lobster cocktail, fillet steak, and peaches in kirsch. We drank wine, coffee and brandy, and took our time.

'Oh!' she said ecstatically at one point. 'It is so long since I had anything like this. My father used to take me out now and then, but since he died . . . well, I can't go to places like this myself . . . I sometimes eat in a café round the corner from my rooms, they know me there . . . it's very good food really, chops, eggs and chips . . . you know . . . things like that.' I could picture her there, sitting alone, with her ravaged head turned to the wall. Lonely unhappy Zanna Martin. I wished I could do something – anything – to help her.

Eventually, when she was stirring her coffee, she said simply, 'It was a rocket, this.' She touched her face. 'A firework. The bottle it was standing in tipped over just as it went off, and came straight at me. It hit me on the cheek bone and exploded . . . It wasn't anybody's fault . . . I was sixteen.'

'They made a good job of it,' I said.

She shook her head, smiling the crooked tragic smile. 'A good job from what it was, I suppose, but . . . they said if the rocket had struck an inch higher it would have gone through my eye into my brain and killed me. I often wish it had.'

She meant it. Her voice was calm. She was stating a fact.

'Yes,' I said.

'It's strange, but I've almost forgotten about it this evening, and that doesn't often happen when I'm with anyone.'

'I'm honoured.'

She drank her coffee, put down her cup, and looked at me thoughtfully.

She said, 'Why do you keep your hand in your pocket all the time?'

I owed it to her, after all. I put my hand palm upward on the table, wishing I didn't have to.

She said 'Oh!' in surprise, and then, looking back at my face, 'So you do know. That's why I feel so . . . so easy with you. You do understand.'

I shook my head. 'Only a little. I have a pocket; you haven't. I can hide.' I rolled my hand over (the back of it was less off-putting), and finally retreated it on to my lap.

'But you can't do the simplest things,' she exclaimed. Her voice was full of pity. 'You can't tie your shoe-laces, for instance. You can't even eat steak in a restaurant without asking someone else to cut it up for you . . .'

'Shut up,' I said abruptly. 'Shut up, Miss Martin. Don't you dare to do to me what you can't bear yourself.'

'Pity . . .' she said, biting her lip and staring at me unhappily. 'Yes, it's so easy to give . . .'

'And embarrassing to receive.' I grinned at her. 'And my shoes don't have shoe-laces. They're out of date, for a start.'

'You can know as well as I do what it feels like, and yet do it to someone else . . .' She was very upset.

'Stop being miserable. It was kindness. Sympathy.'

'Do you think,' she said hesitantly, 'that pity and sympathy are the same thing?'

'Very often, yes. But sympathy is discreet and pity is tactless. Oh . . . I'm sorry.' I laughed. 'Well . . . it was sympathetic of you to feel sorry I can't cut up my own food, and tactless to say so. The perfect example.'

'It wouldn't be so hard to forgive people for just being tactless,' she said thoughtfully.

'No,' I agreed, surprised. 'I suppose it wouldn't.'

'It might not hurt so much . . . just tactlessness?'

'It mightn't . . .'

'And curiosity . . . that might be easier, too, if I just thought of it as bad manners, don't you think? I mean tactlessness and bad manners wouldn't be so hard to stand. In fact *I* could be sorry for *them*, for not knowing better how to behave. Oh why, why didn't I think of that years ago, when it seems so simple now. So sensible.'

'Miss Martin,' I said with gratitude. 'Have some more brandy . . . you're a liberator.'

'How do you mean?'

'Pity is bad manners and can be taken in one's stride, as you said.'

'You said it,' she protested.

'Indeed I didn't, not like that.'

'All right,' she said with gaiety. 'We'll drink to a new era. A bold front to the world. I will put my desk back to where it was before I joined the office, facing the door. I'll let every caller see me. I'll . . .' Her brave voice nearly cracked. 'I'll just think poorly of their manners if they pity me too openly. That's settled.'

We had some more brandy. I wondered inwardly whether she would have the same resolve in the morning, and doubted it. There had been so many years of hiding. She too, it seemed, was thinking along the same lines.

'I don't know that I can do it alone. But if you will promise me something, then I can.'

'Very well,' I said incautiously. 'What?'

'Don't put your hand in your pocket tomorrow. Let everyone see it.'

I couldn't. Tomorrow I would be going to the races. I looked at her, appalled, and really understood only then what she had to bear, and what it would cost her to move her desk. She saw the refusal in my face, and some sort of light died in her own. The gaiety collapsed, the defeated, defenceless look came back, the liberation was over.

'Miss Martin . . .' I swallowed.

'It doesn't matter,' she said tiredly. 'It doesn't matter. And anyway, it's Saturday tomorrow. I only go in for a short while to see to the mail and anything urgent from today's transactions. There wouldn't be any point in changing the desk.'

'And on Monday?'

'Perhaps.' It meant no.

'If you'll change it tomorrow and do it all next week, I'll do what you ask,' I said, quaking at the thought of it.

'You can't,' she said sadly. 'I can see that you can't.'

'If you can, I must.'

'But I shouldn't have asked you . . . you work in a shop.'

'Oh.' That I had forgotten. 'It won't matter.'

An echo of her former excitement crept back.

'Do you really mean it?'

I nodded. I had wanted to do something – anything – to help her. Anything. My God.

'Promise?' she said doubtfully.

'Yes. And you?'

'All right,' she said, with returning resolution. 'But I can only do it if I know you are in the same boat . . . I couldn't let you down then, you see.'

I paid the bill, and although she said there was no need, I took her home. We went on the underground to Finchley. She made straight for the least conspicuous seat and sat presenting the good side of her face to the carriage. Then, laughing at herself, she apologised for doing it.

'Never mind,' I said, 'the new era doesn't start until tomorrow,' and hid my hand like a proper coward.

Her room was close to the station (a deliberately short walk, I guessed) in a large prosperous looking suburban house. At the gate she stopped.

'Will . . . er . . . I mean, would you like to come in? It's not very late . . . but perhaps you are tired.'

She wasn't eager, but when I accepted she seemed pleased.

'This way, then.'

We went through a bare tidy garden to a black painted front door adorned with horrible stained glass panels. Miss Martin fumbled endlessly in her bag for her key and I reflected idly that I could have picked that particular lock as quickly as she opened it legally. Inside there was a warm hall smelling healthily of air freshener, and at the end of a passage off it, a door with a card saying 'Martin'.

Zanna Martin's room was a surprise. Comfortable, large, close carpeted, newly decorated, and alive with colour. She switched on a standard lamp and a rosy table lamp, and drew burnt orange curtains over the black expanse of french windows. With satisfaction she showed me the recently built tiny bathroom leading out of her room, and the suitcase sized kitchen beside it, both of which additions she had paid for herself. The people who owned the house were very understanding, she said. Very kind. She had lived there for eleven years. It was home.

Zanna Martin had no mirrors in her home. Not one.

She bustled in her little kitchen, making more coffee: for something to do, I thought. I sat relaxed on her long comfortable modern sofa and watched how, from long habit, she leant forward most of the time so that the heavy shoulder length dark hair swung down to hide her face. She brought the tray and set it down, and sat on the sofa carefully on my right. One couldn't blame her.

'Do you ever cry?' she said suddenly.

'No.'

'Not . . . from frustration?'

'No.' I smiled. 'Swear.'

She sighed. 'I used to cry often. I don't any more, though. Getting older, of course. I'm nearly forty. I've got resigned now to not getting married . . . I knew I was resigned to it when I had the bathroom and kitchen built. Up to then, you see, I'd always pretended to myself that one day . . . one day, perhaps . . . but I don't expect it any more, not any more.'

'Men are fools,' I said inadequately.

'I hope you don't mind me talking like this? It's so seldom that I have anyone in here, and practically never anyone I can really talk to . . .'

I stayed for an hour, listening to her memories, her experiences, her whole shadowed life. What, I chided myself, had ever happened to me that was one tenth as bad. I had had far more ups than downs.

At length she said, 'How did it happen with you? Your hand . . .'

'Oh, an accident. A sharp bit of metal.' A razor sharp racing horse-shoe attached to the foot of a horse galloping at thirty miles an hour, to be exact. A hard kicking slash as I rolled on the ground from an easy fall. One of those things.

Horses race in thin light shoes called plates, not the heavy ones they normally wear: blacksmiths change them before and after, every time a horse runs. Some trainers save a few shillings by using the same racing plates over and over again, so that the leading edge gradually wears down to the thickness of a knife. But jagged knives, not smooth. They can cut you open like a hatchet.

I'd really known at once when I saw my stripped wrist with the blood spurting out in a jet and the broken bones showing white, that I was finished as a jockey. But I wouldn't give up hope, and insisted on the surgeons sewing it all up, even though they wanted to take my hand off there and then. It would never be any good, they said; and they were right. Too many of the tendons and nerves were severed. I persuaded them to try twice later on to rejoin and graft some of them and both times it had been a useless agony. They had refused to consider it again.

Zanna Martin hesitated on the brink of asking for details, and fortunately didn't. Instead she said, 'Are you married? Do you know, I've talked so much about myself, that I don't know a thing about you.'

'My wife's in Athens, visiting her sister.'

'How lovely,' she sighed. 'I wish . . .'

'You'll go one day,' I said firmly. 'Save up, and go in a year or two. On a bus tour or something. With people anyway. Not alone.'

I looked at my watch, and stood up. 'I've enjoyed this evening a great deal. Thank you so much for coming out with me.'

She stood and formally shook hands, not suggesting another meeting. So much humility, I thought: so little expectation. Poor, poor Miss Martin.

'Tomorrow morning . . .' she said tentatively, at the door.

'Tomorrow,' I nodded. 'Move that desk. And I . . . I promise I won't forget.'

I went home cursing that fate had sent me someone like Zanna Martin. I had expected Charing, Street and King's secretary to be young, perhaps pretty, a girl I could take to a café and the pictures and flirt with, with no great involvement on either side. Instead it looked as if I should have to pay more than I'd meant to for my inside information on Ellis Bolt.

Chapter Nine

'Now look,' said Lord Hagbourne, amidst the bustle of Kempton races, 'I've had a word with Captain Oxon and he's satisfied with the way things are going. I really can't interfere any more. Surely you understand that?'

'No, sir, I don't. I don't think Captain Oxon's feelings are more important than Seabury Racecourse. The course should be put right quickly, even if it means overruling him.'

'Captain Oxon,' he said with a touch of sarcasm, 'knows more about his job than you do. I give more weight to his assurance than to your quick look at the track.'

'Then couldn't you go and see for yourself? While there is still time.'

He didn't like being pushed. His expression said so, plainly. There was no more I could say, either, without risking him ringing up Radnor to cancel the whole investigation.

'I may ... er ... I may find time on Monday,' he said at last, grudgingly. 'I'll see. Have you found anything concrete to support your idea that Seabury's troubles were caused maliciously?'

'Not yet, sir.'

'A bit far-fetched, if you ask me,' he said crossly. 'I said so to begin with, if you remember. If you don't turn something up pretty soon ... it's all expense, you know.'

He was intercepted by a passing Steward who took him off to another problem, leaving me grimly to reflect that so far there was a horrid lack of evidence of any sort. What there was, was negative.

George had still found no chink in Kray's respectability, ex-sergeant Carter had given Bolt clearance, and Chico had come back from Seabury with no results all along the line.

We'd met in the office that morning, before I went to Kempton.

'Nothing,' said Chico. 'I wagged me tongue off, knocking at every front door along that road. Not a soggy flicker. The bit which crosses the racecourse wasn't closed by diversion notices, that's for sure. There isn't much traffic along there, of course. I counted it. Only forty to the hour, average. Still, that's too much for at least some of the neighbours not to notice if there'd been anything out of the ordinary.'

'Did anyone see the tanker, before it overturned?'

'They're always seeing tankers, nowadays. Several complaints about it, I got. No one noticed that one, especially.'

'It can't be coincidence ... just at that spot at that time, where it would do most harm. And the driver packing up and moving a day or two afterwards, with no forwarding address.'

'Well ...' Chico scratched his ear reflectively. 'I got no dice with the hiring of lifting gear either. There isn't much to be had, and what there was was accounted for. None of the little bungalows saw anything in that line, except the breakdown cranes coming to lift the tanker up again.'

'How about the drains?'

'No drains,' he said. 'A blank back to Doomsday.'

'Good.'

'Come again?'

'If you'd found them on a map, the hurdle race accident would have been a genuine accident. This way, they reek of tiger traps.'

'A spot of spade work after dark? Dodgy stuff.'

I frowned. 'Yes. And it had to be done long enough before the race meeting for the ground to settle, so that the line of the trench didn't show . . .'

'And strong enough for a tractor to roll over it.'

'Tractor?'

'There was one on the course yesterday, pulling a trailer of dug up turf.'

'Oh yes, of course. Yes, strong enough to hold a tractor . . . but wheels wouldn't pierce the ground like a horse's legs. The weight is more spread.'

'True enough.'

'How fast was the turf-digging going?' I asked.

'Fast? You're joking.'

It was depressing. So was Lord Hagbourne's shilly-shallying. So, acutely, was the whole day, because I kept my promise to Zanna Martin. Pity, curiosity, surprise, embarrassment and revulsion, I encountered the lot. I tried hard to look on some of the things that were said as tactlessness or bad manners, but it didn't really work. Telling myself it was idiotic to be so sensitive didn't help either. If Miss Martin hadn't kept her side of the bargain, I thought miserably, I would throttle her.

Half way through the afternoon I had a drink in the big upstairs bar with Mark Witney.

'So that's what you've been hiding all this time in pockets and gloves,' he said.

'Yes.'

'Bit of a mess,' he commented.

'I'm afraid so.'

'Does it hurt still?'

'No, only if I knock it. And it aches sometimes.'

'Mm,' he said sympathetically. 'My ankle still aches too. Joints are always like that; they mend, but they never forgive you.' He grinned. 'The other half? There's time; I haven't a runner until the fifth.'

We had another drink, talking about horses, and I reflected that it would be easy if they were all like him.

'Mark,' I said as we walked back to the weighing room, 'do you remember whether Dunstable ran into any sort of trouble before it packed up?'

'That's going back a bit.' He pondered. 'Well, it certainly wasn't doing so well during the last year or two, was it? The attendances had fallen off, and they weren't spending any money on paint.'

'But no specific disasters?'

'The Clerk of the Course took an overdose, if you call that a disaster. Yes, I remember now, the collapse of the place's prosperity was put down to the Clerk's mental illness. Brinton, I think his name was. He'd been quietly going loco and making hopeless decisions all over the place.'

'I'd forgotten,' I said glumly. Mark went into the weighing room and I leant against the rails outside. A suicidal Clerk of the Course could hardly have been the work of Kraye, I thought. It might have given him the idea of accelerating the demise of Seabury, though. He'd had plenty of time over Dunstable, but owing to a recent political threat of nationalisation of building land, he might well be in a hurry to clinch Seabury. I sighed, disregarded as best I could a stare of fascinated horror from the teenage daughter of a man I used to ride for, and drifted over to look at the horses in the parade ring.

At the end of the too-long afternoon I drove back to my flat, mixed a bigger drink than usual, and spent the evening thinking, without any world-shattering results. Late the next morning, when I was similarly engaged, the door bell rang, and I found Charles outside.

'Come in,' I said with surprise: he rarely visited the flat, and was seldom in London at week-ends. 'Like some lunch? The restaurant downstairs is quite good.'

'Perhaps. In a minute.' He took off his overcoat and gloves and accepted some whisky. There was something unsettled in his manner, a ruffling of the smooth urbane exterior, a suggestion of a troubled frown in the high domed forehead.

'O.K.,' I said. 'What's the matter?'

'Er . . . I've just driven up from Aynsford. No traffic at all, for once. Such a lovely morning, I thought the drive would be . . . oh damn it,' he finished explosively, putting down his glass with a bang. 'To get it over quickly . . . Jenny telephoned from Athens last night. She's met some man there. She asked me to tell you she wants a divorce.'

'Oh,' I said. How like her, I thought, to get Charles to wield the axe. Practical Jenny, eager for a new fire, hacking away the dead wood. And if some of the wood was still alive, too bad.

'I must say,' said Charles, relaxing, 'you make a thorough job of it.'

'Of what?'

'Of not caring what happens to you.'

'I do care.'

'No one would suspect it,' he sighed. 'When I tell you your wife wants to divorce you, you must say, "Oh." When that happened,' he nodded to my arm, 'the first thing you said to me afterwards when I arrived full of sorrow and sympathy was, if I remember correctly, and I do, "Cheer up, Charles. I had a good run for my money." '

'Well, so I did.' Always, from my earliest childhood, I had instinctively shied away from too much sympathy. I didn't want it. I distrusted it. It made you soft inside, and an illegitimate child couldn't afford to be soft. One might weep at school, and one's spirit would never recover from so dire a disgrace. So the poverty and the sniggers, and later the lost wife and the smashed career had to be passed off with a shrug, and what one really felt about it had to be locked up tightly inside, out of view. Silly, really, but there it was.

We lunched companionably together downstairs, discussing in civilised tones the mechanics of divorce. Jenny, it appeared, did not want me to use the justified grounds of desertion: I, she said, should 'arrange things' instead. I must know how to do it, working for the agency. Charles was apologetic: Jenny's prospective husband was in the Diplomatic Service like Tony, and would prefer her not to be the guilty party.

Had I, Charles enquired delicately, already been . . . er . . . unfaithful to Jenny? No, I replied, watching him light his cigar, I was afraid I hadn't. For much of the time, owing to one thing and another, I hadn't felt well enough. That, he agreed with amusement, was a reasonable excuse.

I indicated that I would fix things as Jenny wanted, because it didn't affect my future like it did hers. She would be grateful, Charles said. I thought she would very likely take it for granted, knowing her.

When there was little else to say on that subject, we switched to Kraye. I asked Charles if he had seen him again during the week.

'Yes, I was going to tell you. I had lunch with him in the Club on Thursday. Quite accidentally. We both just happened to be there alone.'

'That's where you met him first, in your club?'

'That's right. Of course he thanked me for the week-end, and so on. Talked about the quartz. Very interesting collection, he said. But not a murmur about the St. Luke's Stone. I would have liked to have asked him straight out, just to see his reaction.' He tapped off the ash, smiling. 'I did mention you, though, in passing, and he switched on all the charm and said you had been extremely insulting to him and his wife, but that of course you hadn't spoiled his enjoyment. Very nasty, I thought it. He was causing bad trouble for you. Or at least, he intended to.'

'Yes,' I said cheerfully. 'But I did insult him, and I also spied on him. Anything he says of me is fully merited.' I told Charles how I had taken the photographs, and all that I had discovered or guessed during the past week. His cigar went out. He looked stunned.

'Well, you wanted me to, didn't you?' I said. 'You started it. What did you expect?'

'It's only that I had almost forgotten . . . this is what you used to be like, always. Determined. Ruthless, even.' He smiled. 'My game for convalescence has turned out better than I expected.'

'God help your other patients,' I said, 'if Kraye is standard medicine.'

We walked along the road towards where Charles had left his car. He was going straight home again.

I said, 'I hope that in spite of the divorce I shall see something of you? I should be sorry not to. As your ex-son-in-law, I can hardly come to Aynsford any more.'

He looked startled. 'I'll be annoyed if you don't, Sid. Jenny will be living all round the world, like Jill. Come to Aynsford whenever you want.'

'Thank you,' I said. I meant it, and it sounded like it.

He stood beside his car, looking down at me from his straight six feet.

'Jenny,' he said casually, 'is a fool.'

I shook my head. Jenny was no fool. Jenny knew what she needed, and it wasn't me.

When I went into the office (on time) the following morning, the girl on the switchboard caught me and said Radnor wanted me straight away.

'Good morning,' he said. 'I've just had Lord Hagbourne on the telephone telling me it's time we got results and that he can't go to Seabury today because his car is being serviced. Before you explode, Sid . . . I told him that you would take him down there now, at once, in your own car. So get a move on.'

I grinned. 'I bet he didn't like that.'

'He couldn't think of an excuse fast enough. Get round and collect him before he comes up with one.'

'Right.'

I made a quick detour up to the Racing Section where Dolly was adjusting her lipstick. No cross-over blouse today. A disappointment.

I told her where I was going, and asked if I could use Chico.

'Help yourself,' she said resignedly. 'If you can get a word in edgeways. He's along in Accounts arguing with Jones-boy.'

Chico, however, listened attentively and repeated what I had asked him. 'I'm to find out exactly what mistakes the Clerk of the Course at Dunstable made, and make sure that they and nothing else were the cause of the course losing money.'

'That's right. And dig out the file on Andrews and the case you were working on when I got shot.'

'But that's all dead,' he protested, 'the file's down in records in the basement.'

'Send Jones-boy down for it,' I suggested, grinning. 'It's probably only a coincidence, but there is something I want to check. I'll do it tomorrow morning. O.K.?'

'If you say so, chum.'

Back at my flat, I filled up with Extra and made all speed round to Beauchamp Place. Lord Hagbourne, with a civil but cool good morning, lowered himself into the passenger seat, and we set off for Seabury. It took him about a quarter of an hour to get over having been manoeuvred into something he didn't want to do, but at the end of that time he sighed and moved in his seat, and offered me a cigarette.

'No, thank you, sir. I don't smoke.'

'You don't mind if I do?' He took one out.

'Of course not.'

'This is a nice car,' he remarked, looking round.

'It's nearly three years old now. I bought it the last season I was riding. It's the best I've ever had, I think.'

'I must say,' he said inoffensively, 'that you manage extremely well. I wouldn't have thought that you could drive a car like this with only one effective hand.'

'Its power makes it easier, actually. I took it across Europe last Spring . . . good roads, there.'

We talked on about cars and holidays, then about theatres and books, and he seemed for once quite human. The subject of Seabury we carefully by-passed. I wanted to get him down there in a good mood; the arguments, if any, could take place on the way back; and it seemed as if he was of the same mind.

The state of Seabury's track reduced him to silent gloom. We walked down to the burnt piece with Captain Oxon, who was bearing himself stiffly and being pointedly polite. I thought he was a fool: he should have fallen on the Senior Steward and begged for instant help.

Captain Oxon, whom I had not met before, though he said he knew me by sight, was a slender pleasant looking man of about fifty, with a long pointed chin and a slight tendency to watery eyes. The present offended obstinacy of his expression looked more like childishness than real strength. A colonel manqué, I thought uncharitably, and no wonder.

'I know it's not really my business,' I said, 'but surely a bulldozer would shift what's left of the burnt bit in a couple of hours? There isn't time to settle new turf, but you could cover the whole area with some tons of tan and race over it quite easily, like that. You must be getting tan anyway, to cover the road surface. Surely you could just increase the order?'

Oxon looked at me with irritation. 'We can't afford it.'

'You can't afford another cancellation at the last minute,' I corrected.

'We are insured against cancellations.'

'I doubt whether an insurance company would stand this one,' I said. 'They'd say you could have raced if you'd tried hard enough.'

'It's Monday now,' remarked Lord Hagbourne thoughtfully. 'Racing's due on Friday. Suppose we call in a bulldozer tomorrow; the tan can be unloaded and spread on Wednesday and Thursday. Yes, that seems sound enough.'

'But the cost . . .' began Oxon.

'I think the money must be found,' said Lord Hagbourne. 'Tell Mr. Fotherton when he comes over that I have authorised the expenditure. The bills will be met, in one way or another. But I do think there is no case for not making an effort.'

It was on the tip of my tongue to point out that if Oxon had arranged for the bulldozer on the first day he could have saved the price of casual labour for six hand-diggers for a week, but as the battle was already won, I nobly refrained. I continued to think, however, that Oxon was a fool. Usually the odd custom of giving the managerships of racecourses to ex-army and navy officers worked out well, but conspicuously not in this case.

The three of us walked back up to the stands, Lord Hagbourne pausing and pursing his lips at their dingy appearance. I reflected that it was a pity that Seabury had a Clerk of the Course whose heart and home were far away on the thriving course at Bristol. If I'd been arranging things, I'd have seen to it a year ago, when the profits turned to loss, that Seabury had a new Clerk entirely devoted to its own interests, someone moreover whose livelihood depended on it staying open. The bungle, delay, muddle, too much politeness and failure to take action showed by the Seabury executive had been of inestimable value to the quietly burrowing Kraye.

Mr. Fotherton might have been worried, as he said, but he had done little except mention it in passing to Charles in his capacity as Steward at some other meeting. Charles, looking for something to divert my mind from my stomach, and perhaps genuinely anxious about Seabury, had tossed the facts to me. In his own peculiar way, naturally.

The casualness of the whole situation was horrifying. I basely wondered whether Fotherton himself had a large holding in Seabury shares and therefore a vested interest in its demise. Planning a much closer scrutiny of the list of shareholders, I followed Lord Hagbourne and Captain Oxon round the end of the stands, and we walked the three hundred yards or so through the racecourse gates and down the road to where Captain Oxon's flat was situated above the canteen in the stable block.

On Lord Hagbourne's suggestion he rang up a firm of local contractors while we were still there, and arranged for the urgent earth-moving to be done the following morning. His manner was still ruffled, and it didn't improve things when I declined the well-filled ham and chutney sandwiches he offered, though I would have adored to have eaten them, had he but known. I had been out of hospital for a fortnight, but I had another fortnight to go before things like new bread, ham, mustard and chutney were due back on the agenda. Very boring.

After the sandwiches Lord Hagbourne decided on a tour of inspection, so we all three went first round the stable block, into the lads' hostel, through the canteen to the kitchen, and into all the stable administrative offices. Everywhere the story was the same. Except for the rows of wooden boxes which had been thrown up cheaply after the old ones burned down, there was no recent maintenance and no new paint.

Then we retraced our steps up the road, through the main gate, and across to the long line of stands with the weighing room, dining-rooms, bars and cloakrooms built into the back. At one end were the secretary's office, the press room and the Stewards' room: at the other, the first-aid room and a store. A wide tunnel like a passage ran centrally through the whole length of the building, giving secondary access on one side to many of the rooms, and on the other to the steps of the stands themselves. We painstakingly covered the lot, even down to the boiler room and the oil bunkers, so I had my nostalgic look inside the weighing room and changing room after all.

The whole huge block was dankly cold, very draughty, and smelt of dust. Nothing looked new, not even the dirt. For inducing depression it was hard to beat, but the dreary buildings along in the cheaper rings did a good job of trying.

Captain Oxon said the general dilapidation was mostly due to the sea air, the racecourse being barely half a mile from the shore, and no doubt in essence he was right. The sea air had had a free hand for far too long.

Eventually we returned to where my car was parked inside the gate, and looked back to the row of stands: forlorn, deserted, decaying on a chilly early November afternoon, with a salt-laden drizzle just beginning to blur the outlines.

'What's to be done?' said Lord Hagbourne glumly, as we drove through the rows of bungalows on our way home.

'I don't know.' I shook my head.

'The place is dead.'

I couldn't argue. Seabury had suddenly seemed to me to be past saving. The Friday and Saturday fixtures could be held now, but as things stood the gate money would hardly cover expenses. No company could go on making a loss indefinitely. Seabury could plug the gap at present by drawing on their reserve funds, but as I'd seen from their balance sheets at Company House, the reserves only amounted to a few thousands. Matters were bound to get worse. Insolvency waited round a close corner. It might be more realistic to admit that Seabury had no future and to sell the land at the highest price offered as soon as possible. People were, after all, crying out for flat land at the seaside. And there was no real reason why the shareholders shouldn't be rewarded for their long loyalty and recent poor dividends and receive eight pounds for each one they had invested. Many would gain if Seabury came under the hammer, and no one would lose. Seabury was past saving: best to think only of the people who would benefit.

My thoughts stopped with a jerk. This, I realised, must be the attitude of the Clerk, Mr. Fotherton, and of the Manager, Oxon, and of all the executive. This explained why they had made surprisingly little attempt to save the place. They had accepted defeat easily and seen it not only to be harmless, but to many, usefully profitable. As it had been with other courses, big courses like Hurst Park and Birmingham, so it should be with Seabury.

What did it matter that yet another joined the century's ghost ranks of Cardiff, Derby, Bournemouth, Newport? What did it matter if busy people like Inspector Cornish of Dunstable couldn't go racing much because their local course had vanished? What did it matter if Seabury's holiday makers went to the Bingo halls instead?

Chasing owners, I thought, should rise up in a body and demand that Seabury should be preserved, because no racecourse was better for their horses. But of course they wouldn't. You could tell owners how good it was, but unless they were horsemen themselves, it didn't register. They only saw the rotten amenities of the stands, not the splendidly sited well-built fences that positively invited their horses to jump. They didn't know how their horses relished the short springy turf underfoot, or found the arc and cambers of the bends perfect for maintaining an even speed. Corners at many other racecourses threw horses wide and broke up their stride, but not those at Seabury. The original course builder had been brilliant, and regular visits from the Inspector of Courses had kept his work fairly intact. Fast, true run, unhazardous racing, that's what Seabury gave.

Or had done, before Kraye.

Kraye and the executive's inertia between them . . . I stamped on the accelerator in a surge of anger and the car swooped up the side of the South Downs like a bird. I didn't often drive fast any more: I did still

miss having two hands on the wheel. At the top, out of consideration for
my passenger's nerves, I let the speedometer ribbon slide back to fifty.

He said, 'I feel like that about it too.'

I glanced at him in surprise.

'The whole situation is infuriating,' he nodded. 'Such a good course
basically, and nothing to be done.'

'It could be saved,' I said.

'How?'

'A new attitude of mind . . .' I tailed off.

'Go on,' he said. But I couldn't find the words to tell him politely that
he ought to chuck out all the people in power at Seabury; too many of
them were probably his ex-school chums or personal friends.

'Suppose,' he said after a few minutes, 'that you had a free hand, what
would you do?'

'One would never get a free hand. That's half the trouble. Someone
makes a good suggestion, and someone else squashes it. They end up,
often as not, by doing nothing.'

'No, Sid, I mean you personally. What would you do?'

'I?' I grinned. 'What I'd do would have the National Hunt Committee
swooning like Victorian maidens.'

'I'd like to know.'

'Seriously?'

He nodded. As if he could ever be anything else but serious.

I sighed. 'Very well then. I'd pinch every good crowd-pulling idea that
any other course has thought of, and put them all into operation on the
same day.'

'What, for instance?'

'I'd take the whole of the reserve fund and offer it as a prize for a big
race. I'd make sure the race was framed to attract the really top chasers.
Then I'd go round to their trainers personally and explain the situation,
and beg for their support. I'd go to some of the people who sponsor Gold
Cup races and cajole them into giving five hundred pound prizes for all
the other races on that day. I'd make the whole thing into a campaign.
I'd get Save Seabury discussed on television, and in the sports columns
of newspapers. I'd get people interested and involved. I'd make helping
Seabury the smart thing to do. I'd get someone like the Beatles to come
and present the trophies. I'd advertise free car-parking and free race
cards, and on the day I'd have the whole place bright with flags and
bunting and tubs of flowers to hide the lack of paint. I'd make sure
everyone on the staff understood that a friendly welcome must be given
to the customers. And I'd insist that the catering firm used its imagination.
I'd fix the meeting for the beginning of April, and pray for a sunny
Spring day. That,' I said, running down, 'would do for a start.'

'And afterwards?' He was non-committal.

'A loan, I suppose. Either from a bank or from private individuals.
But the executive would have to show first that Seabury could be a
success again, like it used to be. No one falls over himself to lend to a
dying business. The revival has to come before the money, if you see
what I mean.'

'I do see,' he agreed slowly, 'but . . .'

'Yes. But. It always comes to But. But no one at Seabury is going to bother.'

We were silent for a long way.

Finally I said, 'This meeting on Friday and Saturday . . . it would be a pity to risk another last-minute disaster. Hunt Radnor Associates could arrange for some sort of guard on the course. Security patrols, that kind of thing.'

'Too expensive,' he said promptly. 'And you've not yet proved that it is really needed. Seabury's troubles still look like plain bad luck to me.'

'Well . . . a security patrol might prevent any more of it.'

'I don't know. I'll have to see.' He changed the subject then, and talked firmly about other races on other courses all the way back to London.

Chapter Ten

Dolly lent me her telephone with resignation on Tuesday morning, and I buzzed the switchboard for an internal call to Missing Persons.

'Sammy?' I said. 'Sid Halley, down in Racing. Are you busy?'

'The last teenager has just been retrieved from Gretna. Fire away. Who's lost?'

'A man called Smith.'

Some mild blasphemy sped three storeys down the wire.

I laughed. 'I think his name really is Smith. He's a driver by trade. He's been driving a tanker for Intersouth Chemicals for the last year. He left his job and his digs last Wednesday; no forwarding address.' I told him about the crash, the suspect concussion and the revelry by night.

'You don't think he was planted on purpose on the job a year ago? His name likely wouldn't be Smith in that case . . . make it harder.'

'I don't know. But I think it's more likely he was a bona fide Intersouth driver who was offered a cash payment for exceptional services rendered.'

'O.K., I'll try that first. He might give Intersouth as a reference, in which case they'll know if he applies for another job somewhere, or I might trace him through his union. The wife might have worked, too. I'll let you know.'

'Thanks.'

'Don't forget, when the old man buys you a gold-plated executive desk I want my table back.'

'You'll want for ever,' I said, smiling. It had been Sammy's lunch.

On the table in question lay the slim file on the Andrews case that Jones-boy had unearthed from the basement. I looked round the room.

'Where's Chico?' I asked.

Dolly answered. 'Helping a bookmaker to move house.'

'He's doing *what*?' I goggled.

'That's right. Long-standing date. The bookmaker is taking his safe with him and wants Chico to sit on it in the furniture van. It had to be Chico, he said. No one else would do. The paying customer is always right, so Chico's gone.'

'Damn.'

She reached into a drawer. 'He left you a tape,' she said.

'Undamn, then.'

She grinned and handed it to me, and I took it over to the recorder, fed it through on to the spare reel, and listened to it in the routine office way, through the earphones.

'After wearing my plates down to the ankles,' said Chico's cheerful voice, 'I found out that the worst things your Clerk of the Course did at Dunstable were to frame a lot of races that did the opposite of attract any decent runners, and be stinking rude to all and sundry. He was quite well liked up to the year before he killed himself. Then everyone says he gradually got more and more crazy. He was so rude to people who worked at the course that half of them wouldn't put up with it and left. And the local tradesmen practically spat when I mentioned his name. I'll fill you in when I see you, but there wasn't anything like Seabury – no accidents or damage or anything like that.'

Sighing, I wiped the tape clean and gave it back to Dolly. Then I opened the file on my table and studied its contents.

A Mr. Mervyn Brinton of Reading, Berks., had applied to the agency for personal protection, having had reason to believe that he was in danger of being attacked. He had been unwilling to say why he might be attacked, and refused to have the agency make enquiries. All he wanted was a bodyguard. There was a strong possibility, said the report, that Brinton had tried a little amateurish blackmail, which had backfired. He had at length revealed that he possessed a certain letter, and was afraid of being attacked and having it stolen. After much persuasion by Chico Barnes, who pointed out that Brinton could hardly be guarded for the rest of his life, Brinton had agreed to inform a certain party that the letter in question was lodged in a particular desk drawer in the Racing Section of Hunt Radnor Associates. In fact it was not; and had not at any time been seen by anyone working for the agency. However, Thomas Andrews came, or was sent, to remove the letter, was interrupted by J. S. Halley (whom he wounded by shooting), and subsequently made his escape. Two days later Brinton telephoned to say he no longer required a bodyguard, and as far as the agency was concerned the case was then closed.

The foregoing information had been made available to the police in their investigation into the shooting of Halley.

I shut the file. A drab little story, I thought, of a pathetic little man playing out of his league.

Brinton.

The Clerk of the Course at Dunstable had also been called Brinton.

I sat gazing at the short file. Brinton wasn't an uncommon name. There was probably no connection at all. Brinton of Dunstable had died a good two years before Brinton of Reading had asked for protection.

The only visible connection was that at different ends of the scale both the Dunstable Brinton and Thomas Andrews had earned their living on the racecourse. It wasn't much. Probably nothing. But it niggled.

I went home, collected the car, and drove to Reading.

A nervous grey haired elderly man opened the front door on a safety chain, and peered through the gap.

'Yes?'

'Mr. Brinton?'

'What is it?'

'I'm from Hunt Radnor Associates. I'd be most grateful for a word with you.'

He hesitated, chewing an upper lip adorned with an untidy pepper and salt moustache. Anxious brown eyes looked me up and down and went past me to the white car parked by the kerb.

'I sent a cheque,' he said finally.

'It was quite in order,' I assured him.

'I don't want any trouble . . . it wasn't my fault that that man was shot.' He didn't sound convinced.

'Oh, no one blames you for that,' I said. 'He's perfectly all right now. Back at work, in fact.'

His relief showed, even through the crack. 'Very well,' he said, and pushed the door shut to take off the chain.

I followed him into the front room of his tall terrace house. The air smelt stale and felt still, as if it had been hanging in the same spot for days. The furniture was of the hard-stuffed and brown shellacked substantial type that in my plywood childhood I had thought the peak of living, unobtainable; and there were cases of tropical butterflies on the walls, and carved ornaments from somewhere like Java or Borneo on several small tables. A life abroad, retirement at home, I thought. From colour and heat to suburban respectability in Reading.

'My wife has gone out shopping,' he said, still nervously. 'She'll be back soon.' He looked hopefully out of the lace curtained window, but Mrs. Brinton didn't oblige him by coming to his support.

I said, 'I just wanted to ask you, Mr. Brinton, if you were by any chance related to a Mr. William Brinton, one-time Clerk of Dunstable racecourse.'

He gave me a long agonised stare, and to my consternation sat down on his sofa and began to cry, his shaking hands covering his eyes and the tears splashing down on to his tweed-clad knees.

'Please . . . Mr. Brinton . . . I'm so sorry,' I said awkwardly.

He snuffled and coughed, and dragged a handerkerchief out to wipe his eyes. Gradually the paroxysm passed, and he said indistinctly, 'How did you find out? I told you I didn't want anyone asking questions . . .'

'It was quite accidental. Nobody asked any questions, I promise you. Would you like to tell me about it? Then I don't think any questions will need to be asked at all, from anyone else.'

'The police . . .' he said doubtfully, on a sob. 'They came before. I refused to say anything, and they went away.'

'Whatever you tell me will be in confidence.'

'I've been such a fool . . . I'd like to tell someone, really.'

I pictured the strung up, guilt-ridden weeks he'd endured, and the crying fit became not only understandable but inevitable.

'It was the letter, you see,' he said sniffing softly. 'The letter William began to write to me, though he never sent it . . . I found it in a whole trunk of stuff that was left when he . . . killed himself. I was in Sarawak then, you know, and they sent me a cable. It was a shock . . . one's only brother doing such a . . . a terrible thing. He was younger than me. Seven years. We weren't very close, except when we were children. I wish . . . but it's too late now. Anyway, when I came home I fetched all his stuff round from where it had been stored and put it up in the attic here, all his racing books and things. I didn't know what to do with them, you see. I wasn't interested in them, but it seemed . . . I don't know . . . I couldn't just burn them. It was months before I bothered to sort them out, and then I found the letter . . .' His voice faltered and he looked at me appealingly, wanting to be forgiven.

'Kitty and I had found my pension didn't go anywhere near as far as we'd expected. Everything is so terribly expensive. The rates . . . we decided we'd have to sell the house again though we'd only just bought it, and Kitty's family are all close. And then . . . I thought . . . perhaps I could sell the letter instead.'

'And you got threats instead of money,' I said.

'Yes. It was the letter itself which gave me the idea . . .' He chewed his moustache.

'And now you no longer have it,' I said matter of factly, as if I knew for certain and wasn't guessing. 'When you were first threatened you thought you could still sell the letter if Hunt Radnor kept you safe, and then you got more frightened and gave up the letter, and then cancelled the protection because the threats had stopped.'

He nodded unhappily. 'I gave them the letter because that man was shot . . . I didn't realise anything like that would happen. I was horrified. It was terrible. I hadn't thought it could be so dangerous, just selling a letter . . . I wish I'd never found it. I wish William had never written it.'

So did I, as it happened.

'What did the letter say?' I asked.

He hesitated, his fear showing. 'It might cause more trouble. They might come back.'

'They won't know you've told me,' I pointed out. 'How could they?'

'I suppose not.' He looked at me, making up his mind. There's one thing about being small: no one is ever afraid of you. If I'd been big and commanding I don't think he'd have risked it. As it was, his face softened and relaxed and he threw off the last threads of reticence.

'I know it by heart,' he said. 'I'll write it down for you, if you like. It's easier than saying it.'

I sat and waited while he fetched a ball point pen and a pad of large writing paper and got on with his task. The sight of the letter materialising again in front of his eyes affected him visibly, but whether to fear or remorse or sorrow, I couldn't tell. He covered one side of the page, then tore it off the pad and shakily handed it over.

I read what he had written. I read it twice. Because of these short desperate sentences, I reflected enemotionally, I had come within spitting distance of St. Peter.

'That's fine,' I said. 'Thank you very much.'

'I wish I'd never found it,' he said again. 'Poor William.'

'Did you go to see this man?' I asked, indicating the letter as I put it away in my wallet.

'No, I wrote to him . . . he wasn't hard to find.'

'And how much did you ask for?'

Shame-faced, he muttered, 'Five thousand pounds.'

Five thousand pounds had been wrong, I thought. If he'd asked fifty thousand, he might have had a chance. But five thousand didn't put him among the big-power boys, it just revealed his mediocrity. No wonder he had been stamped on, fast.

'What happened next?' I asked.

'A big man came for the letter, about four o'clock one afternoon. It was awful. I asked him for the money and he just laughed in my face and pushed me into a chair. No money, he said, but if I didn't hand over the letter at once he'd . . . he'd teach me a thing or two. That's what he said, teach me a thing or two. I explained that I had put the letter in my box at the bank and that the bank was closed and that I couldn't get it until the next morning. He said that he would come to the bank with me the next day, and then he went away . . .'

'And you rang up the agency almost at once? Yes. What made you choose Hunt Radnor?'

He looked surprised. 'It was the only one I knew about. Are there any others? I mean, most people have heard of Hunt Radnor, I should think.'

'I see. So Hunt Radnor sent you a bodyguard, but the big man wouldn't give up.'

'He kept telephoning . . . then your man suggested setting a trap in his office, and in the end I agreed. Oh, I shouldn't have let him, I was such a fool. I knew all the time, you see, who was threatening me, but I couldn't tell your agency because I would have had to admit I'd tried to get money . . . illegally.'

'Yes. Well, there's only one more thing. What was he like, the man who came and threatened you?'

Brinton didn't like even the memory of him. 'He was very strong. Hard. When he pushed me it was like a wall. I'm not . . . I mean, I've never been good with my fists, or anything like that. If he'd started hitting me I couldn't have stopped him . . .'

'I'm not blaming you for not standing up to him,' I pointed out. 'I just want to know what he looked like.'

'Very big,' he said vaguely. 'Huge.'

'I know it's several weeks ago now, but can't you possibly remember more than that? How about his hair? Anything odd about his face? How old? What class?'

He smiled for the first time, the sad wrinkles folding for a moment into some semblance of faded charm. If he'd never taken his first useless step into crime, I thought, he might still have been a nice gentle innocuous man, fading without rancour twtowards old age, troubled only by how to make a little pension go a long way. No tearing, destructive guilt.

'It's certainly easier when you ask questions like that. He was beginning to go bald, I remember now. And he had big blotchy freckles on the backs of his hands. It's difficult to know about his age. Not a youth, though; more than thirty, I think. What else did you ask? Oh yes, class. Working class, then.'

'English?'

'Oh yes, not foreign. Sort of cockney, I suppose.'

I stood up, thanked him, and began to take my leave. He said, begging me still for reassurance, 'There won't be any more trouble?'

'Not from me or the agency.'

'And the man who was shot?'

'Not from him either.'

'I tried to tell myself it wasn't my fault . . . but I haven't been able to sleep. How could I have been such a fool? I shouldn't have let that young man set any trap . . . I shouldn't have called in your agency . . . and it cost another chunk of our savings . . . I ought never to have tried to get money for that letter . . .'

'That's true, Mr. Brinton, you shouldn't. But what's done is done, and I don't suppose you'll start anything like that again.'

'No, no,' he said with pain. 'I wouldn't. Ever. These last few weeks have been . . .' His voice died. Then he said more strongly, 'We'll have to sell the house now. Kitty likes it here, of course. But what I've always wanted myself is a little bungalow by the sea.'

When I reached the office I took out the disastrous letter and read it again, before adding it to the file. Being neither the original nor a photocopy, but only a reproduction from memory, it wasn't of the slightest use as evidence. In the older Brinton's small tidy script, a weird contrast to the heart-broken contents, it ran:

Dear Mervy, dear big brother,

I wish you could help me, as you did when I was little. I have spent fifteen years building up Dunstable racecourse, and a man called Howard Kraye is making me destroy it. I have to frame races which nobody likes. Very few horses come now, and the gate receipts are falling fast. This week I must see that the race-card goes to the printers too late, and the Press room telephones will all be out of order. There will be a terrible muddle. People must think I am mad. I can't escape him. He is paying me as well, but I must do as he says. I can't help my nature, you know that. He has found out about a boy I was living with, and I could be prosecuted. He wants the racecourse to sell for housing. Nothing can stop him getting it. My racecourse, I love it.

I know I shan't send this letter. Mervy, I wish you were here. I haven't anyone else. Oh dear God, I can't go on much longer, I really can't.

At five to six that afternoon I opened the door of Zanna Martin's office. Her desk was facing me and so was she. She raised her head, recognised me, and looked back at me in a mixture of pride and embarrassment.

'I did it,' she said. 'If you didn't, I'll kill you.'

She had combed her hair even further forward, so that it hung close round her face, but all the same one could see the disfigurement at first glance. I had forgotten, in the days since Friday, just how bad it was.

'I felt the same about you,' I said grinning.

'You really did keep your promise?'

'Yes, I did. All day Saturday and Sunday, most of yesterday and most of today, and very nasty it is, too.'

She sighed with relief. 'I'm glad you've come. I nearly gave it up this morning. I thought you wouldn't do it, and you'd never come back to see if I had, and that I was being a proper idiot.'

'Well, I'm here,' I said. 'Is Mr. Bolt in?'

She shook her head. 'He's gone home. I'm just packing up.'

'Finished the envelopes?' I said.

'Envelopes? Oh, those I was doing when you were here before? Yes, they're all done.'

'And filled and sent?'

'No, the leaflets haven't come back from the printers yet, much to Mr. Bolt's disgust. I expect I'll be doing them tomorrow.'

She stood up, tall and thin, put on her coat and tied the scarf over her hair.

'Are you going anywhere this evening?' I asked.

'Home,' she said decisively.

'Come out to dinner,' I suggested.

'Aunty's legacy won't last long, the way you spend. I think Mr. Bolt has already invested your money. You'd better save every penny until after settlement day.'

'Coffee, then, and the flicks?'

'Look,' she said hesitantly, 'I sometimes buy a hot chicken on my way home. There's a fish and chip shop next to the station that sells them. Would you . . . would you like to come and help me eat it? In return, I mean, for Friday night.'

'I'd enjoy that,' I said, and was rewarded by a pleased half-incredulous laugh.

'Really?'

'Really.'

As before, we went to Finchley by underground, but this time she sat boldly where her whole face showed. To try to match her fortitude, I rested my elbow on the seat arm between us. She looked at my hand and then at my face, gratefully, amost as if we were sharing an adventure.

As we emerged from the tube station she said, 'You know, it makes a great deal of difference if one is accompanied by a man, even . . .' she stopped abruptly.

'Even,' I finished, smiling, 'if he is smaller than you and also damaged.'

'Oh dear . . . and much younger, as well.' Her real eye looked at me with rueful amusement. The glass one stared stonily ahead. I was getting used to it again.

'Let me buy the chicken,' I said, as we stopped outside the shop. The smell of hot chips mingled with diesel fumes from a passing lorry. Civilisation, I thought. Delightful.

'Certainly not.' Miss Martin was firm and bought the chicken herself. She came out with it wrapped in newspaper. 'I got a few chips and a packet of peas,' she said.

'And I,' I said firmly, as we came to an off-licence, 'am getting some brandy.' What chips and peas would do to my digestion I dared not think.

We walked round to the house with the parcels and went through into her room. She moved with a light step.

'In that cupboard over there,' she said, pointing, as she peeled off her coat and scarf, 'there are some glasses and a bottle of sherry. Will you pour me some? I expect you prefer brandy, but have some sherry if you'd like. I'll just take these things into the kitchen and put them to keep hot.'

White I unscrewed the bottles and poured the drinks I heard her lighting her gas stove and unwrapping the parcels. There was dead quiet as I walked across the room with her sherry, and when I reached the door I saw why. She held the chicken in its piece of greaseproof paper absently in one hand: the bag of chips lay open on the table with the box of peas beside it: and she was reading the newspaper they had all been wrapped in.

She looked up at me in bewilderment.

'You,' she said. 'It's you. This is you.'

I looked down where her finger pointed. The fish and chip shop had wrapped up her chicken in the *Sunday Hemisphere*.

'Here's your sherry,' I said, holding it out to her.

She put down the chicken and took the glass without appearing to notice it.

'Another Halley,' she said. 'It caught my eye. Of course I read it. And it's your picture, and it even refers to your hand. You are Sid Halley.'

'That's right.' There was no chance of denying it.

'Good heavens. I've known about you for years. Read about you. I saw you on television, often. My father loved watching the racing, we always had it on when he was alive ...' She broke off and then said with increased puzzlement, 'Why on earth did you say your name was John and that you worked in a shop? Why did you come to see Mr. Bolt? I don't understand.'

'Drink your sherry, put the chicken in the oven before it freezes and I'll tell you.' There was nothing else to do: I didn't want to risk her brightly passing on the interesting titbit of news to her employer.

Without demur she put the dinner to heat, came to sit on the sofa, opposite to where I apprehensively waited in an arm-chair, and raised her eyebrows in expectation.

'I don't work in a shop,' I admitted. 'I am employed by a firm called Hunt Radnor Associates.'

Like Brinton, she had heard of the agency. She stiffened her whole body and began to frown. As casually as I could, I told her about Kraye

and the Seabury shares; but she was no fool and she went straight to the
heart of things.

'You suspect Mr. Bolt too. That's why you went to see him.'

'Yes, I'm afraid so.'

'And me? You took me out simply and solely to find out about him?'
Her voice was bitter.

I didn't answer at once. She waited, and somehow her calmness was
more piercing than tears of temper could have been. She asked so little
of life.

At last I said, 'I went to Bolt's office as much to take out his secretary
as to see Bolt himself, yes.'

The peas boiled over, hissing loudly. She stood up slowly. 'At least
that's honest.'

She went into the tiny kitchen and turned out the gas under the
saucepan.

I said, 'I came to your office this afternoon because I wanted to look
at those leaflets Bolt is sending to Seabury shareholders. You told me at
once that they hadn't come from the printers. I didn't need to accept your
invitation to supper after that. But I'm here.'

She stood in the kitchen doorway, holding herself straight with an all
too apparent effort.

'I suppose you lied about that too,' she said in a quiet rigidly controlled
voice, pointing to my arm. 'Why? Why did you play such a cruel game
with me? Surely you could have got your information without that. Why
did you make me change my desk round? I suppose you were laughing
yourself sick all day Saturday thinking about it.'

I stood up. Her hurt was dreadful.

I said, 'I went to Kempton races on Saturday.'

She didn't move.

'I kept my promise.'

She made a slight gesture of disbelief.

'I'm sorry,' I said helplessly.

'Yes. Good night Mr. Halley. Good night.'

I went.

Chapter Eleven

Radnor held a Seabury conference the next morning, Wednesday, consisting of himself, Dolly, Chico and me: the result, chiefly, of my having
the previous afternoon finally wrung grudging permission from Lord
Hagbourne to arrange a twenty-four hour guard at Seabury for the
coming Thursday, Friday and Saturday.

The bulldozing had been accomplished without trouble, and a call to
the course that morning had established that the tan was arriving in

regular lorry loads and was being spread. Racing, bar any last minute accidents, was now certain. Even the weather was co-operating. The glass was rising; the forecast was dry, cold and sunny.

Dolly proposed a straight patrol system, and Radnor was inclined to agree. Chico and I had other ideas.

'If anyone intended to sabotage the track,' Dolly pointed out, 'they would be frightened off by a patrol. Same thing if they were planning something in the stands themselves.'

Radnor nodded. 'Safest way of making sure racing takes place. I suppose we'll need at least four men to do it properly.'

I said, 'I agree that we need a patrol tonight, tomorrow night and Friday night, just to play safe. But tomorrow, when the course will be more or less deserted . . . what we need is to pinch them at it, not to frighten them off. There's no evidence yet that could be used in a court of law. If we could catch them in mid-sabotage, so to speak, we'd be much better off.'

'That's right,' said Chico. 'Hide and pounce. Much better than scaring them away.'

'I seem to remember,' said Dolly with a grin, 'that the last time you two set a trap the mouse shot the cheese.'

'Oh God, Dolly, you slay me,' said Chico, laughing warmly and for once accepting her affection.

Even Radnor laughed. 'Seriously, though,' he said, 'I don't see how you can. A racecourse is too big. If you are hiding you can only see a small part of it. And surely if you show yourself your presence would act like any other patrol to stop anything plainly suspicious being done? I don't think it's possible.'

'Um,' I said. 'But there's one thing I can still do better than anyone else in this agency.'

'And what's that?' said Chico, ready to argue.

'Ride a horse.'

'Oh,' said Chico. 'I'll give you that, chum.'

'A horse,' said Radnor thoughtfully. 'Well, that's certainly an idea. Nobody's going to look suspiciously at a horse on a racecourse, I suppose. Mobile, too. Where would you get one?'

'From Mark Witney. I could borrow his hack. Seabury's his local course. His stables aren't many miles away.'

'But can you still . . .?' began Dolly, and broke off. 'Well, don't glare at me like that, all of you. I can't ride with two hands, let alone one.'

'A man called Gregory Philips had his arm amputated very high up,' I said, 'and went on racing in point-to-points for years.'

'Enough said,' said Dolly. 'How about Chico?'

'He can wear a pair of my jodphurs. Protective colouring. And lean nonchalantly on the rails.'

'Stick insects,' said Chico cheerfully.

'That's what you want, Sid?' said Radnor.

I nodded. 'Look at it from the worst angle: we haven't anything on Kraye that will stand up. We might not find Smith, the tanker driver, and even if we do, he has everything to lose by talking and nothing to gain. When the racecourse stables burned down a year ago, we couldn't prove it wasn't an accident; an illicit cigarette end. Stable lads do smoke, regardless of bans.

'The so-called drain which collapsed – we don't know if it was dug a day, a week, or six weeks before it did its work. That letter William Brinton of Dunstable wrote to his brother, it's only a copy from memory that we've got, no good at all for evidence. All it proves, to our own satisfaction, is that Kraye is capable of anything. We can't show it to Lord Hagbourne, because I obtained it in confidence, and he still isn't a hundred per cent convinced that Kraye has done more than buy shares. As I see it, we've just got to give the enemy a chance to get on with their campaign.'

'You think they will, then?'

'It's awfully likely, isn't it? This year there isn't another Seabury meeting until February. A three months' gap. And if I read it right, Kraye is in a hurry now because of the political situation. He won't want to spend fifty thousand buying Seabury and then find building land has been nationalised overnight. If I were him, I'd want to clinch the deal and sell to a developer as quickly as possible. According to the photographs of the share transfers, he already holds twenty-three per cent of the shares. This is almost certainly enough to swing the sale of the company if it comes to a vote. But he's greedy. He'll want more. But he'll only want more if he can get it soon. Waiting for February is too risky. So yes, I do think if we give him a chance that he will organise some more damage this week.'

'It's a risk,' said Dolly. 'Suppose something dreadful happens and we neither prevent it nor catch anyone doing it?'

They kicked it round among the three of them for several minutes, the pros and cons of the straight patrols versus cat and mouse. Finally Radnor turned back to me and said 'Sid?'

'It's your agency,' I said seriously. 'It's your risk.'

'But it's your case. It's still your case. You must decide.'

I couldn't understand him. It was all very well for him to have given me a free hand so far, but this wasn't the sort of decision I would have ever expected him to pass on.

Still . . . 'Chico and I, then,' I said. 'We'll go along tonight and stay all day tomorrow. I don't think we'll let even Captain Oxon know we're there. Certainly not the foreman, Ted Wilkins, or any of the other men. We'll come in from the other side from the stands, and I'll borrow the horse for mobility. Dolly can arrange official patrol guards with Oxon for tomorrow night . . . suggest he gives them a warm room, Dolly. He ought to have the central heating on by then.'

'Friday and Saturday?' asked Radnor, non-committally.

'Full guards, I guess. As many as Lord Hagbourne will sub for. The racecourse crowds make cat and mouse impossible.'

'Right,' said Radnor, decisively. 'That's it, then.'

When Dolly, Chico, and I had got as far as the door he said, 'Sid, you wouldn't mind if I had another look at those photographs? Send Jones-boy down with them if you're not needing them.'

'Sure,' I agreed. 'I've pored over them till I know them by heart. I bet you'll spot something at once that I've missed.'

'It often works that way,' he said, nodding.

The three of us went back to the Racing Section, and via the switchboard I traced Jones-boy, who happened to be in Missing Persons. While he was on his way down I flipped through the packet of photographs yet again. The share transfers, the summary with the list of bank accounts, the letters from Bolt, the ten pound notes, and the two sheets of dates, initials and figures from the very bottom of the attaché case. It had been clear all along that these last were lists either of receipts or expenditure: but by now I was certain they were the latter. A certain W.L.B. had received regular sums of fifty pounds a month for twelve months, and the last date for W.L.B. was four days before William Leslie Brinton, Clerk of Dunstable Racecourse, had taken the quickest way out. Six hundred pounds and a threat; the price of a man's soul.

Most of the other initials meant nothing to me, except the last one, J.R.S., which looked as if they could be the tanker driver's. The first entry for J.R.S., for one hundred pounds, was dated the day before the tanker overturned at Seabury, the day before Kraye went to Aynsford for the week-end.

In the next line, the last of the whole list, a further sum of one hundred and fifty pounds was entered against J.R.S. The date of this was that of the following Tuesday, three days ahead when I took the photographs. Smith had packed up and vanished from his job and his digs on that Tuesday.

Constantly recurring amongst the other varying initials were two christian names, Leo and Fred. Each of these was on the regular pay-roll, it seemed. Either Leo or Fred, I guessed, had been the big man who had visited and frightened Mervyn Brinton. Either Leo or Fred was the 'Big Chap' who had sent Andrews with a gun to the Cromwell Road.

I had a score to settle with either Leo or Fred.

Jones-boy came in for the photographs. I tapped them together back into their box and gave them to him.

'Where, you snotty nosed little coot, is our coffee?' said Chico rudely. We had been downstairs when Jones-boy did his rounds.

'Coots are bald,' observed Dolly dryly, eyeing Jones-boy's luxuriant locks.

Jones-boy unprintably told Chico where he could find his coffee.

Chico advanced a step, saying, 'You remind me of the people sitting on the walls of Jerusalem.' He had been raised in a church orphange, after all.

Jones-boy also knew the more basic bits of Isaiah. He said callously, 'You did it on the doorstep of the Barnes cop shop, I believe.'

Chico furiously lashed out a fist to Jones-boy's head. Jones-boy jumped back, laughed insultingly, and the box he was holding flew high out of his hand, opening as it went.

'Stop it you two, damn you,' shouted Dolly, as the big photographs floated down on to her desk and on to the floor.

'Babes in the Wood,' remarked Jones-boy, in great good humour from having got the best of the slanging match. He helped Dolly and me pick up the photographs, shuffled them back into the box in no sort of order, and departed grinning.

'Chico,' said Dolly severely, 'you ought to know better.'

'The bossy-mother routine bores me sick,' said Chico violently.

Dolly bit her lip and looked away. Chico stared at me defiantly, knowing very well he had started the row and was in the wrong.

'As one bastard to another,' I said mildly, 'pipe down.'

Not being able to think of a sufficiently withering reply fast enough Chico merely scowled and walked out of the room. The show was over. The office returned to normal. Typewriters clattered, someone used the tape recorder, someone else the telephone. Dolly sighed and began to draw up her list for Seabury. I sat and thought about Leo. Or Fred. Unproductively.

After a while I ambled upstairs to Bona Fides, where the usual amount of telephone shouting filled the air. George, deep in a mysterious conversation about moth-balls, saw me and shook his head. Jack Copeland, freshly attired in a patchily faded green sleeveless pullover, took time out between calls to say that they were sorry, but they'd made no progress with Kraye. He had, Jack said, very craftily covered his tracks about ten years back. They would keep digging, if I liked. I liked.

Up in Missing Persons Sammy said it was too soon for results on Smith.

When I judged that Mark Witney would be back in his house after exercising his second lot of horses, I rang him up and asked him to lend me his hack, a pensioned-off old steeplechaser of the first water.

'Sure,' he said. 'What for?'

I explained what for.

'You'd better have my horse box as well,' he commented. 'Suppose it pours with rain all night? Give you somewhere to keep dry, if you have the box.'

'But won't you be needing it? The forecast says clear and dry anyway.'

'I won't need it until Friday morning. I haven't any runners until Seabury. And only one there, I may say, in spite of it being so close. The owners just won't have it. I have to go all the way to Banbury on Saturday. Damn silly with another much better course on my door-step.'

'What are you running at Seabury?'

He told me, at great and uncomplimentary length, about a half blind, utterly stupid, one paced habitual non-jumper with which he proposed to win the novice chase. Knowing him, he probably would. We agreed that Chico and I should arrive at his place at about eight that evening, and I rang off.

After that I left the office, went across London by underground to Company House in the City, and asked for the files of Seabury Racecourse. In a numbered chair at a long table, surrounded by earnest men and women clerks poring over similar files and making copious notes, I studied the latest list of investors. Apart from Kraye and his various aliases, which I now recognised on sight from long familiarity with the share transfer photographs, there were no large blocks in single owner-ship. No one else held more than three per cent of the total: and as three per cent meant that roughly two and a half thousand pounds was lying idle and not bringing in a penny in dividends, it was easy to see why no one wanted a larger holding.

Fotherton's name was not on the list. Although this was not conclusive, because a nominee name like 'Mayday Investments' could be anyone at all, I was more or less satisfied that Seabury's Clerk was not gambling on Seabury's death. All the big share movements during the past year had been to Kraye, and no one else.

A few of the small investors, holding two hundred or so shares each, were people I knew personally. I wrote down their names and addresses, intending to ask them to let me see Bolt's circular letter when it arrived. Slower than via Zanna Martin, but surer.

My mind shied away from Zanna Martin. I'd had a bad night thinking about her. Her and Jenny, both.

Back in the office I found it was the tail-end of the lunch hour, with nearly all the desks still empty. Chico alone was sitting behind his, biting his nails.

'If we're going to be up all night,' I suggested, 'we'd better take the afternoon off for sleep.'

'No need.'

'Every need. I'm not as young as you.'

'Poor old grandpa.' He grinned suddenly, apologising for the morning. 'I can't help it. That Jones-boy gets on my wick.'

'Jones-boy can look after himself. It's Dolly . . .'

'It's not my bloody fault she can't have kids.'

'She wants kids like you want a mother.'

'But I don't . . .' he began indignantly.

'Your own,' I said flatly. 'Like you want your own mother to have kept you and loved you. Like mine did.'

'You had every advantage, of course.'

'That's right.'

He laughed. 'Funny thing is I like old Dolly, really. Except for the hen bit.'

'Who wouldn't?' I said amicably. 'You can sleep on my sofa.'

He sighed. 'You're going to be less easy than Dolly to work for, I can see that.'

'Eh?'

'Don't kid yourself, mate. Sir, I mean.' He was lightly ironic.

The other inmates of the office drifted back, including Dolly, with whom I fixed for Chico to have the afternoon free. She was cool to him and unforgiving, which I privately thought would do them both good.

She said, 'The first official patrol will start on the racecourse tomorrow at six p.m. Shall I tell them to find you and report?'

'No,' I said definitely. 'I don't know where I'll be.'

'It had better be the usual then,' she said. 'They can report to the old man at his home number when they are starting the job, and again at six a.m. when they go off and the next lot take over.'

'And they'll ring him in between if anything happens?' I said.

'Yes. As usual.'

'It's as bad as being a doctor,' I said smiling.

Dolly nodded, and half to herself she murmured, 'You'll find out.'

Chico and I walked round to my flat, pulled the curtains, and did our best to sleep. I didn't find it easy at two-thirty in the afternoon: it was the time for racing, not rest. I seemed to me that I had barely drifted off when the telephone rang: I looked at my watch on my way to answer it in the sittingroom and found it was only ten to five. I had asked for a call at six.

It was not the telephone exchange, however, but Dolly.

'A message has come for you by hand, marked very urgent. I thought you might want it before you go to Seabury.'

'Who brought it?'

'A taxi driver.'

'Shunt him round here, then.'

'He's gone, I'm afraid.'

'Who's the message from?'

'I've no idea. It's a plain brown envelope, the size we use for interim reports.'

'Oh. All right, I'll come back.'

Chico had drowsily propped himself up on one elbow on the sofa.

'Go to sleep again,' I said. 'I've got to go and see something in the office. Won't be long.'

When I reached the Racing Section again I found that whatever had come for me, something else had gone. The shaky lemon coloured table. I was deskless again.

'Sammy said he was sorry,' explained Dolly, 'but he has a new assistant and nowhere to park him.'

'I had things in t.ie drawer,' I complained. Shades of Sammy's lunch, I thought.

'They're here,' Dolly said, pointing to a corner of her desk. 'There was only the Brinton file, a half bottle of brandy, and some pills. Also I found this on the floor.' She held out a flat crackly celophane and paper packet.

'The negatives of those photographs are in here,' I said, taking it from her. 'They were in the box, though.'

'Until Jones-boy dropped it.'

'Oh yes.' I put the packet of negatives inside the Brinton file and pinched a large rubber band from Dolly to snap round the outside.

'How about that mysterious very urgent message?' I asked.

Dolly silently and considerately slit open the envelope in question, drew out the single sheet of paper it contained and handed it to me. I unfolded it and stared at it in disbelief.

It was a circular, headed Charing, Street and King, Stockbrokers, dated with the following day's date, and it ran:

Dear Sir or Madam,

We have various clients wishing to purchase small parcels of shares in the following lists of minor companies. If you are considering selling your interests in any of these, we would be grateful if you would get in touch with us. We would assure you of a good fair price, based on today's quotation.

There followed a list of about thirty companies, of which I had heard of only one. Tucked in about three-quarters of the way down was Seabury Racecourse.

I turned the page over. Zanna Martin had written on the back in a hurried hand.

This is only going to Seabury shareholders. Not to anyone owning shares in the other companies. The leaflets came from the printers this morning, and are to be posted tomorrow. I hope it is what you want. I'm sorry about last night.

                                                              Z.M.

'What is it?' asked Dolly.

'A free pardon,' I said light-heartedly, slipping the circular inside the Brinton file along with the negatives. 'Also confirmation that Ellis Bolt is not on the side of the angels.'

'You're a nut,' she said. 'And take these things off my desk. I haven't room for them.'

I put the pills and brandy in my pocket and picked up the Brinton file.

'Is that better?'

'Thank you, yes.'

'So long, then, my love. See you Friday.'

On the walk back to the flat I decided suddenly to go and see Zanna Martin. I went straight down to the garage for my car without going up and waking Chico again, and made my way eastwards to the City for the second time that day. The rush hour traffic was so bad that I was afraid I would miss her, but in fact she was ten minutes late leaving the office and I caught her up just before she reached the underground station.

'Miss Martin,' I called. 'Would you like a lift home?'

She turned round in surprise.

'Mr. Halley!'

'Hop in.'

She hopped. That is to say, she opened the door, picked up the Brinton file which was lying on the passenger seat, sat down, tidily folded her coat over her knees, and pulled the door shut again. The bad side of her face was towards me, and she was very conscious of it. The scarf and the hair were gently pulled forward.

I took a pound and a ten shilling note out of my pocket and gave them to her. She took them, smiling.

'The taxi-man told our switchboard girl you gave him that for bringing the leaflet. Thank you very much.' I swung out through the traffic and headed for Finchley.

She answered obliquely. 'That wretched chicken is still in the oven, stone cold. I just turned the gas out yesterday, after you'd gone.'

'I wish I could stay this evening instead,' I said, 'but I've got a job on for the agency.'

'Another time,' she said tranquilly. 'Another time, perhaps. I understand that you couldn't tell me at first who you worked for, because you didn't know whether I was an ... er, an accomplice of Mr. Bolt's, and afterwards you didn't tell me for fear of what actually happened, that I would be upset. So that's that.'

'You are generous.'

'Realistic, even if a bit late.'

We went a little way in silence. Then I asked 'What would happen to the shares Kraye owns if it were proved he was sabotaging the company? If he were convicted, I mean. Would his shares be confiscated, or would he still own them when he came out of jail?'

'I've never heard of anyone's shares being confiscated,' she said, sounding interested. 'But surely that's a long way in the future?'

'I wish I knew. It makes a good deal of difference to what I should do now.'

'How do you mean?'

'Well ... an easy way to stop Kraye buying too many more shares would be to tell the racing press and the financial press that a take-over is being attempted. The price would rocket. But Kraye already holds twenty-three per cent, and if the law couldn't take it away from him, he would either stick to that and vote for a sell out, or if he got cold feet he could unload his shares at the higher price and still make a fat profit. Either way, he'd be sitting pretty financially, in jail or out. And either way Seabury would be built on.'

'I suppose this sort of thing's happened before?'

'Take-overs, yes, several. But only one other case of sabotage. At Dunstable. Kraye again.'

'Haven't any courses survived a take-over bid?'

'Only Sandown, publicly. I don't know of any others, but they may have managed it in secrecy.'

'How did Sandown do it?'

'The local council did it for them. Stated loudly that planning permission would not be given for building. Of course the bid collapsed then.'

'It looks as though the only hope for Seabury, in that case, is that the council there will act in the same way. I'd try a strong lobby, if I were you.'

'You're quite a girl, Miss Martin,' I said smiling. 'That's a very good idea. I'll go and dip a toe into the climate of opinion at the Town Hall.'

She nodded approvingly. 'No good lobbying against the grain. Much better to find out which way people are likely to move before you start pushing!'

Finchley came into sight. I said. 'You do realise, Miss Martin, that if I am successful at my job, you will lose yours?'

She laughed. 'Poor Mr. Bolt. He's not at all bad to work for. But don't worry about my job. It's easy for an experienced stockbroker's secretary to get a good one, I assure you.'

I stopped at her gate, looking at my watch. 'I'm afraid I can't come in. I'm already going to be a bit late.'

She opened the door without ado and climbed out. 'Thank you for coming at all.' She smiled, shut the door crisply, and waved me away.

I drove back to my flat as fast as I could, fuming slightly at the traffic. It wasn't until I switched off the engine down in the garage and leaned over to pick it up that discovered the Brinton file wasn't there. And then remembered Miss Martin holding it on her lap during the journey, and me hustling her out of the car. Zanna Martin still had Brinton's file. I hadn't time to go back for it, and I couldn't ring her up because I didn't know the name of the owner of the house she lived in. But surely, I reassured myself, surely the file would be safe enough where it was until Friday.

Chapter Twelve

Chico and I sat huddled together for warmth in some gorse bushes and watched the sun rise over Seabury Racecourse. It had been a cold clear night with a tingle of nought degrees centigrade about it, and we were both shivering.

Behind us, among the bushes and out of sight, Revelation, one-time winner of the Cheltenham Gold Cup, was breakfasting on meagre patches of grass. We could hear the scrunch when he bit down close to the roots, and the faint chink of the bridle as he ate. For some time Chico and I had been resisting the temptation to relieve him of his nice warm rug.

'They might try someting now,' said Chico hopefully. 'First light, before anyone's up.'

Nothing had moved in the night, we were certain of that. Every hour I had ridden Revelation at a careful walk round the whole of the track itself, and Chico had made a plimsole-shod inspection of the stands, at one with the shadows. There had been no one about. Not a sound but the stirring breeze, not a glimmer of light but from the stars and a waning moon.

Our present spot, chosen as the sky lightened and some concealment became necessary, lay at the furthest spot from the stands, at the bottom of the semi-circle of track cut off by the road which ran across the course. Scattered bushes and scrub filled the space between the track and boundary fence, enough to shield us from all but closely prying eyes. Behind the boundary fence were the little back gardens of the first row of bungalows. The sun rose bright and yellow away to our left and the birds sang around us. It was half past seven.

'It's going to be a lovely day,' said Chico.

At ten past nine there was some activity up by the stands and the tractor rolled on to the course pulling a trailer. I unshipped my race glasses, balanced them on my bent up knees, and took a look. The trailer was loaded with what I guessed were hurdles, and was accompanied by three men on foot.

I handed the glasses to Chico without comment, and yawned.

'Lawful occasions,' he remarked, bored.

We watched the tractor and trailer lumber slowly round the far end of the course, pause to unload, and return for a refill. On its second trip it came close enough for us to confirm that it was in fact the spare hurdles that were being dumped into position, four or five at each flight, ready to be used if any were splintered in the races. We watched for a while in silence. Then I said slowly, 'Chico, I've been blind.'

'Huh?'

'The tractor,' I said. 'The tractor. Under our noses all the time.'

'So?'

'So the sulphuric acid tanker was pulled over by a tractor. No complicated lifting gear necessary. Just a couple of ropes or chains slung over the top of the tanker and fastened round the axles. Then you unscrew the hatches and stand well clear. Someone drives the tractor at full power up the course, over goes the tanker and out pours the juice. And Bob's your uncle!'

'Every racecourse has a tractor,' said Chico thoughtfully.

'That's right.'

'So no one would look twice at a tractor on a racecourse. Quite. No one would remark on any tracks it left. No one would mention seeing one on the road. So if you're right, and I'd say you certainly are, it wouldn't necessarily have been that tractor, the racecourse tractor, which was used.'

'I'll bet it was, though.' I told Chico about the photographed initials and payments. 'Tomorrow I'll check the initials of all the workmen here from Ted Wilkins downwards against that list. Any one of them might have been paid just to leave the tractor on the course, lying handy. The tanker went over on the evening before the meeting, like today. The tractor would have been in use then too. Warm and full of fuel. Nothing easier. And afterwards, straight on up the racecourse, and out of sight.'

'It was dusk,' agreed Chico. 'As long as no one came along the road in the minutes it took to unhitch the ropes or chains afterwards, they were clear. No traffic diversions, no detours, nothing.'

We sat watching the tractor lumbering about, gloomily realising we couldn't prove a word of it.

'We'll have to move,' I said presently. 'There's a hurdle just along there, about fifty yards away, where those wings are. They'll be down here over the road soon.'

We adjourned with Revelation back to the horse box half a mile away down the road to the west and took the opportunity to eat our own breakfast. When we had finished Chico went back first, strolling along confidently in my jodphurs, boots and polo-necked jersey, the complete horseman from head to foot. He had never actually sat on a horse in his life.

After a while I followed on Revelation. The men had brought the hurdles down into the semi-circular piece of track and had laid them in place. They were now moving further away up the course, unloading the next lot. Unremarked, I rode back to the bushes and dismounted. Of Chico there was no sign for another half hour, and then he came whistling across from the road with his hands in his pockets.

When he reached me he said, 'I had another look round the stands. Rotten security, here. No one asked me what I was doing. There are some women cleaning here and there, and some are working in the stable block, getting the lads' hostel ready, things like that. I said good morning to them, and they said good morning back.' He was disgusted.

'Not much scope for saboteurs,' I said morosely. 'Cleaners in the stands and workmen on the course.'

'Dusk tonight,' nodded Chico. 'That's the most likely time now.'

The morning ticked slowly away. The sun rose to its low November zenith and shone straight into our eyes. I passed the time by taking a photograph of Revelation and another of Chico. He was fascinated by the tiny camera and said he couldn't wait to get one like it. Eventually I put it back into my breeches pocket, and shading my eyes against the sun took my hundredth look up the course.

Nothing. No men, no tractor. I looked at my watch. One o'clock. Lunch hour. More time passed.

Chico picked up the race-glasses and swept the course.

'Be careful,' I said idly. 'Don't look at the sun with those. You'll hurt your eyes.'

'Do me a favour.'

I yawned, feeling the sleepless night catch up.

'There's a man on the course,' he said. 'One. Just walking.'

He handed me the glasses and I took a look. He was right. One man was walking alone across the racecourse; not round the track but straight across the rough grass in the middle. He was too far away for his features to be distinguishable and in any case he was wearing a fawn duffle coat with the hood up. I shrugged and lowered the glasses. He looked harmless enough.

With nothing better to do we watched him reach the far side, duck under the rails, and move along until he was standing behind one of the fences with only his head and shoulders in our sight.

Chico remarked that he should have attended to nature in the gents before he left the stands. I yawned again, smiling at the same time. The man went on standing behind the fence.

'What on earth is he doing?' said Chico, after about five minutes.

'He isn't doing anything,' I said, watching through the glasses. 'He's just standing there looking this way.'

'Do you think he's spotted us?'

'No, he couldn't. He hasn't any binocs, and we are in the bushes.'

Another five minutes passed in inactivity.

'He must be doing *something*,' said Chico, exasperated.

'Well, he isn't,' I said.

Chico took a turn with the glasses. 'You can't see a damn thing against the sun,' he complained. 'We should have camped up the other end.'

'In the car park?' I suggested mildly. 'The road to the stables and the main gates runs along the other end. There isn't a scrap of cover.'

'He's got a flag,' said Chico suddenly. 'Two flags. One in each hand. White on the left, orange on the right. He seems to be waving them alternately. He's just some silly nit of a racecourse attendant practising calling up the ambulance and the vet.' He was disappointed.

I watched the flags waving, first white, then orange, then white, then orange, with a gap of a second or two between each wave. It certainly wasn't any form of recognisable signalling: nothing like semaphore. They were, as Chico had said, quite simply the flags used after a fall in a race: white to summon the ambulance for the jockey, orange to get attention for a horse. He didn't keep it up very long. After about eight waves altogether he stopped, and in a moment or two began to walk back across the course to the stands.

'Now what,' said Chico, 'do you think all that was in aid of?'

He swept the glasses all round the whole racecourse yet again. 'There isn't a soul about except him and us.'

'He's probably been standing by a fence for months waiting for a chance to wave his flags, and no one has been injured anywhere near him. In the end, the temptation proved too much.'

I stood up and stretched, went through the bushes to Revelation, undid the head collar with which he was tethered to the bushes, unbuckled the surcingle and pulled off his rug.

'What are you doing?' said Chico.

'The same as the man with the flags. Succumbing to an intolerable temptation. Give me a leg up.' He did what I asked, but hung on to the reins.

'You're mad. You said in the night that they might let you do it after this meeting, but they'd never agree to it before. Suppose you smash the fences?'

'Then I'll be in almighty trouble,' I agreed. 'But here I am on a super jumper looking at a heavenly course on a perfect day, with everyone away at lunch.' I grinned. 'Leave go.'

Chico took his hand away. 'It's not like you,' he said doubtfully.

'Don't take it to heart,' I said flippantly, and touched Revelation into a walk.

At this innocuous pace the horse and I went out on to the track and proceeded in the direction of the stands. Anti-clockwise, the way the races were run. Still at a walk we reached the road and went across its uncovered tarmac surface. On the far side of the road lay the enormous dark brown patch of tan, spread thick and firm where the burnt turf had been bulldozed away. Horses would have no difficulty in racing over it.

Once on the other side, on the turf again, Revelation broke into a trot. He knew where he was. Even with no crowds and no noise the fact of being on a familiar racecourse was exciting him. His ears were pricked, his step springy. At fourteen he had been already a year in retirement,

but he moved beneath me like a four-year-old. He too, I guessed fancifully,
was feeling the satanic tug of pleasure about to be illicitly snatched.

Chico was right, of course. I had no business at all to be riding on the
course so soon before a meeting. It was indefensible. I ought to know
better. I did know better. I eased Revelation gently into a canter.

There were three flights of hurdles and three fences more or less side
by side up the straight, and the water jump beyond that. As I wasn't sure
that Revelation would jump the fences in cold blood on his own (many
horses won't), I set him at the hurdles.

Once he had seen these and guessed my intention I doubt if I could
have stopped him, even if I'd wanted to. He fairly ate up the first flight
and stretched out eagerly for the second. After that I gave him a choice,
and of the two obstacles lying ahead, he opted for the fence. It didn't
seem to bother him that he was on his own. They were excellent fences
and he was a Gold Cup winner, born and bred for the job and being
given an unexpected, much missed treat. He flew the fence with all his
former dash and skill.

As for me, my feelings were indescribable. I'd sat on a horse a few
times since I'd given up racing, but never found an opportunity of doing
more than riding out quietly at morning exercise with Mark's string.
And here I was, back in my old place, doing again what I'd ached for
in two and a half years. I grinned with irrepressible joy and got Revelation
to lengthen his stride for the water jump.

He took it with feet to spare. Perfect. There were no irate shouts from
the stands on my right, and we swept away on round the top bend of the
course, fast and free. Another fence at the end of the bend – Revelation
floated it – and five more stretching away down the far side. It was at
the third of these, the open ditch, that the man had been standing and
waving the flags.

It's an undoubted fact that emotions pass from rider to horse, and
Revelation was behaving with the same reckless exhilaration which
gripped me: so after two spectacular helps over the next two fences we
both sped onwards with arms open to fate. There ahead was the guard
rail, the four foot wide open ditch and the four foot six fence rising on
the far side of it. Revelation, knowing all about it, automatically put
himself right to jump.

It came, the blinding flash in the eyes, as we soared into the air. White,
dazzling, brain shattering light, splintering the day into a million fragments and blotting out the world in a blaze as searing as the sun.

I felt Revelation falling beneath me and rolled instinctively, my eyes
open and quite unable to see. Then there was the rough crash on the turf
and the return of vision from light to blackness and up through grey to
normal sight.

I was on my feet before Revelation, and I still had hold of the reins.
He struggled up, bewildered and staggering, but apparently unhurt. I
pulled him forward into an unwilling trot to make sure of his legs, and
was relieved to find them whole and sound. It only remained to remount
as quickly as possible, and this was infuriatingly difficult. With two
hands I could have jumped up easily: as it was I scrambled untidily back

into the saddle at the third attempt, having lost the reins altogether and bashed my stomach on the pommel of the saddle into the bargain. Revelation behaved very well, all things considered. He trotted only fifty yards or so in the wrong direction before I collected myself and the reins into a working position and turned him round. This time we by-passed the fence and all subsequent ones: I cantered him first down the side of the track, slowed to a trot to cross the road, and steered then not on round the bottom semi-circle but off to the right, heading for where the boundary fence met the main London road.

Out of the corner of my eye I saw Chico running in my direction across the rough grass. I waved him towards me with a sweep of the arm and reined in and waited for him where our paths converged.

'I thought you said you could bloody well ride,' he said, scarcely out of breath from the run.

'Yeah,' I said. 'I thought so once.'

He looked at me sharply. 'You fell off. I was watching. You fell off like a baby.'

'If you were watching ... the horse fell, if you don't mind. There's a distinction. Very important to jockeys.'

'Nuts,' he said. 'You fell off.'

'Come on,' I said, walking Revelation towards the boundary fence. 'There's something to find.' I told Chico what. 'In one of those bungalows, I should think. At a window or on the roof, or in a garden.'

'Sods,' said Chico forcefully. 'The dirty sods.'

I agreed with him.

It wasn't very difficult, because it had to be within a stretch of only a hundred yards or so. We went methodically along the boundary fence towards the London road, stopping to look carefully into every separate little garden, and at every separate little house. A fair number of inquisitive faces looked back.

Chico saw it first, propped into a high leafless branch of a tree growing well back in the second to last garden. Traffic whizzed along the London road only ten yards ahead, and Revelation showed signs of wanting to retreat.

'Look,' said Chico, pointing upwards.

I looked, fighting a mild battle against the horse. It was five feet high, three feet wide, and polished to a spotless brillance. A mirror.

'Sods,' said Chico again.

I nodded, dismounted, led Revelation back to where the traffic no longer fretted him, and tied the reins to the fence. Then Chico and I walked along to the London road and round into the road of bungalows. Napoleon Close, it said. Napoleon wasn't *that* close, I reflected, amused.

We rang the door of the second bungalow. A man and a woman both came to the door to open it, elderly, gentle, inoffensive and enquiring.

I came straight to the point, courteously. 'Do you know you have a mirror in your tree?'

'Don't be silly,' said the woman, smiling as at an idiot. She had flat wavy grey hair and was wearing a sloppy black cardigan over a brown wool dress. No colour sense, I thought.

'You'd better take a look,' I suggested.

'It's not a mirror, you know,' said the husband puzzled. 'It's a placard. One of those advertisement things.'

'That's right,' said his wife contrapuntally. 'A placard.'

'We agreed to lend our tree . . .'

'For a small sum, really . . . only our pension . . .'

'A man put up the framework . . .'

'He said he would be back soon with the poster . . .'

'A religious one, I believe. A good cause . . .'

'We wouldn't have done it otherwise . . .'

Chico interrupted. 'I wouldn't have thought it was a good place for a poster. Your tree stands further back than the others. It isn't conspicuous.'

'I did think . . .' began the man doubtfully, shuffling in his checked woolly bedroom slippers.

'But if he was willing to pay rent for your particular tree, you didn't want to put him off,' I finished. 'An extra quid or two isn't something you want to pass on next door.'

They wouldn't have put it so bluntly, but they didn't demur.

'Come and look,' I said.

They followed me round along the narrow path beside their bungalow wall and into their own back garden. The tree stood half way to the racecourse boundary fence, the sun slanting down through the leafless branches. We could see the wooden back of the mirror, and the ropes which fastened it to the tree trunk. The man and his wife walked round to the front, and their puzzlement increased.

'He said it was for a poster,' repeated the man.

'Well,' I said as matter of factly as I could, 'I expect it is for a poster, as he said. But at the moment, you see, it is a mirror. And it's pointing straight out over the racecourse; and you know how mirrors reflect the sunlight? We just thought it might not be too safe, you know, if anyone got dazzled, so we wondered if you would mind us moving it?'

'Why, goodness,' agreed the woman, looking with more awareness at our riding clothes, 'no one could see the racing with light shining in their eyes.'

'Quite. So would you mind if we turned the mirror round a bit?'

'I can't see that it would hurt, Dad,' she said doubtfully.

He made a nondescript assenting movement with his hand, and Chico asked how the mirror had been put up in the tree in the first place. The man had brought a ladder with him, they said, and no, they hadn't one themselves. Chico shrugged, placed me beside the tree, put one foot on my thigh, one on my shoulder, and was up in the bare branches like a squirrel. The elderly couple's mouths sagged open.

'How long ago?' I asked. 'When did the man put up the mirror?'

'This morning,' said the woman, getting over the shock. 'He came back just now, too, with another rope or something. That's when he said he'd be back with the poster.'

So the mirror had been hauled up into the tree while Chico and I had been obliviously sitting in the bushes, and adjusted later when the sun was at the right angle in the sky. At two o'clock. The time, the next day, of the third race, the handicap steeplechase. Some handicap, I thought, a smash of light in the eyes.

White flag: a little bit to the left. Orange flag: a little bit to the right. No flag: dead on target.

Come back tomorrow afternoon and clap a religious poster over the glass as soon as the damage was done, so that even the quickest search wouldn't reveal a mirror. Just another jinx on Seabury racecourse. Dead horses, crushed and trampled jockeys. A jinx. Send my horses somewhere else, Mr. Witney, something always goes wrong at Seabury.

I was way out in one respect. The religious poster was not due to be put in place the following day.

Chapter Thirteen

'I think,' I said gently to the elderly couple, 'that it might be better if you went indoors. We will explain to the man who is coming what we are doing to his mirror.'

Dad glanced up the path towards the road, put his arm protectively round his wife's woolly shoulders, and said gratefully, 'Er ... yes ... yes.'

They shuffled rapidly through the back door into the bungalow just as a large man carrying an aluminium folding ladder and a large rolled up paper came barging through their front gate. There had been the squeak of his large plain dark blue van stopping, the hollow crunch of the handbrake being forcibly applied, the slam of the door and the scrape of the ladder being unloaded. Chico in the tree crouched quite still, watching.

I was standing with my back to the sun, but it fell full on the big man's face when he came into the garden. It wasn't the sort of face one would naturally associate with religious posters. He was a cross between a heavyweight wrestler and Mount Vesuvius. Craggy, brutally strong, and not far off erupting.

He came straight towards me across the grass, dropped the ladder beside him, and said enquiringly, 'What goes on?'

'The mirror,' I said, 'Comes down.'

His eyes narrowed in sudden awareness and his body stiffened. 'There's a poster going over it,' he began quite reasonably, lifting the paper roll. Then with a rush the lava burst out, the paper flew wide, and the muscles bunched into action.

It wasn't much of a fight. He started out to hit my face, changed his mind, and ploughed both fists in below the belt. It was quite a long way down for him. Doubling over in pain on to the lawn, I picked up the ladder, and gave him a swinging swipe behind the knees.

The ground shook with the impact. He fell on his side, his coat swinging open. I lunged forward, snatching at the pistol showing in the holster beside his ribs. It came loose, but he brushed me aside with an arm like a telegraph pole. I fell, sprawling. He rolled into a crouch, picked up the gun from the grass and sneered down into my face. Then he stood up like a released spring and on the way with force and deliberation booted his toe-cap into my navel. He also clicked back the catch on his gun.

Up in the tree Chico yelled. The big man turned and took three steps towards him, seeing him for the first time. With a choice of targets, he favoured the one still in a state to resist. The hand with the pistol pointed at Chico.

'Leo,' I shouted. Nothing happened. I tried again.

'Fred!'

The big man turned his head a fraction back to me and Chico jumped down on to him from ten feet up.

The gun went off with a double crash and again the day flew apart in shining splintering fragments. I sat on the ground with my knees bent up, groaning quietly, cursing fluently, and getting on with my business.

Drawn by the noise, the inhabitants of the bungalows down the line came out into their back gardens and looked in astonishment over the fences. The elderly couple stood palely at their window, their mouths again open. The big man had too big an audience now for murder.

Chico was overmatched for size and nearly equalled in skill. He and the big man threw each other round a bit while I crept doubled up along the path into the front garden as far as the gate, but the battle was a foregone conclusion, bar the retreat.

He came alone, crashing up the path, saw me hanging on to the gate and half raised the gun. But there were people in the road now, and more people peering out of opposite windows. In scorching fury he whipped at my head with the barrel, and I avoided it by leaving go of the gate and collapsing on the ground again. Behind the gate, with the bars nice and comfortingly between me and his boot.

He crunched across the pavement, slammed into the van, cut his cogs to ribbons and disappeared out on to the London road in a cloud of dust.

Chico came down the garden path staggering, with blood sloshing out of a cut eyebrow. He looked anxious and shaken.

'I thought you said you could bloody well fight,' I mocked him.

He came to a halt beside me on his knees. 'Blast you.' He put his fingers to his forehead and winced at the result.

I grinned at him.

'You were running away,' he said.

'Naturally.'

'What have you got here?' He took the little camera out of my hand. 'Don't tell me,' he said, his face splitting into an unholy smile. 'Don't tell me.'

'It's what we came for, after all.'

'How many?'

'Four of him. Two of the van.'

'Sid, you slay me, you really do.'

'Well,' I said, 'I feel sick.' I rolled over and retched what was left of my breakfast on to the roots of the privet hedge. There wasn't any blood. I felt a lot better.

'I'll go and get the horse-box,' said Chico, 'and pick you up.'

'You'll do nothing of the sort,' I said, wiping my mouth on a handkerchief. 'We're going back into the garden. I want that bullet.'

'It's half way to Seabury,' he protested, borrowing my handkerchief to mop the blood off his eyebrow.

'What will you bet?' I said. I used the gate again to get up, and after a moment or two was fairly straight. We presented a couple of reassuring grins to the audience, and retraced our way down the path into the back garden.

The mirror lay in sparkling pointed fragments all over the lawn.

'Pop up the tree and see if the bullet is there, in the wood. It smashed the mirror. It might be stuck up there. If not, we'll have to comb the grass.'

Chico went up the aluminium ladder that time.

'Of all the luck,' he called. 'It's here.' I watched him take a penknife out of his pocket and carefully cut away at a section just off-centre of the back board of the ex-mirror. He came down and held the little misshapen lump out to me on the palm of his hand. I put it carefully away in the small waist pocket of my breeches.

The elderly couple had emerged like tortoises from their bungalow. They were scared and puzzled, understandably. Chico offered to cut down the remains of the mirror, and did, but we left them to clear up the resulting firewood.

As an afterthought, however, Chico went across the garden and retrieved the poster from a soggy winter rosebed. He unrolled it and showed it to us, laughing.

'Blessed are the meek: for they shall inherit the earth.'

'One of them,' said Chico, 'has a sense of humour.'

Much against his wishes, we returned to our observation post in the scrubby gorse.

'Haven't you had enough?' he said crossly.

'The patrols don't get here till six,' I reminded him. 'And you yourself said that dusk would be the likely time for them to try something.'

'But they've already done it.'

'There's nothing to stop them from rigging up more than one booby trap,' I pointed out. 'Especially as that mirror thing wouldn't have been one hundred per cent reliable, even if we hadn't spotted it. It depended on the sun. Good weather forecast, I know, but weather forecasts are as reliable as a perished hot-water bottle. A passing cloud would have wrecked it. I would think they have something else in mind.'

'Cheerful,' he said resignedly. He led Revelation away along the road to stow him in the horse box, and was gone a long time.

When he came back he sat down beside me and said, 'I went all round the stables. No one stopped me or asked what I was doing. Don't they have *any* security here? The cleaners have all gone home, but there's a woman cooking in the canteen. She said I was too early, to come back at half past six. There wasn't anyone about in the stands block except an old geyser with snuffles mucking about with the boiler.'

The sun was lower in the sky and the November afternoon grew colder. We shivered a little and huddled inside our jerseys.

Chico said, 'You guessed about the mirror before you set off round the course.'

'It was a possibility, that's all.'

'You could have ridden along the boundary fence, looking into the gardens like we did afterwards, instead of haring off over all those jumps.'

I grinned faintly. 'Yes. As I told you, I was giving in to temptation.'

'Screwy. You must have known you'd fall.'

'Of course I didn't. The mirror mightn't have worked very effectively. Anyway, it's better to test a theory in a practical way. And I just wanted to ride round there. I had a good excuse if I were hauled up for it. So I went. And it was grand. So shut up.'

He laughed. 'All right.' Restlessly he stood up again and said he would make another tour. While he was gone I watched the racecourse with and without the binoculars, but not a thing moved on it.

He came back quietly and dropped down beside me.

'As before,' he said.

'Nothing here, either.'

He looked at me sideways. 'Do you feel as bad as you look?'

'I shouldn't be surprised,' I said. 'Do you?'

He tenderly touched the area round his cut eyebrow. 'Worse. Much worse. Soggy bad luck, him slugging away at your belly like that.'

'He did it on purpose,' I said idly; 'and it was very informative.'

'Huh?'

'It showed he knew who I was. He wouldn't have needed to have attacked us like that if we'd just been people come over from the racecourse to see if we could shift the mirror. But when he spoke to me he recognised me, and he knew I wouldn't be put off by any poster eyewash. And his sort don't mildly back down and retreat without paying you off for getting in their way. He just hit where he knew it would have most effect. I actually saw him think it.'

'But how did he know?'

'It was he who sent Andrews to the office,' I said. 'He was the man Mervyn Brinton described; big, going a bit bald, freckles on the backs of his hands, cockney accent. He was strong-arming Brinton, and he sent Andrews to get the letter that was supposed to be in the office. Well . . . Andrews knew me, and I knew him. He must have gone back and told our big friend Fred that he had shot me in the stomach. My death wasn't reported in the papers, so Fred knew I was still alive and would put the finger on Andrews at once. Andrews wasn't exactly a good risk to Fred, just a silly spiv with no sense, so Fred, I guess, marched him straight off to Epping Forest and left him for the birds. Who did a fair job, I'll give them that.'

'Do you think,' said Chico slowly, 'that the gun Fred had today . . . is that why you wanted the bullet?'

I nodded. 'That's right. I tried for the gun too, but no dice. If I'm going on with this sort of work, pal, you'll have to teach me a spot of judo.'

He looked down doubtfully. 'With that hand?'

'Invent a new sport,' I said, 'One-armed combat.'

'I'll take you to the club,' he said smiling. 'There's an old Jap there who'll find a way if anyone can.'

'Good.'

Up at the far end of the racecourse a horse box turned in off the main road and trundled along towards the stables. The first of the next day's runners had apparently arrived.

Chico went to have a look.

I sat on in fading daylight, watching nothing happen, hugging myself against the cold and the re-awakened grinding ache in my gut, and thinking evil thoughts about Fred. Not Leo. Fred.

There were four of them, I thought. Kraye, Bolt, Fred and Leo.

I had met Kraye: he knew me only as Sid, a despised hanger-on in the home of a retired admiral he had met at his club and had spent a week-end with.

I had met Bolt: he knew me as John Halley, a shop assistant wanting to invest a gift from an aunt.

I had met Fred: he knew my whole name, and that I worked for an agency, and that I had turned up at Seabury.

I did not know if I had met Leo. But Leo might know *me*. If he had anything to do with racing, he definitely did.

It would be all right, I thought, as long as they did not connect all the Halleys and Sids too soon. But there was my wretched hand, which Kraye had pulled out of my pocket, which Fred could have seen in the garden, and which Leo, whoever he was, might have noticed almost anywhere in the last six days, thanks to my promise to Zanna Martin. Zanna Martin, who worked for Bolt. A proper merry-go-round, I thought wryly.

Chico materialised out of the dusk. 'It was Ping Pong, running in the first tomorrow. All above board,' he said. 'And nothing doing anywhere, stands or course. We might as well go.'

It was well after five. I agreed, and got up stiffly.

'That Fred,' said Chico, casually giving me a hand, 'I've been thinking. I've seen him before, I'm certain. At race meetings. He's not a regular. Doesn't work for a bookie, or anything like that. But he's about. Cheap rings, mostly.'

'Let's hope he doesn't burrow,' I said.

'I don't see why he should,' he said seriously. 'He can't possibly think you'd connect him with Andrews or with Kraye. All you caught him doing was fixing a poster in a tree. If I were him, I'd be sleeping easy.'

'I called him Fred,' I said.

'Oh,' said Chico glumly. 'So you did.'

We reached the road and started along it towards the horse box.

'Fred must be the one who does all the jobs,' said Chico. 'Digs the false drains, sets fire to stables, and drives tractors to pull over tankers. He's big enough for anything.'

'He didn't wave the flags. He was up the tree at the time.'

'Um. Yes. Who did?'

'Not Bolt,' I said. 'It wasn't fat enough for Bolt, even in a duffle coat. Possibly Kraye. More likely Leo, whoever he is.'

'One of the workmen, or the foreman. Yes. Well, that makes two of them for overturning tankers and so on.'

'It would be easier for two,' I agreed.

Chico drove the horse box back to Mark's, and then, to his obvious delight, my Merc back to London.

Chapter Fourteen

Chief-Inspector Cornish was pleased but trying to hide it.

'I suppose you can chalk it up to your agency,' he said, as if it were debatable.

'He walked slap into us, to be fair.'

'And slap out again,' he said dryly.

I grimaced. 'You haven't met him.'

'You want to leave that sort to us,' he said automatically.

'Where were you, then?'

'That's a point,' he admitted, smiling.

He picked up the matchbox again and looked at the bullet. 'Little beauty. Good clear markings. Pity he has a revolver, though, and not an automatic. It would have been nice to have had cartridge cases as well.'

'You're greedy,' I said.

He looked at the aluminium ladder standing against his wall, and at the poster on his desk, and at the rush-job photographs. Two clear prints of the van showing its number plates and four of Fred in action against Chico. Not exactly posed portraits, those, but four different, characteristic and recognisable angles taken in full sunlight.

'With all this lot to go on, we'll trace him before he draws breath.'

'Fine,' I said. And the sooner Fred was immobilised the better, I thought. Before he did any more damage to Seabury. 'You'll need a tiger net to catch him. He's a very tough baby, and knows judo. And unless he has the sense to throw it away, he'll still have that gun.'

'I'll remember,' he said. 'And thanks.' We shook hands amicably as I left.

It was results day at Radnor's, too. As soon as I got back Dolly said Jack Copeland wanted me up in Bona Fides. I made the journey.

Jack gleamed at me over the half moons, pleased with his department. 'George's got him. Kraye. He'll tell you.'

I went over to George's desk. George was fairly smirking, but after he'd talked for two minutes, I allowed he'd earned it.

'On the off chance,' he said, 'I borrowed a bit of smooth quartz Kraye recently handled in the Geology Museum and got Sammy to do the prints on it. Two or three different sets of fingers came out, so we photographed the lot. None of them were on the British files, but I've given them the run around with the odd pal in Interpol and so on, just in case. And brother, have we hit pay dirt or have we.'

'We have?' I prompted, grinning.

'And how. Your friend Kraye is in the ex-con library of the state of New York.'

'What for?'

'Assault.'

'Of a girl?' I asked.

George raised his eyebrows. 'A girl's father. Kraye had beaten the girl, apparently with her permission. She didn't complain. But her father saw the bruises and raised the roof. He said he'd get Kraye on a rape charge, though it seems the girl had been perfectly willing on that count too. But it looked bad for Kraye, so he picked up a chair and smashed it over the father's head and scarpered. They caught him boarding a plane for South America and hauled him back. The father's brain was damaged. There are long medical details, but what it all boils down to is that he couldn't coordinate properly afterwards. Kraye got off on the rape charge, but served four years for attacking the father.

'Three years after that he turned up in England with some money and a new name, and soon acquired a wife. The one who divorced him for cruelty. Nice chap.'

'Yes indeed,' I said. 'What was his real name?'

'Wilbur Potter,' said George sardonically. 'And you'll never guess. He was a geologist by profession. He worked for a construction firm, surveying. Always moving about. Character assessment: slick, a pusher, a good talker. Cut a few corners, always had more money than his salary, threw his weight about, but nothing indictable. The assault on the father was his first brush with the law. He was thirty-four at that time.'

'Messy,' I said. 'The whole thing.'

'Very,' George agreed.

'But sex violence and fraudulent take-overs aren't much related,' I complained.

'You might as well say it is impossible to have boils and cancer at the same time. Something drastically wrong with the constitution, and two separate symptoms.'

'I'll take your word for it,' I said.

Sammy up in Missing Persons had done more than photograph Kraye's fingerprints, he had almost found Smith.

'Intersouth rang us this morning,' he purred. 'Smith gave them as a reference. He's applied for a driving job in Birmingham.'

'Good,' I said.

'We should have his address by this afternoon.'

Downstairs in Racing I reached for Dolly's telephone and got through to Charing, Street and King.

'Mr. Bolt's secretary speaking,' said the quiet voice.

'Is Mr. Bolt in?' I asked.

'I'm afraid not . . . er, who is that speaking, please?'

'Did you find you had a file of mine?'

'Oh . . .' she laughed. 'Yes, I picked it up in your car. I'm so sorry.'

'Do you have it with you?'

'No,' she said. 'I didn't bring it here. I thought it might be better not to risk Mr. Bolt seeing it, as it's got Hunt Radnor Associates printed on the outside along with a red sticker saying "Ex Records, care of Sid Halley".'

'Yes, it would have been a disaster,' I agreed with feeling.

'I left it at home. Do you want it in a hurry?'

'No, not really. As long as it's safe, that's the main thing. How would it be if I came over to fetch it the day after tomorrow – Sunday morning? We could go for a drive, perhaps, and have some lunch?'

There was a tiny pause. Then she said strongly, 'Yes, please. Yes.'

'Have the leaflets gone out?' I asked.

'They went yesterday.'

'See you on Sunday, Miss Martin.'

I put down Dolly's telephone to find her looking at me quizzically. I was again squatting on the corner of her desk, the girl from the typing pool having in my absence reclaimed her chair.

'The mouse got away again, I understand,' she said.

'Some mouse.'

Chico came into the office. The cut on his eyebrow looked red and sore, and all the side of his face showed greyish bruising.

'Two of you,' said Dolly disgustedly, 'and he knocked you about like kids.'

Chico took this a lot better than if she had fussed maternally over his injury.

'It took more than two Lilliputians to peg down Gulliver,' he said with good humour. (They had a large library in the children's orphanage.)

'But only one David to slay Goliath.'

Chico made a face at her, and I laughed.

'And how are our collywobbles today?' he asked me ironically.

'Better than your looks.'

'You know why Sid's best friends don't know him?' said Chico.

'Why?' said Dolly, seriously.

'He suffers from Halley-tosis.'

'Oh God,' said Dolly. 'Take him away someone. Take him away. I can't stand it.'

On the ground floor I sat in a padded maroon arm-chair in Radnor's drawing-room office and listened to him saying there were no out-of-the-ordinary reports from the patrols at Seabury.

'Fison has just been on the telephone. Everything is normal for a race day, he says. The public will start arriving very shortly. He and Thom walked all round the course just now with Captain Oxon for a thorough check. There's nothing wrong with it, that they can see.'

There might be something wrong with it that they couldn't see. I was uneasy.

'I might stay down there tonight, if I can find a room,' I said.

'If you do, give me a ring again at home, during the evening.'

'Sure.' I had disturbed his dinner, the day before, to tell him about Fred and the mirror.

'Could I have those photographs back, if you've finished with them?' I asked. 'I want to check that list of initials against the racecourse workmen at Seabury.'

'I'm sorry, Sid, I haven't got them.'

'Are they back upstairs . . .?'

'No, no, they aren't here at all. Lord Hagbourne has them.'

'But why?' I sat up straight, disturbed.

'He came here yesterday afternoon. I'd say on balance he is almost down on our side of the fence. I didn't get the usual caution about expenses, which is a good sign. Anyway, what he wanted was to see the proofs you told him we held which show it is Kraye who is buying the shares. Photographs of share transfer certificates. He knew about them. He said you'd told him.'

'Yes, I did.'

'He wanted to see them. That was reasonable, and I didn't want to risk tipping him back into indecision, so I showed them to him. He asked me very courteously if he could take them to show them to the Seabury executive. They held a meeting this morning, I believe. He thought they might be roused to some effective action if they could see for themselves how big Kraye's holding is.'

'What about the other photographs? The others that were in the box.'

'He took them all. They were all jumbled up, and he was in a hurry. He said he'd sort them out himself later.'

'He took them to Seabury?' I said uneasily.

'That's right. For the executive meeting this morning.' He looked at his watch. 'The meeting must be on at this moment, I should think. If you want them you can ask him for them as soon as you get there. He should have finished with them by then.'

'I wish you hadn't let him take them,' I said.

'It can't do any harm. Even if he lost them we'd still have the negatives. You could get another print done tomorrow, of your list.'

The negatives, did he but know it, were inaccessibly tucked into a mislaid file in Finchley. I didn't confess. Instead I said, unconvinced, 'All right. I suppose it won't matter. I'll get on down there, then.'

I packed an overnight bag in the flat. The sun was pouring in through the windows, making the blues and greens and blond wood furniture look warm and friendly. After two years the place was at last beginning to feel like home. A home without Jenny. Happiness without Jenny. Both were possible, it seemed. I certainly felt more myself than at any time since she left.

The sun was still shining, too, at Seabury. But not on a very large crowd. The poor quality of the racing was so obvious as to be pathetic: and it was in order that such a rotten gaggle of weedy quadrupeds could stumble and scratch their way round to the winning post, I reflected philosophically, that I tried to pit my inadequate wits against Lord Hagbourne, Captain Oxon, the Seabury executive, Kraye, Bolt, Fred, Leo, old Uncle Tom Cobley and all.

There were no mishaps all day. The horses raced nonchalantly over the tan patch at their speedy crawl, and no light flashed in their eyes as they knocked hell out of the fences on the far side. Round One to Chico and me.

As the fine weather put every one in a good mood a shred of Seabury's former vitality temporarily returned to the place: enough, anyway, for people to notice the dinginess of the stands and remark that it was time something was done about it. If they felt like that, I thought, a revival shouldn't be impossible.

The Senior Steward listened attentively while I passed on Zanna Martin's suggestion that Seabury council should be canvassed, and surprisingly said that he would see it was promptly done.

In spite of these small headways, however, my spine wouldn't stop tingling. Lord Hagbourne didn't have the photographs.

'They are only mislaid, Sid,' he said soothingly. 'Don't make such a fuss. They'll turn up.'

He had put them down on the table round which the meeting had been held, he said. After the official business was over, he had chatted, standing up. When he turned back to pick up the box, it was no longer there. The whole table had been cleared. The ashtrays were being emptied. The table was required for lunch. A white cloth was being spread over it.

What, I asked, had been the verdict of the meeting, anyway? Er, um, it appeared the whole subject had been shelved for a week or two: no urgency was felt. Shares changed hands slowly, very slowly. But they had agreed that Hunt Radnor could carry on for a bit.

I hesitated to go barging into the executive's private room just to look for a packet of photographs, so I asked the caterers instead. They hadn't seen it, they said, rushing round me. I tracked down the man and woman who had cleared the table after the meeting and laid it for lunch.

Any amount of doodling on bits of paper, said the waitress, but no box of photographs, and excuse me love, they're waiting for these sandwiches. She agreed to look for it, looked, and came back shaking her head. It wasn't there, as far as she could see. It was quite big, I said despairingly.

I asked Mr. Fotherton, Clerk of the Course; I asked Captain Oxon, I asked the secretary, and anyone else I could think of who had been at the meeting. None of them knew where the photographs were. All of them, busy with their racing jobs, said much the same as Lord Hagbourne.

'Don't worry, Sid, they're bound to turn up.'
But they didn't.

I stayed on the racecourse until after the security patrols changed over at six o'clock. The incomers were the same men who had been on watch the night before, four experienced and sensible ex-policemen, all middle-aged. They entrenched themselves comfortably in the Press room, which had windows facing back and front, effective central heating, and four telephones; better headquarters than usual on their night jobs, they said.

Between the last race (three-thirty) and six o'clock, apart from hunting without success for the photographs and driving Lord Hagbourne round to Napoleon Close for a horrified first-hand look at the smashed-up mirror, I persuaded Captain Oxon to accompany me on a thorough nook and cranny check-up of all the racecourse buildings.

He came willingly enough, his stiffness of earlier in the week having been thawed, I supposed, by the comparative success of the day; but we found nothing and no one that shouldn't have been there.

I drove into Seabury and booked into the Seafront Hotel, where I had often stayed in the past. It was only half full. Formerly, on racing nights, it had been crammed. Over a brandy in the bar the manager lamented with me the state of trade.

'Race meetings used to give us a boost every three weeks nearly all the winter. Now hardly anyone comes, and I hear they didn't even ask for the January fixture this year. I tell you, I'd like to see that place blooming again, we need it.'

'Ah,' I said. 'Then write to the Town Council and say so.'

'That wouldn't help,' he said gloomily.

'You never know. It might. Do write.'

'All right, Sid. Just to please you then. For old time's sake. Let's have another brandy on the house.'

I had an early dinner with him and his wife and afterwards went for a walk along the seashore. The night was dry and cold and the onshore breeze smelt of seaweed. The banked pebbles scrunched into trickling hollows under my shoes and the winter sand was as hard-packed as rock. Thinking about Kraye and his machinations, I had strolled quite a long way eastwards, away from the racecourse, before I remembered I had said I would ring Radnor at his home during the evening.

There was nothing much to tell him. I didn't hurry, and it was nearly ten o'clock when I got back to Seabury. The modernisations didn't yet run to telephones in all the bedrooms at the hotel, so I used the kiosk outside on the promenade, because I came to it first.

It wasn't Radnor who answered, but Chico, and I knew at once from his voice that things had gone terribly wrong.

'Sid ...' he said. 'Sid ... look, pal, I don't know how to tell you. You'll have to have it straight. We've been trying to reach you all the evening.'

'What ...?' I swallowed.

'Someone bombed your flat.'

'*Bombed*,' I said stupidly.

'A plastic bomb. It blew the street wall right out. All the flats round yours were badly damaged, but yours ... well, there's nothing there. Just a big hole with disgusting black sort of cobwebs. That's how they knew it was a plastic bomb. The sort the French terrorists used ... Sid, are you there?'

'Yes.'

'I'm sorry, pal. I'm sorry. But that's not all. They've done it to the office, too.' His voice was anguished. 'It went off in the Racing Section. But the whole place is cracked open. It's ... it's bloody ghastly.'

'Chico.'

'I know. I know. The old man's round there now, just staring at it. He made me stay here because you said you'd ring, and in case the racecourse patrols want anything. No one was badly hurt, that's the only good thing. Half a dozen people were bruised and cut, at your flats. And the office was empty, of course.'

'What time ...?'

'The bomb in the office went off about an hour and a half ago, and the one in your flat was just after seven. The old man and I were round there with the police when they got the radio message about the office. The police seem to think that whoever did it was looking for something. The people who live underneath you heard someone moving about upstairs for about two hours shortly before the bomb went off, but they just thought it was you making more noise than usual. And it seems everything in your flat was moved into one pile in the sitting-room and the bomb put in the middle. The police said it meant that they hadn't found what they were looking for and were destroying everything in case they had missed it.'

'Everything ...' I said.

'Not a thing was left. God, Sid, I wish I didn't have to ... but there it is. Nothing that was there exists any more.'

The letters from Jenny when she loved me. The only photograph of my mother and father. The trophies I won racing. The lot. I leant numbly against the wall.

'Sid, are you still there?'

'Yes.'

'It was the same thing at the office. People across the road saw lights on and someone moving about inside, and just thought we were working late. The old man said we must assume they still haven't found what they were looking for. He wants to know what it is.'

'I don't know,' I said.

'You must.'

'No. I don't.'

'You can think on the way back.'

'I'm not coming back. Not tonight. It can't do any good. I think I'll go out to the racecourse again, just to make sure nothing happens there too.'

'All right. I'll tell him when he calls. He said he'd be over in Cromwell Road all night, very likely.'

We rang off and I went out of the kiosk into the cold night air. I thought that Radnor was right. It was important to know what it was that the bomb merchants had been looking for. I leaned against the outside of the box, thinking about it. Deliberately not thinking about the flat, the place that had begun to be home, and all that was lost. That had happened before, in one way or another. The night my mother died, for instance. And I'd ridden my first winner the next day.

To look for something, you had to know it existed. If you used bombs, destroying it was more important than finding it. What did I have, which I hadn't had long (or they would have searched before) which Kraye wanted obliterated.

There was the bullet which Fred had accidentally fired into the mirror. They wouldn't find that, because it was somewhere in the police ballistics laboratory. And if they had thought I had it, they would have looked for it the night before.

There was the leaflet Bolt had sent out, but there were hundreds of those, and he wouldn't want the one I had, even if he knew I had it.

There was the letter Mervyn Brinton had re-written for me, but if it were that it meant . . .

I went back into the telephone box, obtain Mervyn Brinton's number from directory enquiries, and rang him up.

To my relief, he answered.

'You are all right, Mr. Brinton?'

'Yes, yes. What's the matter?'

'You haven't had a call from the big man? You haven't told anyone about my visit to you, or that you know your brother's letter by heart?'

He sounded scared. 'No. Nothing's happened. I wouldn't tell anyone. I never would.'

'Fine,' I reassured him. 'That's just fine. I was only checking.'

So it was not Brinton's letter.

The photographs, I thought. They had been in the office all the time until Radnor gave them to Lord Hagbourne yesterday afternoon. No one outside the agency, except Lord Hagbourne and Charles, had known they existed. Not until this morning, when Lord Hagbourne took them to Seabury executive meeting and lost them.

Suppose they weren't lost, but stolen. By someone who knew Kraye, and thought he ought to have them. From the dates on all those documents Kraye would know exactly when the photographs had been taken. And where.

My scalp contracted. I must assume I thought, that they had now connected all the Halleys and Sids.

Suddenly fearful, I rang up Aynsford. Charles himself answered, calm and sensible.

'Charles, please will you do as I ask, at once, and no questions? Grab Mrs. Cross, go out and get in the car and drive well away from the house, and ring me back at Seabury 79411. Got that? Seabury 79411.'

'Yes.' He said, and put down the telephone. Thank God, I thought, for naval training. There might not be much time. The office bomb had exploded an hour and a half ago; London to Aynsford took the same.

Ten minutes later the bell began to ring. I picked up the receiver.

'They say you're in a call box,' Charles said.

'That's right. Are you?'

'No, the pub down in the village. Now, what's it all about?'

I told him about the bombs, which horrified him, and about the missing photographs.

'I can't think what else it can be that they are looking for.'

'But you said that they've got them.'

'The negatives,' I said.

'Oh. Yes. And they weren't in your flat or the office?'

'No. Quite by chance, they weren't.'

'And you think if they're still looking, that they'll come to Aynsford?'

'If they are desperate enough, they might. They might think you would know where I keep things ... And even have a go at making you tell them. I asked you to come out quick because I didn't want to risk it. If they are going to Aynsford, they could be there at any minute now. It's horribly likely they'll think of you. They'll know I took the photos in your house.'

'From the dates. Yes. Right. I'll get on to the local police and ask for a guard on the house at once.'

'Charles, one of them ... well, if he's the one with the bombs, you'll need a squad.' I described Fred and his van, together with its number.

'Right.' He was still calm. 'Why would the photographs be so important to them? Enough to use bombs, I mean?'

'I wish I knew.'

'Take care.'

'Yes,' I said.

I did take care. Instead of going back to the hotel, I rang up.'

The manager said, 'Sid, where on earth are you, people have been trying to reach you all the evening ... the police too.'

'Yes, Joe, I know. It's all right. I've talked to the people in London. Now, has anyone actually called at the hotel, wanting me?'

'There's someone up in your room, yes. Your father-in-law, Admiral Roland.'

'Oh really? Does he look like an Admiral?'

'I suppose so,' he sounded puzzled.

'A gentleman?'

'Yes, of course.' Not Fred, then.

'Well, he isn't my father-in-law. I've just been talking to him in his house in Oxfordshire. You collect a couple of helpers and chuck my visitor out.'

I put down the receiver sighing. A man up in my room meant everything I'd brought to Seabury would very likely be ripped to bits. That left me with just the clothes I stood in, and the car ...

I fairly sprinted round to where I'd left the car. It was locked, silent and safe. No damage. I patted it thankfully, climbed in, and drove out to the racecourse.

Chapter Fifteen

All was quiet as I drove through the gates and switched off the engine. There were lights on – one shining through the windows of the Press room, one outside the weighing room door, one high up somewhere on the stands. The shadows in between were densely black. It was a clear night with no moon.

I walked across to the Press room, to see if the security patrols had anything to report.

They hadn't.

All four of them were fast asleep.

Furious, I shook the nearest. His head lolled like a pendulum, but he didn't wake up. He was sitting slumped into his chair. One of them had his arms on the table and his head on his arms. One of them sat on the floor, his head on the seat of the chair and his arms hanging down. The fourth lay flat, face downwards, near the opposite wall.

The stupid fools, I thought violently. Ex-policemen letting themselves be put to sleep like infants. It shouldn't have been possible. One of the their first rules in guard work was to take their own food and drink with them and not accept sweets from strangers.

I stepped round their heavily breathing hulks and picked up one of the Press telephones to ring Chico for reinforcements. The line was dead. I tried the three other instruments. No contact with the exchange on any of them.

I would have to go back and ring up from Seabury, I thought. I went out of the Press room but in the light pouring out before I shut the door I saw a dim figure walking towards me from the direction of the gate.

'Who's that?' he called imperiously, and I recognised his voice. Captain Oxon.

'It's only me, Sid Halley.' I shouted back. 'Come and look at this.'

He came on into the light, and I stood aside for him to go into the Press room.

'Good heavens. What on earth's the matter with them?'

'Sleeping pills. And the telephones don't work. You haven't seen anyone about who ought not to be?'

'No. I haven't heard anything except your car. I came down to see who had come.'

'How many lads are there staying overnight in the hostel? Could we use some of those to patrol the place while I ring the agency to get some more men?'

'I should think they'd love it,' he said, consideringly. 'There are about five of them. They shouldn't be in bed yet. We'll go over and ask them, and you can use the telephone from my flat to ring your agency.'

'Thanks,' I said. 'That's fine.'

I looked round the room at the sleeping men. 'I think perhaps I ought to see if any of them tried to write a message. I won't be a minute.'

He waited patiently while I looked under the head and folded arms of the man at the table and under the man on the floor, and all round the one with his head on the chair seat, but none of them had even reached for a pencil. Shrugging, I looked at the remains of their supper, lying on the table. Half-eaten sandwiches on grease-proof paper, dregs of coffee in cups and thermos flasks, a couple of apple cores, some cheese sections and empty wrappings, and an unpeeled banana.

'Found anything?' asked Oxon.

I shook my head in disgust. 'Not a thing. They'll have terrible headaches when they wake up, and serve them right.'

'I can understand you being annoyed . . .' he began. But I was no longer really listening. Over the back of the chair occupied by the first man I had shaken was hanging a brown leather binoculars case: and on its lid were stamped three black initials: L.E.O. Leo. *Leo.*

'Something the matter?' asked Oxon.

'No.' I smiled at him and touched the strap of the binoculars. 'Are these yours?'

'Yes. The men asked if I could lend them some. For the dawn, they said.'

'It was very kind of you.'

'Oh. Nothing.' He shrugged, moving out into the night. 'You'd better make the phone call first. We'll tackle the boys afterwards.'

I had absolutely no intention of walking into his flat.

'Right,' I said.

We went out of the door, and I closed it behind us.

A familiar voice, loaded with satisfaction, spoke from barely a yard away. 'So you've got him, Oxon. Good.'

'He was coming . . .' began Oxon in anxious anger, knowing that 'got him' was an exaggeration.

'No,' I said, and turned and ran for the car.

When I was barely ten yards from it someone turned the lights on. The headlights of my own car. I stopped dead.

Behind me one of the men shouted and I heard their feet running. I wasn't directly in the beam, but silhouetted against it. I swerved off to the right, towards the gate. Three steps in that direction, and the headlights of a car turning in through it caught me straight in the eyes.

There were more shouts, much closer, from Oxon and Kraye. I turned, half dazzled, and saw them closing in. Behind me the incoming car rolled forward. And the engine of my Mercedes purred separately into life.

I ran for the dark. The two cars, moving, caught me again in their beams. Kraye and Oxon ran where they pointed.

I was driven across and back towards the stands like a coursed hare, the two cars behind inexorably finding me with their lights and the two men running with reaching, clutching hands. Like a nightmare game of 'He', I thought wildly, with more than a child's forfeit if I were caught.

Across the parade ring, across the flat tarmac stretch beyond it, under the rails of the unsaddling enclosure and along the weighing room wall. Sometimes only a foot from hooking fingers. Once barely a yard from a speeding bumper.

But I made it. Safe, panting, in the precious dark, on the inside of the door into the trainers' luncheon room and through there without stopping into the kitchen. And weaving on from there out into the members' lunch room, round acres of tables with upturned chairs, through the far door into the wide passage which cut like a tunnel along the length of the huge building, across it, and up a steep stone staircase emerging half way up the open steps of the stands, and sideways along them as far as I could go. The pursuit was left behind.

I sank down, sitting with one leg bent to run, in the black shadow where the low wooden wall dividing the Members from Tattersalls cut straight down the steps separating the stands into two halves. On top of the wall wire netting stretched up too high to climb: high enough to keep out the poorer customers from gate-crashing the expensive ring.

At the bottom of the steps lay a large expanse of Members' lawn stretching to another metal mesh fence, chest high, and beyond that lay the whole open expanse of racecourse. Half a mile across it to the London road to Seabury, with yet another barrier, the boundary fence, to negotiate.

It was too far. I knew I couldn't do it. Perhaps once, with two hands for vaulting, with a stomach which didn't already feel as if it were tearing into more holes inside. But not now. Although I always mended fast, it was only two weeks since I had found the short walk to Andrews' body very nearly too much; and Fred's well-aimed attentions on the previous day had not been therapeutic.

Looking at it straight: if I ran, it had to be successful. My kingdom for a horse, I thought. Any reasonable cowboy would have had Revelation hitched to the rails, ready for a flying leap into the saddle and a thundering exit. I had a hundred and fifty mile an hour little white Mercedes: and someone else was sitting in it.

To run and be caught running would achieve nothing and be utterly pointless.

Which left just one alternative.

The security patrol hadn't been drugged for nothing. Kraye wasn't at Seabury for his health. Some more damage had been planned for this night. Might already have been done. There was just a chance, if I stayed to look, that I could find out what it was. Before they found *me*. Naturally.

If I ever have any children, they won't get me playing hide and seek.

Half an hour later the grim game was still in progress. My own car was now parked on the racecourse side of the stands, on the tarmac in Tattersalls where the bookies had called the odds that afternoon. It was facing the stands with the headlights full on. Every inch of the steps was lit by them, and since the car had arrived there I had not been able to use that side of the building at all.

The other car was similarly parked inside the racecourse gates, its headlights shining on the fronts of the weighing room, bars, dining-rooms, cloakrooms and offices.

Presuming that each car still had a watching occupant, that left only Kraye and Oxon, as far as I could guess, to run me to ground: but I became gradually sure that there were three, not two, after me in the stands. Perhaps one of the cars was empty. But which? And it would be unlikely to have its ignition key in place.

Bit by bit I covered the whole enormous block. I didn't know what I was looking for, that was the trouble. It could have been anything from a plastic bomb downwards, but if past form was anything to go by, it was something which could appear accidental. Bad luck. A jinx. Open, recognisable sabotage would be ruinous to the scheme.

Without a surveyor I couldn't be certain that part of the steps would not collapse the following day under the weight of the crowd, but I could find no trace of any structural damage at all, and there hadn't been much time: only five or six hours since the day's meeting ended.

There were no large quantities of food in the kitchen: the caterers appeared to have removed what had been left over ready to bring fresh the next day. A large double-doored refrigerator was securely locked. I discounted the possibility that Kraye could have thought of large scale food poisoning.

All the fire extinguishers seemed to be in their places, and there were no smouldering cigarette ends near tins of paraffin. Nothing capable of spontaneous combustion. I supposed another fire, so soon after the stables, might have been too suspicious.

I went cautiously, carefully, every nerve-racking step of the way, peering round corners, easing through doors, fearing that at any moment one of them would pounce on me from behind.

They knew I was still there, because everywhere they went they turned on lights, and everywhere I went I turned them off. Opening a door from a lighted room on to a dark passage made one far too easy to spot; I turned off the lights before I opened any door. There had been three lights in the passage itself, but I had broken them early on with a broom from the kitchen.

Once when I was in the passage, creeping from the men's lavatories to the Tattersalls bar, Kraye himself appeared at the far end, the Members' end, and began walking my way. He came in through the faint glow from the car's headlights, and he hadn't seen me. One stride took me across the passage, one jump and a wriggle into the only cover available, the help of equipment the bookmakers had left there out of the weather, overnight.

These were only their metal stands, their folded umbrellas, the boxes and stools they stood on: a thin, spiky, precarious heap. I crouched down beside them, praying I wouldn't dislodge anything.

Kraye's footsteps scraped hollowly as he trod toward my ineffective hiding place. He stopped twice, opening doors and looking into the store-rooms which were in places built back under the steps of the stands. They were mostly empty or nearly so, and offered nothing to me. They were too small, and all dead ends: if I were found in one of them, I couldn't get out.

The door of the bar I had been making for suddenly opened, spilling bright light into the passage between me and Kraye.

Oxon's voice said anxiously, 'He can't have got away.'

'Of course not, you fool,' said Kraye furiously. 'But if you'd had the sense to bring your keys over with you we'd have had him long ago.' Their voices echoed up and down the passage.

'It was your idea to leave so much unlocked. I could go back and fetch them.'

'He'd have too much chance of giving us the slip. But we're not getting anywhere with all this dodging about. We'll start methodically from this end and move down.'

'We did that to start with,' complained Oxon. 'And we missed him. Let me go back for the keys. Then as you said before we can lock all the doors behind us and stop him doubling back.'

'No,' said Kraye decisively. 'There aren't enough of us. You stay here. We'll go back to the weighing room and start all together.'

They began to walk away. The bar door was still open, lighting up the passage, which I didn't like. If anyone came in from the other end, he would see me for sure.

I shifted my position to crawl away along the wall for better conceal-ment, and one of the bookmakers' metal tripods slid down and clattered off the side of the pile with an echoing noise like a dozen demented machine guns.

There were shouts from the two men down the passage.

'There he is.'

'Get him.'

I stood up and ran.

The nearest opening in the wall was a staircase up to a suite of rooms above the changing room and Member's dining-room. I hesitated a fraction of a second and then passed it. Up those steps were the executive's rooms and offices. I didn't know my way round up there, but Oxon did. He had a big enough advantage already in his knowledge of the building without my giving him a bonus.

I ran on, past the gent's cloaks, and finally in through the last possible door, that of a long bare dirty room smelling of beer. It was a sort of extra, subsidiary bar, and all it now contained was a bare counter backed by empty shelves. I nearly fell over a bucket full of crinkled metal bottle tops which someone had carelessly left in my way, and then wasted precious seconds to dart back to put the bucket just inside the door I'd come in by.

Kraye and Oxon were running. I snapped off the lights, and with no time to get clear through the far door out into the paddock, where anyway I would be lit by car headlights, I scrambled down behind the bar counter.

The door jerked open. There was a clatter of the bucket and a yell, and the sound of someone falling. Then the light snapped on again, showing me just how tiny my hiding place really was, and two bottle tops rolled across the floor into my sight.

'For God's sake,' yelled Kraye in anger. 'You clumsy, stupid fool. Get up. Get up.' He charged down into the room to the far door, the board floor bouncing slightly under his weight. From the clanking, cursing, and clattering of bottle tops I imagined that Oxon was extricating himself from the bucket and following. If it hadn't been so dangerous it would have been funny.

Kraye yanked the outside door open, stepped outside and yelled across to the stationary car to ask where I had gone. I felt rather than saw Oxon run down to join him. I crawled round the end of the counter, sprinted for the door I had come in by, flipped off the light again, slammed the door, and ran back up the passage. There was a roar from Kraye as he fumbled back into the darkened room, and long before they had emerged into the passage again, kicking bottle tops in all directions, I was safe in the opening of a little off-shoot lobby to the kitchen.

The kitchens were safest to me because there were so many good hiding places and so many exits, but it wasn't much good staying there as I had searched them already.

I was fast runnng out of places to look. The boiler room had given me an anxious two minutes as its only secondary exit was into a dead end store-room containing, as far as I could see, nothing but vast oil-tanks with pipes and gauges. They were hard against the walls: nowhere to hide. The boiler itself roared, keeping the central heating going all through the night.

The weighing room was even worse, because it was big and entirely without cover. It contained nothing it shouldn't have: tables, chairs, notices pinned on the walls, and the weighing machine itself. Beyond, in the changing room, there were rows of pegs with saddles on, the warm, banked-up coke stove in the corner, and a big wicker basket full of helmets, boots, weight cloths and other equipment left by the valets overnight. A dirty cup and saucer. A copy of *Playboy*. Several raincoats. Racing colours on pegs. A row of washed breeches hanging up to dry. It was the most occupied looking part of the stands, the place I felt most at home in and where I wanted to go to ground, like an ostrich in familiar sand. But on the far side of the changing room lay only the wash room, another dead end.

Opening out of the weighing room on the opposite side to the changing room was the Stewards' room, where in the past like all jockeys I'd been involved in cases of objections-to-the-winner. It was a bare room: large table, chairs round it, sporting pictures, small threadbare carpet. A few of the Stewards' personal possessions lay scattered about, but there was no concealment.

A few doors here and there were locked, in spite of Oxon having left the keys in his flat. As usual I had the bunch of lock-pickers in my pocket and with shortened breath I spent several sticky minutes letting myself into one well secured room off the Members' bar. It proved to be the liquor store: crates of spirits, champagne, wine and beer. Beer from floor to ceiling, and a porter's trolly to transport it. It was a temptation to lock myself in there, and wait for the caterers to rescue me in the morning. This was one door that Oxon would not expect to find me on the far side of.

In the liquor store I might be safe. On the other hand, if I were safe the racecourse might not be. Reluctantly I left again; but I didn't waste time locking up. With the pursuit out of sight, I risked a look upstairs. It was warm and quiet, and all the lights were on. I left them on, figuring that if the watchers in the cars saw them go out they would know too accurately where I was.

Nothing seemed to be wrong. On one side of a central lobby there was the big room where the executive held their meetings and ate their lunch. On the other side there was a sort of drawing-room furnished with light armchairs, with two cloakrooms leading off it at the back. At the front, through double glass doors, it led out into a box high up on the stands. The private box for directors and distinguished guests, with a superb view over the whole course.

I didn't go out there. Sabotaging the Royal Box wouldn't stop a race meeting to which royalty weren't going anyway. And besides, whoever was in my car would see me opening the door.

Retreating, I went back, right through the dining-board room and out into the servery on the far side. There I found a storeroom with plates, glass and cutlery, and in the storeroom also a second exit. A small service lift down to the kitchens. It worked with ropes, like the one in the office in the Cromwell Road . . . like the office lift *had* worked, before the bomb.

Kraye and Oxon were down in the kitchen. Their angry voices floated up the shaft, mingled with a softer murmuring voice which seemed to be arguing with them. Since for once I knew where they all were, I returned with some boldness to the ground again. But I was worried. There seemed to be nothing at all going wrong in the main building. If they were organising yet more damage somewhere out on the course itself, I didn't see how I could stop it.

While I was still dithering rather aimlessly along the passage the kitchen door opened, the light flooded out, and I could hear Kraye still talking. I dived yet again for the nearest door and put it between myself and them.

I was, I discovered, in the ladies' room, where I hadn't been before: and there was no second way out. Only a double row of cubicles, all with the doors open, a range of wash-basins, mirrors on the walls with a wide shelf beneath them, a few chairs, and a counter like that in the bar. Behind the counter there was a rail with coat hangers.

There were heavy steps in the passage outside. I slid instantly behind and under the counter and pressed myself into a corner. The door opened.

'He won't be in here,' said Kraye. 'The light's still on.'

'I looked in here not five minutes ago, anyway,' agreed Oxon.

The door closed behind them and their footsteps went away. I began to breathe again and my thudding heart slowed down. But for a couple of seconds only. Across the room, someone coughed.

I froze. I couldn't believe it. The room had been empty when I came in, I was certain. And neither Kraye nor Oxon had stayed . . . I stretched my ears, tense, horrified.

Another cough. A soft, single cough.

Try as I could, I could hear nothing else. No breathing. No rustle of clothing, no movement. It didn't make sense. If someone in the room knew I was behind the counter, why didn't they do something about it? If they didn't know, why were they so unnaturally quiet?

In the end, taking a conscious grip on my nerves, I slowly stood up. The room was empty.

Almost immediately there was another cough. Now that my ears were no longer obstructed by the counter, I got a clearer idea of its direction. I swung towards it. There was no one there.

I walked across the room and stared down at the wash basin. Water was trickling from one of the taps. Even while I looked at it the tap coughed. Almost laughing with relief I stretched out my hand and turned it off.

The metal was very hot. Surprised, I turned the water on again. It came spluttering out of the tap, full of air bubbles and very hot indeed. Steaming. How stupid, I thought, turning it off again, to have the water so hot at this time of night . . .

Christ, I thought. The boiler.

Chapter Sixteen

Kraye and Oxon's so-called methodical end to end search which had just failed to find me in the ladies', was proceeding from the Members' end of the stands towards Tattersalls. The boiler, like myself, was in the part they had already put behind them. I switched out the ladies' room lights, carefully eased into the passage, and via the kitchen, the Members' dining-room, the gentlemen's cloaks and another short strip of passage returned to the boiler room.

Although there was no door through, I knew that on the far side of the inside wall lay to the left the weighing room and to the right the changing room, with the dividing wall between. From both those rooms, when it was quiet, as it was that night, one could quite clearly hear the boiler's muffled roar.

The light that I had switched off was on again in the boiler room. I looked round. It all looked as normal as it had before, except . . . except that away to the right there was a very small pool of water on the floor.

Boilers. We had had a lesson on them at school. Sixteen or seventeen years ago, I thought hopelessly. But I remembered very well the way the master had begun the lesson.

'The first thing to learn about boilers,' he said, 'is that they explode.'

He was an excellent teacher: the whole class of forty boys listened from then on with avid interest. But since then the only acquaintance I'd had with boilers was down in the basement of the flats, where I sometimes drank a cup of orange tea with the caretaker. A tough ex-naval stoker, he was, and a confirmed student of racing form. Mostly we'd talked about horses, but sometimes about his job. There were strict regulations for boilers, he'd said, and regular official inspections every three months, and he was glad of it, working alongside them every day.

The first thing to learn about boilers is that they explode.

It's no good saying I wasn't frightened, because I was. If the boiler burst it wasn't simply going to make large new entrances into the weighing room and changing room, it was going to fill every cranny near it with scalding tornadoes of steam. Not a death I looked on with much favour.

I stood with my back against the door and tried desperately to remember that long ago lesson, and to work out what was going wrong.

It was a big steam boiler. An enormous cylinder nine feet high and five feet in diameter. Thick steel, with dark red anti-rust paint peeling off. Fired at the bottom not by coke, which it had been built for, but by the more modern roaring jet of burning oil. If I opened the fire door I would feel the blast of its tremendous heat.

The body of the cylinder would be filled almost to the top with water. The flame boiled the water. The resulting steam went out of the top under its own fierce pressure in a pipe which – I followed it with my eye – led into a large yellow-painted round-ended cylinder slung horizontally near the ceiling. This tank looked rather like a zeppelin. It was, if I remembered right, a calorifier. Inside it, the steam pipe ran in a spiral, like an immobile spring. The tank itself was supplied direct from the mains with the water which was to be heated, the water going to the central heating radiators, and to the hot taps in the kitchen, the cloakrooms and the jockeys' washrooms. The scorching heat from the spiral steam pipe instantly passed into the mains water flowing over it, so that the cold water entering the calorifier was made very hot in the short time before it left at the other end.

The steam, however, losing its heat in the process, gradually condensed back into water. A pipe led down the wall from the calorifier into a much smaller tank, an ordinary square one, standing on the floor. From the bottom of this yet another pipe tracked right back across the room and up near the boiler itself to a bulbous metal contraption just higher than my head. An electric pump. It finished the circuit by pumping the condensed water up from the tank on the floor and returning it to the boiler, to be boiled, steamed and condensed all over again. Round and round, continuously.

So far, so good. But if you interfered with the circuit so that the water didn't get back into the boiler, and at the same time kept the heat full on at the bottom, all the water inside the cylinder gradually turned to steam. Steam, which was strong enough to drive a liner, or pull a twelve coach train, but could in this case only get out at all through a narrow, closely spiralled pipe.

This type of boiler, built not for driving an engine but only for heating water, wasn't constructed to withstand enormous pressures. It was a toss-up, I thought, whether when all the water had gone the fast expanding air and steam found a weak spot to break out of before the flames burnt through the bottom. In either case, the boiler would blow up.

On the outside of the boiler there was a water gauge, a foot-long vertical glass tube held in brackets. The level of water in the tube indicated the level of water in the boiler. Near the top of the gauge a black line showed what the water level ought to be. Two thirds of the way down a broad red line obviously acted as a warning. The water in the gauge was higher than the red line by half an inch.

To put it mildly, I was relieved. The boiler wasn't bulging. The explosion lay in the future: which gave me more time to work out how to prevent it. As long as it would take Oxon and Kraye to decide on a repeat search, perhaps.

I could simply have turned out the flame, but Kraye and Oxon would notice that the noise had stopped, and merely light it again. Nothing would have been gained. On the other hand, I was sure that the flame was higher than it should have been at night, because the water in the ladies' tap was nearly boiling.

Gingerly I turned the adjusting wheel on the oil line. Half a turn. A full turn. The roaring seemed just as loud. Another turn: and that time there was a definite change. Half a turn more. It was perceptibly quieter. Slowly I inched the wheel around more, until quite suddenly the roar turned to a murmur. Too far. Hastily I reversed. At the point where the murmur was again a roar, I left it.

I looked consideringly at the square tank of condensed water on the floor. It was this, overflowing, which was making the pool of water; and it was overflowing because the contents were not being pumped back into the boiler. If they've broken the pump, I thought despairingly, I'm done. I didn't know the first thing about electric pumps.

Another sentence from that far away school lesson floated usefully through my mind. *For safety's sake, every boiler must have two sources of water.*

I chewed my lower lip, watching the water trickle down the side of the tank on to the floor. Even in the few minutes I had been there the pool had spread. One source of water was obviously knocked out. Where and what was the other?

There were dozens of pipes in the boiler room; not only oil pipes and water pipes, but all the electric cables were installed inside tubes as well. There were about six separate pipes with stop cocks on them. It seemed to me that all the water for the entire building came in through the boiler room.

Two pipes, apparently rising mains, led from the floor up the wall and into the calorifier. Both had stop-cocks, which I tested. Both were safely open. There was no rising main leading direct into the boiler.

By sheer luck I was half way round the huge cylinder looking for an inlet pipe when I saw the lever type door handle move down. I leapt for the only vestige of cover, the space between the boiler and the wall. It was scorching hot there: pretty well unbearable.

Kraye had to raise his voice to make himself heard over the roaring flame.

'You're sure it's still safe?'

'Yes, I told you, it won't blow up for three hours yet. At least three hours.'

'The water's running out already,' Kraye objected.

'There's a lot in there.' Oxon's voice came nearer. I could feel my heart thumping and hear the pulse in my ears. 'The level's not down to the caution mark on the gauge yet,' he said. 'It won't blow for a long time after it goes below that.'

'We've got to find Halley,' Kraye said. 'Got to.' If Oxon moved another step he would see me. 'I'll work from this end; you start again from the other. Look in every cupboard. The little rat has gone to ground somewhere.'

Oxon didn't answer audibly. I had a sudden glimpse of his sleeve as he turned, and I shrank back into my hiding place.

Because of the noise of the boiler I couldn't hear them go away through the door, but eventually I had to risk that they had. The heat where I stood was too appalling. Moving out into the ordinarily hot air in the middle of the room was like diving into a cold bath. And Oxon and Kraye had gone.

I slipped off my jacket and wiped the sweat off my face with my shirt sleeve. Back to the problem: water supply.

The pump *looked* all right. There were no loose wires, and it had an undisturbed, slightly greasy, slightly dirty appearance. With luck, I thought, they hadn't damaged the pump, they'd blocked the pipe where it left the tank. I took off my tie and shirt as well, and put them with my jacket on the grimy floor.

The lid of the tank came off easily enough, and the water, when I tested it, proved to be no more than uncomfortably hot. I drank some in my cupped palm. The running and the heat had made me very thirsty, and although I would have preferred it iced, no water could have been purer; or more tasteless, though I was not inclined to be fussy on that point.

I stretched my arm down into the water, kneeling beside the tank. As it was only about two feet deep I could touch the bottom quite easily, and almost at once my searching fingers found and gripped a loose object. I pulled it out.

It was a fine mesh filter, which should no doubt have been in place over the opening of the outlet pipe.

Convinced now that the pipe was blocked from this end, I reached down again into the water. I found the edge of the outlet, and felt carefully into it. I could reach no obstruction. Bending over further, so that my shoulder was half in the water, I put two fingers as far as they would go into the outlet. I could feel nothing solid, but there did seem to be a piece of string. It was difficult to get it between two fingers firmly enough to pull as hard as was necessary, but gradually with a series of little jerks I managed to move the plug backwards into the tank.

It came away finally so that I nearly overbalanced. There was a burp from the outlet pipe of the tank and on the other side of the room a sharp click from the pump.

I lifted my hand out of the water to see what had blocked the pipe, and stared in amazement. It was a large mouse. I had been pulling its tail.

Accidental sabotage, I thought. The same old pattern. However unlikely it was that a mouse should dive into a tank, find the filter conveniently out of place, and get stuck just inside the outlet pipe, one would have a hard job proving that it was impossible.

I carefully put the sodden little body out of sight in the small gap between the tank and wall. With relief I noticed that the water level was already going down slightly, which meant that the pump was working properly and the boiler would soon be more or less back to normal.

I splashed some more water out of the tank to make a larger pool should Kraye or Oxon glance in again, and replaced the lid. Putting on my shirt and jacket I followed with my eyes the various pipes in and out of the boiler. The lagged steam exit pipe to the calorifier. The vast chimney flue for the hot gases from the burning oil. The inlet pipe from the pump. The water gauge. The oil pipe. There had to be another water inlet somewhere, partly for safety, partly to keep the steam circuit topped up.

I found it in the end running alongside and behind the inlet pipe from the pump. It was a gravity feed from a stepped series of three small unobtrusive tanks fixed high on the wall. Filters, I reckoned, so that the mains water didn't carry its mineral salts into the boiler and fur it up. The filter tanks were fed by a pipe which branched off one of the rising mains and had its own stop cock.

Reaching up, I tried to turn it clockwise. It didn't move. The mains water was cut off. With satisfaction, I turned it on again.

Finally, with the boiler once more working exactly as it should, I took a look at the water gauge. The level had already risen to nearly half way between the red and black marks. Hoping fervently Oxon wouldn't come back for another check on it, I went over to the door and switched off the light.

There was no one in the passage. I slipped through the door, and in the last three inches before shutting it behind me stretched my hand back and put the light on again. I didn't want Kraye knowing I'd been in there.

Keeping close to the wall, I walked softly down the passage towards the Tattersalls end. If I could get clear of the stands there were other buildings out that way to give cover. The barns, cloakrooms and tote buildings in the silver ring. Beyond these lay the finishing straight, the way down to the tan patch and the bisecting road. Along that, bungalows, people, and telephones.

That was when my luck ran out.

Chapter Seventeen

I was barely two steps past the door of the Tattersalls bar when it opened and the lights blazed out on to my tiptoeing figure. In the two seconds it took Oxon to realise what he was seeing I was six running paces down towards the way out. His shouts echoed in the passage mingled with others further back, and I still thought that if Kraye too were behind me I might have a chance. But when I was within ten steps of the end another figure appeared there hurrying, called by the noise.

I skidded nearly to a stop, sliding on one of the scattered bottle tops, and crashed through the only possible door, into the same empty bar as before. I raced across the board floor, kicking bottle tops in all directions, but I never got to the far door. It opened before I reached it: and that was the end.

Doria Kraye stood there, maliciously triumphant. She was dressed theatrically in white slender trousers and a shiny short white jacket. Her dark hair fell smoothly, her face was as flawlessly beautiful as ever: and she held rock steady in one elegant long-fingered hand the little .22 automatic I had last seen in a chocolate box at the bottom of her dressing-case.

'The end of the line, buddy boy,' she said. 'You stay just where you are.'

I hesitated on the brink of trying to rush her.

'Don't risk it,' she said. 'I'm a splendid shot. I wouldn't miss. Do you want a knee-cap smashed?'

There was little I wanted less. I turned round slowly. There were three men coming forward into the long room. Kraye, Oxon and Ellis Bolt. All three of them looked as if they had long got tired of the chase and were going to take it out on the quarry.

'Will you walk,' said Doria behind me, 'or be dragged?'

I shrugged. 'Walk.'

All the same, Kraye couldn't keep his hands off me. When, following Doria's instructions, I walked past him to go back out through the passage he caught hold of my jacket at the back of my neck and kicked my legs. I kicked back, which wasn't too sensible, as I presently ended up on the floor. There was nothing like little metal bottle tops for giving you a feeling of falling on little metal bottle tops, I thought, with apologies to Michael Flanders and Donald Swan.

'Get up,' said Kraye. Doria stood beside him, pointing at me with the gun.

I did as he said.

'Right,' said Doria. 'Now, walk down the passage and go into the weighing room. And Howard, for God's sake wait till we get there, or we'll lose him again. Walk, buddy boy. Walk straight down the middle of the passage. If you try anything, I'll shoot you in the leg.'

I saw no reason not to believe her. I walked down the centre of the passage with her too close behind for escape, and with the two men bringing up the rear.

'Stop a minute,' said Kraye, outside the boiler room.

I stopped. I didn't look round.

Kraye opened the door and looked inside. The light spilled out, adding to that already coming from the other open doors along the way.

'Well?' said Oxon.

'There's more water on the floor.' He sounded pleased, and shut the door without going in for a further look. Not all of my luck had departed, it seemed.

'Move,' he said. I obeyed.

The weighing room was as big and as bare as ever. I stopped in the middle of it and turned round. The four of them stood in a row, looking at me, and I didn't like at all what I read in their faces.

'Go and sit there,' said Doria, pointing.

I went on across the floor and sat where she said, on the chair of the weighing machine. The pointer immediately swung round the clock face to show my weight. Nine stone seven. It was, I was remotely interested to see, exactly ten pounds less than when I last raced. Bullets would solve any jockey's weight problem, I thought.

The four men came closer. It was some relief to find that Fred wasn't among them, but only some. Kraye was emitting the same livid fury as he had twelve days ago at Aynsford. And then, I had merely insulted his wife.

'Hold his arms,' he said to Oxon. Oxon was one of those thin wiry men of seemingly limitless strength. He came round behind me, clamped his fingers round my elbows and pulled them back. With concentration Kraye hit me several times in the face.

'Now,' he said, 'where are they?'

'What,' I said indistinctly.

'The negatives.'

'What negatives?'

He hit me again and hurt his own hand. Shaking it out and rubbing his knuckles, he said, 'You know what negatives. The films you took of my papers.'

'Oh, those.'

'Those.' He hit me again, but less hard.

'In the office,' I mumbled.

He tried a slap to save his knuckles. 'Office,' I said.

He tried with his left hand, but it was clumsy. After that he sucked his knuckles and kept his hands to himself.

Bolt spoke for the first time, in his consciously beautiful voice. 'Fred wouldn't have missed them, especially as there was no reason for them to be concealed. He's too thorough.'

If Fred wouldn't have missed them, the bombs had been pure spite.

I licked the inside of a split lip and thought about what I would like to do to Fred.

'Where in the office?' said Kraye.

'Desk.'

'Hit him,' said Kraye. 'My hand hurts.'

Bolt had a go, but it wasn't his sort of thing.

'Try with this,' said Doria, offering Bolt the gun, but it was luckily so small he couldn't hold it effectively.

Oxon let go of my elbows, came round to the front, and looked at my face.

'If he's decided not to tell you, you won't get it out of him like that,' he said.

'I told you,' I said.

'Why not?' said Bolt.

'You're hurting yourselves more than him. And if you want my opinion, you won't get anything out of him at all.'

'Don't be silly,' said Doria scornfully. 'He's so small.'

Oxon laughed without mirth.

'If Fred said so, the negatives weren't at his office,' asserted Bolt again. 'Nor in his flat. And he didn't bring them with him. Or at least, they weren't in his luggage at the hotel.'

I looked at him sideways, out of an eye which was beginning to swell. And if I hadn't been so quick to have him flung out of my hotel room, I thought sourly, he wouldn't have driven through the racecourse gate at exactly the wrong moment. But I couldn't have foreseen it, and it was too late to help.

'They weren't in his car either,' said Doria. 'But this was.' She put her hand into her shining white pocket and brought out my baby camera. Kraye took it from her, opened the case, and saw what was inside. The veins in his neck and temples became congested with blood. In a paroxysm of fury he threw the little black toy across the room so that it hit the wall with a disintegrating crash.

'Sixteen millimetre,' he said savagely. 'Fred must have missed them.'

Bolt said obstinately, 'Fred would find a needle in a haystack. And those films wouldn't have been hidden.'

'He might have them in his pocket,' suggested Doria.

'Take your coat off,' Kraye said. 'Stand up.'

I stood up, and the base-plate of the weighing machine wobbled under my feet. Oxon pulled my coat down over the back of my shoulders, gave a tug to get the sleeves off, and passed the jacket to Kraye. His own hand he thrust into my trouser pockets. In the right one, under my tie, he found the bunch of lock pickers.

'Sit down,' he said. I did so, exploring with the back of my hand some of the damage to my face. It could have been worse, I thought resignedly, much worse. I would be lucky if that were all.

'What are those?' said Doria curiously, taking the jingling collection from Oxon.

Kraye snatched them from her and slung them after the camera. 'Skeleton keys,' he said furiously. 'What he used to unlock my cases.'

'I don't see how he could,' said Doria, 'with that . . . that . . . *claw*.'
She looked down where it lay on my lap.

A nice line in taunts, I thought, but a week too late. Thanks to Zanna
Martin, I was at last learning to live with the claw. I left it where it was.

'Doria,' said Bolt calmly, 'would you be kind enough to go over to the
flat and wait for Fred to ring? He may already have found what we
want at Aynsford.'   .

I turned my head and found him looking straight at me, assessingly.
There was a detachment in the eyes, an unmoved quality in the rounded
features; and I began to wonder whether his stolid coolness might not in
the end prove even more difficult to deal with than Kraye's rage.

'Aynsford,' I repeated thickly. I looked at my watch. If Fred had really
taken his bombs to Aynsford, he should by now be safely in the bag. One
down, four to go. Five of them altogether, not four. I hadn't thought of
Doria being an active equal colleague of the others. My mistake.

'I don't want to go,' said Doria, staying put.

Bolt shrugged. 'It doesn't matter. I see that the negatives aren't at
Aynsford, because the thought of Fred looking for them doesn't worry
Halley one little bit.'

The thought of what Fred might be doing at Aynsford or to Charles
himself didn't worry any of them either. But more than that I didn't like
the way Bolt was reasoning. In the circumstances, a clear-thinking
opponent was something I could well have done without.

'We must have them,' said Kraye intensely. 'We must. Or be certain
beyond doubt that they were destroyed.' To Oxon he said, 'Hold his
arms again.'

'No,' I said, shrinking back.

'Ah, that's better. Well?

'They were in the office.' My mouth felt stiff.

'Where?'

'In Mr. Radnor's desk, I think.'

He stared at me, eyes narrowed, anger half under control, weighing
up whether I were telling the truth or not. He certainly .couldn't go to
the office and make sure.

'Were,' said Bolt suddenly.

'What?' asked Kraye, impatiently.

'Were,' said Bolt. 'Halley said were. The negatives *were* in the office.
Now that's very interesting indeed, don't you think?'

Oxon said, 'I don't see why.'

Bolt came close to me and peered into my face I didn't meet his eyes,
and anything he could read from my bruised features he was welcome
to.

'I think he knows about the bombs,' he said finally.

'How?', said Doria.

'I should think he was told at the hotel. People in London must have
been trying to contact him. Yes, I think we can take it for granted he
knows about the bombs.'

'What difference does that make?' said Oxon.

Kraye knew. 'It means he thinks he is safe saying the negatives were in the office, because we can't prove they weren't.'

'They were,' I insisted, showing anxiety.

Bolt pursed his full moist lips. 'Just how clever is Halley?' he said.

'He was a jockey,' said Oxon flatly, as if that automatically meant an I.Q. of 70.

Bolt said, 'But they took him on at Hunt Radnor's.'

'I told you before,' said Oxon patiently, 'I asked various people about that. Radnor took him on as an adviser, but never gave him anything special to do, and if that doesn't show that he wasn't capable of much, I don't know what does. Everyone knows that his job is only a face saver. It sounds all right, but it means nothing really. Jobs are quite often given in that way to top jockeys when they retire. No one expects them to *do* much, it's just their name that's useful for a while. When their news value has gone, they get the sack.'

This all too true summing up of affairs depressed me almost as deeply as my immediate prospects.

'Howard?' said Bolt.

'I don't know,' said Kraye slowly. 'He doesn't strike me as being in the least clever. Very much the opposite. I agree he did take those photographs, but I think you are quite right in believing he doesn't know why we want them destroyed.'

That, too, was shatteringly correct. As far as I had been able to see, the photographs proved nothing conclusively except that Kraye had been buying Seabury shares under various names with Bolt's help. Kraye and Bolt could not be prosecuted for that. Moreover the whole of Seabury executive had seen the photographs at the meeting that morning, so their contents were no secret.

'Doria?' Bolt said.

'He's a slimy spying little creep, but if he was clever he wouldn't be sitting where he is.'

You couldn't argue with that, either. It had been fairly certain all along that Kraye was getting help from somebody working at Seabury, but even after knowing about Clerk of the Course Brinton's unwilling collaboration at Dunstable, I had gone on assuming that the helper at Seabury was one of the labourers. I hadn't given more than a second's flicker of thought to Oxon, because it didn't seem reasonable that it should be him. In destroying the racecourse he was working himself out of a job, and good jobs for forty year old ex-army captains weren't plentiful enough to be lost lightly. As he certainly wasn't mentally affected like Brinton, he wasn't being blackmailed into doing it against his will. I had thought him silly and self important, but not a rogue. As Doria said, had I been clever enough to suspect him, I wouldn't be sitting where I was.

Bolt went on discussing me as if I weren't there, and as if the decision they would come to would have ordinary every-day consequences.

He said, 'You may all be right, but I don't think so, because since Halley has been on the scene everything's gone wrong. It was he who persuaded Hagbourne to get the course put right, and he who found the

mirror as soon as it was up. I took him without question for what he said
he was when he came to see me – a shop assistant. You two took him for
a wretched little hanger-on of no account. All that, together with the fact
that he opened your locked cases and took good clear photographs on a
miniature camera, adds up to just one thing to me. Professionalism. Even
the way he sits there saying nothing is professional. Amateurs call you
names and try to impress you with how much they know. All he has said
is that the negatives were in the office. I consider we ought to forget every
previous impression we have of him and think of him only as coming
from Hunt Radnor.'

They thought about this for five seconds. Then Kraye said, 'We'll have
to make sure about the negatives.'

Bolt nodded. If reason hadn't told me what Kraye meant, his wife's
smile would have done. My skin crawled.

'How?' she said interestedly.

Kraye inspected his grazed knuckles. 'You won't beat it out of him,'
said Oxon. 'Not like that. You haven't a hope.'

'Why not?' said Bolt.

Instead of replying, Oxon turned to me. 'How many races did you ride
with broken bones?'

I didn't answer. I couldn't remember anyway.

'That's ridiculous,' said Doria scornfully. 'How could he?'

'A lot of them do,' said Oxon. 'And I'm sure he was no exception.'

'Nonsense,' said Kraye.

Oxon shook his head. 'Collar bones, ribs, forearms, they'll ride with
cracks in any of those if they can keep the owners and trainers from
finding out.'

Why couldn't he shut up, I thought savagely. He was making things
much worse; as if they weren't appalling enough already.

'You mean,' said Doria with sickening pleasure, 'that he can stand a
great deal?'

'No,' I said. 'No.' It sounded like the plea it was. 'You can only ride
with cracked bones if they don't hurt.'

'They must hurt,' said Bolt reasonably.

'No,' I said. 'Not always.' It was true, but they didn't believe it.

'The negatives were in the office,' I said despairingly. 'In the office.'

'He's scared,' said Doria delightedly. And that too was true.

It struck a chord with Kraye. He remembered Aynsford. 'We know
where he's most easily hurt,' he said. 'That hand.'

'No,' I said in real horror.

They all smiled.

My whole body flushed with uncontrollable fear. Racing injuries were
one thing: they were quick, one didn't expect them, and they were part
of the job.

To sit and wait and know that a part of ones self which had already
proved a burden was about to be hurt as much as ever was quite
something else. Instinctively I put my arm up across my face to hide
from them that I was afraid, but it must have been obvious.

Kraye laughed insultingly. 'So there's your brave clever Mr. Halley for you. It won't take much to get the truth.'

'What a pity,' said Doria.

They left her standing in front of me holding the little pistol in an unswerving pink nailed hand while they went out and rummaged for what they needed. I judged the distance to the door, which was all of thirty feet, and wondered whether the chance of a bullet on the way wasn't preferable to what was going to happen if I stayed where I was.

Doria watched my indecision with amusement.

'Just try it, buddy boy. Just try it.'

I had read that to shoot accurately with an automatic pistol took a great deal of skill and practice. It was possible that all Doria had wanted was the power feeling of owning a gun and she couldn't aim it. On the other hand she was holding it high and with a nearly straight arm, close to where she could see along the sights. On balance, I thought her claim to be a splendid shot had too much probability to be risked.

It was a pity Doria had such a vicious soul inside her beautiful body. She looked gay and dashing in her white Courreges clothes, smiling a smile which seemed warm and friendly and was as safe as the yawn of a python. She was the perfect mate for Kraye, I thought. Fourth, fifth, sixth time lucky, he'd found a complete complement to himself. If Kraye could do it, perhaps one day I would too . . . but I didn't know if I would even see tomorrow.

I put the back of my hand up over my eyes. My whole face hurt, swollen and stiff, and I was developing a headache. I decided that if I ever got out of this I wouldn't try any more detecting. I had made a proper mess of it.

The men came back, Oxon from the Steward's room lugging a wooden spoke-backed chair with arms, Kraye and Bolt from the changing room with the yard-long poker from the stove and the rope the wet breeches had been hung on to dry. There were still a couple of pegs clinging to it.

Oxon put the chair down a yard or two away and Doria waved the gun a fraction to indicate I should sit in it. I didn't move.

'God,' she said disappointedly, 'you really are a little worm, just like at Aynsford. Scared to a standstill.'

'He isn't a shop assistant,' said Bolt sharply. 'And don't forget it.'

I didn't look at him. But for him and his rejection of Charles' usefully feeble Halley image, I might not have been faced with quite the present situation.

Oxon punched me on the shoulder. 'Move,' he said.

I stood up wearily and stepped off the weighing machine. They stood close round me. Kraye thrust out a hand, twisted it into my shirt, and pushed me into the chair. He, Bolt and Oxon had a fine old time tying my arms and legs to the equivalent wooden ones with the washing line. Doria watched, fascinated.

I remembered her rather unusual pleasures.

'Like to change places?' I said tiredly.

It didn't make her angry. She smiled slowly, put her gun in a pocket, and leaned down and kissed me long and hard on the mouth. I loathed it. When at length she straightened up she had a smear of my blood on her lip. She wiped it off on to her hand, and thoughtfully licked it. She looked misty-eyed and languorous, as if she had had a profound sexual experience. It made me want to vomit.

'Now,' said Kraye. 'Where are they?' He didn't seem to mind his wife kissing me. He understood her, of course.

I looked at the way they had tied the rope tightly round and round my left forearm, leaving the wrist bare, palm downwards. A hand, I thought. What good, anyway, was a hand that didn't work.

I looked at their faces, one by one. Doria, rapt. Oxon, faintly surprised. Kraye confident, flexing his muscles. And Bolt, calculating and suspicious. None of them within a mile of relenting.

'Where are they?' Kraye repeated, lifting his arm.

'In the office,' I said helplessly.

He hit my wrist with the poker. I'd hoped he might at least try to be subtle, but instead he used all his strength and with that one first blow smashed the whole shooting match to smithereens. The poker broke through the skin. The bones cracked audibly like sticks.

I didn't scream only because I couldn't get enough breath to do it. Before that moment I would have said I knew everything there was to know about pain, but it seems one can always learn. Behind my shut eyes the world turned yellow and grey, like sun shining through mist, and every inch of my skin began to sweat. There had never been anything like it. It was too much, too much. And I couldn't manage any more.

'Where are they?' said Kraye again.

'Don't,' I said. 'Don't do it.' I could hardly speak.

Doria sighed deeply.

I opened my eyes a slit, my head lolling weakly back, too heavy to hold up. Kraye was smiling, pleased with his efforts. Oxon looked sick.

'Well?' said Kraye.

I swallowed, hesitating still.

He put the tip of the poker on my shattered bleeding wrist and gave a violent jerk. Among other things it felt like a fizzing electric shock, up my arm into my head and down to my toes. Sweat started sticking my shirt to my chest and my trousers to my legs.

'Don't,' I said. 'Don't.' It was a croak; a capitulation; a prayer.

'Come on, then,' said Kraye, and jolted the poker again.

I told them. I told them where to go.

Chapter Eighteen

They decided it should be Bolt who went to fetch the negatives.

'What is this place?' he said. He hadn't rcognised the address.

'The home of . . . a . . . girl friend.'

He dispassionately watched the sweat run in trickles down my face. My mouth was dry. I was very thirsty.

'Say . . . I sent you,' I said, between jagged breaths. 'I . . . asked her . . . to keep them safe . . . They . . . are with . . . several other things . . . The package . . . you want . . . has a name on it . . . a make of film . . . Jigoro . . . Kano.'

'Jigoro Kano. Right,' Bolt said briskly.

'Give me . . .' I said, 'some morphine.'

Bolt laughed. 'After all the trouble you've caused us? Even if I had any, I wouldn't. You can sit there and sweat it out.'

I moaned. Bolt smiled in satisfaction and turned away.

'I'll ring you as soon as I have the negatives,' he said to Kraye. 'Then we can decide what to do with Halley. I'll give it some thought on the way up.' From his tone he might have been discussing the disposal of a block of worthless stocks.

'Good,' said Kraye. 'We'll wait for your call over in the flat.'

They began to walk towards the door. Oxon and Doria hung back, Doria because she couldn't tear her fascinated, dilated eyes from watching me, and Oxon for more practical reasons.

'Are you just going to leave him here?' he asked in surprise.

'Yes. Why not?' said Kraye. 'Come on, Doria darling. The best is over.'

Unwilling she followed him, and Oxon also.

'Some water,' I said. 'Please.'

'No,' said Kraye.

They filed past him out of the door. Just before he shut it he gave me a last look compounded of triumph, contempt and satisfied cruelty. Then he switched off all the lights and went away.

I heard the sound of a car starting up and driving off. Bolt was on his way. Outside the windows the night was black. Darkness folded round me like a fourth dimension. As the silence deepened I listened to the low hum of the boiler roaring safely on the far side of the wall. At least, I thought, I don't have to worry about that as well. Small, small consolation.

The back of the chair came only as high as my shoulders and gave no support to my head. I felt deathly tired. I couldn't bear to move: every muscle in my body seemed to have a private line direct to my left wrist, and merely flexing my right foot had me panting. I wanted to lie down flat. I wanted a long cold drink. I wanted to faint. I went on sitting in the chair, wide awake, with a head that ached and weighed a ton, and an arm which wasn't worth the trouble.

I thought about Bolt going to Zanna Martin's front door, and finding that his own secretary had been helping me. I wondered for the hundredth time what he would do about that: whether he would harm her. Poor Miss Martin, whom life had already hurt too much.

Not only her, I thought. In the same file was the letter Mervyn Brinton had written out for me. If Bolt should see that, Mervyn Brinton would be needing a bodyguard for life.

I thought about the people who had borne the beatings and brutalities of the Nazis and the Japanese and had often died without betraying their secrets. I thought about the atrocities still going on throughout the world, and the ease with which man could break man. In Algeria, they said, unbelievable things had been done. Behind the Iron Curtain, brain washing wasn't all. In African jails, who knew?

Too young for World War Two, safe in a tolerant society, I had had no thought that I should ever come to such a test. To suffer or to talk. The dilemma which stretched back to antiquity. Thanks to Kraye, I now knew what it was like at first hand. Thanks to Kraye, I didn't understand how anyone could keep silent unto death.

I thought: I wanted to ride round Seabury racecourse again, and to go back into the weighing room, and to sit on the scales; and I've done all those things.

I thought: a fortnight ago I couldn't let go of the past. I was clinging to too many ruins, the ruins of my marriage and my racing career and my useless hand. They were gone for good now, all of them. There was nothing left to cling to. And every tangible memory of my life had blown away with a plastic bomb. I was rootless and homeless: and liberated.

What I refused to think about was what Kraye might still do during the next few hours.

Bolt had been gone for a good long time when at last Kraye came back. It had seemed half eternity to me, but even so I was in no hurry for it to end.

Kraye put the lights on. He and Doria stood just inside the doorway, staring across at me.

'You're sure there's time?' said Doria.

Kraye nodded, looking at his watch. 'If we're quick.'

'Don't you think we ought to wait until Ellis rings?' she said. 'He might have thought of something better.'

'He's late already,' said Kraye impatiently. They had clearly been arguing for some time. 'He should have rung by now. If we're going to do this, we can't wait any longer.'

'All right,' she shrugged. 'I'll go and take a look.'

'Be careful. Don't go in.'

'No,' she said. 'Don't fuss.'

They both came over to where I sat. Doria looked at me with interest, and liked what she saw.

'He looks ghastly, doesn't he? Serves him right.'

'Are you human?' I said.

A flicker of awareness crossed her lovely face, as if deep down she did indeed know that everything she had enjoyed that night was sinful and obscene, but she was too thoroughly addicted to turn back. 'Shall I help you?' she said to Kraye, not answering me.

'No. I can manage. He's not very heavy.'

She watched with a smile while her husband gripped the back of the chair I was sitting in and began to tug it across the floor towards the wall. The jerks were almost past bearing. I grew dizzy with the effort of not yelling my head off. There was no one close enough to hear me if I did. Not the few overnight stable lads fast asleep three hundred yards away. Only the Krayes, who would find it sweet.

Doria licked her lips, as if at a feast.

'Go on,' said Kraye. 'Hurry.'

'Oh, all right,' she agreed crossly, and went out through the door into the passage.

Kraye finished pulling me across the room, turned the chair round so that I was facing the wall with my knees nearly touching it and stood back, breathing deeply from the exertion.

On the other side of the wall the boiler gently roared. One could hear it more clearly at such close quarters. I knew I had no crashing explosion, no flying bricks, no killing steam to worry about. But the sands were running out fast, all the same.

Doria came back and said in a puzzled voice, 'I thought you said there would be water all down the passage.'

'That's right.'

'Well, there isn't. Not a drop. I looked into the boiler room and it's as dry as a bone.'

'It can't be. It's nearly three hours since it started overflowing. Oxon warned us it must be nearly ready to blow. You must be wrong.'

'I'm not,' she insisted. 'The whole thing looks perfectly normal to me.'

'It can't be.' Kraye's voice was sharp. He went off in a hurry to see for himself, and came back even faster.

'You're right. I'll go and get Oxon. I don't know how the confounded thing works.' He went straight on out of the main door, and I heard his footsteps running. There was no urgency except his own anger. I shivered.

Doria wasn't certain enough of the boiler's safety to spend any time near me, which was about the first really good thing which had happened the whole night. Nor did she find the back of my head worth speaking to: she liked to see her worms squirm. Perhaps she had even lost her appetite, now things had gone wrong. She waited uneasily near the door for Kraye to come back, fiddling with the catch.

Oxon came with him, and they were both running. They charged across the weighing room and out into the passage.

I hadn't much left anyway, I thought. A few tatters of pride, perhaps. Time to nail them to the mast.

The two men walked softly into the room and down to where I sat. Kraye grasped the chair and swung it violently round. The weighing room was quiet, undisturbed. There was only blackness through the window. So that was that.

I looked at Kraye's face, and wished on the whole that I hadn't. It was white and rigid with fury. His eyes were two black pits.

Oxon held the mouse in his hand. 'It must have been Halley,' he said, as if he'd said it before. 'There's no one else.'

Kraye put his right hand down on my left, and systematically began to take his revenge. After three long minutes I passed out.

I clung to the dark, trying to hug it round me like a blanket, and it obstinately got thinner and thinner, lighter and lighter, noisier and noisier, more and more painful, until I could no longer deny that I was back in the world.

My eyes unstuck themselves against my will.

The weighing room was full of people. People in dark uniforms. Policemen. Policemen coming through every door. Bright yellow lights at long last shining outside the window. Policemen carefully cutting the rope away from my leaden limbs.

Kraye and Doria and Oxon looked smaller, surrounded by the dark blue men. Doria in her brave white suit instinctively and unsuccessfully tried to flirt with her captors. Oxon, disconcerted to his roots, faced the facts of life for the first time.

Kraye's fury wasn't spent. His eyes stared in hatred across the room.

He shouted, struggling in strong restraining arms, 'Where did you send him? Where did you send Ellis Bolt?'

'Ah, Mr. Potter,' I said into a sudden oasis of silence. 'Mr. Wilbur Potter. Find out. But not from me.'

Chapter Nineteen

Of course I ended up where I had begun, flat on my back in a hospital. But not for so long, that time. I had a pleasant sunny room with a distant view of the sea, some exceedingly pretty nurses, and a whole stream of visitors. Chico came first, as soon as they would let him, on the Sunday afternoon.

He grinned down at me.

'You look bloody awful.'

'Thanks very much.'

'Two black eyes, a scabby lip, a purple and yellow complexion and a three day beard. Glamorous.'

'It sounds it.'

'Do you want to look?' he asked, picking up a hand mirror from a chest of drawers.

I took the mirror and looked. He hadn't exaggerated. I would have faded into the background in a horror movie.

Sighing, I said, 'X certificate, definitely.'

He laughed, and put the mirror back. His own face still bore the marks of battle. The eyebrow was healing, but the bruise showed dark right down his cheek.

'This is a better room than you had in London,' he remarked, strolling over to the window. 'And it smells O.K. For a hospital, that is.'

'Pack in the small talk and tell me what happened,' I said.

'They told me not to tire you.'

'Don't be an ass.'

'Well, all right. You're a bloody rollicking nit in many ways, aren't you?'

'It depends how you look at it,' I agreed peaceably.

'Oh sure, sure.'

'Chico, give,' I pleaded. 'Come on.'

'Well, there I was harmlessly snoozing away in Radnor's arm-chair with the telephone on one side and some rather good chicken sandwiches on the other, dreaming about a willing blonde and having a ball, when the front door bell rang.' He grinned. 'I got up, stretched and went to answer it. I thought it might be you, come back after all and with nowhere to sleep. I knew it wouldn't be Radnor, unless he'd forgotten his key. And who else would be knocking on his door at two o'clock in the morning? But there was this fat geezer standing on the doorstep in his city pinstripes, saying you'd sent him. 'Come in, then,' I said, yawning my head off. He came in, and I showed him into Radnor's sort of study place, where I'd been sitting.

' "Sid sent you?" I asked him, "What for?"

'He said he understood your girl-friend lived here. God, mate, don't ever try snapping your mouth shut at the top of a yawn. I nearly dislocated my jaw. Could he see her, he said. Sorry it was so late, but it was extremely important.

' "She isn't here," I said. "She's gone away for a few days. Can I help you?"

' "Who are you?" he said, looking me up and down.

'I said I was her brother. He took a sharpish look at the sandwiches and the book I'd been reading, which had fallen on the floor, and he could see I'd been asleep, so he seemed to think everything was O.K., and he said, "Sid asked me to fetch something she is keeping for him. Do you think you could help me find it?"

' "Sure," I said. "What is it?"

'He hesitated a bit but he could see that it would look too weird if he refused to tell me, so he said "It's a packet of negatives. Sid said your sister had several things of his, but the packet I want has a name on it, a make of films, Jigoro Kano."

' "Oh?" I said innocently. "Sid sent you for a packet marked Jigoro Kano?"

' "That's right," he said, looking round the room. "Would it be in here?"'

' "It certainly would," I said.'

Chico stopped, came over beside the bed, and sat on the edge of it, by my right toe.

'How come you know about Jigoro Kano?' he said seriously.

'He invented judo,' I said. 'I read it somewhere.'

Chico shook his head. 'He didn't really invent it. In 1882 he took all the best bits of hundreds of versions of ju-jitsu and put them into a formal sort of order, and called it judo.'

'I was sure you would know,' I said, grinning at him.

'You took a very sticky risk.'

'You had to know. After all, you're an expert. And there were all those years at your club. No risk. I knew you'd know. As long as I'd got the name right, that is. Anyway, what happened next?'

Chico smiled faintly.

'I tied him into a couple of knots. Arm locks and so on. He was absolutely flabbergasted. It was really rather funny. Then I put a bit of pressure on. You know. The odd thumb screwing down to a nerve. God, you should have heard him yell. I suppose he thought he'd wake the neighbours, but you know what London is. No one took a blind bit of notice. So then I asked him where you were, when you sent him. He didn't show very willing, I must say, so I gave him a bit more. Poetic justice, wasn't it, considering what they'd just been doing to you? I told him I could keep it up all night, I'd hardly begun. There was a whole bookful I hadn't touched on. It shook him, it shook him bad.'

Chico stood up restlessly and walked about the room.

'You know?' he said wryly. 'He must have had a lot to lose. He was a pretty tough cookie, I'll give him that. If I hadn't been sure that you'd sent him to me as a sort of S.O.S., I don't think I'd have had the nerve to hurt him enough to bust him.'

'I'm sorry,' I said.

He looked at me thoughtfully. 'We both learnt about it, didn't we? You on the receiving end, and me . . . I didn't like it. Doing it, I mean. I mean, the odd swipe or two and a few threats, that's usually enough, and it doesn't worry you a bit, you don't give it a second thought. But I've never hurt anyone like that before. Not seriously, on purpose, beyond bearing. He was crying, you see. . .'

Chico turned his back to me, looking out of the window.

There was a long pause. The moral problems of being on the receiving end were not so great, I thought. It was easier on the conscience altogether.

At last Chico said, 'He told me, of course. In the end.'

'Yes.'

'I didn't leave a mark on him, you know. Not a scratch . . . He said you were at Seabury racecourse. Well, I knew that was probably right, and that he wasn't trying the same sort of misdirection you had, because you'd told me yourself that you were going there. He said that you were in the weighing room and that the boiler would soon blow up. He said that he hoped it would kill you. He seemed half out of his mind with rage about you. How he should have known better than to believe you, he should have realised that you were as slippery as a snake, he'd been fooled once before . . . He said he'd taken it for granted you were telling the truth when you broke down and changed your story about the negatives being in the office, because you . . . because you were begging for mercy and morphine and God knows what.'

'Yes,' I said. 'I know all about that.'

Chico turned away from the window, his face lightening into a near grin, 'You don't say,' he said.

'He wouldn't have believed it if I'd given in sooner, or less thoroughly. Kraye would have done, but not him. It was very annoying.'

'Annoying,' said Chico. 'I like that word.' He paused, considering. 'At what moment exactly did you think of sending Bolt to me?'

'About half an hour before they caught me,' I admitted. 'Go on. What happened next?'

'There was a ball of string on Radnor's writing desk, so I tied old Fatso up with that in an uncomfortable position. Then there was the dicey problem of who to ring up to get the rescue squads on the way. I mean, the Seabury police might think I was some sort of a nut, ringing up at that hour and telling such an odd sort of story. At the best, they might send a bobby or two out to have a look, and the Krayes would easily get away. And I reckoned you'd want them rounded up red-handed, so to speak. I couldn't get hold of Radnor on account of the office phones being plasticated. So, well, I rang Lord Hagbourne.'

'You didn't!'

'Well, yes. He was O.K., he really was. He listened to what I told him about you and the boiler and the Krayes and so on, and then he said, "Right", he'd see that half the Sussex police force turned up at Seabury racecourse as soon as possible.'

'Which they did.'

'Which they did,' agreed Chico. 'To find that my old pal Sid had dealt with the boiler himself, but was otherwise in a fairly ropy state.'

'Thanks,' I said. 'For everything.'

'Be my guest.'

'Will you do me another favour?'

'Yes, what?'

'I was supposed to take someone out to lunch today. She'll be wondering why I didn't turn up. I'd have got one of the nurses to ring her, but I still don't know her telephone number.'

'Are you talking about Miss Zanna Martin? The poor duck with the disaster area of a face?'

'Yes,' I said, surprised.

'Then don't worry. She wasn't expecting you. She knows you're here.'

'How?'

'She turned up at Bolt's office yesterday morning, to deal with the mail apparently, and found a policeman waiting on the doorstep with a search warrant. When he had gone she put two and two together smartly and trailed over to the Cromwell Road to find out what was going on. Radnor had gone down to Seabury with Lord Hagbourne, but I was

there poking about in the ruins, and we sort of swapped info. She was
a bit upset about you, mate, in a quiet sort of way. Anyhow, she won't
be expecting you to take her out to lunch.'

'Did she say anything about having one of our files?'

'Yes. I told her to hang on to it for a day or two. There frankly isn't
anywhere in the office to put it.'

'All the same, you go over to where she lives as soon as you get back,
and collect it. It's the Brinton file. And take great care of it. The negatives
Kraye wanted are inside it.'

Chico stared. 'You're not serious.'

'Why not?'

'But everyone . . . Radnor, Lord Hagbourne, even Kraye and Bolt,
and the police . . . everyone has taken it for granted that what you said
first was right, that they were in the office and were blown up.'

'It's lucky they weren't,' I said. 'Get some more prints made. We've
still got to find out why they were so hellishly important. And don't tell
Miss Martin they were what Kraye wanted.'

The door opened and one of the pretty nurses came in.

'I'm afraid you'll have to go now,' she said to Chico. She came close
beside the bed and took my pulse. 'Haven't you any sense?' she exclaimed,
looking at him angrily. 'A few quiet minutes was what we said. Don't
talk too much, and don't let Mr. Halley talk at all.'

'You try giving *him* orders,' said Chico cheerfully, 'and see where it
gets you.'

'Zanna Martin's address,' I began.

'No,' said the nurse severely. 'No more talking.'

I told Chico the address.

'See what I mean?' he said to the nurse. She looked down at me and
laughed. A nice girl behind the starch.

Chico went across the room and opened the door.

'So long, then, Sid. Oh, by the way, I brought this for you to read. I
thought you might be interested.'

He pulled a glossy booklet folded lengthwise out of an inner pocket
and threw it over on to the bed. It fell just out of my reach, and the nurse
picked it up to give it me. Then suddenly she held on to it tight.

'Oh no,' she said. 'You can't give him that!'

'Why not?' said Chico. 'What do you think he is, a baby?'

He went out and shut the door. The nurse clung to the booklet, looking
very troubled. I held out my hand for it.

'Come on.'

'I think I ought to ask the doctors . . .'

'In that case,' I said, 'I can guess what it is. Knowing Chico. So be a
dear and hand it over. It's quite all right.'

She gave it to me hesitantly, waiting to see my reaction when I caught
sight of the bold words on the cover.

'Artificial Limbs. The Modern Development.'

I laughed. 'He's a realist,' I said. 'You wouldn't expect him to bring
fairy stories.'

Chapter Twenty

When Radnor came the next day he looked tired, dispirited, and ten years older. The military jauntiness had gone from his bearing, there were deep lines around his eyes and mouth, and his voice was lifeless.

For some moments he stared in obvious distress at the white-wrapped arm which stopped abruptly four inches below the elbow.

'I'm sorry about the office,' I said.

'For God's sake . . .'

'Can it be rebuilt? How bad is it?'

'Sid . . .'

'Are the outside walls still solid, or is the whole place a write-off?'

'I'm too old,' he said, giving in, 'to start again.'

'It's only bricks and mortar that are damaged. You haven't got to start again. The agency is you, not the building. Everyone can work for you just as easily somewhere else.'

He sat down in an arm-chair, rested his head back, and closed his eyes. .

'I'm tired,' he said.

'I don't suppose you've had much sleep since it happened.'

'I am seventy-one,' he said flatly.

I was utterly astounded. Until that day I would have put him in the late fifties.

'You can't be.'

'Time passes,' he said. 'Seventy-one.'

'If I hadn't suggested going after Kraye it wouldn't have happened,' I said with remorse. 'I'm so sorry . . . so sorry . . .'

He opened his eyes. 'It wasn't your fault. If it was anyone's it was my own. You wouldn't have let Hagbourne take those photographs to Seabury, if it had been left to you. I know you didn't like it, that I'd given them to him. Letting the photographs go to Seabury was the direct cause of the bombs, and it was my mistake, not yours.'

'You couldn't possibly tell,' I protested.

'I should have known better, after all these years. I think . . . perhaps I may not see so clearly . . . consequences, things like that.' His voice died to a low, miserable murmur. 'Because I gave the photographs to Hagbourne . . . you lost your hand.'

'No,' I said decisively. 'It's ridiculous to start blaming yourself for that. For heaven's sake snap out of it. No one in the agency can afford to have you in this frame of mind. What are Dolly and Jack Copeland and Sammy and Chico and all the others to do if you don't pick up the pieces?'

He didn't answer.

'My hand was useless, anyway,' I said. 'And if I'd been willing to give in to Kraye I needn't have lost it. It had nothing whatever to do with you.'

He stood up.

'You told Kraye a lot of lies,' he said.

'That's right.'

'But you wouldn't lie to me.'

'Naturally not.'

'I don't believe you.'

'Concentrate on it. It'll come in time.'

'You don't show much respect for your elders.'

'Not when they behave like bloody fools,' I agreed dryly.

He blew down his nostrils, smouldering inwardly. But all he said was, 'And you? Will you still work for me?'

'It depends on you. I might kill us all next time.'

'I'll take the risk.'

'All right then. Yes. But we haven't finished this time, yet. Did Chico get the negatives?'

'Yes. He had two sets of prints done this morning. One for him, and he gave me one to bring to you. He said you'd want them, but I didn't think . . .'

'But you did bring them?' I urged.

'Yes, they're outside in my car. Are you sure . . .?'

'For heaven's sake,' I said in exasperation. 'I can hardly wait.'

By the following day I had acquired several more pillows, a bedside telephone, and a reputation for being a difficult patient.

The agency re-started work that morning, squeezing into Radnor's own small house. Dolly rang to say it was absolute hell, there was only one telephone instead of thirty, the blitz spirit was fortunately in operation, not to worry about a thing, there was a new word going round the office, it was Halley-lujah, and goodbye, someone else's turn now.

Chico rang a little later from a call box.

'Sammy found that driver, Smith,' he said. 'He went to see him in Birmingham yesterday. Now that Kraye's in jug Smith is willing to turn Queen's evidence. He agreed that he did take two hundred and fifty quid, just for getting out of his cab, unclipping the chains when the tanker had gone over, and sitting on the side of the road moaning and putting on an act. Nice easy money.'

'Good,' I said.

'But that's not all. The peach of it is he still has the money, most of it, in a tin box, saving it for a deposit on a house. That's what tempted him, apparently, needing money for a house. Anyway, Kraye paid him the second instalment in tenners, from one of the blocks you photographed in his case. Smith still has one of the actual tenners in the pictures. He agreed to part with that for evidence, but I can't see anyone making him give the rest back, can you?'

'Not exactly!'

'So we've got Kraye nicely tied up on malicious damage.'

'That's terrific,' I said. 'What are they holding him on now?'

'G.B.H. And the others for aiding and abetting.'

'Consecutive sentences, I trust.'

'You'll be lucky.'

I sighed. 'All the same, he still owns twenty-three per cent of Seabury's shares.'

'So he does,' agreed Chico gloomily.

'How bad exactly is the office?' I asked.

'They're surveying it still. The outside walls look all right, it's just a case of making sure. The inside was pretty well gutted.'

'We could have a better lay-out,' I said. 'And a lift.'

'So we could,' he said happily. 'And I'll tell you something else which might interest you.'

'What?'

'The house next door is up for sale.'

I was asleep when Charles came in the afternoon, and he watched me wake up, which was a pity. The first few seconds of consciousness were always the worst: I had the usual hellish time, and when I opened my eyes, there he was.

'Good God, Sid,' he said in alarm. 'Don't they give you anything?'

I nodded, getting a firmer grip on things.

'But with modern drugs, surely . . . I'm going to complain.'

'No.'

'But Sid . . .'

'They do what they can, I promise you. Don't look so upset. It'll get better in a few days. Just now it's a bore, that's all . . . Tell me about Fred.'

Fred had already been at the house when the police guard arrived at Aynsford. Four policeman had gone there, and it took all four to hold him, with Charles going back and helping as well.

'Did he do much damage?' I asked. 'Before the police got there?'

'He was very methodical, and very quick. He had been right through my desk, and all the wardroom. Every envelope, folder and notebook had been ripped apart, and the debris was all in a heap, ready to be destroyed. He'd started on the dining-room when the police arrived. He was very violent. And they found a box of plastic explosive lying on the hall table, and some more out in the van.' He paused. 'What made you think he would come?'

'They knew I took the photographs at Aynsford, but how would they know I got them developed in London? I was afraid they might think I'd had them done locally, and that they'd think you'd know where the negatives were, as it was you who inveigled Kraye down there in the first place.'

He smiled mischievously. 'Will you come to Aynsford for a few days when you get out of here?'

'I've heard that somewhere before,' I said. 'No thanks.'

'No more Krayes,' he promised. 'Just a rest.'

'I'd like to, but there won't be time. The agency is in a dicky state. And I've just been doing to my boss what you did to me at Aynsford.'

'What's that?'

'Kicking him out of depression into action.'

His smile twisted in amusement.

'Do you know how old he is?' I said.

'About seventy, why?'

I was surprised. 'I'd no idea he was that age, until he told me yesterday.'

Charles squinted at the tip of his cigar. He said, 'You always thought I asked him to give you a job, didn't you? And guaranteed your wages.'

I made a face at him, embarrassed.

'You may care to know it wasn't like that at all. I didn't know him personally, only by name. He sought me out one day in the club and asked me if I thought you'd be any good at working with him. I said yes, I thought you would. Given time.'

'I don't believe it.'

He smiled. 'I told him you played a fair game of chess. Also that you had become a jockey simply through circumstances, because you were small and your mother died, and that you could probably succeed at something else just as easily. He said that from what he'd seen of you racing you were the sort of chap he needed. He told me then how old he was. That's all. Nothing else. Just how old he was. But we both understood what he was saying.'

'I nearly threw it away,' I said. 'If it hadn't been for you . . .'

'Oh, yes,' he said wryly. 'You have a lot to thank me for. A lot.'

Before he went I asked him to look at the photographs, but he studied them one by one and handed them back shaking his head.

Chief-Inspector Cornish rang up to tell me Fred was not only in the bag but sewn up.

'The bullets match all right. He drew the same gun on the men who arrested him, but one of them fortunately threw a vase at him and knocked it out of his hand before he could shoot.'

'He was a fool to keep that gun after he had shot Andrews.'

'Stupid. Crooks often are, or we'd never catch them. And he didn't mention his little murder to Kraye and the others, so they can't be pinched as accessories to that. Pity. But it's quite clear he kept it quiet. The Sussex force said that Kraye went berserk when he found out. Apparently he mostly regretted not having known about your stomach while he had you in his clutches.'

'Thank God he didn't!' I exclaimed with feeling.

Cornish's chuckle came down the wire. 'Fred was supposed to look for Brinton's letter at your agency himself, but he wanted to go to a football match up North or something, and sent Andrews instead. He said he didn't think there'd be a trap, or anything subtle like that. Just an errand, about on Andrews' level. He said he only lent him the gun for a lark, he didn't mean Andrews to use it, didn't think he'd be so silly. But then Andrews went back to him scared stiff and said he'd shot you, so Fred says he suggested a country ramble in Epping Forest and the gun went off by accident! I ask you, try that on a jury! Fred says he didn't tell Kraye because he was afraid of him.'

'What! Fred afraid?'

'Kraye seems to have made an adverse impression on him.'

'Yes, he's apt to do that,' I said.

I read Chico's booklet from cover to cover. One had to thank the thalidomide children, it appeared, for the speed-up of modern techniques. As soon as my arm had properly healed I could have a versatile gas-powered tool-hand with a swivelling wrist, activated by small pistons and controlled by valves, and operated by my shoulder muscles. The main snag to that, as far as I could gather, was that one always had to carry the small gas cylinders about, strapped on, like a permanent skin diver.

Much more promising, almost fantastic, was the latest invention of British and Russian scientists, the myo-electric arm. This worked entirely by harnessing the tiny electric currents generated in one's own remaining muscles, and the booklet cheerfully said it was easiest to fit on someone whose amputation was recent. The less one had lost of a limb, the better were one's chances of success. That put me straight in the guinea seats.

Finally, said the booklet with a justifiable flourish of trumpets, at St. Thomas' Hospital they had invented a miraculous new myo-electric hand which could do practically everything a real one could except grow nails.

I missed my real hand, there was no denying it. Even in its deformed state it had had its uses, and I suppose that any loss of so integral a part of oneself must prove a radical disturbance. My unconscious mind did its best to reject the facts: I dreamed each night that I was whole, riding races, tying knots, clapping . . . anything which required two hands. I awoke to the frustrating stump.

The doctors agreed to enquire from St. Thomas's how soon I could go there.

On Wednesday morning I rang up my accountant and asked when he had a free day. Owing to an unexpected cancellation of plans, he said, he would be free on Friday. I explained where I was and roughly what had happened. He said that he would come to see me, he didn't mind the journey, a breath of sea air would do him good.

As I put the telephone down my door opened and Lord Hagbourne and Mr. Fotherton came tentatively through it. I was sitting on the edge of the bed in a dark blue dressing-gown, my feet in slippers, my arm in a cradle inside a sling, chin freshly shaved, hair brushed, and the marks of Kraye's fists fading from my face. My visitors were clearly relieved at these encouraging signs of revival, and relaxed comfortably into the arm-chairs.

'You're getting on well, then, Sid?' said Lord Hagbourne.

'Yes, thank you.'

'Good, good.'

'How did the meeting go?' I asked. 'On Saturday?'

Both of them seemed faintly surprised at the question.

'Well, you did hold it, didn't you?' I said anxiously.

'Why yes,' said Fotherton. 'We did. There was a moderately good gate, thanks to the fine weather.' He was a thin, dry man with a long face moulded into drooping lines of melancholy, and on that morning he kept smoothing three fingers down his cheek as if he were nervous.

Lord Hagbourne said, 'It wasn't only your security men who were drugged. The stable lads all woke up feeling muzzy, and the old man who was supposed to look after the boiler was asleep on the floor in the canteen. Oxon had given them all a glass of beer. Naturally, your men trusted him.'

I sighed. One couldn't blame them too much. I might have drunk with him myself.

'We had the inspector in yesterday to go over the boiler thoroughly,' said Lord Hagbourne. 'It was nearly due for its regular check anyway. They said it was too old to stand much interference with its normal working, and that it was just as well it hadn't been put to the test. Also that they thought that it wouldn't have taken as long as three hours to blow up. Oxon was only guessing.'

'Charming,' I said.

'I sounded out Seabury Council,' said Lord Hagbourne. 'They're putting the racecourse down on their agenda for next month. Apparently a friend of yours, the manager of the Seafront Hotel, has started a petition in the town urging the council to take an interest in the racecourse on the grounds that it gives a seaside town prestige and free advertising and is good for trade.'

'That's wonderful,' I said, very pleased.

Fotherton cleared his throat, looked hesitantly at Lord Hagbourne, and then at me.

'It has been discussed . . .' he began. 'It has been decided to ask you if you . . . er . . . would be interested in taking on . . . in becoming Clerk of the Course at Seabury.'

'Me?' I exclaimed, my mouth falling open in astonishment.

'It's getting too much for me, being Clerk of two courses,' he said, admitting it a year too late.

'You saved the place on the brink of the grave,' said Lord Hagbourne with rare decisiveness. 'We all know it's an unusual step to offer a Clerkship to a professional jockey so soon after he's retired, but Seabury executive are unanimous. They want you to finish the job.'

They were doing me an exceptional honour. I thanked them, and hesitated, and asked if I could think it over.

'Of course, think it over,' said Lord Hagbourne. 'But say yes.'

I asked them then to have a look at the box of photographs, which they did. They both scrutinised each print carefully, one by one, but they could suggest nothing at the end.

Zanna Martin came to see me the next afternoon, carrying some enormous, sweet-smelling bronze chrysanthemums. A transformed Zanna Martin, in a smart dark green tweed suit and shoes chosen for looks more than sturdy walking. Her hair had been re-styled so that it was shorter and curved in a bouncy curl on to her cheek. She had even tried a little lipstick and powder, and had tidied her eyebrows into a shapely line. The scars were just as visible, the facial muscles as wasted as ever, but Miss Martin had come to terms with them at last.

'How super you look,' I said truthfully.

She was embarrassed, but very pleased. 'I've got a new job. I had an interview yesterday, and they didn't even seem to notice my face. Or at least they didn't say anything. In a bigger office, this time. A good bit more than I've earned before, too.'

'How splendid,' I congratulated her sincerely.

'I feel new,' she said.

'I too.'

'I'm glad we met.' She smiled, saying it lightly. 'Did you get that file back all right? Your young Mr. Barnes came to fetch it.'

'Yes, thank you.'

'Was it important?'

'Why?'

'He seemed very odd when I gave it to him. I thought he was going to tell me something about it. He kept starting to, and then he didn't.'

I would have words with Chico, I thought.

'It was only an ordinary file,' I said. 'Nothing to tell.'

On the off-chance, I got her to look at the photographs. Apart from commenting on the many examples of her own typing, and expressing surprise that anybody should have bothered to photograph such ordinary papers, she had nothing to say.

She rose to go, pulling on her gloves. She still automatically leaned forward slightly, so that the curl swung down over her cheek.

'Good-bye, Mr. Halley. And thank you for changing everything for me. I'll never forget how much I owe you.'

'We didn't have that lunch,' I said.

'No.' She smiled, not needing me any more. 'Never mind. Some other time.' She shook hands. 'Good-bye.'

She went serenely out of the door.

'Good-bye, Miss Martin,' I said to the empty room. 'Good-bye, good-bye, good-bye.' I sighed sardonically at myself, and went to sleep.

Noel Wayne came loaded on Friday morning with a bulging brief-case of papers. He had been my accountant ever since I began earning big money at eighteen, and he probably knew more about me than anyone else on earth. Nearly sixty, bald except for a grey fringe over the ears, he was a small, round man with alert black eyes and a slow-moving mills-of-God mind. It was his advice more than my knowledge which had turned my earnings into a modest fortune via the stock markets, and I seldom did anything of any importance financially without consulting him first.

'What's up?' he said, coming straight to the point as soon as he had taken off his overcoat and scarf.

I walked over to the window and looked out. The weather had broken. It was drizzling, and a fine mist lay over the distant sea.

'I've been offered a job,' I said, 'Clerk of the Course at Seabury.'

'No!' he said, as astonished as I had been. 'Are you going to accept?'

'It's tempting,' I said. 'And safe.'

He chuckled behind me. 'Good. So you'll take it.'

'A week ago I definitely decided not to do any more detecting.'

'Ah.'

'So I want to know what you think about me buying a partnership in Radnor's agency.'

He choked.

'I didn't think you even liked the place.'

'That was a month ago. I've changed since then. And I won't be changing back. The agency is what I want.'

'But has Radnor *offered* a partnership?'

'No. I think he might have done eventually, but not since someone let a bomb off in the office. He's hardly likely to ask me to buy a half share of the ruins. And he blames himself for this.' I pointed to the sling.

'With reason?'

'No,' I said rather gloomily. 'I took a risk which didn't come off.'

'Which was?'

'Well, if you need it spelled out, that Kraye would only hit hard enough to hurt, not to damage beyond repair.'

'I see.' He said it calmly, but he looked horrified. 'And do you intend to take similar risks in future?'

'Only if necessary.'

'You always said the agency didn't do much crime work,' he protested.

'It will from now on, if I have anything to do with it. Crooks make too much misery in the world.' I thought of the poor Dunstable Brinton. 'And listen, the house next door is for sale. We could knock the two into one. Radnor's is bursting at the seams. The agency has expanded a lot even in the two years I've been there. There seems more and more demand for his sort of service. Then the head of Bona Fides, that's one of the departments, is a natural to expand as an employment consultant on the managerial level. He has a gift for it. And insurance – Radnor's always neglected that. We don't have an insurance investigation department. I'd like to start one. Suspect insurance claims; you know. There's a lot of work in that.'

'You're sure Radnor will agree, if you suggest a partnership?'

'He may kick me out. I'd risk it though. What do you think?'

'I think you've gone back to how you used to be,' he said thoughtfully. 'Which is good. Nothing but good. But . . . well, tell me what you really think about that.' He nodded at my chopped off arm. 'None of your flippant lies, either. The truth.'

I looked at him and didn't answer.

'It's only a week since it happened,' he said, 'and as you still look the colour of a grubby sheet I suppose it's hardly fair to ask. But I want to know.'

I swallowed. There were some truths which really couldn't be told. I said instead. 'It's gone. Gone, like a lot of other things I used to have. I'll live without it.'

'Live, or exist?'

'Oh live, definitely. Live.' I reached for the booklet Chico had brought, and flicked it at him. 'Look.'

He glanced at the cover and I saw the faint shock in his face. He didn't have Chico's astringent brutality. He looked up and saw me smiling.

'All right,' he said soberly. 'Yes. Invest your money in yourself.'

'In the agency,' I said.

'That's what I mean,' he said. 'In the agency. In yourself.'

He said he'd need to see the agency's books before a definite figure could be reached, but we spent an hour discussing the maximum he thought I should prudently offer Radnor, what return I could hope for in salary and dividends, and what I should best sell to raise the sum once it was agreed.

When we had finished I trotted out once more the infuriating photographs.

'Look them over, will you?' I said. 'I've shown them to everyone else without result. These photographs were the direct cause of the bombs in my flat and the office, and of me losing my hand, and I can't see why. It's driving me ruddy well mad.'

'The police . . .' he suggested.

'The police are only interested in the one photograph of a ten pound note. They looked at the others, said they could see nothing significant, and gave them back to Chico. But Kraye couldn't have been worried about that bank note, it was ten thousand to one we'd come across it again. No, it's something else. Something not obviously criminal, something Kraye was prepared to go to any lengths to obliterate immediately. Look at the time factor . . . Oxon only pinched the photographs just before lunch, down at Seabury. Kraye lived in London. Say Oxon rang him and told him to come and look: Oxon couldn't leave Seabury, it was a race day. Kraye had to go to Seabury himself. Well, he went down and looked at the photographs and saw . . . what? What? My flat was being searched by five o'clock.'

Noel nodded in agreement. 'Kraye was desperate. Therefore there was something to be desperate about.' He took the photographs and studied them one by one.

Half an hour later he looked up and stared blankly out of the window at the wet grey skies. For several minutes he stayed completely still, as if in a state of suspended animation: it was his way of concentrated thinking. Finally he stirred and sighed. He moved his short neck as if it were stiff, and lifted the top photograph off the pile.

'This must be the one,' he said.

I nearly snatched it out of his hand.

'But it's only the summary of the share transfers,' I said in disappointment. It was the sheet headed S.R., Seabury Racecourse, which listed in summary form all Kraye's purchases of Seabury shares. The only noticeable factor in what had seemed to me merely a useful at-a-glance view of his total holding, was that it had been typed on a different typewriter, and not by Zanna Martin. This hardly seemed enough reason for Kraye's hysteria.

'Look at it carefully,' said Noel. 'The three left hand columns you can disregard, because I agree they are simply a tabulation of the share transfers, and I can't see any discrepancies.'

'There aren't,' I said. 'I checked that.'

'How about the last column, the small one on the right?'

'The banks?'

'The banks.'

'What about them?' I said.

'How many different ones are there?'

I looked down the long list, counting. 'Five. Barclays, Piccadilly. Westminster, Birmingham. British Linen Bank, Glasgow. Lloyds, Doncaster. National Provincial, Liverpool.'

'Five bank accounts, in five different towns. Perfectly respectable. A very sensible arrangement in many ways. He can move round the country and always have easy access to his money. I myself have accounts in three different banks: it avoids muddling my clients' affairs with my own.'

'I know all that. I didn't see any significance in his having several accounts. I still don't.'

'Hm,' said Noel. 'I think it's very likely that he has been evading income tax.'

'Is that all?' I said disgustedly.

Noel looked at me in amusement, pursing his lips. 'You don't understand in the least, I see.'

'Well, for heaven's sake, you wouldn't expect a man like Kraye to pay up every penny he was liable for like a good little citizen.'

'You wouldn't,' agreed Noel, grinning broadly.

'I'll agree he might be worried. After all, they sent Al Capone to jug in the end for tax evasion. But over here, what's the maximum sentence?'

'He'd only get a year, at the most,' he said, 'but . . .'

'And he would have been sure to get off with a fine. Which he won't do now, after attacking me. Even so, for that he'll only get three or four years, I should think, and less for the malicious damage. He'll be out and operating again far too soon. Bolt, I suppose, will be struck off, or whatever it is with stockbrokers.'

'Stop talking,' he said, 'and listen. While it's quite normal to have more than one bank account, an Inspector of Taxes, having agreed your tax liability, may ask you to sign a document stating that you have disclosed to him *all* your bank accounts. If you fail to mention one or two, it constitutes a fraud, and if you are discovered you can then be prosecuted. So, suppose Kraye has signed such a document, omitting one or two or even three of the five accounts? And then he finds a photograph in existence of his most private papers, listing all five accounts as undeniably his?'

'But no one would have noticed,' I protested.

'Quite. Probably not. But to him it must have seemed glaringly dangerous. Guilty people constantly fear their guilt will be visible to others. They're vibratingly sensitive to anything which can give them away. I see quite a lot of it in my job.'

'Even so . . . bombs are pretty drastic.'

'It would entirely depend on the sum involved,' he said primly.

'Huh?'

'The maximum fine for income tax evasion is twice the tax you didn't pay. If for example you amassed ten thousand pounds but declared only two, you could be fined a sum equal to twice the tax on eight thousand pounds. With surtax and so on, you might be left with almost nothing. A nasty set-back.'

'To put it mildly,' I said in awe.

'I wonder,' Noel said thoughtfully, putting the tips of his fingers together, 'just how much undeclared loot Kraye has got stacked away in his five bank accounts?'

'It must be a lot,' I said, 'for bombs.'

'Quite so.'

There was a long silence. Finally I said, 'One isn't required either legally or morally to report people to the Inland Revenue.'

He shook his head.

'But we could make a note of those five banks, just in case?'

'If you like,' he agreed.

'Then I think I might let Kraye have the negatives and the new sets of prints,' I said. 'Without telling him I know why he wants them.'

Noel looked at me enquiringly, but didn't speak.

I grinned faintly. 'On condition that he makes a free, complete and outright gift to Seabury Racecourse Company of his twenty-three per cent holding.'

FLYING FINISH

Flying Finish

With my thanks to

THE BRITISH BLOODSTOCK AGENCY

BRUCE DAGLISH
Of Lep Transport

PETER PALMER
Airline Captain

JOHN MERCER
Of C.S.E. Aviation, Oxford Airport

I assure them that everyone in this book is imaginary

Chapter One

'You're a spoilt bad-tempered bastard,' my sister said, and jolted me into a course I nearly died of.

I carried her furious unattractive face down to the station and into the steamed-up compartment of Monday gloom and half done crosswords and all across London to my unloved office.

Bastard I was not: not with parents joined by bishop with half Debrett and Burke in the pews. And if spoilt, it was their doing, their legacy to an heir born accidentally at the last possible minute when earlier intended pregnancies had produced five daughters. My frail eighty-six year old father in his second childhood saw me chiefly as the means whereby a much hated cousin was to be done out of an earldom he had coveted: my father delighted in my existence and I remained to him a symbol.

My mother had been forty-seven at my birth and was now seventy-three. With a mind which had to all intents stopped developing round about Armistice Day 1918, she had been for as long as I could remember completely batty. Eccentric, her aquaintances more kindly said. Anyway, one of the first things I ever learnt was that age had nothing to do with wisdom.

Too old to want a young child around them, they had brought me up and educated me at arms length – nurse-maids, prep school and Eton – and in my hearing had regretted the length of the school holidays. Our relationship was one of politeness and duty, but not of affection. They didn't even seem to expect me to love them, and I didn't. I didn't love anyone. I hadn't had any practice.

I was first at the office as usual. I collected the key from the caretaker's cubbyhole, walked unhurriedly down the long echoing hall, up the gritty stone staircase, down a narrow dark corridor, and at the far end of it unlocked the heavily brown varnished front door of the Anglia Bloodstock Agency. Inside, typical of the old London warren-type blocks of offices, comfort took over from barracks. The several rooms opening right and left from the passage were close carpeted, white painted, each with the occupant's name in neat black on the door. The desks ran to extravagances like tooled leather tops, and there were sporting prints on the wall. I had not yet, however, risen to this success bracket.

The room where I had worked (on and off) for nearly six years lay at the far end, past the reference room and the pantry. 'Transport' it said, on the half-open door. I pushed it wide. Nothing had changed from Friday. The three desks looked the same as usual: Christopher's, with thick uneven piles of papers held down by cricket balls; Maggie's with the typewriter cover askew, carbons screwed up beside it, and a vase of dead chrysanthemums dropping petals into a scummy teacup; and mine, bare.

I hung up my coat, sat down, opened my desk drawers one by one and uselessly straightened the already tidy contents. I checked that it was precisely eight minutes to nine by my accurate watch, which made the office clock two minutes slow. After this activity I stared straight ahead unseeingly at the calendar on the pale green wall.

A spoilt bad-tempered bastard, my sister said.

I didn't like it. I was not bad-tempered, I assured myself defensively. I was not. But my thoughts carried no conviction. I decided to break with tradition and refrain from reminding Maggie that I found her slovenly habits irritating.

Christopher and Maggie arrived together, laughing, at ten past nine.

'Hullo,' said Christopher cheerfully, hanging up his coat. 'I see you lost on Saturday.'

'Yes,' I agreed.

'Better luck next time,' said Maggie automatically, blowing the sodden petals out of the cup on to the floor. I bit my tongue to keep it still. Maggie picked up the vase and made for the pantry, scattering petals as she went. Presently she came back with the vase, fumbled it, and left a dripping trail of Friday's tea across my desk. In silence I took some white blotting paper from the drawer, mopped up the spots, and threw the blotting paper in the waste basket. Christopher watched in sardonic amusement, pale eyes crinkling behind thick spectacles.

'A short head, I believe?' he said, lifting one of the cricket balls and going through the motions of bowling it through the window.

'A short head,' I agreed. All the same if it had been ten lengths, I thought sourly. You got no present for losing, whatever the margin.

'My uncle had a fiver on you.'

'I'm sorry,' I said formally.

Christopher pivoted on one toe and let go: the cricket ball crashed into the wall, leaving a mark. He saw me frowning at it and laughed. He had come straight into the office from Cambridge two months before, robbed of a cricket blue through deteriorating eyesight and having failed his finals into the bargain. He remained always in better spirits than I, who had suffered no similar reverses. we tolerated each other. I found it difficult, as always, to make friends, and he had given up trying.

Maggie came back from the pantry, sat down at her desk, took her nail varnish out of the stationery drawer and begun brushing on the silvery pink. She was a large assured girl from Surbiton with a naturally unkind tongue and a suspect talent for registering remorse immediately after the barbs were in.

The cricket ball slipped out of Christopher's hand and rolled across Maggie's desk. Lunging after it, he brushed one of his heaps of letters into a fluttering muddle on the floor, and the ball knocked over Maggie's bottle of varnish, which scattered pretty pink viscous blobs all over the 'We have received yours of the fourteenth ult.'

'God-damn,' said Christopher with feeling.

Old Cooper who dealt with insurance came into the room at his doddery pace and looked at the mess with cross disgust and pinched nostrils. He held out to me the sheaf of papers he had brought.

'Your pigeon, Henry. Fix it up for the earliest possible.'

'Right.'

As he turned to go he said to Christopher and Maggie in a complaining voice certain to annoy them, 'Why can't you two be as efficient as Henry? He's never late, he's never untidy, his work is always correct and always done on time. Why don't you try to be more like him?'

I winced inwardly and waited for Maggie's inevitable retaliation. She would be in good form: it was Monday morning.

'I wouldn't want to be like Henry in a thousand years,' she said sharply. 'He's a prim, dim, sexless *nothing*. He's not alive.'

Not my day, definitely.

'He rides those races though,' said Christopher in mild defence.

'And if he fell off and broke both his legs, all he'd care about would be seeing they got the bandages straight.'

'The bones,' I said.

'What?'

'The bones straight.'

Christopher blinked and laughed. 'Well, well, what do you know? The still waters of Henry might just possibly be running deep.'

'Deep, nothing,' said Maggie. 'A stagnant pond, more like.'

'Slimy and smelly?' I suggested.

'No . . . oh dear . . . I mean, I'm sorry . . .'

'Never mind,' I said. 'Never mind.' I looked at the paper in my hand and picked up the telephone.

'Henry . . .' said Maggie desperately. 'I didn't mean it.'

Old Cooper tut-tutted and doddered away along the passage, and Christopher began sorting his varnished letters. I got through to Yardman Transport and asked for Simon Searle. 'Four yearlings from the Newmarket sales to go to Buenos Aires as soon as possible,' I said.

'There might be a delay.'

'Why?'

'We've lost Peters.'

'Careless,' I remarked.

'Oh ha-ha.'

'Has he left?'

Simon hesitated perceptibly. 'It looks like it.'

'How do you mean?'

'He didn't come back from one of the trips. Last Monday. Just never turned up for the flight back, and hasn't been seen or heard of since.'

'Hospitals?' I said.

'We checked those, of course. And the morgue, and the jail. Nothing. He just vanished. And as he hasn't done anything wrong the police aren't interested in finding him. No police would be, it isn't criminal to leave your job without notice. They say he fell for a girl, very likely, and decided not to go home.'

'Is he married?'

'No.' He sighed. 'Well, I'll get on with your yearlings, but I can't give you even an approximate date.'

'Simon,' I said slowly. 'Didn't something like this happen before?'

'Er . . . do you mean Ballard?'

'One of your liaison men,' I said.

'Yes. Well . . . I suppose so.'

'In Italy?' I suggested gently.

There was a short silence the other end. 'I hadn't thought of it,' he said. 'Funny coincidence. Well . . . I'll let you know about the yearlings.'

'I'll have to get on to Clarksons if you can't manage it.'

He sighed. 'I'll do my best. I'll ring you back tomorrow.'

I put down the receiver and started on a large batch of customs declarations, and the long morning disintegrated towards the lunch hour. Maggie and I said nothing at all to each other and Christopher cursed steadily over his letters. At one sharp I beat even Maggie in the rush to the door.

Outside, the December sun was shining. On impulse I jumped on to a passing bus, got off at Marble Arch, and walked slowly through the park to the Serpentine. I was still there, sitting on a bench, watching the sun ripple on the water, when the hands on my watch read two o'clock. I was still there at half past. At a quarter to three I threw some stones with force into the lake, and a park keeper told me not to.

A spoilt bad-tempered bastard. It wouldn't have been so bad if she had been used to saying things like that, but she was a gentle see-no-evil person who had been made to wash her mouth out with soap for swearing as a child and had never taken the risk again. She was my youngest sister, fifteen years my elder, unmarried, plain, and quietly intelligent. She had reversed roles with our parents: she ran the house and managed them as her children. She also to a great extent managed me, and always had.

A repressed, quiet, 'good' little boy I had been: and a quiet, withdrawn, secretive man I had become. I was almost pathologically tidy and methodical, early for every appointment, controlled alike in behaviour, hand-writing and sex. A prim dim nothing, as Maggie had said. The fact that for some months now I had not felt in the least like that inside was confusing, and getting more so.

I looked up into the blue gold-washed sky. Only there, I thought with a fleeting inward smile, only there am I my own man. And perhaps in steeplechases. Perhaps there too, sometimes.

She had been waiting for me as usual at breakfast, her face fresh from her early walk with the dogs. I had seen little of her over the week end: I'd been racing on Saturday, and on Sunday I'd left home before breakfast and gone back late.

'Where did you go yesterday?' she asked.

I poured some coffee and didn't answer. She was used to that, however.

'Mother wanted to speak to you.'

'What about?'

'She has asked the Filyhoughs to lunch next Sunday.'

I tidily ate my bacon and egg. I said calmly, 'That coy spotty Angela. It's a waste of time. I won't be here anyway.'

'Angela will inherit half a million,' she said earnestly.

'And we have beetles in the roof,' I agreed dryly.

'Mother wants to see you married.'

'Only to a very rich girl.'

My sister acknowledged that this was true, but saw nothing particularly wrong in it. The family fortunes were waning: as my parents saw it, the swop of a future title for a future fortune was a suitable bargain. They didn't seem to realise that a rich girl nowadays had more sense than to hand over her wealth to her husband, and could leave with it intact if she felt like it.

'Mother told Angela you would be here.'

'That was silly of her.'

'Henry!'

'I do not like Angela,' I said coldly. 'I do not intend to be here for lunch next Sunday. Is that quite clear?'

'But you must . . . you can't leave me to deal with them all alone.'

'You'll just have to restrain Mother from issuing these stupid invitations. Angela is the umpteenth unattractive heiress she's invited this year. I'm fed up with it.'

'We need . . .'

'I am not,' I said stiffly, 'a prostitute.'

She stood up bitterly offended. 'That's unkind.'

'And while we are at it, I wish the beetles good luck. This damp decaying pile of a house eats up every penny we've got and if it fell down tomorrow we'd all be far better off.'

'It's our home,' she said, as if that was the final word.

When it was mine, I would get rid of it; but I didn't say that, and encouraged by my silence she tried persuasion. 'Henry, please be here for the Filyhoughs.'

'No,' I said forcefully. 'I won't. I want to do something else next Sunday. You can count me right out.'

She suddenly and completely lost her temper. Shaking she said, 'I cannot stand much more of your damned autistic behaviour. You're a spoilt, bad-tempered *bastard* . . .'

Hell, I thought by the Serpentine, was I really? And if so, why?

At three, with the air growing cold, I got up and left the park, but the office I went to was not the elegant suite of Anglia Bloodstock in Hanover Square. There, I thought, they could go on wondering why the ever-punctual Henry hadn't returned from lunch. I went instead by taxi to a small dilapidated rubbish-strewn wharf down in the Pool, where the smell of Thames mud at low tide rose earthily into my nostrils as I paid the fare.

At one end of the wharf, on an old bombed site, a small square concrete building had been thrown up shortly after the war and shoddily maintained ever since. Its drab walls, striped by rust from leaking gutters, badly needed a coat of 'Snowcem'; its rectangular metal windows were grimed and flaking, and no one had polished the brass door fittings since my previous visit six months ago. There was no need to put on a plushy front for the customers; the customers were not expected to come.

I walked up the uncarpeted stairs, across the eight foot square of linoleumed landing and through the open door of Simon Searle's room. He looked up from some complicated doodling on a memo pad, lumbered to his feet and greeted me with a large handshake and a wide grin. As he was the only person who ever gave me this sort of welcome I came as near to unbending with him as with anyone. But we had never done more than meet now and again on business and occasionally repair to a pub afterwards. There he was inclined to lots of beer and bonhomie, and I to a single whisky, and that was that.

'You haven't trekked all the way down here about those yearlings?' he protested. 'I told you . . .'

'No,' I said, coming to the point abruptly. 'I came to find out if Yardman would give me a job.'

'*You*,' said Simon, 'want to work *here?*'

'That's right.'

'Well I'm damned.' Simon sat down on the edge of his desk and his bulk settled and spread comfortably around him. He was a vast shambling man somewhere in the doldrums between thirty-five and forty-five, bald on top, bohemian in dress and broad of mind.

'Why, for God's sake?' he said, looking me up and down. A more thorough contrast than me in my charcoal worsted to him in his baggy green corduroys would have been hard to find.

'I need a change.'

'For the worse?' He was sardonic.

'Of course not. And I'd like the chance of a bit of globe-trotting now and then.'

'You can afford to do that in comfort. You don't have to do it on a horse transport.'

Like so many other people, he took it for granted that I had money. I hadn't. I had only my salary from Anglia, and what I could earn by being frankly, almost notoriously, a shamateur jockey. Every penny I got was earmarked. From my father I took only my food and the beetle infested roof over my head, and neither expected nor asked for anything else.

'I imagine I would like a horse transport,' I said equably. 'What are the chances?'

'Oh,' Simon laughed. 'You've only to ask. I can't see him turning you down.'

But Yardman very nearly did turn me down, because he couldn't believe I really meant it.

'My dear boy, now think carefully, I beg you. Anglia Bloodstock is surely a better place for you? However well you might do here, there isn't any power or any prestige . . . We must face facts, we must indeed.'

'I don't particularly care for power and prestige.'

He sighed deeply. 'There speaks one to whom they come by birth. Others of us are not so fortunate as to be able to despise them.'

'I don't despise them. Also I don't want them. Or not yet.'

He lit a dark cigar with slow care. I watched him, taking him in. I hadn't met him before, and as he came from a different mould from the top men at Anglia I found that I didn't instinctively know how his mind worked. After years of being employed by people of my own sort of background, where much that was understood never needed to be stated, Yardman was a foriegn country.

He was being heavily paternal, which somehow came oddly from a thin man. He wore black-rimmed spectacles on a strong beaky nose. His cheeks were hollowed, and his mouth in consequence seemed to have to stretch to cover his teeth and gums. His lips curved downwards strongly at the corners, giving him at times a disagreeable and at times a sad expression. He was bald on the crown of his head, which was not noticeable at first sight, and his skin looked unhealthy. But his voice and his fingers were strong, and as I grew to acknowledge, his will and his character also.

He puffed slowly at the cigar, a slim fierce looking thing with an aroma to match. From behind the glasses his eyes considered me without haste. I hadn't a clue as to what he was thinking.

'All right,' he said at last. 'I'll take you on as an assistant to Searle, and we'll see how it goes.'

'Well . . . thank you,' I answered. 'But what I really came to ask for was Peters's job.'

'*Peters's* . . .' His mouth literally fell open, revealing a bottom row of regular false teeth. He shut it with a snap. 'Don't be silly, my boy. You can't have Peters's job.'

'Searle says he has left.'

'I dare say, but that's not the point, is it?'

I said calmly, 'I've been in the Transport Section of Anglia for more than five years, so I know all the technical side of it, and I've ridden horses all my life, so I know how to look after them. I agree that I haven't any practical experience, but I could learn very quickly.'

'Lord Grey,' he said, shaking his head. 'I don't think you realise just what Peters's job was.'

'Of course I do,' I said. 'He travelled on the planes with the horses and saw they arrived safely and well. He saw that they passed the Customs all right at both ends and that the correct people collected them, and where necessary saw that another load of horses was brought safely back again. It is a responsible job and it entails a lot of travelling and I am seriously applying for it.'

'You don't understand,' he said with some impatience. 'Peters was a travelling head groom.'

'I know.'

He smoked, inscrutable. Three puffs. I waited, quiet and still.

'You're not . . . er . . . in any trouble, at Anglia?'

'No. I've grown tired of a desk job, that's all.' I had been tired of it from the day I started, to be exact.

'How about racing?'

'I have Saturdays off at Anglia, and I take my three weeks annual holiday in seperate days during the winter and spring. And they have been very considerate about extra half-days.'

'Worth it to them in terms of trade, I dare say.' He tapped off the ash absentmindedly into the inkwell. 'Are you thinking of giving it up?'

'No.'

'Mm . . . if you work for me, would I get any increase in business from your racing connections?'

'I'd see you did,' I said.

He turned his head away and looked out of the window. The river tide was sluggishly at the ebb, and away over on the other side a row of cranes stood like red meccano toys in the beginnings of dusk. I couldn't even guess then at the calculations clicking away at high speed in Yardman's nimble brain, though I've often thought about those few minutes since.

'I think you are being unwise, my dear boy. Youth . . . youth . . .' He sighed, straightened his shoulders and turned the beaky nose back in my direction. His shadowed greenish eyes regarded me steadily from deep sockets, and he told me what Peters had been earning; fifteen pounds a trip plus three pounds expenses for each overnight stop. He clearly thought that would deter me; and it nearly did.

'How many trips a week?' I asked frowning.

'It depends on the time of year. You know that, of course. After the yearling sales, and when the brood mares come over, it might be three trips. To France, perhaps even four. Usually two, sometimes none.'

There was a pause. We looked at each other. I learned nothing.

'All right,' I said abruptly. 'Can I have the job?'

His lips twisted in a curious expression which I later came to recognise as an ironic smile.

'You can try it,' he said. 'If you like.'

Chapter Two

A job is what you make it. Three weeks later, after Christmas, I flew to Buenos Aires with twelve yearlings, the four from Anglia and eight more from different bloodstock agencies, all mustered together at five o'clock on a cold Tuesday morning at Gatwick. Simon Searle had organised their arrival and booked their passage with a charter company; I took charge of them when they unloaded from their various horseboxes, installed them in the plane, checked their papers through Customs, and presently flew away.

With me went two of Yardman's travelling grooms, both of them fiercely resenting that I had been given Peter's job over their heads. Each of them had coveted the promotion, and in terms of human relationships the trip was a frost-bitten failure. Otherwise, it went well enough. We arrived in Argentina four hours late, but the new owners' horseboxes had all turned up to collect the cargo. Again I cleared the horses and papers through the Customs, and made sure that each of the five new owners had got the right horses and the certificates to go with them. The following day the plane picked up a load of crated furs for the return journey, and we flew back to Gatwick, arriving on Friday.

On Saturday I had a fall and a winner at Sandown Races, Sunday I spent in my usual way, and Monday I flew with some circus ponies to Germany. After a fortnight of it I was dying from exhaustion; after a month I was acclimatised. My body got used to long hours, irregular food, non-stop coffee, and sleeping sitting upright on bales of hay ten thousand feet up in the sky. The two grooms, Timmie and Conker, gradually got over the worst of their anger, and we developed into a quick, efficient, laconic team.

My family were predictably horrified by my change of occupation and did their best to pry me away from it. My sister anxiously retracted the words I knew I'd earned, my father foresaw the earldom going to the cousin after all, aeroplanes being entirely against nature and usually fatal, and my mother had hysterics over what her friends would say.

'It's a labourer's job,' she wailed.

'A job is what you make it.'

'What will the Filyhoughs think?'

'Who the hell cares what they think?'

'It isn't a *suitable* job for you.' She wrung her hands.

'It's a job I like. It suits me, therefore it *is* suitable.'

'You know that isn't what I mean.'

'I know exactly what you mean, Mother, and I profoundly disagree with you. People should do work they like doing; that's all that should decide them. Whether it is socially O.K. or not shouldn't come into it.'

'But it does,' she cried, exasperated.

'It has for me for nearly six years,' I admitted, 'but not any more. And ideas change. What I am doing now may be the top thing next year. If I don't look out half the men I know will be muscling in on the act. Anyway, it's right for me, and I'm going on with it.'

All the same she couldn't be won over, and could only face her own elderly convention-bound circle by pretending my job was 'for the experience, you know,' and by treating it as a joke.

It was a joke to Simon Searle too, at first.

'You won't stick it, Henry,' he said confidently. 'Not you and all that dirt. You with your spotless dark suits and your snowy white shirts and not a hair out of place. One trip will be enough.'

After a month, looking exactly the same, I turned up for my pay packet late on Friday afternoon, and we sauntered along to his favourite pub, a tatty place with stained glass doors and a chronic smell of fug. He oozed onto a bar stool, his bulk drooping around him. A pint for him, he said. I bought it, and a half for me, and he drank most of his off with one much practised swallow.

'How's the globe-trotting, then?' He ran his tongue over his upper lip for the froth.

'I like it.'

'I'll grant you,' he said, smiling amicably, 'that you haven't made a mess of it yet.'

'Thanks.'

'Though of course since I do all the spade work for you at both ends you bloody well shouldn't.'

'No,' I agreed. He was, in truth, an excellent organiser, which was mainly why Anglia often dealt with Yardman Transport instead of Clarkson Carriers, a much bigger and better known firm. Simon's arrangements were clear, simple, and always twice confirmed: agencies, owners and air-lines alike knew exactly where they stood and at what hours they were expected to be where. No one else in the business, that I had come across at any rate, was as consistently reliable. Being so precise myself, I admired his work almost as a work of art.

He looked me over, privately amused. 'You don't go on trips dressed like that?'

'I do, yes, more or less.'

'What does more or less mean?'

'I wear a sweater instead of my jacket, in and around the aircraft.'

'And hang up your jacket on a hanger for when you land?'

'Yes, I do.'

He laughed, but without mockery. 'You're a rum sort of chap, Henry.' He ordered more beer, shrugged when I refused, and drank deep again. 'Why are you so methodical?'

'It's safer.'

'Safer.' He choked on his beer, coughing and laughing. 'I suppose it doesn't strike you that to many people steeplechasing and air transport might not seem especially safe?'

'That wasn't what I meant.'

'What, then?'

But I shook my head and didn't explain.

'Tell me about Yardman,' I said.

'What about him?'

'Well, where he came from . . . anything.'

Simon hunched his great shoulders protectively around his pint, and pursed his lips.

'He joined the firm after the war, when he left the Army. He was a sergeant in an infantry regiment, I think. Don't know any details: never asked. Anyway he worked his way up through the business. It wasn't called Yardman Transport then, of course. Belonged to a family, the Mayhews, but they were dying out . . . nephews weren't interested, that sort of thing. Yardman had taken it over by the time I got there; don't know how really, come to think of it, but he's a bright lad, there's no doubt of that. Take switching to air, for instance. That was him. He was pressing the advantages of air travel for horses, whilst all the other transport agencies were going entirely by sea.'

'Even though the office itself is on a wharf,' I remarked.

'Yes. Very handy once. It isn't used much at all now since they clamped down on exporting horses to the continent for meat.'

'Yardman was in that?'

'Shipping agent,' he nodded. 'There's a big warehouse down the other end of the wharf where we used to collect them. They'd start being brought in three days before the ship came. Once a fortnight, on average. I can't say I'm sorry it's finished. It was a lot of work and a lot of mess and noise, and not much profit, Yardman said.'

'It didn't worry you, though, that they were going to be slaughtered?'

'No more than cattle or pigs.' He finished his beer. 'Why should it? Everything dies sometime.' He smiled cheerfully and gestured to the glasses. 'Another?'

He had one, I didn't.

'Has anyone heard any more of Peters?' I asked.

He shook his head. 'Not a murmur.'

'How about his cards?'

'Still in the office, as far as I know.'

'It's a bit odd isn't it?'

Simon shrugged. 'You never know, he might have wanted to duck someone, and did it thoroughly.'

'But did anyone ever come looking for him?'

'Nope. No police, no unpaid bookies, no rampaging females, no one.'

'He just went to Italy and didn't come back?'

'That's the size of it,' Simon agreed. 'He went with some brood mares to Milan and he should have come back the same day. But there was some trouble over an engine or something, and the pilot ran out of time and said he'd be in dead trouble if he worked too many hours. So they stayed there overnight and in the morning Peters didn't turn up. They waited nearly all day, then they came back without him.'

'And that's all?'

'That's the lot,' he agreed. 'Just one of life's little mysteries. What's the matter, are you afraid Peters will reappear and take back his job?'

'Something like that.'

'He was an awkward bastard,' he said thoughtfully. 'stood on his rights. Always arguing; that sort of chap. Belligerent. Never stood any nonsense from foreign customs officers.' He grinned. 'I'll bet they're quite glad to see you instead.'

'I dare say I'll be just as cussed in a year or two.'

'A year or two?' He looked surprised. 'Henry, it's all very well you taking Peters's job for a bit of a giggle but you surely can't mean to go on with it permanently?'

'You think it would be more suitable if I was sitting behind a nice solid desk at Anglia?' I asked ironically.

'Yes,' he said seriously. 'Of course it would.'

I sighed. 'Not you too. I thought you at least might understand . . .' I stopped wryly.

'Understand what?'

'Well . . . that who one's father is has nothing to do with the sort of work one is best suited for. And I am not fitted for sitting behind a desk. I came to that conclusion my first week at Anglia, but I stayed there because I'd kicked up a fuss and insisted on getting an ordinary job, and

I wasn't going to admit I'd made a mistake with it. I tried to like it. At any rate I got used to it, but now ... now ... I don't think I could face that nine-to-five routine ever again.'

'Your father's in his eighties, isn't he?' Simon said thoughtfully.

I nodded.

'And do you think that when he dies you will be allowed to go on carting horses around the world? And for how long *could* you do it without becoming an eccentric nut? Like it or not, Henry, it's easy enough to go up the social scale, but damn difficult to go down. And still be respected, that is.'

'And I could be respected sitting behind a desk at Anglia, transferring horses from owner to owner on paper, but not if I move about and do it on aeroplanes?'

He laughed. 'Exactly.'

'The world is mad,' I said.

'You're a romantic. But time will cure that.' He looked at me in a large tolerant friendship, finished his beer, and flowed down from the stool like a green corduroy amoeba.

'Come on,' he said, 'there's time for another along the road at the Saracen's Head.'

At Newbury Races the following afternoon I watched five races from the stands and rode in one.

This inactivity was not mine by choice, but thrust upon me by the Stewards. They had, by the time I was twenty, presented me with their usual ultimatum to regular amateur riders: either turn professional, or ride in only fifty open races each season. In other words, don't undercut the trade: stop taking the bread and butter out of the professionals mouths. (As if jockeys *ate* much bread and butter, to start with.)

I hadn't turned professional when I was twenty because I had been both too conventional and not really good enough. I was still not good enough to be a top rank professional, but I had long been a fully employed amateur. A big fish in a small pond. In the new-found freedom of my Yardman's job I regretted that I hadn't been bolder at twenty. I liked steeplechasing enormously, and with full-time professional application I might just have made a decent success. Earth-bound on the stands at Newbury I painfully accepted that my sister had brought me to my senses a lot too late.

The one horse I did ride was in the 'amateurs only' race. As there were no restrictions on the number of amateur events I could ride in, few were run without me. I rode regularly for many owners who grudged paying professional jockey's fees, for some who reckoned their horses stood more chance in amateur races, and a few who genuinely liked my work.

All of them knew very well that if I won either amateur or open races I expected ten per cent of the prize. The word had got around. Henry Grey rode for money, not love. Henry Grey was the shamateur to end all shamateurs. Because I was silent and discreet and they could trust my tongue, I had even been given cash presents by stewards: and solely because my father was the Earl of Creggan, my amateur permit survived.

In the changing room that afternoon I found that however different I might feel, I could not alter my long set pattern. The easy bantering chat flowed round me and as usual it was impossible to join in. No one expected me to. They were used to me. Half of them took my aloofness to be arrogant snobbery, and the rest shrugged it off as 'just Henry's way.' No one was actively hostile, and it was I, I, who had failed to belong. I changed slowly into my racing clothes and listened to the jokes and the warm earthy language, and I could think of nothing, not one single thing, to say.

I won the race. The well pleased owner gave me a public clap on the shoulder and a drink in the members' bar, and surreptitiously, round a private corner, forty pounds.

On the following day, Sunday, I spent the lot.

I started my little Herald in the garage in the pre-dawn dark, and as quietly as possible opened the doors and drifted away down the drive. Mother had invited yet another well-heeled presumptive virgin for the week-end, together with her slightly forbidding parents, and having dutifully escorted them all to Newbury Races the day before and tipped them a winner – my own – I felt I had done quite enough. They would be gone, I thought coolly, before I got back late that evening, and with a bit of luck my bad manners in disappearing would have discouraged them for ever.

A steady two and a half hours driving northwards found me at shortly before ten o'clock turning in through some inconspicuously signposted gates in Lincolnshire. I parked the car at the end of the row of others, climbed out, stretched, and looked up into the sky. It was a cold clear morning with maximum visibility. Not a cloud in sight. Smiling contentedly I strolled over to the row of white painted buildings and pushed open the glass door into the main hall of the Fenland Flying Club.

The hall was a big room with several passages leading off it and a double door on the far side opening to the airfield itself. Round the walls hung framed charts, Air Ministry regulations, a large map of the surrounding area, do's and don'ts for visiting pilots, a thumb-tacked weather report and a list of people wanting to enter for a ping-pong tournament. There were several small wooden tables and hard chairs at one end, half occupied, and across the whole width of the other end stretched the reception-cum-operations-cum-everything else desk. Yawning behind it and scratching between his shoulder blades stood a plump sleepy man of about my own age, sporting a thick sloppy sweater and a fair sized hangover. He held a cup of strong coffee and a cigarette in his free hand, and he was talking lethargically to a gay young spark who had turned up with a girl-friend he wanted to impress.

'I've told you, old chap, you should have given us a ring. All the planes are booked today. I'm sorry, no can do. You can hang about if you like, in case someone doesn't turn up . . .'

He turned towards me, casually.

'Morning, Harry,' he said. 'How's things?'

'Very O.K.,' I said. 'And you?'

'Ouch,' he grinned, 'don't cut me. The gin would run out.' He turned round and consulted the vast timetable charts covering most of the wall behind him. 'You've got Kilo November today, it's out by the petrol pumps, I think. Cross country again; is that right?'

'Uh-huh,' I nodded.

'Nice day for it.' He put a tick on his chart where it said H. Grey, solo cross.

'Couldn't be better.'

The girl said moodily, 'How about this afternoon, then?'

'No dice. All booked. And it gets dark so early ... there'll be plenty of planes tomorrow.'

I strolled away, out of the door to the airfield and around to the petrol pumps.

There were six single engined aircraft lined up there in two rows of three, with a tall man in white overalls filling one up through the opening on the upper surface of the port wing. He waved when he saw me coming, and grinned.

'Just doing yours next, Harry. The boys have tuned her up special. They say you couldn't have done it better yourself.'

'I'm delighted to hear it,' I said smiling.

He screwed on the cap and jumped down.

'Lovely day,' he said, looking up. There were already two little planes in the air, and four more stood ready in front of the control tower. 'Going far?' he asked.

'Scotland,' I said.

'That's cheating.' He swung the hose away and began to drag it along to the next aircraft. 'The navigation's too easy. you only have to go west till you hit the A.1 and then fly up it.'

'I'm going to Islay,' I smiled. 'No roads, I promise.'

'Islay. That's different.'

'I'll land there for lunch and bring you back a bit of heather.'

'How far is it?'

'Two seventy nautical miles, about.'

'You'll be coming back in the dark.' It was a statement, not a question. He unscrewed the cap of Kilo November and topped up the tanks.

'Most of the way, yes.'

I did the routine checks all round the aircraft, fetched my padded jacket and my charts from the car, filed my flight plan, checked with the control tower for taxy clearance, and within a short while was up in the sky and away.

Air is curious stuff. One tends to think that because it is invisible it isn't there. What you can't see don't exist, sort of thing. But air is tough, elastic and resistant; and the harder you dig into it the more solid it becomes. Air has currents stronger than tides and turbulences which would make Charybdis look like bath water running away.

When I first went flying I rationalised the invisibility thing by thinking of an aircraft being like a submarine: in both one went up and down and sideways in a medium one couldn't see but which was very palpably around. Then I considered that if human eyes had been constructed differently it might have been possible to see the mixture of nitrogen and oxygen we breathe as clearly as the hydrogen and oxygen we wash in. After that I took the air's positive plastic existence for granted, and thought no more about it.

The day I went to Islay was pure pleasure. I had flown so much by then that the handling of the little aircraft was as normal as driving a car, and with the perfect weather and my route carefully worked out and handy on the empty passenger seat behind me, there was nothing to do but enjoy myself. And that I did, because I liked being alone. Specifically I liked being alone in a tiny noisy efficient little capsule at 25,000 revs a minute, four thousand five hundred feet above sea level, speed over the ground one hundred and ten miles an hour, steady on a course 313 degrees, bound north-west towards the sea and a Scottish island.

I found Islay itself without trouble, and tuned my radio to the frequency – 118.5 – of Port Ellen airfield.

I said, 'Port Ellen tower this is Golf Alpha Romeo Kilo November, do you read?'

A Scots accent cracked back, 'Golf Kilo November, good afternoon, go ahead.'

'Kilo November is approaching from the south-east, range fifteen miles, request joining instructions, over.'

'Kilo November is cleared to join right base for runway zero four, QFE 998 millibars. Surface wind zero six zero, ten knots, call field in sight.'

Following his instructions I flew in and round the little airfield on the circuit, cut the engine, turned into wind, glided in at eighty, touched down, and taxied across to the control tower to report.

After eating in a snack bar I went for a walk by the sea, breathing the soft Atlantic air, and forgot to look for some heather to take back with me. The island lay dozing in the sun, shut up close because it was Sunday. It was peaceful and distant and slowed the pulse; soul's balm if you stayed three hours, devitalising if you stayed for life.

The gold had already gone from the day when I started back, and I flew contentedly along in the dusk and the dark, navigating by compass and checking my direction by the radio beacons over which I passed. I dropped down briefly at Carlisle to refuel, and uneventfully returned to Lincolnshire, landing gently and regretfully on the well-known field.

As usual on Sundays the club room next to the main hall was bursting with amateur pilots like myself all talking at once about stalls and spins and ratings and slide slips and allowances for deviations. I edged round the crowd to the bar and aquired some whisky and water, which tasted dry and fine on my tongue and reminded me of where I had been.

Turning round I found myself directly beside the reception desk man and a red-haired boy he was talking to. Catching my eye he said to the boy, 'Now here's someone you ought to have a word with. Our Harry here, he's dead quiet, but don't let that fool you ... He could fly the pants off most of that lot.' He gestured round the room. 'You ask Harry, now. He started just like you, knowing nothing at all, only three or four years ago.'

'Four,' I said.

'There you are, then. Four years. Now he's got a commercial licence and enough ratings to fill a book and he can strip an engine down like a mechanic.'

'That's enough,' I interrupted mildly. The young man looked thoroughly unimpressed anyway, as he didn't understand what he was being told. 'I suppose the point is that once you start, you go on,' I said. 'One thing leads to another.'

'I had my first lesson today,' he said eagerly, and gave me a rev by rev account of it for the next fifteen minutes. I ate two thick ham sandwiches while he got it off his chest, and finished the whisky. You couldn't really blame him, I thought, listening with half an ear: if you liked it, your first flight took you by the throat and you were hooked good and proper. It had happened to him. It had happened to me, one idle day when I passed the gates of the airfield and then turned back and went in, mildly interested in going up for a spin in a baby aircraft just to see what it was like.

I'd been visiting a dying great-aunt, and was depressed. Certainly Mr. ....? 'Grey.' I said. Certainly Mr. Grey could go up with an instructor, the air people said: and the instructor, who hadn't been told I only wanted a sight-seeing flip, began as a matter of course to teach me to fly. I stayed all day and spent a week's salary in fees; and the next Sunday I went back. Most of my Sundays and most of my money had gone the same way since.

The red-head was brought to a full stop by a burly tweed-suited man who said 'Excuse me,' pleasantly but very firmly, and planted himself between us.

'Harry, I've been waiting for you to come back.'

'Have a drink?'

'Yes ... all right, in a minute.'

His name was Tom Wells. He owned and ran a small charter firm which was based on the airfield, and on Sundays, if they weren't out on jobs, he allowed the flying club to hire his planes. It was one of his that I had flown to Islay.

'Have I done something wrong?' I asked.

'Wrong? Why should you, for God's sake? No, I'm in a spot and I thought you might be able to help me out.'

'If I can, of course.'

'I've overbooked next week-end and I'm going to be a pilot short. Will you do a flight for me next Sunday?'

'Yes,' I said: I'd done it before, several times.

He laughed. 'You never waste words, Harry boy. Well, thanks. When can I ring you to give you a briefing?'

I hesitated. 'I'd better ring you, as usual.'

'Saturday morning, then.'

'Right.'

We had a drink together, he talking discontentedly about the growing shortage of pilots and how it was now too expensive for a young man to take it up on his own account, it cost at least three thousand pounds to train a multi-engine pilot, and only the air lines could afford it. They trained their own men and kept them, naturally. When the generation who had learned flying in the R.A.F. during the war got too old, the smaller charter firms were going to find themselves in very sticky straits.

'You know,' he said, and it was obviously what he'd been working round to all along. 'You're an oddity. You've got a commercial licence and all the rest, and you hardly use it. Why not? Why don't you give up that boring old desk job and come and work for me?'

I looked at him for a long, long moment. It was almost too tempting, but apart from everything else, it would mean giving up steeplechasing, and I wasn't prepared to do that. I shook my head slowly, and said not for a few years yet.

Driving home I enjoyed the irony of the situation. Tom Wells didn't know what my desk job was, only that I worked in an office. I hadn't got around to telling him that I no longer did, and I wasn't going to. He didn't know where I came from or anything about my life away from the airfield. No one there did, and I liked it that way. I was just Harry who turned up on Sundays and flew if he had any money and worked on the engines in the hangars if he hadn't.

Tom Wells had offered me a job on my own account, not, like Yardman, because of my father, and that pleased me very much. It was rare for me to be sure of the motive behind things which were offered to me. But if I took the job my anonymity on the airfield would vanish pretty soon, and all the old problems would crowd in, and Tom Wells might very well retract, and I would be left with nowhere to escape to on one day a week to be myself.

My family did not know I was a pilot. I hadn't told them I had been flying that first day because by the time I got home my great-aunt had died and I was ashamed of having enjoyed myself while she did it. I hadn't told them afterwards because I was afraid that they would make a fuss and stop me. Soon after that I realised what a release it was to lead two lives and I deliberately kept them separate. It was quite easy, as I had always been untalkative: I just didn't answer when asked where I went on Sundays, and I kept my books and charts, slide rules and computers, securely locked up in my bedroom. And that was that.

Chapter Three

It was on the day after I went to Islay that I first met Billy.

With Conker and Timmie, once they had bitten down their resentment at my pinching their promotion, I had arrived at a truce. On trips they chatted exclusively to each other, not to me, but that was as usual my fault: and we had got as far as sharing things like sandwiches and chocolate – and the work – on a taken-for-granted basis.

Billy at once indicated that with him it would be quite quite different. For Billy the class war existed as a bloody battlefield upon which he was the most active and tireless warrior alive. Within five seconds of our first meeting he was sharpening his claws.

It was at Cambridge Airport at five in the morning. We were to take two consignments of recently sold racehorses from Newmarket to Chantilly near Paris, and with all the loading and unloading at each end it would be a long day. Locking my car in the car park I was just thinking how quickly Conker and Timmie and I were getting to be able to do things when Yardman himself drove up alongside in a dark Jaguar Mark 10. There were two other men in the car, a large indistinct shape in the back, and in front, Billy.

Yardman stepped out of his car, yawned, stretched, looked up at the sky, and finally turned to me.

'Good-morning my dear boy,' he said with great affability. 'A nice day for flying.'

'Very,' I agreed. I was surprised to see him: he was not given to early rising or to waving us bon voyage. Simon Searle occasionally came if there were some difficulty with papers but not Yardman himself. Yet here he was with his black suit hanging loosely on his too thin frame and the cold early morning light making uncomplimentary shadows on his stretched coarsely pitted skin. The black-framed spectacles as always hid the expression in his deep-set eyes. After a month in his employ, seeing him at the wharf building two or three times a week on my visits for instructions, reports, and pay, I knew him no better than on that first afternoon. In their own way his defence barriers were as good as mine.

He told me between small shut-mouthed yawns that Timmie and Conker weren't coming, they were due for a few days leave. He had brought two men who obligingly substituted on such occasions and he was sure I would do a good job with them instead. He had brought them, he explained, because public transport wasn't geared to five o'clock rendezvous at Cambridge Airport.

While he spoke the front passenger climbed out of his car.

'Billy Watkins,' Yardman said casually, nodding between us.

'Good-morning, Lord Grey,' Billy said. He was about nineteen, very slender, with round cold blue eyes.

'Henry,' I said automatically. The job was impossible on any other terms and these were in any case what I preferred.

Billy looked at me with eyes wide, blank, and insolent. He spaced his words, bit them out and hammered them down.

'Good . . . morning . . . Lord . . . Grey.'

'Good-morning then, Mr. Watkins.'

His eyes flickered sharply and went back to their wide stare. If he expected any placatory soft soaping from me, he could think again.

Yardman saw the instant antagonism and it annoyed him.

'I warned you, Billy,' he began swiftly, and then as quickly stopped. 'You won't, I am sure, my dear boy,' he said to me gently, 'allow any personal ... er ... clash of temperaments to interfere with the safe passage of your valuable cargo.'

'No,' I agreed.

He smiled, showing his greyish regular dentures back to the molars. I wondered idly why, if he could afford such a car, he didn't invest in more natural looking teeth. It would have improved his unprepossessing appearance one hundred per cent.

'Right then,' he said in brisk satisfaction. 'Let's get on.'

The third man levered himself laboriously out of the car. His trouble stemmed from a paunch which would have done a pregnant mother of twins proud. About him flapped a brown storeman's overall which wouldn't do up by six inches, and under that some bright red braces over a checked shirt did a load-bearing job on some plain dark trousers. He was about fifty, going bald, and looked tired, unshaven and sullen, and he did not then or at any time meet my eyes.

What a crew, I thought resignedly, looking from him to Billy and back. So much for a day of speed and efficiency. The fat man, in fact, proved to be even more useless than he looked, and treated the horses with the sort of roughness which is the product of fear. Yardman gave him the job of loading them from their own horse-boxes up the long matting-covered side-walled ramp into the aircraft, while Billy and I inside fastened them into their stalls.

John, as Yardman called him, was either too fat or too scared of having his feet trodden on to walk side by side with each horse up the ramp: he backed up it, pulling the horse after him, stretching its head forward uncomfortably. Not surprisingly they all stuck their toes in hard and refused to budge. Yardman advanced on them from behind, shouting and waving a pitch fork, and prodded them forward again. The net result was some thoroughly upset and frightened animals in no state to be taken flying.

After three of them had arrived in the plane sweating, rolling their eyes and kicking out, I went down the ramp and protested.

Let John help Billy, and I'll lead the horses,' I said to Yardman. 'I don't suppose you'll want them to arrive in such an unnerved state that their owners won't use the firm again? Always supposing that they don't actually kick the aircraft to bits en route.'

He knew very well that this had really happened once or twice in the history of bloodstock transport. There was always the risk that a horse would go berserk in the air at the best of times: taking off with a whole planeload of het-up thoroughbreds would be a fair way to commit suicide.

He hesitated only a moment, then nodded.

'All right. Change over.'

The loading continued with less fuss but no more speed. John was as useless at installing the horses as he was at leading them.

Cargo on aeroplanes has to be distributed with even more care than on ships. If the centre of gravity isn't kept to within fairly close specific limits the plane won't fly at all, just race at high speed to the end of the runway and turn into scrap metal. If the cargo shifts radically in mid-air it keels the plane over exactly as it would a ship, but with less time to put it right, and no lifeboats handy as a last resort.

From the gravity point of view, the horses had to be stowed down the centre of the plane, where for their own comfort and balance they had to face forwards. This meant, in a medium sized aircraft such as Yardman's usually chartered, four pairs of horses standing behind each other. From the balance point of view, the horses had to be fairly immobile, and they also had to be accessible, as one had to be able to hold their heads and soothe them at take-off and landing. Each pair was therefore boxed separately, like four little islands down the centre of the plane. There were narrow gangways between the boxes and up both sides the whole length of the aircraft so that one could easily walk round and reach every individual horse to look after him.

The horses stood on large trays of peat which were bolted to the floor. The boxes of half inch thick wood panels had to be built up round the horses when each pair was loaded: one erected the forward end wall and the two sides, led in the horses and tied them up, added the back wall, and made the whole thing solid with metal bars banding the finished box. The bars were joined at each corner by lynch pins. There were three bars, at the top, centre and bottom. To prevent the boxes from collapsing inwards, each side of each box had to be separately fixed to the floor with chains acting as guy ropes. When the loading was complete, the result looked like four huge packing cases chained down, with the horses' backs and heads showing at the open tops.

As one couldn't afford to have a box fall apart in the air, the making of them, though not difficult, demanded attention and thoroughness. John conspicuously lacked both. He was also unbelievably clumsy at hooking on and tightening the guy chains, and he dropped two lynch pins which we couldn't find again: we had to use wire instead, which wouldn't hold if a strong-minded horse started kicking. By the end Billy and I were doing the boxes alone, while John stood sullenly by and watched: and Billy throughout made my share as difficult as he could.

It all took such a time that at least the three frightened horses had calmed down again before the pilot climbed aboard and started the engines. I closed the first of the big double doors we had loaded the horses through, and had a final view of Yardman on the tarmac, the slipstream from the propellers blowing his scanty hair up round the bald patch like a black sea anemone. The light made silver window panes of his glasses. He lifted his hand without moving his elbow, an awkward little gesture of farewell. I put my own hand up in acknowledgement and reply, and fastened the second door as the plane began to move.

As usual there was a crew of three flying the aircraft, pilot, co-pilot and engineer. The engineer, on all the trips I had so far made, was the one who got landed with brewing the coffee and who could also be reasonably asked to hold a pair of horses' heads during take-off. This one did so with far more familiarity than John.

The trip was a relatively short one and there was a helpful following wind, but we were over an hour late at the French end. When we had landed the airport staff rolled another ramp up to the doors and I opened them from inside. The first people through them were three unsmiling businesslike customs officials. With great thoroughness they compared the horses we had brought against our list and their own. On the papers for each horse were details of its physical characteristics and colour: the customs men checked carefully every star, blaze and sock, guarding against the possibility that some poorer animal had been switched for the good one bought. France proved more hard to satisfy and more suspicious than most other countries.

Content at length that no swindle had been pulled this time, the chief customs man politely gave me back the papers and said that the unloading could begin.

Four horseboxes from French racing stables had turned up to collect the new purchases. The drivers, phlegmatically resigned to all delays, were engaged in digging round their mouths with tooth picks in a solid little group. I went down the ramp and across to them and told them in which order the horses would be unloaded. My French vocabulary, which was shaky on many subjects, covered at least all horse jargon and was fairly idiomatic when it came to racing or bloodstock: at Anglia I had done quite a bit of work on French horses, and after six years knew my way round the French stud book as well as I did the British.

The drivers nodded, sucked their teeth and drove up the boxes in the right order. The first horse off (the last loaded at Cambridge) was a nondescript brown filly who was led into the waiting horse-box by the driver himself. He took her casually from my hand, slapped her rump in a friendly fashion, and by the time I led out the second horse he had already loaded her up and was on his way.

The other drivers had, more usually, brought one or two grooms with them, as they were to collect more than one horse. Billy took over leading the horses from the ramp, and I dismantled the boxes with John. This very nearly meant, in effect, doing it by myself. He dropped the bars, tripped over the anchorages on the floor, caught his fingers in the chains, and because of the paunch could do nothing which entailed bending down. Why Yardman employed him at all, I thought in irritation, was an unfathomable mystery.

We were supposed to be taking four horses back on the return trip, but by the time the last of our cargo had departed, not one of the four had turned up. When they were more than half an hour overdue, I walked over to the airport buildings and rang up one of the trainers concerned. Certainly he was sending two horses today he said, two four-year-old hurdlers which he had sold to an English stable, but they were not due at the airport until three o'clock. Fifteen hundred hours: it was typed clearly on his notice from Yardman Transport. A second trainer, consulted, said the same: and although I had no phone number for the third, I took it for granted that his notice had been identical. Either Simon, or more likely his typist, had written five instead of nought on all three. It was a bore, as it meant unloading at the end of the last trip when we would all be tired.

The day's troubles, however, had barely warmed up. On my way back to the plane I saw Billy and John standing beside it engaged in a furious argument, but they broke off before I was close enough to hear what they were saying. John turned his back and kicked moodily at the bottom of the ramp and Billy gave me his best insulting stare.

'What's the matter?' I said.

Billy pursed his lips into an expression which said clearly that it was none of my business, but after a visible inner struggle he did answer.

'He's got a headache,' he said, nodding at John. 'From the noise.'

A headache. That hardly explained the fat man's hopeless inefficiency, his sullenness, his shifty manner or his row with Billy. Nor, I realised in some surprise, did it explain why he hadn't spoken a single word to me the whole trip. But as repeating the question was unlikely to get a more fruitful answer, I shrugged and didn't bother.

'Get on board,' I said instead. 'We're going back empty. There's been a mix-up and we'll have to take the French horses back next time.'

'—' said Billy calmly. He used a word so obscene that I wondered what he used for when he was annoyed.

'I dare say,' I said dryly. 'Let's not waste any more time.'

John lumbered unwillingly and morosely up the ramp. Billy followed him after a pause, and I too let Billy get well ahead before I started after him. The spaces between us, I thought sardonically, were symbolic.

The airport staff removed the ramp, the plane's crew returned from their coffee break, and we proceeded back to Cambridge. On the way we sat on three separate bales of straw along the length of the aircraft and didn't even look at each other. John put his elbows on his knee and held his head in his hands, and Billy looked steadily and sightlessly at the cloud-dotted sky.

With all the sides of the boxes lying flat and strapped down on the peat trays the body of the aircraft seemed large and empty. In that state it echoed and was much noisier than usual, and I had some small sympathy for John's head. The plane was adapted, by the charter company who owned it, for any purpose that was required. The regularly spaced anchorages on the floor were as often used for fastening passenger seats as boxes for animals, and the airline would fly sixty people on a coach tour type holiday to Europe one day and a load of pigs or cattle the next. In between they merely bolted or unbolted the rows of seats and swept out the relevant debris, either farmyard manure and straw or cigarette packets and bags full of vomit.

One was not allowed to sweep out manure on to foreign soil. The whole lot had to be solemnly carted back to England to comply with quarantine regulations. The odd thing was, I reflected again, that the peat trays never seemed to smell. Not even now that there was no live horse smell to mask it. Of course this plane was unpressurised, so that fresh air continually found its way in, but all the same it smelled less than an ordinary stable, even after a whole day in a hot climate.

The first person on the plane at Cambridge was a cheerful underworked bareheaded excise officer who had come there especially to clear the horses. He bounced in as soon as the cockpit ladder was in position, made a loud rude comment to the pilot and came back through the galley into the main cabin.

'What have you done with them, then?' he said, looking round at the emptiness. 'Dumped them in the Channel?'

I explained the situation.

'Damn,' he said. 'I wanted to get off early. Well, did any of you buy anything in France?'

John didn't answer. I shook my head. Billy said offensively, 'We weren't given a sodding minute to get off the sodding plane.'

The Customs man in his navy blue suit glanced at me sideways in amusement. I gathered that he had met Billy before.

'O.K.' he said. 'See you this afternoon, then.'

He opened the big double doors, beckoned to the men outside who were wheeling up the ramp, and as soon as it was in position walked jauntily down it and back across the tarmac towards the airport building. As we were now more or less up to schedule through not having to load and unload the French hurdlers, John and Billy and I followed him in order to have lunch. I sat at one table and Billy and John ostentatiously moved to another as far away as they could get. But if Billy thought he could distress me in that way, he was wrong. I felt relieved to be alone, not shunned.

By one o'clock the horseboxes bringing the next consignment had arrived, and we started the loading all over again. This time I got the groom who had brought the horses to lead them up to the plane. Billy and I made the boxes, and John belched and got in the way.

When I had finished I went into the airport building, checked the horses' export papers with the customs man and persuaded the pilot away from his fourth cup of coffee. Up we went again into the clear wintry sky, across the grey sea, and down again in France. The same French customs men came on board, checked every horse as meticulously as before, and as politely let them go. We took down the boxes, led out the horses, saw them loaded into their horseboxes, and watched them depart.

This time the French hurdlers for the return journey had already arrived and without a pause we began getting them on board. As there were only four we had only two boxes to set up, which by that point I found quite enough. John's sole contribution towards the fourth journey was to refill and hang the haynets for the hurdlers to pick from on their way, and even at that he was clumsy and slow.

With the horses at length unconcernedly munching in their boxes we went across to the airport buildings, Billy and John ahead, I following. The only word I heard pass between them as they left down the ramp was 'beer.'

There was a technical delay over papers in one of the airport offices. One of the things I had grown to expect in the racehorse export business was technical delays. A journey without one of some sort was a gift. With up to twenty horses sometimes carried on one aeroplane there only had to be a small query about a single animal for the whole load to be kept waiting for hours. Occasionally it was nothing to do with the horses themselves but with whether the airlines owed the airport dues for another plane or another trip: in which case the airport wouldn't clear the horse plane to leave until the dues were paid. Sometimes the quibbling was enough to get one near to jumping out of the window. I was growing very good indeed at keeping my temper when all around were losing theirs and blaming it on me. Kipling would have been proud.

This time it was some question of insurance which I could do nothing to smooth out as it involved the owner of one of the hurdlers, who was fighting a contested claim on a road accident it had been slightly hurt in. The insurance company didn't want the horse to leave France. I said it was a bit late, the horse was sold, and did the insurance company have the right to stop it anyway. No one was quite sure about that. A great deal of telephoning began.

I was annoyed, mainly because the horse in question was in the forward of the two boxes: if we had to take it off the plane it meant dismantling the rear box and unloading the back pair first in order to reach it; and then reloading those two again once we had got it off. And with Billy and John full of all the beer they were having plenty of time to ship, this was likely to be a sticky manoeuvre. The horses' own grooms and motor boxes had long gone home. The hurdlers were each worth thousands. Who, I wondered gloomily, was I going to trust not to let go of them if we had to have them standing about on the tarmac.

The pilot ran me to earth and said that if we didn't take off soon we would be staying all night as after six o'clock he was out of time. We had to be able to be back at Cambridge at six, or he couldn't start at all.

I relayed this information to the arguing officials. It produced nothing but some heavy gallic shrugs. The pilot swore and told me that until twenty to five I would find him having coffee and after that he'd be en route for Paris. And I would have to get another pilot as he had worked for maximum hours for a long spell and was legally obliged now to have forty-eight hours rest.

Looking morosely out of the window across to where the plane with its expensive cargo sat deserted on the apron, I reflected that this was the sort of situation I could do without. And if we had to stay all night, I was going to have to sleep with those horses. A delightful new experience every day, I thought in wry amusement. Join Yardman Transport and see the world, every discomfort thrown in.

With minutes to spare, the insurance company relented: the hurdler could go. I grabbed the papers, murmuring profuse thanks, raced to dig out the pilot, and ran Billy to earth behind a large frothy glass. It was clearly far from his first.

'Get John,' I said shortly. 'We've got to be off within ten minutes.'

'Get him yourself,' he said with sneering satisfaction. 'If you can.'

'Where is he?'

'Half way to Paris.' He drank unconcernedly. 'He's got some whore there. He said he'd come back tomorrow on a regular airline. There isn't a sodding thing you can do about it, so put that in your pipe and smoke it.'

John's presence, workwise, made little difference one way or another. I really cared not a bent sou if he wanted to pay his own fare back. He was free enough. He had his passport in his pocket, as we all did. Mine was already dog-eared and soft from constant use. We had to produce

them whenever asked, though they were seldom stamped as we rarely
went into the passengers' immigration section of airports. We showed
them more like casual passes than weighty official documents, and most
countries were so tolerant of people employed on aircraft that one pilot
told me he had left his passport in a hotel bedroom in Madrid and had
been going unhindered round the world for three weeks without it while
he tried to get it back.

'Ten minutes,' I said calmly to Billy. 'Fifteen, and you'll be paying
your own fare back too.'

Billy gave me his wide-eyed stare. He picked up his glass of beer and
poured it over my foot. The yellow liquid ran away in a pool on the
glossy stone floor, froth bubbles popping round the edges.

'What a waste,' I said, unmoving. 'Are you coming?'

He didn't answer. It was too much to expect him to get up meekly
while I waited, and as I wanted to avoid too decisive a clash with him
if I could I turned away and went back alone, squelching slightly, to the
aircraft. He came as I had thought he would, but with less than two
minutes in hand to emphasize his independence. The engines were
already running when he climbed aboard, and we were moving as soon
as the doors were shut.

As usual during take-off and landing, Billy stood holding the heads of
two horses and I of the other two. After that, with so much space on the
half loaded aircraft, I expected him to keep as far from me as he could,
as he had done all day. But Billy by then was eleven hours away from
Yardman's restraining influence and well afloat on airport beer. The
crew were all up forward in the cockpit, and fat useless John was sex-
bent for Paris.

Billy had me alone, all to himself.

Billy intended to make the most of it.

Chapter Four

'Your kind ought not to be allowed,' he said, with charming directness.
He had to say it very loudly, also, on account of the noise of the aircraft.

I sat on a hay bale with my back against the rear wall of the cabin and
looked at him as he stood ten feet in front of me with his legs apart for
balance.

'Your kind, of course,' I shouted back, 'are the salt of the earth.'

He took a step forward and the plane bumped hard in an air pocket.
It lurched him completely off his balance and he fell rolling on to his
side. With sizzling fury, though it wasn't I who had pushed him, he
raised himself up on one knee and thrust his face close to mine.

'— you,' he said.

At close quarters I could see how very young he was. His skin was still smooth like a child's and he had long thick eyelashes round those vast pale blue-grey searchlight eyes. His hair, a fairish brown, curled softly close to his head and down the back of his neck, cut short and in the shape of a helmet. He had a soft, full lipped mouth and a strong straight nose. A curiously sexless face. Too unlined to be clearly male, too heavily boned to be female.

He wasn't so much a man, not even so much a person, as a force. A wild, elemental, poltergeist force trapped barely controllably in a vigorous steel-spring body. You couldn't look into Billy's cold eyes from inches away and not know it. I felt a weird unexpected primitive tingle away down somewhere in my gut, and at the same time realised on a conscious level that friendliness and reason couldn't help, that there would be no winning over, ever, of Billy.

He began mildly enough.

'Your sort,' he yelled. 'You think you own the bloody earth. You soft lot of out-of-date nincompoops, you and your lah-di-dah bloody Eton.'

I didn't answer. He put his sneering face even nearer.

'Think yourself something special, don't you? You and your sodding ancestors.'

'They aren't very usual,' I yelled in his ear.

'What aren't?'

'Sodding ancestors.'

He had no sense of humour. He looked blank.

'You didn't spring from an acorn,' I said resignedly. 'You've had as many ancestors as I have.'

He stood up and took a step back. 'Bloody typical,' he shouted, 'making fun of people you look down on.'

I shook my head, got to my feet, and went along the plane to check the horses. I didn't care for useless arguments at the best of times, let alone those which strained the larynx. All four hurdlers were standing quiet in the boxes, picking peacefully at the haynets, untroubled by the noise. I patted their heads, made sure everything was secure, hesitated about going forward to the galley and cockpit for more friendly company, and had the matter settled for me by Billy.

'Hey,' he shouted. 'Look at this.' He was pointing downwards with one arm and beckoning me with sweeps of the other. There was anxiety on his face.

I walked back between the last box and the side wall of the aircraft, into the open space at the back, and across to Billy. As soon as I got near enough to see what he was pointing at, the anxiety on his face changed to spite.

'Look at this,' he shouted again, and jabbed his clenched fist straight at my stomach.

The only flicker of talent I had shown in a thoroughly mediocre and undistinguished career at Eton had been for boxing. I hadn't kept it up afterwards, but all the same the defence reflex was still there even after eight years. Billy's unexpected blow landed on a twisting target and my head did not go forward to meet a punch on the jaw. Or more likely in this case, I thought fleetingly, a chop on the back of the neck. Instead,

I gave him back as good as I got, a short hard jolt to the lower ribs. He was surprised, but it didn't stop him. Just the reverse. He seemed pleased.

There are better places for fighting than the back of an aircraft. The floor of that one was banded by the rows of seat anchorages, so that it was only a matter of time before one of us caught his foot in them and overbalanced, and it happened to be me, dodging away from a hand stretched at my throat. I went down flat on my back, unable to stop myself.

Billy fell deliberately and heavily on top of me, grinning fiercely with his own private pleasure, stabbing his elbows sharply into my chest and pressing me down hard on to the rigid anchorages. It hurt, and he meant it to. I kicked and rolled over, trying to get him underneath for a taste of it, but he was off like a cat at the crucial point and already aiming his boot as I stood up. I took that on the thigh and lunged accurately in return at his head. He just shook it briefly and went on punching, hard, quick, and with no respect for convention; but the pleasure left his face when he continued to get everything back with interest.

Thankful at least that he had produced no flick knife or bicycle chain I battled on, knowing in a cold detached part of my brain that I would gain nothing even if I won. Billy's resentment would be greater, not less, for being slogged by what he despised.

I did win in the end, if anyone did, but only because he had a belly full of beer and I hadn't. We were both very near to a standstill. I hit him finally very hard just below the navel, my fist sinking in deep, and he fell against the aft box retching and clutching himself and sliding down on to his knees. I caught hold of one of his wrists and twisted his arm up across his back.

'Now you listen, Billy,' I said loudly in his ear, panting to get enough breath, 'I don't see any point in fighting you, but I will if you make me. You can forget I'm an earl's son, Billy, and take me as I am, and this is what I am ...' I jerked his arm. 'Hard, Billy, not soft. As tough as necessary. Remember it.'

He didn't answer, perhaps because he was showing signs of being sick. I yanked him to his feet, pushed him across to the lavatory compartment in the tail, opened the door for him, and shoved him through. As the only lock was on the inside I couldn't make sure he stayed there, but from the sounds which presently issued from the open door, he was in no state to leave.

My own body ached from head to foot from his punches and kicks and from brisk contact with many sharp and knobbled edges, not least those spaced regularly on the floor. I sat down weakly on a straw bale and rubbed at a few places which didn't do much good, and was suddenly struck by something very odd indeed.

My face was completely unmarked.

I had bashed my head against one of the metal bars on the rear box and there was a tender swelling a little above my right ear. But Billy, I remembered dinstinctly, had not once even aimed at my face; not at any point higher than my throat.

For someone in the grip of obsessive fury, surely that was extraordinary,

I thought. The usual impulse in such a case was to 'smash his face in'. Billy had actually taken pains not to. I didn't understand why. I thought about it all the way to Cambridge.

It was dark when we landed and the cabin lights were on. The cheerful customs man made his way through the plane, raised his eyebrows, and asked where my two mates were.

'Billy is in there,' I nodded towards the lavatory, 'and John stayed in France. He said he was coming back tomorrow.'

'O.K.' He checked through the horses' papers perfunctorily. 'All clear,' he said, and as an afterthought: 'Buy anything?'

I shook my head, and he grinned, helped me open the double doors, and whistled away down the ramp as soon as it was in position.

Billy had locked himself into the lavatory and refused to come out, so I had to get one of the box drivers who had arrived to collect the cargo to help me unload the horses. Unloading was always quicker and easier than loading, but I had begun to stiffen up all over with bruises, and I was glad when it was done. The helpful box driver led out the last horse, an undistinguished brown mare, and before turning back to tidy up I watched them step and slither down the ramp. That mare, I thought idly, was very like the one we had taken across in the morning, though the rug she wore might be misleading. But it couldn't of course be the same. No one would ship a horse out in the morning and back in the afternoon.

I turned away and began slowly to stack the box sides and the bars, wished painfully that Billy hadn't been quite so rough, and forgot about it.

The following day I went down to the wharf building and hooked Simon out for a liquid lunch. We shambled down the road to the usual hideous pub and he buried his face in a pint like a camel at an oasis.

'That's better,' he said, sighing, when a scant inch remained. 'How did yesterday's trip go?'

'All right.'

His eyes considered me thoughtfully. 'Did you have a fall on Saturday?'

'No. A winner. Why?'

'You're moving a bit carefully, that's all.'

I grinned suddenly. 'You should see the other fellow.'

His face melted in comprehension and he laughed. 'I imagine I have,' he said. 'Billy has a sunset of a black eye.'

'You've seen him?' I was surprised.

Simon nodded. 'He was in the office this morning, talking to Yardman.'

'Getting his version in first, I suppose.'

'What happened?' he asked interestedly.

'Billy picked a fight.' I shrugged. 'He resents my existence. It's ridiculous. No one can help what his father is. You can't choose your birth.'

'You feel strongly about it,' Simon observed, ordering another pint. I shook my head to his invitation.

'So would you, if you had to live with it. I mostly get treated as a villain or a nit or a desirable match, and not much else.' I was exaggerating, but not unduly.

'That last doesn't sound too bad,' he grinned.

'You haven't had half the debs' mums in London trying to net you for their daughters,' I said gloomily, 'with your own mother egging them on.'

'It sounds a wow.' He had no sympathy for such a fate.

'It isn't me they want,' I pointed out. 'It's only my name. Which is no fun at all. And on the other end from the wedding ring I get bashed around for exactly the same reason.'

'Very few can feel as strongly as Billy.'

I looked at him. 'There were the French in seventeen eighty-nine, remember? And the Russians in nineteen-seventeen. They all felt as strongly as Billy.'

'The English like their aristocrats.'

'Don't you believe it. They don't mind them from the social point of view because titles make the scandal sheets juicier. But they make damn sure they have no effective power. They say we are a joke, an anachronism, out of date, and weak and silly. They pretend we are these things so that we are kept harmless, so that no one will take us seriously. Think of the modern attitude to the House of Lords, for example. And you – you still think it funny that I want this sort of job, but you wouldn't think so if my father was a ... a farmer, or a pubkeeper, or a school-master. But I'm me, here and now, a man of now, not of some dim glorious past. I am not an anachronism. I'm Henry Grey, conceived and born like everyone else, into this present world. Well, I insist on living in it. I am not going to be shoved off into an unreal playboy existence where my only function is to s're the next in line, which is what my parents want.'

'You could renounce your title, when you get it,' Simon pointed out calmly. He spotted a pin on the bar counter and absent-mindedly tucked it into his lapel. It was such a habit with him that he sported a whole row of them, like a dressmaker.

'I could,' I said, 'but I won't. The only good reason for doing that is to stay in the House of Commons, and I'll never be a politician, I'm not the type. Renouncing for any other reason would be just a retreat. What I want is for people to acknowledge that an earl is as good as the next man, and give him an equal chance.'

'But if you get on, they say it's because of your title, not because you have talent.'

'You are so right. But there's a prince or two, a few dukes' sons, and some others like me, all in the same boat just now, and I reckon that our generation, if we try hard enough, might in the end be treated on our own terms. Have some more beer.'

He laughed and agreed.

'I've never heard you say so much,' he said smiling.

'It's Billy's fault. Forget it.'

'I don't think I will.'

'You know something odd? I'm covered with bruises, and there isn't a single one on my face.'

He considered, drinking.

'He'd have got into trouble if he'd marked you for all to see.'

'I suppose so.'

'I gather you haven't told Yardman?'

'No.'

'Why not?'

I shrugged. 'I think he expected it, or something like it. He was ironic when he gave me the job. He must have known that sooner or later I would come up against Billy. And yesterday, he knew Billy would be after me. He warned me, in his way.'

'What are you going to do about it?'

'Nothing.'

'But what if you find yourself on another trip with Billy? I mean, you're bound to, sometime.'

'Yes, I know. Well, it's up to him entirely. I wouldn't start anything. I didn't yesterday. But I did tell him plainly that I'd fight back any time. And I am not, repeat *not*, leaving here because of him.'

'And you look so quiet and mild.' He smiled one-sidedly, looking down into his again empty glass. 'I think,' he said slowly, almost it seemed to me sadly, 'that one or two people in Yardman Transport have miscalculated about you, Henry.'

But when I pressed him to explain, he wouldn't.

With no more export trips to be flown until Thursday, I went the next day, Wednesday, to the races. Someone offered me a spare ride in the novice chase and for some reason it fretted me more than ever to have to refuse. 'I can't,' I said, explaining thoroughly so that he wouldn't think I was being rude. 'I'm only allowed to ride in fifty open races a season, and I'm already over the forty mark, and I've got mounts booked for Cheltenham and the Whitbread and so on. And if I ride too much now I'll be out of those, but thank you very much for asking me.'

He nodded understandingly and hurried off to find someone else, and in irritation two hours later I watched his horse canter home to a ten lengths win. It was some consolation, however, when immediately afterwards I was buttonholed by a large shrewd-faced man I knew very slightly, the father of another well occupied amateur jockey. Between them, father and son owned and trained half a dozen good hunter 'chasers which they ran only in amateur events with notoriously satisfactory results. But on this particular afternoon Mr. Thackery, a large-scale farmer from Shropshire, showed signs both of worry and indecision.

'Look,' he said, 'I'll not beat about the bush, I'm a blunt man, so I'm told. Now, what do you say to riding all my horses until the end of the season?'

I was astonished. 'But surely Julian . . . I mean, he hasn't had a bad fall or anything, has he?'

He shook his head. The worry stayed in place. 'Not a fall. He's got jaundice. Got it pretty badly, poor chap. He won't be fit again for weeks.

But we've a grand lot of horses this year and he won't hear of them not running just because he can't ride them. He told me to ask you, it's his idea.'

'It's very good of him,' I said sincerely. 'And thank you, I'd like to ride for you very much, whenever I can.'

'Good, then.' He hesitated, and added, 'Er . . . Julian told me to tell you, to ask you, if ten per cent of the prize money would be in order?'

'Thank you,' I said. 'That will be fine.'

He smiled suddenly, his heavy face lightening into wrinkles which made him look ten years younger. 'I wasn't sure about asking you, I'll tell you that, only Julian insisted on it. There's no nonsense about Henry, he said, and I can see he's right. He said Henry don't drink much, don't talk much, gets on with the job and expects to be paid for it. A pro at heart, he says you are. Do you want expenses?'

I shook my head. 'Ten per cent for winning. Nothing else.'

'Fair enough.' He thrust out his hand and I shook it.

'I'm sorry about Julian's jaundice,' I said.

Mr. Thackery's lips twitched. 'He said if you said that, that he hoped for the sake of our horses you were being hypocritical.'

'Oh, subtle stuff.' I pondered. 'Tell him to get up too soon and have a relapse.'

The next afternoon I went on a flight to New York.

With Billy.

The ice between us was as cold as the rarefied air outside the pressurized stratocruiser which took us. Yardman, I reflected, wasn't showing much sense in pushing us off together so soon, and on a two-day journey at that.

The wide cold stare was somewhat marred by the blackish streaks and yellow smudges left by my fist, and Billy was distinctly warier than he had been on the French journeys. There were no elementary taunts this time; but at the end of everything he said to me he tacked on the words 'Lord Grey,' and made them sound like an insult.

He tried nothing so crude as punching to make my trip memorable; instead he smashed down one of the metal bars as I was fixing a guy chain during the loading. I looked up angrily, squeezing four squashed right fingers in my left hand, and met his watchful waiting eyes. He was looking down at me with interest, with faintly sneering calculation, to see what I would do.

If anyone else had dropped the bar, I would have known it was accidental. With Billy, apart from the force with which it had landed, I knew it wasn't. But the day had barely begun, and the cargo was much too valuable to jeopardise for personal reasons, which I dare say he was counting on. When he saw that I was not going to retaliate, or at least not instantly, he nodded in satisfaction, picked up the bar with a small cold private smile, and calmly began putting it into place.

The loading was finished and the plane took off. There were thick dark red marks across my fingers an inch below the nails, and they throbbed all the way to America.

With us on that trip, looking after a full load of twelve horses, we took two other grooms, an elderly deaf one supplied by Yardman, and another man travelling privately with one particular horse. Owners occasionally sent their own grooms instead of entrusting their valued or difficult animals entirely to Yardman's, and far from resenting it I had learned from Timmie and Conker to be glad of the extra help.

The horse involved on this occasion had come from Norway, stayed in England overnight, and was bound for a racing stable in Virginia. The new owner had asked for the Norwegian groom to go all the way, at his expense, so that the horse should have continuous care on the journey. It didn't look worth it, I reflected, looking over at it idly while I checked the horses in the next box. A weak-necked listless chestnut, it had a straggle of hair round the fetlocks which suggested there had been a cart horse not far enough back in its ancestry, and the acute-angled hocks didn't have the best conformation for speed. Norway was hardly famed for the quality of its racing any more, even though it was possibly the Vikings who had invented the whole sport. They placed heaps of valued objects (the prizes) at varying distances from the starting point: then all the competitors lined up, and with wild whoops the race began. The prizes nearest the start were the smallest, the furthest away, the richest, so each rider had to decide what suited his mount best, a quick sprint or a shot at stamina. Choosing wrong meant getting no prize at all. Twelve hundred years ago fast sturdy racing horses had been literally worth a fortune in Norway, but the smooth skinned long legged descendants of those tough shaggy ponies didn't count for much in the modern thoroughbred industry. It was sentiment, I supposed, which caused an American to pay for such an inferior looking animal to travel so far from home.

I asked the middle-aged Norwegian groom if he had everything he wanted, and he said, in halting, heavily accented English, that he was content. I left him sitting on his hay bale staring mindlessly into space, and went on with my rounds. The horses were all travelling quietly, munching peacefully at their haynets, oblivious to rocketing round the world at six hundred miles an hour. There is no sensation of speed if you can't see an environment rushing past.

We arrived without incident at Kennedy airport, where a gum-chewing customs man came on board with three helpers. He spoke slowly, every second word an 'uh', but he was sharply thorough with the horses. All their papers were in order however, and we began the unloading without more ado. There was the extra job of leading all the horses through a tray of disinfectant before they could set foot on American soil, and while I was seeing to it I heard the customs man asking the Norwegian groom about a work permit, and the halting reply that he was staying for a fortnight only, for a holiday, the kindness of the man who owned the horse.

It was the first time I too had been to the States, and I envied him his fortnight. Owing to the five hours time difference, it was only six in the evening, local time, when we landed at Kennedy, and we were due to leave again at six next morning; which gave me about nine free hours in which to see New York. Although to my body mechanism it was already bedtime, I didn't waste any of them in sleeping.

The only snag to this was having to start another full day's work with eyes requiring matchsticks. Billy yawned over making the boxes as much as I did and only the third member of the team, the deaf elderly Alf, had had any rest. Since even if one shouted he could hear very little, the three of us worked in complete silence like robots, isolated in our own thoughts, with gaps as unbridgeable between us as between like poles of magnets. Unlike poles attract, like poles repel. Billy and I were a couple of cold Norths.

There was a full load going back again, as was usual on Yardman trips from one continent to another. He hated wasting space, and was accustomed to telephone around the studs when a long flight was on the books, to find out if they had anything to send or collect. The customers all liked it, for on full long distance loads Yardman made a reduction in the fares. Timmie and Conker had less cheerful views of this practice, and I now saw why. One's body didn't approve of tricks with the clock. But at the point of no return way out over the Atlantic I shed my drowsiness in one leaping heartbeat, and with horror had my first introduction to a horse going berserk in mid-air.

Old Alf shook my shoulder, and the fright in his face brought me instantly to my feet. I went where he pointed, up towards the nose of the aircraft.

In the second to front box a solidly muscled three-year-old colt had pulled his head collar to pieces and was standing free and untied in the small wooden square. He had his head down, his forelegs straddled, and he was kicking out with his hind feet in a fixed, fearful rhythm. White foamy sweat stood out all over him, and he was squealing. The companion beside him was trying in a terrified way to escape, his eyes rolling and his body pushing hard against the wooden side of the box.

The colt's hooves thudded against the back wall of the box like battering rams. The wooden panels shook and rattled and began to splinter. The metal bars banding the sides together strained at the corner lynch pins, and it only needed one to break for the whole thing to start disintegrating.

I found the co-pilot at my elbow, yelling urgently.

'Captain says how do you expect him to fly the aircraft with all this thumping going on. He says to keep that horse still, it's affecting the balance.'

'How?' I asked.

'That's your affair,' he pointed out. 'And for God's sake do something about it quickly.'

The back wall of the colt's box cracked from top to bottom. The pieces were still held in place by the guy chains, but at the present rate they wouldn't hold more than another minute, and then we should have on our minds a maddened animal loose in a pressurised aircraft with certain death to us all if he got a hoof through a window.

'Have you got a humane killer on board?' I said.

'No. This is usually a passenger craft. Why don't you bring your own?'

There were no rules to say one had to take a humane killer in animal transport. There should be. But it was too late to regret it.

'We've got drugs in the first aid kit,' the co-pilot suggested.

I shook my head. 'They're unpredictable. Just as likely to make him worse.' It might even have been a tranquilliser which started him off, I thought fleetingly. They often backfired with horses. And it would be quite impossible in any case to inject even a safe drug through a fine needle designed for humans into a horse as wild as this.

'Get a carving knife or something from the galley,' I said. 'Anything long and sharp. And quick.'

He turned away, stumbling in his haste. The colt's hind feet smashed one broken half of the back wall clean out. He turned round balefully, thrust his head between the top and centre banding bars, and tried to scramble through. The panic in his eyes was pitiful.

From inside his jerkin Billy calmly produced a large pistol and pointed it towards the colt's threshing head.

'Don't be a bloody fool,' I shouted. 'We're thirty thousand feet up.'

The co-pilot came back with a white handled saw-edged bread knife, saw the gun, and nearly fainted.

'D . . . don't,' he stuttered. 'D . . . d . . . don't.'

Billy's eyes were very wide. He was looking fixedly at the heaving colt and hardly seemed to hear. All his mind seemed to be concentrated on aiming the gun that could kill us all.

The colt smashed the first of the lynch pins and lunged forwards, bursting out of the remains of the box like flood water from a dam. I snatched the knife from the co-pilot and as the horse surged towards me stuck the blade into the only place available, the angle where the head joined the neck.

I hit by some miracle the carotid artery. But I couldn't get out of his way afterwards. The colt came down solidly on top of me, pouring blood, flailing his legs and rolling desperately in his attempts to stand up again.

His mane fell in my mouth and across my eyes, and his heaving weight crushed the breath in and out of my lungs like some nightmare form of artificial respiration. He couldn't right himself over my body, and as his struggles weakened he eventually got himself firmly wedged between the remains of his own box and the one directly aft of it. The co-pilot bent down and put his hands under my arm-pits and in jerks dragged me out from underneath.

The blood went on pouring out, hot sticky gallons of it, spreading down the gangways in scarlet streams. Alf cut open one of the hay bales and began covering it up, and it soaked the hay into a sodden crimson brown mess. I don't know how many pints of blood there should be in a horse: the colt bled to death and his heart pumped out nearly every drop.

My clothes were soaked in it, and the sweet smell made me feel sick. I stumbled down the plane into the lavatory compartment and stripped to the skin, and washed myself with hands I found to be helplessly trembling. The door opened without ceremony, and the co-pilot thrust a pair of trousers and a sweater into my arms. His overnight civvies.

'Here,' he said. 'Compliments of the house.'

I nodded my thanks, put them on, and went back up the plane, soothing the restive frightened cargo on the way.

The co-pilot was arguing with Billy about whether Billy would really have pulled the trigger and Billy was saying a bullet from a revolver wouldn't make a hole in a metal aircraft. The co-pilot cursed, said you couldn't risk it, and mentioned richochets and glass windows. But what I wanted to know, though I didn't ask, was what was Billy doing carrying a loaded pistol round with him in an underarm holster as casually as a wallet.

Chapter Five

I slept like the dead when I finally got home, and woke with scant time the next morning to reach Kempton for the amateurs' chase. After such a mangling week I thought it highly probable I would crown the lot by falling off the rickety animal I had in a weak moment promised to ride. But though I misjudged where it was intending to take off at the last open ditch and practically went over the fence before it while it put in an unexpected short one, I did in fact cling sideways like a limpet to the saddle, through sheer disinclination to hit the ground.

Though I scrambled back on top, my mount, who wouldn't have won anyway, had lost all interest, and I trotted him back and apologised to his cantankerous owner, who considered I had spoilt his day and was churlish enough to say so. As he outranked my father by several strawberry leaves he clearly felt he had the right to be as caustic as he chose. I listened to him saying I couldn't ride in a cart with a pig-net over it and wondered how he treated the professionals.

Julian Thackery's father caught the tail end of these remarks as he was passing, and looked amused: and when I came out of the weighing room after changing he was leaning against the rails waiting for me. He had brought the list of entries of his horses, and at his suggestion we adjourned to the bar to discuss them. He bought me some lemon squash without a quiver, and we sat down at a small table on which he spread out several sheets of paper. I realised, hearing him discussing his plans and prospects, that the year by year success of his horses was no accident: he was a very able man.

'Why don't you take out a public licence?' I said finally.

'Too much worry,' he smiled. 'This way it's a hobby. If I make mistakes, I have no one on my conscience. No one to apologise to or smooth down. No need to worry about owners whisking their horses away at an hour's notice. No risk of them not paying my fees for months on end.'

'You know the snags,' I agreed dryly.

'There's no profit in training,' he said. 'I break even most years, maybe finish a little ahead. But I work the stable in with the farm, you see. A lot of the overheads come into the farm accounts. I don't see how half these public trainers stay in business, do you? They either have to be rich to start with, or farmers like me, or else they have to bet, if they want a profit.'

'But they don't give it up,' I pointed out mildly. 'And they all drive large cars. They can't do too badly.'

He shook his head and finished his whisky. 'They're good actors, some of them. They put on a smiling not-a-care-in-the-world expression at the races when they've got the bank manager camping on their door-step back home. Well, now,' he shuffled the papers together, folded them, and tucked them into a pocket. 'You think you can get next Thursday off to go to Stratford?'

'I'm pretty sure of it, yes.'

'Right. I'll see you there, then.'

I nodded and we stood up to go. Someone had left an *Evening Standard* on the next table, and I glanced at it casually as we passed. Then I stopped and went back for a closer look. A paragraph on the bottom of the front page started 'Derby Hope Dead,' and told a few bald words that Okinawa, entered for the Derby, had died on the flight from the United States, and was consequently scratched from all engagements.

I smiled inwardly. From the lack of detail or excitement, it was clear the report had come from someone like the trainer to whom Okinawa had been travelling, not from airport reporters sniffing a sensational story. No journalist who had seen or even been told of the shambles on that plane could have written so starkly. But the horse had been disposed of now, and I had helped wash out the plane myself, and there was nothing to see any more. Okinawa had been well insured, a vet had certified that destroying him was essential, and I had noticed that my name on the crew list was spelled wrongly; H. Gray. With a bit of luck, and if Yardman himself had his way, that was the end of it. 'My dear boy,' he'd said in agitation when hurriedly summoned to the airport, 'it does business no good to have horses go crazy on our flights. We will not broadcast it, will we?'

'We will not,' I agreed firmly, more for my sake than for his.

'It was unfortunate . .' he sighed and shrugged, obviously relieved.

'We should have a humane killer,' I said, striking the hot iron.

'Yes. Certainly. All right. I'll get one.'

I would hold him to that, I thought. Standing peacefully in the bar at Kempton I could almost feel the weight of Okinawa and the wetness of his blood, the twenty-four hour old memory of lying under a dying horse still much too vivid for comfort. I shook myself firmly back into the present and went out with Julian's father to watch a disliked rival ride a brilliant finish.

Saturday night I did my level best to be civil to Mother's youngest female week-end guest, while avoiding all determined manoeuvres to leave me alone with her, and Sunday morning I slid away before dawn northwards to Lincolnshire.

Tom Wells was out on the apron when I arrived, giving his planes a personal check. He had assigned me, as I had learned on the telephone the previous morning, to fly three men to Glasgow for a round of golf. I was to take them in an Aztec and do exactly what they wanted. They were good customers. Tom didn't want to lose them.

'Good-morning, Harry,' he said as I reached him. 'I've given you Quebec Bravo. You planned your route?'

I nodded.

'I've put scotch and champagne on board, in case they forget to bring any,' he said. 'You're fetching them from Coventry – you know that – and taking them back there. They may keep you late at Gleneagles until after dinner. I'm sorry about that.'

'Expensive game of golf,' I commented.

'Hm,' he said shortly. 'That's an alibi. They are three tycoons who like to compare notes in private. They stipulate a pilot who won't repeat what he hears, and I reckon you fit that bill, Harry my lad, because you've been coming here for four years and if a word of gossip has passed your lips in that time I'm a second class gas fitter's mate.'

'Which you aren't.'

'Which I'm not.' He smiled, a pleasant solid sturdy man of forty plus, a pilot himself who knew chartering backwards and ran his own little firm with the minimum of fuss. Ex-R.A.F., of course, as most flyers of his age were: trained on bombers, given a love for the air, and let down with a bang when the service chucked them out as redundant. There were too many pilots chasing too few jobs in the post-war years, but Tom Wells had been good, persistent and lucky, and had converted a toe-hole co-pilot's job in a minor private airline into a seat on the board, and finally, backed by a firm of light aircraft manufacturers, had started his present company on his own.

'Give me a ring when you're leaving Gleneagles,' he said, 'I'll be up in the Tower myself when you come back.'

'I'll try not to keep you too late.'

'You won't be the last.' He shook his head. 'Joe Wilkins is fetching three couples from a week-end in Le Touquet. A dawn job, that'll be, I shouldn't wonder . . .'

I picked up the three impressive business men as scheduled and conveyed them to Scotland. On the way up they drank Tom Wells' Black and White and talked about dividend equalisation reserves, unappropriated profits, and contingent liabilities: none of which I found in the least bit interesting. They moved on to exports and the opportunities available in the European market. There was some discussion about 'whether the one and three-quarters was any positive inducement,' which was the only point of their conversation I really understood.

The one and three quarters, as I had learned at Anglia Bloodstock, was a percentage one could claim from the Government on anything one sold for export. The three tycoons were talking about machine tools and soft drinks, as far as I could gather, but the mechanism worked for bloodstock also. If a stud sold a horse abroad for say twenty thousand pounds, it received not only that sum from the buyer, but also one and three quarters per cent of it – three hundred and fifty pounds – from the Government. A carrot before the export donkey. A bonus. A pat on the head for helping the country's economy. In effect, it did influence some studs to prefer foreign buyers. But racehorses were simple to export: they needed no after sales service, follow-up campaign or multi-lingual advertising, which the tycoons variously argued were or were not worth the trouble. Then they moved on to taxation and I lost them again, the more so as they were some lowish clouds ahead over the Cheviots and at their request I was flying them below three thousand feet so that they could see the countryside.

I went up above the cloud into the quadrantal system operating above three thousand feet, where to avoid collision one had to fly on a steady regulated level according to the direction one was heading: in our case, going north west, four thousand five hundred or six thousand five hundred or eight thousand five hundred, and so on up.

One of the passengers commented on the climb and asked the reason for it, and wanted to know my name.

'Grey.'

'Well, Grey, where are we off to? Mars?'

I smiled. 'High hills, low clouds.'

'My God,' said the weightiest and oldest tycoon, patting me heavily on the shoulder, 'What wouldn't I give for such succinctness in my boardroom.'

They were in good form, enjoying their day as well as making serious use of it. The smell of whisky in the warm luxurious little cabin overcame even that of hot oil, and the expensive cigar smoke swirled huskily in my throat. I enjoyed the journey, and for Tom's sake as well as my own pride, knowing my passengers were connoisseurs of private air travel, put them down on the Gleneagles strip like a whisper on a lake.

They played golf and drank and ate; and repeated the programme in the afternoon. I walked on the hills in the morning, had lunch, and in the late afternoon booked a room in the hotel, and went to sleep. I guess it was a satisfactory day all round.

It was half past ten when the reception desk woke me by telephone and said my passengers were ready to leave, and eleven before we got away. I flew back on a double dogleg, making for the St. Abbs radio beacon on the Northumberland coast and setting a course of one sixty degrees south south east from there on a one five two nautical mile straight course to Ottringham, and then south west across country to Coventry, coming in finally on their 122.70 homer signal.

The tycoons, replete, talked in mellow, rumbling, satisfied voices, no longer about business but about their own lives. The heaviest was having trouble over currency regulations with regard to a villa he had bought on the Costa del Sol: the government had slapped a two thousand pound ceiling on pleasure spending abroad, and two thousand would hardly buy the bath taps . . .

The man sitting directly behind me asked about decent yachts available for charter in the Aegean, and the other two told him. The third said it was really time his wife came back from Gstaad, she had been there for two months, and they were due to go to Nassau for Easter. They made me feel poverty-stricken, listening to them.

We landed safely at Coventry, where they shook my hand, yawning, thanked me for a smooth trip, and ambled off to a waiting Rolls, shivering in the chilly air. I made the last small hop back to Fenland and found Tom, as good as his word on duty in the control tower to help me down. He yelled out of the window to join him, and we drank coffee out of a thermos jug while he waited for his Le Touquet plane to come back. It was due in an hour: earlier than expected. Apparently the client had struck a losing streak and the party had fizzled out.

'Everything go all right with your lot?' Tom said.

'They seemed happy,' I nodded, filling in the flight details on his record chart and copying them into my own log book.

'I suppose you want your fee in flying hours, as usual?'

I grinned. 'How did you guess?'

'I wish you'd change your mind and work for me permanently.'

I put down the pen and stretched, lolling back on the wooden chair with my hands laced behind my head. 'Not yet. Give it three or four years; perhaps then.'

'I need you now.'

Need. The word was sweet. 'I don't know . . . I'll think it over again, anyway.'

'Well, that's something I suppose.' He ruffled his thinning light brown hair and rubbed his hands down over his face, his skin itching with tiredness. 'Sandwich?'

'Thanks.' I took one. Ham, with French mustard, made in their bungalow by Tom's capable wife Janie, not from the airport canteen. The ham was thick and juicy, home cooked in beer. We ate in silence and drank the hot strong coffee. Outside the glass-walled high up square room the sky grew a thick matt black, with clouds drifting in to mask the stars. The wind was slowly backing, the atmospheric pressure falling. It was getting steadily colder. Bad weather on its way.

Tom checked his instruments, frowned, leaned back on his chair and twiddled his pencil. 'The forecast was right,' he said gloomily, 'Snow tomorrow.'

I grunted sympathetically. Snow grounded his planes and caused a hiatus in his income.

'Have to expect it in February, I suppose,' he sighed.

I nodded in agreement. I wondered if Stratford races would be snowed off on Thursday. I wondered if weather interfered much with Yardman's trips. I reflected that Janie Wells made good coffee, and that Tom was a sound sensible man. Untroubled, organised surface thoughts. And it was the last night I ever spent in my calm emotional deep-freeze.

The sky was a sullen orange grey when we took off at eight the next morning from Gatwick, the as yet unshed snow hanging heavily as spawn in a frog's belly. We were carrying eight brood mares in an old unpressurised D.C.4, flying away from the incoming storm, en route to Milan. Timmie and Conker were back to my relief, but neither had had a scintillating holiday, by the sound of it. I overheard Conker, a much harassed small father of seven large hooligans, complaining as he loaded the cargo that he'd done nothing but cook and wash up while his wife curled up in bed with what was, in his opinion, opportunist malingering influenza. Timmie showed his sympathy in his usual way: a hearty gear-changing sniff. A thick-set black haired square little Welshman, he suffered from interminable catarrh and everyone around him suffered also. It had been his sinuses, he unrepentantly said after one particularly repulsive spitting session, which had stopped him going down the mines like his pa. The February holiday, Timmie agreed, was not much cop.

'How many holidays do you have?' I asked, fixing chains.

'A week off every two months,' Conker said. 'Blimey mate, don't tell me you took this job without asking that.'

'I'm afraid I did.'

'You'll be exploited,' Conker said seriously. 'When you start a job, you want your terms cut and dried, wages, overtime, holidays with pay, bonuses, superannuation, the lot. If you don't stand up for your rights, no one else will, there isn't a union for us, you know, bar the agricultural workers, if you care for that which I don't. And old Yardman, he don't give nothing away you know. You want to make sure about your weeks off, mate, or you won't get any. I'm telling you.'

'Well . . . thank you. I'll ask him.'

'Aw, look man,' said Timmie in his soft Welsh voice, 'We get other times off too. You don't want to work yourself to death. Mr. Yardman don't hold you to more than two trips a week, I'll say that for him. If you don't want to go, that is.'

'I see,' I said. 'And if you don't go, Billy and Alf do?'

'That's about it,' agreed Conker. 'I reckon.' He fitted the last lynch pin on the last box and rubbed his hands down the sides of his trousers.

I remembered Simon saying that my predecessor Peters had been a belligerent stand-on-your-rights man, and I supposed that Conker had caught his anti-exploitation attitude from him, because it seemed to me, from what they'd said, that Conker and Timmie both had free time positively lavished up them. A day's return trip certainly meant working a continuous stretch of twelve hours or more, but two of those in seven days wasn't exactly penal servitude. Out of interest I had added up my hours on duty some weeks, and even at the most they had never touched forty. They just don't know when they are well off, I thought mildly, and signalled to the airport staff to take the ramp away.

The D.C.4 was noisy and very cramped. The gangways between and alongside the horses were too narrow for two people to pass, and in addition one had to go forward and backward along the length of the plane bent almost double. It was, as usual, normally a passenger ship, and it had low-hung luggage shelves along its length on both sides. There were catches to hold the racks up out of the way, but they were apt to shake open in flight and it was more prudent to start with all the racks down than have them fall on one's head. This, added to the angled guy chains cutting across at shin level, made walking about a tiresome process and provided the worst working conditions I had yet struck. But Conker, I was interested to notice, had no complaints. Peters, maybe, hadn't been with him on a D.C.4.

After take-off, the horses all being quiet and well behaved, we went forward into the galley for the first cup of coffee. The engineer, a tall thin man with a habit of raising his right eyebrow five or six times rather fast when he asked a question, was already dispensing it into disposable mugs. Two full ones had names pencilled on: Patrick and Bob. The engineer picked them up and took them forward to the pilot and co-pilot in the cockpit. Coming back, the engineer asked our names and wrote us each a mug.

'There aren't enough on board for us to throw them away every time,' he explained, handing me 'Henry'. 'Sugar?' He had a two-pound bag of granulated, and a red plastic spoon. 'I know the way you lot drink coffee. The skipper, too.'

We drank the scalding brown liquid: it didn't taste of coffee, but if you thought of it as a separate unnamed thirst quencher, it wasn't too bad. In the galley the engine noise made it necessary to shout loudly to be heard, and the vibration shook concentric ripples in the coffee. The engineer sipped his gingerly over the scrawled word 'Mike'.

'You've got a right load there,' he commented. 'A ship full of expectant mums, aren't they?'

Conker, Timmie and I nodded in unison.

'Are they Italian?'

Together we shook our heads. Music hall stuff.

'What are they going for, then?'

'They are English mares going to be mated with Italian sires,' explained Conker, who had once worked in a stud and would be positively happy if one of the mares foaled down prematurely on the flight.

'Pull the other one, it's got bells on,' said the engineer.

'No, it's right,' said Conker. 'They have to have the foals they are carrying now in the stud where their next mate is.'

'Why?' The agile eyebrow worked overtime.

'Ah,' said Conker seriously. 'The gestation period for horses is eleven months, right? And a brood mare has a foal every twelve months, right? So there's only four weeks left between production and – er – reproduction, do you see? And in those four weeks the new foal isn't fit for travelling hundreds of miles in the freezing cold, so the mares have to have the foals in the stud of their next mate, Get?'

'I get,' agreed the engineer. 'I get indeed.'

'That one,' said Conker admiringly, pointing out in the foremost box an elegant brown silky head which owing to the general lack of space was almost in the galley, 'that one's going to Molvedo.'

'How do you know?' asked Timmie interestedly.

'Horse box driver told me.'

The co-pilot came back from the cockpit and said the skipper wanted a refill.

'Already? That man's a tank.' The engineer poured into the Patrick mug.

'Here,' said the co-pilot, handing it to me. 'Take it to him, will you? I'm off to see a man about a dog.' He brushed under Molvedo's future wife's inquisitive nose and bent down for the obstructed walk down to the john.

I took the steaming mug forward into the cockpit. The pilot, flying in white-than-white shirtsleeves despite the zero temperature outside, stretched out a languid hand and nodded his thanks. I stayed for a second looking round at the banked instruments, and he glanced up at me and gestured to me to put my ear down to his mouth. The noise there made even ordinary shouting impossible.

'Are you the head chap with the horses?'

'Yes.'

'Like to sit there for a bit?' He pointed to the empty co-pilot's seat.

'Yes, I would.' He gestured permissively, and I edged sideways into the comfortable bucket seat beside him. The cockpit was tiny, considering how much had to be packed into it, and battered and dented with age. It was also, to me, very much my home.

I studied the instruments with interest. I had never flown a four engined craft, only one and two, for the excellent reason that there were no four engined planes at Fenland. As even small two engined jobs like the Aztec I had taken to Gleneagles the day before cost nearly thirty-five pounds per flying hour to hire from Tom, I thought it unlikely I would ever raise enough cash for a course on the really big stuff, even if I could use the qualification once I got it. You couldn't just go up alone for an afternoon's jolly in an airliner: they simply weren't to be had. None of which stopped me for a moment being intent on learning everything I could.

The pilot, Patrick, indicated that I should put on the combined set of earphones and mouthpiece which was hanging over the semi-circular wheel. I slid it on to my head, and through it he began to explain to me what all the switches and dials were for. He was the first pilot I'd flown with on Yardman's trips who had taken such trouble, and I listened and nodded and felt grateful, and didn't tell him I knew already most of what he was saying.

Patrick was a big striking looking man of about thirty, with straight dark auburn hair cut a bit theatrically in duck tails, and light amber eyes like a cat. His mouth turned naturally up at the corners so that even in repose he seemed to be smiling, as if everything in the world was delightful, with no evil to be found anywhere. Nor, I later proved, did the implication of that curve lie: he persisted in believing the best of everybody, even with villainy staring him in the face. He had the illogical faith in human goodness of a probation officer, though in that first half-hour all I learned about him was that he was a gentle, careful, self-assured and eminently safe pilot.

He tuned in to the frequency of the radio beacon at Dieppe, explaining it to me as he went, and took a weather report there before turning on to the course to Paris.

'We'll go down to the Med and fly along the coast,' he said. 'There's too much cloud over the Alps to go straight across. Not being pressurised we ought not to go above ten thousand feet but fourteen thousand or so doesn't hurt unless you've got a bad heart. Even that doesn't give us enough in hand over the Alps in the present conditions, so I'm going the long way round.'

I nodded, thoroughly approving.

He checked the de-icing equipment for a second time in ten minutes and said, 'This bird won't fly with more than a quarter of a ton of ice on her, and the de-icers were U.S. last week.' He grinned. 'It's O.K., I've checked them six times since they were repaired, they're doing all right.'

He peeled and ate one of a large bunch of bananas lying on the ledge over the instrument panel, then calmly unhinged the window beside him a few inches and threw the skin out. I laughed to myself in appreciation and began to like Patrick a good deal.

The co-pilot returned to claim his place, and I went back to the horses for the rest of the journey. Uneventfully we went down across France to Dijon, turned south down the Rhone valley, east at Saint Tropez, and north again at Albenga, landing at Malpensa Airport, Milan, in exactly four hours from Gatwick.

Italy was cold. Shivering as the open doors let in air thirty degrees below the cabin temperature we watched about ten airport men in royal blue battle dress push the wide top-class ramp into position, and waited while three customs men made their way over from the building. They came up the ramp, and the eldest of them said something in his own language.

'Non parlo italiano,' I said apologetically, which useful sentence was all I knew.

'Non importa,' he said. He took from me the mares' temporary import permits which had been made out in both English and Italian, and his two assistants began going from horse to horse calling out their descriptions.

All was in order. He gave me back the papers with a courteous nod of the head, and led his shadows away down the ramp. Again we went through the familiar routine of transferring the cargo from the plane to the waiting horse boxes, Conker making a great fuss of the mare going to Molvedo.

With an hour to spare before we set about loading another cargo of mares bound in the opposite direction for the same reason, Conker, Timmie and I walked across a quarter of a mile of tarmac to the airport building to have lunch. We were met at the door by Patrick, looking very official with gold-braided shoulder tabs on his navy uniform jacket, and wearing an expression of resignation.

'We can't go back today.' he said, 'so you chaps don't need to hurry over your beer.'

'What's up, then?' asked Timmie, sniffing loudly.

'A blizzard. Came down like a burst eiderdown in a wind tunnel after we left this morning. It's raging all over the south and half-way across the channel, and snowing clear up to John o' Groats. The bottom's dropped out of the barometer and . . . well, anyway, my instructions are not to go back.'

'All that pasta,' said Conker philosophically. 'It does my tripes no good.'

He and Timmie went off to the snack bar and Patrick showed me the telegraph office to send 'no go' messages to Yardman and the expectant studs. After that we went back to the aircraft, where he collected his overnight bag and I turned homewards the arriving convoy of Italian mares. He waited for me to finish and helped me shut the big double doors from inside at the top of the ramp, and we walked forward across the flattened dismantled boxes, through the galley, and down the staircase which had been wheeled up to the door just behind the cockpit.

'Where will you stay?' he said.

'Hotel, I suppose,' I said vaguely.

'If you like, you could come with me. There's a family in Milan I berth with when I'm stranded, and there's room for two.'

I had a strong inclination, as usual, to be by myself, but principally because I couldn't even ask for a hotel room in Italian let alone find entertainment except looking at architecture for the rest of the day, I accepted his offer, and thanked him.

'You'll like them,' he said.

We went two hundred yards in silence.

'Is it true,' he said, 'that you're a viscount?'

'No,' I said casually. 'A Boeing 707.'

He chuckled. 'A bleeding viscount, that little Welshman said you were, to be precise.'

'Would it make any difference to you if I were?'

'None whatever.'

'That's all right, then.'

'So you are?'

'On and off.'

We went through the glass doors into the hall of the airport. It was spacious, airy, glass-walled, stone floored. Along one side stretched a long gift counter with souvenir presents crowded in a row of display cases and stacked on shelves at the back. There were silk ties on a stand, and dolls in local dress scattered on the counter, and trays of paper-backed books and local view post-cards. In charge of this display stood a tall dark-haired girl in a smooth black dress. She saw us coming and her coolly solemn face lit into a delicious smile.

'Patrick,' she said. 'Hullo, Patrick, come sta?'

He answered her in Italian, and as an afterthought waved his hand at me and said 'Gabriella, . . . Henry.' He asked her a question, and she looked at me carefully and nodded.

'Si,' she said. 'Henry anche.'

'That's fixed, then,' said Patrick cheerfully.

'You mean,' I said incredulously, 'that we are going to stay with – er – Gabriella?'

He stiffened slightly. 'Do you object?'

I looked at Gabriella, and she at me.

'I think,' I said slowly, 'that it is too good to be true.'

It wasn't for another ten minutes, during which time she talked to Patrick while looking at me, that I realised that I spoke no Italian and the only English word that she knew was 'Hullo'.

Chapter Six

You couldn't say it was reasonable, it was just electric. I found out between one heartbeat and the next what all the poets throughout the ages had been going on about. I understood at last why Roman Anthony threw away his honour for Egyptian Cleopatra, why Trojan Paris caused a ten years war abducting Greek Helen, why Leander drowned on one of his risky nightly swims across the Dardanelles to see Hero. The distance from home, the mystery, the unknownness, were a part of it: one couldn't feel like that for the girl next door. But that didn't explain why it hadn't happened before: why it should be this girl, this one alone who fizzed in my blood.

I stood on the cool stone airport floor and felt as if I'd been struck by lightning: the world had tilted, the air was crackling, the grey February day blazed with light, and all because of a perfectly ordinary girl who sold souvenirs to tourists.

The same thing, fantastically, had happened to her as well. Perhaps it had to be mutual, to happen at all. I don't know. But I watched the brightness grow in her eyes, the excitement and gaiety in her manner, and I knew that against all probability it was for me. Girls were seldom moved to any emotion by my brown haired tidy unobtrusive self, and since I rarely set out to make an impression on them, I even more rarely did so. Even the ones who wanted to marry my title were apt to yawn in my face. Which made Gabriella's instant reaction doubly devastating.

'For God's sake,' said Patrick in amusement, when she didn't answer a twice repeated question, 'will you two stop gawping at each other?'

'Gabriella,' I said.

'Si?'

'Gabriella . . .'

Patrick laughed. 'You're not going to get far like that.'

'Parla francese?' she said anxiously.

Patrick translated. 'Do you speak French.'

'Yes.' I laughed with relief. 'Yes, more or less.'

'E bene,' she sighed smiling. 'E molto molto bene.'

Perhaps because we were unburdened by having to observe any French proprieties and because we both knew already that we would need it later on, we began right away using the intimate form tu instead of vous, for 'you'. Patrick raised his eyebrows and laughed again and said in three languages that we were nuts.

I *was* nuts, there was no getting away from it. Patrick endured the whole afternoon sitting at a table in the snack bar drinking coffee and telling me about Gabriella and her family. We could see her from where we sat, moving quietly about behind her long counter, selling trinkets to departing travellers. She was made of curves, which after all the flat hips, flat stomachs, and more or less flat chests of the skinny debs at home, was as warming as a night-watchman's fire on a snowy night. Her oval pale olive-skinned face reminded me of mediaeval Italian paintings, a type of bone structure which must have persisted through centuries, and her expression, except when she smiled, was so wholly calm as to be almost unfriendly.

It struck me after a while, when I watched her make two or three self-conscious customers nervous by her detached manner, that selling wasn't really suited to her character, and I said so, idly, to Patrick.

'I agree,' he said dryly. 'But there are few places better for a smuggler to work than an airport.'

'A . . . *smuggler?* I don't believe it.' I was aghast.

Patrick enjoyed his effect. 'Smuggler,' he nodded. 'Definitely.'

'No,' I said.

'So am I,' he added smiling.

I looked down at my coffee, very disturbed. 'Neither of you is the type.'

'You're wrong, Henry. I'm only one of many who brings . . . er . . . goods . . . in to Gabriella.'

'What,' I said slowly, fearing the answer, 'are the goods?'

He put his hand into his jacket pocket, pulled out a flat bottle about five inches high, and handed it to me. A printed chemist's label on the front said 'Two hundred aspirin tablets B.P.', and the brown glass bottle was filled to the brim with them. I unscrewed the top, pulled out the twist of cotton wool, and shook a few out on to my hand.

'Don't take one,' said Patrick, still smiling. 'It wouldn't do you any good at all.'

'They're not aspirins.' I tipped them back into the bottle and screwed on the cap.

'No.'

'Then what?'

'Birth control pills,' he said.

'*What?*'

'Italy is a Roman Catholic country,' he observed. 'You can't buy these pills here. But that doesn't stop women wanting to avoid being in a constant state of baby production, does it? And the pills are marvellous for them, they can take them without the devoutest husbands knowing anything about it.'

'Good God,' I said.

'My brother's wife collects them at home from her friends and so on, and when she has a bottle full I bring it to Gabriella and she passes them on at this end. I know for a fact that at least four other pilots do the same, not to mention a whole fleet of air hostesses, and she admitted to me once that a day seldom goes by without some supplies flying in.'

'Do you ... well ... sell ... them to Gabriella?'

He was quite shocked, which pleased me. 'Of course not. She doesn't sell them, either. They are a gift, a service if you like, from the women of one country to the women of another. My sister-in-law and her friends are really keen on it, they don't see why any woman in the world should have to risk having a child if she doesn't want one.'

'I've never thought about it,' I said, fingering the bottle.

'You've never had a sister who's borne six children in six years and collapsed into a shattering nervous break-down when she started the seventh.'

'Gabriella's sister?'

He nodded. 'That's why she got some pills, in the first place. And the demand just grew and grew.'

I gave him back the bottle and he put it in his pocket. 'Well?' he said, with a hint of challenge.

'She must be quite a girl,' I said, 'to do something like this.'

His curving mouth curved wider. 'If she smuggled the Crown Jewels you'd forgive her. Confess it.'

'Whatever she did,' I said slowly.

The amusement died right out of his face and he looked at me soberly. 'I've heard of this sort of thing,' he said. 'But I've never seen it happen before. And you didn't even need to speak to each other. In fact, it's just damn lucky you *can* speak to each other ...'

Three times during the afternoon I made sure of that. She would get into trouble, she said, if she just talked to me when she should be working, so I bought presents, separately, for my father, mother and sister, taking a long time over each choice. Each time she spoke and looked at me in a kaleidoscopic mixture of excitement, caution and surprise, as if she too found falling helplessly in love with a complete stranger an overwhelming and almost frightening business.

'I like that one.'

'It costs six thousand lire.'

'That is too dear.'

'This one is cheaper.'

'Show me some others.'

We began like that, like school-day text books, in careful stilted French, but by the end of the afternoon, when she locked the display cases and left with Patrick and me through the employees' entrance, we could talk with some ease. I perhaps knew most French of the three of us, then Gabriella, then Patrick; but his Italian was excellent, so between us everything could in one language or another be understood.

We left the airport in a taxi, and as soon as we were on the move Patrick gave her the aspirin bottle. She thanked him with a flashing smile and asked him if they were all the same sort. He nodded, and explained they'd come from some R.A.F. wives whose husbands were away on a three months overseas course.

From her large shoulder-sling bag of black leather she produced some of the bright striped wrapping paper from her airport gift shop and a large packet of sweets. The sweets and the aspirin bottle were expertly whisked into a ball shaped parcel with four corners sticking up on top like leaves on a pineapple, and a scrap of sticky tape secured them.

The taxi stopped outside a dilapidated narrow terrace house in a poor looking street. Gabriella climbed out of the taxi, but Patrick waved me back into my seat.

'She doesn't live here,' he said. 'She's just delivering the sweets.'

She was already talking to a tired looking young woman whose black dress accentuated the pallor of her skin, and whose varicose veins were the worst I had seen, like great dark blue knobbed worms networking just under the surface of her legs. Round her clung two small children with two or three more behind in the doorway, but she had a flat stomach in her skimpy dress and no baby in her arms. The look she gave Gabriella and her pretty present were all the reward that anyone would need. The children knew that there were sweets in the parcel. They were jumping up trying to reach it as their mother held it above their heads, and as we left she went indoors with them, and she was laughing.

'Now,' said Patrick, turning away from the window, 'we had better show Henry Milan.'

It was getting dark and was still cold, but not for us. I wouldn't have noticed if it had been raining ice. They began by marching me slowly around the Piazza del Duomo to see the great gothic cathedral and the Palazzo Reale, and along the high glass arcade into the Piazza della Scala to gaze at the opera house, which Gabriella solemnly told me was the second largest theatre in Europe, and could hold three thousand six hundred people.

'Where is the largest?' said Patrick.

'In Naples,' she said smiling. 'It is ours too.'

'I suppose Milan has the biggest cathedral, then,' he teased her.

'No,' she laughed, showing an unsuspected dimple, 'Rome.'

'An extravagant nation, the Italians.'

'We were ruling the world while you were still painting yourselves blue.'

'Hey, hey,' said Patrick.

'Leonardo da Vinci lived in Milan,' she said.

'Italy is undoubtedly the most beautiful country in the world and Milan is its pearl.'

'Patrick, you are a great idiot,' she said affectionately. But she was proud indeed of her native city, and before dinner that evening I learned that nearly a million and a half people lived there and that there were dozens of museums, and music and art schools, and that it was the best manufacturing town in the country, and the richest, and its factories made textiles and paper and railway engines and cars. And, in fact, aeroplanes.

We ate in a quiet warmly lit little restaurant which looked disconcertingly like Italian restaurants in London but smelled quite different, spicy and fragrant. I hardly noticed what I ate: Gabriella chose some sort of veal for us all, and it tasted fine, like everything else that evening. We drank two bottles of red local wine which fizzed slightly on the tongue, and unending little gold cups of black coffee. I knew even then that it was because we were all speaking a language not our own that I felt liberated from my usual self. It was so much easier to be uninhibited away from everything which had planted the inhibitions: another sky, another culture, a time out of time. But that only made the way simpler, it didn't make the object less real. It meant I didn't have chains on my tongue; but what I had said wasn't said loosely, it was still rooted in some unchanging inner core. On that one evening in Milan I learned what it was like to be gay deep into the spirit, and if for nothing else I would thank Gabriella for that all my life.

We talked for hours: not profoundly, I dare say, but companionably: at first about the things we had done and seen that day, then of ourselves, our childhood. Then of Fellini's films, and a little about travel, and then, in ever widening ripples, of religion, and our own hopes, and the state the world was in. There wasn't an ounce of natural reforming zeal among the three of us, as perhaps there ought to have been when so much needed reforming; but faith didn't move mountains any more, it got bogged down by committees, Patrick said, and the saints of the past would be smeared as psychological misfits today.

'Could you imagine the modern French army allowing itself to be inspired and led into battle by a girl who saw visions?' he said. 'You could not.'

It was true. You could not.

'Psychology,' Patrick said, with wine and candle light in his yellow eyes, 'is the death of courage.'

'I don't understand,' protested Gabriella.

'Not for girls,' he said. 'For men. It is now not considered sensible to take physical risks unless you can't avoid them. Ye gods, there's no quicker way to ruin a nation than to teach its young men it's foolish to take risks. Or worse than foolish, they would have you believe.'

'What do you mean?' she said.

'Ask Henry. He'll cheerfully go out and risk his neck on a racehorse any day of the week. Ask him why.'

'Why?' she said, half-serious, half-laughing, the glints of light in her dark eyes outpointing the stars.

'I like it,' I said. 'It's fun.'

Patrick shook his red head. 'You look out, pal, you mustn't go around admitting that sort of thing these days. You've got to say you do it only for the money, or you'll be labelled as a masochistic guilt complex before you can say . . . er . . . masochistic guilt complex.'

'Oh yeah?' I said, laughing.

'Yeah, damn it, and it's not funny. It's deadly serious. The knockers have had so much success that now it's fashionable to say you're a coward. You may not *be* one, mind, but you've got to *say* so, just to prove you're normal. Historically, it's fantastic. What other nation ever went around saying on television and in the press and at parties and things that cowardice is normal and courage is disgusting? Nearly all nations used to have elaborate tests for young men to prove they were brave. Now in England they are taught to settle down and want security. But bravery is built in somewhere in human nature and you can't stamp it out any more than the sex urge. So if you outlaw ordinary bravery it bursts out somewhere else, and I reckon that's what the increase in crime is due to. If you make enjoying danger seem perverted, I don't see how you can complain if it becomes so.'

This was too much for his French; he said it to me in hot English, and repeated it, when Gabriella protested, in cooler Italian.

'But,' she said wonderingly, 'I do not like a man to say he is a coward. Who wants that? A man is for hunting and for defending, for keeping his wife safe.'

'Back to the caves?' I said.

'Our instincts are still the same,' agreed Patrick. 'Basically good.'

'And a man is for loving,' Gabriella said.

'Yes, indeed,' I agreed with enthusiasm.

'If you like to risk your neck, I like that. If you risk it for me, I like it better.'

'You mustn't say so,' said Patrick smiling. 'There's probably some vile explanation for that too.'

We all laughed, and some fresh coffee came, and the talk drifted away to what girls in Italy wanted of life as opposed to what they could have. Gabriella said the gap was narrowing fast, and that she was content, particularly as she was an orphan and had no parental pressure to deal with. We discussed for some time the pros and cons of having parents after adolescence, and all maintained that what we had was best: Gabriella her liberty, Patrick a widowed mother who spoiled him undemandingly, and I, free board and lodging. Patrick looked at me sharply when I said that, and opened his mouth to blow the gaff.

'Don't tell her,' I said in English. 'Please don't.'

'She would like you even more.'

'No.'

He hesitated, but to my relief he left it, and when Gabriella asked, told her we had been arguing as to who should pay the bill. We shared it between us, but we didn't leave for some time after that. We talked, I remember, about loyalty: at first about personal loyalty, and then political.

Gabriella said that Milan had many communists, and she thought that for a Roman Catholic to be a communist was like an Arab saying he wanted to be ruled by Israel.

'I wonder who they would be loyal to, if Russia invaded Italy?' Patrick said.

'That's a big if,' I said smiling. 'Pretty impossible with Germany, Austria and Switzerland in between, not to mention the Alps.'

Gabriella shook her head. 'Communists begin at Trieste.'

I was startled and amused at the same time, hearing an echo of my die-hard father. 'Wogs begin at Calais.'

'Of course they do,' Patrick said thoughtfully. 'On your door-step.'

'But cheer up,' she said laughing. 'Yugoslavia also has mountains, and the Russians will not be arriving that way either.'

'They won't invade any more countries with armies,' I agreed mildly.

'Only with money and technicians. Italian and French and British communists can rely on never having to choose which side to shoot at.'

'And can go on undermining their native land with a clear conscience,' Patrick nodded smiling.

'Let's not worry about it,' I said, watching the moving shadows where Gabriella's smooth hair fell across her cheek. 'Not tonight.'

'It will never touch us, anyway,' Patrick agreed. 'And if we stay here much longer Gabriella's sister will lock us out.'

Reluctantly we went out into the cold street. When we had gone ten paces Patrick exclaimed that he had left his overnight bag behind, and went back for it, striding quickly.

I turned to Gabriella, and she to me. The street lights were reflected in her welcoming eyes, and the solemn mouth trembled on the edge of that transfiguring smile. There wasn't any need to say anything. We both knew. Although I stood with my body barely brushing hers and put my hands very gently on her arms just below the shoulders, she rocked as if I'd pushed her. It was the same for me. I felt physically shaken by a force so primitive and volcanic as to be frightening. How could just touching a girl, I thought confusedly, just touching a girl I'd been longing to touch all afternoon and all evening, sweep one headlong into such an uncivilised turbulence. And on a main street in Milan, where one could do nothing about it.

She let her head fall forward against my shoulder, and we were still standing like that, with my cheek on her hair, when Patrick came back with his bag. Without a word, smiling resignedly, he pulled her round, tucked her arm into his, and said briefly, 'Come on. You'll get run in if you stay here much longer like that.' She looked at him blindly for a moment, and then laughed shakily. 'I don't understand why this has happened,' she said.

'Struck by the Gods,' said Patrick ironically. 'Or chemistry. Take your pick.'

'It isn't sensible.'

'You can say that again.'

He began to walk down the road, pulling her with him. My feet unstuck themselves from the pavement and re-attached themselves to my watery legs and I caught them up. Gabriella put her other arm through mine, and we strolled the mile and a half to where her sister lived, gradually losing the heavy awareness of passion and talking normally and laughing, and finally ending up on her door-step in a fit of giggles.

Lisabetta, Gabriella's sister, was ten years older and a good deal fatter, though she had the same smooth olive skin and the same shaped fine dark eyes. Her husband, Giulio, a softly flabby man approaching forty with a black moustache, bags under his eyes, and less hair than he'd once had, lumbered ungracefully out of his arm-chair when we went into his sitting room and gave us a moderately enthusiastic welcome.

Neither he nor Lisabetta spoke English or French so while the two girls made yet more coffee, and Patrick talked to Giulio, I looked around with some interest at Gabriella's home. Her sister had a comfortable four bedroomed flat in a huge recently built tower, and all the furnishings and fabrics were uncompromisingly modern. The floors were some sort of reconstituted stone heated from underneath and without carpet or rugs, and there were blinds, not curtains, to cover the windows. I thought the total effect rather stark, but reflected idly that Milan in mid-summer must be an oven, and the flat had been planned for the heat.

Several children came and went, all indistinguishable to my eyes. Seven of them, there should be, I remembered. Four boys, three girls, Patrick had said. Although it was nearly midnight, none of them seemed to have gone to bed. They had all been waiting to see Patrick and tumbled about him like puppies.

When Lisabetta had poured the coffee and one of the children had handed it round Giulio asked Patrick a question, looking at me.

'He wants to know what your job is,' Patrick said.

'Tell him I look after the horses.'

'Nothing else?'

'Nothing else.'

Giulio was unimpressed. He asked another question.

Smiling faintly, Patrick said, 'He wants to know how much you earn?'

'My pay for a single trip to Milan is about one fifth of yours.'

'He won't like that.'

'Nor do I.'

He laughed. When he translated Giulio scowled.

Patrick and I slept in a room which normally belonged to two of the boys, now doubling with the other two. Gabriella shared a third bedroom with the two elder girls, while the smallest was in with her parents. There were toys all over the place in our room, and small shoes kicked off and clothes dumped in heaps, and the unchanged sheets on the boys' beds were wrinkled like elephant skins from their restless little bodies. Patrick had from long globe trotting habit come equipped with pyjamas, slippers, washing things, and a clean shirt for the morning. I eyed this splendour with some envy, and slept in my underpants.

'Why,' said Patrick in the dark, 'won't you tell them you have a title?'

'It isn't important.'

'It would be to Giulio.'

'That's the best reason for not telling him.'

'I don't see why you're so keen to keep it a secret.'

'Well, you try telling everyone you're an earl's son, and see what happens.'

'I'd love it. Everyone would be bowing and scraping in all directions. Priorities galore. Instant service. A welcome on every mat.'

'And you'd never be sure if anyone liked you for yourself.'

'Of course you would.'

'How many head grooms have you brought here before?' I asked mildly.

He drew in a breath audibly and didn't answer.

'Would you have offered me this bed if Timmie had kept his big mouth shut?'

He was silent.

I said, 'Remind me to kick your teeth in in the morning.'

But the morning, I found, was a long way off. I simply couldn't sleep. Gabriella's bed was a foot away from me on the far side of the wall, and I lay and sweated for her with a desire I hadn't dreamed possible. My body literally ached. Cold controlled Henry Grey, I thought helplessly. Grey by name and grey by nature. Cold controlled Henry Grey lying in a child's bed in a foreign city biting his arm to stop himself crying out. You could laugh at such hunger: ridicule it away. I tried that, but it didn't work. It stayed with me hour after wretched hour, all the way to the dawn, and I would have been much happier if I'd been able to go to sleep and dream about her instead.

She had kissed me good night in the passage outside her door, lightly, gaily, with Patrick and Lisabetta and about six children approvingly looking on. And she had stopped and retreated right there because it was the same as in the street outside the restaurant; even the lightest touch could start an earthquake. There just wasn't room for an earthquake in that crowded flat.

Patrick lent me his razor without a word, when we got up.

'I'm sorry,' I said.

'You were quite right. I would not have offered to take you with me if the Welshman hadn't said . . .'

'I know.' I put on my shirt and buttoned the cuffs.

'All the same I still wouldn't have asked you if I hadn't thought you looked all right.'

I turned towards him, surprised.

'What you need, Henry, is a bit more self-confidence. Why ever shouldn't people like you for yourself? Gabriella obviously does. So do I.'

'People often don't.' I pulled on my socks.

'You probably don't give them half a chance.' With which devastatingly accurate shot he went out of the door, shrugging his arms into his authoritative Captain's uniform.

Subdued by the raw steely morning, the three of us went back to the airport. Gabriella had dark shadows under her eyes and wouldn't look at me, though I could think of nothing I had done to offend her. She spoke only to Patrick, and in Italian, and he, smiling briefly, answered her in the same language. When we arrived at the airport, she asked me, hurriedly, not to come and talk to her at the gift counter, and almost ran away from me without saying good-bye. I didn't try to stop her. It would be hours before we got the horses loaded, and regardless of what she asked, I intended to see her again before I left.

I hung around the airport all the morning with Conker and Timmie, and about twelve Patrick came and found me and with a wide grin said I was in luck, traffic at Gatwick was restricted because of deep snow, and unessential freight flights were suspended for another day.

'You'd better telephone the studs again, and tell them we are taking the mares to England tomorrow at eight,' he said. 'Weather permitting.'

Gabriella received the news with such a flash of delight that my spirits rose to the ionosphere. I hesitated over the next question, but she made it easy for me.

'Did you sleep well?' she asked gravely, studying my face.

'I didn't sleep at all.'

She sighed, almost blushing. 'Nor did I.'

'Perhaps,' I said tentatively, 'if we spent the evening together, we could sleep tonight.'

'Henry!' She was laughing. 'Where?'

Where proved more difficult than I had imagined, as she would not consider a hotel, as we must not sleep there, but go back to her sister's before midnight. One must not be shameless, she said. She could not stay out all night. We ended up, of all unlikely places, inside the D.C.4, lying in a cosy nest hollowed in a heap of blankets stacked in the luggage bay alongside the galley.

There, where no one would ever find us, and with a good deal of the laughter of total happiness, we spent the whole of the evening in the age-old way: and were pleased and perhaps relieved to find that we suited each other perfectly.

Lying quietly cradled in my arms, she told me hesitantly that she had had a lover before, which I knew anyway by then, but that it was odd making love anywhere except in bed. She felt the flutter in my chest and lifted her head up to peer at my face in the dim reflected moonlight.

'Why are you laughing?' she said.

'It so happens that I have never made love *in* bed.'

'Where then?'

'In the grass.'

'Henry! Is that the custom in England?'

'Only at the end of parties in the summer.'

She smiled and put her head down contentedly again, and I stroked her hair and thought how wholesome she was, and how dreadful in comparison seemed the half-drunk nymphs taken casually down the deb-dance garden path. I would never do that again, I thought. Never again.

'I was ashamed, this morning,' she said, 'of wanting this so much. Ashamed of what I had been thinking all night.'

'There is no shame in it.'

'Lust is one of the seven deadly sins.'

'Love is a virtue.'

'They get very mixed up. Are we this evening being virtuous or sinful?' She didn't sound too worried about it.

'Doing what comes naturally.'

'Then it's probably sinful.'

She twisted in my arms, turning so that her face was close to mine. Her eyes caught a sheen in the soft near-darkness. Her teeth rubbed gently against the bare skin on the point of my shoulder.

'You taste of salt,' she said.

I moved my hand over her stomach and felt the deep muscles there contract. Nothing, I thought, shaken by an echoing ripple right down my spine, nothing was so impossibly potent as being wanted in return. I kissed her, and she gave a long soft murmuring sigh which ended oddly in a laugh.

'Sin,' she said, with a smile in her voice, 'is O.K.'

We went back to her sister's and slept soundly on each side of the wall. Early in the morning, in her dressing-gown, with tousled hair and dreaming eyes, she made coffee for Patrick and me before we set off for the airport.

'You'll come back?' she said almost casually, pouring my cup.

'As soon as I can.'

She knew I meant it. She kissed me good-bye without clinging, and Patrick also. 'For bringing him,' she said.

In the taxi on the way to the airport Patrick said, 'Why don't you just stay here with her? You easily could.'

I didn't answer him until we were turning into the airport road.

'Would you? Stay, I mean.'

'No. But then, I need to keep my job.'

'So do I. For different reasons, perhaps. But I need to keep it just the same.'

'It's none of my business,' he said, 'but I'm glad.'

We loaded the Italian mares and flew them to snowy England without another hitch. I soothed them on their way and thought about Gabriella, who seemed to have established herself as a warming knot somewhere under my diaphragm.

I thought about her with love and without even the conventional sort of anxiety, for as she had said with a giggle, it would be a poor smuggler who couldn't swallow her own contraband.

Chapter Seven

Stratford Races were off because of snow, which was just as well as Yardman squeezed in an extra trip on that day at very short notice. Seven three-year-olds to France, he said; but at loading time there were eight.

I was held up on the way to Cambridge by a lorry which had skidded sideways and blocked the icy road, and when I reached the airport all the cargo had already arrived, with the box drivers stamping their feet to keep warm and cursing me fluently. Billy, and it was Billy again, not Conker and Timmie, stood about with his hands in his pockets and a sneer permanently fixed like epoxy resin, enjoying the disapproval I had brought on myself. He had not, naturally, thought of beginning the work before I arrived.

We loaded the horses, he, I, and deaf old Alf, whom Billy had brought with him, and we worked in uncompanionable silence. There was a fourth groom on the trip, a middle-aged characterless man with a large straggly moustache and a bad cold, but he had come with one particular horse from an upper crust stud, and he refrained from offering to help with any others. Neither did he lend a hand on the journey, but sat throughout beside his own protégée, guarding it carefully from no visible danger. Billy dropped a handful of peat in my coffee and later poured his own, which was half full of sugar, over my head. I spent the rest of the journey in the washroom, awkwardly rinsing the stickiness out of my hair and vowing to get even with Billy one day when I hadn't thousands of pounds worth of bloodstock in my care.

During the unloading I looked closely at one inconspicuous brown mare, trying to memorise her thoroughly unmemorable appearance. She was definitely not a three-year-old, like all the others on the trip, and she was, I was sure, almost identical to the one we had taken to France the first day I flew with Billy. And very like the one we had brought back that afternoon on the second trip. Three mares, all alike . . . well, it was not impossible, especially as they had no distinct markings between them, none at all.

The special groom left us in Paris, escorting his own horse right through to its new home. He had been engaged, he said, to bring another horse back, a French stallion which his stud had bought, and we would be collecting him again the next week. We duly did collect him, the next Tuesday, complete with the stallion, a tight-muscled butty little horse with a fiery eye and a restless tail. He was squealing like a colt when we stored him on board, and this time there was some point in his straggly moustached keeper staying beside him all the way.

Among the cargo there was yet another undistinguished brown mare. I was leaning on the starboard side of her box, gazing over and down at her, not able to see her very clearly against the peat she stood on and the brown horse on her other side, when Billy crept up behind me and hit me savagely across the shoulders with a spare tethering chain. I turned faster than he expected and got in two hard quick kicks on his thigh. His lips went back with the pain and he furiously swung his arm, the short chain flickering and bending like an angry snake. I dodged it by ducking into one of the cross-way alleys between the boxes, and the chain wrapped itself with a vicious clatter round the corner where I had been standing. Unhesitatingly I skipped through to the port side of the plane and went forward at top speed to the galley. Hiding figuratively under the engineer's skirts may not have been the noblest course, but in the circumstances by far the most prudent, and I stayed with him, drinking coffee, until we were on the final approach to Cambridge.

I did a good deal of hard thinking that night and I didn't like my thought.

In the morning I waited outside Yardman's office, and fell into step with Simon as he shambled out to lunch.

'Hullo,' he said, beaming. 'Where did you spring from? Come and have a warmer up at the Angel.'

I nodded and walked beside him, shuffling on the thawing remains of the previous week's snow. Our breaths shot out in small sharp clouds. The day was misty and overcast; the cold, raw, damp, and penetrating, exactly matched my mood.

Simon pushed the stained glass and entered the fug; swam on to his accustomed stool, tugged free his disreputable corduroy jacket and hustled the willing barmaid into pouring hot water on to rum and lemon juice, a large glass each. There was a bright new modern electric fire straining at its kilowatts in the old brick fireplace, and the pulsating light from its imitation coal base lit warmly the big smiling face opposite me, and shone brightly on the friendliness in his eyes.

I had so few friends. So few.

'What's the matter then?' he said, sipping his steaming drink. 'You're excessively quiet today, even for you.'

I watched the fake flames for a while, but it couldn't be put off for ever.

'I have found out,' I said slowly, 'about the brown mare.'

He put down his glass with a steady hand but the smile drained completely away.

'What brown mare?'

I didn't answer. The silence lengthened hopelessly.

'What do you mean?' he said at last.

'I escorted a brown mare to France and back twice in a fortnight. The same brown mare every time.'

'You must be mistaken.'

'No.'

There was a pause. Then he said again, but without conviction, 'You are mistaken.'

'I noticed her the day she went over in the morning and came back the same afternoon. I wondered when she went over again last Thursday ... and I was certain it was the same horse yesterday, when she came back.'

'You've been on several other trips. You couldn't remember one particular mare out of all those you dealt with ...'

'I know horses,' I said.

'You're too quick,' he said, almost to himself. 'Too quick.'

'No,' I shook my head. 'You were. You shouldn't have done it again so soon; then I might not have realised ...'

He shook himself suddenly, the bulk quivering in folds. 'Done what?' he said more firmly. 'What if a horse did go over and back twice? And what's it got to do with me?'

'There's no point in telling you what you already know.' ·

'Henry,' he leaned forward. 'I know what I know, but I don't know what you think you know. You've got some damn-fool notion in your head and I want to hear what it is.'

I watched the steam rise gently from my untouched drink and wished I hadn't come.

'Nice little fiddle,' I sighed. 'A sweet, neat little fraud. Easy as shelling peas. A few hundred quid every time you send the mare to France.'

He looked at me without speaking, waiting, making me say it all straight out.

'All right then. You sell a horse – the brown mare – to an accomplice in France. He arranges for his bank to transfer the purchase price to England and the bank over here certifies that it has been received. You put in a claim to the government that one thoroughbred has been exported

for x thousand francs: part of the great bloodstock industry. The grateful
government pays you the bonus, the one and three quarters per cent
bonus on exports, and you put it in your pocket. Meanwhile you bring
the horse back here and smuggle the money back as cash to France and
you're ready to start again.'

Simon sat like a stone, staring at me.

'All you really need is the working capital,' I said. 'A big enough sum
to make the one and three quarters per cent worth the trouble. Say twenty
thousand pounds, for argument's sake. Three hundred and fifty pounds
every time the mare goes across. If she went only once a month that
would make an untaxed dividend of over 20 per cent on the year. Four
thousand or more, tax free. You'd have a few expenses, of course, but
even so . . .'

'Henry!' his voice was low and stunned.

'It's not a big fraud,' I said. 'Not big. But pretty safe. And it had to
be you, Simon, because it's all a matter of filling up the right forms, and
you fill the forms at Yardman's. If anyone else, an outsider, tried it, he'd
have to pay the horse's air passage each way, which would make the
whole business unprofitable. No one would do it unless they could send
the horse for nothing. You can send one for nothing, Simon. You just put
one down on the flying list, but not on the office records. Every time
there's room on a flight to France, you send the mare. Yardman told me
himself there would be seven three-year-olds going over last Thursday,
but we took eight horses, and the eighth wasn't a three-year old, it was
the brown mare.

'The day we did two trips, when we took her over in the morning and
brought her back in the afternoon, that day it was no accident the return
horses weren't at the airport to come back on the first trip. Not even you
could risk unloading the mare and promptly loading her up again straight
away. So you made a "mistake" and put fifteen hundred hours on the
trainers' travelling instructions instead of ten hundred hours, you, who
never make such mistakes, whose accuracy is so phenomenal usually that
no one queries or checks up on what you do . . .'

'How,' he said dully. 'How did you work it out?'

'I came from Anglia Bloodstock,' I said gently. 'Don't you remember?
I used to fill up the same export forms as you do. I used to send them
to you from the transport section. But I might not have remembered
about the government bonus if I hadn't heard three business men
discussing it ten days ago, and last night while I was wondering how
anyone could gain from shuffling that mare over and back, the whole
thing just clicked.'

'Clicked,' he said gloomily.

I nodded. 'No markings on the mare, either. You couldn't keep sending
her in her own name, someone would have noticed at once. I would have
done, for a start. But all you had to do was go through the stud book, and
choose other unmarked mares of approximately the same age and fill up
the export forms accordingly. The customs certify a brown mare was
actually exported from here, and the French customs certify it was
imported there. No trouble at all. No one bothers to check with an owner

that he has sold his horse. Why ever should they? And coming back, you go through the same process with the French stud book, only this time you have to be a bit careful your faked mare isn't too well bred because you can't spend more than two thousand in sterling abroad without searching enquiries, which you couldn't risk.'

'Got it all buttoned up, haven't you?' he said bitterly.

'I was thinking about it nearly all night.'

'Who are you going to tell?'

I glanced at him and away, uncomfortably.

'Yardman?' he asked.

I didn't answer.

'The police?'

I looked at the flickering fire. I wouldn't have told anyone had it not been for . . .

'Did you,' I said painfully, 'did you *have* to get Billy to knock me about?'

'Henry!' He looked shattered. 'I didn't. How can you think I did that?'

I swallowed. 'He's been on all the trips with the mare, and he's never given me a moment's peace on any of them, except perhaps the first. He's punched me and poured syrupy coffee on my hair, and yesterday when I was looking at the mare he hit me with a chain. He's not doing it because he dislikes me . . . or not only. It's a smoke screen to keep me away from looking too closely at the horses. That's why he didn't smash my face in . . . he was fighting for a purpose, not from real fury.'

'Henry, I promise you, it isn't true.' He seemed deeply distressed. 'I wouldn't hurt you, for God's sake.'

He put out his hand for his drink and took a long swallow. There was no more steam: drink and friendship were both cold.

'Don't look like that,' he said shivering. 'Like an iceberg.' He drank again. 'All right, you've got it right about the mare. I'll admit that, but as God's my judge, I didn't put Billy on to you. I can't stand him. He's a young thug. Whatever he's been doing to you, it's from his own bloody nature. I promise you, Henry, I promise you . . .'

I looked at him searchingly, wanting very much to believe him, and feeling I'd merely be fooling myself if I did.

'Look,' he said anxiously, leaning forward, 'would you have sicked him on to me?'

'No.'

'Well, then.' He leaned back again. 'I didn't either.'

There was a long, long pause.

'What do you do with the money?' I asked, shelving it.

He hesitated. 'Pay my gambling debts.'

I shook my head. 'You don't gamble.'

'I do.'

'No.'

'You don't know everything.'

'I know that,' I said tiredly. 'I know that very well. You're not interested in racing. You never ask me for tips, never even ask me if I expect to win myself. And don't say you gamble at cards or something feeble like that . . . if you gambled enough to have to steal to pay your debts, you'd gamble on anything, horses as well. Compulsively.'

He winced. 'Steal is a hard word.' He leaned forward, picked up my untasted drink, and swallowed the lot.

'There's no pension at Yardman's,' he said.

I looked into his future, into his penurious retirement. I would have the remains of the Creggan fortune to keep me in cars and hot rums. He would have what he'd saved.

'You've banked it?'

'Only a third,' he said. 'A third is my cousin's. He's the one who keeps the mare on his small-holding and drives her to the airport at this end. And a third goes to a chap with a horse dealing business in France. He keeps the mare when she is over there, and drives her back and fore to the planes. They put up most of the stake, those two, when I thought of it. I hadn't anything like enough on my own.'

'You don't really make much out of it, then, yourself, considering the risks.'

'Double my salary,' he observed dryly. 'Tax free. And you underestimate us. We have two horses, and they each go about fifteen times a year.'

'Have I seen the other one?'

'Yes,' he nodded. 'There and back.'

'Once?'

'Once.'

'And how do you get the money back to France?'

'Send it in magazines. Weeklies. The *Horse and Hound*, things like that.'

'English money?'

'Yes. The chap in France has a contact who exchanges it.'

'Risky, sending it by post.'

'We've never lost any.'

'How long have you been doing it?'

'Since they invented the bonus. Shortly after, anyway.'

There was another long silence. Simon fiddled with his empty glass and didn't look like an embezzler. I wondered sadly if it was priggish to want one's friends to be honest, and found that I did still think of him as a friend, and could no longer believe that he had paid Billy to give me a bad time. Billy quite simply hated my pedigreed guts: and I could live with that.

'Well,' he said in the end. 'What are you going to do about it?'

He knew as well as I did that he'd have no chance in an investigation. Too many records of his transactions would still exist in various government and banking files. If I started any enquiry he would very likely end up in gaol. I stood up stiffly off the bar stool and shook my head.

'Nothing . . .' I hesitated.

'Nothing . . . as long as we stop?'

'I don't know.'

He gave me a twisted smile. 'All right, Henry. We'll pack it in.'

We went out of the pub and walked together through the slush back to the office, but it wasn't the same. There was no trust left. He must have been wondering whether I would keep my mouth shut permanently, and I knew, and hated the knowledge, that he could probably go on with his scheme in spite of saying he wouldn't. The brown mare wouldn't go again, but he could change her for another, and there was his second horse, which I hadn't even noticed. If he was careful, he could go on. And he was a careful man.

The travel schedules in the office, checked again, still showed no more trips to Milan till the Wednesday of the following week. Nor, as far as I could see, were there any flights at all before then; only a couple of sea passages booked for polo ponies, which weren't my concern. I knocked on Yardman's door, and went in and asked him if I could have the rest of the week off: my rights, Conker would have said.

'Milan next Wednesday,' he repeated thoughtfully. 'And there's nothing before that? Of course, my dear boy, of course you can have the time off. If you don't mind if I bring you back should an urgent trip crop up?'

'Of course not.'

'That's good, that's good.' The spectacles flashed as he glanced out of the window, the tight skin around his mouth lifting fleetingly into a skeletal smile. 'You still like the job, then?'

'Yes, thank you,' I said politely.

'Well, well, my dear boy, and I won't say that you're not good at it, I won't say that at all. Very reliable, yes, yes. I admire you for it, dear boy, I do indeed.'

'Well . . . thank you, Mr. Yardman.' I wasn't sure that underneath he wasn't laughing at me, and wondered how long it would be before he understood that I didn't look on my job as the great big joke everyone else seemed to think it.

I wrote to Gabriella to tell her I would be coming back the following week, and drove moderately home, thinking alternately of her and Simon in an emotional see-saw.

There was a message for me at home to ring up Julian Thackery's father, which I did. The weather forecast was favourable, he said, and it looked as though there would be racing on Saturday. He was planning to send a good hunter chaser up to Wetherby, and could I go and ride it.

'I could,' I said. 'Yes.'

'That's fine. She's a grand little mare, a real trier, with the shoulders of a champion and enough behind the saddle to take you over the best.'

'Wetherby fences are pretty stiff,' I commented.

'She'll eat them,' he said with enthusiasm. 'And she's ready. We gave her a mile gallop this morning, thinking she'd be backward after the snow, and she was pulling like a train at the end of it. Must thrive on being held up.'

'Sounds good.'

'A snip,' he said. 'I'll see you in the weighing room, just before the first. Right?'

I assured him I would be there, and was glad to be going, as I learned from a letter of acceptance lying beside the telephone that the Filyhoughs were again expected for the week-end. My sister Alice came along while I held the letter in my hand.

'I'm going up to Wetherby on Saturday,' I said, forestalling her.

'Sunday . . .' she began.

'No, Alice dear, no. I have no intention whatsoever of marrying Angela Fillyhough and there's no point in seeing her. I thought that we had agreed that Mother should stop this heiress hunting.'

'But you must marry someone, Henry,' she protested.

I thought of Gabriella, and smiled. Maybe her, once I was sure she'd be a friend for life, not just a rocket passion with no embers.

'I'll marry someone, don't you worry.'

'Well,' Alice said, 'if you're going as far north as Wetherby you might as well go on and see Louise and cheer her up a bit.'

'Cheer her up?' I said blankly. Louise was the sister just older than Alice. She lived in Scotland, nearly twice as far from Wetherby, as it happened, as Wetherby from home, but before I could point that out Alice replied.

'I told you yesterday evening,' she said in exasperation. 'Weren't you listening?'

'I'm afraid not.' I'd been thinking about brown mares.

'Louise has had an operation. She goes home from hospital today and she'll be in bed for two or three weeks more.'

'What's wrong with her?' But Alice either didn't know or wouldn't tell me, and though I hardly knew Louise in any deep sense I thought she would be far preferable to Angela Filyhough, and I agreed to go. Deciding, as I would be driving a long way after the races, to go up to Yorkshire on the Friday and spend the Saturday morning lazily, I set off northward at lunchtime and made a detour out of habit to Fenland.

'Hey, Harry, you're just the man I want. A miracle.' Tom Wells grabbed my arm as I walked in. 'Do me a short flight tomorrow? Two trainers and a jockey from Newmarket to Wetherby races.'

I nearly laughed. 'I'm awfully sorry. I can't, Tom. I really called in to cancel my booking for Sunday. I can't come then either. Got to go and visit a sick sister in Scotland. I'm on my way now.'

'Blast,' he said forcibly. 'Couldn't you put it off?'

'Afraid not.'

'You can have a plane to fly up, on Sunday.' He was cunning, looking at me expectantly. 'Free.'

I did laugh then. 'I can't.'

'I'll have to tell the trainers I can't fix them up.'

'I'm really sorry.'

'Yeah. Damn it all. Well, come and have a cup of coffee.'

We sat in the canteen for an hour and talked about aircraft, and I continued my journey to Wetherby thinking in amusement that my life was getting more and more like a juggling act, and that it would need skill to keep the racing, flying, horse-ferrying and Gabriella all spinning round safely in separate orbits.

At Wetherby the struggling sunshine lost to a fierce east wind, but the going was perfect, a surprise after the snow. Mr. Thackery's mare was all that he had promised, a tough workmanlike little chestnut with a heart as big as a barn, a true racer who didn't agree with giving up. She took me over the first two fences carefully, as she'd not been on the course before, but then with confidence attacked the rest. I'd seldom had a more solid feeling ride and enjoyed it thoroughly, finding she needed the barest amount of help when meeting a fence wrong and was not too pigheaded to accept it. Coming round the last bend into the straight she was as full of running as when she started, and with only a flicker of encouragement from me she began working her way up smoothly past the four horses ahead of us. She reached the leader coming into the last, pecked a bit on landing, recovered without breaking up her stride, and went after the only horse in sight with enviable determination. We caught him in time, and soared past the winning post with the pleasure of winning coursing like wine in the blood.

'Not bad,' said Julian's father beaming. 'Not bad at all,' and he gave me a sealed envelope he'd had the faith to prepare in advance.

With about three hundred and fifty miles to go I left soon after the race, and on the empty northern roads made good time to Scotland. My sister Louise lived in a dreary baronial hall near Elgin, a house almost as big as ours at home and just as inadequately heated. She had pleased our parents by marrying for money, and hadn't discovered her husband's fanatical tightfistedness until afterwards. For all she'd ever had to spend since, she'd have been better off in a semi-detached in Peckham. Her Christmas gifts to me as a child had been Everyman editions of the classics. I got none at all now.

Even so, when I went in to see her in the morning, having arrived after she was sleeping the night before, it was clear that some of her spirit had survived. We looked at each other as at strangers. She, after a seven-year gap, was much older looking than I remembered, older than forty-three, and pale with illness, but her eyes were bright and her smile truly pleased.

'Henry, my little brother, I'm so glad you've come . . .'

One had to believe her. I was glad too, and suddenly the visit was no longer a chore. I spent all day with her, looking at old photographs and playing Chinese chequers, which she had taught me as a child, and listening to her chat about the three sons away at boarding school and how poor the grouse had been this winter and how much she would like to see London again, it was ten years since she had been down. She asked me to do various little jobs for her, explaining that 'dear James' was apt to be irritated and the maids had too much else to do, poor things. I fetched things for her, packed up a parcel, tidied her room, filled her hot water bottle and found her some more toothpaste. After that she wondered if we couldn't perhaps turn out her medicine drawer while we had the opportunity.

The medicine drawer could have stocked a dispensary. Half of them, she said with relief, she would no longer need. 'Throw them away.' She sorted the bottles and boxes into two heaps. 'Put all those in the wastepaper basket.' Obediently I picked up a handful. One was labelled

'Conovid,' with some explanatory words underneath, and it took several seconds before the message got through. I picked that box out of the rubbish and looked inside. There was a strip of foil containing pills, each packed separately. I tore one square open and picked out the small pink tablet.

'Don't you want these?' I asked.

'Of course not. I don't need them any more, after the operation.'

'Oh . . . I see. No, of course not. Then may I have them?'

'What on earth for?'

'Don't be naïve, Louise.'

She laughed. 'You've got a girl friend at last? Of course you can have them. There's a full box lying around somewhere too, I think. In my top drawer, perhaps? Maybe some in the bathroom too.'

I collected altogether enough birth control pills to fill a bottle nearly as big as the one Patrick had given Gabriella, a square cornered brown bottle four inches high, which had held a prescription for penicillin syrup for curing the boys' throat infections. Louise watched with amusement while I rinsed it out, baked it dry in front of her electric fire, and filled it up, stuffing the neck with cotton wool before screwing on the black cap.

'Marriage?' she said. As bad as Alice.

'I don't know.' I put the drawer she had tidied back into the bedside table. 'And don't tell Mother.'

Wednesday seemed a long time coming, and I was waiting at Gatwick a good hour before the first horses turned up. Not even the arrival of Billy and Alf could damp my spirits and we loaded the horses without incident and faster than usual, as two of the studs had sent their own grooms as well, and for once they were willing.

It was one of the mornings that Simon came with last minute papers, and he gave them to me warily in the charter airline office when the plane was ready to leave.

'Good morning, Henry.'

'Good morning.'

One couldn't patch up a friendship at seven-thirty in the morning in front of yawning pilots and office staff. I took the papers with a nod, hesitated, and went out across the tarmac, bound for the aircraft and Milan.

There were running steps behind me and a hand on my arm.

'Lord Grey? You're wanted on the telephone. They say it's urgent.'

I picked up the receiver and listened, said 'All right,' and slowly put it down again. I was not, after all, going to see Gabriella. I could feel my face contract into lines of pain.

'What is it?' Simon said.

'My father . . . my father has died . . . sometime during the night. They have just found him . . . he was very tired, yesterday evening . . .'

There was a shocked silence in the office. Simon looked at me with great understanding, for he knew how little I wanted this day.

'I'm sorry,' he said, his voice thick with sincerity.

I spoke to him immediately, without thinking, in the old familiar way. 'I've got to go home.'

'Yes, of course.'

'But the horses are all loaded, and there's only Billy . . .'

'That's easy. I'll go myself.' He fished in his brief case and produced his passport.

It was the best solution. I gave him back the papers and took the brown bottle of pills out of my pocket. With a black ball point I wrote on the label, 'Gabriella Barzini, Souvenir Shop, Malpensa Airport.'

'Will you give this to the girl at the gift counter, and tell her why I couldn't come, and say I'll write?'

He nodded.

'You won't forget?' I said anxiously.

'No, Henry.' He smiled as he used to. 'I'll see she gets it, and the message. I promise.'

We shook hands, and after a detour through the passport office he shambled across the tarmac and climbed up the ramp into the plane. I watched the doors shut. I watched the aircraft fly away, taking my job, my friend and my gift, but not me.

Simon Searle went to Italy instead of me, and he didn't come back.

Chapter Eight

It was over a week before I found out. I went straight up to his room when I reached the wharf, and it was empty and much too tidy.

The dim teen-age secretary next door, in answer to my questions, agreed that Mr. Searle wasn't in today, and that no one seemed to know when he would be in at all . . . or whether.

'What do you mean?'

'He hasn't been in for a week. We don't know where he's got to.'

Disturbed, I went downstairs and knocked on Yardman's door.

'Come in.'

I went in. He was standing by the open window, watching colliers' tugs pulling heavy barges up the river. A Finnish freighter, come up on the flood, was manoeuvring alongside across the river under the vulture-like meccano cranes. The air was alive with hooter signals and the bang and clatter of dock work, and the tide was carrying the garbage from the lower docks steadily upstream to the Palace of Westminster. Yardman turned, saw me, carefully closed the window, and came across the room with both hands outstretched.

'My dear boy,' he said, squeezing one of mine. 'My condolences on your sad loss, my sincere condolences.'

'Thank you,' I said awkwardly. 'You are very kind. Do you . . . er . . . know where Simon Searle is?'

'Mr. Searle?' he raised his eyebrows so that they showed above the black spectacle frames.

'He hasn't been in for a week, the girl says.'

'No . . .' he frowned. 'Mr. Searle, for reasons best known to himself, chose not to return to this country. Apparently he decided to stay in Italy, the day he went to Milan in your place.'

'But why?' I said.

'I really have no idea. It is very inconvenient. Very. I am having to do his work until we hear from him.'

He shook his head. 'Well, my dear boy, I suppose our troubles no longer concern you. You'd better have your cards, though I don't expect you'll be needing them.' He smiled the twisted ironic smile and stretched out his hand to the inter-office phone.

'You're giving me the sack, then?' I said bluntly.

He paused, his hand in mid-air. 'My dear boy,' he protested. 'My dear boy. It simply hadn't occurred to me that you would want to stay on.'

'I do.'

He hesitated, and then sighed. 'It's against my better judgment, it is indeed. But with Searle and you both away, the agency has had to refuse business, and we can't afford much of that. No, we certainly can't. No, we certainly can't. Very well then, if you'll see us through at least until I hear from Searle, or find someone to replace him, I shall be grateful, very grateful indeed.'

If that was how he felt, I thought I might as well take advantage of it. 'Can I have three days off for Cheltenham races in a fortnight? I've got a ride in the Gold Cup.'

He nodded calmly. 'Let me have the exact dates, and I'll avoid them.'

I gave them to him then and there, and went back to Simon's room thinking that Yardman was an exceptionally easy employer, for all that I basically understood him as little as on our first meeting. The list of trips on Simon's wall showed that the next one scheduled was for the following Tuesday, to New York. Three during the past and present week had been crossed out, which as Yardman had said, was very bad for business. The firm was too small to stand much loss of its regular customers.

Yardman confirmed on the intercom that the Tuesday trip was still on, and he sounded so pleased that I guessed that he had been on the point of cancelling it when I turned up. I confirmed that I would fetch the relevant papers from the office on Monday afternoon, and be at Gatwick on the dot on Tuesday morning. This gave me a long week-end free and unbeatable ideas on how to fill it. With some relief the next day I drove determinedly away from the gloomy gathering of relations at home, sent a cable, picked up a stand-by afternoon seat with Alitalia, and flew to Milan to see Gabriella.

Three weeks and three days apart had changed nothing. I had forgotten the details of her face, shortened her nose in my imagination and lessened the natural solemnity of her expression, but the sight of her again and instantly did its levitation act. She looked momentarily anxious that I wouldn't feel the same, and then smiled with breathtaking brilliance when she saw that I did.

'I got your cable,' she said. 'One of the girls has changed her free day with me, and now I don't have to keep the shop tomorrow or Sunday.'

'That's marvellous.'

She hesitated, almost blushing. 'And I went home at lunch time to pack some clothes, and I have told my sister I am going to stay for two days with a girl friend near Genoa.'

'Gabriella!'

'Is that all right?' she asked anxiously.

'It's a miracle,' I said fervently, having expected only snatched unsatisfactory moments by day, and nights spent each side of a wall. 'It's unbelievable.'

When she had finished for the day we went to the station and caught a train, and on the principle of not telling more lies than could be helped, we did in fact go to Genoa. We booked separately into a large impersonal hotel full of incurious business men, and found our rooms were only four doors apart.

Over dinner in a warm obscure little restaurant she said, 'I'm sorry about your father, Henry.'

'Yes . . .' Her sympathy made me feel a fraud. I had tried to grieve for him, and had recognised that my only strong emotion was an aversion to being called by his name. I wished to remain myself. Relations and family solicitors clearly took it for granted, however, that having sown a few wild oats I would now settle down into his pattern of life. His death, if I wasn't careful, would be my destruction.

'I was pleased to get your letter,' Gabriella said, 'because it was awful when you didn't come with the horses. I thought you had changed your mind about me.'

'But surely Simon explained?'

'Who is Simon?'

'The big fat bald man who went instead of me. He promised to tell you why I couldn't come, and to give you a bottle . . .' I grinned, 'a bottle of pills.'

'So they were from you!'

'Simon gave them to you. I suppose he couldn't explain why I hadn't come, because he doesn't know Italian. I forgot to tell him to speak French.'

She shook her head.

'One of the crew gave them to me. He said he'd found them in the toilet compartment just after they had landed, and he brought them across to see if I had lost them. He is a tall man, in uniform. I've seen him often. It was not your bald, fat Simon.'

'And Simon didn't try to talk to you at all?'

'No.' She shook her head. 'I don't think so. I see hundreds of bald fat travellers, but no one tried to speak to me about you.'

'A friendly big man, with kind eyes,' I said. 'He was wearing a frightful old green corduroy jacket, with a row of pins in one lapel. He has a habit of picking them up.'

She shook her head again. 'I didn't see him.'

Simon had promised to give her my message and the bottle. He had done neither, and he had disappeared. I hadn't liked to press Yardman too hard to find out where Simon had got to because there was always the chance that too energetic spadework would turn up the export bonus fraud: and I had vaguely assumed that it was because of the fraud that Simon had chosen not to come back. But even if he had decided on the spur of the moment to duck out, he would certainly have kept his promise to see Gabriella. Or didn't a resuscitated friendship stretch that far?

'What's the matter?' Gabriella asked.

I explained.

'You are worried about him?'

'He's old enough to decide for himself . . .' But I was remembering like a cold douche that my predecessor Peters hadn't come back from Milan, and before him the liaison man Ballard.

'Tomorrow morning,' she said firmly, 'you will go back to Milan and find him.'

'I can't speak Italian.'

'Undoubtedly you will need an interpreter,' she nodded. 'Me.'

'The best,' I agreed, smiling.

We walked companionably back to the hotel.

'Were the pills all right?' I asked.

'Perfect, thank you very much. I gave them to the wife of our baker . . . She works in the bakery normally, but when she gets pregnant she's always sick for months, and can't stand the sight of dough, and he gets bad-tempered because he has to pay a man to help him instead. He is not a good Catholic.' She laughed. 'He makes me an enormous cake oozing with cream when I take the pills.'

No one took the slightest notice of us in the hotel. I went along the empty passage in my dressing-gown and knocked on her door, and she opened it in hers to let me in. I locked it behind me.

'If my sister could see us,' she said smiling, 'she'd have a fit.'

'I'll go away . . . if you like.'

'Could you?' She put her arms round my neck.

'Very difficult.'

'I don't ask it.'

I kissed her. 'It would be impossible to go now,' I said.

She sighed happily. 'I absolutely agree. We will just have to make the best of it.'

We did.

We went back to Milan in the morning sitting side by side in the railway carriage and holding hands surreptitiously under her coat, as if by this tiny area of skin contact we could keep alive the total union of the night. I had never wanted to hold hands with anyone before: never realised that it could feel like being plugged into a small electric current, warm, comforting, and vibrant, all at the same time.

Apart from being together, it was a depressing day. No one had seen Simon.

'He couldn't just vanish,' I said in exasperation, standing late in the afternoon in a chilly wind outside the last of the hospitals. We had drawn a blank there as everywhere else, though they had gone to some trouble to make sure for us. No man of his description had been admitted for any illness or treated for any accident during the past ten days.

'Where else can we look?' she said, the tiredness showing in her voice and in the droop of her rounded body. She had been splendid all day, asking questions unendingly from me and translating the replies, calm and business-like and effective. It wasn't her fault the answers had all been negative. Police, government departments, undertakers, we had tried them all. We had rung up every hotel in Milan and asked for him: he had stayed in none.

'I suppose we could ask the taxi drivers at the airport . . .' I said finally.

'There are so many . . . and who would remember one passenger after so long?'

'He had no luggage,' I said as I'd said a dozen times before. 'He didn't know he was coming here until fifteen minutes before he took off. He couldn't have made any plans. He doesn't speak Italian. He hadn't any Italian money. Where did he go? What did he do?'

She shook her head dispiritedly. There was no answer. We took a tram back to the station and with half an hour to wait made a few last enquiries from the station staff. They didn't remember him. It was hopeless.

Over dinner at midnight in the same café as the night before we gradually forgot the day's frustration; but the fruitless grind, though it hadn't dug up a trace of Simon, had planted foundations beneath Gabriella and me.

She drooped against me going back to the hotel, and I saw with remorse how exhausted she was. 'I've tired you too much.'

She smiled at the anxiety in my voice. 'You don't realise how much energy you have.'

'Energy?' I repeated in surprise.

'Yes. It must be that.'

'What do you mean?'

'You don't look energetic. You're quiet, and you move like machinery, oiled and smooth. No effort. No jerks. No awkwardness. And inside somewhere is a dynamo. It doesn't run down. I can feel its power. All day I've felt it.'

I laughed. 'You're too fanciful.'

'No. I'm right.'

I shook my head. There were no dynamos ticking away inside me. I was a perfectly ordinary and not too successful man, and the smoothness she saw was only tidiness.

She was already in bed and half asleep when I went along to her room. I locked the door and climbed in beside her, and she made a great effort to wake up for my sake.

'Go to sleep,' I said, kissing her lightly. 'There is always the morning.'

She smiled contentedly and snuggled into my arms, and I lay there cradling her sweet soft body, her head on my chest and her hair against

my mouth, and felt almost choked by the intensity with which I wanted
to protect her and share with her everything I had: Henry Grey, I
thought in surprise in the dark, was suddenly more than half way down
the untried track to honest-to-goodness love.

Sunday morning we strolled aimlessly round the city, talking and
looking at the mountains of leather work in the shops in the arcades;
Sunday afternoon we went improbably to a football match, an unexpected
passion of Gabriella's; and Sunday night we went to bed early because,
as she said with her innocent giggle, we would have to be up at six to
get her back to start work in the shop on time. But there was something
desperate in the way she clung to me during that night, as if it were our
last for ever instead of only a week or two, and when I kissed her there
were tears on her cheeks.

'Why are you crying?' I said, wiping them away with my fingers.
'Don't cry.'

'I don't know why.' She sniffed, half laughing. 'The world is a sad
place. Beauty bursts you. An explosion inside. It can only come out as
tears.'

I was impossibly moved. I didn't deserve her tears. I kissed them away
in humility and understood why people said love was painful, why Cupid
was invented with arrows. Love did pierce the heart, truly.

It wasn't until we were on the early train to Milan the next morning
that she said anything about money, and from her hesitation in beginning
I saw that she didn't want to offend me.

'I will repay you what you lent me for my bill,' she said matter of
factly, but a bit breathlessly. I had pushed the notes into her hand on the
way downstairs, as she hadn't wanted me to pay for her publicly, and
she hadn't enough with her to do it herself.

'Of course not,' I said.

'It was a much more expensive place than I'd thought of . . .'

'Big hotels ignore you better.'

She laughed. 'All the same . . .'

'No.'

'But you don't earn much. You can't possibly afford it all. The hotel
and the train fares, and the dinners.'

'I earned some money winning a race.'

'Enough?'

'I'll win another race . . . then it will be enough.'

'Giulio doesn't like it that you work with horses.' She laughed. 'He
says that if you were good enough to be a jockey you'd do it all the time
instead of being a groom.'

'What does Giulio do?'

'He works for the government in the taxation office.'

'Ah,' I said, smiling. 'Would it help if you told him my father has left
me some money? Enough to come to see you, anyway, when I get it.'

'I'm not sure I'll tell him. He judges people too much by how much
money they've got.'

'Do you want to marry a rich man?'

'Not to please Giulio.'

'To please yourself?'

'Not rich necessarily. But not too poor. I don't want to worry about how to afford shoes for the children.'

I smoothed her fingers with my own.

'I think I will have to learn Italian,' I said.

She gave me the flashing smile. 'Is English very difficult?'

'You can practise on me.'

'If you come back often enough. If your father's money should not be saved for the future.'

'I think,' I said slowly, smiling into her dark eyes, 'that there will be enough left. Enough to buy the children's shoes.'

I went to New York with the horses the following day in the teeth of furious opposition from the family. Several relatives were still staying in the house, including my three sharp tongued eldest sisters, none of whom showed much reserve in airing their views. I sat through a depressing lunch, condemned from all sides. The general opinion was, it seemed, that my unexplained absence over the week-end was disgraceful enough, but that continuing with my job was scandalous. Mother cried hysterical tears and Alice was bitterly reproving.

'Consider your *position*,' they all wailed, more or less in chorus.

I considered my position and left for Yardman's and Gatwick three hours after returning from Milan.

Mother had again brought up the subject of my early marriage to a suitable heiress. I refrained from telling her I was more or less engaged to a comparatively penniless Italian girl who worked in a gift shop, smuggled birth control pills, and couldn't speak English. It wasn't exactly the moment.

The outward trip went without a hitch. Timmie and Conker were along, together with a pair of grooms with four Anglia Bloodstock horses, and in consequence the work went quickly and easily. We were held up for thirty-six hours in New York by an engine fault, and when I rang up Yardman to report our safe return on the Friday morning he asked me to stay at Gatwick, as another bunch of brood mares was to leave that afternoon.

'Where for?'

'New York again,' he said briskly. 'I'll come down with the papers myself, early in the afternoon. You can send Timms and Chestnut home. I'm bringing Billy and two others to replace them.'

'Mr. Yardman . . .' I said.

'Yes?'

'If Billy tries to pick a fight, or molests me at all on the way, my employment with you ceases the instant we touch down in New York, and I will not help unload the horses or accept any responsibility for them.'

There was a shocked silence. He couldn't afford to have me do what I threatened, in the present sticky state of the business.

'My dear boy . . .' he protested sighing. 'I don't want you to have troubles. I'll speak to Billy. He's a thoughtless boy. I'll tell him not everyone is happy about his little practical jokes.'

'I'd appreciate it,' I said with irony at his view of Billy's behaviour.

Whatever Yardman said to him worked. Billy was sullen, unhelpful, and calculatingly offensive, but for once I completed a return trip with him without a bruise to show for it.

On the way over I sat for a time on a hay bale beside Alf and asked him about Simon's last trip to Milan. It was hard going, as the old man's deafness was as impenetratable as seven eighths cloud.

'Mr. Searle,' I shouted. 'Did he say where he was going?'

'Eh?'

After about ten shots the message got through, and he nodded.

'He came to Milan with us.'

'That's right, Alf. Where did he go then?'

'Eh?'

'Where did he go then?'

'I don't rightly know,' he said. 'He didn't come back.'

'Did he *say* where he was going?'

'Eh?'

I yelled again.

'No. He didn't say. Perhaps he told Billy. He was talking to Billy, see?'

I saw. I also saw that it was no use my ever asking Billy anything about anything. Yardman would have asked him, anyway, so if Simon had told Billy where he was going Yardman would have known. Unless, of course, Simon had asked Billy not to tell, and he hadn't. But Simon didn't like Billy and would never trust him with a secret.

'Where did Mr. Searle go, when you left the plane?'

I was getting hoarse before he answered.

'I don't know where he went. He was with Billy and the others. I went across on my own, like, to get a beer. Billy said they were just coming. But they never came.'

'None of them came?'

There had been the two grooms from the stud beside Simon and Billy, on that trip.

Eventually Alf shook his head. 'I finished my beer and went back to the plane. There was no one there as I ate my lunch.'

I left it at that because my throat couldn't stand any more.

Coming back we were joined by some extra help in the shape of a large pallid man who didn't know what to do with his hands and kept rubbing them over the wings of his jodhpurs as if he expected to find pockets there. He was ostensibly accompanying a two-year-old, but I guessed tolerantly he was some relation of the owner or trainer travelling like that to avoid a transatlantic fare. I didn't get around to checking on it, because the double journey had been very tiring, and I slept soundly nearly all the way back. Alf had to shake me awake as we approached Gatwick. Yawning I set about the unloading – it was by then well into Sunday morning – and still feeling unusually tired, drove home afterwards in a bee line to bed. A letter from Gabriella stopped me in the hall, and I went slowly upstairs reading it.

She had, she said, asked every single taxi driver and all the airport bus drivers if they had taken anywhere a big fat Englishman who couldn't speak Italian, had no luggage, and was wearing a green corduroy jacket. None of them could remember anyone like that. Also, she said, she had checked with the car hire firms which had agencies at the airport, but none of them had dealt with Simon. She had checked with all the airlines' passenger lists for the day he went to Milan, and the days after: he had not flown off anywhere.

I lay in a hot bath and thought about whether I should go on trying to find him. Bringing in any professional help, even private detectives, would only set them searching in England for a reason for his disappearance, and they'd all too soon dig it up. A warrant out for his arrest was not what I wanted. It would effectively stop him coming back at all. Very likely he didn't want to be found in the first place, or he wouldn't have disappeared so thoroughly, or stayed away so long. But supposing something had happened to him ... though what, I couldn't imagine. And I wouldn't have thought anything could have happened at all, were it not for Peters and Ballard.

There were Simon's partners in the fraud. His cousin, and the man in France. Perhaps I could ask them if they had heard from him ... I couldn't ask them, I thought confusedly: I didn't know their names. Simon had an elderly aunt somewhere, but I didn't know her name either ... the whole thing was too much ... and I was going to sleep in the bath.

I went to the wharf building the next morning at nine thirty to collect my previous week's pay and see what was on the schedule for the future. True to his word, Yardman had arranged no air trips for the following three days of Cheltenham races. There was a big question mark beside a trip for six circus horses for Spain that same afternoon, but no question mark, I was glad to see, about a flight to Milan with brood mares on Friday.

Yardman, when I went down to see him, said the circus horses were postponed until the following Monday owing to their trainer having read in his stars that it was a bad week to travel. Yardman was disgusted. Astrology was bad for business.

'Milan on Friday, now,' he said, sliding a pencil to and fro through his fingers. 'I might come on that trip myself, if I can get away. It's most awkward, with Searle's work to be done. I've advertised for someone to fill his place ... anyway, as I was saying, if I can get away I think I'd better go and see our opposite numbers out there. It always pays you know, my dear boy. I go to all the countries we export to. About once a year. Keeps us in touch, you know.'

I nodded. Good for business, no doubt.

'Will you ask them ... our opposite numbers ... if they saw Simon Searle any time after he landed?'

He looked surprised, the taut skin stretched over his jaw.

'I could, yes. But I shouldn't think he told them where he was going, if he didn't have the courtesy to tell me.'

'It's only an outside chance,' I agreed.

'I'll ask, though.' He nodded. 'I'll certainly ask.'

I went upstairs again to Simon's room, shut his door, sat in his chair, and looked out of his window. His room, directly over Yardman's, had the same panoramic view of the river, from a higher angle. I would like to live there, I thought idly. I liked the shipping, the noise of the docks, the smell of the river, the coming and going. Quite simply, I supposed, I liked the business of transport.

The Finnish ship had gone from the berth opposite and another small freighter had taken her place. A limp flag swung fitfully at her mast head, red and white horizontal stripes with a navy blue triangle and a white star. I looked across at the nationality chart on Simon's wall. Puerto Rico. Well, well, one lived and learned. Three alphabetical flags lower down, when checked, proved to be E, Q and M. Mildly curious, I turned them up in the international code of signals. 'I am delivering.' Quite right and proper. I shut the book, twiddled my thumbs, watched a police launch swoop past doing twenty knots on the ebb, and reflected not for the first time that the London river was a fast rough waterway for small boats.

After a while I picked up the telephone and rang up Fenland to book a plane for Sunday.

'Two o'clock?'

'That'll do me fine,' I said. 'Thanks.'

'Wait a minute, Harry. Mr. Wells said if you rang that he wanted a word with you.'

'O.K.'

There were some clicks, and then Tom's voice.

'Harry? Look, for God's sake, what is this job of yours?'

'I work for . . . a travel agency.'

'Well, what's so special about it? Come here, and I'll pay you more.' He sounded worried and agitated, not casually inviting as before.

'What's up?' I said.

'Everything's up except my planes. I've landed an excellent contract with a car firm in Coventry ferrying their executives, technicians, salesmen and so on all round the shop. They've a factory in Lancashire and tie-ups all over Europe, and they're fed-up with the airfield they've been using. They're sending me three planes. I'm to maintain them, provide pilots and have them ready when wanted.'

'Sounds good,' I said. 'So what's wrong?'

'So I don't want to lose them again before I've started. And not only can I not find any out-of-work pilots worth considering, but one of my three regulars went on a ski-ing holiday last week and broke his leg, the silly bastard. So how about it?'

'It's not as easy as you make it sound,' I said reluctantly.

'What's stopping you?'

'A lot of things . . . if you'll be around on Sunday, anyway, we could talk it over.'

He sighed in exasperation. 'The planes are due here at the end of the month, in just over a fortnight.'

'Get someone else, if you can,' I said.

'Yeah . . . if I can.' He was depressed. 'And if I can't?'

'I don't know. I could do a day a week to help out, but even then . . .'

'Even then, what?'

'There are difficulties.'

'Nothing to mine, Harry. Nothing to mine. I'll break you down on Sunday.'

Everyone had troubles, even with success. The higher the tougher, it seemed. I wiggled the button, and asked for another number, the charter airline which Patrick worked for. The Gatwick office answered, and I asked them if they could tell me how to get hold of him.

'You're in luck. He's actually here, in the office. Who's speaking?'

'Henry Grey, from Yardman Transport.'

I waited, and he came on the line.

'Hullo . . . how's things? How's Gabriella?'

'She,' I said, 'is fine. Other things are not. Could you do me a favour?'

'Shoot.'

'Could you look up for me the name of the pilot who flew a load of horses to Milan for us a fortnight last Thursday? Also the names of the co-pilot and engineer, and could you also tell me how or when I could talk to one or all of them?'

'Trouble?'

'Oh, no trouble for your firm, none at all. But one of our men went over on that trip and didn't come back, and hasn't got in touch with us since. I just wanted to find out if the crew had any idea what became of him. He might have told one of them where he was going . . . anyway, his work is piling up here and we want to find out if he intends to come back.'

'I see. Hang on then. A fortnight last Thursday?'

'That's it.'

He was away several minutes. The cranes got busy on the freighter from Puerto Rico. I yawned.

'Henry? I've got them. The pilot was John Kyle, co-pilot G. L. Rawlings, engineer V. N. Brede. They're not here, though; they've just gone to Arabia, ferrying mountains of luggage from London after some oil chieftain's visit. He brought about six wives, and they all went shopping.'

'Wow,' I said. 'When do they get back?'

He consulted someone in the background.

'Sometime Wednesday. They have Thursday off, then another trip to Arabia on Friday.'

'Some shopping,' I said gloomily. 'I can't get to see them on Wednesday or Thursday. I'm racing at Cheltenham. But I could ring them up on Wednesday night, if you can give me their numbers.'

'Well . . .,' said Patrick slowly. 'John Kyle likes his flutter on the horses.'

'You don't think he'd come to Cheltenham, then?'

'He certainly might, if he isn't doing anything else.'

'I'll get him a member's badge, and the others too, if they'd like.'

'Fair enough. Let's see. I'm going to Holland twice tomorrow. I should think I could see them on Wednesday, if we all get back reasonably on schedule. I'll tell them what you want, and ring you. If they go to Cheltenham you'll see them, and if not you can ring them. How's that?'

'Marvellous. You'll find me at the Queen's Hotel at Cheltenham. I'll be staying there.'

'Right ... and oh, by the way, I see I'm down for a horse transport flight on Friday to Milan. Is that your mob, or not?'

'Our mob,' I agreed. 'What's left of it.'

We rang off, and I leaned back in Simon's chair, pensively biting my thumbnail and surveying the things on his desk: telephone, tray of pens, blank notepad, and a pot of paper clips and pins. Nothing of any help. Then slowly, methodically, I searched through the drawers. They were predictably packed with export forms of various sorts, but he had taken little of a personal nature to work. Some indigestion tablets, a screwdriver, a pair of green socks, and a plastic box labelled 'spare keys'. That was the lot. No letters, no bills, no private papers of any sort.

I opened the box of keys. There were about twenty or more, the silt of years. Suitcase keys, a heavy old iron key, car keys. I stirred them up with my finger. A Yale key. I picked it out and looked at it. It was a duplicate, cut for a few shillings from a blank, and had no number. The metal had been dulled by time, but not smoothed, from use. I tapped it speculatively on the edge of the desk, thinking that anyway there would be no harm in trying.

Chapter Nine

Simon's home address, obtained off his insurance card via the dim typist, proved to be located in a dingy block of flats in the outer reaches of St. John's Wood. The grass on patchy lawns had remained uncut from about the previous August, which gave the graceless buildings a mournful look of having been thoughtlessly dumped in a hayfield. I walked through spotted glass entrance doors, up an uninspiring staircase, met no one, and came to a halt outside number fifteen in white twopenny plastic letters screwed on to cheap green painted deal.

The Yale key slid raspingly into the lock as if it had never been there before, but it turned under my pressure and opened the door. There was a haphazard foot-high pile of newspapers and magazines just inside. When I pushed the door against them they slithered away, and I stepped in and round them, and shut the door behind me.

The flat consisted only of a tiny entrance hall, a small bedroom, poky kitchen and bathroom and a slightly larger sitting-room. The prevailing colour was maroon, which I found depressing, and the furniture looked as if it had been bought piece by piece from second-class second-hand shops. The total effect could have been harmonious, but it wasn't: not so much through lack of taste as lack of imagination. He had spent the minimum trouble on his surroundings, and the result was gloomy. Cold dead air and a smell of mustiness seeped up my nose. There were unwashed, mould-growing dishes on the draining board in the kitchen, and crumpled thrown-back bedclothes on the bed. He had left his shaving water in the washbasin and the scum had dried into a hard grey line round the edge. Poor Simon, I thought forlornly, what an existence. No wife, no warmth: no wonder he liked pubs.

One wall in the sitting-room was lined with bookcases, and the newest, most obviously luxurious object in the flat was a big stereophonic radiogram standing behind the door. No television. No pictures on the dull coffee walls. Not a man of visual pleasures. Beside a large battered arm-chair, handy to perpetual reach, stood a wooden crate of bottled beer.

Wandering round his flat I realised what a fearful comment it was on myself that I had never been there before. This big tolerant dishonest man I would have counted my only real friend, yet I'd never seen where he lived. Never been asked; never thought of asking him to my own home. Even where I had wanted friendship, I hadn't known how to try. I felt as cold inside as Simon's flat; as uninhabited. Gabriella seemed very far away.

I picked up the heap of papers inside the front door and carried them into the sitting-room. Sorted into piles, they consisted of sixteen dailies, three Sundays, three *Horse and Hounds*, three *Sporting Life* weeklies and one *Stud and Stable*. Several letters in brown unstuck envelopes looked unpromising and with very little hesitation I opened all the rest. There were none from France, and none from the accomplice cousin. The only one of any help was written in spiky black hand on dark blue paper. It began 'Dear Simon,' thanked him for a birthday present, and was signed 'your loving aunt Edna.' The handwritten address at the top said 3 Gordon Cottages, East Road, Potter's Green, Berks., and there was no telephone number.

There was no desk as such in his flat. He kept his bills and papers clipped into labelled categories in the top drawer of a scratched chest in his bedroom, but if his cousin's name and address was among them, I couldn't recognise them. Alongside the papers lay a *Horse and Hound* rolled tightly into a tube and bound with wide brown sticky paper, ready to be posted. I picked it up and turned it round in my hands. It bore no address. The thick layers of brown sticky paper were tough, and even though I was careful with my penknife it looked as though a tiger had been chewing it when I finally hacked my way through. The magazine unrolled reluctantly, and I picked it up and shook it. Nothing happened. It wasn't until one looked at it page by page that the money showed, five pound notes stuck on with sellotape. They were used notes, not new, and there were sixty of them. I rolled the *Horse and Hound* up again and laid it back in the drawer, seeing a vivid mental picture, as I picked up the brown pieces of gummed strips and put them in the wastbasket, of Simon listening to his radiogram and sticking his money into the journals, night after night, an endless job, working for his old age.

Potter's Green turned out to be a large village spreading out into tentacles of development around the edges. East Road was a new one, and Gordon Cottages proved to be one of several identical strips of council-built bungalows for old people. Number three like all the rest still looked clean and fresh, with nothing growing yet in the bathmat sized flower bed under the front window. There was bright yellow paint clashing with pale pink curtains and a bottle of milk standing on the concrete doorstep.

I rang the bell. The pink curtains twitched, and I turned my head to see myself being inspected by a pair of mournful, faded eyes set in a large pale face. She flapped a hand at me in a dismissing movement, shooing me away, so I put my finger on the bell and rang again.

I heard her come round to the other side of the door.

'Go away,' she said. 'I don't want anything.'

'I'm not selling,' I said through the letter-box. 'I'm a friend of Simon's, your nephew Simon Searle.'

'Who are you? I don't know you.'

'Henry Grey . . . I work with Simon at Yardman's. Could I please talk to you inside, it's very difficult like this, and your neighbours will wonder what's going on.' There were in truth several heads at the front windows already, and it had its effect. She opened the door and beckoned me in.

The tiny house was crammed with the furniture she must have brought with her from a much larger place, and every available surface was covered with useless mass-produced ornaments. The nearest to me as I stood just inside the doorway was a black box decorated with 'A present from Brighton' in shells. And next to that a china donkey bore panniers of dried everlasting flowers. Pictures of all sorts crowded the walls, interspersed by several proverbs done in poker-work on wood. 'Waste not, Want not' caught my eye, and further round there was 'Take care of the pence and the pounds will take care of you'; an improvement on the original.

Simon's stout aunt had creaking corsets and wheezing breath and smelled of mentholated cough pastilles. 'Simon isn't here, you know. He lives in London, not here.'

'I know, yes.' Hesitatingly, I told her about Simon going away and not coming back. 'I wondered,' I finished, 'if by any chance he has written to you. Sent you a picture postcard. That sort of thing.'

'He will do. He's sure to.' She nodded several times. 'He always does, and brings me a little souvenir when he's been away. Very considerate is Simon.'

'But you haven't had a postcard yet.'

'Not yet. Soon, I expect.'

'If you do, would you write to me and let me know? You see, he hasn't said when he'll be back, and Mr. Yardman is advertising for someone to fill his job.'

'Oh, dear.' She was troubled. 'I hope nothing has happened to him.'

'I don't expect so: but if you hear from him, you will let us know?'

'Yes, yes, of course. Dear oh dear, I wonder what he is up to.'

Her choice of phrase reminded me of what in fact he was up to, and I asked her if she knew Simon's cousin's name and address. Unhesitatingly she reeled it off. 'He's my poor dead sister's son,' she said. 'But a surly man. I don't get on with him at all. Not easy, like Simon, now. Simon stayed with m e a lot when he was little, when I kept the village shop. He never forgets my birthday, and always brings me nice little mementoes like these.' She looked proudly round her overflowing possessions. 'Simon's very kind. I've only my old age pension, you know, and a little bit put by and Simon's the only one who bothers with me much. Oh I've got my two daughters, of course, but one's married in Canada and the other's got enough troubles of her own. Simon's given me a hundred pounds for my birthday every year for the last three years; what do you think of that?'

'Absolutely splendid.' A hundred pounds of tax payers' money. Robin Hood stuff. Oh well.

'You'll let me know, then,' I said, turning to go. She nodded, creaking as she moved round me to open the street door. Facing me in the little hall hung more time-worn poker work. 'See a pin and pick it up, all the day you'll have good luck. See a pin and let it lie, you will want before you die.' So there, I thought, smiling to myself, was the origin of Simon's pin tidying habit, a proverb stretching back to childhood. He didn't intend to want before he died.

The accomplice cousin farmed in Essex, reasonably handy for Cambridge airport, but a long haul for Gatwick. It was evident at once, however, that I could expect no easy help from him.

'You,' he said forcefully, 'you're the interfering bastard who's fouled up the works, aren't you? Well you can damn well clear off, that's what you can do. It's no business of yours where Simon's gone and in future you keep your bloody nose out of things that don't concern you.'

'If,' I said mildly, 'you prefer me to ask the police to find him, I will.'

He looked ready to explode, a large red faced man in khaki clothes and huge gum boots, standing four square in a muddy yard. He struggled visibly between the pleasure of telling me to go to hell and fear of the consequences if he did so. Prudence just won.

'All right. All right. I don't know where he is and that's straight. He didn't tell me he was going, and I don't know when he's coming back.'

Depressed, I drove home to Bedfordshire. The bulk and grandeur of the great house lay there waiting as I rolled slowly up the long drive. History in stone; the soul of the Creggans. Earl upon earl had lived there right back to the pirate who brought Spanish gold to Queen Bess, and since my father died I had only to enter to feel the chains fall heavily on me like a net. I stopped in the sweep of gravel in front instead of driving round to the garages as usual, and looked at what I had inherited. There was beauty, I admitted, in the great façade with its pillars and pediments and the two wide flights of steps sweeping up to meet at the door. The Georgian Palladian architect who had grafted a whole new mansion on to the Elizabethan and Stuart one already existing had produced a curiously satisfactory result, and as a Victorian incumbent had luckily confined his Gothic urges to a ruined folly in the garden, the only late addition had been a square red-bricked block of Edwardian plumbing. But for all its splendid outer show it had those beetles in the roof, miles of draughty passages, kitchens in the basement and twenty bedrooms mouldering into dust. Only a multi-millionaire could maintain and fill such a place now with servants and guests, whereas after death duties I would be hard put to it to find a case of champagne once the useless pile had voraciously gulped what it cost just to keep standing.

Opening it to the public might have been a solution if I had been any sort of a showman. But to someone solitary by nature that way meant a lifetime of horrifying square-peggery. Slavery to a building. Another human sacrifice on the altar of tradition. I simply couldn't face it. The very idea made me wilt.

Since it was unlikely anyone would simply let me pull the whole thing down, the National Trust, I thought, was the only hope. They could organise the sight-seeing to their heart's content and they might let Mother live there for the rest of her life, which she needed.

Mother usually used the front entrance while Alice and I drove on and went in through one of the doors at the side, near the garages. That early evening, however, I left my little car on the gravel and walked slowly up the shallow steps. At the top I leaned against the balustrade and looked back over the calm wide fields and bare branched trees just swelling into bud. I didn't really own all this, I thought. It was like the baton in a relay race, passed on from one, to be passed on to the next, belonging to none for more than a lap. Well, I wasn't going to pass it on. I was the last runner. I would escape from the track at a tangent and give the baton away. My son, if I ever had one, would have to lump it.

I pushed open the heavy front door and stepped into the dusk-filled house. I, Henry Grey, descendant of the sea pirate, of warriors and explorers and empire builders and of a father who'd been decorated for valour on the Somme, I, the least of them, was going to bring their way of life to an end. I felt one deep protesting pang for their sakes, and that was all. If they had anything of themselves to pass on to me, it was already in my genes. I carried their inheritance in my body, and I didn't need their house.

Not only did John Kyle and his engineer come to Cheltenham, but Patrick as well.

'I've never been before,' he said, his yellow eyes and auburn hair shining as he stood in the bright March sun. 'These two are addicts. I just came along for the ride.'

'I'm glad you did,' I said, shaking hands with the other two. John Kyle was a bulky battered looking young man going prematurely thin on top. His engineer, tall and older, had three racing papers and a form sheet tucked under his arm.

'I see,' he said, glancing down at them, 'th . . . that you won the United Hunts Ch . . . Challenge Cup yesterday.' He managed his stutter unselfconsciously. 'W . . . w . . . well done.'

'Thank you,' I said. 'I was a bit lucky. I wouldn't have won if Century hadn't fallen at the last.'

'It d . . . d . . . d . . . does say that, in the p . . . p . . . paper,' he agreed disarmingly.

Patrick laughed and said, 'What are you riding in today?'

'The Gold Cup and the Mildmay of Flete Challenge Cup.'

'Clobber and Boathook,' said John Kyle readily.

'I'll back you,' Patrick said.

'M . . . m . . . money down the drain b . . . backing Clobber,' said the engineer seriously.

'Thanks very much,' I said with irony.

'F . . . form's all haywire. V . . . v . . . very inconsistent,' he explained.

'Do you think you've got a chance?' Patrick asked.

'No, not much. I've never ridden him before. The owner's son usually rides him, but he's got jaundice.'

'N . . . not a b . . . betting proposition,' nodded the engineer.

'For God's sake don't be so depressing, man,' protested Kyle.

'How about Boathook?' I asked, smiling.

The engineer consulted the sky. The result wasn't written there, as far as I could see.

'B . . . B . . . Boathook,' he remarked, coming back to earth, 'm . . . m . . . might just do it. G . . . good for a p . . . place anyway.'

'I shall back them both, just the same,' said Patrick firmly.

I took them all to lunch and sat with them while they ate.

'Aren't you having any?' said Patrick.

'No. It makes you sick if you fall after eating.'

'How often do you fall then?' asked Kyle curiously, cutting into his cold red beef.

'On average, once in a dozen rides, I suppose. It varies. I've never really counted.'

'When did you fall last?'

'Day before yesterday.'

'Doesn't it bother you?' asked Patrick, shaking salt. 'The prospect of falling?'

'Well, no. You never think you're going to, for a start. And a lot of falls are easy ones; you only get a bruise, if that. Sometimes when the horse goes right down you almost step off.'

'And sometimes you break your bones,' Kyle said dryly.

I shook my head. 'Not often.'

Patrick laughed. I passed him the butter for his roll, looked at my watch, and said, 'I'll have to go and change soon. Do you think we could talk about the day you took Simon Searle to Milan?'

'Shoot,' said Kyle. 'What do you want to know?'

'Everything you can think of that happened on the way there and after you landed.'

'I don't suppose I'll be much help,' he said apologetically. 'I was in the cockpit most of the time, and I hardly spoke to him at all. I went aft to the karzy once, and he was sitting in one of those three pairs of sets that were bolted on at the back.'

I nodded. I'd bolted the seats on to the anchorages myself, after we had loaded all the horses. There was usually room for a few seats, and they made a change from hay bales.

'Was he alone?'

'No, there was a young fellow beside him. Your friend Searle was on the inside by the window, I remember, because this young chap had his legs sprawled out in the gangway and I had to step over them. He didn't move.'

'Billy,' I nodded.

'After I came out I asked them if they were O.K. and said we'd be landing in half an hour. The young one said "thanks Dad" as if he was bored to death, and I had to step over his legs again to get past. I can't say I took to him enormously.'

'You surprise me,' I said sardonically. 'Did Simon say anything?'

He hesitated. 'It's three weeks ago. I honestly can't remember, but I don't think so. Nothing special, anyway.'

I turned to the engineer. 'How about you?'

He chewed, shook his head, swallowed, and took a sip of beer.

'D . . . d . . . don't think I'm much better. I w . . . w . . . was talking to him q . . . q . . . quite a lot at the beginning. In the g . . . g . . . galley. He said he'd come at the l . . . l . . . last minute instead of you. He t . . . t . . . talked about you quite a lot.'

The engineer took a mouthful of salad and stuttered through it without embarrassment. A direct man, secure in himself. 'He's . . . said you were ice on a v . . . volcano. I said th . . . th . . . that didn't make sense, and he said it w . . . was the only w . . . way to describe you.'

Without looking up from his plate Patrick murmured, 'In a nutshell.'

'That's no help at all,' I said, disregarding him. 'Didn't he say anything about where he was going, or what he might do, when you got to Milan?'

The engineer shook his head. 'He m . . . m . . . meant to come straight back with us, in the afternoon, I'm sure of th . . . th . . . that.'

'We didn't come straight back, of course,' said Kyle matter-of-factly.

'You didn't?' I was surprised. 'I didn't know that.'

'We were supposed to. They got the return load of horses loaded up and then discovered there were no papers for one of the two they'd put in first. They had to get the whole lot out again, and they weren't very quick because there were only two of them, and by that time I said it was pointless loading again, as it would be too late to start, I'd be out of hours.'

'They should have checked they had all the papers before they loaded,' I said.

'Well, they didn't.'

'Only two of them,' I said, frowning.

'That's right. The young one – Billy, did you say? – and one other. Not you friend Simon. A deaf old fellow.'

'Alf,' I said. 'That's Alf. What about the two others who went over?

They were two specials going with horses from the studs they worked in.'

'From what I could make out from the old man, those two were going on with their horses right to their destination, somewhere further south.'

I thought it over. Simon obviously hadn't intended to come back at all, and it hadn't been the unexpected overnight stop which had given him the idea.

'You didn't see where Simon was headed, I suppose, when you got to Milan?' I spoke without much hope, and they both shook their heads.

'We got off the plane before him,' Kyle said.

I nodded. The crew didn't have customs and unloading to see to.

'Well . . . that's that. Thank you for coming today, anyway. And thank you,' I said directly to the engineer, 'for delivering that bottle of pills to the girl in the souvenir shop.'

'P . . . pills? Oh yes, I remember.' He was surprised. 'How on earth d . . . d . . . did you know about that?'

'She told me a tall crew member brought them over for her.'

'I f . . . f . . . found them on the plane, standing on the w . . . w . . . washbasin in the k . . . k . . . karzy. I th . . . th . . . thought I might as well give them to her, as I was g . . . going across anyway. I did . . . didn't see how they got there, b . . . b . . . but they had her name on them.'

'Simon was taking them to her from me,' I explained.

'Oh, I s . . . see.'

Patrick said, grinning, 'Were they . . .?'

'Yes, they were.'

'He didn't go over to the airport building at all, then,' said Patrick flatly. 'He left the pills on board, hoping they would get to Gabriella somehow, and scooted from there.'

'It looks like it,' I agreed gloomily.

'You can get off that end of the airfield quite easily, of course. It's only that scrubland and bushes, and if you walk down that road leading away from the unloading area, the one the horseboxes often use, you're off the place in no time. I should think that explains pretty well why no one saw him.'

'Yes,' I sighed, 'that's what he must have done.'·

'But it doesn't explain why he went,' said Patrick gently.

There was a pause.

'He had . . . troubles,' I said at last.

'*In* trouble?' said Kyle.

'Looming. It might be because of something I discovered that he went. I wanted to find him, and tell him it was . . . safe . . . to come back.'

'On your conscience,' said Patrick.

'You might say so.'

They all nodded, acknowledging their final understanding of my concern for a lost colleague. The waiter brought their cheese and asked whether they would like coffee. I stood up.

'I'll see you again,' I said. 'How about after the fifth, outside the weighing room? After I've changed.'

'Sure thing,' said Patrick.

I ambled off to the weighing room and later got dressed in Mr. Thackery's red and blue colours. I'd never ridden in the Gold Cup before, and although I privately agreed with the engineer's assessment of the situation, there was still something remarkably stirring in going out in the best class race of the season. My human opponents were all handpicked professionals and all Clobber's bunch looked to have the beating of him, but nevertheless my mouth grew dry and my heart thumped.

I suspected Mr. Thackery had entered Clobber more for the prestige of having a Gold Cup runner than from any thought that he would win, and his manner in the parade ring confirmed it. He was enjoying himself enormously, untouched by the sort of anxious excitement characteristic of the hopeful.

'Julian's regards,' he said, beaming and shaking hands vigorously. 'He'll be watching on T.V.'

T.V. There was always the fair chance that one of the people I knew at Fenland might be watching television, though none that I'd heard of was interested in racing. I turned my back on the cameras, as usual.

'Just don't disgrace me,' said Mr. Thackery happily. 'Don't disgrace me, that's all I ask.'

'You could have got a professional,' I pointed out.

'Oh, eh, I could. But frankly, it hasn't done me any harm, here and there, for folks to know you're riding my horses.'

'A mutually satisfactory arrangement, then,' I said dryly.

'Yes,' said Mr. Thackery contentedly. 'That's about it.'

I swung up on his horse, walked out in the parade, and cantered down to the start. Clobber, an eight year old thoroughbred chestnut hunter, had only once won (thanks to being low in the handicap) in the company he was taking on now at level weights, but he shone with condition and his step was bursting with good feeling. Like so many horses, he responded well to spring air and sun on his back and my own spirits lifted with his. It was not, after all, going to be a fiasco.

We lined up and the tapes went up, and Clobber set off to the first fence pulling like a train. As he hadn't a snowball's hope in hell of winning, I thought Mr. Thackery might as well enjoy a few moments in the limelight, and I let Clobber surge his way to the front. Once he got there he settled down and stopped trying to run away with me and we stayed there, surprisingly leading the distinguished field for over two and a half of the three and a quarter miles.

Clobber had never been run in front before, according to the form book, but from his willingness it was evidently to his liking. Holding him up against his inclination, I thought, probably accounted for his inconsistency: he must have lost interest on many occasions when thwarted, and simply packed up trying.

The others came up to him fast and hard going into the second last fence, and three went ahead before the last: but Clobber jumped it cleanly and attacked the hill with his ears still pricked good temperedly, and he finished fourth out of eight with some good ones still behind him. I was pleased with the result myself, having thoroughly enjoyed the whole race, and so it appeared was Mr. Thackery.

'By damn,' he said, beaming, 'that's the best he's ever run.'

'He likes it in front.'

'So it seems, yes. We've not tried that before, I must say.'

A large bunch of congratulating females advanced on him and I rolled the girths round my saddle and escaped to the weighing room to change for the next race. The colours were those of Old Strawberry Leaves, who had commented sourly that it was disgraceful of me to ride in public only three weeks after my father's death, but had luckily agreed not to remove me from his horse. The truth was that he begrudged paying professionals when he could bully the sons of his friends and acquaintances for nothing. Boathook was his best horse, and for the pleasure of winning on him I could easily put up with the insults I got from losing on the others. On that day, however, there was one too good for him from Ireland, and for being beaten by half a length I got the customary bawling out. Not a good loser by any means, Old Strawberry Leaves.

All in all I'd had a good Cheltenham, I thought, as I changed into street clothes: a winner, a second, an also ran, one harmless fall, and fourth in the Gold Cup. I wouldn't improve on it very easily.

Patrick and the other two were waiting for me outside, and after we'd watched the last race together, I drove them down to the station to catch the last train to London. They had all made a mint out of the engineer's tips and were in a fine collective state of euphoria.

'I can see why you like it,' Patrick said on the way. 'It's a magnificent sport. I'll come again.'

'Good,' I said, stopping at the station to let them out. 'I'll see you tomorrow, then.'

He grinned. 'Milan first stop.'

'Arabia again for us,' said Kyle resignedly, shutting the door.

They waved their thanks and began to walk away into the station. An elderly man tottered slowly across in front of my car, and as I was waiting for him to pass the engineer's voice floated back to me, clear and unmistakable.

'It's f . . . funny,' he said, 'you qu . . . quite forget he's a L . . . Lord.'

I turned my head round to them, startled. Patrick looked over his shoulder and saw that I had heard, and laughed. I grinned sardonically in return, and drove off reflecting that I was much in favour of people like him who could let me forget it too.

Chapter Ten

Fire can't burn without air. Deprived of an oxygen supply in a sealed space, it goes out. There existed a state of affairs like a smouldering room which had been shuttered and left to cool down in safety. Nothing much would have happened if I hadn't been trying to find Simon: but when I finally came on a trace of him, it was like throwing wide the door. Fresh air poured in and the whole thing banged into flames.

The fine Cheltenham weather was still in operation on the Friday, the day after the Gold Cup. The met reports in the charter company's office showed clear skies right across Europe, with an extended high pressure area almost stationary over France. No break up of the system was expected for at least twenty-four hours. Someone tapped me on the shoulder and I half turned to find Patrick reading over my shoulder.

'Trouble free trip,' he commented with satisfaction. 'Piece of cake.'

'We've got that old D.C.4 again, I see,' I said, looking out of the window across to where it stood on the tarmac.

'Nice reliable old bus.'

'Bloody uncomfortable old bus.'

Patrick grinned. 'You'll be joining a union next.'

'Workers unite,' I agreed.

He looked me up and down. 'Some worker. You remind me of Fanny Cradock.'

'Of *who?*' I said.

'That woman on television who cooks in a ball gown without marking it.'

'Oh.' I looked down at my neat charcoal worsted, my black tie, and the fraction of white showing at the cuffs. Beside me, in the small overnight bag I now carried everywhere, was the high necked black jersey I worked in, and a hanger for my jacket. Tidiness was addictive: one couldn't kick it, even when it was inappropriate.

'You're no slouch yourself,' I pointed out defensively. He wore his navy gold-braided uniform with the air of authority, his handsome good natured face radiating confidence. A wonderful bedside manner for nervous passengers, I thought. An inborn conviction that one only had to keep to the rules for everything to be all right. Fatal.

'Eight each way, today?' he said.

'Eight out, four back. All brood mares.'

'Ready to drop?'

'Let's hope not too ready.'

'Let's indeed.' He grinned and turned away to check over his flight plan with one of the office staff. 'I suppose,' he said over his shoulder, 'you'd like me to organise an overnight delay at Milan?'

'You suppose correctly.'

'You could do it yourself.'

'How?'

'Load up all the horses and then "lose" the papers for a front one. Like John Kyle said, by the time they'd unloaded and reloaded, it was too late to take off.'

I laughed. 'An absolutely brilliant idea. I shall act on it immediately.'

'That'll be the day.' He smiled over his papers, checking the lists.

The door opened briskly and Yardman came in, letting a blast of cold six-thirty air slip past him.

'All set?' he said, impressing on us his early hour alertness.

'The horses haven't arrived yet,' I said mildly. 'They're late again.'

'Oh.' He shut the door behind him and came in, putting down his briefcase and rubbing his thin hands together for warmth. 'They were due at six.' He frowned and looked at Patrick. 'Are you the pilot?'

'That's right.'

'What sort of trip are we going to have?'

'Easy,' said Patrick. 'The weather's perfect.'

Yardman nodded in satisfaction. 'Good, good.' He pulled out a chair and sat down, lifting and opening his brief case. He had brought all the brood mares' papers with him, and as he seemed content to check them with the airline people himself I leaned lazily against the office wall and thought about Gabriella. The office work went steadily on, regardless of the hour. No nine-to-five about an airline. As usual, some of the flying staff were lying there fast asleep, one on a canvas bed under the counter Patrick was leaning on, another underneath the big table where Yardman sat, and a third on my right, stretched along the top of a row of cupboards. They were all wrapped in blankets, heads and all, and were so motionless that one didn't notice them at first. They managed to sleep solidly through the comings and goings and telephoning and typing, and even when Yardman inadvertently kicked the one under the table he didn't stir.

The first of the horseboxes rolled past the window and drove across to the waiting plane. I peeled myself off the wall, temporarily banished Gabriella, and touched Yardman's arm.

'They're here,' I said.

He looked round and glanced through the window. 'Ah, yes. Well here you are, my dear boy, here's the list. You can load the first six, they are all checked. There's just one more to do . . . it seems there's some query of insurance on this one . . .' He bent back to his work, riffling through his brief case for more papers.

I took the list and walked across to the plane. I had expected Timmie and Conker to arrive in a horsebox as they lived near the stud one lot of horses had come from, but when I got over there I found it was to be Billy and Alf again. They had come with Yardman, and were already sitting on the stacked box sides in the plane, eating sandwiches. With them sat a third man in jodhpurs and a grubby tweed jacket a size too small. He was wearing an old greenish cap and he didn't bother to look up.

'The horses are here,' I said.

Billy turned his wide insolent glare full on and didn't answer. I bent down and touched Alf's knee, and pointed out of the oval window. He saw the horseboxes, nodded philosophically, and began to wrap up his remaining sandwiches. I left them and went down the ramp again, knowing very well that Billy would never obey an instruction of mine if I waited over him to see he did it.

The horsebox drivers said they'd had to make a detour because of roadworks. A detour into a transport café, more like.

Two grooms who had travelled with the mares gave a hand with the loading, which made it easy. The man who had come with Billy and Alf, whose name was John, was more abstracted than skilful, but with six of us it was the quickest job I had done when Billy was along. I imagined that it was because he knew Yardman was within complaining distance that he left me alone.

Yardman came across with the all clear for the other two mares, and we stowed them on board. Then as always we trooped along to the Immigration Office in the main passenger building where a bored official collected our dog-eared passports, flipped through them, and handed them back. Mine still had Mr. on it, because I'd originally applied for it that way, and I intended to put off changing it as long as possible.

'Four grooms and you,' he said to Yardman. 'That's the lot?'

'That's the lot.' Yardman stifled a yawn. Early starts disagreed with him.

A party of bleary-eyed passengers from a cut rate night flight shuffled past in an untidy crocodile.

'O.K. then.' The passport man flicked the tourists a supercilious glance and retired into his office. Not everyone was at his best before breakfast.

Yardman walked back to the plane beside me.

'I've arranged to meet our opposite numbers for lunch,' he said. 'You know what business lunches are, my dear boy. I'm afraid it may drag on a little, and that you'll be kicking your heels about the airport for a few hours. Don't let any of them get ... er ... the worse for wear.'

'No,' I agreed insincerely. The longer his lunch, the better I'd be pleased. Billy drunk couldn't be worse than Billy sober, and I didn't intend to waste my hours at Malpensa supervising his intake.

Patrick and his crew were ready out by the plane, and had done their checks. The mobile battery truck stood by the nose cone with its power lead plugged into the aircraft: Patrick liked always to start his engines from the truck, so that he took off with the plane's own batteries fully charged.

Yardman and I followed Billy, Alf and John up the ramp at the rear, and Patrick with his co-pilot Bob, and the engineer, Mike, climbed the forward stairs into the nose. The airport staff wheeled away the stairs and unfastened and removed the two long sections of ramp. The inner port propeller began to grind slowly round as I swung shut the double doors, then sparked into life with a roar, and the plane came alive with vibration. The moment of the first engine firing gave me its usual lift of the spirits and I went along the cabin checking the horses with a smile in my mind.

Patrick moved down the taxi track and turned on to the apron set aside for power checks, the airframe quivering against the brakes as he pushed the throttles open. Holding two of the horses by their head collars I automatically followed him in imagination through the last series of checks before he closed the throttles, released the brakes and rolled round to Gatwick's large single runway. The engine's note deepened and the plane began to move, horses and men leaning against the thrust as the speed built up to a hundred over the tarmac. We unstuck as per schedule and climbed away in a great wheeling turn, heading towards the channel on course to the radio beacon at Dieppe. The heavy mares took the whole thing philosophically, and having checked round the lot of them I went forward into the galley, bending under the luggage racks and stepping over the guy chains as always in the cramped D.C.4.

Mike, the engineer, was already writing names on disposable cups with a red·felt pen.

'All O.K.?' he asked, the eyebrow going up and down like a yo-yo.

'All fine,' I said.

He wrote 'Patrick' and 'Bob' and 'Henry' and asked me the names of the others. 'Mr. Y', 'Billy', 'Alf' and 'John' joined the roll. He filled the crew's cups and mine, and I took Patrick's and Bob's forward while he went back to ask the others if they were thirsty. The rising sun blazed into the cockpit, dazzling after the comparative gloom of the cabin. Both pilots were wearing dark glasses, and Patrick already had his jacket off, and had started on the first of his attendant bunch of bananas. The chart lay handy, the usual unlikely mass of half-inch circles denoting radio stations connected by broad pale blue areas of authorised airlines, with the normal shape of the land beneath only faintly drawn in and difficult to distinguish. Bob pulled a tuft of cotton wool off a shaving cut, made it bleed again, and swore, his exact words inaudible against the racket of the engines. Both of them were wearing head-sets, earphones combined with a microphone mounted on a metal band which curved round in front of the mouth. They spoke to each other by means of a transmitting switch set into the wheel on the control column, since normal speech in that noise was impossible. Giving me a grin and a thumbs up sign for the coffee, they went on with their endless attention to the job in hand. I watched for a bit, then strolled back through the galley, picking up 'Henry' en route, and relaxed on a hay bale to drink, looking down out of the oval window and seeing the coast of France tilt underneath as we passed the Dieppe beacon and set course for Paris.

A day like any other day, a flight like any other flight. And Gabriella waiting at the other end of it. Every half hour or so I checked round the mares, but they were a docile lot and travelled like veterans. Mostly horses didn't eat much in the air, but one or two were picking at their haynets, and a chestnut in the rearmost box was fairly guzzling. I began to untie her depleted net to fill it again for her from one of the bales when a voice said in my ear, 'I'll do that.'

I looked round sharply and found Billy's face two feet from my own.

'You?' The surprise and sarcasm got drowned by the engine noise.

He nodded, elbowed me out of the way, and finished untying the haynet. I watched with astonishment as he carried it away into the narrow starboard gangway and began to stuff it full again. He came back pulling the drawstring tight round the neck, slung it over to hang inside the box, and re-tied its rope on to the cleat. Wordlessly he treated me to a wide sneering glare from the searchlight eyes, pushing past, and flung himself with what suddenly looked like pent-up fury into one of the seats at the back.

In the pair of seats immediately behind him Yardman and John sat side by side. Yardman was frowning crossly at Billy, though to my mind he should have been giving him a pat on the head and a medal for self control.

Yardman turned his head from Billy to me and gave me his graveyard smile. 'What time do we arrive?' he shouted.

'About half an hour.'

He nodded and looked away through the window. I glanced at John and saw that he was dozing, with his grubby cap pushed back on his head and his hands lying limp on his lap. He opened his eyes while I was looking at him, and his relaxed facial muscles sharply contracted so that suddenly he seemed familiar to me, though I was certain I hadn't met him before. It puzzled me for only a second because Billy, getting up again, managed to kick my ankle just out of Yardman's sight. I turned away from him, lashed backwards with my heel, and felt a satisfactory clunking jar as it landed full on his shin. One day, I thought, smiling to myself as I squeezed forward along the plane, one day he'll get tired of it.

We joined the circuit at Malpensa four hours from Gatwick; a smooth, easy trip. Holding the mares' heads I saw the familiar red and white chequered huts near the edge of the airfield grow bigger and bigger as we descended, when they were suddenly behind us at eye level as Patrick levelled out twenty feet from the ground at about a hundred and ten miles an hour. The bump from the tricycle undercarriage as we touched down will full flaps at a fraction above stalling speed wasn't enough to rock the mares on their feet. Top of the class, I thought.

The customs man with his two helpers came on board, and Yardman produced the mares' papers from his briefcase. The checking went on without a hitch, brisk but thorough. The customs man handed the papers back to Yardman with a small bow and signed that the unloading could begin.

Yardman ducked out of any danger of giving a hand with that by saying that he'd better see if the opposite numbers were waiting for him inside the airport. As it was barely half past eleven, it seemed doubtful, but all the same he marched purposefully down the ramp and away across the tarmac, a gaunt black figure with sunshine flashing on his glasses.

The crew got off at the sharp end and followed him, a navy blue trio in peaked caps. A large yellow Shell tanker pulled up in front of the aircraft, and three men in white overalls began the job of refuelling.

We unloaded into the waiting horseboxes in record time, Billy seemingly being as anxious as me to get it done quickly, and within half an hour of landing I had changed my jersey for my jacket and was pushing open the glass doors of the airport. I stood just inside, watching Gabriella. She was selling a native doll, fluffing up the rich dark skirt to show the petticoats underneath, her face solemn and absorbed. The heavy dark club-cut hair swung forward as she leaned across the counter, and her eyes were cool and quiet as she shook her head gently at her customer, the engineer Mike. My chest constricted at the sight of her, and I wondered how I was possibly going to bear leaving again in three hours time. She looked up suddenly as if she felt my gaze, and she saw me and smiled, her soft mouth curving sweet and wide.

Mike looked quite startled at the transformation and turned to see the reason.

'Henry,' said Gabriella, with welcome and gaiety shimmering in her voice. 'Hullo, darling.'

'Darling?' exclaimed Mike, the eyebrow doing its stuff.

Gabriella said in French, 'I've doubled my English vocabulary, as you see. I know two words now.'

'Essential ones, I'm glad to say.'

'Hey,' said Mike. 'If you can talk to her, Henry, ask her about this doll. It's my elder girl's birthday tomorrow, and she's started collecting these things, but I'm damned if I know whether she'll like this one.'

'How old is she?'

'Twelve.'

I explained the situation to Gabriella, who promptly produced a different doll, much prettier and more colourful, which she wrapped up for him while he sorted out some lire. Like Patrick's his wallet was stuffed with several different currencies, and he scattered a day's pay in deutschmarks over the merchandise before finding what he wanted. Collecting his cash in an untidy handful he thanked her cheerfully in basic French, picked up his parcel and walked off upstairs into the restaurant. There were always lunches provided for us on the planes, tourist class lunches packed in boxes, but both Mike and Bob preferred eating on the ground, copiously and in comfort.

I turned back to Gabriella and tried to satisfy my own sort of hunger by looking at her and touching her hand. And I could see in her face that to her too this was like a bowl of rice to the famine of India.

'When do you go?' she said.

'The horses arrive at two thirty. I have to go then to load them. I might get back for a few minutes afterwards, if my boss dallies over his coffee.'

She sighed, looking at the clock. It was ten past noon. 'I have an hour off in twenty minutes. I'll make it two hours . . .' She turned away into swift chatter with the girl along on the duty free shop, and came back smiling. 'I'm doing her last hour today, and she'll do the gift shop in her lunch hour.'

I bowed my thanks to the girl and she laughed back with a flash of teeth, very white against the gloom of her bottle shop.

'Do you want to have lunch up there?' I suggested to Gabriella pointing where Mike and Bob had gone.

She shook her head. 'Too public. Everyone knows me so well. We've time to go to Milan, if you can do that?'

'If the horses get here early, they can wait.'

'Serve them right.' She nodded approvingly her lips twitching.

A crowd of outgoing passengers erupted into the hall and swarmed round the gift counter. I retired to the snack bar at the far end to wait out the twenty minutes, and found Yardman sitting alone at one of the small tables. He waved me to join him, which I would just as soon not have done, and told me to order myself a double gin and tonic, like his.

'I'd really rather have coffee.'

He waved a limp hand permissively. 'Have whatever you like, my dear boy.'

I looked casually round the big airy place, at the glass, the polished wood, the terrazza. Along one side, next to a stall of sweets and chocolates, stretched the serving counter with coffee and beer rubbing shoulders with milk and gin. And down at the far end, close-grouped round another little table and clutching pint glasses, sat Alf and Billy, and with his back to us, John. Two and a half hours of that, I thought wryly, and we'd have a riotous trip home.

'Haven't your people turned up?' I asked Yardman.

'Delayed,' he said resignedly. 'They'll be here about one, though.'

'Good,' I said, but not for his sake. 'You won't forget to ask them about Simon?'

'Simon?'

'Searle.'

'Searle . . . oh yes. Yes, all right, I'll remember.'

Patrick walked through the hall from the office department, exchanged a greeting with Gabriella over the heads of her customers and came on to join us.

'Drink?' suggested Yardman, indicating his glass. He only meant to be hospitable, but Patrick was shocked.

'Of course not.'

'Eh?'

'Well . . . I thought you'd know. One isn't allowed to fly within eight hours of drinking alcohol.'

'Eight hours,' repeated Yardman in astonishment.

'That's right. Twenty-four hours after a heavy party, and better not for forty-eight if you get paralytic.'

'I didn't know,' said Yardman weakly.

'Air Ministry regulations,' Patrick explained. 'I'd like some coffee, though.'

A waitress brought him some, and he unwrapped four sugars and stirred them in. 'I enjoyed yesterday,' he said, smiling at me with his yellow eyes. 'I'll go again. When do you race next?'

'Tomorrow.'

'That's out for a start. When else?'

I glanced at Yardman. 'It depends on the schedules.'

Patrick turned to him in his usual friendly way. 'I went to Cheltenham yesterday and saw our Henry here come forth in the Gold Cup. Very interesting.'

'You know each other well, then?' Yardman asked. His deep set eyes were invisible behind the glasses, and the slanting sunlight showed up every blemish in his sallow skin. I still had no feeling for him either way, not liking, nor disliking. He was easy to work for. He was friendly enough. He was still an enigma.

'We know each other,' Patrick agreed. 'We've been on trips together before.'

'I see.'

Gabriella came down towards us, wearing a supple brown suede coat over her black working dress. She had flat black round-toed patent leather shoes and swung a handbag with the same shine. A neat, composed, self-reliant, nearly beautiful girl who took work for granted and a lover for fun.

I stood up as she came near, trying to stifle a ridiculous feeling of pride, and introduced her to Yardman. He smiled politely and spoke to her in slow Italian, which surprised me a little, and Patrick translated for me into one ear.

'He's telling her he was in Italy during the war. Rather tactless of him, considering her grandfather was killed fighting off the invasion of Sicily.'

'Before she was born,' I protested.

'True.' He grinned. 'She's pro-British enough now, anyway.'

'Miss Barzini tells me you are taking her to lunch in Milan,' Yardman said.

'Yes,' I agreed. 'If that's all right with you? I'll be back by two-thirty when the return mares come.'

'I can't see any objection,' he said mildly. 'Where do you have in mind?'

'Trattoria Romana,' I said promptly. It was where Gabriella, Patrick and I had eaten on our first evening together.

Gabriella put her hand in mine. 'Good. I'm very hungry.' She shook hands with Yardman and waggled her fingers at Patrick. 'Arrivederci.'

We walked away up the hall, the voltage tingling gently through our joined palms. I looked back once, briefly, and saw Yardman and Patrick watching us go. They were both smiling.

Chapter Eleven

Neither of us had much appetite, when it came to the point. We ate half our lasagne and drank coffee, and needed nothing else but proximity. We didn't talk a great deal, but at one point, clairvoyantly reading my disreputable thoughts, she said out of the blue that we cduldn't go to her sister's flat as her sister would be in, complete with two or three kids.

'I was afraid of that,' I said wryly.

'It will have to be next time.'

'Yes.' We both sighed deeply in unison, and laughed.

A little later, sipping her hot coffee, she said, 'How many pills were there in the bottle you sent with Simon Searle?'

'I don't know. Dozens. I didn't count them. The bottle was over three-quarters full.'

'I thought so.' She sighed. 'The baker's wife rang up last night to ask me whether I could let her have some more. She said the bottom of the bottle was all filled up with paper, but if you ask me she's given half of them away to a friend, or something, and now regrets it.'

'There wasn't any paper in the bottle. Only cotton wool on top.'

'I thought so.' She frowned, wrinkling her nose in sorrow. 'I wish she'd told me the truth.'

I stood up abruptly. 'Come on,' I said. 'Leave the coffee.'

'Why?' She began to put on her coat.

'I want to see that bottle.'

She was puzzled. 'She'll have thrown it away.'

'I hope to God she hasn't,' I said urgently, paying the bill. 'If there's paper in the bottle, Simon put it there.'

'You mean . . . it could matter?'

'He thought I was giving the pills to you. He didn't know they'd go to someone else. And I forgot to tell him you didn't speak English. Perhaps he thought when you'd finished the pills you'd read the paper and tell me what it said. Heaven knows. Anyway, we must find it. It's the first and only trace of him we've had.'

We hurried out of the restaurant, caught a taxi, and sped to the bakery. The baker's wife was fat and motherly and looked fifty, though she was probably only thirty-five. Her warm smile for Gabriella slowly turned anxious as she listened, and she shook her head and spread her hands wide.

'It's in the dustbin,' Gabriella said. 'She threw it away this morning.'

'We'll have to look. Ask her if I can look for it.'

The two women consulted.

'She says you'll dirty your fine suit.'

'Gabriella . . .'

'She says the English are mad, but you can look.'

There were three dustbins in the backyard, two luckily empty and one full. We turned this one out and I raked through the stinking contents with a broom handle. The little brown bottle was there, camouflaged by wet coffee grounds and half a dozen noodles. Gabriella took it and wiped it clean on a piece of newspaper while I shovelled the muck back into the dustbin and swept the yard.

'The paper won't come out,' she said. She had the cap off and was poking down the neck of the bottle with her finger. 'It's quite right. There is some in there.' She held it out to me.

I looked and nodded, wrapped the bottle in newspaper, put it on the ground, and smashed it with the shovel. She squatted beside me as I unfolded the paper and watched me pick out from the winking fragments of brown glass the things which had been inside.

I stood up slowly, holding them. A strip torn off the top of a piece of Yardman's stationery. A bank note of a currency I did not recognise, and some pieces of hay. The scrap of writing paper and the money were pinned together, and the hay had been folded up inside them.

'They are nonsense,' said Gabriella slowly.

'Do you have any idea where this comes from?' I touched the note. She flicked it over to see both sides.

'Yugoslavia. One hundred dinars.'

'Is that a lot?'

'About five thousand one hundred lire.'

Three pounds. Wisps of hay. A strip of paper. In a bottle.

Gabriella took the money and paper out of my hands and removed the pin which joined them.

'What do they mean?' she asked.

'I don't know.'

A message in a bottle.

'There are some holes in the paper.'

'Where he put the pin.'

'No. More holes than that. Look.' She held it up to the sky. 'You can see the light through.'

The printed heading said in thick red letters 'Yardman Transport Ltd., Carriers.' The strip of paper was about six inches across and two inches deep from the top smooth edge to the jagged one where it had been torn off the page. I held it up to the light.

Simon had pinpricked four letters. S.M.E.N. I felt the first distant tremor of cold apprehension.

'What is it?' she asked. 'What does it say?'

'Yardman Transport.' I showed her. 'See where he has added to it. If you read it with the pin hole letters tacked on, it says. "Yardman Transports MEN".'

She looked frightened by the bleakness in my voice, as if she could feel the inner coldness growing. 'What does it mean?'

'It means he didn't have a pencil,' I said grimly, evading the final implication. 'Only pins in his coat.'

A message in a bottle, washed ashore.

'I've got to think it out,' I said. 'I've got to remember.'

We perched on a pile of empty boxes stacked in one corner of the baker's yard, and I stared sightlessly at the whitewashed wall opposite and at the single bush in a tub standing in one corner.

'Tell me,' Gabriella said. 'Tell me. You look so . . . so terrible.'

'Billy,' I said. 'Billy put up a smoke screen, after all.'

'Who is Billy?'

'A groom. At least, he works as one. Men . . . Every time Billy has been on a trip, there has been a man who didn't come back.'

'Simon?' she said incredulously.

'No, I don't mean Simon, though he went with Billy . . . No, Someone who went as a groom, but wasn't a groom at all. And didn't come back. I can't remember any of their faces, not to be sure, because I never talked to any of them much. Billy saw to that.'

'How?'

'Oh, by insults and . . .' I stopped, concentrating back. 'The first time I went with Billy, there was a very fat man called John. At least, that was what I was told he was called. He was absolutely useless. Didn't know how to handle horses at all. We did two trips to France that day, and I think he wanted to vanish after the first. I saw him arguing furiously with Billy just before we came back the first time. But Billy made him do the double journey . . . and when he told me John had gone to Paris instead of coming back with us, he poured beer over my foot, so that I'd think about that, and not about John. And he made sure of it by picking a fight on the plane coming back . . .'

'But who was this John?'

I shook my head. 'I've no idea.'

'And were there others?'

'Yes . . . we went to New York next, he and I. There was a groom travelling with a half-bred Norwegian horse. He hardly talked at all, said he didn't speak English much. I understood he was staying in the States for a fortnight; but who knows if he came back? And on that trip Billy smashed a bar across my fingers so that they hurt all the way across, and I thought about them, not the Norwegian groom.'

'Are you sure?' She was frowning.

'Oh yes, I'm sure. I thought once before that Billy had done it for a purpose. I just got the purpose wrong.' I pondered. 'There was a day we took a man with a large bushy moustache to France, and a fornight later we brought a man with a large bushy moustache back again. I never looked beyond the moustache . . . I think it could have been two different men.'

'What did Billy do, those times?'

'On the way over he poured syrupy coffee on my head, and I spent nearly all the time in the washroom getting it out. And on the way back he hit me with a chain, and I went up into the galley all the way with the engineer to avoid any more.'

She looked at me very gravely. 'Is that . . . is that the lot?'

I shook my head. 'We went to New York last week. I told Yardman if Billy didn't leave me alone I'd quit. The journey out went quite all right, but coming back ... there was a man who was plainly not a horseman. He wasn't even comfortable in the riding clothes he had on. I thought at the time he was the owner's nephew or something, cadging a free ride, but again I didn't talk to him much. I slept all the way back. All ten hours ... I don't usually get tired like that, but I thought it was only because it was my fourth Atlantic crossing in six days ...'

'A sleeping pill?' she said slowly.

'It might have been. Alf brought some coffee back for me soon after we left. There was a restive colt in the aft box and I was trying to soothe him ... It could have been in that.'

'Alf?'

'An old deaf man, who always goes with Billy.'

'Do you think it *was* a sleeping pill?'

'It could ... I was still tired long after I got home. I even went to sleep in the bath.'

'It's serious,' she said.

'Today,' I said. 'There's a stranger with us today. His name is John too. I've never met him before, but there's something about him ... I was looking at him on the plane and wondering what it was, and Billy kicked me on the ankle. I kicked him back, but I went away, and stopped thinking about that man.'

'Can you think now?'

'Well ... his hands are wrong for one thing. Stablemen's hands are rough and chafed from being wet so often in cold weather, with washing tack and so on, but his are smooth, with well shaped nails.'

She picked up one of my hands and looked at it, running the tips of her fingers over the roughnesses which had developed since I left my desk job.

'They are not like yours, then.'

'Not like mine. But it's expression really. I watched him wake up. It was what came into his face with consciousness ...' I could remember that moment vividly, in spite of Billy's kick. I knew that expression very well ... so what was it? 'Oh,' I exclaimed in enlightenment, half laughing at my own stupidity, 'I know what it is ... he went to the same school as I did.'

'You do know him then, I mean, you've seen him before, if you were at school together.'

'Not together. He's older. He must have left about five years before I went. No, I've never seen him before, but the look he has is typical of some of the boys there. Not the nicest ones ... only the ones who think they are God's gift to mankind and everyone else is a bit inferior. He's one of those. Definitely *not* a groom. He looked as if wearing the grubby riding clothes he's got on was a kick in the dignity.'

'But you don't wear riding clothes,' she pointed out. 'It isn't necessary for him if he doesn't like them.'

'It is though. Alf wears jodhpurs, Billy wears jeans. The two grooms who travel turn about with these two, Timmie and Conker, they both wear breeches to work in. It's a sort of badge of office ... No one would think twice about a man arriving on a horse transport dressed in breeches or jodhpurs.'

'No, I see that.'

'No one bothers much about our passports,' I said. 'Look how simply I came out into Milan today, through the airport staff door. Hardly any airports, especially the very small ones, take much notice of you, if you work on aeroplanes. It's dead easy just to walk off most airfields round at the loading bays without ever being challenged. The Americans are strictest, but even they are used to our comings and goings.'

'But people do look at your passports sometimes, surely,' she protested.

I produced mine, battered and dogeared in the last three months after several years of dark blue stiffness. 'Look at it. It gets like that from always being in my pocket, but it doesn't get stamped much.' I turned through the pages. 'American visa, certainly. But look, the only stamp from Milan is the time I came on a scheduled flight and went through immigration with the other passengers. Hardly a mark for France, and I've been over there several times . . . of course it gets looked at, but never very thoroughly. It must be easy to fake one in this condition, and even travelling without one wouldn't be impossible. A pilot told me he'd done it for three weeks once, all over the world.'

'People who work on aircraft would go mad if everyone started checking their passports thoroughly every time they walked in or out.'

'Well . . . normally there's no need for it. It isn't all that easy to get on a single one way flight as a worker. Impossible, if you haven't a strong pull somewhere or other. Just any odd person who fancies a quiet trip to foreign parts wouldn't have a hope of getting himself into a horse transport. But if the transport agency itself, or someone working for it, is ready to export people illegally along with the horses, then it's easy.'

'But . . . what people?'

'What indeed! Billy can hardly advertise his service in the daily press. But he has no shortage of customers.'

'Crooks, do you think?' Gabriella asked frowning.

I fingered the bank-note and twisted the small pieces of hay.

'Hay,' I said. 'Why hay?'

Gabriella shrugged. 'Perhaps he found the money in some hay.'

'Of course!' I exclaimed. 'You're dead right. Haynets. Carried openly on and off the planes and never searched by customs officers. Perhaps they're transporting currency as well as men.' I told her about Billy refilling the net for me on the trip over, and how astonished I had been.

'But Henry darling, what I really do not understand is why you were not astonished all along at the unpleasant things Billy has been doing to you. I would have thought it utterly extraordinary, and I would have made a very big fuss about it.' She looked solemn and doubtful.

'Oh, I thought it was simply because I . . .' I stopped.

'Because you what?'

I smiled slightly. 'Because I belong to a sort of people he thinks should be exterminated.'

'Henry!' Her mouth lost its severity. 'What sort of people?'

'Well . . . you have counts and countesses still in Italy . . .'

'But you're not . . . you're not, are you . . . a count?'

'Sort of. Yes.'

She looked at me doubtfully, halfway to laughing, not sure that I was not teasing her.

'I don't believe you.'

'The reason I wasn't astonished at Billy knocking me about was that I knew he hated my guts for having a title.'

'That makes sense, I suppose.' She managed to frown and smile at the same time, which looked adorable. 'But if you have a title, Henry, why are you working in a horse transport?'

'You tell me why,' I said.

She looked at me searchingly for a moment, then she put her arms round my neck and her cheek on mine, with her mouth against my ear.

'It isn't enough for you to have a title,' she said. 'It isn't enough for anyone. It is necessary to show also that you are . . .' She fished around in her French vocabulary, and came up with a word: '. . . véritable. Real.'

I took a deep breath of relief and overspilling love, and kissed her neck where the dark hair swung below her ear.

'My wife will be a countess,' I said. 'Would you mind that?'

'I could perhaps bear it.'

'And me? Could you bear me? For always?'

'I love you,' she said in my ear. 'Yes. For always. Only, Henry . . .'

'Only what?'

'You won't stop being real?'

'No,' I said sadly.

She pulled away from me, shaking her head.

'I'm stupid. I'm sorry. But if even I can doubt you . . . and so quickly . . . you must always be having to prove . . .'

'Always,' I agreed.

'Still, you don't have to go quite so far.'

My heart sank.

'It's not everyone,' she said, 'who gets proposed to in a baker's backyard surrounded by dustbins.' Her mouth trembled and melted into the heart-wrenching smile.

'You wretch, my love.'

'Henry,' she said, 'I'm so happy I could burst.'

I kissed her and felt the same, and lived another half minute of oblivion before I thought again of Simon.

'What is it?' she said, feeling me straighten.

'The time . . .'

'Oh.'

'And Simon . . .'

'I fear for him,' she said, half under her breath.

'I too.'

She took the piece of paper out of my hand and looked at it again.

'We've been trying to avoid realising what this means.'

'Yes,' I said softly.

'Say it, then.'

'This was the only message he had a chance of sending. The only way he could send it.' I paused, looking into her serious dark eyes. After ten seconds I finished it. 'He is dead.'

She said in distress, 'Perhaps he is a prisoner.'

I shook my head. 'He's the third man who's disappeared. There was a man called Ballard who used to arrange trips from this end, and the man who used to have my own job, a man called Peters. They both vanished, Ballard over a year ago, and no one's heard of them since.'

'This Billy . . .' she said slowly, her eyes anxious.

'This Billy,' I said, 'is young and heartless, and carries a loaded revolver under his left arm.'

'Please . . . don't go back with him.'

'It will be quite safe as long as I keep quiet about this.' I took the hurried, desperate, pinpricked message back, folded it up with the banknote and the hay, and put them all in my wallet. 'When I get back to England, I'll find out who I have to tell.'

'The police,' she said, nodding.

'I'm not sure . . .' I thought about the Yugoslav currency and remembered Gabriella saying on our first evening 'Communists begin at Trieste.' I felt like someone who had trodden through a surface into a mole run underneath, and had suddenly realised that it was part of a whole dark invisible network. I thought it very unlikely that the men I'd flow with were ordinary crooks. They were couriers, agents . . . heaven knew what. It seemed fantastic to me to have brushed so closely with people I had known must exist but never expected to see; but I supposed the suburban people who had lived next door to Peter and Helen Kroger in Cranley Drive, Ruislip, had been pretty astonished too.

'Billy must have unloaded whatever he brought over in the haynet today,' I said. 'But going back . . .'.

'No,' Gabriella said vehemently. 'Don't look. That's what Simon must have done. Found the money. And Billy saw him.'

It might have been like that. And there had been two extra grooms on that trip, men I'd never seen before. Somehow, on the way, Simon had come across something I'd been blind to: perhaps because there was one more man than he'd arranged for; perhaps because Billy couldn't distract his attention by the methods he'd used on me; perhaps because of other happenings in the past which I didn't know about. In any case. Simon had found Billy out, and had let Billy know it. I thought drearily of Simon suddenly realising towards the end of that flight that Ballard and Peters had never come back, and that he wouldn't get a chance to put Billy in gaol. Billy the young thug, with his ready gun. A few minutes in the lavatory, that was all the time he'd had. No pencil. Only his pins, and the little bottle I'd given him in the privacy of the airline office; the bottle Billy didn't know existed, with Gabriella's name on it. Pills into loo. Banknote and paper with its inadequate message into bottle. Simon into eternity.

'Please don't search the haynets,' Gabriella said again.

'No,' I agreed. 'Someone official had better do it, next time Billy goes on a trip.'

She relaxed with relief. 'I'd hate you to disappear.'

I smiled. 'I won't do that. I'll go back most of the way up front with the crew, with Patrick and the man who bought the doll. And when I get to England I'll telephone you to let you know I arrived safely. How's that?'

'It would be wonderful. I could stop worrying.'

'Don't start,' I said confidently. 'Nothing will go wrong.'

How the local gods must have laughed their Roman heads off.

Chapter Twelve

We went through the baker's shop and out into the street I looked somewhat anxiously at my watch and calculated a dead heat with the brood mares.

'We need a taxi,' I said.

Gabriella shook her head. 'Very unlikely to find one in this quarter. We'd better catch a tram back to the centre, and take one on from there.'

'All right,' I agreed. 'Tram or taxi, whichever comes first.'

The trams ran along the busy street at the end of the quiet empty road where the baker lived, and we began to walk towards them with some dispatch.

'I didn't realise how late it is,' Gabriella said, catching sight of a clock with the hands together pointing north-east.

'And that one's slow. It's a quarter past.'

'Oh dear.'

One of the long green and cream single decker trams rolled across the end of the road, not far ahead.

'Run,' Gabriella said. 'The stop's just round the corner. We must catch it.'

We ran, holding hands. It couldn't have been more than ten strides to the corner. Not more.

Gabriella cried out suddenly and stumbled, whirling against me as I pulled her hand. There was a sharp searing stab in my side and we fell down on the pavement, Gabriella's weight pulling me over as I tried to save her from hurting herself.

Two or three passers by stopped to help her up, but she didn't move. She was lying face down, crumpled. Without belief, I stared at the small round hole near the centre of the back of her coat. Numbly, kneeling beside her, I put my left hand inside my jacket against my scorching right side, and when I brought it out it was covered in blood.

'Oh no,' I said in English. 'Oh dear God, no.'

I bent over her and rolled her up and on to her back in my arms. Her eyes were open. They focused on my face. She was alive. It wasn't much.

'Henry,' her voice was a whisper. 'I can't . . . breathe.'

The three passers by had grown to a small crowd. I looked up desperately into their enquiring faces.

'Doctor,' I said. 'Medico.' That was Spanish. 'Doctor.'

'Si si,' said a small boy at my elbow. 'Un dottore, si.'

There was a stir in the crowd and a great deal of speculation of which I understood only one word. 'Inglese,' they said, and I nodded. 'Inglese.'

I opened gently the front of Gabriella's brown suede coat. There was a jagged tear in the right side, nearest me, and the edges of it were dark. Underneath, the black dress was soaking. I waved my arm wildly round at the people to get them to stand back a bit, and they did take one pace away. A motherly looking women produced a pair of scissors from her handbag and knelt down on Gabriella's other side. She pointed at me to open the coat again, and when I'd tucked it back between Gabriella's body and my own she began to cut away the dress. Gentle as she was, Gabriella moved in my arms and gave a small gasping cry.

'Hush,' I said, 'my love, it's all right.'

'Henry . . .' She shut her eyes.

I held her in anguish while the woman with the scissors carefully cut and peeled away a large piece of dress. When she saw what lay underneath her big face filled with overwhelming compassion, and she began to shake her head. 'Signor,' she said to me, 'mi dispiace molto. Molto.'

I took the clean white handkerchief out of my top pocket, folded it inside out, and put it over the terrible wound. The bullet had smashed a rib on its way out. There were splinters of it showing in the bleeding area just below her breast. The bottom edge of her white bra had a new scarlet border. I gently untucked the coat and put it over her again to keep her warm and I thought in utter agony that she would die before the doctor came.

A carabiniere in glossy boots and greenish khaki breeches appeared beside us, but I doubt if I could have spoken to him even if he'd known the same language. The crowd chattered to him in subdued voices and he left me alone.

Gabriella opened her eyes. Her face was grey and wet with the sweat of appalling pain.

'Henry . . .'.

'I'm here.'

'I can't . . . breathe.'

I raised her a little more so that she was half sitting, supported by my arm and my bent knee. The movement was almost too much for her. Her pallor became pronounced. The short difficult breaths passed audibly through her slackly open mouth.

'Don't . . . leave me.'

'No,' I said. 'Hush, my dearest love.'

'What . . . happened?'

'You were shot,' I said.

'Shot . . .'. She showed no surprise. 'Was it . . . Billy?'

'I don't know. I didn't see. Don't talk, my sweet love, don't talk. The doctor will be here soon.'

'Henry . . .'. She was exhausted, her skin the colour of death. 'Henry . . . I love you.'

Her eyes flickered shut again, but she was still conscious, her left hand moved spasmodically and restlessly on the ground beside her and the lines of suffering deepening in her face.

I would have given anything, anything on earth, to have had her whole again, to have taken that pain away.

The doctor, when at last he came, was young enough to have been newly qualified. He had thick black curly hair and thin clever hands: this was what I most saw of him as he bent over Gabriella, and all I remembered. He looked briefly under my white handkerchief and turned to speak to the policeman.

I heard the words 'auto ambulanza' and 'pallota,' and eager information from the crowd.

The young doctor went down on one knee and felt Gabriella's pulse. She opened her eyes, but only a fraction.

'Henry . . .'.

'I'm here. Don't talk.'

'Mm . . .'.

The young doctor said something soothing to her in Italian, and she said faintly 'Si.' He opened his case beside him on the ground and with quick skilful fingers prepared an injection, made a hole in her stocking, swabbed her skin with surgical spirit, and pushed the needle firmly into her thigh. Again he spoke to her gently, and again felt her pulse. I could read nothing but reassurance in his manner, and the reassurance was for her, not me.

After a while she opened her eyes wider and looked at me, and a smile struggled on to her damp face.

'That's better,' she said. Her voice was so weak as to be scarcely audible, and she was growing visibly more breathless. Nothing was better, except the pain.

I smiled back. 'Good. You'll be all right soon, when they get you to hospital.'

She nodded a fraction. The doctor continued to hold her pulse, checking it on his watch.

Two vehicles drove up and stopped with a screech of tyres. A Citroen police car and an ambulance like a large estate car. Two carabinieri of obvious seniority emerged from one, and stretcher bearers from the other. These last, and the doctor, lifted Gabriella gently out of my arms and on to the stretcher. They piled blankets behind her to support her, and I saw the doctor take a look at what he could see of the small hole in her back. He didn't try to take off her coat.

One of the policeman said, 'I understand you speak French.'

'Yes,' I said, standing up. I hadn't felt the hardness of the pavement until that moment. The leg I'd been kneeling on was numb.

'What are the young lady's name and address?'

I told him. He wrote them down.

'And your own?'

I told him.

'What happened?' he said, indicating the whole scene with a flickering wave of the hand.

'We were running to catch the tram. Someone shot at us from back there.' I pointed down the empty street towards the baker's.

'Who?'

'I didn't see.' They were lifting Gabriella into the ambulance. 'I must go with her,' I said.

The policeman shook his head. 'You can see her later. You must come with us, and tell us exactly what happened.'

'I said I wouldn't leave her . . .' I couldn't bear to leave her. I took a quick stride and caught the doctor by the arm. 'Look,' I said, pulling open my jacket.

He looked. He tugged my bloodstained shirt out of my trousers to inspect the damage more closely. A ridged furrow five inches long along my lowest rib. Not very deep. It felt like a burn. The doctor told the policeman who also looked.

'All right,' said the one who spoke French, 'I suppose you'd better go and have it dressed.' He wrote an address on a page of his notebook, tore it off and gave it to me. 'Come here, afterwards.'

'Yes.'

'Have you your passport with you?'

I took it out of my pocket and gave it to him, and put the address he'd given me in my wallet. The doctor jerked his head towards the ambulance to get in, and I did.

'Wait,' said the policeman as they were shutting the door. 'Did the bullet go through the girl into you?'

'No,' I said. 'Two bullets. She was hit first, me after.'

'We will look for them,' he said.

Gabriella was still alive when we reached the hospital. Still alive when they lifted her, stretcher and all, on to a trolley. Still alive while one of the ambulance men explained rapidly to a doctor what had happened, and while that doctor and another took in her general condition, left my handkerchief undisturbed, and whisked her away at high speed.

'Inglese.' I shook my head. 'Non parlo italiano.'

'Sit down,' he said in English. His accent was thick, his vocabulary tiny, but it was a relief to be able to talk to him at all. He led me into a small white cubicle containing a hard, high narrow bed and a chair. He pointed to the chair and I sat on it. He went away and returned with a nurse carrying some papers.

'The name of the miss?'

I told him. The nurse wrote it down, name, address and age, gave me a comforting smile, took the papers away and came back with a trolley of equipment and a message.

She told it to the doctor, and he translated, as it was for me.

'Telephone from carabinieri. Please go to see them before four.'

I looked at my watch, blank to the time. It was still less than an hour since Gabriella and I had run for the tram. I had lived several ages.

'I understand,' I said.

'Please now, remove the coat,' the doctor said.

I stood up, took off my jacket and slid my right arm out of my shirt. He put two dressings over the bullet mark, an impregnated gauze one and a slightly padded one with adhesive tape. He pressed the tapes firmly into my skin and stood back. I put my arm back into my shirt sleeve.

'Don't you feel it?' he said. He seemed surprised.

'No.'

His rugged face softened. 'E sua moglie?'

I didn't understand.

'I am sorry . . . is she your wife?'

'I love her,' I said. The prospect of losing her was past bearing. There were tears suddenly in my eyes and on my cheeks. 'I love her.'

'Yes.' He nodded, sympathetic and unembarrassed, one of a nation who saw no value in stiff upper lips. 'Wait here. We will tell you . . .' He left the sentence unfinished and went away, and I didn't know whether it was because he didn't want to tell me she was dying or because he simply didn't know enough English to say what he meant.

I waited an hour I couldn't endure again. At the end of it another doctor came, a tall grey haired man with a fine boned face.

'You wish to know about Signora Barzini?' His English was perfect, his voice quiet and very precise.

I nodded, unable to ask.

'We have cleaned and dressed her wound. The bullet passed straight through her lung, breaking a rib on the way out. The lung was collapsed. The air from it, and also a good deal of blood, had passed into the chest cavity. It was necessary to remove the air and blood at once so that the lung would have room to inflate again, and we have done that.' He was coolly clinical.

'May I . . . may I see her?'

'Later,' he said, without considering it. 'She is unconscious from the anaesthetic and she is in the post-operative unit. You may see her later.'

'And . . . the future?'

He half smiled. 'There is always danger in such a case, but with good care she could certainly recover. The bullet itself hit nothing immediately fatal; none of the big blood vessels. If it had, she would have died soon, in the street. The longer she lived, the better were her chances.'

'She seemed to get worse,' I said, not daring to believe him.

'In some ways that was so,' he explained patiently. 'Her injury was very painful, she was bleeding internally, and she was suffering from the onset of shock, which as you may know is a physical condition often as dangerous as the original damage.'

I nodded, swallowing.

'We are dealing with all those things. She is young and healthy, which is good, but there will be more pain and there may be difficulties. I can give you no assurances. It is too soon for that. But hope, yes definitely, there is considerable hope.'

'Thank you,' I said dully, 'for being so honest.'

He gave his small smile again. 'Your name is Henry?'

I nodded.

'You have a brave girl,' he said.

If I couldn't see her yet I thought, I would have to go and talk to the police. They had said to be with them by four and it was already twenty past; not that that mattered a jot.

I was so unused to thinking in the terms of the strange half world into which I had stumbled that I failed to take the most elementary precautions. Distraught about Gabriella, it didn't even cross my mind that if I had been found and shot at in a distant back street I was equally vulnerable outside the hospital.

There was a taxi standing in the forecourt, the driver reading a newspaper. I waved an arm at him, and he folded the paper, started the engine and drove over. I gave him the paper with the address the policeman had written out for me, and he looked at it in a bored sort of way and nodded. I opened the cab door and got in. He waited politely till I was settled, his head half turned, and then drove smoothly out of the hospital gates. Fifty yards away he turned right down a tree-lined secondary road beside the hospital, and fifty yards down there he stopped. From a tree one yard from the curb a lithe figure peeled itself, wrenched open the nearest door, and stepped inside.

He was grinning fiercely, unable to contain his triumph. The gun with the silencer grew in his hand as if born there. I had walked right into his ambush.

Billy the Kid.

'You took your bloody time, you stinking bastard,' he said.

I looked at him blankly, trying to keep the shattering dismay from showing. He sat down beside me and shoved his gun into my ribs, just above the line it had already drawn there.

'Get cracking Vittorio,' he said. 'His effing Lordship is late.'

The taxi rolled smoothly away and gathered speed.

'Four o'clock we said,' said Billy, grinning widely. 'Didn't you get the message?'

'The police . . .' I said weakly.

'Hear that, Vittorio?' Billy laughed. 'The hospital thought you were the police. Fancy that. How extraordinary.'

I looked away from him, out of the window on my left.

'You just try it,' Billy said. 'You'll have a bullet through you before you get the door open.'

I looked back at him.

'Yeah,' he grinned. 'Takes a bit of swallowing, don't it, for you to have to do what I say. Sweet, I call it. And believe me, matey, you've hardly bloody started.'

I didn't answer. It didn't worry him. He sat sideways, the gloating grin fixed like a rictus.

'How's the bird . . . Miss what's her name?' He flicked his fingers. 'The girl friend.'

I did some belated thinking.

I said stonily, 'She's dead.'

'Well, well,' said Billy gleefully. 'How terribly sad. Do you hear that, Vittorio? His Lordship's bit of skirt has passed on.'

Vittorio's head nodded. He concentrated on his driving, mostly down side streets, avoiding heavy traffic. I stared numbly at the greasy back of his neck and wondered what chance I had of grabbing Billy's gun before he pulled the trigger. The answer to that, I decided, feeling its steady pressure against my side, was none.

'Come on now, come on,' said Billy. 'Don't you think I'm clever.'

I didn't answer. Out of the corner of my eye I sensed the grin change from triumph to vindictiveness.

'I'll wipe that bloody superior look off your face,' he said. 'You sodding blue-arsed—'

I said nothing. He jerked the gun hard into my ribs.

'You just wait, your high and mighty Lordship, you just bloody well wait.'

There didn't in fact seem to be much else I could do. The taxi bowled steadily on, leaving the city centre behind.

'Hurry it up, Vittorio,' said Billy. 'We're late.'

Vittorio put his foot down and we drove on away from the town and out into an area of scrubland. The road twisted twice and then ran straight, and I stared in astonishment and disbelief at what lay ahead at the end of it. It was the broad open sweep of Malpensa Airport. We had approached it from the side road leading away from the loading bay, the road the horseboxes sometimes took.

The D.C.4 stood there on the tarmac less than a hundred yards away, still waiting to take four mares back to England. Vittorio stopped the taxi fifty yards from the loading area. 'Now,' said Billy to me, enjoying himself again. 'You listen and do as you are told, otherwise I'll put a hole in you. And it'll be in the breadbasket, not the heart. That's a promise.' I didn't doubt him. 'Walk down the road, straight across to the plane, up the ramp and into the toilet. Get it? I'll be two steps behind you, all the way.'

I was puzzled, but greatly relieved. I had hardly expected such a mild end to the ride. Without a word I opened the door and climbed out. Billy wriggled agilely across and stood up beside me, the triumphant sneer reasserting itself on his babyish mouth.

'Go on,' he said.

There was no one about at that side of the airfield. Four hundred yards ahead there were people moving round the main building, but four hundred yards across open tarmac looked a very long way. Behind lay scrubland and the taxi. Mentally shrugging, I followed Billy's instructions: walked down the short stretch of road, across to the plane, and up the ramp. Billy stalked a steady two paces behind me, too far to touch, too near to miss.

At the top of the ramp stood Yardman. He was frowning heavily, though his eyes were as usual inscrutable behind the glasses, and he was tapping his watch.

'You've cut it very fine,' he said in annoyance. 'Another quarter of an hour and we'd have been in trouble.'

My chief feeling was still of astonishment and unreality. Billy broke the bubble, speaking over my shoulder.

'Yeah, he was dead late coming out of the hospital. Another five minutes, and we'd have had to go in for him.'

My skin rose in goose pimples. The ride had after all led straight to the heart of things. The pit yawned before me.

'Get in then,' Yardman said. 'I'll go and tell the pilot our wandering boy has at last returned from lunch and we can start back for England.' He went past us and down the ramp, hurrying.

Billy sniggered. 'Move, your effing Lordship,' he said. 'Open the toilet door and go in. The one on the left.' The pistol jabbed against the bottom of my spine. 'Do as you're told.'

I walked the three necessary steps, opened the left hand door, and went in.

'Put your hands on the wall,' said Billy. 'Right there in front of you, so that I can see them.'

I did as he said. He swung the door shut behind him and leaned against it. We waited in silence. He sniggered complacently from time to time, and I considered my blind stupidity.

Yardman. Yardman transports men. Simon had fought through to a conclusion, where I had only gone halfway. Billy's smoke screen had filled my eyes. I hadn't seen beyond it to Yardman. And instead of grasping from Simon's message and my own memory that it had to be Yardman too, I had kissed Gabriella and lost the thread of it. And five minutes later she had been bleeding on the pavement . . .

I shut my eyes and rested my forehead momentarily against the wall. Whatever the future held it meant nothing to me if Gabriella didn't live.

After a while Yardman returned. He rapped on the door and Billy moved over to give him room to come in.

'They're all coming across, now,' he said. 'We'll be away shortly. But before we go . . . how about the girl?'

'Croaked,' said Billy laconically.

'Good,' Yardman said. 'One less job for Vittorio.'

My head jerked.

'My dear boy,' said Yardman. 'Such a pity. Such a nice girl too.' In quite a different voice he said to Billy, 'Your shooting was feeble. You are expected to do better than that.'

'Hey,' there was a suspicion of a whine in Billy's reply. 'They started running.'

'You should have been closer.'

'I *was* close. Close enough. Ten yards at the most. I was waiting in a doorway, ready to pump it into them just after they'd passed me. And then they just suddenly started running. I got the girl all right, though, didn't I? I mean, I got her, even if she lingered a bit, like. As for him, well, granted I did miss him, but she sort of swung round and knocked him over just as I pulled the trigger.'

'If Vittorio hadn't been with you,' Yardman began coldly.

'Well, he was with me, then, wasn't he?' Billy defended himself. 'After all, it was me that told him to worm into that crowd round the girl and keep his ears flapping. Granted it was Vittorio who heard the police telling this creep to go and see them straight from the hospital, but it was me that thought of ringing up the hospital and winkling him out. And anyway, when I rang you up the second time, didn't you say it was just as well, you could do with him back here alive as you'd got a use for him?'

'All right,' said Yardman. 'It's worked out all right, but it was still very poor shooting.'

He opened the door, letting in a brief murmur of people moving the ramp away, and closed it behind him. Billy sullenly delivered a long string of obscenity, exclusively concerned with the lower part of the body. Not one to take criticism sweetly.

The aircraft trembled as the engines started one after the other. I glanced at my watch, on a level with my eyes. If it had been much later, Patrick would have refused to take off that day. As it was, there was little enough margin for him to get back to Gatwick within fifteen hours of going on duty that morning. It was the total time which mattered, not just flying hours, with enquiries and fines to face for the merest minutes over.

'Kneel down.' Billy said, jabbing me in the spine. 'Keep your hands on the wall. And don't try lurching into me accidental like when we take off. It wouldn't do you an effing bit of good.'

I didn't move.

'You'll do as you're ruddy well told, matey,' said Billy, viciously kicking the back of one of my knees. 'Get down.'

I knelt down on the floor. Billy said 'There's a good little earl,' with a pleased sneer in his voice, and rubbed the snout of his pistol up and down the back of my neck.

The plane began to taxi, stopped at the perimeter for power checks, rolled forward on to the runway, and gathered speed. Inside the windowless lavatory compartment it was impossible to tell the exact moment of unstick, but the subsequent climb held me close anyway against the wall, as I faced the tail, and Billy stopped himself from overbalancing on to me by putting his gun between my shoulder blades and leaning on it. I hoped remotely that Patrick wouldn't strike an air pocket.

Up in the cockpit, as far away in the plane as one could get and no doubt furious with me for coming back so late, he would be drinking his first coffee, and peeling his first banana, a mile from imagining I could need his help. He completed a long climbing turn and after a while levelled off and reduced power. We were well on the first leg south to the Mediterranean.

The Mediterranean. A tremor as nasty as the one I'd had on finding Yardman at the heart of things fluttered through my chest. The D.C.4 was unpressurised. The cabin doors could be opened in flight. Perhaps Billy had simply opened the door and pushed Simon out.

The traceless exit. Ten thousand feet down to the jewel blue sea.

Chapter Thirteen

Yardman came back, edging round the door.

'It's time,' he said.

Billy sniggered. 'Can't be too soon.'

'Stand up, stand up, my dear boy,' Yardman said. 'You look most undignified down there. Face the wall all the time.'

As I stood up he reached out, grasped my jacket by the collar, and pulled it backwards and downwards. Two more jerks and it was off.

'I regret this, I do indeed,' he said. 'But I'm afraid we must ask you to put your hands together behind your back.'

I thought that if I did that I was as good as dead. I didn't move. Billy squeezed round into the small space between me and the washbasin and put the silencer against my neck.

Yardman's unhurried voice floated into my ear. 'I really must warn you, my dear boy, that your life hangs by the merest thread. If Billy hadn't clumsily missed you in the street, you would be in the Milan morgue by now. If you do not do as we ask, he will be pleased to rectify his mistake immediately.'

I put my hands behind my back.

'That's right,' Yardman said approvingly. He tied them together with a rough piece of rope.

'Now, my dear boy,' he went on. 'You are going to help us. We have a little job for you.'

'Billy's searchlight eyes were wide and bright, and I didn't like his smile.

'You don't ask what it is,' Yardman said. 'So I will tell you. You are going to persuade your friend the pilot to alter course.'

Alter course. Simple words. Premonition shook me to the roots. Patrick wasn't strong enough.

I said nothing. After a moment Yardman continued conversationally, 'We were going to use the engineer originally, but as I find you and the pilot are goods friends I am sure he will do as you ask.'

I still said nothing.

'He doesn't understand,' Billy sneered.

I understood all right. Patrick would do what they told him. Yardman opened the washroom door. 'Turn round,' he said.

I turned. Yardman's eyes fell immediately to the dried bloodstains on my shirt. He reached out a long arm, pulled the once white poplin out of my trousers and saw the bandage underneath.

'You grazed him,' he said to Billy, still critical.

'Considering he was running and falling at the same time that isn't bad, not with a silencer.'

'Inefficient.' Yardman wasn't letting him off the hook.

'I'll make up for it,' Billy said viciously.

'Yes, you do that.'

Yardman turned his head back to me. 'Outside, dear boy.'

I followed him out of the washroom into the cabin, and stopped. It looked utterly normal. The four mares stood peacefully in the two middle boxes, installed, I presumed, by Yardman and Alf. The foremost and aft boxes were strapped down flat. There were the normal bales of hay dotted about. The noise was the normal noise, the air neither hotter nor colder than usual. All familiar. Normal. As normal as a coffin.

Yardman walked on.

'This way,' he said. He crossed the small area at the back of the plane, stepped up on to the shallow platform formed by the flattened rear box, walked across it, and finished down again on the plane's floor, against the nearest box containing mares. Billy prodded his gun into my back. I joined Yardman.

'So wise, my dear boy,' nodded my employer. 'Stand with your back to the box.'

I turned round to face the tail of the aircraft. Yardman took some time fastening my tied hands to the centre banding bar round the mare's box. Billy stood up on the flattened box and amused himself by pointing his gun at various parts of my anatomy. He wasn't going to fire it. I took no notice of his antics but looked beyond him, to the pair of seats at the back. There was a man sitting there, relaxed and interested. The man who had flown out with us, whose name was John. Milan hadn't been the end of his journey, I thought. Yardman wanted to land him somewhere else.

He stood up slowly, his pompous manner a complete contradiction to his grubby ill-fitting clothes.

'Is this sort of thing really necessary?' he asked, but with curiosity, not distress. His voice was loud against the beat of the engine.

'Yes,' said Yardman shortly. I turned my head to look at him. He was staring gravely at my face, the bones of his skull sharp under the stretched skin. 'We know our business.'

Billy got tired of waving his gun about to an unappreciative audience. He stepped off the low platform and began dragging a bale of hay into the narrow alleyway between the standing box and the flattened one, settling it firmly longways between the two. On top of that bale he put another, and on top of that another and another. Four bales high. Jammed against these, on top of the flattened box, he raised three more, using all the bales on the plane. Together, they formed a solid wall three feet away on my left. Yardman, John and I watched him in silence.

'Right,' Yardman said when he'd finished it. He checked the time and looked out of the window. 'Ready?'

Billy and John said they were. I refrained from saying that I wasn't, and never would be.

All three of them went away up the plane, crouching under the luggage racks and stumbling over the guy chains. I at once discovered by tugging that Yardman knew his stuff with a rope. I couldn't budge my hands.

Jerking them in vain, I suddenly discovered Alf watching me. He had come back from somewhere up front, and was standing on my right with his customary look of missing intelligence.

'Alf,' I shouted. 'Untie me.'

He didn't hear. He simply stood and looked at me without surprise. Without feeling. Then he slowly turned and went away. Genuinely deaf; but it paid him to be blind too, I thought bitterly. Whatever he saw he didn't tell. He had told me nothing about Simon.

I thought achingly of Gabriella hanging on to life in Milan. She must still be alive, I thought. She must. Difficulties, the doctor had said. There might be difficulties. Like infection. Like pneumonia. Nothing would matter if she died . . . but she wouldn't . . . she couldn't. Anxiety for her went so deep that it pretty well blotted out the hovering knowledge that I should spare some for myself. The odds on her survival were about even: I wouldn't have taken a hundred to one on my own.

After ten eternal minutes Yardman and Billy came back, with Patrick between them. Patrick stared at me, his face tight and stiff with disbelief. I knew exactly how he felt. Billy pushed him to the back with his gun, and Yardman pointed to the pair of seats at the back. He and Patrick sat down on them, side by side, fifteen feet away. A captive audience, I reflected sourly. Front row of the stalls.

Billy put his mouth close to my ear. 'He doesn't fancy a detour, your pilot friend. Ask him to change his mind.'

I didn't look at Billy, but at Patrick. Yardman was talking to him unhurriedly, but against the engine noise I couldn't hear what he said. Patrick's amber eyes looked dark in the gauntness of his face, and he shook his head slightly, staring at me beseechingly. Beseech all you like, I thought, but don't give in. I knew it was no good. He wasn't tough enough.

'Ask him,' Billy said.

'Patrick,' I shouted.

He could hear me. His head tilted to listen. It was difficult to get urgency and conviction across when one had to shout to be heard at all, but I did my best. 'Please . . . fly back to Milan.'

Nothing happened for three seconds. Then Patrick tried to stand up and Yardman pulled him back, saying something which killed the beginning of resolution is his shattered face. Patrick, for God's sake, I thought, have some sense. Get up and go.

Billy unscrewed the silencer from his gun and put in in his pocket. He carefully unbuttoned my shirt, pulled the collar back over my shoulders, and tucked the fronts round into the back of my trousers. I felt very naked and rather silly. Patrick's face grew, if anything, whiter.

Billy firmly cutched the dressing over the bullet mark and with one wrench pulled the whole thing off.

'Hey,' he shouted to Yardman, 'I don't call that a miss.'

Yardman's reply got lost on the way back.

'Want to know something?' Billy said, thrusting his sneering face close to mine. 'I'm enjoying this.'

I saved my breath.

He put the barrel of his revolver very carefully against my skin, laying it flat along a rib just above the existing cut. Then he pushed me round until I was half facing the wall he had made of the hay bales. 'Keep still,' he said. He drew the revolver four inches backwards with the barrel still touching me and pulled the trigger. At such close quarters, without the silencer, the shot was a crashing explosion. The bullet sliced through the skin over my ribs and embedded itself in the wall of hay. The spit of flame from the barrel scorched in its wake. In the box behind me, the startled mares began making a fuss. It would create a handy diversion, I thought, if they were frightened into dropping their foals.

Patrick was on his feet, aghast and swaying. I heard him shouting something unintelligible to Billy, and Billy shouting back, 'Only you can stop it, mate.'

'Patrick,' I yelled. 'Go to Milan.'

'That's bloody enough,' Billy said. He put his gun back on my side, as before. 'Keep still.'

Yardman couldn't afford me dead until Patrick had flown where they wanted. I was all for staying alive as long as possible, and jerking around in the circumstances could cut me off short. I did as Billy said, and kept still. He pulled the trigger.

The flash, the crash, the burn, as before.

I looked down at myself, but I couldn't see clearly because of the angle. There were three long furrows now, parallel and fiery. The top two were beginning to bleed.

Patrick sat down heavily as if his knees had given way and put his hands over his eyes. Yardman was talking to him, clearly urging him to save me any more. Billy wasn't for waiting. He put his gun in position, told me to keep still, and shot.

Whether he intended it or not, that one went deeper, closer to the bone. The force of it spun me round hard against the mares' box and wrenched my arms, and my feet stumbed as I tried to keep my balance. The mares whinnied and skittered around, but on the whole they were getting less agitated, not more. A pity.

I had shut my eyes, that time. I opened them slowly to see Patrick and Yardman much nearer, only eight feet away on the far side of the flattened box. Patrick was staring with unreassuring horror at Billy's straight lines. Too soft-hearted, I thought despairingly. The only chance we had was for him to leave Billy to get on with it and go and turn back to Milan. We weren't much more than half an hour out. In half an hour we could be back. Half an hour of this . . .

I swallowed and ran my tongue round my dry lips.

'If you go where they say,' I said urgently to Patrick, 'they will kill us all.'

He didn't believe it. It wasn't in his nature to believe it. He listened to Yardman instead.

'Don't be silly, my dear boy. Of course we won't kill you. You will land, we will disembark, and you can all fly off again, perfectly free.'

'Patrick,' I said desperately. 'Go to Milan.'

Billy put his gun along my ribs.

'How long do you think he can keep still?' he asked, as if with genuine interest. 'What'll you bet?'

I tried to say, 'They shot Gabriella,' but Billy was waiting for that. I got the first two words out but he pulled the trigger as I started her name, and the rest of it got lost in the explosion and my own gasping breath.

When I opened my eyes that time, Patrick and Yardman had gone.

For a little while I clung to a distant hope that Patrick would turn back, but Billy merely blew across the top of his hot revolver and laughed at me, and when the plane banked it was to the left, and not a one eighty degree turn. After he had straightened out I looked at the acute angle of the late afternoon sun as it sliced forwards in narrow slivers of brilliance through the row of oval windows on my right.

No surprise, I thought drearily.

We were going east.

Billy had a pocket full of bullets. He sat on the flattened box, feeding his gun. The revolving cylinder broke out sideways with its axis still in line with the barrel, and an ejector rod, pushed back towards the butt, had lifted the spent cartridges out into his hand. The empty cases now lay beside him in a cluster, rolling slightly on their rims. When all the chambers were full again he snapped the gun shut and fondled it. His eyes suddenly switched up to me, the wide stare full of malice.

'Stinking earl,' he said.

A la lanterne, I thought tiredly. And all that jazz.

He stood up suddenly and spoke fiercely, with some sort of inner rage.

'I'll make you,' he said.

'What?'

'Ask.'

'Ask what?'

'Something ... anything. I'll make you bloody well ask me for something.'

I said nothing.

'Ask,' he said savagely.

I stared past him as if he wasn't there. Fights, I thought with some chill, weren't always physical.

'All right,' he said abruptly. 'All right. You'll ask in the end. You bloody sodding well will.'

I didn't feel sure enough to say I bloody sodding well wouldn't. The taunting sneer reappeared on his face, without the same infallible confidence perhaps, but none the less dangerous for that. He nodded sharply, and went off along the alleyway towards the nose, where I hoped he'd stay.

I watched the chips of sunshine grow smaller and tried to concentrate on working out our course, more for distraction than from any hope of needing the information for a return journey. The bullets had hurt enough when Billy fired them, but the burns, as burns do, had hotted up afterwards. The force generated inside the barrel of a pistol was, if I remembered correctly, somewhere in the region of five tons. A bullet left a revolver at a rate of approximately seven hundred feet per second and if not stopped carried about five hundred yards. The explosion which drove the bullet spinning on its way also shot out flames, smoke, hot propulsive gases and burning particles of gunpowder, and at close quarters they made a very dirty mess. Knowing these charming facts was of no comfort at all. The whole ruddy area simply burnt and went on burning, as if someone had stood an electric iron on it and had forgotten to switch off.

After Billy went away it was about an hour before I saw anyone again, and then it was Alf. He shuffled into my sight round the corner of the box I was tied to, and stood looking at me with one of the disposable mugs in his hand. His lined old face was, as usual, without expression.

'Alf,' I shouted. 'Untie me.'

There wasn't anywhere to run to. I just wanted to sit down. But Alf either couldn't hear, or wouldn't. He looked unhurriedly at my ribs, a sight which as far as I could see produced no reaction in him at all. But something must have stirred somewhere, because he took a slow step forward, and being careful not to touch me, lifted his mug. It had 'Alf' in red where Mike had written it that morning, in that distant sane and safe lost world or normality.

'Want some?' he said.

I nodded, half afraid he'd pour it out on the floor, as Billy would have done; but he held it up to my mouth, and let me finish it all. Lukewarm, oversweet neo-coffee. The best drink I ever had.

'Thank you,' I said.

He nodded, produced the nearest he could do to a smile, and shuffled away again. Not an ally. A non-combatant, rather.

More time passed. I couldn't see my watch or trust my judgment, but I would have guessed it was getting on for two hours since we had turned. I had lost all sense of direction. The sun had gone, and we were travelling into dusk. Inside the cabin the air grew colder. I would have liked to have had my shirt on properly, not to mention a jersey, but the mares behind my back provided enough warmth to keep me from shivering. On a full load in that cramped plane eight horses generated a summer's day even with icing conditions outside, and we seldom needed the cabin heaters. It was far too much to hope in the circumstances that Patrick would think of switching them on.

Two hours flying. We must, I thought, have been down near Albenga when we turned, which meant that since then, if we were still going east and the winds were the same as in the morning, we could have been crossing Italy somewhere north of Florence. Ahead lay the Adriatic, beyond that, Yugoslavia, and beyond that, Roumania.

It didn't matter a damn where we went, the end would be the same.

I shifted wearily, trying to find some ease, and worried for the thousandth time whether Gabriella was winning, back in Milan. The police there, I supposed, wrenching my mind away from her, would be furious I hadn't turned up. They still had my passport. There might at least be a decent investigation if I never went back for it, and Gabriella

knew enough to explain what I'd inadvertently got caught up in. If she
lived. If she lived . . .

The plane banked sharply in a steep turn to the left. I leant against
the roll and tried to gauge its extent. Ninety degrees turn, I thought. No;
more. It didn't seem to make much sense. But if – if – we had reached
the Adriatic I supposed it was possible we were now going up it, north
west, back towards Venice . . . and Trieste. I admitted gloomily to myself
that it was utter guesswork; that I was lost, and in more than one sense.

Ten minutes later the engine note changed and the volume of noise
decreased. We had started going down. My heart sank with the plane.
Not much time left. Oncoming night and a slow descent, the stuff of
death.

There were two rows of what looked like car headlights marking each
end of a runway. We circled once so steeply that I caught a glimpse of
them through the tipped window, and then we levelled out for the
approach and lost speed, and the plane bumped down on to a rough
surface. Grass, not tarmac. The plane taxied round a bit, and then
stopped. One by one the four engines died. The plane was quiet and
dark, and for three long deceptive minutes at my end of it there was
peace.

The cabin lights flashed on, bright overhead. The mares behind me
kicked the box. Further along, the other pair whinnied restlessly. There
was a clatter in the galley, and the noise of people coming back through
the plane, stumbling over the chains.

Patrick came first, with Billy after. Billy had screwed the silencer back
on his gun.

Patrick went past the flattened box into the small area in front of the
two washroom doors. He moved stiffly, as if he couldn't feel his feet on
the floor, as if he were sleep walking.

Billy had stopped near me, on my right.

'Turn round, pilot,' he said.

Patrick turned, his body first and his legs untwisting after. He staggered
slightly, and stood swaying. If his face had been white before, it was
leaden grey now. His eyes were stretched and glazed with shock, and his
good-natured mouth trembled.

He stared at me with terrible intensity.

'He . . . shot . . . them,' he said. 'Bob . . . and Mike. Bob and Mike.'
His voice broke on the horror of it.

Billy sniggered quietly.

'You said . . . they would kill us all.' A tremor shook him. 'I didn't
. . . believe it.'

His eyes went down to my side. 'I couldn't . . .' he said. 'They said
they'd go on and on . . .'

'Where are we?' I said sharply.

His eyes came back in a snap, as if I'd kicked his brain.

'Italy,' he began automatically. 'South west of . . .'　　Billy raised his
gun, aiming high for the skull.

'No.' I yelled at him in rage and horror at the top of my voice. 'No.'

He jumped slightly, but he didn't even pause. The gun coughed through the silencer and the bullet hit its target. Patrick got both his hands half-way to his head before the blackness took him. He spun on his collapsing legs and crashed headlong, face down, his long body still and silent, the auburn hair brushing against the washroom door. The soles of his feet were turned mutely up, and one of his shoes needed mending.

Chapter Fourteen

Yardman and John edged round Billy and the flattened box and stood in the rear area, looking down at Patrick's body.

'Why did you do it back here?' John said.

Billy didn't answer. His gaze was fixed on me.

Yardman said mildly, 'Billy, Mr. Rous-Wheeler wants to know why you brought the pilot here to shoot him?'

Billy smiled and spoke to me. 'I wanted you to watch,' he said.

John – Rous-Wheeler – said faintly 'My God,' and I turned my head and found him staring at my ribs.

'Pretty good shooting,' said Billy complacently, following the direction of his eyes and taking his tone as a compliment. 'There's no fat on him and the skin over his ribs is thin. See where I've got every shot straight along a bone? Neat, that's what it is. A bit of craftsmanship I'd say. These lines are what I'm talking about,' he was anxious to make his point, 'not all that black and red around them. That's only dried blood and powder burn.'

Rous-Wheeler, to do him justice, looked faintly sick.

'All right, Billy,' Yardman said calmly. 'Finish him off.'

Billy lifted his gun. I had long accepted the inevitability of that moment, and I felt no emotion but regret.

'He's not afraid,' Billy said. He sounded disappointed.

'What of it?' Yardman asked.

'I want him to be afraid.'

Yardman shrugged. 'I can't see what difference it makes.'

To Billy it made all the difference in the world. 'Let me take a little time over him, huh? We've got hours to wait.'

Yardman sighed. 'All right, Billy, if that's what you want. Do all the other little jobs first, eh? Shut all the curtains on the plane first, we don't want to advertise ourselves. And then go down and tell Giuseppe to turn those landing lights off, the stupid fool's left them on. He'll have ladders and paint waiting for us. He and you and Alf can start straight away on painting out the airline's name and the plane's registration letters.'

'Yeah,' said Billy. 'O.K. And while I'm doing it I'll think of something.' He put his face close to mine, mocking. 'Something special for your effing Lordship.'

He put the gun in its holster and the silencer in his pocket, and drew all the curtains in the back part of the plane, before starting forward to do the rest.

Rous-Wheeler stepped over Patrick's body, sat down in one of the seats, and lit a cigarette. His hands were shaking.

'Why do you let him?' he said to Yardman. 'Why do you let him do what he likes?'

'He is invaluable,' Yardman sighed. 'A natural killer. They're not at all common, you know. That combination of callousness and enjoyment, it's unbeatable. I let him have his way if I can as a sort of reward, because he'll kill anyone I tell him to. I couldn't do what he does. He kills like stepping on a beetle.'

'He's so young,' Rous-Wheeler protested.

'They're only any good when they're young,' Yardman said. 'Billy is nineteen. In another seven or eight years, I wouldn't trust him as I do now. And there's a risk a killer will turn maudlin any time after thirty.'

'It sounds,' Rous-Wheeler cleared his throat, trying to speak as unconcernedly as Yardman, 'it sounds rather like keeping a pet tiger on a leash.'

He began to cross his legs and his shoes knocked against Patrick's body. With an expression of distaste he said, 'Can't we cover him up?'

Yardman nodded casually and went away up the plane. He came back with a grey blanket from the pile in the luggage bay, opened it out, and spread it over, covering head and all. I spent the short time that he was away watching Rous-Wheeler refuse to meet my eyes and wondering just who he was, and why he was so important that taking him beyond Milan was worth the lives of three totally uninvolved and innocent airmen.

An unremarkable looking man of about thirty-five, with incipient bags under his eyes, and a prim mouth. Unused to the violence surrounding him, and trying to wash his hands of it. A man with his fare paid in death and grief.

When Yardman had covered Patrick, he perched himself down on the edge of the flattened box. The overhead lights shone on the bald patch on his skull and the black spectacle frames made heavy bars of shadow on his eyes and cheeks.

'I regret this, my dear boy, believe me, I regret it sincerely,' he said, eyeing the result of Billy's target practice. Like Rous-Wheeler he took out a cigarette and lit it. 'He really has made a very nasty mess.'

But only skin deep, if one thought about it. I thought about it. Not much good.

'Do you understand what Billy wants?' Yardman said, shaking out his match.

I nodded.

He sighed. 'Then couldn't you ... er ... satisfy him, my dear boy? You will make it so hard for yourself, if you don't.'

I remembered the stupid boast I'd made to Billy the first day I'd met him, that I could be as tough as necessary. Now that I looked like having to prove it, I had the gravest doubts.

When I didn't answer Yardman shook his head sorrowfully. 'Foolish boy, whatever difference would it make, after you are dead?'

'Defeat . . .' I cleared my throat and tried again. 'Defeat on all levels.'

He frowned. 'What do you mean?'

'Communists are greedy,' I said.

'Greedy,' he echoed. 'You're wandering, my dear boy.'

'They like to . . . crumble . . . people, before they kill them. And that's . . . gluttony.'

'Nonsense,' said Rous-Wheeler in a vintage Establishment voice.

'You must have read newspaper accounts of trials in Russia,' I said, raising an eyebrow. 'All those "confessions".'

'The Russians,' he said stiffly, 'are a great warm-hearted simple people.'

'Oh, sure,' I agreed. 'And some are like Billy.'

'Billy is English.'

'So are you,' I said. 'And where are you going?'

He compressed his lips and didn't answer.

'I hope,' I said, looking at the blanket which covered Patrick, 'that your travel agents have confirmed your belief in the greatness, warm-heartedness and simplicity of the hemisphere you propose to join.'

'My dear boy,' interrupted Yardman smoothly, 'what eloquence!'

'Talking,' I explained, 'takes the mind off . . . this and that.'

A sort or recklessness seemed to be running in my blood, and my mind felt clear and sharp. To have even those two to talk to was suddenly a great deal more attractive than waiting for Billy on my own.

'The end justifies the means,' said Rous-Wheeler pompously, as if he'd heard it somewhere before.

'Crap,' I said inelegantly. 'You set yourself too high.'

'I am . . .' he began angrily, and stopped.

'Go on,' I said. 'You are what? Feel free to tell me. Moriturus, and all that.'

It upset him, which was pleasant. He said stiffly, 'I am a civil servant.'

'Were,' I pointed out.

'Er, yes.'

'Which ministry?'

'The Treasury,' he said, with the smugness of those accepted in the inner of inner sanctums.

The Treasury. It was a stopper, that one.

'What rank?' I asked.

'Principal.' There was a grudge in his voice. He hadn't risen.

'And why are you defecting?'

The forthcomingness vanished. 'It's none of your business.'

'Well it is rather,' I said in mock apology, 'since your change of allegiance looks like having fairly decisive effect on my future.'

He looked mulish and kept silent.

'I suppose,' I said with mild irony, 'you are going where you think your talents will be appreciated.'

For a second he looked almost as spiteful as Billy. A petty-minded man I thought, full of imagined slights, ducking the admission that he wasn't as brilliant as he thought he was. None of that lessened one jot the value of the information he carried in his head.

'And you,' I said to Yardman. 'Why do you do it? All this.'

He looked back gravely, the tight skin pulling over his shut mouth.

'Ideology?' I suggested.

He tapped ash off his cigarette, made a nibbling movement with his lip, and said briefly, 'Money.'

'The brand of goods doesn't trouble you, as long as the carriage is paid?'

'Correct,' he said.

'A mercenary soldier. Slaughter arranged. Allegiance always to the highest bidder?'

'That,' he said, inclining his head, 'is so.'

It wasn't so strange, I thought inconsequentially, that I'd never been able to understand him.

'But believe me, my dear boy,' he said earnestly, 'I never really intended you any harm. Not you.'

'Thanks,' I said dryly.

'When you asked me for a job I nearly refused you ... but I didn't think you'd stay long, and your name gave my agency some useful respectability, so I agreed.' He sighed. 'I must admit, you surprised me. You were very good at that job, if it's of any comfort to you. Very good. Too good. I should have stopped it when your father died, when I had the chance, before you stumbled on anything ... it was selfish of me. Selfish.'

'Simon Searle stumbled,' I reminded him. 'Not me.'

'I fear so,' he agreed without concern. 'A pity. He too was invaluable. An excellent accurate man. Very hard to replace.'

'Would you be so good as to untuck my shirt?' I said. 'I'm getting cold.'

Without a word he stood up, came round, tugged the bunched cloth out of the back of my trousers and pulled the collar and shoulders back to their right place. The shirt fronts fell together edge to edge, the light touch of the cloth on the burns being more than compensated by the amount of cool air shut out.

Yardman sat down again where he had been before and lit another cigarette from the stub of the first, without offering one to Rous-Wheeler.

'I didn't mean to bring you on this part of the trip,' he said. 'Believe me, my dear boy, when we set off from Gatwick I intended to organise some little delaying diversion for you in Milan, so that you wouldn't embark on the trip back.'

I said bleakly, 'Do you call sh ... shooting my girl a little diversion.'

He looked distressed. 'Of course not. Of course not. I didn't know you had a girl until you introduced her. But then I thought it would be an excellent idea to tell you to stay with her for a day or two, that we could easily manage without you on the way back. 'He,' he nodded at Patrick's shrouded body, 'told me you were ... er ... crazy about her. Unfortunately for you, he also told me how assiduous you had been in searching for Searle. He told me all about that bottle of pills. Now, my dear boy, that was a risk we couldn't take.'

'Risk,' I said bitterly.

'Oh yes, my dear boy, of course. Risk is something we can't afford in this business. I always act on risk. Waiting for certain knowledge may be fatal. And I was quite right in this instance, isn't that so? You had told me yourself where you were going to lunch, so I instructed Billy to go and find you and follow you from there, and make sure it was all love's young dream and no excitement. But you went bursting out of the restaurant and off at high speed to an obscure little bakery. Billy followed you in Vittorio's cab and rang me up from near there.' He spread his hands. 'I told him to kill you both and search you under cover of helping, as soon as you came out.'

'Without waiting to find out if there was anything in the bottle except pills?'

'Risk,' he nodded. 'I told you. We can't afford it. And that reminds me; where is Searle's message?'

'No message,' I said wearily.

'Of course there was, my dear boy,' he chided. 'You've shown so little surprise, asked so few questions. It was clear to me at once that you knew far too much when Billy brought you back to the plane. I have experience in these things, you see.'

I shrugged a shoulder. 'In my wallet,' I said.

He drew on his cigarette, gave me an approving look, stepped over Patrick, and fetched my jacket from the washroom. He took everything out of the wallet and spread them beside him on the flattened box. When he picked out the hundred dinar note and unfolded it, the pieces of writing paper and hay fell out.

He fingered the note. 'It was plain carelessness on Billy's part,' he said. 'He didn't hide the canisters properly.'

'There was a lot of money, then, on the plane?'

'Wheels have to be oiled,' Yardman said reasonably, 'and it's no good paying Yugoslavs in sterling. All agents insist on being paid in the currency they can spend without arousing comment. I do, myself.'

I watched him turn the scrap of his stationery over and over, frowning. He saw the pin holes in the end, and held them up to the light. After a few seconds he put it down and looked from me to Rous-Wheeler.

'Men,' he said without inflection. 'And when you read that, my dear boy, you understood a great deal.' A statement, not a question.

Gabriella, I thought dumbly, for God's sake live. Live and tell. I shut my eyes and thought of her as she had been at lunch. Gay and sweet and vital. Gabriella my dearest love . . .

'Dear boy,' said Yardman in his dry unconcerned voice, 'are you feeling all right?'

I opened my eyes and shut Gabriella away out of reach of his frightening intuition.

'No,' I said with truth.

Yardman actually laughed. 'I like you, my dear boy, I really do. I shall miss you very much in the agency.'

'Miss . . .' I stared at him. 'You are going back?'

'Of course.' He seemed surprised, then smiled his bony smile. 'How could you know, I was forgetting. Oh yes, of course we're going back. My transport system . . . is . . . er . . . much needed, and much appreciated. Yes. Only the plane and Mr. Rous-Wheeler are going on.'

'And the horses?' I asked.

'Those too,' he nodded. 'They carry good blood lines, those mares. We expected to have to slaughter them, but we have heard they will be acceptable alive, on account of their foals. No, my dear boy, Billy and I go back by road, half way with Giuseppe, the second half with Vittorio.'

'Back to Milan?'

'Quite so. And tomorrow morning we learn the tragic news that the plane we missed by minutes this afternoon has disappeared and must be presumed lost with all souls, including yours, my dear boy, in the Mediterranean.'

'There would be a radar trace . . .' I began.

'My dear boy, we are professionals.'

'Oiled wheels?' I said ironically.

'So quick,' he said nodding. 'A pity I can't tempt you to join us.'

'Why can't you?' said Rous-Wheeler truculently.

Yardman answered with slightly exaggerated patience. 'What do I offer him?'

'His life,' Rous-Wheeler said with an air of triumph.

Yardman didn't even bother to explain why that wouldn't work. The Treasury, I thought dryly, really hadn't lost much.

Billy's voice suddenly spoke from the far end of the plane.

'Hey, Mr. Yardman,' he called. 'Can't you and Mr. Rous-flipping-Wheeler come and give us a hand? This ruddy aeroplane's bloody covered with names and letters. We're practically having to paint the whole sodding crate.'

Yardman stood up. 'Yes, all right,' he said.

Rous-Wheeler didn't want to paint. 'I don't feel . . .' he began importantly.

'And you don't want to be late,' Yardman said flatly.

He stood aside to let the deflated Rous-Wheeler pass, and they both made their way up past the two boxes, through the galley, and down the telescopic ladder from the forward door.

Desperation can move mountains. I'd never hoped to have another minute alone to put it to the test, but I'd thought of a way of detaching myself from the mare's box, if I had enough strength. Yardman had had difficulty squeezing the rope down between the banding bar and the wooden box side when he'd tied me there: he'd had to push it through with the blade of his penknife. It wouldn't have gone through at all I thought, if either the box side wasn't a fraction warped or the bar a shade bent. Most of the bars lay flat and tight along the boxes, with no space at all between them.

I was standing less than two feet from the corner of the box: and along at the corner the bar was fastened by a lynch pin.

I got splinters in my wrists, and after I'd moved along six inches I thought I'd never manage it. The bar and the box seemed to come closer together the further I went, and jerking the rope along between them grew harder and harder, until at last it was impossible. I shook my head in bitter frustration. Then I thought of getting my feet to help, and bending my knee put my foot flat on the box as high behind me as I could get leverage. Thrusting back with my foot, pulling forward on the bar with my arms, and jerking my wrists sideways at the same time, I moved along a good inch. It worked. I kept at it grimly and finally arrived at the last three inches. From there, twisting, I could reach the lynch pin with my fingers. Slowly, agonisingly slowly, I pushed it up from the bottom, transferred my weak grip to the rounded top, slid it fraction by fraction up in my palm, and with an enormous sense of triumph felt it come free. The iron bands parted at the corner, and it required the smallest of jerks to tug the rope out through the gap.

Call that nothing, I said to myself with the beginnings of a grin. All that remained was to free my hands from each other.

Yardman had left my jacket lying on the flattened box, and in my jacket pocket was a small sharp penknife. I sat down on the side of the shallow platform, trying to pretend to myself that it wasn't because my legs were buckling at the knees but only the quickest way to reach the jacket. The knife was there, slim and familiar. I clicked open the blade, gripped it firmly, and sawed away blindly at some unseen point between my wrists. The friction of dragging the rope along had frayed it helpfully, and before I'd begun to hope for it I felt the strands stretch and give, and in two more seconds my hands were free. With stiff shoulders I brought them round in front of me. Yardman had no personal brutality and hadn't tied tight enough to stop the blood. I flexed my fingers and they were fine.

Scooping up wallet and jacket I began the bent walk forward under the luggage rack and over the guy chains, stepping with care so as not to make a noise and fetch the five outdoor decorators in at the double. I reached the galley safely and went through it. In the space behind the cockpit I stopped dead for a moment. The body of Mike the engineer lay tumbled in a heap against the left hand wall.

Tearing both mind and eyes away from him I edged towards the way out. On my immediate right I came first to the luggage bay, and beyond that lay the door. The sight of my overnight bag in the bay made me remember the black jersey inside it. Better than my jacket, I thought. It had a high neck, was easier to move in, and wouldn't be so heavy on my raw skin. In a few seconds I had it on, and had transferred my wallet to my trousers.

Five of them round the plane, I thought. The exit door was ajar, but when I opened it the light would spill out, and for the time it took to get on to the ladder they would be able to see me clearly. Unless by some miracle they were all over on the port side, painting the tail. Well, I thought coldly, I would just be unlucky if the nearest to me happened to be Billy with his gun.

It wasn't Billy, it was the man I didn't know, Giuseppe. He was standing at the root of the starboard wing painting out the airline's name on the fuselage, and he saw me as soon as I opened the door not far below him. I pulled the door shut behind me and started down the ladder, hearing Giuseppe shouting and warning all the others. They had ladders to get down too, I thought. I could still make it.

Giuseppe was of the hard core, a practising militant communist. He was also young and extremely agile. Without attempting to reach a ladder he ran along the wing to its tip, put his hands down, swung over the edge, and dropped ten feet to the ground. Seeing his running form outlined on the wing against the stars I veered away to the left as soon as I had slid down the ladder, and struck out forwards, more or less on the same axis as the plane.

My eyes weren't accustomed to the light as theirs were. I couldn't see where I was going. I heard Giuseppe shouting in Italian, and Yardman answering. Billy tried a shot which missed by a mile. I scrambled on, holding my arms up defensively and hoping I wouldn't run into anything too hard. All I had to do, I told myself, was to keep going. I was difficult to see in black and moved silently over the grass of the field. If I got far enough from the plane they wouldn't be able to find me, not five of them with Alf no better than a snail. Keep going and get lost. After that I'd have all night to search out a bit of civilisation and someone who could speak English.

The field seemed endless. Endless. And running hurt. What the hell did that matter, I thought dispassionately, with Billy behind me. I had also to refrain from making a noise about it in case they should hear me, and with every rib-stretching breath that got more difficult. In the end I stopped, went down on my knees, and tried to get air in shallow silent gulps. I could hear nothing behind but a faint breeze, see nothing above but the stars, nothing ahead but the dark. After a few moments I stood up again and went on, but more slowly. Only in nightmares did fields go on for ever. Even airfields.

At the exact second that I first thought I'd got away with it, bright white lights blazed out and held me squarely in their beams. A distant row of four in front, a nearer row of four behind, and I a black figure in the flarepath. Sick devastating understanding flooded through me. I had been trying to escape down the runway.

Sharply, almost without missing a step, I wheeled left and sprinted; but Giuseppe wasn't very far behind after all. I didn't see or hear him until the last moment when he closed in from almost in front. I swerved to avoid him, and he threw out his leg at a low angle and tripped me up.

Even though I didn't fall very heavily, it was enough. Giuseppe very slickly put one of his feet on each side of my head and closed them tight on my ears. Grass pressed into my eyes, nose and mouth, and I couldn't move in the vice.

Billy came up shouting as if with intoxication, the relief showing with the triumph.

'What you got there then, my friend? A bleeding aristocrat, then? Biting the dust, too, ain't that a gas?'

I guessed with a split second to spare what he would do, and caught his swinging shoe on my elbow instead of my ribs.

Yardman arrived at a smart military double.

'Stop it,' he said. 'Let him get up.'

Giuseppe stepped away from my head and when I put my hands up by my shoulders and began to push myself up, Billy delivered the kick I had avoided before. I rolled half over, trying not to care. The beams from the runway lights shone through my shut eyelids, and the world seemed a molten river of fire, scarlet and gold.

Without, I hoped, taking too long about it I again started to get up. No one spoke. I completed the incredibly long journey to my feet and stood there, quiet and calm. We were still on the runway between the distant lights, Yardman close in front of me, Giuseppe and Billy behind, with Rous-Wheeler struggling breathlessly up from the plane. Yardman's eyes, level with mine, were lit into an incandescent greenness by the glow. I had never clearly seen his eyes before. It was like drawing back curtains and looking into a soul.

A soldier without patriotism. Strategy, striking power and transport were skills he hired out, like any other craftsman. His pride was to exercise his skill to the most perfect possible degree. His pride overrode all else.

I think he probably meant it when he said he liked me. In a curious way, though I couldn't forgive him Gabriella, I felt respect for him, not hatred. Battle against him wasn't personal or emotional, as with Billy. But I understood that in spite of any unexpected warmth he might feel, he would be too prudent to extend foolish mercy to the enemy.

We eyed each other in a long moment of cool appraisal. Then his gaze slid past me, over my shoulder, and he paid me what was from his point of view a compliment.

'You won't crack him, Billy. Kill him now. One shot, nice and clean.'

Chapter Fifteen

I owed my life to Billy's greed. He was still hungry, still unsatisfied, and he shook his head to Yardman's request. Seeing the way Yardman delicately deferred to Billy's wishes it struck me that Rous-Wheeler's simile of a tiger on a leash might not be too far off the mark. In any case for the first time I was definitely glad of Billy's lust to spill my blue blood ounce by ounce, as I really was most averse to being shot down on the spot; and I acknowledged that I already had him to thank that I was still breathing at all. If I'd been anyone but who I was I would have died with the crew.

We walked back up the runway, I in front, the other four behind. I could hear Rous-Wheeler puffing, the only one not physically fit. Fit ... It was only yesterday, I thought incredulously, that I rode in the Gold Cup.

The plane was a faintly lit shape to the left of the end of the runway. A hundred yards short of it Yardman said, 'Turn left, dear boy. That's it. Walk straight on. You will see a building. Go in.'

There was, in fact, a building. A large one. It resembled an outsize prefabricated garage, made of asbestos sheets on a metal frame. The door was ajar and rimmed by light. I pushed it open, and with Billy's gun touching my back, walked in.

The right hand two-thirds of the concrete floor space was occupied by a small four-seater single-engined aeroplane, a new looking high winged Cessna with an Italian registration. On its left stood a dusty black Citroen, its bonnet towards me. Behind the car and the plane the whole far wall consisted of sliding doors. No windows anywhere. Three metal girders rose from floor to ceiling on the left of the car, supporting the flat roof and dividing the left hand part of the hangar into a kind of bay. In that section stood Alf.

'Right,' said Yardman briskly. 'Well done, Alf, turn them off now.' His voice echoed hollowly in space.

Alf stared at him without hearing.

Yardman went up to him and shouted in his ear. 'Turn the runway lights off.'

Alf nodded, walked up to the wall on the left of the door I had come in by, and pushed up a heavy switch beside a black fuse box. A second similar box worked, I suppose, the fluorescent strips across the ceilings and the low-powered radiant heaters mounted high on both side walls. Beside the switches stood a mechanic's bench with various tools and a vice, and further along two sturdy brackets held up a rack of gardening implements; spades, fork, rake, hoe and shears. Filling all the back of the bay was a giant motor mower with a seat for the driver, and dotted about there were some five gallon petrol cans, funnels, tins of paint, an assortment of overalls and several greasy looking metal chairs.

That Cessna, I thought briefly; I could fly it like riding a bicycle. And the car . . . if only I had known they were there.

Yardman searched among the clutter on the bench and produced a length of chain and two padlocks, one large, one small. Billy had shut the door and was standing with his back to it, the gun pointing steadily in my direction. Alf, Rous-Wheeler and Giuseppe had prudently removed themselves from his line of fire.

Yardman said, 'Go over to that first girder, my dear boy, and sit down on the floor.'

To say I was reluctant to be tied again is to put it mildly. It wasn't only that it was the end of any hope of escape, but I had a strong physical repugnance to being attached to things, the result of having been roped to a fir in a Scottish forest one late afternoon in a childhood game by some cousins I was staying with: they had run away to frighten me and got lost themselves, and it had been morning before the subsequent search had found me.

When I didn't obey at once, Yardman, Giuseppe and Billy all took a step forward as if moved by the same mind. There was no percentage in having them jump on me: I was sore enough already. I walked over to the girder and sat down facing them, leaning back idly against the flat metal surface.

'That's better,' Yardman said. He came round and knelt down on the ground at my back. 'Hands behind, my dear boy.'

He twined the chain round my wrists and clicked on both padlocks. Tossing the keys on his palm he stood up and came round in front of me. All five of them stared down with varying degrees of ill-feeling and I stared glassily back.

'Right,' said Yardman after a pause. 'We'd better get out and finish the painting. But this time we must leave someone with him, just in case.' He reviewed his available troops, and alighted on Rous-Wheeler. 'You sit here,' he said to him, picking up a chair and taking it over beside the switches, 'and if he does anything you aren't sure about, switch on the runway lights and we'll come at once. Clear?'

Rous-Wheeler was delighted to avoid any more painting and accepted his new task with enthusiasm.

'Good.' Yardman looked at his watch. 'Go on then, Billy.' Billy, Alf and Giuseppe filed out and Yardman stopped as he followed them to say to Rous-Wheeler, 'The cargo will be arriving soon. Don't be alarmed.'

'Cargo?' said Rous-Wheeler in surprise.

'That's right,' Yardman said. 'Cargo. The reason for this ... um ... operation.'

'But I thought I ...' began Rous-Wheeler.

'My dear Rous-Wheeler, no,' said Yardman. 'Had it been just you, I could have sent you down the usual discreet pipeline from Milan. Your journey would have been just as secret as it is now. No, we needed the plane for a rather special cargo, and as you know, my dear boy,' he swung round to speak directly to me with a small ironic smile, 'I do hate wasting space on flights. I always try to make up a full load, so as not to neglect an opportunity.'

'What is this cargo, then?' asked Rous-Wheeler with a damaged sense of self-importance.

'Mm?' said Yardman, putting the padlock keys down on the bench. 'Well now, it's the brain child of a brilliant little research establishment near Brescia. A sort of machine. An interesting little development, one might say. Broadly speaking, it's a device for emitting ultrasonic rays on the natural frequency of any chosen mineral substance.'

'Ultrasonics have been extensively researched,' Rous-Wheeler said testily.

Yardman smiled tightly. 'Take it from me, dear fellow, this particular development has great possibilities. Our friends have been trying to arrange photographs of the drawings and specifications, but these have been too well guarded. It proved easier in the end to ... er ... remove some vital parts of the device itself. But that of course presented a transport problem, a difficult transport problem, requiring my own personal supervision.' He was talking for my benefit as much as Rous-Wheeler's: letting me know how expert he was at his job. 'Once we were committed to the plane, of course it was the easiest way to take you too.'

No opportunity wasted. But he hadn't originally intended to take me as well: to give him his due.

Yardman went out of the hangar. Rous-Wheeler sat on his hard chair and I on the hard concrete and again my presence and/or predicament embarrassed him.

'Played any good wall games lately?' I said at length.

A hit, a palpable hit. He hadn't expected any needling school chums on his little trip. He looked offended.

'Have you been to ... er ... wherever you're going ... before?' I asked.

'No,' he said shortly. He wouldn't look at me.

'And do you speak the language?'

He said stiffly, 'I am learning.'

'What are they offering you?'

Some heavy smugness crept into his manner. 'I am to have a flat and a car, and a better salary. I will of course be in an important advisory position.'

'Of course,' I said dryly.

He flicked me his first glance. Disapproving.

'I am to be a consultant interpreter of the British way of life ... I pride myself that in my own small way I shall be promoting better understanding between two great peoples and making a positive contribution to the establishment of fruitful relations.'

He spoke as if he really meant it; and if he were as self-satisfied as that, he wouldn't consider turning round and going back. But Yardman had left the padlock keys on the bench ...

'Your actions may be misunderstood, back home,' I said.

'At first. That has been explained to me. But in time ...'

'You're wrong,' I said roughly. 'They'll call you a traitor. A plain stinking common or garden traitor.'

'No,' he said uneasily.

'What you need is someone to put your views forward, to explain what you are doing, so that your former colleagues admire you, and wish they had made more use of your undoubted abilities while they had the chance ...' I thought I'd laid it on too thick, but not so. He was looking seriously pensive.

'You mean ... you? You would represent me?' He pursed his lips.

'I don't always look so dirty,' I said earnestly. 'I could pull a certain amount of weight with my father's friends, and ... er ... I have an uncle who more or less lives in the Reform Club.'

He was nodding, taking it all in.

'A word in the right ear,' he said judiciously.

'Recognition,' I put in gently.

He looked modest. 'That's too much to hope for.'

'In time,' I insinuated.

'Do you really think so?'

'Well, of course.' I paused. 'I would be happy to clear up any ... er ... bad feelings which your ... move ... may have left.'

'Uncommonly kind of you,' he said pompously.

'At the moment, however, I don't look like being able to.'

He looked disappointed. 'I suppose not.' He frowned. 'You could have done me an excellent . . . as I see it now, an essential . . . service.'

I said casually, 'A great pity, yes. Of course . . . the keys are just beside you . . . if you felt like it.'

He looked at the keys and at me. He stood up. He took the keys into his hand. I could feel my heart thudding as I tried to look unconcerned. He took a step in my direction. Then, looking uneasily round, his glance fell on the runway lights switch. He stared at it, transfixed.

'Yardman said to put the light on, if you tried anything.' There was consternation in his voice. He turned and put the keys back on the bench as if they were suddenly hot. 'Yardman considers it essential for you to remain here. It would not be an auspicious start for me with my new friends if the first thing I did was so exactly contrary to their wishes.'

'Yardman's wishes.'

He used a modicum of brain. 'If I let you go back to England, Yardman wouldn't be able to. His invaluable transport service would have come to an end . . .' He looked horrified at the abyss he had almost stepped into. 'I would have been most unpopular.'

I didn't say anything. Down the snakes and back to square one. I tried again without success to do a Houdini on Yardman's chain job, and Rous-Wheeler sat down again and watched me with a mixture of anxiety and annoyance.

'What branch of the Treasury?' I said, giving it up.

'Initial finance,' he replied stiffly.

'What does that mean?'

'Grants.'

'You mean, your department settles who gets grants of public money, and how much?'

'That is so.'

'Development, research, defence, and so on?'

'Precisely.'

'So that you personally would know what projects are in hand . . . or contemplated?'

'Yes.'

They wouldn't have bothered with him, I supposed, for any less.

After a pause, I said, 'What about this ultrasonic transmitter?'

'What about it? It isn't a British project, if that's what you mean.'

'Did I get it right . . . that it will emit waves on the natural frequency of any mineral substance?'

'I believe that's what Yardman said,' he agreed stiffly.

'It would break things . . . like sound breaks glass?'

'I am not a scientist. I've no idea.' And from the tone of his voice he didn't care.

I stared gloomily at the floor and wondered what made a man change his allegiance. Rous-Wheeler might have been self-important and disappointed and have refused to face his own limitations, but thousands of men were like that, and thousands of men didn't give away a slice of their nation's future in return for a flat, a car, and a pat on the back.

There had to be more to it. Deep obsessive murky convoluted motives I couldn't guess at, pushing him irresistibly over. But he would be the same man wherever he went: in five years or less, again disgruntled and passed over. A useless dispensable piece of flotsam.

He, it appeared, took as pessimistic a view of my future as I of his.

'Do you think,' he cleared his throat. 'Do you think Billy will really kill you?'

'Be your age,' I said. 'You saw what he did to the crew.'

'He keeps putting it off,' he said.

'Saving the icing till last.'

'How can you be so frivolous?' he exclaimed. 'Your position is very serious.'

'So is yours,' I said. 'And I wouldn't swop.'

He gave me a small pitying smile of contemptuous disbelief, but it was true enough. Everyone dies sometime, as Simon had once said, and one was probably as little eager at eighty as at twenty-six. And there really were, I reflected with a smile for Victorian melodramas, fates worse than death.

A heavy van or lorry of some sort pulled up with a squeak of brakes somewhere near the door and after a few moments its driver came into the hangar. He was like Giuseppe, young, hard, cold-eyed and quick. He looked at me without apparent surprise and spoke to Rous-Wheeler in rapid Italian, of which the only intelligible word as far as I was concerned was Brescia.

Rous-Wheeler held up a hand, palm towards the driver. 'I don't understand you, my good fellow. Wait until I fetch Yardman.'

This proved unnecessary as my ex-employer had already seen the lorry's arrival. Followed by his entourage carrying ladders, paint pots, brushes and overalls, Yardman came forward into the hangar and exchanged some careful salutations with the driver.

'Right,' Yardman said in English to Billy. 'There should be several small light cases and one large heavy one. It will be easiest to load the light cases up through the forward door and stow them in the luggage bay. Then we will open the back doors, haul the heavy case in on the block and tackle, and stand it in the peat tray of the last box, the one that's now flattened. Clear?'

Billy nodded.

I opened my mouth to speak, and shut it again.

Yardman noticed. 'What is it?' he said sharply.

'Nothing.' I spoke listlessly.

He came over to me and looked down. Then he squatted on his haunches to peer on a level with my face.

'Oh yes, my dear boy, there is something. Now what, what?'

He stared at me as if he could read my thoughts while the calculations ticked over in his own. 'You were going to tell me something, and decided not to. And I feel I really should know what it is. I feel it must be to my disadvantage, something definitely to my disadvantage, as things stand between us.'

'I'll shoot it out of him,' Billy offered.

'It'll be quicker if I guess it . . . Now, what is wrong with stowing the cases the way I suggested? Ah yes, my dear boy, you know all about loading aeroplanes, don't you? You know what I said was wrong . . .' He snapped his fingers and stood up. 'The heavy case at the back is wrong. Billy, move the mares forward so that they occupy the two front boxes, and put the heavy case in the second to back box, and leave the rear one as it is.'

'Move the mares?' Billy complained.

'Yes, certainly. The centre of gravity is all-important, isn't that right, my dear boy?' He was pleased with himself, smiling. Quick as lightning. If I gave him even a thousandth of a second of suspicion that Gabriella was still alive . . .

Billy came over and stood looking down at me with a revoltingly self-satisfied smile.

'Not long now,' he promised.

'Load the plane first,' Yardman said. 'The van has to go back as soon as possible. You can . . . er . . . have your fun when I go to fetch the pilot. And be sure he's dead by the time I get back.'

'O.K.' Billy agreed. He went away with Alf, Giuseppe and the driver, and the van ground away on the short stretch to the D.C.4.

'What pilot?' Rous-Wheeler asked.

'My dear Rous-Wheeler,' Yardman explained with a touch of weary contempt. 'How do you think the plane is going on?'

'Oh . . . Well, why did you kill the other one? He would have flown on to wherever you said.'

Yardman sighed. 'He would have done no such thing without Billy at hand to shoot pieces off our young friend here. And frankly, my dear fellow, quite apart from the problem of Billy's and my return journey, it would have been embarrassing for us to kill the crew in your new country. Much better here. Much more discreet, don't you think?'

'Where exactly . . . where are we?' asked Rous-Wheeler. A good question if ever there was one.

'A private landing field,' Yardman said. 'An elderly respected nobleman lets us use it from time to time.'

Elderly and respected: Yardman's voice held some heavy irony.

'The usual sort of blackmail?' I asked. 'Filmed in a bed he had no right in?'

Yardman said 'No,' unconvincingly.

'What's he talking about?' Rous-Wheeler asked testily.

'I'm talking about the methods employed by your new friends,' I said. 'If they can't get help and information by bamboozling and subverting people like you, they do it by any form of blackmail or intimidation that comes to hand.'

Rous-Wheeler was offended. 'I haven't been bamboozled.'

'Nuts,' I said. 'You're a proper sucker.'

Yardman took three threatening steps towards me with the first anger he had shown. 'That's enough.'

'Nothing's enough,' I said mildly. 'What the hell do you think I have to lose?'

Yardman's glasses flashed in the light, and Rous-Wheeler said self-righteously, 'He tried to get me to free him, while you were painting the plane. He asked me to unlock him. I didn't, of course.'

'You nearly did,' I said. 'Anyone can reach you; your overgrown self-esteem makes you permanently gullible.'

Yardman looked from me to him with a taut mouth. 'I have to go over to the plane, Mr. Rous-Wheeler, and I think it would be best if you came with me.'

'But I wouldn't let him go,' he said, like a scolded schoolboy.

'All the same . . .' Yardman came behind me and bent down to check that his chains were still effective, which unfortunately they were. 'You look so gentle, dear boy,' he said into my ear. 'So misleading, isn't it?'

They went away and left me alone. I had another go at the chains, tantalised by the Cessna standing so close behind me: but this time Yardman had been more careful. The girder was rooted in concrete, the chain wouldn't fray like rope, and try as I might I couldn't slide my hands out.

Little time to go, I thought. And no questions left. There wasn't much profit in knowing the answers, since in a very short while I would know nothing at all. I thought about that too. I didn't believe in any form of after life. To die was to finish. I'd been knocked out several times in racing falls, and death was just a knockout from which one didn't awake. I couldn't honestly say that I much feared it. I never had. Undoubtedly on my part a defect of the imagination, a lack of sensitivity. All I felt was a strong reluctance to leave the party so soon when there was so much I would have liked to do. But there was the messy business of Billy to be got through first . . . and I admitted gloomily to myself that I would have avoided that if I could have dredged up the smallest excuse.

Alf shuffed into the hangar, went across to the rack of gardening tools and took down a spade. I shouted to him, but he showed no sign of having heard, and disappeared as purposefully as he'd come.

More minutes passed. I spent them thinking about Gabriella. Gabriella alive and loving, her solemnity a crust over depths of warmth and strength. A girl for always. For what was left of always.

The lorry came back, halted briefly outside, and rumbled away into the distance. Yardman and all his crew except Alf trooped into the hangar. Giuseppe walked past me across to the sliding doors at the back and opened a space behind the Citroen. A cool draught blew in and sent the dust round in little squirls on the concrete floor, and outside the sky was an intense velvety black.

Yardman said, 'Right Billy. If the new crew are on time, we'll be back with them in a little over an hour. I want you ready to go then, immediately the plane has taken off. All jobs done. Understood?'

'O.K.' Billy nodded. 'Relax.'

Yardman walked over and paused in front of me, looking down with a mixture of regret and satisfaction.

'Good-bye, my dear boy.'

'Good-bye,' I answered politely.

His taut mouth twisted. He looked across at Billy. 'Take no chances,

Billy, do you understand? You underestimate this man. He's not one of your fancy nitwits, however much you may want him to be. You ought to know that by now. And Billy, I'm warning you, I'm warning you my dear Billy, that if you should let him escape at this stage, knowing everything that he does, you may as well put one of your little bullets through your own brain, because otherwise, rest assured, my dear Billy, I will do it for you.'

Even Billy was slightly impressed by the cold menace in Yardman's usually uninflected voice. 'Yeah,' he said uneasily. 'Well he won't bloody escape, not a chance.'

'Make sure of it.' Yardman nodded, turned, and went and sat in the front passenger seat of the Citroen. Giuseppe beside him started the engine, reversed the car out of the hangar, and drove smoothly away, Yardman facing forwards and not looking back. Billy slid the door shut again behind them and came slowly across the concrete, putting his feet down carefully and silently like a stalker. He stopped four paces away, and the silence slowly thickened.

Rous-Wheeler cleared his throat nervously, and it sounded loud.

Billy flicked him a glance. 'Go for a walk,' he said.

'A ... walk?'

'Yeah, a walk. One foot in front of the other.' He was offensive. 'Down the runway and back should just about do it.'

Rous-Wheeler understood. He wouldn't meet my eyes and he hadn't even enough humanity to plead for me. He turned his back on the situation and made for the exit. So much for the old school tie.

'Now,' said Billy. 'Just the two of us.'

Chapter Sixteen

He walked cat-footed round the hangar in his quiet shoes, looking for things. Eventually he came back towards me carrying an old supple broken bicycle chain and a full flat five gallon tin of petrol. I looked at these objects with what I hoped was fair impassiveness and refrained from asking what he intended to do with them. I supposed I would find out soon enough.

He squatted on his haunches and grinned at me, his face level with mine, the bicycle chain in one hand and the petrol can on the floor in the other. His gun was far away, on the bench.

'Ask me nicely,' he said. 'And I'll make it easy.'

I didn't believe him anyway. He waited through my silence and sniggered.

'You will,' he said. 'You'll ask all right, your sodding lordship.'

He brought forward the bicycle chain, but instead of hitting me with it as I'd expected he slid it round my ankle and tied it there into two half hitches. He had difficulty doing this but once the knots were tied the links looked like holding for ever. The free end he led through the handle of the petrol can and again bent it back on itself into knots. When he had finished there was a stalk of about six inches between the knots on my ankle and those on the can. Billy picked up the can and jerked it. My leg duly followed, firmly attached. Billy smiled, well satisfied. He unscrewed the cap of the can and let some of the petrol run out over my feet and make a small pool on the floor. He screwed the cap back on, but looser.

Then he went round behind the girder and unlocked both the padlocks on my wrists. The chain fell off, but owing to a mixture of surprise and stiffened shoulders I could do nothing towards getting my hands down to undo the bicycle chain before Billy was across the bay for his gun and turning with it at the ready.

'Stand up,' he said. 'Nice and easy. If you don't, I'll throw this in the petrol.' This, in his left hand, was a cigarette lighter: a gas lighter with a top which stayed open until one snapped it shut. The flame burned bright as he flicked his thumb.

I stood up stiffly, using the girder for support, the sick and certain knowledge of what Billy intended growing like a lump of ice in my abdomen. So much for not being afraid of death. I had changed my mind about it. Some forms were worse than others.

Billy's mouth curled. 'Ask, then,' he said.

I didn't. He waved his pistol slowly towards the floor. 'Outside, matey. I've a little job for you to do. Careful now, we don't want a bleeding explosion in here if we can help it.' His face was alight with greedy enjoyment. He'd never had such fun in his life. I found it definitely irritating.

The can was heavy as I dragged it along with slow steps to the door and through on to the grass outside. Petrol slopped continuously in small amounts through the loosened cap, leaving a highly inflammable trail in my wake. The night air was sweet and the stars were very bright. There was no moon. A gentle wind. A beautiful night for flying.

'Turn right,' Billy said behind me. 'That's Alf along there where the light is. Go there, and don't take too bloody long about it, we haven't got all night.' He sniggered at his feeble joke.

Alf wasn't more than a tennis court away, but I was fed up with the petrol can before I got there. He had been digging, I found. A six or seven foot square of grass had been cut out, the turf lying along one edge in a tidy heap, and about a foot of earth had been excavated into a crumbling mound. A large torch standing on the pile of turf shone on Alf's old face as he stood in the shallow hole. He held the spade loosely and looked at Billy enquiringly.

'Go for a walk,' Billy said loudly. Alf interpreted the meaning if not the words, nodded briefly, leaned the spade against the turf, stepped up on to the grass and shuffled away into the engulfing dark.

'O.K., then,' said Billy. 'Get in there and start digging. Any time you want to stop, you've only got to ask. Just ask.'

'And if I do?'

The light shone aslant on Billy's wide bright eyes and his jeering delighted mouth. He lifted the pistol a fraction. 'In the head,' he said. 'And I'll have bloody well beaten you, your effing bloody lordship. And it's a pity I haven't got the whole lot like you here as well.'

'We don't do any harm,' I said, and wryly knew that history gave me the lie. There'd been trampling enough done in the past, and resentment could persist for centuries.

'Keep both hands on the spade,' he said. 'You try and untie the bicycle chain, and you've had it.'

He watched me dig, standing safely out of reach of any slash I might make with the spade and snapping his lighter on and off. The smell of petrol rose sharply into my nostrils as it oozed drop by drop through the leaking cap and soaked into the ground I stood on. The earth was soft and loamy, not too heavy to move, but Billy hadn't chosen this task without careful malice aforethought. Try as I might, I found I could scarcely shift a single spadeful without in some way knocking or rubbing my arm against my side. Jersey and shirt were inadequate buffers, and every scoop took its toll. The soreness increased like a geometrical progression.

Billy watched and waited. The hole grew slowly deeper. I told myself severely that a lot of other people had had to face far worse than this, that others before me had dug what they knew to be their own graves, that others had gone up in flames for a principle . . . that it was possible, even if not jolly.

Billy began to get impatient. 'Ask,' he said. I threw a spadeful of earth at him in reply and very nearly ended things there and then. The gun barrel jerked up fiercely at my head, and then slowly subsided. 'You'll be lucky,' he said angrily. 'You'll have to go down on your bloody knees.'

When I was sure my feet must be below his line of sight I tugged my foot as far away from the petrol can as the chain would allow, and jammed the spade down hard on the six inches of links between the knots. It made less noise than I'd feared on the soft earth. I did it again and again with every spadeful, which apart from being slightly rough on my ankle produced no noticeable results.

'Hurry up,' Billy said crossly. He flicked the lighter. 'Hurry it up.'

Excellent advice. Time was fast running out and Yardman would be back. I jammed the spade fiercely down and with a surge of long dead hope felt the battered links begin to split. It wasn't enough. Even if I got free of the petrol can I was still waist deep in a hole, and Billy still had his revolver: but even a little hope was better than none at all. The next slice of the spade split the chain further. The one after that severed it: but I had hit it with such force that when it broke I fell over, sprawing on hands and knees.

'Stand up,' Billy said sharply. 'Or I'll . . .'

I wasn't listening to him. I was acknowledging with speechless horror that the grave which was big enough for Patrick and Mike and Bob as well as myself was already occupied. My right hand had closed on a piece of cloth which flapped up through the soil. I ran my fingers along it, burrowing, and stabbed them into something sharp. I felt, and knew. A row of pins.

I stood up slowly and stared at Billy. He advanced nearly to the edge of the hole, looked briefly down, and back to me.

'Simon,' I said lifelessly. 'It's . . . Simon.'

Billy smiled. A cold, terrible, satisfied smile.

There were no more time. Time was only the distance from his gun to my head, from his gas lighter to my petrol-soaked shoes and the leaking can at my feet. He'd only been waiting for me to find Simon. His hunger was almost assuaged.

'Well,' he said, his eyes wide. 'Ask. It's your last chance.'

I said nothing.

'Ask,' he repeated furiously. 'You must.'

I shook my head. A fool, I thought. I'm a bloody fool. I must be mad.

'All right,' he said, raging. 'If I had more time you'd ask. But if you won't . . .' His voice died, and he seemed suddenly almost as afraid as I was at what he was going to do. He hesitated, half lifting the gun instead: but the moment passed and his nerve came back, renewed and pitiless.

He flicked the lighter. The flame shot up, sharp and blazing against the night sky. He poised it just for a second so as to be sure to toss it where I couldn't catch it on the way: and in that second I bent down, picked up the petrol can, and flung it at him. The loose cap unexpectedly came right off on the way up, and the petrol splayed out in a great glittering volatile stream, curving round to meet the flame.

A split second for evasion before the world caught fire.

The flying petrol burnt in the air with a great rushing noise and fell like a fountain over both the spots where Billy and I had just been standing. The can exploded with a gust of heat. The grave was a square blazing pit and flames flickered over the mound of dug out soil like brandy on an outsize plum pudding. Five gallons made dandy pyrotechnics.

I rolled out on my back over the lip of the grave with nothing to spare before it became a crematorium, and by some blessed miracle my feet escaped becoming part of the general holocaust. More than I had hoped.

Billy was running away screaming with his coat on fire along the left shoulder and down his arm. He was making frantic efforts to get it off but he was still clinging to his gun and this made it impossible. I had to have the gun and would have fought for it, but as I went after him I saw him drop it and stagger on, tearing at his jacket buttons in panic and agony: and my spine and scalp shuddered at the terror I had escaped.

With weak knees I half stumbled, half ran for the place where the revolver had fallen. The light of the flames glinted on it in the grass, and I bent and took it into my hand, the bulbous silencer heavy on the barrel and the butt a good fit in my palm.

Billy had finally wrenched his jacket off and it lay on the ground ahead in a deserted smouldering heap. Billy himself was still on his feet and making for the hangar, running and staggering and yelling for Alf.

I went after him.

Alf wasn't in the hangar. When I reached it Billy was standing with his back to me in the place where the car had been, rocking on his feet and still yelling. I stepped through the door and shut it behind me.

Billy swung round. The left sleeve of his shirt had burned into ribbons and his skin was red and glistening underneath. He stared unbelievingly at me and then at his gun in my hand. His mouth shut with a snap; and even then he could still raise a sneer.

'You won't do it,' he said, panting.

'Earls' sons,' I said, 'learn to shoot.'

'Only birds.' He was contemptuous. 'You haven't the guts.'

'You're wrong, Billy. You've been wrong about me from the start.'

I watched the doubt creep in and grow. I watched his eyes and then his head move from side to side as he looked for escape. I watched his muscles bunch to run for it. And when I saw that he finally realised in a moment of stark astonishment that I was going to, I shot him.

Chapter Seventeen

The Cessna had full tanks. Hurriedly I pressed the master switch in the cockpit and watched the needles swing round the fuel gauges. All the instruments looked all right, the radio worked, and the latest date on the maintenance card was only three days old. As far as I could tell from a cursory check, the little aircraft was ready to fly. All the same . . .

Alf and Rous-Wheeler came bursting in together through the door, both of them startled and wild looking and out of breath. Back from their little walks and alarmed by the bonfire. Alf gave an inarticulate cry and hurried over to Billy's quiet body. Rous-Wheeler followed more slowly, not liking it.

'It's Billy,' he said, as if stupefied. 'Billy.'

Alf gave no sign of hearing. They stood looking down at Billy as he lay on his back. There was a small scarlet star just left of his breastbone, and he had died with his eyes wide open, staring sightlessly up to the roof. Alf and Rous-Wheeler looked lost and bewildered.

I climbed quickly and quietly out of the Cessna and walked round its tail. They turned after a moment or two and saw me standing there not six paces away, holding the gun. I wore black. I imagine my face was grim. I frightened them.

Alf backed away two steps, and Rous-Wheeler three. He pointed a shaking arm at Billy.

'You . . . you killed him.'

'Yes.' My tone gave him no comfort. 'And you too, if you don't do exactly as I say.'

He had less difficulty in believing it than Billy. He made little protesting movements with his hands, and when I said, 'Go outside. Take Alf,' he complied without hesitation.

Just outside the door I touched Alf's arm, pointed back at Billy and then down to where the grave was. The flames had burnt out.

'Bury Billy,' I shouted in his ear.

He heard me, and looked searchingly into my face. He too found no reassurance: and he was used to doing what I said. Accepting the situation with only a shade more dumb resignation than usual he went slowly back across the concrete. I watched him shut the glazing eyes with rough humane fingers, and remembered the cup of coffee he'd given me when I badly needed it. He had nothing to fear from me as long as he stayed down by the grave. He picked Billy up, swung him over his shoulder in a fireman's lift, and carried him out and away across the grass, a sturdy old horseman who should never have got caught up in this sort of thing. Any more than I should.

I stretched an arm back into the hangar and pulled down the lever which controlled the runway lights. At each end of the long strip the four powerful beams sprang out, and in that glow Alf could see where he was going and what he was going to do.

That Cessna, I thought, glancing at it, probably had a range of about six or seven hundred miles . . .

'You,' I said abruptly to Rous-Wheeler. 'Go and get into the plane we came in. Go up the forward steps, back through the galley, right back through the cabin, and sit down on those seats. Understand?'

'What . . .?' He began nervously.

'Hurry up.'

He gave me another frightened glance and set off to the plane, a lumbering grey shape behind the runway lights. I walked three steps behind him and unsympathetically watched him stumble in his fear.

'Hurry.' I said again, and he stumbled faster. The thought of the Citroen returning was like a devil on my tail. I was just not going to be taken again. There was five bullets left in the gun. The first for Rous-Wheeler, the next for Yardman, and after that . . . he would have Giuseppe with him, and at least two others. Not nice.

'Faster.' I said.

Rous-Wheeler reached the ladder and stumbled up it, tripping over half the steps. He went awkwardly back through the plane just as I had said and flopped down panting on one of the seats. I followed him. Someone, Alf I supposed, had given the mares some hay, and one of the bales from Billy's now dismantled wall had been clipped open and split. The binding wire from it lay handy on the flattened aft box. I picked it up to use on Rous-Wheeler, but there was nothing on the comfortable upholstered double seat I could tie him to.

He made no fuss when I bound his wrists together. His obvious fear made him flabby and malleable, and his eyes looked as if he could feel shock waves from the violence and urgency which were flowing through me.

'Kneel down,' I said, pointing to the floor in front of the seats. He didn't like that. Too undignified.

'Kneel,' I said. 'I haven't time to bother about your comfort.'

With a pained expression that at any other time would have been funny he lowered himself on to his knees. I slid the ends of the wire through one of the holes in the seat anchorages on the floor, and fastened him there securely by the wrists.

'I ss . . . say,' he protested.

'You're bloody lucky to be alive at all, so shut up.'

He shut up. His hands were tied only a couple of feet away from the blanket which covered Patrick. He stared at the quiet mound and he didn't like that either. Serve him right, I thought callously.

'What . . . what are you going to do?' he said.

'I didn't answer. I went back up the cabin, looking at the way they'd re-stored the cargo. Aft box still flat. The walls of the next one, dismantled, had been stacked in the starboard alley. On the peat tray now stood a giant packing case six feet long, four feet wide, and nearly five feet tall. Chains ran over it in both directions, fastening it down to the anchorages. It had rope handles all the way round, and Yardman had said something about using a block and tackle, but all the same manoeuvring it into its present position must have been a tricky sweaty business. However, for the sake of forwarding the passage of this uninformative crate Yardman had also been prepared to steal a plane and kill three airmen. Those who had no right to it wanted it very badly.

I went up further. The four mares were unconcernedly munching at full haynets and paid me scant attention. Through the galley and into the space behind the cockpit, where Mike's body still lay. Burial had been the last of the jobs. Uncompleted.

The luggage compartment held four more crates, the size of tea chests. They all had rope handles and no markings.

Beyond them was the open door. It represented to me a last chance of not going through with what I had in mind. Yardman hadn't yet come back, and the Cessna was ready. If I took it, with its radio and full tanks, I would undoubtedly be safe, and Yardman's transport business would be busted. But he'd still have the D.C.4 and the packing cases . . .

Abruptly I pulled up the telescopic ladder and shut the door with a clang. Too much trouble, I told myself, to change my mind now. I'd have to take Rous-Wheeler all the way back to the Cessna or shoot him, and neither course appealed. But the situation I found in the cockpit nearly defeated me before I began.

Billy had shot Bob as he sat, through the back of the head. The upper part of him had fallen forward over the wheel, the rest held firmly in the seat by the still fastened safety strap across his thighs. In the ordinary way even stepping into the co-pilot's seat in the cramped space was awkward enough, and lifting a dead man out of it bodily was beyond me. Blacking my mind to the sapping thought that this was a man I had known, and considering him solely as an object which spelled disaster to me if I didn't move it I undid the seat belt, heaved the pathetic jack-knifed figure round far enough to clear his feet and head from the controls, and fastened the belt tight across him again in his new position, his back half towards me.

With the same icy concentration I sat in Patrick's place and set about starting the plane. Switches. Dozens of switches everywhere: On the control panel, on the roof, in the left side wall and in the bank of throttles

on my right. Each labelled in small metal letters, and too many having
to be set correctly before the plane would fly.

Patrick had shown me how. Quite different from doing it. I pared the
pre-starting checks down to the barest minimum; fuel supply on, mixture
rich, propeller revs maximum, throttle just open, brakes on, trimmer
central, direction indicator synchronised with the compass.

My boats were burned with the first ignition switch, because it worked.
The three bladed propeller swung and ground and the inner port engine
roared into action with an earsplitting clatter. Throttle too far open.
Gently I pulled the long lever with its black knob down until the engine
fell back to warming up speed, and after that in quick succession and
with increasing urgency I started the other three. Last, I switched on the
headlights: Alf might not have heard the engines, but he would certainly
see the lights. It couldn't be helped. I had to be able to see where I was
going. With luck he wouldn't know what do do, and do nothing.

I throttled back a bit and took the brakes off and the plane began to
roll. Too fast. Too fast. I was heading straight for the runway lights and
could smash them, and I needed them alight. I pulled the two starboard
throttles back for a second and the plane slewed round in a sort of skid
and missed the lights and rolled forward on to the runway.

The wind was behind me, which meant taxi-ing to the far end and
turning back to take off. No one ever taxied a D.C.4 faster. And at the
far end I skipped all the power checks and everything else I'd been taught
and swung the plane round facing the way I'd come and without a pause
pushed forward all the four throttles wide open.

The great heavy plane roared and vibrated and began to gather speed
with what seemed to me agonising slowness. The runway looked too
short. Grass was slower than tarmac, the strip was designed for light
aircraft, and heaven alone knew the weight of that packing case . . . For
short runways, lower flaps. The answer came automatically from the
subconscious, not as a clear coherent thought. I put my hand on the lever
and lowered the trailing edges of the wings. Twenty degrees. Just under
half-way. Full slaps were brakes . . .

Yardman came back.

Unlike Alf, he knew exactly what to do, and wasted no time doing it.
Towards the far end the Citroen was driven straight out on to the centre
line of the runway, and my headlights shone on distant black figures
scrambling out and running towards the hangar. Swerve wide enough
to miss the car, I thought, and I'll get unbalanced on rough ground and
pile up. Go straight up the runway and not be able to lift off in time, and
I'll hit it either with the wheels or the propellers . . .

Yardman did what Alf hadn't. He switched off the runway lights.
Darkness clamped down like a sack over the head. Then I saw that the
plane's bright headlights raised a gleam on the car now frighteningly
close ahead and at least gave me the direction to head for. I was going
far too fast to stop, even if I'd felt like it. Past the point of no return, and
still on the ground. I eased gently back on the control column, but she
wouldn't come. The throttles were wide; no power anywhere in reserve.
I ground my teeth and with the car coming back to me now at a hundred

miles an hour hung on for precious moments I couldn't spare, until it was then or never. No point in never. I hauled back on the control column and at the same time slammed up the lever which retracted the undercarriage. Belly flop or car crash; I wasn't going to be around to have second thoughts. But the D.C.4 flew. Unbelievably there was no explosive finale, just a smooth roaring upward glide. The plane's headlights slanted skywards, the car vanished beneath, the friction of the grass fell away. Airborne was the sweetest word in the dictionary.

Sweat was running down my face; part exertion, part fear. The D.C.4 was heavy, like driving a fully loaded pantechnicon after passing a test on empty minis, and the sheer muscle power needed to hold it straight on the ground and get it into the air was in the circumstances exhausting. But it was up, and climbing steadily at a reasonable angle, and the hands were circling reassuringly round the clock face of the altimeter. Two thousand, three thousand, four thousand feet. I levelled out at that and closed the throttles a little as the airspeed increased to two twenty knots. A slow old plane, built in nineteen-forty-five. Two twenty was the most it could manage.

The little modern Cessna I'd left behind was just about as fast. Yardman had brought a pilot. If he too took off without checks, he could be only scant minutes behind.

Get lost, I thought, I'd the whole sky to get lost in. The headlights were out, but from habit I'd switched on the navigation lights on the wing tips and tail and also the revolving beacon over the cockpit. The circling red beam from it washed the wings alternately with pale pink light. I switched it out, and the navigation lights too. Just one more broken law in a trail of others.

The runway had been laid out from due east to west. I had taken off to the west and flown straight on, urgent to get out, regardless of where. Too easy for them. I banked tentatively to the left and felt the plane respond cumbrously, heavy on my arms. South-west, into the wind. I straightened up and flew on, an invisible shell in the darkness, and after five minutes knew they wouldn't find me. Not with the Cessna, anyway.

The tight-strung tension of my nerves relaxed a little: with most uncomfortable results. I was suddenly far too aware of the wicked square of burn over my ribs, and realised that I hadn't really felt it since the moment I found Simon. Under the pressure of events its insistent message hadn't got through. Now it proceeded to rectify that with enthusiasm.

Weakness seeped down my limbs. I shivered, although I was still sweating from exertion. My hands started trembling on the wheel, and I began to realise the extent to which I was unfit to fly anything, let alone take a first try at an airliner way out of my normal class. But far worse than the physical stress was the mental let-down which accompanied it. It was pride which had got me into that plane and up into the air. Nothing but pride. I was still trying to prove something to Billy, even though he was dead. I hadn't chosen the D.C.4 because of any passionate conviction that the ultrasonic gadget needed saving at all costs, but simply to show them, Yardman and Billy's ghost, that there wasn't much I couldn't do. Childish, vainglorious, stupid, ridiculous: I was the lot.

And now I was stuck with it. Up in the air in thundering tons of metal, going I didn't know where.

I wiped the sleeve of my jersey over my face and tried to think. Direction and height were vital if I were ever to get down again. Four thousand feet, I thought, looking at the altimeter; at that height I could fly straight into a mountain . . . if there were any. South west steady: but south west from where? I hunted round the cockpit for a map of any sort, but there wasn't one to be found.

Patrick had said we were in Italy, and Giuseppe was Italian, and so was the registration on the Cessna, and the ultrasonic device had been driven straight from Brescia. Conclusive, I thought. Northern Italy, probably somewhere near the east cost. Impossible to get closer than that. If I continued south-west, in the end I'd be over the Mediteranean. And before that . . . new sweat broke out on my forehead. Between the northern plain and the Mediterranean lay the Apennines, and I couldn't remember at all how high they were. But four thousand was much too low . . . and for all I knew they were only a mile ahead . . .

I put the nose up and opened the throttles and slowly gained height. Five thousand, six thousand, seven thousand, eight. That ought to be enough . . . The Alps only reached above twelve thousand at the peaks, and the Apennines were a good deal lower. I was guessing. They might be higher than I thought. I went up again to ten thousand.

At that height I was flying where I had no business to be, and at some point I'd be crossing the airways to Rome. Crossing a main road in the dark, without lights. I switched the navigation lights on again, and the revolving beacon too. They wouldn't give much warning to a jetliner on a collision course, but possibly better than none.

The thunderous noise of the engines was tiring in itself. I stretched out a hand for Patrick's headset and put it on, the padded earphones reducing the din to a more manageable level. I had taken it for granted from the beginning that Yardman would have put the radio out of order before ever asking Patrick to change course, and some short tuning with the knobs confirmed it. Not a peep or crackle from the air. There had been just a chance that he wouldn't have disconnected the V.O.R. - Very high frequency Omni-range - by which one navigated from one radio beacon to the next: it worked independently of two-way ground to air communication, and he might have needed to use it to find the airfield we had landed on. But that too was dead.

Time, I thought. If I didn't keep track of the time I'd be more lost than ever. I looked at my watch. Half-past eleven. I stared at the hands blankly. If they'd said half nine or half one it would have felt the same. The sort of time one measured in minutes and hours had ceased to exist in a quite street in Milan. I shook myself. Half past eleven. From now on it was important. Essential. Without maps or radio, time and the compass were going to decide my fate. Like all modern pilots I had been taught to stick meticulously to using all the aids and keeping all the regulations. The 'seat of the pants' stuff of the pioneers was held to be unscientific and no longer necessary. This was a fine time to have to learn it from scratch.

If I'd been up for a quarter of an hour, I thought, and if I'd started from the northern plain, and if I could only remember within a hundred miles how broad Italy was, then I might have some idea of when I'd be over the sea. Not yet, anyway. There were pinpricks of lights below me, and several small clusters of towns. No conveniently lit airports with welcoming runways.

If I'd taken the Cessna, I thought wretchedly, it would have been easy. Somewhere, by twiddling the knobs, I'd have raised radio contact with the ground. The international air language was English. A piece of cake. They'd have told me my position, what course to set, how to get down, everything. But if I'd taken the Cessna, I would have had to leave the D.C.4 intact, because of the mares. I'd thought at first of piling a couple more five gallon cans under the big plane and putting a match to it, and then remembered the living half of the cargo. Yardman might be cold-bloodedly prepared to kill airmen, but I baulked at roasting alive four horses. And I couldn't get them out, because the plane carried no ramp. With time I could have put the engines out of action . . . and with time they could have mended them again. But I hadn't had time. If I'd done that, I couldn't have got the Cessna out and away before Yardman's return.

I could have taken Rous-Wheeler in the Cessna and landed safely and put Yardman Transport out of business. But I was as greedy as Billy: half wasn't enough. It had to be all. I could choke on all, as Billy had.

The useless thoughts squirrelled round and round, achieving nothing. I wiped my face again on the sleeve of my jersey and understood why Patrick had nearly always flown in shirt sleeves, even though it was winter.

Italy couldn't be much wider than England. If as wide. A hundred and twenty, a hundred and forty nautical miles. Perhaps more. I hadn't looked at the time when I took off. I should have done. It was routine. I hadn't a hope if I couldn't concentrate better than that. A hundred and forty miles of two twenty knots . . . say a hundred and sixty miles to be sure . . . it would take somewhere between forty and forty-five minutes. If I'd had the sense to look at my watch earlier I would have known how far I'd gone.

The lights below grew scarcer and went out. It was probably too soon to be the sea . . . it had to be mountains. I flew on for some time, and then checked my watch. Midnight. And still no lights underneath. The Apennines couldn't be so broad . . . but if I went down too soon, I'd hit them. I gave it another five minutes and spent them wishing Billy's burns would let up again. They were a five star nuisance.

Still no lights. I couldn't understand it. I couldn't possibly still be over the narrow Apennines. It was no good. I'd have to go down for a closer look. I throttled back, let the nose go down, and watched the altimeter hands go anti-clockwise through seven, six, five, four. At four thousand feet I levelled out again, and the night was as black as ever. I'd certainly hit no mountains, but for all I could see I was a lost soul in Limbo. It wasn't a safe feeling, not at all.

When at last I saw lights ahead I was much more uneasy than reassured. It was twelve fifteen by my watch, which meant I had come nearly two hundred miles already, and Italy couldn't be as wide as that. Or at least I wouldn't have thought so. .

The lights ahead resolved themselves into little clusters strung out in a horizontal line. I knew the formation too well to mistake it. I was approaching a coastline. Incredulity swamped me. I was approaching *from the sea*.

Nightmares weren't in it. I felt a great sense of unreality, as if the world had spun and rearranged its face, and nothing was ever going to be familiar again. I must be somewhere, I thought, taking a fierce grip on my escaping imagination. But where on earth, where literally on earth, was I?

I couldn't go on flying blindly south-west for ever. The coast line must have a shape. About three miles short of it I banked to the right, wheeling northwards, guided by nothing more rational than instinct, and flew along parallel with the few and scattered lights on the shore. The sea beneath was black but the land was blacker. The line where they met was like ebony against coal, a shadowy change of texture, a barely perceptible rub of one mass against another.

I couldn't, I thought, bullying my mind into some sort of order, I couldn't possibly have flown straight across the Gulf of Genoa and now be following the Italian coast northwards from Alassio. There weren't enough lights, even for that time of night. And I knew that coastline well. This one, I didn't. Moreover, it ran due north for far too long. I had already been following it for fifteen minutes: fifty-five miles.

It had to be faced that I'd been wrong about where I started from. Or else the directional gyro was jammed. It couldn't be . . . I'd checked it twice against the remote reading compass, which worked independently. I checked again: they matched. They couldn't both be wrong. But I *must* have started in Italy. I went right back in my mind to the flight out, when Patrick had first turned east. It had been east. I was still sure of that: and that was all.

There was a flashing light up aheal, on the edge of the sea. A lighthouse. Very useful if I'd had a nautical chart, which I hadn't. I swept on past the lighthouse and stopped dead in my mental tracks. There was no land beyond.

I banked the plane round to the left and went back. The light-house stood at the end of a long narrow finger of land pointing due north. I flew southwards along the western side of it for about twenty miles until the sporadic lights spread wider and my direction swung again to the south-west. A fist pointing north.

Supposing I'd been right about starting from Italy, but wrong about being so far east. Then I would have been over the sea when I thought I was over the mountains. Supposing I'd been going for longer than a quarter of an hour when I first looked at my watch: then I would have gone further than I guessed. All the same, there simply wasn't any land this shape in the northern Mediterranean, not even an island.

An island of this size . . .

Corsica.

It couldn't be, I thought. I couldn't be so far south. I wheeled the plane round again and went back to the lighthouse. If it was Corsica and I flew north-west I'd reach the south of France and be back on the map. If it was Corsica I'd started from right down on the southern edge of the northern plain, not near Trieste or Venice as I'd imagined. It wasn't impossible. It made sense. The world began to fall back into place. I flew north-west over the black invisible sea. Twenty-seven minutes. About a hundred miles.

The strings and patterns of lights along the French coast looked like lace sewn with diamonds, and were just as precious. I turned and followed them westwards, looking for Nice airport. It was easy to spot by day: the runways seemed to be almost on the beach, as the airfield had been built on an outward curve of the shoreline. But either I was further west than I thought, or the airport had closed for the night, because I missed it. The first place I was sure of was Cannes with its bay of embracing arms, and that was so close to Nice that if the runway had been lit I must have seen it.

A wave of tiredness washed through me, along with a numb feeling of futility. Even if I could find one, which was doubtful, I couldn't fly into a major airport without radio, and all the minor ones had gone to bed. I couldn't land anywhere in the dark. All I looked like being able to do was fly around in circles until it got light again and land at Nice . . . and the fuel would very likely give out before then.

It was at that depressing point that I first thought about trying to go all the way to England. The homing instinct in time of trouble. Primitive. I couldn't think of a thing against it except that I was likely to go to sleep from tiredness on the way, and I could do that even more easily going round in circles outside Cannes.

Committed from the moment I'd thought of it, I followed the coast until it turned slightly north again and the widespread lights of Marseilles lay beneath. The well-known way home from there lay up the Rhone Valley over the beacons at Montélimar and Lyons, with a left wheel at Dijon to Paris. But though the radio landmarks were unmistakable the geographical ones weren't, and I couldn't blindly stumble into the busy Paris complex without endangering every other plane in the area. North of Paris was just as bad, with the airlanes to Germany and the East. South, then. A straight line across France south of Paris. It would be unutterably handy to have known where Paris lay; what precise bearing. I had to guess again . . . and my first guesses hadn't exactly been a riotous triumph.

Three-twenty degrees, I thought. I'd try that. Allow ten degrees for wind drift from the south-west. Three ten. And climb a bit . . . the centre of France was occupied by the Massif Central and it would be fairly inefficient to crash into it. I increased the power and went back up to ten thousand feet. That left fuel, the worst problem of all.

I'd taken off on the main tanks and the gauges now stood in half full. I switched over to the auxiliaries and they also were half full. And half empty, too. The plane had been refuelled at Milan that morning, ten centuries ago. It carried ... I thought searchingly back to Patrick's casually thrown out snippets of information the first day I flew with him ... it carried twelve hundred United States gallons, giving a range of approximately eighteen hundred miles in normal conditions with a normal load. The load, though unconventional, was normal enough in weight. The condition of the weather was perfect, even if the condition of the pilot wasn't. Nine hundred miles from Marseilles would see me well over England, but it wouldn't take much more than four hours at the present speed until the tanks ran dry and it would still be too dark ...

There was just one thing to be done about that. I put my hand on the throttle levers and closed them considerably. The airspeed fell back from two-twenty, back through two hundred, one-eighty, steadied on one-fifty. I didn't dare go any slower than that because one thing Patrick hadn't told me was the stalling speed, and a stall I could do without. The nose wanted to go down heavily with the decreased airspeed and I was holding it up by brute strength, the wheel of the control column lodged against my whole left forearm. I stretched my right hand up to the trimmer handle in the roof and gave it four complete turns, and cursed as a piece of shirt which was sticking to the furrows and burns unhelpfully unstuck itself. The nose of the plane steadied; ten thousand feet at one-fifty knots; and blood oozed warmly through my jersey.

A hundred and fifty knots should reduce the petrol consumption enough for me to stay in the air until long enough after dawn to find an airfield. I hoped. It also meant not four hours ahead, but more than five: and I'd had enough already. Still, now that I knew roughly where I was going, the plane could fly itself. I made small adjustments to the trimmer until the needle on the instrument which showed whether she was climbing or descending pointed unwaveringly to level, and then switched in the automatic pilot. I took my hands off the wheel and learned back. The D.C.4 flew straight on. Very restful.

Nothing happened for several minutes except that I developed a thirst and remembered Rous-Wheeler for the first time since takeoff. Still on his knees, I supposed, and extremely uncomfortable. His bad luck.

There was water in the galley only five or six steps behind me, cold and too tempting. Gingerly I edged out of my seat. The plane took no notice. I took two steps backwards. The instruments didn't quiver. I went into the galley and drew a quick cup of water, and went back towards the cockpit drinking it. Clearly the plane was doing splendidly without me. I returned to the galley for a refill of the cold delicious liquid, and when I'd got it, nearly dropped it.

Even above the noise of the engines I could hear Rous-Wheeler's scream. Something about the raw terror in it raised the hair on my neck. That wasn't pain, I thought, not the sort he'd get from cramp anyway. It was fear.

He screamed again, twice.

One of the horses, I thought immediately. If Billy hadn't boxed them properly ... My newly irrigated mouth went dry again. A loose horse was just too much.

I went back to the cockpit, hurrying. Nothing had moved on the instrument panel. I'd have to risk it.

The plane had never seemed longer, the chains and racks more obstructing. And none of the mares was loose. They weren't even fretting, but simply eating hay. Half relieved, half furious. I went on past the packing case. Rous-Wheeler was still there, still kneeling. His eyes protruded whitely and his face was wet. The last of his screams hung like an echo in the air.

'What the hell's the matter?' I shouted o him angrily.

'He ...' his voice shrieked uncontrollably. 'He ... moved.'

'Who moved?'

'Him.' His eyes were staring fixedly at the blanket covering Patrick.

He couldn't have moved. Poor, poor Patrick. I went across and pulled the rug off and stood looking down at him, the tall silent body, the tumbled hair, the big pool of blood under his downturned face.

Pool of blood.

It was impossible. He hadn't had time to bleed as much as that. I knelt down beside him and rolled him over, and he opened his yellow eyes.

Chapter Eighteen

He'd been out cold for six hours and he was still unconscious. Nothing moved in his eyes, and after a few seconds they fell slowly shut again.

My fingers were clumsy on his wrist and for anxious moments I could feel nothing; but his pulse was there. Slow and faint, but regular. He was on his way up from the depths. I was so glad that he wasn't dead that had Rous-Wheeler not been there I would undoubtedly have wept. As it was, I fought against the flooding back of the grief I'd suppressed when Billy shot him. Odd that I should be tumbled into such intense emotion only because the reason for it was gone.

Rous-Wheeler stuttered 'What ... what is it?' with a face the colour and texture of putty, and I glanced at him with dislike.

'He's alive,' I said tersely.

'He can't be.'

'Shut up.'

Billy's bullet had hit Patrick high, above the hairline and at a rising angle, and instead of penetrating his skull had slid along outside it. The long, swollen and clotted wound looked dreadful, but was altogether beautiful in comparison with a neat round hole. I stood up and spread the blanket over him again, to keep him warm. Then, disregarding Rous-Wheeler's protest, I went away up the plane.

In the cockpit nothing had changed. The plane roared steadily on its three ten heading and all the instruments were like rocks. I touched the back of the co-pilot, awake again to his presence. The silence in him was eternal: he wouldn't feel my sympathy, but he had it.

Turning back a pace or two, I knelt down beside Mike. He too had been shot in the head, and about him too there was no question. The agile eyebrow was finished. I straightened him out from his crumpled position and laid him flat on his back. It wouldn't help any, but it seemed to give him more dignity. That was all you could give the dead, it seemed; and all you could take away.

The four packing cases in the luggage bay were heavy and had been thrust in with more force than finesse, pushing aside and crushing most of the things already there. Shifting the first case a few inches I stretched a long arm past it and tugged out a blanket, which I laid over Mike. Armed with a second one I went back into the galley. Sometime in the past I'd seen the first-aid box in one of the cupboards under the counter, and to my relief it was still in the same place.

Lying on top of it was a gay parcel wrapped in the stripped paper of Malpensa Airport. The doll for Mike's daughter. I felt the jolt physically. Nothing could soften the facts. I was taking her a dead father for her birthday.

And Gabriella . . . anxiety for her still hovered in my mind like a low cloud ceiling, thick, threatening and unchanged. I picked up the parcel she had wrapped and put it on the counter beside the plastic cups and the bag of sugar. People often did recover from bullets in the lungs: I knew they did. But the precise Italian doctor had only offered hope, and hope had tearing claws. I was flying home to nothing if she didn't live.

Taking the blanket and the first aid kid I went back to Patrick. In the lavatory compartment I washed my filthy hands and afterwards soaked a chunk of cotton wool with clean water to wipe his blood-streaked face. Dabbing dry with more cotton wool I found a large hard lump on his forehead where it had hit the floor: two heavy concussing shocks within seconds, his brain had received. His eyelids hadn't flickered while I cleaned him, and with a new burst of worry I reached for his pulse: but it was still there, faint but persevering.

Sighing with relief I broke open the wrapping of a large sterile wound dressing, laid it gently over the deep gash in his scalp, and tied it on with the tape. Under his head I slid the second blanket, folded flat, to shield him a little from the vibration in the aircraft's metal skin. I loosened his tie and undid the top button of his shirt and also the waistband of his trousers: and beyond that there was no help I could give him. I stood up slowly with the first aid kit and turned to go.

With anxiety bordering on hysteria Rous-Wheeler shouted, 'You aren't going to leave me like this again, are you?'

I looked back to him. He was half sitting, half kneeling, with his hands still fastened to the floor in front of him. He'd been there for nearly three hours, and his flabby muscles must have been cracking. It was probably too cruel to leave him like that for the rest of the trip. I put the first aid kid down on the flattened box, pulled a bale of hay along on the starboard side and lodged it against the untrasonic packing case. Then with Alf's cutter I clipped through the wire round his wrists and pointed to the bale.

'Sit there.'

He got up slowly and stiffly, crying out. Shuffling, half-falling, he sat where I said. I picked up another piece of wire and in spite of his protests bound his wrists together again and fastened them to one of the chains anchoring the crate. I didn't want him bumbling all over the plane and breathing down my neck.

'Where are we going?' he said, the pomposity reawakening now that he'd got something from me.

I didn't answer.

'And who is flying the plane?'

'George,' I said, finishing his wrists with a twirl he'd never undo. 'Naturally.'

'George who?'

'A good question,' I said, nodding casually.

He was beautifully disconcerted. I left him to stew in it, picked up the first aid kit, checked again that Patrick's pulse was plodding quietly along, and made my way back to the galley.

There were a number of dressings in the first aid box, including several especially for burns, and I wasn't keen on my shirt sticking and tearing away again. Gingerly I pulled my jersey up under my arms and tucked the side of the shirt away under it. No one except Billy would have found the view entertaining, and the air at once started everything going again at full blast. I opened one of the largest of the burn dressings and laid it in place with that exquisite kind of gentleness you only give to yourself. Even so, it was quite enough. After a moment I fastened it on and pulled my shirt and jersey down on top. It felt so bad for a bit that I really wished I hadn't bothered.

I drank another cup of water, which failed to put out the fire. The first aid kit, on further inspection, offered a three-way choice in pain killers: a bottle each of aspirin and codeine tablets, and six ampoules of morphine. I shook out two of the codeines, and swallowed these. Then I packed everything back into the box, shut the lid, and left it on the counter.

Slowly I went up to the cockpit and stood looking at the instruments. All working fine. I fetched a third blanket from the luggage bay and tucked it over and round the body of Bob. He became immediately less of a harsh reality, and I wondered if that was why people always covered the faces of the dead.

I checked the time. An hour from Marseilles. Only a hundred and fifty miles, and a daunting way still to go. I learned against the metal wall and shut my eyes. It was no good feeling the way I did with so much still to do. Parts of Air Ministry regulations drifted ironically into my mind ... 'Many flying accidents have occurred as a result of pilots flying while medically unfit ... and the more exacting the flying task the more likely are minor indispositions to be serious ... so don't go up at all if you are ill enough to need drugs . . . and if coffee isn't enough to keep you awake you are not fit to fly.'

Good old Air Ministry I thought: they'd hit the nail on the head. Where they would have me be was down on the solid earth, and I wholeheartedly agreed.

The radio, I thought inconsequentially. Out of order. I opened my eyes, pushed myself off the wall, and set about finding out why. I hadn't far to look. Yardman had removed all the circuit breakers, and the result was like an electric light system with no fuses in the fuse box. Every plane carried spares, however. I located the place where the spares should have been, and there weren't any. The whole lot in Yardman's pockets, no doubt.

Fetching a fresh cup of water, I climbed again into Patrick's seat and put on the headset to reduce the noise. I leaned back in the comfortable leather upholstery and rested my elbows on the stubby arms, and after a while the codeine and the bandage turned in a reasonable job.

Outside the sky was still black and dotted with brilliant stars, and the revolving anti-collision beacon still skimmed pinkly over the great wide span of the wings, but there was also a new misty greyish quality in the light. Not dawn. The moon coming up. Very helpful of it, I thought appreciatively. Although it was well on the wane I would probably be able to see what I was doing the next time I flew out over the coastline. I began to work out what time I would get there. More guesses. North-west across France coast to coast had to be all of five hundred miles. It had been one-forty when I left Marseilles; was three-ten now. E.T.A. English Channel, somewhere about five.

Patrick's being alive made a lot of difference to everything. I was now thankful without reservation that I had taken the D.C.4 however stupid my motive at the time, for if I'd left it, and Yardman had found him alive, they would simply have pumped another bullet into him, or even buried him as he was. The tiring mental merry-go-round of whether I should have taken the Cessna troubled me no more.

I yawned. Not good. Of all things I couldn't afford to go to sleep. I shouldn't have taken those pills, I thought: there was nothing like the odd spot of agony for keeping you awake. I rubbed my hand over my face and it felt as if it belonged to someone else.

I murdered Billy, I thought.

I could have shot him in the leg and left him to Yardman, and I'd chosen to kill him myself. Choice and those cold-blooded seconds of revenge . . . they made it murder. An interesting technical point, where self-defence went over the edge into something else. Well . . . no one would ever find out; and my conscience didn't stir.

I yawned again more deeply, and thought about eating one of Patrick's bananas. A depleted bunch of them lay on the edge by the windscreen, with four blackening stalks showing where he had fended off starvation on the morning trip. But I imagined the sweet pappiness of them in my mouth, and left them alone. I wasn't hungry enough. The last thing I'd eaten had been the lasagne with Gabriella.

Gabriella . . .

After a while I got up and went through the plane to look at Patrick. He lay relaxed and unmoving, but his eyes were open again. I knelt beside him and felt his pulse. Unchanged.

'Patrick,' I said. 'Can you hear?'

There was no response of any sort.

I stood up slowly and looked at Rous-Wheeler sitting on the bale of hay. He seemed to have shrunk slightly as if the gas had leaked out, and there was a defeated sag to his whole body which showed that he realised his future was unlikely to be rosy. I left him without speaking and went back to the cockpit.

Four o'clock. France had never seemed so large. I checked the fuel gauges for the hundredth time and saw that the needles on the auxiliary tanks were knocking uncomfortably near zero. The plane's four engines used a hundred and fifty gallons an hour at normal speed and even with the power reduced they seemed to be drinking the stuff. Fuel didn't flow automatically from the main tanks when the auxiliaries were empty: one had to switch over by hand. And I simply couldn't afford to use every drop in the auxiliaries, because the engines would stop without warning the second the juice dried up. My fingers hovered on the switch until I hadn't the nerve to wait any longer, and then flipped it over to the mains.

Time passed, and the sleeping country slipped by underneath. When I got to the coast, I thought wearily, I was going to have the same old problem. I wouldn't know within two hundred miles where I was, and the sky was ruthless to the lost. One couldn't stop to ask the way. One couldn't stop at all. A hundred and fifty an hour might be slow in terms of jetliners, but it was much too fast in the wrong direction.

In Patrick's briefcase there would be not only a thick book of radio charts but also some topographical ground maps: they weren't needed for ordinary aerial navigation, but they had to be carried in case of radio failure. The briefcase was almost certainly somewhere under or behind the four packing cases in the luggage bay. I went to have a look, but I already knew. The heavy cases were jammed in tight, and even if there had been room to pull them all out into the small area behind the cockpit I hadn't enough strength to do it.

At about half past four I went back for another check on Patrick, and found things very different. He had thrown off the blanket covering him and was plucking with lax uncoordinated hands at the bandage on his head. His eyes were open but unfocused still, and his breath came out in short regular groans.

'He's dying,' Rous-Wheeler shouted unhelpfully.

Far from dying, he was up close to the threshold of consciousness, and his head was letting him know it. Without answering Rous-Wheeler I went back along the alley and fetched the morphine from the first aid kit.

There were six glass ampoules in a flat box, each with its own built-in hypodermic needle enclosed in a glass cap. I read the instruction leaflet carefully and Rous-Wheeler shouted his unasked opinion that I had no right to give an injection, I wasn't a doctor, I should leave it for someone who knew how.

'Do you?' I said.

'Er, no.'

'Then shut up.'

He couldn't. 'Ask the pilot, then.'

I glanced at him. 'I'm the pilot.'

That did shut him up. His jaw dropped to allow a clear view of his tonsils and he didn't say another word.

While I was rolling up his sleeve Patrick stopped groaning. I looked quickly at his face and his eyes moved slowly round to meet mine.

'Henry,' he said. His voice didn't reach me, but the lip movement was clear.

I bent down and said, 'Yes, Patrick. You're O.K. Just relax.'

His mouth moved. I put my ear to his lips, and he said 'My bloody head hurts.'

I nodded, smiling. 'Not for long.'

He watched me snap the glass to uncover the needle and didn't stir when I pushed it into his arm, though I'd never been on the delivering end of an injection before and I must have been clumsy. When I'd finished he was talking again. I put my head down to hear.

'Where . . . are . . . we?'

'On your way to a doctor. Go to sleep.'

He lay looking vaguely at the roof for a few minutes and then gradually shut his eyes. His pulse was stronger and not so slow. I put the blanket over him again and tucked it under his legs and arms and with barely a glance for Rous-Wheeler went back to the cockpit.

A quarter to five. Time to go down. I checked all the gauges, found I was still carrying the box of ampoules, and put it up on the ledge beside the bananas and the cup of water. I switched out the cockpit lights so that I could see better outside, leaving the round dial faces illuminated only by rims of red, and finally unlocked the automatic pilot.

It was when I'd put the nose down and felt again the great weight of the plane that I really doubted that I could ever land it, even if I found an airfield. I wasn't a mile off exhaustion and my muscles were packing up, and not far beyond this point I knew the brain started missing on a cylinder or two, and haze took the place of thought. If I couldn't think in crystalline terms and at reflex speed I was going to make an irretrievable mistake, and for Patrick's sake, quite apart from my own, I couldn't afford it.

Four thousand feet. I levelled out and flew on, looking down through the moonlit blackness, searching for the sea. Tiredness was insidious and crept up like a tide, I thought, until it drowned you. I shouldn't have taken that codeine, it was probably making me sleepy . . . though I'd had some at other times after racing injuries, and never noticed it. But that was on the ground, and nothing to do but recover.

There. There was the sea. A charcoal change from black, the moonlight just reflecting enough to make it certain. I flew out a little way, banked the plane to the right and began to follow the shore. Compass heading, east-south-east. This seemed extra-ordinary, but it certainly had to be the north-east coast of France somewhere, and I wasn't going to lose myself again. There were lighthouses, flashing their signals. No charts to interpret them. The biggest port along that coast, I thought, was Le Havre. I couldn't miss that. There would be a lot of lights even at five in the morning. If I turned roughly north from there I couldn't help but reach England. Roughly was just the trouble. The map in my head couldn't be trusted. Roughly north could find me barging straight into the London Control Zone, which would be even worse than Paris.

It wouldn't be light until six at the earliest. Sunrise had been about a quarter to seven, the day before.

The lights of Le Havre were ahead and then below me before I'd decided a thing. Too slow, I thought numbly, I was already too slow. I'd never get down.

The coast swung northwards, and I followed. Five twenty a.m. The fuel gauges looked reasonable with dawn not far ahead. But I'd got to decide where I was going. I'd got to.

If I simply went on for a bit I'd reach Calais. It still wouldn't be light. Somewhere over in Kent were Lympne, Lydd and Manston airports. Somewhere. My mind felt paralysed.

I went on and on along the French coast like an automaton until at last I knew I'd gone too far. I hadn't watched the compass heading closely enough and it had crept round from north to nearly east. That light I'd passed a while back, I thought vaguely, the light flashing at five second intervals, that must have been Gris Nez. I'd gone past Calais. I was nearly round to Belgium. I'd simply got to decide . . .

The sky was definitely lighter. With surprise I realised that for several minutes the coastline had been easier to see, the water beneath lightening to a flat dark grey. Soon I could look for an airport: but not in Belgium. The explanations would be too complicated. Back to Kent, perhaps . . .

In a way, the solution when it came was simple. I would go to the place I knew best. To Fenland. In daylight I could find my way unerringly there from any direction, which meant no anxious circling around, and familiarity would cancel out a good deal of the tiredness. The flying club used grass runways which were nothing like long enough for a D.C.4, but its buildings had once been part of an old Air Force base, and the concrete runways the bombers had used were still there. Grass grew through the cracks in them and they weren't maintained, but they were marked at the ends with a white cross over a white bar, air traffic signal for a safe enough landing in an emergency.

My mental fog lifted. I banked left and set off North Seawards, and only after five decisive minutes remembered the fuel.

The burns were hurting again and my spirits fell to zero. Would I never get it right? I was an amateur, I thought despairingly. Still an amateur. The jockey business all over again. I had never achieved anything worthwhile and I certainly hadn't built the solid life I wanted. Simon had been quite right, I couldn't have gone on carting racehorses all my life; and now that Yardman Transport no longer existed I wouldn't look for the same job again.

It was a measure of my exhausted state that having once decided to go to Fenland I hadn't the will to plunge back into uncertainty. The fuel margin was far too small for it to be prudent to go so far. Prudence in the air was what kept one alive. If I went to Fenland I'd be landing on a thimbleful, and if the engines stopped five miles away it would be too late to wish I hadn't.

Streaks of faint red crept into the sky and the sea turned to grey pearl. The sky wasn't so clear any more: there were layers of hazy cloud on the horizon, shading from dark grey-blue to a wisp of silver. The moment before dawn had always seemed to me as restoring as sleep, but that time when I really needed it, it had no effect. My eyes felt gritty and my limbs trembled under every strain. And the codeine had worn off.

The coast of East Anglia lay like a great grey blur ahead on my left. I would follow it round, I thought, and go in over the Wash . . .

A swift dark shape flashed across in front of the D.C.4 and my heart jumped at least two beats. A fighter, I thought incredulously. It had been a jet fighter. Another came over the top of me ridiculously close and screamed away ahead leaving me bumping horribly in the turbulence he left in his wake. They both turned a long way ahead and roared back towards me, flying level together with their wing tips, almost touching. Expert formation pilots: and unfriendly. They closed at something like the speed of sound and swept over the D.C.4 with less than a hundred feet between. To them I must have seemed to be standing still. To me, the trail they left me was very nearly the clincher.

Yardman couldn't have found me, I thought desperately. Not after the wavering roundabout route I'd taken. They couldn't have followed me and wouldn't have guessed I'd go up the North Sea . . . it couldn't be Yardman's doing. So who?

I looked out at East Anglia away on my left, and didn't know whether to laugh or die of fear. Americans. East Anglia was stiff with American air bases. They would have picked me up on their radar, an unidentified plane flying in at dawn and not answering to radio. Superb watchdogs, they would send someone to investigate . . . and they'd found a plane without registration numbers of markings of any sort. A plane like that couldn't be up to any good . . . had to be hostile. One could almost hear them think it.

They wouldn't start shooting, not without making sure . . . not yet. If I just went straight on and could deal with the buffeting, what would they do? I wouldn't let them force me down . . . I had only to plod straight on . . . They swept past on each side and threw the D.C.4 about like a cockleshell.

I couldn't do it, I thought, not this on top of everything else. My hands were slipping on the wheel with sweat. If the fighters went on much longer the sturdy old plane would shake to bits. They came past twice more and proved me wrong. They also reduced me to a dripping wreck. But after that they vanished somewhere above me, and when I looked up I saw them still circling overhead like angry bees. They were welcome to accompany me home, I thought weakly, if that was only where they'd stay.

I could see the lightship off Cromer still flashing its group of four every fifteen seconds. The first real sign of home. Only sixty miles to go. Fifteen minutes to the lightship in the Wash, and the sun rose as I went over it. I turned the plane on to the last leg to Fenland, and up above the escorts came with me.

The fuel gauges looked horrible. I drove what was left of my mind into doing some vital checks. Pitch fully fine, brakes off, mixture rich, fuel pumps on. There must have been a list somewhere, but heaven knew where. I had no business to be flying the plane at all, I didn't know its drill ... The Air Ministry could take away my licence altogether and I was liable for a prison sentence as well. Except, I thought suddenly with a flicker of amusement, that Patrick was qualified to fly it, and he might be said to be technically in charge. Resident, anyway.

I throttled back and began to go down. If I managed it, I thought, I would be a professional. The decision was suddenly standing there full-blown like a certainty that had been a long time growing. This time it wasn't too late. I would take Tom Wells' job and make him stick to it when he inevitably found out my name. I would fly his car firm executives around and earn the sort of life I wanted, and if it meant giving up racing ... I'd do that too.

The airspeed indicator stood at a hundred and thirty knots on the slow descent, and I could see the airfield ahead. The fighters were there already, circling high. The place would be crawling with investigators before my wheels stopped rolling. Questions, when I could do with sleep.

The distant orange wind sock blew out lazily, still from the south west. There wasn't enough fuel for frills like circuits, the gauges registered empty. I'd have to go straight in, and get down first time ... get down. If I could.

I was close now. The club building developed windows, and there was Tom's bungalow ...

A wide banking turn to line up with the old concrete runway ... It looked so narrow, but the bombers had used it. Six hundred feet. My arms were shaking. I pushed down the lever of the undercarriage and the light went green as it locked. Five hundred ... I put on full flap, maximum drag ... retrimmed ... felt the plane get slower and heavier, soft on the controls ... I could stall and fall out of the sky ... a shade more power ... still some fuel left ... the end of the runway ahead with its white cross coming up to meet me, rushing up ... two hundred feet ... I was doing a hundred and twenty ... I'd never landed a plane with a cockpit so high off the ground ... allow for that ... One hundred ... lower ... I seemed to be holding the whole plane up ... I closed the throttles completely and levelled out as the white cross and the bar slid underneath, and waited an agonised few seconds while the air speed fell down and down until there was too little lift to the wings and the whole mass began to sink ...

The wheels touched and bounced, touched and stayed down, squeaking and screeching on the rough surface. With muscles like jelly, with only tendons, I fought to keep her straight. I couldn't crash now ... I wouldn't. The big plane rocketted along the bumpy concrete ... I'd never handled anything so powerful ... I'd misjudged the speed and landed too fast and she'd never stop ...

A touch of brake ... agonising to be gentle with them and fatal if I wasn't ... They gripped and tugged and the plane stayed straight ... more brake, heavier ... it was making an impression ... she wouldn't flip over on to her back, she had a tricycle undercarriage with a nose wheel ... I'd have to risk it ... I pulled the brakes on hard and the plane shuddered with the strain, but the tyres didn't burst and I hadn't dipped and smashed a wing or bent the propellers and there wasn't going to be a scratch on the blessed old bus ... She slowed to taxi-ing speed with a hundred yards to spare before the runway tapered off into barbed wire and gorse bushes. Anything would have been enough. A hundred yards was a whole future.

Trembling, feeling sick, I wheeled round in a circle and rolled slowly back up the runway to where it ran closest to the airport buildings. There I put the brakes full on and stretched out a hand which no longer seemed part of me, and stopped the engines. The roar died to a whisper, and to nothing. I slowly pulled off the headset and listened to the cracking noises of the hot metal cooling.

It was done. And so was I. I couldn't move from my seat. I felt disembodied. Burnt out. Yet in a sort of exhausted peace I found myself believing that as against all probability I had survived the night, so had Gabriella ... that away back in Milan she would be breathing safely through her damaged lung. I had to believe it. Nothing else would do.

Through the window I saw Tom Wells come out of his bungalow, staring first up at the circling fighters and then down at the D.C.4. He shrugged his arms into his old sheepskin jacket and began to run towards me over the grass.

BONECRACK

Chapter One

They both wore thin rubber masks.

Identical.

I looked at the two identical faceless faces in tingling disbelief. I was not the sort of person to whom rubber-masked individuals up to no good paid calls at twenty to midnight. I was a thirty-four-year-old sober-minded businessman quietly bringing up to date the account books at my father's training stables in Newmarket.

The pool of light from the desk lamp shone squarely upon me and the work I had been doing, and the two rubber faces moved palely against the near-black panelling of the dark room like alien moons closing in on the sun. I had looked up when the latch clicked, and there they were, two dim figures calmly walking in from the hall of the big house, silhouetted briefly against the soft lighting behind them and then lost against the panelling as they closed the door. They moved without a squeak, without a scrape, on the bare polished floor. Apart from the unhuman faces, they were black from head to foot.

I picked up the telephone receiver and dialled the first of three nines.

One of them closed in faster, swung his arm, and smashed downwards on the telephone. I removed my finger fractionally in time with the second nine all but complete, but no one was ever going to achieve the third. The black gloved hand slowly disentangled a heavy police truncheon from the mangled remains of the Post Office's property.

'There's nothing to steal,' I remarked.

The second man had reached the desk. He stood on the far side of it, facing me, looking down to where I still sat. He produced an automatic pistol, without silencer, which he pointed unwaveringly at the bridge of my nose. I could see quite a long way into the barrel.

'You,' he said. 'You will come with us.'

His voice was flat, without tone, deliberate. There was no identifiable accent, but he wasn't English.

'Why?'

'You will come.'

'Where to?'

'You will come.'

'I won't, you know,' I said pleasantly, and reached out and pressed the button which switched off the desk lamp.

The sudden total darkness got me two seconds advantage. I used them to stand up, pick up the heavy angled lamp, and swing the base of it round in an arc in the general direction of the mask which had spoken.

There was a dull thump as it connected, and a grunt. Damage, I thought, but no knock-out.

Mindful of the truncheon on my left I was out from behind the desk and sprinting towards the door. But no one was wasting time batting away in the darkness in the hope of hitting me. A beam of torchlight snapped out from his hand, swung round, dazzled on my face, and bounced as he came after me.

I swerved. Dodged. Lost my straight line to the door and saw sideways the rubber-face I'd hit with the lamp was purposefully on the move.

The torch beam flickered away, circled briefly, and steadied like a rock on the light switch beside the door. Before I could reach it the black gloved hand swept downwards and clicked on the five double wall brackets, ten naked candle bulbs coldly lighting the square wood-lined room.

There were two windows with green floor length curtains. One rug from Istanbul. Three unmatched William and Mary chairs. One sixteenth century oak chest. One flat walnut desk. Nothing else. An austere place, reflection of my father's austere and spartan soul.

I had always agreed that the best time to foil an abduction was at the moment it started: that merely obeying marching orders could save present pain but not long-term anxiety: that abductors might kill later but not at the beginning, and that if no one else's safety was at risk, it would be stupid to go without a fight.

Well, I fought.

I fought for all of ninety seconds more, during which time I failed to switch off the lights, to escape through the door, or to crash out through the windows. I had only my hands and not much skill against the truncheon of one of them and the threat of a crippling bullet from the other. The identical rubber faces came towards me with an unnerving lack of human expression, and although I tried, probably unwisely, to rip one of the masks off, I got no further than feeling my fingers slip across the tough slippery surface.

They favoured in-fighting, with their quarry pinned against the wall. As there were two of them, and they appeared to be experts in their craft, I got such a hammering in that eternal ninety seconds that I soundly wished that I had not put my abduction-avoiding theories into practice.

It ended with a fist in my stomach, the pistol slamming into my face, my head crashing back against the panelling, and the truncheon polishing the whole thing off somewhere behind my right ear. When I was next conscious of anything, time had all too clearly passed. Otherwise I should not have been lying face down along the back seat of a moving car with my hands tied crampingly behind my back.

For a good long time I believed I was dreaming. Then my brain came further awake and made it clear that I wasn't I was revoltingly uncomfortable and also extremely cold, as the thin sweater I had been wearing indoors was proving a poor barrier to a freezing night.

My head ached like a steam hammer. Bang, bang, bang.

If I could have raised the mental energy I would have been furious with myself for having proved such a pushover. As it was, only uncomplicated responses were getting anywhere, like dumb unintelligent endurance and a fog-like bewilderment. Of all the candidates for abduction, I would have put myself among the most unlikely.

There was a lot to be said for a semi-conscious brain in a semi-conscious body. *Mens blotto in corpore ditto* ... the words dribbled inconsequentially through my mind and a smile started along the right nerve but didn't get as far as my mouth. My mouth anyway was half in contact with some imitation leather upholstery which smelled of dogs. They say many grown men call out for their mothers in moments of fatal agony, and then upon their God: but anyway I hadn't had a mother since I was two, and from then until seven I had believed God was someone who had run off with her and was living with her somewhere else ... (God took your mother, dear, because he needed her more than you do) which had never endeared him to me, and in any case this was no fatal agony, this was just a thumping concussion and some very sore places and maybe a grisly future at the end of the ride. The ride meanwhile went on and on. Nothing about it improved. After several years the car stopped with a jerk. I nearly fell forwards off the seat. My brain came alert with a jolt and my body wished it hadn't.

The two rubber faces loomed over me, lugged me out, and literally carried me up some steps and into a house. One of them had his hands under my armpits and the other held my ankles. My hundred and sixty pounds seemed to be no especial burden.

The sudden light inside the door was dazzling, which seemed as good a reason as any for shutting ones eys. I shut them. The steam hammer had not by any means given up.

They dumped me presently down on my side, on a wooden floor. Polished. I could smell the polish. Scented. Very nasty. I opened my eyes a slit, and verified. Small intricately squared parquet, modern. Birch veneer, wafer thin. Nothing great. A voice awakening towards fury and controlled with audible effort spoke from a short distance above me.

'*And who exactly is this?*'

There was a long pin-dropping silence during which I would have laughed, if I could. The rubber faces hadn't even pinched the right man. All that battering for bloody nothing. And no guarantee they would take me home again, either.

I squinted upwards against the light. The man who had spoken was sitting in an upright leather armchair with his fingers laced rigidly together over a swelling paunch. His voice was much the same as Rubber Mask's: without much accent, but not English. His shoes, which were more on my level, were supple, handmade, and of Genoese leather.

Italian shape. Not conclusive: they sell Italian shoes from Hong Kong to San Francisco.

One of the rubber-faces cleared his throat. 'It is Griffon.'

The remains of laughter died coldly away. Griffon was indeed my name. If I was not the right man, they must have come for my father. Yet that made no more sense: he was, like me, in none of the abduction-prone professions.

The man in the armchair, with the same reined-in anger, said through his teeth. 'It is not Griffon.'

'It is,' persisted Rubber Face faintly.

The man stood up out of his armchair and with his elegant toe rolled me over on to my back.

'Griffon is an old man,' he said. The sting in his voice sent both rubber-faces back a pace as if he had physically hit them.

'You didn't *tell* us he was old.'

The other rubber-face backed up his colleague in a defensive whine and a different accent. This time, down-the-scale American. 'We watched him all evening. He went round the stables, looking at the horses. At every horse. The men, they treated him as boss. He is the trainer. He is Griffon.'

'Griffon's assistant,' he said furiously. He sat down again and held on to the arms with the same effort as he was holding on to his temper.

'Get up,' he said to me abruptly.

I struggled up nearly as far as my knees, but the rest was daunting, and I thought, why on earth should I bother, so I lay gently down again. It did nothing to improve the general climate.

'Get up,' he said furiously.

I shut my eyes.

There was a sharp blow on my thigh. I opened my eyes again in time to see the American-voiced rubber-face draw back his foot for another kick. All one could say was that he was wearing shoes and not boots.

'Stop it.' The sharp voice arrested him mid-kick. 'Just put him in that chair.'

American rubber-face picked up the chair in question and placed it six feet from the armchair, facing it. Mid-Victorian, I assessed automatically. Mahogany. Probably once had a caned seat, but was upholstered now in pink flowered glazed chintz. The two rubber-faces lifted me up bodily and draped me around so that my tied wrists were behind the back of the chair, When they had done that they stepped away, just as far as one pace behind each of my shoulders.

From that elevation I had a better view of their master, if not of the total situation.

'Griffon's assistant,' he repeated. But this time the anger was secondary: he'd accepted the mistake and was working out what to do about it.

It didn't take him long.

'Gun,' he said, and Rubber Face gave it to him.

He was plump and bald, and I guessed he would take no pleasure from looking at old photographs of himself. Under the rounded cheeks, the heavy chin, the folds of eyelids, there lay an elegant bone structure. It still showed in the strong clear beak of the nose and in the arch above the eye sockets. He had the basic equipment of a handsome man, but he looked, I thought fancifully, like a Caesar gone self-indulgently to seed: and one might have taken the fat as a sign of mellowness had it not been for the ill will that looked unmistakably out of his narrowed eyes.

'Silencer,' he said acidly. He was contemptuous, irritated and not suffering his rubber-faced fools gladly.

One rubber-face produced a silencer from his trouser pocket and Caesar began screwing it on. Silencers meant business where naked barrels might not. He was about to bury his employees' mistake.

My future looked decidedly dim. Time for a few well-chosen words, especially if they might prove to be my last.

'I am not Griffon's assistant,' I said. 'I am his son.'

He had finished screwing on the silencer and was beginning to raise it in the direction of my chest.

'I am Griffon's son,' I repeated. 'And just what is the point of all this?'

The silencer reached the latitude of my heart.

'If you're going to kill me,' I said, 'you might at least tell me why.'

My voice sounded more or less all right. He couldn't see, I hoped, that all my skin was prickling into sweat.

An eternal time passed. I stared at him: he stared back. I waited. Waited while the tumblers clicked over in his brain: waited for three thumbs-down to slot into a row on the fruit machine.

Finally, without lowering the gun a millimetre, he said, 'Where is your father?'

'In hospital.'

Another pause.

'How long will he be there?'

'I don't know. Two or three months, perhaps.'

'Is he dying?'

'No.'

'What is the matter with him?'

'He was in a car crash. A week ago. He has a broken leg.'

Another pause. The gun was still steady. No one, I thought wildly, should die so unfairly. Yet people did die unfairly. Probably only one in a million deserved it. All death was intrinsically unfair: but in some forms more unfair than in others. Murder, it forcibly seemed to me, was the most unfair of all.

In the end, all he said, and in a much milder tone, was 'Who will train the horses this summer, if your father is not well enough?'

Only long experience of wily negotiators who thundered big threats so that they could achieve their real aims by presenting them as a toothless anticlimax kept me from stepping straight off the precipice. I nearly, in relief at so harmless an enquiry, told him the truth: that no one had yet decided. If I had done, I discovered later, he would have shot me, because his business was exclusively with the resident trainer at Rowley Lodge. Temporary substitutes, abducted in error, were too dangerous to leave chattering around.

So from instinct I answered, 'I will be training them myself,' although I had not the slightest intention of doing so for longer than it took to find someone else.

It had indeed been the crucial question. The frightening black circle of the silencer's barrel dipped a fraction: became an ellipse: disappeared altogether. He lowered the gun and balanced it on one well-padded thigh.

A deep breath trickled in and out of my chest in jerks, and the relief from immediate tension made me feel sick. Not that total safety loomed very loftily on the horizon. I was still tied up in an unknown house, and I still had no idea for what possible purpose I could be a hostage.

The fat man went on watching me. Went on thinking. I tried to ease the stiffness which was creeping into my muscles, to shift away the small pains and the throbbing headache, which I hadn't felt in the slightest when faced with a bigger threat.

The room was cold. The rubber-faces seemed to be snug enough in their masks and gloves, and the fat man was insulated and impervious, but the chill was definitely adding to my woes. I wondered whether he had planned the cold as a psychological intimidation for my elderly father, or whether it was simply accidental. Nothing in the room looked cosily lived in.

In essence it was a middle class sitting-room in a smallish middle class house, built, I guess, in the nineteen thirties. The furniture had been pushed back against striped cream wallpaper to give the fat man clear space for manoeuvre: furniture which consisted of an uninspiring three piece suite swathed in pink chintz, a gate-legged table, a standard lamp with parchment coloured shade, and a display cabinet displaying absolutely nothing. There were no rugs on the highly polished birch parquet, no ornaments, no books or magazines, nothing personal at all. As bare as my father's soul, but not to his taste.

The room did not in the least fit what I had so far seen of the fat man's personality.

'I will release you,' he said, 'on certain conditions.'

I waited. He considered me, still taking his time.

'If you do not follow my instructions exactly, I will put your father's training stables out of business.'

I could feel my mouth opening in astonishment. I shut it with a snap.

'I suppose you doubt that I can do it. Do not doubt. I have destroyed better things than your father's little racing stables.'

He got no reaction from me to the slight in the word 'little'. It was years since I had learned that to rise to slights was to be forced into a defensive attitude which only benefited my opponent. In Rowley Lodge, as no doubt he knew, stood eighty-five aristocrats whose aggregate worth topped six million pounds.

'How?' I asked flatly.

He shrugged. 'What is important to you is not how I would do it, but how to prevent me from doing it. And that, of course, is comparatively simple.'

'Just run the horses to your instructions?' I suggested neutrally. 'Just lose to order?'

A spasm of renewed anger twisted the chubby features and the gun came six inches off his knee. The hand holding it relaxed slowly, and he put it down again.

'I am not,' he said heavily, 'a petty crook.'

But you do, I thought, rise to an insult, even to one that was not intended, and one day, if the game went on long enough, that could give me an advantage.

'I apologise,' I said without sarcasm. 'But those rubber masks are not top level.'

He glanced up in irritation at the two figures standing behind me.

'The masks are their own choice. They feel safer if they cannot be recognised.'

Like highwaymen, I thought: who swung in the end.

'You may run your horses as you like. You are free to choose entirely . . . save in one special thing.'

I made no comment. He shrugged, and went on.

'You will employ someone who I will send you.'

'No.' I said.

'Yes.' He stared at me unwinkingly. 'You will employ this person. If you do not, I will destroy the stable.'

'That's lunacy,' I insisted. 'It's pointless.'

'No, it is not,' he said. 'Furthermore, you will tell no one that you are being forced to employ this person. You will assert that it is your own wish. You will particularly not complain to the police, either about tonight, or about anything else which may happen. Should you act in any way to discredit this person, or to get him evicted from your stables, your whole business will be destroyed.' He paused. 'Do you understand? If you act in any way against this person, your father will have nothing to return to, when he leaves the hospital.'

After a short, intense silence, I asked, 'In what capacity do you want this person to work for me?'

He answered with care. 'He will ride the horses,' he said. 'He is a jockey.'

I could feel the twitch round my eyes. He saw it, too. The first time he had really reached me.

It was out of the question. He would not need to tell me every time he wanted a race lost. He had simply to tell his man.

'We don't need a jockey,' I said. 'We already have Tommy Hoylake.'

'Your new jockey will gradually take his place.'

Tommy Hoylake was the second best jockey in Britain and among the top dozen in the world. No one could take his place.

'The owners wouldn't agree,' I said.

'You will persuade them.'

'Impossible.'

'The future existence of your stable depends on it.'

There was another longish pause. One of the rubber-faces shifted on his feet and sighed as if from boredom, but the fat man seemed to be in no hurry. Perhaps he understood very well that I was getting colder and more uncomfortable minute by minute. I would have asked him to untie my hands if I hadn't been sure he would count himself one up when he refused.

Finally I said, 'Equipped with your jockey, the stable would have no future existence anyway.'

He shrugged. 'It may suffer a little, perhaps, but it will survive.'

'It is unacceptable,' I said.

He blinked. His hand moved the gun gently to and fro across his well filled trouser leg.

He said, 'I see that you do not entirely understand the position. I told you that you could leave here upon certain conditons.' His flat tone made the insane sound reasonable. 'They are, that you employ a certain jockey, and that you do not seek aid from anyone, including the police. Should you break either of these agreements the stable will be destroyed. But . . .' He spoke more slowly, and with emphasis, '. . . if you do not agree to these conditions in the first place, you will not be freed.'

I said nothing.

'Do you understand?'

I sighed. 'Yes.'

'Good.'

'Not a petty crook, I think you said.'

His nostrils flared. 'I am a manipulator.'

'And a murderer.'

'I never murder unless the victim insists.'

I stared at him. He was laughing inside at his own jolly joke, the fun creeping out in little twitches to his lips and tiny snorts of breath.

This victim, I supposed, was not going to insist. He was welcome to his amusement.

I moved my shoulders slightly, trying to ease them. He watched attentively and offered nothing.

'Who then,' I said, 'is this jockey?'

He hesitated.

'He is eighteen,' he said.

'*Eighteen* . . .'

He nodded. 'You will give him the good horses to ride. He will ride Archangel in the Derby.'

Impossible. Totally impossible. I looked at the gun lying so quiet on the expensive tailoring. I said nothing. There was nothing to say.

When he next spoke there was the satisfaction of victory in his voice alongside the careful non-accent.

'He will arrive at the stable tomorrow. You will hire him. He has not yet much experience in races. You will see he gets it.'

An inexperienced rider on Archangel . . . ludicrous. So ludicrous, in fact, that he had used abduction and the threat of murder to make it clear he meant it seriously.

'His name is Alessandro Rivera,' he said.

After interval for consideration, he added the rest of it.

'He is my son.'

Chapter Two

When I next woke up I was lying face down on the bare floor of the oak panelled room in Rowley Lodge. Too many bare boards everywhere. Not my night.

Facts oozed back gradually. I felt woolly, cold, semiconscious, anaesthetised . . .

Anaesthetised.

For the return journey they had had the courtesy not to hit my head. The fat man had nodded to the American rubber-face, but instead of flourishing the truncheon he had given me a sort of quick pricking thump in the upper arm. After that we had waited around for about a quarter of an hour during which no one said anything at all, and then quite suddenly I had lost consciousness. I remembered not a flicker of the journey home.

Creaking and groaning I tested all articulated parts. Everything present, correct, and in working order. More or less, that is, because having clanked to my feet it became advisable to sit down again in the chair by the desk. I put my elbows on the desk and my head in my hands, and let time pass.

Outside, the beginnings of a damp dawn were turning the sky to grey flannel. There was ice round the edges of the windows, where condensed warm air had frozen solid. The cold went through to my bones.

In the brain department things were just as chilly. I remembered all too clearly that Alessandro Rivera was that day to make his presence felt. Perhaps he would take after father, I thought tiredly, and would be so overweight that the whole dilemma would fold its horns and quietly steal away. On the other hand, if not, why should his father use a sledgehammer to crack a peanut. Why not simply apprentice his son in the normal way? Because he wasn't normal, because his son wouldn't be a normal apprentice, and because no normal apprentice would expect to start his career on a Derby favourite.

'I wondered how my father would now be reacting, had he not been slung up in traction with a complicated fracture of tibia and fibula. He would not, for certain, be feeling as battered as I was, because he would, with supreme dignity, have gone quietly. But he would none the less have also been facing the same vital questions: which were, firstly, did the fat man seriously intend to destroy the stable if his son did not get the job, and secondly, how could he do it.

And the answer to both was a king-sized blank.

It wasn't my stable to risk. They were not my six million pounds worth of horses. They were not my livelihood, nor my life's work.

I could not ask my father to decide for himself; he was not well enough to be told, let alone to reason out the pros and cons.

I could not now transfer the stable to anyone else, because passing this situation to a stranger would be like handing him a grenade with the pin out.

I was already due back at my own job and was late for my next assignment, and I had only stop-gapped at the stable at all because my father's capable assistant, who had been driving the Rolls when the lorry jack-knifed into it, was now lying in the same hospital in a coma.

All of which added up to a fair sized problem. But then problems, I reflected ironically, were my business. The problems of sick businesses were my business.

Nothing at that moment looked sicker than my prospects at Rowley Lodge.

Shivering violently, I removed myself bit by bit from the desk and chair, went out to the kitchen, and made myself some coffee. Drank it. Moderate improvement only.

Inched upstairs to the bathroom. Scraped off the night's whiskers and dispassionately observed the dried blood down one cheek. Washed it off. Gun barrel graze, dry and already healing.

Outside, through the leafless trees, I could see the lights of the traffic thundering as usual up and down Bury Road. These drivers in their warm moving boxes, they were in another world altogether, a world where abduction and extortion were something that only happened to others. Incredible to think that I had in fact joined the others.

Wincing from an all over feeling of soreness, I looked at my smudge-eyed reflection and wondered how long I would go on doing what the fat man had told me to. Saplings who bent before the storm lived to grow into oaks.

Long live oaks.

I swallowed some aspirins, stopped shivering, tried to marshal a bit more sense into my shaky wits, and struggled into jodhpurs, boots, two more pullovers, and a windproof jacket. Whatever had happened that night, or whatever might happen in the future, there were still those eighty-five six million quids worth downstairs waiting to be seen to.

They were housed in a yard that had been an inspiration of spacious design when it was built in 1870 and which still, a hundred-plus years later, worked as an effective unit. Originally there had been two blocks facing each other, each block consisting of three bays, and each bay being made up to ten boxes. Across the far end, forming a wall joining the two blocks, were a large feed-store room, a pair of double gates, and an equally large tack room. The gates had originally led into a field, but early on in his career, when success struck him, my father had built on two more bays, which formed another small enclosed yard of twenty-five boxes. More double gates opened from these, now, into a small railed paddock.

Four final boxes had been built facing towards Bury Road, on to the outside of the short west wall at the end of the north block. It was in the furthest of these four boxes that a full blown disaster had just been discovered.

My appearance through the door which led directly from the house to the yard galvanised the group which had been clustered round the outside boxes into returning into the main yard and advancing in ragged but purposeful formation. I could see I was not going to like their news. Waited in irritation to hear it. Crises, on that particular morning, were far from welcome.

'It's Moonrock, sir,' said one of the lads anxiously, 'Got cast in his box, and broke his leg.'

'All right,' I said abruptly. 'Get back to your own horses, then. It's nearly time to pull out.'

'Yessir,' they said, and scattered reluctantly round the yard to their charges, looking back over their shoulders.

'Damn and bloody hell,' I said aloud, but I can't say it did much good. Moonrock was my father's hack, a pensioned-off star-class steeplechaser of which he was uncharacteristically fond. The least valuable inmate of the yard in many terms, but the one he would be most upset to lose. The others were also insured. No one, though, could insure against painful emotion.

I plodded round to the box. The elderly lad who looked after him was standing at the door with the light from inside falling across the deep worried wrinkles in his tortoise skin and turning them to crevasses. He looked round towards me at my step. The crevasses shifted and changed like a kaleidoscope.

'Ain't no good, sir. He's broke his hock.'

Nodding, and wishing I hadn't, I reached the door and went in. The old horse was standing up, tied in his usual place by his head-collar. At first sight there was nothing wrong with him: he turned his head towards me and pricked his ears, his liquid black eyes showing nothing but his customary curiosity. Five years in headline limelight had given him the sort of presence which only intelligent highly successful horses seem to develop; a sort of consciousness of their own greatness. He knew more about life and about racing than any of the golden youngsters round in the main yard. He was fifteen years old and had been a friend of my father's for five.

The hind leg on his near side, towards me, was perfect. He bore his weight on it. The off-hind looked slightly tucked up.

He had been sweating: there were great dark patches on his neck and flanks; but he looked calm enough at that moment. Pieces of straw were caught in his coat, which was unusually dusty.

Soothing him with her hand, and talking to him in a common sense voice, was my father's head stable hand, Etty Craig. She looked up at me with regret on her pleasant weather-beaten face.

'I've sent for the vet, Mr. Neil.'

'Of all damn things,' I said.

She nodded. 'Poor old fellow. You'd think he'd know better after all these years.'

I made a sympathetic noise, went in and fondled the moist black muzzle, and took as good a look at his hind leg as I could without moving him. There was absolutely no doubt: the hock joint was out of shape.

Horses occasionally rolled around on their backs in the straw in their boxes. Sometimes they rolled over with too little room and wedged their legs against the wall, then thrashed around to get free. Most injuries from getting cast were grazes and strains, but it was possible for a horse to twist or lash out with a leg strongly enough to break it. Incredibly bad luck when it happened, which luckily wasn't often.

'He was still lying down when George came in to muck him out,' Etty said. 'He got some of the lads to come and pull the old fellow into the centre of the box. He was a bit slow, George says, standing up. And then of course they could see he couldn't walk.'

'Bloody shame,' George said, nodding in agreement.

I sighed. 'Nothing we can do, Etty.'

'No, Mr. Neil.'

She called me Mr. Neil religiously during working hours, though I'd been plain Neil to her in my childhood. Better for discipline in the yard, she said to me once, and on matters of discipline I would never contradict her. There had been quite a stir in Newmarket when my father had promoted her to head lad, but as he had explained to her at the time, she was loyal, she was knowledgeable, she would stand no nonsense from anyone, she deserved it from seniority alone, and had she been a man the job would have been hers automatically. He had decided, as he was a just and logical person, that her sex was immaterial. She became the only female head lad in Newmarket, where girl lads anyway were rare, and the stable had flourished through all the six years of her reign.

I remembered the days when her parents used to turn up at the stables and accuse my father of ruining her life. I had been about ten when she first came to the yard, and she was nineteen and had been privately educated at an expensive boarding school. Her parents with increasing bitterness had arrived and complained that the stable was spoiling her chances of a nice suitable marriage; but Etty had never wanted marriage. If she had ever experimented with sex she had not made a public mess of it, and I thought it likely that she had found the whole process uninteresting. She seemed to like males well enough, but she treated them as she did her horses, with brisk friendliness, immense understanding, and cool unsentimentality.

Since my father's accident she had to all intents been in complete charge. The fact that I had been granted a temporary licence to hold the fort made mine the official say-so, but both Etty and I knew I would be lost without her.

It occurred to me, as I watched her capable hands moving quietly across Moonrock's bay hide, that the fat man might find me a pushover, but as an apprentice his son Alessandro was going to run into considerable difficulties with Miss Henrietta Craig.

'You better go out with the string, Etty,' I said. 'I'll stay and wait for the vet.'

'Right,' she said, and I guessed she had been on the point of suggesting it herself. As a distribution of labour it was only sense, as the horses were well along in their preparation for the coming racing season, and she knew better than I what each should be doing.

She beckoned to George to come and hold Moonrock's headcollar and keep him soothed. To me she said, stepping out of the box, 'What about this frost? It seems to me it may be thawing.'

'Take the horses over to Warren Hill and use your own judgement about whether to canter.'

She nodded. 'Right.' She looked back at Moonrock and a momentary softness twisted her mouth. 'Mr. Griffon will be sorry.'

'I won't tell him yet.'

'No.' She gave me a small businesslike smile and then walked off into the yard, a short neat figure, hardy and competent.

Moonrock would be quiet enough with George. I followed Etty back into the main yard and watched the horses pull out: thirty-three of them in the first lot. The lads led their charges out of the boxes, jumped up into the saddles, and rode away down the yard, through the first double gates, across the lower yard, and out through the far gates into the collecting paddock beyond. The sky lightened moment by moment and I thought Etty was probably right about the thaw.

After ten minutes or so, when she had sorted them out as she wanted them, the horses moved away out beyond the paddock, through the trees and the boundary fence and straight out on to the Heath.

Before the last of them had gone there was a rushing scrunch in the drive behind me and the vet halted his dusty Land Rover with a spray of gravel. Leaping out with his bag he said breathlessly, 'Every bloody horse on the Heath this morning has got colic or ingrowing toenails ... You must be Neil Griffon ... sorry about your father ... Etty says it's old Moonrock ... still in the same box?' Without drawing breath he turned on his heel and strode along the outside boxes. Young, chubby, purposeful, he was not the vet I had expected. The man I knew was an older version, slower, twinkly, just as chubby, and given to rubbing his jaw while he thought things over.

'Sorry about this,' the young vet said, having given Moonrock three full seconds examination. 'Have to put him down, I'm afraid.'

'I suppose that hock couldn't just be dislocated?' I suggested, clinging to straws.

He gave me a brief glance full of the expert's forgiveness for a layman's ignorance. 'The joint is shattered,' he said succinctly.

He went about his business, and splendid old Moonrock quietly folded down on to the straw. Packing his bag again he said, 'Don't look so depressed. He had a better life than most. And be glad it wasn't Archangel.'

I watched his chubby back depart at speed. Not so very unlike his father, I thought. Just faster.

I went slowly into the house and telephoned to the people who removed dead horses. They would come at once, they said, sounding cheerful. And within half an hour, they came.

Another cup of coffee. Sat down beside the kitchen table and went on feeling unwell. Abduction didn't agree with me in the least.

The string came back from the Heath without Etty, without a two-year-old colt called Lucky Lindsay, and with a long tale of woe.

I listened with increasing dismay while three lads at once told me that Lucky Lindsay had whipped round and unshipped little Ginge over by Warren Hill, and had then galloped off loose and seemed to be making for home, but had diverted down Moulton Road instead, and had knocked over a man with a bicycle and had sent a woman with a pram into hysterics, and had ended up by the clock tower, disorganising the traffic. The police, added one boy, with more relish than regret, were currently talking to Miss Etty.

'And the colt?' I asked. Because Etty could take care of herself, but Lucky Lindsay had cost thirty thousand guineas and could not.

'Someone caught him down the High Street outside Woolworths.'

I sent them off to their horses and waited for Etty to come back, which she presently did, riding Lucky Lindsay herself and with the demoted and demoralised Ginge slopping along behind on a quiet three-year-old mare.

Etty jumped down and ran an experienced hand down the colt's chestnut legs.

'Not much harm done,' she said. 'He seems to have a small cut there ... I think he probably did it on the bumper of a parked car.'

'Not on the bicycle?' I asked.

She looked up, and then straightened. 'Shouldn't think so.'

'Was the cyclist hurt?'

'Shaken,' she admitted.

'And the woman with the pram?'

'Anyone who pushes a baby and drags a toddler along Moulton Road during morning exercise should be ready for loose horses. The stupid woman wouldn't stop screaming. It upset the colt thoroughly, of course. Someone had caught him at that point, but he backed off and broke free and went down into the town ...'

She paused and looked at me. 'Sorry about all this.'

'It happens,' I said. I stifled the small inward smile at her relative placing of colts and babies. Not surprising. To her, colts were in sober fact more important than humans.

'We had finished the canters,' she said. 'The ground was all right. We went right through the list we mapped out yesterday. Ginge came off as we turned for home.'

'Is the colt too much for him?'

'Wouldn't have thought so. He's ridden him before.'

'I'll leave it to you, Etty.'

'Then maybe I'll switch him to something easier for a day or two ...' She led the colt away and handed him over to the lad who did him, having come as near as she was likely to admitting she had made an error in putting Ginge on Lucky Lindsay. Anyone, any day, could be thrown off. But some were thrown off more than others.

Breakfast. The lads put straight the horses they had just ridden and scurried round to the hostel for porridge, bacon sandwiches and tea. I went back into the house and didn't feel like eating.

It was still cold indoors. There were sad mounds of fir cones in the fireplaces of ten dust-sheeted bedrooms, and a tapestry fire screen in front of the hearth in the drawing-room. There was a two-tier electric fire in the cavernous bedroom my father used and an undersized convector heater in the oak panelled room where he sat at his desk in the evenings. Not even the kitchen was warm, as the cooker fire had been out for repairs for a month. Normally, having been brought up in it, I did not notice the chill of the house in winter: but then, normally I did not feel so physically wretched.

A head appeared round the kitchen door. Neat dark hair coiled smoothly at the base, to emerge in a triumphant arrangement of piled curls on the crown.

'Mr. Neil?'

'Oh . . . good morning, Margaret.'

A pair of fine dark eyes gave me an embracing once-over. Narrow nostrils moved in a small quiver, testing the atmosphere. As usual I could see no further than her neck and half a cheek, as my father's secretary was as economical with her presence as with everything else.

'It's cold in here,' she said.

'Yes.'

'Warmer in the office.'

The half-head disappeared and did not come back. I decided to accept what I knew had been meant as an invitation, and retraced my way towards the corner of the house which adjoined the yard. In that corner were the stable office, a cloakroom, and the one room furnished for comfort, the room we called the owner's room, where owners and assorted others were entertained on casual visits to the stable.

The lights were on in the office, bright against the grey day outside. Margaret was taking off her sheepskin coat, and hot air was blowing busily out of a mushroom shaped heater.

'Instructions?' she asked briefly.

'I haven't opened the letters yet.'

She gave me a quick comprehensive glance.

'Trouble?'

I told her about Moonrock and Lucky Lindsay. She listened attentively, showed no emotion, and asked how I had cut my face.

'Walked into a door.'

Her expression said plainly 'I've heard that one before,' but she made no comment.

In her way she was as unfeminine as Etty, despite her skirt, her hairdo, and her efficient make-up. In her late thirties, three years widowed and bringing up a boy and a girl with masterly organisation, she bristled with intelligence and held the world at arm's length from her heart.

Margaret was new at Rowley Lodge, replacing mouselike old Robinson who had finally scratched his way at seventy into unwilling retirement. Old Robinson had liked his little chat, and had frittered away hours of working time telling me in my childhood about the days when Charles II rode in races himself, and made Newmarket the second capital of England, so that ambassadors had to go there to see him, and how the

Prince Regent had left the town for ever because of an enquiry into the running of his colt Escape, and refused to go back even though the Jockey Club apologised and begged him to, and how in 1905 King Edward VII was in trouble with the police for speeding down the road to London – at forty miles an hour on the straight bits.

Margaret did old Robinson's work more accurately and in half the time, and I understood after knowing her for six days why my father found her inestimable. She demanded no human response, and he was a man who found most relationships boring. Nothing tired him quicker than people who constantly demanded attention for their emotions and problems, and even social openers about the weather irritated him. Margaret seemed to be a matched soul, and they got on excellently.

I slouched down in my father's revolving office armchair and told Margaret to open the letters herself. My father never let anyone open his letters, and was obsessive about it. She simply did as I said without comment, either spoken or implied. Marvellous.

The telephone rang. Margaret answered it.

'Mr. Bredon? Oh yes. He'll be glad you called. I'll put you on to him.' She handed me the receiver across the desk, and said, 'John Bredon.'

'Thanks.'

I took the receiver with none of the eagerness I would have shown the day before. I had spent three intense days trying to find someone who was free at short notice to take over Rowley Lodge until my father's leg mended, and of all the people whom helpful friends had suggested, only John Bredon, an elderly recently-retired trainer, seemed to be of the right experience and calibre. He had asked for time to think it over and had said he would le met know as soon as he could.

He was calling to say he would be happy to come. I thanked him and uncomfortably apologised as I put him off. 'The fact is that after thinking it over I've decided to stay on myself . . .'

I set the receiver down slowly, aware of Margaret's astonishment. I didn't explain. She didn't ask. After a pause she went back to opening the letters.

The telephone rang again. This time, with schooled features, she asked if I would care to speak to Mr. Russell Arletti.

Silently I stretched out a hand for the receiver.

'Neil?' a voice barked. 'Where the hell have you got to? I told Grey and Cox you'd be there yesterday. They're complaining. How soon can you get up there?'

Grey and Cox in Huddersfield were waiting for Arletti Incorporated to sort out why their once profitable business was going down the drain. Arletti Incorporated's sorter was sitting disconsolately in a stable office in Newmarket wishing he was dead.

'You'll have to tell Grey and Cox that I can't come.'

'You *what*?'

'Russell . . . count me out for a while. I've got to stay on here.'

'For God's sake why?'

'I can't find anyone to take over.'

'You said it wouldn't take you more than a week.'

'Well, it has. There isn't anyone suitable. I can't go and sort out Grey and Cox and leave Rowley Lodge rudderless. There is six million involved here. Like it or not, I'll have to stay.'

'Damn it, Neil . . .'

'I'm really sorry.'

'Grey and Cox will be livid.' He was exasperated.

'Go up there yourself. It'll only be the usual thing. Bad costing. Underpricing their product at the planning stage. Rotten cash flow. They say they haven't any militants, so it's ninety per cent to a cornflake that it's lousy finance.'

He sighed. 'I don't have quite your talent. Better ones, mind you. But not the same.' He paused for thought. 'Have to send James, when he gets back from Shoreham. If you're sure?'

'Better count me out for three months at least.'

'Neil!'

'Better say, in fact, until after the Derby . . .'

'Legs don't take that long,' he protested.

'This one is a terrible mess. The bones were splintered and came through the skin, and it was touch and go whether they amputated.'

'Oh *hell*.'

'I'll give you a call,' I said. 'As soon as I look like being free.'

After he had rung off I sat with the receiver in my hand, staring into space. Slowly I put it back in its cradle.

Margaret sat motionless, her eyes studiously downcast, her mouth showing nothing. She made no reference at all to the lie I had told.

It was, I reflected, only the first of the many.

Chapter Three

Nothing about that day got any better.

I rode out with the second lot on the Heath and found there were tender spots I hadn't even known about. Etty asked if I had toothache. I looked like it, she said. Sort of drawn, she said.

I said my molars were in good crunching order and how about starting the canters. The canters were started, watched, assessed, repeated, discussed. Archangel, Etty said, would be ready for the Guineas.

When I told her I was going to stay on myself as the temporary trainer she looked horrified.

'But you *can't*.'

'You are unflattering, Etty.'

'Well, I mean . . . You don't know the horses.' She stopped and tried again. 'You hardly ever go racing. You've never been interested, not since you were a boy. You don't know enough about it.'

'I'll manage,' I said, 'with your help.'

But she was only slightly reassured, because she was not vain, and she never overestimated her own abilities. She knew she was a good head lad. She knew there was a lot to training that she wouldn't do so well. Such self knowledge in the Sport of Kings was rare, and facing it rarer still. There were always thousands of people who knew better, on the stands.

'Who will do the entries?' she asked astringently, her voice saying quite clearly that I couldn't.

'Father can do them himself when he's a bit better. He'll have a lot of time.'

At this she nodded with more satisfaction. The entering of horses in races suited to them was the most important skill in training. All the success and prestige of a stable started with the entry forms, where for each individual horse the aim had to be not too high, not too low, but just right. Most of my father's success had been built on his judgement of where to enter, and when to run, each horse.

One of the two-year-olds pranced around, lashed out, and caught another two-year-old on the knee. The boys' reactions had not been quick enough to keep them apart, and the second colt was walking lame. Etty cursed them coldly and told the second boy to lead his charge home.

I watched him following on foot behind the string, the horse's head ducking at every tender step. The knee would swell and fill and get hot, but with a bit of luck it would right itself in a few days. If it did not, someone would have to tell the owner. The someone would be me.

That made one horse dead and two damaged in one morning. If things went on at that rate there would soon be no stable left for the fat man to bother about.

When we got back there was a small police car in the drive and a large policeman in the office. He was sitting in my chair and staring at his boots, and rose purposefully to his feet as I came through the door.

'Mr. Griffon?'

'Yes.'

He came to the point without preliminaries.

'We've had a complaint, sir, that one of your horses knocked over a cyclist on the Moulton Road this morning. Also a young woman has complained to us that this same horse endangered her life and that of her children.'

He was a uniformed sergeant, about thirty, solidly built, uncompromising. He spoke with the aggressive politeness that in some policemen is close to rudeness, and I gathered that his sympathies were with the complainants.

'Was the cyclist hurt sergeant?'

'I understand he was bruised, sir.'

'And his bicycle?'

'I couldn't say, sir.'

'Do you think that a ... er ... a settlement out of court, so to speak, would be in order?'

'I couldn't say, sir,' he repeated flatly. His face was full of negative attitude which erects a barrier against sympathy or understanding. Into my mind floated one of the axioms that Russell Arletti lived by: in business matters with trade unions, the press, or the police, never try to make them like you. It arouses antagonism instead. And never make jokes: they are anti jokes.

I gave the sergeant back a stare of equal indifference and asked if he had the cyclist's name and address. After only the slightest hesitation he flicked over a page or two of notebook and read it out to me. Margaret took it down.

'And the young woman's?'

He provided that too. He then asked if he might take a statement from Miss Craig and I said certainly sergeant, and took him out into the yard. Etty gave him a rapid adding-up inspection and answered his questions in an unemotional manner. I left them together and went back to the office to finish the paper work with Margaret, who preferred to work straight through the lunch hour and leave at three to collect her children from school.

'Some of the account books are missing,' she observed.

'I had them last night,' I said. 'They're in the oak room . . . I'll go and fetch them.'

The oak room was quiet and empty. I wondered what reaction I would get from the sergeant if I brought him in there and said that last night two faceless men had knocked me out, tied me up, and removed me from my home by force. Also they had threatened to kill me, and had punched me full of anaesthetic to bring me back.

'Oh yes sir? And do you want to make a formal allegation?'

I smiled slightly. It seemed ridiculous. The sergeant would produce a stare of top-grade disbelief, and I could hardly blame him. Only my depressing state of health and the smashed telephone lying on the desk made the night's events seem real at all.

The fat man, I reflected, hardly needed to have warned me away from the police. The sergeant had done the job for him.

Etty came into the office fuming while I was returning the account books to Margaret.

'Of all the pompous clods . . .'

'Does this sort of thing happen often?' I asked.

'Of course not,' Etty said positively. 'Horses get loose, of course, but things are usually settled without all this fuss. And I told that old man that you would see he didn't suffer. Why he had to go complaining to the police beats me.'

'I'll go and see him this evening.' I said.

'Now, the old sergeant, Sergeat Chubb,' Etty said forcefully, 'he would have sorted it out himself. He wouldn't have come round taking down statements. But this one, this one is new here. They've posted him here from Ipswich and he doesn't seem to like it. Just promoted, I shouldn't wonder. Full of his own importance.'

'The stripes were new,' Margaret murmured in agreement.

'We always have good relations with the police here,' Etty said gloomily. 'Can't think what they're doing, sending the town someone who doesn't understand the first thing about horses.'

The steam had all blown off. Etty breathed sharply through her nose, shrugged her shoulders, and produced a small resigned smile.

'Oh well . . . worse things happen at sea.'

She had very blue eyes, and light brown hair that went frizzy when the weather was damp. Middle age had roughened her skin without wrinkling it, and as with most undersexed women there was much in her face that was male. She had thin dry lips and bushy unkempt eyebrows, and the handsomeness of her youth was only something I remembered. Etty seemed a sad, wasted person to many who observed her, but to herself she was fulfilled, and was busily content.

She stamped away in her jodhpurs and boots and we heard her voice raised at some luckless boy caught in wrong doing.

Rowley Lodge needed Etty Craig. But it needed Alessandro Rivera like a hole in the head.

He came late that afternoon.

I was out in the yard looking round the horses at evening stables. With Etty alongside I had got as far round as bay five, from where we would go round the bottom yard before working up again towards the house.

One of the fifteen-year-old apprentices nervously appeared as we came out of one box and prepared to go into the next.

'Someone to see you, sir.'

'Who?'

'Don't know, sir.'

'An owner?'

'Don't know, sir.'

'Where is he?'

'Up by the drive, sir.'

I looked up, over his head. Beyond the yard, out on the gravel, there was parked a large white Mercedes with a uniformed chauffeur standing by the bonnet.

'Take over, Etty, would you?' I said.

I walked up through the yard and out into the drive. The chauffeur folded his arms and his mouth like barricades against fraternisation. I stopped a few paces away from him and looked towards the inside of the car.

One of the rear doors, the one nearest to me, opened. A small black-shod foot appeared, and then a dark trouser leg, and then, slowly straightening, the whole man.

It was clear at once who he was, although the resemblance to his father began and ended with the autocratic beak of the nose and the steadfast stoniness of the black eyes. The son was a little shorter, and emaciated instead of chubby. He had sallow skin that looked in need of a sun-tan, and strong thick black hair curving in springy curls round his ears. Over all he wore an air of disconcerting maturity, and the determination in the set of his mouth would have done credit to a steel trap. Eighteen he might be, but it was a long time since he had been a boy.

I guessed that his voice would be like his father's; definite, unaccented, and careful.

It was.

'I am Rivera,' he announced. 'Alessandro.'

'Good evening,' I said, and intended it to sound polite, cool and unimpressed.

He blinked.

'Rivera,' he repeated. 'I am Rivera.'

'Yes,' I agreed. 'Good evening.'

He looked at me with narrowing attention. If he expected from me a lot of grovelling, he was not going to get it. And something of this message must have got across to him from my attitude, because he began to look faintly surprised and a shade more arrogant.

'I understand you wish to become a jockey,' I said.

'Intend.'

I nodded casually, 'No one succeeds as a jockey without determination,' I said, and made it sound patronising.

He detected the flavour immediately. He didn't like it. I was glad. But it was a small pin-pricking resistance that I was showing, and in his place I would have taken it merely as evidence of frustrated surrender.

'I am accustomed to succeed,' he said.

'How very nice,' I replied dryly.

It sealed between us an absolute antagonism. I felt him shift gear into overdrive, and it seemed to me that he was mentally gathering himself to fight on his own account a battle he believed his father had already won.

'I will start at once,' he said.

'I am in the middle of evening stables,' I said matter-of-factly. 'If you will wait, we will discuss your position when I have finished.' I gave him the politeness of an inclination of the head which I would have given to anybody, and without waiting around for him to throw any more of his slight weight about, I turned smoothly away and walked without haste back to Etty.

When we had worked our way methodically round the whole stable, discussing briefly how each horse was progressing, and planning the work programme for the following morning, we came finally to the four outside boxes, three only busy now, and the fourth full of Moonrock's absence.

The Mercedes still stood on the gravel, with both Rivera and the chauffeur sitting inside it. Etty gave them a look of regulation curiosity and asked who they were.

'New customer,' I said economically.

She frowned in surprise. 'But surely you shouldn't have kept him waiting!'

'This one,' I reassured her with private, rueful irony, 'will not go away.'

But Etty knew how to treat new clients, and making them wait in their car was not it. She hustled me along the last three boxes and anxiously pushed me to return to the Mercedes. Tomorrow, no doubt, she would not be so keen.

I opened the rear door and said to him, 'Come along in to the office.'

He climbed out of the car and followed me without a word. I switched on the fan heater, sat in Margaret's chair behind the desk, and pointed to the swivel armchair in front of it. He made no issue of it, but merely did as I suggested.

'Now,' I said in my best interviewing voice, 'You want to start tomorrow.'

'Yes.'

'In what capacity?'

He hesitated. 'As a jockey.'

'Well, no,' I said reasonably. 'There are no races yet. The season does not start for about four weeks.'

'I know that,' he said stiffly.

'What I meant was, do you want to work in the stable? Do you want to look after two horses, as the others do?'

'Certainly not.'

'Then what?'

'I will ride the horses at exercise two or three times a day. Every day. I will not clean their boxes or carry their food. I wish only to ride.'

Highly popular, that was going to be, with Etty and the other lads. Apart from all else, I was going to have a shop floor management confrontation, or in plain old terms, a mutiny, on my hands in no time at all. None of the other lads was going to muck out and groom a horse for the joy of seeing Rivera ride it.

However, all I said was, 'How much experience, exactly, have you had so far?'

'I can ride,' he said flatly.

'Racehorses?'

'I can ride.'

This was getting nowhere. I tried again. 'Have you ever ridden in any sort of race?'

'I have ridden in amateur races.'

'Where?'

'In Italy, and in Germany.'

'Have you won any?'

He gave me a black stare. 'I have won two.'

I supposed that that was something. At least it suggested that he could stay on. Winning itself, in his case, had no significance. His father was the sort to buy the favourite and nobble the opposition.

'But you want now to become a professional?'

'Yes.'

'Then I'll apply for a licence for you.'

'I can apply myself.'

I shook my head. 'You will have to have an apprentice licence, and I will have to apply for it for you.'

'I do not wish to be an apprentice.'

I said patiently, 'Unless you become an apprentice you will be unable to claim a weight allowance. In England in flat races the only people who can claim weight allowances are apprentices. Without a weight allowance the owners of the horses will all resist to the utmost any suggestion that you should ride. Without a weight allowance, in fact, you might as well give up the whole idea.'

'My father . . .' he began.

'Your father can threaten until he's blue in the face,' I interrupted. 'I cannot *force* the owners to employ you, I can only persuade. Without a weight allowance, they will never be persuaded.'

He thought it over, his expression showing nothing.

'My father,' he said, 'told me that anyone could apply for a licence and that there was no need to be apprenticed.'

'Technically, that is true.'

'But practically, it is not.' It was a statement more than a question: he had clearly understood what I had said.

I began to speculate about the strength of his intentions. It certainly seemed possible that if he read the Deed of Apprenticeship and saw to what he would be binding himself, he might simply step back into his car and be driven away. I fished in one of Margaret's tidy desk drawers, and drew out a copy of the printed agreement.

'You will need to sign this,' I said casually, and handed it over.

He read it without a flicker of an eyelid, and considering what he was reading, that was remarkable.

The familiar words trotted through my mind '. . . the Apprentice will faithfully, diligently and honestly serve the Master and obey and perform all his lawful commands . . . and will not absent himself from the service of the Master, nor divulge any of the secrets of the Master's business . . . and shall deliver to the Master all such monies and other things that shall come into his hands for work done . . . and will in all matters and things whatsoever demean and behave himself as a good true and faithful Apprentice ought to do . . .'

He put the form down on the desk and looked across at me.

'I cannot sign that.'

'Your father will have to sign it as well,' I pointed out.

'He will not.'

'Then that's an end to it,' I said, relaxing back in my chair.

He looked down at the form. 'My father's lawyers will draw up a different agreement,' he said.

I shrugged. 'Without a recognisable apprenticeship deed you won't get an apprentice's licence. That form there is based on the articles of apprenticeship common to all trades since the Middle Ages. If you alter its intentions, it won't meet the licensing requirements.'

After a packed pause he said, 'That part about delivering all monies to the Master . . . does that mean I would have to give to you all money I might earn in races?' He sounded incredulous, as well he might.

'It does say that,' I agreed, 'but it is normal nowadays for the Master to return half of race earnings to the apprentice. In addition, of course, to giving him a weekly allowance.'

'If I win the Derby on Archangel, you would take half. Half of the fee and half of the present?'

'That's right.'

'It's wicked!'

'You've got to win it before you start worrying,' I said flippantly, and watched the arrogance flare up like a bonfire.

'If the horse is good enough, I will.'

You kid yourself, mate, I thought; and didn't answer.

He stood up abruptly, picked up the form, and without another word walked out of the office, and out of the house, out of the yard, and into his car. The Mercedes purred away with him down the drive, and I stayed sitting back in Margaret's chair, hoping I had seen the last of him, wincing at the energy of my persisting headache, and wondering whether a treble brandy would restore me to instant health.

I tried it.

It didn't.

There was no sign of him in the morning, and on all counts the day was better. The kicked two-year-old's knee had gone up like a football but he was walking pretty sound on it, and the cut on Lucky Lindsay was as superficial as Etty had hoped. The elderly cyclist, the evening before, had accepted my apologies and ten pounds for his bruises and had left me with the impression that we could knock him down again, any time, for a similar supplement to his income. Archangel worked a half speed six furlongs on the Sidehill gallop, and in me a night's sleep had ironed out some creases.

But Alessandro Rivera did come back.

He rolled up the drive in the chauffeur-driven Mercedes just as Etty and I finished the last three boxes at evening stables, timing it so accurately that I wondered if he had been waiting and watching from out on Bury Road.

I jerked my head towards the office, and he followed me in. I switched on the heater, and sat down, as before; and so did he.

He produced from an inner pocket the apprenticeship form and passed it towards me across the desk. I took it and unfolded it, and turned it over.

There were no alterations. It was the deed in the exact form he had taken it. There were, however, four additions.

The signatures of Alessandro Rivera and Enso Rivera, with an appropriate witness in each case, sat squarely in the spaces designed for them.

I looked at the bold heavy strokes of both the Riveras' signatures and the nervous elaborations of the witnesses. They had signed the agreement without filling in any of the blanks: without even discussing the time the apprenticeship was to run for, or the weekly allowance to be paid.

He was watching me. I met his cold black eyes.

'You and your father signed it like this,' I said slowly, 'because you have not the slightest intention of being bound by it.'

His face didn't change. 'Think what you like,' he said.

And so I would. And what I thought was that the son was not as criminal as his father. The son had taken the legal obligations of the apprenticeship form seriously. But his father had not.

Chapter Four

The small private room in the North London hospital where my father had been taken after the crash seemed to be almost entirely filled with the frames and ropes and pulleys and weights which festooned his high bed. Apart from all that there was only a high-silled window with limp floral curtains and a view of half the back of another building and a chunk of sky, a chest-high wash basin with lever type taps designed to be turned on by elbows, a bedside locker upon which reposed his lower teeth in a glass of water, and an armchair of sorts, visitors for the use of.

There were no flowers glowing against the margarine coloured walls, and no well-wishing cards brightening the top of the locker. He did not care for flowers, and would have dispatched any that came straight along to other wards, and I doubted that anyone at all would have made the error of sending him a glossy or amusing get-well, which he would have considered most frightfully vulgar.

The room itself was meagre compared with what he would have chosen and could afford, but to me during the first critical days the hospital itself had seemed effortlessly efficient. It did after all, as one doctor had casually explained to me, have to deal constantly with wrecked bodies prised out of crashes on the A.1. They were used to it. Geared to it. They had a higher proportion of accident cases than of the normally sick.

He had said he thought I was wrong to insist on private treatment for my father and that he would find time hanging less heavy in a public ward where there was a lot going on, but I had assured him that he did not know my father. He had shrugged and acquiesced, but said that the private rooms weren't much. And they weren't. They were for getting out of quickly, if one could.

When I visited him that evening, he was asleep. The ravages of the pain he had endured during the past week had deepened and darkened the lines round his eyes and tinged all his skin with grey, and he looked defenceless in a way he never did when awake. The dogmatic set of his mouth was relaxed, and with his eyes shut he no longer seemed to be disapproving of nineteen twentieths of what occurred. A lock of grey-white hair curved softly down over his forehead, giving him a friendly gentle look which was hopelessly misleading.

He had not been a kind father. I had spent most of my childhood fearing him and most of my teens loathing him, and only in the past very few years had I come to understand him. The severity with which he had used me had not after all been rejection and dislike, but lack of imagination and an inability to love. He had not believed in beating, but he had lavishly handed out other punishments of deprivation and solitude, without realising that what would have been trifling to him was torment to me. Being locked in one's bedroom for three or four days at a time might not have come under the heading of active cruelty, but it had dumped me into agonies of humiliation and shame: and it had not been possible, although I had tried until I was the most repressed child in Newmarket, to avoid committing anything my father could interpret as a fault.

He had sent me to Eton, which in its way had proved just as callous, and on my sixteenth birthday I ran away.

I knew that he had never forgiven me. An aunt had relayed to me his furious comment that he had provided me with horses to ride and taught me obedience, and what more could any father do for his son?

He had made no effort to get me back, and during all the years of my commercial success we had not once spoken to each other. In the end, after fourteen years absence, I had gone to Ascot races knowing that he would be there and wanting finally to make peace.

When I said 'Mr. Griffon ...' he had turned to me from a group of people, raised his eyebrows, and looked at me enquiringly. His eyes were cool and blank. He hadn't known me.

I had said, with more amusement than awkwardness, 'I am your son ... I am Neil.'

Apart from surprise he had shown no emotion whatsoever, and on the tacit understanding that none would be expected on either side, he had suggested that any day I happened to be passing through Newmarket, I could call in and see him.

I had called three or four times every year since then, sometimes for a drink, sometimes for lunch, but never staying; and I had come to see him from a much saner perspective in my thirties than I had at fifteen. His manner to me was still for the most part forbidding, critical, and punitive, but as I no longer depended solely upon him for approval, and as he could no longer lock me in my bedroom for disagreeing with him, I found a perverse sort of pleasure in his company.

I had thought when I was called in a hurry to Rowley Lodge after the accident that I wouldn't sleep again in my old bed, that I'd choose any other. But in fact in the end I did sleep in it, because it was the room that had been prepared for me, and there were dust-sheets still over all the rest.

Too much had crowded back when I looked at the unchanged furnishings and the fifty-times read books on the small bookshelf; and smile at myself as cynically as I would, on that first night back I hadn't been able to lie in there in the dark with the door shut.

I sat down in the armchair and read the copy of *The Times* which rested on his bed. His hand, yellowish, freckled, and with thick knotted veins, lay limply on the sheets, still half entwined in the black-framed spectacles he had removed before sleeping. I remembered that when I was seventeen I had taken to wearing frames like those, with plain glass in, because to me they stood for authority, and I had wanted to present an older and weightier personality to my clients. Whether it was the frames or not which did the trick, the business had flourished.

He stirred, and groaned, and the lax hand closed convulsively into a fist with almost enough force to break the lenses.

I stood up. His face was screwed up with pain and beads of sweat stood out on his forehead, but he sensed that there was someone in the room and opened his eyes sharp and wide as if there were nothing the matter.

'Oh . . . it's you.'

'I'll fetch a nurse,' I said.

'No. Be better . . . in a minute.'

But I went to fetch one anyway, and she looked at the watch pinned upside down on her bosom and remarked that it was time for his pills, near enough.

After he had swallowed them and the worst of it had passed I noticed that during the short time I was out of the room he had managed to replace his lower teeth. The glass of water stood empty on the locker. A great one for his dignity, my father.

'Have you found anyone to take over the licence?' he asked.

'Can I make your pillows more comfortable?' I suggested.

'Leave them alone,' he snapped. 'Have you found anyone to take charge?' He would go on asking, I knew, until I gave him a direct answer.

'No,' I said. 'There's no need.'

'What do you mean?'

'I've decided to stay on, myself.'

His mouth opened, just as Etty's had done, and then shut again with equal vigour.

'You can't. You don't know a damn thing about it. You couldn't win a single race.'

'The horses are good, Etty is good, and you can sit here and do the entries.'

'You will not take over. You will get someone who is capable, someone I approve of. The horses are far too valuable to have amateurs messing about. You will do as I say. Do you hear? You will do as I say.'

The pain-killing drug had begun to act on his eyes, if not yet on his tongue.

'The horses will come to no harm,' I said, and thought of Moonrock and Lucky Lindsay and the kicked two-year-old, and wished with all my heart I could hand the whole lot over to Bredon that very day.

'If you think,' he said with a certain malice, 'that because you sell antiques you can run a racing stable, you are over-estimating yourself.'

'I no longer sell antiques,' I pointed out calmly. As he knew perfectly well.

'The principles are different,' he said.

'The principles of all businesses are the same.'

'Rubbish.'

'Get the costs right and supply what the customer wants.'

'I can't see you supplying winners.' He was contemptuous.

'Well,' I said moderately, 'I can't see why not.'

'Can't you?' he asked acidly. 'Can't you, indeed?'

'Not if you will give me your advice.'

He gave me instead a long wordless stare while he searched for an adequate answer. The pupils in his grey eyes had contracted to micro-dots. There was no tension left in the muscles which had stiffened his jaw.

'You must get someone else,' he said: but the words had begun to slur. I made a non-committal movement of my head halfway between a nod and a shake, and the argument was over for that day. He asked after that merely about the horses. I told him how they had each performed during their workouts, and he seemed to forget that he didn't believe I understood what I had seen. When I left him, a short while later, he was again on the edge of sleep.

I rang the door bell of my own flat in Hampstead, two long and two short, and got three quick buzzes back, which meant come on in. So I fitted my key into the latch and opened the door.

Gillie's voice floated disembodiedly across the hall.

'I'm in your bedroom.'

'Convenient,' I said to myself with a smile. But she was painting the walls.

'Didn't expect you tonight,' she said, when I kissed her. She held her arms away from me so as not to smear yellow ochre on my jacket. There was a yellow streak on her forehead and a dusting of it on her shining chestnut hair and she looked companionable and easy. Gillie at thirty-six had a figure no model would have been seen dead in, and an attractive lived-in face with wisdom looking out of grey-green eyes. She was sure and mature and much travelled in spirit, and had left behind her one collapsed marriage and one dead child. She had answered an advertise-ment for a tenant which I had put in *The Times*, and for two and a half years she had been my tenant and a lot else.

'What do you think of this colour?' she said. 'And we're having a cinnamon carpet and green and shocking pink striped curtains.'

'You can't mean it.'

'It will look ravishing.'

'Ugh,' I said, but she simply laughed. When she had taken the flat it had had white walls, polished furniture and blue fabrics. Gillie had retained only the furniture, and Sheraton and Chippendale would have choked over their new settings.

'You look tired,' she said. 'Want some coffee?'

'And a sandwich, if there's any bread.'

She thought. 'There's some crisp-bread, anyway.'

She was permanently on diets and her idea of dieting was not to buy food. This led to a lot of eating out, which completely defeated the object.

Gillie had listened attentively to my wise dictums about laying in suitable protein like eggs and cheese and then continued happily in the same old ways, which brought me early on to believe that she really did not lust after a beauty contest figure, but was content as long as she did not burst out of her forty-inch hip dresses. Only when they got tight did she actually shed half a stone. She could if she wanted to. She didn't obsessively want.

'How is your father?' she asked, as I crunched my way through a sandwich of rye crisp-bread and slices of raw tomato.

'It's still hurting him.'

'I would have thought they could have stopped that.'

'Well they do, most of the time. And the sister in charge told me this evening that he will be all right in a day or two. They aren't worried about his leg any more. The wound has started healing cleanly, and it should all be settling down soon and giving him an easier time.'

'He's not young, of course.'

'Sixty-seven,' I agreed.

'The bones will take a fair time to mend.'

'Mm.'

'I suppose you've found someone to hold the fort.'

'No,' I said, 'I'm staying there myself.'

'Oh boy, oh boy,' she said, 'I might have guessed.'

I looked at her enquiringly with my mouth full of bits.

'Anything which smells of challenge is your meat and drink.'

'Not this one,' I said with feeling.

'It will be unpopular with the stable,' she diagnosed, 'and apoplectic to your father, and a riotous success.'

'Correct on the first two, way out on the third.'

She shook her head with the glint of a smile. 'Nothing is impossible for the whiz kids.'

She knew I disliked the journalese term, and I knew she liked to use it. 'My lover is a whiz kid,' she said once into a hush at a sticky party: and the men mobbed her.

She poured me a glass of the marvellous Château Lafite 1961 which she sacrilegiously drank with anything from caviare to baked beans. It had seemed to me when she moved in that her belongings consisted almost entirely of fur coats and cases of wine, all of which she had precipitously inherited from her mother and father respectively when they died together in Morocco in an earthquake. She had sold the coats because she thought they made her look fat, and had set about drinking her way gradually through the precious bins that wine merchants were wringing their hands over.

'That wine is an *investment*,' one of them had said to me in agony.

'But *someone's* got to drink it,' said Gillie reasonably, and pulled out the cork on the second of the Cheval Blanc 61.

Gillie was so rich, because of her grandmother, that she found it more pleasing to drink the super-duper than to sell it at a profit and develop a taste for Brand X. She had been surprised that I had agreed until I had pointed out that that flat was filled with precious pieces where painted deal would have done the same job. So we sat sometimes with our feet up on a sixteenth century Spanish walnut refectory table which had brought dealers sobbing to their knees and drank her wine out of eighteenth century Waterford glass, and laughed at ourselves, because the only safe way to live with any degree of wealth was to make fun of it.

Gillie had said once, 'I don't see why that table is so special, just because it's been here since the Armada. Just look at those moth-eaten legs ...' She pointed to four feet which were pitted, stripped of polish, and worn untidily away.

'In the sixteenth century they used to sluice the stone floors with beer because it whitened them. Beer was fine for the stone, but a bit unfortunate for any wood which got continually splashed.'

'Rotten legs proves it's genuine?'

'Got it in one.'

I was fonder of that table than of anything else I possessed, because on it had been founded all my fortunes. Six months out of Eton, on what I had saved out of sweeping the floors at Sotheby's, I set up in business on my own by pushing a barrow round the outskirts of flourishing country towns and buying anything worthwhile that I was offered. The junk I sold to secondhand shops and the best bits to dealers, and by the time I was seventeen I was thinking about a shop.

I saw the Spanish table in the garage of a man from whom I had just bought a late Victorian chest of drawers. I looked at the wrought iron crossed spars bracing the solid square legs under the four inch thick top, and felt unholy butterflies in my guts.

He had been using it as a trestle for paper hanging, and it was littered with pots of paint.

'I'll buy that, too, if you like,' I said.

'It's only an old work table.'

'Well ... how much would you want for it?'

He looked at my barrow, on to which he had just helped me lift the chest of drawers. He looked at the twenty pounds I had paid him for it, and he looked at my shabby jeans and jerkin, and he said kindly, 'No lad, I couldn't rob you. And anyway, look, its legs are all rotten at the bottom.'

'I could afford another twenty,' I said doubtfully. 'But that's about all I've got with me.'

He took a lot of persuading, and in the end would only let me give him fifteen. He shook his head over me, telling me I'd better learn a bit more before I ruined myself. But I cleaned up the table and repolished the beautiful slab of walnut, and I sold it a fortnight later to a dealer I knew from the Sotheby days for two hundred and seventy pounds.

With those proceeds swelling my savings I had opened the first shop, and things never looked back. When I sold out twelve years later to an American syndicate there was a chain of eleven, all bright and clean and filled with treasures.

A short time afterwards, on a sentimental urge, I traced the Spanish table, and bought it back. And I sought out the handyman with his garage and gave him two hundred pounds, which almost caused a heart attack; so I reckoned if anyone was going to put their feet up on that expensive plank, no one had a better right.

* * *

'Where did you get all those bruises?' Gillie said, sitting up in the spareroom bed and watching me undress.

I squinted down at the spatter of mauve blotches.

'I was attacked by a centipede.'

She laughed. 'You're hopeless.'

'And I've got to be back at Newmarket by seven tomorrow morning.'

'Stop wasting time, then. It's midnight already.'

I climbed in beside her, and lying together in naked companionship we worked our way through *The Times* crossword.

It was always better like that. By the time we turned off the light we were relaxed and entwined, and we turned to each other for an act that was a part but not the whole of a relationship.

'I quite love you,' Gillie said. 'Believe it or not.'

'Oh, I believe you,' I said modestly. 'Thousands wouldn't.'

'Stop biting my ear, I don't like it.'

'The books say the ear is an AI erogenous zone.'

'The books can go stuff themselves.'

'Charming.'

'And all those women's lib publications about "The Myth of the Vaginal Orgasm". So much piffle. Of course it isn't a myth.'

'This is not supposed to be a public meeting,' I said, 'This is supposed to be a spot of private passion.'

'Oh well . . . if you insist.'

She wriggled more comfortably into my arms.

'I'll tell you something, if you like,' she said.

'If you absolutely must.'

'The answer to four down isn't hallucinated, it's hallucinogen.'

I shook. 'Thanks very much.'

'Thought you'd like to know.'

I kissed her neck and laid my hand on her stomach.

'That makes it a g, not a t, in twenty across,' she said.

'Stigma?'

'Clever old you.'

'Is that the lot?'

'Mm.'

After a bit she said, 'Do you really loathe the idea of green and shocking pink curtains?'

'Would you mind just concentrating on the matter in hand?'

I could feel her grin in the darkness.

'O.K.' she said.

And concentrated.

She woke me up like an alarm clock at five o'clock. It was not so much the pat she woke me up with, but where she chose to plant it. I came back to the surface laughing.

'Good morning, little one,' she said.

She got up and made some coffee, her chestnut hair in a tangle and her skin pale and fresh. She looked marvellous in the mornings. She stirred a dollop of heavy cream into the thick black coffee and sat opposite me across the kitchen table.

'Someone really had a go at you, didn't they?' she said casually.

I buttered a piece of rye crunch and reached for the honey.

'Sort of,' I agreed.

'Not telling?'

'Can't,' I said briefly. 'But I will when I can.'

'You may have a mind like teak,' she said, 'but you've a vulnerable body, just like anyone else.'

I looked at her in surprise, with my mouth full. She wrinkled her nose at me.

'I used to think you mysterious and exciting,' she said.

'Thanks.'

'And now you're about as exciting as a pair of old bedroom slippers.'

'So kind,' I murmured.

'I used to think there was something magical about the way you disentangled all those nearly bankrupt businesses . . . and then I found out that it wasn't magic but just uncluttered common sense . . .'

'Plain, boring old me,' I agreed, washing down the crumbs with a gulp of coffee.

'I know you well, now,' she said. 'I know how you tick . . . And all those bruises . . .' She shivered suddenly in the warm little room.

'Gillie,' I said accusingly, 'You are suffering from intuition;' and that remark in itself was a dead giveaway.

'No . . . from interpretation,' she said. 'And just you watch out for yourself.'

'Anything you say.'

'Because,' she explained seriously, 'I do not want to have the bother of hunting for another ground floor flat with cellars to keep the wine in. It took me a whole month to find this one.'

Chapter Five

It was drizzling when I got back to Newmarket. A cold wet horrible morning on the Heath. Also the first thing I saw when I turned into the drive of Rowley Lodge was the unwelcome white Mercedes.

The uniformed chauffeur sat behind the wheel. The steely young Alessandro sat in the back. When I stopped not far away from him he was out of his car faster than I was out of mine.

'Where have you been?' he demanded, looking down his nose at my silver-grey Jenson.

'Where have you?' I said equably, and received the full freeze of the Rivera speciality in stares.

'I have come to begin,' he said fiercely.

'So I see.'

He wore superbly cut jodhpurs and glossy brown boots. His waterproof anorak had come from an expensive ski shop and his string gloves were clean and pale yellow. He looked more like an advertisement in *Country Life* than a working rider.

'I have to go in and change,' I said. 'You can begin when I come out.'

'Very well.'

He waited again in his car and emerged from it immediately I reappeared. I jerked my head at him to follow, and went down into the yard wondering just how much of a skirmish I was going to have with Etty.

She was in a box in bay three helping a very small lad to saddle a seventeen hand filly, and with Alessandro at my heels I walked across to talk to her. She came out of the box and gave Alessandro a widening look of speculation.

'Etty,' I said matter-of-factly, 'This is Alessandro Rivera. He has signed his indentures. He starts today. Er, right now, in fact. What can we give him to ride?'

Etty cleared her throat. 'Did you say *apprenticed*?'

'That's right.'

'But we don't need any more lads,' she protested.

'He won't be doing his two. Just riding exercise.'

She gave me a bewildered look. 'All apprentices do their two.'

'Not this one,' I said briskly. 'How about a horse for him?'

She brought her scattered attention to bear on the immediate problem. 'There's Indigo,' she said doubtfully. 'I had him saddled for myself.'

'Indigo will do beautifully,' I nodded. Indigo was a quiet ten-year-old gelding which Etty often rode as lead horse to the two-year-olds, and upon which she liked to give completely untrained apprentices their first riding lessons. I stifled the urge to show Alessandro up by putting him on something really difficult: couldn't risk damaging expensive property.

'Miss Craig is the head lad,' I told Alessandro. 'And you will take your orders from her.'

He gave her a black unfathomable stare which she returned with uncertainty.

'I'll show him where Indigo is,' I reassured her. 'Also the tackroom, and so on.'

'I've given you Cloud Cuckoo-land this morning, Mr. Neil,' she said hesitantly. 'Jock will have got him ready.'

I pointed out the tackroom, feedroom, and the general lay-out of the stable to Alessandro and led him back towards the drive.

'I do not take orders from a woman,' he said.

'You'll have to,' I said without emphasis.

'No.'

'Goodbye, then.'

He walked one pace behind me in fuming silence, but he followed me round to the outside boxes and did not peel off towards his car. Indigo's box was the one next to Moonrock's, and he stood there patiently in his saddle and bridle, resting his weight on one leg and looking round lazily when I unbolted his door.

Alessandro's gaze swept him from stem to stern and he turned to me with unrepressed anger.

'I do not ride nags. I wish to ride Archangel.'

'No one lets an apprentice diamond cutter start on the Kohinoor,' I said.

'I can ride any racehorse on earth. I can ride exceptionally well.'

'Prove it on Indigo, then, and I'll give you something better for second lot.'

He compressed his mouth. I looked at him with the complete lack of feeling that always seemed to calm tempers in industrial negotiations; and after a moment or two it worked on him as well. His gaze dropped away from my face; he shrugged, untied Indigo's headcollar, and led him out of his box. He jumped with ease up into the saddle, slipped his feet into the stirrups, and gathered up the reins. His movements were precise and unfussy, and he settled on to old Indigo's back with an appearance of being at home. Without another word he started walking away down the yard, shortening the stirrup leathers as he went, for Etty rode long.

Watching his backview I followed him on foot, while from all the bays the lads led out the horses for the first lot. Down in the collecting paddock they circled round the outer cinder track while Etty on the grass in the centre began the ten minute task of swapping some of the riders. The lads who did the horses did not necessarily ride their own charges out at exercise: each horse had to be ridden by a rider who could at the least control him and at the most improve him. The lowliest riders usually got the task of walking any unfit horses round the paddock at home: Etty seldom let them loose in canters on the Heath.

I joined her in the centre as she referred to her list. She was wearing a bright yellow sou'wester down which the drizzle trickled steadily, and she looked like a diminutive American fireman. The scrawled list in her hand was slowly degenerating into pulp.

'Ginge, get up on Pullitzer,' she said.

Ginge did as he was told in a sulk. Pullitzer was a far cry from Lucky Lindsay, and he considered that he had lost face.

Etty briefly watched Alessandro plod round on Indigo, taking in with a flick of a glance that he could at least manage him with no problems. She looked at me in a baffled questioning way but I merely steered her away from him by asking who she was putting up on our problem colt Traffic.

She shook her head in frustration. 'It'll still have to be Andy . . . He's a right little devil, that Traffic. All that breed, you can't trust one of them.' She turned and called to him 'Andy . . . Get up on Traffic.'

Andy, middle-aged, tiny, wrinkled, could ride the sweetest of training gallops: but when years ago he had been given his chance in races his wits had flown out of the window, and his grasp of tactics was nil. He was given a leg-up on to the dark irritable two-year-old, which jigged and fidgeted and buck-jumped under him without remission.

Etty had switched herself to Lucky Lindsay, who wore a shield over the cut knee and although sound would not be cantering, and in Cloud Cuckoo-land had given me the next best to a hack, a strong five-year-old handicapper up to a man's weight. With everyone mounted, the gates to the Heath were opened, and the whole string wound out on to the walking ground . . . colts as always in front, fillies behind.

Bound for the Southfield gallops beside the racecourse we turned right out of the gate and walked down behind the other stables which were strung out along the Bury Road. Passed the Jockey Club notice board announcing which training areas could be used that day. Crossed the A 11, holding up heavy lorries with their windscreen wipers twitching impatiently. Wound across the Severals, along the Watercourse, through St Mary's Square, along The Rows, and so finally to Southfields. No other town in England provided a special series of roads upon which the only traffic allowed was horses; but one could go from one end of Newmarket to the other, only yards behind its bustling High Street, and spend only a fraction of the journey on the public highway.

We were the only string on Southfields that morning, and Etty wasted no time in starting the canters. Up on the road to the racecourse stood the two usual cars, with two men standing out in the damp in the unmistakable position which meant they were watching us through binoculars.

'They never miss a day,' Etty said sourly. 'And if they think we've brought Archangel down here they're in for a disappointment.'

The touts watched steadfastly, though what they could see from half a mile away through unrelenting drizzle was anyone's guess. They were employed not by bookmakers but by racing columnists, who relied on their reports for the wherewithal to fill their pages. I thought it might be a very good thing if I could keep Alessandro out of their attention for as long as possible.

He could handle Indigo right enough, though the gelding was an undemanding old thing within the powers of the Pony Club. All the same, he sat well on him and had quiet hands. 'Here, you,' Etty said, beckoning to him with her whip. 'Come over here.'

To me she said, as she slid to the ground from Lucky Lindsay, 'What is his name?'

'Alessandro.'

'Aless . . .? Far too long.'

Indigo was reined to a halt beside her. 'You, Alex,' she said. 'Jump down and hold this horse.'

I thought he would explode. His furious face said plainly that no one had any right to call him Alex, and that no one, but no one, was going to order him about. Especially not a woman.

He saw me watching him and suddenly wiped all expression from his own face as if with a sponge. He shook his feet out of the irons, swung his leg agilely forward over Indigo's withers, and slid to the ground facing us. He took the reins of Lucky Lindsay, which Etty held out to him, and gave her those of Indigo. She lengthened the stirrup leathers, climbed up into the saddle, and rode away without comment to give a lead to the six two-year-olds we had brought with us.

Alessandro said like a throttled volcano, 'I am not going to take any more orders from that woman.'

'Don't be so bloody silly,' I said.

He looked up at me. The fine rain had drenched his black hair so that the curls had tightened and clung close to his head. With the arrogant nose, the back tilted skull, the close curling hair, he looked like a Roman statue come to life.

'Don't talk to me like that. No one talks to me like that.'

Cloud Cuckoo-land stood patiently, pricking his ears to watch some seagulls fly across the Heath.

I said, 'You are here because you want to be. No one asked you to come, no one will stop you going. But just so long as you do stay here, you will do what Miss Craig says, and you will do what I say, and you will do it without arguing. Is that clear?'

'My father will not let you treat me like this.' He was rigid with the strength of his outrage.

'Your father,' I said coldly, 'must be overjoyed to have a son who needs to shelter behind his skirts.'

'You will be sorry,' he threatened furiously.

I shrugged. 'Your father said I was to give you good horses to ride in races. Nothing was mentioned about bowing down to a spoiled little tin god.'

'I will tell him . . .'

'Tell him what you like. But the more you run to him the less I'll think of you.'

'I don't care what you think of me,' he said vehemently.

'You're a liar,' I said flatly, and he gave me a long tightlipped stare until he turned abruptly away. He led Lucky Lindsay ten paces off, and stopped and watched the canters that Etty was directing. Every line of the slender shape spoke of injured pride and flaming resentment, and I wondered whether his father would indeed think that I had gone too far. And if I had, what was he going to do about it?

Mentally shrugging off the evil until the day thereof, I tried to make some assessment of the two-year-olds' relative abilities. Scoff as people might about me taking over my father's licence, I had found that childhood skills came back after nineteen years as naturally as riding a bicycle; and few lonely children could grow up in a racing stable without learning the trade from the muck-heap up. I'd had the horses out of doors for company, and the furniture indoors, and I reckoned if I could build one business out of the dead wood I could also try to keep things rolling with the live muscles. But for only as long, I reminded myself, as it took me to get rid of Alessandro.

Etty came back after the canters and changed horses again.

'Give me a leg-up,' she said briskly to Alessandro; for Lucky Lindsay like most young thoroughbreds did not like riders climbing up to mount them.

For a moment I thought the whole pantomime was over. Alessandro drew himself up to his full height, which topped Etty's by at least two inches, and dispatched at her a glare which should have cremated her. Etty genuinely didn't notice.

'Come on,' she said impatiently, and held out her leg backwards, bent at the knee.

Alessandro threw a glance of desperation in my direction, then took a visibly deep breath, looped Indigo's reins over his arm, and put his two hands under Etty's shin. He gave her quite a respectable leg-up, though I wouldn't have been surprised if it had been the first time in his life that he had done it.

I carefully didn't laugh, didn't sneer, didn't show that I thought there was anything to notice. Alessandro swallowed his capitulation in private. But there was nothing to indicate that it would be permanent.

We rode back through the town and into the yard, where I gave Cloud Cuckoo-land back to Jock and walked into the office to see Margaret. She had the mushroom heater blowing full blast, but I doubted that I would have properly dried through by the time we pulled out again for second lot.

'Morning,' she said economically.

I nodded, half smiled, slouched into the swivel chair. 'I've opened the letters again . . . was that right,' she said.

'Absolutely. And answer them yourself, if you can.'

She looked surprised. 'Mr. Griffon always dictates everything.'

'Anything you have to ask about, ask. Anything I need to know, tell me. Anything else, deal with it yourself.'

'All right,' she said, and sounded pleased.

I sat in my father's chair, and stared down at his boots, which I had usurped, and thought seriously about what I had seen in his account books. Alessandro wasn't the only trouble the stable was running into.

There was a sudden crash as the door from the yard was forcibly opened, and Etty burst into the office like a stampeding ballistic missile.

'That bloody boy you've taken on . . . He'll have to go. I'm not standing for it. I'm not.'

She looked extremely annoyed, with eyes blinking fiercely and her mouth pinched into a slit.

'What has he done?' I asked resignedly.

'He's gone off in that stupid white car and left Indigo in his box still with his saddle and bridle on. George says he just got down off Indigo, led him into the box, and came out and shut the door, and got into the car and the chauffeur drove him away. Just like that!' She paused for breath. 'And who does he think is going to take the saddle off and dry the rain off Indigo and wash out his feet and rug him up and fetch his hay and water and make his bed?'

'I'll go out and see George,' I said. 'And ask him to do it.'

'I've asked him already,' Etty said furiously. 'But that's not the point. We're not keeping that wretched little Alex. Not one more minute.'

She glanced at me with her chin up, making an issue of it. Like all head lads she had a major say in the hiring and firing of the help. I had not consulted her over the hiring of Alessandro, and clear as a bell she was telegraphing that I was to acknowledge her authority and get rid of him.

'I'm afraid that we'll have to put up with him, Etty,' I said sympathetically. 'And hope to teach him better ways.'

'He must go,' she insisted vehemently.

'Alessandro's father,' I lied sincerely, 'is paying through the nose to have his son taken on here as an apprentice. It is very much worth the stable's while financially to put up with him. I'll have a talk with him when he comes back for second lot and see if I can get him to be more reasonable.'

'I don't like the way he stares at me,' Etty said, unmollified.

'I'll ask him not to.'

'Ask!' Etty said exasperatedly. 'Whoever heard of *asking* an apprentice to behave with respect to the head lad.'

'I'll tell him,' I said.

'And tell him to stop being so snooty with the other lads, they are already complaining. And tell him he is to put his horse straight after he has ridden it, the same as all the others.'

'I'm sorry, Etty. I don't think he'll put his horse straight. We'll have to get George to do it regularly. For a bonus, of course.'

Etty said angrily, 'It's not a yard man's job to act as a . . . a . . . *servant* . . . to an *apprentice*. It just isn't right.'

'I know, Etty,' I agreed. 'I know it isn't right. But Alessandro is not an ordinary apprentice, and it might be easier all round if you could let all the other lads know that his father is paying for him to be here, and that he has some romantic notion of wanting to be a jockey, which he'll get out of his system soon enough, and when he has gone, we can all get back to normal.'

She looked at me uncertainly. 'It isn't a proper apprenticeship if he doesn't look after his horses.'

'The details of an apprenticeship are a matter for agreement between the contracting parties,' I said regretfully. 'If I agree that he doesn't have to do his two, then he doesn't have to. And I don't really approve of him not doing them, but there you are, the stable will be richer if he doesn't.'

Etty had calmed down but she was not pleased. 'I think you might have consulted me before agreeing to all this.'

'Yes, Etty. I'm very sorry.'

'And does your father know about it?'

'Of course,' I said.

'Oh well, then.' She shrugged. 'If your father wants it, I suppose we must make the best of it. But it won't be at all good for discipline.'

'The lads will be used to him within a week.'

'They won't like it if he looks like getting any chance in races which they think should be theirs.'

'The season doesn't start for a month,' I said soothingly. 'Let's see how he makes out, shall we?'

And put off the day when he got the chances however bad he was, and however much they should have gone to someone else.

Etty put him on a quiet four-year-old mare which didn't please him but was a decided step up from old Indigo. He had received with unyielding scorn my request that he should stop staring so disquietingly at Etty, and sneered at my suggestion that he should let it be understood that his father was paying for him to be there.

'It is not true,' he said superciliously.

'Believe me,' I said with feeling, 'if it were true, you wouldn't be here tomorrow. Not if he paid a pound a minute.'

'Why not?'

'Because you are upsetting Miss Craig and upsetting the other lads, and a stable seething with resentment is not going to do its best by its horses. In fact, if you want the horses here to win races for you, you'll do your best to get along without arousing ill-feeling in the staff.'

He had given me the black stare and hadn't answered, but I noticed that he looked steadfastly at the ground when Etty detailed him to the mare. He rode her quietly along towards the back of the string and completed his allotted half-speed four-furlong canter without incident. On our return to the yard George met him and took the mare away to the box, and Alessandro without a backward glance walked into his Mercedes and was driven away.

The truce lasted for two more mornings. On each of them Alessandro arrived punctually for the first exercise, disappeared presumably for breakfast, came back for the second lot, and departed for the rest of the day. Etty gave him middling horses to ride, all of which he did adequately enough to wring from her the grudging comment: 'If he doesn't give us any more trouble, I suppose it could be worse.'

But on his fourth morning, which was Saturday, the defiant attitude was not only back but reinforced. We survived through both lots without a direct confrontation between him and Etty only because I purposely kept parting them. For the second lot, in fact, I insisted on taking him with me and a party of two-year-olds along to the special two-year-old training ground while Etty led the bulk of the string over to Warren Hill.

We got back before Etty so that he should be gone before she returned, but instead of striding away to his Mercedes he followed me to the office door.

'Griffon,' he said behind me.

I turned; regarded him. The arrogant stare was much in evidence. His eyes were blacker than space.

'I have been to see my father,' he said. 'He says that you should be treating me with deference. He says I should not take orders from a woman and that you must arrange that I do not. If necessary, Miss Craig must leave. He says I must be given better horses to ride, and in particular, Archangel. He says that if you do not see to these things immediately, he will show you that he meant what he said. And he told me to give you this. He said it was a promise of what he could do.'

He produced a flat tin box from an inner pocket of his anorak, and held it out to me.

I took it. I said, 'Do you know what it contains?'

He shook his head, but I was sure he did know.

'Alessandro,' I said, 'Whatever your father threatens, or whatever he does, your only chance of success is to leave the stable unharmed. If your father destroys it, there will be nothing for you to ride.'

'He will make another trainer take me,' he asserted.

'He will not,' I said flatly, 'Because should he destroy this stable I will put all the facts in front of the Jockey Club and they will take away your licence and stop you riding in any races whatsoever.'

'He would kill you,' he said matter-of-factly. The thought of it did not surprise or appal him.

'I have already lodged with my solicitor a full account of my interview with your father. Should he kill me, they will open that letter. He could find himself in great trouble. And you, of course, would be barred for life from racing anywhere in the world.'

A lot of the starch had turned to frustration. 'He will have to talk to you himself,' he said. 'You do not behave as he tells me you will. You confuse me . . . He will talk to you himself.'

He turned on his heel and took himself stiffly away to the attendant Mercedes. He climbed into the back, and the patient chauffeur, who waited always in the car all the time that his passenger was on the horses, started the purring engine and with a scrunch of his Michelins, carried him away.

I took the flat tin with me into the house, through into the oak-panelled room, and opened it there on the desk.

Between the layers of cotton wool it contained a small carved wooden model of a horse. Round its neck was tied a label, and on the label was written one word: Moonrock.

I picked the little horse out of the tin. It was necessary to lift it out in two pieces, because the off-hind leg was snapped through at the hock.

Chapter Six

I sat for quite a long time turning the little model over in my hands, and its significance over in my mind, wondering whether Enso Rivera could possibly have organised the breaking of Moonrock's leg, or whether he was simply pretending that what had been a true accident was all his own work.

I did not on the whole believe that he had destroyed Moonrock. What did become instantly ominous, though, was his repeated choice of that word, destroy.

Almost every horse which broke a leg had to be destroyed, as only in exceptional cases was mending them practicable. Horses could not be kept in bed. They would scarcely ever even lie down. To take a horse's weight off a leg meant supporting him in slings. Supporting him in slings for the number of weeks that it took a major bone to mend incurred debility and gut troubles. Racehorses, always delicate creatures, could die of the inactivity, and if they survived were never as good afterwards; and only in the case of valuable stallions and brood mares was any attempt normally made to keep them alive.

If Enso Rivera broke a horse's leg, it would have to be destroyed. If he broke enough of them, the owners would remove their survivors in a panic, and the stable itself would be destroyed.

Alessandro had said his father had sent the tin as a promise of what he could do.

If he could break horses's legs, he could indeed destroy the stable.

But it wasn't as easy as all that, to break a horse's leg.

Fact or bluff.

I fingered the little maimed horse. I didn't know, and couldn't decide, which it represented. But I did decide at least to turn a bit of my own bluff into fact.

I wrote a full account of the abduction, embellished with every detail I could remember. I packed the little wooden horse back into its tin and wrote a short explanation of its possible significance. Then I enclosed everything in a strong manilla envelope, wrote on it the time honoured words, 'To be opened in the event of my death', put it into a larger envelope with a covering letter and posted it to my London solicitor from the main post office in Newmarket.

'You've done *what*?' my father exclaimed.

'Taken on a new apprentice.

He looked in fury at all the junk anchoring him to his bed. Only the fact that he was tied down prevented him from hitting the ceiling.

'It isn't up to you to take on new apprentices. You are not to do it. Do you hear?'

I repeated my fabrication about Enso paying well for Alessandro's privilege. The news percolated through my father's irritation and the voltage went out of it perceptibly. A thoughtful expression took over, and finally a grudging nod.

He knows, I thought. He knows that the stable will before long be short of ready cash.

I wondered whether he were well enough to discuss it, or whether even if he were well enough he would be able to talk to me about it. We had never in our lives discussed anything: he had told me what to do, and I either had or hadn't done it. The divine right of kings had nothing on his attitude, which he applied also to most of the owners. They were all in varying degrees in awe of him and a few were downright afraid: but they kept their horses in his stable because year after year he brought home the races that counted.

He asked how the horses were working. I told him at some length and he listened with a sceptical slant to his mouth and eyebrows, intended to show doubt of the worth of any or all of my assessments. I continued without rancour through everything of any interest, and at the end he said, 'Tell Etty I want a list of the work done by each horse, and its progress.'

'All right,' I agreed readily. He searched my face for signs of resentment and seemed a shade disappointed when he didn't find any. The antagonism of an ageing and infirm father towards a fully grown healthy son was a fairly universal manifestation throughout nature, and I wasn't fussed that he was showing it. But all the same I was not going to give him the satisfaction of feeling he had scored over me; and he had no idea of how practised I was at taking the prideful flush out of people's ill-natured victories.

I said merely, 'Shall I take a list of the entries home, so that Etty will know which races the horses are to be prepared for?'

His eyes narrowed and his mouth tightened, and he explained that it had been impossible for him to do the entries: treatment and X-rays took up so much of his time and he was not left alone long enough to concentrate.

'Shall Etty and I have a go, between us?'

'Certainly not. I will do them . . . when I have more time.'

'All right,' I said equably. 'How is the leg feeling? You are certainly looking more your own self now . . .'

'It is less troublesome,' he admitted. He smoothed the already wrinkle-free bed clothes which lay over his stomach, engaged in his perennial habit of making his surroundings as orderly, as dignified, as starched as his soul.

I asked if there was anything I could bring him. 'A book,' I suggested. 'Or some fruit? Or some champagne?' Like most racehorse trainers he saw champagne as a sort of superior Coca Cola, best drunk in the mornings if at all, but he knew that as a pick-me-up for the sick it had few equals.

He inclined his head sideways, considering. 'There are some half bottles in the cellar at Rowley Lodge.'

'I'll bring some,' I said.

He nodded. He would never, whatever I did, say thank you. I smiled inwardly. The day my father thanked me would be the day his personality disintegrated.

Via the hospital telephone I checked whether I would be welcome at Hampstead, and having received a warming affirmative, headed the Jensen along the further eight miles south.

Gillie had finished painting the bedroom but its furniture was still stacked in the hall.

'Waiting for the carpet,' she explained. 'Like Godot.'

'Godot never came,' I commented.

'That,' she agreed with exaggerated patience, 'is what I mean.'

'Send up rockets, then.'

'Fire crackers have been going off under backsides since Tuesday.'

'Never mind,' I said soothingly. 'Come out to dinner.'

'I'm on a grapefruit day,' she objected.

'Well I'm not. Positively not. I had no lunch and I'm hungry.'

'I've got a really awfully nice grapefruit recipe. You put the halves in the oven doused in saccharine and Kirsch and eat it hot . . .'

'No,' I said definitely. 'I'm going to the Empress.'

That shattered the grapefruit programme. She adored the Empress.

'Oh well . . . it would be so boring for you to eat alone,' she said. 'Wait a mo while I put on my tatty black.'

Her tatty black was a long-sleeved St. Laurent dress that made the least of her curves. There was nothing approaching tatty about it, very much on the contrary, and her description was inverted, as if by diminishing its standing she could forget her guilt over its price. She had recently developed some vaguely socialist views, and it had mildly begun to bother her that what she had paid for one dress would have supported a ten-child family throughout Lent.

Dinner at the Empress was its usual quiet, spacious, superb self. Gillie ordered curried prawns to be followed by chicken in a cream and brandy sauce, and laughed when she caught my ironic eye.

'Back to the grapefruit,' she agreed. 'But not until tomorrow.'

'How are the suffering orphans?' I asked. She worked three days a week for an adoption society which because of the Pill and easy abortion was running out of its raw materials.

'You don't happen to want two-year-old twins, Afro-Asian boys, one of them with a squint?' she said.

'Not all that much, no.'

'Poor little things.' She absent-mindedly ate a bread roll spread with enjoyable chunks of butter. 'We'll never place them. They don't look even averagely attractive . . .'

'Squints can be put right,' I said.

'Someone has to care enough first, to get it done.'

We drank a lesser wine than Gillie's but better than most.

'Do you realise,' Gillie said, 'that a family of ten could live for a week on what this dinner is costing?'

'Perhaps the waiter has a family of ten,' I suggested. 'And if we didn't eat it, what would they live on?'

'Oh . . . Blah,' Gillie said, but looking speculatively at the man who brought her chicken.

She asked how my father was. I said better, but by no means well.

'He said he would do the entries,' I explained, 'but he hasn't started. He told me it was because he isn't given time, but the Sister says he sleeps a great deal. He had a frightful shaking and his system hasn't recovered yet.'

'What will you do, then, about the entries? Wait until he's better?'

'Can't. The next lot have to be in by Wednesday.'

'What happens if they aren't?'

'The horses will go on eating their heads off in the stable when they ought to be out on a racecourse trying to earn their keep. It's now or never to put their names down for some of the races at Chester and Ascot and the Craven meeting at Newmarket.'

'So you'll do them yourself,' she said matter-of-factly, 'And they'll all go and win.'

'Almost any entry is better than no entry at all,' I sighed. 'And by the law of averages, some of them must be right.'

'There you are, then. No more problems.'

But there were two more problems, and worse ones, sticking up like rocks on the fairway. The financial problem, which I could solve if I had to; and that of Alessandro, which I didn't yet know how to.

The following morning, he arrived late. The horses for first lot were already plodding round the cinder track, while I stood with Etty in the centre as she changed the riders, when Alessandro appeared through the gate from the yard. He waited for a space between the passing horses and then crossed the cinder track and came towards us.

The finery of the week before was undimmed. The boots shone as glossily, the gloves as palely, and the ski jacket and jodhpurs were still immaculate. On his head, however, he wore a blue and white striped woolly cap with a pompom, the same as most of the other lads: but on Alessandro this cosy protection against the stinging March wind looked as incongruous as a bowler hat on the beach.

I didn't even smile. The black eyes regarded me with their customary chill from features that were more gaunt than delicate. The strong shape of the bones showed clearly through the yellowish skin, and more so, it seemed to me, than a week ago.

'What do you weigh?' I asked abruptly.

He hesitated a little. 'I will be able to ride at six stone seven when the races begin. I will be able to claim all the allowances.'

'But now? What do you weigh now?'

'A few pounds more. But I will lose them.'

Etty fumed at him but forbore to point out to him that he wouldn't get any rides if he weren't good enough. She looked down at her list to see which horse she had allotted him, opened her mouth to tell him, and then shut it again, and I literally saw the impulse take hold of her.

'Ride Traffic,' she said. 'You can get up on Traffic.'

Alessandro stood very still.

'He doesn't have to,' I said to Etty; and to Alessandro, 'You don't have to ride Traffic. Only if you choose.'

He swallowed. He raised his chin and his courage, and said, 'I choose.'

With a stubborn set to her mouth Etty beckoned to Andy, who was already mounted on Traffic, and told him of the change.

'Happy to oblige,' Andy said feelingly, and gave Alessandro a leg-up into his unrestful place. Traffic lashed out into a few preliminary bucks, found he had a less hardbitten customer than usual on his back, and started off at a rapid sideways trot across the paddock.

Alessandro didn't fall off, which was the best that could be said. He hadn't the experience to settle the sour colt to obedience, let alone to teach him to be better, but he was managing a great deal more efficiently than I could have done.

Etty watched him with disfavour and told everyone to give him plenty of room.

'That nasty little squirt needs taking down a peg,' she said in unnecessary explanation.

'He isn't doing too badly,' I commented.

'Huh.' There was a ten ton lorry-load of scorn in her voice. 'Look at the way he's jabbing him in the mouth. You wouldn't catch Andy doing that in a thousand years.'

'Better not let him out on the Heath,' I said.

'Teach him a lesson,' Etty said doggedly.

'Might kill the goose, and then where would we be for golden eggs?'

She gave me a bitter glance. 'The stable doesn't need that sort of money.'

'The stable needs any sort of money it can get.'

But Etty shook her head in disbelief. Rowley Lodge had been in the top division of the big league ever since she had joined it, and no one would ever convince her that its very success was leading it into trouble.

I beckoned to Alessandro and he came as near as his rocking horse permitted.

'You don't have to ride him on the Heath,' I said.

Traffic turned his quarters towards us and Alessandro called over his shoulder: 'I stay here. I choose.'

Etty told him to ride fourth in the string and everyone else to keep out of his way. She herself climbed into Indigo's saddle, and I into Cloud Cuckoo-land's, and George opened the gates. We turned right on to the walking ground, bound for the canter on Warren Hill, and nothing frantic happened on the way except that Traffic practically backed into an incautious tout when crossing Moulton Road. The tout retreated with curses, calling the horse by name. The Newmarket touts knew every horse on the Heath by sight. A remarkable feat, as there were about two thousand animals in training there, hundreds of them two-year-olds which altered shape as they developed month by month. Touts learned horses like headmasters learned new boys, and rarely made a mistake. All I hoped was that this one had been too busy getting himself to safety to take much notice of the rider.

We had to wait our turn on Warren Hill as we were the fourth stable to choose to work there that morning. Alessandro walked Traffic round in circles a little way apart – or at least tried to walk him. Traffic's idea of walking would have tired a bucking bronco.

Eventually Etty sent the string off up the hill in small clusters, with me sitting half way up the slope on Cloud Cuckoo-land, watching them as they swept past. At the top of the hill they stopped, peeled off to the left, and went back down the central walking ground to collect again at the bottom. Most mornings each horse cantered up the hill twice, the sharpish incline getting a lot of work into them in a comparatively short distance.

Alessandro started up the hill in the last bunch, one of only four.

Long before he drew level with me I could see that of the two it was the horse who had control. Galloping was hard labour up Warren Hill, but no one had given Traffic the message.

As he passed me he was showing all the classic signs of the bolter in action: head stretched horizontally forward, bit gripped between his teeth, eyes showing the whites. Alessandro, with as much hope of dominating the situation as a virgin in a troop ship, hung grimly on to the neckstrap and appeared to be praying.

The top of the rise meant nothing to Traffic. He swerved violently to the left and set off sideways towards Bury Hill, not even having the sense to make straight for the stable but swinging too far north and missing it by half a mile. On he charged, his hooves thundering relentlessly over the turf, carrying Alessandro inexorably away in the general direction of Lowestoft.

Stifling the unworthy thought that I wouldn't care all that much if he plunged straight on into the North Sea, I reflected with a bit more sense that if Traffic damaged himself, Rowley Lodge's foundations would feel the tremor. I set off at a trot after him as he disappeared into the distance, but when I reached the Bury St. Edmunds Road there was no sign of him. I crossed the road and reined in there, wondering which direction to take.

A car came slowly towards me with a shocked looking driver poking his head out of the window.

'Some bloody madman nearly ploughed straight into me, he yelled. 'Some bloody madman on the road on a mad horse.'

'How very upsetting,' I shouted back sympathetically, but he glared at me balefully and nearly ran into a tree.

I went on along the road, wondering whether it would be a dumped-off Alessandro I saw first, and if so, how long it would take to find and retrieve the wayward Traffic.

From the next rise there was no sign of either of them: the road stretched emptily ahead. Beginning to get anxious, I quickened Cloud Cuckoo-land until we were trotting fast along the soft ground edging the tarmac.

Past the end of the Limekilns, still no trace of Alessandro. The road ran straight, down and up its inclines. No Alessandro. It was a good two miles from the training ground that I finally found him.

He was standing at the cross roads, dismounted, holding Traffic's reins. The colt had evidently run himself to a standstill, as he drooped there with his head down, his sides heaving, and sweat streaming from him all over. Flecks of foam spattered his neck, and his tongue lolled exhaustedly out.

I slid down from Cloud Cuckoo-land and ran my hand down Traffic's legs. No tenderness. No apparent strain. Sighing with relief, I straightened up and looked at Alessandro. His face was stiff, his eyes expressionless.

'Are you all right?' I asked.

He lifted his chin. 'Of course.'

'He's a difficult horse,' I remarked.

Alessandro didn't answer. His self-pride might have received a body blow, but he was not going to be so soft as to accept any comfort.

'You'd better walk back with him,' I said, 'Walk until he's thoroughly cooled down. And keep him out of the way of the cars.'

Alessandro tugged the reins and Traffic sluggishly turned, not moving his legs until he absolutely had to.

'What's that?' Alessandro said, pointing to a mound in the grass at the corner of the cross roads where he had been standing. He shoved Traffic further away so that I could see; but I had no need to.

'It's the boy's grave,' I said.

'What boy?' He was startled. The small grave was known to everyone in Newmarket, but not to him. The mound, about four feet long, was outlined with overlapping wire hoops, like the edges of lawns in parks. There were some dirty looking plastic daffodils entwined in the hoops, and a few dying flowers scattered in the centre. Also a white plastic drinking mug which someone had thrown there. The grave looked forlorn, yet in a futile sort of way, cared for.

'There are a lot of legends,' I said. 'The most likely is that he was a shepherd boy who went to sleep in charge of his flock. A wolf came and killed half of them, and when he woke up he was so remorseful that he hanged himself.'

'They used to bury suicides at cross roads,' Alessandro said, nodding. 'It is well known.'

There didn't seem to be any harm in trying to humanise him, so I went on with the story.

'The grave is always looked after, in a haphazard sort of way. It is never overgrown, and fresh flowers are often put there . . . No one knows exactly who puts them there, but it is supposed to be the gypsies. And there is also a legend that in May the flowers on the grave are in the colours that will win the Derby.'

Alessandro stared down at the pathetic little memorial.

'There are no black flowers,' he said slowly: and Archangel's colours were black, pale blue, and gold.

'The gypsies will solve that if they have to,' I said dryly: and thought that they would opt for an easier-to-stage nap selection.

I turned Cloud Cuckoo-land in the direction of home and walked away. When presently I looked back, Alessandro was walking Traffic quietly along the side of the road, a thin straight figure in his clean clothes and bright blue and white cap. It was a pity, I thought, that he was as he was. With a different father, he might have been a different person.

But with a different father, so would I. And who wouldn't.

I thought about it all the way back to Rowley Lodge. Fathers, it seemed to me, could train, feed or warp their young plants, but they couldn't affect their basic nature. They might produce a stunted oak or a luxuriant weed, but oak and weed were inborn qualities, which would prevail in the end. Alessandro, on such a horticultural reckoning, was like a cross between holly and deadly nightshade; and if his father had his way the red berries would lose out to the black.

Alessandro bore Etty's strongly implied scorn with a frozen face, but few of the other lads teased him on his return, as they would have done to one of their own sort. Most of them seemed to be instinctively afraid of him, which to my mind showed their good sense, and the other, less sensitive types had drifted into the defence mechanism of ignoring his existence.

George took Traffic off to his box, and Alessandro followed me into the office. His glance swept over Margaret, sitting at her desk in a neat navy blue dress with the high curls piled as elaborately as ever, but he saw her as no bar to giving me the benefit of the thoughts that he, evidently, had also had time for on the way back.

'You should not have made me ride such a badly trained horse,' he began belligerently.

'I didn't make you. You chose to.'

'Miss Craig told me to ride it to make a fool of me.'

True enough.

'You could have refused,' I said.

'I could not.'

'You could have said that you thought you needed more practice before taking on the worst ride in the yard.'

His nostrils flared. So self-effacing an admission would have been beyond him.

'Anyway,' I went on. 'I personally don't think riding Traffic is going to teach you most. So you won't be put on him again.'

'But I insist,' he said vehemently.

'You insist what?'

'I insist I ride Traffic again.' He gave me the haughtiest of his selection of stares, and added, 'Tomorrow.'

'Why?'

'Because if I do not, everyone will think it is because I cannot, or that I am afraid to.'

'So you do care,' I said matter-of-factly, 'What the others think of you.'

'No, I do not.' He denied it strongly.

'Then why ride the horse?'

He compressed his strong mouth stubbornly. 'I will answer no more questions. I will ride Traffic tomorrow.'

'Well, O.K.,' I said casually. 'But I'm not sending him on the Heath tomorrow. He'll hardly need another canter. Tomorrow he'll only be walking round the cinder track in the paddock, which will be very boring for you.'

He gave me a concentrated, suspicious, considering stare, trying to work out if I was meaning to undermine him. Which I was, if one can call taking the point out of a Grand Gesture, undermining.

'Very well,' he said grudgingly. 'I will ride him round the paddock.'

He turned on his heel and walked out of the office. Margaret watched him go with a mixed expression I couldn't read.

'Mr. Griffon would never stand for him talking like that,' she said.

'Mr. Griffon doesn't have to.'

'I can see why Etty can't bear him,' she said. 'He's insolent. There's no other word for it. Insolent.' She handed me three opened letters across the desk. 'These need your attention, if you don't mind.' She reverted to Alessandro: 'But all the same, he's beautiful.'

'He's no such thing,' I protested mildly. 'If anything, he's ugly.'

She smiled briefly. 'He's absolutely loaded with sex appeal.'

I lowered the letters. 'Don't be silly. He has the sex appeal of a bag of rusty nails.'

'You wouldn't notice,' she said judiciously, 'Being a man.'

I shook my head. 'He's only eighteen.'

'Age has nothing to do with it,' she said. 'Either you've got it, or you haven't got it, right from the start. And he's got it.'

I didn't pay much attention: Margaret herself had so little sex appeal that I didn't think her a reliable judge. When I'd read through the letters and agreed with her how she should answer them, I went along to the kitchen for some coffee.

The remains of the night's work lay littered about: the various dregs of brandy, cold milk, coffee, and masses of scribbled-on bits of paper. It had taken me most of the night to do the entries; a night I would far rather have spent lying warmly in Gillie's bed.

The entries had been difficult, not only because I had never done them before, and had to read the conditions of each race several times to make sure I understood them, but also because of Alessandro. I had to make a balance of what I would have done without him, and what I would have to let him ride if he were still there in a month's time.

I was taking his father's threats seriously. Part of the time I thought I was foolish to do so; but that abduction a week ago had been no playful joke, and until I was certain Enso would not let loose a thunderbolt it was more prudent to go along with his son. I still had nearly a month before the Flat season started, still nearly a month to see a way out. But, just in case, I had put down some of the better prospects for apprentice races, and had duplicated the entries in many open races, because if two ran there would be one for Alessandro. Also I entered a good many in the lesser meetings, particularly those in the north: because whether he liked it or not, Alessandro was not going to start his career in a glaze of limelight. After all that I dug around in the office until I found the book in which old Robinson had recorded all the previous years' entries, and I checked my provisional list against what my father had done. After subtracting about twenty names, because I had been much too lavish, and shuffling things around a little, I made the total number of entries for that week approximately the same as those for the year before, except that I still had more in the north. But I wrote the final list on to the official yellow form, in block letters as requested, and double checked again to make sure I hadn't entered two-year-olds in handicaps, or fillies in colts-only, and made any other such giveaway gaffs.

When I gave the completed form to Margaret to record and then post, all she said was, 'This isn't your father's writing.'

'No,' I said. 'He dictated the entries. I wrote them down.'

She nodded non-committally, and whether she believed me or not I had no idea.

Alessandro rode Pullitzer competently next day at first lot, and kept himself to himself. After breakfast he returned with a stony face that forbade comment, and when the main string had started out for the Heath, was given a leg-up on to Traffic. Looking back from the gate I saw the fractious colt kicking away at shadows as usual, and noticed that the two other lads detailed to stay in and walk their charges were keeping well away from him.

When we returned an hour and a quarter later, George was holding Traffic's reins, the other lads had dismounted, and Alessandro was lying on the ground in an unconscious heap.

Chapter Seven

'Traffic just bucked him off, sir,' one of the lads said. 'Just bucked him clean off, sir. And he hit his head on the paddock rail, sir.'

'Just this minute, sir,' added the other anxiously.

They were both about sixteen, both apprentices, both tiny, neither of them very bold. I thought it unlikely they would have done anything purposely to upset Traffic further and bring the stuck-up Alessandro literally down to earth, but one never knew. What I did know was that Alessandro's continuing health was essential to my own.

'George,' I said, 'Put Traffic away in his box, and Etty ...' she was at my shoulder, clicking her tongue but not looking over-sorry, 'Is there anything we can use as a stretcher?'

'There's one in the tackroom,' she said, nodding, and told Ginge to go and get it.

The stretcher turned out to be a minimal affair of a piece of grubby green canvas slung between two uneven shaped poles, which looked as though they might once have been a pair of oars. By the time Ginge returned with it my heart-beat had descended from Everest: Alessandro was alive and not in too deep a coma, and Enso's pistol would not yet be popping me off in revenge to kingdom come.

As far as I could tell, none of his bones was broken, but I took exaggerated care over lifting him on to the stretcher. Etty disapproved: she would have had George and Ginge lift him up by his wrists and ankles and sling him on like a sack of corn. I, more moderately, told George and Ginge to lift him gently, carry him down to the house, and put him on the sofa in the owner's room. Following, I detoured off into the office and asked Margaret to telephone for a doctor.

Alessandro was stirring when I went into the owners' room. George and Ginge stood looking down at him, one elderly and resigned, one young and pugnacious, neither of them feeling any sympathy with the patient.

'O.K.,' I said to them. 'That's the lot. The doctor's coming for him.'

Both of them looked as if they would like to say a lot, but they ambled out tight-lipped and aired their opinions in the yard.

Alessandro opened his eyes, and for the first time looked a little vulnerable. He didn't know what had happened, didn't know where he was or how he had got there. The puzzlement formed new lines on his face; made it look younger and softer. Then his eyes focused on my face and in one bound a lot of memory came back. The dove dissolved into the hawk. It was like watching the awakening of a spastic, from loose-limbed peace up to tightness and jangle.

'What happened?' he asked.

'Traffic threw you.'

'Oh,' he said more weakly than he liked. He shut his eyes and through his teeth emitted one heartfelt word. 'Sod.'

There was a sudden commotion at the door and the chauffeur plunged into the room with Margaret trying to cling to one arm. He threw her effortlessly out of his way and shaped up to do the same to me.

'What has happened?' he demanded threateningly. 'What are you doing to the son?' His voice set up a shiver in my spine. If he wasn't one of the rubber-faces, he sounded exactly like it.

Alessandro spoke from the sofa with tiredness in his voice: and he spoke in Italian, which thanks to a one-time girl friend I more or less understood.

'Stop, Carlo. Go back to the car. Wait for me. The horse threw me. Neil Griffon will not harm me. Go back to the car, and wait for me.'

Carlo moved his head to and fro like a baffled bull, but finally subsided and did as he was told. Three sotto voce cheers for the discipline of the Rivera household.

'A doctor is coming to see you,' I said.

'I do not want a doctor.'

'You're not leaving that sofa until I'm certain there is nothing wrong with you.'

He sneered, 'Afraid of my father?'

'Think what you like,' I said; and he obviously did.

The doctor, when he came, turned out to be the same one who had once diagnosed my mumps, measles and chickenpox. Old now, with overactive lacrymal glands and hesitant speech, he did not in the least appeal to his present patient. Alessandro treated him rudely, and got back courtesy where he deserved a smart kick.

'Nothing much wrong with the lad,' was the verdict. 'But he'd better stay in bed today, and rest tomorrow. That'll put you right, young man, eh?'

The young man glared back ungratefully and didn't answer. The old doctor turned to me, gave me a tolerant smile and said to let him know if the lad had any after effects, like dizziness or headaches.

'Old fool,' said the lad audibly, as I showed the doctor out; and when I went back he was already on his feet.

'Can I go now?' he asked sarcastically.

'As far and for as long as you like,' I agreed.

His eyes narrowed. 'You are not getting rid of me.'

'Pity,' I said.

After a short furious silence he walked a little unsteadily past me and out of the door. I went into the office and with Margaret watched through the window while the chauffeur bustled around, settling him comfortably into the back seat of the Mercedes; and presently, without looking back, he drove 'the son' away.

'Is he all right?' Margaret asked.

'Shaken, not stirred,' I said flippantly, and she laughed. But she followed the car with her eyes until it turned left down Bury Road.

He stayed away the following day but came back on the Thursday morning in time for the first lot. I was up in the top part of the yard talking to Etty when the car arrived. Her pleasant expression changed to the one of tight-lipped dislike which she always wore when Alessandro was near her, and when she saw him erupting athletically from the back seat and striding purposefully towards us she discovered something that urgently needed seeing to in one of the bays further down.

Alessandro noted her flight with a twist of scorn on his lips, and widened it into an irritating smirk as a greeting to me. He held out a small flat tin box, identical with the one he had presented before.

'Message for you,' he said. All the cockiness was back fortissimo, and I would have known even without the tin that he had again been to see his father. He had recharged his malice like a battery plugged into the mains.

'Do you know what is in it, this time?'

He hesitated. 'No,' he said. And this time I believed him, because his ignorance seemed to annoy him. The tin was fastened round the edge with adhesive tape. Alessandro with the superior smirk still in place watched me pull it off. I rolled the tape into a small sticky ball and put it in my pocket: then carefully I opened the tin.

There was another little wooden horse between two thin layers of cotton wool.

It had a label round its neck.

It had a broken leg.

I didn't know what exactly was in my face when I looked up at Alessandro, but the smirk deteriorated into a half-anxious bravado.

'He said you wouldn't like it,' he remarked defiantly.

'Come with me, then,' I said abruptly. 'And see if you do.' I set off up the yard towards the drive, but he didn't follow: and before I reached my destination I was met by George hurrying towards me with a distressed face and worried eyes.

'Mr. Neil . . . Indigo's got cast and broken a leg in his box . . . same as Moonrock . . . you wouldn't think it could happen, not to two old'uns like them, not ten days apart.'

'No, you wouldn't,' I said grimly, and walked back with him into Indigo's box stuffing the vicious message in its tin into my jacket pocket.

The nice-natured gelding was lying in the straw trying feebly to stand up. He kept lifting his head and pushing at the floor with one of his forefeet, but all strength seemed to have left him. The other forefoot lay uselessly bent at an unnatural angle, snapped through just above the pastern.

I squatted down beside the poor old horse and patted his neck. He lifted his head again and thrashed to get back on to his feet, then flopped limply back into the straw. His eyes looked glazed, and he was dribbling.

'Nothing to be done, George,' I said. 'I'll go and telephone the vet.' I put only regret into my voice and kept my boiling fury to myself. George nodded resignedly but without much emotion: like every older stableman he had seen a lot of horses die.

The young chubby Dainsee got out of his bath to answer the telephone. 'Not another one!' he exclaimed, when I explained.

'I'm afraid so. And would you bring with you any gear you need for doing a blood test?'

'Whatever for?'

'I'll tell you when you get here . . .'

'Oh,' he sounded surprised, but willing to go along. 'All right then. Half a jiffy while I swop the bath towel for my natty suiting.'

He came in jeans, his dirty Land-Rover, and twenty minutes. Bounced out on to the gravel, nodded cheerfully, and turned at once towards Indigo's box. George was along there with the horse, but the rest of the yard stood quiet and empty. Etty, showing distress at the imminent loss of her lead horse, had taken the string down to Southfields on the racecourse side, and Alessandro presumably had gone with her, as he was nowhere about, and his chauffeur was waiting as usual in the car.

Indigo was up on his feet. George, holding him by the headcollar, said that the old boy just suddenly seemed to get his strength back and stood up, and he'd been eating some hay since then, and it was a right shame he'd got cast, that it was. I nodded and took the headcollar from him, and told him I'd see to Indigo, and he could go and get on with putting the oats through the crushing machine ready for the morning feeds.

'He makes a good yard man,' Dainsee said. 'Old George, he was deputy head gardener once at the Viceroy's palace in India. It accounts for all those tidy flower beds and tubs of pretty shrubs which charm the owners when they visit the yard.'

I was surprised. 'I didn't know that . . .'

'Odd world.' He soothed Indigo with a touch, and peered closely at the broken leg. 'What's all this about a blood test?' he asked, straightening up and eyeing me with speculation.

'Do vets have a keep-mum tradition?'

His gaze sharpened into active curiosity. 'Professional secrets, like doctors and lawyers? Yes, sure we do. As long as it's not a matter of keeping quiet about a spot of foot and mouth.'

'Nothing like that.' I hesitated. 'I'd like you to run a private blood test . . . could that be done?'

'How private? It'll have to go to the Equine Research Labs. I can't do it myself, haven't got the equipment.'

'Just a blood sample with no horse's name attached.'

'Oh sure. That happens all the time. But you can't really think anyone *doped* the poor old horse!'

'I think he was given an anaesthetic,' I said. 'And that his leg was broken on purpose.'

'Oh glory.' His mouth was rounded into an O of astonishment, but the eyes flickered with the rapidity of his thoughts. 'You seem sane enough,' he said finally, 'So let's have a look see.'

He squatted down beside the affected limb and ran his fingers very lightly down over the skin. Indigo shifted under his touch and ducked and raised his head violently.

'All right, old fellow,' Dainsee said, standing up again and patting his neck. He raised his eyebrows at me, 'Can't say you're wrong, can't say you're right.' He paused, thinking it over. The eyebrows rose and fell several times, like punctuations. 'Tell you what,' he said at length. 'I've got a portable X-ray machine back home. I'll bring it along, and we'll take a picture. How's that?'

'Very good idea,' I said, pleased.

'Right.' He opened his case, which he had parked just inside the door. 'Then I'll just freeze that leg, so he'll be in no discomfort until I come back.' He brought out a hypodermic and held it up against the light, beginning to press the plunger.

'Do the blood test first,' I said.

'Eh?' He blinked at me. 'Oh yes, of course. Golly, yes of course. Silly of me.' He laughed gently, laid down the first syringe and put together a much larger one, empty.

He took the sample from the jugular vein, which he found and pierced efficiently first time of asking. 'Bit of luck,' he murmured in self deprecation, and drew half a tumbler full of blood into the syringe. 'Have to give the Lab people enough to work on, you know,' he said, seeing my surprise. 'You can't get reliable results from a thimbleful.'

'I suppose not . . .'

He packed the sample into his case, shot the freezing local into Indigo's near fore, nodded and blinked with undiminished cheerfulness, and smartly departed. Indigo, totally unconcerned, went back contentedly to his haynet, and I with bottled anger went into the house.

The label on the little wooden horse had 'Indigo' printed in capitals on one side of it, and on the other, also in capitals, a short sharp message.

'To hurt my son is to invite destruction.'

Neither George nor Etty saw any sense in the vet going away without putting Indigo down.

'Er . . .' I said. 'He found he didn't have the humane killer with him after all. He thought it was in his bag, but it wasn't.'

'Oh,' they said, satisfied, and Etty told me that everything had gone well on the gallops and that Lucky Lindsay had worked a fast five furlongs and afterwards wouldn't have blown out a candle.

'I put that bloody little Alex on Clip Clop and told him to take him along steadily, and he damn well disobeyed me. He shook him into a full gallop and left Lancat standing, and the touts' binoculars were working overtime.

'Stupid little fool,' I agreed. 'I'll speak to him.'

'He takes every opportunity he can to cross me,' she complained. 'When you aren't there he's absolutely insufferable.' She took a deep, troubled breath, considering. 'In fact, I think you should tell Mr. Griffon that we can't keep him.'

'Next time I go to the hospital, I'll see what he says,' I said. 'What are you giving him to ride, second lot?'

'Pullitzer,' she replied promptly. 'It doesn't matter so much if he doesn't do as he's told on that one.'

'When you get back, tell him I want to see him before he leaves.'

'Aren't you coming?'

I shook my head. 'I'll stay and see to Indigo.'

'I rather wanted your opinion of Pease Pudding. If he's to run in the Lincoln we ought to give him a trial this week or next. The race is only three weeks on Saturday, don't forget.'

'We could give him a half speed gallop tomorrow and see if he's ready for a full trial,' I suggested, and she grudgingly agreed that one more day would do no harm.

I watched the trim jodhpured figure walk off towards her cottage for breakfast, and would have felt flattered that she wanted my opinion had I not known why. Under an umbrella, she worked marvellously: out in the open, she felt rudderless. Even though in her heart she knew she knew more than I did, her shelter instinct had cast me as decision maker. What I needed now was a crash course in how to tell when a horse was fit ... and that old joke about a crash course for pilots edged itself into a corner of my mind, like a thin gleam in the gloom.

Dainsee came back in his Land-Rover when the string had gone out for second lot, and we ran the cable for the X-ray machine through the office window and plugged it into the socket which served the mushroom heater. There seemed to be unending reinforcements of cable: it took four lengths plugged together to reach to Indigo's box, but their owner assured me that he could manage a quarter of a mile, if pushed.

He took three X-rays of the dangling leg, packed everything up again, and almost as a passing thought, put poor old Indigo out of his troubles.

'You'll want evidence for the police,' Dainsee said, shaking hands and blinking rapidly.

'No ... I shan't bother the police. Not yet, anyway.' He opened his mouth to protest, so I went straight on, 'There are very good reasons. I can't tell you them ... but they do exist.'

'Oh well, it's up to you.' His eyes slid sideways towards Moonrock's box, and his eyebrows asked the question.

'I don't know,' I said. 'What do you think? Looking back.'

He thought for several seconds, which meant he was serious, and then said 'It would have taken a good heavy blow to smash the hock. Wouldn't have thought anyone would bother, when a pastern like Indigo's would be simple.'

'Moonrock just provided the idea for Indigo?' I suggested.

'I should think so.' He grinned. 'Mind it doesn't become an epidemic.'

'I'll mind,' I said lightly; and knew I would have to.

Alessandro showed no sign that Etty had given him my message about wanting to see him. He strode straight out of the yard towards his waiting car and it was only because I happened to be looking out of the office window that I caught him.'

I opened the window and called to him. 'Alessandro, come here a minute . . .'

He forged straight on as if he hadn't heard, so I added 'To talk about your first races.'

He stopped in one stride with a foot left in the air in indecision, then changed direction and came more slowly towards the window.

'Go round into the owners' room,' I said. 'Where you were lying on the sofa . . .' I shut the window, gave Margaret a whimsical rueful placating smile which could mean whatever she thought it did, and removed myself from earshot.

Alessandro came unwillingly into the owners' room, knowing that he had been hooked. I played fair, however.

'You can have a ride in an apprentice race at Catterick four weeks today. On Pullitzer. And on condition that you don't go bragging about it in the yard and antagonising all the other boys.'

'I want to ride Archangel,' he said flatly.

'It sometimes seems to me that you are remarkably intelligent and with a great deal of application might become a passable jockey,' I said, and before his self-satisfaction smothered him, added, 'And sometimes, like today, you behave so stupidly and with such little understanding of what it takes to be what you want to be, that your ambitions look pathetic.'

The thin body stiffened rigidly and the black eyes glared. Since I undoubtedly had his full attention, I made the most of it.

'These horses are here to win races. They won't win races if their training programme is hashed up. If you are told to do a half speed gallop on Clip Clop and you work him flat out and tire him beyond his capacity, you are helping to make sure he takes longer to prepare. You won't win races unless the stable does, so it is in your interest to help train the horses to the best of your ability. Disobeying riding orders is therefore just plain stupid. Do you follow?'

The black eyes looked blacker and sank into the sockets. He didn't answer.

'Then there is this fixation of yours about Archangel. I'll let you ride him on the Heath as soon as you show you are good enough, and in particular responsible enough to look after him. Whether you ever ride him in a race is up to you, more than me. But I'm doing you a favour in starting you off on less well known horses at smaller meetings. You may think you are brilliant, but you have only ridden against amateurs. I am giving you a chance to prove what you can do against professionals in private, and lessening the risk of you falling flat on your face at Newbury or Kempton.'

The eyes were unwavering. He still said nothing.

'And Indigo,' I went on, taking a grip on my anger and turning it out cold and biting, 'Indigo may have been of no use to you because he no longer raced, but if you cause the death of any more of the horses there will be just one less for you to win on.'

He moved his jaw as if with an effort.

'I didn't . . . cause the death of Indigo.'

I took the tin out of my pocket and gave it to him. He opened it slowly, compressed his mouth at the contents, and read the label.

'I didn't want . . . I didn't mean him to kill Indigo.' The supercilious smile had all gone. He was still hostile, but defensive. 'He was angry because Traffic had thrown me.'

'Did you mean him to kill Traffic, then?'

'No, I did not,' he said vehemently. 'As you said, what would be the point of killing a horse I could win a race on?'

'But to kill harmless old Indigo because you bumped your head off a horse you yourself insisted on riding . . .' I protested with bitter sarcasm.

His gaze, for the first time, switched to the carpet. Somewhere, deep down, he was not too proud of himself.

'You didn't tell him,' I guessed. 'You didn't tell him that you insisted on riding Traffic.'

'Miss Craig told me to,' he said sullenly.

'Not the time he threw you.'

He looked up again, and I would have sworn he was unhappy. 'I didn't tell my father I was knocked out.'

'Who did?'

'Carlo. The chauffeur.'

'You could have explained that I did not try to harm you.'

The unhappiness turned to a shade of desperation.

'You have met him,' he said. 'It isn't always possible to tell him things, especially when he is angry. He will give me anything I ask for, but I cannot talk to him.'

He went away and left me speechless.

He couldn't talk to his father.

Enso would give Alessandro anything he wanted . . . would smash a path for him at considerable trouble to himself and would persist as long as Alessandro hungered, but they couldn't talk.

And I . . . I could lie and scheme and walk a tightrope to save my father's stables for him.

But talk with him, no, I couldn't.

Chapter Eight

'Did you know,' Margaret said, looking up casually from her typewriter, 'That Alessandro is living down the road at the Forbury Inn?'

'No, I didn't,' I said, 'But it doesn't surprise me. It goes with a chauffeur-driven Mercedes, after all.'

'He has a double room to himself with a private bathroom, and doesn't eat enough to keep a bird alive.'

'How do you know all this?'

'Susie brought a friend home from school for tea yesterday and she turned out to be the daughter of the resident receptionist at the Forbury Inn.'

'Any more fascinating intimate details?' I asked.

She smiled. 'Alessandro puts on a track suit every afternoon and goes off in the car and when he comes back he is all sweaty and has a very hot bath with nice smelly oil in it.'

'The receptionist's daughter is how old?'

'Seven.'

'Proper little snooper.'

'All children are observant ... And she also said that he never talks to anyone if he can avoid it except to his chauffeur in a funny language ...'

'Italian,' I murmured.

'... and that nobody likes him very much because he is pretty rude, but they like the chauffeur still less because he is even ruder.'

I pondered. 'Do you think,' I said, 'That via your daughter, via her school chum, via her receptionist parent, we could find out if Alessandro gave any sort of home address when he registered?'

'Why don't you just ask him?' she said reasonably.

'Ah,' I said. 'But our Alessandro is sometimes a mite contrary. Didn't you ask him, when you completed his indentures?'

'He said they were moving, and had no address.'

'Mm,' I nodded.

'How extraordinary ... I can't see why he won't tell you. Well, yes, I'll ask Susie's chum if she knows.'

'Great,' I said, and pinned little hope on it.

Gillie wanted to come and stay at Rowley Lodge.

'How about the homeless orphans?' I said.

'I could take some weeks off. I always can. You know that. And now that you've stopped wandering round industrial towns living in one hotel after another, we could spend a bit more time together.'

I kissed her nose. Ordinarily I would have welcomed her proposal. I looked at her with affection.

'No,' I said. 'Not just now.'

'When, then?'

'In the summer.'

She made a face at me, her eyes full of intelligence. 'You never like to be cluttered when you are deeply involved in something.'

'You're not clutter,' I smiled.

'I'm afraid so ... That's why you've never married. Not like most bachelors because they want to be free to sleep with any offered girl, but because you don't like your mind to be distracted.'

'I'm here,' I pointed out, kissing her again.

'For one night in seven. And only then because you had to come most of the way to see your father.'

'My father gets visited because he's on the way to you.'

'Liar,' she said equably. 'The best you can say is that it's two cats with one stone.'

'Birds.'

'Well, birds, then.'

'Let's go eat,' I said; opened the front door and closed it behind us, and packed her into the Jensen.

'Did you know that Aristotle Onassis had earned himself a whole million by the time he was twenty-eight?'

'No, I didn't know,' I said.

'He beat you,' she said. 'By four times as much.'

'He's four times the man.'

Her eyes slid sideways towards me and a smile hovered in the air. 'He may be.'

We stopped for a red light and then turned left beside a church with a notice board saying 'These doth the Lord hate: a proud look, a lying tongue. Proverbs 6. 16-17'.

'Which proverb do you think is the most stupid?' she asked.

'Um . . . Bird in the hand is worth two in the bush.'

'Why ever?'

'Because if you build a cage round the bush you get a whole flock.'

'As long as the two birds aren't both the same sex.'

'You think of everything,' I said admiringly.

'Oh, I try. I try.'

We went up to the top of the Post Office Tower and revolved three and a half times during dinner.

'It said in *The Times* today that that paper firm you advised last autumn has gone bust,' she said.

'Well . . .' I grinned. 'They didn't take my advice.'

'Silly old them . . . What was it?'

'To sack ninety per cent of the management, get some new accountants, and make peace with the unions.'

'So simple, really.' Her mouth twitched.

'They said they couldn't do it, of course.'

'And you said?'

'Prepare to meet thy doom.'

'How biblical.'

'Or words to that effect.'

'Think of all those poor people thrown out of work,' she said. 'It can't be funny when a firm goes bust.'

'The firm had hired people all along in the wrong proportions. By last autumn they had only two productive workers for every one on the clerical, executive and maintenance staff. Also the unions were vetoing automation, and insisting that every time a worker left another should be hired in his place.'

She pensively bit into paté and toast. 'It doesn't sound as if it could have been saved at all.'

'Yes, it could,' I said reflectively, 'But it often seems to me that people in a firm would rather see the whole ship sink than throw out half of the crew and stay afloat.'

'Fairer to everyone if they all drown?'

'Only the firm drowns. The people swim off and make sure they overload someone else's raft.'

She licked her fingers. 'You used to find sick firms fascinating.'

'I still do,' I said, surprised.

She shook her head. 'Disillusion has been creeping in for a long time.'

I looked back, considering. 'It's usually quite easy to see what's wrong. But there's often a stone-wall resistance on both sides to putting it right. Always dozens of reasons why change is impossible.'

'Russell Arletti rang me up yesterday,' she said casually.

'Did he really?'

She nodded. 'He wanted me to persuade you to leave Newmarket and do a job for him. A big one, he said.'

'I can't,' I said positively.

'He's taking me out to dinner on Tuesday evening to discuss, as he put it, how to wean you from the gee-gees.'

'Tell him to save himself the price of a meal.'

'Well no . . . she wrinkled her nose. 'I might just be hungry again by Tuesday. I'll go out with him. I like him. But I think I'll spend the evening preparing him for the worst.'

'What worst?'

'That you won't ever be going back to work for him.'

'Gillie . . .'

'It was only a phase,' she said, looking out of the window at the sparkle of the million lights slowly sliding by below us. 'It was just that you'd cashed in your antique chips and you weren't exactly starving, and Russell netted you on the wing, so to speak, with an interesting diversion. But you've been getting tired of it recently. You've been restless, and too full of . . . I don't know . . . too full of power. I think that after you've played with the gee-gees you'll break out in a great gust and build a new empire . . . much bigger than before.'

'Have some wine?' I said ironically.

'. . . and you may scoff, Neil Griffon, but you've been letting your Onassis instinct go to rust.'

'Not a bad thing, really.'

'You could be creating jobs for thousands of people, instead of trotting round a small town in a pair of jodhpurs.'

'There's six million quid's worth in that stable,' I said slowly; and felt the germ of an idea lurch as it sometimes did across the ganglions.

'What are you thinking about?' she demanded. 'What are you thinking about at this moment?'

'The genesis of ideas.'

She gave a sigh that was half a laugh. 'And that's exactly why you'll never marry me, either.'

'What do you mean?'

'You like *The Times* crossword more than sex.'

'Not more,' I said. 'First.'

'Do you want me to marry you?'

She kissed my shoulder under the sheet.

'Would you?'

'I thought you were fed up with marriage.' I moved my mouth against her forehead. 'I thought Jeremy had put you off it for life.'

'He wasn't like you.'

He wasn't like you ... She said it often. Any time her husband's name cropped up. He wasn't like you.

The first time she said it, three months after I met her, I asked the obvious question.

'What was he like?'

'Fair, not dark. Willowy, not compact. A bit taller; six feet two. Outwardly more fun; inwardly, infinitely more boring. He didn't want a wife so much as an admiring audience ... and I got tired of the play.' She paused. 'And when Jennifer died ...'

She had not talked about her ex-husband before, and had always shied painfully away from the thought of her daughter. She went on in a careful emotionless quiet voice, half muffled against my skin.

'Jennifer was killed in front of me ... by a youth in a leather jacket on a motor-cycle. We were crossing the road. He came roaring round the corner doing sixty in a built-up area. He just ... ploughed into her ...' A long shuddering pause. 'She was eight ... and super.' She swallowed. 'The boy had no insurance ... Jeremy raved on and on about it, as if money could have compensated ... and we didn't need money, he'd inherited almost as much as I had ...' Another pause. 'So, anyway, after that, when he found someone else and drifted off, I was glad, really ...'

Though passing time had done its healing, she still had dreams about Jennifer. Sometimes she cried when she woke up, because of Jennifer.

I smoothed her shining hair. 'I'd make a lousy husband.'

'Oh ...' She took a shaky breath. 'I know that. Two and a half years I've known you, and you've blown in every millennium or so, to say Hi.'

'But stayed a while.'

'I'll grant you.'

'So what do you want?' I asked. 'Would you rather be married?'

She smiled contentedly. 'We'll go on as we are ... if you like.'

'I do like.' I switched off the light.

'As long as you prove it now and again,' she added unnecessarily.

'I wouldn't let anyone else,' I said, 'Hang pink and green curtains against ochre walls in my bedroom.'

'My bedroom. I rent it.'

'You're in arrears. By at least eighteen months.'

'I'll pay up tomorrow ... Hey, what are you doing?'

'I'm a business man,' I murmured, 'Getting down to business.'

Neville Knollys Griffon did not make it easy for me to start a new era in father-son relationships.

He told me that as I did not seem to be making much progress in engaging someone else to take over the stable, he was going to find someone himself. By telephone.

He said he had done some of the entries for the next two weeks, and that Margaret was to type them out and send them off.

He said that Pease Pudding was to be taken out of the Lincoln.

He said that I had brought him the '64 half bottles of Bollinger, and he preferred the '61.

'You are feeling better, then,' I said into the first real gap of the monologue.

'What? Oh yes, I suppose I am. Now did you hear what I said? Pease Pudding is not to go in the Lincoln.'

'Why ever not?'

He gave me an irritated look. 'How do you expect him to be ready?'

'Etty is a good judge. She says he will be.'

'I will not have Rowley Lodge made to look stupid by running hopelessly under-trained horses in important races.'

'If Pease Pudding runs badly, people will only say that it shows how good a trainer you are yourself.'

'That is not the point,' he said repressively.

I opened one of the half bottles and poured the golden bubbles into his favourite Jacobean glass, which I had brought for the purpose. Champagne would not have tasted right to him from a tooth mug. He took a sip and evidently found the '64 was bearable after all, though he didn't say so.

'The point,' he explained as if to a moron, 'Is the stud fees. If he runs badly, his future value at stud is what will be affected.'

'Yes, I understand that.'

'Don't be silly, how can you? You know nothing about it.'

I sat down in the visitors' armchair, leant back, crossed my legs, and put into my voice all the reasonableness and weight which I had learned to project into industrial discussions, but which I had never before had the sense to use on my father.

'Rowley Lodge is heading for some financial rocks,' I said, 'And the cause of it is too much prestige-hunting. You are scared of running Pease Pudding in the Lincoln because you own a half share in him, and if he runs badly it will be your own capital investment, as well as Lady Vector's, that will suffer.'

He spilled some champagne on his sheet, and didn't notice it.

I went on, 'I know that it is quite normal for people to own shares in the horses they train. At Rowley Lodge just now, however, you own too many part shares for safety. I imagine you collected so many because you could not bear to see rival stables acquiring what you judged to be the next crop of world beaters, so that you probably said to your owners something like "If Archangel goes for forty thousand at auction and that's too much for you, I'll put up twenty thousand towards it." So you've gathered together one of the greatest strings in the country, and their potential stud value is enormous.'

He gazed at me blankly, forgetting to drink.

'This is fine,' I said, 'As long as the horses do win as expected. And year after year, they do. You've been pursuing this policy in moderation for a very long time, and it's made you steadily richer. But now, this year, you've over-extended. You've bought too many. As all the part owners only pay part training fees, the receipts are not now covering the expenses. Not by quite a long way. As a result the cash balance at the bank is draining away like bath-water, and there are still three weeks to go before the first race let alone the resale of the successful animals for stud. This dicey situation is complicated by your broken leg, your assistant being still in a coma from which he is unlikely to recover, and your stable apparently stagnating in the hands of a son who doesn't know how to train the horses; and all that is why you are scared silly of running Pease Pudding at the Lincoln.'

I stopped for reactions. There weren't any. Just shock.

'You can on the whole stop worrying,' I said, and knew that things would never again be quite as they had been between us. Thirty-four, I thought ruefully; I had to be thirty-four before I entered this particular arena on equal terms. 'I could sell your half share before the race.'

Wheels slowly began to turn again behind his eyes. He blinked. Stared at his sloping champagne and straightened the glass. Tightened the mouth into an echo of the old autocracy.

'How . . . how do you know all this?' There was more resentment in his voice than anxiety.

'I looked at the account books.'

'No . . . I mean, who told you?'

'No one needed to tell me. My job for the last six years has involved reading account books and doing sums.'

He recovered enough to take some judicious sips.

'At least you do understand why it is imperative we get an experienced trainer to take over until I can get about again.'

'There's no need for one,' I said incautiously. 'I've been there for three weeks now . . .'

'And do you suppose that you can learn how to train racehorses in three weeks?' he asked with reviving contempt.

'Since you ask,' I said. 'Yes.' And before he turned purple, tacked on, 'I was born to it, if you remember . . . I grew up there. I find, much to my own surprise, that it is second nature.'

He saw this statement more as a threat than as a reassurance. 'You're not staying on after I get back.'

'No,' I smiled. 'Nothing like that.'

He grunted. Hesitated. Gave in. He didn't say in so many words that I could carry on, but just ignored the whole subject from that point.

'I don't want to sell my half of Pease Pudding.'

'Draw up a list of those you don't mind selling, then,' I said. 'About ten of them, for a start.'

'And just who do you think is going to buy them? New owners don't grow on trees, you know. And half shares are harder to sell . . . owners like to see their names in the race cards and in the press.'

'I know a lot of business men,' I said, 'Who would be glad to have a racehorse but who actively shun the publicity. You pick out ten horses, and I'll sell your half shares.'

He didn't say he would, but he did, then and there. I ran my eye down the finished list and saw only one to disagree with.

'Don't sell Lancat,' I said.

He bristled. 'I know what I'm doing.'

'He's going to be good as a three-year-old,' I said. 'I see from the form book that he was no great shakes at two, and if you sell now you'll not get back what you paid. He's looking very well, and I think he'll win quite a lot.'

'Rubbish. You don't know what you're talking about.'

'All right . . . how much would you accept for your half?'

He pursed his lips, thinking about it. 'Four thousand. You should be able to get four, with his breeding. He cost twelve, altogether, as a yearling.'

'You'd better suggest prices for all of them,' I said. 'If you wouldn't mind.'

He didn't mind. I folded the list, put it in my pocket, picked up the entry forms he had written on, and prepared to go. He held out to me the champagne glass, empty.

'Have some of this . . . I can't manage it all.'

I took the glass, refilled it, and drank a mouthful. The bubbles popped round my teeth. He watched. His expression was as severe as ever, but he nodded, sharply, twice. Not as symbolic a gesture as a pipe of peace, but just as much of an acknowledgment, in its way.

On Monday morning, tapping away, Margaret said, 'Susie's friend's mum says she has just happened to see Alessandro's passport.'

'Which just happened,' I said dryly, 'To be well hidden away in Alessandro's bedroom.'

'Let us not stare at gift horses.'

'Let us not,' I agreed.

'Susie's friend's mum says that the address on the passport was not in Italy, but in Switzerland. A place called Bastagnola. Is that any use?'

'I hope Susie's friend's mum won't lose her job.'

'I doubt it,' Margaret said. 'She hops into bed with the manager, when his wife goes shopping in Cambridge.'

'How do you know?'

Her eyes laughed. 'Susie's friend told me.'

I telephoned to an importer of cameras who owed me a favour and asked him if he had any contacts in the town of Bastagnola.

'Not myself. But I could establish one, if it's important.'

'I want any information anyone can dig up about a man called Enso Rivera. As much information as possible.'

He wrote it down and spelled it back. 'See what I can do,' he said.

He rang two days later and sounded subdued.

'I'll be sending you an astronomical bill for European phone calls.'

'That's all right.'

'An awful lot of people didn't want to talk about your man. I met an exceptional amount of resistance.'

'Is he Mafia, then?' I asked.

'No. Not Mafia. In fact, he and the Mafia are not on speaking terms. On stabbing terms, maybe, but not speaking. There seems to be some sort of truce between them.' He paused.

'Go on,' I said.

'Well . . . As far as I can gather . . . and I wouldn't swear to it . . . he is a sort of receiver of stolen property. Most of it in the form of currency, but some gold and silver and precious stones from melted down jewellery. I heard . . . and it was at third hand from a high-up policeman, so you can believe it or not as you like . . . that Rivera accepts the stuff, sells or exchanges it, takes a large commission, and banks the rest in Swiss accounts which he opens up for his clients. They can collect their money any time they like . . . and it is believed that he has an almost world-wide connection. But all this goes on behind a supposedly legitimate business as a dealer in watches. They've never managed to bring him to court. They can never get witnesses to testify.'

'You've done marvels,' I said.

'There's a bit more.' He cleared his throat. 'He has a son, apparently, that no one cares to cross. Rivera has been known to ruin people who don't immediately do what the son wants. He only has this one child. He is reputed to have deserted his wife . . . well, a lot of Italian men do that . . .'

'He is Italian, then?'

'By birth, yes. He's lived in Switzerland for about fifteen years, though. Look, I don't know if you're intending to do business with him, but I got an unmistakable warning from several people to steer clear of him. They say he's dangerous. They say if you fall foul of him you wake up dead. Either that, or . . . well, I know you'll laugh . . . but there's a sort of superstition that if he looks your way you'll break a bone.'

I didn't laugh. Not a chuckle.

Almost as soon as I put the receiver down the telephone rang again. Dainsee.

'I've got your X-ray pictures in front of me,' he said. 'But they're inconclusive, I'm afraid. It just looks a pretty ordinary fracture. There's a certain amount of longitudinal splitting, but then there often is with cannon bones.'

'What would be the simplest way to break a bone on purpose?' I asked.

'Twist it,' he said promptly. 'Put it under stress. A bone under stress would snap quite easily if you gave it a bang. Ask any footballer or any skater. Stress, that's what does it.'

'You can't see stress on the X-rays . . .'

'Afraid not. Can't rule it out, though. Can't rule it in, either. Sorry.'

'It can't be helped.'

'But the blood test,' he said. 'I've had the results, and you were bang on target.'

'Anaesthetic?'

'Yep. Some brand of promazine. Sparine, probably.'

'I'm no wiser,' I said. 'How would you give it to a horse?'

'Injection,' Dainsee said promptly. 'Very simple intramuscular injection, nothing difficult. Just punch the needle in anywhere handy. It's often used to shoot into mania patients in mental hospitals, when they're raving. Puts them out for hours.'

Something about promazine rung a highly personal note.

'Does the stuff work instantly?' I asked.

'If you give it intravenously, it would. But intramuscularly, what it's equally designed for, it would take a few minutes, probably. Ten to fifteen minutes on a human; don't know for a horse.'

'If you injected it into a human, could you do it through clothes?'

'Oh sure. Like I said. They use it as a standby in mental hospitals. They wouldn't get people in a manic state to sit nice and quiet and roll their sleeves up.'

Chapter Nine

For three weeks the status at Rowley Lodge remained approximately quo.

I heavily amended my father's entry forms and sent them in, and sold six of the half shares to various acquaintances, without offering Lancat to any of them.

Margaret took to wearing green eye shadow, and Susie's friend reported that Alessandro had made a telephone call to Switzerland and didn't wear pyjamas. Also that the chauffeur always paid for everything, as Alessandro didn't have any money.

Etty grew more tense as the beginning of the season drew nearer, and lines of anxiety seldom left her forehead. I was leaving a great deal more to her judgement than my father did, and she was in consequence feeling insecure. She openly ached for his return.

The horses all the same were working well. We had no further mishaps except that a two-year-old filly developed severe sinus trouble, and as far as I could judge from watching the performances of the other forty-five stables using Newmarket Heath, the Rowley Lodge string was as forward as any.

Alessandro turned up day after day and silently rode what and how Etty told him to, though with a ramrod spine of protest. He said no more about not taking orders from a woman, and I imagined that even he could see that without Etty there would be fewer winners on the horizon. She herself had almost stopped complaining about him and was watching him with a more objective eye; because there was no doubt that after a month's concentrated practice he was riding better than the other apprentices.

He was also growing visibly thinner, and no longer looked well.

Small-framed though he might be, the six stone seven pounds that he was aiming to shrink his body down to was punitive for five foot four.

Alessandro's fanaticism was an awkward factor. If I had imagined that by making the going as rough as I dared he would give up his idle fancy and depart, I had been wrong. This was no idle fancy. It was revealing itself all too clearly as a consuming ambition: an ambition strong enough to make him starve himself, take orders from a woman, and perform what were evidently miracles of self-discipline, considering that it was probably the first time in his life that he had had to use any.

Against Etty's wishes I put him up one morning on Archangel.

'He's not ready for that,' she protested, when I told her I was going to.

'There isn't another lad in the yard who will take more care of him,' I said.

'But he hasn't the experience.'

'He has, you know. Archangel is only more valuable, not more difficult to ride, than the others.'

Alessandro received the news not with joy but with an 'at last' expression, more scorn than patience. We went down to the Waterhall canter, away from public gaze, and there Archangel did a fast six furlongs and pulled up looking as if he had just walked out of his box.

'He had him balanced,' I said to Etty. 'All the way.'

'Yes, he did,' she said grudgingly. 'Pity he's such an obnoxious little squirt.'

Alessandro returned with an 'I told you so' face which I wiped off by saying he would be switched to Lancat tomorrow.

'Why?' he demanded furiously. 'I rode Archangel very well.'

'Well enough,' I agreed. 'And you can ride him again, in a day or two. But I want you to ride Lancat in a trial on Wednesday, so you can go out on him tomorrow as well, and get used to him. And after the trial I want you to tell me your opinion of the horse and how he went. And I don't want one of your short sneering comments but a thought-out assessment. It is almost as important for a jockey to be able to analyse what a horse has done in a race as ride it. Trainers depend quite a lot on what their jockeys can tell them. So you can tell me about Lancat, and I'll listen.'

He gave me a long concentrating stare, but for once without the habitual superciliousness.

'All right,' he said. 'I will.'

We held the trial on the Wednesday afternoon on the trial ground past the Limekilns, a long way out of Newmarket. Much to Etty's disgust, because she wanted to watch it on television, I had timed the trial to start at exactly the same moment as the Champion Hurdle at Cheltenham. But the stratagem worked. We achieved the well-nigh impossible, a full scale trial without an observer or a tout in sight.

Apart from the two Etty and I rode, we took only four horses along there: Pease Pudding, Lancat, Archangel, and one of the previous year's most prolific winners, a four-year-old colt called Subito, whose best distance was a mile. Tommy Hoylake drove up from his home in

Berkshire to ride Pease Pudding, and we put Andy on Archangel and a taciturn lad called Faddy on the chestnut Subito.

'Don't murder them,' I said, before they started. 'If you feel them falter, just ease off.'

Four nods. Four fidgeting colts, glossy and eager.

Etty and I hacked round to within a hundred yards of where the trial ground ended and when we had pulled up a useful position for watching, she waved a large white handkerchief above her head. The horses started towards us, moving fast and still accelerating, with the riders crouched forward on their withers, heads down, reins very short, feet against the horses' moving shoulders.

They passed us still going all out, and pulled up a little further on. Archangel and Pease Pudding ran the whole gallop stride for stride and finished together. Lancat, from starting level, lost ten lengths, made up eight, lost two again, but still move easily. Subito was ahead of Lancat at the beginning, behind him when he moved up quickly, and alongside when they passed Etty and me.

She turned to me with a deeply worried expression.

'Pease Pudding can't be ready for the Lincoln if Lancat can finish so near him. In fact the way Lancat finished means that neither Archangel or Subito are as far on as I thought.'

'Calm down, Etty,' I said. 'Relax. Take it easy. Just turn it the other way round.'

She frowned. 'I don't understand you. Mr. Griffon will be very worried when he hears . . .'

'Etty,' I interrupted. 'Did Pease Pudding, or did he not, seem to you to be moving fast and easily?'

'Well, yes, I suppose so,' she said doubtfully.

'Then it may be Lancat who is much better than you expected, not the others which are worse.'

She looked at me with a face screwed up with indecision. 'But Alex is only an apprentice, and Lancat was useless last year.'

'In what way was he useless?'

'Oh . . . sprawly. Babyish. Had no action.'

'Nothing sprawly about him today,' I pointed out.

'No,' she admitted slowly. 'You're right. There wasn't.'

The riders walked towards us, leading the horses, and Etty and I both dismounted to hear more easily what they had to say. Tommy Hoylake, built like a twelve-year-old boy with a forty-three-year-old man's face sitting incongruously on top, said in his comfortable Berkshire accent that he had thought that Pease Pudding had run an excellent trial until he saw Lancat pulling up so close behind him. He had ridden Lancat a good deal the previous year, and hadn't thought much of him.

Andy said Archangel went beautifully, considering the Guineas was nearly six weeks away, and Faddy in his high pitched finicky voice said Subito had only been a pound or two behind Pease Pudding last year in his opinion, and he could have been nearer to him if he had really tried. Tommy and Andy shook their heads. If they had really tried, they too could have gone faster.

'Alessandro?' I said.

He hesitated. 'I . . . I lost ground at the beginning because I didn't realise . . . I didn't expect them to go so fast. When I asked him, Lancat just shot forward . . . and I could have kept him nearer to Archangel at the end, only he did seem to tire a bit, and you said . . .' He stopped with his voice, so to speak, on one foot.

'Good,' I said. 'You did right.' I hadn't expected him to be so honest. For the first time since his arrival he had made an objective self-assessment, but my faint and even slightly patronising praise was enough to bring back the smirk. Etty looked at him with uncontrolled dislike, which didn't disturb Alessandro one little bit.

'I hardly need to remind you,' I said to all of them, ignoring the displayed emotions, 'To keep this afternoon's doing to yourselves. Tommy, you can count on Pease Pudding in the Lincoln and Archangel in the Guineas, and if you'll come back to the office now we'll go through your other probable rides for the next few weeks.'

Alessandro's smirk turned sour, and the look he cast on Tommy was pure Rivera. Actively dangerous: inured to murder. Any appearance he might have given of being even slightly tamed was suddenly as reliable as sunlight on quicksand. I remembered the unequivocal message of Enso's gun pointing at my chest; that if killing seemed desirable, killing would quite casually be done. I had put Tommy Hoylake in jeopardy, and I'd have to get him out.

I sent the others on ahead and told Alessandro to stay for a minute. When the others were too far away to hear, I said, 'You will have to accept that Tommy Hoylake will be riding as first jockey to the stable.'

I got the full stare treatment, black, wide, and ill intentioned. I could almost feel the hate which flowed out of him like hot waves across the cool March air.

'If Tommy Hoylake breaks his leg,' I said clearly, 'I'll break yours.'

It shook him, though he tried not to show it.

'Also it would be pointless to put Tommy Hoylake out of action, as I would then engage someone else. Not you. Is that clear?'

He didn't answer.

'If you want to be a top jockey, you've got to do it yourself. You've got to be good enough. You've got to fight your own battles. It's no good thinking your father will destroy everyone who stands in your way. If you are good enough, no one will stand in your way; and if you are not, no amount of ruining others will make you.'

Still no sound. But fury, yes. Signifying all too much.

I said seriously, 'If Tommy Hoylake comes to any harm whatsoever, I will see that you never ride in another race. At whatever consequence to myself.'

He removed the stare from my face and scattered it over the wide windy spread of the Heath.

'I am accustomed . . .' he began arrogantly, and then stopped.

'I know to what you are accustomed,' I said. 'To having your own way at any expense to others. Your own way, bought in misery, pain and fear. Well . . . you should have settled for something which could be paid for. No amount of death and destruction will buy you ability.'

'All I wanted was to ride Archangel in the Derby,' he said defensively.

'Just like that? Just a whim?'

He turned his head towards Lancat and gathered together the reins. 'It started like that,' he said indistinctly, and walked away from me in the direction of Newmarket.

He came and rode out as usual the following morning, and all the days after. News that the trial had taken place got around, and I heard that I had chosen the time of the Champion Hurdle so that I could keep the unfit state of Pease Pudding decently concealed. The ante-post price lengthened and I put a hundred pounds on him at twenty to one.

My father shook the *Sporting Life* at me in a rage and insisted that the horse should be withdrawn.

'Have a bit on him instead,' I said. 'I have.'

'You don't know what you're doing.'

'Yes, I do.'

'It says here . . .' He was practically stuttering with the frustration of not being able to get out of bed and thwart me. 'It says here that if the trial was unsatisfactory, nothing more could be expected, with me away.'

'I read it,' I agreed. 'That's just a guess. And it wasn't unsatisfactory, if you want to know. It was very encouraging.'

'You're crazy,' he said loudly. 'You're ruining the stable. I won't have it. I won't have it, do you hear?'

He glared at me. A hot amber glare, not a cold black one. It made a change.

'I'll send Tommy Hoylake to see you,' I said. 'You can ask him what he thinks.'

Three days before the racing season started I walked into the office at two-thirty to see if Margaret wanted me to sign any letters before she left to collect her children, and found Alessandro in there with her, sitting on the edge of her desk. He was wearing a navy-blue track suit and heavy white running shoes, and his black hair had crisped into curls from the dampness of his own sweat.

She was looking up at him with obvious arousal, her face slightly flushed as if someone had given all her senses a friction rub.

She caught sight of me before he did, as he had his back to the door. She looked away from him in confusion, and he turned to see who had disturbed them.

There was a smile on the thin sallow face. A real smile, warm and uncomplicated, wrinkling the skin round the eyes and lifting the upper lip to show good teeth. For two seconds I saw an Alessandro I wouldn't have guessed existed, and then the light went out inside and the facial muscles gradually reshaped themselves into the familiar lines of wariness and annoyance.

He slid his slight weight to the ground and wiped away with a thumb some of the sweat which stood out on his forehead and trickled down in front of his ears.

'I want to know what horses I am going to ride this week at Doncaster,' he said. 'Now that the season is starting, you can give me horses to race.'

Margaret looked at him in astonishment, for he had sounded very much the boss. I answered him in a manner and tone carefully lacking in both apology and aggression.

'We have only one entry at Doncaster, which is Pease Pudding in the Lincoln on Saturday, and Tommy Hoylake rides it,' I said. 'And the reason we have only one entry,' I went straight on, as I saw the anger stoking up at what he believed to be a blocking movement on my part, 'Is that my father was involved in a motor accident the week these entries should have been made, and they were never sent in.'

'Oh,' he said blankly.

'Still,' I said, 'It would be a good idea for you to go every day to the races, to see what goes on, so that you don't make any crashing mistakes next year.'

I didn't add that I intended to do the same myself. It never did to show all your weaknesses to the opposition.

'You can start on Pullitzer on Wednesday at Catterick,' I said. 'And after that, it's up to you.'

There was a flash of menace in the black eyes.

'No,' he said, a bite in his voice. 'It's up to my father.'

He turned abruptly on one toe and without looking back trotted out of the office into the yard, swerved left and set off at a steady jog up the drive towards Bury Road. We watched him through the window, Margaret with a smile tinged with puzzlement and I with more apprehension than I liked.

'He ran all the way to the Boy's Grave and back,' she said. 'He says he weighed six stone twelve before he set off today, and he's lost twenty-two pounds since he came here. That sounds an awful lot, doesn't it? Twenty-two pounds, for someone as small as him.'

'Severe,' I said, nodding.

'He's strong, though. Like wire.'

'You like him,' I said, making it hover on the edge of a question.

She gave me a quick glance. 'He's interesting.'

I slouched into the swivel chair and read through the letters she pushed across to me. All of them in economic, good English, perfectly typed.

'If we win the Lincoln,' I said. 'You can have a raise.'

'Thanks very much.' A touch of irony. 'I hear the *Sporting Life* doesn't think much of my chances.'

I signed three of the letters and started reading the fourth. 'Does Alessandro often call in?' I asked casually.

'First time he's done it.'

'What did he want?' I asked.

'I don't think he wanted anything, particularly. He said he was going past, and just came in.'

'What did you talk about?'

She looked surprised at the question but answered without comment.

'I asked him if he liked the Forbury Inn and he said he did, it was much more comfortable than a house his father had rented on the outskirts of Cambridge. He said anyway his father had given up that house now and gone back home to do some business.' She paused thinking back, the memory of his company making her eyes smile, and I reflected that the house at Cambridge must have been where the rubber-faces took me, and that there was now no point in speculating more about it.

'I asked him if he had always liked riding horses and he said yes, and I asked him what his ambitions were and he said to win the Derby and to be Champion Jockey, and I said that there wasn't an apprentice born who didn't want that.'

I turned my head to glance at her. 'He said he wanted to be Champion Jockey?'

'That's right.'

I stared gloomily down at my shoes. The skirmish had been a battle, the battle was in danger of becoming war, and now it looked as if hostilities could crackle on for months. Escalation seemed to be setting in in a big way.

'Did he,' I asked, 'Ask *you* anything?'

'No. At least . . . yes, I suppose he did.' She seemed surprised, thinking about it.

'What?'

'He asked if you or your father owned any of the horses . . . I told him your father had half shares in some of them, and he said did he own any of them outright. I said Buckram was the only one . . . and he said . . .' She frowned, concentrating, 'He said he supposed it would be insured like the others, and I said it wasn't actually, because Mr. Griffon had cut back on his premiums this year, so he'd better be extra careful with it on the roads . . .' She suddenly sounded anxious. 'There wasn't any harm in telling him, was there? I mean, I didn't think there was anything secret about Mr. Griffon owning Buckram.'

'There isn't,' I said comfortingly. 'It runs in his name, for a start. It's public knowledge, that he owns it.'

She looked relieved and the lingering smile crept back round her eyes, and I didn't tell her that it was the bit about insurance that I found disturbing.

One of the firms I had advised in their troubles were assemblers of electronic equipment. Since they had in fact reorganised themselves from top to bottom and were now delighting their shareholders, I rang up their chief executive and asked for help for myself.

Urgently, I said. In fact, today. And it was half past three already.

A sharp 'phew' followed by some tongue clicking, and the offer came. If I would drive towards Coventry, their Mr. Wallis would meet me at Kettering. He would bring what I wanted with him, and explain how I was to install it, and would that do?

It would do very well indeed, I said: and did the chief executive happen to be in need of half a racehorse?

He laughed. On the salary cut I had persuaded him to take? I must be joking, he said.

Our Mr. Wallis, all of nineteen, met me in a businesslike truck and blinded me with science. He repeated the instructions clearly and twice, and then obviously doubted whether I could carry them out. To him the vagaries of the photoelectric effect were home ground, but he also realised that to the average fool they were not. He went over it again to make sure I understood.

'What is your position with the firm?' I asked in the end.

'Deputy Sales Manager,' he said happily, 'And they tell me I have you to thank.'

I quite easily, after the lecture, installed the early warning system at Rowley Lodge: basically a photoelectric cell linked to an alarm buzzer. After dark, when everything was quiet, I hid the necessary ultra-violet light source in the flowering plant in a tub which stood against the end wall of the four outside boxes, and the cell itself I camouflaged in a rose bush outside the office window. The cable from this led through the office window, across the lobby and into the owners' room, with a switch box handy to the sofa.

Soon after I had finished rigging it, Etty walked into the yard from her cottage for her usual last look round before going to bed, and the buzzer rasped out loud and clear. Too loud, I thought. A silent intruder might just hear it. I put a cushion over it, and the muffled buzz sounded like a bumble bee caught in a drawer.

I switched the noise off. When Etty left the yard it started again immediately. Hurrah for the Deputy Sales Manger, I thought, and slept in the owners' room with my head on the cushion.

No one came.

Stiffly at six o'clock I got up and rolled up the cable, and collected and stowed all the gear in a cupboard in the owners' room; and when the first of the lads ambled yawning into the yard, I headed directly to the coffee pot.

Tuesday night, no one came.

Wednesday, Margaret mentioned that Susie's friend had reported two Swiss phone calls, one outgoing by Alessandro, one incoming to the chauffeur.

Etty, more anxious than ever with the Lincoln only three days away, was snapping at the lads, and Alessandro stayed behind after second exercise and asked me if I had reconsidered and would put him up on Pease Pudding in place of Tommy Hoylake.

We were outside in the yard, with the late morning bustle going on all around. Alessandro looked tense and hollow eyed.

'You must know I can't,' I said reasonably.

'My father says I am to tell you that you must.'

I slowly shook my head. 'For your own sake, you shouldn't. If you rode it, you would make a fool of yourself. Is that what your father wants?'

'He says I must insist.' He was adamant.

'O.K.,' I said. 'You've insisted. But Tommy Hoylake is going to ride.'

'But you must do what my father says,' he protested.

I smiled at him faintly, but didn't answer, and he did not seem to know what to say next.

'Next week, though,' I said matter-of-factly. 'You can ride Buckram in a race at Aintree. I entered him there especially for you. He won first time out last year, so he should have a fair chance again this time.'

He just stared; didn't even blink. If there was anything to be given away, he didn't give it.

At three o'clock Thursday morning the buzzer went off with enthusiasm three inches from my ear drum and I nearly fell off the sofa. I switched off the noise and got to my feet, and took a look into the yard through the owners' room window.

Moving quickly through the moonless night went one single small light, very faint, directed at the ground. Then, as I watched, it swung round, paused on some of the boxes in bay four, and settled inexorably on the one which housed Buckram.

Treacherous little bastard, I thought. Finding out which horse he could kill without the owner wailing a complaint; an uninsured horse, in order to kick Rowley Lodge the harder in the financial groin.

Telling him Buckram might win him a race hadn't stopped him. Treacherous, callous little bastard . . .

I was out through the ready left-ajar doors and down the yard, moving silently on rubber shoes. I heard the bolts drawn quietly back and the doors squeak in their hinges, and homed on the small flicking light with far from charitable intentions.

No point in wasting time. I swept my hand down on the switch and flooded Buckram's box with a hundred watts.

I took in at a glance the syringe held in a stunned second of suspended animation in the gloved hand, and noticed the truncheon lying on the straw just inside the door.

It wasn't Alessandro. Too heavy. Too tall. The figure turning purposefully towards me, dressed in black from neck to foot, was one of the rubber-faces.

In his rubber-face.

Chapter Ten

This time I didn't waste my precious advantage. I sprang straight at him and chopped with all my strength at the wrist of the hand that held the syringe.

A direct hit. The hand flew backwards, the fingers opened, and the syringe spun away through the air.

I kicked his shin and punched him in the stomach, and when his head came forward I grabbed hold of it and swung him with a crash against the wall.

Buckram kicked up a fuss and stamped around loose, as rubber-face had not attempted to put the headcollar on. When rubber-face rushed me with jabbing fists I caught hold of his clothes and threw him against Buckram, who snapped at him with his teeth.

A muffled sound came through the rubber, which I declined to interpret as an appeal for peace. Once away from the horse he came at me again, shoulders hunched, head down, arms stretching forwards. I stepped straight into his grasp, ignored a bash in my short ribs, put my arm tight round his neck, and banged his head on the nearest wall. The legs turned to latex to match the face, and the lids palely shut inside the eyeholes. I gave him another small crack against the wall to remove any lingering doubts, and stood back a pace. He lay feebly in the angle between floor and wall, one hand twisting slowly forwards and backwards across the straw.

I tied up Buckram, who by some miracle had not pushed his way out of the unbolted door and roused the neighbourhood, and in stepping away from the tethering ring nearly put my foot down on the scattered syringe. It lay under the manger, in the straw, and had survived undamaged through the rumpus.

Picking it up I tossed it lightly in my hand and decided that the gifts of the gods should not be wasted. Pulling up the sleeve of rubber-face's black jersey, I pushed the needle firmly into his arm and gave him the benefit of half the contents. Prudence, not compassion, stopped me from squirting in the lot: it might be that what the syringe held was a flattener for a horse but curtains for a man, and murdering was not going to help.

I pulled off rubber-face's rubber face. Underneath it was Carlo. Surprise, surprise.

The prizes of war now amounted to one rubber mask, one half empty syringe, and one bone-breaking truncheon. After a slight pause for thought I wiped my fingerprints off the syringe, removed Carlo's gloves, and planted his all over it; both hands. A similar liberal sprinkling went on to the truncheon: then, using the gloves to hold them with, I took the two incriminating articles up to the house and hid them temporarily in a lacquered box under a dust-sheet in one of the ten unused bedrooms.

From the window on the stairs on the way down I caught an impression of a large pale shape in the drive near the gate. Went to look, to make sure. No mistake; the Mercedes.

Back in Buckram's box, Carlo slept peacefully, totally out. I felt his pulse, which was slow but regular, and looked at my watch. Not yet three thirty. Extraordinary.

Carrying Carlo to the car looked too much of a chore, so I went and fetched the car to Carlo. The engine started with a click and a purr, and made too little noise in the yard even to disturb the horses. Leaving the engine running I opened both rear doors and lugged Carlo in backwards. I had intended to do him the courtesy of the back seat, since he had done as much for me, but he fell limply to the floor. I bent his knees up, as he lay on his back, and gently shut him in.

As far as I could tell no one saw our arrival at the Forbury Inn. I parked the Mercedes next to the other cars near the front door, switched off the engine and the side lights, and quietly went away.

By the time I had walked the near mile home, collected the rubber mask from Buckram's box and taken off his headcollar, and dismantled the electronic eye and stowed it in the cupboard, it was too late to bother with going to bed. I slept for an hour or so more on the sofa and woke up feeling dead tired and not a bit full of energy for the first day of the races.

Alessandro arrived late, on foot, and worried.

I watched him, first through the office window and then from the owners' room, as he made his way down into the yard. He hovered in indecision in bay four, and with curiosity overcoming caution, made a crablike traverse over to Buckram's box. He unbolted the top half of the door, looked inside, and then bolted the door again. Unable from a distance to read his reaction, I walked out of the house into his sight without appearing to take any notice of him.

He removed himself smartly from bay four and pretended to be looking for Etty in bay three, but finally his uncertainty got the better of him and he turned to come and meet me.

'Do you know where Carlo is?' he asked without preamble.

'Where would you expect him to be?' I said.

He blinked. 'In his room . . . I knock on his door when I am ready . . . but he wasn't there. Have you . . . have you seen him?'

'At four o'clock this morning,' I said casually. 'He was fast asleep in the back of your car. I imagine he is still there.'

He turned his head away as if I'd punched him.

'He came, then,' he said, and sounded hopeless.

'He came,' I agreed.

'But you didn't . . . I mean . . . kill him?'

'I'm not your father,' I said astringently. 'Carlo got injected with some stuff he brought for Buckram.'

His head snapped back and his eyes held a fury that was for once not totally directed at me.

'I told him not to come,' he said angrily. 'I told him not to.'

'Because Buckram could win for you next week?'

'Yes . . . no . . . You confuse me.'

'But he disregarded you,' I suggested, 'And obeyed your father?'

'I told him not to come,' he repeated.

'He wouldn't dare disobey your father,' I said dryly.

'No one disobeys my father,' he stated automatically and then looked at me in bewilderment. 'Except you,' he said.

'The knack with your father,' I explained, 'Is to disobey within the area where retaliation becomes progressively less profitable, and to widen that area at every opportunity.'

'I don't understand.'

'I'll explain it to you on the way to Doncaster,' I said.

'I am not coming with you,' he said stiffly. 'Carlo will drive me in my own car.'

'He'll be in no shape to. If you want to go to the races I think you'll find you either have to drive yourself or come with me.'

He gave me an angry stare and didn't admit he couldn't drive. But he couldn't resist the attraction of the races either, and I had counted on it.

'Very well. I will come with you.'

After we had ridden back from Racecourse side with the first lot I told him to talk to Margaret in the office while I changed into race-going clothes, and then I drove him up to the Forbury Inn for him to do the same.

He bounded out of the Jensen almost before it stopped rolling and wrenched open one of the Mercedes' rear doors. Inside the car a hunched figure sitting on the back seat showed that Carlo was at least partially awake, if not a hundred per cent receptive of the Italian torrent of abuse breaking over him.

I tapped Alessandro on the back and when he momentarily stopped cursing, said, 'If he feels anything like I did after similar treatment, he will not be taking much notice. Why don't you do something constructive, like getting ready to go to the races?'

'I'll do what I please,' he said fiercely, but the next minute it appeared that what pleased him was to change for the races.

While he was indoors, Carlo made one or two remarks in Italian which stretched my knowledge of the language too far. The gist, however, was clear. Something to do with my ancestors.

Alessandro reappeared wearing the dark suit he had first arrived in, which was now a full size too large. It made him look even thinner, and a good deal younger, and almost harmless. I reminded myself sharply that a lowered guard invited the uppercut, and jerked my head for him to get into the Jensen.

When he had closed the door, I spoke to Carlo through the open window of the Mercedes. 'Can you hear what I say?' I said. 'Are you listening?'

He raised his head with an effort and gave me a look which showed that he was, even if he didn't want to.

'Good,' I said. 'Now, take this in. Alessandro is coming with me to the races. Before I bring him back, I intend to telephone to the stables to make quite sure that no damage of any kind has been done there . . . that all the horses are alive and well. If you have any idea of going back today to finish off what you didn't do last night, you can drop it. Because if you do any damage you will not get Alessandro back tonight . . . or for many nights . . . and I cannot think that Enso Rivera would be very pleased with you.'

He looked as furious as his sorry state would let him.

'You understand?' I said.

'Yes.' He closed his eyes and groaned. I left him to it with reprehensible satisfaction.

'What did you say to Carlo?' Alessandro demanded as I swept him away down the drive.

'Told him to spend the day in bed.'

'I don't believe you.'

'Words to that effect.'

He looked suspiciously at the beginnings of a smile I didn't bother to repress, and then, crossly, straight ahead through the windscreen.

After ten silent miles I said, 'I've written a letter to your father. I'd like you to send it to him.'

'What letter?'

I took an envelope out of my inner pocket and handed it to him.

'I want to read it,' he stated aggressively.

'Go ahead. It isn't stuck. I thought I would save you the trouble.'

He compressed his mouth and pulled out the letter.

He read:

Enso Rivera,

The following points are for your consideration.

1. While Alessandro stays, and wishes to stay, at Rowley Lodge, the stable cannot be destroyed.

Following any form or degree of destruction, or of attempted destruction, of the stables, the Jockey Club will immediately be informed of everything that has passed, with the result that Alessandro would be banned for life from riding races anywhere in the world.

2. Tommy Hoylake.

Should any harm of any description come to Tommy Hoylake, or to any other jockey employed by the stable, the information will be laid, and Alessandro will ride no more races.

3. Moonrock, Indigo and Buckram.

Should any further attempts be made to injure or kill any of the horses at Rowley Lodge, information will be laid, and Alessandro will ride no more races.

4. The information which would be laid consists at present of a full account of all pertinent events, together with (a) the two model horses and their handwritten labels; (b) the results of an analysis done at the Equine Research Establishment on a blood sample taken from Indigo, showing the presence of the anaesthetic promazine; (c) X-ray pictures of the fracture of Indigo's near foreleg; (d) one rubber mask, worn by Carlo; (e) one hypodermic syringe containing traces of anaesthetic, and (f) one truncheon, both bearing Carlo's fingerprints.

These items are all lodged with a solicitor, who has instructions for their use in the event of my death.

Bear in mind that the case against you and your son does not have to be proved in a court of law, but only to the satisfaction of the Stewards of the Jockey Club. It is they who take away jockeys' licences.

If no further damage is done or attempted at Rowley Lodge, I will agree on my part to give Alessandro every reasonable opportunity of becoming a proficient and successful jockey.

* * *

He read the letter through twice. Then he slowly folded it and put it back in the envelope.

'He won't like it,' he said. 'He never lets anyone threaten him.'

'He shouldn't have tried threatening me,' I said mildly.

'He thought it would be your father . . . and old people frighten more easily, my father says.'

I took my eyes off the road for two seconds to glance at him. He was no more disturbed by what he had just said than when he had said his father would kill me. Frightening and murdering had been the background to his childhood, and he still seemed to consider them normal.

'Do you really have all those things?' he asked. 'The blood test result . . . and the syringe?'

'I do indeed.'

'But Carlo always wears gloves . . .' He stopped.

'He was careless,' I said.

He brooded over it. 'If my father makes Carlo break any more horses' legs, will you really get me warned off?'

'I certainly will.'

'But after that you would have no way of stopping him from destroying the stables in revenge.'

'Would he do that?' I asked. 'Would he bother?'

Alessandro gave me a pitying, superior smile. 'My father would be revenged if someone ate the cream cake he wanted.'

'So you approve of vengeance?' I said.

'Of course.'

'It wouldn't get you back your licence,' I pointed out, 'And anyway I doubt whether he could actually do it, because there would then be no bar to police protection and the loudest possible publicity.'

He said stubbornly, 'There wouldn't be any risk at all if you would agree to my riding Pease Pudding and Archangel.'

'It never was possible for you to ride them without any experience, and if you'd had any sense you would have known it.'

The haughty look flooded back, but diluted from the first time I'd seen it.

'So,' I went on, 'Although there's always a risk in opposing extortion, in some cases it is the only thing to do. And starting from there, it's just a matter of finding ways of opposing that don't land you in the morgue empty-handed.'

There was another long pause while we skirted Grantham and Newark. It started raining. I switched on the wipers and the blades clicked like metronomes over the glass.

'It's seems to me,' Alessandro said glumly, 'As if you and my father have been engaged in some sort of power struggle, with me being the pawn that both of you push around.'

I smiled, surprised both at his perception and that he should have said it aloud.

'That's right,' I agreed, 'that's how it's been from the beginning.'

'Well, I don't like it.'

'It only happened because of you. And if you give up the idea of being a jockey, it will all stop.'

'But I *want* to be a jockey,' he said, as if that were the end of it. And as far as his doting father was concerned, it was. The beginning of it, and the end of it.

Ten wet miles further on, he said, 'You tried to get rid of me, when I came.'

'Yes, I did.'

'Do you still want me to leave?'

'Would you?' I sounded hopeful.

'No,' he said.

I twisted my mouth. 'No,' he said again, 'Because between you, you and my father have made it impossible for me to go to any other stable and start again.'

Another long pause. 'And anyway,' he said. 'I don't want to go to any other stable. I want to stay at Rowley Lodge.'

'And be Champion Jockey?' I murmured.

'I only told Margaret . . .' he began sharply, and then put a couple of things together. 'She told you I asked about Buckram,' he said bitterly. 'And that's how you caught Carlo.'

In justice to Margaret I said, 'She wouldn't have told me if I hadn't directly asked her what you wanted.'

'You don't trust me,' he complained.

'Well, no,' I said ironically. 'I would be a fool to.'

The rain fell more heavily against the windscreen. We stopped at a red light in Bawtry and waited while a lollipop man shepherded half a school across in front of us.

'That bit in your letter about helping me to be a good jockey . . . do you mean it?'

'Yes, I do,' I said. 'You ride well enough at home. Better than I expected, to be honest.'

'I told you . . .' he began, lifting the arching nose.

'That you were brilliant,' I finished, nodding. 'So you did.'

'Don't laugh at me.' The ready fury boiled up.

'All you've got to do is win a few races, keep your head, show a judgement of pace and an appreciation of tactics, and stop relying on your father.'

He was unpacified. 'It is natural to rely on one's father,' he said stiffly.

'I ran away from mine when I was sixteen.'

He turned his head. I could see out of the corner of my eye that he was both surprised and unimpressed.

'Obviously he did not, like mine, give you everything you wanted.'

'No,' I agreed. 'I wanted freedom.'

I judged that freedom was the one thing that Enso wouldn't give his son for the asking: the obsessively generous were often possessive as well. There was no hint of freedom in the fact that Alessandro carried no money, couldn't drive, and had Carlo around to supervise and report on every move. But then freedom didn't seem to be high on Alessandro's list of desirables. The perks of serfdom were habit-forming, and sweet.

I spent most of the afternoon meeting the people who knew my father: other trainers, jockeys, officials, and some of the owners. They were all without exception helpful and informative, so that by the end of the day I had learned what I would be expected (and just as importantly, not expected) to do in connection with Pease Pudding for the Lincoln.

Tommy Hoylake, with an expansive grin, put it succinctly. 'Declare it, saddle it, watch it win, and stick around in case of objections.'

'Do you think we have any chance?'

'Oh, must have,' he said. 'It's an open race, anything could win. Lap of the Gods, you know. Lap of the Gods.' By which I gathered that he still hadn't made up his mind about the trial, whether Lancat was good or Pease Pudding bad.

I drove Alessandro back to Newmarket and asked how he had got on. As his expression whenever I caught sight of him during the afternoon had been a mixture of envy and pride, I knew without him telling me that he had been both titillated to be recognisable as a jockey, because of his size, and enraged that a swarm of others should have started the season without him. The look he had given the boy who had won the apprentice race would have frightened a rattlesnake.

'I cannot wait until next Wednesday,' he said. 'I wish to begin tomorrow.'

'We have no runners before next Wednesday,' I said calmly.

'Pease Pudding.' He was fierce. 'On Saturday.'

'We've been through all that.'

'I wish to ride him.'

'No.'

He seethed away in the passenger seat. The actual sight and sound and smell of the races had excited him to the pitch where he could scarcely keep still. The approach to reasonableness which had been made on the way up had all blown away in the squally wind on Doncaster's Town Moor, and the first half of the journey back was a complete waste, as far as I was concerned. Finally, though, the extreme tenseness left him, and he slumped back in his seat in some species of gloom.

At that stage, I said, 'What sort of a race do you think you should ride on Pullitzer?'

His spine straightened again instantly and he answered with the same directness as he had after the trial.

'I looked up his last year's form,' he said. 'Pullitzer was consistent, he came third or fourth or sixth, mostly. He was always near the front for most of the race but then faded out in the last furlong. Next Wednesday at Catterick it is seven furlongs. It says in the book that the low numbers are the best to draw, so I would hope for one of those. Then I will try to get away well at the start and take a position next to the rails, or with only one other horse inside me, and I will not go too fast, but not too slow either. I will try to stay not further back than two and a half lengths behind the leading horse, but I will not try to get to the front until right near the end. The last sixty yards, I think. And I will try to be in front only about fifteen yards before the winning post. I think he does not race his best if he is in front, so he mustn't be in front very long.'

To say I was surprised is to get nowhere near the queer excitement which rose sharply and unexpectedly in my brain. I'd had years of practice in sorting the genuine from the phoney, and what Alessandro had said rang of pure sterling.

'O.K.,' I said casually. 'That sounds all right. You ride him just like that. And how about Buckram . . . you'll be riding him in the apprentice race at Liverpool the day after Pullitzer. Also you can ride Lancat at Teesside two days later, on the Saturday.'

'I'll look them up, and think about them,' he said seriously.

'Don't bother with Lancat's form,' I reminded him. 'He was no good as a two-year-old. Work from what you learned during the trial.'

'Yes,' he said. 'I see.'

His eagerness had come back, but more purposefully, more controlled. I understood to some degree his hunger to make a start: he was reaching out to race riding as a starving man to bread, and nothing would deflect him. I found, moreover, that I no longer needed to deflect him, that what I had said about helping him to become a jockey was more true than I had known when I had written it.

As far as Enso was concerned, and as far as Alessandro was concerned, they were both still forcing me to give him opportunities against my will. It privately and sardonically began to amuse me that I was beginning to give him opportunities because I wanted to.

The battle was about to shift to different ground. I thought about Enso, and about the way he regarded his son . . . and I could see at last how to make him retract his threats. But it seemed to me that very likely the future would be more dangerous than the past.

Chapter Eleven

Every evening during the week before the Lincoln I spent hours answering the telephone. One owner after another rang up, and without exception sounded depressed. This, I discovered, after the fourth in a row had said in more or less identical words, 'can't expect much with your father chained to his bed', was because the invalid in question had been extremely busy on the blower himself.

He had rung them all up, apologised for my presence, told them to expect nothing, and promised then that everything would be restored to normal as soon as he got back. He had also told his co-owner of Pease Pudding, a Major Barnette, that in his opinion the horse was not fit to run; and it had taken me half an hour of my very best persuasive tongue to convince the Major that as my father hadn't seen the horse for the past six weeks, he didn't actually know.

Looking into his activities more closely, I found that my father had also written privately every week to Etty for progress reports and had told her not to tell me she was sending them. I practically bullied this last gem out of her on the morning before the Lincoln, having cottoned on to what was happening only through mentioning that my father had told all the owners the horses were unfit. Something guilty in her expression had given her away, but she fended off my bitterness by claiming that she hadn't actually said they were unfit: that was just the way my father had chosen to interpret things.

I went into the office and asked Margaret if my father had telephoned or written to her for private reports. She looked embarrassed and said that he had.

When I spoke about race tactics to Tommy Hoylake that Friday, he said not to worry, my father had rung him up and given him his instructions.

'And what were they?' I asked, with a great deal more restraint than I was feeling.

'Oh . . . just to keep in touch with the field and not drop out of the back door when he blows up.'

'Um . . . If he hadn't rung you up, how would you have planned to ride?' I said.

'Keep him well up all the time,' he said promptly. 'When he's fit, he's one of those horses who likes to make the others try to catch him. I'd pick him up two furlongs out, take him to the front, and just pray he'd stay there.'

'Ride him like that, then,' I said. 'I've got a hundred pounds on him, and I don't usually bet.'

His mouth opened in astonishment. 'But your father . . .'

'Promise you'll ride the horse to win,' I said pleasantly, 'or I'll put someone else up.'

I was insulting him. No one ever suggested replacing Tommy Hoylake. He looked uncertainly at my open expression and came to the conclusion that because of my inexperience I didn't realise the enormity of what I'd said.

He shrugged. 'All right. I'll give it a whirl. Though what your father will say . . .'

My father had not finished saying, not by six or more calls, mostly, it appeared, to the Press. Three papers on the morning of the Lincoln quoted his opinion that Pease Pudding had no chance. He'd have me in before the Stewards, I grimly reflected, if the horse did any good.

Among all this telephonic activity he rang me only once. Although the overpowering bossiness had not returned to his voice, he sounded stilted and displeased, and I gathered that the champagne truce had barely seen me out of the door.

He rang on the Thursday evening after I got back from Doncaster, and I told him how helpful everyone had been.

'Hmph,' he said, 'I'll ring the Clerk of the Course tomorrow, and ask him to keep an eye on things.'

'Have you entirely cornered the telephone trolley?' I asked.

'Telephone trolley? Could never get hold of it for long enough. Too many people asking for it all the time. No, no. I told them I needed my own private extension, here in this room, and after a lot of fuss and delay they fixed one up. I insisted, of course, that I had a business to run.'

'And you insisted often?'

'Of course,' he said without humour, and I knew from long experience that the hospital had had as much chance as an egg under a steamroller.

'The horses aren't as backward as you think,' I told him. 'You don't really need to be so pessimistic.'

'You're no judge of a horse,' he said dogmatically; and it was the day after that that he talked to the Press.

Major Barnette gloomed away in the parade ring and poured scorn and pity on my hefty bet.

'Your father told me not to throw good money after bad,' he said. 'And I can't think why I let you persuade me to run.'

'You can have fifty of my hundred, if you like,' I offered it with the noblest of intentions, but he took it as a sign that I wanted to get rid of my losses.

'Certainly not,' he said resentfully.

He was a spare, elderly man of middle height, who stood at the slightest provocation upon his dignity. Sign of basic failure, I diagnosed uncharitably, and remembered the old adage that some owners were harder to train than their horses.

The twenty-nine runners for the Lincoln were stalking long-leggedly round the parade ring, with all the other owners and trainers standing about in considering groups. Strong, cold north-west winds had blown the clouds away and the sun shone brazenly from a brilliant high blue sky. When the jockeys trickled through the crowd and emerged in a sunburst into the parade ring their glossy colours gleamed and reflected the light like children's toys.

The old-young figure of Tommy Hoylake in bright green bounced towards us with a carefree aura of play-it-as-it-comes, which did nothing to persuade Major Barnette that his half share of the horse would run well.

'Look,' he said heavily to Tommy. 'Just don't get tailed off. If it looks as if you will be, pull up and jump off, for God's sake, and pretend the horse is lame or the saddle's slipped. Anything you like, but don't let it get around that the horse is no good, or its stud value will sink like a stone.'

'I don't think he'll actually be tailed off, sir.' Tommy said judiciously, and cast an enquiring glance up at me.

'Just ride him as you suggested,' I said, 'And don't leave it all in the lap of the gods.'

He grinned. Hopped on the horse. Flicked his cap to Major Barnette. Went on his light-hearted way.

The Major didn't want to watch the race with me, which suited me fine. My mouth felt dry. Suppose after all that my father was right . . . that I couldn't tell a fit horse from a letter-box, and that he in his hospital bed was a better judge. Fair enough, if the horse ran stinkingly badly I would acknowledge my mistake and do a salutary spot of grovelling.

Pease Pudding didn't run stinkingly badly.

The horses had cantered a straight mile away from the stands, circled, sorted, lined up, and started back at a flat gallop. Unused to holding race glasses and to watching races head-on from a mile away, I couldn't for a long time see Tommy at all, even though I knew vaguely where to look for him: drawn number twenty-one, almost midfield. I put the glasses down after a while and just watched the mass making its distant way towards the stands, a multi-coloured charge dividing into two sections, one each side of the course. Each section narrowed until the centre of the track was bare, and it looked as though two separate races were being held at the same time.

I heard his name on the commentary before I spotted the colours.

'And now on the stands' side it's Pease Pudding coming to take it up. With two furlongs to go, Pease Pudding on the rails with Gossamer next and Badger making up ground now behind them, and Willy Nilly on the far side followed by Thermometer, Student Unrest, Manganeta ...' He rattled off a long string of names to which I didn't listen.

That he had been fit enough to hit the front two furlongs from home was all that mattered. I honestly didn't care from that moment whether he won or lost. But he did win. He won by a short head from Badger, holding his muzzle stubbornly in front when it looked impossible that he shouldn't be caught, with Tommy Hoylake moving rhythmically over the withers and getting out of him the last milligram of balance, of stamina, of utter bloody-minded refusal to be beaten.

In the winner's unsaddling enclosure Major Barnette looked more stunned than stratospheric, but Tommy Hoylake jumped down with the broadest of grins and said, 'Hey, what about that, then? He had the goods in the parcel after all.'

'So he did,' I said, and told the discountenanced pressmen that anyone could win the Lincoln any old day of the week: any old day, given the horse, the luck, the head lad, my fathers' stable routine, and the second best jockey in the country.

About twenty people having suddenly developed a close friendship with Major Barnette, he drifted off more or less at their suggestion to the bar to lubricate their hoarse-from-cheering throats. He asked me lamely to join him, but as I had caught his eye just when, recovering from his surprise, he had been telling the world that he always knew Pease Pudding had it in him, I saved him embarrassment and declined.

When the crowd round the unsaddling enclosure had dispersed and the fuss had died away, I somehow found myself face to face with Alessandro, who had been driven to Doncaster that day, and the previous day, by a partially revitalised chauffeur.

His face was as white as his yellowish skin could get, and his black eyes were as deep as pits. He regarded me with a shaking, strung up intensity, and seemed to have difficulty in actually saying what was hovering on the edge. I looked back at him without emotion of any sort, and waited.

'All right,' he said jerkily, after a while. 'All right. Why don't you say it? I expect you to say it.'

'There's no need,' I said neutrally. 'And no point.'

Some of the jangle drained out of his face. He swallowed with difficulty.

'I will say it for you, then,' he said. 'Pease Pudding would not have won if you had let me ride it.'

'No, he wouldn't,' I agreed.

'I could see,' he said, still with a shake in his voice, 'That I couldn't have ridden like that. I could see . . .'

Humility was a torment for Alessandro.

I said, in some sort of compassion, 'Tommy Hoylake has no more determination than you have, and no better hands. But what he does have is a marvellous judgement of pace and tremendous polish in a tight finish. Your turn will come, don't doubt it.'

Even if his colour didn't come back, the rest of the rigidity disappeared. He looked more dumbfounded than anything else.

He said slowly, 'I thought . . . I thought you would . . . what is it Miss Craig says . . .? rub my nose in it.'

I smiled at the sound of the colloquialism in his careful accent.

'No, I wouldn't do that.'

He took a deep breath and involuntarily stretched his arms out sideways.

'I want . . .' he said, and didn't finish it.

You want the world, I thought. And I said, 'Start on Wednesday.'

When the horsebox brought Pease Pudding back to Rowley Lodge that night the whole stable turned out to greet him. Etty's face was puckered with a different emotion from worry, and she fussed over the returning warrior like a mother hen. The colt himself clattered stiff legged down the ramp into the yard and modestly accepted the melon sized grins and the earthy comments (you did it, you old bugger) which were directed his way.

'Surely every winner doesn't get this sort of reception,' I said to Etty, after I'd come out of the house to investigate the bustle. I had reached the house half an hour before the horse, and found everything quiet: the lads had finished evening stables and gone round to the hostel for their tea.

'It's the first of the season,' she said, her eyes shining in her good plain face. 'And we didn't expect . . . well, I mean . . . without Mr. Griffon and everything . . .'

'I told you to have more faith in yourself, Etty.'

'It's bucked the lads up no end,' she said, ducking the compliment. 'Everyone was watching on TV. They made such a noise in the hostel they must have heard them at the Forbury Inn . . . .'

The lads were all spruced up for their Saturday evening out. When they'd seen Pease Pudding safely stowed away, they set off in a laughing and cheering bunch to make inroads into the stocks of the Golden Lion; and until I saw the explosive quality of their pleasure, I hadn't realised the extent of their depression. But they had after all, I reflected, read the papers. And they were used to believing my father rather than their own eyes.

'Mr. Griffon will be so pleased,' Etty said, with genuine, unsophisticated certainty.

But Mr. Griffon, predictably, was not.

I drove down to see him the following afternoon and found several of the Sunday newspapers in the waste basket. He greeted me with a face that made agate look putty, and was watchfully determined that I shouldn't have a chance of crowing.

He needn't have worried. Nothing made for worse future relations in any field whatsoever than crowing over losers; and if I knew nothing else, I knew how to negotiate for the best long term results.

I congratulated him on the win.

He didn't quite know how to deal with that, but at least it got him out of the embarrassment of having to admit he'd been made to look foolish. 'Tommy Hoylake rode a brilliant race,' he stated, and ignored the fact that he had given him directly opposite instructions.

'Yes, he did,' I agreed wholeheartedly, and repeated that all the rest of the credit lay with Etty and with his own stable routine, which we had faithfully followed.

He unbent a little more, but I found, slightly to my dismay, that in contrast I admired Alessandro for the straightforwardness of his apology, and for the moral courage which had nerved him to offer it. Moral courage was not something I had ever associated with Alessandro, before that moment.

Since my last visit, my father's room had taken on the appearance of an office. The regulation bedside locker had been replaced by a much larger table which pushed around easily on huge wheel castors, like the bed. On the table was the telephone on which he had broadcast so much blight, also a heap of *Racing Calendars*, copies of the *Sporting Life*, entry forms, a copy of *Horses in Training*, the three previous years' form books and, half hidden, the reports from Etty in her familiar schoolgirl handwriting.

'What, no typewriter?' I said flippantly, and he said stiffly that he was arranging for a local girl to come in and take dictation some time in the next week.

'Fine,' I said encouragingly; but he refused to be friendly. He saw the winning of the Lincoln as a serious threat to his authority, and his manner said plainly that that authority was not passing to me or even to Etty, while he could do anything to prevent it.

He was putting himself in a very ambivalent position. Every winner would be to him personally excruciating, yet at the same time he needed it desperately from the financial angle. Too much of his fortune for safety was still invested in half shares: and if the horses all ran as badly as it seemed he would like them to, their value would curl up like dahlias in a frost.

Understanding him was one thing: sorting him out, quite another.

'I can't wait for you to get back,' I said, but that didn't work either. It seemed that the bones were not mending as fast as had been hoped, and the reminder of the delay simply switched him into a different sort of aggravation.

'Some tommy-rot about elderly bones taking longer to knit,' he said irritably. 'All these weeks . . . and they can't say when I can get out of all these confounded pulleys. I told them I want a plaster cast I can walk on . . . damn it, enough people have them . . . but they say there are lots of cases where it isn't possible, and that I'm one of them.'

'You're lucky to have a leg at all,' I pointed out. 'At first they thought they would have to take it off.'

'Better if they had,' he snorted. 'Then I would have been back at Rowley Lodge by now.'

I had brought some more champagne, but he refused to drink any. Afraid it might look too much like a celebration, I supposed.

Gillie gave me an uncomplicated hug, and it was she who said, 'I told you so.'

'So you did,' I agreed contentedly. 'And since I won two thousand pounds on your convictions, I'll take you to the Empress.'

The tatty black, however, was tight.

'Just look,' she wailed, pressing in her abdomen with her fingers, 'I wore it only ten days ago and it was perfectly all right. And now, it's impossible.'

'I'm not over addicted to flat chested ladies with hip bones sticking up like Mont Blanc,' I said comfortingly.

'No . . . but voluptuous plenty can go too far.'

'Grapefruit, then?'

She sighed, considered, went to fetch a cream trench coat which covered a multitude of bulges, and said cheerfully, 'Whoever could do justice to Pease Pudding on a grapefruit?'

We toasted the victory in Château Figeac 1964, but out of respect for the tatty black seams ate melon and steak and averted our eyes strong mindedly from the puddings.

Gillie said over the coffee that owing to the continued shortage of orphans she was more or less having time off thrust upon her, and couldn't I think again and let her come to Newmarket.

'No,' I said, more positively than I intended.

She looked a little hurt, which was unusual enough in her to bother me considerably.

'You remember those bruises I had, about five weeks ago?' I said.

'Yes, I do.'

'Well . . . they were the beginning of a rather unpleasant argument I am still having with a man who has a strong line in threats. So far I have resisted some of the threats, and at present there's a sort of stalemate.' I paused. 'I don't want to upset that balance. I don't want to give him any levers. I've no wife, no children, and no near relatives except a father well protected in hospital. There's no one the enemy can threaten . . . no one for whose sake I will do anything he says. But you see . . . if you come to Newmarket, there would be.'

She looked at me for a long time, taking it in, but the hurt went away at once.

Finally she said, 'Archimedes said that if he could find somewhere to stand he could shift the world.'

'Huh?'

'With a lever,' she said, smiling. 'You uneducated goose.'

'Let's not give Archimedes a foothold.'

'No.' She sighed. 'Set your tiny mind at rest. I'll pay you no visits until invited.'

Back at the flat, lying side by side in bed and reading the Sunday papers in companionable quiet, she said, 'You do see what follows from allowing him no levers?'

'What?'

'More bruises.'

'Not if I can help it.'

She rolled her head on the pillow and looked at me. 'You know damn well. You're no great fool.'

'It won't come to that,' I said.

She turned back to the *Sunday Times*. 'There's an advertisement here for travel on a cargo boat to Australia . . . Would you feel safer if I went on a cruise on a cargo boat to Australia? Would you like me to go?'

'Yes, I would,' I said. 'And no I wouldn't.'

'Just an offer.'

'Declined.'

She smiled. 'Don't leave this address lying about, then.'

'I haven't.'

She put the paper down. 'Just how much of a lever do you suppose I am?'

I threw the *Observer* on the floor. 'I'll show you, if you like.'

'Please do,' she said; and switched off the light.

Chapter Twelve

'I would like you to come in my car to the races,' I said to Alessandro on Wednesday morning, when he turned up for the first lot. 'Give Carlo a day off.'

He looked back dubiously to where Carlo sat as usual in the Mercedes, staring watchfully down the yard.

'He says I talk with you too much. He will object.'

I shrugged. 'All right,' I said, and walked off to mount Cloud Cuckoo-land. We took the string down to Waterhall, where Alessandro rode a pipe opener on both Buckram and Lancat, and Etty grudgingly said that they both seemed to be going well for him. The thirty or so others that we took along there didn't seem to be doing so badly either, and the Lincoln booster was still fizzing around in grins and good humour. The whole stable, that week, had come alive.

Pullitzer had set off to Catterick early in the smaller of the stable's two horse-boxes, accompanied by his own lad and the travelling head lad, Vic Young, who supervised the care of the horses while they were away from home. Second in command to Etty, he was a resourceful, quick-witted Londoner grown too heavy in middle age to ride most of the young stable inmates; but the weight came in useful for throwing around. Vic Young was a great one for getting his own way, and it was just good luck that his own way, was usually to the stable's advantage. He was, like all the best older lads, deeply partisan.

When I went out after changing, ready to follow to the races, I found Alessandro waiting beside the Jensen, with Carlo glowering in the Mercedes six feet away.

'I will come in your car,' announced Alessandro firmly. 'But Carlo will follow us.'

'Very well,' I nodded.

I slid down into the driving seat and waited while he got in beside me. Then I started up, moved down the drive, and turned out of the gate with Carlo following in convoy.

'My father ordered him to drive me everywhere ...' Alessandro explained.

'And he doesn't care to disobey your father,' I finished for him.

'That is right. My father also ordered him to make sure I am safe.'

I slid a glance sideways.

'Don't you feel safe?'

'No one would dare to hurt me,' he said simply.

'It would depend what there was to gain,' I said, speeding away from Newmarket.

'But my father ...'

'I know,' I said. 'I know. And I have no wish to harm you. None at all.'

Alessandro subsided, satisfied. But I reflected that levers could work both ways, and Enso unlike me did have someone for whose sake he could be forced to do things against his will. Suppose, I daydreamed idly, that I abducted Alessandro and shut him up in the convenient cellar in the flat in Hampstead. I would then have Enso by the short and curlies in a neat piece of tit for tat.

I sighed briefly. Too many problems that way. And since all I wanted from Enso was for him to get off my back and out of my life before my father came out of hospital, abducting Alessandro didn't seem the quickest way of doing it. The quickest way to the dissolution of Rowley Lodge, more like. Pity, though ...

Alessandro was impatient for the journey to be over, but was otherwise calmer than I had feared. Determination, however, shouted forth from the arrogant carriage of his head down to the slender hands which clenched and unclenched at intervals on his knees.

I avoided an oncoming oil tanker whose driver seemed to think he was in France, and said casually, 'You won't be able to threaten the other apprentices with reprisals if you don't get it all your own way. You do understand that, don't you?'

He looked almost hurt. 'I will not do that.'

'The habits of a lifetime,' I said without censure, 'Are apt to rear their ugly heads at moments of stress.'

'I will ride to win,' he asserted.

'Yes . . . But do remember that if you win by pushing someone else out of the way, the Stewards will take the race away from you, and you'll gain nothing.'

'I will be careful,' he said, with his chin up.

'That's all that is required,' I confirmed. 'Generosity is not.'

He looked at me with suspicion. 'I do not always know if you are meaning to make jokes.'

'Usually,' I said.

We drove steadily north.

'Did it never occur to your father to buy you a Derby prospect, rather than to insert you into Rowley Lodge by force?' I enquired conversationally, as we sped past Wetherby.

He looked as if the possibility were new to him. 'No,' he said. 'It was Archangel I wanted to ride. The favourite. I want to win the Derby, and Archangel is the best. And all the money in Switzerland would not buy Archangel.'

That was true, because the colt belonged to a great sportsman, an eighty-year-old merchant banker, whose life-long ambition it had been to win the great race. His horses had in years gone by finished second and third, and he had won every other big race in the Calendar, but the ultimate peak had always eluded him. Archangel was the best he had ever had, and time was running short.

'Besides,' Alessandro added, 'My father would not spend the money if a threat would do instead.'

As usual when referring to his father's modus operandi, he took it entirely for granted and saw nothing in it but logic.

'Do you ever think objectively about your father?' I asked. 'About how he achieves his ends, and about whether the ends themselves are of any merit?'

He looked puzzled. 'No . . .' he said uncertainly.

'Where did you go to school, then?' I said, changing tack.

'I didn't go to school,' he said. 'I had two teachers at home. I did not want to go to school. I did not want to be ordered about and to have to work all day . . .'

'So your two teachers spent a lot of time twiddling their thumbs?'

'Twiddling . . .? Oh, yes. I suppose so. The English one used to go off and climb mountains and the Italian one chased the local girls.' There was no humour, however, in his voice. There never was. 'They both left when I was fifteen. They left because I was then riding my two horses all day long and my father said there was no point in paying for two tutors instead of one riding master . . . so he hired one old Frenchman who had been an instructor in the cavalry, and he showed me how to ride better. I used to go and stay with a man my father knew and go hunting on his horse . . . and that is when I rode a bit in races. Four or five races. There were not many for amateurs. I liked it, but I didn't feel as I do now . . . And then, one day at home when I was saying I was bored, my father said, very well, Alessandro, say what you want and I will get it for you, and into my head came Archangel, and I just said, just like that, without really thinking, 'I want to win the English Derby on Archangel . . .' and he just laughed, how he sometimes does, and said, so I should.' He paused. 'After that, I asked him if he meant it, because the more I thought about it the more I knew there was nothing on earth I wanted more. Nothing on earth I wanted at all. He kept saying all in good time, but I was impatient to come to England and start, so when he had finished some business, we came.'

For about the tenth time he twisted round in his seat to look out of the back window. Carlo was still there, faithfully following.

'Tomorrow,' I said, 'He can follow us again, to Liverpool. After Buckram for you tomorrow we have five other horses running at the meeting, and I'm staying there for the three days. I won't be coming with you to Teesside for Lancat.'

He opened his mouth to protest, but I said, 'Vic Young is going up with Lancat. He will do all the technical part. It's the big race of the afternoon, as you know, and you'll be riding against very experienced jockeys. But all you've got to do is get quietly up on that colt, point it in the right direction, and tell it where to accelerate. And if it wins, for God's sake don't brag about how brilliant you are. There's nothing puts backs up quicker than a boastful jockey, and if you want the Press on your side, which you most certainly do, you will give the credit to the horse. Even if you don't feel in the least modest, it will pay to act it.'

He digested this with a stubborn look which gradually softened into plain thoughtfulness. I deemed I might as well take advantage of a receptive mood, so I went on with the pearls of wisdom.

'Don't despair if you make a right mess of any race. Everyone does, sometime. Just admit it to yourself. Never fool yourself, ever. Don't get upset by criticism . . . and don't get swollen-headed from praise . . . and keep your temper on a racecourse, all of the time. You can lose it as much as you like on the way home.'

After a while he said, 'You have given me more instructions on behaviour than on how to win races.'

'I trust your social manners less than your horsemanship.'

He worked it out, and didn't know whether to be pleased or not.

After the glitter of Doncaster, Catterick Bridge racecourse disappointed him. His glance raked the simple stands, the modest weighing room, the small-meeting atmosphere, and he said bitterly, 'Is this . . . all?'

'Never mind,' I said, though I hadn't myself known what to expect. 'Down there on the course are seven important furlongs, and they are all that matters.'

The parade ring itself was attractive with trees dotted all around. Alessandro came out there in yellow and blue silks, one of a large bunch of apprentices, most of whom looked slightly smug or self-conscious or nervous, or all of them at once.

Alessandro didn't. His face held no emotion whatsoever. I had expected him to be excited, but he wasn't. He watched Pullitzer plod round the parade ring as if he were of no more interest to him than a herd of cows. He settled into the saddle casually, and without haste gathered the reins to his satisfaction. Vic Young stood holding Pullitzer's rug and gazing up at Alessandro doubtfully.

'Jump him off, now,' he said admonishingly. 'You've got to keep him up there as long as you can.'

Alessandro met my eyes over Vic's head. 'Ride the way you've planned,' I said, and he nodded.

He went away without fuss on to the course and Vic Young, watching him go, exclaimed to me, 'I never did like that sooty little sod, and now he doesn't look as though he's got his heart in the job.'

'Let's wait and see,' I said soothingly. And we waited. And we saw.

Alessandro rode the race exactly as he'd said he would. Drawn number five of sixteen runners he made his way over to the rails in the first two furlongs, stayed steadfastly in fifth or sixth place for the next three, moved up slightly after that, and in the last sixty yards found an opening and some response from Pullitzer, and shot through the leading pair of apprentices not more than ten strides from the post. The colt won by a length and a half, beginning to waver.

He hadn't been backed and he wasn't much cheered, but Alessandro didn't seem to need it. He slid off the horse in the unsaddling enclosure and gave me a cool stare quite devoid of the arrogant self-satisfaction I had been expecting. Then suddenly his face dissolved into the smile I'd only seen him give that once to Margaret, a warm, confident, uncomplicated expression of delight.

'I did it,' he said, and I said, 'You did it beautifully,' and he could certainly see that I was as pleased as he was.

Pullitzer's win was not popular with the lads. No one had had a penny on it, and when Vic got back and reported that the old horse must have developed a lot with age as Alessandro hadn't ridden to instructions, they were all quick to deny him any credit. As he seldom talked to any of them, however, I doubted whether he knew.

He was highly self-contained when he came to Rowley Lodge the following morning. Etty had gone down to the Flat on Racecourse side with the first lot to give them some longish steady canters, which because of the distance I had to drive, I couldn't stay to watch. She seemed content to be left in charge for the three days, and had assured me that Lancat and Lucky Lindsay, (bound for a two-year-old five furlongs with an experienced northern jockey), would arrive safely at Teesside on the Saturday.

Alessandro came with me in the Jensen, with Carlo following as before. On the way we mostly discussed the tactics he would need on Buckram and Lancat, and again there was that odd lack of excitement, only this time more marked. Where I would have expected him to be strung up and passionate, he was totally relaxed. Now that he was actually racing, it seemed as if his impatient fever had evaporated.

Buckram didn't win for him, but not because he didn't ride the race he had meant to. Buckram finished third because two other horses were faster, and Alessandro accepted it with surprising resignation.

'He did his best,' he explained simply. 'But we couldn't get there.'

'I saw,' I said; and that was that.

During the rest of the three day meeting I came to know a great many more racing people and began to get the feel of the industry. I saddled our other four runners, which Tommy Hoylake rode, and congratulated him when one of them won.

'Funny thing,' he said, 'The horses are as forward this year as I've ever known them.'

'Is that good or bad?' I asked.

'Are you kidding? But the next trick will be to keep them going till September.'

'My father will be back to do that,' I assured him.

'Oh . . . yes. I suppose he will,' Tommy said without the enthusiasm I would have expected, and took himself off to weigh out for the next race.

On Saturday Lancat cruised home by four lengths at Teesside at twenty-five to one, which increased my season's winnings from two thousand to four thousand five hundred. And that, I imagined, would be the last of the easy pickings: Lancat was the third winner from the stable out of nine runners, and no one was any longer going to suppose that Rowley Lodge was in the doldrums.

Alessandro's and Vic Young's accounts of what had happened at Teesside were predictably different.

Alessandro said, 'You remember, in the trial, that I made up a lot of ground . . . but I did it too soon, because I had been left behind, and then he got tired . . . well, he did produce that burst of speed again, just as we thought, and it worked well. I got him going a little before the last furlong pole and he simply zoomed past the others. It was terrific.'

But Vic Young said, 'He left it nearly too late. Got shut in. The others could ride rings round him, of course. That Lancat must be something special, winning in spite of being ridden by an apprentice having only his third race.'

During the next week we had eight more runners, of which Alessandro rode three. Only one of his was in an apprentice race, and none of them won. In one race he was quite clearly outridden in a tight finish by the champion jockey, but all he said about that was that he would improve, he supposed, with practice.

The owners of all three horses turned up to watch, and raised not a grumble between them. Alessandro behaved towards them with sense and civility, though I gathered from an unguarded sneer that he let loose when he thought no one was looking, that he was acting away like crazy.

One of the owners was an American who turned out to be one of the subscribers to the syndicate which had bought out my shops. It amused him greatly to find I was Neville Griffon's son, and he spent some time in the parade ring before the race telling Alessandro that this young fellow here, meaning me, could teach everyone he knew a thing or two about how to run a business.

'Never forgot how you summed up your recipe for success, when we bought you out. "Put an eyecatcher in the window, and deal fair." We'd asked you, remember? And we were expecting a whole dose of the usual management-school jargon, but that was all you said. Never forgot it.'

It was his horse on which Alessandro lost by a head, but he had owned racehorses for a long time and knew what he was seeing, and he turned to me on the stands immediately they had passed the post, and said, 'Never a disgrace to be beaten by the champion . . . and that boy of yours, he's going to be good.'

The following week, Alessandro rode in four races and won two of them, both against apprentices. On the second occasion he beat the previous season's star apprentice discovery on the home ground at Newmarket, and the Press began to ask questions. Four wins in three weeks had put him high on the apprentice list . . . Where had he come from, they wanted to know. One or two of them spoke to Alessandro himself, and to my relief he answered them quietly. Strictly eyes down, even if tongue in cheek. The old habitual arrogance was kept firmly out of sight.

He usually came to the races in the Jensen, but Carlo never gave up following. The arrangement had become routine.

He talked quite a lot on the journeys. Talked naturally, unselfconsciously, without strain. Mostly we discussed the horses and their form and possibilities in relation to the opposition, but sometimes I had another glimpse or two of his extraordinary home life.

He had not seen his mother since he was about six, when she and his father had had a last appalling row which had seemed to him to go on for days. He said he had been frightened because they were both so violent, and he hadn't understood what it was all about. She kept shouting one word at his father, taunting him, he said, and he had remembered it, though for years he didn't know what it meant. Sterile, he said. That had been the word. His father was sterile. He had had some sort of illness shortly after Alessandro's birth, to which his mother had constantly referred. He couldn't remember her features, only her voice beginning sentences to his father, bitterly and often, with, 'since your illness . . .'

He had never asked his father about it, he added. It would be impossible, he said, to ask.

I reflected that if Alessandro was the only son Enso could ever have, it explained in some measure the obsessive side of his regard for him. Alessandro was special to Enso in a psychologically disturbing way, and Enso, with well developed criminal characteristics, was not a normal character in the first place.

As Alessandro's riding successes became more than coincidences, Etty unbent to him a good deal: and Margaret unbent even more. For a period of about four days there was an interval of peaceful, constructive teamwork in a friendly atmosphere. Something which looking back to the day of his arrival one would have said was as likely as snow in Singapore.

Four days, it lasted. Then he arrived one morning with a look of almost apprehension, and said that his father was coming to England. Was flying over, that same afternoon. He had telephoned, and he hadn't sounded pleased.

Chapter Thirteen

Enso moved into the Forbury Inn and the very next day the prickles were back in Alessandro's manner. He refused to go to Epsom with me in the Jensen: he was going with Carlo.

'Very well,' I said calmly, and had a distinct impression that he wanted to say something, to explain, to entreat . . . perhaps something like that . . . but that loyalty to his father was preventing it. I smiled a bit ruefully at him and added, 'But any day you like, come with me.'

There was a flicker in the black eyes, but he turned away without answering and walked off to where Carlo was waiting: and when we arrived at Epsom I found that Enso had travelled with him as well.

Enso was waiting for me outside the weighing room, a shortish chubby figure standing harmlessly in the April sunshine. No silenced pistol. No rubberfaced henchmen. No ropes round my wrists, needles in my arm. Yet my scalp contracted and the hairs on my legs rose on end.

He held in his hand the letter I had written him, and the hostility in his puffy lidded eyes beat anything Alessandro had ever conjured up by a good twenty lengths.

'You have disobeyed my instructions,' he said, in the sort of voice which would have sent bolder men than I scurrying for shelter. 'I told you that Alessandro was to replace Hoylake. I find that he has not done so. You have given my son only crumbs. You will change that.'

'Alessandro,' I said, with as unmoved an expression as I could manage, 'has had more opportunities than most apprentices get in their first six months.'

The eyes flashed with a thousand kilowatt sizzle. 'You will not talk to me in that tone. You will do as I say. Do you understand? I will not tolerate your continued disregard of my instructions.'

I considered him. Where on the night he had abducted me he had been deliberate and cool, he was now fired by some inner strong emotion. It made him no less dangerous. More, possibly.

'Alessandro is riding a very good horse in the Dean Swift Handicap this afternoon,' I said.

'He tells me this race is not important. It is the Great Metropolitan which is important. He is to ride in that race as well.'

'Did he say he wanted to?' I asked curiously, because our runner in the Great Met was the runaway Traffic, and even Tommy Hoylake regarded the prospect without joy.

'Of course,' Enso insisted, but I didn't wholly believe him. I thought he had probably bullied Alessandro into saying it.

'I'm afraid,' I said with insincere regret, 'That the owner could not be persuaded. He insists that Hoylake should ride. He is adamant.'

Enso smouldered, but abandoned the lost cause. He said instead, 'You will try harder in future. Today, I will overlook. But there is to be no doubt, no shadow of doubt, do you understand, that Alessandro is to ride this horse of yours in the Two Thousand Guineas. Next week he is to ride Archangel, as he wishes. Archangel.'

I said nothing. It was still as impossible for Alessandro to be given the ride on Archangel as ever it was, even if I wanted to, which I didn't. The merchant banker was never going to agree to replacing Tommy Hoylake with an apprentice of five weeks' experience, not on the starriest Derby prospect he had ever owned. And for my father's sake also, Archangel had to have the best jockey he could. Enso took my continuing silence for acceptance, began to look less angry and more satisfied, and finally turned his back on me in dismissal.

Alessandro rode a bad race in the Handicap. He knew the race was the Derby distance, and he knew I was giving him practice at the mile and a half because I hoped he would win the big apprentice race of that length two days later: but he hopelessly misjudged things, swung really wide at Tattenham Corner, failed to balance his mount in and out of the dip, and never produced the speed that was there for the asking.

He wouldn't meet my eyes when he dismounted, and after Tommy Hoylake won the Great Met (as much to Traffic's surprise as to mine) I didn't see him for the rest of the day.

Alessandro rode four more races that week, and in none of them showed his former flair. He lost the apprentices' race at Epsom by a glaringly obvious piece of mistiming, letting the whole field slip him half a mile from home and failing to reach third place by a neck, though travelling faster than anything else at the finish.

At Sandown on the Saturday the two owners he rode for both told me after he trailed in mid-field on their fancied and expensive three-year-olds that they did not agree that he was as good as I had made out, that my father would have known better, and that they would like a different jockey next time.

I relayed these remarks to Alessandro by sending into the changing room for him and speaking to him in the weigh-room itself. I was now given little opportunity to talk to him anywhere else. He was wooden in the mornings and left the instant he dismounted, and at the races he was continuously flanked by Enso and Carlo, who accompanied him everywhere like guards.

He listened to me with desperation. He knew he had ridden badly, and made no attempt to justify himself. All he said, when I had finished, was, 'Can I ride Archangel in the Guineas?'

'No,' I said.

His black eyes burned in his distressed face.

'Please,' he said with intensity, 'Please say I can ride him. I beg you.'

I shook my head.

'You don't understand.' It was an entreaty; but I wouldn't and couldn't give him what he wanted.

'If your father will give you anything you ask,' I said slowly, 'Ask him to go back to Switzerland and leave you alone.'

It was he then who shook his head, but helplessly, not in disagreement.

'Please,' he said again, but without any hope in his voice, 'I must . . . ride Archangel. My father believes that you are going to let me, even though I told him you wouldn't . . . I am so afraid that if you don't, he really will destroy the stable . . . and then I will not be able to race again . . . and I can't . . . bear . . .' He limped to a stop.

'Tell him,' I suggested without emphasis, 'That if he destroys the stable you will hate him for ever.'

He looked at me numbly. 'I think I would,' he said.

'Then tell him so, before he does it.'

'I'll . . .' He swallowed. 'I'll try.'

He didn't turn up to ride out the next morning, the first he had missed since his bump on the head. Etty suggested it was time some of the other apprentices had more chances than the very few I had given them, and indicated that their earlier ill-feeling towards Alessandro had all returned with interest.

I agreed with her for the sake of peace, and drove off for my Sunday visit south.

My father was bearing the stable's successes with fortitude and finding some comfort in its losses. He did however seem genuinely to want Archangel to win the Guineas, and told me he had had long telephone talks with Tommy Hoylake about how it should be ridden.

He said that his assistant trainer was finally showing signs of coming out of his coma, though the doctors feared irreparable brain damage. He thought he would have to find a replacement.

His own leg also was mending properly at last, he said. He hoped to be home in time for the Derby; and he wouldn't be needing me after that.

The hours spent with Gillie were the usual oasis of peace and amusement, and bed-time was even more satisfactory than usual.

Most of the newspapers that day carried summings-up of the Guineas, with varying assessments of Archangel's chances. They all agreed that Hoylake's big race temperament was a considerable asset.

I wondered if Enso read the English papers.

I hoped he didn't.

There were to be no race meetings for the next two days, not until Ascot and Catterick on Wednesday, followed by the Newmarket Guineas meeting on Thursday, Friday and Saturday.

Monday morning, Alessandro appeared on leaden feet with charcoal shadows round his eyes, and said his father was practically raving because Tommy Hoylake was still down to ride Archangel.

'I told him,' he said, 'That you wouldn't let me ride him. I told him I understood why you wouldn't. I told him I would never forgive him if he did any more harm here. But he doesn't really listen. I don't know . . . he's different, somehow. Not how he used to be.'

But Enso, I imagined, was what he had always been. It was Alessandro himself who had changed.

I said merely, 'Stop fretting over it and bend your mind to a couple of races you had better win for your own sake.'

'What?' he said vaguely.

'Wake up, you silly nit. You're throwing away all you've worked so hard for. It soon won't matter a damn if you're warned off for life, you're riding so atrociously you won't get any rides anyway.'

He blinked, and the old fury made a temporary come-back. 'You will not speak to me like that.'

'Want to bet?'

'Oh . . .' he said in exasperation. 'You and my father, you tear me apart.'

'You'll have to choose your own life,' I said matter-of-factly. 'And if it still includes being a jockey, mind you win at Catterick. I'm running Buckram there in the apprentice race, and I should give one of the other lads the chance, but I'm putting you up again, and if you don't win they will likely lynch you.'

The ghost of the arrogant lift of the nose did its best. His heart was no longer in it.

'And on Thursday, here at Newmarket, you can ride Lancat in the Heath Handicap. It's a straight mile, for three-year-olds only, and I reckon he should win it, on his Teesside form. So get cracking, study those races and know approximately what the opposition might do. And you bloody well win them both. Understand?'

He gave me a long stare in which there was all of the old intensity but none of the old hostility.

'Yes,' he said finally. 'I understand. I am to bloody well win them both.' A faint smile rose and died in his eyes over the first attempt at a joke I had ever heard him make.

Etty was tight-lipped and angry over Buckram. My father would not approve, she said; and another private report was clearly on its way.

I sent Vic Young up to Catterick and went myself with three other horses to Ascot, telling myself that I was in duty bound to escort the owners at the bigger meeting, and that it had nothing to do with wanting to avoid Enso.

Out on the Heath during the wait at the bottom of Side Hill for two other stables to complete their canters, I discussed with Alessandro the tactics he proposed using. Apart from the shadows which persisted round his eyes he seemed to have regained some of his former race-day icy calm. It had yet to survive a long drive in his father's company, but it was a hopeful sign.

Buckram finished second. I felt distinctly disappointed when I saw his name on the 'Results from Other Meetings' board at Ascot, but when I got back to Rowley Lodge Vic Young was just returning with Buckram, and he was, for him, enthusiastic.

'He rode a good race,' he said, nodding. 'Intelligent, you might say. Not his fault he got beat. Not like those stinking efforts last week. He didn't look the same boy, not at all.'

The boy walked into the Newmarket parade ring the following afternoon with all the inward-looking self-possession I could want.

'It's a straight mile,' I said, 'Don't get tempted by the optical illusion that the winning post is much nearer than it really is. You'll know where you are by the furlong posts. Don't pick him up until you've passed the one with two on it, by the bushes, even if you think it looks wrong.'

'I won't,' he said seriously. And he didn't.

He rode a copybook race, cool, well paced, unflustered. From looking boxed-in two furlongs out he suddenly sprinted through a split-second opening and reached the winning post an extended length ahead of his nearest rival. With his 5 lb. apprentice allowance and his Teesside form he had carried a lot of public money, and he earned his cheers.

When he slid down from Lancat in the winner's unsaddling enclosure he gave me again the warm rare smile, and I reckoned that as well as too much weight and too much arrogance, he was going to kick the worst problem of too much father.

But his focus shifted to somewhere behind me and the smile changed and disintegrated, first into a deprecating smirk and then into plain apprehension.

I turned round.

Enso stood inside the small white railed enclosure.

Enso, staring at me with the towering venom of the dispossessed.

I stared back. Nothing else to do. But for the first time, I feared I couldn't contain him.

For the first time, I was afraid.

I dare say it was asking for trouble to work at the desk in the oak room after I'd seen round the stables and poured myself a modest scotch. But this time it was a fine light evening on the last day in April, not midnight in a freezing February.

The door opened with an aggressive crash and Enso walked through it with his two men behind him, the stony faced familiar Carlo and another with a long nose, small mouth and no evidence of loving-kindness.

Enso was accompanied by his gun, and the gun was accompanied by its silencer.

'Stand up' he said.

I slowly stood.

He waved the gun towards the door.

'Come,' he said.

I didn't move.

The gun steadied on the central area of my chest. He handled the wicked looking thing as coolly, as familiarly, as a toothbrush.

'I am close to killing you,' he said in such a way that I saw no reason not to believe him. 'If you do not come at once, you will go nowhere.'

This time there were no little jokes about only killing people if they insisted. But I remembered; and I didn't insist. I moved out from behind the desk and walked woodenly towards the door.

Enso moved back to let me pass, too far away from me for me to jump him. But with the two now barefaced helpers at hand, I would have had no chance at all if I had tried.

Across the large central hall of Rowley Lodge the main front door stood open. Outside, through the lobby and the further doors, stood a Mercedes. Not Alessandro's. This one was maroon, and a size larger.

I was invited inside it. The American ex-rubber face drove. Enso sat on my right side in the back, and Carlo on the left. Enso held his gun in his right hand, balancing the silencer on his rounded knee, and his fingers never relaxed. I could feel the angry tension in all his muscles whenever the moving car swayed his weight against me.

The American drove the Mercedes northwards along the Norwich road, but only for a short distance. Just past the Limekilns and before the bridge over the railway line he swung off to the left into a small wood, and stopped as soon as the car was no longer in plain sight of the road.

He had stopped on one of the regular and often highly populated walking grounds. The only snag was that as all horses had to be off the Heath by four o'clock every afternoon, there was unlikely to be anyone at that hour along there to help.

'Out,' Enso said economically; and I did as he said.

There was a short pause while the American, who seemed to be known as Cal to his friends, walked around to the back of the car and opened the boot. From it he took first a canvas grip, which he handed to Carlo. Next he produced a long darkish grey gaberdine raincoat, which he put on although the weather was as good as the forecast. Finally he picked out with loving care a Lee Enfield 303.

Protruding from its underside was a magazine for ten bullets. He very deliberately worked the bolt to bring the first of them into the breach. Then he pulled back the short lever which locked the firing mechanism in the safety position.

I looked at the massive rifle which he handled so carefully yet with such accustomed precision. It was a gun to frighten with as much as to kill, though from what I knew of it, a bullet from it would blow a man to pieces at a hundred yards, would pierce the brick walls of an average house like butter, would penetrate fifteen feet into sand, and if unimpeded would carry acurately for five miles. Compared with a shotgun, which wasn't reliably lethal at a range of more than thirty yards, the Lee Enfield 303 was a dambuster to a peashooter. Compared with the silenced pistol, which couldn't be counted on even as far as a shotgun, it gave making a dash for it over the Heath as much chance of success as a tortoise in the Olympics.

I raised my eyes from the source of these unprofitable thoughts and met the unwinking gaze of its owner. He was obscurely amused, enjoying the effect his pet had had on me. I had never as far as I knew met an assassin before; but without any doubt, I knew then.

'Walk along there,' Enso said, pointing with his pistol up the walking ground. So I walked, thinking that a Lee Enfield made a lot of noise, and that someone would hear, if they shot me with it. The only thing was, the bullet travelled one and a half times as fast as sound, so that you'd be dead before you heard the bang.

Cal had calmly put the big gun under the long raincoat and was carrying it upright with his hand through what was clearly a slit, not a pocket. From even a very short distance away, one would not have known he had it with him.

Not that there was anyone to see. My gloomiest assessments were quite right: we emerged from the little wood on to the narrow end of the Railway Land, and there wasn't a horse or a rider in sight.

Across the field, alongside the railway, there was a fence made of wooden posts with a wooden top rail and plain wire strands below. There were a few bushes bursting green round about, and a calm peaceful late spring evening sunshine touching everything with red gold.

When we reached the fence, Enso said to stop.

I stopped.

'Fasten him up,' he said to Carlo and Cal; and he himself stayed quietly pointing his pistol at me while Cal laid his deadly treasure flat on the ground and Carlo unzipped the canvas hold-all.

From it he produced nothing more forbidding than two narrow leather belts, with buckles. He gave one of them to Cal, and without allowing me the slightest hope of escape, they turned my back towards the fence and each fastened one of my wrists to the top wooden rail.

It didn't seem much. It wasn't even uncomfortable, as the rail was barely more than waist high. It just seemed professional, as I couldn't even turn my hands inside the straps, let alone slide them out.

They stepped away, behind Enso, and the sunlight threw my shadow on the ground in front of me . . . Just a man leaning against a fence on an evening stroll.

Away in the distance on my left I could see the cars going over the railway bridge on the Norwich road, and further still, down towards Newmarket on my right, there were glimpses of the traffic in and out of the town.

The town, the whole area, was bursting with thousands of visitors to the Guineas meeting. They might as well have been at the South Pole. From where I stood, there wasn't a soul within screaming distance.

Just Enso and Carlo and Cal.

I had watched Cal in his efforts on my right wrist, but it seemed to me shortly after they had finished that it was Carlo who had been rougher.

I turned my head and understood why I thought so. He had somehow turned my arm over the top of the rail and strapped it so that my palm was half facing backwards. I could feel the strain taking shape right up through my shoulder and I thought at first he had done it by accident.

Then with unwelcome clarity I remembered what Dainsee had said: the easiest way to break a bone is to twist it, to put it under stress.

Oh Christ, I thought: and my mind cringed.

Chapter Fourteen

I said, 'I thought this sort of thing went out with the Middle Ages.'

Enso was not in the mood for flippant comment.

Enso was stoking himself up into a proper fury.

'I hear everywhere today on the racecourse that Tommy Hoylake is going to win the Two Thousand Guineas on Archangel. Everywhere, Tommy Hoylake, Tommy Hoylake.'

I said nothing.

'You will correct that. You will tell the newspapers that it is to be Alessandro. You will let Alessandro ride Archangel on Saturday.'

Slowly I said, 'Even if I wanted to, I could not put Alessandro on the horse. The owner will not have it.'

'You must find a way,' Enso said. 'There is to be no more of this blocking of my orders, no more of these tactics of producing unsurmountable reasons why you are not able to do as I say. This time, you will do it. This time you will work out how you *can* do it, not how you cannot.'

I was silent.

Enso warmed to his subject.

'Also you will not entice my son away from me.'

'I have not.'

'Liar.' The hatred flared up like magnesium and his voice rose half an octave. 'Everything Alessandro says is Neil Griffon this and Neil Griffon that and Neil Griffon says, and I have heard your name so much that I could cut ... your ... throat.' He was almost shouting as he bit out the last three words. His hands were shaking, and the gun barrel wavered round its target. I could feel the muscles tighten involuntarily in my stomach, and my wrists jump uselessly against the straps.

He took a step nearer and his voice was loud and high.

'What my son wants, I will give him. *I* ... I ... will give him. I will give him what he wants.'

'I see,' I said, and reflected that comprehending the situation went no way at all towards getting me out of it.

'There is no one who does not do as I say,' he shouted. 'No one. When Enso Rivera tells people to do things, they do them.'

Whatever I said was as likely to enrage as to calm him, so I said nothing at all. He took a further step near me, until I could see the glint of gold-capped back teeth and smell the sweet heavy scent of his aftershave.

'You too,' he said. 'You too will do what I say. There is no one who can boast he disobeyed Enso Rivera. There is no one alive who has disobeyed Enso Rivera.' The pistol moved in his grasp and Cal picked up his Lee Enfield, and it was quite clear what had become of the disobedient.

'You would be dead now,' he said. 'And I want to kill you.' He thrust his head forward on his short neck, the strong nose standing out like a beak and the black eyes as dangerous as napalm. 'But my son . . . my son says he will hate me for ever if I kill you . . . And for that I want to kill you more than I have ever wanted to kill anyone . . .'

He took another step and rested the silencer against my thin wool sweater shirt, with my heart thumping away only a couple of inches below it. I was afraid he would risk it, afraid he would calculate that Alessandro would in time get over the loss of his racing career, afraid he would believe that things would somehow go back and be the same as on the day his son casually said, 'I want to ride Archangel in the Derby.'

I was afraid.

But Enso didn't pull the trigger. He said, as if the one followed inexorably from the other, as I suppose in a way it did, 'So I will not kill you . . . but I will make you do what I say. I cannot afford for you not to do what I say. I am going to make you . . .'

I didn't ask how. Some questions are so silly they are better unsaid. I could feel the sweat prickling out on my body and I was sure he could read the apprehension on my face: and he had done nothing at all yet, nothing but threaten.

'Alessandro will ride Archangel,' he said. 'The day after tomorrow. In the Two Thousand Guineas.'

His face was close enough for me to see the blackheads in the unhealthy putty skin.

I said nothing. He wasn't asking for a promise. He was telling me.

He took a pace backwards and nodded his head at Carlo. Carlo picked up the holdall and produced from it a truncheon very like the one I had removed from him in Buckram's box.

Promazine first?

No promazine.

They didn't mess around making things easy, as they had for the horses. Carlo simply walked straight up to me, lifted his right arm with truncheon attached, and brought it down with as much force as he could manage. He seemed to be taking a pride in his work. He concentrated on getting the direction just right. And it wasn't any of the fearsome things like my twisted elbow that he hit, but my collar-bone.

Not too bad, I thought confusedly in the first two seconds of numbness, and anyway steeplechase jockeys broke their collar-bones any bloody day of the week, and didn't make a fuss of it . . . but the difference between a racing fall and Carlo's effort lay in the torque and tension all the way up my arm. They acted like one of Archimedes' precious levers and pulled the ends of my collar-bone apart. When sensation returned with ferocity, I could feel the tendons in my neck tighten into strings and stand out taut with the effort of keeping my mouth shut.

I saw on Enso's face a grey look of suffering: narrow eyes, clamped lips, anxious, contracted muscles, lines showing along his forehead and round his eyes: and realised with extraordinary shock that what I saw on his face was a mirror of my own.

When his jaw relaxed a fraction I knew it was because mine had. When his eyes opened a little and some of the overall tension slackened, it was because the worst had passed with me.

It wasn't sympathy, though, on his part. Imagination, rather. He was putting himself in my place, to savour what he'd caused. Pity he couldn't do it more thoroughly. I'd break a bone for him any time he asked.

He nodded sharply several times, a message of satisfaction. There was still a heavy unabated anger in his manner and no guarantee that he had finished his evening's work. But he looked regretfully at the pistol, unscrewed the silencer, and handed both bits to Cal, who stowed them away under the raincoat.

Enso stepped close to me. Very close. He ran his finger down my cheek and rubbed the sweat from it against his thumb.

'Alessandro will ride Archangel in the Guineas,' he said. 'Because if he doesn't, I will break your other arm. Just like this.'

I didn't say anything. Couldn't, really.

Carlo unfastened the strap from my right wrist and put it with the truncheon in the holdall, and they all three turned their backs on me and walked away across the field and through the wood to the waiting Mercedes.

It took a long inch-by-inch time to get my right hand round to my left, to undo the other strap. After that I sat on the ground with my back against one of the posts, to wait until things got better. They didn't seem to, much.

I looked at my watch. Eight o'clock. Time for dinner, down at the Forbury Inn. Enso probably had his fat knees under the table, tucking in with a good appetite.

In theory it had seemed reasonable that the most conclusive way to defeat him had been to steal his son away. In practice, as I gingerly hugged to my chest my severely sore left arm, I doubted if Alessandro's soul was worth the trouble. Arrogant, treacherous, spoilt little bastard ... but with guts and determination and talent. A mini battlefield, torn apart by loyalty to his father and the lure of success on his own. A pawn, pushed around in a power struggle. But this pawn was all ... and whoever captured the pawn, won the game.

I sighed, and slowly, wincing, got back on my feet. No one except me was going to get me home and bandaged up.

I walked. It was less than a mile. But far enough.

The elderly doctor was fortunately at home when I telephoned.

'What do you mean, you fell off a horse and broke your collar-bone?' he demanded. 'At this hour? I thought all horses had to be off the Heath by four.'

'Look,' I said wearily. 'I've broken my collar-bone. Would you come and deal with it?'

'Mm,' he grunted. 'All right.'

He came within half an hour, equipped with what looked like a

couple of rubber quoits. Clavicle rings, he said, as he proceeded to push
one up each of my shoulders and tie them together behind my back.

'Bloody uncomfortable,' I said.

'Well, if you will fall off horses . . .'

His heavy eyes assessed his handiwork with impassive professionalism.
Tying up broken collar-bones in Newmarket was as regular as
dispensing coughdrops.

'Take some codeine,' he said. 'Got any?'

'I don't know.'

He clicked his tongue and produced a packet from his bag 'Two every
four hours.'

'Thank you. Very much.'

'That's all right,' he said, nodding. He shut his bag and flipped the
clips.

'Have a drink?' I suggested, as he helped me into my shirt.

'Thought you'd never ask,' he said smiling, and dealt with a large
whisky as familiarly as with his bandages. I kept him company, and the
spirit helped the codeine along considerably.

'As a matter of interest,' I said as he reached the second half of his
glassful, 'What illnesses cause sterility?'

'Eh?' He looked surprised, but answered straightforwardly. 'Only two,
really. Mumps and venereal disease. But mumps very rarely causes
complete sterility. Usually affects one testicle only, if it affects any at all.
Syphilis is the only sure sterility one. But with modern treatment, it
doesn't progress that far.'

'Would you tell me more about it?'

'Hypothetical?' he asked. 'I mean, you don't think you yourself may
be infected? Because if so . . .'

'Absolutely not,' I interrupted. 'Strictly hypothetical.'

'Good . . .' He drank efficiently. 'Well. Sometimes people contract both
syphilis and gonorrhoea at once. Say they get treated and cured of
gonorrhoea, but the syphilis goes unsuspected . . . Right? Now syphilis
is a progressive disease, but it can lie quiet for years, doing its slow
damage more or less unknown to its host. Sterility could occur a few
years after infection. One couldn't say exactly how many years, it varies
enormously. But before the sterility occurs, any number of infected
children could be conceived. Mostly, they are stillborn. Some live, but
there's almost always something wrong with them.'

Alessandro had said his father had been ill after he was born, which
seemed to put him in the clear. But venereal disease would account for
Enso's wife's extreme bitterness, and the violent break up of the marriage.

'Henry VIII,' the doctor said, as if it followed naturally on.

'What?' I said.

'Henry VIII,' he repeated patiently. 'He had syphilis. Katherine of
Aragon had about a dozen stillborn children and her one surviving child,
Mary, was barren. His sickly son Edward died young. Don't know about
Elizabeth, not enough data.' He polished off the last drop in his glass.

I pointed to the bottle. 'Would you mind helping yourself?'

He got to his feet and refilled my glass, too. 'He went about blaming his poor wives for not producing sons, when it was his fault all the time. And that extreme fanaticism about having a son . . . and cutting off heads right and left to get one . . . that's typical obsessive syphilitic behaviour.'

'How do you mean?'

'The pepper king,' he said, as if that explained all.

'What had he got to do with pepper, for heaven's sake?'

'Not Henry VIII,' he said impatiently. 'The pepper king was someone else . . . Look, in the medical text books, in the chapter on the advanced complications which can arise from syphilis, there's this bit about the pepper king. He was a chap who had megalomania in an interim stage of G.P.I., and he got this obsession about pepper. He set out to corner all the pepper in the world and make himself into a tycoon, and because of his compulsive fanaticism, he managed it.'

I sorted my way through the maze. 'Are you saying that at a further stage than sterility, our hypothetical syphilitic gent can convince himself that he can move mountains?'

'Not only convince himself,' he agreed, nodding. 'But actually do it. There is literally no one more likely to move mountains than your megalomaniac syphilitic. Not that it lasts for ever, of course. Twenty years, perhaps, in that stage, once it's developed.'

'And then what?'

'G.P.I.' He took a hefty swallow. 'General paralysis of the insane. In other words, descent to cabbage.'

'Inevitable?'

'After this megalomania stage, yes. But not everyone who gets syphilis gets G.P.I., and not everyone who gets G.P.I. gets megalomania first. They're only branch lines . . . fairly rare complications.'

'They would need to be,' I said with feeling.

'Indeed yes. If you meet a syphilitic megalomania, duck. Duck quickly, because they can be dangerous. There's a theory that Hitler was one . . .' He looked at me thoughtfully over the top of his glass, and his old damp eyes slowly widened. His gaze focused on the sling he had put round my arm, and he said as if he couldn't believe what he was thinking, 'You didn't duck quick enough . . .'

'A horse threw me,' I said.

He shook his head. 'It was a direct blow. I could see that . . . but I couldn't believe it. Thought it very puzzling, as a matter of fact.'

'A horse threw me,' I repeated.

He looked at me in awakening amusement. 'If you say so,' he said. 'A horse threw you. I'll write that in my notes.' He finished his drink and stood up. 'Don't stand in his path any more, then. And I'm serious, young Neil. Just remember that Henry VIII chopped off a lot of heads.'

'I'll remember,' I said.

As if I could forget.

I rethought the horse-threw-me story and substituted a fall down the stairs for Etty's benefit.

'What a damn nuisance,' she said in brisk sympathy, and obviously thought me clumsy. 'I'll drive you along to Waterhall in the Land-Rover, when we pull out.'

I thanked her, and while we were waiting for the lads to lead the horses out of the boxes ready for the first lot, we walked round into bay one to check on Archangel. Checking on Archangel had become my most frequent occupation.

He was installed in the most secure of the high security boxes, and since Enso's return to England I had had him guarded day and night. Etty thought my care excessive, but I had insisted.

By day bay one was never left unattended. By night the electric eye was positioned to trap unwanted visitors. Two specially engaged security men watched all the time, in shifts, from the owners' room, whose window looked out towards Archangel's box: and their Alsatian dog on a long tethering chain crouched on the ground outside the box and snarled at everyone who approached.

The lads had complained about the dog, because each time they had to see to any horse in bay one, they had to fetch the security guard to help them. All other stables, they had pointed out, only had a dog on duty at night.

Etty waved an arm to the guard in the window. He nodded, came out into the yard, and held his dog on a short leash so that we could walk by safely. Archangel came over to the door when I opened the top half, and poked his nose out into the soft Mayday morning. I rubbed his muzzle and patted his neck, admiring the gloss on his coat and thinking that he hadn't looked better in all the weeks I'd been there.

'Tomorrow,' Etty said to him with a gleam in her eyes, 'We'll see what you can do, boy, tomorrow.' She smiled at me in partnership, acknowledging finally that I had taken some share in getting him ready. During the past month, since the winners had begun mounting up, her constant air of worry had mostly disappeared, and the confidence I had remembered in her manner had all come back. 'And we'll see how much more we'll have to do with him, to win the Derby.'

'My father will be back for that,' I said, intending to reassure her. But the spontaneity went out of her smile, and she looked blank.

'So he will,' she said. 'Do you know . . . I'd forgotten.'

She turned away from his box and walked out into the main yard. I thanked the large ex-policeman guard and begged him and his mate to be especially vigilant for the next thirty-four hours.

'Safe as the Bank of England, sir. Never you fear, sir.' He was easy with certainty, but I thought him optimistic.

Alessandro didn't turn up to ride out, not for either lot. But when I climbed stiffly out of the Land-Rover after the second dose of Etty's jolting driving, he was standing waiting for me at the entrance to the yard. When I walked towards the door to the office he came to meet me and stopped in my way.

I stopped also, and looked at him. He held himself rigidly, and his face was thin and white with strain.

'I am sorry,' he said jerkily. 'I am sorry. He told me what he had done . . . I did not want it. I did not ask it.'

'Good,' I said casually. I thought about the way I was carrying my head on one side because it was less painful like that. I felt it was time to straighten up. I straightened.

'He said you would now agree to me riding Archangel tomorrow.'

'And what do you think?' I asked.

He looked despairing, but he answered without doubt. 'I think you will not.'

'You've grown up a lot,' I said.

'I have learned from you . . .' He shut his mouth suddenly and shook his head. 'I mean . . . I beg you to let me ride Archangel.'

I said mildly, 'No.'

The words burst out of him, 'But he will break your other arm. He said so, and he always does what he says. He'll break your arm again, and I . . . and I . . .' He swallowed and took a grip on his voice, and said with much more control, 'I told him this morning that it is right that I do not ride Archangel. I told him that if he hurt you any more you would tell the Stewards about everything, and I would be warned off. I told him I do not want him to do any more. I want him to leave me here with you, and let me get on on my own.'

I took a slow deep breath. 'And what did he say to that?'

He seemed bewildered as well as distraught. 'I think it made him even more angry.'

I said in explanation, 'He doesn't so much care about whether or not you ride Archangel in the Guineas. He cares only about making me let you ride it. He cares about proving to you that he can give you everything you ask, just as he always has.'

'But I ask him now to leave you alone. Leave me here. And he will not listen.'

'You are asking him for the only thing he won't give you,' I said.

'And what is that?'

'Freedom.'

'I don't understand,' he said.

'Because he did not want you to have freedom, he gave you everything else. Everything . . . to keep you with him. As he sees it, I have recently been holding out to you the one thing he doesn't want you to have. The power to make a success of life on your own. So his fight with me now is not really about who rides Archangel tomorrow, but about you.'

He understood all right. It drenched him like a revelation.

'I will tell him he has no fear of losing me,' he said passionately. 'Then he will do you no more harm.'

'Don't you do that. His fear of losing you is all that's keeping me alive.'

His mouth opened. He stared at me with the black eyes, a pawn lost between the rooks.

'Then what . . . what am I to do?'

'Tell him that Tommy Hoylake rides Archangel tomorrow.'

His gaze wandered down from my face to the hump made by the clavicle rings and the outline of my arm in its sling inside my jersey.

'I cannot,' he said.

I half smiled. 'He will find out soon enough.'

Alessandro shivered slightly. 'You don't understand. I have seen ...' His voice trailed away and he looked back to my face with a sort of awakening on his own. 'I have seen people he has hurt. Afterwards, I've seen them. There was fear in their faces. And shame, too. I just thought ... how clever he was ... to know how to make people do what he wanted. I've seen how everyone fears him ... and I thought he was marvellous ...' He took a shaky breath. 'I don't want him to make you look like those others.'

'He won't,' I said, with more certainty than I felt.

'But he will not just let Tommy ride Archangel, and do nothing about it. I know him ... I know he will not. I know he means what he says. You don't know what he can be like ... You must believe it. You must.'

'I'll do my best,' I said dryly, and Alessandro almost danced with frustration.

'Neil,' he said, and it was the only time he had used my first name, 'I am afraid for you.'

'That makes two of us,' I said without seriousness, but he was not at all cheered. I looked at him with compassion. 'Don't take it so hard, boy.'

'But you don't ... you don't understand.'

'I do indeed understand,' I said.

'But you don't seem to care.'

'Oh I care,' I said truthfully. 'I'm not mad keen on another smashing up session with your father. But I'm even less keen on crawling along the ground to lick his boots. So Tommy rides Archangel, and we keep our fingers crossed.'

He shook his head, intensely troubled. 'I know him,' he said, 'I know him ...'

'Next week at Bath,' I said, 'You can ride Pullitzer in the apprentice race, and Clip Clop at Chester.'

His expression said plainly that he doubted we would ever reach next week.

'Did you ever have any brothers or sisters?' I asked abruptly.

He looked bewildered at the unconnected question. 'No ... My mother had two more children after me, but they were both born dead.'

Chapter Fifteen

Saturday morning, 2nd May. Two Thousand Guineas day.

The sun rose to another high golden journey over the Heath, and I inched myself uncomfortably out of bed with less fortitude than I would have admired. The thought that Enso could inflict yet more damage was one I hastily shied away from: yet I myself had blocked all his tangents and left him with only one target to aim at. Having engineered the full frontal confrontation, so to speak, it was too late to wish I hadn't.

I sighed. Were eighty-five thoroughbreds, my father's livelihood, the stable's future, and perhaps Alessandro's liberation, worth one broken collar-bone?

Well, yes, they were.

But *two* broken collar-bones?

God forbid.

Through the buzz of my electric razor I considered the pros and cons of the quick getaway. A well organised, unfollowed retreat to the fastnesses of Hampstead. Simple enough to arrange. The trouble was, sometime or other I would have to come back; and while I was away the stable would be too vulnerable.

Perhaps I could fill the house with guests and make sure I was never alone ... but the guests would depart in a day or two, and Enso's idea of vengeance would be like Napoleon brandy, undiluted by passing time.

I struggled into a sweater and went down into the yard hoping that even Enso would see that revenge was useless if it lost you what you prized most on earth. If he harmed me any more, he would lose his son.

It had long been arranged that Tommy Hoylake should take the opportunity of his overnight stay in Newmarket to ride a training gallop in the morning. Accordingly at seven o'clock he drove his Jaguar up the gravel and stopped with a jerk outside the office window.

'Morning,' he said, stepping out.

'Morning.' I looked at him closely. 'You don't look terribly well.'

He made a face. 'Had a stomach ache all night. Threw up my dinner, too. I get like that, sometimes. Nerves, I guess. Anyway, I'm a bit better now. And I'll be fine by this afternoon, don't worry about that.'

'You're sure?' I asked with anxiety.

'Yeah.' He gave a pale grin. 'I'm sure. Like I told you, I get this upset now and again. Nothing to worry about. But look, would you mind if I don't ride this gallop this morning?'

'No,' I said. 'Of course not. I'd much rather you didn't ... We don't want anything to stop you being all right for this afternoon.'

'Tell you what, though. I could give Archangel his pipe-opener. Nice and quiet. How about that?'

'If you're sure you're all right?' I said doubtfully.

'Yeah. Good enough for that. Honest.'

'All right, then,' I said, and he took Archangel out accompanied by Clip Clop, and they cantered a brisk four furlongs, watched by hundreds of the thousands who would yell for him down on the racecourse that afternoon.

Etty was taking the rest of the string along to Waterhall, where several were due for a three-quarter speed mile along the Line gallop.

'Who shall we put on Lucky Lindsay, now we haven't got Tommy?' Etty said. And it presented a slight problem, because we were short of enough lads with good hands.

'I suppose we had better swop them around,' I said, 'And put Andy on Lucky Lindsay and Faddy on Irrigate, and . . .'

'No need,' Etty interrupted, looking towards the drive. 'Alex is good enough, isn't he?'

I turned round. Alessandro was walking down the yard, dressed for work. Long gone were the dandified clothes and the pale washed gloves: he now appeared regularly in a camel coloured sweater with a blue shirt beneath, an outfit he had copied from Tommy Hoylake on the basis that if that was what a top jockey wore to ride out in, it was what Alessandro Rivera should wear too.

There was no Mercedes waiting behind him in the drive. No watchful Carlo staring down the yard. Alessandro saw my involuntary search for the faithful attendant and he said awkwardly, 'I skipped out. They said not to come, but Carlo's gone off somewhere, so I thought I would. May I . . . I mean, will you let me ride out?'

'Why ever not?' said Etty, who didn't know why ever not.

'Go ahead,' I agreed. 'You can ride the gallop on Lucky Lindsay.'

He was surprised. 'But it said in all the papers that Tommy was riding that gallop this morning.'

'He's got a stomach ache,' I said, and as I saw the wild hope leap in his face, added, 'And don't get excited. He's better, and he will definitely be O.K. for this afternoon.'

'Oh.'

He smothered the shattered hope as best he could and went off to fetch Lucky Lindsay. Etty was riding Cloud Cuckoo-land along with the string, but I had arranged to have George drive me down later in the Land-Rover in time to watch the gallops. The horses pulled out, circled in the paddock to sort out the riders, and went away out of the gate, turning left along the walking ground towards Waterhall.

With them went Lancat, but he, after his hard race two days earlier, was just to go as far as the main road crossing, and then turn back.

I watched them all go, glossy and elegant creatures on one of those hazy May mornings like the beginning of the world. I took a deep regretful breath. It was strange . . . but in spite of Enso and his son, I had enjoyed my spell as a race-horse trainer. I was going to be sorry when I had to leave. Sorrier than I had imagined. Odd, I thought. Very odd.

I walked back up the yard, talked for a few minutes to Archangel's security guard, who was taking the opportunity of his absence to go off to the canteen for his breakfast, went into the house, made some coffee, and took it into the office. Margaret didn't come on Saturdays. I drank some of the coffee and opened the morning's mail by holding the envelopes between my knees and slitting them with a paper-knife.

I heard a car on the gravel, and the slam of a door, and just missed seeing who was passing the window through misjudging the speed at which I could turn my head. Any number of people would be coming to visit the stable on Guineas' morning. Any of the owners who were staying in Newmarket for the meeting. Anyone.

It was Enso who had come. Enso with his silenced leveller. He was waving it about as usual. So early in the morning, I thought frivolously. Guns before breakfast. Damn silly.

The end of the road, I thought. The end of the damn bloody road.

If Enso had looked angry before, he now looked explosive. The short thick body moved like a tank round the desk towards where I sat, and I knew what Alessandro meant about knowing what he could be like. Enso up in Railway Field had been an appetiser: this one was a holocaust.

He waded straight in with a fierce right jab onto the elderly doctor's best bandaging, which took away at one stroke my breath, my composure and most of my resistance. I made a serious stab at him with the paper-knife and got my wrist bashed against the edge of the filing cabinet in consequence. He was strong and energetic and frightening, and I was not being so much beaten by Enso as overwhelmed. He hit me on the side of my head with his pistol and then swung it by the silencer and landed the butt viciously on my shoulder, and by that time I was half sick and almost past caring.

'Where is Alessandro?' he shouted, two centimetres from my right ear.

I sagged rather spinelessly against the desk. I had my eyes shut. I was doing my tiny best to deal with an amount of feeling that was practically beyond my control.

He shook me. Not nice. 'Where is Alessandro?' he yelled.

'On a horse,' I said weakly. 'Where else? On a horse.'

'You have abducted him,' he yelled. 'You will tell me where he is. Tell me . . . or I'll break your bones. All of them.'

'He's out riding a horse,' I said.

'He's not,' Enso shouted. 'I told him not to.'

'Well . . . he is.'

'What horse?'

'What does it matter?'

'*What horse?*' He was practically screaming in my ear.

'Lucky Lindsay,' I said. As if it made any difference. I pushed myself upright in the chair and got my eyes open. Enso's face was only inches away and the look in his eyes was a death warrant.

The gun came up. I waited numbly.

'Stop him,' he said. 'Get him back.'

'I can't.'

'You must. Get him back or I'll kill you.'

'He's been gone twenty minutes.'

'*Get him back.*' His voice was hoarse, high-pitched, and terrified. It finally got through to me that his rage had turned into agony. The fury had become fear. The black eyes burnt with some unimaginable torment.

'What have you done?' I said rigidly.

'Get him back,' he repeated, as if shouting alone would achieve it. 'Get him back.' He lifted the gun, but I don't think even he knew if he intended to shoot me or to hit me with it.

'I can't,' I said flatly. 'Whatever you do, I can't.'

'He will be killed,' he yelled wildly. 'My son . . . my son will be killed.' He waved his arms wide and his whole body jerked uncontrollably. 'Tommy Hoylake . . . It says in the newspapers that Tommy Hoylake is riding Lucky Lindsay this morning . . .'

I shifted to the front of the chair, tucked my legs underneath it, and made the cumbersome shift up on to my feet. Enso didn't try to shove me back. He was too preoccupied with the horror trotting through his mind.

'Tommy Hoylake . . . Hoylake is riding Lucky Lindsay.'

'No,' I said roughly. 'Alessandro is.'

'Tommy Hoylake . . . Hoylake . . . It has to be, it has to be . . .' His eyes were stretching wider and his voice rose higher and higher.

I lifted my hand and slapped him hard in the face.

His mouth stayed open but the noise coming out of it stopped as suddenly as if it had been switched off.

Muscles in his cheeks twitched. His throat moved continuously. I gave him no time to get going again.

'You were planning to kill Tommy Hoylake.'

No answer.

'How?' I said.

No answer. I slapped his face again, with everything I could manage. It wasn't very much.

'*How?*'

'Carlo . . . and Cal . . .' The words were barely distinguishable.

Horses on the Heath, I thought. Tommy Hoylake riding Lucky Lindsay. Carlo, who knew every horse in the yard, who watched all the horses every day and knew Lucky Lindsay by sight as infallibly as any tout. And Cal. . . I felt my own gut contract much as Enso's must have done. Cal had the Lee Enfield 303.

'Where are they?' I said.

'I . . . don't . . . know.'

'You'd better find them.'

'They . . . are . . . hiding.'

'Go and find them,' I said. 'Go out and find them. It's your only chance. It's Alessandro's only chance. Find him before they shoot him . . . you stupid murdering sod.'

He stumbled as if blind round the desk and made for the door. Still holding the pistol he bashed into the frame and rocked on his feet. He righted himself, crashed down the short passage and out through the door into the yard, and half ran on unsure legs to his dark red Mercedes. He took three shots at starting the engine before it fired. Then he swept round in a frantic arc, roared away up the drive and turned right on to the Bury Road with a shriek of tyres.

Bloody, murdering sod . . . I followed him out of the office but turned down the yard.

Couldn't run. The new hammering he'd given my shoulder made even walking a trial. Stupid, mad, murdering bastard . . . Twenty minutes since Alessandro rode out on Lucky Lindsay . . . twenty minutes, and the rest. They'd be pretty well along at Waterhall. Circling round at the end of the Line gallop, forming up into groups. Setting off . . .

Damn it, I thought. Why don't I just go and sit down and wait for whatever happens. If Enso kills his precious son, serve him right.

I went faster down the yard. Through the gates into the bottom bays. Through the far gate. Across the little paddock. Out through the gate to the Heath. Turned left.

Just let him be coming back, I thought. Let him be coming back. Lancat, coming back from his walk, saddled and bridled and ready to go. He was there, coming towards me along the fence, led by one of the least proficient riders, sent back by Etty as he was little use in the gallops.

'Help me take this jersey off,' I said urgently.

He looked surprised, but lads my father had trained never argued. He helped me take off the jersey. He was no Florence Nightingale. I told him to take the sling off as well. No one could ride decently in a sling.

'Now give me a leg up.'

He did that too.

'O.K.' I said. 'Go on in. I'll bring Lancat back later.'

'Yes, sir,' he said. And if I'd told him to stand on his head he would have said yes, sir, just the same.

I turned Lancat back the way he had come. I made him trot along the walking ground. Too slow. Much too slow. Started to canter, breaking the Heath rules. It felt horrible. I twitched him out on to the Bury Hill ground which wasn't supposed to be used for another fortnight and pointed him straight at the Bury Road crossing.

Might as well gallop . . . I did the first five furlongs on the gallop and the next three along the walking ground without slowing down much, and frightened a couple of early morning motorists as I crossed the main road.

Too many horses on Waterhall. I couldn't from more than half a mile away distinguish the Rowley Lodge string from others. All I could see was that it wasn't yet too late. The morning scene was peaceful and orderly. No appalled groups bending over bleeding bodies.

I kept Lancat going. He'd had a hard race two days earlier and shouldn't have been asked for the effort I was urging him into . . . he was fast and willing, but I was running him into the ground.

It was technically difficult, riding in clavicle rings, let alone anything else. However, the ground looked very hard and too far down. I stayed in the saddle as the lesser of two considerable evils. I did wish most fervently that I had stayed at home. I knew all about steeplechase jockeys riding races with broken collar-bones. They were crazy. It was for the birds.

I could see Etty. See some of the familiar horses.

I could see Alessandro on Lucky Lindsay.

I was too far away to be heard even if I'd had any breath for shouting, and neither of them looked behind them.

Alessandro kicked Lucky Lindsay into a fast canter and with two other horses accelerated quickly up the Line gallop.

A mile away, up the far end of it, there were trees and scrub, and a small wood.

And Carlo. And Cal.

I had a frightful feeling of inevitable disaster, like trying to run away through treacle in a nightmare. Lancat couldn't possibly catch the fresh Lucky Lindsay up the gallop. Interception was the only possibility, yet I could misjudge it so terribly easily.

I set off straight across Waterhall, galloping across the cantering ground and then charging over the Middle Canter in the opposite direction to the horses working there. Furious yells from all sides didn't deter me. I hoped Lancat had enough sense not to run head on into another horse, but apart from that my only worry, my sole, embracing, consuming worry, was to get to Alessandro before a bullet did.

Endless furlongs over the grass . . . only a mile, give or take a little . . . but endless. Lancat was tiring, finding every fresh stride a deeper effort . . . his fluid rhythm had broken into bumps . . . he wouldn't be fit again to race for months . . . I was asking him for the reserves, the furthest stores of power . . . and he poured them generously out.

Endless furlongs . . . and I wasn't getting the angle right . . . Lancat was slowing and I'd reach the Line gallop after Alessandro had gone past. I swerved more to the right . . . swayed perilously in the saddle, couldn't even hold the reins in my left hand and I wanted to hold on to the neck-strap with my right, wanted to hold on for dear life, and if I held on, I couldn't steer . . . It wasn't far, not really. No distance at all on a fresh horse. No distance at all for Lucky Lindsay.

All the trees and bushes up ahead . . . somewhere in there lay Carlo and Cal . . . and if Enso didn't know where, he wasn't going to find them. People didn't lie about in full sight, not with a Lee Enfield aimed at a galloping horse; and Cal would have to be lying down. Have to be, to be accurate enough. A Lee Enfield was as precise as any gun ever made, but only if one aimed and fired while lying down. It kicked too much to be reliable if one was standing up.

Enso wouldn't find them. He might find the car. Alessandro's Mercedes. But he wouldn't find Carlo and Cal until the thunderous noise gave away their position . . . and no one but Enso would find them even then, before they reached the car and drove away. Everyone would be concentrating on Alessandro with a hole torn in his chest, Alessandro in his camel jersey and blue shirt which were just like Tommy Hoylake's.

Carlo and Cal knew Alessandro . . . they knew him well . . . but they thought he had obeyed his father and stayed in the hotel . . . and one jockey looked very like another, from a distance, on a galloping horse . . .

Alessandro, I thought. Galloping along in the golden May morning . . . straight to his death.

I couldn't go any faster. Lancat couldn't go any faster. Didn't know about the horse's breath, but mine was coming out in great gulps. Nearer to sobs, I dare say. I really should have stayed at home.

Shifted another notch to the right and kicked Lancat. Feeble kick. Didn't increase the speed.

We were closing. The angle came sharper suddenly as the Line gallop began its sweep round to the right. Lucky Lindsay came round the corner to the most vulnerable stretch . . . Carlo and Cal would be there . . . they would be ahead of him, because Cal would be sure of hitting a man coming straight towards him . . . there weren't the same problems as in trying to hit a crossing target . . .

They must be able to see me too, I thought. But if Cal was looking down his sights, levelling the blade in the ring over Alessandro's brown sweater and black bent head, he wouldn't notice me . . . wouldn't anyway see any significance in just another horse galloping across the Heath.

Lancat swerved of his own volition towards Lucky Lindsay and took up the race . . . a born and bred competitor bent even in exhaustion on getting his head in front.

Ten yards, ten feet . . . and closing.

Alessandro was several lengths ahead of the two horses he had started out with. Several lengths ahead, all on his own.

Lancat reached Lucky Lindsay at an angle and threw up his head to avoid a collision . . . and Alessandro turned his face to me in wide astonishment . . . and although I had meant to tell him to jump off and lie flat on the ground until his father succeeded in finding Carlo and Cal, it didn't happen quite like that.

Lancat half rose up into the air and threw me, twisting, on to Lucky Lindsay, and I put my right arm out round Alessandro and scooped him off, and we fell like that down on to the grass. And Lancat fell too, and lay across our feet, because brave, fast, determined Lancat wasn't going anywhere any more.

Half of Lancat's neck was torn away, and his blood and his life ran out on to the bright green turf.

Alessandro tried to twist out of my grasp and stand up.

'Lie still,' I said fiercely. 'Just do as I say, and lie still.'

'I'm hurt,' he said.

'Don't make me laugh.'

'I have hurt my leg,' he protested.

'You'll have a hole in your heart if you stand up.'

'You are mad,' he said.

'Look at Lancat . . . What do you think is wrong with him? Do you think he is lying there for fun?' I couldn't keep the bitterness out of my voice, and I didn't try. 'Cal did that. Cal and his big bloody rifle. They came out here to shoot Tommy Hoylake, and you rode Lucky Lindsay instead, and they couldn't tell the difference, which should please you . . . and if you stand up now they'll have another go.'

He lay still. Speechless. And quite, quite still.

I rolled away from him and stuffed my fist against my teeth, for if the truth were told I was hurting far more than I would have believed possible. Him and his damn bloody father ... the free sharp ends of collar-bone were carving new and unplanned routes for themselves through several protesting sets of tissue.

A fair amount of fuss was developing around us. When the ring of shocked spectators had grown solid and thick enough I let him get up, but he only got as far as his knees beside Lancat, and there were smears of the horse's blood on his jodhpurs and jersey.

'Lancat ...' he said hopelessly, with a sort of death in his voice. He looked across at me as a couple of helpful onlookers hauled me to my feet, and the despair on his face was bottomless and total.

'Why?' he said. 'Why did he do it?'

I didn't answer. Didn't need to. He already knew.

'I hate him,' he said.

The people around us began to ask questions but neither Alessandro nor I answered them.

From somewhere away to our right there was another loud unmistakable crack. I and half the gathering crowd involuntarily ducked, but the bullet would already have reached us if it had been coming our way.

One crack, then silence. The echoes died quickly over Waterhall, but they shivered for ever through Alessandro's life.

Chapter Sixteen

Enso had found Carlo and Cal hidden in a clump of bushes near the Boy's Grave crossroads.

We found them there too, when we walked along to the end of the Line gallop to flag down a passing motorist to take Etty quickly into Newmarket. Etty, who had arrived frantic up the gallop, had at first like all the other onlookers taken it for granted that the shooting had been an accident. A stray bullet loosed off by someone being criminally careless with a gun.

I watched the doubt appear on her face when she realised that my transport had been Lancat and not the Land-Rover, but I just asked her matter-of-factly to buzz down to Newmarket and ring up the dead horse removers, then to drive herself back. She sent Andy off with instructions to the rest of the string, and the first car that came along stopped to pick her up.

Alessandro walked off the training ground into the road with a stunned, stony face, and came towards me. He was leading Lucky Lindsay, which someone had caught, but as automatically as if unaware he was there. Three or four paces away, he stopped.

'What am I to do?' he said. His voice was without hope or anxiety. Lifeless. I didn't answer immediately, and it was then that we heard the noise.

A low distressed voice calling unintelligibly.

Startled, I walked along the road a little and through a thin belt of bushes, and there I found them.

Three of them, Enso and Carlo and Cal.

It was Cal who had called out. He was the only one capable of it. Carlo lay sprawled on his back with his eyes open to the sun and a splash of drying scarlet trickling from a hole in his forehead.

Cal had a wider, wetter, spreading stain over the front of his shirt. His breath was shallow and quick, and calling out loud enough to be found had used up most of his energy.

The Lee Enfield lay across his legs. His hand moved convulsively towards the butt, but he no longer had the strength to pick it up.

And Enso . . . Cal had shot Enso with the Lee Enfield at a range of about six feet. It wasn't so much the bullet itself, but the shock wave of its velocity: at that short distance it had dug an entrance as large as a plate.

The force of it had flung Enso backwards, against a tree. He sat there now at the foot of it with the silenced pistol still in his hand and his head sunk forward on his chest. There was a soul-sickening mess where his paunch had been, and his back was indissoluble from the bark.

I would have stopped Alessandro seeing, but I didn't hear him come. I heard only the moan beside me, and I turned abruptly to see the nausea spring out in sweat on his face.

For Cal his appearance there was macabre.

'You . . .' he said. 'You . . . are dead.'

Alessandro merely stared at him, too shocked to understand, too shocked to speak.

Cal's eyes opened wide and his voice grew stronger with a burst of futile anger.

'He said . . . I had killed you. Killed his son. He was . . . out of his senses. He said . . . I should have known it was you . . .' He coughed, and frothy blood slid over his lower lip.

'You did shoot at Alessandro,' I said. 'But you hit a horse.'

Cal said with visibly diminishing strength, 'He shot Carlo . . . and he shot me . . . so I let him have it . . . the son of a bitch . . . he was out . . . of his senses . . .'

The voice stopped. There was nothing anyone could do for him, and presently, imperceptibly, he died.

He died where he had lain in wait for Tommy Hoylake. When I knelt beside him to feel his pulse, and lifted my head to look along the gallop, there in front of me was the view he had had: a clear sight of the advancing horses, from through the sparse low branches of a concealing bush. The dark shape of Lancat lay like a hump on the grass three hundred yards away, and another batch of horses, uncaring, were sweeping round the far bend and turning towards me.

An easy shot, it had been, for a marksman. He hadn't bothered even with a telescopic sight. At that range, with a Lee Enfield, one didn't need one. One didn't need to be of pinpoint accuracy: anywhere on the head or trunk would do the trick. I sighed. If he had used a telescopic sight, he would probably have realised that what he was aiming at was Alessandro.

I stood up. Clumsily, painfully, wishing I hadn't got down.

Alessandro hadn't fainted. Hadn't been sick. The sweat had dried on his face, and he was looking steadfastly at his father.

When I moved towards him he turned, but he needed two or three attempts before he could get his throat to work.

He managed it, finally. His voice was strained; different; hoarse: and what he said was as good an epitaph as any.

'He gave me everything,' he said.

We went back to the road, where Alessandro had tethered Lucky Lindsay to a fence. The colt had his head down to the grass, undisturbed.

Neither of us said anything at all.

Etty clattered up in the Land-Rover, and I got her to turn it round and take me straight down to the town.

'I'll be right back,' I said to Alessandro, but he stared silently at nothing with eyes that had seen too much.

When I went back, it was with the police. Etty stayed behind at Rowley Lodge to see to the stables, because it was, still, and incredibly, Guineas day, and we had Archangel to look to. Also, in the town, I made a detour to the doctor, where I bypassed an outraged queue waiting in his surgery, and got him to put the ends of my collar-bone back into alignment. After that it was a bit more bearable, though nothing still to raise flags about.

I spent most of the morning up at the crossroads. Answered some questions and didn't answer others. Alessandro listened to me telling the highest up of the police who had arrived from Cambridge that Enso had appeared to me to be unbalanced.

The police surgeon was sceptical of a layman's opinion.

'In what way?' he said without deference.

I paused to consider. 'You could look for spirochaetes,' I said, and his eyes widened abruptly before he disappeared back into the bushes.

They were considerate to Alessandro. He sat on somebody's raincoat on the grass at the side of the road, and later on the police surgeon gave him a sedative.

It was an injection, and Alessandro didn't want it. They wouldn't pay attention to his objections, and when the needle went into his arm I found him staring fixedly at my face. He knew that I too was thinking about too many other injections; about myself, and Carlo, and Moonrock and Indigo and Buckram. Too many needles. Too much death.

The drug didn't put him out, just made him look even more dazed than before. The police decided he should go back to the Forbury Inn and sleep, and steered him towards one of their cars.

He stopped in front of me before he reached it, and gazed at me in awe from hollow dark sockets in a grey gaunt face.

'Look at the flowers,' he said. 'On the Boy's Grave.'

When he had gone I walked over to the raincoat where he had been sitting, close to the little mound.

There were pale yellow polyanthus, and blue forget-me-nots coming into flower round the edge: and all the centre was filled with pansies. Dark dark purple velvet pansies, shining black in the sun.

It was cynical of me to wonder if he could have planted them himself.

Enso was in the mortuary and Alessandro was asleep when Archangel and Tommy Hoylake won the Guineas.

Not what they had planned.

A heaviness like thunder persisted with me all afternoon, even though there was by then no reason for it. The defeat of Enso no longer directed half my actions, but I found it impossible in one bound to throw off his influence. It was not until then that I understood how intense it had become.

What I should have felt was relief that the stable was safe. What I did feel was depression.

The merchant banker, Archangel's owner, was practically incandescent with happiness. He glowed in the unsaddling enclosure and joked with the Press in shaky pride.

'Well done, my boy, well done indeed,' he said to me, to Tommy, and to Archangel impartially, and looked ready to embrace us all.

'And now, my boy, now for the Derby, eh?'

'Now for the Derby,' I nodded, and wondered how soon my father would be back at Rowley Lodge.

I went to see him, the next day.

He was looking even more forbidding than usual because he had heard all about the multiple murders on the gallops. He blamed me for letting anything like that happen. It saved him, I reflected sourly, from having to say anything nice about Archangel.

'You should never have taken on that apprentice.'

'No,' I said.

'The Jockey Club will be seriously displeased.'

'Yes.'

'The man must have been mad.'

'Sort of.'

'Absolutely mad to think he could get his son to ride Archangel by killing Tommy Hoylake.'

I had had to tell the police something, and I had told them that. It had seemed enough.

'Obsessed,' I agreed.

'Surely you must have noticed it before? Surely he gave some sign?'

'I suppose he did,' I agreed neutrally.

'Then surely you should have been able to stop him.'

'I did stop him . . . in a way.'

'Not very efficiently,' he complained.

'No,' I said patiently, and thought that the only one who had stopped Enso efficiently and finally had been Cal.

'What's the matter with your arm?'

'Broke my collar-bone,' I said.

'Hard luck.'

He looked down at his still suspended leg, almost but not quite saying aloud that a collar-bone was chicken feed compared with what he had endured. What was more, he was right.

'How soon will you be out?' I asked.

He answered in a smug satisfaction tinged with undisguisable malice. 'Sooner than you'd like, perhaps.'

'I couldn't wish you to stay here,' I protested.

He looked faintly taken aback: faintly ashamed.

'No . . . well . . . They say not long now.'

'The sooner the better,' I said, and tried to mean it.

'Don't do any more work with Archangel. And I see from the Calendar that you have made entries on your own. I don't want you to do that. I am perfectly capable of deciding where my horses should run.'

'As you say,' I said mildly, and with surprisingly little pleasure realised that I now no longer had any reason for amending his plans.

'Tell Etty that she did very well with Archangel.'

'I will,' I said. 'In fact, I have.'

The corners of his mouth turned down. 'Tell her that I said so.'

'Yes,' I said.

Nothing much, after all, had changed between us. He was still what I had run away from at sixteen, and it would take me a lot less time to leave him again. I couldn't possibly have stayed on as his assistant, even if he had asked me to.

'He gave me everything,' Alessandro had said of his father. I would have said of mine that he gave me not very much. And I felt for him something that Alessandro had never through love or hate felt for his.

I felt . . . apathy.

'Go away, now,' he said. 'And on your way out, find a nurse. I need a bedpan. They take half an hour, sometimes, if I ring the bell. And I want it now, at once.'

The driver of the car I had hired in Newmarket was quite happy to include Hampstead in the itinerary.

'A couple of hours?' I suggested, when I had hauled myself out on to the pavement outside the flat.

'Sure,' he said. 'Maybe there's somewhere open for tea, even on Sunday.' He drove off hopefully, optimistic soul that he was.

Gillie said she had lost three pounds, she was painting the bathroom sludge green, and how did I propose to make love to her looking like a washed out edition of a terminal consumptive.

'I don't,' I said. 'Propose.'

'Ah,' she said wisely. 'All men have their limits.'

'And just change that description to looking like a race-horse trainer who has just won his first Classic.'

She opened her mouth and obviously was not going to come across with the necessary compliment.

'O.K.,' I interrupted resignedly. 'So it wasn't me. Everyone else, but not me. I do so agree. Wholeheartedly.'

'Self-pity is disgusting,' she said.

'Mm.' I sat gingerly down in a blue armchair, put my head back, and shut my eyes. Didn't get much sympathy for that, either.

'So you collected the bruises,' she observed.

'That's right.'

'Silly old you.'

'Yes.'

'Do you want some tea?'

'No thank you,' I said politely. 'No sympathy, no tea.'

She laughed. 'Brandy, then?'

'If you have some.'

She had enough for the cares of the world to retreat a pace: and she came across, in the end, with her own brand of fellow-feeling.

'Don't wince,' she said, 'When I kiss you.'

'Don't kiss so damned hard.'

After a bit she said, 'Is this shoulder the lot? Or will there be more to come?'

'It's the lot,' I said, and told her all that had happened. Edited, and flippantly; but more or less all.

'And does your own dear dad know all about this?'

'Heaven forbid,' I said.

'But he will, won't he? When you get this Alessandro warned off? And then he will understand how much he owes you?'

'I don't want him to understand,' I said. 'He would loathe it.'

'Charming fellow, your dad.'

'He is what he is,' I said.

'And was Enso what he was?'

I smiled lopsidedly. 'Same principle, I suppose.'

'You're a nut, Neil Griffon.'

I couldn't dispute it.

How long before he gets out of hospital?' she asked.

'I don't know. He hopes to be on his feet soon. Then a week or two for physiotherapy and walking practice with crutches, or whatever. He expects to be home before the Derby.'

'What will you do then?'

'Don't know,' I said. 'But he'll be three weeks at least, and leverage no longer applies . . . so would you still like to come to Rowley Lodge?'

'Um,' she said, considering. 'There's a three-year-old Nigerian girl I'm supposed to be settling with a family in Dorset . . .'

I felt very tired. 'Never mind, then.'

'I could come on Wednesday.'

When I got back to Newmarket I walked round the yard before I went indoors. It all lay peacefully in the soft light of sundown, the beginning of dusk. The bricks looked rosy and warm, the shrubs were out in flower, and behind the green painted doors the six million quids' worth were safely chomping on their evening oats. Peace in all the bays, winners in many of the boxes, and an air of prosperity and timelessness over the whole.

I would be gone from there soon; and Enso had gone, and Alessandro. When my father came back it would be as if the last three months had never happened. He and Etty and Margaret would go on as they had been before; and I would read about the familiar horses in the newspapers.

I didn't yet know what I would do. Certainly I had grown to like my father's job, and maybe I could start a stable of my own, somewhere else. I wouldn't go back to antiques, and I knew by then that I wasn't going to work any more for Russell Arletti.

Build a new empire, Gillie had said.

Well, maybe I would.

I looked in at Archangel, now no longer guarded by men, dogs and electronics. The big brown colt lifted his head from his manger and turned on me an enquiring eye. I smiled at him involuntarily. He still showed the effects of his hard race the day before, but he was sturdy and sound, and there was a very good chance he would give the merchant banker his Derby.

I stifled a sigh and went indoors, and heard the telephone ringing in the office.

Owners often telephoned on Sunday evenings, but it wasn't an owner, it was the hospital.

'I'm very sorry,' the voice said several times at the other end. 'We've been trying to reach you for some hours now. Very sorry. Very sorry.'

'But he *can't* be dead,' I said stupidly. 'He was all right when I left him. I was with him this afternoon, and he was all right.'

'Just after you left,' they said. 'Within half an hour.'

'But how?' My mind couldn't grasp it. 'He only had a broken leg . . . and that had mended.'

Would I like to talk to the doctor in charge, they said. Yes, I would.

'He was all right when I left him,' I protested. 'In fact he was yelling for a bedpan.'

'Ah. Yes. Well,' said a high pitched voice loaded with professional sympathy. 'That's . . . er . . . that's a very common preliminary to a pulmonary embolus. Calling for a bedpan . . . very typical. But do rest assured, Mr. Griffon, your father died very quickly. Within a few seconds. Yes, indeed.'

'What,' I said with a feeling of complete unreality, 'Is a pulmonary embolus?'

'Blood clot,' he said promptly. 'Unfortunately not uncommon in elderly people who have been bedridden for some time. And your father's fracture . . . well, it's tragic, tragic, but not uncommon, I'm afraid. Death sitting up, some people say. Very quick, Mr. Griffon. Very quick. There was nothing we could do, do believe me.'

'I believe you.'

But it was impossible, I thought. He couldn't be dead. I had been talking to him just that afternoon . . .

The hospital would like instructions, they delicately said.

I would send someone from Newmarket, I said vaguely. An undertaker from Newmarket, to fetch him home.

Monday I spent in endless chat. Talked to the police. Talked to the Jockey Club. Talked to a dozen or so owners who telephoned to ask what was going to happen to their horses.

Talked and talked.

Margaret dealt with the relentless pressure as calmly as she did with Susie and her friend. And Susie's friend, she said, had incidentally reported that Alessandro had not left his room since the police took him there on Saturday morning. He hadn't eaten anything, and he wouldn't talk to anyone except to tell them to go away. Susie's chum's mum said it was all very well, but Alessandro never had any money, and his bill had only been paid up to the previous Saturday, and they were thinking of asking him to go.

'Tell Susie's chum's mum that Alessandro has money here, and also that in Switzerland he will be rich.'

'Will do,' she said, and rang the Forbury Inn at once.

Etty took charge of both lots out at exercise, and somehow or other the right runners got dispatched to Bath. Vic Young went in charge of them and said later that the apprentice who had the ride on Pullitzer instead of Alessandro was no effing good.

To the police I told the whole of what had occurred on Saturday morning, but nothing of what had occurred before it. Enso had recently arrived in England, I said, and had developed this extraordinary fixation. There was no reason for them not to accept this abbreviated version, and nothing to be gained by telling them more.

Down at the Jockey Club I had a lengthy session with a committee of Members and a couple of Stewards left over on purpose from the Guineas meeting, and the outcome of that was equally peaceful.

After that I told Margaret to let all enquiring owners know that I would be staying on a Rowley Lodge for the rest of the season, and they could leave or remove their horses as they wished.

'Are you really?' she said. 'Are you staying?'

'Not much else to do, is there?' I said. But we were both smiling.

'Ever since you told that lie about not being able to find anyone to take over, when you had John Bredon lined up all the time, ever since then I've known you liked it here.'

I didn't disillusion her.

'I'm glad you're staying,' she said. 'I suppose it's very disloyal to your father, as he only died yesterday, but I have much preferred working for you.'

I was not so autocratic, that was all. She would have worked efficiently for anyone.

Before she left at three, she said that none of the owners who had so far telephoned were going to remove their horses; and that included Archangel's merchant banker.

When she had gone I wrote to my solicitors in London and asked them to send back to me at Newmarket the package I had instructed them to open in case of my sudden death.

After that I swallowed a couple of codeines and wondered how soon everything would stop aching, and from five to six thirty I walked round at evening stables with Etty.

We passed by Lancat's empty box.

'Damn that Alex,' Etty said, but with a retrospective anger. The past was past. Tomorrow's races were all that mattered. Tomorrow at Chester. She talked of plans ahead. She was contented, fulfilled, and busy. The transition from my father to me had been too gradual to need now any sudden adjustment.

I left her supervising as usual the evening feeds for the horses and walked back towards the house. Something made me look up along the drive, and there, motionless and only half visible against the tree trunks, stood Alessandro.

It was as if he had got half way down the drive before his courage deserted him. I walked without haste out of the yard and went to meet him.

Strain had aged him so that he now looked nearer forty than eighteen. Bones stood out sharply under his skin, and there was little in the black eyes except no hope at all.

'I came,' he started. 'I need . . . I mean, you said, at the beginning, that I could have half the money I earned racing . . . Can I still . . . have it?'

'You can,' I said. 'Of course.'

He swallowed. 'I am sorry to come, I had to come. To ask you about the money.'

'You can have it now,' I said. 'Come along into the office.'

I half turned away from him but he didn't move.

'No. I . . . can't.'

'I'll send it along to the Forbury Inn for you,' I said.

He nodded. 'Thank you.'

'Do you have any plans?' I asked him.

The shadows in his face if anything deepened.

'No.'

He visibly gathered every shred of resolution, clamped his teeth together, and asked me the question which was tearing him to shreds.

'When will I be warned off?'

Neil Griffon was a nut, as Gillie said.

'You won't be warned off,' I told him. 'I talked to the Jockey Club this morning. I told them that you shouldn't lose your licence because your father had gone mad, and they saw that point of view. You may not of course like it that I stressed your father's insanity, but it was the best I could do.'

'But . . .' he said in bewilderment, and then in realisation, 'Didn't you tell them about Moonrock and Indigo . . . and about your shoulder?'

'No.'

'I don't understand . . . why you didn't.'

'I don't see any point in revenging myself on you for what your father did.'

'But . . . he only did it . . . in the beginning . . . because I asked.'

'Alessandro,' I said. 'Just how many fathers would do as he did? How many fathers, if their sons said they wanted to ride Archangel in the Derby, would go as far as murder to achieve it?'

After a long pause, he said, 'He was mad, then. He really was.' It was clearly no comfort.

'He was ill,' I said. 'That illness he had after you were born. It affected his brain.'

'Then I . . . will not . . .?'

'No,' I said. 'You can't inherit it. You're as sane as anyone. As sane as you care to be.'

'As I care to be,' he repeated vaguely. His thoughts were turned inward. I didn't hurry him. I waited most patiently, because what he cared to be was the final throw in the game.

'I care to be a jockey,' he said faintly. 'To be a good one.'

I took a breath. 'You are free to ride races anywhere you like,' I said. 'Anywhere in the world.'

He stared at me with a face from which all the arrogance had gone. He didn't look the same boy as the one who had come from Switzerland three months ago, and in fact he wasn't. All of his values had been turned upside-down, and the world as he had known it had come to an end.

To defeat the father, I had changed the son. Changed him at first only as a solution to a problem, but later also because the emerging product was worth it. It seemed a waste, somehow, to let him go.

I said abruptly, 'You can stay on at Rowley Lodge, if you like.'

Something shattered somewhere inside him, like glass breaking. When he turned away I could have sworn that against all probability there were tears in his eyes.

He took four paces, and stopped.

'Well?' I said.

He turned round. The tears had drained back into the ducts, as they do in the young.

'What as?' he said apprehensively, looking for snags.

'Stable jockey,' I said. 'Second to Tommy.'

He walked six more paces away down the drive as if his ankles were springs.

'Come back,' I called. 'What about tomorrow?'

He looked over his shoulder.

'I'll be here to ride out.'

Three more bouncing steps.

'You won't,' I shouted. 'You get a good sleep and a good breakfast and be here at eleven. We're flying over to Chester.'

'Chester?' He turned and shouted in surprise, and went two more steps, backwards.

'Clip Clop,' I yelled. 'Ever heard of him?'

'Yes,' he yelled back, and the laughter took him uncontrollably, and he turned and ran away down the drive, leaping into the air as if he were six.

IN THE FRAME

In The Frame

My thanks to two professional artists

MICHAEL JEFFERY
of Australia
and
JOSEF JIRA
of Czechoslovakia

who generously showed me their studios, their methods, their minds and their lives.

Also to the many art galleries whose experts gave me information and help, and particularly to Peter Johnson of Oscar and Peter Johnson, London, SW1, and to the Stud and Stable gallery, Ascot.

FOR CAROLINE
Sound Asleep

Chapter One

I stood on the outside of disaster, looking in.

There were three police cars outside my cousin's house, and an ambulance with its blue turret light revolving ominously, and people bustling in seriously through his open front door. The chill wind of early autumn blew dead brown leaves sadly on to the driveway, and harsh scurrying clouds threatened worse to come. Six o'clock, Friday evening, Shropshire, England.

Intermittent bright white flashes from the windows spoke of photography in progress within. I slid my satchel from my shoulder and dumped both it and my suitcase on the grass verge, and with justifiable foreboding completed my journey to the house.

I had travelled by train to stay for the week-end. No cousin with car to meet me as promised, so I had started to walk the mile and a half of country road, sure he would come tearing along soon in his muddy Peugeot, full of jokes and apologies and plans.

No jokes.

He stood in the hall, dazed and grey. His body inside his neat business suit looked limp, and his arms hung straight down from the shoulders as if his brain had forgotten they were there. His head was turned slightly towards the sittingroom, the source of the flashes, and his eyes were stark with shock.

'Don?' I said. I walked towards him. 'Donald!'

He didn't hear me. A policeman, however, did. He came swiftly from the sittingroom in his dark blue uniform, took me by the arm and swung me strongly and unceremoniously back towards the door.

'Out of here, sir,' he said. 'If you please.'

The strained eyes slid uncertainly our way.

'Charles . . .' His voice was hoarse.

The policeman's grip loosened very slightly. 'Do you know this man, sir?' he asked Donald.

'I'm his cousin,' I said.

'Oh.' He shook his hand off, told me to stay where I was and look after Mr. Stuart, and returned to the sittingroom to consult.

'What's happened?' I said.

Don was past answering. His head turned again towards the sitting-room door, drawn to a horror he could no longer see. I disobeyed the police instructions, took ten quiet steps, and looked in.

The familiar room was unfamiliarly bare. No pictures, no ornaments, no edge-to-edge floor covering of oriental rugs. Just bare grey walls, chintz-covered sofas, heavy furniture pushed awry, and a great expanse of dusty wood-block flooring.

And on the floor, my cousin's young wife, bloody and dead.

The big room was scattered with busy police, measuring, photograph-ing, dusting for fingerprints. I knew they were there; didn't see them. All I saw was Regina lying on her back, her face the colour of cream.

Her eyes were half open, still faintly bright, and her lower jaw had fallen loose, outlining brutally the shape of the skull. A pool of urine lay wetly on the parquet around her sprawled legs, and one arm was flung out sideways with the dead white fingers curling upwards as if in supplication.

There had been no mercy.

I looked at the scarlet mess of her head and felt the blood draining from my own.

The policeman who had grabbed me before turned round from his consultation with another, saw me swaying in the doorway, and took quick annoyed strides back to my side.

'I told you to wait outside, sir,' he said with exasperation, stating clearly that my faintness was my own fault.

I nodded dumbly and went back into the hall. Donald was sitting on the stairs, looking at nothing. I sat abruptly on the floor near him and put my head between my knees.

'I . . . f . . . found . . . her,' he said.

I swallowed. What could one say? It was bad enough for me, but he had lived with her, and loved her. The faintness passed away slowly, leaving a sour feeling of sickness. I leaned back against the wall behind me and wished I knew how to help him.

'She's . . . never . . . home . . . on F . . . Fridays,' he said.

'I know.'

'S . . . six. S . . . six o'clock . . . she comes b . . . back. Always.'

'I'll get you some brandy,' I said.

'She shouldn't . . . have been . . . here . . .'

I pushed myself off the floor and went into the diningroom, and it was there that the significance of the bare sittingroom forced itself into consciousness. In the diningroom too there were bare walls, bare shelves, and empty drawers pulled out and dumped on the floor. No silver ornaments. No silver spoons or forks. No collection of antique china. Just a jumble of table mats and napkins and broken glass.

My cousin's house had been burgled. And Regina . . . Regina, who was never home on Fridays . . . had walked in . . .

I went over the plundered sideboard, flooding with anger and wanting to smash in the heads of all greedy, callous, vicious people who cynically devastated the lives of total strangers. Compassion was all right for saints. What I felt was plain hatred, fierce and basic.

I found two intact glasses, but all the drink had gone. Furiously I stalked through the swing door into the kitchen and filled the electric kettle.

In that room too, the destruction had continued, with stores swept wholesale off the shelves. What valuables, I wondered, did thieves expect to find in kitchens? I jerkily made two mugs of tea and rummaged in Regina's spice cupboard for the cooking brandy, and felt unreasonably triumphant when it proved to be still there. The sods had missed that, at least.

Donald still sat unmoving on the stairs. I pressed the cup of strong sweet liquid into his hands and told him to drink, and he did, mechanically.

'She's never home . . . on Fridays,' he said.

'No,' I agreed, and wondered just how many people knew there was no one home on Fridays.

We both slowly finished the tea. I took his mug and put it with mine on the floor, and sat near him as before. Most of the hall furniture had gone. The small Sheraton desk . . . the studded leather chair . . . the nineteenth century carriage clock . . .

'Christ, Charles,' he said.

I glanced at his face. There were tears, and dreadful pain. I could do nothing, nothing, to help him.

The impossible evening lengthened to midnight, and beyond. The police, I suppose, were efficient, polite, and not unsympathetic, but they left a distinct impression that they felt their job was to catch criminals, not to succour the victims. It seemed to me that there was also, in many of their questions, a faint hovering doubt, as if it were not unknown for householders to arrange their own well-insured burglaries, and for smooth-seeming swindles to go horrifically wrong.

Donald didn't seem to notice. He answered wearily, automatically, with long pauses sometimes between question and answer.

Yes, the missing goods were well-insured.

Yes, they had been insured for years.

Yes, he had been to his office all day as usual.

Yes, he had been out to lunch. A sandwich in a pub.

He was a wine shipper.

His office was in Shrewsbury.

He was thirty-seven years old.

Yes, his wife was much younger. Twenty-two.

He couldn't speak of Regina without stuttering, as if his tongue and lips were beyond his control. She always s . . . spends F . . . Fridays . . . working . . . in a f . . . friend's . . . f . . . flower . . . shop.

'Why?'

Donald looked vaguely at the Detective Inspector, sitting opposite him across the diningroom table. The matched antique dining chairs had gone. Donald sat in a garden armchair brought from the sunroom. The Inspector, a constable and I sat on kitchen stools.

'What?'

'Why did she work in a flower shop on Fridays?'

'She . . . she . . . l . . . likes . . .'

I interrupted brusquely. 'She was a florist before she married Donald. She liked to keep her hand in. She used to spend Fridays making those table arrangement things for dances and weddings and things like that . . .' And wreaths, too, I thought, and couldn't say it.

'Thank you, sir, but I'm sure Mr. Stuart can answer for himself.'

'And I'm sure he can't.'

The Detective Inspector diverted his attention my way.

'He's too shocked,' I said.

'Are you a doctor, sir?' His voice held polite disbelief, which it was entitled to, no doubt. I shook my head impatiently. He glanced at Donald, pursed his lips, and turned back to me. His gaze wandered briefly over my jeans, faded denim jacket, fawn polo-neck, and desert boots, and returned to my face, unimpressed.

'Very well, sir. Name?'

'Charles Todd.'

'Age?'

'Twenty-nine.'

'Occupation?'

'Painter.'

The constable unemotionally wrote down these scintillating details in his pocket-sized notebook.

'Houses or pictures?' asked the Inspector.

'Pictures.'

'And your movements today, sir?'

'Caught the two-thirty from Paddington and walked from the local station.'

'Purpose of visit?'

'Nothing special. I come here once or twice a year.'

'Good friends, then?'

'Yes.'

He nodded non-committally. Turned his attention again to Donald and asked more questions, but patiently and without pressure.

'And what time do you normally reach home on Fridays, sir?'

Don said tonelessly, 'Five. About.'

'And today?'

'Same.' A spasm twitched the muscles of his face. 'I saw . . . the house had been broken into . . . I telephoned . . .'

'Yes, sir. We received your call at six minutes past five. And after you had telephoned, you went into the sittingroom, to see what had been stolen?'

Donald didn't answer.

'Our sergeant found you there, sir, if you remember.'

'*Why?*' Don said in anguish. 'Why did she come home?'

'I expect we'll find out, sir.'

The careful exploratory questions went on and on, and as far as I could see achieved nothing except to bring Donald ever closer to all-out breakdown.

I, with a certain amount of shame, grew ordinarily hungry, having not bothered to eat earlier in the day. I thought with regret of the dinner I had been looking forward to, with Regina tossing in unmeasured ingredients and herbs and wine and casually producing a gourmet feast. Regina with her cap of dark hair and ready smile, chatty and frivolous and anti-bloodsports. A harmless girl, come to harm.

At some point during the evening her body was loaded into the ambulance and driven away. I heard it happen, but Donald gave no sign of interpreting the sounds. I thought that probably his mind was raising barriers against the unendurable, and one couldn't blame him.

The Inspector rose finally and stretched the kinks caused by the kitchen stool out of legs and spine. He said he would be leaving a constable on duty at the house all night, and that he would return himself in the morning. Donald nodded vaguely, having obviously not listened properly to a word, and when the police had gone still sat like an automaton in the chair, with no energy to move.

'Come on,' I said. 'Let's go to bed.'

I took his arm, persuaded him to his feet, and steered him up the stairs. He came in a daze, unprotesting.

His and Regina's bedroom was a shambles, but the twin-bedded room prepared for me was untouched. He flopped full-length in his clothes and put his arm up over his eyes, and in appalling distress asked the unanswerable question of all the world's sufferers.

'*Why?* Why did it have to happen to *us?*'

I stayed with Donald for a week, during which time some questions, but not that one, were answered.

One of the easiest was the reason for Regina's premature return home. She and the flower-shop friend, who had been repressing annoyance with each other for weeks, had erupted into a quarrel of enough bitterness to make Regina leave at once. She had driven away at about two-thirty, and had probably gone straight home, as it was considered she had been dead for at least two hours by five o'clock.

This information, expressed in semi-formal sentences, was given to Donald by the Detective Inspector on Saturday afternoon. Donald walked out into the autumnal garden and wept.

The Inspector, Frost by name and cool by nature, came quietly into the kitchen and stood beside me watching Donald with his bowed head among the apple trees.

'I would like you to tell me what you can about the relationship between Mr. and Mrs. Stuart.'

'You'd like *what?*'

'How did they get on?'

'Can't you tell for yourself?'

He answered neutrally after a pause. 'The intensity of grief shown is not always an accurate indication of the intensity of love felt.'

'Do you always talk like that?'

A faint smile flickered and died. 'I was quoting from a book on psychology.'

' "Not always" means it usually is,' I said.

He blinked.

'Your book is bunk,' I said.

'Guilt and remorse can manifest themselves in an excess of mourning.'

'Dangerous bunk,' I added. 'And as far as I could see, the honeymoon was by no means over.'

'After three years?'

'Why not?'

He shrugged and didn't answer. I turned away from the sight of Donald and said, 'What are the chances of getting back any of the stuff from this house?'

'Small, I should think. Where antiques are involved, the goods are likely to be halfway across the Atlantic before the owner returns from his holidays.'

'Not this time, though,' I objected.

He sighed. 'Next best thing. There have been hundreds of similar break-ins during recent years and very little has been recovered. Antiques are big business these days.'

'Connoisseur thieves?' I said sceptically.

'The prison library service reports that all their most requested books are on antiques. All the little chummies boning up to jump on the bandwagon as soon as they get out.'

He sounded suddenly quite human. 'Like some coffee?' I said.

He looked at his watch, raised his eyebrows, and accepted. He sat on a kitchen stool while I fixed the mugs, a fortyish man with thin sandy hair and a well-worn grey suit.

'Are you married?' he asked.

'Nope.'

'In love with Mrs. Stuart?'

'You do try it on, don't you?'

'If you don't ask, you don't find out.'

I put the milk bottle and a sugar basin on the table and told him to help himself. He stirred his coffee reflectively.

'When did you visit this house last?' he said.

'Last March. Before they went off to Australia.'

'Australia?'

'They went to see the vintage there. Donald had some idea of shipping Australian wine over in bulk. They were away for at least three months. Why didn't their house get robbed *then*, when they were safely out of the way?'

He listened to the bitterness in my voice. 'Life is full of nasty ironies.' He pursed his lips gingerly to the hot coffee, drew back, and blew gently across the top of the mug. 'What would you all have been doing today? In the normal course of events?'

I had to think what day it was. Saturday. It seemed totally unreal.

'Going to the races,' I said. 'We always go to the races when I come to stay.'

'Fond of racing, were they?' The past tense sounded wrong. Yet so much was now past. I found it a great deal more difficult than he did, to change gear.

'Yes . . . but I think they only go . . . went . . . because of me.'

He tried the coffee again and managed a cautious sip. 'In what way do you mean?' he asked.

'What I paint,' I said, 'is mostly horses.'

Donald came in through the back door, looking red-eyed and exhausted.

'The Press are making a hole in the hedge,' he said leadenly.

Inspector Frost clicked his teeth, got to his feet, opened the door to the hall and the interior of the house, and called out loudly.

'Constable? Go and stop those reporters from breaking into the garden.'

A distant voice replied 'Sir', and Frost apologised to Donald. 'Can't get rid of them entirely, you know, sir. They have their editors breathing down their necks. They pester the life out of us at times like these.'

All day long the road outside Donald's house had been lined with cars, which disgorged crowds of reporters, photographers and plain sensation-seekers every time anyone went out of the front door. Like a hungry wolf pack they lay in wait, and I supposed that they would eventually pounce on Donald himself. Regard for his feelings was nowhere in sight.

'Newspapers listen to the radio on the police frequencies,' Frost said gloomily. 'Sometimes the Press arrive at the scene of a crime before we can get there ourselves.'

At any other time I would have laughed, but it wouldn't have been much fun for Donald if it had happened in his case. The police, of course, had thought at first that it more or less had, because I had heard that the constable who had tried to eject me forcibly had taken me for a spear-heading scribbler.

Donald sat down heavily on a stool and rested his elbows wearily on the table.

'Charles,' he said, 'If you wouldn't mind heating it, I'd like some of that soup now.'

'Sure,' I said, surprised. He had rejected it earlier as if the thought of food revolted him.

Frost's head went up as if at a signal, and his whole body straightened purposefully, and I realised he had merely been coasting along until then, waiting for some such moment. He waited some more while I opened a can of Campbell's condensed, sloshed it and some water and cooking brandy into a saucepan, and stirred until the lumps dissolved. He drank his coffee and waited while Donald disposed of two platefuls and a chunk of brown bread. Then, politely, he asked me to take myself off, and when I'd gone he began what Donald afterwards referred to as 'serious digging'.

It was three hours later, and growing dark, when the Inspector left. I watched his departure from the upstairs landing window. He and his attendant plain-clothes constable were intercepted immediately outside the front door by a young man with wild hair and a microphone, and before they could dodge round him to reach their car the pack on the road were streaming in full cry into the garden and across the grass.

I went methodically round the house drawing curtains, checking windows, and locking and bolting all the outside doors.

'What are you doing?' Donald asked, looking pale and tired in the kitchen.

'Pulling up the drawbridge.'

'Oh.'

In spite of his long session with the Inspector he seemed a lot calmer and more in command of himself, and when I had finished Fort-Knoxing the kitchen-to-garden door he said, 'The police want a list of what's gone. Will you help me make it?'

'Of course.'

'It'll give us something to do . . .'

'Sure.'

'We did have an inventory, but it was in that desk in the hall. The one they took.'

'Damn silly place to keep it,' I said.

'That's more or less what *he* said. Inspector Frost.'

'What about your insurance company? Haven't they got a list?'

'Only of the more valuable things, like some of the paintings, and her jewellery.' He sighed. 'Everything else was lumped together as "contents".'

We started on the diningroom and made reasonable progress, with him putting the empty drawers back in the sideboard while trying to remember what each had once contained, and me writing down to his dictation. There had been a good deal of solid silver tableware, acquired by Donald's family in its affluent past and handed down routinely. Donald, with his warmth for antiques, had enjoyed using it, but his pleasure in owning it seemed to have vanished with the goods. Instead of being indignant over its loss, he sounded impersonal, and by the time we had finished the sideboard, decidedly bored.

Faced by the ranks of empty shelves where once had stood a fine collection of early nineteenth century porcelain, he baulked entirely.

'What does it matter?' he said drearily, turning away. 'I simply can't be bothered . . .'

'How about the paintings, then?'

He looked vaguely round the bare walls. The site of each missing frame showed unmistakably in lighter oblong patches of palest olive. In this room they had mostly been works of modern British painters: a Hockney, a Bratby, two Lowrys, and a Spear for openers, all painted on what one might call the artists' less exuberant days. Donald didn't like paintings which he said 'jumped off the wall and made a fuss'.

'You probably remember them better than I do,' he said. 'You do it.'

'I'd miss some.'

'Is there anything to drink?'

'Only the cooking brandy,' I said.

'We could have some of the wine.'

'What wine?'

'In the cellar.' His eyes suddenly opened wide. 'Good God, I'd forgotten about the cellar.'

'I didn't even know you had one.'

He nodded. 'Reason I bought the house. Perfect humidity and temperature for long-term storage. There's a small fortune down there in claret and port.'

There wasn't, of course. There were three floor-to-ceiling rows of empty racks, and a single cardboard box on a plain wooden table.

Donald merely shrugged. 'Oh well . . . that's that.'

I opened the top of the cardboard box and saw the elegant corked shapes of the tops of wine bottles.

'They've left these, anyway,' I said. 'In their rush.'

'Probably on purpose,' Don smiled twistedly. 'That's Australian wine. We brought it back with us.'

'Better than nothing,' I said disparagingly, pulling out a bottle and reading the label.

'Better than most, you know. A lot of Australian wine is superb.'

I carried the whole case up to the kitchen and dumped it on the table. The stairs from the cellar led up into the utility room among the washing machines and other domesticities, and I had always had an unclear impression that its door was just another cupboard. I looked at it thoughtfully, an unremarkable white painted panel merging inconspicuously into the general scenery.

'Do you think the burglars *knew* the wine was there?' I asked.

'God knows.'

'I would never have found it.'

'You're not a burglar, though.'

He searched for a corkscrew, opened one of the bottles, and poured the deep red liquid into two kitchen tumblers. I tasted it and it was indeed a marvellous wine, even to my untrained palate. *Wynn's Coonawarra Cabernet Sauvignon.* You could wrap the name round the tongue as lovingly as the product. Donald drank his share absentmindedly as if it were water, the glass clattering once or twice against his teeth. There was still an uncertainty about many of his movements, as if he could not quite remember how to do things, and I knew it was because with half his mind he thought all the time of Regina, and the thoughts were literally paralysing.

The old Donald had been a man of confidence, capably running a middle-sized inherited business and adding his share to the passed-on goodies. He had a blunt uncompromising face lightened by amber eyes which smiled easily, and he had considered his money well-spent on shapely hair-cuts.

The new Donald was a tentative man shattered with shock, a man trying to behave decently but unsure where his feet were when he walked upstairs.

We spent the evening in the kitchen, talking desultorily, eating a scratch meal, and tidying all the stores back on to the shelves. Donald made a good show of being busy but put half the tins back upside down.

The front door bell rang three times during the evening but never in the code pre-arranged with the police. The telephone, with its receiver lying loose beside it, rang not at all. Donald had turned down several offers of refuge with local friends and visibly shook at the prospect of talking to anyone but Frost and me.

'Why don't they go away?' he said despairingly, after the third attempt on the front door.

'They will, once they've seen you,' I said. And sucked you dry, and spat out the husk, I thought.

He shook his head tiredly. 'I simply can't.'

It felt like living through a siege.

We went eventually again upstairs to bed, although it seemed likely that Donald would sleep no more than the night before, which had been hardly at all. The police surgeon had left knock-out pills, which Donald wouldn't take. I pressed him again on that second evening, with equal non-results.

'No, Charles. I'd feel I'd deserted her. D . . . ducked out. Thought only of myself, and not of . . . of how awful it was for her . . . dying like that . . . with n . . . no one near who 1 . . . loved her.'

He was trying to offer her in some way the comfort of his own pain. I shook my head at him, but tried no more with the pills.

'Do you mind,' he said diffidently, 'if I sleep alone tonight?'

'Of course not.'

'We could make up a bed for you in one of the other rooms.'

'Sure.'

He pulled open the linen-cupboard door on the upstairs landing and gestured indecisively at the contents. 'Could you manage?'

'Of course,' I said.

He turned away and seemed struck by one particular adjacent patch of empty wall.

'They took the Munnings,' he said.

'What Munnings?'

'We bought it in Australia. I hung it just there . . . only a week ago. I wanted you to see it. It was one of the reasons I asked you to come.'

'I'm sorry,' I said. Inadequate words.

'Everything,' he said helplessly. 'Everything's gone.'

Chapter Two

Frost arrived tirelessly again on Sunday morning with his quiet watchful eyes and non-committal manner. I opened the front door to his signal, and he followed me through to the kitchen, where Donald and I seemed to have taken up permanent residence. I gestured him to a stool, and he sat on it, straightening his spine to avoid future stiffness.

'Two pieces of information you might care to have, sir,' he said to Donald, his voice at its most formal. 'Despite our intensive investigation of this house during yesterday and the previous evening, we have found no fingerprints for which we cannot account.'

'Would you expect to?' I asked.

He flicked me a glance. 'No, sir. Professional housebreakers always wear gloves.'

Donald waited with a grey patient face, as if he would find whatever Frost said unimportant. Nothing, I judged, was of much importance to Donald any more.

'Second,' said Frost, 'our investigations in the district reveal that a removal van was parked outside your front door early on Friday afternoon.'

Donald looked at him blankly.

'Dark coloured, and dusty, sir.'

'Oh,' Donald said, meaninglessly.

Frost sighed. 'What do you know of a bronze statuette of a horse, sir? A horse rearing up on its hind legs?'

'It's in the hall,' Donald said automatically; and then, frowning slightly, 'I mean, it used to be. It's gone.'

'How do you know about it?' I asked Frost curiously, and guessed the answer before I'd finished the question. 'Oh no . . .' I stopped, and swallowed. 'I mean, perhaps you found it . . . fallen off the van . . .?'

'No, sir.' His face was calm. 'We found it in the sittingroom, near Mrs. Stuart.'

Donald understood as clearly as I had done. He stood up abruptly and went to the window, and stared out for a while at the empty garden.

'It is heavy,' he said at last. 'The base of it.'

'Yes, sir.'

'It must have been . . . quick.'

'Yes, sir,' Frost said again, sounding more objective than comforting.

'P . . . poor Regina.' The words were quiet, the desolation immense. When he came back to the table, his hands were trembling. He sat down heavily and stared into space.

Frost started another careful speech about the sittingroom being kept locked by the police for a few days yet and please would neither of us try to go in there.

Neither of us would.

Apart from that, they had finished their enquiries at the house, and Mr. Stuart was at liberty to have the other rooms cleaned, if he wished, where the fingerprint dust lay greyish-white on every polished surface.

Mr. Stuart gave no sign of having heard.

Had Mr. Stuart completed the list of things stolen?

I passed it over. It still consisted only of the diningroom silver and what I could remember of the paintings. Frost raised his eyebrows and pursed his lips.

'We'll need more than this, sir.'

'We'll try again today,' I promised. 'There's a lot of wine missing, as well.'

'Wine?'

I showed him the empty cellar and he came up looking thoughtful.

'It must have taken hours to move that lot,' I said.

'Very likely, sir,' he said primly.

Whatever he was thinking, he wasn't telling. He suggested instead that Donald should prepare a short statement to read to the hungry reporters still waiting outside, so that they could go away and print it.

'No,' Don said.

'Just a short statement,' Frost said reasonably. 'We can prepare it here and now, if you like.'

He wrote it himself, more or less, and I guessed it was as much for his own sake as Donald's that he wanted the Press to depart, as it was he who had to push through them every time. He repeated the statement aloud when he had finished. It sounded like a police account, full of jargon, but because of that so distant from Donald's own raw grief that my cousin agreed in the end to read it out.

'But no photographs,' he said anxiously, and Frost said he would see to it.

They crowded into the hall, a collection of dry-eyed fact-finders, all near the top of their digging profession and inured from sensitivity by a hundred similar intrusions into tragedy. Sure, they were sorry for the guy whose wife had been bashed, but news was news and bad news sold papers, and if they didn't produce the goods they'd lose their jobs to others more tenacious. The Press Council had stopped the brutal bullying of the past, but the leeway still allowed could be a great deal too much for the afflicted.

Donald stood on the stairs, with Frost and myself at the foot, and read without expression, as if the words applied to someone else.

'. . . I returned to the house at approximately five p.m. and observed that during my absence a considerable number of valuable objects had been removed . . . I telephoned immediately for assistance . . . My wife, who was normally absent from the house on Fridays, returned unexpectedly . . . and, it is presumed, disturbed the intruders.'

He stopped. The reporters dutifully wrote down the stilted words and looked disillusioned. One of them, clearly elected by pre-arrangement, started asking questions for them all, in a gentle, coaxing, sympathetic tone of voice.

'Could you tell us which of these closed doors is the one to the room where your wife . . .'

Donald's eyes slid briefly despite himself towards the sittingroom. All the heads turned, the eyes studied the uninformative white painted panels, the pencils wrote.

'And could you tell us what exactly was stolen?'

'Silver. Paintings.'

'Who were the paintings by?'

Donald shook his head and began to look even paler.

'Could you tell us how much they were worth?'

After a pause Don said 'I don't know.'

'Were they insured?'

'Yes.'

'How many bedrooms are there in your house?'

'What?'

'How many bedrooms?'

Donald looked bewildered. 'I suppose . . . five.'

'Do you think you could tell us anything about your wife? About her character, and about her job? And could you let us have a photograph?'

Donald couldn't. He shook his head and said 'I'm sorry,' and turned and walked steadily away upstairs.

'That's all,' Frost said with finality.

'It's not much,' they grumbled.

'What do you want? Blood?' Frost said, opening the front door and encouraging them out. 'Put yourselves in his position.'

'Yeah,' they said cynically; but they went.

'Did you see their eyes?' I said. 'Sucking it all in?'

Frost smiled faintly. 'They'll all write long stories from that little lot.'

The interview, however, produced to a great extent the desired results. Most of the cars departed, and the rest, I supposed, would follow as soon as fresher news broke.

'Why did they ask about the bedrooms?' I said.

'To estimate the value of the house.'

'Good grief.'

'They'll all get it different.' Frost was near to amusement. 'They always do.' He looked up the stairs in the direction Donald had taken, and, almost casually, said 'Is your cousin in financial difficulties?'

I knew his catch-them-off-guard technique by now.

'I wouldn't think so,' I said unhurriedly. 'You'd better ask him.'

'I will, sir.' He switched his gaze sharply to my face and studied my lack of expression. 'What do you know?'

I said calmly, 'Only that the police have suspicious minds.'

He disregarded that. 'Is Mr. Stuart worried about his business?'

'He's never said so.'

'A great many middle-sized private companies are going bankrupt these days.'

'So I believe.'

'Because of cash flow problems,' he added.

'I can't help you. You'll have to look at his company's books.'

'We will, sir.'

'And even if the firm turns out to be bust, it doesn't follow that Donald would fake a robbery.'

'It's been done before,' Frost said dryly.

'If he needed money he could simply have sold the stuff,' I pointed out.

'Maybe he had. Some of it. Most of it, maybe.'

I took a slow breath and said nothing.

'That wine, sir. As you said yourself, it would have taken a long time to move.'

'The firm is a limited company,' I said. 'If it went bankrupt, Donald's own house and private money would be unaffected.'

'You know a good deal about it, don't you?'

I said neutrally, 'I live in the world.'

'I thought artists were supposed to be unworldly.'

'Some are.'

He peered at me with narrowed eyes as if he were trying to work out a possible way in which I too might have conspired to arrange the theft.

I said mildly, 'My cousin Donald is an honourable man.'

'That's an out of date word.'

'There's quite a lot of it about.'

He looked wholly disbelieving. He saw far too much in the way of corruption, day in, day out, all his working life.

Donald came hesitantly down the stairs and Frost took him off immediately to another private session in the kitchen. I thought that if Frost's questions were to be as barbed as those he'd asked me, poor Don was in for a rough time. While they talked I wandered aimlessly round the house, looking into storage spaces, opening cupboards, seeing the inside details of my cousin's life.

Either he or Regina had been a hoarder of empty boxes. I came across dozens of them, all shapes and sizes, shoved into odd corners of shelves or drawers: brown cardboard, bright gift-wrap, beribboned chocolate boxes, all too potentially useful or too pretty to be thrown away. The burglars had opened a lot but had thrown more unopened on the floor. They must, I thought, have had a most frustrating time.

They had largely ignored the big sunroom, which held few antiques and no paintings, and I ended up there sitting on a bamboo armchair among sprawling potted plants looking out into the windy garden. Dead leaves blew in scattered showers from the drying trees and a few late roses clung hardily to thorny stems.

I hated autumn. The time of melancholy, the time of death. My spirits fell each year with the soggy leaves and revived only with crisp winter frost. Psychiatric statistics proved that the highest suicide rate occurred in the spring, the time for rebirth and growth and stretching in the sun. I could never understand it. If ever I jumped over a cliff, it would be in the depressing months of decay.

The sunroom was grey and cold. No sun, that Sunday.

I went upstairs, fetched my suitcase, and brought it down. Over years of wandering journeys I had reversed the painter's traditional luggage: my suitcase now contained the tools of my trade, and my satchel, clothes. The large toughened suitcase, its interior adapted and fitted by me, was in fact a sort of portable studio, containing besides paints and brushes a light collapsible metal easel, unbreakable containers of linseed oil and turpentine, and a rack which would hold four wet paintings safely apart. There were also a dust sheet, a large box of tissues, and generous amounts of white spirit, all designed for preventing mess and keeping things clean. The organisation of the suitcase had saved and made the price of many a sandwich.

I untelescoped the easel and set out my palette, and on a middling-sized canvas laid in the beginnings of a melancholy landscape, a mixture of Donald's garden as I saw it, against a sweep of bare fields and gloomy woods. Not my usual sort of picture, and not, to be honest, the sort to make headline news a century hence; but it gave me at least something to do. I worked steadily, growing ever colder, until the chillier Frost chose to depart; and he went without seeing me again, the front door closing decisively on his purposeful footsteps.

Donald, in the warm kitchen, looked torn to rags. When I went in he was sitting with his arms folded on the table and his head on his arms, a picture of absolute despair. When he heard me he sat up slowly and wearily, and showed a face suddenly aged and deeply lined.

'Do you know what he thinks?' he said.

'More or less.'

He stared at me sombrely. 'I couldn't convince him. He kept on and on. Kept asking the same questions, over and over. Why doesn't he believe me?'

'A lot of people lie to the police. I think they grow to expect it.'

'He wants me to meet him in my office tomorrow. He says he'll be bringing colleagues. He says they'll want to see the books.'

I nodded. 'Better be grateful he didn't drag you down there today.'

'I suppose so.'

I said awkwardly, 'Don, I'm sorry. I told him the wine was missing. It made him suspicious . . . It was a good deal my fault that he was so bloody to you.'

He shook his head tiredly. 'I would have told him myself. I wouldn't have thought of not telling him.'

'But . . . I even pointed out that it must have taken a fair time to move so many bottles.'

'Mm. Well, he would have worked that out for himself.'

'How long, in fact, do you think it would have taken?'

'Depends how many people were doing it,' he said, rubbing his hand over his face and squeezing his tired eyes. 'They would have to have had proper wine boxes in any case. That means they had to know in advance that the wine was there, and didn't just chance on it. And that means . . . Frost says . . . that I sold it myself some time ago and am now saying it is stolen so I can claim fraudulent insurance, or, if it was stolen last Friday, that I told the thieves they'd need proper boxes, which means that I set up the whole frightful mess myself.'

We thought it over in depressed silence. Eventually, I said, 'Who *did* know you had the wine there? And who knew the house was always empty on Fridays? And was the prime target the wine, the antiques, or the paintings?'

'God, Charles, you sound like Frost.'

'Sorry.'

'Every business nowadays,' he said defensively, 'is going through a cash crisis. Look at the nationalised industries, losing money by the million. Look at the wage rises and the taxes and the inflation . . . How can any small business make the profit it used to? Of *course* we have a cash flow problem. Whoever hasn't?'

'How bad is yours?' I said.

'Not critical. Bad enough. But not within sight of liquidation. It's illegal for a limited company to carry on trading if it can't cover its costs.'

'But it could . . . if you could raise more capital to prop it up?'

He surveyed me with the ghost of a smile. 'It surprises me still that you chose to paint for a living.'

'It gives me a good excuse to go racing whenever I like.'

'Lazy sod.' He sounded for a second like the old Donald, but the lightness passed. 'The absolutely last thing I would do would be to use my own personal assets to prop up a dying business. If my firm was that rocky, I'd wind it up. It would be mad not to.'

I sucked my teeth. 'I suppose Frost asked if the stolen things were insured for more than their worth?'

'Yes, he did. Several times.'

'Not likely you'd tell him, even if they were.'

'They weren't, though.'

'No.'

'Under-insured, if anything.' He sighed. 'God knows if they'll pay up for the Munnings. I'd only arranged the insurance by telephone. I hadn't actually sent the premium.'

'It should be all right, if you can give them proof of purchase, and so on.'

He shook his head listlessly. 'All the papers to do with it were in the desk in the hall. The receipt from the gallery where I bought it, the letter of provenance, and the customs and excise receipt. All gone.'

'Frost won't like that.'

'He doesn't.'

'Well ... I hope you pointed out that you would hardly be buying expensive pictures and going on world trips if you were down to your last farthing.'

'He said it might be *because* of buying expensive pictures and going on world trips that I might be down to my last farthing.'

Frost had built a brick wall of suspicion for Donald to batter his head against. My cousin needed hauling away before he was punch drunk.

'Have some spaghetti,' I said.

'What?'

'It's about all I can cook.'

'Oh ...' He focused unclearly on the kitchen clock. It was half past four and long past feeding time according to my stomach.

'If you like,' he said.

The police sent a car the following morning to fetch him to his ordeal in the office. He went lifelessly, having more or less made it clear over coffee that he wouldn't defend himself.

'Don, you must,' I said. 'The only way to deal with the situation is to be firm and reasonable, and decisive, and accurate. In fact, just your own self.'

He smiled faintly. 'You'd better go instead of me. I haven't the energy. And what does it matter?' His smile broke suddenly and the ravaging misery showed deeply like black water under cracked ice. 'Without Regina ... there's no point making money.'

'We're not talking about making money, we're talking about suspicion. If you don't defend yourself, they'll assume you can't.'

'I'm too tired. I can't be bothered. They can think what they like.'

'Don,' I said seriously, 'They'll think what you let them.'

'I don't really care,' he said dully: and that was the trouble. He really didn't.

He was gone all day. I spent it painting.

Not the sad landscape. The sunroom seemed even greyer and colder that morning, and I had no mind any more to sink into melancholy. I left the half-finished canvas on the table there and removed myself and trappings to the source of warmth. Maybe the light wasn't so good in the kitchen, but it was the only room in the house with the pulse of life.

I painted Regina standing beside her cooker, with a wooden spoon in one hand and a bottle of wine in the other. I painted the way she held her head back to smile, and I painted the smile, shiny-eyed and guileless and unmistakably happy. I painted the kitchen behind her as I literally saw it in front of my eyes, and I painted Regina herself from the clearest of inner visions. So easily did I see her that I looked up once or twice from her face on the canvas to say something to her, and was disconcerted to find only empty space. An extraordinary feeling of the real and unreal disturbingly tangled.

I seldom ever worked for more than four hours at a stretch because for one thing the actual muscular control required was tiring, and for another the concentration always made me cold and hungry; so I knocked off at around lunch-time and dug out a tin of corned beef to eat with pickles on toast, and after that went for a walk, dodging the front-gate watchers by taking to the apple trees and wriggling through the hedge.

I tramped aimlessly for a while round the scattered shapeless village, thinking about the picture and working off the burst of physical energy I often felt after the constraint of painting. More burnt umber in the folds of the kitchen curtains, I thought; and a purplish shadow on the saucepan. Regina's cream shirt needed yellow ochre under the collar, and probably a touch of green. The cooking stove needed a lot more attention, and I had broken my general rule of working the picture as a whole, background and subject pace by pace.

This time, Regina's face stood out clearly, finished except for a gloss on the lips and a line of light along inside the lower eyelids, which one couldn't do until the under paint was dry. I had been afraid of seeing her less clearly if I took too long, but because of it the picture was now out of balance and I'd have to be very careful to get the kitchen into the same key, so that the whole thing looked harmonious and natural and as if it couldn't have been any other way.

The wind was rawly cold, the sky a hurrying jumbled mass of darkening clouds. I huddled my hands inside my anorak pockets and slid back through the hedge with the first drops of rain.

The afternoon session was much shorter because of the light, and I frustratingly could not catch the right mix of colours for the tops of the kitchen fitments. Even after years of experience, what looked right on the palette looked wrong on the painting. I got it wrong three times and decided to stop.

I was cleaning the brushes when Donald came back. I heard the scrunch of the car, the slam of the doors, and, to my surprise, the ring of the front door bell. Donald had taken his keys.

I went through and opened the door. A uniformed policeman stood there, holding Don's arm. Behind, a row of watching faces gazed on hungrily. My cousin, who had looked pale before, now seemed bloodlessly white. The eyes were as lifeless as death.

'Don!' I said, and no doubt looked as appalled as I felt.

He didn't speak. The policeman learnt forward, said, 'There we are,

sir,' and transferred the support of my cousin from himself to me: and
it seemed to me that the action was symbolic as much as practical, because
he turned immediately on his heel and methodically drove off in his
waiting car.

I helped Donald inside and shut the door. I had never seen anyone in
such a frightening state of disintegration.

'I asked,' he said, 'about the funeral.'

His face was stony, and his voice came out in gasps.

'They said . . .' He stopped, dragged in air, tried again. 'They said
. . . no funeral.'

'Donald . . .'

'They said . . . she couldn't be buried until they had finished their
enquiries. They said . . . it might be months. They said . . . they will
keep her . . . refrigerated . . .'

The distress was fearful.

'They said . . .' He swayed slightly. 'They said . . . the body of a
murdered person belongs to the State.'

I couldn't hold him. He collapsed at my feet in a deep and total faint.

Chapter Three

For two days Donald lay in bed, and I grew to understand what was
meant by prostration.

Whether he liked it or not, this time he was heavily sedated, his doctor
calling morning and evening with pills and injections. No matter that I
was a hopeless nurse and a worse cook, I was appointed, for lack of
anyone else, to look after him.

'I want Charles,' Donald in fact told the doctor. 'He doesn't *fuss.*'

I sat with him a good deal when he was awake, seeing him struggle
dazedly to face and come to terms with the horrors in his mind. He lost
weight visibly, the rounded muscles of his face slackening and the contours
changing to the drawn shape of illness. The grey shadows round his eyes
darkened to a permanent charcoal, and all normal strength seemed to
have vanished from arms and legs.

I fed us both from tins and frozen packets, reading the instructions
and doing what they said. Donald thanked me punctiliously and ate what
he could, but I doubt if he tasted a thing.

In between times, while he slept, I made progress with both the
paintings. The sad landscape was no longer sad but merely Octoberish,
with three horses standing around in a field, one of them eating grass.
Pictures of this sort, easy to live with and passably expert, were my bread
and butter. They sold quite well, and I normally churned one off the
production line every ten days or so, knowing that they were all technique
and no soul.

The portrait of Regina, though, was the best work I'd done for months. She laughed out of the canvas, alive and glowing, and to me at least seemed vividly herself. Pictures often changed as one worked on them, and day by day the emphasis in my mind had shifted, so that the kitchen background was growing darker and less distinct and Regina herself more luminous. One could still see she was cooking, but it was the girl who was important, not the act. In the end I had painted the kitchen, which was still there, as an impression, and the girl, who was not, as the reality.

I hid that picture in my suitcase whenever I wasn't working on it. I didn't want Donald to come face to face with it unawares.

Early Wednesday evening he came shakily down to the kitchen in his dressing-gown, trying to smile and pick up the pieces. He sat at the table, drinking the Scotch I had that day imported, and watching while I cleaned my brushes and tidied the palette.

'You're always so neat,' he said.

'Paint's expensive.'

He waved a limp hand at the horse picture which stood drying on the easel. 'How much does it cost, to paint that?'

'In raw materials, about ten quid. In heat, light, rates, rent, food, Scotch and general wear and tear on the nervous system, about the amount I'd earn in a week if I chucked it in and went back to selling houses.'

'Quite a lot, then,' he said seriously.

I grinned. 'I don't regret it.'

'No. I see that.'

I finished the brushes by washing them in soap and water under the tap, pinching them into shape, and standing them upright in a jar to dry. Good brushes were at least as costly as paint.

'After the digging into the company accounts,' Donald said abruptly, 'they took me along to the police station and tried to prove that I had actually killed her myself.'

'I don't believe it!'

'They'd worked out that I could have got home at lunch time and done it. They said there was time.'

I picked up the Scotch from the table and poured a decent sized shot into a tumbler. Added ice.

'They must be crazy,' I said.

'There was another man, besides Frost. A Superintendent. I think his name was Wall. A thin man, with fierce eyes. He never seemed to blink. Just stared and said over and over that I'd killed her because she'd come back and found me supervising the burglary.'

'For God's sake!' I said disgustedly. 'And anyway, she didn't leave the flower shop until half past two.'

'The girl in the flower shop now says she doesn't know to the minute when Regina left. Only that it was soon after lunch. And I didn't get back from the pub until nearly three. I went to lunch late. I was hung up with a client all morning . . .' He stopped, gripping his tumbler as if it were a support to hold on to. 'I can't tell you . . . how awful it was.'

The mild understatement seemed somehow to make things worse.

'They said,' he added, 'that eighty per cent of murdered married women are killed by their husbands.'

That statement had Frost stamped all over it.

'They let me come home, in the end, but I don't think . . .' His voice shook. He swallowed, visibly trying to keep tight control on his hard-won calm. 'I don't think they've finished.'

It was five days since he'd walked in and found Regina dead. When I thought of the mental hammerings he'd taken on top, the punishing assault on his emotional reserves, where common humanity would have suggested kindness and consoling help, it seemed marvellous that he had remained as sane as he had.

'Have they got anywhere with catching the thieves?' I said.

He smiled wanly. 'I don't even know if they're trying.'

'They must be.'

'I suppose so. They haven't said.' He drank some whisky slowly. 'It's ironic, you know. I've always had a regard for the police. I didn't know they could be . . . the way they are.'

A quandary, I thought. Either they leaned on a suspect in the hope of breaking him down, or they asked a few polite questions and got nowhere: and under the only effective system the innocent suffered more than the guilty.

'I see no end to it.' Donald said. 'No end at all.'

By mid-day Friday the police had called twice more at the house, but for my cousin the escalation of agony seemed to have slowed. He was still exhausted, apathetic, and as grey as smoke, but it was as if he were saturated with suffering and could absorb little more. Whatever Frost and his companion said to him, it rolled off without destroying him further.

'You're supposed to be painting someone's horse, aren't you?' he said suddenly, as we shaped up to lunch.

'I told them I'd come later.'

He shook his head. 'I remember you saying, when I asked you to stay, that it would fit in fine before your next commission.' He thought a bit. 'Tuesday. You should have gone to Yorkshire on Tuesday.'

'I telephoned and explained.'

'All the same, you'd better go.'

He said he would be all right alone, now, and thanks for everything. He insisted I look up the times of trains, order a taxi, and alert the people at the other end. I could see in the end that the time had indeed come for him to be by himself, so I packed up my things to depart.

'I suppose,' he said diffidently, as we waited for the taxi to fetch me, 'that you never paint portraits? People, that is, not horses.'

'Sometimes,' I said.

'I just wondered . . . Could you, one day . . . I mean, I've got quite a good photograph of Regina . . .'

I looked searchingly at his face. As far as I could see, it could do no harm. I unclipped the suitcase and took out the picture with its back towards him.

'It's still wet,' I warned. 'And not framed, and I can't varnish it for at least six months. But you can have it, if you like.'

'Let me see.'

I turned the canvas round. He stared and stared, but said nothing at all. The taxi drove up to the front door.

'See you,' I said, propping Regina against a wall.

He nodded and punched my arm, opened the door for me, and sketched a farewell wave. Speechlessly, because his eyes were full of tears.

I spent nearly a week in Yorkshire doing my best to immortalise a patient old steeplechaser, and then went home to my noisy flat near Heathrow airport, taking the picture with me to finish.

Saturday I downed tools and went to the races, fed up with too much nose-to-the-grindstone.

Jump racing at Plumpton, and the familiar swelling of excitement at the liquid movement of racehorses. Paintings could never do justice to them: never. The moment caught on canvas was always second best.

I would love to have ridden in races, but hadn't had enough practice or skill; nor, I dare say, nerve. Like Donald, my childhood's background was of middle-sized private enterprise, with my father an auctioneer in business on his own account in Sussex. I had spent countless hours in my growing years watching the horses train on the Downs round Findon, and had drawn and painted them from about the age of six. Riding itself had been mostly a matter of begging the wherewithal for an hour's joy from indulgent aunts, never of a pony of my own. Art school later had been fine, but at twenty-two, alone in the world with both parents newly dead, I'd had to face the need to eat. It had been a short meant-to-be-temporary step to the estate agents across the street, but I'd liked it well enough to stay.

Half the horse painters in England seemed to have turned up at Plumpton, which was not surprising, as the latest Grand National winner was due to make his first appearance of the new season. It was a commercial fact that a picture called for instance 'Nijinsky on Newmarket Heath' stood a much better chance of being sold than one labelled 'A horse on Newmarket Heath', and 'The Grand National winner at the start' won hands down over 'A runner at Plumpton before the Off'. The economic facts of life had brought many a would-be Rembrandt down to market research.

'Tod!' said a voice in my ear. 'You owe me fifteen smackers.'

'I bloody don't,' I said.

'You said Seesaw was a certainty for Ascot.'

'Never take sweets from a stranger.'

Billy Pyle laughed extravagantly and patted me heavily on the shoulder. Billy Pyle was one of those people you met on racecourses who greeted you as a bosom pal, plied you with drinks and bonhomie, and bored you to death. On and off I'd met Billy Pyle at the races for umpteen years, and had never yet worked out how to duck him without positive rudeness.

Ordinary evasions rolled off his thick skin like mercury off glass, and I found it less wearing on the whole to get the drink over quickly than dodge him all afternoon.

I waited for him to say 'how about a beverage', as he always did.

'How about a beverage?' he said.

'Er . . . sure,' I agreed, resignedly.

'Your father would never forgive me if I neglected you.' He always said that, too. They had been business acquaintances, I knew, but I suspected the reported friendship was posthumous.

'Come along, laddie.'

I knew the irritating routine by heart. He would meet his Auntie Sal in the bar, as if by accident, and in my turn I would buy them both a drink. A double brandy and ginger forAuntie Sal.

'Why, there's Auntie Sal,' Billy said, pushing through the door. Surprise, surprise.

Auntie Sal was a compulsive racegoer in her seventies with a perpetual cigarette dangling from the corner of her mouth and one finger permanently inserted in her form book, keeping her place.

'Know anything for the two-thirty?' she demanded.

'Hello,' I said.

'What? Oh, I see. Hello. How are you? Know anything for the two-thirty?'

''Fraid not.'

'Huh.'

She peered into the form book. 'Treetops is well in at the weighs, but can you trust his leg?' She looked up suddenly and with her free hand prodded her nephew, who was trying to attract service from the bar. 'Billy, get a drink for Mrs. Matthews.'

'Mrs. Who?'

'Matthews. What do you want, Maisie?'

She turned to a large middle-aged woman who had been standing in the shadows behind her.

'Oh . . . gin and tonic, thanks.'

'Got that, Billy? Double brandy and ginger for me, gin and tonic for Mrs. Matthews.'

Maisie Matthews' clothes were noticeably new and expensive, and from laquered hair via crocodile handbag to gold-trimmed shoes she shouted money without saying a word. The hand which accepted the drink carried the weight of a huge opal set in diamonds. The expression on her expertly painted face showed no joy at all.

'How do you do?' I said politely.

'Eh?' said Auntie Sal. 'Oh yes, Maisie, this is Charles Todd. What do you think of Treetops?'

'Moderate,' I said.

Auntie Sal peered worriedly into the form book and Billy handed round the drinks.

'Cheers,' Maisie Matthews said, looking cheerless.

'Down the hatch,' said Billy, raising his glass.

'Maisie's had a bit of bad luck,' Auntie Sal said.

Billy grinned. 'Backed a loser, then, Mrs. Matthews?'

'Her house burned down.'

As a light conversation-stopper, it was a daisy.

'Oh . . . I say . . .' said Billy uncomfortably. 'Hard luck.'

'Lost everything, didn't you, Maisie?'

'All but what I stand up in,' she agreed gloomily.

'Have another gin,' I suggested.

'Thanks, dear.'

When I returned with the refills she was in full descriptive flood.

'. . . I wasn't there, of course, I was staying with my sister Betty up in Birmingham, and there was this policeman on the doorstep telling me what a job they'd had finding me. But by that time it was all over, of course. When I got back to Worthing there was just a heap of cinders with the chimney-breast sticking up in the middle. Well, I had a real job finding out what happened, but anyway they finally said it was a flash fire, whatever that is, but they didn't know what started it, because there'd been no one in the house of course for two days.'

She accepted the gin, gave me a brief unseeing smile, and returned to her story.

'Well, I was spitting mad, I'll tell you, over losing everything like that, and I said why hadn't they used sea water, what with the sea being only the other side of the tamarisk and down the shingle, because of course they said they hadn't been able to save a thing because they hadn't enough water, and this fireman, the one I was complaining to, he said they couldn't use sea water because for one thing it corroded everything and for another the pumps sucked up sea-weed and shells and things, and in any case the tide was out.'

I smothered an unseemly desire to laugh. She sensed it, however.

'Well, dear, it may seem funny to you, of course, but then you haven't lost all your treasures that you'd been collecting since heaven knows when.'

'I'm really sorry, Mrs. Matthews. I don't think it's funny. It was just . . .'

'Yes, well, dear. I suppose you can see the funny side of it, all that water and not a drop to put a fire out with, but I was that mad, I can tell you.'

'I think I'll have a bit on Treetops,' Auntie Sal said thoughtfully.

Maisie Matthews looked at her uncertainly and Billy Pyle, who had heard enough of disaster, broke gratefully into geniality, clapped me again on the shoulder, and said yes, it was time to see the next contest.

Duty done, I thought with a sigh, and took myself off to watch the race from the top of the stands, out of sight and earshot.

Treetoops broke down and finished last, limping. Too bad for its owner, trainer, and Auntie Sal. I wandered down to the parade ring to see the Grand National winner walk round before his race, but without any thought of drawing him. I reckoned he was just about played out as a subject, and there would shortly be a glut.

The afternoon went quickly, as usual. I won a little, lost a little, and filled my eyes with something better than money. On the stands for the last race, I found myself approached by Maisie Matthews. No mistaking the bright red coat, the air of gloss, and the big, kind-looking, worldly face. She drew to a halt on the step below me, looking up. Entirely self-confident, though registering doubt.

'Aren't you,' she said, 'the young man I had a drink with, with Sal and Billy?'

'Yes, that's right.'

'I wasn't sure,' she said, the doubt disappearing. 'You look older out here.'

'Different light,' I said, agreeing. She too looked older, by about ten years. Fifty-something, I thought. Barlight always flattered.

'They said you were an artist.' Their mild disapproval coloured the way she spoke.

'Mm,' I said, watching the runners canter past on the way to the post.

'Not very well paid, is it, dear?'

I grinned at her, liking her directness. 'It depends who you are. Picasso didn't grumble.'

'How much would you charge to paint a picture for me?'

'What sort of picture?'

'Well, dear, you may say it sounds morbid and I dare say it is, but I was just thinking this morning when I went over there, and really it makes me that mad every time I see it, well, I was thinking actually that it makes a crazy picture, that burnt ruin with the chimney sticking up, and the burnt hedge behind and all that sea, and I was thinking of getting the local photographer who does all the weddings and things to come along and take a colour picture, because when it's all cleared away and rebuilt, no one will believe how awful it was, and I want to hang it in the new house, just to show them.'

'But . . .'

'So how much would you charge? Because I dare say you can see I am not short of the next quid but if it would be hundreds I might as well get the photographer of course.'

'Of course,' I agreed gravely. 'How about if I came up see the house, or what's left of it, and gave you an estimate?'

She saw nothing odd in that. 'All right, dear. That sounds very businesslike. Of course, it will have to be soon, though, because once the insurance people have been I am having the rubble cleared up.'

'How soon?'

'Well, dear, as you're half-way there, could you come today?'

We discussed it. She said she would drive me in her Jaguar as I hadn't a car, and I could go home by train just as easily from Worthing as from Plumpton.

So I agreed.

One takes the most momentous steps unawares.

The ruin was definitely paintagenic, if there is such a word. On the way there, more or less non-stop, she had talked about her late husband, Archie, who had looked after her very well, dear.

'Well, that's to say, I looked after him, too, dear, because of course I was a nurse. Private of course. I nursed his first wife all through her illness, cancer it was, dear, of course, and then I stayed on for a bit to look after him, and, well, he asked me to stay on for life, dear, and I did. Of course he was much older, he's been gone more than ten years now. He looked after me very well, Archie did.'

She glanced fondly at the huge opal. Many a man would have liked to have been remembered as kindly.

'Since he went, and left me so well off, dear, it seemed a shame not to get some fun out of it, so I carried on with what we were doing when we were together those few years, which was going round to auction sales in big houses, dear, because you pick up such nice things there, quite cheap sometimes, and of course it's ever so much more interesting when the things have belonged to someone well known or famous.' She changed gear with a jerk and aggressively passed an inoffensive little van. 'And now all those things are burnt to cinders, of course, and all the memories of Archie and the places we went together, and I'll tell you, dear, it makes me mad.'

'It's really horrid for you.'

'Yes, dear, it is.'

I reflected that it was the second time in a fortnight that I'd been cast in the role of comforter; and I felt as inadequate for her as I had for Donald.

She stamped on the brakes outside the remains of her house and rocked us to a standstill. From the opulence of the minor mansions on either side, her property had been far from a slum; but all that was left was an extensive sprawling black heap, with jagged pieces of outside wall defining its former shape, and the thick brick chimney, as she'd said, pointing sturdily skywards from the centre. Ironic, I thought fleetingly, that the fireplace alone had survived the flames.

'There you are, dear,' Maisie said. 'What do you think?'

'A very hot fire.'

She raised her pencilled eyebrows. 'But yes, dear, all fires are hot, aren't they? And of course there was a lot of wood. So many of these old seaside houses were built with a lot of wood.'

Even before we climbed out of her big pale blue car, I could smell the ash.

'How long ago . . .?' I asked.

'Last week-end, dear. Sunday.'

While we surveyed the mess for a moment in silence a man walked slowly into view from behind the chimney. He was looking down, concentrating, taking a step at a time and then bending to poke into the rubble.

Maisie, for all her scarlet-coated bulk, was nimble on her feet.

'Hey,' she called, hopping out of the car and advancing purposefully. 'What do you think you're doing?'

The man straightened up, looking startled. About forty, I judged, with a raincoat, a crisp-looking trilby and a down-turning moustache.

He raised his hat politely. 'Insurance, madam.'

'I thought you were coming on Monday.'

'I happened to be in the district. No time like the present, don't you think?'

'Well, I suppose not,' Maisie said. 'And I hope there isn't going to be any shilly-shallying over you paying up, though of course nothing is going to get my treasures back and I'd rather have them than any amount of money, as I've got plenty of that in any case.'

The man was unused to Maisie's brand of chat.

'Er . . .' he said. 'Oh yes. I see.'

'Have you found out what started it?' Maisie demanded.

'No, madam.'

'Found anything at all?'

'No, madam.'

'Well, how soon can I get all this cleared away?'

'Any time you like, madam.'

He stepped carefully towards us, picking his way round clumps of blackened debris. He had steady greyish eyes, a strong chin, and an overall air of intelligence.

'What's your name?' Maisie asked.

'Greene, madam.' He paused slightly, and added 'With an "e" '.

'Well, Mr. Greene with an "e",' Maisie said good-humouredly. 'I'll be glad to have all that in writing.'

He inclined his head. 'As soon as I report back.'

Maisie said 'Good,' and Greene, lifting his hat again, wished her good afternoon and walked along to a white Ford parked a short way along the road.

'That's all right, then,' Maisie said with satisfaction, watching him go. 'Now, how much for that picture?'

'Two hundred plus two nights' expenses in a local hotel.'

'That's a bit steep, dear. *One* hundred, and two nights, and I've got to like the results, or I don't pay.'

'No foal, no fee?'

The generous red mouth smiled widely. 'That's it, dear.'

We settled on one-fifty if she liked the picture, and fifty if she didn't, and I was to start on Monday unless it was raining.

Chapter Four

Monday came up with a bright breezy day and an echo of summer's warmth. I went to Worthing by train and to the house by taxi, and to the interest of the neighbours set up my easel at about the place where the front gates would have been, had they not been unhinged and transplanted by the firemen. The gates themselves lay flat on the lawn, one of them still pathetically bearing a neat painted nameboard.

'*Treasure Holme.*'

Poor Archie. Poor Maisie.

I worked over the whole canvas with an unobtrusive coffee-coloured underpainting of raw umber much thinned with turpentine and linseed oil, and while it was still wet drew in, with a paintbrushful of a darker shade of the same colour, the shape of the ruined house against the horizontals of hedges, shingle, sea and sky. It was easy with a tissue to wipe out mistakes of composition at that stage, and try again: to get the proportions right, and the perspective, and the balance of the main masses.

That done and drying, I strolled right round the whole garden, looking at the house from different angles, and staring out over the blackened stumps of the tamarisk hedge which had marked the end of the grass and the beginning of the shingle. The sea sparkled in the morning sunshine, with the small hurrying cumulus clouds scattering patches of dark slate-grey shadow. All the waves had white frills: distant, because the tide again had receded to the far side of a deserted stretch of wet-looking, waverippled sand.

The sea wind chilled my ears. I turned to get back to my task and saw two men in overcoats emerge from a large station wagon and show definite signs of interest in what was left of *Treasure Holme*.

I walked back towards them, reaching them where they stood by the easel appraising my handiwork.

One, heavy and fiftyish. One lean, in the twenties. Both with firm self-confident faces and an air of purpose.

The elder raised his eyes as I approached.

'Do you have permission to be here?' he asked. An enquiry; no belligerence in sight.

'The owner wants her house painted,' I said obligingly.

'I see.' His lips twitched a fraction.

'And you?' I enquired.

He raised his eyebrows slightly. 'Insurance,' he said, as if surprised that anyone should ask.

'Same company as Mr. Greene?' I said.

'Mr. Who?'

'Greene. With an "e".'

'I don't know who you mean,' he said. 'We are here by arrangement with Mrs. Matthews to inspect the damage to her house, which is insured with us.' He looked with some depression at the extent of the so-called damage, glancing about as if expecting Maisie to materialise Phoenix-like from the ashes.

'No Greene?' I repeated.

'Neither with nor without an "e".'

I warmed to him. Half an ounce of a sense of humour, as far as I was concerned, achieved results where thumbscrews wouldn't.

'Well ... Mrs. Matthews is no longer expecting you, because the aforesaid Mr. Greene, who said he was in insurance, told her she could roll in the demolition squad as soon as she liked.'

His attention sharpened like a tightened violin string.

'Are you serious?'

'I was here, with her. I saw him and heard him, and that's what he said.'

'Did he show you a card?'

'No, he didn't.' I paused. 'And ... er ... nor have you.'

He reached into an inner pocket and did so, with the speed of a conjuror. Producing cards from pockets was a reflex action, no doubt.

'Isn't it illegal to insure the same property with two companies?' I asked idly, reading the card.

Foundation Life and Surety.

D. F. Lagland. Area Manager

'Fraud.' He nodded.

'Unless of course Mr. Greene with an "e" had nothing to do with insurance.'

'Much more likely.'

I put the card in my trouser pocket, Arran sweaters not having been designed noticeably for business transactions. He looked at me thoughtfully, his eyes observant but judgement suspended. He was the same sort of man my father had been, middle-aged, middle-of-the-road, expert at his chosen job but unlikely to set the world on fire.

Or *Treasure Holme*, for that matter.

'Gary,' he said to his younger side-kick, 'go and find a telephone and ring the Beach Hotel. Tell Mrs. Matthews we're here.'

'Will do,' Gary said. He was that sort of man.

While he was away on the errand, D. J. Lagland turned his attention to the ruin, and I, as he seemed not to object, tagged along at his side.

'What do you look for?' I asked.

He shot me a sideways look. 'Evidence of arson. Evidence of the presence of the goods reported destroyed.'

'I didn't expect you to be so frank.'

'I indulge myself, occasionally.'

I grinned. 'Mrs. Matthews seems pretty genuine.'

'I've never met the lady.'

Treat in store, I thought. 'Don't the firemen,' I said, 'look for signs of arson?'

'Yes, and also the police, and we ask them for guidance.'

'And what did they say?'

'None of your business, I shouldn't think.'

'Even for a wooden house,' I said, 'it is pretty thoroughly burnt.'

'Expert, are you?' he said with irony.

'I've built a lot of Guy Fawkes bonfires, in my time.'

He turned his head.

'They burn a lot better,' I said, 'if you soak them in paraffin. Especially round the edges.'

'I've been looking at fires since before you were born,' he said. 'Why don't you go over there and paint?'

'What I've done is still wet.'

'Then if you stay with me, shut up.'

I stayed with him, silent, and without offence. He was making what appeared to be a preliminary reconnaissance, lifting small solid pieces of debris, inspecting them closely, and carefully returning them to their former positions. None of the things he chose in that way were identifiable to me from a distance of six feet, and as far as I could see none of them gave him much of a thrill.

'Permission to speak?' I said.

'Well?'

'Mr. Greene was doing much what you are, though in the area behind the chimney breast.'

He straightened from replacing yet another black lump. 'Did he take anything?' he said.

'Not while we were watching, which was a very short time. No telling how long he'd been there.'

'No.' He considered. 'Wouldn't you think he was a casual sight-seer, poking around out of curiosity?'

'He hadn't the air.'

D. J. Frowned. 'Then what did he want?'

A rhetorical question. Gary rolled back, and soon after him, Maisie. In her Jaguar. In her scarlet coat. In a temper.

'What do you mean,' she said, advancing upon D. J. with eyes flashing fortissimo, 'the question of arson isn't yet settled? Don't tell me you're trying to wriggle out of paying my cheque, now. Your man said on Saturday that everything was all right and I could start clearing away and rebuilding, and anyway even if it had been arson you would still have to pay up because the insurance covered arson of course.'

D. J. opened and shut his mouth several times and finally found his voice.

'Didn't our Mr. Robinson tell you that the man you saw here on Saturday wasn't from us?'

Our Mr. Robinson, in the shape of Gary, nodded vigorously.

'He ... Mr. Greene ... distinctly said he *was*,' Maisie insisted.

'Well ... what did he look like?'

'Smarmy,' said Maisie without hesitation. 'Not as young as Charles ...' she gestured towards me, 'Or as old as you.' She thought, then shrugged. 'He looked like an insurance man, that's all.'

D. J. swallowed the implied insult manfully.

'About five feet ten,' I said. 'Suntanned skin with a sallow tinge, grey eyes with deep upper eyelids, widish nose, mouth straight under heavy drooping dark moustache, straight brown hair brushed back and retreating from the two top corners of his forehead, ordinary eyebrows, greeny-brown trilby of smooth felt, shirt, tie, fawn unbuttoned raincoat, gold signet ring on little finger of right hand, suntanned hands.'

I could see him in memory as clearly as if he still stood there in the ashes before me, taking off his hat and calling Maisie 'madam.'

'Good God,' D. J. said.

'An artist's eye, dear,' said Maisie admiringly. 'Well I never.'

D. J. said he was certain they had no one like that in their poking-into-claims department, and Gary agreed.

'Well,' said Maisie, with a resurgence of crossness, 'I suppose that still means you are looking for arson, though why you think that anyone in his right senses would want to burn down my lovely home and all my treasures is something I'll never understand.'

Surely Maisie, worldly Maisie, could not be so naïve. I caught a deep glimmer of intelligence in the glance she gave me, and knew that she certainly wasn't. D. J. however, who didn't know, made frustrated little motions with his hands and voted against explaining. I smothered a few more laughs, and Maisie noticed.

'Do you want your picture,' I asked, 'To be sunny like today, or cloudy and sad?'

She looked up at the bright sky.

'A bit more dramatic, dear,' she said.

D. J. and Gary inch-by-inched over the ruin all afternoon, and I tried to infuse it with a little Gothic romance. At five o'clock, on the dot, we all knocked off.

'Union hours?' said D. J. sarcastically, watching me pack my suitcase.

'The light gets too yellow in the evenings.'

'Will you be here tomorrow?'

I nodded. 'And you?'

'Perhaps.'

I went by foot and bus along to the Beach Hotel, cleaned my brushes, thought a bit, and at seven met Maisie downstairs in the bar, as arranged.

'Well, dear,' she said, as her first gin and tonic gravitated comfortably, 'Did they find anything?'

'Nothing at all, as far as I could see.'

'Well, that's good, dear.'

I tackled my pint of draught. Put the glass down carefully.

'Not altogether, Maisie.'

'Why not?'

'What exactly were your treasures, which were burned?'

'I dare say you wouldn't think so much of them of course, but we had ever such fun buying them, and so have I since Archie's gone, and well, dear, things like an antique spear collection that used to belong to old Lord Stequers whose niece I nursed once, and a whole wall of beautiful butterflies, which professors and such came to look at, and a wrought iron gate from Lady Tythe's old home, which divided the hall from the sittingroom, and six warming pans from a castle in Ireland, and two tall vases with eagle on the lids signed by Angelica Kaufman, which once belonged to a cousin of Mata Hari, they really did, dear, and a copper firescreen with silver bosses which was a devil to polish, and a marble table from Greece, and a silver tea urn which was once used by Queen Victoria, and really, dear, that's just the beginning, if I tell you them all I'll go on all night.'

'Did the Foundation insurance company have a full list?'

'Yes, they did, dear, and why do you want to know?'

'Because,' I said regretfully, 'I don't think many of those things were inside the house when it burned down.'

'*What?*' Maisie, as far as I could tell, was genuinely astounded. 'But they must have been.'

'D. J. as good as told me they were looking for traces of them, and I don't think they found any.'

'D. J.?'

'Mr. Lagland. The elder one.'

Alternate disbelief and anger kept Maisie going through two more double gins. Disbelief, eventually, won.

'You got it wrong, dear,' she said finally.

'I hope so.'

'Inexperience of youth, of course.'

'Maybe.'

'Because of course everything was in its place, dear, when I went off last Friday week to stay with Betty, and I only went to Betty's with not having seen her for so long while I'd been away, which is ironic when you think of it, but of course you can't stay at home for ever on the off-chance your house is going to catch fire and you can save it, can you dear, or you'd never go anywhere and I would have missed my trip to Australia.'

She paused for breath. Coincidence, I thought.

'All I can say, dear, is that it's a miracle I took most of my jewellery with me to Betty's, because I don't always, except that Archie always said it was safer and of course he was always so sensible and thoughtful and sweet.'

'Australia?' I said.

'Well, yes, dear, wasn't that nice? I went out there for a visit to Archie's sister who's lived there since Heaven knows when and was feeling lonely since she'd been widowed, poor dear, and I went out for a bit of fun, dear, because of course I'd never really met her, only exchanged postcards of course, and I was out there for six weeks with her. She wanted me to stay, and of course we got on together like a house on fire . . . oh dear, I didn't mean that exactly . . . well, anyway, I said I wanted to come back to my little house by the sea and think it over, and of course I took my jewellery with me on that trip too, dear.'

I said idly, 'I don't suppose you bought a Munnings while you were there.'

I didn't know why I'd said it, apart from thinking of Donald in Australia. I was totally unprepared for her reaction.

Astounded she had been before: this time, pole-axed. Before, she had been incredulous and angry. This time, incredulous and frightened.

She knocked over her gin, slid off her bar stool, and covered her open mouth with four trembling red-nailed fingers.

'You didn't!' I said disbelievingly.

'How do you know?'

'I don't . . .'

'Are you from Customs and Excise?'

'Of course not.'

'Oh dear. Oh dear . . .' She was shaking, almost as shattered as Donald.

I took her arm and led her over to an armchair beside a small bar table.

'Sit down,' I said coaxingly, 'and tell me.'

It took ten minutes and a refill double gin.

'Well, dear, I'm not an art expert, as you can probably guess, but there was this picture by Sir Alfred Mannings, signed and everything, dear, and it was such a bargain really, and I thought how tickled Archie would have been to have a real Munnings on the wall, what with us both liking the races, of course, and, well, Archie's sister egged me on a bit, and I felt quite . . . I suppose you might call it *high*, dear so I bought it.'

She stopped.

'Go on,' I said.

'Well, dear, I suppose you've guessed from what I said just now.'

'You brought it into this country without declaring it?'

She sighed. 'Yes, dear, I did. Of course it was silly of me but I never gave customs duty a thought when I bought the painting, not until just before I came home, a week later, that was, and Archie's sister asked if I was going to declare it, and well, dear, I really *resent* having to pay duty on things, don't you? So any way I thought I'd better find out just how much the duty would be, and I found it wasn't duty at all in the ordinary way, dear, there isn't duty on second-hand pictures being brought in from Australia, but would you believe it they said I would have to pay Value Added Tax, sort of tax on buying things, you know, dear, and I would have to pay eight per cent on whatever I had bought the picture for. Well, I ask you! I was that mad, dear, I can tell you. So Archie's sister said why didn't I leave the painting with her, because then if I went back to Australia I would have paid the tax for nothing, but I wasn't sure I'd go back and anyway I did want to see Sir Alfred Munnings on the wall where Archie would have loved it, so, well, dear, it was all done up nicely in boards and brown paper so I just camouflaged it a bit with my best nightie and popped it in my suitcase, and pushed it through the 'Nothing to Declare' lane at Heathrow when I got back, and nobody stopped me.'

'How much would you have had to pay?' I said.

'Well, dear, to be precise, just over seven hundred pounds. And I know that's not a fortune, dear, but it made me so mad to have to pay tax here because I'd bought something nice in Australia.'

I did some mental arithmetic. 'So the painting cost about nine thousand?'

'That's right, dear. Nine thousand.' She looked anxious. 'I wasn't done, was I? I've asked one or two people since I got back and they say lots of Munningses cost fifteen or more.'

'So they do,' I said absently. And some could be got for fifteen hundred, and others, I dared say, for less.

'Well, anyway, dear, it was only when I began to think about insurance that I wondered if I would be found out, if say, the insurance people wanted a *receipt* or anything, which they probably would, of course, so I didn't do anything about it, because of course if I *did* go back to Australia I could just take the picture with me and no harm done.'

'Awkward,' I agreed.

'So now it's burnt, and I dare say you'll think it serves me right, because the nine thousand's gone up in smoke and I won't see a penny of it back.'

She finished the gin and I bought her another.

'I know it's not my business, Maisie, but how did you happen to have nine thousand handy in Australia? Aren't there rules about exporting that much cash?'

She giggled. 'You don't know much about the world, do you, dear? But anyway, this time it was all hunky dory. I just toddled along with Archie's sister to a jewellers and sold him a brooch I had, a nasty sort of *toad*, dear, with a socking big diamond in the middle of its forehead, something to do with Shakespeare, I think, though I never got it clear, anyway I never wore it, it was so ugly, but of course I'd taken it with me because of it being worth so much, and I sold it for nine thousand five, though in Australian dollars of course, so there was no problem, was there?'

Maisie took it for granted I would be eating with her, so we drifted in to dinner. Her appetite seemed healthy, but her spirits were damp.

'You won't *tell* anyone, will you, dear, about the picture?'

'Of course not, Maisie.'

'I could get into such trouble, dear.'

'I know.'

'A fine, of course,' she said. 'And I suppose that might be the least of it. People can be so beastly about a perfectly innocent little bit of smuggling.'

'No one will find out if you keep quiet.' A thought struck me. 'Unless, that is, you've told anyone already that you'd bought it?'

'No, dear, I didn't, because of thinking I'd better pretend I'd had it for years, and of course I hadn't even hung it on the wall yet because one of the rings was loose in the frame and I thought it might fall down and be damaged, and I couldn't decide who to ask to fix it.' She paused for a mouthful of prawn cocktail. 'I expect you'll think me silly, dear, but I suppose I was feeling a bit scared of being found out, not guilty exactly because I really don't see why we *should* pay that irritating tax but anyway I didn't not only not hang it up, I hid it.'

'You hid it? Still wrapped up?'

'Well, yes, dear, more or less wrapped up. Of course I'd opened it when I got home, and that's when I found the ring coming loose with the cord through it, so I wrapped it up again until I'd decided what to do.'

I was fascinated. 'Where did you hide it?'

She laughed. 'Nowhere very much, dear. I mean, I was only keeping it out of sight to stop people asking about it, of course, so I slipped it behind one of the radiators in the lounge, and don't look so horrified dear, the central heating was turned off.'

I painted at the house all the next day, but neither D. J. nor anyone else turned up.

In between stints at the easel I poked around a good deal on my own account, searching for Maisie's treasures. I found a good many recognisable remains, durables like bed-frames, kitchen machines and radiators, all of them twisted and buckled not merely by heat but by the weight of the whole edifice from roof downwards having collapsed inwards. Occasional remains of heavy rafters lay blackly in the thick ash, but apart from these, everything combustible had totally, as one might say, combusted.

Of all the things Maisie had described, and of all the dozens she hadn't, I found only the wrought iron gate from Lady Tythe's old home, which had divided the hall from the sittingroom. Lady Tythe would never have recognised it.

No copper warming pans, which after all had been designed to withstand red-hot coals. No metal fire screen. No marble table. No antique spears.

Naturally, no Munnings.

When I took my paint-stained fingers back to the Beach at five o'clock I found Maisie waiting for me in the hall. Not the kindly, basically cheerful Maisie I had come to know, but a belligerent woman in a full-blown state of rage.

'I've been waiting for you,' she said, fixing me with a furious eye.

I couldn't think how I could have offended her.

'What's the matter?' I said.

'The bar's shut,' she said. 'So come upstairs to my room. Bring all your stuff with you.' She gestured to the suitcase. 'I'm so *mad* I think I'll absolutely *burst*.'

She did indeed, in the lift, look in danger of it. Her cheeks were bright red with hard outlines of colour against the pale surrounding skin. Her blonde-rinsed hair, normally lacquered into sophistication, stuck out in wispy spikes, and for the first time since I'd met her her mouth was not glistening with lipstick.

She threw open the door of her room and stalked in. I followed, closing it after me.

'You'll never believe it,' she said forcefully, turning to face me and letting go with all guns blazing. 'I've had the police here half the day, and those insurance men here the other half, and *do you know what they're saying?*'

'Oh, Maisie.' I sighed inwardly. It had been inevitable.

'What do you think I am, I asked them,' she said. 'I was so *mad*. There they were, having the nerve to suggest I'd sold all my treasures and over-insured my house, and was trying to take the insurance people for a ride. I told them, I told them over and over, that everything was in its place when I went to Betty's and if it was over-insured it was to allow for inflation and anyway the brokers had advised me to put up the amount pretty high, and I'm glad I took their advice, but that Mr. Lagland says they won't be paying out until they have investigated further and he was proper sniffy about it, and no sympathy at all for me having lost everything. They were absolute *beastly*, and I *hate* them all.'

She paused to regather momentum, vibrating visibly with the strength of her feelings. 'They made me feel so *dirty*, and maybe I *was* screaming at them a bit, I was so mad, but they'd no call to be so *rude*, and making out I was some sort of criminal, and just what *right* have they to tell me to pull myself together when it is because of *them* and their bullying that I am yelling at them at the top of my voice?'

It must, I reflected, have been quite an encounter. I wondered in what state the police and D.J. had retired from the field.

'They say it was definitely arson and I said why did they think so now when they hadn't thought so at first, and it turns out that it was because that Lagland couldn't find any of my treausres in the ashes or any trace of them at all, and they said even if I hadn't sold the things first I had arranged for them to be stolen and the house burnt to cinders while I was away at Betty's, and they kept on and on asking me who I'd paid to do it, and I got more and more furious and if I'd had anything handy I would have *hit* them, I really would.'

'What you need is a stiff gin,' I said.

'I told them they ought to be out looking for whoever had done it instead of hounding helpless women like me, and the more I thought of someone walking into *my* house and stealing *my* treasures and then callously setting fire to everything the madder I got, and somehow that made me even *madder* with those stupid men who couldn't see any further than their stupid noses.'

It struck me after a good deal more of similar diatribe that genuine though Maisie's anger undoubtedly was, she was stoking herself up again every time her temper looked in danger of relapsing to normal. For some reason, she seemed to need to be in the position of the righteous wronged.

I wondered why; and in a breath-catching gap in the flow of hot lava, I said, 'I don't suppose you told them about the Munnings.'

The red spots on her cheeks burned suddenly brighter.

'I'm not *crazy*,' she said bitingly. 'If they found out about that, there would have been a fat chance of convincing them I'm telling the truth about the rest.'

'I've heard,' I said tentatively, 'That nothing infuriates a crook more than being had up for the one job he didn't do.'

It looked for a moment as if I'd just elected myself as the new target for hatred, but suddenly as she glared at me in rage her sense of humour reared its battered head and nudged her in the ribs. The stiffness round her mouth relaxed, her eyes softened and glimmered, and after a second or two, she ruefully smiled.

'I dare say you're right, dear, when I come to think of it.' The smile grew into a giggle. 'How about that gin?'

Little eruptions continued all evening through drinks and dinner, but the red-centred volcano had subsided to manageable heat.

'You didn't seem surprised, dear, when I told you what the police thought I've done.' She looked sideways at me over her coffee cup, eyes sharp and enquiring.

'No.' I paused. 'You see, something very much the same has just happened to my cousin. Too much the same, in too many ways. I think, if you will come, and he agrees, that I'd like to take you to meet him.'

'But why, dear?'

I told her why. The anger she felt for herself burned up again fiercely for Donald.

'How *dreadful*. How *selfish* you must think *me*, after all that that poor man has suffered.'

'I don't think you're selfish at all. In fact, Maisie, I think you're a proper trouper.'

She looked pleased and almost kittenish, and I had a vivid impression of what she had been like with Archie.

'There's one thing, though, dear,' she said awkwardly. 'After today, and all that's been said, I don't think I want that picture you're doing. I don't any more want to remember the house as it is now, only like it used to be. So if I give you just fifty pounds, do you mind?'

Chapter Five

We went to Shropshire in Maisie's Jaguar, sharing the driving.

Donald on the telephone had sounded unenthusiastic at my suggested return, but also too lethargic to raise objections. When he opened his front door to us, I was shocked.

It was two weeks since I'd left him to go to Yorkshire. In that time he had shed at least fourteen pounds and aged ten years. His skin was tinged with blue-ish shadows, the bones in his face showed starkly, and even his hair seemed speckled with grey.

The ghost of the old Donald put an obvious effort into receiving us with good manners.

'Come in,' he said. 'I'm in the diningroom now. I expect you'd like a drink.'

'That would be very nice, dear,' Maisie said.

He looked at her with dull eyes, seeing, as I saw, a large good-natured lady with glossy hair and expensive clothes, her smart appearance walking a tightrope between vulgarity and elegance and just making it to the safer side.

He waved to me to pour the drinks, as if it would be too much for him, and invited Maisie to sit down. The diningroom had been roughly refurnished, containing now a large rug, all the sunroom armchairs, and a couple of small tables from the bedrooms. We sat in a fairly close group round one of the tables, because I had come to ask questions, and I wanted to write down the answers. My cousin watched the production of notebook and ballpoint with no show of interest.

'Don,' I said, 'I want you to listen to a story.'

'All right.'

Maisie, for once, kept it short. When she came to the bit about buying a Munnings in Australia, Donald's head lifted a couple of inches and he looked from her to me with the first stirring of attention. When she stopped, there was a small silence.

'So,' I said finally, 'you both went to Australia, you both bought a Munnings, and soon after your return you both had your houses burgled.'

'Extraordinary coincidence,' Donald said: but he meant simply that, nothing more. 'Did you come all this way just to tell me that?'

'I wanted to see how you were.'

'Oh. I'm all right. Kind of you, Charles, but I'm all right.'

Even Maisie, who hadn't known him before, could see that he wasn't.

'Where did you buy your picture, Don? Where exactly, I mean.'

'I suppose . . . Melbourne. In the Hilton Hotel. Opposite the cricket ground.'

I looked doubtful. Although hotels quite often sold pictures by local artists, they seldom sold Munnings.

'Fellow met us there,' Don added. 'Brought it up to our room. From the gallery where we saw it first.'

'Which gallery?'

He made a slight attempt to remember. 'Might have been something like Fine Arts.'

'Would you have it on a cheque stub, or anything?'

He shook his head. 'The wine firm I was dealing with paid for it for me, and I sent a cheque to their British office when I got back.'

'Which wine firm?'

'Monga Vineyards Proprietary Limited of Adelaide and Melbourne.'

I wrote it all down.

'And what was the picture like? I mean, could you describe it?'

Donald looked tired. 'One of those "Going Down to the Start" things. Typical Munnings.'

'So was mine,' said Maisie, surprised. 'A nice long row of jockeys in their colours against a darker sort of sky.'

'Mine had only three horses,' Donald said.

'The biggest, I suppose you might say the *nearest* jockey in my picture had a purple shirt and green cap,' Maisie said, 'and I expect you'll think I was silly but that was one of the reasons I bought it, because when Archie and I were thinking what fun it would be to buy a horse and go to the races as owners, we decided we'd like purple with a green cap for our colours, if no one else already had that, of course.'

'Don?' I said.

'Mm? Oh . . . three bay horses cantering . . . in profile . . . on in front, two slightly overlapping behind. Bright colours on the jockeys. I don't remember exactly. White racetrack rails and a lot of sunny sky.'

'What size?'

He frowned slightly. 'Not very big. About twenty-four inches by eighteen, inside the frame.'

'And yours, Maisie?'

'A bit smaller, dear, I should think.'

'Look,' Donald said. 'What are you getting at?'

'Trying to make sure that there are no more coincidences.'

He stared, but without any particular feeling.

'On the way up here,' I said, 'Maisie told me everything' (but *everything*) 'of the way she came to buy her picture. So could you possibly tell us how you came to buy yours. Did you, for example, deliberately go looking for a Munnings?'

Donald passed a weary hand over his face, obviously not wanting the bother of answering.

'Please, Don,' I said.

'Oh . . .' A long sigh. 'No. I wasn't especially wanting to buy anything at all. We just went into the Melbourne Art Gallery for a stroll round. We came to the Munnings they have there . . . and while we were looking at it we just drifted into conversation with a woman near us, as one does in art galleries. She said there was another Munnings, not far away, for sale in a small commercial gallery, and it was worth seeing even if one didn't intend to buy it. We had time to spare, so we went.'

Maisie's mouth had fallen open. 'But, dear,' she said, recovering 'that was *just* the same as us, my sister-in-law and me, though it was Sydney Art Gallery, not Melbourne. They have this marvellous picture there, "The Coming Storm", and we were admiring it when this man sort of drifted up to us and joined in . . .'

Donald suddenly looked a great deal more exhausted, like a sick person overdone by healthy visitors.

'Look . . . Charles . . . you aren't going to the police with all this? Because I . . . I don't think . . . I could stand . . . a whole new lot . . . of questions.'

'No, I'm not,' I said.

'Then what . . . does it matter?'

Maisie finished her gin and tonic and smiled a little too brightly.

'Which way to the little girls' room, dear?' she asked, and disappeared to the cloakroom.

Donald said faintly, 'I can't concentrate . . . I'm sorry, Charles, but I can't seem to do anything . . . while they still have Regina . . . unburied . . . just *stored* . . .'

Time, far from dulling the agony, seemed to have preserved it, as if the keeping of Regina in a refrigerated drawer had stopped dead the natural progression of mourning. I had been told that the bodies of murdered people could be held in that way for six months or more in unsolved cases. I doubted whether Donald would last that long.

He stood suddenly and walked away out of the door to the hall. I followed. He crossed the hall, opened the door of the sittingroom, and went in.

Hesitantly, I went after him.

The sittingroom still contained only the chintz-covered sofas and chairs, now ranged over-tidily round the walls. The floor where Regina had laid was clean and polished. The air was cold.

Donald stood in front of the empty fireplace looking at my picture of Regina, which was propped on the mantelpiece.

'I stay in here with her, most of the time,' he said. 'It's the only place I can bear to be.'

He walked to one of the armchairs and sat down, directly facing the portrait.

'You wouldn't mind seeing yourselves out, would you, Charles?' he said. 'I'm really awfully tired.'

'Take care of yourself.' Useless advice. One could see he wouldn't.

'I'm all right,' he said. 'Quite all right. Don't you worry.'

I looked back from the door. He was sitting immobile, looking at Regina. I didn't know whether it would have been better or worse if I hadn't painted her.

Maisie was quiet for the whole of the first hour of the return journey, a record in itself.

From Donald's house we had driven first to one of the neighbours who had originally offered refuge, because he clearly needed help more now than ever.

Mrs. Neighbour had listened with sympathy, but had shaken her head.

'Yes, I know he should have company and get away from the house, but he won't. I've tried several times. Called. So have lots of people round here. He just tells us he's all right. He won't let anyone help him.'

Maisie drove soberly, mile after mile. Eventually she said, 'We shouldn't have bothered him. Not so soon after . . .'

Three weeks, I thought. Only three weeks. To Donald it must have seemed like three months, stretched out in slow motion. You could live a lifetime in three weeks' pain.

'I'm going to Australia,' I said.

'You're very fond of him, dear, aren't you?' Maisie said.

Fond? I wouldn't have used that word, I thought: but perhaps after all it was accurate.

'He's eight years older than me, but we've always got on well together.' I looked back, remembering. 'We were both only children. His mother and mine were sisters. They used to visit each other, with me and Donald in tow. He was always pretty patient about having a young kid under his feet.'

'He looks very ill, dear.'

'Yes.'

She drove another ten miles in silence. Then she said, 'Are you sure it wouldn't be better to tell the police? About the paintings, I mean? Because you do think they had something to do with the burglaries, don't you, dear, and the police might find out things more easily than you.'

I agreed. 'I'm sure they would, Maisie. But how can I tell them? You heard what Donald said, that he couldn't stand a new lot of questions. Seeing him today, do you think he could? And as for you, it wouldn't just be confessing to a bit of smuggling and paying a fine, but of having a conviction against your name for always, and having the customs search your baggage every time you travelled, and all sorts of other complications and humiliations. Once you get on any blacklist nowadays it is just about impossible to get off.'

'I didn't know you cared, dear.' She tried a giggle, but it didn't sound right.

We stopped after a while to exchange places. I liked driving her car, particularly as for the last three years, since I'd given up a steady income, I'd owned no wheels myself. The power purred elegantly under the pale blue bonnet and ate up the southward miles.

'Can you afford the fare, dear?' Maisie said. 'And hotels, and things?'

'I've a friend out there. Another painter. I'll stay with him.'

She looked at me doubtfully. 'You can't get there by hitch-hiking, though.'

I smiled. 'I'll manage.'

'Yes, well, dear, I dare say you can, but all the same, and I don't want any silly arguments, I've got a great deal of this world's goods thanks to Archie, and you haven't, and as because it's partly because of me having gone in for smuggling that you're going yourself at all, I am insisting that you let me buy your ticket.'

'No, Maisie.'

'Yes, dear. Now be a good boy, dear, and do as I say.'

You could see, I thought, why she'd been a good nurse. Swallow the medicine, dear, there's a good boy. I didn't like accepting her offer but the truth was that I would have had to borrow anyway.

'Shall I paint your picture, Maisie, when I get back?'

'That will do very nicely, dear.'

I pulled up outside the house near Heathrow whose attic was my home, and from where Maisie had picked me up that morning.

'How do you stand all this noise, dear?' she said, wincing as a huge jet climbed steeply overhead.

'I concentrate on the cheap rent.'

She smiled, opening the crocodile handbag and producing her cheque-book. She wrote out and gave me the slip of paper which was far more than enough for my journey.

'If you're so fussed, dear,' she said across my protests, 'you can give me back what you don't spend.' She gazed at me earnestly with grey-blue eyes. 'You will be careful dear, won't you?'

'Yes, Maisie.'

'Because of course, dear, you might turn out to be a nuisance to some really *nasty* people.

I landed at Mascot airport at noon five days later, wheeling in over Sydney and seeing the harbour bridge and the opera house down below, looking like postcards.

Jik met me on the other side of Customs with a huge grin and a waving bottle of champagne.

'Todd the sod,' he said. 'Who'd have thought it?' His voice soared easily over the din. 'Come to paint Australia red!'

He slapped me on the back with an enthusiastic horny hand, not knowing his own strength. Jik Cassavetes, long-time friend, my opposite in almost everything.

Bearded, which I was not. Exuberant, noisy, extravagant, unpredictable; qualities I envied. Blue eyes and sun-blond hair. Muscles which left mine gasping. An outrageous way with girls. An abrasive tongue; and a wholehearted contempt for the things I painted.

We had met at Art School, drawn together by mutual truancy on racetrains. Jik compulsively went racing, but strictly to gamble, never to admire the contestants, and certainly not to paint them. Horse-painters, to him, were the lower orders. No *serious* artist, he frequently said, would be seen dead painting horses.

Jik's paintings, mostly abstract, were the dark reverse of the bright mind: fruits of depression, full of despair at the hatred and pollution destroying the fair world.

Living with Jik was like a toboggan run, downhill, dangerous, and exhilarating. We'd spent the last two years at Art School sharing a studio flat and kicking each other out for passing girls. They would have chucked him out of school except for his prodigious talent, because he'd missed weeks in the summer for his other love, which was sailing.

I'd been out with him, deep sea, several times in the years afterwards. I reckoned he'd taken us on several occasions a bit nearer death than was strictly necessary, but it had been a nice change from the office. He was a great sailor, efficient, neat, quick and strong, with an instinctive feeling for wind and waves. I had been sorry when one day he had said he was setting off singlehanded round the world. We'd had a paralytic farewell party on his last night ashore; and the next day, when he'd gone, I'd given the estate agent my notice.

He had brought a car to fetch me: his car, it turned out. A British M.G. Sports, dark blue. Both sides of him right there, extrovert and introvert, the flamboyant statement in a sombre colour.

'Are there many of these here?' I asked, surprised, loading suitcase and satchel into the back. 'It's a long way from the birth pangs.'

He grinned. 'A few. They're not popular now because petrol passes through them like salts.' The engine roared to life, agreeing with him, and he switched on the windscreen wiper against a starting shower. 'Welcome to sunny Australia. It rains all the time here. Puts Manchester in the sun.'

'But you like it?'

'Love it, mate. Sydney's like rugger, all guts and go and a bit of grace in the line-out.'

'And how's business?'

'There are thousands of painters in Australia. It's a flourishing cottage industry.' He glanced at me sideways. 'A hell of a lot of competition.'

'I haven't come to seek fame and fortune.'

'But I scent a purpose,' he said.

'How would you feel about harnessing your brawn?'

'To your brain? As in the old days?'

'Those were pastimes.'

His eyebrows rose. 'What are the risks?'

'Arson and murder, to date.'

'Jesus.'

The blue car swept gracefully into the centre of the city. Skyscrapers grew like beanstalks.

'I live right out on the other side,' Jik said. 'God, that sounds banal. Suburban. What has become of me?'

'Contentment oozing from every pore,' I said smiling.

'Yes. So O.K., for the first time in my life I've been actually happy. I dare say you'll soon put that right.'

The car nosed on to the expressway, pointing towards the bridge.

'If you look over your right shoulder,' Jik said, 'You'll see the triumph of imagination over economics. Like the Concorde. Long live madness, it's the only thing that gets us anywhere.'

I looked. It was the opera house, glimpsed, grey with rain.

'Dead in the day,' Jik said. 'It's a night bird. Fantastic.'

The great arch of the bridge rose above us, intricate as steel lace. 'This is the only flat bit of road in Sydney,' Jik said. We climbed again on the other side.

To our left, half-seen at first behind other familiar-looking high-rise blocks, but then revealed in its full glory, stood a huge shiny red-orange building, all its sides set with regular rows of large curve-cornered square windows of bronze-coloured glass.

Jik grinned. 'The shape of the twenty-first century. Imagination and courage. I love this country.'

'Where's your natural pessimism?'

'When the sun sets, those windows glow like gold.' We left the gleaming monster behind. 'It's the water-board offices,' Jik said sardonically. 'The guy at the top moors his boat near mine.'

The road went up and down out of the city through close-packed rows of one-storey houses, whose roofs, from the air, had looked like a great red-squared carpet.

'There's one snag,' Jik said. 'Three weeks ago, I got married.'

The snag was living with him aboard his boat, which was moored among a colony of others near a headland he called The Spit: and you could see why, temporarily at least, the glooms of the world could take care of themselves.

She was not plain, but not beautiful. Oval-shaped face, mid-brown hair, so-so figure and a practical line in clothes. None of the style or instant vital butterfly quality of Regina. I found myself the critically inspected target of bright brown eyes which looked out with impact-making intelligence.

'Sarah,' Jik said. 'Todd. Todd, Sarah.'

We said hi and did I have a good flight and yes I did. I gathered she would have preferred me to stay at home.

Jik's thirty-foot ketch, which had set out from England as a cross between a studio and a chandler's warehouse, now sported curtains, cushions, and a flowering plant. When Jik opened the champagne he poured it into shining tulip glasses, not plastic mugs.

'By God,' he said. 'It's good to see you.'

Sarah toasted my advent politely, not sure that she agreed. I apologised for gatecrashing the honeymoon.

'Nuts to that,' Jik said, obviously meaning it. 'Too much domestic bliss is bad for the soul.'

'It depends,' said Sarah neutrally, 'on whether you need love or loneliness to get you going.'

For Jik, before, it had always been loneliness. I wondered what he had painted recently; but there was no sign, in the now comfortable cabin, of so much as a brush.

'I walk on air,' Jik said. 'I could bound up Everest and do a handspring on the summit.'

'As far as the galley will do,' Sarah said, 'if you remembered to buy the crayfish.'

Jik, in our shared days, had been the cook; and times, it seemed, had not changed. It was he, not Sarah, who with speed and efficiency chopped open the crayfish, covered them with cheese and mustard, and set them under the grill. He who washed the crisp lettuce and assembled crusty bread and butter. We ate the feast round the cabin table with rain pattering on portholes and roof and the sea water slapping against the sides in the freshening wind. Over coffee, at Jik's insistence, I told them why I had come to Australia.

They heard me out in concentrated silence. Then Jik, whose politics had not changed much since student pink, muttered darkly about 'pigs', and Sarah looked nakedly apprehensive.

'Don't worry,' I told her. 'I'm not asking for Jik's help, now that I know he's married.'

'You have it. You have it,' he said explosively.

I shook my head. 'No.'

Sarah said, 'What precisely do you plan to do first?'

'Find out where the two Munnings came from.'

'And after?'

'If I knew what I was looking for I wouldn't need to look.'

'That doesn't follow,' she said absently.

'Melbourne,' Jik said suddenly. 'You said one of the pictures came from Melbourne. Well, that settles it. Of course we'll help. We'll go there at once. It couldn't be better. Do you know what next Tuesday is?'

'No,' I said. 'What is it?'

'The day of the Melbourne Cup!'

His voice was triumphant. Sarah stared at me darkly across the table.

'I wish you hadn't come,' she said.

Chapter Six

I slept that night in the converted boathouse which constituted Jik's postal address. Apart from a bed alcove, new-looking bathroom, and rudimentary kitchen, he was using the whole space as studio.

A huge old easel stood in the centre, with a table to each side holding neat arrays of paints, brushes, knives, pots of linseed and turpentine and cleaning fluid: all the usual paraphernalia.

No work in progress. Everything shut and tidy. Like its counterpart in England, the large rush mat in front of the easel was black with oily dirt, owing to Jik's habit of rubbing his roughly rinsed brushes on it between colours. The tubes of paint were characteristically squeezed flat in the middles, impatience forbidding an orderly progress from the bottom. The palette was a small oblong, not needed any larger because he used most colours straight from the tube and got his effects by overpainting. A huge box of rags stood under one table, ready to wipe clean everything used to apply paint to picture, not just brushes and knives, but fingers, palms, nails, wrists, anything which took his fancy. I smiled to myself. Jik's studio was as identifiable as his pictures.

Along one wall a two-tiered rack held rows of canvasses, which I pulled out one by one. Dark, strong, dramatic colours, leaping to the eye. Still the troubled vision, the perception of doom. Decay and crucifixions, obscurely horrific landscapes, flowers wilting, fish dying, everything to be guessed, nothing explicit.

Jik hated to sell his paintings and seldom did, which I thought was just as well, as they made uncomfortable roommates, enough to cause depression in a skylark. They had a vigour, though, that couldn't be denied. Everyone who saw his assembled work remembered it, and had their thoughts modified, and perhaps even their basic attitudes changed. He was a major artist in a way I would never be, and he would have looked upon easy popular acclaim as personal failure.

In the morning I walked down to the boat and found Sarah there alone.

'Jik's gone for milk and newspapers,' she said. 'I'll get you some breakfast.'

'I came to say goodbye.'

She looked at me levelly. 'The damage is done.'

'Not if I go.'

'Back to England?'

I shook my head.

'I thought not.' A dim smile appeared briefly in her eyes. 'Jik told me last night that you were the only person he knew who had a head cool enough to calculate a ship's position for a Mayday call by dead reckoning at night after tossing around violently for four hours in a force ten gale with a hole in the hull and the pumps packed up, and get it right.'

I grinned. 'But he patched the hull and mended the pump, and we cancelled the Mayday when it got light.'

'You were both stupid.'

'Better to stay safely at home?' I said.

She turned away. '*Men*,' she said. 'Never happy unless they're risking their necks.'

She was right, to some extent. A little healthy danger wasn't a bad feeling, especially in retrospect. It was only the nerve-breakers which gave you the shakes and put you off repetition.

'Some women, too,' I said.

'Not me.'

'I won't take Jik with me.'

Her back was still turned. 'You'll get him killed,' she said.

Nothing looked less dangerous than the small suburban gallery from which Maisie had bought her picture. It was shut for good. The bare premises could be seen nakedly through the shop-front window, and a succinct and unnecessary card hanging inside the glass door said 'Closed'.

The little shops on each side shrugged their shoulders.

'They were only open for a month or so. Never seemed to do much business. No surprise they folded.'

Did they, I asked, know which estate agent was handling the letting? No, they didn't.

'End of enquiry,' Jik said.

I shook my head. 'Let's try the local agents.'

We split up and spent a fruitless hour. None of the firms on any of the 'For Sale' boards in the district admitted to having the gallery on its books.

We met again outside the uninformative door.

'Where now?'

'Art Gallery?'

'In the Domain,' Jik said, which turned out to be a chunk of park in the city centre. The Art Gallery had a suitable façade of six pillars outside and the Munnings, when we ran it to earth, inside.

No one else was looking at it. No one approached to fall into chat and advise us we could buy another one cheap in a little gallery in an outer suburb.

We stood there for a while with me admiring the absolute mastery which set the two grey ponies in the shaft of pre-storm light at the head of the darker herd, and Jik grudgingly admitted that at least the man knew how to handle paint.

Absolute nothing else happened. We drove back to the boat in the M.G., and lunch was an anti-climax.

'What now?' Jik said.

'A spot of work with the telephone, if I could borrow the one in the boathouse.'

It took nearly all afternoon, but alphabetically systematic calls to every estate agent as far as Holloway and Son in the classified directory produced the goods in the end. The premises in question, said Holloway and Son, had been let to 'North Sydney Fine Arts' on a short lease.

How short?

Three months, dating from September first.

No, Holloway and Son did not know the premises were now empty. They could not re-let them until December first, because North Sydney Fine Arts had paid all the rent in advance; and they did not feel able to part with the name of any individual concerned. I blarneyed a bit, giving a delicate impression of being in the trade myself, with a client for the empty shop. Holloway and Son mentioned a Mr. John Grey, with a post-office box number for an address. I thanked them. Mr. Grey, they said, warming up a little, had said he wanted the gallery for a short private exhibition, and they were not really surprised he had already gone.

How could I recognise Mr. Grey if I met him? They really couldn't say: all the negotiations had been done by telephone and post. I could write to him myself, if my client wanted the gallery before December first.

Ta ever so, I thought.

All the same, it couldn't do much harm. I unearthed a suitable sheet of paper, and in twee and twirly lettering in black ink told Mr. Grey I had been given his name and box number by Holloway and Son, and asked him if he would sell me the last two weeks of his lease so that I could mount an exhibition of a young friend's *utterly meaningful* water-colours. Name his own price, I said, within reason. Yours sincerely, I said; Peregrine Smith.

I walked down to the boat to ask if Jik or Sarah would mind me putting their own box number as a return address.

'He won't answer,' Sarah said, reading the letter. 'If he's a crook. I wouldn't.'

'The first principle of fishing,' Jik said, 'is to dangle a bait.'

'This wouldn't attract a starving pirhana.'

I posted it anyway, with Sarah's grudging consent. None of us expected it to bring forth any result.

Jik's own session on the telephone proved more rewarding. Melbourne, it seemed, was crammed to the rooftops for the richest race meeting of the year, but he had been offered last-minute cancellations. Very lucky indeed, he insisted, looking amused.

'Where?' I asked suspiciously.

'In the Hilton,' he said.

I couldn't afford it, but we went anyway. Jik in his student days had lived on cautious hand-outs from a family trust, and it appeared that the source of bread was still flowing. The boat, the boathouse, the M.G. and the wife were none of them supported by paint.

We flew south to Melbourne the following morning, looking down on the Snowy Mountains en route and thinking our own chilly thoughts. Sarah's disapproval from the seat behind froze the back of my head, but she had refused to stay in Sydney. Jik's natural bent and enthusiasm for dicey adventure looked like being curbed by love, and his reaction to danger might not henceforth be uncomplicatedly practical. That was, if I could find any dangers for him to react to. The Sydney trail was dead and cold, and maybe Melbourne too would yield an un-looked-at public Munnings and a gone-away private gallery. And if it did, what then? For Donald the outlook would be bleaker than the strange puckered ranges sliding away underneath.

If I could take home enough to show beyond doubt that the plundering of his house had its roots in the sale of a painting in Australia, it should get the police off his neck, the life back to his spirit, and Regina into a decent grave.

If.

And I would have to be quick, or it would be too late to matter. Donald, staring hour after hour at a portrait in an empty house . . . Donald, on the brink.

Melbourne was cold and wet and blowing a gale. We checked gratefully into the warm plushy bosom of the Hilton, souls cossetted from the door onwards by rich reds and purples and blues, velvety fabrics, copper and gilt and glass. The staff smiled. The lifts worked. There was polite shock when I carried my own suitcase. A long way from the bare boards of home.

I unpacked, which is to say, hung up my one suit, slightly crumpled from the squashy satchel, and then went to work again on the telephone.

The Melbourne office of the Monga Vineyards Proprietary Limited cheerfully told me that the person who dealt with Mr. Donald Stuart from England was the managing director, Mr. Hudson Taylor, and he could be found at present in his office at the vineyard itself, which was north of Adelaide. Would I like the number?

Thanks very much.

'No sweat,' they said, which I gathered was Australian shorthand for 'It's no trouble, and you're welcome.'

I pulled out the map of Australia I'd acquired on the flight from England. Melbourne, capital of the state of Victoria, lay right down in the south-east corner. Adelaide, capital of South Australia, lay about four hundred and fifty miles north west. Correction, seven hundred and thirty kilometres: the Australians had already gone metric, to the confusion of my mental arithmetic.

Hudson Taylor was not in his vineyard office. An equally cheerful voice there told me he'd left for Melbourne to go to the races. He had a runner in the Cup. Reverence, the voice implied, was due.

Could I reach him anywhere, then?

Sure, if it was important. He would be staying with friends. Number supplied. Ring at nine o'clock.

Sighing a little I went two floors down and found Jik and Sarah bouncing around their room with gleeful satisfaction.

'We've got tickets for the races tomorrow and Tuesday,' he said, 'And a car pass, and a car. And the West Indies play Victoria at cricket on Sunday opposite the hotel and we've tickets for that too.'

'Miracles courtesy of the Hilton,' Sarah said, looking much happier at this programme. 'The whole package was on offer with the cancelled rooms.'

'So what do you want us to do this afternoon?' finished Jik expansively.

'Could you bear the Arts Centre?'

It appeared they could. Even Sarah came without forecasting universal doom, my lack of success so far having cheered her. We went in a taxi to keep her curled hair dry.

The Victoria Arts Centre was huge, modern, inventive and endowed with the largest stained-glass roof in the world. Jik took deep breaths as if drawing the living spirit of the place into his lungs and declaimed at the top of his voice that Australia was the greatest, the greatest, the only adventurous country left in the corrupt, stagnating, militant, greedy, freedom-hating, mean-minded, strait-jacketed, rotting, polluted world. Passers-by stared in amazement and Sarah showed no surprise at all.

We ran the Munnings to earth, eventually, deep in the labyrinth of galleries. It glowed in the remarkable light which suffused the whole building; the *Departure of the Hop Pickers*, with its great wide sky and the dignified gypsies with their ponies, caravans and children.

A young man was sitting at an easel slightly to one side, painstakingly working on a copy. On a table beside him stood large pots of linseed oil and turps, and a jar with brushes in cleaning fluid. A comprehensive box of paints lay open to hand. Two or three people stood about, watching him and pretending not to, in the manner of gallery-goers the world over.

Jik and I went round behind him to take a look. The young man glanced at Jik's face, but saw nothing there except raised eyebrows and blandness. We watched him squeeze flake white and camium yellow from tubes on to his palette and mix them together into a nice pale colour with a hogshair brush.

On the easel stood his study, barely started. The outlines were there, as precise as tracings, and a small amount of blue had been laid on the sky.

Jik and I watched in interest while he applied the pale yellow to the shirt of the nearest figure.

'Hey,' Jik said loudly, suddenly slapping him on the shoulder and shattering the reverent gallery hush into kaleidoscopic fragments, 'You're a fraud. If you're an artist I'm a gas-fitter's mate.'

Hardly polite, but not a hanging matter. The faces of the scattered onlookers registered embarrassment, not affront.

On the young man, though, the effect was galvanic. He leapt to his feet, overturning the easel and staring at Jik with wild eyes: and Jik, with huge enjoyment put in the clincher.

'What you're doing is *criminal*,' he said.

The young man reacted to that with ruthless reptilian speed, snatching up the pots of linseed and turps and flinging the liquids at Jik's eyes.

I grabbed his left arm. He scooped up the paint-laden palette in his right hand and swung round fiercely, aiming at my face. I ducked instinctively. The palette missed me and struck Jik, who had his hands to his eyes and was yelling very loudly.

Sarah rushed towards him, knocking into me hard in her anxiety and loosening my grip on the young man. He tore his arm free, ran precipitously for the exit, dodgèd round behind two open-mouthed middle-aged spectators who were on their way in, and pushed them violently into my chasing path. By the time I'd disentangled myself, he had vanished from sight. I ran through several halls and passages, but couldn't find him. He knew his way, and I did not: and it took me long enough, when I finally gave up the hunt, to work out the route back to Jik.

A fair-sized crowd had surrounded him, and Sarah was in a roaring fury based on fear, which she unleashed on me as soon as she saw me return.

'Do something,' she screamed. 'Do something, he's going blind . . . He's going *blind* . . . I knew we should never have listened to you . . .'

I caught her wrists as she advanced in near hysteria to do at least some damage to my face in payment for Jik's. Her strength was no joke.

'Sarah,' I said fiercely. 'Jik is *not* going blind.'

'He is. He is,' she insisted, kicking my shins.

'Do you *want* him to?' I shouted.

She gasped sharply in outrage. What I'd said was at least as good as a slap in the face. Sense reasserted itself suddenly like a drench of cold water, and the manic power receded back to normal angry girl proportions.

'Linseed oil will do no harm at all,' I said positively. 'The turps is painful, but that's all. It absolutely will not affect his eyesight.'

She glared at me, pulled her wrists out of my grasp, and turned back to Jik, who was rocking around in agony and cupping his fingers over his eyes with rigid knuckles. Also, being Jik, he was exercising his tongue.

'The slimy little bugger . . . wait till I catch him . . . Jesus Christ Almighty I can't bloody see . . . Sarah . . . where's that bloody Todd . . . I'll strangle him . . . get an ambulance . . . my eyes are burning out . . . bloody buggering hell . . .'

I spoke loudly in his ear. 'Your eyes are O.K.'

'They're my bloody eyes and if I say they're not O.K. they're bloody not.'

'You know damn well you're not going blind, so stop hamming it up.'

'They're not your eyes, you sod.'

'And you're frightening Sarah,' I said.

That message got through. He took his hands away and stopped rolling about.

At the sight of his face a murmur of pleasant horror rippled through the riveted audience. Blobs of bright paint from the young man's palette had streaked one side of his jaw yellow and blue: and his eyes were red with inflammation and pouring with tears, and looked very sore indeed.

'Jesus, Sarah,' he said blinking painfully. 'Sorry, love. The bastard's right. Turps never blinded anybody.'

'Not permanently,' I said, because to do him justice he obviously couldn't see anything but tears at the moment.

Sarah's animosity was unabated. 'Get him an ambulance, then.'

I shook my head. 'All he needs is water and time.'

'You're a stupid heartless *pig*. He obviously needs a doctor, and hospital care.'

Jik, having abandoned histrionics, produced a handkerchief and gently mopped his streaming eyes.

'He's right, love. Lots of water, as the man said. Washes the sting away. Lead me to the nearest gents.'

With Sarah unconvinced but holding one arm, and a sympathetic male spectator the other, he was solicitously helped away like an amateur production of Samson. The chorus in the shape of the audience bent reproachful looks on me, and cheerfully awaited the next act.

I looked at the overturned mess of paints and easel which the young man had left. The onlookers looked at them too.

'I suppose,' I said slowly, 'that no one here was talking to the young artist before any of this happened?'

'We were,' said one woman, surprised at the question.

'So were we,' said another.

'What about?'

'Munnings,' said one, and 'Munnings,' said the other, both looking immediately at the painting on the wall.

'Not about his own work?' I said, bending down to pick it up. A slash of yellow lay wildly across the careful outlines, result of Jik's slap on the back.

Both of the ladies, and also their accompanying husbands, shook their heads and said they had talked with him about the pleasure of hanging a Munnings on their own walls, back home.

I smiled slowly.

'I suppose,' I said, 'That he didn't happen to know where you could get one?'

'Well, yeah,' they said. 'As a matter of fact, he sure did.'

'Where?'

'Well, look here, young fellow ...' The elder of the husbands, a seventyish American with the unmistakable stamp of wealth, began shushing the others to silence with a practised damping movement of his right hand. Don't give information away, it said, you may lose by it.

'... You're asking a lot of questions.'

'I'll explain,' I said. 'Would you like some coffee?'

They all looked at their watches and said doubtfully they possibly would.

'There's a coffee shop just down the hall,' I said. 'I saw it when I was trying to catch that young man ... to make him tell why he flung turps in my friend's eyes.'

Curiosity sharpened in their faces. They were hooked.

The rest of the spectators drifted away, and I, asking the others to wait a moment, started moving the jumbled painting stuff off the centre of the floor to a tidier wallside heap.

None of it was marked with its owner's name. All regulation kit, obtainable from art shops. Artists' quality, not students' cheaper equivalents. None of it new, but not old, either. The picture itself was on a standard sized piece of commercially prepared hardboard, not on stretched canvas. I stacked everything together, added the empty jars which had held linseed and turps, and wiped my hands on a piece of rag.

'Right,' I said. 'Shall we go?'

They were all Americans, all rich, retired, and fond of racing. Mr. and Mrs. Howard K. Petrovitch of Ridgeville, New Jersey, and Mr. and Mrs. Wyatt L. Minchless from Carter, Illinois.

Wyatt Minchless, the one who had shushed the others, called the meeting to order over four richly creamed iced coffees and one plain black. The black was for himself. Heart condition, he murmured, patting the relevant area of suiting. A white-haired man, black-framed specs, pale indoor complexion, pompous manner.

'Now, young fellow, let's hear it from the top.'

'Um,' I said. Where exactly was the top? 'The artist boy attacked my friend Jik because Jik called him a criminal.'

'Yuh,' Mrs. Petrovitch nodded, 'I heard him. Just as we were leaving the gallery. Now why would he do that?'

'It isn't criminal to copy good painting,' Mrs. Minchless said knowledgeably. 'In the Louvre in Paris, France, you can't get near the Mona Lisa for those irritating students.'

She had blue-rinsed puffed-up hair, uncreasable navy and green clothes, and enough diamonds to attract a top-rank thief. Deep lines of automatic disapproval ran downwards from the corner of her mouth. Thin body. Thick mind.

'It depends what you are copying *for*,' I said. 'If you're going to try to pass your copy off as an original, then that definitely is a fraud.'

Mrs. Petrovitch began to say, 'Do you think the young man was *forging* ...' but was interrupted by Wyatt Minchless, who smothered her question both by the damping hand and his louder voice.

'Are you saying that this young artist boy was painting a Munnings he later intended to sell as the real thing?'

'Er ...' I said.

Wyatt Minchless swept on. 'Are you saying that the Munnings picture he told us we might be able to buy is itself a forgery?'

The others looked both horrified at the possibility and admiring of Wyatt L. for his perspicacity.

'I don't know,' I said. 'I just thought I'd like to see it.'

'You don't want to buy a Munnings yourself? You are not acting as an agent for anyone else?' Wyatt's questions sounded severe and inquisitorial.

'Absolutely not,' I said.

'Well, then.' Wyatt looked round the other three, collected silent assents. 'He told Ruthie and me there was a good Munnings racing picture at a very reasonable price in a little gallery not far away ...' He fished with forefinger and thumb into his outer breast pocket. 'Yes, here we are. *Yarra River Fine Arts.* Third turning off Swanston Street, about twenty yards along.'

Mr. and Mrs. Petrovitch looked resigned. 'He told us, exactly the same.'

'He seemed such a nice young man,' Mrs. Petrovitch added sadly. 'So interested in our trip. Asked us what we'd be betting on in the Cup.'

'He asked where we would be going after Melbourne,' Mr. Petrovitch nodded. 'We told him Adelaide and Alice Springs, and he said Alice Springs was a Mecca for artists and to be sure to visit the Yarra River gallery there. The same firm, he said. Always had good pictures.'

Mr. Petrovitch would have misunderstood if I had leaned across and hugged him. I concentrated on my fancy coffee and kept my excitement to myself.

'We're going on to Sydney,' pronounced Wyatt L. 'He didn't offer any suggestions for Sydney.'

The tall glasses were nearly empty. Wyatt looked at his watch and swallowed the last of his plain black.

'You didn't tell us,' Mrs. Petrovitch said, looking puzzled, 'why your friend called the young man a criminal. I mean . . . I can see why the young man attacked your friend and ran away if he *was* a criminal, but why did your friend *think* he was?'

'Just what I was about to ask,' said Wyatt, nodding away heavily. Pompous liar, I thought.

'My friend Jik,' I said, 'is an artist himself. He didn't think much of the young man's effort. He called it criminal. He might just as well have said lousy.'

'Is that all?' said Mrs. Petrovitch, looking disappointed.

'Well . . . the young man was painting with paints which won't really mix. Jik's a perfectionist. He can't stand seeing paint misused.'

'What do you mean, won't mix?'

'Paints are chemicals,' I said apologetically. 'Most of them don't have any effect on each other, but you have to be careful.'

'What happens if you aren't?' demanded Ruthie Minchless.

'Um . . . nothing explodes,' I said, smiling. 'It's just that . . . well, if you mix flake white, which is lead, with cadmium yellow, which contains sulphur, like the young man was doing, you get a nice pale colour to start with but the two minerals react against each other and in time darken and alter the picture.'

'And your friend called this criminal?' Wyatt said in disbelief. 'It couldn't possibly make that much difference.'

'Er . . .' I said. 'Well, Van Gogh used a light bright new yellow made of chrome when he painted a picture of sunflowers. Cadmium yellow hadn't been developed then. But chrome yellow has shown that over a couple of hundred years it decomposes and in the end turns greenish black, and the sunflowers are already an odd colour, and I don't think anyone has found a way of stopping it.'

'But the young man wasn't painting for posterity,' said Ruthie with irritation. 'Unless he's another Van Gogh, surely it doesn't matter.'

I didn't think they'd want to hear that Jik hoped for recognition in the twenty-third century. The permanence of colours had always been an obsession with him, and he'd dragged me along once to a course on their chemistry.

The Americans got up to go.

'All very interesting,' Wyatt said with a dismissive smile. 'I guess I'll keep my money in regular stocks.'

Chapter Seven

Jik had gone from the gents, gone from the whole Arts Centre. I found him back with Sarah in their hotel room, being attended by the Hilton's attractive resident nurse. The door to the corridor stood open, ready for her to leave.

'Try not to rub them, Mr. Cassavetes,' she was saying. 'If you have any trouble, call the reception desk, and I'll come back.'

She gave me a professional half-smile in the open doorway and walked briskly away, leaving me to go in.

'How are the eyes?' I said, advancing tentatively.

'Ruddy awful.' They were bright pink, but dry. Getting better.

Sarah said with tight lips, 'This has all gone far enough. I know that this time Jik will be all right again in a day or two, but we are not taking any more risks.'

Jik said nothing and didn't look at me.

It wasn't exactly unexpected. I said, 'O.K. . . . Well, have a nice week-end, and thanks anyway.'

'Todd . . .' Jik said.

Sarah leapt in fast. 'No, Jik. It's not our responsibility. Todd can think what he likes, but his cousin's troubles are nothing to do with us. We are not getting involved any further. I've been against all this silly poking around all along, and this is where it stops.'

'Todd will go on with it,' Jik said.

'Then he's a fool.' She was angry, scornful, biting.

'Sure,' I said. 'Anyone who tries to right a wrong these days is a fool. Much better not to meddle, not to get involved, not to think it's your responsibility. I really ought to be painting away safely in my attic at Heathrow, minding my own business and letting Donald rot. Much more sensible, I agree. The trouble is that I simply can't do it. I see the hell he's in. How can I just turn my back? Not when there's a chance of getting him out. True enough, I may not manage it, but what I can't face is not having tried.'

I came to a halt.

A blank pause.

'Well,' I said, raising a smile. 'Here endeth the lesson according to the world's foremost nit. Have fun at the races. I might go too, you never know.'

I sketched a farewell and eased myself out. Neither of them said a word. I shut the door quietly and took the lift up to my own room.

A pity about Sarah, I thought. She would have Jik in cottonwool and slippers if he didn't look out; and he'd never paint those magnificent brooding pictures any more, because they sprang from a torment he would no longer be allowed. Security, to him, would be a sort of abdication; a sort of death.

I looked at my watch and decided the *Yarra River Fine Arts* set-up might still have its doors open. Worth trying.

I wondered, as I walked along Wellington Parade and up Swanston Street, whether the young turps-flinger would be there, and if he was, whether he would know me. I'd seen only glimpses of his face, as I'd mostly been standing behind him. All one could swear to was light-brown hair, acne on the chin, a round jaw-line and a full-lipped mouth. Under twenty. Perhaps not more than seventeen. Dressed in blue jeans, white tee-shirt, and tennis shoes. About five-foot-eight, a hundred and thirty pounds. Quick on his feet, and liable to panic. And no artist.

The gallery was open, brightly lit, with a horse painting on a gilt display easel in the centre of the window. Not a Munnings. A portrait picture of an Australian horse and jockey, every detail sharp-edged, emphatic, and, to my taste, overpainted. Beside it a notice, gold embossed on black, announced a special display of distinguished equine art; and beside that, less well-produced but with larger letters, stood a display card saying 'Welcome to the Melbourne Cup'.

The gallery looked typical of hundreds of others round the world; narrow frontage, with premises stretching back a good way from the street. Two or three people were wandering about inside, looking at the merchandise on the well-lit neutral grey walls.

I had gone there intending to go in. To go in was still what I intended, but I hesitated outside in the street feeling as if I were at the top of a ski jump. Stupid, I thought. Nothing venture, nothing gain, and all that. If you don't look, you won't see.

I took a ruefully deep breath and stepped over the welcoming threshold.

Greeny-grey carpet within, and an antique desk strategically placed near the door, with a youngish woman handing out small catalogues and large smiles.

'Feel free to look around,' she said. 'More pictures downstairs.'

She handed me a catalogue, a folded glazed white card with several typed sheets clipped into it. I flipped them over. One hundred and sixty-three items, numbered consecutively, with titles, artists' names, and asking price. A painting already sold, it said, would have a red spot on the frame.

I thanked her. 'Just passing by,' I said.

She nodded and smiled professionally, eyes sliding in a rapid summing up over my denim clothes and general air of not belonging to the jet set. She herself wore the latest trendy fashion with careless ease and radiated tycoon-catching sincerity. Australian, assured, too big a personality to be simply a receptionist.

'You're welcome anyway,' she said.

I walked slowly down the long room, checking the pictures against their notes. Most were by Australian artists, and I could see what Jik had meant about the hot competition. The field was just as crowded as at home, if not more so, and the standard in some respects better. As usual when faced with other people's flourishing talents I began to have doubts of my own.

At the far end of the ground-floor display there was a staircase leading downwards, adorned with a large arrow and a notice repeating 'More Pictures Downstairs'. ·

I went down. Same carpet, same lighting, but no scatter of customers looking from pictures to catalogues and back again.

Below stairs, the gallery was not one straight room but a series of small rooms off a long corridor, apparently the result of not being able to knock down all the dividing and load-bearing walls. A room to the rear of the stairs was an office, furnished with another distinguished desk, two or three comfortable chairs for prospective clients, and a civilised row of teak-faced filing cabinets. Heavily framed pictures adorned the walls, and an equally substantial man was writing in a ledger at the desk.

He raised his head, conscious of my presence outside his door.

'Can I help you?' he said.

'Just looking.'

He gave me an uninterested nod and went back to his work. He, like the whole place, had an air of permanence and respectability quite unlike the fly-by-night suburban affair in Sydney. This reputable business, I thought, could not be what I was looking for. I had got the whole thing wrong. I would have to wait until I could get Hudson Taylor to look up Donald's cheque and point me in a new direction.

Sighing, I continued down the line of rooms, thinking I might as well finish taking stock of the opposition. A few of the frames were adorned with red spots, but the prices on everything good were a mile from a bargain and a deterrent to all but the rich.

In the end room, which was larger than the others, I came across the Munnings. Three of them. All with horses; one racing scene, one hunting, one of gypsies.

They were not in the catalogue.

They hung without ballyhoo in a row of similar subjects, and to my eyes stuck out like thoroughbreds among hacks.

Prickles began up my spine. It wasn't just the workmanship, but one of the pictures itself. Horses going down to the start. A long line of jockeys, bright against a dark sky. The silks of the nearest rider, purple with a green cap.

Maisie's chatty voice reverberated in my inner ear, describing what I saw. '. . . I expect you'll think I was silly but that was one of the reasons I bought it . . . because Archie and I decided we'd like purple with a green cap for our colours, if no one already had that . . .'

Munnings had always used a good deal of purple and green in shadows and distances. All the same . . . This picture, size, subject, and colouring, was exactly like Maisie's, which had been hidden behind a radiator, and, presumably, burned.

The picture in front of me looked authentic. The right sort of patina for the time since Munnings' death, the right excellence of draughtsmanship, the right indefinable something which separated the great from the good. I put out a gentle finger to feel the surface of canvas and paint. Nothing there that shouldn't be.

An English voice from behind me said, 'Can I help you?'

'Isn't that a Munnings?' I said casually, turning round.

He was standing in the doorway, looking in, his expression full of the guarded helpfulness of one whose best piece of stock is being appraised by someone apparently too poor to buy it.

I knew him instantly. Brown receding hair combed back, grey eyes, down-drooping moustache, suntanned skin: all last on view thirteen days ago beside the sea in Sussex, England, prodding around in a smoky ruin.

Mr. Greene. With an 'e'.

It took him only a fraction longer. Puzzlement as he glanced from me to the picture and back, then the shocking realisation of where he'd seen me. He took a sharp step backwards and raised his hand to the wall outside.

I was on my way to the door, but I wasn't quick enough. A steel mesh gate slid down very fast in the doorway and clicked into some sort of bolt in the floor. Mr. Greene stood on the outside, disbelief still stamped on every feature and his mouth hanging open. I revised all my easy theories about danger being good for the soul and felt as frightened as I'd ever been in my life.

'What's the matter?' called a deeper voice from up the corridor.

Mr. Greene's tongue was stuck. The man from the office appeared at his shoulder and looked at me through the imprisoning steel.

'A thief?' he asked with irritation.

Mr. Greene shook his head. A third person arrived outside, his young face bright with curiosity, and his acne showing like measles.

'Hey,' he said in loud Australian surprise. 'He was the one at the Art Centre. The one who chased me. I swear he didn't follow me. I swear it.'

'Shut up,' said the man from the office briefly. He stared at me steadily. I stared back.

I was standing in the centre of a brightly lit room of about fifteen feet square. No windows. No way out except through the guarded door. Nowhere to hide, no weapons to hand. A long way down the ski jump and no promise of a soft landing.

'I say,' I said plaintively. 'Just what is all this about?' I walked up to the steel gate and tapped on it. 'Open this up, I want to get out.'

'What are you doing here?' the office man said. He was bigger than Greene and obviously more senior in the gallery. Heavy dark spectacle frames over unfriendly eyes, and a blue bow tie with polka dots under a double chin. Small mouth with a full lower lip. Thinning hair.

'Looking,' I said, trying to sound bewildered. 'Just looking at pictures.' An innocent at large, I thought, and a bit dim.

'He chased me in the Art Centre,' the boy repeated.

'You threw some stuff in that man's eyes,' I said indignantly. 'You might have blinded him.'

'Friend of yours, was he?' the office man said.

'No,' I said. 'I was just there, that was all. Same as I'm here. Just looking at pictures. Nothing wrong in that, is there? I go to lots of galleries, all the time.'

Mr. Greene got his voice back. 'I saw him in England,' he said to the office man. His eyes returned to the Munnings, then he put his hand on the office man's arm and pulled him up the corridor out of my sight.

'Open the door,' I said to the boy, who still gazed in.

'I don't know how,' he said. 'And I don't reckon I'd be popular, somehow.'

The two other men returned. All three gazed in. I began to feel sympathy for creatures in cages.

'Who *are* you?' said the office man.

'Nobody. I mean, I'm just here for the racing, of course, and the cricket.'

'Name?'

'Charles Neil.' Charles Neil Todd.

'What were you doing in England?'

'I live there!' I said. 'Look,' I went on, as if trying to be reasonable under great provocation. 'I saw this man here,' I nodded to Greene, 'at the home of a woman I know slightly in Sussex. She was giving me a lift home from the races, see, as I'd missed my train to Worthing and was thumbing along the road from the Members' car park. Well, she stopped and picked me up, and then said she wanted to make a detour to see her house which had lately been burnt, and when we got there, this man was there. He said his name was Greene and that he was from an insurance company, and that's all I know about him. So what's going on?'

'It is a coincidence that you should meet here again, so soon.'

'It certainly is,' I agreed fervently. 'But that's no bloody reason to lock me up.'

I read indecision on all their faces. I hoped the sweat wasn't running visibly down my own.

I shrugged exasperatedly. 'Fetch the police or something, then,' I said. 'If you think I've done anything wrong.'

The man from the office put his hand to the switch on the outside wall and carefully fiddled with it, and the steel gate slid up out of sight, a good deal more slowly than it had come down.

'Sorry,' he said perfunctorily. 'But we have to be careful, with so many valuable paintings on the premises.'

'Well, I see that,' I said, stepping forward and resisting a strong impulse to make a dash for it. 'But all the same . . .' I managed an aggrieved tone. 'Still, no harm done, I suppose.' Magnanimous, as well.

They all walked behind me along the corridor and up the stairs and through the upper gallery, doing my nerves no slightest good. All the other visitors seemed to have left. The receptionist was locking the front door.

My throat was dry beyond swallowing.

'I thought everyone had gone,' she said in surprise.

'Slight delay,' I said, with a feeble laugh.

She gave me the professional smile and reversed the locks. Opened the door. Held it, waiting for me.

Six steps.

Out in the fresh air.

God almighty, it smelled good. I half turned. All four stood in the gallery watching me go. I shrugged and nodded and trudged away into the drizzle, feeling as weak as a fieldmouse dropped by a hawk.

I caught a passing tram and travelled a good way into unknown regions of the huge city, conscious only of an urgent desire to put a lot of distance between myself and that basement prison.

They would have second thoughts. They were bound to. They would wish they had found out more about me before letting me go. They couldn't be certain it wasn't a coincidence that I'd turned up at their gallery, because far more amazing coincidences did exist, like Lincoln at the time of his assassination having a secretary called Kennedy and Kennedy having a secretary called Lincoln; but the more they thought about it the less they would believe it.

If they wanted to find me, where would they look? Not at the Hilton, I thought in amusement. At the races: I had told them I would be there. On the whole I wished I hadn't.

At the end of the tramline I got off and found myself opposite a small interesting-looking restaurant with B.Y.O. in large letters on the door. Hunger as usual rearing its healthy head, I went in and ordered a steak, and asked for a look at the wine list.

The waitress looked surprised. 'It's B.Y.O.,' she said.

'What's B.Y.O.?'

Her eyebrows went still higher. 'You a stranger? Bring Your Own. We don't sell drinks here, only food.'

'Oh.'

'If you want something to drink, there's a drive-in bottle shop a hundred yards down the road that'll still be open. I could hold the steak until you get back.'

I shook my head and settled for a teetotal dinner, grinning all through coffee at a notice on the wall saying 'We have an arrangement with our bank. They don't fry steaks and we don't cash cheques.'

When I set off back to the city centre on the tram, I passed the bottle shop, which at first sight looked so like a garage that if I hadn't known I would have thought the line of cars was queuing for petrol. I could see why Jik liked the Australian imagination: both sense and fun.

The rain had stopped. I left the tram and walked the last couple of miles through the bright streets and dark parks, asking the way. Thinking of Donald and Maisie and Greene with an 'e', and of paintings and burglaries and violent minds.

The overall plan had all along seemed fairly simple: to sell pictures in Australia and steal them back in England, together with everything else lying handy. As I had come across two instances within three weeks, I had been sure there had to be more, because it was surely impossible that I could have stumbled on the *only* two, even given the double link of racing and painting. Since I'd met the Petrovitches and the Minchlesses, it seemed I'd been wrong to think of all the robberies taking place in England. Why not in America? Why not anywhere that was worth the risk?

Why not a mobile force of thieves shuttling containerfuls of antiques from continent to continent, selling briskly to a ravenous market. As Inspector Frost had said, few antiques were ever recovered. The demand was insatiable and the supply, by definition, limited.

Suppose I were a villain, I thought, and I didn't want to waste weeks in foreign countries finding out exactly which houses were worth robbing. I could just stay quietly at home in Melbourne selling paintings to rich visitors who could afford an impulse-buy of ten thousand pounds or so. I could chat away with them about their picture collections back home, and I could shift the conversation easily to their silver and china and objets d'art.

I wouldn't want the sort of customers who had Rembrandts or Fabergés or anything well-known and unsaleable like that. Just the middling wealthy with Georgian silver and lesser Gauguins and Chippendale chairs.

When they bought my paintings, they would give me their addresses. Nice and easy. Just like that.

I would be a supermarket type of villain, with a large turnover of small goods. I would reckon that if I kept the victims reasonably well scattered, the fact that they had been to Australia within the past year or so would mean nothing to each regional police force. I would reckon that among the thousands of burglary claims they had to settle, Australia visits would bear no significance to insurance companies.

I would not, though, reckon on a crossed wire like Charles Neil Todd. If I were a villain, I thought, with a well-established business and a good reputation, I wouldn't put myself at risk by selling fakes. Forged oil paintings were almost always detectable under a microscope, even if one discounted that the majority of experienced dealers could tell them at a glance. A painter left his signature all over a painting, not just in the corner, because the way he held his brush was as individual as handwriting. Brush strokes could be matched as conclusively as grooves on bullets.

If I were a villain I'd wait in my spider's web with a real Munnings, or maybe a real Picasso drawing, or a genuine work by a recently dead good artist whose output had been voluminous, and along would come the rich little flies, carefully steered my way by talkative accomplices who stood around in the States' Capitals' art galleries for the purpose. Both Donald and Maisie had been hooked that way.

Supposing when I'd sold a picture to a man from England and robbed him, and got my picture back again, I then sold it to someone from

America. And then robbed him, and got it back, and so on round and round.

Suppose I sold a picture to Maisie in Sydney, and got it back, and started to sell it again in Melbourne ... My supposing stopped right there, because it didn't fit.

If Maisie had left her picture in full view it would have been stolen like her other things. Maybe it even had been, and was right now glowing in the Yarra River Fine Arts, but if so, why had the house been burnt, and why had Mr. Greene turned up to search the ruins?

It only made sense if Maisie's picture had been a copy, and if the thieves hadn't been able to find it. Rather than leave it aroun d, they'd burned the house. But I'd just decided that I wouldn't risk fakes. Except that ... would Maisie know an expert copy if she saw one? No, she wouldn't.

I sighed. To fool even Maisie you'd have to find an accomplished artist willing to copy instead of pressing on with his own work, and they weren't that thick on the ground. All the same, she'd bought her picture in the short-lived Sydney gallery, not in Melbourne, so maybe in other places besides Melbourne they would take a risk with fakes.

The huge bulk of the hotel rose ahead of me across the last stretch of park. The night air blew cool on my head. I had a vivid feeling of being disconnected, a stranger in a vast continent, a speck under the stars. The noise and warmth of the Hilton brought the expanding universe down to imaginable size.

Upstairs, I telephoned to Hudson Taylor at the number his secretary had given me. Nine o'clock on the dot. He sounded mellow and full of good dinner, his voice strong, courteous and vibrantly Australian.

'Donald Stuart's cousin? Is it true about little Regina being killed?'

'I'm afraid so.'

'It's a real tragedy. A real nice lass, that Regina.'

'Yes.'

'Lookee here, then, what can I do for you? Is it tickets for the races?'

'Er, no,' I said. It was just that since the receipt and provenance letter of the Munnings had been stolen along with the picture, Donald would like to get in touch with the people who had sold it to him, for insurance purposes, but he had forgotten their name. And as I was coming to Melbourne for the Cup ... .

'That's easy enough,' Hudson Taylor said pleasantly. 'I remember the place well. I went with Donald to see the picture there, and the guy in charge brought it along to the Hilton afterwards, when we arranged the finance. Now let's see ...' There was a pause for thought. 'I can't remember the name of the place just now. Or the manager. It was some months ago, do you see? But I've got him on record here in the Melbourne office, and I'm calling in there anyway in the morning, so I'll look them up. You'll be at the races tomorrow?'

'Yes,' I said.

'How about meeting for a drink, then? You can tell me about poor Donald and Regina, and I'll have the information he wants.'

I said that would be fine, and he gave me detailed instructions as to where I would find him, and when. 'There will be a huge crowd,' he said, 'But if you stand on that exact spot I shouldn't miss you.'

The spot he had described sounded public and exposed. I hoped that it would only be he who found me on it.

'I'll be there,' I said.

Chapter Eight

Jik called through on the telephone at eight next morning.

'Come down to the coffee shop and have breakfast.'

'O.K.'

I went down in the lift and along the foyer to the hotel's informal restaurant. He was sitting at a table alone, wearing dark glasses and making inroads into a mountain of scrambled egg.

'They bring you coffee,' he said, 'But you have to fetch everything else from that buffet.' He nodded towards a large well-laden table in the centre of the breezy blue and sharp green decor. 'How's things?'

'Not what they used to be.'

He made a face. 'Bastard.'

'How are the eyes?'

He whipped off the glasses with a theatrical flourish and leaned forward to give me a good look. Pink, they were, and still inflamed, but on the definite mend.

'Has Sarah relented?' I asked.

'She's feeling sick.'

'Oh?'

'God knows,' he said. 'I hope not. I don't want a kid yet. She isn't overdue or anything.'

'She's a nice girl,' I said.

He slid me a glance. 'She says she's got nothing against you personally.'

'But,' I said.

He nodded. 'The mother hen syndrome.'

'Wouldn't have cast you as a chick.'

He put down his knife and fork. 'Nor would I, by God. I told her to cheer up and get this little enterprise over as soon as possible and face the fact she hadn't married a marshmallow.'

He gave a twisted grin. 'From my performance in bed last night, that she had.'

I wondered idly about the success or otherwise of their sex life. From the testimony of one or two past girls who had let their hair down to me while waiting hours in the flat for Jik's unpredictable return, he was a moody lover, quick to arousal and easily put off. 'It only takes a dog barking, and he's gone.' Not much, I dared say, had changed.

'Anyway,' he said. 'There's this car we've got. Damned silly if you didn't come with us to the races.'

'Would Sarah . . .' I asked carefully, '. . . scowl?'

I accepted this offer and inwardly sighed. It looked as if he wouldn't take the smallest step henceforth without the nod from Sarah. When the wildest ones got married, was it always like that? Wedded bliss putting nets over the eagles.

'Where did you get to, last night?' he said.

'Aladdin's cave,' I said. 'Treasures galore and damned lucky to escape the boiling oil.'

I told him about the gallery, the Munnings, and my brief moment of captivity. I told him what I thought of the burglaries. It pleased him. His eyes gleamed with humour and the familiar excitement rose.

'How are we going to prove it?' he said.

He heard the 'we' as soon as he said it. He laughed ruefully, the fizz dying away. 'Well, how?'

'Don't know yet.'

'I'd like to help,' he said apologetically.

I thought of a dozen sarcastic replies and stifled the lot. It was I who was the one out of step, not them. The voice of the past had no right to break up the future.

'You'll do what pleases Sarah,' I said with finality, and as an order, not a prodding satire.

'Don't sound so bloody bossy.'

We finished breakfast amicably trying to build a suitable new relationship on the ruins of the old, and both knowing well what we were about.

When I met them later in the hall at setting-off time it was clear that Sarah too had made a reassessment and put her mind to work on her emotions. She greeted me with an attempted smile and an outstretched hand. I shook the hand lightly and also gave her a token kiss on the cheek. She took it as it was meant.

Truce made, terms agreed, pact signed. Jik the mediator stood around looking smug.

'Take a look at him,' he said, flapping a hand in my direction. 'The complete stockbroker. Suit, tie, leather shoes. If he isn't careful they'll have him in the Royal Academy.'

Sarah looked bewildered. 'I thought that was an honour.'

'It depends,' said Jik, sneering happily. 'Passable artists with polished social graces get elected in their thirties. Masters with average social graces, in their forties; masters with no social graces, in their fifties. Geniuses who don't give a damn about being elected are ignored as long as possible.'

'Putting Todd in the first category and yourself in the last?' Sarah said.

'Of course.'

'Stands to reason,' I said. 'You never hear about Young Masters. Masters are always Old.'

'For God's sake,' Sarah said. 'Let's go to the races.'

We went slowly, on account of a continuous stream of traffic going the same way. The car park at Flemington racecourse, when we arrived, looked like a giant picnic ground, with hundreds of full-scale lunch parties going on between the cars. Tables, chairs, cloths, china, silver, glass. Sun umbrellas optimistically raised in defiance of the rain-clouds threatening above. A lot of gaiety and booze and a giant overall statement that 'This Was The Life'.

To my mild astonishment Jik and Sarah had come prepared. They whipped out table, chairs, drinks and food from the rented car's boot and said it was easy when you knew how, you just ordered the whole works.

'I have an uncle,' Sarah said, 'who holds the title of Fastest Bar in the West. It takes him roughly ten seconds from putting the brakes on to pouring the first drink.'

She was really trying, I thought. Not just putting up with an arrangement for Jik's sake, but actually trying to make it work. If it was an effort, it didn't show. She was wearing an interesting olive green linen coat, with a broad brimmed hat of the same colour, which she held on from time to time against little gusts of wind. Overall, a new Sarah, prettier, more relaxed, less afraid.

'Champagne?' Jik offered, popping the cork. 'Steak and oyster pie?'

'How will I go back to cocoa and chips?'

'Fatter.'

We demolished the goodies, repacked the boot, and with a sense of taking part in some vast semi-religious ritual, squeezed along with the crowd through the gate to the Holy of Holies.

'It'll be much worse than this on Tuesday,' observed Sarah, who had been to these junkets several times in the past. 'Melbourne Cup day is a public holiday. The city has three million inhabitants and half of them will try to get here.' She was shouting above the crowd noises and holding grimly on to her hat against the careless buffeting all around.

'If they've got any sense they'll stay at home and watch it on the box,' I said breathlessly, receiving a hefty kidney punch from the elbow of a man fighting his way into a can of beer.

'It won't be on the television in Melbourne, only on the radio.'

'Good grief. Why ever not?'

'Because they want everyone to come. It's televised all over the rest of Australia, but not on its own doorstep.'

'Same with the golf and the cricket,' Jik said with a touch of gloom. 'And you can't even have a decent bet on those.'

We went through the bottleneck and, by virtue of the inherited badges, through a second gate and round into the calmer waters of the green oblong of Members' lawn. Much like on many a Derby Day at home, I thought. Same triumph of will over weather. Bright faces under grey skies. Warm coats over the pretty wilks, umbrellas at the ready for the occasional top hat. When I painted pictures of racegoers in the rain, which I sometimes did, most people laughed. I never minded. I reckoned it meant they understood that the inner warmth of a pleasure couldn't be externally damped: that they too might play a trumpet in a thunderstorm.

Come to think of it, I thought, why didn't I paint a racegoer playing a trumpet in a thunderstorm? It might be symbolic enough even for Jik.

My friends were deep in a cross-talking assessment of the form of the first race. Sarah, it appeared, had a betting pedigree as long as her husband's, and didn't agree with him.

'I know it was soft going at Randwick last week. But it's pretty soft here too after all this rain, and he likes it on top.'

'He was only beaten by Boyblue at Randwick, and Boyblue was out of sight in the Caulfield Cup.'

'Please your silly self,' Sarah said loftily. 'But it's still too soft for Grapevine.'

'Want to bet?' Jik asked me.

'Don't know the horses.'

'As if that mattered.'

'Right.' I consulted the racecard. 'Two dollars on Generator.'

They both looked him up, and they both said 'Why?'

'If in doubt, back number eleven. I once went nearly through the card on number eleven.'

They made clucking and pooh-poohing noises and told me I could make a gift of my two dollars to the bookies or the T.A.B.

'The what?'

'Totalisator Agency Board.'

The bookmakers, it seemed, were strictly on-course only, with no big firms as in England. All off-course betting shops were run by the T.A.B., which returned a good share of the lolly to racing. Racing was rich, rock-solid, and flourishing. Bully for Australia, Jik said.

We took our choice and paid our money, and Generator won at twenty-fives.

'Beginners' luck,' Sarah said.

Jik laughed. 'He's no beginner. He got kicked out of playschool for running a book.'

They tore up their tickets, set their minds to race two, and made expeditions to place their bets. I settled for four dollars on number one.

'Why?'

'Double my stake on half of eleven.'

'Oh God,' said Sarah. 'You're something else.'

One of the more aggressive clouds started scattering rain, and the less hardy began to make for shelter.

'Come on,' I said. 'Let's go and sit up there in the dry.'

'You two go,' Sarah said. 'I can't.'

'Why not?'

'Because those seats are only for men.'

I laughed. I thought she was joking, but it appeared it was no joke. Very unfunny, in fact. About two thirds of the best seats in the Members' stands were reserved for males.

'What about their wives and girl friends?' I said incredulously.

'They can go up on the roof.'

Sarah, being Australian, saw nothing very odd in it. To me, and surely to Jik, it was ludicrous.

He said with a carefully straight face, 'On a lot of the bigger courses the men who run Australian racing give themselves leather armchairs behind glass to watch from, and thick-carpeted restaurants and bars to eat and drink like kings in, and let their women eat in the cafeterias and sit on hard plastic chairs on the open stands among the rest of the crowd. They consider this behaviour quite normal. All anthropological groups consider their most bizarre tribal customs quite normal.'

'I thought you were in love with all things Australian.'

Jik sighed heavily. 'Nowhere's perfect.'

'I'm getting wet,' Sarah said.

We escalated to the roof which had a proportion of two women to one man and was windy and damp, with bench seating.

'Don't worry about it,' Sarah said, amused at my aghastness on behalf of womenkind. 'I'm used to it.'

'I thought this country made a big thing about equality for all.'

'For all except half the population,' Jik said.

We could see the whole race superbly from our eyrie. Sarah and Jik screamed encouragement to their fancies but Number One finished in front by two lengths, at eight to one.

'It's disgusting,' Sarah said, tearing up more tickets. 'What number do you fancy for the third?'

'I won't be with you for the third. I've got an appointment to have a drink with someone who knows Donald.'

She took it in, and the lightness went out of her manner. 'More ... investigating?'

'I have to.'

'Yes.' She swallowed and made a visible effort. 'Well ... Good luck.'

'You're a great girl.'

She looked surprised that I should think so and suspicious that I was intending sarcasm, and also partly pleased. I returned earthwards with her multiple expressions amusing my mind.

The Members' lawn was bounded on one long side by the stands and on the opposite side by the path taken by the horses on their way from the saddling boxes to the parade ring. One short side of the lawn lay alongside part of the parade ring itself: and it was at the corner of lawn where the horses' path reached the parade ring that I was to meet Hudson Taylor.

The rain had almost stopped, which was good news for my suit. I reached the appointed spot and stood there waiting, admiring the brilliant scarlet of the long bedful of flowers which lined the railing between horse-walk and lawn. Cadmium red mixtures with highlights of orange and white and maybe a streak or two of expensive vermilion ...

'Charles Todd?'

'Yes ... Mr. Taylor?'

'Hudson. Glad to know you.' He shook hands, his grip dry and firm. Late forties, medium height, comfortable build, with affable, slightly sad eyes sloping downwards at the outer corners. He was one of the minority of men in morning suits, and he wore it as comfortably as a sweater.

'Let's find somewhere dry,' he said. 'Come this way.'

He led me steadily up the bank of steps, in through an entrance door, down a wide interior corridor running the whole length of the stands, past a uniformed guard and a notice saying 'Committee Only', and into a large square comfortable room fitted out as a small-scale bar. The journey had been one long polite push through expensively dressed cohorts, but the bar was comparatively quiet and empty. A group of four, two men, two women, stood chatting with half-filled glasses held close to their chests, and two women in furs were complaining loudly of the cold.

'They love to bring out the sables,' Hudson Taylor chuckled, fetching two glasses of Scotch and gesturing to me to sit by a small table. 'Spoils their fun, the years it's hot for this meeting.'

'Is it usually hot?'

'Melbourne's weather can change twenty degrees in an hour.' He sounded proud of it. 'Now then, this business of yours.' He delved into an inner breast pocket and surfaced with a folded paper. 'Here you are, typed out for Donald. The gallery was called Yarra River Fine Arts.'

I would have been astounded if it hadn't been.

'And the man we dealt with was someone called Ivor Wexford.'

'What did he look like?' I asked.

'I don't remember very clearly. It was back in April, do you see?'

I thought briefly and pulled a small slim sketchbook out of my pocket.

'If I draw him, might you know him?'

He looked amused. 'You never know.'

I drew quickly in soft pencil a reasonable likeness of Greene, but without the moustache.

'Was it him?'

Hudson Taylor looked doubtful. I drew in the moustache. He shook his head decisively. 'No, that wasn't him.'

'How about this?'

I flipped over the page and started again. Hudson Taylor looked pensive as I did my best with the man from the basement office.

'Maybe,' he said.

I made the lower lip fuller, added heavy-framed spectacles, and a bow tie with spots.

'That's him,' said Hudson in surprise. 'I remember the bow tie, anyway. You don't see many of those these days. How did you know? You must have met him.'

'I walked round a couple of galleries yesterday afternoon.'

'That's quite a gift you have there,' he said with interest, watching me put the notebook away.

'Practice, that's all.' Years of seeing people's faces as matters of shapes and proportions and planes, and remembering which way the lines slanted. I could already have drawn Hudson's eyes from memory. It was a knack I'd had from childhood.

'Sketching is your hobby?' Hudson asked.

'And my work. I mostly paint horses.'

'Really?' He glanced at the equine portraits decorating the wall. 'Like these?'

I nodded, and we talked a little about painting for a living.

'Maybe I can give you a commission, if my horse runs well in the Cup.' He smiled, the outer edges of his eyes crinkling finely. 'If he's down the field, I'll feel more like shooting him.'

He stood up and gestured me still to follow. 'Time for the next race. Care to watch it with me?'

We emerged into daylight in the prime part of the stands, overlooking the big square enclosure which served both for parading the runners before the race and unsaddling the winners after. I was amused to see that the front rows of seats were all for men: two couples walking in front of us split like amoebas, the husbands going down left, the women up right.

'Down here,' Hudson said, pointing.

'May we only go up there if accompanied by a lady?' I asked.

He glanced at me sideways, and smiled. 'You find our ways odd? We'll go up, by all means.'

He led the way and settled comfortably among the predominantly female company, greeting several people and introducing me companionably as his friend Charles from England. Instant first names, instant acceptance, Australian style.

'Regina hated all this division of the sexes, poor lass,' he said. 'But it has interesting historical roots.' He chuckled. 'Australia was governed nearly all last century with the help of the British Army. The officers and gentlemen left their wives back in England, but such is nature, they all set up liaisons here with women of low repute. They didn't want their fellow officers to see the vulgarity of their choice, so they invented a rule that the officers' enclosures were for men only, which effectively silenced their popsies' pleas to be taken.'

I laughed 'Very neat.'

'It's easier to establish a tradition,' Hudson said, 'than to get rid of it.'

'You're establishing a great tradition for fine wines, Donald says.'

The sad-looking eyes twinkled with civilized pleasure. 'He was most enthusiastic. He travelled round all the big vineyards, of course, besides visiting us.'

The horses for the third race cantered away to the start, led by a fractious chestnut colt with too much white about his head.

'Ugly brute,' Hudson said. 'But he'll win.'

'Are you backing it?'

He smiled. 'I've a little bit on.'

The race started and the field sprinted, and Hudson's knuckles whitened so much from his grip as he gazed intently through his binoculars that I wondered just how big the little bit was. The chestnut colt was beaten into fourth place. Hudson put his race-glasses down slowly and watched the unsatisfactory finish with a blank expression.

'Oh well,' he said, his sad eyes looking even sadder. 'Always another day.' He shrugged resignedly, cheered up, shook my hand, told me to remember him to Donald, and asked if I could find my own way out.

'Thank you for your help,' I said.

He smiled. 'Any time. Any time.'

With only a couple of wrong turnings I reached ground level, listening on the way to fascinating snippets of Australian conversation.

'. . . They say he's an embarrassment as a Committee man. He only opens his mouth to change feet . . .'

'. . . a beastly stomach wog, so he couldn't come . . .'

'. . . told him to stop whingeing like a bloody Pommie, and get on with it . . .'

'. . . won twenty dollars? Good on yer, Joanie . . .'

And everywhere the diphthong vowels which gave the word 'No' about five separate sounds, defying my attempts to copy it. I'd been told on the flight over, by an Australian, that all Australians spoke with one single accent. It was about as true as saying all Americans spoke alike, or all British. English was infinitely elastic; and alive, well and living in Melbourne.

Jik and Sarah, when I rejoined them, were arguing about their fancies for the Victoria Derby, next race on the card.

'Ivory Ball is out of his class and has as much chance as a blind man in a blizzard.'

Sarah ignored this. 'He won at Moonee Valley last week and two of the tipsters pick him.'

'Those tipsters must have been drunk.'

'Hello Todd,' Sarah said, 'Pick a number, for God's sake.'

'Ten.'

'Why ten?'

'Eleven minus one.'

'Jesus,' Jik said. 'You used to have more sense.'

Sarah looked it up. 'Royal Road. Compared with Royal Road, Ivory Ball's a certainty.'

We bought our tickets and went up to the roof, and none of our bets came up. Sarah disgustedly yelled at Ivory Ball who at least managed fifth, but Royal Road fell entirely by the wayside. The winner was number twelve.

'You should have *added* eleven and one,' Sarah said. 'You make such silly mistakes.'

'What are you staring at?' Jik said.

I was looking attentively down at the crowd which had watched the race from ground level on the Members' lawn.

'Lend me your raceglasses . . .'

Jik handed them over. I raised them, took a long look, and slowly put them down.

'What is it?' Sarah said anxiously. 'What's the matter?'

'That,' I said, 'has not only torn it, but ripped the bloody works apart.'

'What has?'

'Do you see those two men . . . about twenty yards along from the parade ring railing . . . one of them in a grey morning suit?'

'What about them?' Jik said.

'The man in the morning suit is Hudson Taylor, the man I just had a drink with. He's the managing director of a wine-making firm, and he saw a lot of my cousin Donald when he was over here. And the other man is called Ivor Wexford, and he's the manager of the Yarra River Fine Arts gallery.'

'So what?' Sarah said.

'So I can just about imagine the conversation that's going on down there,' I said. 'Something like, "Excuse me, sir, but didn't I sell a picture to you recently?" "Not to me, Mr. Wexford, but to my friend Donald Stuart." "And who was that young man I saw you talking to just now?" "That was Donald Stuart's cousin, Mr. Wexford." "And what do you know about him?" "That he's a painter by trade and drew a picture of you, Mr. Wexford, and asked me for your name." '

I stopped. 'Go on,' Jik said.

I watched Wexford and Hudson Taylor stop talking, nod casually to each other, and walk their separate ways.

'Ivor Wexford now knows he made a horrible mistake in letting me out of his gallery last night.'

Sarah looked searchingly at my face. 'You really do think that's very serious.'

'Yes I really do.' I loosened a few tightened muscles and tried a smile. 'At the least, he'll be on his guard.'

'And at the most,' Jik said, 'he'll come looking for you.'

'Er . . .' I said thoughtfully. 'What do either of you feel about a spot of instant travel?'

'Where to?'

'Alice Springs?' I said.

Chapter Nine

Jik complained all the way to the airport on various counts. One, that he would be missing the cricket. Two, that I hadn't let him go back to the Hilton for his paints. Three, that his Derby clothes would be too hot in Alice. Four, that he wasn't missing the Melbourne Cup for any little ponce with a bow tie.

None of the colourful gripes touched on the fact that he was paying for all our fares with his credit card, as I had left my travellers cheques in the hotel.

It had been Sarah's idea not to go back there.

'If we're going to vanish, let's get on with it,' she said. 'It's running back into fires for handbags that gets people burnt.'

'You don't have to come,' I said tentatively.

'We've been through all that. What do you think the rest of my life would be like if I stopped Jik helping you, and you came to grief?'

'You'd never forgive me.'

She smiled ruefully. 'You're dead right.'

As far as I could tell we had left the racecourse unobserved, and certainly no one car had followed us to the airport. Neither Greene with an 'e' nor the boy non-artist appeared underfoot to trip us up, and we travelled uneventfully on a half-full aircraft on the first leg to Adelaide, and an even emptier one from there to Alice Springs.

The country beneath us from Adelaide northwards turned gradually from fresh green to grey-green, and finally to a fierce brick red.

'Gaba,' said Jik, pointing downwards.

'What?'

'G.A.B.A.,' he said. 'Gaba. Stands for Great Australian Bugger All.'

I laughed. The land did indeed look baked, deserted, and older than time, but there were track-like roads here and there, and incredibly isolated homesteads. I watched in fascination until it grew dark, the purple shadows rushing in like a tide as we swept north into the central wastelands.

The night air at Alice was hot, as if someone had forgotten to switch off the oven. The luck which had presented us with an available flight as soon as we reached Melbourne airport seemed still to be functioning: a taciturn taxi driver took us sraight to a new-looking motel which proved to have room for us.

'The season is over,' he grunted, when we congratulated and thanked him. 'It will soon be too hot for tourists.'

Our rooms were air-conditioned, however. Jik and Sarah's was down on the ground floor, their door opening directly on to a shady covered walk which bordered a small garden with a pool. Mine, in an adjacent wing across the car park, was two tall floors up, reached by an outside tree-shaded staircase and a long open gallery. The whole place looked greenly peaceful in the scattered spotlights which shone unobtrusively from palms and gums.

The motel restaurant had closed for the night at eight o'clock, so we walked along the main street to another. The road surface itself was tarmacadamed, but some of the side roads were not, nor were the footpaths uniformly paved. Often enough we were walking on bare fine grit, and we could see from the dust haze in the headlights of passing cars that the grit was bright red.

'Bull dust,' Sarah said. 'I've never seen it before. My aunt swore it got inside her locked trunk once when she and my uncle drove out to Ayers Rock.'

'What's Ayers Rock?' I said.

'Ignorant pommie,' Sarah said. 'It's a chunk of sandstone two miles long and a third of a mile high left behind by some careless glacier in the ice-age.'

'Miles out in the desert,' Jik added. 'A place of ancient magic regularly desecrated by the plastic society.'

'Have you been there?' I asked dryly.

He grinned. 'Nope.'

'What difference does that make?' Sarah asked.

'He means,' Jik said, 'our pompous friend here means that one shouldn't make judgments from afar.'

'You haven't actually got to be swallowed by a shark before you believe it's got sharp teeth,' Sarah said. 'You can believe what other people see.'

'It depends from where they're looking.'

'Facts are not judgments, and judgments are not facts,' Jik said. 'A bit of Todd's Law from way back.'

Sarah gave me a glance. 'Have you got iced water in that head?'

'Emotion is a rotten base for politics. He used to say that too,' Jik said. 'Envy is the root of all evil. What have I left out?'

'The most damaging lies are told by those who believe they're true.'

'There you are,' Jik said. 'Such a pity you can't paint.'

'Thanks very much.'

We reached the restaurant and ate a meal of such excellence that one wondered at the organisation it took to bring every item of food and clothing and everyday life to an expanding town of thirteen and a half thousand inhabitants surrounded by hundreds of miles of desert in every direction.

'It was started here, a hundred years ago, as a relay station for sending cables across Australia,' Sarah said. 'And now they're bouncing messages off the stars.'

Jik said, 'Bet the messages aren't worth the technology. Think of "See you Friday, Ethel", chattering round the eternal spheres.'

With instructions from the restaurant we walked back a different way and sought out the Yarra River Fine Arts gallery, Alice Springs variety.

It was located in a paved shopping arcade closed to traffic, one of several small but prosperous-looking boutiques. There were no lights on in the gallery, nor in the other shops. From what we could see in the single dim street light the merchandise in the gallery window consisted of two bright orange landscapes of desert scenes.

'Crude,' said Jik, whose own colours were not noted for pastel subtlety.

'The whole place,' he said, 'will be full of local copies of Albert Namatjira. Tourists buy them by the ton.'

We strolled back to the motel more companionably than at any time since my arrival. Maybe the desert distances all around us invoked their own peace. At any rate when I kissed Sarah's cheek to say goodnight it was no longer as a sort of pact, as in the morning, but with affection.

At breakfast she said, 'You'll never guess. The main street here is Todd Street. So is the river. Todd River.'

'Such is fame,' I said modestly.

'And there are eleven art galleries.'

'She's been reading the Alice Springs Tourist Promotion Association Inc.'s handout,' Jik explained.

'There's also a Chinese Takeaway.'

Jik made a face. 'Just imagine all this lot dumped down in the middle of the Sahara.'

The daytime heat, in fact, was fierce. The radio was cheerfully forecasting a noon temperature of thirty-nine, which was a hundred and two in the old fahrenheit shade. The single step from a cool room to the sun-roasting balcony was a sensuous pleasure, but the walk to the Yarra River gallery, though less than half a mile, was surprisingly exhausting.

'I suppose one would get used to it, if one lived here,' Jik said. 'Thank God Sarah's got her hat.'

We dodged in and out of the shadows of overhanging trees and the local inhabitants marched around bare-headed as if the branding-iron in the sky was pointing another way. The Yarra River gallery was quiet and air conditioned and provided chairs near the entrance for flaked-out visitors.

As Jik has prophesied, all visible space was knee deep in the hard clear watercolour paintings typical of the disciples of Namatjira. They were fine if you liked that sort of thing, which on the whole I didn't. I prefrred the occasional fuzzy outline, indistinct edge, shadows encroaching, suggestion, impression, and ambiguity. Namatjira, given his due as the first and greatest of the Aboriginal artists, had had a vision as sharp as a diamond. I vaguely remembered reading somewhere that he'd produced more than two thousand paintings himself, and certainly his influence on the town where he'd been born had been extraordinary. Eleven art galleries. Mecca for artists. Tourists buying pictures by the ton. He had died, a plaque on the wall said, in Alice Springs hospital on August 8, 1959.

We had been wandering around for a good five minutes before anyone came. Then the plastic strip curtain over a recessed doorway parted, and the gallery keeper came gently through.

'See anything you fancy?' he said.

His voice managed to convey an utter boredom with tourists and a feeling that we should pay up quickly and go away. He was small, languid, long-haired and pale, and had large dark eyes with drooping tired-looking lids. About the same age as Jik and myself, though a lot less robust.

'Do you have any other pictures?' I asked.

He glanced at our clothes. Jik and I wore the trousers and shirts in which we'd gone to the races: no ties and no jackets, but more promising to picture-sellers than denims. Without discernible enthusiasm he held back half of the strip curtain, inviting us to go through.

'In here,' he said.

The inner room was bright from skylights, and its walls were almost entirely covered with dozens of pictures which hung closely together. Our eyes opened wide. At first sight we were surrounded by an incredible feast of Dutch interiors, French impressionists and Gainsborough portraits. At second blink one could see that although they were original oil paintings, they were basically second rate. The sort sold as 'school of' because the artists hadn't bothered to sign them.

'All European, in this room,' the gallery keeper said. He still sounded bored. He wasn't Australian, I thought. Nor British. Maybe American. Difficult to tell.

'Do you have any pictures of horses?' I asked.

He gave me a long steady peaceful gaze. 'Yes we do, but this month we are displaying works by native Australians and lesser Europeans.' His voice had the faintest of lisps. 'If you wish to see horse paintings, they are in racks through there.' He pointed to a second plastic strip curtain directly opposite the first. 'Are you looking for anything in particular?'

I murmured the names of some of the Australians whose work I had seen in Melbourne. There was a slight brightening of the lack-lustre eyes.

'Yes, we do have a few by those artists.'

He led us through the second curtain into the third, and from our point of view, most interesting room. Half of it, as promised, was occupied by well-filled double tiers of racks. The other half was the office and packing and framing department. Directly ahead a glass door led out to a dusty parched-looking garden, but most of the lighting in here too came from the roof.

Beside the glass door stood an easel bearing a small canvas with its back towards us. Various unmistakable signs showed work currently in progress and recently interrupted.

'Your own effort?' asked Jik inquisitively, walking over for a look.

The pale gallery keeper made a fluttering movement with his hand as if he would have stopped Jik if he could, and something in Jik's expression attracted me to his side like a magnet.

A chestnut horse, three-quarters view, its elegant head raised as if listening. In the background, the noble lines of a mansion. The rest, a harmonious composition of trees and meadow. The painting, as far as I could judge, was more or less finished.

'That's great,' I said with enthusiasm. 'Is that for sale? I'd like to buy that.'

After the briefest hesitation he said, 'Sorry. That's commissioned.'

'What a pity! Couldn't you sell me that one, and paint another?'

He gave me a small regretful smile. 'I'm afraid not.'

'Do tell me your name,' I said earnestly.

He was unwillingly flattered. 'Harley Renbo.'

'Is there anything else of yours here?'

He gestured towards the racks. 'One or two. The horse paintings are all in the bottom row, against the wall.'

We all three of us pulled out the paintings one by one, making amateur-type comments.

'That's nice,' said Sarah, holding a small picture of a fat grey pony with two old-fashioned country boys. 'Do you like that?' She showed it to Jik and me.

We looked at it.

'Very nice,' I said kindly.

Jik turned away as if uninterested. Harley Renbo stood motionless.

'Oh well,' Sarah said, shrugging. 'I just thought it looked nice.' She put it back in the rack and pulled out the next. 'How about this mare and foal? I think it's pretty.'

Jik could hardly bear it. 'Sentimental tosh,' he said.

Sarah looked downcast. 'It may not be Art, but I like it.'

We found one with a flourishing signature; Harley Renbo. Large canvas, varnished, unframed.

'Ah,' I said appreciatively. 'Yours.'

Harley Renbo inclined his head. Jik, Sarah and I gazed at his acknowledged work.

Derivative Stubbs-type. Elongated horses set in a Capability Brown landscape. Composition fair, anatomy poor, execution good, originality nil.

'Great,' I said. 'Where did you paint it?'

'Oh . . . here.'

'From memory?' Sarah said admiringly. 'How clever.'

Harley Renbo, at our urging, brought out two more examples of his work. Neither was better than the first, but one was a great deal smaller.

'How much is this?' I asked.

Jik glanced at me sharply, but kept quiet.

Harley Renbo mentioned a sum which had me shaking my head at once.

'Awfully sorry,' I said. 'I like your work, but . . .'

The haggling continued politely for quite a long time, but we came to the usual conclusion, higher than the buyer wanted, lower than the painted hoped. Jik resignedly lent his credit card and we bore our trophy away.

'Jesus Christ,' Jik exploded when we were safely out of earshot. 'You could paint better than that when you were in your cradle. Why the hell did you want to buy that rubbish?'

'Because,' I said contentedly, 'Harley Renbo is the copier.'

'But this,' Jik pointed to the parcel under my arm, 'Is his own abysmal original work.'

'Like fingerprints?' Sarah said. 'You can check other things he paints against this?'

'Got brains, my wife,' Jik said. 'But that picture he wouldn't sell was nothing like any Munnings I've ever seen.'

'You never look at horse paintings if you can help it.'

'I've seen more of your pathetic daubs than I care to.'

'How about Raoul Millais?' I said.

'Jesus.'

We walked along the scorching street almost without feeling it.

'I don't know about you two,' Sarah said. 'But I'm going to buy a bikini and spend the rest of the day in the pool.'

We all bought swimming things, changed into them, splashed around for ages, and laid ourselves out on towels to dry. It was peaceful and quiet in the shady little garden. We were the only people there.

'That picture of a pony and two boys, that you thought was nice,' I said to Sarah.

'Well, it was,' she repeated defensively. 'I liked it.'

'It was a Munnings.'

She sat up abruptly on her towel.

'Why ever didn't you say so?'

'I was waiting for our friend Renbo to tell us, but he didn't.'

'A real one?' Sarah asked. 'Or a copy?'

'Real,' Jik said, with his eyes shut against the sun dappling through palm leaves.

I nodded lazily. 'I thought so, too,' I said. 'An old painting. Munnings had that grey pony for years when he was young, and painted it dozens of times. It's the same one you saw in Sydney in "The Coming Storm".'

'You two do know a lot,' Sarah said, sighing and lying down again.

'Engineers know all about nuts and bolts,' Jik said. 'Do we get lunch in this place?'

I looked at my watch. Nearly two o'clock. 'I'll go and ask,' I said.

I put shirt and trousers on over my sun-dried trunks and ambled from the outdoor heat into the refrigerated air of the lobby. No lunch, said the reception desk. We could buy lunch nearby at a takeaway and eat in the garden. Drink? Same thing. Buy your own at a bottle shop. There was an ice-making machine and plastic glasses just outside the door to the pool.

'Thanks,' I said.

'You're welcome.'

I looked at the ice-making machine on the way out. Beside it swung a neat notice: 'We don't swim in your toilet. Please don't pee in our pool.' I laughed across to Jik and Sarah and told them the food situation.

'I'll go and get it,' I said. 'What do you want?'

Anything, they said.

'And drink?'

'Cinzano,' Sarah said, and Jik nodded. 'Dry white.'

'O.K.'

I picked up my room key from the grass and set off to collect some cash for shopping. Walked along to the tree-shaded outside staircase, went up two storeys, and turned on to the blazing hot balcony.

There was a man walking along it towards me, about my own height, build and age; and I heard someone else coming up the stairs at my back.

Thought nothing of it. Motel guests like me. What else?

I was totally unprepared both for the attack itself, and for its ferocity.

Chapter Ten

They simply walked up to me, one from in front, one from behind.

They reached me together. They sprang into action like cats. They snatched the dangling room key out of my hand.

The struggle, if you could call it that, lasted less than five seconds. Between them, with Jik's type of strength, they simply picked me up by my legs and armpits and threw me over the balcony.

It probably takes a very short time to fall two storeys. I found it long enough for thinking that my body, which was still whole, was going to be smashed. That disaster, not yet reached, was inevitable. Very odd, and very nasty.

What I actually hit first was one of the young trees growing round the staircase. Its boughs bent and broke and I crashed on through them to the hard driveway beneath.

The monstrous impact was like being wiped out. Like fusing electrical circuits. A flash into chaos. I lay in a semi-conscious daze, not knowing if I were alive or dead.

I felt warm. Simply a feeling, not a thought.

I wasn't aware of anything else at all. I couldn't move any muscle. Couldn't remember I had muscles to move. I felt like pulp.

It was ten minutes, Jik told me later, before he came looking for me: and he came only because he wanted to ask me to buy a lemon to go with the Cinzano, if I had not gone already.

'Jesus Christ Almighty,' Jik's voice, low and horrified, near my ear. I heard him clearly. The words made sense.

I'm alive, I thought. I think, therefore I exist.

Eventually, I opened my eyes. The light was brilliant. Blinding. There was no one where Jik's voice had been. Perhaps I'd imagined it. No I hadn't. The world began coming back fast, very sharp and clear.

I knew also that I hadn't imagined the fall. I knew, with increasing insistence, that I hadn't broken my neck and hadn't broken my back. Sensation, which had been crushed out, came flooding back with vigour from every insulted tissue. It wasn't so much a matter of which bits of me hurt, as of finding out which didn't. I remembered hitting the tree. Remembered the ripping of its branches. I felt both torn to shreds and pulverised. Frightfully jolly.

After a while I heard Jik's voice returning. 'He's alive,' he said, 'and that's about all.'

'It's impossible for anyone to fall off our balcony. It's more than waist high.' The voice of the reception desk, sharp with anger and anxiety. A bad business for motels, people falling off their balconies.

'Don't . . . panic,' I said. It sounded a bit coaky.

'Todd!' Sarah appeared, kneeling on the ground and looking pale.

'If you give me time . . .' I said. '. . . I'll fetch . . . the Cinzano.' How much time? A million years should be enough.

'You sod,' Jik said, standing at my feet and staring down. 'You gave us a shocking fright.' He was holding a broken-off branch of tree.

'Sorry.'

'Get up, then.'

'Yeah . . . in a minute.'

'Shall I cancel the ambulance?' said the reception desk hopefully.

'No,' I said. 'I think I'm bleeding.'

Alice Springs hospital, even on a Sunday, was as efficient as one would expect from a Flying Doctor base. They investigated and X-rayed and stitched, and presented me with a list.

One broken shoulder blade. (Left).
Two broken ribs. (Left side. No lung puncture).
Large contusion, left side of head. (No skull fracture).
Four jagged tears in skin of trunk, thigh, and left leg. (Stitched).
Several other small cuts.

Grazes and contusions on practically all of left side of body.

'Thanks,' I said, sighing.

'Thank the tree. You'd've been in a right mess if you'd missed it.'

They suggested I stop there for the rest of the day and also all night. Better, they said, a little too meaningfully.

'O.K.' I said resignedly. 'Are my friends still here?'

They were. In the waiting room. Arguing over my near-dead body about the favourite for the Melbourne Cup.

'Newshound *stays* . . .'

'Stays in the same place . . .'

'Jesus,' Jik said, as I shuffled stiffly in. 'He's on his feet.'

'Yeah.' I perched gingerly on the arm of a chair, feeling a bit like a mummy, wrapped in bandages from neck to waist with my left arm totally immersed, as it were, and anchored firmly inside.

'Don't damn well laugh,' I said.

'No one but a raving lunatic would fall off that balcony,' Jik said.

'Mm,' I agreed. 'I was pushed.'

Their mouths opened like landed fish. I told them exactly what had happened.

'Who were they?' Jik said.

'I don't know. Never seen them before. They didn't introduce themselves.'

Sarah said, definitely, 'You must tell the police.'

'Yes,' I said. 'But . . . I don't know your procedures here, or what the police are like. I wondered . . . if you would explain to the hospital, and start things rolling in an orderly and unsensational manner.'

'Sure,' she said, 'if anything about being pushed off a balcony could be considered orderly and unsensational.'

'They took my room key first,' I said. 'Would you see if they've pinched my wallet?'

They stared at me in awakening unwelcome awareness.

I nodded. 'Or that picture,' I said.

Two policemen came, listened, took notes, and departed. Very noncommittal. Nothing like that had happened in The Alice before. The locals wouldn't have done it. The town had a constant stream of visitors so, by the law of averages, some would be muggers. I gathered that there would have been much more fuss if I'd been dead. Their downbeat attitude suited me fine.

By the time Jik and Sarah came back I'd been given a bed, climbed into it, and felt absolutely rotten. Shivering. Cold deep inside. Gripped by the system's aggrieved reaction to injury, or in other words, shock.

'They did take the painting,' Jik said. 'And your wallet as well.'

'And the gallery's shut,' Sarah said. 'The girl in the boutique opposite said she saw Harley close early today, but she didn't see him actually leave. He goes out the back way, because he parks his car there.'

'The police've been to the motel,' Jik said. 'We told them about the picture being missing, but I don't think they'll do much more about it unless you tell them the whole story.'

'I'll think about it,' I said.

'So what do we do now?' Sarah asked.

'Well . . . there's no point in staying here any more. Tomorrow we'll go back to Melbourne.'

'Thank God,' she said, smiling widely. 'I thought you were going to want us to miss the Cup.'

In spite of a battery of pills and various ministering angels I spent a viciously uncomfortable and wideawake night. Unable to lie flat. Feverishly hot on the pendulum from shock. Throbbing in fifteen places. Every little movement screechingly sticky, like an engine without oil. No wonder the hospital had told me it would be better to stay.

I counted my blessings until daybreak. It could have been so very much worse.

What was most alarming was not the murderous nature of the attackers, but the speed with which they'd found us. I'd known ever since I'd seen Regina's head that the directing mind was ruthlessly violent. The acts of the team always reflected the nature of the boss. A less savage attitude would have left Regina gagged and bound, not brutally dead.

I had to conclude that it was chiefly this pervading callousness which had led to my being thrown over the balcony. As a positive means of murder, it was too chancy. It was quite possible to survive a fall from such a height, even without a cushioning tree. The two men had not as far as I could remember bothered to see whether I was alive or dead, and they had not, while I lay half-unconscious and immobile, come along to finish the job.

So it had either been simply a shattering way of getting rid of me while they robbed my room, or they'd had the deliberate intention of injuring me so badly that I would have to stop poking my nose into their affairs.

Or both.

And how had they found us?

I puzzled over it for some time but could arrive at no definite answer. It seemed most likely that Wexford or Greene had telephoned from Melbourne and told Harley Renbo to be on his guard in case I turned up. Even the panic which would have followed the realisation that I'd seen the Munnings and the fresh Millais copy, and actually carried away a specimen of Renbo's work, could not have transported two toughs from Melbourne to Alice Springs in the time available.

There had only been about four hours between purchase and attack, and some of that would have had to be spent on finding out which motel we were in, and which rooms, and waiting for me to go upstairs from the pool.

Perhaps we had after all been followed all the way from Flemington racecourse, or traced from the aeroplane passenger lists. But if that were the case, surely Renbo would have been warned we were on the way, and would never have let us see what we had.

I gave it up. I didn't even know if I would recognise my attackers again if I saw them. Certainly not the one who had been behind me, because I hadn't had a single straight look at him.

They could, though, reasonably believe they had done a good job of putting me out of action: and indeed, if I had any sense, they had.

If they wanted time, what for?

To tighten up their security, and cover their tracks, so that any investigation I might persuade the police to make into a paintings-robbery link would come up against the most respectable of brick walls.

Even if they knew I'd survived, they would not expect any action from me in the immediate future: therefore the immediate future was the best time to act.

Right.

Easy enough to convince my brain. From the neck down, a different story.

Jik and Sarah didn't turn up until eleven, and I was still in bed. Sitting up, but not exactly perky.

'God,' Sarah said, 'You look much worse than yesterday.'

'So kind.'

'You're never going to make it to Melbourne.' She sounded despondent. 'So goodbye Cup.'

'Nothing to stop you going,' I said.

She stood beside the bed. 'Do you expect us just to leave you here . . . like this . . . and go and enjoy ourselves?'

'Why not?'

'Don't be so bloody stupid.'

Jik sprawled in a visitor's chair. 'It isn't our responsibility if he gets himself thrown from heights,' he said.

Sarah whirled on him. 'How *can* you say such a thing?'

'We don't want to be involved,' Jik said.

I grinned. Sarah heard the sardonic echo of what she'd said so passionately herself only three days ago. She flung out her arms in exasperated realisation.

'You absolutely bloody beast,' she said.

Jik smiled like a cream-fed cat. 'We went round to the gallery,' he said. 'It's still shut. We also found our way round into the back garden, and looked in through the glass door, and you can guess what we saw.'

'Nothing.'

'Dead right. No easel with imitation Millais. Everything dodgy carefully hidden out of sight. Everything else, respectable and normal.'

I shifted a bit to relieve one lot of aches, and set up protests from another. 'Even if you'd got in, I doubt if you'd've found anything dodgy. I'll bet everything the least bit incriminating disappeared yesterday afternoon.'

Jik nodded. 'Sure to.'

Sarah said, 'We asked the girl in the reception desk at the motel if anyone had been asking for us.'

'And they had?'

She nodded. 'A man telephoned. She thought it was soon after ten o'clock. He asked if a Mr. Charles Todd was staying there with two friends, and when she said yes, he asked for your room number. He said he had something to deliver to you.'

'Christ.' Some delivery. Express. Downwards.

'She told him the room number but said if he left the package at the desk, she would see you got it.'

'He must have laughed.'

'He wouldn't have that much sense of humour,' Jik said.

'Soon after ten?' I said, considering.

'While we were out,' Sarah said, nodding. 'It must have been fairly soon after we'd left the gallery . . . and while we were buying the swimming things.'

'Why didn't the girl tell us someone had been enquiring for us?'

'She went off for a coffee break, and didn't see us when we came back. And after that, she forgot. She hadn't anyway thought it of any importance.'

'There aren't all that many motels in Alice,' Jik said. 'It wouldn't have taken long to find us, once they knew we were in the town. I suppose the Melbourne lot telephoned Renbo, and that set the bomb ticking.'

'They must have been apoplectic when they heard you'd bought that picture.'

'I wish I'd hidden it,' I said. The words reminded me briefly of Maisie, who had hidden her picture, and had her house burnt.

Sarah sighed. 'Well . . . what are we going to do?'

'Last chance to go home,' I said.

'Are you going?' she demanded.

I listened briefly to the fierce plea from my battered shell, and I thought too of Donald in his cold house. I didn't actually answer her at all.

She listened to my silence. 'Quite,' she said. 'So what do we do next?'

'Well . . .' I said. 'First of all, tell the girl in the reception desk at the motel that I'm in a pretty poor state and likely to be in hospital for at least a week.'

'No exaggeration,' Jik murmured.

'Tell her it's O.K. to pass on that news, if anyone enquires. Tell her you're leaving for Melbourne, pay all our bills, confirm your bookings on the afternoon flight, and cancel mine, and make a normal exit to the airport bus.'

'But what about you?' Sarah said. 'When will you be fit to go?'

'With you,' I said. 'If between you you can think of some unobtrusive way of getting a bandaged mummy on to an aeroplane without anyone noticing.'

'Jesus,' Jik said. He looked delighted. 'I'll do that.'

'Telephone the airport and book a seat for me under a different name.'

'Right.'

'Buy me a shirt and some trousers. Mine are in the dustbin.'

'It shall be done.'

'And reckon all the time that you may be watched.'

'Put on sad faces, do you mean?' Sarah said.

I grinned. 'I'd be honoured.'

'And after we get to Melbourne, what then?' Jik said.

I chewed my lip. 'I think we'll have to go back to the Hilton. All our clothes are there, not to mention my passport and money. We don't know if Wexford and Greene ever knew we were staying there, so it may well be a hundred per cent safe. And anyway, where else in Melbourne are we likely to get beds on the night before the Melbourne Cup?'

'If you get thrown out of the Hilton's windows, you won't be alive to tell the tale,' he said cheerfully.

'They don't open far enough,' I said. 'It's impossible.'

'How reassuring.'

'And tomorrow,' Sarah said. 'What about tomorrow?'

Hesitantly, with a pause or two, I outlined what I had in mind for Cup day. When I had finished, they were both silent.

'So now,' I said. 'Do you want to go home?'

Sarah stood up. 'We'll talk it over,' she said soberly. 'We'll come back and let you know.'

Jik stood also, but I knew from the jut of his beard which way he'd vote. It had been he who'd chosen the bad-weather routes we'd taken into the Atlantic and the North Sea. At heart he was more reckless than I.

They came back at two o'clock lugging a large fruit-shop carrier with a bottle of scotch and a pineapple sticking out of the top.

'Provisions for hospitalised friend,' said Jik, whisking them out and putting them on the end of the bed. 'How do you feel?'

'With every nerve ending.'

'You don't say. Well, Sarah says we go ahead.'

I looked searchingly at her face. Her dark eyes stared steadily back, giving assent without joy. There was no antagonism, but no excitement. She was committed, but from determination, not conviction.

'O.K.,' I said.

'Item,' said Jik, busy with the carrier, 'One pair of medium grey trousers. One light blue cotton shirt.'

'Great.'

'You won't be wearing those, though, until you get to Melbourne. For leaving Alice Springs, we bought something else.'

I saw the amusement in both their faces. I said with misgiving, 'What else?'

With rising glee they laid out what they had brought for my unobtrusive exit from Alice Springs.

Which was how I came to stroll around the little airport, in the time-gap between signing in and boarding, with the full attention of everyone in the place. Wearing faded jeans cut-off and busily frayed at mid-calf. No socks. Flip-flop rope-soled sandals. A brilliant orange, red and magenta poncho-type garment which hung loosely over both arms like a cape from shoulders to crutch. A sloppy white T-shirt underneath. A large pair of sunglasses. Artificial suntan on every bit of skin. And to top it all, a large straw sunhat with a two inch raffia fringe round the brim, the sort of hat in favour out in the bush for keeping flies away.

Flies were the torment of Australia. The brushing-away-of-flies movement of the right hand was known as The Great Australian Salute.

On this hat there was a tourist-type hat-band, bright and distinctly legible. It said 'I Climbed Ayers Rock'.

Accompanying all this jazz I carried the Trans-Australian airline bag Sarah had bought on the way up. Inside it, the garments of sanity and discretion.

'No one,' Jik had said with satisfaction, laying out my wardrobe, 'will guess you're a walking stretcher case, if you're wearing these.'

'More like a nut case.'

'Not far out,' Sarah said dryly.

They were both at the airport, sitting down and looking glum, when I arrived. They gave me a flickering glance and gazed thereafter at the floor, both of them, they told me later, fighting off terrible fits of giggles at seeing all that finery on the march.

I walked composedly down to the postcard stand and waited there on my feet, for truth to tell it was more comfortable than sitting. Most of the postcards seemed to be endless views of the huge crouching orange monolith out in the desert: Ayers Rock at dawn, at sunset, and every five minutes in between.

Alternatively with inspecting the merchandise I took stock of the room. About fifty prospective passengers, highly assorted. Some airline ground-staff, calm and unhurried. A couple of aborigines with shadowed eyes and patient black faces, waiting for the airport bus back to dreamtime. Air-conditioning doing fine, but everyone inside still moving with the slow walk of life out in the sun.

No one remotely threatening.

The flight was called. The assorted passengers, including Jik and Sarah, stood up, picked up their hand luggage and straggled out to the tarmac.

It was then, and then only, that I saw him.

The man who had come towards me on the balcony to throw me over.

I was almost sure at once, and then certain. He had been sitting among the waiting passengers, reading a newspaper which he was now folding up. He stood still, watching Jik and Sarah present their boarding passes at the door and go through to the tarmac. His eyes followed them right across to the aircraft. When they'd filed up the steps and vanished, he peeled off and made a bee-line in my direction.

My heart lurched painfully. I absolutely could not run.

He looked just the same. Exactly the same. Young, strong, purposeful, as well-co-ordinated as a cat. Coming towards me.

As Jik would have said, *Jesus.*

He didn't even give me a glance. Three yards before he reached me he came to a stop beside a wall telephone, and fished in his pocket for coins.

My feet didn't want to move. I was still sure he would see me, look at me carefully, recognise me . . . and do something I would regret. I could feel the sweat prickling under the bandages.

'Last call for flight to Adelaide and Melbourne.'

I would have to, I thought. Have to walk past him to get to the door.

I unstuck my feet. Walked. Waiting with every awful step to hear his voice shouting after me. Or even worse, his heavy hand.

I got to the door, presented the boarding pass, made it out on to the tarmac.

Couldn't resist glancing back. I could see him through the glass, earnestly telephoning, and not even looking my way.

The walk to the aircraft was all the same quite far enough. God help us all, I thought, if the slightest fright is going to leave me so weak.

Chapter Eleven

I had a window seat near the rear of the aircraft, and spent the first part of the journey in the same sort of fascination as on the way up, watching the empty red miles of the ancient land roll away underneath. A desert with water underneath it in most places; with huge lakes and many rock pools. A desert which could carry dormant seeds for years in its burning dust, and bloom like a garden when it rained. A place of pulverising heat, harsh and unforgiving, and in scattered places, beautiful.

GABA, I thought. I found it awesome, but it didn't move me in terms of paint.

After a while I took off the exaggerated hat, laid it on the empty seat beside me, and tried to find a comfortable way to sit, my main frustration being that if I leaned back in the ordinary way my broken shoulder blade didn't care for it. You wouldn't think, I thought, that one *could* break a shoulder blade. Mine, it appeared, had suffered from the full thud of my five-eleven frame hitting terra extremely firma.

Oh well . . . I shut my eyes for a bit and wished I didn't still feel so shaky.

My exit from hospital had been the gift of one of the doctors, who had said he couldn't stop me if I chose to go, but another day's rest would be better.

'I'd miss the Cup,' I said, protesting.

'You're crazy.'

'Yeah . . . Would it be possible for you to arrange that the hospital said I was 'satisfactory', and 'progressing' if anyone telephones to ask, and not on any account to say that I'd left?'

'Whatever for?'

'I'd just like those muggers who put me here to think I'm still flat out. For several days, if you don't mind. Until I'm long gone.'

'But they won't try again.'

'You never know.'

He shrugged. 'You mean you're nervous?'

'You could say so.'

'All right. For a couple of days, anyway. I don't see any harm in it, if it will set your mind at rest.'

'It would indeed,' I said gratefully.

'Whatever are these?' He gestured to Jik's shopping, still lying on the bed.

'My friend's idea of suitable travelling gear.'

'You're having me on?'

'He's an artist,' I said, as if that explained any excesses.

He returned an hour later with a paper for me to sign before I left, Jik's credit card having again come up trumps, and at the sight of me, nearly choked. I had struggled slowly into the clothes and was trying on the hat.

'Are you going to the airport dressed like that?' he said incredulously.

'I sure am.'

'How?'

'Taxi, I suppose.'

'You'd better let me drive you,' he said, sighing. 'Then if you feel too rotten I can bring you back.'

He drove carefully, his lips twitching. 'Anyone who has the courage to go around like that shouldn't worry about a couple of thugs.' He dropped me solicitously at the airport door, and departed laughing.

Sarah's voice interrupted the memory.

'Todd?'

I opened my eyes. She had walked towards the back of the aeroplane and was standing in the aisle beside my seat.

'Are you all right?'

'Mm.'

She gave me a worried look and went on into the toilet compartment. By the time she came out, I'd assembled a few more wits, and stopped her with the flap of the hand. 'Sarah ... You were followed to the airport. I think you'll very likely be followed from Melbourne. Tell Jik ... tell Jik to take a taxi, spot the tail, lose him, and take a taxi back to the airport, to collect the hired car. O.K.?'

'Is this ... this tail ... on the aeroplane?' She looked alarmed at the thought.

'No. He telephoned ... from Alice.'

'All right.'

She went away up front to her seat. The aeroplane landed at Adelaide, people got off, people got on, and we took off again for the hour's flight to Melbourne. Halfway there, Jik himself came back to make use of the facilities.

He too paused briefly beside me on the way back.

'Here are the car keys,' he said. 'Sit in it, and wait for us. You can't go into the Hilton like that, and you're not fit enough to change on your own.'

'Of course I am.'

'Don't argue. I'll lose any tail, and come back. You wait.'

He went without looking back. I picked up the keys and put them in my jeans pocket, and thought grateful thoughts to pass the time.

I dawdled a long way behind Jik and Sarah at disembarkation. My gear attracted more scandalised attention in this solemn financial city, but I didn't care in the least. Nothing like fatigue and anxiety for killing off embarrassment.

Jik and Sarah, with only hand-baggage, walked without ado past the suitcase-unloading areas and straight out towards the waiting queue of taxis. The whole airport was bustling with Cup eve arrivals, but only one person, that I could see, was bustling exclusively after my fast-departing friends.

I smiled briefly. Young and eel-like, he slithered through the throng, pushing a young woman with a baby out of the way to grab the next taxi behind Jik's. They'd sent him, I supposed, because he knew Jik by sight. He'd flung turps in his eyes at the Arts Centre.

Not too bad, I thought. The boy wasn't over-intelligent, and Jik should have little trouble in losing him. I wandered around for a bit looking gormless, but as there was no one else who seemed the remotest threat, I eventually eased out to the car park.

The night was chilly after Alice Springs. I unlocked the car, climbed into the back, took off the successful hat, and settled to wait for Jik's return.

They were gone nearly two hours, during which time I grew stiffer and ever more uncomfortable and started swearing.

'Sorry,' Sarah said breathlessly, pulling open the car door and tumbling into the front seat.

'We had the devil's own job losing the little bugger,' Jik said, getting in beside me in the back. 'Are you all right?'

'Cold, hungry, and cross.'

'That's all right, then,' he said cheerfully. 'He stuck like a bloody little leech. That boy from the Arts Centre.'

'Yes, I saw him.'

'We hopped into the Victoria Royal, meaning to go straight out again by the side door and grab another cab, and there he was following us in through the front. So we peeled off for a drink in the bar and he hovered around in the lobby looking at the bookstall.'

'We thought it would be better not to let him know we'd spotted him, if we could,' Sarah said. 'So we did a re-think, went outside, called another taxi, and set off to The Naughty Ninety, which is about the only noisy big dine, dance and cabaret place in Melbourne.'

'It was absolutely packed.' Jik said. 'It cost me ten dollars to get a table. Marvellous for us, though. All dark corners and psychedelic coloured lights. We ordered and paid for some drinks, and read the menu, and then got up and danced.'

'He was still there, when we saw him last, standing in the queue for tables just inside the entrance door. We got out through an emergency exit down a passage past some cloakrooms. We'd dumped our bags there when we arrived, and simply collected them again on the way out.'

'I don't think he'll know we ducked him on purpose,' Jik said. 'It's a proper scrum there tonight.'

'Great.'

With Jik's efficient help I exchanged Tourist, Alice Style, for Racing Man, Melbourne Cup. He drove us all back to the Hilton, parked in its car park, and we walked into the front hall as if we'd never been away.

No one took any notice of us. The place was alive with pre-race excitement. People in evening dress flooding downstairs from the ballroom to stand in loud-talking groups before dispersing home. People returning from eating out, and calling for one more nightcap. Everyone discussing the chances of the next day's race.

Jik collected our room keys from the long desk.

'No messages,' he said. 'And they don't seem to have missed us.'

'Fair enough.'

'Todd,' Sarah said. 'Jik and I are going to have some food sent up. You'll come as well?'

I nodded. We went up in the lift and along to their room, and ate a subdued supper out of collective tiredness.

'Night,' I said eventually, getting up to go. 'And thanks for everything.'

'Thank us tomorrow,' Sarah said.

The night passed. Well, it passed.

In the morning I did a spot of one-handed shaving and some highly selective washing, and Jik came up, as he'd insisted, to help with my tie. I opened the door to him in underpants and dressing gown and endured his comments when I took the latter off.

'Jesus God Almighty, is there any bit of you neither blue nor patched?'

'I could have landed face first.'

He stared at the thought. '*Jesus.*'

'Help me rearrange these bandages,' I said.

'I'm not touching that lot.'

'Oh come on, Jik. Unwrap the swaddling bands. I'm itching like hell underneath and I've forgotten what my left hand looks like.'

With a variety of blasphemous oaths he undid the expert handiwork of the Alice hospital. The outer bandages proved to be large strong pieces of linen, fastened with clips, and placed so as to support my left elbow and hold my whole arm statically in one position, with my hand across my chest and pointing up towards my right shoulder. Under the top layer there was a system of crepe bandages tying my arm in that position. Also a sort of tight cummerbund of adhesive strapping, presumably to deal with the broken ribs. Also, just below my shoulder blade, a large padded wound dressing, which, Jik kindly told me after a delicate inspection from one corner, covered a mucky looking bit of darning.

'You damn near tore a whole flap of skin off. There are four lots of stitching. Looks like Clapham Junction.'

'Fasten it up again.'

'I have, mate, don't you worry.'

There were three similar dressings, two on my left thigh and one, a bit smaller, just below my knee: all fastened both with adhesive strips and tapes with clips. We left them all untouched.

'What the eye doesn't see doesn't scare the patient,' Jik said. 'What else do you want done?'

'Untie my arm.'

'You'll fall apart.'

'Risk it.'

He laughed and undid another series of clips and knots. I tentatively straightened my elbow. Nothing much happened except that the hovering ache and soreness stopped hovering and came down to earth.

'That's not so good,' Jik observed.

'It's my muscles as much as anything. Protesting about being stuck in one position all that time.'

'What now, then?'

From the bits and pieces we designed a new and simpler sling which gave my elbow good support but was less of a strait-jacket. I could get my hand out easily, and also my whole arm, if I wanted. When we'd finished, we had a small heap of bandages and clips left over.

'That's fine,' I said.

We all met downstairs in the hall at ten-thirty.

Around us a buzzing atmosphere of anticipation pervaded the chattering throng of would-be winners, who were filling the morning with celebratory drinks. The hotel, I saw, had raised a veritable fountain of champagne at the entrance to the bar-lounge end of the lobby, and Jik, his eyes lighting up, decided it was too good to be missed.

'Free booze,' he said reverently, picking up a glass and holding it under the prodigal bubbly which flowed in delicate gold streams from a pressure-fed height. 'Not bad, either,' he added, tasting. He raised his glass. 'Here's to Art. God rest his soul.'

'Life's short. Art's long,' I said.

'I don't like that,' Sarah said, looking at me uneasily.

'It was Alfred Munnings's favourite saying. And don't worry, love, he lived to be eighty plus.'

'Let's hope you do.'

I drank to it. She was wearing a cream dress with gold buttons; neat, tailored, a touch severe. An impression of the military for a day in the front line.

'Don't forget,' I said. 'If you think you see Wexford or Greene, make sure they see you.'

'Give me another look at their faces,' she said.

I pulled the small sketch book out of my pocket and handed it to her again, though she'd studied it on and off all the previous evening through supper.

'As long as they look like this, maybe I'll know them,' she said, sighing. 'Can I take it?' She put the sketch book in her handbag.

Jik laughed. 'Give Todd his due, he can catch a likeness. No imagination, of course. He can only paint what he sees.' His voice as usual was full of disparagement.

Sarah said, 'Don't you mind the awful things Jik says of your work, Todd?'

I grinned. 'I know exactly what he thinks of it.'

'If it makes you feel any better,' Jik said to his wife, 'He was the star pupil of our year. The Art School lacked judgment, of course.'

'You're both crazy.'

I glanced at the clock. We all finished the champagne and put down the glasses.

'Back a winner for me,' I said to Sarah, kissing her cheek.

'Your luck might run out.'

I grinned. 'Back number eleven.'

Her eyes were dark with apprehension. Jik's beard was at the bad-weather angle for possible storms ahead.

'Off you go,' I said cheerfully. 'See you later.'

I watched them through the door and wished strongly that we were all three going for a simple day out to the Melbourne Cup. The effort ahead was something I would have been pleased to avoid. I wondered if others ever quaked before the task they'd set themselves, and wished they'd never thought of it. The beginning, I supposed, was the worst. Once you were in, you were committed. But before, when there was still time to turn back, to rethink, to cancel, the temptation to retreat was demoralising.

Why climb Everest if at its foot you could lie in the sun.

Sighing, I went to the cashier's end of the reception desk and changed a good many travellers' cheques into cash. Maisie's generosity had been far-sighted. There would be little enough left by the time I got home.

Four hours to wait. I spent them upstairs in my room calming my nerves by drawing the view from the window. Black clouds still hung around the sky like cobwebs, especially in the direction of Flemington racecourse. I hoped it would stay dry for the Cup.

Half an hour before it was due to be run I left the Hilton on foot, walking unhurriedly along towards Swanston Street and the main area of shops. They were all shut, of course. Melbourne Cup day was a national public holiday. Everything stopped for the Cup.

I had taken my left arm out of its sling and threaded it gingerly through the sleeves of my shirt and jacket. A man with his jacket hunched over one shoulder was too memorable for sense. I found that by hooking my thumb into the waistband of my trousers I got quite good support.

Swanston Street was far from its usual bustling self. People still strode along with the breakneck speed which seemed to characterise all Melbourne pedestrians, but they strode in tens, not thousands. Trams ran up and down the central tracks with more vacant seats than passengers. Cars sped along with the drivers, eyes down, fiddling dangerously with radio dials. Fifteen minutes to the race which annually stopped Australia in its tracks.

Jik arrived exactly on time, driving up Swanston Street in the hired grey car and turning smoothly round the corner where I stood waiting. He stopped outside the Yarra River Fine Arts gallery, got out, opened the boot, and put on a brown coat-overall, of the sort worn by storemen.

I walked quietly along towards him. He brought out a small radio, switched it on, and stood it on top of the car. The commentator's voice emerged tinnily, giving details of the runners currently walking round the parade ring at Flemington races.

'Hello,' he said unemotionally, when I reached him. 'All set?' I nodded, and walked to the door of the gallery. Pushed it. It was solidly shut. Jik dived again into the boot, which held further fruits of his second shopping expedition in Alice Springs.

'GLoves,' he said, handling me some, and putting some on himself. They were of white cotton, with ribbed wristbands, and looked a lot too new and clean. I wiped the backs of mine along the wings of Jik's car, and he gave me a glance and did the same with his.

'Handles and impact adhesive.'

He gave me the two handles to hold. They were simple chromium plated handles, with flattened pieces at each end, pierced by screw holes for fixing. Sturdy handles, big enough for gripping with the whole hand. I held one steady, bottom side up, while Jik covered the screw-plate areas at each end with adhesive. We couldn't screw these handles where we wanted them. They had to be stuck.

'Now the other. Can you hold it in your left hand?'

I nodded. Jik attended to it. One or two people passed, paying no attention. We were not supposed to park there, but no one told us to move.

We walked across the pavement to the gallery. Its frontage was not one unbroken line across its whole width, but was recessed at the right-hand end to form a doorway. Between the front-facing display window and the front-facing glass door, there was a joining window at right angles to the street.

To this sheet of glass we stuck the handles, or rather, Jik did, at just above waist height. He tested them after a minute, and he couldn't pull them off. We returned to the car.

One or two more people passed, turning their heads to listen to the radio on the car roof, smiling in brotherhood at the universal national interest. The street was noticeably emptying as the crucial time drew near.

' . . . *Vinery carries the colours of Mr. Hudson Taylor of Adelaide and must be in with a good outside chance. Fourth in the Caulfield Cup and before that, second at Randwick against Brain-Teaser, who went on to beat Afternoon Tea . . .*'

'Stop listening to the damn race!' Jik said sharply.

'Sorry.'

'Ready?'

'Yes.'

We walked back to the entrance to the gallery, Jik carrying the sort of glass-cutter used by, among others, picture framers. Without casting a glance around for possible onlookers, he applied the diamond cutting edge to the matter in hand, using considerable strength as he pushed the professional tool round the outside of the pane. I stood behind him to block any passing curious glances.

'Hold the right-hand handle,' he said, as he started on the last of the four sides, the left-hand vertical.

I stepped past him and slotted my hand through the grip. None of the few people left in the street paid the slightest attention.

'When it goes,' Jik said. 'for God's sake don't drop it.'

'No.'

'Put your knee against the glass. Gently, for God's sake.'

I did what he said. He finished the fourth long cut.

'Press smoothly.'

I did that. Jik's knee, too, was firmly against the glass. With his left hand he gripped the chromium handle, and with the palm of his right he began jolting the top perimeter of the heavy pane.

Jik had cut a lot of glass in his time, even if not in exactly these circumstances. The big flat sheet cracked away evenly all round under our pressure and parted with hardly a splinter. The weight fell suddenly on to the handle I held in my right hand, and Jik steadied the now free sheet of glass with hands and knees and blasphemy.

'Jesus, don't let go.'

'No.'

The heavy vibrations set up in the glass by the breaking process subsided, and Jik took over the right-hand handle from me. Without any seeming inconvenience he pivoted the sheet of glass so that it opened like a door. He stepped through the hole, lifted the glass up wholesale by the two handles, carried it several feet, and propped it against the wall to the right of the more conventional way in.

He came out, and we went over to the car. From there, barely ten feet away, one could not see that the gallery was not still securely shut. There were by now in any case very few to look.

'. . . *Most jockeys have now mounted and the horses will soon be going out onto the course . . .*'

I picked up the radio. Jik exchanged the glass-cutter for a metal saw, a hammer and a chisel, and shut the boot, and we walked through the unorthodox entrance as if it was all in the day's work. Often only the furtive manner gave away the crook. If you behaved as if you had every right to, it took longer for anyone to suspect.

It would really have been best had we next been able to open the real door, but a quick inspection proved it impossible. There were two useful locks, and no keys.

'The stairs are at the back,' I said.

'Lead on.'

We walked the length of the plushy green carpet and down the beckoning stairs. There was a bank of electric switches at the top: we pressed those lighting the basement and left the upstairs lot off.

Heart-thumping time, I thought. It would take only a policeman to walk along and start fussing about a car parked in the wrong place to set Cassavetes and Todd on the road to jail.

'. . . *horses are now going out on to the course. Foursquare in front, sweating up and fighting jockey Ted Nester for control . . .*'

We reached the front of the stairs. I turned back towards the office, but Jik took off fast down the corridor.

'Come back,' I said urgently. 'If that steel gate shuts down . . .'

'Relax,' Jik said. 'You told me.' He stopped before reaching the threshold of the furthest room. Stood still, and looked. Came back rapidly.

'O.K. The Munnings are all there. Three of them. Also something else which will stun you. Go and look while I get this door open.'

'. . . *cantering down to the start, and the excitement is mounting here now . . .*'

With a feeling of urgency I trekked down the passage, stopped safely short of any electric gadgets which might trigger the gate and set off alarms, and looked into the Munnings room. The three paintings still hung there, as they had before. But along the row from them was something which, as Jik had said, stunned me. Chestnut horse with head raised, listening. Stately home in the background. The Raoul Millais picture we'd seen in Alice.

I went back to Jik who with hammer and chisel had bypassed the lock on the office door.

'Which is it?' he said. 'Original or copy?'

'Can't tell from that distance. Looks like real.'

He nodded. We went into the office and started work.

'. . . *Derriby and Special Bet coming down to the start now, and all the runners circling while the girths are checked . . .*'

I put the radio on Wexford's desk, where it sat like an hourglass, ticking away the minutes as the sands ran out.

Jik turned his practical attention to the desk drawers, but they were all unlocked. One of the waist-high line of filing cabinets, however, proved to be secure. Jik's strength and knowhow soon ensured that it didn't remain that way.

In his wake I looked through the drawers. Nothing much in them except catalogues and stationery.

In the broken-open filing cabinet, a gold mine.

Not that I realised it at first. The contents looked merely like ordinary files with ordinary headings.

'. . . *moved very freely coming down to the start and is prime fit to run for that hundred and ten thousand dollar prize . . .*'

There were a good many framed pictures in the office, some on the walls but even more standing in a row on the floor. Jik began looking through them at high speed, almost like flicking through a rack of record albums.

'. . . *handlers are beginning to load the runners into the starting stalls, and I see Vinery playing up . . .*'

Half of the files in the upper of the two drawers seemed to deal in varying ways with insurance. Letters, policies, revaluations and security. I didn't really know what I was looking for, which made it all a bit difficult.

'Jesus Almighty,' Jik said.

'What is it?'

'Look at this.'

'. . . *more than a hundred thousand people here today to see the twenty-three runners fight it out over the three thousand two hundred metres . . .*'

Jik had reached the end of the row and was looking at the foremost of three unframed canvasses tied loosely together with string. I peered over his shoulder. The picture had Munnings written all over it. It had Alfred Munnings written large and clear in the right hand bottom corner. It was a picture of four horses with jockeys cantering on a racecourse: and the paint wasn't dry.

'What are the others?' I said.

Jik ripped off the string. The two other pictures were exactly the same.

'God Almighty,' Jik said in awe.

'. . . *Vinery carries only fifty-one kilograms and has a good barrier position so it's not impossible* . . .'

'Keep looking,' I said, and went back to the files.

Names. Dates. Places. I shook my head impatiently. We needed more than those Munnings copies and I couldn't find a thing.

'Jesus!' Jik said.

He was looking inside the sort of large flat two-foot by three-foot folder which was used in galleries to store prints.

'. . . *only Derriby now to enter the stalls* . . .'

The print-folder had stood between the end of the desk and the nearby wall. Jik seemed transfixed.

Overseas Customers. My eyes flicked over the heading and then went back. Overseas Customers. I opened the file. Lists of people, sorted into countries. Pages of them. Names and addresses.

England.

A long list. Not alphabetical. Too many to read through in the shortage of time.

A good many of the names had been crossed out.

'. . . *They're running! This is the moment you've all been waiting for, and Special Bet is out in front* . . .'

'Look at this,' Jik said.

Donald Stuart. Donald Stuart, crossed out. Shropshire, England. Crossed out.

I practically stopped breathing.

'. . . *as they pass the stands for the first time it's Special Bet, Foursquare, Newshound, Derriby, Wonderbug, Vinery* . . .'

'Look at this,' Jik said again, insistently.

'Bring it,' I said. 'We've got less than three minutes before the race ends and Melbourne comes back to life.'

'But—'

'Bring it,' I said. 'And also those three copies.'

'. . . *Special Bet still making it, from Newshound close second, then Wonderbug* . . .'

I shoved the filing-drawer shut.

'Put this file in the print-folder and let's get out.'

I picked up the radio and Jik's tools, as he himself had enough trouble managing all three of the untied paintings and the large-print folder.

'. . . *down the backstretch by the Maribyrnong River it's still Special Bet with Vinery second now* . . .'

We went up the stairs. Switched off the lights. Eased round into a view of the car.

It stood there, quiet and unattended, just as we'd left it. No policeman. Everyone elsewhere, listening to the race.

Jik was calling on the Deity under his breath.

'. . . *rounding the turn towards home Special Bet is dropping back now and its Derriby with Newshound . . .*'

We walked steadily down the gallery.

The commentator's voice rose in excitement against a background of shouting crowds.

'. . . *Vinery in third with Wonderbug, and here comes Ringwood very fast on the stands side . . .*'

Nothing stirred out on the street. I went first through our hole in the glass and stood once more, with a great feeling of relief, on the outside of the beehive. Jik carried out the plundered honey and stacked it in the boot. He took the tools from my hands and stored them also.

'Right?'

I nodded with a dry mouth. We climbed normally into the car. The commentator was yelling to be heard.

'. . . *Coming to the line it's Ringwood by a length from Wonderbug, with Newshound third, then Derriby, then Vinery . . .*'

The cheers echoed inside the car as Jik started the engine and drove away.

'. . . *Might be a record time. Just listen to the cheers. The result again. The result of the Melbourne Cup. In the frame . . . first Ringwood, owned by Mr. Robert Khami . . . second Wonderbug . . .*'

'Phew,' Jik said, his beard jaunty and a smile stretching to show an expanse of gum. 'That wasn't a bad effort. We might hire ourselves out some time for stealing politicians' papers.' He chuckled fiercely.

'It's an overcrowded field,' I said, smiling broadly myself.

We were both feeling the euphoria which follows the safe deliverance from danger. 'Take it easy,' I said. 'We've a long way to go.'

He drove to the Hilton, parked, and carried the folder and pictures up to my room. He moved with his sailing speed, economically and fast, losing as little time as possible before returning to Sarah on the racecourse and acting as if he'd never been away.

'We'll be back here as soon as we can,' he promised, sketching a farewell.

Two seconds after he'd shut my door there was a knock on it.

I opened it. Jik stood there.

'I'd better know,' he said, 'What won the Cup?'

Chapter Twelve

When he'd gone I looked closely at the spoils.

The more I saw, the more certain it became that we had hit the absolute jackpot. I began to wish most insistently that we hadn't wasted time in establishing that Jik and Sarah were at the races. It made me nervous, waiting for them in the Hilton with so much dynamite in my hands. Every instinct urged immediate departure.

The list of Overseas Customers would to any other eyes have seemed the most harmless of documents. Wexford would not have needed to keep it in better security than a locked filing-cabinet, for the chances of anyone seeing its significance in ordinary circumstances were millions to one against.

Donald Stuart, Wrenstone House, Shropshire.

Crossed out.

Each page had three columns, a narrow one at each side with a broad one in the centre. The narrow left-hand column was for dates and the centre for names and addresses. In the narrow right-hand column, against each name, was a short line of apparently random letters and numbers. Those against Donald's entry, for instance, were MM3109T: and these figures had not been crossed out with his name. Maybe a sort of stock list, I thought, identifying the picture he'd bought.

I searched rapidly down all the other crossed-out names in the England sector. Maisie Matthews' name was not among them.

Damn, I thought. Why wasn't it?

I turned all the papers over rapidly. As far as I could see all the overseas customers came from basically English-speaking countries, and the proportion of crossed-out names was about one in three. If every crossing-out represented a robbery, there had been literally hundreds since the scheme began.

At the back of the file I found there was a second and separate section, again divided into pages for each country. The lists in this section were much shorter.

England.

Half way down. My eyes positively leapt at it.

Mrs. M. Matthews, Treasure Holme, Worthing, Sussex.

Crossed out.

I almost trembled. The date in the left-hand column looked like the date on which Maisie had bought her picture. The uncrossed-out numbers in the right hand column were SMC29R.

I put down the file and sat for five minutes staring unseeingly at the wall, thinking.

My first and last conclusions were that I had a great deal to do before

Jik and Sarah came back from the races, and that instincts were not always right.

The large print-folder, which had so excited Jik, lay on my bed. I opened it flat and inspected the contents.

I daresay I looked completely loony standing there with my mouth open. The folder contained a number of simplified line drawings like the one the boy-artist had been colouring in the Arts Centre. Full-sized outline drawings, on flat white canvas, as neat and accurate as tracings.

There were seven of them, all basically or horses. As they were only black and white line drawings I couldn't be sure, but I guessed that three were Munnings, two Raoul Millais, and the other two . . . I stared at the old-fashioned shapes of the horses . . . They couldn't be Stubbs, he was too well documented . . . How about Herring? Herring, I thought, nodding. The last two had a look of Herring.

Attached to one of these two canvases by an ordinary paper clip was a small handwritten memo on a piece of scrap paper.

'Don't forget to send the original. Also find out what palette he used, if different from usual.'

I looked again at the three identical finished paintings which we had also brought away. These canvases, tacked on to wooden stretchers, looked very much as if they might have started out themselves as the same sort of outlines. The canvas used was of the same weave and finish.

The technical standard of the work couldn't be faulted. The paintings did look very much like Munnings' own, and would do much more so after they had dried and been varnished. Different coloured paints dried at different speeds, and also the drying time of paints depended very much on the amount of oil or turps used to thin them, but at a rough guess all three pictures had been completed between three and six days earlier. The paint was at the same stage on all of them. They must, I thought, have all been painted at once, in a row, like a production line. Red hat, red hat, red hat . . . It would have saved time and paint.

The brushwork throughout was painstaking and controlled. Nothing slapdash. No time skimped. The quality of care was the same as in the Millais copy at Alice.

I was looking, I knew, at the true worth of Harley Renbo.

All three paintings were perfectly legal. It was never illegal to copy: only to attempt to sell the copy as real.

I thought it all over for a bit longer, and then set rapidly to work.

The Hilton, when I went downstairs an hour later, were most amiable and helpful.

Certainly, they could do what I asked. Certainly, I could use the photo-copying machine, come this way. Certainly, I could pay my bill now, and leave later.

I thanked them for their many excellent services.

'Our pleasure,' they said: and, incredibly, they meant it.

Upstairs again, waiting for Jik and Sarah, I packed all my things. That done, I took off my jacket and shirt and did my best at rigging the spare bandages and clips back into something like the Alice shape, with my hand inside across my chest. No use pretending that it wasn't a good deal more comfortable that way than the dragging soreness of letting it all swing free. I buttoned my shirt over the top and calculated that if the traffic was bad Jik might still be struggling out of the racecourse.

A little anxiously, and still faintly feeling unwell, I settled to wait.

I waited precisely five minutes. Then the telephone by the bed rang, and I picked up the receiver.

Jik's voice, sounding hard and dictatorial.

'Charles, will you please come down to our room at once.'

'Well . . .' I said hesitantly. 'Is it important?'

'Bloody chromic oxide!' he said explosively. 'Can't you do anything without arguing?'

Christ, I thought.

I took a breath. 'Give me ten minutes,' I said. 'I need ten minutes. I'm . . . er . . . I've just had a shower. I'm in my underpants.'

'Thank you, Charles,' he said. The telephone clicked as he disconnected.

A lot of Jik's great oaths galloped across my mind, wasting precious time. If ever we needed divine help, it was now.

Stifling a gut-twisting lurch of plain fear I picked up the telephone and made a series of internal calls.

'Please could you send a porter up right away to room seventeen eighteen to collect Mr. Cassavetes' bags?'

'Housekeeper . . . ? Please will you send someone along urgently to seventeen eighteen to clean the room as Mr. Cassavetes has been sick . . .'

'Please will you send the nurse along to seventeen eighteen at once as Mr. Cassavetes has a severe pain . . .'

'Please will you send four bottles of your best champagne and ten glasses up to seventeen eighteen immediately . . .'

'Please bring coffee for three to seventeen eighteen at once . . .'

'Electrician? All the electrics have fused in room seventeen eighteen, please come at once.'

'. . . the water is overflowing in the bathroom, please send the plumber urgently.'

Who else was there? I ran my eye down the list of possible services. One wouldn't be able to summon chiropodists, masseuses, secretaries, barbers or clothes-pressers in a hurry . . . but television, why not?

'. . . Please would you see to the television in room seventeen eighteen. There is smoke coming from the back and it smells like burning . . .'

That should do it, I thought. I made one final call for myself, asking for a porter to collect my bags. Right on, they said. Ten dollar tip I said if the bags could be down in the hall within five minutes. No sweat, an Australian voice assured me happily. Coming right that second.

I left my door ajar for the porter and rode down two storeys in the lift to floor seventeen. The corridor outside Jik and Sarah's room was still a broad empty expanse of no one doing anything in a hurry.

The ten minutes had gone.

I fretted.

The first to arrive was the waiter with the champagne, and he came not with a tray but a trolley, complete with ice buckets and spotless white cloths. It couldn't possibly have been better.

As he slowed to a stop outside Jik's door, two other figures turned into the corridor, hurrying, and behind them, distantly, came a cleaner slowly pushing another trolley of linen and buckets and brooms.

I said to the waiter, 'Thank you so much for coming so quickly.' I gave him a ten dollar note, which surprised him. 'Please go and serve the champagne straight away.'

He grinned, and knocked on Jik's door.

After a pause, Jik opened it. He looked tense and strained.

'Your champagne, sir,' said the waiter.

'But I didn't . . .' Jik began. He caught sight of me suddenly, where I stood a little back from his door. I made waving-in motions with my hand, and a faint grin appeared to lighten the anxiety.

Jik retreated into the room followed by trolley and waiter.

At a rush, after that, came the electrician, the plumber and the television man. I gave them each ten dollars and thanked them for coming so promptly. 'I had a winner,' I said. They took the money with more grins and Jik opened the door to their knock.

'Electrics . . . plumbing . . . television . . .' His eyebrows rose. He looked across to me in rising comprehension. He flung wide his door and invited them in with all his heart.

'Give them some champagne,' I said.

'God Almighty.'

After that, in quick succession, came the porter, the man with the coffee, and the nurse. I gave them all ten dollars from my mythical winnings and invited them to join the party. Finally came the cleaner, pushing her top-heavy-looking load. She took the ten dollars, congratulated me on my good fortune, and entered the crowded and noisy fray.

It was up to Jik, I thought. I couldn't do any more.

He and Sarah suddenly popped out like the corks from the gold-topped bottles, and stood undecided in the corridor. I gripped Sarah's wrist and tugged her towards me.

'Push the cleaning trolley through the door, and turn it over,' I said to Jik.

He wasted no time deliberating. The brooms crashed to the carpet inside the room, and Jik pulled the door shut after him.

Sarah and I were already running on our way to the lifts. She looked extremely pale and wild-eyed, and I knew that whatever had happened in their room had been almost too much for her.

Jik sprinted along after us. There were six lifts from the seventeenth floor, and one never had to wait more than a few seconds for one to arrive. The seconds this time seemed like hours but were actually very few indeed. The welcoming doors slid open, and we leapt inside and pushed the 'doors closed' button like maniacs.

The doors closed.

The lift descended, smooth and fast.

'Where's the car?' I said.

'Car park.'

'Get it and come round to the side door.'

'Right.'

'Sarah . . .'

She stared at me in fright.

'My satchel will be in the hall. Will you carry it for me?'

She looked vaguely at my one-armed state, my jacket swinging loosely over my left shoulder.

'Sarah!'

'Yes . . . all right.'

We erupted into the hall, which had filled with people returning from the Cup. Talkative groups mixed and mingled, and it was impossible to see easily from one side to the other. All to the good, I thought.

My suitcase and satchel stood waiting near the front entrance, guarded by a young man in porter's uniform.

I parted with the ten dollars. 'Thank you very much,' I said.

'No sweat,' he said cheerfully. 'Can I get you a taxi?'

I shook my head. I picked up the suitcase and Sarah the satchel and we headed out of the door.

Turned right. Hurried. Turned right again, round to the side where I'd told Jik we'd meet him.

'He's not here,' Sarah said with rising panic.

'He'll come,' I said encouragingly. 'We'll just go on walking to meet him.'

We walked. I kept looking back nervously for signs of pursuit, but there were none. Jik came round the corner on two wheels and tore millimetres off the tyres stopping beside us. Sarah scrambled into the front and I and my suitcase filled the back. Jik made a hair-raising U turn and took us away from the Hilton at an illegal speed.

'Wowee,' he said, laughing with released tension. 'Whatever gave you that idea?'

'The Marx brothers.'

He nodded. 'Pure crazy comedy.'

'Where are we going?' Sarah said.

'Have you noticed,' Jik said, 'How my wife always brings us back to basics?'

The city of Melbourne covered a great deal of land.

We drove randomly north and east through seemingly endless suburban developments of houses, shops, garages and light industry, all looking prosperous, haphazard, and, to my eyes, American.

'Where are we?' Jik said.

'Somewhere called Box Hill,' I said, reading it on shopfronts.

'As good as anywhere.'

We drove a few miles further and stopped at a modern middle-rank motel which had bright coloured strings of triangular flags fluttering across the forecourt. A far cry from the Hilton, though the rooms we presently took were cleaner than nature intended.

There were plain divans, a square of thin carpet nailed at the edges, and a table lamp screwed to an immovable table. The looking glass was stuck flat to the wall and the swivelling armchair was bolted to the floor. Apart from that, the curtains were bright and the hot tap ran hot in the shower.

'They don't mean you to pinch much,' Jik said. 'Let's paint them a mural.'

'No!' Sarah said, horrorstruck.

'There's a great Australian saying,' Jik said. 'If it moves, shoot it, and if it grows, chop it down.'

'What's that got to do with it?' Sarah said.

'Nothing. I just thought Todd might like to hear it.'

'Give me strength.'

We were trying to, in our inconsequential way.

Jik sat in the arm chair in my room, swivelling. Sarah sat on one of the divans, I on the other. My suitcase and satchel stood side by side on the floor.

'You do realise we skipped out of the Hilton without paying,' Sarah said.

'No we didn't,' Jik said. 'According to our clothes, we are still resident. I'll ring them up later.'

'But Todd . . .'

'I did pay,' I said. 'Before you got back.'

She looked slightly happier.

'How did Greene find you?' I said.

'God knows,' Jik said gloomily.

Sarah was astonished. 'How did you know about Greene? How did you know there was anyone in our room besides Jik and me? How did you know we were in such awful trouble?'

'Jik told me.'

'But he couldn't! He couldn't risk warning you. He just had to tell you to come. He really did . . .' Her voice quivered. The tears weren't far from the surface. 'They made him . . .'

'Jik told me,' I said matter-of-factly. 'First, he called me Charles, which he never does, so I knew something was wrong. Second, he was rude to me, and I know you think he is most of the time, but he isn't, not like that. And third, he told me the name of the man who I was to guess was in your room putting pressure on you both to get me to come down and walk into a nasty little hole. He told me it was chromic oxide, which is the pigment in green paint.'

'Green paint!' The tearful moment passed. 'You really are both extra ordinary,' she said.

'Long practice,' Jik said cheerfully.

'Tell me what happened,' I said.

'We left before the last race, to avoid the traffic, and we just came back normally to the Hilton. I parked the car, and we went up to our room. We'd only been there about a minute when there was this knock on the door, and when I opened it they just pushed in . . .'

'They?'

'Three of them. One was Greene. We both knew him straight away, from your drawing. Another was the boy from the Arts Centre. The third was all biceps and beetle brows, with his brains in his fists.'

He absentmindedly rubbed an area south of his heart.

'He punched you?' I said.

'It was all so quick . . .' he said apologetically. 'They just crammed in . . . and biff bang . . . The next thing I knew they'd got hold of Sarah and were twisting her arm and saying that she wouldn't just get turps in her eyes if I didn't get you to come at once.'

'Did they have a gun?' I asked.

'No . . . a cigarette lighter. Look, I'm sorry, mate. I guess it sounds pretty feeble, but Beetle-brows had her in a pretty rough grasp and the boy had this ruddy great cigarette lighter with a flame like a blow torch just a couple of inches from her cheek . . . and I was a bit groggy . . . and Greene said they'd burn her if I didn't get you . . . and I couldn't fight them all at once.'

'Stop apologising,' I said.

'Yeah . . . well, so I rang you. I told Greene you'd be ten minutes because you were in your underpants, but I think he heard you anyway because he was standing right beside me, very wary and sharp. I didn't know really whether you'd cottoned on, but I hoped to God . . . and you should have seen their faces when the waiter pushed the trolley in. Beetle-brows let go of Sarah and the boy just stood there with his mouth open and the cigarette lighter flaring up like an oil refinery . . .'

'Greene said we didn't want the champagne and to take it away,' Sarah said. 'But Jik and I said yes we did, and Jik asked the waiter to open it at once.'

'Before he got the first cork out the others all began coming . . . and then they were all picking up glasses . . . and the room was filling up . . . and Greene and the boy and Beetle-brows were all on the window side of the room, sort of pinned in by the trolley and all those people . . . and I just grabbed Sarah and we ducked round the edge. The last I saw, Greene and the others were trying to push through, but our guests were pretty thick on the ground by then and keen to get their champagne . . . and I should think the cleaning trolley was just about enough to give us that start to the lift.'

'I wonder how long the party lasted,' I said.

'Until the bubbles ran out.'

'They must all have thought you mad,' Sarah said.

'Anything goes on Cup day,' I said, 'and the staff of the Hilton would be used to eccentric guests.'

'What if Greene had had a gun?' Sarah said.

I smiled at her twistedly. 'He would have had to wave it around in front of a hell of a lot of witnesses.'

'But he might have done.'

'He might . . . but he was a long way from the front door.' I bit my thumbnail. 'Er . . . how did he know I was in the Hilton?'

There was a tangible silence.

'I told him,' Sarah said finally, in a small mixed outburst of shame and defiance. 'Jik didn't tell you it all, just now. At first they said . . .

Greene said . . . they'd burn my face if Jik didn't tell them where you were. He didn't want to . . . but he had to . . . so I told them, so that it wouldn't be him . . . I suppose that sounds stupid.'

I thought it sounded extraordinarily moving. Love of an exceptional order, and a depth of understanding.

I smiled at her. 'So they didn't know I was there, to begin with?'

Jik shook his head. 'I don't think they knew you were even in Melbourne. They seemed surprised when Sarah said you were upstairs. I think all they knew was that you weren't still in hospital in Alice Springs.'

'Did they know about our robbery?'

'I'm sure they didn't.'

I grinned. 'They'll be schizophrenic when they find out.'

Jik and I both carefully shied away from what would have happened if I'd gone straight down to their room, though I saw from his eyes that he knew. With Sarah held as a hostage I would have had to leave the Hilton with Greene and taken my chance. The uncomfortable slim chance that they would have let me off again with my life.

'I'm hungry,' I said.

Sarah smiled. 'Whenever are you not?'

We ate in a small Bring Your Own restaurant nearby, with people at tables all around us talking about what they'd backed in the Cup.

'Good heavens,' Sarah exclaimed. 'I'd forgotten about that.'

'About what?'

'Your winnings,' she said. 'On Ringwood.'

'But . . .' I began.

'It was number eleven!'

'I don't believe it.'

She opened her handbag and produced a fat wad of notes. Somehow, in all the mêlée in the Hilton, she had managed to emerge from fiery danger with the cream leather pouch swinging from her arm. The strength of the instinct which kept women attached to their handbags had often astounded me, but never more than that day.

'It was forty to one,' she said. 'I put twenty dollars on for you, so you've got eight hundred dollars, and I think it's disgusting.'

'Share it,' I said, laughing.

She shook her head. 'Not a cent . . . To be honest, I thought it had no chance at all, and I thought I'd teach you not to bet that way by losing you twenty dollars, otherwise I'd only have staked you ten.'

'I owe most of it to Jik, anyway,' I said.

'Keep it,' he said. 'We'll add and subtract later. Do you want me to cut your steak?'

'Please.'

He sliced away neatly at my plate, and pushed it back with the fork placed ready.

'What else happened at the races?' I said, spearing the first succulent piece. 'Who did you see?' The steak tasted as good as it looked, and I realised that in spite of all the sore patches I had at last lost the overall feeling of unsettled shaky sickness. Things were on the mend, it seemed.

'We didn't see Greene,' Jik said. 'Or the boy, or Beetle-brows.'

'I'd guess they saw you.'

'Do you think so?' Sarah said worriedly.

'I'd guess,' I said, 'That they saw you at the races and simply followed you back to the Hilton.'

'Jesus,' Jik groaned. 'We never spotted them. There was a whole mass of traffic.'

I nodded. 'And all moving very slowly. If Greene was perhaps three cars behind you, you'd never have seen him, but he could have kept you in sight easily.'

'I'm bloody sorry, Todd.'

'Don't be silly. And no harm done.'

'Except for the fact,' Sarah said, 'That I've still got no clothes.'

'You look fine,' I said absently.

'We saw a girl I know in Sydney,' Sarah said. 'We watched the first two races together and talked to her aunt. And Jik and I were talking to a photographer we both knew just after he got back . . . so it would be pretty easy to prove Jik was at the races all afternoon, like you wanted.'

'No sign of Wexford?'

'Not if he looked like your drawing,' Sarah said. 'Though of course he might have been there. It's awfully difficult to recognise a complete stranger just from a drawing, in a huge crowd like that.'

'We talked to a lot of people,' Jik said. 'To everyone Sarah knew even slightly. She used the excuse of introducing me as her newly-bagged husband.'

'We even talked to that man you met on Saturday,' Sarah agreed, nodding. 'Or rather, he came over and talked to us.'

'Hudson Taylor?' I asked.

'The one you saw talking to Wexford,' Jik said.

'He asked if you were at the Cup,' Sarah said. 'He said he'd been going to ask you along for another drink. We said we'd tell you he'd asked.'

'His horse ran quite well, didn't it?' I said.

'We saw him earlier than that. We wished him luck and he said he'd need it.'

'He bets a bit,' I said, remembering.

'Who doesn't?'

'Another commission down the drain,' I said. 'He would have had Vinery painted if he'd won.'

'You hire yourself out like a prostitute,' Jik said. 'It's obscene.'

'And anyway,' added Sarah cheerfully, 'You won more on Ringwood than you'd've got for the painting.'

I looked pained, and Jik laughed.

We drank coffee, went back to the motel, and divided to our separate rooms. Five minutes later Jik knocked on my door.

'Come in,' I said, opening it.

He grinned. 'You were expecting me.'

'Thought you might come.'

He sat in the armchair and swivelled. His gaze fell on my suitcase, which lay flat on one of the divans.

'What did you do with all the stuff we took from the gallery?'

I told him.

He stopped swivelling and sat still.

'You don't mess about, do you?' he said eventually.

'A few days from now,' I said, 'I'm going home.'

'And until then?'

'Um . . . until then, I aim to stay one jump ahead of Wexford, Greene, Beetle-brows, the Arts·Centre boy, and the tough who met me on the balcony at Alice.'

'Not to mention our copy artist, Harley Renbo.'

I considered it. 'Him too,' I said.

'Do you think we can?'

'Not we. Not from here on. This is where you take Sarah home.'

He slowly shook his head. 'I don't reckon it would be any safer than staying with you. We're too easy to find. For one thing, we're in the Sydney 'phone book. What's to stop Wexford from marching on to the boat with a bigger threat than a cigarette lighter?'

'You could tell him what I've just told you.'

'And waste all your efforts.'

'Retreat is sometimes necessary.'

He shook his head. 'If we stay with you, retreat may never be necessary. It's the better of two risks. And anyway . . .' the old fire gleamed in his eye . . . 'It will be a great game. Cat and mouse. With cats who don't know they are mice chasing a mouse who knows he's a cat.'

More like a bull fight, I thought, with myself waving the cape to invite the charge. Or a conjuror, attracting attention to one hand while he did the trick with the other. On the whole I preferred the notion of the conjuror. There seemed less likelihood of being gored.

Chapter Thirteen

I spent a good deal of the night studying the list of Overseas Customers, mostly because I still found it difficult to lie comfortably to sleep, and partly because I had nothing else to read.

It became more and more obvious that I hadn't really pinched *enough*. The list I'd taken was fine in its way, but would have been doubly useful with a stock list to match the letters and numbers in the right hand column.

On the other hand, all stock numbers were a form of code, and if I looked at them long enough, maybe some sort of recognisable pattern might emerge.

By far the majority began with the letter M, particularly in the first and much larger section. In the smaller section, which I had found at the back of the file, the M prefixes were few, and S, A, W and B were much commoner.

Donald's number began with M. Maisie's began with S.

Suppose, I thought, that the M simply stood for Melbourne, and the S for Sydney, the cities where each had bought their pictures.

Then A, W and B were where? Adelaide, Wagga Wagga and Brisbane? Alice?

In the first section the letters and numbers following the initial M seemed to have no clear pattern. In the second section, though, the third letter was always C, the last letter always R, and the numbers, divided though they were between several different countries, progressed more or less consecutively. The highest number of all was 54, which had been sold to a Mr. Norman Updike, living in Auckland, New Zealand. The stock number against his name was WHC54R. The date in the left hand column was only a week old, and Mr. Updike had not been crossed out.

All the pictures in the shorter section had been sold within the past three years. The first dates in the long first section were five and a half years old.

I wondered which had come first, five and a half years ago: the gallery or the idea. Had Wexford originally been a full-time crook deliberately setting up an imposing front, or a formerly honest art dealer struck by criminal possibilities? Judging from the respectable air of the gallery and what little I'd seen of Wexford himself, I would have guessed the latter. But the violence lying just below the surface didn't match.

I sighed, put down the lists, and switched off the light. Lay in the dark, thinking of the telephone call I'd made after Jik had gone back to Sarah.

It had been harder to arrange from the motel than it would have been from the Hilton, but the line had been loud and clear.

'You got my cable?' I said.

'I've been waiting for your call for half an hour.'

'Sorry.'

'What do you want?'

'I've sent you a letter,' I said. 'I want to tell you what's in it.'

'But . . .'

'Just listen,' I said. 'And talk after.' I spoke for quite a long time to a response of grunts from the far end.

'Are you sure of all this?'

'Positive about most,' I said. 'Some of it's a guess.'

'Repeat it.'

'Very well.' I did so, at much the same length.

'I have recorded all that.'

'Good.'

'Hm . . . What do you intend doing now?'

'I'm going home soon. Before that, I think I'll keep looking into things that aren't my business.'

'I don't approve of that.'

I grinned at the telephone. 'I don't suppose you do, but if I'd stayed in England we wouldn't have got this far. There's one other thing . . . Can I reach you by telex if I want to get a message to you in a hurry?'

'Telex? Wait a minute.'

I waited.

'Yes, here you are.' A number followed. I wrote it down. 'Address any message to me personally and head it urgent.'

'Right,' I said. 'And could you get answers to three questions for me?' He listened, and said he could. 'Thank you very much,' I said. 'And goodnight.'

Sarah and Jik both looked heavy-eyed and languorous in the morning. A successful night, I judged.

We checked out of the motel, packed my suitcase into the boot of the car, and sat in the passenger seats to plan the day.

'Can't we please get our clothes from the Hilton?' Sarah said, sounding depressed.

Jik and I said 'No' together.

'I'll ring them now,' Jik said. 'I'll get them to pack all our things and keep them safe for us, and I'll tell them I'll send a cheque for the bill.' He levered himself out of the car again and went off on the errand.

'Buy what you need out of my winnings,' I said to Sarah.

She shook her head. 'I've got some money. It's not that. It's just . . . I wish all this was over.'

'It will be, soon,' I said neutrally. She sighed heavily. 'What's your idea of a perfect life?' I asked.

'Oh . . .' she seemed surprised. 'I suppose right now I just want to be with Jik on the boat and have fun, like before you came.'

'And for ever?'

She looked at me broodingly. 'You may think, Todd, that I don't know Jik is a complicated character, but you've only got to look at his paintings . . . They make me shudder. They're a side of Jik I don't know because he hasn't painted anything since we met. You may think that this world will be worse off if Jik is happy for a bit, but I'm no fool, I know that in the end whatever it is that drives him to paint like that will come back again . . . I think these first few months together are frantically precious . . . and it isn't just the physical dangers you've dragged us into that I hate, but the feeling that I've lost the rest of that golden time . . . that you remind him of his painting, and that after you've gone he'll go straight back to it . . . weeks and weeks before he might have done.'

'Get him to go sailing,' I said. 'He's always happy at sea.'

'You don't care, do you?'

I looked straight into her clouded brown eyes. 'I care for you both, very much.'

'Then God help the people you hate.'

And God help me, I thought, if I became any fonder of my oldest friend's wife. I looked away from her, out of the window. Affection wouldn't matter. Anything else would be a mess.

Jik came back with a satisfied air. 'That's all fixed. They said there's a letter for you, Todd, delivered by hand a few minutes ago. They asked me for a forwarding address.'

'What did you say?'

'I said you'd call them yourself.'

'Right . . . Well, let's get going.'

'Where to?'

'New Zealand, don't you think?'

'That should be far enough,' Jik said dryly.

He drove us to the airport, which was packed with people going home from the Cup.

'If Wexford and Greene are looking for us,' Sarah said, 'They will surely be watching at the airport.'

If they weren't, I thought, we'd have to lay a trail: but Jik, who knew that, didn't tell her.

'They can't do much in public,' he said comfortingly.

We bought tickets and found we could either fly to Auckland direct at lunchtime, or via Sydney leaving within half an hour.

'Sydney,' said Sarah positively, clearly drawing strength from the chance of putting her feet down on her own safe doorstep.

I shook my head. 'Auckland direct. Let's see if the restaurant's still open for breakfast.'

We squeezed in under the waitresses' pointed consultation of clocks and watches and ordered bacon and eggs lavishly.

'Why are we going to New Zealand?' Sarah said.

'To see a man about a painting and advise him to take out extra insurance.'

'Are you actually making sense?'

'Actually,' I said, 'yes.'

'I don't see why we have to go so far, when Jik said you found enough in the gallery to blow the whole thing wide open.'

'Um . . .' I said. 'Because we don't want to blow it wide open. Because we want to hand it to the police in full working order.'

She studied my face. 'You are very devious.'

'Not on canvas,' Jik said.

After we'd eaten we wandered around the airport shops, buying yet more toothbrushes and so on for Jik and Sarah, and another airline bag. There was no sign of Wexford or Greene or the boy or Beetle-brows or Renbo, or the tough who'd been on watch at Alice Springs. If they'd seen us without us seeing them, we couldn't tell.

'I think I'll ring the Hilton,' I said.

Jik nodded. I put the call through with him and Sarah sitting near, within sound and sight.

'I called about a forwarding address . . .' I told the reception desk. 'I can't really give you one. I'll be in New Zealand. I'm flying to Auckland in an hour or two.'

They asked for instructions about the hand-delivered letter.

'Er . . . Would you mind opening it, and reading it to me?'

Certainly, they said. Their pleasure. The letter was from Hudson Taylor saying he was sorry to have missed me at the races, and that if while I was in Australia I would like to see round a vineyard, he would be pleased to show me his.

Thanks, I said. Our pleasure, sir, they said. If anyone asked for me, I said, would they please mention where I'd gone. They would. Certainly. Their pleasure.

During the next hour Jik called the car-hire firm about settling their account and leaving the car in the airport carpark, and I checked my suitcase through with Air New Zealand. Passports were no problem: I had mine with me in any case, but for Jik and Sarah they were unnecessary, as passage between New Zealand and Australia was as unrestricted as between England and Ireland.

Still no sign of Wexford or Greene. We sat in the departure bay thinking private thoughts.

It was again only when our flight was called that I spotted a spotter. The prickles rose again on my skin. I'd been blind, I thought. Dumb and blind.

Not Wexford, nor Greene, nor the boy, nor Renbo, nor any rough set of muscles. A neat day dress, neat hair, unremarkable handbag and shoes. A calm concentrated face. I saw her because she was staring at Sarah. She was standing outside the departure bay, looking in. The woman who had welcomed me into the Yarra River Fine Arts, and given me a catalogue, and let me out again afterwards.

As if she felt my eyes upon her she switched her gaze abruptly to my face. I looked away instantly, blankly, hoping she wouldn't know I'd seen her, or wouldn't know at least that I'd recognised her.

Jik, Sarah and I stood up and drifted with everyone else towards the departure doors. In their glass I could see the woman's reflection: standing still, watching us go. I walked out towards the aircraft and didn't look back.

Mrs. Norman Updike stood in her doorway, shook her head, and said that her husband would not be home until six.

She was thin and sharp-featured and talked with tight New Zealand vowels. If we wanted to speak to her husband, we would have to come back.

She looked us over; Jik with his rakish blond beard, Sarah in her slightly crumpled but still military cream dress, I with my arm in its sling under my shirt, and jacket loose over my shoulder. Hardly a trio one would easily forget. She watched us retreat down her front path with a sharply turned-down mouth.

'Dear gentle soul,' murmured Jik.

We drove away in the car we had hired at the airport.

'Where now?' Jik said.

'Shops.' Sarah was adamant. 'I must have some clothes.'

The shops, it appeared, were in Queen Street, and still open for another half hour. Jik and I sat in the car, waiting and watching the world go by.

'The dolly-birds fly out of their office cages about now,' Jik said happily.

'What of it?'

'I sit and count the ones with no bras.'

'And you a married man.'

'Old habits die hard.'

We had counted eight definites and one doubtful by the time Sarah returned. She was wearing a light olive skirt with a pink shirt, and reminded me of pistachio ice cream.

'That's better,' she said, tossing two well-filled carriers onto the back seat. 'Off we go, then.'

The therapeutic value of the new clothes lasted all the time we spent in New Zealand and totally amazed me. She seemed to feel safer if she looked fresh and clean, her spirits rising accordingly. Armourplated cotton, I thought. Drip-dry bullet-proofing. Security is a new pin.

We dawdled back to the hill overlooking the bay where Norman Updike's house stood in a crowded suburban street. The Updike residence was large but squashed by neighbours, and it was not until one was inside that one realised that the jostling was due to the view. As many houses as could be crammed on to the land had been built to share it. The city itself seemed to sprawl endlessly round miles of indented coastline, but all the building plots looked tiny.

Norman Updike proved as expansive as his wife was closed in. He had a round shiny bald head on a round short body, and he called his spouse Chuckles without apparently intending satire.

We said Jik and I, that we were professional artists who would be intensely interested and grateful if we could briefly admire the noted picture he had just bought.

'Did the gallery send you?' he asked, beaming at the implied compliments to his taste and wealth.

'Sort of,' we said, and Jik added: 'My friend here is well known in England for his painting of horses, and is represented in many top galleries, and has been hung often at the Royal Academy . . .'

I thought he was laying it on a bit too thick, but Norman Updike was impressed and pulled wide his door.

'Come in then. Come in. The picture's in the lounge. This way, lass, this way.'

He showed us into a large over-stuffed room with dark ankle-deep carpet, big dark cupboards, and the glorious view of sunlit water.

Chuckles, sitting solidly in front of a television busy with a moronic British comic show, gave us a sour look and no greeting.

'Over her,' Norman Updike beamed, threading his portly way round a battery of fat armchairs. 'What do you think of that, eh?' He waved his hand with proprietorial pride at the canvas on his wall.

A smallish painting, fourteen inches by eighteen. A black horse, with an elongated neck curving against a blue and white sky; a chopped-off tail; the grass in the foreground yellow; and the whole covered with an old-looking varnish.

'Herring,' I murmured reverently.

Norman Updike's beam broadened. 'I see you know your stuff. Worth a bit, that is.'

'A good deal,' I agreed.

'I reckon I got a bargain. The gallery said I'd always make a profit if I wanted to sell.'

'May I look at the brushwork?' I asked politely.

'Go right ahead.'

I looked closely. It was very good. It did look like Herring, dead since 1865. It also, indefinably, looked like the meticulous Renbo. One would need a microscope and chemical analysis, to make sure.

I stepped back and glanced round the rest of the room. There was nothing of obvious value, and the few other pictures were all prints.

'Beautiful,' I said admiringly, turning back to the Herring. 'Unmistakable style. A real master.'

Updike beamed.

'You'd better beware of burglars,' I said.

He laughed. 'Chuckles, dear, do you hear what this young man says? He says we'd better beware of burglars!'

Chuckles' eye gave me two seconds' sour attention and returned to the screen.

Updike patted Sarah on the shoulder. 'Tell your friend not to worry about burglars.'

'Why not?' I said.

'We've got alarms all over this house,' he beamed. 'Don't you worry, a burglar wouldn't get far.'

Jik and Sarah, as I had done, looked round the room and saw nothing much worth stealing. Nothing, certainly, worth alarms all over the house. Updike watched them looking and his beam grew wider.

'Shall I show these young people our little treasures, Chuckles?' he said.

Chuckles didn't even reply. The television cackled with tinned laughter.

'We'd be most interested,' I said.

He smiled with the fat anticipatory smirk of one about to show what will certainly be admired. Two or three steps took him to one of the big dark cupboards which seemed built into the walls, and he pulled open the double doors with a flourish.

Inside, there were about six deep shelves, each bearing several complicated pieces of carved jade. Pale pink, creamy white and pale green, smooth, polished, intricate, expensive; each piece standing upon its own heavy-looking black base-support. Jik, Sarah and I made appreciative noises and Norman Updike smiled ever wider.

'Hong Kong, of course,' he said. 'I worked there for years, you know. Quite a nice little collection, eh?' He walked along to the next dark cupboard and pulled open a duplicate set of doors. Inside, more shelves, more carvings, as before.

'I'm afraid I don't know much about jade,' I said, apologetically. 'Can't appreciate your collection to the full.'

He told us a good deal more about the ornate goodies than we actually wanted to know. There were four cupboards full in the lounge and overflows in bedroom and hall.

'You used to be able to pick them up very cheap in Hong Kong,' he said. 'I worked there more than twenty years, you know.'

Jik and I exchanged glances. I nodded slightly.

Jik immediately shook Norman Updike by the hand, put his arm round Sarah, and said we must be leaving. Updike looked enquiringly at Chuckles, who was still glued to the telly and still abdicating from the role of hostess. When she refused to look our way he shrugged good-humouredly and came with us to his front door. Jik and Sarah walked out as soon as he opened it, and let me alone with him in the hall.

'Mr. Updike,' I said. 'At the gallery . . . which man was it who sold you the Herring?'

'Mr. Grey,' he said promptly.

Mr. Grey . . . Mr. Grey . . .

I frowned.

'Such a pleasant man,' nodded Updike, beaming. 'I told him I knew very little about pictures, but he assured me I would get as much pleasure from my little Herring as from all my jade.'

'You did tell him about your jade, then?'

'Naturally I did. I mean . . . if you don't know anything about one thing, well . . . you try and show you do know about something else. Don't you? Only human, isn't it?'

'Only human,' I agreed, smiling. 'What was the name of Mr. Grey's gallery?'

'Eh?' He looked puzzled. 'I thought you said he sent you, to see my picture.'

'I go to so many galleries, I've foolishly forgotten which one it was.'

'Ruapehu Fine Arts,' he said. 'I was down there last week.'

'Down . . .?'

'In Wellington.' His smile was slipping. 'Look here, what is all this?' Suspicion flitted across his rounded face. 'Why did you come here? I don't think Mr. Grey sent you at all.'

'No,' I said. 'But Mr. Updike, we mean you no harm. We really are painters, my friend and I. But . . . now we've seen your jade collection . . . we do think we must warn you. We've heard of several people who've bought paintings and had their houses burgled soon after. You say you've got burglar alarms fitted, so if I were you I'd make sure they are working properly.'

'But . . . good gracious . . .'

'There's a bunch of thieves about,' I said, 'who follow up the sales of paintings and burgle the houses of those who buy. I suppose they reckon that if anyone can afford, say, a Herring, they have other things worth stealing.'

He looked at me with awakening shrewdness. 'You mean, young man, that I told Mr. Grey about my jade . . .'

'Let's just say,' I said, 'That it would be sensible to take more precautions than usual.'

'But . . . for how long?'

I shook my head. 'I don't know Mr. Updike. Maybe for ever.'

His round jolly face looked troubled.

'Why did you bother to come and tell me all this?' he said.

'I'd do a great deal more to break up this bunch.'

He asked 'Why?' again, so I told him. 'My cousin bought a painting. My cousin's house was burgled. My cousin's wife disturbed the burglars, and they killed her.'

Norman Updike took a long slow look at my face. I couldn't have stopped him seeing the abiding anger, even if I'd tried. He shivered convulsively.

'I'm glad you're not after *me*,' he said.

I managed a smile. 'Mr. Updike . . . please take care. And one day, perhaps, the police may come to see your picture, and ask where you bought it . . . anyway, they will if I have anything to do with it.'

The round smile returned with understanding and conviction. 'I'll expect them,' he said.

Chapter Fourteen

Jik drove us from Auckland to Wellington; eight hours in the car.

We stopped overnight in a motel in the town of Hamilton, south of Auckland, and went on in the morning. No one followed us, molested us or spied on us. As far as I could be, I was sure no one had picked us up in the northern city, and no one knew we had called at the Updikes.

Wexford must know, all the same, that I had the Overseas Customers list, and he knew there were several New Zealand addresses on it. He couldn't guess which one I'd pick to visit, but he could and would guess that any I picked with the prefix W would steer me straight to the gallery in Wellington.

So in the gallery in Wellington, he'd be ready . . .

'You're looking awfully grim, Todd,' Sarah said.

'Sorry.'

'What were you thinking?'

'How soon we could stop for lunch.'

She laughed. 'We've only just had breakfast.'

We passed the turning to Rotorua and the land of hot springs. Anyone for a boiling mud pack, Jik asked. There was a power station further on run by steam jets from underground, Sarah said, and horrid black craters stinking of sulphur, and the earth's crust was so thin in places that it vibrated and sounded hollow. She had been taken round a place called

Waiotapu when she was a child, she said, and had had terrible nightmares afterwards, and she didn't want to go back.

'Pooh,' Jik said dismissively. 'They only have earthquakes every other Friday.'

'Somebody told me they have so many earthquakes in Wellington that all the new office blocks are built in cradles,' Sarah said.

'Rock-a-bye skyscraper . . .' sang Jik, in fine voice.

The sun shone bravely, and the countryside was green with leaves I didn't know. There were fierce bright patches and deep mysterious shadows; gorges and rocks and heaven-stretching tree trunks; feathery waving grasses, shoulder high. An alien land, wild and beautiful.

'Get that chiaroscuro,' Jik said, as we sped into one particularly spectacular curving valley.

'What's chiaroscuro?' Sarah said.

'Light and shade,' Jik said. 'Contrast and balance. Technical term. All the world's a chiaroscuro, and all the men and women merely blobs of light and shade.'

'Every life's a chiaroscuro,' I said.

'And every soul.'

'The enemy,' I said, 'is grey.'

'And you get grey,' Jik nodded, 'by muddling together red, white and blue.'

'Grey lives, grey deaths, all levelled out into equal grey nothing.'

'No one,' Sarah sighed, 'would ever call you two grey.'

'Grey!' I said suddenly. 'Of bloody course.'

'What are you on about?' Jik said.

'Grey was the name of the man who hired the suburban art gallery in Sydney, and Grey is the name of the man who sold Updike his quote Herring unquote.'

'Oh dear.' Sarah's sigh took the lift out of the spirits and the dazzle from the day.

'Sorry,' I said.

There were so many of them, I thought. Wexford and Greene. The boy. The woman. Harley Renbo. Two toughs at Alice Springs, one of whom I knew by sight, and one, (the one who'd been behind me) whom I didn't. The one I didn't know might, or might not, be Beetle-brows. If he wasn't, Beetle-brows was extra.

And now Grey. And another one, somewhere.

Nine at least. Maybe ten. How could I possibly tangle all that lot up without getting crunched. Or worse, getting Sarah crunched, or Jik. Every time I moved, the serpent grew another head.

I wondered who did the actual robberies. Did they send their own two (or three) toughs overseas, or did they contract out to local labour, so to speak?

If they had sent their own toughs, was it one of them who had killed Regina?

Had I already met Regina's killer? Had he thrown me over the balcony at Alice?

I pondered uselessly, and added one more twist . . .
Was he waiting ahead in Wellington?

We reached the capital in the afternoon and booked into the Townhouse
Hotel because of its splendid view over the harbour. With such marvellous
coastal scenery, I thought it would have been a disgrace if the cities of
New Zealand had been ugly. I still thought there were no big towns
more captivating than flat old marshy London, but that was another
story. Wellington, new and cared for, had life and character to spare.

I looked up the Ruapehu Fine Arts in the telephone directory and
asked the hotel's reception desk how to get there. They had never heard
of the gallery, but the road it was in, that must be up past the old town,
they thought: past Thorndon.

They sold me a local area road map, which they said would help, and
told me that Mount Ruapehu was a (with luck) extinct volcano, with a
warm lake in its crater. If we'd come from Auckland, we must have
passed nearby.

I thanked them and carried the map to Jik and Sarah upstairs in their
room.

'We could find the gallery,' Jik said. 'But what would we do when we
got there?'

'Make faces at them through the window?'

'You'd be crazy enough for that, too,' Sarah said.

'Let's just go and look,' I said. 'They won't see us in the car, if we
simply drive past.'

'And after all,' Jik said incautiously, 'we do want them to know we're
here.'

'Why?' asked Sarah in amazement.

'Oh Jesus,' Jik said.

'Why?' she demanded, the anxiety crowding back.

'Ask Todd, it's his idea.'

'You're a sod,' I said.

'Why, Todd?'

'Because,' I said, 'I want them to spend all their energies looking for
us over here and not clearing away every vestige of evidence in Melbourne.
We do want the police to deal with them finally, don't we, because we
can't exactly arrest them ourselves? Well . . . when the police start
moving, it would be hopeless if there was no one left for them to find.'

She nodded. 'That's what you meant by leaving it all in working order.
But . . . you didn't say anything about deliberately enticing them to follow
us.'

'Todd's got that list, and the pictures we took,' Jik said, 'and they'll
want them back. Todd wants them to concentrate exclusively on getting
them back, because if they think they can get them back and shut us
up . . .'

'Jik,' I interrupted. 'You do go on a bit.'

Sarah looked from me to him and back again. A sort of hopeless calm
took over from the anxiety.

'If they think they can get everything back and shut us up,' she said, 'they will be actively searching for us in order to kill us. And you intend to give them every encouragement. Is that right?'

'No,' I said. 'Or rather, yes.'

'They'd be looking for us anyway,' Jik pointed out.

'And we are going to say "Coo-ee, we're over here"?'

'Um,' I said. 'I think they may know already.'

'God give me strength,' she said. 'All right. I see what you're doing, and I see why you didn't tell me. And I think you're a louse. But I'll grant you you've been a damn sight more successful than I thought you'd be, and here we all still are, safe and moderately sound, so all right, we'll let them know we're definitely here. On the strict understanding that we then keep our heads down until you've fixed the police in Melbourne.'

I kissed her cheek. 'Done,' I said.

'So how do we do it?'

I grinned at her. 'We address ourselves to the telephone.'

In the end Sarah herself made the call, on the basis that her Australian voice would be less remarkable than Jik's Englishness, or mine.

'Is that the Ruapehu Fine Arts gallery? It is? I wonder if you can help me . . .' she said. 'I would like to speak to whoever is in charge. Yes, I know, but it is important. Yes, I'll wait.' She rolled her eyes and put her hand over the mouthpiece. 'She sounded like a secretary. New Zealand, anyway.'

'You're doing great,' I said.

'Oh . . . Hello? Yes. Could you tell me your name, please?' Her eyes suddenly opened wide. '*Wexford*. Oh, er . . . Mr. Wexford, I've just had a visit from three extraordinary people who wanted to see a painting I bought from you some time ago. Quite extraordinary people. They said you'd sent them. I didn't believe them. I wouldn't let them in. But I thought perhaps I'd better check with you. Did you send them to see my painting?'

There was some agitated squawking from the receiver.

'Describe them? A young man with fair hair and a beard, and another young man with an injured arm, and a bedraggled looking girl. I sent them away. I didn't like the look of them.'

She grimaced over the 'phone and listened to some more squawks.

'No of course I didn't give them any information. I told you I didn't like the look of them. Where do I live? Why, right here in Wellington. Well, thank you so much Mr. Wexford, I am so pleased I called you.'

She put the receiver down while it was still squawking.

'He was asking me for my name,' she said.

'What a girl,' Jik said. 'What an actress, my wife.'

Wexford. Wexford himself.

It had *worked*.

I raised a small internal cheer.

'So now that they know we're here,' I said, 'would you like to go off somewhere else?'

'Oh no,' Sarah said instinctively. She looked out of the window across the busy harbour. 'It's lovely here, and we've been travelling all day already.'

I didn't argue. I thought it might take more than a single telephone call to keep the enemy interested in Wellington, and it had only been for Sarah's sake that I would have been prepared to move on.

'They won't find us just by checking the hotels by telephone,' Jik pointed out. 'Even if it occurred to them to try the Townhouse, they'd be asking for Cassavetes and Todd, not Andrews and Peel.'

'Are we Andrews and Peel?' Sarah asked.

'We're Andrews. Todd's Peel.'

'So nice to know,' she said.

Mr. and Mrs. Andrews and Mr. Peel took dinner in the hotel restaurant without mishap, Mr. Peel having discarded his sling for the evening on the grounds that it was in general a bit too easy to notice. Mr. Andrews had declined, on the same consideration, to remove his beard.

We went in time to our separate rooms, and so to bed. I spent a jolly hour unsticking the Alice bandages from my leg and admiring the hemstitching. The tree had made tears that were far from the orderly cuts of operations, and as I inspected the long curving railway lines on a ridged backing of crimson, black and yellow skin, I reckoned that those doctors had done an expert job. It was four days since the fall, during which time I hadn't exactly led an inactive life, but none of their handiwork had come adrift. I realised I had progressed almost without noticing it from feeling terrible all the time to scarcely feeling anything worth mentioning. It was astonishing, I thought, how quickly the human body repaired itself, given the chance.

I covered the mementoes with fresh adhesive plaster bought that morning in Hamilton for the purpose, and even found a way of lying in bed that drew no strike action from mending bones. Things, I thought complacently as I drifted to sleep, were altogether looking up.

I suppose one could say that I underestimated on too many counts. I underestimated the desperation with which Wexford had come to New Zealand. Underestimated the rage and the thoroughness with which he searched for us.

Underestimated the effect of our amateur robbery on professional thieves. Underestimated our success. Underestimated the fear and the fury we had unleashed.

My picture of Wexford tearing his remaining hair in almost comic frustration was all wrong. He was pursuing us with a determination bordering on obsession, grimly, ruthlessly, and fast.

In the morning I woke late to a day of warm windy spring sunshine and made coffee from the fixings provided by the hotel in each room; and Jik rang through on the telephone.

'Sarah says she *must* wash her hair today. Apparently it's sticking together.'

'It looks all right to me.'

His grin came down the wire. 'Marriage opens vast new feminine horizons. Anyway, she's waiting down in the hall for me to drive her to the shops to buy some shampoo, but I thought I'd better let you know we were going.'

I said uneasily, 'You will be careful . . .'

'Oh sure,' he said. 'We won't go anywhere near the gallery. We won't go far. Only as far as the nearest shampoo shop. I'll call you as soon as we get back.'

He disconnected cheerfully, and five minutes later the bell rang again. I lifted the receiver.

It was the girl from the reception desk. 'Your friends say would you join them downstairs in the car.'

'O.K.' I said.

I went jacketless down in the lift, left my room key at the desk, and walked out through the front door to the sun-baked and windy car park. I looked around for Jik and Sarah; but they were not, as it happened, the friends who were waiting.

It might have been fractionally better if I hadn't had my left arm slung up inside my shirt. As it was they simply clutched my clothes, lifted me off balance and off my feet, and ignominiously bundled me into the back of their car.

Wexford was sitting inside it; a one-man reception committee. The eyes behind the heavy spectacles were as hostile as forty below, and there was no indecision this time in his manner. This time he as good as had me again behind his steel mesh door, and this time he was intent on not making mistakes.

He still wore a bow tie. The jaunty polka-dots went oddly with the unfunny matter in hand.

The muscles propelling me towards him turned out to belong to Greene with an 'e', and to a thug I'd never met but who answered the general description of Beetle-brows.

My spirits descended faster than the Hilton lifts. I ended up sitting between Beetle-brows and Wexford, with Greene climbing in front into the driving seat.

'How did you find me?' I said.

Greene, with a wolfish smile, took a polaroid photograph from his pocket and held it for me to see. It was a picture of the three of us, Jik, Sarah and me, standing by the shops in Melbourne airport. The woman from the gallery, I guessed, had not been wasting the time she spent watching us depart.

'We went round asking the hotels,' Greene said. 'It was easy.'

There didn't seem to be much else to say, so I didn't say anything. A slight shortage of breath might have had something to do with it.

None of the others, either, seemed over-talkative. Greene started the car and drove out into the city. Wexford stared at me with a mixture of anger and satisfaction: and Beetle-brows began twisting my free right arm behind my back in a grip which left no room for debate. He wouldn't let me remain upright. My head went practically down to my knees. It was all most undignified and excruciating.

Wexford said finally, 'We want our list back.'

There was nothing gentlemanly in his voice. He wasn't making light conversation. His heavy vindictive rage had no trouble at all in communicating itself to me without possibility of misunderstanding.

Oh Christ, I thought miserably; I'd been such a bloody fool, just walking into it like that.

'Do you hear? We want our list back, and everything else you took.'

I didn't answer. Too busy suffering.

From external sounds I guessed we were travelling through busy workaday Friday morning city streets, but as my head was below window-level, I couldn't actually see.

After some time the car turned sharply left and ground uphill for what seemed like miles. The engine sighed from overwork at the top, and the road began to descend.

Almost nothing was said on the journey. My thoughts about what very likely lay at the end of it were so unwelcome that I did my best not to allow them houseroom. I could give Wexford his list back, but what then? What then, indeed.

After a long descent the car halted briefly and then turned to the right. We had exchanged city sounds for those of the sea. There were also no more Doppler-effects from cars passing us from the opposite direction. I came to the sad conclusion that we had turned off the highway and were on our way along an infrequently used side road.

The car stopped eventually with a jerk.

Beetle-brows removed his hands. I sat up stiffly, wrenched and unenthusiastic.

They could hardly have picked a lonelier place. The road ran along beside the sea so closely that it was more or less part of the shore, and the shore was a jungle of sharply pointed rough black rocks, with frothy white waves slapping among them, a far cry from the gentle beaches of home.

On the right rose jagged cliffs, steeply towering. Ahead, the road ended blindly in some workings which looked like a sort of quarry. Slabs had been cut from the cliffs, and there were dusty clearings, and huge heaps of small jagged rocks, and graded stones, and sifted chips. All raw and harsh and blackly volcanic.

No people. No machinery. No sign of occupation.

'Where's the list?' Wexford said.

Greene twisted round in the driving seat and looked seriously at my face.

'You'll tell us,' he said. 'With or without a beating. And we won't hit you with our fists, but with pieces of rock.'

Beetle-brows said aggrievedly, 'What's wrong with fists?' But what was wrong with Greene's fists was the same as with mine: I would never have been able to hit anyone hard enough to get the desired results. The local rocks, by the look of them, were something else.

'What if I tell you?' I said.

They hadn't expected anything so easy. I could see the surprise on their faces, and it was flattering, in a way. There was also a furtiveness in their expressions which boded no good at all. Regina, I thought. Regina, with her head bashed in.

I looked at the cliffs, the quarry, the sea. No easy exit. And behind us, the road. If I ran that way, they would drive after me, and mow me down. If I could run. And even that was problematical.

I swallowed and looked dejected, which wasn't awfully difficult.

'I'll tell you . . .' I said. 'Out of the car.'

There was a small silence while they considered it; but as they weren't anyway going to have room for much crashing around with rocks in that crowded interior, they weren't entirely against.

Greene leaned over towards the glove compartment on the passenger side, opened it, and drew out a pistol. I knew just about enough about firearms to distinguish a revolver from an automatic, and this was a revolver, a gun whose main advantage, I had read, was that it never jammed.

Greene handled it with a great deal more respect than familiarity. He showed it to me silently, and returned it to the glove compartment, leaving the hinged flap door open so that we all had a clear view of his ultimate threat.

'Get out, then,' Wexford said.

We all got out, and I made sure that I ended up on the side of the sea. The wind was much stronger on this exposed coast, and chilling in the bright sunshine. It lifted the thin carefully combed hair away from Wexford's crown, and left him straggly bald, and intensified the stupid look of Beetle-brows. Greene's eyes stayed as watchful and sharp as the harsh terrain around us.

'All right then,' Wexford said roughly, shouting a little to bring his voice above the din of sea and sky. 'Where's the list?'

I whirled away from them and did my best to sprint for the sea.

I thrust my right hand inside my shirt and tugged at the sling-forming bandages.

Wexford, Greene and Beetle-brows shouted furiously and almost trampled on my heels.

I pulled the lists of Overseas Customers out of the sling, whirled again with them in my hand, and flung them with a bowling action as far out to sea as I could manage.

The pages fluttered apart in mid air, but the off shore winds caught most of them beautifully and blew them like great leaves out to sea.

I didn't stop at the water's edge. I went straight on into the cold inhospitable battlefield of shark-teeth rocks and green water and white foaming waves. Slipping, falling, getting up, staggering on, finding that the current was much stronger than I'd expected, and the rocks more abrasive, and the footing more treacherous. Finding I'd fled from one deadly danger to embrace another.

For one second, I looked back.

Wexford had followed me a step or two into the sea, but only, it seemed, to reach one of the pages which had fallen shorter than the others. He was standing there with the frothy water swirling round his trouser legs, peering at the sodden paper.

Greene was beside the car, leaning in; by the front passenger seat.

Beetle-brows had his mouth open.

I reapplied myself to the problem of survival.

The shore shelved, as most shores do. Every forward step led into a stronger current, which sucked and pulled and shoved me around like a piece of flotsam. Hip-deep between waves, I found it difficult to stay on my feet, and every time I didn't I was in dire trouble, because of the black needle-sharp rocks waiting in ranks above and below the surface to scratch and tear.

The rocks were not the kind I was used to: not the hard familiar lumpy rocks of Britain, polished by the sea. These were the raw stuff of volcanoes, as scratchy as pumice. One's groping hand didn't slide over them: one's skin stuck to them, and tore off. Clothes fared no better. Before I'd gone thirty yards I was running with blood from a dozen superficial grazes: and no blood vessels bleed more convincingly than the small surface capillaries.

My left arm was still tangled inside the sling, which had housed the Overseas Customers since Cup day as an insurance against having my room robbed, as at Alice. Soaking wet, the bandages now clung like leeches, and my shirt also. Muscles weakened by a fracture and inactivity couldn't deal with them. I rolled around a lot from not having two hands free.

My foot stepped awkwardly on the side of a submerged rock and I felt it scrape my shin: lost my balance, fell forward, tried to save myself with my hand, failed, crashed chest first against a small jagged peak dead ahead, and jerked my head sharply sideways to avoid connecting with my nose.

The rock beside my cheek splintered suddenly as if exploding. Slivers of it prickled in my face. For a flicker of time I couldn't understand it: and then I struggled round and looked back to the shore with a flood of foreboding.

Greene was standing there, aiming the pistol, shooting to kill.

Chapter Fifteen

Thirty to thirty-five yards is a long way for a pistol; but Greene seemed so close.

I could see his drooping moustache and the lanky hair blowing in the wind. I could see his eyes and the concentration in his body. He was standing with his legs straddled and his arms out straight ahead, aiming the pistol with both hands.

I couldn't hear the shots above the crash of the waves on the rocks. I couldn't see him squeeze the trigger. But I did see the upward jerk of the arms at the recoil, and I reckoned it would be just plain silly to give him a stationary target.

I was, in all honesty, pretty frightened. I must have looked as close to him as he to me. He must have been quite certain he would hit me, even though his tenderness with the pistol in the car had made me think he was not an expert.

I turned and stumbled a yard or two onwards, though the going became even rougher, and the relentless fight against current and waves and rocks was draining me to dish-rags.

There would have to be an end to it.

Have to be.

I stumbled and fell on a jagged edge and gashed the inside of my right forearm, and out poured more good red life. Christ, I thought, I must be scarlet all over, leaking from a hundred tiny nicks.

It gave me at least an idea.

I was waist-deep in dangerous green water, with most of the shore-line rocks now submerged beneath the surface. Close to one side a row of bigger rock-teeth ran out from the shore like a nightmarish breakwater, and I'd shied away from it, because of the even fiercer waves crashing against it. But it represented the only cover in sight. Three stumbling efforts took me nearer; and the current helped.

I looked back at Greene. He was reloading the gun. Wexford was practically dancing up and down beside him, urging him on; and Beetle-brows, from his disinclination to chase me, probably couldn't swim.

Greene slapped shut the gun and raised it again in my direction.

I took a frightful chance.

I held my fast-bleeding forearm close across my chest: and I stood up, swaying in the current, visible to him from the waist up.

I watched him aim, with both arms straight. It would take a marksman, I believed, to hit me with that pistol from that distance, in that wind. A marksman whose arms didn't jerk upwards when he fired.

The gun was pointing straight at me.

I saw the jerk as he squeezed the trigger.

For an absolutely petrifying second I was convinced he had shot accurately; but I didn't feel or see or even hear the passing of the flying death.

I flung my own right arm wide and high, and paused there facing him for a frozen second, letting him see that most of the front of my shirt was scarlet with blood.

Then I twisted artistically and fell flat, face downwards, into the water; and hoped to God he would think he had killed me.

The sea wasn't much better than bullets. Nothing less than extreme fear of the alternative would have kept me down in it, tumbling and crashing against the submerged razor edges like a piece of cheese in a grater.

The waves themselves swept me towards the taller breakwater teeth, and with a fair amount of desperation I tried to get a grip on them, to avoid being alternately sucked off and flung back, and losing a lot more skin.

There was also the problem of not struggling too visibly. If Wexford or Greene saw me threshing about, all my histrionics would have been in vain.

As much by luck as trying I found the sea shoving me into a wedge-shaped crevice between the rocks, from where I was unable to see the shore. I clutched for a hand-hold, and then with bent knees found a good foothold, and clung there precariously while the sea tried to drag me out again. Every time the wave rolled in it tended to float my foot out of the niche it was lodged in, and every time it receded it tried to suck me with it, with a syphonic action. I clung, and see-sawed in the chest-high water, and clung, and see-sawed, and grew progressively more exhausted.

I could hear nothing except the waves on the rocks. I wondered forlornly how long Wexford and Greene would stay there, staring out to sea for signs of life. I didn't dare to look, in case they spotted my moving head.

The water was cold, and the grazes gradually stopped bleeding, including the useful gash on my forearm. Absolutely nothing, I thought, like having a young strong healthy body. Absolutely nothing like having a young strong healthy body on dry land with a paintbrush in one hand and a beer in the other, with the nice friendly airliners thundering overhead and no money to pay the gas.

Fatigue, in the end, made me look. It was either that or cling like a limpet until I literally fell off nervelessly, too weak to struggle back to life.

To look, I had to leave go. I tried to find other holds, but they weren't as good. The first out-going wave took me with it in no uncertain terms; and its incoming fellow threw me back.

In the tumbling interval I caught a glimpse of the shore.

The road, the cliffs, the quarry, as before. Also the car. Also people.

Bloody damn, I thought.

My hand scrambled for its former hold. My fingers were cramped, bleeding again, and cold. Oh Christ, I thought. How much longer.

It was a measure of my tiredness that it took the space of three in and out waves for me to realise that it wasn't Wexford's car, and it wasn't Wexford standing on the road.

If it wasn't Wexford, it didn't matter who it was.

I let go again of the hand-hold and tried to ride the wave as far out of the crevice as possible, and to swim away from the return force flinging me back. All the other rocks were still there under the surface. A few yards was a heck of a long way.

I stood up gingerly, feeling for my footing more carefully than on the outward flight, and took a longer look at the road.

A grey-white car. A couple beside it, standing close, the man with his arms round the girl.

A nice quiet spot for it, I thought sardonically. I hoped they would drive me somewhere dry.

They moved apart and stared out to sea.

I stared back.

For an instant it seemed impossible. Then they started waving their arms furiously and ran towards the water; and it was Sarah and Jik.

Throwing off his jacket, Jik ploughed into the waves with enthusiasm, and came to a smart halt as the realities of the situation scraped his legs. All the same, he came on after a pause towards me, taking care.

I made my slow way back. Even without haste driving like a fury, any passage through those wave-swept rocks was ruin to the epidermis. By the time we met we were both streaked with red.

We looked at each other's blood. Jik said 'Jesus' and I said 'Christ', and it occurred to me that maybe the Almighty would think we had been calling for His help a bit too often.

Jik put his arm round my waist and I held on to his shoulders, and together we stumbled slowly to land. We fell now and then. Got up gasping. Reclutched, and went on.

He let go when we reached the road. I sat down on the edge of it with my feet pointing out to sea, and positively drooped.

'Todd,' Sarah said anxiously. She came nearer. '*Todd.*' Her voice was incredulous. 'Are you *laughing?*'

'Sure.' I looked up at her, grinning. 'Why ever not?'

Jik's shirt was torn, and mine was in tatters. We took them off and used them to mop up the grazes which were still persistently oozing. From the expression on Sarah's face, we must have looked crazy.

'What a damn silly place to bathe,' Jik said.

'Free back-scratchers,' I said.

He glanced round behind me. 'Your Alice Springs dressing has come off.'

'How're the stitches?'

'Intact.'

'Bully for them.'

'You'll both get penumonia, sitting there,' Sarah said.

I took off the remnants of sling. All in all, I thought, it had served me pretty well. The adhesive rib-supporting cummerbund was still more or less in place, but had mostly come unstuck through too much immersion. I pulled that off also. That only left the plasters on my leg, and they too, I found, had floated off in the mêlée. The trousers I'd worn over them had windows everywhere.

'Quite a dust-up,' Jik observed, pouring water out of his shoes and shivering.

'We need a telephone,' I said, doing the same.

'Give me strength,' Sarah said. 'What you need is hot baths, warm clothes, and half a dozen psychiatrists.'

'How did you get here?' I asked.

'How come you aren't dead?' Jik said.

'You first.'

'I came out of the shop where I'd bought the shampoo,' Sarah said, 'and I saw Greene drive past. I nearly died on the spot. I just stood still, hoping he wouldn't look my way, and he didn't . . . The car turned to the left just past where I was . . . and I could see there were two other people in the back . . . and I went back to our car and told Jik.'

'We thought it damn lucky he hadn't spotted her,' Jik said, dabbing at persistent scarlet trickles. 'We went back to the hotel, and you weren't there, so we asked the girl at the desk if you'd left a message, and she said you'd gone off in a car with some friends . . . With a man with a droopy moustache.'

'Friends!' Sarah said.

'Anyway,' Jik continued, 'Choking down our rage, sorrow, indignation and what not, we thought we'd better look for your body.'

'Jik!' Sarah protested.

He grinned. 'And who was crying?'

'Shut up.'

'Sarah hadn't seen any sign of you in Greene's car but we thought you might be imitating a sack of potatoes in the boot or something, so we got out the road map, applied our feet to the accelerator, and set off in pursuit.

Turned left where Greene had gone, and found ourselves climbing a ruddy mountain.'

I surveyed our extensive grazes and scratches. 'I think we'd better get some disinfectant,' I said.

'We could bath in it.'

'Good idea.'

I could hear his teeth chattering even above the din of my own.

'Let's get out of this wind,' I said. 'And bleed in the car.'

We crawled stiffly into the seats. Sarah said it was lucky the upholstery was plastic. Jik automatically took his place behind the wheel.

'We drove for miles,' he said. 'Growing, I may say, a little frantic. Over the top of the mountain and down this side. At the bottom of the hill the road swings round to the left and we could see from the map that it follows the coastline round a whole lot of bays and eventually ends up right back in Wellington.'

He started the car, turned it, and rolled gently ahead. Naked to the waist, wet from there down, and still with beads of blood forming and overflowing, he looked an unorthodox chauffeur. The beard, above, was undaunted.

'We went that way,' Sarah said. 'There was nothing but miles of craggy rocks and sea.'

'I'll paint those rocks,' Jik said.

Sarah glanced at his face, and then at me. She'd heard the fervour in that statement of intent. The golden time was almost over.

'After a bit we turned back,' Jik said. 'There was this bit of road saying "no through road", so we came down it. No you, of course. We stopped here on this spot and Sarah got out of the car and started bawling her eyes out.'

'You weren't exactly cheering yourself,' she said.

'Huh,' he smiled. 'Anyway, I kicked a few stones about, wondering what to do next, and there were those cartridges.'

'Those what?'

'On the edge of the road. All close together. Maybe dropped out of one of those spider-ejection revolvers, or something like that.'

'When we saw them,' Sarah said, 'we thought . . .'

'It could have been anyone popping off at seabirds,' I said. 'And I think we might go back and pick them up.'

'Are you serious?' Jik said.

'Yeah.'

We stopped, turned again, and retraced our tyre-treads.

'No one shoots sea-birds with a revolver,' he said. 'But bloody awful painters of slow horses, that's different.'

The quarry came in sight again. Jik drew up and stopped, and Sarah, hopping out quickly, told us to stay where we were, she would fetch the bullet cases.

'They really did shoot at you?' Jik said.

'Greene. He missed.'

'Inefficient.' He shifted in his seat, wincing. 'They must have gone back over the hill while we were looking for you round the bays.' He glanced at Sarah as she searched along the side of the road. 'Did they take the list?'

'I threw it in the sea.' I smiled lopsidedly. 'It seemed too tame just to hand it over . . . and it made a handy diversion. They salvaged enough to see that they'd got what they wanted.'

'It must all have been a bugger.'

'Hilarious.'

Sarah found the cases, picked them up, and came running back. 'Here they are . . . I'll put them in my handbag.' She slid into the passenger seat. 'What now?'

'Telephone,' I said.

'Like that?' She looked me over. 'Have you any idea . . .' She stopped. 'Well,' she said. 'I'll buy you each a shirt at the first shop we come to.' She swallowed. 'And don't say what if it's a grocery.'

'What if it's a grocery?' Jik said.

We set off again, and at the intersection turned left to go back over the hill, because it was about a quarter of the distance.

Near the top there was a large village with the sort of store which sold everything from hammers to hairpins. Also groceries. Also, upon enquiry, shirts. Sarah made a face at Jik and vanished inside.

I pulled on the resulting navy tee-shirt and made wobbly tracks for the telephone, clutching Sarah's purse.

'Operator . . . which hotels have a telex?'

She told me three. One was the Townhouse. I thanked her and rang off.

I called the Townhouse. Remembered, with an effort, that my name was Peel.

'But, Mr. Peel . . .' said the girl, sounding bewildered. 'Your friend . . . the one with the moustache, not the one with the beard . . . He paid your account not half an hour ago and collected all your things . . . Yes, I suppose it is irregular, but he brought your note, asking us to let him have your room key . . . I'm sorry but I didn't know you hadn't written it . . . Yes, he took all your things, the room's being cleaned at this minute . . .'

'Look,' I said, 'Can you send a telex for me? Put it on my friend Mr. . . . er . . . Andrew's bill.'

She said she would. I dictated the message. She repeated it, and said she would send it at once.

'I'll call again soon for the reply,' I said.

Sarah had bought jeans for us, and dry socks. Jik drove out of the village to a more modest spot, and we put them on: hardly the world's best fit, but they hid the damage.

'Where now?' he said. 'Intensive Care Unit?'

'Back to the telephone.'

'Jesus God Almighty.'

He drove back and I called the Townhouse. The girl said she'd received an answer, and read it out. 'Telephone at once, reverse charges,' she said, 'And there's a number . . .' She read it out, twice. I repeated it. 'That's right.'

I thanked her.

'No sweat,' she said. 'Sorry about your things.'

I called the international exchange and gave them the number. It had a priority rating, they said. The call would be through in ten minutes. They would ring back.

The telephone was on the wall of a booth inside the general store. There was nothing to sit on. I wished to God there was.

The ten minutes dragged slowly by. Nine and a half, to be exact.

The bell rang, and I picked up the receiver.

'Your call to England . . .'

The modern miracle. Half-way round the world, and I was talking to Inspector Frost as if he were in the next room. Eleven-thirty in the morning at Wellington: eleven-thirty at night in Shropshire.

'Your letter arrived today, sir,' he said. 'And action has already been started.'

'Stop calling me sir. I'm used to Todd.'

'All right. Well, we telexed Melbourne to alert them and we've started checking on all the people on the England list. The results are already incredible. All the crossed-out names we've checked so far have been the victims of break-ins. We're alerting the police in all the other countries concerned. The only thing is, we see the list you sent us is a photo-copy. Do you have the original?'

'No . . . Most of it got destroyed. Does it matter?'

'Not really. Can you tell us how it came into your possession?'

'Er . . . I think we'd better say it just did.'

A dry laugh travelled twelve thousand miles.

'All right. Now what's so urgent that you're keeping me from my bed?'

'Are you at home?' I said contritely.

'On duty, as it happens. Fire away.'

'Two things . . . One is, I can save you time with the stock list numbers. But first . . .' I told him about Wexford and Greene being in Wellington, and about them stealing my things. 'They've got my passport and travellers' cheques, and also my suitcase which contains painting equipment.'

'I saw it at your cousin's,' he said.

'That's right. I think they may also have a page or two of the list . . .'

'Say that again.'

I said it again. 'Most of it got thrown into the sea, but I know Wexford regained at least one page. Well . . . I thought . . . they'd be going back to Melbourne, probably today, any minute really, and when they land there, there's a good chance they'll have at least some of those things with them . . .'

'I can fix a Customs search,' he said. 'But why should they risk stealing . . . ?'

'They don't know I know,' I said. 'I think they think I'm dead.'

'Good God. Why?'

'They took a pot shot at me. Would bullet cases be of any use? Fortunately I didn't collect a bullet, but I've got six shells.'

'They may be . . .' He sounded faint. 'What about the stock list?'

'In the shorter list . . . Got it?'

'Yes, in front of me.'

'Right. The first letter is for the city the painting was sold in; M for Melbourne, S for Sydney, W for Wellington. The second letter identifies the painter; M for Munnings, H for Herring, and I think R for Raoul Millais. The letter C stands for copy. All the paintings on that list are copies. All the ones on the longer list are originals. Got that?'

'Yes. Go on.'

'The numbers are just numbers. They'd sold 54 copies when I . . . er . . . when the list reached me. The last letter R stands for Renbo. That's Harley Renbo, who was working at Alice Springs. If you remember, I told you about him last time.'

'I remember,' he said.

'Wexford and Greene have spent the last couple of days chasing around in New Zealand, so with a bit of luck they will not have destroyed anything dodgy in the Melbourne gallery. If the Melbourne police can arrange a search, there might be a harvest.'

'It's their belief that the disappearance of the list from the gallery will have already led to the immediate destruction of anything else incriminating.'

'They may be wrong. Wexford and Greene don't know I photo-copied the list and sent it to you. They think the list is floating safely out to sea, and me with it.'

'I'll pass your message to Melbourne.'

'There's also another gallery here in Wellington, and an imitation Herring they sold to a man in Auckland . . .'

'For heaven's sake . . .'

I gave him the Ruapehu address, and mentioned Norman Updike.

'There's also a recurring B on the long stock list, so there's probably another gallery. In Brisbane, maybe. There may also be another one in Sydney. I shouldn't think the suburban place I told you about had proved central enough, so they shut it.'

'Stop,' he said.

'Sorry,' I said. 'But the organisation is like a mushroom . . . it burrows along underground and pops up everywhere.'

'I only said stop so I could change the tape on the recorder. You can carry right on now.'

'Oh.' I half laughed. 'Well . . . did you get any answers from Donald to my questions?'

'Yes, we did.'

'Carefully?'

'Rest assured,' he said dryly. 'We carried out your wishes to the letter. Mr. Stuart's answers were "Yes of course" to the first question, and "No, whyever should I" to the second, and "Yes" to the third.'

'Was he absolutely certain?'

'Absolutely.' He cleared his throat. 'He seems distant and withdrawn. Uninterested. But quite definite.'

'How is he?' I asked.

'He spends all his time looking at a picture of his wife. Every time we call at his house, we can see him through the front window, just sitting there.'

'He is still . . . sane?'

'I'm no judge.'

'You can at least let him know that he's no longer suspected of engineering the robbery and killing Regina.'

'That's a decision for my superiors,' he said.

'Well, kick them into it,' I said. 'Do the police positively yearn for bad publicity?'

'You were quick enough to ask our help,' he said tartly.

To do your job, I thought. I didn't say it aloud. The silence spoke for itself.

'Well . . .' his voice carried a mild apology. 'Our co-operation, then.' He paused. 'Where are you now? When I've telexed Melbourne, I may need to talk to you again.'

'I'm in a 'phone booth in a country store in a village on the hills above Wellington.'

'Where are you going next?'

'I'm staying right here. Wexford and Greene are still around in the city and I don't want to risk the outside chance of their seeing me.'

'Give me the number, then.'

I read it off the telephone.

'I want to come home as soon as possible,' I said. 'Can you do anything about my passport?'

'You'll have to find a consul.'

Oh ta, I thought tiredly. I hung up the receiver and wobbled back to the car.

'Tell you what,' I said, dragging into the back seat, 'I could do with a double hamburger and a bottle of brandy.'

We sat in the car for two hours.

The store didn't sell liquor or hot food. Sarah bought a packet of biscuits. We ate them.

'We can't stay here all day,' she said explosively, after a lengthy glum silence.

I couldn't be sure that Wexford wasn't out searching for her and Jik with murderous intent, and I didn't think she'd be happy to know it.

'We're perfectly safe here,' I said.

'Just quietly dying of blood-poisoning,' Jik agreed.

'I left my pills in the Hilton,' Sarah said.

Jik stared. 'What's that got to do with it?'

'Nothing. I just thought you might like to know.'

'*The* pill?' I asked.

'Yes.'

'Jesus,' Jik said.

A delivery van struggled up the hill and stopped outside the shop. A man in an overall opened the back, took out a large bakery tray, and carried it in.

'Food,' I said hopefully.

Sarah went in to investigate. Jik took the opportunity to unstick his tee-shirt from his healing grazes, but I didn't bother.

'You'll be glued to those clothes, if you don't,' Jik said, grimacing over his task.

'I'll soak them off.'

'All those cuts and things didn't feel so bad when we were in the sea.'

'No.'

'Catches up with you a bit, doesn't it?'

'Mm.'

He glanced at me. 'Why don't you just scream or something?'

'Can't be bothered. Why don't you?'

He grinned. 'I'll scream in paint.'

Sarah came back with fresh doughnuts and cans of Coke. We made inroads, and I at least felt healthier.

After another half hour, the store keeper appeared in the doorway, shouting and beckoning.

'A call for you . . .'

I went stiffly to the telephone. It was Frost, clear as a bell.

'Wexford, Greene and Snell have booked a flight to Melbourne. They will be met at Melbourne airport . . .'

'Who's Snell?' I said.

'How do I know? He was travelling with the other two.'

Beetle-brows, I thought.

'Now listen,' Frost said. 'The telex has been red-hot between here and Melbourne, and the police there want your co-operation, just to clinch things . . .' He went on talking for a long time. At the end he said, 'Will you do that?'

I'm tired, I thought. I'm battered, and I hurt. I've done just about enough.

'All right.'

Might as well finish it, I supposed.

'The Melbourne police want to know for sure that the three Munnings copies you . . . er . . . acquired from the gallery are still where you told me.'

'Yes, they are.'

'Right. Well . . . good luck.'

Chapter Sixteen

We flew Air New Zealand back to Melbourne, tended by angels in sea-green. Sarah looked fresh, Jik definitely shop-worn, and I apparently like a mixture (Jik said) of yellow ochre, Payne's grey, and white, which I didn't think was possible.

Our passage had been oiled by telexes from above. When we arrived at the airport after collecting Sarah's belongings in their carrier bags from the Townhouse, we found ourselves whisked into a private room, plied with strong drink, and subsequently taken by car staight out across the tarmac to the aeroplane.

A thousand miles across the Tasman Sea and an afternoon tea later we were driven straight from the aircraft's steps to another small airport room, which contained no strong drink but only a large hard Australian plain-clothes policeman.

'Porter,' he said, introducing himself and squeezing our bones in a blacksmith's grip. 'Which of you is Charles Todd?'

'I am.'

'Right on, Mr. Todd.' He looked at me without favour. 'Are you ill, or something?' He had a strong rough voice and a strong rough manner, natural aids to putting the fear of God into chummy and bringing on breakdowns in the nervous. To me, I gradually gathered, he was grudgingly offering the status of temporary inferior colleague.

'No,' I said, sighing slightly. Time and airline schedules waited for no man. If I'd spent time on first aid we'd have missed the only possible flight.

'His clothes are sticking to him,' Jik observed, giving the familiar phrase the usual meaning of being hot. It was cool in Melbourne. Porter looked at him uncertainly.

I grinned. 'Did you manage what you planned?' I asked him. He decided Jik was nuts and switched his gaze back to me.

'We decided not to go ahead until you had arrived,' he said, shrugging. 'There's a car waiting outside.' He wheeled out of the door without holding it for Sarah and marched briskly off.

The car had a chauffeur. Porter sat in front, talking on a radio, saying in stiltedly guarded sentences that the party had arrived and the proposals should be implemented.

'Where are we going?' Sarah said.

'To reunite you with your clothes,' I said.

Her face lit up. 'Are we really?'

'And what for?' Jik asked.

'To bring the mouse to the cheese.' And the bull to the sword, I thought: and the moment of truth to the conjuror.

'We got your things back, Todd,' Porter said with satisfaction. 'Wexford, Greene and Snell were turned over on entry, and they copped them with the lot. The locks on your suitcase were scratched and dented but they hadn't burst open. Everything inside should be O.K. You can collect everything in the morning.'

'That's great,' I said. 'Did they still have any of the lists of customers?'

'Yeah. Damp but readable. Names of guys in Canada.'

'Good.'

'We're turning over that Yarra gallery right this minute, and Wexford is there helping. We've let him overhear what we wanted him to, and as soon as I give the go-ahead we'll let him take action.'

'Do you think he will?' I said.

'Look, mister, wouldn't you?'

I thought I might be wary of gifts from the Greeks, but then I wasn't Wexford, and I didn't have a jail sentence breathing down my neck.

We pulled up at the side door of the Hilton. Porter raised himself agilely to the pavement and stood like a solid pillar, watching with half-concealed impatience while Jik, Sarah, and I eased ourselves slowly out. We all went across the familiar red-and-blue opulence of the great entrance hall, and from there through a gate in the reception desk, and into the hotel manager's office at the rear.

A tall dark-suited member of the hotel staff there offered us chairs, coffee, and sandwiches. Porter looked at his watch and offered us an indeterminate wait.

It was six o'clock. After ten minutes a man in shirt and necktie brought a two-way personal radio for Porter, who slipped the ear-plug into place and began listening to disembodied voices.

The office was a working room, lit by neon strips and furnished functionally, with a wall-papering of charts and duty rosters. There were no outside windows: nothing to show the fade of day to night.

We sat, and drank coffee, and waited. Porter ate three of the sandwiches simultaneously. Time passed.

Seven o'clock.

Sarah was looking pale in the artificial light, and tired also. So was Jik, his beard on his chest. I sat and thought about life and death and polka dots.

At seven eleven Porter clutched his ear and concentrated intently on the ceiling. When he relaxed, he passed to us the galvanic message.

'Wexford did just what we reckoned he would, and the engine's turning over.'

'What engine?' Sarah said.

Porter stared at her blankly. 'What we planned,' He said painstakingly, 'is happening.'

'Oh.'

Porter listened again to his private ear and spoke directly to me. 'He's taken the bait.'

'He's a fool,' I said.

Porter came as near to a smile as he could. 'All crooks are fools, one way or another.'

Seven-thirty came and went. I raised my eyebrows at Porter. He shook his head.

'We can't say too much on the radio,' he said. 'Because you get all sorts of ears listening in.'

Just like England, I thought. The Press could turn up at a crime before the police; and the mouse might hear of the trap.

We waited. The time dragged. Jik yawned and Sarah's eyes were dark with fatigue. Outside, in the lobby, the busy rich life of the hotel chattered on unruffled, with guests' spirits rising towards the next day's race meeting, the last of the carnival.

The Derby on Saturday, the Cup on Tuesday, the Oaks (which we'd missed) on Thursday, and the International on Saturday. No serious racegoers went home before the end of things, if they could help it.

Porter clutched his ear again, and stiffened.

'He's here,' he said.

My heart, for some unaccountable reason, began beating overtime. We were in no danger that I could see, yet there it was, thumping away like a steam organ.

Porter disconnected himself from the radio, put it on the manager's desk, and went out into the foyer.

'What do we do?' Sarah said.

'Nothing much except listen.'

We all three went over to the door and held it six inches open. We

listened to people asking for their room keys, asking for letters and
messages, asking for Mr. and Mrs. So-and-So, and which way to Toorak,
and how did you get to Fanny's.

Then suddenly, the familiar voice, sending electric fizzes to my finger
tips. Confident: not expecting trouble. 'I've come to collect a package left
here last Tuesday by a Mr. Charles Todd. He says he checked it into
the baggage room. I have a letter here from him, authorising you to
release it to me.'

There was a crackle of paper as the letter was handed over. Sarah's
eyes were round and startled.

'Did you write it?' she whispered.

I shook my head. 'No.'

The desk clerk outside said, 'Thank you, sir. If you'll just wait a
moment I'll fetch the package.'

There was a long pause. My heart made a lot of noise, but nothing
much else happened.

The desk clerk came back. 'Here you are, sir. Paintings, sir.'

'That's right.'

There were vague sounds of the bundle of paintings and the print-
folder being carried along outside the door.

'I'll bring them round for you,' said the clerk, suddenly closer to us.
'Here we ir, sir.' He went past the office, through the door in the desk,
and round to the front. 'Can you manage them, sir?'

'Yes. Yes. Thank you.' There was haste in his voice, now that he'd got
his hands on the goods. 'Thank you. Goodbye.'

Sarah had begun to say 'Is that all?' in disappointment when Porter's
loud voice chopped into the Hilton velvet like a hatchet.

'I guess we'll take care of those paintings, if you don't mind,' he said.
'Porter, Melbourne city police.'

I opened the door a little, and looked out. Porter stood four square in
the lobby, large and rough, holding out a demanding hand.

At his elbows, two plain-clothes policemen. At the front door, two
more, in uniform. There would be others, I supposed, at the other exits.
They weren't taking any chances.

'Why . . . er . . . Inspector . . . I'm only on an errand . . . er . . . for my
young friend, Charles Todd.'

'And these paintings?'

'I've no idea what they are. He asked me to fetch them for him.'

I walked quietly out of the office, through the gate and round to the
front. I leaned a little wearily against the reception desk. He was only
six feet away, in front of me to my right. I could have stretched forward
and touched him. I hoped Porter would think it near enough, as requested.

A certain amount of unease had pervaded the Hilton guests. They
stood around in an uneven semi-circle, eyeing the proceedings sideways.

'Mr. Charles Todd asked you to fetch them?' Porter said loudly.

'Yes, that's right.'

Porter's gaze switched abruptly to my face.

'Did you ask him?'

'No,' I said.

The explosive effect was all that the Melbourne police could have asked, and a good deal more than I expected. There was no polite quiet identification followed by a polite quiet arrest. I should have remembered all my own theories about the basic brutality of the directing mind.

I found myself staring straight into the eyes of the bull. He realised that he'd been tricked. Had convicted himself out of his own mouth and by his own presence on such an errand. The fury rose in him like a geyser and his hands reached out to grab my neck.

'*You're dead*,' he yelled. '*You're fucking dead.*'

His plunging weight took me off balance and down on to one knee, smothering under his choking grip and two hundred pounds of city suiting; trying to beat him off with my fists and not succeeding. His anger poured over me like lava. Heaven knows what he intended, but Porter's men pulled him off before he did bloody murder on the plushy carpet. As I got creakily to my feet, I heard the handcuffs click.

He was standing there, close to me, quivering in the restraining hands, breathing heavily, dishevelled and bitter-eyed. Civilised exterior all stripped away by one instant of ungovernable rage. The violent core plain to see.

'Hello, Hudson,' I said.

'Sorry,' Porter said perfunctorily. 'Didn't reckon he'd turn wild.'

'Revert,' I said.

'Uh?'

'He always was wild,' I said, 'Underneath.'

'You'd know,' he said. 'I never saw the guy before.' He nodded to Jik and Sarah and finally to me, and hurried away after his departing prisoner.

We looked at each other a little blankly. The hotel guests stared at us curiously and began to drift away. We sat down weakly on the nearest blue velvet seat, Sarah in the middle.

Jik took her hand and squeezed it. She put her fingers over mine.

It had taken nine days.

It had been a long haul.

'Don't know about you,' Jik said. 'But I could do with a beer.'

'Todd,' said Sarah, 'Start talking.'

We were upstairs in a bedroom (mine) with both of them in a relaxed mood, and me in Jik's dressing gown and he and I in a cloud of Dettol.

I yawned. 'About Hudson.'

'Who else? And don't go to sleep before you've told us.'

'Well ... I was looking for him, or someone like him, before I ever met him.'

'But why?'

'Because of the wine,' I said. 'Because of the wine which was stolen from Donald's cellar. Whoever stole it not only knew it was there, down some stairs behind an inconspicuous cupboard-like door ... and I'd stayed several times in the house and never knew the cellar existed ...

but according to Donald they would have had to come prepared with proper cases to pack it in. Wine is usually packed twelve bottles in a case . . . and Donald had two thousand or more bottles stolen. In bulk alone it would have taken a lot of shifting. A lot of time, too, and time for house-breakers is risky. But also it was special wine. A small fortune, Donald said. The sort of wine that's bought and sold as an asset and ends up at a week's wage a bottle, if it's ever drunk at all. Anyway, it was the sort of wine that needed expert handling and marketing if it was to be worth the difficulty of stealing it in the first place . . . and as Donald's business is wine, and the reason for his journey to Australia was wine, I started looking right away for someone who knew Donald, knew he'd bought a Munnings, and knew about good wine and how to sell it. And there, straightaway, was Hudson Taylor, who matched like a glove. But it seemed too easy . . . because he didn't *look* right.'

'Smooth and friendly,' said Sarah, nodding.

'And rich,' Jik added.

'Probably a moneyholic,' I said, pulling open the bed and looking longingly at the cool white sheets.

'A what?'

'Moneyholic. A word I've just made up to describe someone with an uncontrollable addiction to money.'

'The world's full of them,' Jik said, laughing.

I shook my head. 'The world is full of drinkers, but alcoholics are obsessive. Moneyholics are obsessive. They never have enough. They *cannot* have enough. However much they have, they want more. And I'm not talking about the average hard-up man, but about real screw-balls. Money, money, money. Like a drug. Moneyholics will do anything to get it . . . Kidnap, murder, cook the computer, rob banks, sell their grandmothers . . . You name it.'

I sat on the bed with my feet up, feeling less than fit. Sore from too many bruises, on fire from too many cuts. Jik too, I guessed. They had been wicked rocks.

'Moneyholism,' Jik said, like a lecturer to a dimmish class, 'is a widespread disease easily understood by everyone who has ever felt a twinge of greed, which is everyone.'

'Go on about Hudson,' Sarah said.

'Hudson had the organising ability . . . I didn't know when I came that the organisation was so huge, but I did know it was *organised*, if you see what I mean. It was an overseas operation. It took some doing. Knowhow.'

Jik tugged the ring off a can of beer and passed it to me, wincing as he stretched.

'But he convinced me I was wrong about him,' I said, drinking through the triangular hole. 'Because he was so careful. He pretended he had to look up the name of the gallery where Donald bought his picture. He didn't think of me as a threat, of course, but just as Donald's cousin. Not until he talked to Wexford down on the lawn.'

'I remember,' Sarah said. 'When you said it had ripped the whole works apart.'

'Mm . . . I thought it was only that he had told Wexford I was Donald's cousin, but of course Wexford also told *him* that I'd met Greene in Maisie's ruins in Sussex and then turned up in the gallery looking at the original of Maisie's burnt painting.'

'Jesus Almighty,' Jik said. 'No wonder we beat it to Alice Springs.'

'Yes, but by then I didn't think it could be Hudson I was looking for. I was looking for someone brutal, who passed on his violence through his employees. Hudson didn't look or act brutal.' I paused. 'The only slightest crack was when his gamble went down the drain at the races. He gripped his binoculars so hard that his knuckles showed white. But you can't think a man is a big-time thug just because he gets upset over losing a bet.'

Jik grinned. 'I'd qualify.'

'In spades, redoubled,' Sarah said.

'I was thinking about it in the Alice Springs hospital . . . There hadn't been time for the musclemen to get to Alice from Melbourne between us buying Renbo's picture and me diving off the balcony, but there had been time for them to come from *Adelaide*, and Hudson's base was at Adelaide . . . but it was much too flimsy.'

'They might have been in Alice to start with,' Jik said reasonably.

'They might, but what for?' I yawned. 'Then on the night of the Cup you said Hudson had made a point of asking you about me . . . and I wondered how he knew you.'

'Do you know,' Sarah said, 'I did wonder too at the time, but it didn't seem important. I mean, *we'd* seen *him* from the top of the stands, so it didn't seem impossible that somewhere he'd seen you with us.'

'The boy knew you,' I said. 'And he was at the races, because he followed you, with Greene, to the Hilton. The boy must have pointed you out to Greene.'

'And Greene to Wexford, and Wexford to Hudson?' Jik asked.

'Quite likely.'

'And by then,' he said, 'They all knew they wanted to silence you pretty badly, and they'd had a chance and muffed it . . . I'd love to have heard what happened when they found we'd robbed the gallery.' He chuckled, tipping up his beer can to catch the last few drops.

'On the morning after,' I said, 'a letter from Hudson was delivered by hand to the Hilton. How did he know we were there?'

They stared. 'Greene must have told him,' Jik said. 'We certainly didn't. We didn't tell anybody. We were careful about it.'

'So was I,' I said. 'That letter offered to show me round a vineyard. Well . . . if I hadn't been so doubtful of him, I might have gone. He was a friend of Donald's . . . and a vineyard would be interesting. From his point of view, anyway, it was worth a try.'

'Jesus!'

'On the night of the Cup, when we were in that motel near Box Hill, I telephoned the police in England and spoke to the man in charge of Donald's case, Inspector Frost. I asked him to ask Donald some questions . . . and this morning outside Wellington I got the answers.'

'This morning seems several light years away,' Sarah said.

'Mm . . .'

'What questions and what answers?' Jik said.

'The questions were, did Donald tell Hudson all about the wine in his cellar, and did Donald tell *Wexford* about the wine in the cellar, and was it Hudson who had suggested to Donald that he and Regina should go and look at the Munnings in the Arts Centre. And the answers were "Yes, of course", and "No, whyever should I?", and "Yes".'

They thought about it in silence. Jik fiddled with the dispenser in the room's in-built refrigerator and liberated another can of Fosters.

'So what then?' Sarah said.

'So the Melbourne police said it was too insubstantial, but if they could tie Hudson in definitely with the gallery they might believe it. So they dangled in front of Hudson the pictures and stuff we stole from the gallery, and along he came to collect them.'

'How? How did they dangle them?'

'They let Wexford accidentally overhear snippets from a fake report from several hotels about odd deposits in their baggage rooms, including the paintings at the Hilton. Then after we got here they gave him an opportunity to use the telephone when he thought no one was listening, and he rang Hudson at the house he's been staying in here for the races, and told him. So Hudson wrote himself a letter to the Hilton from me, and zoomed along to remove the incriminating evidence.'

'He must have been crazy.'

'Stupid. But he thought I was dead . . . and he'd no idea anyone suspected him. He should have had the sense to know that Wexford's call to him would be bugged by the police . . . but Frost told me that Wexford would think he was using a public 'phone booth.'

'Sneaky,' Sarah said.

I yawned. 'It takes a sneak to catch a sneak.'

'You'd never have thought Hudson would blaze up like that,' she said. 'He looked so . . . so dangerous.' She shivered. 'You wouldn't think people could hide such really frightening violence under a friendly public face.'

'The nice Irish bloke next door,' Jik said, standing up, 'can leave a bomb to blow the legs off children.'

He pulled Sarah to her feet. 'What do you think I paint?' he said. 'Vases of flowers?' He looked down at me. 'Horses?'

We parted the next morning at Melbourne airport, where we seemed to have spent a good deal of our lives.

'It seems strange, saying goodbye,' Sarah said.

'I'll be coming back,' I said.

They nodded.

'Well . . .' We looked at watches.

It was like all partings. There wasn't much to say. I saw in their eyes, as they must have seen in mine, that the past ten days would quickly become a nostalgic memory. Something we did in our crazy youth. Distant.

'Would you do it all again?' Jik said.

I thought inconsequentially of surviving wartime pilots looking back from forty years on. Had their achievements been worth the blood and sweat and risk of death: did they regret?

I smiled. Forty years on didn't matter. What the future made of the past was its own tragedy. What we ourselves did on the day was all that counted.

'I guess I would.'

I leaned forward and kissed Sarah, my oldest friend's wife.

'Hey,' he said. 'Find one of your own.'

Chapter Seventeen

Maisie saw me before I saw her, and came sweeping down like a great scarlet bird, wings outstretched.

Monday lunchtime at Wolverhampton races, misty and cold.

'Hello, dear, I'm so glad you've come. Did you have a good trip back, because of course it's such a long way, isn't it, with all that wretched jet lag?' She patted my arm and peered acutely at my face. 'You don't really look awfully well, dear, if you don't mind me saying so, and you don't seem to have collected any sun-tan, though I suppose as you haven't been away two weeks it isn't surprising, but those are nasty gashes on your hand, dear, aren't they, and you were walking very *carefully* just now.'

She stopped to watch a row of jockeys canter past on their way to the start. Bright shirts against the thin grey mist. A subject for Munnings.

'Have you backed anything, dear? And are you sure you're warm enough in that anorak? I never think jeans are good for people in the winter, they're only cotton, dear, don't forget, and how did you get on in Australia? I mean, dear, did you find out anything useful?'

'It's an awfully long story . . .'

'Best told in the bar, then, don't you think, dear?'

She bought us immense brandies with ginger ale and settled herself at a small table, her kind eyes alert and waiting.

I told her about Hudson's organisation, about the Melbourne gallery, and about the list of robbable customers.

'Was I on it?'

I nodded. 'Yes, you were.'

'And you gave it to the police?' she said anxiously.

I grinned. 'Don't look so worried, Maisie. Your name was crossed out already. I just crossed it out more thoroughly. By the time I'd finished, no one could ever disentangle it, particularly on a photo-copy.'

She smiled broadly. 'No one could call you a fool, dear.'

I wasn't so sure about that. 'I'm afraid, though,' I said, 'that you've lost your nine thousand quid.'

'Oh yes, dear,' she said cheerfully. 'Serves me right, doesn't it, for trying to cheat the Customs, though frankly, dear, in the same circumstances I'd probably do it again, because that tax makes me so mad, dear. But I'm ever so glad, dear, that they won't come knocking on my door this time, or rather my sister Betty's, because of course I'm staying with her again up here at the moment, as of course the Beach told you, until my house is ready.'

I blinked. 'What house?'

'Well, dear, I decided not to rebuild the house at Worthing because it wouldn't be the same without the things Archie and I bought together, so I'm selling that plot of sea-side land for a fortune, dear, and I've chosen a nice place just down the road from Sandown Park racecourse.'

'You're not going to live in Australia?'

'Oh no, dear, that would be too far away. From Archie, you see, dear.'

I saw. I liked Maisie very much.

'I'm afraid I spent all your money,' I said.

She smiled at me with her well-kept head on one side and absent-mindedly stroked her crocodile handbag.

'Never mind, dear. You can paint me *two* pictures. One of me, and one of my new house.'

I left after the third race, took the train along the main line to Shrewsbury, and from there travelled by bus to Inspector Frost's official doorstep.

He was in an office, chin deep in papers. Also present, the unblinking Superintendent Wall, who had so unnerved Donald, and whom I'd not previously met. Both men shook hands in a cool and businesslike manner, Wall's eyes traversing the anorak, jeans and desert boots, and remaining unimpressed. They offered me a chair, moulded plastic and armless.

Frost said, faintly smiling, 'You sure kicked open an ant-hill.'

Wall frowned, disliking such frivolity. 'It appears you stumbled on an organisation of some size.'

The gaze of both men swept the mountain of paper.

'What about Donald?' I asked.

Frost kept his eyes down. His mouth twitched.

Wall said, 'We have informed Mr. Stuart that we are satisfied the break-in at his house and the death of Mrs. Stuart were the work of outside agencies, beyond his knowledge or control.'

Cold comfort words. 'Did he understand what he was hearing?'

The Wall eyebrows rose. 'I went to see him myself, this morning. He appeared to understand perfectly.'

'And what about Regina?'

'The body of Mrs. Stuart,' Wall said correctively.

'Donald wants her buried,' I said.

Frost looked up with an almost human look of compassion. 'The difficulty is,' he said, 'that in a murder case, one has to preserve the victim's body in case the defence wishes to call for its own post mortem. In this case, we have not been able to accuse anyone of her murder, let alone get as far as them arranging a defence.' He cleared his throat. 'We'll release Mrs. Stuart's body for burial as soon as official requirements have been met.'

I looked at my fingers, interlacing them.

Frost said, 'Your cousin already owes you a lot. You can't be expected to do more.'

I smiled twistedly and stood up. 'I'll go and see him,' I said.

Wall shook hands again, and Frost came with me through the hall and out into the street. The lights shone bright in the early winter evening.

'Unofficially,' he said, walking slowly with me along the pavement, 'I'll tell you that the Melbourne police found a list of names in the gallery which it turns out are of known housebreakers. Divided into countries, like the Overseas Customers. There were four names for England. I suppose I shouldn't guess and I certainly ought not to be saying this to you, but there's a good chance Mrs. Stuart's killer may be one of them.'

'Really?'

'Yes. But don't quote me.' He looked worried.

'I won't,' I said. 'So the robberies were local labour?'

'It seems to have been their normal method.'

Greene, I thought. With an 'e'. Greene could have recruited them. And checked afterwards, in burnt houses, on work done.

I stopped walking. We were standing outside the flower shop where Regina had worked. Frost looked at the big bronze chrysanthemums in the brightly lit window, and then enquiringly at my face.

I put my hand in my pocket and pulled out the six revolver shell cases. Gave them to Frost.

'These came from the gun which the man called Greene fired at me,' I said. 'He dropped them when he was reloading. I told you about them on the telephone.'

He nodded.

'I don't imagine they're of much practical use,' I said. 'But they might persuade you that Greene is capable of murder.'

'Well . . . what of it?'

'It's only a feeling . . .'

'Get on with it.'

'Greene,' I said, 'was in England at about the time Regina died.'

He stared.

'Maybe Regina knew him,' I said. 'She had been in the gallery in Australia. Maybe she saw him helping to rob her house . . . supervising, perhaps . . . and maybe that's why she was killed, because it wouldn't have been enough just to tie her up and gag her . . . she could identify him for certain if she was alive.'

He looked as if he was trying to draw breath.

'That's all . . . guessing,' he said.

'I know for certain that Greene was in England two weeks after Regina's death. I know for certain he was up to his neck in selling paintings and stealing them back. I know for certain that he would kill someone who could get him convicted. The rest . . . well . . . it's over to you.'

'My God,' Frost said. 'My God.'

I started off again, towards the bus-stop. He came with me, looking glazed.

'What everyone wants to know,' he said, 'is what put you on to the organisation in the first place.'

I smiled. 'A hot tip from an informer.'

'What informer?'

A smuggler in a scarlet coat, glossy hair-do and crocodile handbag. 'You can't grass on informers,' I said.

He sighed, shook his head, stopped walking, and pulled a piece of torn-off telex paper out of his jacket.

'Did you meet an Australian policeman called Porter?'

'I sure did.'

'He sent you a message.' He handed me the paper. I read the neatly typed words.

'*Tell that Pommie painter Thanks.*'

'Will you send a message back?'

He nodded. 'What is it?'

'No sweat,' I said.

I stood in the dark outside my cousin's house, looking in.

He sat in his lighted drawingroom, facing Regina, unframed on the mantelshelf. I sighed, and rang the bell.

Donald came slowly. Opened the door.

'Charles!' He was mildly surprised. 'I thought you were in Australia.'

'Got back yesterday.'

'Come in.'

We went into the kitchen, where at least it was warm, and sat one each side of the table. He looked gaunt and fifty, a shell of a man, retreating from life.

'How's business?' I said.

'Business?'

'The wine trade.'

'I haven't been to the office.'

'If you didn't have a critical cash flow problem before,' I said. 'You'll have one soon.'

'I don't really care.'

'You've got stuck,' I said. 'Like a needle in a record. Playing the same little bit of track over and over again.'

He looked blank.

'The police know you didn't fix the robbery,' I said.

He nodded slowly. 'That man Wall . . . came and told me so. This morning.'

'Well, then.'

'It doesn't seem to make much difference.'

'Because of Regina?'

He didn't answer.

'You've got to stop it, Donald,' I said. 'She's dead. She's been dead five weeks and three days. Do you want to see her?'

He looked absolutely horrified. 'No! Of course not.'

'Then stop thinking about her body.'

'Charles!' He stood up violently, knocking over his chair. He was somewhere between outrage and anger, and clearly shocked.

'She's in a cold drawer,' I said, 'And you want her in a box in the cold ground. So where's the difference?'

'Get out,' he said loudly. 'I don't want to hear you.'

'The bit of Regina you're obsessed about,' I said, not moving, 'is just a collection of minerals. That . . . that *shape* lying in storage isn't Regina. The real girl is in your head. In your memory. The only life you can give her is to remember her. That's her immortality, in your head. You're killing her all over again with your refusal to go on living.'

He turned on his heel and walked out. I heard him go across the hall, and guessed he was making for the sittingroom.

After a minute I followed him. The white-panelled door was shut.

I opened the door. Went in.

He was sitting in his chair, in the usual place.

'Go away,' he said.

What did it profit a man, I thought, if he got flung over balconies and shot at and mangled by rocks, and couldn't save his cousin's soul.

'I'm taking that picture with me to London,' I said.

He was alarmed. He stood up. 'You're *not*.'

'I am.'

'You can't. You gave it to me.'

'It needs a frame,' I said. 'Or it will warp.'

'You can't take it.'

·'You can come as well.'

'I can't leave here,' he said.

'Why not?'

'Don't be stupid,' he said explosively. 'You know why not. Because of . . .' His voice died away.

I said, 'Regina will be with you wherever you are. Whenever you think of her, she'll be there.'

Nothing.

'She isn't in this room. She's in your head. You can go out of here and take her with you.'

Nothing.

'She was a great girl. It must be bloody without her. But she deserves the best you can do.'

Nothing.

I went over to the fireplace and picked up the picture. Regina's face smiled out, vitally alive. I hadn't done her left nostril too well, I thought.

Donald didn't try to stop me.

I put my hand on his arm.

'Let's get your car out,' I said, 'And drive down to my flat. Right this minute.'

A little silence.

'Come on,' I said.

He began, with difficulty, to cry.

I took a long breath and waited. 'O.K.,' I said. 'How are you off for petrol?'

'We can get some more . . .' he said, sniffing, '. . . on the motorway.'

Erle Stanley Gardner
Perry Mason in the Case of
The Gilded Lady
The Daring Decoy
The Fiery Fingers
The Lucky Loser
The Calendar Girl
The Deadly Toy
The Mischievous Doll
The Amorous Aunt

Richard Gordon
Doctor in the House
Doctor at Sea
Doctor at Large
Doctor in Love
Doctor in Clover
The Facemaker
The Medical Witness

Graham Greene
Brighton Rock
The End of the Affair
It's a Battlefield
England Made Me
The Ministry of Fear
Our Man in Havana

Graham Greene
The Heart of the Matter
Stamboul Train
A Burnt-out Case
The Third Man
Loser Takes All
The Quiet American
The Power and the Glory

Ernest Hemingway*
For Whom the Bell Tolls
The Snows of Kilimanjaro
Fiesta
The Short Happy Life of Francis
  Macomber
Across the River and into the Trees
The Old Man and the Sea

James Herriot
If Only They Could Talk
It Shouldn't Happen to a Vet
Let Sleeping Vets Lie
Vet in Harness
Vets Might Fly
Vet in a Spin

Georgette Heyer
These Old Shades
Sprig Muslin
Sylvester
The Corinthian
The Convenient Marriage

Henry James
The Europeans
Daisy Miller
Washington Square
The Aspern Papers
The Turn of the Screw
The Portrait of a Lady

Franz Kafka*
The Trial
America
In the Penal Settlement
Metamorphosis
The Castle
The Great Wall of China
Investigations of a Dog
Letter to his Father
The Diaries 1910-1923

Rudyard Kipling
The Jungle Book
The Second Jungle Book
Just So Stories
Puck of Pook's Hill
Stalky and Co.
Kim

D. H. Lawrence
Sons and Lovers
St. Mawr
The Fox
The White Peacock
Love among the Haystacks
The Virgin and the Gipsy
Lady Chatterley's Lover

D. H. Lawrence
Women in Love
The Ladybird
The Man Who Died
The Captain's Doll
The Rainbow

Norah Lofts
Jassy
Bless This House
Scent of Cloves
How Far to Bethlehem?

Robert Ludlum*
The Scarlatti Inheritance
The Osterman Weekend
The Matlock Paper
The Gemini Contenders

Thomas Mann*
Death in Venice
Tristan
Tonio Kröger
Doctor Faustus
Mario and the Magician
A Man and His Dog
The Black Swan
Confessions of Felix Krull,
    Confidence Man

W. Somerset Maugham
Cakes and Ale
The Painted Veil
Liza of Lambeth
The Razor's Edge
Theatre
The Moon and Sixpence

W. Somerset Maugham
Sixty-five Short Stories

Ed McBain*
Cop Hater
Give the Boys a Great Big Hand
Doll
Eighty Million Eyes
Hail, Hail, the Gang's All Here!
Sadie When She Died
Let's Hear it for the Deaf Man

James A. Michener*
The Source
The Bridges at Toko-Ri
Caravans
Sayonara

George Orwell
Animal Farm
Burmese Days
A Clergyman's Daughter
Coming up for Air
Keep the Aspidistra Flying
Nineteen Eighty-four

George Orwell
Down and Out in Paris & London
Homage to Catalonia
Selections from Essays and Journalism:
    1931-1949
The Road to Wigan Pier

Jean Plaidy
St. Thomas's Eve
Royal Road to Fotheringay
The Goldsmith's Wife
Perdita's Prince

Nevil Shute
A Town Like Alice
Pied Piper
The Far Country
The Chequer Board
No Highway

Georges Simenon
Ten Maigret Stories

Wilbur Smith
When the Lion Feeds
The Diamond Hunters
Eagle in the Sky
Gold Mine
Shout at the Devil

Wilbur Smith
Hungry as the Sea
The Sound of Thunder
The Eye of the Tiger

John Steinbeck*
The Grapes of Wrath
The Moon is Down
Cannery Row
East of Eden
Of Mice and Men

Mary Stewart
The Crystal Cave
The Hollow Hills
Wildfire at Midnight
Airs Above the Ground

Mary Stewart
Touch Not The Cat
The Gabriel Hounds
Nine Coaches Waiting
Madam, Will You Talk?

Evelyn Waugh
Decline and Fall
Black Mischief
A Handful of Dust
Scoop
Put Out More Flags
Brideshead Revisited

H. G. Wells
The Time Machine
The Island of Dr. Moreau
The Invisible Man
The First Men in the Moon
The Food of the Gods
In the Days of the Comet
The War of the Worlds

Morris West
The Devil's Advocate
The Second Victory
Daughter of Silence
The Salamander
The Shoes of the Fisherman

Dennis Wheatley
The Devil Rides Out
The Haunting of Toby Jugg
Gateway to Hell
To the Devil—A Daughter

John Wyndham
The Day of the Triffids
The Kraken Wakes
The Chrysalids
The Seeds of Time
Trouble With Lichen
The Midwich Cuckoos

***Not currently available in
Canada for copyright reasons**